THE YEAR'S BEST

SCIENCE FICTION

ALSO BY GARDNER DOZOIS

ANTHOLOGIES

A DAY IN THE LIFE

ANOTHER WORLD

BEST SCIENCE FICTION STORIES OF THE
 YEAR #6–10

THE BEST OF ISAAC ASIMOV'S SCIENCE
 FICTION MAGAZINE

TIME-TRAVELERS FROM ISAAC ASIMOV'S
 SCIENCE FICTION MAGAZINE

TRANSCENDENTAL TALES FROM ISAAC
 ASIMOV'S SCIENCE FICTION MAGAZINE

ISAAC ASIMOV'S ALIENS

ISAAC ASIMOV'S MARS

ISAAC ASIMOV'S SF LITE

ISAAC ASIMOV'S WAR

ROADS NOT TAKEN (with Stanley Schmidt)

THE YEAR'S BEST SCIENCE FICTION, #1–32

FUTURE EARTHS: UNDER AFRICAN SKIES
 (with Mike Resnick)

FUTURE EARTHS: UNDER SOUTH AMERICAN
 SKIES (with Mike Resnick)

RIPPER! (with Susan Casper)

MODERN CLASSIC SHORT NOVELS OF
 SCIENCE FICTION

MODERN CLASSICS OF FANTASY

KILLING ME SOFTLY

DYING FOR IT

THE GOOD OLD STUFF

THE GOOD NEW STUFF

EXPLORERS

THE FURTHEST HORIZON

WORLDMAKERS

SUPERMEN

COEDITED WITH SHEILA WILLIAMS

ISAAC ASIMOV'S PLANET EARTH

ISAAC ASIMOV'S ROBOTS

ISAAC ASIMOV'S VALENTINES

ISAAC ASIMOV'S SKIN DEEP

ISAAC ASIMOV'S GHOSTS

ISAAC ASIMOV'S VAMPIRES

ISAAC ASIMOV'S MOONS

ISAAC ASIMOV'S CHRISTMAS

ISAAC ASIMOV'S CAMELOT

ISAAC ASIMOV'S WEREWOLVES

ISAAC ASIMOV'S SOLAR SYSTEM

ISAAC ASIMOV'S DETECTIVES

ISAAC ASIMOV'S CYBERDREAMS

COEDITED WITH JACK DANN

ALIENS!

UNICORNS!

MAGICATS!

MAGICATS 2!

BESTIARY!

MERMAIDS!

SORCERERS!

DEMONS!

DOGTALES!

SEASERPENTS!

DINOSAURS!

LITTLE PEOPLE!

DRAGONS!

HORSES!

UNICORNS 2

INVADERS!

ANGELS!

DINOSAURS II

HACKERS

TIMEGATES

CLONES

NANOTECH

IMMORTALS

FICTION

STRANGERS

THE VISIBLE MAN (collection)

NIGHTMARE BLUE
 (with George Alec Effinger)

SLOW DANCING THROUGH TIME
 (with Jack Dann, Michael Swanwick,
 Susan Casper and Jack C. Haldeman II)

THE PEACEMAKER

GEODESIC DREAMS (collection)

NONFICTION

THE FICTION OF JAMES TIPTREE, JR.

THE YEAR'S BEST

SCIENCE FICTION

thirty-fifth annual collection

edited by **Gardner Dozois**

st. Martin's griffin ✻ New York

THE YEAR'S BEST SCIENCE FICTION THIRTY-FIFTH ANNUAL COLLECTION. Copyright © 2018 by Gardner Dozois. All rights reserved. Printed in the United States of America. For information, address St. Martin's Press, 175 Fifth Avenue, New York, N.Y. 10010.

www.stmartins.com

The Library of Congress Cataloging-in-Publication Data is available upon request.

ISBN 978-1-250-16462-9 (hardcover)
ISBN 978-1-250-16463-6 (trade paperback)
ISBN 978-1-250-16464-3 (ebook)

Our books may be purchased in bulk for promotional, educational, or business use. Please contact your local bookseller or the Macmillan Corporate and Premium Sales Department at 1-800-221-7945, extension 5442, or by email at MacmillanSpecialMarkets@macmillan.com.

First Edition: July 2018

10 9 8 7 6 5 4 3 2 1

contents

permissions

acknowledgments

The editor would like to thank the following people for their help and support: Jonathan Strahan, Sean Wallace, Neil Clarke, Gordon Van Gelder, C. C. Finlay, Andy Cox, John Joseph Adams, Ellen Datlow, Sheila Williams, Trevor Quachri, Nick Gevers, Peter Crowther, Bryan Thomas Schmidt, William Shaffer, Ian Whates, Paula Guran, Liza Trombi, Robert Wexler, Patrick Nielsen Hayden, Joseph Eschrich, Jonathan Oliver, Stephen Cass, Lynne M. Thomas, Gavin Grant, Kelly Link, Katherine Canfield, Ian Redman, Wendy S. Delmater, Beth Wodzinski, E. Catherine Tobler, Carl Rafala, Emily Hockaday, Edmund R. Schubert, Alma Alexander, Atena Andreads, Nick Wood, Joanne Merriam, Mike Allen, David Brin, Richard Thomas, Rich Horton, Mark R. Kelly, Tehani Wessely, Navah Wolfe, Lucus Law, Dominik Parisien, Aliette de Bodard, Robert Reed, Alastair Reynolds, Lavie Tidhar, Rich Larson, Bill Johnson, Carter Scholz, Ian McHugh, Eleanor Arnason, Katherine Canfield, Michael F. Flynn, R. S. Benedict, Kelly Robson, Indrapramit Das, Nancy Kress, Michael Swanwick, Greg Egan, James S. A. Corey, Naomi Kritzer, Maureen F. McHugh, Linda Nagata, Ray Nayler, Jessica Barber and Sara Saab, Jaine Fenn, Silvia Moreno-Garcia, Harry Turtledove, Bruce Sterling, Suzanne Palmer, Kelly Jennings, Jack Skillingstead and Burt Courier, Sean Mc-Mullen, Tobias S. Buckell, Vina Jie-Min Prasad, Alec Nevala-Lee, Madeline Ashby, Finbarr O'Reilly, Karl Schroeder, Kathleen Ann Goonan, James Van Pelt, Gregory Frost, Sean Wallace, Brenda Cooper, Maggie Clark, Martin L. Shoemaker, Joe Pitkin, David Hutchinson, Gregor Hartmann, Sam J. Miller, Gwyneth Jones, Sarah Pinsker, Yoon Ha Lee, Jack McDevitt, Damien Broderick, Eric Brown, Jim Burns, Vaughne Lee Hansen, Mark Watson, Sean Swanwick, Jamie Coyne, and special thanks to my own editor, Marc Resnick.

Thanks are also due to the late, lamented Charles N. Brown, and to all his staff, whose magazine *Locus* [Locus Publications, P.O. Box 13305, Oakland, CA 94661. $63 in the U.S. for a one-year subscription (twelve issues) via periodical mail; $76 for a one-year (twelve issues) via first-class credit card orders (510) 339-9198] was used as an invaluable reference source throughout the Summation; *Locus Online* (www.locusmag.com), edited by Mark R. Kelly, has also become a key reference source.

Like last year, 2017 was another relatively quiet year in the SF publishing world, once the reverberations from last year's restructuring of Penguin Random House, which had included mergers with Berkley, Putnam, and Dutton, had mostly settled down, although aftershocks and consequences will probably be felt for some time to come.

Penguin Random House phased out their Roc imprint, while Hachette axed Weinstein Books in the wake of the Harvey Weinstein scandal. Amanda Ridout resigned as CEO of Head of Zeus, replaced by Anthony Cheetham. Tim Hely Hutchinson retired as CEO of Hachette UK, replaced by David Shelley. Jane Friedman stepped down as board chair and executive publisher of Open Road Integrated Media. Emma Coode left her position as editorial director of Voyager. Navah Wolfe was promoted to senior editor at Saga Press. Jennifer Heddle was promoted to executive director at Disney/Lucasfilm Publishing. Brit Hvide was promoted to senior editor at Orbit. Sam Bradbury joined Hodder as an editor. Nancy Miller was promoted to associate publisher at Bloomsbury, and Mary Kate Castellani was promoted to executive editor at Bloomsbury Children's, with Hali Baumstein promoted to associate editor. Kaelyn Considine joined Parvus Press as an editor. Lucille Rettino joined Tom Doherty Associates as vice president of marketing and publicity. David Pomerico was promoted to executive director of publicity for Tor, Forge, Tor Teen, and Starscape.

The year 2017 was again fairly stable in the professional print magazine market; the magazines didn't register spectacular gains, but neither did they suffer the precipitous decline in subscriptions and circulation of some other years.

Asimov's Science Fiction had a strong year this year, their first as a bimonthly publication after years of publishing ten issues a year, publishing good work by Rich Larson, Ray Nayler, Harry Turtledove, Suzanne Palmer, Ian McHugh, R. Garcia y Robertson, Michael Swanwick, Kristine Kathryn Rusch, Carrie Vaughn, Tom Purdom, Damien Broderick, and others. As usual, their SF was considerably stronger than their fantasy, usually the reverse of *The Magazine of Fantasy & Science Fiction*. *Asimov's Science Fiction* registered a 4.2 percent gain in overall circulation, up to 18,043 copies. There were 7,627 print subscriptions and 8,155 digital subscriptions, for a total of 15,782, up from 2016's 15,269. Newsstand sales were up to 2,261 from 2016's 2,044. Sell-through rose to 39 percent, up from 2016's at 37 percent. Sheila Williams completed her fourteenth year as *Asimov's* editor.

Analog Science Fiction and Fact; also in its first year as a bimonthly magazine, had good work by Michael F. Flynn, Alec Nevala-Lee, Bill Johnson, Maggie Clark, Rich Larson, Joe Pitkin, James Van Pelt, and others. *Analog* registered a 2.7 percent loss in overall circulation, down to 18,278 from 2016's 18,800. There were 12,249 print subscriptions, and 6,029 digital subscriptions. Newsstand sales were down slightly to 2,711 from 2016's 2,773. Sell-through fell to 38 percent from 2016's 43 percent. Editor Trevor Quachri completed his fourth full year as editor, and is doing a good job of widening the definition of what's usually thought of as "an Analog story," and bringing new writers into the magazine.

It will be interesting to see what affect, if any, the switch to bimonthly format has next year on the sales figures for *Asimov's* and *Analog*.

The Magazine of Fantasy & Science Fiction had a stronger than usual year for science fiction, publishing good work by R. S. Benedict, Michael Swanwick, Samuel R. Delany, Matthew Hughes, Rachel Pollack, Kelly Jennings, Larry Niven, Robert Reed, Naomi Kritzer, and others. *F&SF* registered a 7.3 loss in overall circulation from 10,055 to 9,322. Subscriptions dropped slightly from 7,247 to 6,935, with 2,387 copies sold on the newsstands as compared to 2016's 2,808; sell-through was 25 percent. Since digital sales figures for *F&SF* are not available since they switched to Kindle subscriptions, there's no way to be certain what the magazine's overall circulation figures actually are. Charles Coleman Finlay completed his second full year as *F&SF* editor, having taken over from Gordon Van Gelder, who had edited the magazine for eighteen years, with the March/April 2015 issue. Van Gelder remains as the magazine's owner and publisher, as he has been since 2014. Finlay is doing a good job of getting good stories by new authors into the magazine, and seems to be especially strengthening the quality of the magazine's science fiction content.

Interzone is technically not a "professional magazine," by the definition of *the Science Fiction Writers of America* (SFWA), because of its low rates and circulation, but the literary quality of the work published there is so high that it would be ludicrous to omit it. *Interzone* had a weakish year in 2017, but still managed to publish good stuff by Sean McMullen, Malcom Devlin, Erica L. Satifka, T. R. Napper, Laura Mauro, and others. Exact circulation figures not available, but is guessed to be in the 2,000 copy range. TTA Press, *Interzone's* publisher, also publishes a straight horror or dark suspense magazine *Black Static*, which is beyond our purview here, but of a similar level of professional quality. *Interzone* and *Black Static* changed to a smaller trim size in 2011, but maintained their slick look, switching from the old 7 ¾"-by-10 ¾" saddle-stitched semigloss color cover sixty-four page format to a 6 ½"-by-9 ¼" perfect-bound glossy color cover ninety-six page format. The editor and publisher is Andy Cox.

If you'd like to see lots of good SF and fantasy published every year, the survival of these magazines is essential, and one important way that you can help them survive is by subscribing to them. It's never been easier to do so, something that these days can be done with just the click of a few buttons, nor has it ever before been possible to subscribe to the magazines in as many different formats, from the traditional print copy arriving by mail to downloads for your desktop or laptop available from places like Amazon (www.amazon.com), to versions you can read on your Kindle, Nook, or iPad. You can also now subscribe from overseas just as easily as you can from the United States, something formerly difficult to impossible.

So in hopes of making it easier for you to subscribe, I'm going to list both the internet sites where you can subscribe online and the street addresses where you can subscribe by mail for each magazine: *Asimov's* site is at www.asimovs.com, and subscribing online might be the easiest thing to do, and there's also a discounted rate for online subscriptions; its subscription address is *Asimov's Science Fiction*, Dell Magazines, 267 Broadway, Fourth Floor, New York, N.Y. 10007–2352—$34.97 for annual subscription in the U.S., $44.97 overseas. *Analog's* site is at www.analogsf .com; its subscription address is *Analog Science Fiction and Fact*, Dell Magazines, 267 Broadway, Fourth Floor, New York, N.Y. 10007–2352—$34.97 for annual subscription in the U.S., $44.97 overseas. *The Magazine of Fantasy & Science Fiction's* site is at www.sfsite.com/fsf; its subscription address is *The Magazine of Fantasy & Science Fiction*, Spilogale, Inc., P.O. Box 3447, Hoboken, N.J., 07030—annual subscription—$34.97 in the U.S., $44.97 overseas. *Interzone* and *Black Static* can be subscribed to online at www.ttapress.com/onlinestore1.html; the subscription address for both is TTA Press, 5 Martins Lane, Witcham, Ely, Cambs CB6 2LB, England, UK, 42.00 Pounds Sterling each for a twelve-issue subscription, or there is a reduced rate dual subscription offer of 78.00 Pounds Sterling for both magazines for twelve issues; make checks payable to "TTA Press."

Most of these magazines are also available in various electronic formats through the Kindle, the Nook, and other handheld readers.

With more and more of the print semiprozines departing to the digital realm, there isn't a lot left of either the print fiction semiprozine market or the print critical magazine market. (It's also getting a bit problematical to say which are print semiprozines and which are ezines, since some markets, like *Galaxy's Edge*, are offering both print versions and electronic versions of their issues at the same time. I'm tempted to just merge the surviving print fiction and critical magazines into the section covering online publication, but for now I'll keep it as a separate section.

The Canadian *On Spec*, the longest running of all the print fiction semiprozines, which is edited by a collective under general editor Diane L. Walton, again brought out three out of four scheduled issues; there have been rumors about them making the jump to digital format, but so far that hasn't happened. There was only one issue of *Lady Churchill's Rosebud Wristlet*, the long-running slipstream magazine edited by Kelly Link and Gavin Grant. *Space and Time Magazine* (whose future may be in doubt) managed two issues, and *Neo-opsis* managed two. There didn't seem to be any issues of Ireland's long-running *Albedo One* released this year. Australian semiprozines *Aurealis* and *Andromeda Spaceways* have departed the print realm for digital formats.

For general-interest print magazines about SF and fantasy, about the only one left is the venerable newszine *Locus: The Magazine of the Science Fiction and Fantasy Field*, a multiple Hugo winner, for decades an indispensable source of news, information, and reviews, now in its fifty-first year of publication, operating under the guidance of a staff of editors headed by Liza Groen Trombi, and including Kirsten Gong-Wong, Carolyn Cushman, Tim Pratt, Jonathan Strahan, Francesca Myman, Heather Shaw, and many others.

One of the few other remaining popular critical print magazines is newcomer *The Cascadia Subduction Zone: A Literary Quarterly* (www.thecz.com), a feminist magazine of reviews and critical essays, edited by Arrate Hidalgo, L. Timmel Duch-amp, Nisi Shawl, and Kath Wilham, which published three issues in 2017. Most of the other surviving print critical magazines are professional journals more aimed at academics than at the average reader, including the long-running British critical zine *Foundation*, *Science Fiction Studies*, *Extrapolation*, and *Vector*.

Subscription addresses are: **Locus: The Magazine of the Science Fiction and Fantasy Field**, Locus Publications, Inc., 1933 Davis Street, Suite 297, San Leandro, CA 94577, $76.00 for a one-year first-class subscription, twelve issues; *Foundation*, Science Fiction Foundation, Roger Robinson (SFF), 75 Rosslyn Avenue, Harold Wood, Essex RM3 ORG, UK, $37.00 for a three-issue subscription in the U.S.; **On Spec, The Canadian Magazine of the Fantastic**, P.O. Box 4727, Edmonton, AB, Canada T6E 5G6, for subscription information, go to website www.onspec.ca; **Neo-opsis Science Fiction Magazine**, 4129 Carey Rd., Victoria, BC, V8Z 4G5, $25.00 for a three-issue subscription; **Lady Churchill's Rosebud Wristlet**, Small Beer Press, 150 Pleasant Street, #306, Easthampton, MA 01027, $20.00 for four issues; **The Cascadia Subduc-tion Zone: A Literary Quarterly**, subscription and single issues online at www .thecsz.com, $16 annually for a print subscription, print single issues $5, electronic subscription—PDF format—$10 per year, electronic single issue $3, to order by check, make them payable to Aqueduct Press, P.O. Box 95787, Seattle, WA 9845–2787.

The world of online-only electronic magazines now rivals—and often surpasses—the traditional print market as a place to find good new fiction.

The electronic magazine *Clarkesworld* (www.clarkesworldmagazine.com), edited by Neil Clarke, had another very strong year, publishing first-rate work by Kelly Robson, Naomi Kritzer, Rich Larson, Jack Skillingstead and Burt Courtier, Jess Barber and Sara Saab, Vina Jie-Min Prasad, Finbarr O'Reilly, and others. They also host monthly podcasts of stories drawn from each issue. Clarkesworld has won three Hugo Awards as best semiprozine. In 2014, *Clarkesworld* co-editor Sean Wallace, along with Jack Fisher, launched a new online horror magazine, *The Dark Maga-zine* (www.thedarkmagazine.com). Neil Clarke has also launched a monthly reprint ezine, *Forever* (forever-magazine.com).

Lightspeed (www.lightspeedmagazine.com), edited by John Joseph Adams, had a somewhat weak year, but still managed to publish good work by Indrapramit Das, Mari Ness, Cadwell Turnbull, Pat Murphy, Susan Palwick, Lina Rather, Greg Kurzawa, and others. *Lightspeed* won back-to-back Hugo Awards as Best Semipro-zine in 2014 and 2015. Late in 2013, a new electronic companion horror magazine, *Nightmare* (www.nightmare-magazine.com), also edited by John Joseph Adams, was added to the *Lightspeed* stable.

Tor.com (www.tor.com), edited by Patrick Neilsen Hayden and Liz Gorinsky, with additional material purchased by Ellen Datlow, Ann VanderMeer, and others, published a mix of SF, fantasy, dark fantasy, soft horror, and more unclassifiable stuff this year, with good work by Greg Egan, Linda Nagata, Stephen Baxter, Allen M. Steele, Jo Walton, Julianna Baggott, Lavie Tidhar, Yoon Ha Lee, and others. They also launched a new program, Tor.com Publishing, which brought out many of the year's novellas in chapbook form.

An ezine devoted to "literary adventure fantasy," *Beneath Ceaseless Skies* (www.beneath-ceaseless-skies.com), edited by Scott H. Andrews, published good stuff by Richard Parks, Stephen Case, Carrie Vaughn, Sarah Saab, Tony Pi, M. Bennardo, Marissa Lingen, Rose Lemberg, Kameron Hurley, Jeremy Sim, and others.

Strange Horizons (www.strangehorizons.com), the oldest continually running electronic genre magazine on the internet, started in 2000. Niall Harrison stepped down as editor-in-chief, to be replaced by Jane Crowley and Kate Dollarhyde. There wasn't a lot of SF to be found in *Strange Horizons* this year, which seems to have swerved back to mostly slipstream, but they did publish interesting work by Ana Hurtado, Helena Bell, Iona Sharma, Su-Yee Lin, and others.

Newish magazine *Uncanny* (uncannymagazine.com), edited by Lynne M. Thomas and Michael Damian Thomas, which has won the best semiprozine Hugo two years in a row in 2016 and 2017, had entertaining stories by Naomi Kritzer, Sarah Pinsker, Sam J. Miller and Lara Elena Donnelly, Seanan McGuire, Vina Jie-Min Prasad, Sarah Monette, N. K. Jemisin, Fran Wilde, Tina Connelly, and others.

Galaxy's Edge (www.galaxysedge.com), edited by Mike Resnick, reached its fifth year of publication, and is still going strong; it's available in various downloadable formats, although a print edition is available from BN.com and Amazon.com for $5.99 per issue. They continued to publish entertaining original stuff this year, although the reprint stories here are still stronger than the original stories.

The quality of the fiction seemed to go up at *Apex Magazine* this year, (www.apex-magazine.com) which published good work by Rich Larson, Lavie Tidhar, Nisi Shawl, Tobias S. Buckell, S. B. Divya, Silvia Moreno-Garcia, Ken MacLeod, Nick Mamatas and Tim Pratt, and others. Jason Sizemore is the new editor, having taken over the position last year.

Abyss & Apex (www.abyssapexzine.com) ran interesting work by Rich Larson, James Van Pelt, Jon Rollins, Angus McIntyre. Jordan Taylor, and others, although little of it could be considered to be core science fictiton. Wendy S. Delmater, the former longtime editor, has returned to the helm, replacing Carmelo Rafala.

Kaleidotrope (www.kaleidotrope.net), edited by Fred Coppersmith, which started in 2006 as a print semiprozine but transitioned to digital in 2012, published interesting work by Cat Sparks, Octavia Cade, Ken Brady, and others.

Long-running sword and sorcery print magazine *Black Gate*, edited by John O'Neill, transitioned into an electronic magazine in September of 2012 and can be found at www.blackgate.com. They no longer regularly run new fiction, although they will be regularly refreshing their nonfiction content, essays, and reviews, and the occasional story will continue to appear.

Other ezines that published worthwhile, if not often memorable stuff, included *Ideomancer Speculative Fiction* (www.ideomancer.com), edited by Leah Bobet; *Orson Scott Card's Intergalactic Medicine Show* (www.intergalacticmedicineshow.com), now edited by Scott R. Roberts under the direction of Card himself; SF/fantasy ezine *Daily Science Fiction* (dailysciencefiction.com) edited by Michele-Lee Barasso and Jonathan Laden, which publishes one new SF or fantasy story *every single day* for the entire year; *Shimmer Magazine* (www.shimmezine.com), edited by E. Catherine Tobler, which leans heavily toward fantasy, and *GigaNotoSaurus* (giganotosaurus.org), edited by Rashida J. Smith, which publishes one story a month.

The World SF Blog (worldsf.wordpress.com), edited by Lavie Tidhar, was a good place to find science fiction by international authors, and also published news, links, round-table discussions, essays, and interviews related to "science fiction, fantasy, horror, and comics from around the world." The site is no longer being updated, but an extensive archive is still accessible there.

A similar site is *International Speculative Fiction* (http://internationalSF.wordpress .com), edited by Roberto Mendes.

Weird Fiction Review (weirdfictionreview.com), edited by Ann VanderMeer and Jeff VanderMeer, which occasionally publishes fiction, bills itself as "an ongoing exploration into all facets of the weird," including reviews, interviews, short essays, and comics.

Other newcomers include *Omenana Magazine of Africa's Speculative Fiction* (omenana.com), edited by Chinelo Onwualu and Chiagozie Fred Nwonwu; *Persistent Visions* (persistentvisionsmag.com), edited by Heather Shaw; *Shoreline of Infinity* (www.shorelineofinfinity.com), edited by Noel Chidwick; *Terraform* (motherboard .vice.com/terraform),edited by Claire Evans and Brian Merchant; and *Fiyah: Magazine of Black Speculative Fiction* (www.fiyahlitmag.com), edited by Justina Ireland.

Below this point, it becomes harder to find center-core SF, or even genre fantasy/ horror, with most magazines featuring slipstream or literary surrealism instead. Such sites include *Fireside Magazine* (firesidefiction.com), edited by Brian White; *Revolution SF* (www.revolutionsf.com); *Heliotrope* (www.heliotropemag.com); and *Interfictions Online* (interfictions.com/), executive editor Delila Sherman, fiction editors Christopher Barzak and Meghan McCarron.

Original fiction is not the only thing available to be read on the internet, though. Lots of good *reprint* SF and fantasy can be found there as well, sites where you can access formerly published stories for free. Such sites include *Strange Horizons, Tor .com, Clarkesworld, Lightspeed, Subterranean, Abyss & Apex, Beyond Ceaseless Skies, Apex Magazine*; most of the sites that are associated with existent print magazines, such as *Asimov's, Analog*, and *The Magazine of Fantasy & Science Fiction*, make previously published fiction and nonfiction available for access on their sites as well, and also regularly run teaser excerpts from stories coming up in forthcoming issues. Hundreds of out-of-print titles, both genre and mainstream, are also available for free download from *Project Gutenberg* (www.gutenberg.org), and a large selection of novels, collections, and anthologies, can either be bought or be accessed for free, to be either downloaded or read on-screen, at the *Baen Free Library* (www.baen.com/library). Sites such as *Infinity Plus* (www.infinityplus.co.uk) and *The Infinite Matrix* (www.infinitematrix.net) may have died as active sites, but their extensive archives of previously published material are still accessible (an extensive line of *Infinity Plus* Books can also be ordered from the *Infinity Plus* site).

But beyond the search for good stories to read, there are plenty of other reasons for SF/fantasy fans to go on the internet. There are many general genre-related sites of interest to be found, most of which publish reviews of books as well as of movies and TV shows, sometimes comics or computer games or anime, many of which also feature interviews, critical articles, and genre-oriented news of various kinds. The best such site is *Locus Online* (www.locusmag.com), the online version of the newsmagazine *Locus*, where you can access an incredible amount of information—including book reviews, critical lists, obituary lists, links to reviews and essays appearing outside the genre, and links to extensive database archives such as the Locus Index to Science Fiction and the Locus Index to Science Fiction Awards. The previously mentioned *Tor.com* is also one of the most eclectic genre-oriented sites on the internet, a website that, in addition to its fiction, regularly publishes articles, comics, graphics, blog entries, print and media reviews, book "rereads" and episode-by-episode "rewatches" of television shows, as well as commentary on all the above. The long-running and eclectic *The New York Review of Science Fiction* has ceased print publication, but can be purchased in PDF, epub, mobi formats, and POD editions through Weightless Press (weightlessbooks.com; see also www.nyrsf.com for information). Other major general-interest sites include *Io9* (www.io9.com), *SF Site* (www.sfsite.com), although it's no longer being regularly updated, *SFRevu* (www.sfsite.com/sfrevu), *SFCrowsnest* (www.sfcrowsnest.com), *SFScope* (www.sfscope.com), *Green Man Review* (greenmanreview.com), *The Agony Column* (trashotron.com/agony), *SFFWorld* (www.sffworld.com), *SFReader* (forums.sfreader.com), and *Pat's Fantasy Hotlist* (www.fantasyhotlist.blogspot.com). A great research site, invaluable if you want bibliographic information about SF and fantasy writers, is *Fantastic Fiction* (www.fantasticfiction.co.uk). Another fantastic research site is the searchable online update of the Hugo-winning *The Encyclopedia of Science Fiction* (www.sf-encyclopedia.com), where you can access almost four million words of information about SF writers, books, magazines, and genre themes; there is also *The Encyclopedia of Fantasy*, with similar articles about fantasy and fantasy writers. Reviews of short fiction as opposed to novels are very hard to find anywhere, with the exception of *Locus* and *Locus Online*, but you can find reviews of both current and past short fiction at *Best SF* (www.bestsf.net), as well as at pioneering short-fiction review site *Tangent Online* (www.tangentonline.com).

Other sites of general interest include: *Ansible* (news.ansible.co.uk/Ansible), the online version of multiple Hugo-winner David Langford's long-running fanzine *Ansible*; *Book View Café* (www.bookviewcafe.com) is a "consortium of over twenty professional authors," including Vonda N. McIntyre, Laura Ann Gilman, Sarah Zittel, Brenda Clough, and others, who have created a website where work by them—mostly reprints, and some novel excerpts—is made available for free.

Sites where podcasts and SF-oriented radio plays can be accessed have also proliferated in recent years: at *Audible* (www.audible.com), *Escape Pod* (www.escapepod.org, podcasting mostly SF), *SF Squeecast* (sfsqueecast.com/), *The Coode Street Podcast* (jonathanstrahan.podbean.com/), *The Drabblecast* (www.drabblecast.org), *StarShipSofa* (www.starshipsofa.com), *Far Fetched Fables* (www.farfetchedfables.com), new companion to *StarShipSofa*, concentrating on fantasy, *SF Signal Podcast* (www.sfsignal.com), *Pseudopod* (www.pseudopod.org, podcasting mostly fantasy), *Podcastle* (www.podcastle.org), podcasting mostly fantasy, and *Galactic Suburbia* (galacticsuburbia.podbean.com). *Clarkesworld* routinely offers podcasts of stories from the ezine, and *The Agony Column* (agonycolumn.com) also hosts a weekly podcast. There's also a site that podcasts nonfiction interviews and reviews, *Dragon Page Cover to Cover* (www.dragonpage.com).

Last year I mentioned that most of the stories I was seeing were of short-story length, with few long novelettes or novellas. Although perhaps most of this year's stories were still of short-story length, this year saw a dramatic resurgence of novellas. By one count, there were more than eighty novellas published in the SF/fantasy/horror genres in 2017. Most of these were published as stand-alone chapbooks, and the ambitious new program from Tor.com Publishing can account for a lot of these chapbooks; there were also many released by a wide array of small presses, as Kickstarter projects, and in electronic formats. Industry stalwarts such as *Asimov's* and *Analog* and *F&SF* continued to publish novellas as well, as they've always done, and even electronic magazines such as *Clarkesworld*, which had formerly had strict word limits, seem to be loosening up and increasing the length of stories that they're willing to accept.

The odd result of this is that you have a lot of novellas on one end of the scale and a lot of short stories on the opposite end, with fewer novelettes in between. Perhaps, like the midlist in book publishing, novelettes are becoming marginalized. It'll be interesting to see where this goes in the future.

There were a lot of original anthologies published in 2017. The SF anthologies divided up into two rough groups, the space opera/military SF anthologies (with the balance between the two forms varying from book to book), and the futurology anthologies, many of them with corporate or government sponsors, leading Jonathan Strahan to dub them "think-tank fiction." The strongest original SF anthology of the year was Jonathan Strahan's *Infinity Wars* (Solaris), ostensibly a collection of military SF, although in some ways it's actually a kind of stealth antiwar anthology, with character after character wrestling with doubts about the morality of the war and the orders they've been given and whether or not they should comply with them and sicke of the slaughter involved, particularly of civilians. The best stories here are Indrapramit Das's "The Moon is Not a Battlefield" and Nancy Kress's "Dear Sarah," although there are also strong stories by Eleanor Arnason, Peter Watts, Rich Larson, Carrie Vaughn, An Owomoyela, Elizabeth Bear, David D. Levine, E. J. Swift, and others.

In this grouping, the next two strongest anthologies are probably Nick Gever's *Extrasolar—Postscripts 38* (PS Publishing) and John Joseph Adams's *Cosmic Powers: The Saga Anthology of Far-Away Galaxies* (Saga). *Extrasolar's* premise is that its writers are going to take us on a "tour of the stars in our galactic neighborhood," drawing on the knowledge about exotic stars and extrasolar planets derived from more than twenty years of observation by the Kepler telescope and other space telescopes, knowledge that paints a very different picture of what a solar system can be like than that which was gained by observing our own—and which has thrown new fuel on the fire of the debate about the Fermi paradox. As such, it fits a bit uneasily into the space opera/military SF grouping, although stories here by Alastair Reynolds, Aliette de Bodard, and others could easily be considered to be military SF. Best stories here, in addition to the above-mentioned Reynolds and de Bodard stories, are "Canoe," by Nancy Kress and "The Residue of Fire," by Robert Reed, although *Extrasolar* also featured strong work from Kathleen Ann Goonan, Jack McDevitt, Gregory Benford, Paul Di Filippo, Terry Dowling, Ian Watson, Lavie Tidhar, Ian R. MacLeod, and others. *Cosmic Powers* is much more of a space opera anthology, unsurprising in an anthology where the editor asked for stories in the spirit of the Marvel movie *Guardians of the Galaxy*—and that's pretty much exactly what he got. The best stories here are *"Zen and the Art of Starship Maintenance,"* by Tobias S. Buckell, "The Dragon that Flew Out of the Sun," by Aliette de Bodard, "Golden Ring," by Karl Schroeder, "The Chameleon's Gloves," by Yoon Ha Lee, and "Diamond and the World Breaker," by Linda Nagata, there's also strong work here by Seanan McGuire, Charlie Jane Anders, and Kameron Hurley, as well as reprints by Vylar Kaftan, Caroline M. Yoachim, and others. Bryan Thomas Schmidt's *Infinite Stars: The Definitive Anthology of Space Opera and Military SF* (Titan) is the anthology in this grouping the most oriented toward military SF. A mixed original/reprint anthology, the best of the original stories here are Alastair Reynolds's "Revolution Space: Night Passage" and Linda Nagata's "Red: Region Five," but there's also good work here by Charles E. Gannon, David Weber, Jody Lynn Nye, David Drake, Jack Campbell, and Elizabeth Moon. Adding substantially to the value of *Infinite Stars* is a strong list of reprint stories by Poul Anderson, Cordwainer Smith, Leigh Brackett and Edmond Hamilton, Robert Silverberg, Lois McMaster Bujold, Larry Niven and Jerry Pournelle, Nnedi Okorafor, A. C. Crispin, and Anne McCaffrey,

Of the futurology/think tank anthologies (collections of near-future futurology stories dealing with technological change, often sponsored by writers assembled and commissioned for the task by some major corporation), the strongest was *Visions, Ventures, Escape Velocities: A Collection of Space Futures* (Arizona State University), edited by Ed Finn and Joey Eschrich, a mixed fiction/nonfiction anthology about space futures from Arizona State University, sponsored by the National Aeronautics and Space Administration, which featured strong stories by Carter Scholz, Madeline Ashby, Eileen Gunn, Vandana Singh, Ramez Naam, and Steven Barnes. Also strong is another mixed fiction/nonfiction anthology, *Chasing Shadows: Visions of Our Coming Transparent World* (Tor), edited by David Brin and Stephen W. Potts. Best of the original stories here are "Elephant on Table," by Bruce Sterling, "First Presentation," by Aliette de Bodard, and "Eminence," by Karl Schroeder, but the anthology also features good work by Nancy Fulda, Jack Skillingstead, Gregory Benford, Cat Rambo, and Brenda Cooper. Good reprints in *Chasing Shadows* include work by Damon Knight, Robert Silverberg, Kathleen Ann Goonan, Vernor Vinge, William Gibson, Neal Stephenson, Brin himself, and others. Another fairly strong futurology anthology is *Sunvault: Stories of Solarpunk and Eco-Speculation* (Upper Rubber Boot), edited by Phoebe Wagner and Brontë Christopher Wieland. *Sunvault* features strong stories by Lavie Tidhar, A. C. Wise, Nisi Shawl, Jess Barber, and Tyler Young, as well as reprints by Daniel José Older and Nick Wood.

Many of the year's other think tank anthologies don't have physical copies available, but are available online, including *A Flight to the Future* (seat 14c.com), edited by Kathryn Cramer, sponsored by an X Prize and by the Japanese airline company Ana; *Wired: The Fiction Issue—Tales from an Uncertain Future* (www.wired.com) Scott Dadich, editor in chief: *Stories in the Stratosphere* (Arizona State University), edited by Michael G. Bennett, Joey Eschrich, and Ed Finn; and *Megatech*, sponsored by *The Economist* magazine, edited by Daniel Franklin. A subset of futurology anthologies is dystopian anthologies, and there were two this year, *Global Dystopias*

(MIT Press), a special section of the *Boston Review* newspaper, edited by Junot Díaz, featuring strong if rather grim and brutal work by Charlie Jane Anders, Tananarive Due, and Maureen F. McHugh, and *Welcome to Dystopia* (O/R Books), edited by Gordon Van Gelder, a *very* near future anthology (with some stories set next year and few more than ten years on, concentrating mostly on negative results of President Trump's policies), featuring worthwhile work by Geoff Ryman, Janis Ian, Ruth Nestvold, Marguerite Reed, Elizabeth Bourne, Paul Witcover, and others.

A bit harder to categorize are some of the year's other anthologies. *Children of a Different Sky* (Kos Books), edited by Alma Alexander, is a mixed SF and fantasy anthology about refugees and immigrants, with part of the profits being donated to various charitable institutions that help refugees; there is good work here by Aliette de Bodard, Jacey Bedford, Brenda Cooper, Seanan McGuire, and others. *Where the Stars Rise: Asian Science Fiction and Fantasy* (Laska Media Group), edited by Lucas K. Law and Derwin Mak, is a mixed SF/fantasy anthology featuring good stuff by S. B. Divya, Priya Sridhar, Tony Pi, Jeremy Szal, Amanda Sun, and others. *Shadows & Reflections: Stories from the Worlds of Roger Zelazny* (Positronic Publications), edited by Trent Zelazny and Warren Lapine, is a tribute anthology that offers other writers the chance to play with Roger Zelazny's worlds and characters; good stuff here by Steven Brust, Gerald Hausman, Lawrence Watt-Evans, Sharianne Lewitt, and others.

There were only a few original fantasy anthologies this year. One of the most acclaimed was *The Djinn Falls in Love and Other Stories* (Solaris), edited by Mahvesh Murad and Jared Shurin, which featured strong work by Helene Wecker, K. J. Parker, E. J. Swift, Nnedi Okorafor, Catherine Faris King, J. Y. Yang, Maria Dahvana Headley, and others. Noted without comment is *The Book of Swords* (Random House), edited by Gardner Dozois. Although there are streaks of darkness in it, the subject matter of *Mad Hatters and March Hares: All-new Stories from the World of Lewis Carroll's* Alice in Wonderland (Tor), edited by Ellen Datlow, tends to make the stories more whimsical than horrific, so I'm going to list it here in fantasy rather than horror; there are good stories here by Andy Duncan, Ysabeau S. Wilce, Richard Bowes, Seanan McGuire, Jane Yolen, Jeffrey Ford, Delia Sherman, and others.

I don't pay close attention to the horror field, considering it out of my purview, but the original horror anthologies that got the most attention seemed to be *Black Feathers: Dark Avian Tales: An Anthology* (Pegasus), edited by Ellen Datlow, and *Haunted Nights* (Anchor), edited by Ellen Datlow and Lisa Morton.

There were two shared-world anthologies this year, *Missisipi Roll: A Wild Cards Novel* (Tor), edited by George R. R. Martin, and *Treemontaine* (Saga), edited by Ellen Kushner.

L. Ron Hubbard Presents Writers of the Future Volume 33 (Galaxy), edited by David Farland, is the most recent in a long-running series featuring novice work by beginning writers, some of whom may later turn out to be important talents.

There were also a number of anthologies from Fiction River (www.fictionriver .com), which in 2013 launched a continuing series of original SF, fantasy, and mystery anthologies, with Kristine Kathryn Rusch and Dean Wesley Smith as overall series editors, and individual editions edited by various hands. This year, they published *Pulse Pounders: Adrenaline* (WMG), edited by Kevin J. Anderson; *No Humans*

Allowed (WMG), edited by John Helfers; *Feel the Fear* (WMG), edited by Mark Leslie; *Tavern Tales* (WMG), edited by Kerrie L. Hughes; *Editor's Choice* (WMG), edited by Mark Leslie; and *Superpowers* (WMG), edited by Rebecca Moesta. These can be purchased in Kindle versions from Amazon and other online vendors, or from the publisher at wmgpublishinginc.com.

These days to find up-to-date contact information for almost any publisher, however small, you can just Google it. Nevertheless, as a courtesy, I'm going to reproduce here the addresses I have for small presses that may have been mentioned in the various sections of the Summation. If any of them are out-of-date, quite possible, just Google the publisher.

Addresses: **PS Publishing**, Grosvener House, 1 New Road, Hornsea, West Yorkshire, HU18 1PG, England, UK, www.pspublishing.co.uk; **Golden Gryphon Press**, 3002 Perkins Road, Urbana, IL 61802, www.goldengryphon.com ; **NESFA Press**, P.O. Box 809, Framingham, MA 01701–0809, www.nesfa.org; **Subterranean Press**, P.O. Box 190106, Burton, MI 48519, www.subterraneanpress.com; **Old Earth Books**, P.O. Box 19951, Baltimore, MD 21211–0951, www.oldearthbooks.com; **Tachyon Press**, 1459 18th St. #139, San Francisco, CA 94107, www.tachyonpublications.com; **Night Shade Books**, 1470 NW Saltzman Road, Portland, OR 97229, www.nightshadebooks.com; **Five Star Books**, 295 Kennedy Memorial Drive, Waterville, ME 04901, www.galegroup.com/fivestar; **NewCon Press**, via www.newconpress.com; **Small Beer Press**, 176 Prospect Ave., Northampton, MA 01060, www.smallbeerpress.com; **Locus Press**, P.O. Box 13305, Oakland, CA 94661; **Crescent Books**, Mercat Press Ltd., 10 Coates Crescent, Edinburgh, Scotland EH3 7AL, www.crescentfiction.com; **Wildside Press/ Borgo Press**, P.O. Box 301, Holicong, PA 18928–0301, or go to www.wildsidepress.com for pricing and ordering; **Edge Science Fiction and Fantasy Publishing, Inc. and Tesseract Books, Ltd.**, P.O. Box 1714, Calgary, Alberta, T2P 2L7, Canada, www.edgewebsite.com; **Aqueduct Press**, P.O. Box 95787, Seattle, WA 98145–2787, www.aqueductpress.com; **Phobos Books**, 200 Park Avenue South, New York, NY 10003, www.phobosweb.com; **Fairwood Press**, 5203 Quincy Ave. SE, Auburn, WA 98092, www.fairwoodpress.com; **BenBella Books**, 6440 N. Central Expressway, Suite 508, Dallas, TX 75206, www.benbellabooks.com; **Darkside Press**, 13320 27th Ave. NE, Seattle, WA 98125, www.darksidepress.com; **Haffner Press**, 5005 Crooks Rd., Suite 35, Royal Oak, MI 48073–1239, www.haffnerpress.com; **North Atlantic Press**, P.O. Box 12327, Berkeley, CA, 94701; **Prime Books**, P.O. Box 36503, Canton, OH, 44735, www.primebooks.net; **Fairwood Press**, 5203 Quincy Ave SE, Auburn, WA 98092, www.fairwoodpress.com; **MonkeyBrain Books**, 11204 Crossland Drive, Austin, TX 78726, www.monkeybrainbooks.com; **Wesleyan University Press**, University Press of New England, Order Dept., 37 Lafayette St., Lebanon NH 03766-1405, www.wesleyan.edu/wespress; **Agog! Press**, P.O. Box U302, University of Wollongong, NSW 2522, Australia, www.uow.ed.au/~rhood/agogpress; **Wheatland Press**, via www.wheatlandpress.com; **MirrorDanse Books**, P.O. Box 3542, Parramatta NSW 2124 Australia, www.tabula-rasa.info/MirrorDanse; **Arsenal Pulp Press**, 103–1014 Homer Street, Vancouver, BC, Canada V6B 2W9, www.arsenalpress.com; **DreamHaven Books**, 912 W. Lake Street,

Minneapolis, MN 55408; **Elder Signs Press/Dimensions Books**, order through www.dimensionsbooks.com; **Chaosium**, via www.chaosium.com; **Spyre Books**, P.O. Box 3005, Radford, VA 24143; **SCIFI, Inc.**, P.O. Box 8442, Van Nuys, CA 91409–8442; **Omnidawn Publishing**, order through www.omnidawn.com; **CSFG**, Canberra Speculative Fiction Guild, via www.csfg.org.au/publishing/anthologies /the_outcast; **Hadley Rille Books**, via www.hadleyrillebooks.com; **Suddenly Press**, via suddenlypress@yahoo.com; **Sandstone Press**, P.O. Box 5725, One High St., Dingwall, Ross-shire, IV15 9WJ; **Tropism Press**, via www.tropismpress.com; **SF Poetry Association/Dark Regions Press**, via www.sfpoetry.com, checks to Helena Bell, SFPA Treasurer, 1225 West Freeman St., Apt. 12, Carbondale, IL 62401; **DH Press**, via diamondbookdistributors.com; **Kurodahan Press**, via website www .kurodahan.com; **Ramble House**, 443 Gladstone Blvd., Shreveport, LA 71104; **Interstitial Arts Foundation**, via www.interstitialarts.org; **Raw Dog Screaming**, via www.rawdogscreaming.com; **Three Legged Fox Books**, 98 Hythe Road, Brighton, BN1 6JS, UK; **Norilana Books**, via www.norilana.com; **coeur de lion**, via coeurdelion.com.au; **PARSECink**, via www.parsecink.org; **Robert J. Sawyer Books**, via wwww.sfwriter.com/rjsbooks.htm; **Candlewick**, via www.candlewick .com; **Zubaan**, via www.zubaanbooks.com; **Utter Tower**, via www.threeleggedfox .co.uk; **Spilt Milk Press**, via www.electricvelocipede.com; **Paper Golem**, via www.papergolem.com; **Galaxy Press**, via www.galaxypress.com; **Twelfth Planet Press**, via www.twelfhplanetpress.com; **Five Senses Press**, via www.sensefive.com; **Elastic Press**, via www.elasticpress.com; **Lethe Press**, via www.lethepressbooks .com; **Two Cranes Press**, via www.twocranespress.com; **Wordcraft of Oregon**, via www.wordcraftoforegon.com; **Down East**, via www.downeast.com; **ISFiC Press**, 456 Douglas Ave., Elgin, IL 60120 or www.isficpress.com.

According to the newsmagazine *Locus*, there were 2,694 books "of interest to the SF field" published in 2017, down 6 percent from 2,858 titles in 2016. New titles were down 7 percent to 1,820 from 2016's 1,957, while reprints dropped 3 percent to 874 titles from 2016's 910. Hardcovers dropped by 5 percent to 883 titles from 2016's record high of 856. Trade paperbacks dropped to 1,433 titles, down 7 percent from 2016's 1,539. Mass-market paperbacks, the format facing the most competition from ebooks, continued to drop for the ninth year in a row, down 2 percent to 378 titles from 2016's 385. The number of new SF novels was down 7 percent to 396 titles from 2016's 425 titles. The number of new fantasy novels was down 6 percent to 694 titles from 2016's 737, which climbed up 8 percent from 2015's 682 titles, with 246 of those titles being YA fantasy novels. Horror novels were down 10 percent to 154 from 2016's 171 titles. Paranormal romances rose to 122 titles from 2016's 107, still down considerably from 2011's 416 titles at the height of the paranormal romance boom.

It's legitimate to say that 2017 saw a drop across all novel categories—but those drops were minor. Yet 2,694 books "of interest to the SF field" is still an enormous number of books, probably more than some small-town libraries contain of books in general. Even if you consider only the 396 new SF titles, that's still a lot of books, more than 2009's total of 232 titles, and considerably larger than the total number of

SF novels published in prior decades—probably more than most people are going to have time to read (or the desire to read, either). And these totals don't count many ebooks, media tie-in novels, gaming novels, novelizations of genre movies, print-on-demand books, or self-published novels—all of which would swell the overall total by hundreds if counted.

As usual, busy with all the reading I have to do at shorter lengths, I didn't have time to read many novels myself this year, so I'll limit myself to mentioning those novels that received a lot of attention and acclaim in 2017.

Luna: Wolf Moon, by Ian McDonald (Tor); *Austral*, by Paul McAuley (Gollancz); *New York 2140*, by Kim Stanley Robinson (Orbit); *The House of Binding Thorns*, by Aliette de Bodard (Ace); *The Moon and the Other*, by John Kessel (Saga); *Tomorrow's Kin*, by Nancy Kress (Tor); *Persepolis Rising* (Orbit), by James S. A. Corey; *Convergence*, by C. J. Cherryh (DAW); *Ka: Dar Oakley in the Ruin of Ymr* (Saga), by John Crowley; *The Corporation Wars: Emergence* (Orbit), by Ken MacLeod; *Guomon* (Heinemann), by Nick Harkaway; *The Wrong Stars* (Angry Robot), by Tim Pratt; *The Stone in the Skull*, by Elizabeth Bear (Tor); *Akata Warrior*, by Nndi Okorafor (Viking); *Tool of War*, by Paolo Bacigalupi (Little, Brown); *The Real-Town Murders*, by Adam Roberts (Gollancz); *Provenance*, by Ann Leckie (Orbit); *Quillifer*, by Walter Jon Williams (Saga); *The Stone Sky*, by N. K. Jemisin (Orbit); *Raven Stratagem*, by Yoon Ha Lee (Solaris); *The Uploaded*, by Ferrett Steinmetz (Angry Robot); *Spoonbenders*, by Daryl Gregory (Knopf); *Bannerless*, by Carrie Vaughn (John Joseph Adams); *The Masacre of Mankind*, by Stephen Baxter (Gollancz); *The Man in the Tree*, by Sage Walker (Tor); *The Collapsing Empire*, by John Scalzi (Tor); *Cold Welcome*, by Elizabeth Moon (Del Rey); *Assassin's Fate*, by Robin Hobb (Del Ray); *Walkaway*, by Cory Doctorow (Tor); and *Empire Games* (Tor), by Charles Stross.

It's worth noting that in spite of decades of fretting about how fantasy is going to drive all SF from the bookshelves, in the list above the McDonald, the McAuley, the Kessel, the Robinson, the Cherryh, the Corey, the Leckie, the Yoon Ha Lee, the Scalzi, the Baxter, and many others are pure-quill center-core SF.

For a long time, small presses published mostly short-story collections, but in recent years they've begun publishing novels as well. Novels by well-known authors published by small presses this year included: *Mother Go*, by James Patrick Kelly (Audible); *The River Bank*, by Kij Johnson (Small Beer Press); *Infinity Engine*, by Neal Asher (Night Shade); *Fire*, by Elizabeth Hand (PM Press); *Upon This Rock: Book 1—First Contact*, by David Marusek (A Stack of Firewood Press); *The Last Good Man*, by Linda Nagata (Mythic Island Press); *In Evil Times*, by Melinda Snodgrass (Titan); and *The Rift* (Titan) by Nina Allan.

The year's first novels included: *The Art of Starving*, by Sam J. Miller (HarperTeen), *Autonomous*, by Annalee Newitz (Tor), *The Strange Case of the Alchemist's Daughter*, by Theodora Goss (Saga), *Lotus Blue*, by Cat Sparks (Talos), *Tropic of Kansas*, by Christopher Brown (Harper Voyager), *Amatka*, by Karin Tidbeck (Vintage), *The City of Brass*, by S. A. Chakraborty (Harper Voyager), *Amberlough*, by Lara Elena Donnelly (Tor), *Hunger Makes the Wolf*, by Alex Wells (Angry Robot), *Blackwing*, by Ed McDonald (Gollancz), *Wintersong*, by S. Jae-Jones (Thomas Dunne Books), *Found Audio*, by N. J Cambell (Two Dollar Radio), *Aberrant*, by Marek Sindelka and translated by Nathan Fields (Twisted Spoon), *Weave a Circle*

Round: A Novel, by Kari Maaren (Tor), *The Tiger's Daughter*, by K. Arsenault Rivera (Tor), *An Unkindness of Ghosts*, by Rivers Solomon (Akashic), *All Our Wrong Todays*, by Elan Mastai (Dutton), *An Excess Male*, by Maggie Shen King (Harper Voyager), *Ghost Garages*, by Erin M. Hartshorn (Eimarra), *Strange Practice*, by Vivian Shaw (Orbit), *The Bear and the Nightingale*, by Katherine Arden (Del Rey), *The Prey of Gods*, by Nicky Drayden (Harper Voyager), *The Guns Above*, by Robyn Bennis (Tor), *An Alchemy of Masques and Mirrors*, by Curtis Craddock (Tor), *Knucklebones*, by Marni Scofidio (PS Publishing), *Starfire: A Red Peace*, by Spencer Ellsworth (Tor), *The Mercy of the Tide*, by Keith Rosson (Meerkat), *The Space Between the Stars*, by Anne Corlett (Berkley), *Three Years with the Rat: A Novel*, by Jay Hosking (Thomas Dunne Books), and *Witchy Eye*, by D. J. Butler (Baen).

None of these seemed to draw any large amount of attention.

The few novel omnibuses available this year included: *The Hainish Novels and Stories* (Library of America), by Ursula K. Le Guin; *The Dosadi Experiment and The Eyes of Heisenberg* (Tor), by Frank Herbert; and *Armageddon—2419 A.D and The Airlords of Han* (Dover), by Philip Francis Nowlan.

Novel omnibuses are also frequently made available through the Science Fiction Book Club.

Not even counting print on demand books and the availability of out-of-print books as ebooks or as electronic downloads from internet sources, a lot of long out-of-print stuff has come back into print in the last couple of years in commercial trade editions. Here's some out-of-print titles that came back into print this year, although producing a definitive list of reissued novels is probably impossible.

Gollancz reissued *Neuromancer*, *Count Zero*, and *Mona Lisa Overdrive*, all by William Gibson; Tor reissued *Inferno*, by Larry Niven and Jerry Pournelle, *From the Two Rivers: The Eye of the World, Part One*, by Robert Jordan, *Old Man's War*, by John Scalzi, *Whiteout*, by Sage Walker, *Icehenge*, by Kim Stanley Robinson, and *The Age of Wonders: Exploring the World of Science Fiction*, by David G. Hartwell; Penguin Classics reissued *Ice*, by Anna Kavan; Baen reissued *None But Man*, by Gordon R. Dickson, *Wolfling*, by Gordon R. Dickson, *Honor Among Enemies*, by David Weber, and *Borders of Infinity*, by Lois McMaster Bujold; DAW reissued *The Storm Lord*, *Anackire*, *The White Serpent*, *Night's Sorceries*, *Redder than Blood*, *Delirium's Mistress*, and *Delusion's Master*, all by Tanith Lee; Valancourt Books reissued *One*, by David Karp; Harper Classics reissued *The Graveyard Book*, by Neil Gaiman; Dover reissued *The Ant-Men*, by Eric North, *The Mindwarpers*, by Eric Frank Russell, *Eclipse*, by John Shirley, *The Ghost Pirates*, by William Hope Hodgson, *Worlds of the Imperium*, by Keith Laumer, and *In the Drift*, by Michael Swanwick; Fairwood Press reissued *Transfigurations*, by Michael Bishop; Angry Robot reissued *Infernal Devices*, *Fiendish Schemes*, and released *Grim Expectations*, all by K. W. Jeter; Open Road reissued *Bring the Jubilee*, by Ward Moore; Pegasus reissued *Rosemary's Baby*, by Ira Levin; Chicago Review Press reissued *Monday Starts on Saturday*, by Arkady Strugatsky and Boris Strugatsky; CreateSpace reissued *The Star*

Rover, by Jack London; Simon & Schuster reissued *Gloriana: Or, the Unfulfill'd Queen,* by Michael Moorcock and *Something Wicked This Way Comes,* by Ray Bradbury; and Tachyon reissued *The Forgotten Beasts of Eld,* by Patricia A. McKillip.

Many authors are now reissuing their old backtitles as ebooks, either through a publisher or all by themselves, so many that it's impossible to keep track of them all here. Before you conclude that something from an author's backlist is unavailable, though, check with the Kindle and Nook stores, and with other online vendors.

It was a weaker year in 2017 for short-story collections than 2016 had been, although there was still some good stuff.

The year's best collections included: *Cat Pictures Please and Other Stories* (Fairwood), by Naomi Kritzer; *Lost Among the Stars* (WordFire), by Paul Di Filippo; *Telling the Map: Stories* (Small Beer), by Christopher Rowe; *Wicked Wonders* (Tachyon), by Ellen Klages; *Norse Mythology* (Norton), by Neil Gaiman; *Dear Sweet Filthy World* (Subterranean), by Caitlin R. Kiernan; *Down and Out in Purgatory* (Baen), by Tim Powers; *Up the Rainbow: The Complete Short Fiction of Susan Casper* (Fantastic Books); *Concentration* (PS Publishing), by Jack Dann; and *Six Months, Three Days, Five Others* (Tor.com Publishing), by Charlie Jane Anders.

Also good were: *Totalitopia* (PM Press), by John Crowley; *Fire* (PM Press), by Elizabeth Hand; *The Overneath* (Tachyon), by Peter S. Beagle; *The Unorthodox Dr. Draper and Other Stories* (Subterranean), by William Browning Spencer; *Emerald Circus* (Tachyon), by Jane Yolen; *The Refrigerator Monologues* (Saga), by Catherynne M. Valente; and *Tender: Stories* (Small Beer), by Sofia Samatar.

Career-spanning retrospective collections this year included: *The Man with the Speckled Eyes* (Centipede), by R. A. Lafferty; *Tanith By Choice* (NewCon Publishing), by Tanith Lee; *The Best of Bova, Volume III* (Baen), by Ben Bova; *The Thing in the Stone and Other Stories* (Open Road), by Clifford D. Simak; *The Shipshape Miracle and Other Stories* (Open Road), by Clifford D. Simak; *Dusty Zebra and Other Stories* (Open Road), by Clifford D. Simak; *The Hole in the Moon and Other Tales* (Dover), by Margaret St. Clair; *The Horror on the Links: The Complete Tales of Jules de Grandin, Volume One* (Night Shade), edited by Seabury Quinn; *The Devil's Rosary: The Complete Tales of Jules de Grandin, Volume Two* (Night Shade), edited by George A. Vanderburgh; *The Boats of the "Glen Carrig" and Other Nautical Adventures* (Night Shade), by William Hope Hodgson; *The Ghost Pirates* (Dover), by William Hope Hodgson; *The Best of Richard Matheson* (Penguin Classics), edited by Victor LaValle; *The Last Hieroglyph: The Collected Fantasies of Clark Ashton Smith, Volume 5* (Night Shade); *Philip K. Dick's Electric Dreams* (Houghton Mifflin Harcourt); *The Complete Psychotechnic League, Volume 1* (Baen), by Poul Anderson; *First-Person Singularities: Stories* (Three Rooms), by Robert Silverberg, and *The Hainish Novels and Stories* (Library of America), by Ursula K. Le Guin. (*The Hainish Novels and Stories* comes in two volumes, one an omnibus of Le Guin's Hainish novels and the other a collection of her Hainish stories, but the story part alone is probably the strongest short-story collection of the year.)

As usual, small presses dominated the list of short-story collections, with trade collections having become rare.

A wide variety of "electronic collections," often called "fiction bundles," too many to individually list here, are also available for downloading online at many sites. The Science Fiction Book Club continues to issue new collections as well.

Also as usual, the most reliable buys in the reprint anthology market are the various best of the year anthologies, the number of which continues to fluctuate. David G. Hartwell's *Year's Best SF* series was lost with the tragic death of its editor in 2016. There was no edition this year of *The Year's Best Military SF and Space Opera* (Baen), edited by David Afsharirad, but a new volume has been announced for June 2018. There also didn't seem to be a volume this year of *The Year's Best Science Fiction and Fantasy Novellas* (Prime Books), edited by Paula Guran, and this series may have died. There was a new best series launched this year, *Best of British Science Fiction 2016* (NewCon Press), edited by Donna Scott, but since it covers 2016 rather than 2017, we can't count it here. Continuing best series include: *The Best American Science Fiction and Fantasy 2017* (Houghton Mifflin Harcourt), this volume edited by Charles Yu, with the overall series editor being John Joseph Adams; *Year's Best Weird Fiction Volume Four* (Undertow), edited by Helen Marshall, series editor Michael Kelly; *The Best Science Fiction of the Year Volume Two* (Night Shade Books), edited by Neil Clarke *The Year's Best Science Fiction* series (St. Martin's Press), edited by Gardner Dozois, now up to its thirty-fifth annual collection; *The Best Science Fiction and Fantasy of the Year: Volume Eleven* (Solaris), edited by Jonathan Strahan; *The Year's Best Science Fiction and Fantasy: 2017 Edition* (Prime Books), edited by Rich Horton; *The Best Horror of the Year: Volume Nine* (Night Shade Books), edited by Ellen Datlow; *The Year's Best Dark Fantasy and Horror: 2017* (Prime Books), edited by Paula Guran; and *Best New Horror, Number 27* (Drugstore Indian), edited by Stephen Jones.

That means that this year's science fiction was covered by two dedicated best of the year anthologies, my own and the Clarke, plus four separate half anthologies, the science fiction halves of the Strahan, Horton, and Yu books, which in theory adds up to one and a half additional anthologies (in practice, of course, the contents of those books probably won't divide that neatly, with exactly half with their coverage going to each genre, and there'll likely to be more of one thing than another). There is no dedicated fantasy anthology anymore, fantasy only being covered by the fantasy halves of the Strahan, Horton, and Yu books. Horror is now being covered by two dedicated volumes, the Datlow and the Jones, and the "horror" half of Guran's *The Year's Best Dark Fantasy and Horror*. It's hard to tell where *The Year's Best Weird Fiction* fits in, "weird fiction" being a term that could fit anything, depending on the whim of the editor; it's possible that it may have some fantasy in it, but I suspect that it will lean toward horror instead. The annual Nebula Awards anthology, which covers science fiction as well as fantasy of various sorts, functions as a defacto "best of the year" anthology, although it's not usually counted among them; this year's edition was *Nebula Awards Showcase 2017* (Pyr), edited by Julie E. Czerneda. More specialized best of the year anthologies are *Wilde Stories 2017* (Lethe Press), edited by Steve Berman, and *Transcendent 2: The Year's Best Transgender Speculative Fiction* (Lethe Press), edited by Bogi Takács.

There was no really prominent single title in the stand-alone reprint anthology market this year. The best of the stand-alone reprint antholgies were probably *Galactic Empires* (Night Shade), edited by Neil Clarke, and *The Best of Subterranean* (Subterranean Press), edited by William Schafer. More reprint SF anthologies included *Jim Baen Memorial Award: The First Decade* (Baen), edited by William Ledbetter, *If This Goes Wrong . . .* (Baen), edited by Hank Davis, *Go Forth and Multiply: Twelve Tales of Repopulation* (Surinam Turtle Press), edited by Gordon Van Gelder, and *Frankenstein Dreams: A Connoisseur's Collection of Victorian Science Fiction* (Bloomsbury), edited by Michael Sims. Other reprint anthologies, all fantasy, included *Swords Against Darkness* (Prime) and *New York Fantastic: Fantasy Stories from the City that Never Sleeps* (Night Shade), both edited by Paula Guran, *The Best of Beneath Ceaseless Skies Online Magazine, Year Eight* (Firkin Press), edited by Scott H. Andrews, and *The New Voices of Fantasy* (Tachyon), edited by Peter S. Beagle.

The genre-oriented nonfiction was somewhat weak this year. There were a lot of biographies, autobiographies, and critical studies of SF writers, including: *A Lit Fuse: The Provocative Life of Harlan Ellison* (NESFA Press), by Nat Segaloff; *Not So Good a Gay Man: A Memoir* (Tor), by Frank M. Robinson; *Star-Begotten: A Life Lived in Science Fiction* (McFarland), by James Gunn; *J. G. Ballard* (University of Illinois Press), by D. Harlan Wilson; *Luminescent Threads: Connections to Octavia E. Butler* (Twelfth Planet); edited by Alexandra Pierce and Mimi Mondal; *Saving the World Through Science Fiction: James Gunn, Writer, Teacher and Scholar* (McFarland), by Michael R. Page; *Patricia A. McKillip and the Art of Fantasy World-Building* (McFarland), by Audrey Isabel Taylor; *Iain M. Banks* (University of Illinois Press), by Paul Kincaid; and *The Invention of Angela Carter: A Biography* (Oxford University Press), by Edmund Gordon.

Of these, by far the most attention, and the most controversy, was generated by *A Lit Fuse*.

Most of the rest of the year's genre-oriented nonfiction books were more academically oriented, or else overviews of the field: *Science Fiction and the Moral Imagination: Visions, Minds, Ethics* (Springer), by Russell Blackford; *Gender Identity and Sexuality in Fantasy and Science Fiction* (Luna), by Francesca T. Barbini; *Sleeping with Monsters: Readings and Reactions in Science Fiction and Fantasy* (Aqueduct) by Liz Bourke; *Science Fiction Criticism: An Anthology of Essential Writings* (Bloomsbury Academic), by Rob Latham; *Celestrial Empire: The Emergence of Chinese Science Fiction* (Wesleyan University Press), by Nathaniel Isaacson; *Science Fiction: A Literary History* (British Library), by Roger Luckhurst; and *Dis-Orienting Planets: Racial Representations of Asia in Science Fiction* (University Press of Mississippi), by Isiah Lavender.

It was also a weak year for art books. As usual, your best bet here is a sort of a best of the year anthology for fantastic art: *Spectrum 24: The Best in Contemporary Fantastic Art* (Flesk), edited by John Fleskes. Also out in 2017 were *Line of Beauty: The Art* of *Wendy Pini* (Flesk), by Richard and Wendy Peni; *The Art of the Pulps: An Illustrated History* (IDW), edited by Douglas Ellis, Ed Hulse, and Robert Weinberg; *The Movie Art of Syd Mead: Visual Futurist* (Titan), by Craig Hodgetts and Syd Mead; *Familiars/Flora & Fauna/Viscera* (Flesk), by J.A.W. Cooper; *Ink & Paint: The Women of Walt Disney's Animation* (Disney Editions), by Mindy Johnson; *Marvel's Thor: Ragnarok—The Art of the Movie* (Marvel Universe), edited by Jeff Youngquist; *Terry Pratchett's Discworld Imaginarium* (Gollancz), by Paul Kidby; *Classic Storybook Fables* (Artisan), by Scott Gustafson; *Norse Myths: Tales of Odin, Thor, and Loki* (Candlewick Studio), by Kevin Crossley-Holland and illustrated by Jeffrey Alan Love; *Celtic Faeries: The Secret Kingdom* (Goblin's Way), by Jean-Baptiste Monge; *Infected by Art, Volume 5* (ArtOrder), edited by Todd Spoor and Bill Cox; *David Wiesner and the Art of Wordless Storytelling* (Santa Barbara Museum of Art), by Eik Kahng, Ellen Keiter, Katherine Roeder, and David Wiesner; and *The Art of Magic: The Gathering—Kaladesh* (Viz), by James Wyatt.

According to the Box Office Mojo site (www.boxofficemojo.com), for the second year in a row, all ten of the year's ten top-earning movies were genre films of one sort or another (if you're willing to count animated films and superhero movies as being "genre films"). Not only were all of the top ten movies genre films of one sort or another, but by my count, although I may have missed a few, seventeen out of the top twenty, and forty out of the one hundred top-grossing movies were genre films. In the past eighteen years, genre films have been number one at the box office sixteen out of eighteen times, with the only exceptions being *American Sniper* in 2014 and *Saving Private Ryan* in 1998. This year, you have to go down to the twelfth and fourteenth places on the list before you run into any non-genre films, *The Fate of the Furious* and *Dunkirk* respectively.

This year's number one on the list of top ten box-office champs, in spite of a lot of controversy over it in social media, is *Star Wars: The Last Jedi*, which racked up a worldwide box-office total of $1, 331,832.651 (and that's before the profits from DVD sales, action figures, lunch boxes, T-shirts, and other kinds of accessories kick in, it's worth noting).

Disney Studios obviously had a good year, with a stake in many of the year's other top ten movies. Number two on the top ten list, for instance, is Disney's live-action remake of *Beauty and the Beast*.

Superhero movies, which seemed a bit down last year, made a strong resurgence in 2017. Warner Brothers's *Wonder Woman* finished in third place, but there were also a number of Marvel movies as well, in which Disney also has a stake—*Guardians of the Galaxy Volume 2*, which finished in fifth place, *Spider-Man: Homecoming*, which finished in sixth place, and *Thor: Ragnarok*, which finished in eighth place. Other superhero movies made it on to the top ten list as well: *Logan* (featuring Marvel character Wolverine, but not made by Marvel Studios) in eleventh place, and Warner Brothers's *Justice League*, in tenth place.

Animated film *Despicable Me 3* took ninth place on the top ten list, and other animated films showed up in the top twenty list, such as *Coco*, in thirteenth place, *The LEGO Batman Movie*, in sixteenth place, and *The Boss Baby*, in seventeenth place.

Horror movie *It*, based on the novel by Stephen King, took seventh place on the top ten list.

The most critically acclaimed of 2017's genre films were probably *Logan*, an autumnal farewell to the character of Wolverine, *Wonder Woman*, the highest-earning DC superhero movie to date, which seems to have successfully started a new franchise, and *The Shape of Water*, an unacknowledged sequel of sorts to the old horror movie *The Creature from the Black Lagoon*. Critical opinion and fan reaction was sharply split on *Blade Runner 2049*, the long-awaited sequel to the original *Blade Runner*, with some calling it the best genre movie of the year, although it underperformed at the box office, only managing to come in at thirty-fourth place in the top one hundred list.

Other attempts to establish new franchises or reboot old ones also failed, with the ambitious space opera *Valerian and the City of a Thousand Planets* coming in at sixty-sixth place in the top hundred list, the long-anticipated *The Dark Tower*, drawn from a series of novels by Stephen King, taking fifty-fifth place, a reboot of *The Mummy* franchise (one of the most critically savaged movies of the year) coming in at fortieth place, and a reboot of *Power Rangers* finishing at thirty-seventh place.

Coming up in 2018 is another flood of genre movies of one sort or another, including a slew of superhero movies. The most anticipatory buzz is probably being generated by *Avengers: Infinity War* and *Black Panther*, although there's also a movie about the early life of Han Solo, *Solo: A Star Wars Story*; a sequel to *The Incredibles*, *The Incredibles 2*; a sequel to *Fantastic Beasts and Where to Find Them*, *Fantastic Beasts: The Crimes of Grindelwald*; a sequel to *Pacific Rim*, *Pacific Rim Uprising*; a reboot of *Tomb Raider*; a film version of Madeleine L'Engle's children's classic *A Wrinkle in Time*; another X-Men movie, *X-Men: Dark Phoenix* and another *Jurassic World* movie, *Jurassic World: Fallen Kingdom*; a sequel to *Ant-Man*, *Ant-Man and the Wasp*; and a reboot of *Mary Poppins*, *Mary Poppins Returns* (I'm kind of hoping that Mary Poppins is played by Yondu from *Guardians of the Galaxy*, but I wouldn't count on it). There will also be attempts to establish new franchises with *Ready Player One*, *Mortal Engines*, and *Annihilation*.

There are so many genre shows of one sort or another on television these days (after decades when there were few or none of them) that it's becoming difficult to find a show that *isn't* a genre show. As there are almost a hundred of them now available in one form or another, I'm obviously going to be able to list only some of the more prominent ones; my apologies if I miss your favorites.

HBO's *A Game of Thrones*, based on the best-selling fantasy series by George R. R. Martin, is still the most prestigious and successful fantasy show on television, but its last season has been postponed until 2019, so you'll have to wait until then to see who ultimately gets to sit on the Iron Throne. *The Handmaid's Tale* was a huge critical success, as was *American Gods*, based on the novel by Neil Gaiman, although the abrupt departure of the series' showrunners has left the second season of *American Gods* in doubt. There will be another season of the also critically acclaimed series *Westworld*, a complex and tricky series version of the old SF movie of the same name, as well as new seasons of *The Man in the High Castle*, based on the

Hugo-winning alternate history novel by Philip K. Dick, *The Magicians*, based on the best-selling novel by Lev Grossman, and *Outlander*, based on a series of novels by Diana Gabaldon.

The Expanse, based on a series of space opera novels by James S. A. Corey, is about the closest thing to "hard science fiction" available on television, and one of the few series that can be counted as SF rather than superhero shows or fantasy, along with *Westworld*. *Marvel's Agents of S.H.I.E.L.D.* mixes SF concepts with the superhero stuff, especially in the last couple of seasons, featuring androids, cyborgs, rogue A.I.s, virtual reality worlds, alternate history scenarios, alien invasions, visits to other planets, and other SF tropes; the entire current season so far, for instance, has taken place on a space station far in the future, after Earth has been destroyed. A new *Star Trek* series, *Star Trek: Discovery*, and a semisatiric *Star Trek* clone, *The Orville*, have been established, and both have their enthusiastic supporters, although I didn't warm to either of them very much. Anthology show *Black Mirror* sometimes features SF storylines, and there's a new series called *Philip K. Dick's Electric Dreams* that I haven't caught up with. Other SF shows, coming up later in the year, include *Altered Carbon* and *Stargate Origins*, and a miniseries version of George R. R. Martin's novella *Nightflyers*.

An area that didn't even exist a few years ago, more and more shows are becoming available only as streaming video from servers such as Amazon, Netflix, Roku, and Hulu, and it's clear that the floodgates are only just starting to swing open for this form of entertainment delivery, with Disney and others promising to stream shows of their own. An early pioneer in this area, Marvel Studios has already established four solid hits with *Daredevil*, *Jessica Jones*, *Luke Cage*, and *The Punisher* (*Iron Fist* was widely critically savaged and less successful, as was a superhero team-up show, *The Defenders*, largely because of the presence in it of the charisma-less Iron Fist). Meanwhile, in case anybody had any doubt that this is the golden age of television superhero shows, a solid block of superhero shows has been established on regular television by DC, including *Arrow*, *The Flash*, *Supergirl*, *Legends of Tomorrow*, *Gotham*, and *Black Lightning*, with *Krypton*, a show set on Superman's home planet before it was destroyed, coming up later this year. Other superhero shows, largely featuring characters from Marvel Comics, include *Legion*, *The Runaways*, *Inhumans*, and *The Gifted*.

Of the flood of other genre shows that hit the air in the last few years, still surviving (I think, it's sometimes hard to tell) are: *Once Upon a Time*, *Grimm*, *Sleepy Hollow*, *Stranger Things*, *The Librarians*, *The 100*, *Ash vs Evil Dead*, *Dark Matter*, *Lucifer*, *The Good Place*, *Killjoys*, and *Star Wars Rebels*. The reaction to the reboot of *The X-Files*, now in its second season, has been largely unenthusiastic, and its future may be in doubt.

Perennial favorites such as *Doctor Who*, *The Walking Dead*, *Supernatural*, *The Vampire Diaries*, and *The Simpsons* continue to roll on as usual, with *Doctor Who* generating controversy over the selection of a woman to play the next doctor.

Of the upcoming shows, the most buzz seems to be being generated by the return of *Star Trek* to television, with a new series, *Star Trek: Discovery*. Some excitement is also being generated by the revival of *Twin Peaks* and *Mystery Science Theater 3000*. Also ahead are miniseries versions of Neil Gaiman's *American Gods* and *Anansi Boys*, and miniseries versions of Kim Stanley Robinson's *Red Mars*, Len Deighton's *SS-GB*, John Scalzi's *Old Man's War*, Philip José Farmer's *Riverworld*, Robert Holdstock's *Mythago Cycle*, and Joe Haldeman's *The Forever War* continue to be rumored—although how many of these promised shows actually show up is anyone's guess.

Upcoming are TV versions of *Galaxy Quest* and a reboot of **Lost in Space**, both of which I'm pretty sure are going to prove to be bad ideas, paticularly the *Galaxy Quest* remake.

The 75th World Science Fiction Convention, Worldcon 75, was held in Helsinki, Finland, from August 9th to August 13th, 2017. The 2017 Hugo Awards, presented at Worldcon 75, were: Best Novel, *The Obelisk Gate*, by N. K. Jemisin; Best Novella, "Every Heart a Doorway," by Seanan McGuire; Best Novelette, "The Tomato Thief," by Ursula Vernon; Best Short Story, "Seasons of Glass and Iron," by Amal El-Mohtar; Best Graphic Story, *Monstress, Volume 1: Awakening*, by Marjorie Liu, art by Sana Takeda; Best Related Work, *Words Are My Matter: Writings About Life and Books, 2000–2016*, by Ursula K. Le Guin; Best Professional Editor, Long Form, Liz Gorinsky; Best Professional Editor, Short Form, Ellen Datlow; Best Professional Artist, Julie Dillon; Best Dramatic Presentation (short form), *The Expanse*: "Leviathan Wakes"; Best Dramatic Presentation (long form), *Arrival*; Best Semiprozine, *Uncanny*; Best Fanzine, *Lady Business*; Best Fancast, *Tea and Jeopardy*; Best Fan Writer, Abigail Nussbaum; Best Fan Artist, Elizabeth Leggett; Best Series, *The Vorkosigan Saga*, by Lois McMaster Bujold; plus the John W. Campbell Award for Best New Writer to Ada Palmer.

The 2016 Nebula Awards, presented at a banquet at the Pittsburgh Marriott City Center in Pittsburgh, Pennsylvania, on May 20, 2017, were: Best Novel, *All the Birds in the Sky*, by Charlie Jane Anders; Best Novella, "Every Heart a Doorway," by Seanan McGuire; Best Novelette, "The Long Fall Up," by William Ledbetter; Best Short Story, "Seasons of Glass and Iron," by Amal El-Mohtar; Ray Bradbury Award, *Arrival*; the Andre Norton Award to *Arabella of Mars*, by David D. Levine; the Kate Wilhelm Solstice Award to Toni Weisskopf and Peggy Rae Sapienza; the Kevin O' Donnell Jr. Service to SFWA Award to Jim Fiscus; and the Damon Knight Memorial Grand Master Award to Jane Yolen.

The 2017 World Fantasy Awards, presented at a banquet on November 5, 2017, at the Wyndham Riverwalk in San Antonio, Texas, during the Forty-third Annual World Fantasy Convention, were: Best Novel, *The Sudden Appearance of Hope*, by Claire North; Best Long Fiction, *The Dream-Quest of Vellitt Boe*, by Kij Johnson; Best Short Fiction, "Das Steingeschöpf," by G. V. Anderson; Best Collection, *A Natural History of Hell*, by Jeffrey Ford; Best Anthology, *Dreaming in the Dark*, edited by Jack Dann; Best Artist, Jeffrey Alan Love; Special Award (Professional), to Michael Levy and Farah Mendlesohn for *Children's Fantasy in Literature: An Introduction*; Special Award (Non-Professional), to Neile Graham, for fostering excellence in the genre through her role as Workshop Director, Clarion West. Plus Lifetime Achievement Awards to Terry Brooks and Marina Warner.

The 2016 Bram Stoker Awards, presented by the Horror Writers Association on

April 29, 2017, during StokerCon 2017, in a gala aboard the *Queen Mary* in Long Beach, California, were: Superior Achievement in a Novel, *The Fisherman*, by John Langan; Superior Achievment in a First Novel, *Haven*, by Tom Deady; Superior Achievement in a Young Adult Novel, *Snowed*, by Maria Alexander; Superior Achievement in Long Fiction, *The Winter Box*, by Tim Waggoner; Superior Achievement in Short Fiction, "The Crawl Space," by Joyce Carol Oates; Superior Achievment in a Fiction Collection, *The Doll-Master and Other Tales of Terror*, by Joyce Carol Oates; Superior Achievement in an Anthology, *Borderlands 6*, edited by Oliva F. Monteleone and Thomas F. Monteleone; Superior Achievement in Non-Fiction, *Shirley Jackson: A Rather Haunted Life*, by Ruth Franklin; Superior Achievement in a Poetry Collection, *Brothel*, by Stephanie M. Wytovich; Superior Achievement in a Graphic Novel, *Kolchak the Night Stalker: The Forgotten Lore of Edgar Allan Poe*, by James Chambers; Superior Achievment in a Screenplay, *The Witch*.

The 2016 John W. Campbell Memorial Award was won by: *Central Station*, by Lavie Tidhar.

The 2016 Theodore Sturgeon Memorial Award for Best Short Story was won by: "The Future is Blue," by Catherynne M. Valente.

The 2017 Philip K. Dick Memorial Award went to: *The Mercy Journals*, by Claudia Casper.

The 2017 Arthur C. Clarke Award was won by: *The Underground Railroad*, by Colson Whitehead.

The 2016 James Tiptree, Jr. Memorial Award was won by: *When the Moon Was Ours*, by Anna-Marie McLemore.

The 2017 Sidewise Award for Alternate History went to (Long Form): *Underground Airlines*, by Ben H. Winters and (Short Form): "Treasure Fleet," by Daniel M. Bensen and "What If the Jewish State Had Been Established in East Africa," by Adam Rovner (tie).

Dead in 2017 or early 2018 were:

URSULA K. LE GUIN, 88, winner of six Nebula Awards, including SFWA's Grand Master Award, four Hugos, three World Fantasy Awards, including the Lifetime Achievement Award, and three James Tiptree, Jr. Memorial Awards, perhaps the best SF writer of the late twentieth and early twenty-first century, author of such classic novels as *The Left Hand of Darkness*, *The Dispossessed*, *The Lathe of Heaven*, the fantasy Earthsea series, and others, much of whose best work is collected in the recent omnibus *The Hainish Novels and Stories*; **BRIAN W. ALDISS**, 92, one of the giants of twentieth-century science fiction, winner of SFWA's Grand Master Award, author, anthologist, critic, and genre historian, author of many novels and short stories, among them classics such as *The Long Afternoon of Earth*, *Non-stop*, *The Malacia Tapestry*, *Greybeard*, and the Helliconia trilogy; **JERRY POUR-NELLE**, 84, Campbell Award winner, technical writer and SF author, best known to genre audiences for his collaborative novels with Larry Niven, such as *The Mote in God's Eye* and *Footfall*, although he also wrote solo novels such as *A Spaceship for the King* and *The Mercenary*, as well as a long-running column for computer magazine *Byte*; **WILLIAM SANDERS**, 75, SF, mystery, fantasy, and Alternate History author, winner of two Sidewise Awards for alternate history, whose numerous and critically acclaimed short stories were collected in *East of the Sun and West of Fort Smith*, author as well of novels such as *Journey to Fusang* and *The Wild Blue and Gray*, as well as many mystery novels, and nonfiction historical study *Conquest: Hernando de Soto and the Indians: 1539–1543*; **EDWARD BRYANT**, 71, winner of two Nebula Awards, prolific short story writer whose short stories were collected in *Cinnabar, Particle Theory, Predators and Other Stories*, and others, a friend for many years; **SUSAN CASPER**, 69, anthologist and SF/fantasy/horror writer, co-editor of *Ripper!*, whose many short stories were posthumously collected in *Up the Rainbow: The Complete Short Fiction of Susan Casper*, wife and companion for forty-seven years of SF editor Gardner Dozois; **LEN WEIN**, 69, a giant of the comics industry, co-creator of Wolverine, Swamp Thing, Storm, and many other comics characters, husband of photographer and fan Christine Valada, a friend for many years; **BERNIE WRIGHTSON**, 68, famous comics and horror illustrator, co-creator of Swamp Thing; **KIT REED**, 85, prolific SF writer whose novels include *Armed Camps, Little Sisters of the Apocalypse, The Night Children, Where*, and *Mormama*, and whose numerous stories were collected in *Mister Da V. and Other Stories, The Attack of the Giant Baby, The Story Until Now*, and others; **JULIAN MAY**, 86, SF writer, author of *The Many-Colored Land, The Golden Torc, The Nonborn King, Jack the Bodiless, Orion Arm, Conqueror's Moon*, and many other novels; author and scientist **YOJI KONDO**, 84, who wrote SF as **ERIC KOTANI**, author of the Island Worlds series (written with John Maddox Roberts), *Act of God, The Island Worlds*, and *Between the Stars*, as well as nonfiction such as *Interstellar Travel and Multi-Generation Space Ships*; **COLIN DEXTER**, 86, famous British mystery writer, best known for his long-running series about the cases of Inspector Morse, which inspired a series of the same name on British television, as well as two series spun-off from the original series later on; **J. P. DONLEAVY**, 91, Irish American writer, best known for his novel *The Ginger Man*; **GRANIA DAVIS**, 73, author and anthologist, author of *The Rainbow Annals* and *Moonbird*, perhaps best known in the genre for co-editing posthumous collections of the short work of her late husband, Avram Davidson, such as *The Avram Davidson Treasury*, a friend; **HILARY BAILEY**, 80, British author and editor, co-edited Volume 7 of the *New Worlds* anthology series with Charles Platt, perhaps best known for her story "The Fall of Frenchy Steiner"; **WILLIAM PETER BLATTY**, 89, horror writer, author of *The Exorcist*; **JEFF CARLSON**, 47, SF author of *Plague Year, Plague War*, and *Plague Zone*; **MARIE JOKOBER**, 75, Canadian author of historical, SF, and fantasy fiction; **MUSTAFA IBN ALI KANSO**, 57, Arab Brazilian SF writer; **NANCY WILLARD**, 80, who wrote more than seventy books of fiction and poetry, some SF; **PAULA FOX**, 93, children's book writer; **ANNE R. DICK**, 90, writer and poet, widow of the late Philip K. Dick; **MIKE LEVY**, 66, SF scholar, founder of British critical zine *Foundation*; **JOHN HURT**, 77, acclaimed movie actor, known for his roles in *A Man for All Seasons, Alien, 1984, The Elephant Man*, and, most recently, as Ollivander the wand maker in the Harry Potter films; **HARRY DEAN STANTON**, 91, movie actor known for his roles in *Alien, Escape from New York*, and *Paris, Texas*; **BILL PAXTON**, 61, actor, best known for his roles in *Aliens, Titanic, Twister, Apollo 13*, and television's *Big*

Love; **MARTIN LANDAU**, 89, television and movie actor, known for his roles in the original *Mission: Impossible* and the movie *Ed Wood*; **ROBERT HARDY**, 91, actor best known for playing Cornelius Fudge in the Harry Potter movies; **ADAM WEST**, 88, famous as television's Batman in the 1960s; **ROGER MOORE**, 89, played James Bond in seven James Bond films, also known as TV's *The Saint*; **POWERS BOOTHE**, 68, actor, best known for his roles in television's *Deadwood* and as the villainous head of Hydra in *Marvel's Agents of S.H.I.E.L.D.*; **MIGUEL FERRER**, 61, known for his roles in television's *Twin Peaks* and *NCIS: Los Angeles*; **JERRY LEWIS**, 91, comedian and actor once famous as half of the Martin and Lewis comedy duo with Dean Martin, also made solo movies such as the original *The Nutty Professor* **NELSAN ELLIS**, 39, famous for his role as Lafayette Reynold's in HBO's *True Blood*; **RICHARD HATCH**, 71, star of the original *Battlestar Galactica*, also had a role in the remake; **STEPHEN FURST**, 63, actor, best known for his role as Flounder in *Animal House*; **BARBARA HALE**, 94, who played Perry Mason's secretary Della Street in the original *Perry Mason* TV series, as well as in all the many Perry Mason TV movies that followed; **IRWIN COREY**, 102, comedian, known as "the world's foremost authority"; **NEIL FINGLETON**, 36, known as the giant Mag the Mighty on HBO's *Game of Thrones*; **JUNE FORAY**, 99, voice actor who provided the voice of Rocky the Flying Squirrel as well as many other animated characters; **PETER SALLIS**, 96, voice actor who provided the voice of Wallace in *Wallace and Gromit*; **JONATHAN DEMME**, 73, writer, director, and producer of *The Silence of the Lambs*; **GEORGE A. ROMERO**, 77, filmmaker, best known for *Night of the Living Dead*; **TOBE HOOPER**, 74, director of *The Texas Chain Saw Massacre* and *Poltergeist*; scientist, fan, folksinger **JORDIN KARE**, 60; bookseller and fan **DWAIN KAISER**, 69; British con runner and fan **MIKE DICKINSON**, 69; **JOAN LEE**, 93, wife of comics industry giant Stan Lee.

THE YEAR'S BEST

SCIENCE FICTION

The Moon is Not a Battlefield

Indrapramit Das

Indrapramit Das is a writer and artist from Kolkata, India. His short fiction has appeared in Clarkesworld, Asimov's Science Fiction, Apex Magazine, Redstone Science Fiction, The World SF Blog, Flash Fiction Online, *and the anthology* Breaking the Bow: Speculative Fiction Inspired by the Ramayana. *He is a grateful graduate of the 2012 Clarion West Writers Workshop and a recipient of the Octavia E. Butler Memorial Scholarship Award. He completed his MFA at the University of British Columbia and currently lives in Vancouver, working as a freelance writer, artist, editor, game tester, tutor, would-be novelist, and aspirant to adulthood. Follow him on Twitter @IndrapramitDas.*

In the story that follows, he paints an unsettling portrait of an injured soldier, hurt in combat on the Moon, who lives in poverty in a cardboard slum, his service seemingly forgotten by just about everybody . . . including the force he served.

W*e're recording.*

I was born in the sky, for war. This is what we were told.

I think when people hear this, they think of ancient Earth stories. Of angels and superheroes and gods, leaving destruction between the stars. But I'm no superhero, no Kalel of America-Bygone with the flag of his dead planet flying behind him. I'm no angel Gabreel striking down Satan in the void or blowing the trumpet to end worlds. I'm no devi Durga bristling with arms and weapons, chasing down demons through the cosmos and vanquishing them, no Kali with a string of heads hanging over her breasts black as deep space, making even the other gods shake with terror at her righteous rampage.

I was born in the sky, for war. What does it mean?

I was actually born on Earth, not far above sea level, in the Greater Kolkata Megapolis. My parents gave me away to the Government of India when I was still a small child, in exchange for enough money for them to live off frugally for a year—an unimaginable amount of wealth for two Dalit street-dwellers who scraped shit out of sewers for a living, and scavenged garbage for recycling—sewers sagging with centuries worth of shit, garbage heaps like mountains. There was another child I played with the most in our slum. The government took her as well. Of the few memories I have left of those early days on Earth, the ones of us playing are clearest, more than the ones of my parents, because they weren't around much. But she was always there. She'd bring me hot jalebis snatched from the hands of hapless pedestrians, her hands covered in syrup, and we'd share them. We used to climb and run along the huge sea-wall that holds back the rising Bay of Bengal, and spit in the churning sea. I haven't seen the sea since, except from space—that roiling mass of water feels like a dream. So do those days, with the child who would become the soldier most often by my side. The government told our parents that they would cleanse us of our names, our untouchability, give us a chance to lead noble lives as astral defenders of the Republic of India. Of course they gave us away. I don't blame them. Aditi never blamed hers, either. That was the name my friend was given by the Army. You've met her. We were told our new names before training even began. Single-names, always. Usually from the Mahabharata or Ramayana, we realized later. I don't remember the name my parents gave me. I never asked Aditi if she remembered hers.

That, then, is when the life of asura Gita began.

I was raised by the state to be a soldier, and borne into the sky in the hands of the Republic to be its protector, before I even hit puberty.

The notion that there could be war on the Moon, or anywhere beyond Earth, was once a ridiculous dream.

So are many things, until they come to pass.

I've lived for thirty-six years as an infantry soldier stationed off-world. I was deployed and considered in active duty from eighteen in the Chandnipur Lunar Cantonment Area. I first arrived in Chandnipur at six, right after they took us off the streets. I grew up there. The Army raised us. Gave us a better education than we'd have ever gotten back on Earth. Right from childhood, me and my fellow asuras—Earthbound Indian infantry soldiers were jawans, but we were always, always asuras, a mark of pride—we were told that we were stationed in Chandnipur to protect the intrasolar gateway of the Moon for the greatest country on that great blue planet in our black sky—India. India, which we could see below the clouds if we squinted during Earthrise on a surface patrol (if we were lucky, we could spot the white wrinkle of the Himalayas through telescopes). We learned the history of our home: after the United States of America and Russia, India was the third Earth nation to set foot on the Moon, and the first to settle a permanent base there. Chandnipur was open to scientists, astronauts, tourists and corporations of all countries, to do research, develop space travel, take expensive holidays and launch inter-system mining drones to asteroids. The generosity and benevolence of Bharat Mata, no? But we were to protect Chandnipur's sovereignty as Indian territory at all costs, because other countries were beginning to develop their own lunar expeditions to start bases. Chandnipur, we were told, was a part of India. The only part of India not on Earth. We were to make sure it remained that way. This was our mission. Even though, we were told, the rest of the world didn't officially recognize any land on the moon to belong to any country, back then. Especially because of that.

Do you remember Chandnipur well?

It was where I met you, asura Gita. Hard to forget that, even if it hadn't been my first trip to the Moon. I was very nervous. The ride up the elevator was peaceful. Like . . . being up in the mountains, in the Himalayas, you know? Oh—I'm so sorry. Of course not. Just, the feeling of being high up—the silence of it, in a way, despite all the people in the elevator cabins. But then you start floating under the seat belts, and there are the safety instructions on how to move around the platform once you get to the top, and all you feel like doing is pissing. That's when you feel untethered. The shuttle to the Moon from the top of the elevator wasn't so peaceful. Every blast of the craft felt so powerful out there. The g's just raining down on you as you're strapped in. I felt like a feather.

Like a feather. Yes. I imagine so. There are no birds in Chandnipur, but us asuras always feel like feathers. Felt. Now I feel heavy all the time, like a stone, like a— hah—a moon, crashing into its world, so possessed by gravity, though I'm only skin and bones. A feather on a moon, a stone on a planet.

You know, when our Havaldar, Chamling his name was, told me that asura Aditi and I were to greet and guide a reporter visiting the Cantonment Area, I can't tell you how shocked we were. We were so excited. We would be on the feeds! We never got reporters up there. Well, to be honest, I wanted to show off our bravery, tell you horror stories of what happens if you wear your suit wrong outside the Cantonment Area on a walk, or get caught in warning shots from Chinese artillery kilos away, or what happens if the micro-atmosphere over Chandnipur malfunctions and becomes too thin while you're out and about there (you burn or freeze or asphyxiate). Civilians like horror stories from soldiers. You see so many of them in the media feeds in the pods, all these war stories. I used to like seeing how different it is for soldiers on Earth, in the old wars, the recent ones. Sometimes it would get hard to watch, of course.

Anyway, asura Aditi said to me, "Gita, they aren't coming here to be excited by a war movie. We aren't even at war. We're in *territorial conflict*. You use the word war and it'll look like we're boasting. We need to make them feel at home, not scare the shit out of them. We need to show them the hospitality of asuras on our own turf."

Couldn't disagree with that. We wanted people on Earth to see how well we do our jobs, so that we'd be welcomed with open arms when it was time for the big trip back—the promised pension, retirement, and that big old heaven in the sky where we all came from, Earth. We wanted every Indian up there to know we were protecting their piece of the Moon. Your piece of the Moon.

I thought soldiers would be frustrated having to babysit a journalist following them around. But you and asura Aditi made me feel welcome.

I felt bad for you. We met civilians in Chandnipur proper, when we got time off, in the Underground Markets, the bars. But you were my first fresh one, Earth-fresh. Like the imported fish in the Markets. Earth-creatures, you know, always delicate, expensive, mouth open gawping, big eyes. Out of water, they say.

Did I look "expensive"? I was just wearing the standard issue jumpsuits they give visitors.

Arre, you know what I mean. In the Markets we soldiers couldn't buy Earth-fish or Earth-lamb or any Earth-meat, when they showed up every six months. We only ever tasted the printed stuff. Little packets, in the stalls they heat up the synthi for you in the machine. Nothing but salt and heat and protein. Imported Earth-meat was too expensive. Same for Earth-people, expensive. Fish out of water. Earth meant paradise. You came from heaven. No offense.

None taken. You and asura Aditi were very good to me. That's what I remember.

After Aditi reminded me that you were going to show every Indian on their feeds our lives, we were afraid of looking bad. You looked scared, at first. Did we scare you?

I wouldn't say scared. Intimidated. You know, everything you were saying earlier, about gods and superheroes from the old Earth stories. The stuff they let you watch and read in the pods. That's what I saw, when you welcomed us in full regalia, out on the surface, in your combat suits, at the parade. You gleamed like gods. Like devis, asuras, like your namesakes. Those weapon limbs, when they came out of the backs of your suit during the demonstration, they looked like the arms of the goddesses in the epics, or the wings of angels, reflecting the sunlight coming over the horizon—the light was so white, after Earth, not shifted yellow by atmosphere. It was blinding, looking at you all. I couldn't imagine having to face that, as a soldier, as your enemy. Having to face you. I couldn't imagine having to patrol for hours, and fight, in those suits—just my civilian surface suit was so hot inside, so claustrophobic. I was shaking in there, watching you all.

Do you remember, the Governor of Chandnipur Lunar Area came out to greet you, and shake the hands of all the COs. A surface parade like that, on airless ground, that never happened—it was all for you and the rest of the reporters, for the show back on Earth. We had never before even seen the Governor in real life, let alone in a surface suit. The rumours came back that he was trembling and sweating when he shook their hands—that he couldn't even pronounce the words to thank them for their service. So you weren't alone, at least.

Then when we went inside the Cantonment Area, and we were allowed to take off our helmets right out in the open—I waited for you and Aditi to do it first. I didn't believe I wouldn't die, that my face wouldn't freeze. We were on that rover, such a bumpy ride, but open air like those vehicles in the earliest pictures of people on the Moon—just bigger. We went through the Cantonment airlock gate, past the big yellow sign that reads "Chandnipur, Gateway to the Stars," and when we emerged from the other side Aditi told me to look up and see for myself, the different sky. From deep black to that deep, dusky blue, it was amazing, like crossing over into another world. The sunlight still felt different, blue-white instead of yellow, filtered by the nanobot haze, shimmering in that lunar dawn coming in over the hilly rim of Daedalus crater. The sun felt tingly, raw, like it burned even though the temperature was cool. The Earth was half in shadow—it looked fake, a rendered backdrop in a veeyar sim. And sometimes the micro-atmosphere would move just right and the bots would be visible for a few seconds in a wave across that low sky, the famous flocks of "lunar fireflies." The rover went down the suddenly smooth lunarcrete road, down the main road of the Cantonment—

New Delhi Avenue.

Yes, New Delhi Avenue, with the rows of wireframed flags extended high, all the state colours of India, the lines and lines of white barracks with those tiny windows on both sides. I wanted to stay in those, but they put us civilians underground, in a hotel. They didn't want us complaining about conditions. As we went down New Delhi

Avenue and turned into the barracks for the tour, you and Aditi took off your helmets and breathed deep. Your faces were covered in black warpaint. Greasepaint. Full regalia, yes? You both looked like Kali, with or without the necklace of heads. Aditi helped me with the helmet, and I felt lunar air for the first time. The dry, cool air of Chandnipur. And you said "Welcome to chota duniya. You can take off the helmet." Chota duniya, the little world. Those Kali faces, running with sweat, the tattoos of your wetware. You wore a small beard, back then, and a crew-cut. Asura Aditi had a ponytail, I was surprised that was allowed.

You looked like warriors, in those blinding suits of armour.

Warriors. I don't anymore, do I. What do I look like now?

I see you have longer hair. You shaved off your beard.

Avoiding the question, clever. Did you know that jawan means "young man"? But we were asuras. We were proud of our hair, not because we were young men. We, the women and the hijras, the not-men, told the asuras who were men, why do you get to keep beards and moustaches and we don't? Some of them had those twirly moustaches like the asuras in the myths. So the boys said to us: we won't stop you. Show us your beards! From then it was a competition. Aditi could hardly grow a beard on her pretty face, so she gave up when it was just fuzz. I didn't. I was so proud when I first sprouted that hair on my chin, when I was a teenager. After I grew it out, Aditi called it a rat-tail. I never could grow the twirly moustaches. But I'm a decommissioned asura now, so I've shaved off the beard.

What do you think you look like now?

Like a beggar living in a slum stuck to the side of the space elevator that took me up to the sky so long ago, and brought me down again not so long ago.

Some of my neighbours don't see asuras as women or men. I'm fine with that. They ask me: do you still bleed? Did you menstruate on the Moon? They say, menstruation is tied to the Moon, so asuras must bleed all the time up there, or never at all down here. They think we used all that blood to paint ourselves red because we are warriors. To scare our enemies. I like that idea. Some of them don't believe it when I say that I bleed the same as any Earthling with a cunt. The young ones believe me, because they help me out, bring me rags, pads when they can find them, from down there in the city—can't afford the meds to stop bleeding altogether. Those young ones are a blessing. I can't exactly hitch a ride on top of the elevator up and down every day in my condition.

People in the slum all know you're an asura?

I ask again: what do I look like now?

A veteran. You have the scars. From the wetware that plugged you into the suits. The lines used to be black, raised—on your face, neck. Now they're pale, flat.

The mark of the decommissioned asura—everyone knows who you are. The government plucks out your wires. Like you're a broken machine. They don't want you selling the wetware on the black market. They're a part of the suits we wore, just a part we wore all the time inside us—and the suits are property of the Indian Army, Lunar Command.

I told you why the suits are so shiny, didn't I, all those years ago? Hyper-reflective surfaces so we didn't fry up in them like the printed meat in their heating packets when the sun comes up. The suits made us easy to spot on a lunar battlefield. It's why we always tried to stay in shadow, use infrared to spot enemies. When we went on recon, surveillance missions, we'd use lighter stealth suits, nonmetal, non-reflective, dark grey like the surface. We could only do that if we coordinated our movements to land during nighttime.

When I met you and asura Aditi then you'd been in a few battles already. With Chinese and Russian troops. Small skirmishes.

All battles on the moon are small skirmishes. You can't afford anything bigger. Even the horizon is smaller, closer. But yes, our section had seen combat a few times. But even that was mostly waiting, and scoping with infra-red along the shadows of craters. When there was fighting, it was between long, long stretches of walking and sitting. But it was never boring. Nothing can be boring when you've got a portioned ration of air to breathe, and no sound to warn you of a surprise attack. Each second is measured out and marked in your mind. Each step is a success. When you do a lunar surface patrol outside Chandnipur, outside regulated atmosphere or Indian territory, as many times as we did, you do get used to it. But never, ever bored. If anything, it becomes hypnotic—you do everything you need to do without even thinking, in that silence between breathing and the words of your fellow soldiers.

You couldn't talk too much about what combat was like on the Moon, on that visit.

They told us not to. Havaldar Chamling told us that order came all the way down from the Lieutenant General of Lunar Command. It was all considered classified information, even training maneuvers. It was pretty silent when you were in Chandnipur. I'm sure the Russians and the Chinese had news of that press visit. They could have decided to put on a display of might, stage some shock and awe attacks, missile strikes, troop movements to draw us out of the Cantonment Area.

I won't lie—I was both relieved and disappointed. I've seen war, as a field reporter. Just not on the Moon. I wanted to see firsthand what the asuras were experiencing.

It would have been difficult. Lunar combat is not like Earth combat, though I don't know much about Earth combat other than theory and history. I probably know less than you do, ultimately, because I've never experienced it. But I've read things, watched things about wars on Earth. Learned things, of course, in our lessons. It's different on the Moon. Harder to accommodate an extra person when each battle is like a game of chess. No extra pieces allowed on the board. Every person needs their own air. No one can speak out of turn and clutter up comms. The visibility of each person needs to be accounted for, since it's so high.

The most frightening thing about lunar combat is that you often can't tell when it's happening until it's too late. On the battlefields beyond Chandnipur, out on the magma seas, combat is silent. You can't hear anything but your own footsteps, the *thoom-thoom-thoom* of your suit's metal boots crunching dust, or the sounds of your own weapons through your suit, the rattle-kick of ballistics, the near-silent hum of lasers vibrating in the metal of the shell keeping you alive. You'll see the flash of a mine or grenade going off a few feet away but you won't hear it. You won't hear anything coming down from above unless you look up—be it ballistic missiles or a meteorite hurtling down after centuries flying through outer space. You'll feel the shockwave knock you back but you won't hear it. If you're lucky, of course.

Laser weapons are invisible out there, and that's what's we mostly used. There's no warning at all. No muzzle-flash, no noise. One minute you're sitting there thinking you're on the right side of the rocks giving you cover, and the next moment you see a glowing hole melting into the suit of the soldier next to you, like those time-lapse videos of something rotting. It takes less than a second if the soldier on the other side of the beam is aiming properly. Less than a second and there's the flash and pop, blood and gas and superheated metal venting into the thin air like an aerosol spray, the scream like static in the mics. Aditi was a sniper, she could've told you how lethal the long-range lasers were. I carried a semiauto, laser or ballistic; those lasers were as deadly, just lower range and zero warm-up. When we were in battles closer to settlements, we'd switch to the ballistic weaponry, because the buildings and bases are mostly better protected from that kind of damage, bulletproof. There was kind of a silent agreement between all sides to keep from heavily damaging the actual bases. Those ballistic fights were almost a relief—our suits could withstand projectile damage better, and you could see the tracers coming from kilometers away, even if you couldn't hear them. Like fire on oil, across the jet sky. Bullets aren't that slow either, especially here on the Moon, but somehow it felt better to see it, like you could dodge the fire, especially if we were issued jetpacks, though we rarely used them because of how difficult they were to control. Aditi was better at using hers.

She saved my life once.

I mean, she did that many times, we both did for each other, just by doing what we needed to do on a battlefield. But she directly saved my life once, like an Earth movie hero. Rocket propelled grenade on a quiet battlefield. Right from up above and behind us. I didn't even see it. I just felt asura Aditi shove me straight off the ground from behind and blast us off into the air with her jetpack, propelling us both twenty feet above the surface in a second. We twirled in mid-air, and for a little moment, it felt like we were free of the Moon, hovering there between it and the blazing blue Earth, dancing together. As we sailed back down and braced our legs for landing without suit damage, Aditi never let me go, kept our path back down steady. Only then did I see the cloud of lunar dust and debris hanging where we'd been seconds earlier, the aftermath of an explosion I hadn't heard or seen, the streaks of light as the rest of the fireteam returned fire ballistic, spreading out in leaps with short bursts from their jetpacks. No one died in that encounter. I don't even remember whose troops we were fighting in that encounter, which lunar army. I just remember that I didn't die because of Aditi.

Mostly, we never saw the enemy close up. They were always just flecks of light on the horizon, or through our infrared overlay. Always ghosts, reflecting back the light of sun and Earth, like the Moon itself. It made it easier to kill them, if I'm being honest. They already seemed dead. When you're beyond Chandnipur, out on the mara under that merciless black sky with the Earth gleaming in the distance, the only colour you can see anywhere, it felt like we were already dead too. Like we were all just ghosts playing out the old wars of humanity, ghosts of soldiers who died far, far down on the ground. But then we'd return to the city, to the warm bustle of the Underground Markets on our days off, to our chota duniya, and the Earth would seem like heaven again, not a world left behind but one to be attained, one to earn, the unattainable paradise rather than a distant history of life that we'd only lived through media pods and lessons.

And now, here you are. On Earth.

Here I am. Paradise attained. I have died and gone to heaven.

It's why I'm here, isn't it? Why we're talking.

You could say that. Thank you for coming, again. You didn't have any trouble coming up the elevator shaft, did you? I know it's rough clinging to the top of the elevator.

I've been on rougher rides. There are plenty of touts down in the elevator base station who are more than willing to give someone with a few rupees a lending hand up the spindle. So. You were saying. About coming back to Earth. It must have been surprising, the news that you were coming back, last year.

FTL changed everything. That was, what, nine years ago?

At first it brought us to the edge of full-on lunar war, like never before, because the Moon became the greatest of all jewels in the night sky. It could become our first FTL port. Everyone wanted a stake in that. Every national territory on the Moon closed off its borders while the Earth governments negotiated. We were closed off in our bunkers, looking at the stars through the small windows, eating nothing but thin parathas from emergency flour rations. We made them our personal heating coils with synthi butter—no food was coming through because of embargo, mess halls in the main barracks were empty. We lived on those parathas and caffeine infusion. Our stomachs were like balloons, full of air.

Things escalated like never before, in that time. I remember a direct Chinese attack on Chandnipur's outer defences, where we were stationed. One bunker window was taken out by laser. I saw a man stuck to the molten hole in the pane because of depressurization, wriggling like a dying insect. Asura Jatayu, a quiet, skinny soldier with a drinking problem. People always said he filled his suit's drinking water pods with diluted moonshine from the Underground Markets, and sucked it down during patrols. I don't know if that's true, but people didn't trust him because of it, even though he never really did anything to fuck things up. He was stone cold sober that day. I know, because I was with him. Aditi, me and two other asuras ripped him off the broken window, activated the emergency shutter before we lost too much pressure. But he'd already hemorrhaged severely through the laser wound, which had blown blood out of him and into the thin air of the Moon. He was dead. The Chinese had already retreated by the time we recovered. It was a direct response to our own overtures before the embargo. We had destroyed some nanobot anchors of theirs in disputed territory, which had been laid down to expand the micro-atmosphere of Yueliang Lunar Area.

That same tech that keeps air over Chandnipur and other lunar territories, enables the micro-atmospheres, is what makes FTL work—the q-nanobots. On our final patrols across the mara, we saw some of the new FTL shipyards in the distance. The ships—half-built, they looked like the Earth ruins from historical pictures, of palaces and cities. We felt like we were looking at artifacts of a civilization from the future. They sparked like a far-off battle, bots building them tirelessly. They will sail out to outer space, wearing quenbots around them like cloaks. Like the superheroes! The quenbot cloud folds the space around the ship like a blanket, make a bubble that shoots through the universe. I don't really understand. Is it like a soda bubble or a blanket? We had no idea our time on the Moon was almost over on those patrols, looking at the early shipyards.

After one of the patrols near the shipyards, asura Aditi turned to me and said, "We'll be on one of those ships one day, sailing to other parts of the galaxy. They'll need us to defend Mother India when she sets her dainty feet on new worlds. Maybe we'll be able to see Jupiter and Saturn and Neptune zoom by like cricket balls, the Milky Way spinning far behind us like a chakra."

"I don't think that's quite how FTL works," I told her, but obviously she knew that. She looked at me, low dawn sunlight on her visor so I couldn't see her face. Even though this patrol was during a temporary ceasefire, she had painted her face like she so loved to, so all you could see anyway were the whites of her eyes and her teeth. Kali Ma through and through, just like you said. "Just imagine, maybe we'll end up on a world where we can breathe everywhere. Where there are forests and running water and deserts like Earth. Like in the old Bollywood movies, where the heroes and the heroines run around trees and splash in water like foolish children with those huge mountains behind them covered in ice."

"Arre, you can get all that on Earth. It's where those movies come from! Why would you want to go further away from Earth? You don't want to return home?"

"That's a nice idea, Gita," she said. "But the longer we're here, and the more news and movies and feeds I see of Earth, I get the idea it's not really waiting for us."

That made me angry, though I didn't show it. "We've waited all our lives to go back, and now you want to toss off to another world?" I asked, as if we had a choice in the matter. The two of us, since we were children in the juvenile barracks, had talked about moving to a little house in the Himalayas once we went back, somewhere in Sikkim or northern Bengal (we learned all the states as children, and saw their flags along New Delhi Avenue) where it's not as crowded as the rest of Earth still, and we could see those famously huge mountains that dwarfed the Moon's arid hills.

She said, "Hai Ram, I'm just dreaming like we always have. My dear, what you're not getting is that we have seen Earth on the feeds since we came to the Moon. From expectation, there is only disappointment."

So I told her, "When you talk about other worlds out there, you realize those are expectations too. You're forgetting we're soldiers. We go to Earth, it means our battle is over. We go to another world, you think they'd let us frolic like Bollywood stars in alien streams? Just you and me, Gita and Aditi, with the rest of our division doing backup dancing?" I couldn't stay angry when I thought of this, though I still felt a bit hurt that she was suggesting she didn't want to go back to Earth with me, like the sisters in arms we were.

"True enough," she said. "Such a literalist. If our mission is ever to play Bollywood on an exoplanet, you can play the man hero with your lovely rat-tail beard. Anyway, for now all we have is this grey rock where all the ice is underneath us instead of prettily on the mountains. Not Earth or any other tarty rival to it. *This* is home, Gita beta, don't forget it."

How right she was.

Then came peacetime.

We saw the protests on Earth feeds. People marching through the vast cities, more people than we'd ever see in a lifetime in Chandnipur, with signs and chants.

No more military presence on the Moon. The Moon is not an army base. Bring back our soldiers. The Moon is not a battlefield.

But it was, that's the thing. We had seen our fellow asuras die on it.

With the creation of the Terran Union of Spacefaring Nations (T.U.S.N.) in anticipation of human expansion to extrasolar space, India finally gave up its sovereignty over Chandnipur, which became just one settlement in amalgamated T.U.S.N. Lunar territory. There were walled-off Nuclear Seclusion Zones up there on Earth still hot from the last World War, and somehow they'd figured out how to stop war on the Moon. With the signing of the International Lunar Peace Treaty, every nation that had held its own patch of the Moon for a century of settlement on the satellite agreed to lay down their arms under Earth, Sol, the gods, the goddesses, and the God. The Moon was going to be free of military presence for the first time in decades.

When us asuras were first told officially of the decommissioning of Lunar Command in Chandnipur, we celebrated. We'd made it—we were going to Earth, earlier than we'd ever thought, long before retirement age. Even our COs got shit-faced in the mess halls. There were huge tubs of biryani, with hot chunks of printed lamb and gobs of synthi dalda. We ate so much, I thought we'd explode. Even Aditi, who'd been dreaming about other worlds, couldn't hold back her happiness. She asked me, "What's the first thing you're going to do on Earth?" her face covered in grease, making me think of her as a child with another name, grubby cheeks covered in syrup from stolen jalebis. "I'm going to catch a train to a riverside beach or a sea-wall, and watch the movement of water on a planet. Water, flowing and thrashing for kilometers and kilometers, stretching all the way to the horizon. I'm going to fall asleep to it. Then I'm going to go to all the restaurants, and eat all the real foods that the fake food in the Underground Markets is based on."

"Don't spend all your money in one day, okay? We need to save up for that house in the Himalayas."

"You're going to go straight to the mountains, aren't you," I said with a smile.

"Nah. I'll wait for you, first, beta. What do you think."

"Good girl."

After that meal, a handful of us went out with our suits for an unscheduled patrol for the first time—I guess you'd call it a moonwalk, at that point. We saluted the Earth together, on a lunar surface where we had no threat of being silently attacked from all sides. The century-long Lunar Cold War was over—it had cooled, frozen, bubbled, boiled at times, but now it had evaporated. We were all to go to our paradise in the black sky, as we'd wished every day on our dreary chota duniya.

We didn't stop to think what it all really meant for us asuras, of course. Because as Aditi had told me—the Moon was our home, the only one we'd ever known, really. It is a strange thing to live your life in a place that was never meant for human habitation. You grow to loathe such a life—the gritty dust in everything from your food to your teeth to your weapons, despite extensive air filters, the bitter aerosol meds to get rid of infections and nosebleeds from it. Spending half of your days exercising and drinking carefully rationed water so your body doesn't shrivel up in sub-Earth grav or dry out to a husk in the dry, scrubbed air of controlled atmospheres. The deadening beauty of grey horizons with not a hint of water or life or vegetation in sight except for the sharp lines and lights of human settlement, which we compared so unfavorably to the dazzling technicolour of images and video feeds from Earth, the richness of its life and variety. The constant, relentless company of the same people you grow to love with such ferocity that you hate them as well, because there is no one else for company but the occasional civilian who has the courage to talk to a soldier in Chandnipur's streets, tunnels and canteens.

Now the Moon is truly a gateway to the stars. It is pregnant with the vessels that will take humanity to them, with shipyards and ports rising up under the limbs of robots. I look up at our chota duniya, and its face is crusted in lights, a crown given to her by her lover. Like a goddess it'll birth humanity's new children. We were born in the sky, for war, but we weren't in truth. We were asuras. Now they will be devas, devis. They will truly be like gods, with FTL. In Chandnipur, they told us that we must put our faith in Bhagavan, in all the gods and goddesses of the pantheon. We were given a visiting room, where we sat in the veeyar pods and talked directly to their avatars, animated by the machines. That was the only veeyar we were allowed—no sims of Earth or anything like that, maybe because they didn't want us to get too distracted from our lives on the Moon. So we talked to the avatars, dutifully, in those pods with their smell of incense. Every week we asked them to keep us alive on chota duniya, this place where humanity should not be and yet is.

And now, we might take other worlds, large and small.

Does that frighten you?

I . . . don't know. You told us all those years ago, and you tell me now, that we asuras looked like gods and superheroes when you saw us. In our suits, which would nearly crush a human with their weight if anyone wore them on Earth, let alone walked or fought in them. And now, imagine the humans who will go out there into the star-lit darkness. The big ships won't be ready for a long time. But the small ones—they already want volunteers to take one-way test trips to exoplanets. I don't doubt some of those volunteers will come from the streets, like us asuras. They need people who don't have anything on Earth, so they can leave it behind and spend their lives in the sky. They will travel faster than light itself. Impossible made possible. Even the asuras of the Lunar Command were impossible once.

The Moon was a lifeless place. Nothing but rock and mineral and water. And we still found a way to bring war to it. We still found a way to fight there. Now, when the new humans set foot on other worlds, what if there is life there? What if there is god-given life that has learned to tell stories, make art, fight and love? Will we bring an Earth Army to that life, whatever form it takes? Will we send out this new humanity to discover and share, or will we take people like me and Aditi, born in the streets with nothing, and give them a suit of armour and a ship that sails across the cosmos faster than the light of stars, and send them out to conquer? In the myths, asuras can be both benevolent or evil. Like gods or demons. If we have the chariots of the gods at our disposal, what use is there for gods? What if the next soldiers who go forth into space become demons with the power of gods? What if envy strikes their hearts, and they take fertile worlds from other life forms by force? What if we bring war to a peaceful cosmos? At least we asuras only killed other humans.

One could argue that you didn't just fight on the Moon. You brought life there, for the first time. You, we, humans—we loved there, as well. We still do. There are still humans there.

Love.

I've never heard anyone tell me they love me, nor told anyone I love them. People on Earth, if you trust the stories, say it all the time. We asuras didn't really know what the word meant, in the end.

But. I did love, didn't I? I loved my fellow soldiers. I would have given my life for them. That must be what it means.

I loved Aditi.

That is the first time I've ever said that. I loved Aditi, my sister in arms. I wonder what she would have been, if she had stayed on Earth, never been adopted by the Indian government and given to the Army. A dancer? A Bollywood star? They don't like women with muscles like her, do they? She was bloody graceful with a jetpack, I'll tell you that much. And then, when I actually stop to think, I realize, that she would have been a beggar, or a sweeper, or a sewer-scraper if the Army hadn't given us to the sky. Like me. Now I live among beggars, garbage-pickers, and sweepers, and sewer-scrapers, in this slum clinging to what they call the pillar to heaven. To heaven, can you believe that? Just like we called Earth heaven up there. These people here, they take care of me. In them I see a shared destiny.

What is that?

To remind us that we are not the gods. This is why I pray still to the gods, or the one God, whatever is out there beyond the heliosphere. I pray that the humans who will sail past light and into the rest of the universe find grace out there, find a way to bring us closer to godliness. To worlds where we might start anew, and have no need for soldiers to fight, only warriors to defend against dangers that they themselves are not the harbingers of. To worlds where our cities have no slums filled with people whose backs are bent with the bravery required to hold up the rest of humanity.

Can I ask something? How . . . how did asura Aditi die?

Hm. Asura Aditi of the 8th Lunar Division—Chandnipur, Indian Armed Forces, survived thirty-four years of life and active combat duty as a soldier on the Moon, to be decommissioned and allowed to return to planet Earth. And then she died right here in New Delhi Megapolis walking to the market. We asuras aren't used to this gravity, to these crowds. One shove from a passing impatient pedestrian is all it takes. She fell down on the street, shattered her Moon-brittled hip because, when we came here to paradise, we found that treatment and physio for our weakened bodies takes money that our government does not provide. We get a pension, but it's not much— we have to choose food and rent, or treatment. There is no cure. We might have been bred for war in the sky, but we were not bred for life on Earth. Why do you think there are so few volunteers for the asura program? They must depend on the children of those who have nothing.

Aditi fell to Earth from the Moon, and broke. She didn't have money for a fancy private hospital. She died of an infection in a government hospital.

She never did see the Himalayas. Nor have I.

I'm sorry.

I live here, in the slums around Akash Mahal Space Elevator-Shaft, because of

Aditi. It's dangerous, living along the spindle. But it's cheaper than the subsidized rent of the Veterans Arcologies. And I like the danger. I was a soldier, after all. I like living by the stairway to the sky, where I once lived. I like being high up here, where the wind blows like it never did on the Moon's grey deserts, where the birds I never saw now fly past me every morning and warm my heart with their cries. I like the sound of the nanotube ecosystem all around us, digesting all our shit and piss and garbage, turning it into the light in my one bulb, the heat in my one stove coil, the water from my pipes, piggybacking on the charge from the solar panels that power my little feed-terminal. The way the walls pulse, absorbing sound and kinetic energy, when the elevator passes back and forth, the rumble of Space Elevator Garuda-3 through the spindle all the way to the top of the atmosphere. I don't like the constant smell of human waste. I don't like wondering when the police will decide to cast off the blinders and destroy this entire slum because it's illegal. I don't like going with a half-empty stomach all the time, living off the kindness of the little ones here who go up and down all the time and get my flour and rice. But I'm used to such things—Chandnipur was not a place of plenty either. I like the way everyone takes care of each other here. We have to, or the entire slum will collapse like a rotten vine slipping off a tree-trunk. We depend on each other for survival. It reminds me of my past life.

And I save the money from my pension, little by little, by living frugally. To one day buy a basic black market exoskeleton to assist me, and get basic treatment, physio, to learn how to walk and move like a human on Earth.

Can . . . I help, in any way?

You have helped, by listening. Maybe you can help others listen as well, as you've said.

Maybe they'll heed the words of a veteran forced to live in a slum. If they send soldiers to the edge of the galaxy, I can only hope that they will give those soldiers a choice this time.

I beg the ones who prepare our great chariots: if you must take our soldiers with you, take them—their courage, their resilience, their loyalty will serve you well on a new frontier. But do not to take war to new worlds.

War belongs here on Earth. I should know. I've fought it on the Moon, and it didn't make her happy. In her cold anger, she turned our bodies to glass. Our chota duniya was not meant to carry life, but we thrust it into her anyway. Let us not make that mistake again. Let us not violate the more welcoming worlds we may find, seeing their beauty as acquiescence.

With FTL, there will be no end to humanity's journey. If we keep going far enough, perhaps we will find the gods themselves waiting behind the veil of the universe. And if we do not come in peace by then, I fear we will not survive the encounter.

I clamber down the side of the column of the space elevator, winding down through the biohomes of the slum towards one of the tunnels where I can reach the internal shaft and wait for the elevator on the way down. Once it's close to the surface of the planet, it slows down a lot—that's when people jump on to hitch a ride up or down. We're only about one thousand feet up, so it's not too long a ride down, but the wait for it could be much longer. The insides of the shaft are always lined with slum-dwellers and eleva-tor station hawkers, rigged with gas masks and cling clothes, hanging on to the nano-cable chords and sinews of the great spindle. I might just catch a ride on the back of one of the gliders who offer their solar wings to travelers looking for a quick trip back to the ground. Bit more terrifying, but technically less dangerous, if their back harness and propulsion works.

The eight-year-old boy guiding me down through the steep slum, along the pipes and vines of the NGO-funded nano-ecosystem, occasionally looks up at me with a gap-toothed smile. "I want to be an asura like Gita," he says. "I want to go to the stars."

"Aren't you afraid of not being able to walk properly when you come back to Earth?"

"Who said I want to come back to Earth?"

I smile, and look up, past the fluttering prayer flags of drying clothes, the pulsing wall of the slum, at the dizzying stairway to heaven, an infinite line receding into the blue. At the edge of the spindle, I see asura Gita poised between the air and her home, leaning precariously out to wave goodbye to me. Her hair ripples out against the sky, a smudge of black. A pale, late evening moon hovers full and pale above her head, twin-kling with lights.

I wave back, overcome with vertigo. She seems about to fall, but she doesn't. She is caught between the Earth and the sky in that moment, forever.

My English Name

R. S. Benedict

Here's a creepy yet ultimately quite moving story about a man with a secret so deeply buried that even he no longer knows what it is. . . .

R. S. Benedict spent three years teaching English to rich kids in China, before returning to her native New York to become a bureaucrat. Her work can be found in The Magazine of Fantasy & Science Fiction *and Upper Rubber Boot's upcoming anthology* Broad Knowledge: 35 Women Up To No Good.

I want you to know that you are not crazy.

What you saw in the back of the ambulance was real.

What wasn't real was Thomas Majors.

You have probably figured out by now that I wasn't born in London like I told you I was, and that I did not graduate from Oxford, and that I wasn't baptized in the Church of England, as far as I know.

Here is the truth: Thomas Majors was born in room 414 of the Huayuan Bin-guan, a cheap hotel which in defiance of its name contained neither flowers nor any sort of garden.

If the black domes in the ceiling of the fourth-floor corridor had actually contained working cameras the way they were supposed to, a security guard might have noticed Tingting, a dowdy maid from a coal village in Hunan, enter room 414 without her cleaning cart. The guard would have seen Thomas Majors emerge a few days later dressed in a blue suit and a yellow scarf.

A search of the room would have returned no remnant of Tingting.

Hunan Province has no springtime, just alternating winter and summer days. When Tingting enters room 414 it's winter, gray and rainy. The guest room has a heater, at least, unlike the sleeping quarters Tingting shares with three other maids.

Tingting puts a Do Not Disturb sign on the door and locks it. She shuts the curtains. She covers the mirrors. She takes off her maid uniform. Her skin is still new. She was supposed to be invisible: she has small eyes and the sort of dumpy figure you find in a peasant who had too little to eat as a child and too much to eat as an adult. But prying hands found their way to her anyway, simply because she was there. Still, I know it won't be hard for a girl like her to disappear. No one will look for her.

I pull Tingting off, wriggling out of her like a snake. I consider keeping her in case of emergency, but once she's empty I feel myself shift and stretch. She won't fit anymore. She has to go.

I will spare you the details of how that task is accomplished.

It takes a while to make my limbs the right length. I've narrowed considerably. I check the proportions with a measuring tape; all the ratios are appropriate.

But Thomas Majors is not ready. The room's illumination, fluorescent from the lamps, haze-strangled from the sky, isn't strong enough to tan this new flesh the way it is meant to be.

You thought I was handsome when you met me. I wish you could have seen what I was supposed to be. In my plans, Thomas was perfect. He had golden hair and a complexion like toast. But the light is too weak, and instead I end up with flesh that's not quite finished.

I can't wait anymore. I only have room 414 for one week. It's all Tingting can afford.

So I put on Thomas as carefully as I can, and only when I'm certain that not a single centimeter of what lies beneath him can be seen, I uncover the mirrors.

He's tight. Unfinished skin usually is. I smooth him down and let him soften. I'm impatient, nervous, so I turn around to check for lumps on Thomas's back. When I do, the flesh at his neck rips. I practice a look of pain in the mirror.

Then I stitch the gash together as well as I can. It fuses but leaves an ugly ridge across Thomas's throat. I cover it with a scarf Tingting bought from a street vendor. It's yellow, imitation silk with a recurring pattern that reads *Liu Viuttor*.

The next week I spend in study and practice: how to speak proper English, how to stand and sit like a man, how to drink without slurping, how to hold a fork, how to bring my brows together in an expression of concern, how to laugh, how to blink at semi-regular intervals.

It's extraordinary how much one can learn when one doesn't have to eat or sleep.

I check out on time carrying all of Thomas Majors's possessions in a small bag: a fake passport, a hairbrush, a hand mirror, a wallet, a cell phone, and a single change of clothes.

It takes me under twenty-four hours to find a job. A woman approaches me on the sidewalk. She just opened an English school, she says. Would I like to teach there?

The school consists of an unmarked apartment in a gray complex. The students are between ten and twelve years of age, small and rowdy. I'm paid in cash. They don't notice that my vowels are a bit off; Thomas's new tongue can't quite wrap itself around English diphthongs just yet.

On weekday mornings I take more rent-a-whitey gigs. A shipping company pays me to wear a suit, sit at board meetings, nod authoritatively, and pretend to be an executive. A restaurant pays me to don a chef's hat and toss pizza dough in the air on its opening day. Another English training center, unable to legally hire foreigners in its first year of operation, pays me 6000 RMB per month to wander through the halls and pretend to work there.

I model, too: for a travel brochure, for a boutique, for a university's foreign language department. The photographer tells his clients that I was a finalist on *America's Next Top Model*. They don't question it.

China is a perfect place for an imitation human like myself. Everything is fake here. The clothes are designer knockoffs. The DVDs are bootlegs. The temples are replicas of sites destroyed during the Great Leap Forward and the Cultural Revolution. The markets sell rice made from plastic bags, milk made from melamine, and lamb skewers made from rat meat. Even the internet is fake, a slow, stuttering, pornless thing whose search engines are programed not to look in politically sensitive directions.

It was harder in the West. Westerners demand authenticity even though they don't really want it. They cry out for meat without cruelty, war without casualties, thinness without hunger. But the Chinese don't mind artifice.

I make friends in China quickly and easily. Many are thrilled to have a tall, blond Westerner to wave around as a status symbol.

I wait a few weeks before I associate with other *waiguoren*, terrified they'll pick up on my fake accent or ask me a question about London that I can't answer.

But none of that turns out to be a problem. Very few expats in China ask questions about what one did back home, likely because so few of them want to answer that question themselves. Generally, they are not successful, well-adjusted members of their native countries. But if they have fair skin and a marginal grasp of English, they can find an ESL job to pay for beer and a lost girl to tell them how clever and handsome they are.

I learn quickly that my Englishman costume is not lifelike. Most of the Brits I meet in China are fat and bald, with the same scraggly stubble growing on their faces, their necks, and the sides of their heads. They wear hoodies and jeans and ratty trainers. Thomas wears a suit every day. He's thin, too thin for a Westerner. His accent is too aristocratic, nothing at all like the working-class mumbles coming from the real Brits' mouths. And the scarf only highlights his strangeness.

I think for sure I will be exposed, until one day at a bar a real Englishman jabs a sausage-like finger into my chest and says, "You're gay, aren't you, mate?"

When I only stutter in reply, he says, "Ah, it's all right. Don't worry about it. You might want to tone it down, though. The scarf's a bit much."

And so Thomas Majors's sexuality is decided. It proves useful. It hides me from the expats the way Thomas's whiteness hides me from the Chinese.

It's in a *waiguoren* bar that New Teach English spots me. A tiny woman not even five feet tall swims through a sea of beery pink bodies to find me sitting quietly in a corner, pretending to sip a gin and tonic. She offers me a job.

"I don't have a TOEFL certification," I tell her.

"We'll get you one. No problem," she says. And it's true; a friend of hers owns a printshop that can produce such a document with ease.

"I'm not sure I'll pass the medical exam required for a foreign expert certificate," I tell her.

"My brother-in-law works at the hospital," she says. "If you give him a bottle of cognac, you'll pass the health exam."

And that's how I get my residence permit.

You arrive in my second year at New Teach in Changsha with your eyes downcast and your mouth shut. I recognize you. You're a fellow impostor, but a more mundane sort than myself. Though hired as an ESL teacher, you can hardly say, "Hello, how are you?"

We introduce ourselves by our English names. I am Thomas Majors and you are Daniel Liu. "Liu. Like my scarf," I joke. I give you a smile copied from Pierce Brosnan.

I lie to you and tell you that I'm from London and my name is Thomas. Your lies are those of omission: you do not mention that you are the son of New Teach's owner, and that you had the opportunity to study in the United States but flunked out immediately.

Somehow being the only child of rich parents hasn't made you too spoiled. In your first year at New Teach you sit close to me, studying my counterfeit English as I talk to my students. Meanwhile, I sit close to Sarah, a heavyset Canadian girl, trying to glean real English from her as best I can.

Somehow, my *waiguoren* status doesn't spoil me, either. Unlike most Western men in China, I bathe regularly and dress well and arrive to work on time without a hangover every morning, and I don't try to sleep with my students. My humanity requires work to maintain. I don't take it for granted.

For these reasons, I am declared the star foreign instructor at New Teach English. I stand out like a gleaming cubic zirconium in a rubbish heap. The students adore me. Parents request me for private lessons with their children. They dub me *Da Huang* (Big Yellow).

Every six to twelve months, the other foreign teachers leave and a new set takes their place. Only I remain with you. You stay close to me, seeking me out for grammar help and conversation practice. There's more you want, I know, but you are too timid to ask for it outright, and I am unable to offer it.

We slowly create each other like a pair of half-rate Pygmalions. I fix the holes in your English, teach you how to look others in the eye, how to shake hands authoritatively, how to approach Western women, how to pose in photographs, how to project confidence ("fake it till you make it"), how to be the sort of man you see in movies.

Your questions prod me to quilt Thomas Majors together from little scraps stolen from overheard conversations in expat bars. Thomas Majors traveled a lot as a child, which is why his accent is a bit odd. (That came from an American girl who wore red-framed glasses.) Thomas Majors has an annoying younger brother and an eccentric older sister. (This I took from old television sitcoms.) His father owned a stationery shop (based on an ESL listening test), but his sister is set to inherit the business (from a BBC period piece), so Thomas moved to China to learn about calligraphy (that came from you, when I saw you carrying your ink brush).

Your questions and comments nudge me into playing the ideal Englishman: polite, a little silly at times, but sophisticated and cool. Somehow I become the sort of man that other men look up to. They ask Thomas for advice on dating and fashion and fitness and education. They tell him he's tall and handsome and clever. I say "thank you" and smile, just as I practiced in the mirror.

I liked Thomas. I wish I could have kept on being him a little longer.

In Shenzhen, I nearly tell you the truth about myself. New Teach has just opened a center there and sends you out to manage it. You want to bring me to work there and help keep the foreign teachers in line.

"I don't know if I can pass the medical examination," I tell you.

"You look healthy," you reply.

I choose my words carefully. "I have a medical condition. I manage it just fine, but I'm afraid the doctors will think I am too sick."

"What condition? Is it di . . ." You struggle with the pronunciation.

"It's not diabetes. The truth is—" and what follows is at least partially true "—I don't know what it is, exactly."

"You should see a doctor," you tell me.

"I have," I say. "They did a lot of tests on me for a long time but they still couldn't figure it out. I got sick of it. Lots of needles in my arms and painful surgeries." I mime nurses and doctors jabbing and cutting me. "So now I don't go to doctors anymore."

"You should still have an examination," you tell me.

"No," I say.

Physicians are not difficult to fool, especially in China, overworked and sleep-deprived as they are. But their machines, their scanners, and their blood tests are things I cannot deceive. I do not want to know what they might find beneath Thomas Majors's skin.

I tell you I won't go with you if I have to submit to a medical exam, knowing full well how badly you want me to come. And so phone calls are made, red envelopes are stuffed, favors are cashed in, and banquets are arranged.

We feast with Shenzhen hospital administrators. They stare at me as I eat with chopsticks. "You're very good with . . . ah . . ." The hospital director points at the utensils in my hand, unable to dig up the English word.

"*Kuaizi*," I say. They applaud.

We go out to KTV afterward. The KTV bar has one David Bowie song and two dozen from the Backstreet Boys. The men like the way I sing. They order further snacks, more beer, and a pretty girl to sit on our laps and flirt with us. "So handsome," she says, stroking my chin. By then I have mastered the art of blushing.

You present a bottle of liquor: "It's very good *baijiu*," you say, and everyone nods in agreement. We toast. They fill my glass with liquor over and over again. Each time they clink it and say, "*Gan bei!*" And to me they add, "For England!" Now I have no choice but to drain my glass to make my fake mother country proud.

For most foreigners, *baijiu* is a form of torture. I've heard them say it's foul-tasting, that it gives monstrous hangovers, that you'll find yourself burping it up two days later. But for me, it's no more noxious than any other fluid. So I throw down enough liquor to show our guests that I am healthy and strong. We finish the bottle, then a second, and when I realize that the other men are putting themselves in agony to keep up with me I cover my mouth, run to the nearby lavatory, and loudly empty my stomach. Our guests love it. They cheer.

The winner of the drinking contest is a short, fat, toad-like man with a wide mouth. He's the director of the hospital, which is easy to guess by his appearance; powerful men in Hunan often look a bit like toads. You tell me later that I made him very happy by drinking with him, and that he was extremely pleased to have defeated a Westerner.

And that is how I pass my health examination in Shenzhen.

Your grandmother recognizes me during the following Spring Festival.

Going home with you is a bad idea. I should spend those two weeks enjoying the relative quiet of the empty city, drinking myself into oblivion with the leftover handful of expats.

The idea starts as a lark, a jocular suggestion on your part, but once it seizes me it will not let me go. I can't remember the last time I was in a home, with a family. I want to know what it's like.

You are too embarrassed to try to talk me out of it, so home we go.

Your mother is surprised to see me. She takes you aside and scolds you. Tingting's *Changshahua* has faded. Now my new English brain is still struggling to learn proper Mandarin, so I only get the gist of the conversation. I know *meiyou* (without) and *nü pengyou* (girlfriend), and my understanding of the culture fills in the rest. You're supposed to have brought home a woman. You're not getting any younger; you're just a few years shy of turning thirty unmarried, a bare-branch man. Your parents can't bear it. They don't understand. You're tall, rich, and handsome. Why don't you have a girlfriend?

The question is repeated several times over the next ten days, by your mother, your father, your grandfather, and your aunt.

The only person who doesn't denounce your bachelordom is your grandmother. She likes me. When she sees me, she smiles and says, "*Cao didi.*"

"Grass brother?" I ask.

"It's a nickname for an actor she really likes," you explain. "American."

She asks me another question, but Tingting is too far gone. I'm a Westerner now. "*Ting bu dong,*" I say politely. *I hear you, but I don't understand.*

I ask her to repeat herself, but something the old woman said has embarrassed your mother, for she escorts *Nainai* up to her room.

"She's old," you tell me.

Your mother and grandfather and aunt are not as accustomed to the sight of foreigners as you are. They, too, marvel at my chopstick ability as though I am a cat that has learned to play the piano. At all times I am a walking exhibition. In most places, I'm the *waiguoren*, the foreigner. In expat bars, I'm That Bloke with the Scarf, famed for his habit of always appearing well groomed. And around you, I'm Thomas Majors, though for some reason I don't mind it when you look at me.

I have no trouble with chopsticks. But putting food in my mouth, chewing it, and swallowing it are not actions that come naturally to me. This tongue of mine does not have working taste buds. My teeth are not especially secure in their gums, having been inserted one by one with a few taps of a hammer. This stomach of mine is only a synthetic sack that dangles in the recesses of my body. It has no exit. It leads nowhere.

Eating, for me, is purely a ritual to convince others that I am in fact human. I take no pleasure in it and personally find the act distasteful, especially when observing the oil lingering on others' lips, the squelching sounds of food being slurped and smacked between moist mucous membranes in the folds of fleshy human mouths.

I'm not entirely sure how I gain sustenance. I have found certain habits are necessary to keep me intact. As to each one's precise physiological function, I am unclear.

Your mother thinks I don't eat enough. "My stomach is a little weak," I say. "I'm sorry."

"Is that why you're not fat like most foreigners?" your aunt asks. Her English is surprisingly good.

"I guess so," I tell her.

"My mother is from Hunan," you tell me. "Her food is a little spicy for you, maybe."

"It's good," I say.

"I'll tell her less spicy next time," you promise.

"You don't have to," I say. I hate making the woman inconvenience herself to please an artificial stomach.

After the feast, we watch the annual pageant on television. There's Dashan the Canadian smiling and laughing as the other presenters tease him about the length of his nose. Your relatives point at my face and make unflattering comparisons.

At midnight, we watch the sky light up with fireworks.

Then it's time for bed. I sleep in the guest room with your flatulent uncle. I suspect your mother placed me with him as some form of punishment.

I hadn't anticipated sharing a room. I hadn't even brought nightclothes. I don't own any.

"I usually sleep naked," is my excuse when I sheepishly ask you for a spare set of pajamas.

I wonder what it's like to sleep. It strikes me as a strange way to pass the time.

I pull the covers up to my chin, ignoring your uncle when he scolds me for wearing a scarf to bed. I shut my eyes. I practice breathing slowly and loudly as I've seen real people do. Eventually, your uncle falls asleep. He snores like a chainsaw but sleeps like a stone. The hourly bursts of fireworks don't waken him. Neither does the light from my smartphone when I turn it on to look up Cao Didi. That's only his nickname in the Chinese press, of course. His English name is Maxwell Stone, but that's not his real name, either. In his nation of origin, he was called Maksimilian Petrovsky.

Here is Maxwell Stone's biography: born in Russia in 1920, he moved to the United States in the late '30s, where he began working as an extra for Hammerhead Studios. He worked as a stuntman in adventure films, but he got his first speaking role as a torch-wielding villager in 1941's *The Jigsaw Man*, a low-budget knockoff of *Frankenstein* made without the permission of Mary Shelley's estate. Maxwell Stone never attained fame in the United States or in his native Russia, but his only starring role in 1948's *The White Witch of the Amazon* somehow gained him a cult following in China, where audiences dubbed him "Cao Didi" (Grass Brother) after an iconic scene in which Stone evades a tribe of headhunters by hiding in the underbrush. The McCarthy era killed Stone's career in Hollywood. In 1951, he left Los Angeles and never returned.

Thomas Majors does not resemble Maxwell Stone. Maxwell was dark and muscular with a moustache and a square jaw, the perfect early-twentieth-century man: rugged yet refined.

I don't know how your grandmother recognizes Maxwell Stone in Thomas Majors. I have mostly forgotten Stone. There's hardly any of him left in me, just a few acting lessons and a couple of tips on grooming and posing for photographs.

I spend the next few days and nights dredging up Tingting's *Changshahua*. When I speak Chinese at the table, your mother blanches. She didn't realize I could understand the things she has been saying about me.

I don't get the opportunity to talk to your grandmother privately until the fifth day of the lunar New Year. It's late at night, and I hear her hobble down to the living room by herself and turn on the television. There's a burst of fireworks outside, but everyone is too full of *baijiu* and *jiaozi* to wake up. The only two people in the house still conscious are me and *Nainai*.

I turn off the telly and kneel in front of her. In Tingting's old *Changshahua* I ask, "How did you know I was Cao Didi?"

She smiles blankly and says, in accented English, "How did you recognize me under all these feathers?"

It takes a moment for the memory to percolate. It's 1947, on a cheap jungle set in a sound studio in Los Angeles. Maxwell Stone is wearing a khaki costume and a Panama hat and I'm wearing Maxwell Stone. Maxwell is a craftsman, not an artist: dependable and humble. He always remembers his lines. Now I remember them, too.

Your grandmother is reciting dialog from one of Stone's movies. She's playing the lost heiress whom Stone's character was sent to rescue. I can't quite recall the original actress's name. Margot or something like that.

Lights. Camera. Action. "Feathers or no feathers," I recite. "A dame's a dame. Now it's time to go home." Thomas's mouth tries on a mid-Atlantic accent.

"But I can't go back." Your grandmother touches her forehead with the back of her hand. "I won't. This is where I belong now."

"Knock it off with this nonsense, will you?" says an American adventurer played by a Russian actor played by an entity as-of-yet unclassified. "Your family's paying me big money to bring you back to civilization."

"Tell them I died! Tell them Catherine DuBlanc was killed." A melodramatic pause, just like in the film. ". . . Killed by the White Witch of the Amazon."

Then your grandmother goes quiet again, like a toy whose batteries have run out. She says nothing more.

I thought she knew me. But she only knows Maxwell. The performance was all she wanted.

I have worn so many people. I don't know how many. I don't remember most of them. I ought to keep a record of some kind, but most of them strike me as dull or loathsome in retrospect.

I played a scientist once or twice, but I could not figure myself out. In the 1960s I was a graduate student; I sought myself out in folklore and found vague references to creatures called changelings, shapeshifters, but the descriptions don't quite fit me. I do not have a name.

I do not know how old I am or where I came from or what made me or why I came to be. I try on one person after another, hoping that someday I'll find one that fits and I'll settle into it and some biological process or act of magic will turn me into that person.

I have considered leaving civilization, but the wilds are smaller than they used to be. Someone would stumble across me and see me undisguised. It has happened before.

I will not submit to scientific examination. Though the tools have advanced considerably over the course of my many lifetimes, the human method of inquiry remains the same: tear something apart until it confesses its secrets, whether it's a heretic or a frog's nervous system or the atom.

I do experience something akin to pain, and I prefer to avoid it.

I like being Thomas Majors. I enjoy making money, getting promoted, living as a minor celebrity. I appreciate the admiration others heap upon my creation.

And I confess I like your admiration most of all. It's honest and schoolboyish and sweet.

Wearing Thomas grants me the pleasure of your company, which I treasure, though it probably doesn't show. I am fond of so many things about you, such as that little nod you give when you try to look serious, or the way your entire face immediately turns red when you drink. At first, I studied these traits in the hopes of replicating them someday in a future incarnation. I memorized them. I practiced them at home until they were perfect. But even after I've perfected them, I still can't stop watching you.

I would like to be closer to you. I know you want the same thing. I know the real reason you insist on bringing me with you every time you open a new branch in a new city. I know the real reason you always invite me when you go out to dine with new school administrators and government officials and investors.

But I am a creature that falls to pieces terribly often, and you can't hold on to a thing like that. Every instance of physical touch invites potential damage to my artificial skin and the risk of being discovered.

It is difficult to maintain a safe distance in an overcrowded country where schoolboys sit on each other's laps without embarrassment and *ayis* press their shopping baskets into your legs when you queue up at a market.

When you or anyone else stands too near or puts an arm around my shoulders, I step back and say, "Westerners like to keep other people at arm's length."

You have your own reasons not to get too close. You have familial obligations, filial piety. You must make your parents happy. They paid for your education, your clothes, your food, your new apartment. They gave you your job. You owe them a marriage and a child. You have no reason to be a bachelor at the age of twenty-eight.

Your mother and father choose a woman for you. She's pretty and kind. You can think of no adequate excuses to chase her away. You can tolerate a life with her, you decide. You're a businessman. You will travel a lot. She doesn't mind.

You announce your impending marriage less than a year later. The two of you look perfect in your engagement photos, and at your wedding you beam so handsomely that even I am fooled. I'm not jealous. I'm relieved that she has taken your focus from me, and I do love to see you smile.

A few months later, we travel to Beijing. New Teach is opening a training center there, so we have another series of banquets and *gan bei* and KTV with our new business partners.

By the end of the night, you're staggering drunk, too drunk to walk straight, so I stoop low to let you put your arm across Thomas Majors's shoulders in order to save you from tipping onto the pavement. I hope that you're too drunk to notice there's something not quite right with Thomas's limbs, or at least too drunk to remember it afterward.

I help you into a cab. The driver asks me the standard *waiguoren* questions (*Where are you from? How long have you lived in China? Do you like it here? What is your job? Do you eat hamburgers?*) but I ignore him. I only want to listen to you.

You rub your stomach as the taxi speeds madly back to our hotel. "Are you going to vomit?" I ask.

You're quiet for a moment. I try to roll down the window nearest you, but it's broken. Finally, you mutter, "I'm getting fat. Too much beer."

"You look fine," I say.

"I'm gaining weight," you insist.

"You sound like a woman," I tease you.

"Why don't you get fat?" you say. "You're a Westerner. How are you so slim?"

"Just lucky, I guess," I say.

I pay the cab fare and drag you out, back up to your hotel suite. I give you water to drink and an ibuprofen to swallow so you won't get a hangover. You take your medicine like a good boy, but you refuse to go to sleep.

I sit at the edge of your bed. You lean forward and grab my scarf. "You always wear this," you say.

"Always," I agree.

"What would happen if you took it off?" you ask.

"I can't tell you," I reply.

"Come on," you say, adding a line from a song: "Come on, baby, don't be shy." Then you laugh until tears flow down your red cheeks, until you fall backward onto the bed, and when you fall you drag me by the scarf down with you.

"Be careful!" I tell you. "Ah, *xiao xin!*"

But instead you pull on the scarf as though reeling in a fish.

"You never take it off," you say, holding one end of the scarf before your eyes. "I have never seen your neck."

I know I'm supposed to say something witty but I can't think of it, so I smile bashfully instead. It's a gesture I stole from Hugh Grant films.

"What would happen if I take it off?" you ask. You try to unwrap it, but fortunately you're too clumsy with drink.

"My head would fall off," I say.

Then you laugh, and I laugh. Looming over you is awkward, so I lie beside you and prop my head up on Thomas Majors's shoulder. You turn onto your left side to face me.

"Da Huang," you say, still playing with the scarf. "That's your Chinese name."

"What's your Chinese name?" I ask. "Your real name, I mean? You never told me."

"Chengwei," you say.

"Chengwei," I repeat, imperfectly.

"No," you say. "Not Chéngwéi." You raise your hand, then make a dipping motion to indicate the second and third tones. "Chéngwěi."

"Chéngwěi," I say, drawing the tones in the air with Thomas's graceful fingers.

"*Hen hao,*" you say. *Very good.*

"*Nali,*" I say, a modest denial.

You smile. I notice for the first time that one of your front teeth is slightly crooked. It's endearing, though, one of those little flaws which, through some sort of alchemy I have yet to learn to replicate, only serve to flatter the rest of the picture rather than mar it.

"Da Huang is not a good name," you say.

"What should I be called?" I ask.

You study Thomas Majors's face carefully, yet somehow fail to find its glaring faults.

"Shuai," you say. You don't translate the word, but I know what it means. *Handsome.*

You touch Thomas's cheek. I can feel your warmth through the false skin.

Again, I don't know what to say. This hasn't come up in the etiquette books I studied.

I realize that you're waiting for me to be the brash Westerner who shoves his way forward and does what he wants. This hunger of yours presses on Thomas Majors, pinches and pulls at him to resculpt his personality.

I want to be the man who can give you these things. But I'm terrified. When you run your fingers through Thomas's hair, I worry that the scalp might come loose, or that your hand will skate across a bump that should not be there.

You grab me by the scarf again and pull me closer to you. I shut my eyes. I don't want you to see them at this distance; you might find something wrong in them. But that's not what you're looking for.

Then you kiss me, a clumsy, drunk kiss. You cling to me like one of Harlow's monkeys to a cloth mother.

I can't remember the last time I was kissed.

I vaguely remember engaging in the act of coitus in some previous incarnation. It did not go well.

The mechanics of sexuality, of blood redistributing itself and tissue contracting and flesh reddening and appendages hardening and fluids secreting, are marvelously difficult to imitate with any verisimilitude.

This is the climax of every story. In romance novels, the lovers kiss in the rain, and it's all over. In fairy tales, the kiss breaks the spell: the princess awakens, the frog becomes a man. But that doesn't happen, not now, not the last time I was kissed, and not the next time I will be kissed.

But I enjoy it all the same. Your body is warm and right and real: self-heating skin, hair that grows in on its own, a mouth that lubricates itself.

I study your body and memorize it for future reference. At the moment there is little I can learn and so much that I want to know. I wish I could taste you.

You remove yourself from my lips and drunkenly smear your mouth against my cheek, my jaw, what little of my neck is not covered by the scarf. You press your nose against me and try vainly to smell Thomas Majors under the cologne I have chosen for him. You rest your head on my arm for a moment. I stroke your hair—not because it seems appropriate, but because I want to.

Then you close your eyes. They stay closed. Soon I hear the slow, loud breathing of a man asleep.

That's as far as it goes between you and Thomas Majors.

My arms don't fall asleep so I can let you use Thomas Majors as your pillow for as long as you like. I watch your eyelashes flutter as you fall into REM sleep. I wonder what you're dreaming about. I press my fingers against your neck to feel your pulse.

Without waking you, I move my head down and lay it upon your chest. I shut my eyes. I listen to your heartbeat and the slow rhythm of your breath. Your stomach gurgles. The sounds are at once recognizably natural and alien to me, like deep-sea creatures. I find them endlessly fascinating.

I try very hard to fall asleep, but I have no idea how to go about it. Still, I wait, and I imitate your breathing and hope that I'll begin to lose track of each individual thump of your heart, and that I'll slip out of consciousness and maybe even dream, and that I'll wake up next to you.

Hours pass this way. The light through the window turns pale gray as the sun rises in Beijing's smoggy sky. You roll over to face the shade and lie still again.

I slip from the bed and head to the bathroom where I examine myself. I look very much the same as I did the day before.

I take the elevator down to the dining room. It's 8:36 a.m. Breakfast time. I serve myself from the buffet, selecting the sort of things I think a Westerner is supposed to eat at breakfast: bread, mostly, with coffee, tea, and a glass of milk. I sit alone at a little table with this meal before me and let its steam warm my face. I wait for the aroma to awaken a sense of hunger in me. It doesn't.

I eat it anyway so as not to cause suspicion. I can't taste any of it, as usual.

You're still asleep when I get back. It has only been about five hours since you flopped onto my bed. In the bathroom, I empty Thomas Majors's stomach and turn on the shower. Even though the door is locked, I do not remove the yellow scarf. I tape a plastic bag around it to keep it dry.

The grime of last night's drinking and duck neck slides off, along with a few hairs I'll have to replace later.

The water hits me with a muffled impact. I don't feel wet. Thomas's skin keeps me dry like a raincoat. It isn't my flesh.

I wonder if the state you invoke in me can accurately be called love. I know only that I am happier in your presence than out of it, and that I care desperately what you think of me. If that is love, then I suppose it can be said that I love you, with all the shapeless mass I have instead of a heart.

I don't believe that you love me, but I know that you love Thomas Majors, and that's close enough.

I've heard stories like this, hundreds of them, in languages I've long forgotten. The ending is always the same. Galatea's form softens and turns to flesh. The Velveteen Rabbit sprouts fur and whiskers. But I am still myself, whatever that is, and my puppet Thomas Majors has not become a real boy.

I don't know what I am, but at least now I know something I am not: I am not a creature of fairy tales.

Your cell phone wakes you a little after 10 a.m. It's your wife. I'm dressed by then in a navy-blue suit and working on my cell phone in one of the easy chairs. You finish the conversation before you're quite conscious.

"Do you remember last night?" I ask.

You scratch your head. "No," you groan.

"Do you have a hangover?" I ask.

I take your miserable grunt as a yes.

Your daughter is born seven months later. You leave Beijing for a while to tend to your wife. After a few weeks of your unbearable absence, a student invites me to dinner with her family. "I can't," I tell her. "I'm taking a trip this weekend."

"Are you going to see your *giiiirlfriend*?" she asks in a singsong voice. She's in high school, too busy from fifteen-hour school days seven days a week to have a boyfriend of her own, but she has immense interest in the love lives of her more attractive teachers.

"No," I tell her. The expats know that Thomas Majors is gay but his students and colleagues do not. "I'm going to visit my boss, Mr. Liu. I can have dinner with you next week."

I take the bullet train to Shenzhen. As the countryside blurs past my window, I notice that Thomas's fingernails have become brittle. It's too soon. I blame the cold, dry air of Beijing and resolve to buy a bottle of clear nail polish and apply it at the first opportunity.

You're not home when I come to your door. Your mother-in-law thanks me for the gift I have brought (a canister of imported milk powder), invites me in, and explains that you're on a shopping trip in Hong Kong and will be back soon. In the meantime, I sit in the living room and sip warm water.

Your wife isn't finished with her post-partum month of confinement. She does not invite me to her room. It's probably because she's in pajamas and hasn't washed her hair, or she's simply tired, but the suspicion that she knows something unsavory about me crawls on my back.

There's a dog in the apartment, a shaggy little thing that doesn't go up to my knee. It doesn't quite know what to make of me. It barks and skitters around in circles. It can smell me—not Thomas, but *me*—and it knows that something is slightly off.

But dogs are not terribly bright. I sneak to the kitchen, find a piece of bacon, and put it in my pocket. The dog likes me well enough after that.

You return home that afternoon, laden with bags. You weren't expecting me, but you're happy to see me.

"I bought something for you," you tell me. "A gift."

"You didn't have to," I insist.

"I already had to buy gifts for my whole extended family," you say, "so one more doesn't matter. Here."

You pull a small box out of a suitcase.

"Can I open it?" I ask.

You nod.

I peel off the tape. The paper does not tear at all as I remove it. The box shimmers. I open it and can't help but cry out.

"A new scarf!" I hold it up. It's beautiful, gleaming yellow silk with brocade serpents. I try on an expression of overwhelming gratitude. Until now, I haven't had a chance to use it. "Snakes."

"That's your birth year," you say.

"You remembered," I say. "This is wonderful. Thank you so much."

"Put it on," you tell me.

"In a little while."

"Come on, baby. Don't be shy," you say. You couch your demand in humor and a smile. "Go ahead."

I try to think of an excuse not to. A scar on my neck. A skin condition. It's cold. None of them will work.

Your baby saves me. She starts screaming in the bedroom, and neither your wife nor her mother can calm her down. Your wife soon starts crying, too, and your mother-in-law starts shouting at her.

"I think maybe you should get in there and say hello," I tell you.

You groan, but you comply.

I dash to the lavatory. Quickly, I unwind the counterfeit *Liu Viuttor* scarf from around my neck. It sticks to Thomas's flesh like a bandage. I peel it off slowly but the damage is done. The skin of Thomas Majors's neck has gone ragged, like moth-eaten cloth. I wrap the new scarf around it snugly. Then I unwrap it. The damage is still there. Somehow, I thought this new totem would fix me.

I tie my new scarf around Thomas's neck and return to the living room.

To spare your wife further agitation, her mother banishes the baby from the bedroom. You carry her out with you. She's a fat little thing, all lumpy pink pajamas and chubby cheeks gone red from crying. When she sees me, she quiets herself and stares. She's had limited experience of the world, but even she knows that this creature before her is different.

"She's never seen a foreigner before," you say with a smile. "Do you want to hold her?"

You thrust her into my arms before I can resist. She does not cry anymore, just looks at me with big, dark eyes. Her little body is warm and surprisingly heavy.

"Chinese babies like to stare at handsome faces," you say.

I smile at her. She doesn't smile back. She hasn't learned yet that she's supposed to. Everything about her is unpracticed and new and utterly authentic. I find it unnerving.

"You made this," I said. "You made a person. A real person."

"Yeah," you say, probably filing my remark under *foreigners say strange things.* "Do you think you'll have children?" you ask me.

"Probably not," I say.

Your daughter clutches at my new scarf.

A few days later, we take the bullet train back to Beijing together. You nap most of the way with your head on my shoulder. When you wake up, you tell me, "You should sleep more. You look tired."

"So do you," I reply.

"I have a baby," you say. "You don't."

The only reply I have for him is a nervous Colin Firth smile. Underneath it, I am panicking.

"You look a little gray. Maybe it's the air," you say. "Do you use a mask?"

"Of course," I say.

"You need to drink more water," you tell me. I know by now that nagging is an expression of love in China, but the advice still irritates me. It's useless.

Our train plunges deeper and deeper into miasma as we approach the city. The sky darkens even as the sun rises. It's late autumn and the coal plants are blazing in preparation for winter.

Maybe it *is* the air. Maybe it's bad enough to affect even me. Maybe the new skin wasn't ready when I put it on. Maybe it's just the standard decay that conquers every Westerner who spends too much time in China. Whatever the reason, Thomas Majors is beginning to come apart.

We don air filters as we leave the train station. Outside, we pass people in suits, women in brightly colored minidresses, children in school uniforms, all covering their faces. Those of us who can afford it wear enormous, clunky breathing masks. Those who can't, or who don't understand the risk, wear thin surgical masks made of paper, or little cloth masks with cartoon characters on them, or they just tie a bandana around their mouths and noses. A short, stocky man squats on the pavement, removing his mask every so often to suck on a cigarette.

We take separate taxis. I don't go home, though. I visit a beauty shop, pharmacy, and apothecary, and I buy every skincare product I can find. Expensive moisturizer from France. A mud-mask treatment from Korea. Cocoa butter from South America. Jade rollers. Pearl powder. Caterpillar fungus. Back in my apartment, I slather them on Thomas Majors to see if they will make him tight and bright again. They don't.

The skin is looser, thinner, and when that happens the center cannot hold. I feel around for muscles that have slipped out of place, joints that have shifted, limbs trying to lengthen or widen. I have not lost my shape just yet, but I know it is only a matter of time.

I unravel the scarf you gave me and look again. The skin underneath is even worse. There's an open gash along it that threatens to creep even wider. I can see bits of myself through it, brackish and horrible. Sewing it shut won't do anything; the flesh is too fragile. So I tape it up and wrap the scarf around it even tighter. Silk is strong. Silk will hold it, at least for a while.

I make phone calls to forgers, to chemists, to printers, to tanners, to all the sorts of people who can help me make someone new. This time, at least, I have money to spend and privacy in which to work. I can do it right. I can make somebody who will last longer and fit better and maybe won't come apart again.

The smog provides a convenient excuse for my absence over the next few weeks. It traps most of us in our homes with our air purifiers. But at times a strong wind comes to blow it away, at least for a while, and there you are again inviting me out to KTV bars and business lunches and badminton. I can't go. I want to go, but Thomas Majors is fragile and thin, liable to split apart at any moment. His hair is coming out. His gums are getting soft. Speaking is difficult; I feel the gash in Thomas's throat grow wider and wider under the scarf.

I cite my health as a reason not to renew my contract, but you refuse to accept it. You won't let Thomas Majors go. I remind you of my unnamed medical condition. I tell you that I've been to dozens of doctors and even some traditional Chinese healers. I promise to see another specialist.

I promise I'll keep in touch. I promise I'll come back again once I'm better.

Then I sequester myself in my apartment. I don't know what my next form will be. I'd like to build myself another Thomas Majors, one that will last forever, but I feel my body pulling in different directions. It wants to shift in a dozen different ways, all of them horrible: too squat, or insect-thin, or with limbs at angles that don't make sense in human physiology.

My human costume is slipping off me too quickly. I don't go outside anymore. I only wait for the men to come with the documents and the materials. There's a knock at the door. It's you.

I know I shouldn't open it, but I also know that you can hear me moving around in my apartment, and that you'll be hurt if I don't let you in, and even though I don't want you to see me as I am, I still want to see you. I adjust Thomas's face and throw a heavy robe on over the blue suit.

The expression of horror in your eyes is remarkable. I memorize it to use in a future incarnation.

"*Ni shenti bu hao,*" you say, in that blunt Chinese way. *Your body is not good.* You take off your breathing mask and come inside.

"Thanks," I say.

You try to give me a hug.

"Don't," I say. "I could be contagious." The truth is I'm terrified you might feel me moving around underneath Thomas Majors, or you'll squeeze tight enough to leave a dent.

You sit down without invitation.

"What is it?" you ask.

"I think I caught food poisoning, on top of everything else. Probably shouldn't have eaten *shaokao.*"

"Are you going to be healthy enough for the ride home?" you ask.

"I'll be all right," I say. "I just need rest is all."

"Have you been to the hospital?"

"Of course," I tell you. "The doctor gave me a ton of antibiotics and said to avoid cold water."

"Which hospital was it? Which doctor? Maybe he wasn't a good one. My friend knows one of the best doctors for stomach problems. I can take you to him. They have very good equipment. A big laboratory."

"I'll be all right."

You head to the kitchen to boil water. "Wait a moment," you instruct me over the sound of the electric kettle. Then you return with a steaming mug of something dark and greenish. "Drink this," you tell me. "Chinese medicine. For your stomach."

"I can't," I insist.

"Come on," you say. "You look really bad."

"It's too hot," I complain. I feel the steam softening the insides of Thomas's nasal passages.

You return to the kitchen to retrieve some ice from the freezer. I never use ice, but I always make sure to have some in my home because I am a Westerner for the time being.

You drop a few cubes of ice into my mug. "There," you say. "Drink it."

"I'm sick to my stomach," I complain. "I might vomit."

"This will fix it," you insist.

I know I shouldn't listen to you, but I want to make you happy, and some part of me still half-believes that stupid fairy-tale fantasy that your love will make me real somehow. So I put the mug to my lips and slurp down some of its contents, and soon I feel the artificial stomach lining thinning and turning to fizz inside me.

"Excuse me," I rasp. The vocal cords feel loose. I bolt to the bathroom to vomit.

Thomas's stomach lining makes its way up and out. It hangs from my mouth, still attached somewhere around my chest. Your medicine has burned holes into it. I don't blame you. I'm sure it works properly on real human stomachs. I bite through the fake esophagus to free myself from the ruined organ, losing a tooth in the process. Then I flush the mess down the squat toilet.

Evidently, the noise is alarming. "I'm calling you an ambulance!" you shout from the living room.

It takes me much too long to cram the esophagus back in so I can say, "Don't.

I'm quite all right. I just needed to vomit. I'm feeling better now. Really." But the vocal cords are so loose by this point that the words come out slurred and gravelly.

The call is quick; the arrival of the ambulance less so. I lie on the bathroom floor in a fetal position, contemplating my options. My strength is gone. I can't make it to the front door without you tackling me. I could get to a window and throw myself out, perhaps; I could drop through twenty stories of pollution and crawl away from Thomas Majors after he hits the ground. But I can't do something so horrible in front of you.

You punch through the bathroom door, undo the lock, and put your arms around my shoulders. I can feel your hands shake. You tell me over and over again that I'm going to be all right, and you're going to help me. I want to believe you.

The ambulance finally arrives. You pay the driver and help carry me out. "You're so light," you say.

I don't try to fight you.

You should have called a taxi, or maybe flagged down an e-bike instead, because the bulky ambulance gets stuck in traffic. You slap the insides of it as if trying to beat Beijing into submission. You curse the other cars, the ambulance driver, the civil engineers who planned the roadways, the population density, the asphalt for not being wide enough.

You curse the EMTs for the deplorable condition of the ambulance and the black soot on the gauze they've applied to my face, unaware that the filth is coming from the man you're trying to save. Thomas has sprung a leak; now I am pouring out.

They put a respirator of some sort over Thomas Majors's face. They attach devices to him to monitor a heart and lungs that do not exist. You notice the way the technician fiddles with the wires and pokes the electronic box, unable to get a proper reading from the patient, and you curse the defective equipment. You see the other technician jab me over and over again, unable to find a vein in which to stick an IV, and you curse his incompetence.

They get out their scissors. They open the robe and cut through its sleeves. Then they start cutting through my blue suit. I make little sounds of protest. I can't speak anymore.

"I'll buy you a new one," you say.

I try to crawl away, but you hold one arm and a technician grabs the other. Soon you can see what has happened to Thomas's torso—misshapen, discolored, with thick scars where I've had to stich darts as the skin became too loose.

Your hand moves to your mouth. "You were sick how long?" you ask. Your English is slipping.

I know what's coming. There is nothing I can do to stop it but lie here like a damsel tied to the railroad tracks and wait for it to hit me.

It's time to remove the scarf.

I've tied it too tight to slip the scissors underneath it, so they have to cut through the knots. Frustrated by how slowly the technicians work, you lean in and grab the silk.

Your hands shake harder and harder as you unwind the fabric. I watch the silk growing darker the closer you get to me. I'm sorry I ruined such a beautiful thing.

I can't see what's beneath. I don't want to. There's a reason I keep the mirrors covered when I go through a shift. But I can see the reaction on your face and on the technicians' faces, too. They've doubtless encountered horrible things in their line of work, and yet this still alarms them.

Thomas Majors's larynx comes apart. My neck is exposed. I feel cold.

You can't speak anymore either. You only make a strange panting sound and stare. Terror has stolen your voice. What's left is something primitive, an instinct going back millions of years. It must be wonderful to know who your ancestors were and that they were something as benign as apes.

One of the technicians is on his cell phone with the hospital, explaining the situation as best he can. I hear the doctor's voice telling them to bring me in through the basement entrance so the other patients won't see me.

I know what he wants. Physicians here are required to publish research on top of their grueling schedules and the doctor realizes that he has found an extraordinary case study. He's already thinking of fame, research grants, possibly another Nobel Prize for China. He won't have any trouble keeping me in a lab. There are no human rights standards to stop scientific progress here, and my fake UK citizenship will not protect me.

With nothing left to hold him together, Thomas Majors comes undone. The skin of his head shrinks from the skin of his shoulders. His face is loose. A seam opens at his armpit and runs down his torso.

You grab his hand. You can feel me underneath it, squirming. Your wrist jerks but you don't let go. Thomas's hand slips off me like a glove. It takes you a moment to understand what just happened, what you're holding, and when the realization hits, you scream and scream and scream.

The technicians can't pin me down anymore. They don't want to. It's impossible to tell what they can grab on to and whether or not it's safe to touch. So now they're trying to get away, pressing themselves against the walls of the ambulance, trying to clamber up to the front. The driver has already fled.

You're paralyzed. You've wedged yourself into a corner. Your eyes whirl about the ambulance, skipping upon me, upon what's left of Thomas Majors, upon the rear-door latch that's not quite close enough for you to open, upon the ceiling and the machines and all these things that don't make sense anymore.

I stand up. The last scraps of the man I wanted so badly to be fall to the floor. You shrink down, down, trying to disappear, but you don't have as much practice as I do.

You cover your eyes, uncover them, look at me, shut them again. I grab the door latch, averting my gaze from the sight of my own hand.

You're muttering something over and over again like a Buddhist chant. I listen carefully. My hearing is not what it was just a few minutes ago, but I can recognize the words, "Ni shi shenme?" What are you?

I don't have a larynx anymore and my tongue can no longer accommodate human language, so even though I want to, I can't answer "wo bu zhidao" or "ouk oida" or "nga nu-zu" or "I don't know."

I get the door open. The outside world is an endless polluted twilight. The driver behind us doesn't look up from his cell phone to glance in my direction. Two car-lengths away, all I can see are vague shapes and headlights. The smog will hide me well.

I climb out of the ambulance and into the haze. I don't look back.

I saw you once after that. It wasn't long ago, I think. I was wearing someone new, a girl with black hair and a melon-seed face. Pretty girls are easy for me. I can slather on makeup if the skin isn't right, and I don't have to bother with a backstory or a personality. No one really wants it.

It was at an auto show in Shanghai. I was draped across a green Ferrari, wearing a bikini that matched the paint. I hadn't expected to see you, but there you were with a group of businessmen smoking Marlboros and ogling the models.

You were older. I'm not sure by how much. Time passes differently for me, and maybe time alone was not responsible for how much you had aged.

I would like to say I will never forget you, but I can't promise you that. This shapeless matter inside my head shifts and dies and regenerates, and as it does so, memories fade and old incarnations of myself are discarded. Maxwell Stone had lovers, most likely, but I can't recall their faces, and someday I will lose yours as well.

Your group strolled by my Ferrari, making the obligatory lewd remarks, flashing their brown teeth in leery grins. I wore my generic smile and offered up a vacant titter. I told them about the car.

You stood a little ways behind the other men with your hands in your pockets. I knew that look: you were too tired to pretend to be having a good time.

I smiled at you as hard as I could. Finally, you looked up. I thought maybe you would recognize me somehow. Maybe you would cry out, "It's you!" and take me in your arms. Or maybe, at the very least, you'd let your gaze linger on me a little longer than normal.

But you didn't. You made that nervous grimace you do whenever a woman pays too much attention to you. Then you ambled off to look at a Lexus—a four-door with lots of cabin space. Good for families.

I watched you move. Your shoulders were slumped as though you carried something very heavy.

Then more bodies flowed between us, wealthy men and their school-aged mistresses, nouveau riche wives and their spoiled bachelor sons searching for a car to attract a pretty bride, broke students in designer knockoffs come to take selfies in front of BMWs so they can pretend to be rich on Weixin.

I lost you among them. I did not find you again.

an evening with severyn grimes

RICH LARSON

Rich Larson was born in West Africa, has studied in Rhode Island and Edmonton, Alberta, and worked in a small Spanish town outside Seville. He now lives in Grande Prairie, Alberta. He won the 2014 Dell Award and the 2012 Rannu Prize for Writers of Speculative Fiction. In 2011 his cyberpunk novel Devolution *was a finalist for the Amazon Breakthrough Novel Award. His short work appears or is forthcoming in* Lightspeed, Daily Science Fiction, Strange Horizons, Apex Magazine, Beneath Ceaseless Skies, AE, *and many others, including the anthologies* Upgraded, Futuredaze, *and* War Stories. *Coming up is his first collection,* Tomorrow Factory. *Find him online at richwlarson.tumblr.com.*

Here he delivers a suspenseful, fast-paced tale in which a kidnapped billionaire has to try to outwit his kidnappers while in captivity, and at the same time deal with an angry young woman who has some very real personal reasons for wanting him dead.

Do you have to wear the Fawkes in here?" Girasol asked, sliding into the orthochair. Its worn wings crinkled, leaking silicon, as it adjusted to her shape. The plastic stuck cold to her shoulder blades, and she shivered.

"No." Pierce made no move to pull off the smirking mask. "It makes you nervous," he explained, groping around in the guts of his open Adidas track-bag, his tattooed hand emerging with the hypnotic. "That's a good enough reason to wear it."

Girasol didn't argue, just tipped her dark head back, positioning herself over the circular hole they'd punched through the headrest. Beneath it, a bird's nest of circuitry, mismatched wiring, blinking blue nodes. And in the center of the nest: the neural jack, gleaming wet with disinfectant jelly.

She let the slick white port at the top of her spine snick open.

"No cheap sleep this time," Pierce said, flicking his nail against the inky vial. "Get ready for a deep slice, Sleeping Beauty. Prince Charming's got your shit. Highest-grade Dozr a man can steal." He plugged it into a battered needler, motioned for her arm. "I get a kiss or what?"

Girasol proffered her bruised wrist. Let him hunt around collapsed veins while she said, coldly, "Don't even think about touching me when I'm under."

Pierce chuckled, slapping her flesh, coaxing a pale blue worm to stand out in her white skin. "Or what?"

Girasol's head burst as the hypnotic went in, flooding her capillaries, working over her neurotransmitters. "Or I'll cut your fucking balls off."

The Fawkes's grin loomed silent over her; a brief fear stabbed through the descending drug. Then he laughed again, barking and sharp, and Girasol knew she had not forgotten how to speak to men like Pierce. She tasted copper in her mouth as the Dozr settled.

"Just remember who got you out of Correctional," Pierce said. "And that if you screw this up, you'd be better off back in the freeze. Sweet dreams."

The mask receded, and Girasol's eyes drifted up the wall, following the cabling that crept like vines from the equipment under her skull, all the way through a crack gouged in the ceiling, and from there to whatever line Pierce's cronies had managed to splice. The smartpaint splashed across the grimy stucco displayed months of preparation: shifting sat-maps, decrypted dossiers, and a thousand flickering image loops of one beautiful young man with silver hair.

Girasol lowered the chair. Her toes spasmed, kinking against each other as the thrumming neural jack touched the edge of her port. The Dozr kept her breathing even. A bone-deep rasp, a meaty click, and she was synched, simulated REM brainwave flowing through a current of code, flying through wire, up and out of the shantytown apartment, flitting like a shade into Chicago's dark cityscape.

Severyn Grimes felt none of the old heat in his chest when the first round finished with a shattered nose and a shower of blood, and he realized something: the puppet shows didn't do it for him anymore.

The fighters below were massive, as always, pumped full of HGH and Taurus and various combat chemicals, sculpted by a lifetime in gravity gyms. The fight, as always, wouldn't end until their bodies were mangled heaps of broken bone and snapped tendon. Then the technicians would come and pull the digital storage cones from the slick white ports at the tops of their spines, so the puppeteers could return to their own bodies, and the puppets, if they were lucky, woke up in meat repair with a paycheck and no permanent paralysis.

It seemed almost wasteful. Severyn stroked the back of his neck, where silver hair was shorn fashionably around his own storage cone. Beneath him, the fighters hurtled from their corners, grappled, broke, and collided again. He felt nothing. Severyn's adrenaline only ever seemed to spike in boardrooms now. Primate aggression through power broking.

"I'm growing tired of this shit," he said, and his bodyguard carved a clear exit through the baying crowd. Follow-cams drifted in his direction, foregoing the match for a celeb-spotting opportunity: the second-wealthiest bio-businessman in Chicago, 146 years old but plugged into a beautiful young body that played well on cam. The godlike Severyn Grimes slumming at a puppet show, readying for a night of downtown debauchery? The paparazzi feed practically wrote itself.

A follow-cam drifted too close; Severyn raised one finger, and his bodyguard swatted it out of the air on the way out the door.

Girasol jolted, spiraled down to the floor. She'd drifted too close, too entranced by the geometry of his cheekbones, his slate gray eyes and full lips, his swimmer's build swathed in Armani and his graceful hands with Nokia implants glowing just under the skin. A long way away, she was dimly aware of her body in the orthochair in the decrepit apartment. She scrawled a message across the smartpaint:

HE'S LEAVING EARLY. ARE YOUR PEOPLE READY?

"They're, shit, they're on their way. Stall him." Pierce's voice was distant, an insect hum, but she could detect the sound of nerves fraying.

Girasol jumped to another follow-cam, triggering a fizz of sparks as she seized its motor circuits. The image came in upside down: Mr. Grimes clambering into the limo, the bodyguard scanning the street. Springy red hair and a brutish face suggested Neanderthal gene-mixing. Him, they would have to get rid of.

The limousine door glided shut. From six blocks away, Girasol triggered the crude mp4 file she'd prepared—sometimes the old tricks worked best—and wormed inside the vehicle's CPU on a sine wave of sound.

Severyn vaguely recognized the song breezing through the car's sponge speakers, but outdated protest rap was a significant deviation from his usual tastes.

"Music off."

Silence filled the backseat. The car took an uncharacteristically long time calculating their route before finally jetting into traffic. Severyn leaned back to watch the dark street slide past his window, lit by lime green neon and the jittering ghosts of holograms. A moment later he turned to his bodyguard, who had the Loop's traffic reports scrolling across his retinas.

"Does blood excite you, Finch?"

Finch blinked, clearing his eyes back to a watery blue. "Not particularly, Mr. Grimes. Comes with the job."

"I thought having reloaded testosterone would make the world . . . visceral again." Severyn grabbed at his testicles with a wry smile. "Maybe an old mind overwrites a young body in more ways than the technicians suspect. Maybe mortality is escapable, but old age inevitable."

"Maybe so," Finch echoed, sounding slightly uncomfortable. First-lifers often found it unsettling to be reminded they were sitting beside a man who had bought off Death itself. "Feel I'm getting old myself, sometimes."

"Maybe you'd like to turn in early," Severyn offered.

Finch shook his head. "Always up for a jaunt, Mr. Grimes. Just so long as the whorehouses are vetted."

Severyn laughed, and in that moment the limo lurched sideways and jolted to a halt. His face mashed to the cold glass of the window, bare millimeters away from an autocab that darted gracefully around them and back into its traffic algorithm.

Finch straightened him out with one titanic hand.

"What the fuck was that?" Severyn asked calmly, unrumpling his tie.

"Car says there's something in the exhaust port," Finch said, retinas replaced by schematic tracery. "Not an explosive. Could just be debris."

"Do check."

"Won't be a minute, Mr. Grimes."

Finch pulled a pair of wire-veined gloves from a side compartment and opened the door, ushering in a chilly undertow, then disappeared around the rear end of the limousine. Severyn leaned back to wait, flicking alternately through merger details and airbrushed brothel advertisements in the air above his lap.

"Good evening, Mr. Grimes," the car burbled. "You've been hacked."

Severyn's nostrils flared. "I don't pay you for your sense of humor, Finch."

"I'm not joking, parasite."

Severyn froze. There was a beat of silence, then he reached for the door handle. It might as well have been stone. He pushed his palm against the sunroof and received a static charge for his trouble.

"Override," he said. "Severyn Grimes. Open doors." No response. Severyn felt his heartbeat quicken, felt a prickle of sweat on his palms. He slowly let go of the handle. "Who am I speaking to?"

"Take a look through the back window. Maybe you can figure it out."

Severyn spun, peering through the dark glass. Finch was hunched over the exhaust port, only a slice of red hair in sight. The limousine was projecting a yellow hazard banner, cleaving traffic, but as Severyn watched an unmarked van careened to a halt behind them.

Masked men spilled out. Severyn thumped his fist into the glass of the window, but it was soundproof; he sent a warning spike to his security, but the car was shielded against adbombs, and theoretically against electronic intrusion, and now it was walling off his cell signal.

All he could do was watch. Finch straightened up, halfway through peeling off one smartglove when the first black-market Taser sparked electric blue. He jerked, convulsed, but still somehow managed to pull the handgun from his jacket. Severyn's fist clenched. Then the second Taser went off, painting Finch a crackling halo. The handgun dropped.

The masked men bull-rushed Finch as he crumpled, sweeping him up under the arms, and Severyn saw the wide leering smiles under their hoods: Guy Fawkes. The mask had been commandeered by various terror-activist groups over the past half-century, but Severyn knew it was the Priesthood's clearest calling card. For the first time in a long time, he felt a cold corkscrew in his stomach. He tried to put his finger on the sensation.

"He has a husband." Severyn's throat felt tight. "Two children."

"He still will," the voice replied. "He's only a wage-slave. Not a blasphemer."

Finch was a heavy man and his knees scraped along the tarmac as the Priests hauled him toward the van's sliding door. His head lolled to his chest, but Severyn saw his blue eyes were slitted open. His body tensed, then—

Finch jerked the first Priest off-balance and came up with the subcutaneous blade flashing out of his forearm, carving the man open from hip to rib cage. Blood foamed and spat and Severyn felt what he'd missed at the puppet show, a burning flare in his chest. Finch twisted away from the other Priest's arm, eyes roving, glancing off the black glass that divided them, and then a third Taser hit him. He fell with his jaws spasming; a Priest's heavy boot swung into him as he toppled.

The flare died inside Severyn's pericardium. The limousine started to move.

"He should not have done that," the voice grated, as the bleeding Priest and then Finch and then the other Priests disappeared from sight.

Severyn watched through the back window for a moment longer. Faced forward. "I'll compensate for any medical costs incurred by my employee's actions," he said. "I won't tolerate any sort of retribution to his person."

"Still talking like you've got cards. And don't pretend like you care. He's an ant to you. We all are."

Severyn assessed. The voice was synthesized, distorted, but something in the cadence made him think female speaker. Uncommon, for a Priest. He gambled.

"What is your name, madam?"

"I'm a man, parasite."

Only a split second of hesitation before the answer, but it was more than enough to confirm his guess. Severyn had staked astronomical shares on such pauses, pauses that couldn't be passed off as lag in the modern day. Signs of unsettledness. Vulnerability. It made his skin thrum. He imagined himself in a boardroom.

"No need for pretenses," Severyn said. "I merely hoped to establish a more personable base for negotiation."

"Fuck you." A warble of static. Maybe a laugh. "Fuck you. There's not going to be any negotiation. This isn't a funding op. We just caught one of the biggest parasites on the planet. The Priesthood's going to make you an example. Hook you to an autosurgeon and let it vivisect you on live feed. Burn what's left of you to ash. No negotiations."

Severyn felt the icy churn in his stomach again. Fear. He realized he'd almost missed it.

Girasol was dreaming many things at once. Even as she spoke to her captive in real-time, she perched in the limousine's electronic shielding, shooting down message after desperate message he addressed to his security detail, his bank, his associates.

It took her nearly a minute to realize the messages were irrelevant. Grimes was trying to trigger an overuse fail-safe in his implants, generate an error message that could sneak through to Nokia.

Such a clever bastard. Girasol dipped into his implants and shut them down, leaving him half-blind and stranded in realtime. She felt a sympathetic lurch as he froze, gray eyes clearing, clipped neatly away from his data flow. If only it was that easy to reach in and drag him out of that pristine white storage cone.

"There aren't many female Priests," Grimes said, as if he hadn't noticed the severance. "I seem to recall their creed hates the birth control biochip almost as much as they hate neural puppeteering." He flashed a beatific smile that made Girasol ache. "So much love for one sort of parasite, so much ichor for the other."

"I saw the light," Girasol said curtly, even though she knew she should have stopped talking the instant he started analyzing, prying, trying to break her down.

"My body is, of course, a volunteer." Grimes draped his lean arms along the backseat. "But the Priesthood does have so many interesting ideas about what individuals should and should not do with their own flesh and bone."

"Volunteers are as bad as the parasites themselves," Girasol recited from one of Pierce's Adderall-fueled rants. "Selling their souls to a digital demon. The tainted can't enter the kingdom of heaven."

"Don't tell me a hacker riding sound waves still believes in souls."

"You lost yours the second you uploaded to a storage cone."

Grimes replied with another carefully constructed probe, but Girasol's interest diverted from their conversation as Pierce's voice swelled from far away. He was shouting. Someone else was in the room. She cross-checked the limo's route against a staticky avalanche of police scanners, then dragged herself back to the orthochair, forcing her eyes open.

Through the blur of code, she saw Pierce's injured crony, the one who'd been sliced belly to sternum, being helped through the doorway. His midsection was swathed in bacterial film, but the blood that hadn't been coagulated and eaten away left a dripping carmine trail on the linoleum.

"You don't bring him here," Pierce grated. "You lobo, if someone saw you—"

"I'm not going to take him to a damn hospital." The man pulled off his Fawkes, revealing a pale and sweat-slick face. "I think it's, like, shallow. Didn't get any organs. But he's bleeding bad, need more cling film—"

"Where's the caveman?" Pierce snapped. "The bodyguard, where is he?"

The man waved a blood-soaked arm towards the doorway. "In the parking garage. Don't worry, we put a clamp on him and locked the van." His companion moaned and he swore. "Now where's the aid kit? Come on, Pierce, he's going to, shit, he's going to bleed out. Those stairs nearly did him in."

Pierce stalked to the wall and snatched the dented white case from its hook. He caught sight of Girasol's gummy eyes half-open.

"How close are you to the warehouse?" he demanded.

"You know how the Loop gets on weekends," Girasol said, feeling her tongue move inside her mouth like a phantom limb. "Fifteen. Twenty."

Pierce nodded. Chewed his lips. Agitated. "Need another shot?"

"Yeah."

Girasol monitored the limo at the hazy edge of her mind as Pierce handed off the aid kit and prepped another dose of hypnotic. She thought of how soon it would be her blood on the floor, once he realized what she was doing. She thought of slate gray eyes as she watched the oily black Dozr mix with her blood, and when Pierce hit the plunger, she closed her own and plunged with it.

Severyn was methodically peeling back flooring, ruining his manicured nails, humming protest rap, when the voice came back.

"Don't bother. You won't get to the brake line that way."

He paused, staring at the miniscule tear he'd made. He climbed slowly back onto the seat and palmed open the chiller. "I was beginning to think you'd left me," he said, retrieving a glass flute.

"Still here, parasite. Keeping you company in your final moments."

"Parasite," Severyn echoed as he poured. "You know, if it weren't for people like you, puppeteering might have never developed. Religious zealots are the ones who axed cloning, after all. Just think. If not for that, we might have been uploading to fresh blank bodies instead of those desperate enough to sell themselves whole."

He looked at his amber reflection in the flute, studying the beautiful young face he'd worn for nearly two years. He knew the disembodied hacker was seeing it too, and it was an advantage, no matter how she might try to suppress it. Humans loved beauty and underestimated youth. It was one reason Severyn used young bodies instead of the thickset middle-aged Clooneys favored by most CEOs.

"And now it's too late to go back," Severyn said, swirling his drink. "Growing a clone is expensive. Finding a volunteer is cheap." He sipped and held the stinging Perdue in his mouth.

Silence for a beat.

"You have no idea what kind of person I am."

Severyn felt his hook sink in. He swallowed his drink. "I do," he replied. "I've been thinking about it quite fucking hard, what with my impending evisceration. You're no Priest. Your familiarity with my security systems and reticence to kill my bodyguard makes me think you're an employee, former or current."

"People like you assume everyone's working for them."

"Whether you are or not, you've done enough research to know I can easily triple whatever the Priesthood is paying for your services."

"There's not going to be any negotiation. You're a dead man."

Severyn nodded, studying his drink, then slopped it out across the upholstery and smashed the flute against the window. The crystal crunched. Severyn shook the now-jagged stem, sending small crumbs to the floor. It gleamed scalpel-sharp. Running his thumb along it raised hairs on the nape of his neck.

"What are you doing?" the voice blared.

"My hand slipped," Severyn said. "Old age." A fat droplet of blood swelled on his thumb, and he wiped it away. He wasn't one to mishandle his bodies or rent zombies for recreational suicide in drowning tanks, free falls. No, Severyn's drive to survive had always been too strong for him to experiment with death. As he brought the edge to his throat he realized that killing himself would not be easy.

"That won't save you." Another static laugh, but this one forced. "We'll upload your storage cone to an artificial body within the day. Throw you into a pleasure doll with the sensitivity cranked to maximum. Imagine how much fun they'd have with that."

The near-panic was clarion clear, even through a synthesizer. Intuition pounded at Severyn's temples. The song was still in there, too.

"You played yourself in on a music file," Severyn said. "I searched it before you shut off my implants. *Decapitate the state / wipe the slate / create.* Banal, but so very catchy, wasn't it? Swan song of the Anticorp Movement."

"I liked the beat."

"Several of my employees became embroiled in those protests. They were caught trying to coordinate a viral strike on my bank." Severyn pushed the point into the smooth flesh of his throat. "Nearly five years ago, now. I believe the chief conspirator was sentenced to twenty years in cryogenic storage."

"Stop it. Put that down."

"You must have wanted me to guess," Severyn continued, worming the glass gently, like a corkscrew. He felt a warm trickle down his neck. "Why keep talking, otherwise? You wanted me to know who got me in the end. This is your revenge."

"Do you even remember my name?" The voice was warped, but not by static. "And put that down."

The command came so fierce and raw that Severyn's hand hesitated without his meaning to. He slowly set the stem in his lap. "Or you kept talking," he said, "because you missed hearing his voice."

"Fucking parasite." The hacker's voice was tired and suddenly brittle. "First you steal twenty years of my life and then you steal my son."

"Girasol Fletcher." There it was. Severyn leaned back, releasing a long breath. "He came to me, you know." He racked his digital memory for another name, the name of his body before it was his body. "Blake came to me."

"Bullshit. You always wanted him. Had a feed of his swim meets like a pedophile."

"I helped him. Possibly even saved him."

"You made him a puppet."

Severyn balled a wipe and dabbed at the blood on Blake's slender neck. "You left him with nothing," he said. "The money drained off to pay for your cryo. And Blake fell off, too. He was a full addict when he came to me. Hypnotics. Spending all his time in virtual dreamland. You'd know about that." He paused, but the barb drew no response. "It couldn't have been for sex fantasies. I imagine he got anything he wanted in realtime. I think maybe he was dreaming his family whole again."

Silence. Severyn felt a dim guilt, but he pushed through. Survival.

"He was desperate when he found me," Severyn continued. "I told him I wanted his body. Fifteen-year contract, insured for all organic damage. It's been keeping your cryo paid off, and when the contract's up he'll be comfortable for the rest of his life."

"Don't. Act." A stream of static. "Like you did him a favor."

Severyn didn't reply for a moment. He looked at the window, but the glass was still black, opaqued. "I'm not being driven to an execution, am I?"

Girasol wound the limousine through the grimy labyrinth of the industrial district, guiding it past the agreed-upon warehouse where a half-dozen Priests were awaiting the delivery of Severyn Grimes, Chicago's most notorious parasite. Using the car's external camera, she saw the lookout's confused face emerging from behind his mask.

On the internal camera, she couldn't stop looking into Blake's eyes, hoping they would be his own again soon.

"There's a hydrofoil waiting on the docks," she said through the limousine speakers. "I hired a technician to extract you. Paid him extra to drop your storage cone in the harbor."

"The Priesthood wasn't open to negotiations concerning the body."

Far away, Girasol felt the men clustered around her, watching her prone body like predatory birds. She could almost smell the fast-food grease and sharp chemical sweat.

"No," she said dully. "Volunteers are as bad as the parasites themselves. Blake sold his soul to a digital demon. To you."

"When they find out you betrayed their interests?"

Girasol considered. "Pierce will rape me," she said. "Maybe some of the others, too. Then they'll pull some amateur knife-and-pliers interrogation shit, thinking it's some kind of conspiracy. And then they may. Or may not. Kill me." Her voice was steady until the penultimate word. She calculated distance to the pier. It was worth it. It was worth it. Blake would be free, and Grimes would be gone.

"You could skype in CPD."

Girasol had already considered. "No. With what I pulled to get out of the freeze, if they find me I'm back in permanently."

"Skype them in to wherever my bodyguard is being held."

He was insistent about the caveman. Almost as if he gave a shit. Girasol felt a small slink of self-doubt before she remembered Grimes had amassed his wealth by manipulating emotions. He'd been a puppeteer long before he uploaded. Still trying to pull her strings.

"I would," Girasol said. "But he's here with me."

Grimes paused, frowning. Girasol zoomed. She'd missed Blake's face so much, the immaculate bones of it, the wide brow and curved lips. She could still remember him chubby and always laughing.

"Can you contact him without the Priests finding out?" Grimes asked.

Girasol fluttered back to the apartment. She was guillotining texts and voice-calls as they poured in from the warehouse, keeping Pierce in the dark for as long as possible, but one of them would slip through before long. She triangulated on the locked van using the parking garage security cams.

"Maybe," she said.

"If you can get him free, he might be able to help you. I have a non-duress passcode. I could give it to you." Grimes tongued the edges of his bright white teeth. "In exchange, you call off the extraction."

"Thought you might try to make a deal."

"It is what I do." Grimes's lips thinned. "You lack long-term perspective, Ms. Fletcher. Common enough among first-lifers. The notion of sacrificing yourself to free your progeny must seem exceptionally noble and very fucking romantic to you. But if the Priesthood does murder you, Blake wakes up with nobody. Nothing. Again."

"Not nothing," Girasol said reflexively.

"The money you were paid for this job?" Grimes suggested. "He'll have to go into hiding for as long as my disappearance is under investigation. The sort of people who can help him lay low are the sort of people who'll have him back on Sandman or Dozr before the month is out. He might even decide to go puppet again."

Girasol's fury boiled over, and she nearly lost her hold on the steering column. "He made a mistake. Once. He would never agree to that again."

"Even if you get off with broken bones, you'll be a wanted fugitive as soon as Correctional try to thaw you for a physical and find whatever suckerfish the Priests convinced to take your pod." Grimes flattened his hands on his knees. "What I'm proposing is that you cancel the extraction. My bodyguard helps you escape. We meet up to renegotiate terms. I could have your charges dropped, you know. I could even rewrite Blake's contract."

"You really don't want to die, do you?" Girasol's suspicion battled her fear, her fear of Pierce and his pliers and his grinning mask. "You're digital. You saying you don't have a backup of your personality waiting in the wings?"

She checked the limo's external cams and swore. A carload of Priests from the warehouse was barreling up the road behind them, guns already poking through the windows. She reached for the in-built speed limits and deleted them.

"I do," Grimes conceded, bracing himself as the limo accelerated. "But he's not me, is he?"

Girasol resolved. She bounced back to the apartment, where the Priests were growing agitated. Pierce was shaking her arm, even though he should have known better than to shake someone on a deep slice, asking her how close she was to the warehouse. She flashed TWO MINUTES across the smartpaint.

Then she found the electronic signature of the clamp that was keeping Grimes's bodyguard paralyzed inside the van. She hoped he hadn't suffered any long-term nerve damage. Hoped he would still move like quicksilver with that bioblade of his.

"Fair enough," Girasol said, stretching herself thin, reaching into the empty parking garage. "All right. Tell me the passcode and I'll break him out."

Finch was focused on breathing slowly and ignoring the blooming damp spot where piss had soaked through his trousers. The police-issue clamp they'd stuck to his shoulder made most other activities impossible. Finch had experience with the spidery devices. They were designed to react to any arousal in the central nervous system by sending a paralyzing jolt through the would-be agitator's muscles. More struggle, more jolt. More panic, more jolt.

The only thing to do with a clamp was relax and not get upset about anything.

Finch used the downtime to reflect on his situation. Mr. Grimes had fallen victim to a planned ambush, that much was obvious. Electronic intrusion, supposedly impossible, must have been behind the limo's exhaust port diagnostic.

And now Mr. Grimes was being driven to an unknown location, while Finch was lying on the floor of a van with donair wrappers and rumpled anti-puppetry tracts for company. A decade ago, he might have been paranoid enough to think he was a target himself. Religious extremists had not taken kindly to Neanderthal gene mixing at first, but they also had a significant demographic overlap with people overjoyed to see pale-faced and blue-eyed athletes dominating the NFL and NBA again.

Even the flailing Bulls front office had managed to sign that half-thally power forward from Duke. Finch couldn't remember his name. Cletus something. Finch had played football, himself. Sometimes he wished he'd kept going with it, but his fiancé had cared more about intact gray matter than money. Of course, he hadn't been thrilled when Finch chose security as an alternative source of income, but . . .

In a distant corner of his mind, Finch felt the clamp loosening. He kept breathing steadily, kept his heartbeat slow, kept thinking about anything but the clamp loosening. Cletus Rivas. That was the kid's name. He'd pulled down twenty-six rebounds in the match-up against Arizona. Finch brought his hand slowly, slowly up toward his shoulder. Just to scratch. Just because he was itchy. Closer. Closer.

His fingers were millimeters from the clamp's burnished surface when the van's radio blared to life. His hand jerked; the clamp jolted. Finch tried to curse through his lockjaw and came up with mostly spit. So close.

"Listen up," came a voice from the speaker.

Finch had no alternative.

"I can turn off the clamp and unlock the van, but I need you to help me in exchange," the voice said. "I'm in apartment 401, sitting in an orthochair, deep sliced. There are three men in the room. The one you cut up, the one who Tasered you, and one more. They've still got the Tasers, and the last one has a handgun in an Adidas bag. I don't know where your gun is."

Finch felt the clamp fall away and went limp all over. His muscles ached deep like he'd done four hours in the weight room on methamphetamine—a bad idea, he knew from experience. He reached to massage his shoulder with one trembling hand.

"Grimes told me a non-duress passcode to give you," the voice continued. "So you'd know to trust me. It's Atticus."

Finch had almost forgotten that passcode. He'd wikied to find out why it made Mr. Grimes smirk but lost interest halfway through a text on Roman emperors.

"You have to hurry. They might kill me soon."

Hurrying did not sound like something Finch could do. He took three tries to push himself upright on gelatin arms. "Is Mr. Grimes safe?" he asked thickly, tongue sore and swollen from him biting it.

"He's on a leisurely drive to a waiting ferry. He'll be just fine. If you help me."

Finch crawled forward, taking a moment to drive one kneecap into the inactive clamp for a satisfying crunch, then hoisted himself between the two front seats and palmed the glove compartment. His Mulcher was waiting inside, still assembled, still loaded. He was dealing with some real fucking amateurs. The handgun molded to his grip, licking his thumb for DNA confirmation like a friendly cat. He was so glad to find it intact he nearly licked it back.

"Please. Hurry."

"Apartment 401, three targets, one incapacitated, three weapons, one lethal," Finch recited. He tested his wobbling legs as the van door slid open. Crossing the dusty floor of the parking garage looked like crossing the Gobi Desert.

"One other thing. You'll have to take the stairs. Elevator's out."

Finch was hardly even surprised. He stuck the Mulcher in his waistband and started to hobble.

Half the city away, Severyn wished, for the first time, that he'd had his cars equipped with seatbelts instead of only impact foam. Trying to stay seated while the limousine slewed corners and caromed down alleyways was impossible. He was thrown from one side to the other with every jolting turn. His kidnapper had finally cleared the windows and he saw, in familiar flashes, grimy red Southside brick and corrugated steel. The decades hadn't changed it much, except now the blue-green blooms of graffiti were animated.

"Pier's just up ahead. I told my guy there's been a change of plans." Girasol's voice was strained to breaking. Too many places at once, Severyn suspected.

"How long before the ones you're with know what's going on?" he asked, bracing himself against the back window to peer at their pursuers. One Priest was driving manually, and wildly. He was hunched over the steering wheel, trying to conflate what he'd learned in virtual racing sims with reality. His partner in the passenger's seat was hanging out the window with some sort of recoilless rifle, trying to aim.

"A few minutes, max."

A dull crack spiderwebbed the glass a micrometer from Severyn's left eyeball. He snapped his head back as a full barrage followed, smashing like a hailstorm into the reinforced window.

By the time they burst from the final alley, aligned for a dead sprint toward the hazard-sign-decorated pier, the limousine's rear was riddled with bullet holes. Up ahead, Severyn could make out the shape of a hydrofoil sliding out into the oil-slick water. The technician had lost his nerve.

"He's pulling away," Severyn snapped, ducking instinctively as another round raked across the back of the car with a sound of crunching metal.

"Told him to. You're going to have to swim for it."

Severyn's stomach churned. "I don't swim."

"You don't swim? You were All-State."

"Blake was." Severyn pried off his Armani loafers, peeled off his jacket, as the limousine rattled over the metal crosshatch of the pier. "I never learned."

"Just trust the muscle memory." Girasol's voice was taut and pleading. "He knows what to do. Just let him. Let his body."

They skidded to a halt at the lip of the pier. Severyn put his hand on the door and found it blinking blue, unlocked at last.

"If you can tell him things." She sounded ragged now. Exhausted. "Tell him I love him. If you can."

Severyn considered lying for a moment. A final push to solidify his position. "It doesn't work that way," he said instead, and hauled the door open as the Priests screeched to a stop behind him. He vaulted out of the limo, assaulted by unconditioned air, night wind, the smell of brine and oiled machinery.

Severyn sucked his lungs full and ran full-bore, feeling a hurricane of adrenaline that no puppet show or whorehouse could have coaxed from his glands. His bare feet pounded the cold pier, shouts came from behind him, and then he hurled himself into the grimy water. An ancient panic shot through him as ice flooded his ears, his eyes, his nose. He felt his muscles seize. He remembered, in a swath of old memory code, that he'd nearly drowned in Lake Michigan once.

Then nerve pathways that he'd never carved for himself fired, and he found himself cutting up to the surface. His head broke the water; he twisted and saw the gaggle of Priests at the edge of the water, Fawkes masks grinning at him even as they cursed and reloaded the rifle. Severyn grinned back, then pulled away with muscles moving in perfect synch, cupped hands biting the water with every stroke.

The slap of his body on the icy surface, the tug of his breath, the water in his ears—alive, alive, alive. The whine of a bullet never came. Severyn slopped over the side of the hydrofoil a moment later. Spread-eagled on the slick deck, chest working like a bellows, he started to laugh.

"That was some dramatic shit," came a voice from above him.

Severyn squinted up and saw the technician, a twitchy-looking man with gray whiskers and extra neural ports in his shaved skull. There was a tranq gun in his hand.

"There's been a change of plans," Severyn coughed. "Regarding the extraction."

The technician nodded, leveling the tranq. "Girasol told me you'd say that. Said you're a world-class bullshit artist. I'd expect no less from Severyn fucking Grimes."

Severyn's mouth fished open and shut. Then he started to laugh again, a long gurgling laugh, until the tranq stamped through his wet skin and sent him to sleep.

Girasol saw hot white sparks when they ripped her out of the orthochair and realized it was sheer luck they hadn't shut off her brain stem. You didn't tear someone out of a deep slice. Not after two hits of high-grade Dozr. She hoped, dimly, that she wasn't going to go blind in a few days' time.

"You bitch." Pierce's breath was scalding her face. He must have taken off his mask. "You bitch. Why? Why would you do that?"

Girasol found it hard to piece the words together. She was still out of body, still imagining a swerving limousine and marauding cell signals and electric sheets of code. Her hand blurred into view, and she saw her veins were taut and navy blue.

She'd stretched herself thinner than she'd ever done before, but she hadn't managed to stop the skype from the end of the pier. And now Pierce knew what had happened.

"Why did you help him get away?"

The question came with a knee pushed into her chest, under her ribs. Girasol thought she felt her lungs collapse in on themselves. Her head was coming clear.

She'd been a god only moments ago, gliding through circuitry and sound waves, but now she was small, and drained, and crushed against the stained linoleum flooring.

"I'm going to cut your eyeballs out," Pierce was deciding. "I'm going to do them slow. You traitor. You puppet."

Girasol remembered her last flash from the limousine's external cams: Blake diving into the dirty harbor with perfect form, even if Grimes didn't know it. She was sure he'd make it to the hydrofoil. It was barely a hundred meters. She held onto the novocaine thought as Pierce's knife snicked and locked.

"What did he promise you? Money?"

"Fuck off," Girasol choked.

Pierce was straddling her now, the weight of him bruising her pelvis. She felt his hands scrabbling at her zipper. The knife tracing along her thigh. She tamped down her terror.

"Oh," she said. "You want that kiss now?"

His backhand smashed across her face, and she tasted copper. Girasol closed her eyes tight. She thought of the hydrofoil slicing through the bay. The technician leaning over Blake's prone body with his instruments, pulling the parasite up and away, reawakening a brain two years dormant. She'd left him messages. Hundreds of them. Just in case.

"Did he promise to fuck you?" Pierce snarled, finally sliding her pants down her bony hips. "Was that it?"

The door chimed. Pierce froze, and in her peripheral Girasol could see the other Priests' heads turning toward the entryway. Nobody ever used the chime. Girasol wondered how Grimes's bodyguard could possibly be so stupid, then noticed that a neat row of splintery holes had appeared all across the breadth of the door.

Pierce put his hand up to his head, where a bullet had clipped the top of his scalp, carving a furrow of matted hair and stringy flesh. It came away bright red. He stared down at Girasol, angry, confused, and the next slug blew his skull open like a shattering vase.

Girasol watched numbly as the bodyguard let himself inside. His fiery hair was slick with sweat and his face was drawn pale, but he moved around the room with practiced efficiency, putting two more bullets into each of the injured Priests before collapsing to the floor himself. He tucked his hands under his head and exhaled.

"One hundred and twelve," he said. "I counted."

Girasol wriggled out from under Pierce and vomited. Wiped her mouth. "Repairman's in tomorrow." She stared down at the intact side of Pierce's face.

"Where's Mr. Grimes?"

"Nearly docking by now. But he's not in a body." Girasol pushed damp hair out of her face. "He's been extracted. His storage cone is safe. Sealed. That was our deal."

The bodyguard was studying her intently, red brows knitted. "Let's get going, then." He picked his handgun up off the floor. "Gray eyes," he remarked. "Those contacts?"

"Yeah," Girasol said. "Contacts." She leaned over to give Pierce a bloody peck on the cheek, then got shakily to her feet and led the way out the door.

Severyn Grimes woke up feeling rested. His last memory was laughing on the deck of a getaway boat, but the soft cocoon of sheets made him suspect he'd since been moved. Something else had changed, too. His proprioception was sending an avalanche of small error reports. Limbs no longer the correct length. New body proportions. By the feel of it, he was in something artificial.

"Mr. Grimes?"

"Finch." Severyn tried to grimace at the tinny sound of his voice, but the facial myomers were relatively fixed. "The *mise á jour*, please."

Finch's craggy features loomed above him, blank and professional as ever. "Girasol Fletcher had you extracted from her son's body. After we met her technician, I transported your storage cone here to Lumen Technohospital for diagnostics. Your personality and memories came through completely intact and they stowed you in an interim avatar to speak with your lawyers. Of which there's a horde, sir. Waiting in the lobby."

"Police involvement?" Severyn asked, trying for a lower register.

"There are a few Priests in custody, sir," Finch said. "Girasol Fletcher and her son are long gone. CPD requested access to the enzyme trackers in Blake's body. It looks like she hasn't found a way to shut them off yet. Could triangulate and maybe find them if it happens in the next few hours."

Severyn blinked, and his eyelashes scraped his cheeks. He tried to frown. "What the fuck am I wearing, Finch?"

"The order was put in for a standard male android." Finch shrugged. "But there was an electronic error."

"Pleasure doll?" Severyn guessed. Electronic error seemed unlikely.

His bodyguard nodded stonily. "You can be uploaded in a fresh volunteer within twenty-four hours," he said. "They've done up a list of candidates. I can link it."

Severyn shook his head. "Don't bother," he said. "I think I want something clone-grown. See my own face in the mirror again."

"And the trackers?"

Severyn thought of Blake and Girasol tearing across the map, heading somewhere sun-drenched where their money could stretch and their faces couldn't be plucked off the news feeds. She would do small-time hackwork. Maybe he would start to swim again.

"Shut them off from our end," Severyn said. "I want a bit of a challenge when I hunt her down and have her uploaded to a waste disposal."

"Will do, Mr. Grimes."

But Finch left with a ghost of a smile on his face, and Severyn suspected his employee knew he was lying.

vanguard 2.0

CARTER SCHOLZ

Carter Scholz is the author of Palimpsests *(with Glenn Harcourt);* Kafka
Americana *(with Jonathan Lethem); and* Radiance, *which was a New York*
Times *Notable Book; as well as the story collection* The Amount to Carry.
His novella Gypsy *was a finalist for the Theodore Sturgeon Memorial Award.
His electronic and computer music compositions are available from the
composer's collective Frog Peak Music (www.frogpeak.org) as scores and on
the CD* 8 Pieces. *He is an avid backpacker and amateur astronomer and
telescope builder. He plays jazz piano around the San Francisco Bay Area
with The Inside Men (www.theinsidemen.com).*

    *Here he shows us that no matter how high you go, you can't entirely shake
a connection to the ground. . . .*

From the cupola, Sergei Sergeiivitch Ivashchenko looked down on Petersburg. It
was night and the gloomy city sparkled. Around it curved the northern breast of the
Earth, under a thin gauze of atmosphere.

Today would have been his father's sixtieth birthday. Sergei *père* had been prin-
cipal bassist for the St. Petersburg Symphony. He'd died 15 years ago, from multiple
aggressive cancers. It happened to a lot of Russian men his age. He'd been a young
teen at the time of Chernobyl, living in Kyiv.

Vera, Sergei's mother, was a beautiful young singer when she married his father.
She promptly retired, at twenty-three. Never a pleasant person, Vera grew more unpleasant as her looks faded. When his father got his diagnosis, she immediately filed
for divorce, moved out, and took up with one of his colleagues in the woodwinds.
She said, "I have to protect myself." Sergei himself was sixteen, an only child.

Two months later his father was dead. Sergei filed for an extension on the apartment, and was turned down. He'd been playing the part of the rebellious punk
nekulturny, which didn't help. (His band was called *Alyona Ivanovna,* after Raskol-
nikov's victim in *Crime and Punishment.*)

They sold his father's instruments. Vera took most of the proceeds, but Sergei's
own share kept him going for a drunken while. He couch-surfed with friends for
most of a year. He had scholarships and grants and no other options. So he straight-

ened up, and blazed almost contemptuously through math, compsci, and astrody-namics. He had his *kandidat nauk* at twenty-three. But there were no jobs, not in Russia, and competition in the EU and U.S. and India was fierce.

So he switched tracks, took commercial astronaut training, and ended up in Uber's NSLAM Division: Near Space Logistics and Asset Management. The work was menial—glorified trash collection and traffic management—but the pay was good, and he liked being off-Earth.

NSLAM employed about twenty astronauts, in shifts, to staff its two inflatable hab-itats. Apart from the Chinese and European space stations, theirs was the only ongo-ing human presence in orbital space. All told there were several hundred astronauts worldwide, working for nations or militaries or private industry, but few stayed in orbit.

Sergei was in the hab for three or four months at a time, then back on Earth for the same. Up here he sat in his cubby and remotely managed ion-thrust drones to deorbit space debris, or to refuel satellites. The drones would be out for weeks or months at a time on their various missions.

Once in a great while he left the hab in a spacecraft, to work on more complex projects. One such task, still ongoing, was dismantling the International Space Sta-tion. It was decommissioned in 2024 and sold to NSLAM in 2027. They were still salvaging parts—recycling some, selling some on eBay as memorabilia. He made a side income from that.

But crewed missions were rare, because they used so much fuel, and that was fine with Sergei. He liked being off-Earth but he didn't like leaving the hab. There were too many ways to die in space. Debris, for one. NSLAM tracked one million objects one centimeter or larger. Smaller untracked objects numbered over a hundred million. And it was all moving up to 7 times as fast as a bullet, carrying 50 times the kinetic energy. A fleck of paint had put a divot the size of a golf ball in a Space Shuttle back in the day. The habs were made of dozens of layers of super-kevlar and foam, which flexed and absorbed small impacts, but they were still vulnerable to larger objects.

Then there were solar flares. There was usually sufficient warning, but unpro-tected astronauts had died. Even inside, he wasn't crazy about the minimal shield-ing in the habs. During serious solar events, he'd seen flashes behind his closed eyelids. Often he felt like he was following his father to the same early grave.

Petersburg drifted out of view across the northern horizon as the hab orbited south. They'd be back in 90 minutes, but farther west, as the Earth rotated under them.

Below, a meteor flashed over the blackness of the Baltic Sea. Nearer the Earth's limb, over Finland, a green veil of aurora flickered. He'd see Izumi in Helsinki next week; his shift was almost done.

He swiveled and opened the cupola hatch. Cold LED light streamed in from the central shaft. He pushed gently to propel himself feet first down the shaft.

She'd hugged him goodbye, kissed him, and said:

Who will take care of your heart and soul?

He shrugged.

She pointed at him. *You* will. Promise me.

He'd promised, but he wasn't sure he knew how. He could take care of himself, but that was mere survival. The self is not the soul. The soul is what you were as a child, until you learned to protect it, enclosing that fluttering, vulnerable moth in the fist of the self.

As he drifted past Boyle's cubby he heard his name called. He grabbed a stanchion.

Sergei's job title was orbital supervisor, which made him the most important person on the hab, responsible for the launch registry, collision avoidance alerts, and flight plans. But Boyle, the shift boss, was his superior. Competent enough, Boyle tended to see nothing beyond his position, so Sergei played his own to type: the stolid Ukie who kept to himself and loved his *wode-ka*. In truth Sergei hadn't seen the Ukraine since his father moved them to Petersburg in 2010, and his drink was single malt. Talisker 18 Year, for preference.

What's up, Geoff?

We're going to have a visitor. A civilian.

Civilian? Why is he up?

He's Gideon Pace.

Gideon Pace was Uber's CEO. He was one of the world's ten or twenty newly minted trillionaires. The exact number changed daily with the markets, but they were still rare as unicorns, already persistent as myth. This tiny cohort controlled about 5 percent of the world's wealth.

Uber ran a diverse portfolio of businesses on Earth. Package delivery, autonomous transport, data archived in DNA—all hugely profitable.

NSLAM was an indulgence, a pet project of Pace's. He was a space nut who wanted a presence out here at any price. So far, Sergei knew, that presence had bled oceans of money, and not a few lives. But now governments were signing on to underwrite the core mission of cleaning up space debris—enough to have launched a second hab.

All four crew turned out to greet Pace and his pilot: Boyle, Sergei, Kiyoshi, and Sheila. Kiyoshi and Sheila had coupled a few weeks into the shift. Sergei liked Kiyoshi; he was a jazz fan, and had hipped Sergei to Kenny Barron. Sheila, the hab medic, was a petite Canadian blonde with chiseled features. She looked like Vera in her youth, which put Sergei off getting to know her. She'd cropped her hair close to keep it from floating in a halo around her head. Sergei himself shaved his; he hated their no-rinse shampoo.

Their visitor had a weasel's face: dark straight hair in bangs, pinched cheeks, thin sloped nose, pointed dimpled chin, eyes slanting slightly upward. About Sergei's age, but he looked younger.

Fantastic! Fantastic! I've been in space before, but only suborbital. I had to see this for myself.

Welcome to NSLAM Hab One.

You must be Sergei. Chief Boyle tells me you're the most experienced astronaut here.

He wasn't looking quite at Sergei. Sergei guessed he was wearing augmented contacts with a headsup display, clocking Sergei's vitals and recording everything.

Sergei dialed back his English to a cute and unthreatening level.

You gather data on me.

Of course.

Right now. In real time. What don't you know already?

Ah, I see. Well . . . how you are. I don't know that. How are you?

Sergei put on a blank look, but it didn't approach the blankness of Pace's.

Pace smiled thinly. It's what humans do, Sergei.

How would you know? Sergei almost said, but didn't. Pace's headsup probably picked up the subvocalization; his smile twitched.

Boyle grabbed a stanchion. Let's show you around.

I've got work, said Sergei.

Join us later, Sergei, said Pace. I brought some goodies from Earth.

He had indeed. The six of them gathered in what Boyle quaintly called the "mess hall," a multifunction common space packed with gear on every surface—left, right, up, down. The "mess hall" housed some hydrator nozzles and a fold-down table with bungees and velcro to secure plates and feet. It was seldom used. They tended to dine separately.

Pace had brought Kobe beef *tournedos* in vacuum pouches and a bottle of wine. Sergei would have preferred fresh vegetables.

2013 Napa cabernet sauvignon, Pace said. Heitz Cellar, Martha's Vineyard. A wine like this you don't want to suck out of a bulb.

His pilot passed a case, and Pace drew out six glasses and an opener. As he applied the opener to the bottle he let the glasses float. Their cross-section was tear-shaped.

An old NASA guy designed these glasses. The shape creates surface tension to hold the liquid in. Neat, huh?

Pace held one of the glasses while a trigger on the opener let compressed nitrogen into the bottle and forced wine out the spout. The wine sloshed but stayed put in the glass. He drifted glasses one by one to their recipients, lifted his own to his nose, let it twirl slowly while he inhaled. Sergei guessed he'd practiced all this in suborbital.

Enjoy. I want to thank you all for the incredible job you're doing up here. NSLAM is now the most trusted actor in near-Earth space. It's all because we stepped up to do something about the Kessler Effect, and you've all executed flawlessly.

Sergei wasn't sure he believed in the Kessler Effect, that a cascade of debris could destroy satellites to produce more debris to destroy more, et cetera. Noisy disaster movies had been made about it, but if it was truly happening, it was proceeding so slowly that only spreadsheets detected it.

The oven chimed. They all bungeed in and began to eat. Sergei had to admit it was pretty good.

So let me tell you why I'm here. It's not just to sightsee. I want Sergei to do me a favor.

Hm?

You know Vanguard 1?

No idea.

Launched by the U.S. in 1958. Still in orbit, though long defunct. It's the oldest human thing in space.

And?

I want it for my collection. I'd like you to steal it for me. He smiled at the others.

Why not use drone?

I don't want to wait for a drone. I want to take it home with me tomorrow.

Sergei shrugged. Let me run numbers. He returned to his *tournedos*.

Pace was crazy, but that didn't bother him. Everyone in the world was crazy, no exceptions. One managed one's condition in more or less socially acceptable ways, according to one's capacities and resources. He'd once blamed the situation on the overwhelming complexity of modernity, yadda yadda, but he'd come to believe the condition was ancient and fundamental.

His own way of coping involved these long months off-Earth. Pace's, well, who could say. He knew Pace was a believer in the Singularity—the omega point at which machine intelligence was supposed to reach a critical mass and become self-sustaining and independent of humans. To Sergei that was bonus crazy. But Sergei had a parallel notion about what happened to money, when you put enough of it in one place. These guys were as separate from normal humanity, and as alien, as AIs were supposed to be. But they weren't the intelligence: the money ran them.

The mission looked doable. A Hohmann Transfer would take a little over an hour to reach Vanguard's orbit at its apogee. Changing orbital planes was, as always, the bitch; the delta-v budget for that alone was almost four kilometers per second each way. That's why they almost never ran crewed missions like this.

Kestrel One was the only vehicle with enough thrust. It was scarily minimal, about three meters in diameter and four meters long. The forward half tapered to a blunt point. The rear half was for fuel. It would never have passed a design review at any national space agency. Among other shortcuts, it had no life support, relying on the astronaut's spacesuit instead. Sergei figured the suit's eight hours would be enough, but he'd take extra oxygen, in case. *Kestrel* was docked at the propellant depot orbiting behind them. He programmed it to dock with Port Two after fueling itself.

The tricky bit would be locating his tiny target once he got into its orbit. He had its orbital data, but in TLEs, two-line element sets. The format was archaic. Futile editorials periodically appeared in *Orbital Debris News* calling for an overhaul of the system, but it was too entrenched.

The TLEs were tailored to a general perturbation model that was accurate to a kilometer at best. He'd have to get in the neighborhood, scan with radar, then grab it. That'd take how long?

He wanted sunlight for that, so he adjusted his start time. Coming back, the two orbits weren't so good for rendezvous. He'd have some stay time.

There were other, non-orbital considerations, but they weren't really his. *Kestrel* would be picked up by ground radars, but the radars were almost all managed by NSLAM, and the company's manifests were private. If anyone happened to ask what he'd been doing out there, which was unlikely, the company would make something up.

OK. What does this thing look like? How big?

I'll show you.

Pace popped the latches of a Pelican case. The released force spun the case in the air. Pace steadied himself against the wall and got hold of it. From die-cut black foam he drew a small metal sphere, then plucked six thin rods about half a meter long from the case and screwed them into the object's threaded bushings. Finally he drew his hands away and let the small thing float between them. He tapped a vane and the model slowly spun, a silvery seedpod.

Very small.

Pace gazed past it and his eyes twitched. Six and a half inches in diameter, three and a half pounds. Khrushchev called it the grapefruit. It was the first of four Vanguards, sent mainly to test the launch vehicle. It's the only one still in orbit, brave little guy.

Why is this grapefruit so important to you?

You kidding? It's historic.

How so?

Know anything about space law? Once upon a time, the sky was "free." After aircraft came along, it was said that a nation "controlled" its "airspace." Then satellites came along. They crossed all airspaces. There was no legal regime. The U.S. knew the Soviets would object to a military satellite, so they crafted Vanguard, a very public "scientific" mission with no military objectives. Except for establishing the precedent that space was beyond national boundaries. I want this little guy hanging in my office to remind me how elegant that strategy was.

There was a lot Sergei could have replied to that but he controlled himself, and said, I need to launch in twenty-four hours, when Vanguard is in best position relative to us.

Pace reached out and stopped the model's slow spin.

Take this with you. When you've got the real thing, insert this back into its orbit.

They were over Australia in daylight when Kiyoshi stuck his head in.

Dobroe utro, Sergei.

Ohayou gozaimasu, Yoshisan.

English was the lingua franca, but they'd each learned a few words of the other's tongue as a formality, to show respect. It didn't hurt that Sergei had already picked up some Japanese from Izumi.

Sheila and I need a flight plan to Hab Two. They've got some problem with their water recycler. We need to bring a spare.

Both of you?

Boyle says as long as I'm using fuel, Sheila should come along and give them a checkup. Here's our launch window.

Yoshi showed him a tablet.

OK, I'll upload a flight plan.
Spasibo.
Douitashimashite.
Same time window as Sergei. Leaving Boyle and Pace and his pilot alone on the hab.

Sergei watched the hab dwindle against the ocean, positioned between Patagonia and the Antarctic Peninsula. He could see Pace's vehicle, docked at Port One, surprisingly big, as big as the hab itself.

One kilometer out, he yawed and started the transfer burn. Thrust was about half a G. It felt good. How he would welcome gravity when he went down! And fresh air and blue skies. After four and a half minutes, he ended the burn as *Kestrel* passed over the Sahara.

He'd be over Petersburg in fifteen minutes, this time in daylight. Summer was coming to the Northern Hemisphere. He'd relish the long days, the white nights, of Helsinki in July. Izumi and he had been together for almost two years, though he'd been in space most of that time. She was a few years older than him, had been married once, to a Finn. She worked in IT for a comprehensive school. She was also a singer, classical and cabaret. They'd met in Petersburg at a concert. Shostakovich string quartets.

He didn't know where it was going, the two of them, or where he was going, solo or not. He had a sometimes-piercing dread that one day soon she was going to lose patience with him.

Hell, he was losing patience with himself. His smell in the spacesuit was rank. Water was too precious up here to use for washing, especially clothes. When they grew too foul, they were thrown out. He changed his socks and shorts about once a week, his shirt about once a month. They were past due. So was he. The self was too much with him.

He was now over Vladivostok. He'd gained almost 4,000 kilometers in altitude and the Earth was palpably smaller. South across the Sea of Japan was Kyoto, Izumi's birthplace. She'd taken him there once, for a week. They visited Ryoanji temple one morning, arriving very early, before it opened, to avoid the tourists. It had rained in the night but the day was sunny, the road vacant. They hurried past an old woman on their way. Black birds stared at them from the roof of the locked gate. The old woman caught them up, and she looked to them in concern: What time is it? She was the gatekeeper, worried she was late.

Over the South Pacific, in darkness now, he burned to shift his orbital plane into Vanguard's. Ten more minutes of welcome gravity, its force steadily increasing from half a G to over a G as the ship burned fuel and lost mass. When it ceased, he checked his bearings. He was now in Vanguard's orbit.

But nothing was out there. Lots of nothing. More nothing, and more nothing. Then S-band radar bounced back from something about two kilometers ahead of him. He burned briefly into a lower orbit to phase up on it. At 100 meters' separation, he burned back up to stationkeeping. There: a point of light drifting against the stars. After long, fussy minutes of edging up, he had it, closed the arm on it, and brought it into the bay. Mission time: 3 hours, 39 minutes.

It wasn't tarnished or pitted, but the metal bore a slight patina, weathered by solar radiation and micrometeor abrasion. He cupped it in his gloved hand. It was that
small. He felt a mild revulsion at the thought of handing this storied thing over to
Pace.

But he secured it, then loaded the imposter into the bay and launched it. He
checked his position against the hab's, and ran both coordinates through the flight
computer. He'd have to stay for 42 minutes until ship and hab were aligned.

While he waited he played the second Shostakovich string quartet through his
suit's phones. It was what he'd been hearing when he first saw Izumi, two rows in
front of him in the shadows of the concert hall. That elegant profile. He'd studied
the shape of her left ear as she moved her head so slightly.

This quartet had been his father's favorite. Sergei could see him seated at the
north-facing window with his cello between his knees, practicing in the pale light,
occasionally stopping to mark the score.

The final chords resounded, an angry but halfway resigned lament against the
shortness of life, its futile complications, the thwarting of joy.

Sergei checked the flight computer. It was time. He watched the countdown, then
burned for two minutes as thrust climbed steadily to over two Gs. His heart labored.

Another hour passed in silence as the ship followed its new trajectory to the lower
hab orbit. The curvature of the Earth's limb slowly flattened, and the Moon, half-
full, rose above it.

It stared at him and its glory pierced him. The intricate Sun-Moon-Earth system
was best felt from here.

Something hit.

Blyad!

The vehicle jolted. Or maybe it was him who jolted. He thought he'd heard the
hit—a faint crack, something you might hear underwater.

For a moment the world was pure falling. A crowded emptiness. Millions of
specks streaked through this vastness of orbit. Thoughts in a void of unmeaning.
Subatomics in a space of forces. In that maelstrom, once in a great while, two specks
collide: a neutron lodges in a nucleus, and changes its nature.

In the center of the window was a pock: an irregular, finely terraced crater about
five centimeters across. Sunlight raked it into fine relief. The particle, whatever it
was, had vaporized on impact. A little larger or a little faster and it would have continued straight through his visor.

He smelled the sharpness of fresh sweat over his stale miasma. At least he hadn't
shit himself.

The rest of the way back his eyes were on the radar. Not that he would see anything coming before it hit him. It was just magical thinking.

But as he approached the hab he did see something. Four bogeys, faint echoes,
inconsistent returns, in parallel orbits.

Kiyoshi stopped by.

I heard. You okay?

Ah, yeah. You know.

Kiyoshi did know. He'd almost run out of oxygen on an EVA. How are they on the other hab?

Kiyoshi frowned. Their water filter was fine. Sheila ran her tests. They're all good.

Sergei shrugged.

Two pointless EVAs in one day. You could have been killed.

I'm fine. *Arigatou gozaimasu.*

·*Beregi sebya.*

He thought that would be it. It wasn't.

Sergei, my friend. May I come in?

In one hand Pace held two of the tear-shaped glasses. In the other was a bottle: Talisker 18 Year.

It wasn't worth getting upset over, but it annoyed him. Pace didn't need to parade his research.

I want to thank you. I heard you almost got centerpunched out there.

Sergei watched the glasses float while Pace scooped whiskey into them. Now he was almost angry. As far as he was concerned, it was over. What more did Pace want? He meant to keep his mouth shut, but he saw that sunlit pock in the glass again, heard that distant crack, felt himself jolt. He wanted to make Pace jolt.

You launched something while I was gone. You and Boyle. Four objects.

Pace looked at him with interest. Why yes. Yes we did. It was awesome.

Why send me away?

Pace regarded him carefully through the lenses of his headsup. What was he reading there? Sergei's pulse, BP, skin temperature—what else was he tracking? Pace was like a windup toy that never ran down. It was tiring. Sergei didn't want to be sitting here drinking with him.

Well, I truly did want my Vanguard. But I also wanted my objects off the registry. If you were onboard, you would be the one to record them.

What are they?

Pace seemed to think about this.

You know about the Outer Space Treaty. Bans nuclear weapons in outer space. I mean, this goddamn piece of paper is from 1967, but nations still take it seriously, or at least they have to seem to. But we're a private company. That piece of paper means nothing to us.

United States company. Subject to U.S. jurisdiction.

Listen to the space lawyer! No no. They were launched into space by an LLC doing business in the Maldives—which is not a signatory to the treaty.

Maldives? Practically underwater.

We built a seawall and shored up our island.

Why not put objects into orbit direct from Earth? Why from space?

Maldives are still a UN member. They'd have to register my objects with the UN. The fucking *UN*! Isn't that quaint?

They register your launch?

Sure, but that launch didn't put the objects into orbit. Orbit was accomplished up here.

What are they?

Oh, so far, nothing. They're platforms.

Platforms for what?

Pace took a silence, looked troubled, but he was enjoying it.

Let's say that I worry about mankind. We had a close call with an asteroid a few years ago, you may remember. It'll be back soon. We need assets out here to help us with that problem.

And so, you want to put on these platforms . . .

Nuclear weapons. What else has enough push for an asteroid?

Bad idea. Could end up with hundreds of small asteroids instead of one big one.

You know what would be a much worse idea? Doing nothing.

Why you?

Nobody else is doing it, that's why.

Where you going to get nukes?

Oh, look, it doesn't have to be nukes. Use giant lasers if you want, whatever. I'm offering these platforms to any nation that wants to contribute to the long-term survival of mankind. I've got interest at NASA and DoD.

No pushback?

NASA? They've already ceded Earth space. DoD? SecDef is ours, a former Uber VP. The Joint Chiefs are mostly on board, and for the whiners there's always early retirement. I don't need to own their weapons. They'd simply be under our management.

Hard to believe they give you control.

Pace tapped his glass into a slight spin. A small blob of whiskey escaped. He sucked it into his mouth, and swallowed. Smiled.

They let us manage their satellites. We're a trusted actor. DoD would love a way to bypass the Outer Space Treaty. I offer us as a beard, that's perfect for them. Get a few allies on board, even better.

At this point, Sergei knew it would be wise to shut up, finish his drink, say goodnight. He didn't feel wise.

What is your long game?

Pace squinted at him. What makes you think I have a long game?

You are smart guy.

Sergei let the silence stretch. Pace was compelled to dominate a conversation, to fill up the social space. That went against the solitary, obsessive nature that Sergei recognized, but he saw how Pace had learned to deploy that nature tactically. Now he saw Pace shift out of the social space, back into his own mind. He squinted as he manipulated his headsup. It was like watching a lizard.

You've read Max Weber? Pace said at last.

Some.

Pace's eyes flickered as he quoted: "A state is a human community that successfully claims the monopoly of the legitimate use of physical force."

So?

Here's my long game: I want to redefine "human community" for the better. My method is to redefine who's "legitimate."

Yes?

The nation-state as a form of political organization is recent. Treaty of Westphalia, 1648. There's no reason it needs to persist. There are better alternatives.

Sergei gave him more silence. Pace shifted back into his public mode.

See, I'm big on dual use. Once these platforms are armed, they can also protect against dangers from below. I mean, look at the data. Nation-states have very bad metrics. You know that. So many wars, so many killed. So much property damage. We can do better. We will. We can build and manage the defense cloud.

Platforms are vulnerable.

I'm an optimist. These platforms are stealthy and maneuverable. Anyway, ASAT's a non-starter, Kessler Effect and all, that's unwritten but fundamental. It's why we're up here, am I right? Soon I'll have memoranda of understanding with certain public and private actors, which will make any action against the platforms a lot more complicated. Let's say that I foresee a regime in which it's in everyone's interest to leave them the hell alone.

Meanwhile they are traffic hazard.

Oh, they'll be no trouble. The orbital elements are in your database. You have what you need to protect *all* our assets.

All our assets?

Pace held out his hands in a kind of embrace.

Everything that's up here under our management. To quote one of my heroes: They're *our* assets now, and we're not giving them back.

Why tell me?

You're smarter than you like to let on. There could be a place for you in our ground operations.

Sergei shrugged. Pace shook his head.

Hate to see expertise go to waste. Here's my private email. Let me know if you're interested.

That night, strapped in his sleeping bag after Pace and his pilot had departed the hab, Sergei thought it over.

In 2029, the asteroid Apophis had crossed Earth's orbit. A scary close approach, closer than many geosynchronous satellites. The thing was 350 meters across. Not extinction-level, but many times Tunguska. A one-gigaton impact was nothing to sneeze at.

Sergei had been in space then, had watched it fly by. It brightened to third magnitude, moved through about 40 degrees of sky in an hour, faded, was gone. It was due back in 2036. Odds of impact were only a few in a million, but Sergei saw how useful that recent near miss and impending return could be to a system selling itself as asteroid defense. The nuclear option against asteroids made no sense, but politics made no sense. The meme of "protection" was more powerful than reason.

As to Pace's longer game, he didn't buy it for a couple of reasons. First, the U.S. would never hand over control of nukes. They'd invented them; they'd become the global hegemon with them, and more or less remained so because of them. But: that "more or less." Pace was lying, but his lie had exposed a deeper truth that eroded Sergei's faith that the U.S. was the U.S. of his imagination.

Second, it made no strategic sense to station weapons in space. Launch costs were high, platforms vulnerable, delivery difficult. Earth-based systems were the better choice.

Unless the weapons were assembled in orbit. But why do that?

He remembered a job he'd done months ago, EVA, in person, servicing an orbital nanofactory which produced microscopic pellets—flecks of material embedded in zero-G-perfected beads of glass. Manifests identified the material as LiDT: lithium deuteride and tritium. Mildly radioactive. He'd been curious, but had forgotten about it once he was safely back.

Now he logged onto SIPRNet and searched classified scientific papers. Soon he found "Typical number of antiprotons necessary for fast ignition in LiDT." Primary author: R. Fry, Lawrence Livermore National Laboratory. The paper detailed the results of the first break-even fusion reaction a few years back.

That was it, then. The Livermore Lab had worked on fusion since its founding, eighty years ago. Its founding purpose was nuclear weapons, and its grail was a pure fusion weapon. This bomb could be small and light and still hugely destructive. Sergei was no nuclear scientist, but those pellets were clearly nuclear fuel. They were being produced in orbit; and so could bombs that used them.

What about delivery? Uber already had a thriving Earthside business in package delivery using small drones. Suppose you mounted a few dozen fusion bomblets on drones, packed those drones in a cheap capsule, dropped it from orbit, popped it open in the troposphere, where you could then MIRV the drones to individual targets. The only defense would be to destroy the capsule before it opened. If the capsule were small and stealthed, could it get through? He didn't know.

He could be wrong. Maybe they weren't working on bombs. Maybe they wouldn't succeed. Maybe it would take a long time. Maybe he should forget the whole thing.

Kiyoshi and Sheila's alcove was near his. Sergei could hear the thumps and moans of their tangled bodies through the thin walls. He allowed himself to think of Izumi, of tracing his finger slowly along the arch of her foot, hearing the intake of her breath, taking her big toe in his mouth and hearing her gasp.

His heart and soul didn't buy his maybes.

Two days later he was on the way back to Earth. They would touch down in Kazakhstan. Kiyoshi and Sheila were also ending their shifts, while Boyle stayed on. Sergei looked away from the couple, strapped in across from him, their hands intertwined.

It would make sense to take Pace's offer. It had come wrapped in a veiled threat. Pace even had a point. Sergei had no sentiment for the nation-state. During World War II, Petersburg had been under siege for nine hundred days. Shostakovich had been there. The population went from 3.5 million to 600,000. In his lifetime, the endless Chechen wars. Was any of that right?

Out the small window, sun slanted across a long wall of cumulonimbus over the coast of Venezuela. Somewhere below the clouds, American troops were liberating oil fields.

"The right thing." Who could know what that was? Imagine all the damned souls who believed they had done the right thing. Who may in fact have done the right thing, and found themselves damned anyway.

And Sergei was ready, maybe, to finally stay below the clouds. To keep his feet on the ground, to have a normal life.

But that was mere survival. There was a Russian saying, *vsyo normal'no*, "everything is normal." No matter how screwed up: "everything is normal." Also that American saying: "the new normal." Universal surveillance was the new normal. Resource wars were the new normal. Climate refugees by the millions were the new normal. And if Pace got his way, his executive monopoly of "legitimate" violence would be the new normal.

Sergei shut his eyes as the faint whistle of reentry grew to a thunder and the capsule juddered. Soon they'd be at four Gs. Pure falling, again, but now into the burning force of the still-living planet's atmosphere. Still living for how much longer?

Izumi had said to him once: *You think a lot, but you follow your heart.* He wasn't sure he did, but he was glad she thought so, or at least that she said she did. He let the memory of that gladness echo in him. Maybe it was time to be sure.

Who will take care of your heart and soul?

The self is not the soul. The soul is what you were as a child, until you learned to protect it, enclosing that fluttering, vulnerable moth in the fist of the self.

Outside, the heatshield roared and burned. A firedrake of plasma, the capsule passed over Helsinki, Petersburg, Moscow, specks in a crowded emptiness. He opened his eyes.

He saw that both his fists were clenched tight. Very slowly he allowed his hands to open.

starlight express

MICHAEL SWANWICK

Here's a melancholy and evocative story about a man in a far-future Rome who encounters a mysterious woman from very, very far away. . . .

Michael Swanwick made his debut in 1980 and, in the thirty-eight years that have followed, has established himself as one of science fiction's most prolific and consistently excellent writers at short lengths, as well as one of the premier novelists of his generation. He has won the Theodore Sturgeon Memorial Award and the Asimov's Readers' Award poll. In 1991, his novel Stations of the Tide *won him a Nebula Award as well, and in 1995 he won the World Fantasy Award for his story* "Radio Waves." *He won the Hugo Award five times between 1999 and 2006, for his stories* "The Very Pulse of the Machine," "Scherzo with Tyrannosaur," "The Dog Said Bow-Wow," "Slow Life," *and* "Legions in Time." *His other books include the novels* In the Drift, Vacuum Flowers, The Iron Dragon's Daughter, Jack Faust, Bones of the Earth, The Dragons of Babel, Dancing with Bears, *and* Chasing the Phoenix. *His short fiction has been assembled in* Gravity's Angels, A Geography of Unknown Lands, Slow Dancing Through Time, Moon Dogs, Puck Aleshire's Abecedary, Tales of Old Earth, Cigar-Box Faust and Other Miniatures, Michael Swanwick's Field Guide to the Mesozoic Megafauna, The Periodic Table of Science Fiction, *and the massive retrospective collection* The Best of Michael Swanwick. *Coming up is a new novel,* The Iron Dragon's Mother. *Swanwick lives in Philadelphia with his wife, Marianne Porter. He has a website at www .michaelswanwick.com and maintains a blog at floggingbabel.blogspot.com.*

F laminio the water carrier lived in the oldest part of the ancient city of Roma among the *popolo minuto,* the clerks and artisans and laborers and such who could afford no better. His apartment overlooked the piazza dell'Astrovia, which daytimes was choked with tourists from four planets who came to admire the ruins and revenants of empire. They coursed through the ancient transmission station, its stone floor thrumming gently underfoot, the magma tap still powering the energy road, even though the stars had shifted in their positions centuries ago and anyone stepping into the projector would be translated into a complex wave front of neutrinos and shot away from the Earth to fall between the stars forever.

Human beings had built such things once. Now they didn't even know how to turn it off.

On hot nights, Flaminio slept on a pallet on the roof. Sometimes, staring up at the sparkling line of ionization that the energy road sketched through the atmosphere, he followed it in his imagination past Earth's three moons and out to the stars. He could feel its pull at such times, the sweet yearning tug that led suicides to converge upon it in darkness, furtive shadows slipping silently up the faintly glowing steps like lovers to a tryst.

Flaminio wished then that he had been born long ago when it was possible to ride the starlight express away from the weary old Republic to impossibly distant worlds nestled deep in the galaxy. But in the millennia since civilization had fallen, countless people had ridden the Astrovia off the planet, and not one had ever returned.

Except, maybe, the woman in white.

Flaminio was coming home from the baths when he saw her emerge from the Astrovia. It was election week and a ward heeler had treated him to a sauna and a blood scrub in exchange for his vote. When he stepped out into the night, every glint of light was bright and every surface slick and shiny, as if his flesh had been turned to glass and offered not the least resistance to the world's sensations. He felt genuinely happy.

Then there was a pause in the constant throb underfoot, as if the great heart of the world had skipped a beat. Something made Flaminio look up, and he thought he saw the woman step down from the constant light of the landing stage.

An instant only, and then he realized he had to be wrong.

The woman wore a white gown of a cloth unlike any Flaminio had ever seen before. It was luminously cool, and with every move she made it slid across her body with simple grace. Transfixed, he watched her step hesitantly out of the Astrovia and seize the railing with both hands.

She stared out across the plaza, looking confused and troubled, as if gazing into an unfamiliar new world.

Flaminio had seen that look before on the future suicides. They came to the Astrovia during the daylight first, accompanying tours that stopped only briefly on their way to the Colosseum and the Pantheon and the Altair Gate, but later returned alone and at night, like moths compulsively circling in on death and transformation in smaller and more frenzied loops before finally cycling to a full stop at the foot of the Aldebaranian Steps, quivering and helpless as a wren in a cat's mouth.

That, Flaminio decided, was what must be happening here. The woman had gotten as far as the transmission beam, hesitated, and turned around. As he watched, she raised a hand to her mouth, the pale blue gems on her silver bracelet gleaming. She was very lovely, and he felt terribly sorry for her.

Impulsively, Flaminio took the woman's arm and said, "You're with me, babe."

She looked up at him, startled. Where Flaminio had the ruddy complexion and coarse face of one of Martian terraformer ancestry, the woman had aristocratic features, the brown eyes and high cheekbones and wide nose of antique African blood.

He grinned at her as if he had all the carefree confidence in the world, thinking: Come on. You are too beautiful for death. Stay, and rediscover the joy in life.

For a breath as long as all existence, the woman did not react. Then she nodded and smiled.

He led her away.

Back at his room, Flaminio was at a loss as to what to do. He had never brought a woman home for anything other than romantic purposes and, further, to his astonishment, discovered he felt not the least desire to have sex with this one. So he gave her his narrow bed and a cup of herbal tea. He himself lay down on a folded blanket by the door, where she would have to step over him if she tried to return to the Astrovia. They both went to sleep.

In the morning he rose before dawn and made his rounds. Flaminio had a contract with a building seven stories high and though the denizens of the upper floors were poor as poor, everybody needed water. When he got home, he made his guest breakfast.

"*Stat grocera?*" she asked, holding up a sausage squash. Then, when Flaminio shook his head and spread his hands to indicate incomprehension, she took a little bite and spat it out in disgust. The bread she liked, however, and she made exclamations of surprise and pleasure over the oranges and pomegranolos. The espresso she drank as if it were exactly what she were used to.

Finally, because he could think of nothing else to do, he took her to see the Great Albino.

The Great Albino was being displayed in a cellar off of via Dolorosa. Once he had been able to draw crowds large enough that he was displayed in domes and other spaces where he could stand and stretch out his limbs to their fullest. But that was long ago. Now he crouched on all fours in a room that was barely large enough to accommodate him. There were three rows of wooden bleachers, not entirely filled, from which tourists asked questions, which he courteously answered.

Flaminio was able to visit the Great Albino as often as he liked, because when he was young he had discovered that Albino knew things that no one else did. Thirteen times in a single month he had managed to scrape together a penny so he could pepper the giant with questions. On the last visit, Albino had said, "Let that one in free from now."

So of course, the first question the young Flaminio had asked on being let in was "Why?"

"Because you don't ask the same questions as everyone else," Albino had said. "You make me call up memories I thought I had forgotten."

Today, however, the tourists were asking all the same dreary questions as usual. "How old are you?" a woman asked.

"I am three thousand eight hundred forty seven years and almost eleven months old," Albino said gravely.

"No!" the tourist shrieked. "Really?"

"I was constructed so that I would never age, back when humanity had the power to do such things."

"My tutor-mentor says there are no immortals," a child said, frowning seriously.

"Like any man, I am prone to accident and misfortune so I am by no means immortal. But I do not age, nor am I susceptible to any known diseases."

"I hear that and I think you are the very luckiest man in the world," a man with a strong Russikan accent said. "But then I reflect that there are no women your size, and I think maybe not."

The audience laughed. Albino waited for the laughter to subside and with a gentle smile said, "Ah, but think how many fewer times I have to go to confession than you do."

They laughed again.

Flaminio stood, and the woman in white did likewise. "Have you brought your bride-to-be for me to meet, water carrier?" Albino asked. "If so, I am honored."

"No, I have rather brought you a great puzzle—a woman who speaks a language that I have never heard before, though all the peoples of the worlds course through Roma every day."

"Does she?" Albino's great head was by itself taller than the woman was. He slowly lowered it, touching his tremendous brow to the floor before her. "Madam."

The woman looked amused. "*Vuzet gentdom.*"

"*Graz mairsy, dama.*"

Hearing her own language spoken, woman gasped. Then she began talking, endlessly it seemed to Flaminio, gesturing as she did so: at Flaminio, in the direction of the Astrovia, up at the sky. Until finally Albino held up a finger for silence. "Almost, I think she must be mad," he said. "But then . . . she speaks a language that before this hour I believed to be dead. So who is to say? Whatever the truth may be, it is not something I believed possible a day ago."

"What does she say?" one of the audience members asked.

"She says she is not from this planet or any other within the Solar System. She says she comes from the stars."

"No one has come back from the stars for many centuries," the man scoffed.

"Yes. And yet here she is."

The woman's name was Szette, Albino said. She claimed to come from Opale, the largest of three habitable planets orbiting Achernar. When asked whether she had been contemplating suicide, Szette looked shocked and replied that suicide was a sin, for to kill oneself was to despair of God's mercy. Then she had asked what planet this was, and when Albino replied "Earth," adamantly shook her head.

Much later, in Flaminio's memory, the gist of the conversation, stripped of the torrents of foreign words and the hesitant translation, which was curtailed because the paying customers found it boring but continued at some length after the show was over, was as follows:

"That is not possible. It was Earth I meant to visit. So I studied it beforehand and it is not like this. It is all very different."

"Perhaps," Albino said, "you studied a different part of Earth. There is a great variety of circumstance in a planet."

"No. Earth is a rich world, one of the richest in the galaxy. This place is very poor. It must have been named after Earth so long ago that you have forgotten that the human race was not born here."

At last, gently, Albino said, "Perhaps. I think, however, that there is a simpler explanation."

"What explanation? Tell me!"

But Albino only shook his head, as ponderously and stubbornly as an elephant. "I do not wish to get involved in this puzzle. You may go now. However, leave me here with my small friend for a moment, if you would. I have something of a personal nature to say to him."

Then, when he and Flaminio were alone, Albino said, "Do not become emotionally involved with this Szette. There is no substance to her. She is only a traveler—wealthy, by your standards, but a butterfly who flits from star to star, without purpose or consequence. Do you honestly think that she is worthy of your admiration?"

"Yes!" The words were torn from the depths of Flaminio's soul. "Yes, I do!"

Albino had said that he did not wish to be involved. But apparently he cared enough to notify the *protettori*, for later that day they came to arrest Szette and take her to the city courts. There, she was duly charged, declared a pauper, issued a living allowance, and released on Flaminio's recognizance. During the weeks while her trial was pending, he taught her how to speak Roman. She rented a suite of rooms which Flaminio found luxurious, though she clearly did not, and moved them both into it. Daytimes, after work, he showed her all the sights.

At night, they slept apart.

This was a baffling experience for Flaminio, who had never shared quarters with a woman other than his mother on anything but intimate terms. He thought about her constantly when they were apart but in her physical presence, he found it impossible to consider her romantically.

Their conversations, however, were wonderful. Sitting at the kitchen table, Flaminio would ask Szette questions, while she practiced her new language by telling him about the many worlds she had seen.

Achernar, she said, spun so rapidly that it bulged out at the equator and looked like a great blue egg in the skies of Opale. Its companion was a yellow dwarf and when the planet and both stars were all in a line, a holiday was declared in which everyone dressed in green and drank green liqueurs and painted their doors and cities green and poured green dye in their rivers and canals. But such alignments were rare—she had seen only one in all her lifetime.

Snowfall was an ice world, in orbit around a tight cluster of three white dwarfs so dim they were all but indistinguishable from the other stars in a sky that was eternally black. Their mountains had been carved into delicate lacy fantasias, in which were tangled habitats where the air was kept so warm that their citizens wore jewelry and very little else.

The people of Typhonne, a water world whose surface was lashed by almost continuous storms, had so reshaped their bodies that they could no longer be considered human. They built undersea cities in the ocean shallows and when they felt the approach of death would swim into the cold, dark depths of the trenches, to be heard from no more. Their sun was a red dwarf, but not one in a hundred of them knew that fact.

On and on, into the night, Szette's words flew, like birds over the tiled roofs of the Eternal City. Listening, occasionally correcting her grammar or providing a word she did not know, Flaminio traveled in his imagination from star to star, from Algol to Mira to Zaniah.

The day of Szette's trial arrived at last. Because Albino was a necessary witness and the city courts could not hold his tremendous bulk, the judges came to him. The bleachers were dismantled to make room for their seven-chaired bench, from which they interviewed first Flaminio, then Albino, and then Szette. The final witness was an engineer-archivist from the Astrovia.

"This has happened before," the woman said. She was old, scholarly, stylishly dressed. "But not in our lifetimes. Well . . . in his of course." She nodded toward Albino and more than one judge smiled. "It is a very rare occurrence and for you to understand it, I must first explain some of the Astrovia's workings.

"It is an oversimplification to say that the body of a traveler is transformed from matter to energy. It is somewhat closer to the truth to say that the traveler's body is read, recorded, disassembled, and then transmitted as a signal upon a carrier beam. When the beam reaches—or, rather, reached—its destination, the signal is read, recorded, and then used to recreate the traveler. The recordings are retained against the possibility of an interrupted transmission. In which case, the traveler can simply be sent again. As a kind of insurance, you see."

The engineer-archivist paused for questions. There being none, she continued. "I have examined our records. Roughly two thousand years ago, a woman identical to the one you see before you came to Earth. She stayed for a year, and then she left. What she thought of our world we do not know. She is, no doubt, long dead. Recently, there was an earth tremor, too small to be noticed by human senses, which seems to have disrupted something in the workings of the Astrovia. It created a duplicate of that woman as she was when she first arrived in Roma and released her onto the streets. This duplicate is the woman whose fate you are now deciding."

One of the judges leaned forward. "You say this has happened before. How many times?"

"Three that we know of. It is of course possible there were more."

As the testimony went on, Szette had grown paler and paler. Now she clutched Flaminio's arm so tightly that he thought her nails would break.

The judges consulted in unhurried whispers. Finally, one said, "Will the woman calling herself Szette stand forth?"

She complied.

"We are agreed that, simply by being yourself—or, more precisely, a simulacrum of yourself—you know a great deal about an ancient era and the attitudes of its people that would be of interest to the historians at the *Figlia della Sapienze*. You will make yourself available to be interviewed there by credentialed scholars, three days a week. For this you will be paid adequately."

"Two days," snapped the lawyer that the Great Albino had hired for Szette. "More than adequately."

The judges consulted again. "Two," their spokeswoman conceded. "Adequately."

The lawyer smiled.

That night, Szette took off her bracelet, which Flaminio had never seen her without, opened her arms to him, and said, "Come."

He did.

The way that Szette clutched Flaminio as they made love, as if he were a log and she a sailor in danger of drowning, and the unsettling intensity with which she studied his face afterwards, her own expression as unreadable as a moon of ice, told Flaminio that something had changed within her, though he could not have said exactly what.

All that Flaminio knew of Szette was this: That she came from a world called Opale orbiting the stars Achernar A and B. That she loved the darkness of the night sky and the age of Roma's ruins. That she would not eat meat. That she was very fond of him, but nothing more.

This last hurt Flaminio greatly, for he was completely in love with her.

Flaminio was a light sleeper. In the middle of the night, he heard a noise—a footstep on the landing, perhaps, or a door closing—and his eyes flew open.

Szette was gone.

All the rooms of the apartment were empty and when Flaminio went to look for her on the balcony, she wasn't there either. He stared up at the battle-scarred moons and they looked down on him with contempt. Then all the sounds of the city at night drew away from him and in that bubble of silence a sizzle of terror ran up his spine. For he knew where Szette had gone.

It was not difficult to catch up with her. Szette did not hurry and Flaminio ran as hard as he could. But when he stood, panting, before her, she held up a hand in warning. The pale blue stones on her bracelet flashed bright.

He could not move.

He could not speak.

"You have been so very kind to me," Szette said. "I hope you will not hate me too much when you realize why."

She turned her back on him. With casual grace, she climbed the steps. Like many another before her, she hesitated. Then, with sudden resolution, Szette plunged into the beam.

There was nothing Flaminio could have done to stop her. But simultaneous with the dematerialization of Szette's body, he heard an extraordinary noise, a scream, issuing from his own mouth.

What Flaminio did next could not be called an impulsive act. He thought it through carefully, and though that took him only an instant, his resolve was firm.

He ran up the steps toward the beam, determined to join Szette in her endless voyage to nowhere. He would offer his body to the universe and his soul to oblivion. He would not, he was certain, hesitate when he reached the beam.

A shoulder in his chest stopped him cold. A hand gripped his shoulder and another his elbow. Three *protettori* closed in upon him, scowling. "You must come with us, sir," said one, "to have this suicidal impulse removed."

"I'm a citizen! I know my rights! You can't stop me without a contract!"

"Sir, we have a contract."

They dragged him to a *cellular*. It closed about him and took him away.

When he was released from therapy, incapable then or ever after of ending his own life, Flaminio went to see the only individual in all the world who might have taken out a contract on him and asked, "Why wouldn't you let me die?"

"To me, your lives are as those of mayflies," the Great Albino said. "Enjoy what precious seconds remain."

"And the bracelet? Why didn't you tell me about Szette's bracelet?"

"Until that night, I had forgotten about them. Such things were commonly worn by travelers back when the world was rich. To protect themselves from molestation. To enlist aid when in need. But they were a small and unimportant detail in a complex and varied age."

Flaminio had only one more question to pose: "If I was only doing the bracelet's bidding, then why haven't these feelings gone away?"

Albino looked terribly sad. "Alas, my friend, it seems you really did fall in love with her."

That same day, Flaminio left Roma to become a wanderer. He never married, though he took many lovers, both paid and not. Nor did he ever settle down in one place for any length of time. In his old age he frequently claimed to have been around the world forty-eight times and to have seen everything there was to see on all four occupied planets of the Solar System, and much else as well. All of which was verifiably true, were one to search through the records for his whereabouts over the decades. But, in his cups, he would admit to having never gone anywhere or seen anything worth seeing at all.

the martian obelisk

LINDA NAGATA

Here's a look at a project of building a bittersweet memorial to humanity's now-failed attempt to spread beyond the Earth, one which is interrupted by an unexpected emergency that may change everything.

Linda Nagata is a Nebula and Locus Award–winning author. She has spent most of her life in Hawaii, where she's been a writer, a mom, and a programmer of database-driven websites. She lives with her husband in their longtime home on the island of Maui. Her most recent work is The Red Trilogy, *a series of near-future military thrillers published by Saga Press/Simon & Schuster. The first book in the trilogy,* The Red: First Light, *was named a* Publishers Weekly Best Book of 2015. *She maintains a website at www .mythicisland.com.*

T he end of the world required time to accomplish—and time, Susannah reflected, worked at the task with all the leisurely skill of a master torturer, one who could deliver death either quickly or slowly, but always with excruciating pain.

No getting out of it.

But there were still things to do in the long, slow decline; final gestures to make. Susannah Li-Langford had spent seventeen years working on her own offering-for-the-ages, with another six and half years to go before the Martian Obelisk reached completion. Only when the last tile was locked into place in the obelisk's pyramidal cap, would she yield.

Until then, she did what was needed to hold onto her health, which was why, at the age of eighty, she was out walking vigorously along the cliff trail above the encroaching Pacific Ocean, determined to have her daily exercise despite the brisk wind and the freezing mist that ran before it. The mist was only a token moisture, useless to revive the drought-stricken coastal forest, but it made the day cold enough that the fishing platforms at the cliff's edge were deserted, leaving Susannah alone to contemplate the mortality of the human world.

It was not supposed to happen like this. As a child she'd been promised a swift conclusion: duck and cover and nuclear annihilation. And if not annihilation, at least the nihilistic romance of a gun-toting, leather-clad, fight-to-the-death anarchy. That hadn't happened either.

Things had just gotten worse, and worse still, and people gave up. Not everyone, not all at once—there was no single event marking the beginning of the end—but there was a sense of inevitability about the direction history had taken. Sea levels rose along with average ocean temperatures. Hurricanes devoured coastal cities and consumed low-lying countries. Agriculture faced relentless drought, flood, and temperature extremes. A long run of natural disasters made it all worse—earthquakes, landslides, tsunamis, volcanic eruptions. There had been no major meteor strike yet, but Susannah wouldn't bet against it. Health care faltered as antibiotics became useless against resistant bacteria. Surgery became an art of the past.

Out of the devastation, war and terrorism erupted like metastatic cancers.

We are a brilliant species, Susannah thought. *Courageous, creative, generous—as individuals. In larger numbers we fail every time.*

There were reactor meltdowns, poisoned water supplies, engineered plagues, and a hundred other, smaller horrors. The Shoal War had seen nuclear weapons used in the South China Sea. But even the most determined ghouls had failed to ignite a sudden, brilliant cataclysm. The master torturer would not be rushed.

Still, the tipping point was long past, the future truncated. Civilization staggered on only in the lucky corners of the world where the infrastructure of a happier age still functioned. Susannah lived in one of those lucky corners, not far from the crumbling remains of Seattle, where she had greenhouse food, a local network, and satellite access all supplied by her patron, Nathaniel Sanchez, who was the money behind the Martian Obelisk.

When the audio loop on her ear beeped a quiet tone, she assumed the alert meant a message from Nate. There was no one else left in her life, nor did she follow the general news, because what was the point?

She tapped the corner of her wrist-link with a finger gloved against the cold, signaling her personal AI to read the message aloud. Its artificial, androgynous voice spoke into her ear:

"Message sender: Martian Obelisk Operations. Message body: Anomaly sighted. All operations automatically halted pending supervisory approval."

Just a few innocuous words, but weighted with a subtext of disaster.

A subtext all too familiar.

For a few seconds, Susannah stood still in the wind and the rushing mist. In the seventeen-year history of the project, construction had been halted only for equipment maintenance, and that, on a tightly regulated schedule. She raised her wrist-link to her lips. "What anomaly, Alix?" she demanded, addressing the AI. "Can it be identified?"

"It identifies as a homestead vehicle belonging to Red Oasis."

That was absurd. Impossible.

Founded twenty-one years ago, Red Oasis was the first of four Martian colonies, and the most successful. It had outlasted all the others, but the Mars Era had ended nine months ago when Red Oasis succumbed to an outbreak of "contagious asthma"—a made-up name for an affliction evolved on Mars.

Since then there had been only radio silence. The only active elements on the planet were the wind, and the machinery that had not yet broken down, all of it operated by AIs.

"Where is the vehicle?" Susannah asked.

"Seventeen kilometers northwest of the obelisk."

So close!

How was that possible? Red Oasis was over 5,000 kilometers distant. How could an AI have driven so far? And who had given the order?

Homestead vehicles were not made to cover large distances. They were big, slow, and cumbersome—cross-country robotic crawlers designed to haul equipment from the landing site to a colony's permanent location, where construction would commence (and ideally be completed) long before the inhabitants arrived. The vehicles had a top speed of fifteen kilometers per hour which meant that even with the light-speed delay, Susannah had time to send a new instruction set to the AIs that inhabited her construction equipment.

Shifting abruptly from stillness to motion, she resumed her vigorous pace—and then she pushed herself to walk just a little faster.

Nathaniel Sanchez was waiting for her, pacing with a hobbling gait on the front porch of her cottage when she returned. His flawless electric car, an anomaly from another age, was parked in the gravel driveway. Nate was eighty-five and rail-thin, but the electric warmth of his climate-controlled coat kept him comfortable even in the biting wind. She waved at him impatiently. "You know it's fine to let yourself in. I was hoping you'd have coffee brewing by now."

He opened the door for her, still a practitioner of the graceful manners instilled in him by his mother eight decades ago—just one of the many things Susannah admired about him. His trustworthiness was another. Though Nate owned every aspect of the Martian Obelisk project—the equipment on Mars, the satellite accounts, this house where Susannah expected to live out her life—he had always held fast to an early promise never to interfere with her design or her process.

"I haven't been able to talk to anyone associated with Red Oasis," he told her in a voice low and resonant with age. "The support network may have disbanded."

She sat down in the old, armless chair she kept by the door, and pulled off her boots. "Have the rights to Red Oasis gone on the market yet?"

"No." Balancing with one hand against the door, he carefully stepped out of his clogs. "If they had, I would have bought them."

"What about a private transfer?"

He offered a hand to help her up. "I've got people looking into it. We'll find out soon."

In stockinged feet, she padded across the hardwood floor and the hand-made carpets of the living room, but at the door of the Mars room she hesitated, looking back at Nate. Homesteads were robotic vehicles, but they were designed with cabs that could be pressurized for human use, with a life-support system that could sustain two passengers for many days. "Is there any chance some of the colonists at Red Oasis are still alive?" Susannah asked.

Nate reached past her to open the door, a dark scowl on his worn face. "No detectable activity and radio silence for nine months? I don't think so. There's no one in that homestead, Susannah, and there's no good reason for it to visit the obelisk, especially without any notice to us that it was coming. When my people find out who's issuing the orders we'll get it turned around, but in the meantime, do what you have to do to take care of our equipment."

Nate had always taken an interest in the Martian Obelisk, but over the years, as so many of his other aspirations failed, the project had become more personal. He had begun to see it as his own monument and himself as an Ozymandias whose work was doomed to be forgotten, though it would not fall to the desert sands in this lifetime or any other.

"What can I do for you, Susannah?" he had asked, seventeen years ago.

A longtime admirer of her architectural work, he had come to her after the ruin of the Holliday Towers in Los Angeles—her signature project—two soaring glass spires, one 84 floors and the other 104, linked by graceful sky bridges. When the Hollywood Quake struck, the buildings had endured the shaking just as they'd been designed to do, keeping their residents safe, while much of the city around them crumbled. But massive fires followed the quake and the towers had not survived that.

"Tell me what you dream of, Susannah. What you would still be willing to work on."

Nathaniel had been born into wealth, and through the first half of his life he'd grown the family fortune. Though he had never been among the wealthiest individuals of the world, he could still indulge extravagant fancies.

The request Susannah made of him had been, literally, outlandish.

"Buy me the rights to the Destiny Colony."

"On Mars?" His tone suggested a suspicion that her request might be a joke.

"On Mars," she assured him.

Destiny had been the last attempt at Mars colonization. The initial robotic mission had been launched and landed, but money ran out and colonists were never sent. The equipment sat on Mars, unused.

Susannah described her vision of the Martian Obelisk: a gleaming, glittering white spire, taking its color from the brilliant white of the fiber tiles she would use to construct it. It would rise from an empty swell of land, growing more slender as it reached into the sparse atmosphere, until it met an engineering limit prescribed by the strength of the fiber tiles, the gravity of the Red Planet, and by the fierce ghost-fingers of Mars' storm winds. Calculations of the erosional force of the Martian wind led her to conclude that the obelisk would still be standing a hundred thousand years hence and likely far longer. It would outlast all buildings on Earth. It would outlast her bloodline, and all bloodlines. It would still be standing long after the last human had gone the way of the passenger pigeon, the right whale, the dire wolf. In time, the restless Earth would swallow up all evidence of human existence, but the Martian Obelisk would remain—a last monument marking the existence of humankind, excepting only a handful of tiny, robotic spacecraft faring, lost and unrecoverable, in the void between stars.

Nate had listened carefully to her explanation of the project, how it could be done, and the time that would be required. None of it fazed him and he'd agreed, without hesitation, to support her.

The rights to the colony's equipment had been in the hands of a holding company that had acquired ownership in bankruptcy court. Nathaniel pointed out that no one was planning to go to Mars again, that no one any longer possessed the wealth or resources to try. Before long, he was able to purchase Destiny Colony for a tiny fraction of the original backers' investment.

When Susannah received the command codes, Destiny's homestead vehicle had not moved from the landing site, its payload had not been unpacked, and construction on its habitat had never begun. Her first directive to the AI in charge of the vehicle was to drive it three hundred kilometers to the site she'd chosen for the obelisk, at the high point of a rising swell of land.

Once there, she'd unloaded the fleet of robotic construction equipment: a mini-dozer, a mini-excavator, a six-limbed beetle cart to transport finished tiles, and a synth—short for synthetic human although the device was no such thing. It was just a stick figure with two legs, two arms, and hands capable of basic manipulation.

The equipment fleet also included a rolling factory that slowly but continuously produced a supply of fiber tiles, compiling them from raw soil and atmospheric elements. While the factory produced an initial supply of tiles, Susannah prepared the foundation of the obelisk, and within a year she began to build.

The Martian Obelisk became her passion, her reason for life after every other reason had been taken from her. Some called it a useless folly. She didn't argue: what meaning could there be in a monument that would never be seen directly by human eyes? Some called it graffiti: *Kilroy was here!* Some called it a tombstone and that was the truth too.

Susannah just called it better-than-nothing.

The Mars room was a circular extension that Nathaniel had ordered built onto the back of the cottage when Susannah was still in the planning stages of the obelisk's construction. When the door was closed, the room became a theater with a 360-degree floor-to-ceiling flex-screen. A high-backed couch at the center rotated, allowing easy viewing of the encircling images captured in high resolution from the construction site.

Visually, being in this room was like being at Destiny, and it did not matter at all that each red-tinted image was a still shot, because on the Red Planet, the dead planet, change came so slowly that a still shot was as good as video.

Until now.

As Susannah entered the room, she glimpsed an anomalous, bright orange spot in a lowland to the northwest. Nathaniel saw it too. He gestured and started to speak but she waved him to silence, taking the time to circle the room, scanning the entire panorama to assess if anything else had changed.

Her gaze passed first across a long slope strewn with a few rocks and scarred with wheel tracks. Brightly colored survey sticks marked the distance: yellow at 250 meters, pink at 500, green for a full kilometer, and bright red for two.

The red stick stood at the foot of a low ridge that nearly hid the tile factory. She could just see an upper corner of its bright-green, block shape. The rest of it was out of sight, busy as always, processing raw ore dug by the excavator from a pit beyond the ridge, and delivered by the mini-dozer. As the factory slowly rolled, it left a trail of tailings, and every few minutes it produced a new fiber tile.

Next in the panorama was a wide swath of empty land, more tire tracks the only sign of human influence all the way out to a hazy pink horizon. And then, opposite the door and appearing no more than twenty meters distant, was Destiny's homestead vehicle. It was the same design as the approaching crawler: a looming cylindrical cargo container resting on dust-filled tracks. At the forward end, the cab, its windows dusty and lightless, its tiny bunkroom never used. Susannah had long ago removed the equipment she wanted, leaving all else in storage. For over sixteen years, the homestead had remained in its current position, untouched except by the elements.

Passing the Destiny homestead, her gaze took in another downward slope of lifeless desert and then, near the end of her circuit, she faced the tower itself.

The Martian Obelisk stood alone at the high point of the surrounding land, a gleaming-white, graceful, four-sided, tapering spire, already 170-meters high, sharing the sky with no other object. The outside walls were smooth and unadorned, but on the inside, a narrow stairway climbed around the core, rising in steep flights to the tower's top, where more fiber tiles were added every day, extending its height. It was a path no human would ever walk, but the beetle cart, with its six legs, ascended every few hours, carrying in its cargo basket a load of fiber tiles. Though she couldn't see the beetle cart, its position was marked as inside the tower, sixty percent of the way up the stairs. The synth waited for it at the top, its headless torso just visible over the rim of the obelisk's open stack, ready to use its supple hands to assemble the next course of tiles.

All this was as expected, as it should be.

Susannah steadied herself with a hand against the high back of the couch as she finally considered the orange splash of color that was the intruding vehicle. "Alix, distance to the Red Oasis homestead?"

The same androgynous voice that inhabited her ear loop spoke now through the room's sound system. "Twelve kilometers."

The homestead had advanced five kilometers in the twenty minutes she'd taken to return to the cottage—though in truth it was really much closer. Earth and Mars were approaching a solar conjunction, when they would be at their greatest separation, on opposite sides of the Sun. With the lightspeed delay, even this new image was nineteen minutes old. So she had only minutes left to act.

Reaching down to brace herself against the armrest of the couch, she sat with slow grace. "Alix, give me a screen."

A sleeve opened in the armrest and an interface emerged, swinging into an angled display in front of her.

The fires that had destroyed the Holliday Towers might have been part of the general inferno sparked by the Hollywood earthquake, but Susannah suspected otherwise. The towers had stood as a symbol of defiance amid the destruction—

which might explain why they were brought low. The Martian Obelisk was a symbol too, and it had long been a target both for the media and for some of Destiny's original backers who had wanted the landing left undisturbed, for the use of a future colonization mission that no one could afford to send.

"Start up our homestead," Nate urged her. "It's the only equipment we can afford to risk. If you drive it at an angle into the Red Oasis homestead, you might be able to push it off its tracks."

Susannah frowned, her fingers moving across the screen as she assembled an instruction set. "That's a last resort option, Nate, and I'm not even sure it's possible. There are safety protocols in the AIs' core training modules that might prevent it."

She tapped *send*, launching the new instruction set on its nineteen-minute journey. Then she looked at Nate. "I've ordered the AIs that handle the construction equipment to retreat and evade. We cannot risk damage or loss of control."

He nodded somberly. "Agreed—but the synth and the beetle cart are in the tower."

"They're safe in there, for now. But I'm going to move the homestead—assuming it starts. After seventeen years, it might not."

"Understood."

"The easiest way for someone to shut down our operation is to simply park the Red Oasis homestead at the foot of the obelisk, so that it blocks access to the stairway. If the beetle cart can't get in and out, we're done. So I'm going to park our homestead there first."

He nodded thoughtfully, eyeing the image of the obelisk. "Okay. I understand."

"Our best hope is that you can find out who's instructing the Red Oasis homestead and get them to back off. But if that fails, I'll bring the synth out, and use it to try to take manual control."

"The Red Oasis group could have a synth too."

"Yes."

They might also have explosives—destruction was so much easier than creation—but Susannah did not say this aloud. She did not want Nate to inquire about the explosives that belonged to Destiny. Instead she told him, "There's no way we can know what they're planning. All we can do is wait and see."

He smacked a frustrated fist into his palm. "Nineteen minutes! Nineteen minutes times two before we know what's happened!"

"Maybe the AIs will work it out on their own," she said dryly. And then it was her turn to be overtaken by frustration. "Look at us! Look what we've come to! Invested in a monument no one will ever see. Squabbling over the possession of ruins while the world dies. This is where our hubris has brought us." But that was wrong, so she corrected herself. "*My* hubris."

Nate was an old man with a lifetime of emotions mapped on his well-worn face. In that complex terrain it wasn't always easy to read his current feelings, but she thought she saw hurt there. He looked away, before she could decide. A furtive movement.

"Nate?" she asked in confusion.

"This project matters," he insisted, gazing at the obelisk. "It's art, and it's memory, and it *does* matter."

Of course. But only because it was all they had left.

"Come into the kitchen," she said. "I'll make coffee."

Nate's tablet chimed while they were still sitting at the kitchen table. He took the call, listened to a brief explanation from someone on his staff, and then objected. "That can't be right. No. There's something else going on. Keep at it."

He scowled at the table until Susannah reminded him she was there. "Well?"

"That was Davidson, my chief investigator. He tracked down a Red Oasis share-holder who told him that the rights to the colony's equipment had *not* been traded or sold, that they couldn't be, because they had no value. Not with a failed commu-nications system." His scowl deepened. "They want us to believe they can't even talk to the AIs."

Susannah stared at him. "But if that's true—"

"It's not."

"Meaning you don't want it to be." She got up from the table.

"Susannah—"

"I'm not going to pretend, Nate. If it's not an AI driving that homestead, then it's a colonist, a survivor—and that changes everything."

She returned to the Mars room, where she sat watching the interloper's approach. The wall screen refreshed every four minutes as a new image arrived from the other side of the sun. Each time it did, the bright orange homestead jumped a bit closer. It jumped right past the outermost ring of survey sticks, putting it less than two kilo-meters from the obelisk—close enough that she could see a faint wake of drifting dust trailing behind it, giving it a sense of motion.

Then, thirty-eight minutes after she'd sent the new instruction set, the Destiny AI returned an acknowledgement.

Her heart beat faster, knowing that whatever was to happen on Mars had already happened. Destiny's construction equipment had retreated and its homestead had started up or had failed to start, had moved into place at the foot of the tower or not. No way to know until time on Earth caught up with time on Mars.

The door opened.

Nate shuffled into the room.

Susannah didn't bother to ask if Davidson had turned up anything. She could see from his grim expression that he expected the worst.

And what was the worst?

A slight smile stole onto her lips as Nate sat beside her on the couch.

The worst case is that someone has lived.

Was it any wonder they were doomed?

Four more minutes.

The image updated.

The 360-degree camera, mounted on a steel pole sunk deep into the rock, showed

Destiny profoundly changed. For the first time in seventeen years, Destiny's homestead had moved. It was parked by the tower, just as Susannah had requested. She
twisted around, looking for the bright green corner of the factory beyond the distant
ridge—but she couldn't see it.

"Everything is as ordered," Susannah said.

The Red Oasis homestead had reached the green survey sticks.

"An AI has to be driving," Nate insisted.

"Time will tell."

Nate shook his head. "Time comes with a nineteen minute gap. Truth is in the
radio silence. It's an AI."

Four more minutes of silence.

When the image next refreshed, it showed the two homesteads, nose to nose.

Four minutes.

The panorama looked the same.

Four minutes more.

No change.

Four minutes.

Only the angle of sunlight shifted.

Four minutes.

A figure in an orange pressure suit stood beside the two vehicles, gazing up at
the tower.

Before the Martian Obelisk, when Shaun was still alive, two navy officers in dress
uniforms had come to the house, and in formal voices explained that the daughter
Susannah had birthed and nurtured and shaped with such care was gone, her future
collapsed to nothing by a missile strike in the South China Sea.

"We must go on," Shaun ultimately insisted.

And they had, bravely.

Defiantly.

Only a few years later their second child and his young wife had vanished into
the chaos brought on by an engineered plague that decimated Hawaii's population, turning it into a state under permanent quarantine. Day after excruciating
day as they'd waited for news, Shaun had grown visibly older, hope a dying light,
and when it was finally extinguished he had nothing left to keep him moored to
life.

Susannah was of a different temper. The cold ferocity of her anger had nailed
her into the world. The shape it took was the Martian Obelisk: one last creative act
before the world's end.

She knew now the obelisk would never be finished.

"It's a synth," Nate said. "It has to be."

The AI contradicted him. "Text message," it announced.

"Read it," Susannah instructed.

Alix obeyed, reading the message in an emotionless voice. "Message sender: Red Oasis resident Tory Eastman. Message body as transcribed audio: Is anyone out there? Is anyone listening? My name is Tory Eastman. I'm a refugee from Red Oasis. Nineteen days in transit with my daughter and son, twins, three years old. We are the last survivors."

These words induced in Susannah a rush of fear so potent she had to close her eyes against a dizzying sense of vertigo. There was no emotion in the AI's voice and still she heard in it the anguish of another mother:

"The habitat was damaged during the emergency. I couldn't maintain what was left and I had no communications. So I came here. Five thousand kilometers. I need what's here. I need it all. I need the provisions and I need the equipment and I need the command codes and I need the building materials. I need to build my children a new home. Please. Are you there? Are you an AI? Is anyone left on Earth? Respond. Respond please. Give me the command codes. I will wait."

For many seconds—and many, many swift, fluttering heartbeats—neither Nate nor Susannah spoke. Susannah wanted to speak. She sought for words, and when she couldn't find them, she wondered: am I in shock? Or is it a stroke?

Nate found his voice first: "It's a hoax, aimed at you, Susannah. They know your history. They're playing on your emotions. They're using your grief to wreck this project."

Susannah let out a long breath, and with it, some of the horror that had gripped her. "We humans are amazing," she mused, "in our endless ability to lie to ourselves."

He shook his head. "Susannah, if I thought this was real—"

She held up a hand to stop his objection. "I'm not going to turn over the command codes. Not yet. If you're right and this is a hoax, I can back out. But if it's real, that family has pushed the life support capabilities of their homestead to the limit. They can move into our vehicle—that'll keep them alive for a few days—but they'll need more permanent shelter soon."

"It'll take months to build a habitat."

"No. It'll take months to make the tiles to build a habitat—but we already have a huge supply of tiles."

"All of our tiles are tied up in the obelisk."

"Yes."

He looked at her in shock, struck speechless.

"It'll be okay, Nate."

"You're abandoning the project."

"If we can help this family survive, we have to do it—and that will be the project we're remembered for."

"Even if there's no one left to remember?"

She pressed her lips tightly together, contemplating the image of the obelisk. Then she nodded. "Even so."

Knowing the pain of waiting, she sent a message of assurance to Destiny Colony before anything else. Then she instructed the synth and the beetle cart to renew their work, but this time in reverse: the synth would unlink the fiber tiles beginning at the top of the obelisk and the beetle would carry them down.

After an hour—after she'd traded another round of messages with a grateful Tory Eastman and begun to lay out a shelter based on a standard Martian habitat—she got up to stretch her legs and relieve her bladder. It surprised her to find Nate still in the living room. He stood at the front window, staring out at the mist that never brought enough moisture into the forest.

"They'll be alone forever," he said without turning around. "There are no more missions planned. No one else will ever go to Mars."

"I won't tell her that."

He looked at her over his shoulder. "So you are willing to sacrifice the obelisk? It was everything to you yesterday, but today you'll just give it up?"

"She drove a quarter of the way around the planet, Nate. Would you ever have guessed that was possible?"

"No," he said bitterly as he turned back to the window. "No. It should not have been possible."

"There's a lesson for us in that. We assume we can see forward to tomorrow, but we can't. We can't ever really know what's to come—and we can't know what we might do, until we try."

When she came out of the bathroom, Nate was sitting down in the rickety old chair by the door. With his rounded shoulders and his thin white hair, he looked old and very frail. "Susannah—"

"Nate, I don't want to argue—"

"Just *listen*. I didn't want to tell you before because, well, you've already suffered so many shocks and even good news can come too late."

"What are you saying?" she said, irritated with him now, sure that he was trying to undermine her resolve.

"Hawaii's been under quarantine because the virus can be latent for—"

She guessed where this was going. "For years. I know that. But if you're trying to suggest that Tory and her children might still succumb to whatever wiped out Red Oasis—"

"They *might*," he interrupted, sounding bitter. "But that's not what I was going to say."

"Then what?"

"Listen, and I'll tell you. Are you ready to listen?"

"Yes, yes. Go ahead."

"A report came out just a few weeks ago. The latest antivirals worked. The quarantine in Hawaii will continue for several more years, but all indications are the virus is gone. Wiped out. No sign of latent infections in over six months."

Her hands felt numb; she felt barely able to shuffle her feet as she moved to take a seat in an antique armchair. "The virus is gone? How can they know that?"

"Blood tests. And the researchers say that what they've learned can be applied to other contagions. That what happened in Hawaii doesn't ever have to happen again."

Progress? A reprieve against the long decline?

"There's more, Susannah."

The way he said it—his falling tone—it was a warning that set her tired heart pounding.

"You asked me to act as your agent," he reminded her. "You asked me to screen all news, and I've done that."

"Until now."

"Until now," he agreed, looking down, looking frightened by the knowledge he had decided to convey. "I should have told you sooner."

"But you didn't want to risk interrupting work on the obelisk?"

"You said you didn't want to hear anything." He shrugged. "I took you at your word."

"Nate, will you just say it?"

"You have a granddaughter, Susannah."

She replayed these words in her head, once, twice. They didn't make sense.

"DNA tests make it certain," he explained. "She was born six months after her father's death."

"No." Susannah did not dare believe it. It was too dangerous to believe. "They both died. That was confirmed by the survivors. They posted the IDs of all the dead."

"Your daughter-in-law lived long enough to give birth."

Susannah's chest squeezed tight. "I don't understand. Are you saying the child is still alive?"

"Yes."

Anger rose hot, up out of the past. "And how long have you known? How long have you kept this from me?"

"Two months. I'm sorry, but . . ."

But we had our priorities. The tombstone. The Martian folly.

She stared at the floor, too stunned to be happy, or maybe she'd forgotten how. "You should have told me."

"I know."

"And I . . . I shouldn't have walled myself off from the world. I'm sorry."

"There's more," he said cautiously, as if worried how much more she could take.

"What else?" she snapped, suddenly sure this was just another game played by the master torturer, to draw the pain out. "Are you going to tell me that my grand-daughter is sickly? Dying? Or that she's a mad woman, perhaps?"

"No," he said meekly. "Nothing like that. She's healthy, and she has a healthy two-year-old daughter." He got up, put an age-marked hand on the door knob. "I've sent you her contact information. If you need an assistant to help you build the habitat, let me know."

He was a friend, and she tried to comfort him. "Nate, I'm sorry. If there was a choice—"

"There isn't. That's the way it's turned out. You will tear down the obelisk, and this woman, Tory Eastman, will live another year, maybe two. Then the equipment will break and she will die and we won't be able to rebuild the tower. We'll pass on, and the rest of the world will follow—"

"We can't know that, Nate. Not for sure."

He shook his head. "This all looks like hope, but it's a trick. It's fate cheating us, forcing us to fold our hand, level our pride, and go out meekly. And there's no choice in it, because it's the right thing to do."

He opened the door. For a few seconds, wind gusted in, until he closed it again. She heard his clogs crossing the porch and a minute later she heard the crunch of tires on the gravel road.

You have a granddaughter. One who grew up without her parents, in a quarantine zone, with no real hope for the future and yet she was healthy, with a daughter already two years old.

And then there was Tory Eastman of Mars, who had left a dying colony and driven an impossible distance past doubt and despair, because she knew you have to do everything you can, until you can't do anymore.

Susannah had forgotten that, somewhere in the dark years.

She sat for a time in the stillness, in a quiet so deep she could hear the beating of her heart.

This all looks like hope.

Indeed it did and she well knew that hope could be a duplicitous gift from the master torturer, one that opened the door to despair.

"But it doesn't have to be that way," she whispered to the empty room. "I'm not done. Not yet."

we who live in the heart

KELLY ROBSON

Here's an intense and vivid adventure that tells the story of malcontents who grow tired of living in underground colonies on an alien planet that consists mostly of vast oceans, and who opt instead for a more adventurous and much more uncertain life by taking control of and moving into what amount to immense organic submarines, enabling them to roam the seas at will—but also meaning that they must live in constant danger of losing control of their "ship."

New writer Kelly Robson is a graduate of the Taos Toolbox writing workshop. Her first fiction appeared in 2015 at Tor.com, Clarkesworld, and Asimov's Science Fiction, and in the anthologies New Canadian Noir, In the Shadow of the Towers, *and* Licence Expired. *She lives in Toronto with her wife, science fiction writer A. M. Dellamonica.*

Ricci slipped in and out of consciousness as we carried her to the anterior sinus and strapped her into her hammock. Her eyelids drooped but she kept forcing them wide. After we finished tucking her in, she pulled an handheld media appliance out of her pocket and called her friend Jane.

"You're late," Jane said. The speakers flattened her voice slightly. "Are you okay?"

Ricci was too groggy to speak. She poked her hand through the hammock's electrostatic membrane and panned the appliance around the sinus. Eddy and Chara both waved as the lens passed over them, but Jane was only interested in one thing.

"Show me your face, Ricci. Talk to me. What's it like in there?"

Ricci coughed, clearing her throat. "I dunno. It's weird. I can't really think." Her voice slurred from the anesthetic.

I could have answered Jane, if she'd asked me. The first thing newbies notice is how strange it smells. Human olfaction is primal; scents color our perceptions even when they're too faint to describe. Down belowground, the population crush makes it impossible to get away from human funk. Out here, it's the opposite, with no scents our brains recognize. That's why most of us fill our habs with stinky things—pheromone misters, scented fabrics, ablative aromatic gels.

Eventually, Ricci would get around to customizing the scentscape in her big new hab, but right then she was too busy trying to stay awake. Apparently she'd promised Jane she'd check in as soon as she arrived, and not just a quick ping. She was definitely hurting but the call was duty.

"There's people. They're taking care of me." Ricci gazed blearily at our orang. "I was carried in by a porter bot. It's orange and furry. Long arms."

"I don't care about the bot. Tell me about you."

"I'm fine, but my ears aren't working right. It's too noisy."

We live with a constant circulatory thrum, gassy gurgles and fizzes, whumps, snaps, pops, and booms. Sound waves pulse through every surface, a deep hum you feel in your bones.

Jane took a deep breath, let it out with a whoosh. "Okay. Go to sleep. Call me when you wake up, okay?"

Ricci's head lolled back, then she jerked herself awake.

"You should have come with me."

Jane laughed. "I can't leave my clients. And anyway, I'd be bored."

Ricci squeezed her eyes shut, blinked a few times, then forced them wide.

"No you wouldn't. There's seven other people here, and they're all nuts. You'd already be trying to fix them."

Vula snorted and stalked out of the sinus, her long black braids slapping her back. The rest of us just smiled and shook our heads. You can't hold people responsible for what they say when they're half-unconscious. And anyway, it's true—we're not your standard moles. We don't want to be.

Only a mole would think we'd be bored out here. We have to take care of every necessity of life personally—nobody's going to do it for us. Tapping water is one example. Equipment testing and maintenance is another. Someone has to manage the hygiene and maintenance bots. And we all share responsibility for health and safety. Making sure we can breathe is high on everyone's priority list, so we don't leave it up to chance. Finally, there's atmospheric and geographical data gathering. Mama's got to pay the bills. We're a sovereign sociopolitical entity, population: eight, and we negotiate our own service contracts for everything.

But other than that, sure, we have all the free time in the world. Otherwise what's the point? We came out here to get some breathing room—mental and physical. Unlike the moles, we've got plenty of both.

Have you ever seen a tulip? It's a flowering plant. No nutritional value, short bloom. Down belowground, they're grown in decorative troughs for special occasions—ambassadorial visits, arts festivals, sporting events, that sort of thing.

Anyway. Take a tulip flower and stick an ovoid bladder where the stem was and you've got the idea. Except big. Really big. And the petals move. Some of us call it Mama. I just call it home.

The outer skin is a transparent, flexible organic membrane. You can see right through to the central organ systems. The surrounding bladders and sinuses provide structure and protection. Balloons inside a bigger balloon, filled with helium and hydrogen. The whole organism ripples with iridescence.

We live in the helium-filled sinuses. If you get close enough, you can see us moving around inside. We're the dark spots.

While Ricci slept, I called everyone to the rumpus room for a quick status check. All seven of us lounged in the netting, enjoying the free flowing oxygen/hydrogen mix, goggles and breathers dangling around our necks.

I led the discussion, as usual. Nobody else can ever be bothered.

"Thoughts?" I asked.

"Ricci seems okay," said Eddy. "And I like what's-her-name. The mole on the comm."

"Jane. Yeah, pretty smile," said Bouche. "Ricci's fine. Right Vula?"

Vula frowned and crossed her arms. She'd hooked into the netting right next to the hatch and looked about ready to stomp out.

"I guess," she said. "Rude, though."

"She was just trying to be funny," said Treasure. "I can never predict who'll stick and who'll bounce. I thought Chara would claw her way back down belowground. Right through the skin and nose-dive home."

Chara grinned. "I still might."

We laughed, but the camaraderie felt forced. Vula had everyone on edge.

"We'll all keep an eye on Ricci until she settles in," Eleanora said. "Are we good here? I need to get back to training. I got a chess tournament, you know."

"You always have a tournament." I surveyed the faces around me, but it didn't look like anyone wanted to chat.

"As long as nobody hogs the uplink, I never have any problems," said Bouche. "Who's training Ricci?"

"Who do you think?" I said. We have a rule. Whoever scared off the last one has to train the replacement.

We all looked at Vula.

"Shit," she said. "I hate training newbies."

"Stop running them off then," said Chara. "Be nice."

Vula scowled, fierce frown lines scoring her forehead. "I've got important work to do."

No use arguing with Vula. She was deep in a creative tangle, and had been for a while..

"I'll do it," I said. "We better train Ricci right if we want her to stick."

When Ricci woke up, I helped her out of the hammock and showed her how to operate the hygiene station. As soon as she'd hosed off the funk, she called Jane on her appliance.

"Take off your breather for a moment," Jane said. "Goggles too. I need to see your face."

Ricci wedged her fingernails under the seal and pried off her breather. She lifted her goggles. When she grinned, deep dimples appeared on each cheek.

. Jane squinted at her through the screen. She nodded, and Ricci replaced the breather. It attached to her skin with a slurp.

"How do I look?" Ricci asked. "Normal enough for you?"

"What's the failure rate on that thing?"

"Low," Ricci said.

Point two three percent. Which *is* low unless you're talking about death. Then it's high. But we have spares galore. Safety nests here, there, and everywhere. I could have chimed in with the info but Jane didn't want to hear from me. I stayed well back and let Ricci handle her friend.

"Has anyone ever studied the long-term effects of living in a helium atmosphere?" Jane asked. "It can't be healthy."

"Eyes are a problem." Ricci tapped a finger on a goggle lens. "Corneas need oxygen so that's why we wear these. The hammocks are filled with air, so we basically bathe in oxygen while we're sleeping. But you're right. Without that the skin begins to slough."

Jane made a face. "Ugh."

"There's air in the common area, too—they call it the rumpus room. That's where they keep the fab and extruder. I'm supposed to be there now. I have to eat and then do an orientation session. Health, safety, all that good stuff."

"Don't forget to take some time to get to know your hab-mates, okay?"

"I met them when I got here."

"One of them is Vula, the artist, right? The sculptor. She's got to be interesting."

Ricci shrugged. "She looked grumpy."

I was impressed. Pretty perceptive for someone who'd been half-drowned in anesthetic.

"What's scheduled after training?"

"Nothing. That's the whole point of coming here, right?"

"I wondered if you remembered." A smile broke over Jane's face, star-bright even when glimpsed on a small screen at a distance. "You need rest and recreation."

"Relaxation and reading," Ricci added.

"Maybe you'll take up a hobby."

"Oh, I will," said Ricci. "Count on it."

Yes, I was spying on Ricci. We all were. She seemed like a good egg, but with no recourse to on-the-spot conflict intervention, we play it safe with newbies until they settle in. Anyone who doesn't like it can pull down a temporary privacy veil to shield themselves from the bugs, but most don't bother. Ricci didn't.

Plus we needed a distraction.

Whether it's half a million moles in a hole down belowground or eight of us floating around in the atmosphere, every hab goes through ups and downs. We'd been down for a while. Some of it was due to Vula's growly mood, the worst one we'd seen for a while, but really, we just needed a shake-up. Whether we realized it or not, we were all looking to Ricci to deliver us from ourselves.

During orientation, Ricci and I had company. Bouche and Eddy claimed they needed a refresher and tagged along for the whole thing. Chara, Treasure, and Eleanora joined us halfway through. Even Vula popped out of her hab for a few moments, and actually made an effort to look friendly.

With all the chatter and distraction, I wasn't confident Ricci's orientation had stuck, so I shadowed her on her first maintenance rotation. The workflow is fully documented, every detail supported by nested step-by-steps and supervised by dedicated project management bugs that help take human error out of the equation. But I figured she deserved a little extra attention.

Life support is our first priority, always. We clear the air printers, run live tests on the carbon dioxide digesters, and ground-truth the readings on every single sensor. It's a tedious process, but not even Vula complains. She likes to breathe as much as any of us.

Ricci was sharp. Interested. Not just in the systems that keep us alive, but in the whole organism, its biology, behavior, and habitat. She was even interested in clouds around and the icy, slushy landscape below. She wanted to know about the weather patterns, wind, atmospheric layers—everything. I answered as best I could, but I was out of the conversational habit.

That, and something about the line of her jaw had me tongue-tied.

"Am I asking too many questions, Doc?" she asked as we stumped back to the rumpus room after checking the last hammock.

"Let's keep to the life-and-death stuff for now," I said.

Water harvesting is the next priority. To get it, we have to rise to the aquapause. There, bright sunlight condenses moisture on the skin and collects in the dorsal runnels, where we tap it for storage.

Access to the main inflation gland is just under the rumpus room. Ricci squeezed through the elasticized access valve. The electrostatic membrane pulled her hair into spikes that waved at the PM bots circling her head. I stayed outside and watched her smear hormone ointment on the marbled surface of the gland. Sinuses creaked as bladders began to expand. As we walked through the maze of branching sinuses, I showed her how to brace against the roll and use the momentum to pull herself through the narrow access slots. Once we got to the ring-shaped fore cavity, we hooked our limbs into the netting and waited.

Rainbows rippled across the expanded bladder surfaces. We were nearly spherical, petals furled, and the wind rolled us like an untethered balloon. The motion makes some newbies sick, and they have to dial up anti-nauseant. Not Ricci. She looked around with anticipation, as if she were expecting to see something amazing rise over the vast horizon.

"Do you ever run into other whales?" she asked.

"I don't much care for that term," I said. It came out gruffer than I intended.

A dimple appeared at the edge of her breather. "Have you been out here long, Doc?"

"Yes. Ask me an important question."

"Okay." She waved her hand at the water kegs nested at the bottom of the netting, collapsed into a pile of honeycomb folds. "Why don't you carry more water?"

"That's a good question. You don't need me to tell you though. You can figure it out. Flip through your dash."

The dimple got deeper. Behind her darkened goggles, her eyelids flickered as she reviewed her dashboards. Naturally it took a little while; our setup was new to her. I rested my chin on my forearms and waited.

She surfaced quicker than I expected.

"Mass budget, right? Water is heavy."

"Yes. The mass dashboard also tracks our inertia. If we get too heavy, we can't maneuver. And heavy things are dangerous. Everything's tethered and braced, and we have safety nets. But if something got loose, it could punch through a bladder wall. Even through the skin, easy."

Ricci looked impressed. "I won't tell Jane about that."

We popped into the aquapause. The sun was about twenty degrees above the horizon. Its clear orange light glanced across the thick violet carpet of helium clouds below. Overhead, the indigo sky rippled with stars.

Bit of a shock for a mole. I let Ricci ogle the stars for a while. Water ran off the skin, a rushing, cascading sound like one of the big fountains down belowground. I cleared my throat. Ricci startled, eyes wide behind her goggles, then she climbed out of the netting and flipped the valve on the overhead tap. Silver water dribbled through the hose and into the battery of kegs, slowly expanding the pleated walls.

Ricci didn't always fill the quiet spaces with needless chatter. I liked that. We worked in silence until the kegs were nearly full, and when she began to question me again, I welcomed it.

"Eddy said you were one of the first out here," Ricci said. "You figured out how to make this all work."

I answered with a grunt, and then cursed myself. If I scared her away Vula would never let me forget it.

"That's right. Me and a few others."

"You took a big risk."

"Moving into the atmosphere was inevitable," I said. "Humans are opportunistic organisms. If there's a viable habitat, we'll colonize it."

"Takes a lot of imagination to see this as viable."

"Maybe. Or maybe desperation. It's not perfect but it's better than down belowground. Down there, you can't move without stepping on someone. Every breath is measured and every minute is optimized for resource resilience. That might be viable, but it's not human."

"I'm not arguing." Ricci's voice pitched low, thick with emotion as she gazed at the stars in that deep sky. "I love it here."

Yeah, she wasn't a mole anymore. She was one of us already.

One by one, the kegs filled and began flexing through their purification routine. We called in the crab-like water bots and ran them through a sterilization cycle.

Water work done, the next task was spot-checking the equipment nests. I let Ricci take the lead, stayed well back as she jounced through the cavities and sinuses. She was enthusiastic, confident. Motivated, even. Most newbies stay hunkered in their hammocks for a lot longer than her.

We circled back to the rumpus room, inventoried the nutritional feedstock, and began running tests on the hygiene bots. I settled into the netting and watched Ricci pull a crispy snack out of the extruder.

"You must know all the other crews. The ones who live in the . . ." Ricci struggled to frame the concept without offending me.

"You can call them whales if you want. I don't like it, but I've never managed to find a better word."

She passed me a bulb of cold caffeine.

"How often do you talk to the people who live in the other whales, Doc?"

"We don't have anything to do with them. Not anymore."

"How come?"

"The whole reason we came out here is so we don't have to put up with anyone else's crap."

"You never see the other whales at all? Not even at a distance?"

I drained the bulb. "These organisms don't have any social behavior."

"But you must have to talk to them sometimes, don't you? Share info or troubleshoot?"

I collapsed the bulb in my fist and threw it to a hygiene bot.

"You lonely already?"

Ricci tossed her head back and laughed, a full belly guffaw. "Come on, Doc. You have to admit that's weird."

She was relentless. "Go ahead and make friends with the others if you want," I growled. "Just don't believe everything they say. They've got their own ways of doing things, and so do we."

We checked the internal data repeaters and then spent the rest of the shift calibrating and testing the sensor array—all the infrastructure that traps the data we sell to the atmospheric monitoring firms. I kept my mouth shut. Ricci maintained an aggressive cheerfulness even though I was about as responsive as a bot. But my glacier-like chilliness—more than ten years in the making—couldn't resist her. My hermit heart was already starting to thaw.

If I'd been the one calling Jane every day, I would have told her the light is weird out here. We stay within the optimal thermal range, near the equator where the winds are comparatively warm and the solar radiation helps keep the temperature in our habitat relatively viable. That means we're always in daylight, running a race against nightfall, which is good for Mama but not so good for us. Humans evolved to exist in a day-night cycle and something goes haywire in our brains when we mess with that. So our goggles simulate our chosen ratio of light and dark.

Me, I like to alternate fifty-fifty but I'll fool with the mix every so often just to shake things up. Vula likes the night so she keeps things dimmer than most. Everyone's different. That's what the moles don't realize, how different some of us are.

"I did a little digging, and what I found out scared me," Jane said the next time Ricci checked in. "Turns out there's huge gaps in atmospheric research. The only area that's really well monitored is the equator, and only around the beanstalk. Everywhere else, analysis is done by hobbyists who donate a few billable hours here and there."

Ricci nodded. "That's what Doc said."

Hearing my name perked me right up. I slapped down two of my open streams and gave their feed my whole attention.

"Nobody really knows that much about the organism you're living inside. Even less about the climate out there, and nearly nothing about the geography, not in detail. I never would have supported this decision if I'd realized how . . ." Jane's pretty face contorted as she searched for the word. "How *willy-nilly* the whole situation is. It's not safe. I can't believe it's even allowed."

"Allowed? Who can stop us? People go where they want."

"Not if it's dangerous. You can't just walk into a sewage treatment facility or air purification plant. It's unethical to allow people to endanger themselves."

Ricci snorted, fouling the valves on her breather and forcing her to take a big gulp of helium through her mouth.

"Not all of us want to be safe, Jane." The helium made her voice squeaky.

Jane's expression darkened. "Don't mock me. I'm worried about you."

"I know. I'm sorry," Ricci squeaked. She exhaled to clear her lungs and took a deep slow breath through her nose. Her voice dropped to its normal register. "Listen, I've only been here a few days."

"Six," Jane said.

"If I see anything dangerous, you'll be the first to know. Until then, don't worry. I'm fine. Better than fine. I'm even sleeping. A lot."

That was a lie. The air budget showed Ricci hadn't seen much of the inside of her hammock. But I wasn't worried. Exhaustion would catch up with her eventually.

"There's something else," Jane said. "I've been asking around about your habmates."

"Vula's okay. It's just that lately none of her work has turned out the way she wants. You know artists. Their professional standards are always unreachable. Set themselves up to fail."

"It's not about Vula, it's Doc."

Ricci bounced in her netting. "Oh yeah? Tell me. Because I can't get a wink out of that one. Totally impervious."

I maximized the feed to fill my entire visual field. In the tiny screen in Ricci's hand, Jane's dark hair trailed strands across her face and into her mouth. She pushed them back with an impatient flick of her fingers. She was in an atrium, somewhere with stiff air circulation. I could just make out seven decks of catwalk arching behind her, swarming with pedestrians.

"Pull down a veil," Jane said. "You might have lurkers."

"I do," Ricci answered. "Four at least. I'm the most entertaining thing inside Mama for quite a while. It doesn't bother me. Let them lurk."

But Jane insisted, so Ricci pulled down a privacy veil and the bug feed winked out.

I told myself whatever Jane had found out didn't matter. It would bear no relation to reality. That's how gossip works—especially gossip about ancient history. But even so, a little hole opened up under my breastbone, and it ached.

Only six days and I already cared what Ricci thought. I wanted her to like me. So I set about trying to give her a reason.

A few days later, we drifted into a massive storm system. Ricci's first big one. I didn't want her to miss it, so I bounced aft and hallooed to her at a polite distance from her hab. She was lounging in her netting, deep in multiple streams, twisting a lock of her short brown hair around her finger.

She looked happy enough to see me. No wariness behind her gaze, no chill.

We settled in to watch the light show. It was an eye-catcher. Bolts zagged to the peaks of the ice towers below, setting the fog alight with expanding patches of emerald green and acid magenta.

Two big bolts forked overhead with a mighty *whump*. Ricci didn't even jump.

"What was that?" she asked.

I was going to stay silently mysterious, but then remembered I was trying to be friendly.

"That," I said, "was lunch."

A dark splotch began to coalesce at the spot where the two bolts had caressed each other, a green and violet pastel haze in the thin milky fog. We banked slowly, bladders groaning, massive sinus walls clicking as we changed shape to ride the wind currents up, up, and then the massive body flexed just enough to reveal two petals reaching into the coalescing bacteria bloom.

Ricci launched herself out of the netting and clung to the side of her hab, trying to get a better view of the feeding behavior. When the bloom dissipated, she turned to me.

"That's all it does, this whale? Just search for food?"

"Eat, drink, and see the sights," I said. "What else does anyone need from life?"

Good company, I thought, but I didn't say it.

The light show went on for hours. Ricci was fascinated from start to finish. Me, I didn't see it. I spent the whole storm watching the light illuminate her face.

What else does anyone need from life? That was me trying to be romantic. Clumsy. Also inaccurate.

When we first moved out here, my old friends and I thought our habs would eventually become self-contained. Experience killed that illusion pretty quick. We're almost as dependent on the planetary civil apparatus as anyone.

Without feedstock, for example, we'd either starve or suffocate—not sure which would happen first. It has a lot of mass, so we can't stockpile much.

Then there's power. Funding it is a challenge when you're supplying eight people as opposed to eight million. No economy of scale in a hab this size. It's not the power feed itself that's the problem, but the infrastructure. We're always on the move, so the feed has to follow us around and provide multiple points of redundancy. Our ambient power supply costs base market value plus a massive buy-back on the research and development.

Data has to follow us around too, but we don't bother with redundancy. It's not critical. You'd think it was more important than air, though, if you saw us when the data goes down. Shrieking. Curses. Bouche just about catatonic (she's a total media junkie). Eleanora wall-eyed with panic especially if she's in the middle of a tournament (chess is her drug of choice). Vula, Eddy, and me in any state from suave to suicidal depending on what we're doing when the metaphorical umbilical gets yanked out of our guts.

Treasure and Chara are the only ones who don't freak out. Usually they're too busy boning each other.

Without data, we couldn't stay here, either. If we only had each other to talk to, it'd be a constant drama cycle, but we're all plugged into the hab cultures down belowground. We've got hobbies to groom, projects to tend, performances to cheer, games to play, friends to visit.

Finally, as an independent political entity, we need brokers and bankers to handle our economic transactions and lawyers to vet our contracts. We all need the occasional look-in from medtechs and physical therapists. And when we need a new crew member, we contract a recruiter.

"You look tired," Jane said the next time Ricci called. "I thought you said you were sleeping."

Ricci hung upside down in her netting. She'd made friends with the orang. It squatted in front of her, holding the appliance while she chatted with Jane.

"I've been digging through some old work." She dangled her arms, hooked her fingers in the floor grid, and stretched. "I came up with a new approach to my first dissertation."

Jane gaped. Her mouth worked like she was blowing bubbles.

"I know," Ricci added. "I'll never change, right?"

"Don't you try that with me." Jane's eyes narrowed. "You have a choice—"

Ricci raised her hands in mock surrender. "Okay. Take it easy."

"—you can keep working on getting better, or you can go back to your old habits."

"It's not your fault, Jane. You're a great therapist."

"This isn't about me, you idiot!" Jane yelled. "It's about you."

"I tried, Jane." Ricci's voice was soft, ardent. "I really tried. So hard."

"I know you did." Jane sucked in a deep breath. "Don't throw away all your progress."

They went on and on like that. I didn't listen, just checked in now and then to see if they were still at it. I knew Ricci's story. I'd read the report from the recruiter. The privacy seal had timed out but I remembered the details.

Right out of the crèche she'd dived into an elite chemical engineering program, the kind every over-fond crèche manager wants for their favorite little geniuses. Sound good, doesn't it? Isn't that where you'd want to put your little Omi or Occam, little Carey or Karim? But what crèche managers don't realize—because their world is full of guided discovery opportunities and subconscious learning stimuli—is that high-prestige programs are grinders. Go ahead, dump a crèche-full of young brilliants inside. Some of them won't come out whole.

I know; I went through one myself.

When Ricci crashed out of the chem program within spitting distance of an advanced degree, she bounced to protein engineering. She did a lot of good work there before she cracked. Then she moved into pharmaceutical modeling. A few more years of impressive productivity before it all went up in smoke. By that time she wasn't young anymore. The damage had accumulated. Her endocrinologist suggested intensive peer counselling might stop the carnage, so in stepped Jane, who applied her pretty smile, her patience, and all her active listening skills to try to gently guide Ricci along a course of life that didn't include cooking her brain until it scrambled.

At the end of that long conversation through the appliance, Ricci agreed to put her old work under lockdown so she could concentrate on the here-and-now. Which meant all her attention was focused on us.

Ricci got into my notes. I don't keep them locked down; anyone can access them. Free and open distribution of data is a primary force behind the success of the human species, after all. Don't we all learn that in the crèche?

Making data available doesn't guarantee anyone will look at it, and if they do, chances are they won't understand it. Ricci tried. She didn't just skim through, she really studied. Shift after shift, she played with the numbers and gamed my simulation models. Maybe she slept. Maybe not.

I figured Ricci would come looking for me if she got stumped, so I de-hermited, banged around in the rumpus room, put myself to work on random little maintenance tasks.

When Ricci found me, I was in the caudal stump dealing with the accumulated waste pellets. Yes, that's exactly what it sounds like: half-kilogram plugs of dry solid waste covered in wax and transferred from the lavs by the hygiene bots. Liquid waste is easy. We vaporize it, shunt it into the gas exchange bladder, and flush it through gill-like permeable membranes. Solid waste, well, just like anyone we'd rather forget about it as long as possible. We rack the pellets until there's about two hundred, then we jettison them.

Ricci pushed up her goggles and scrubbed knuckles over her red-rimmed eyes.

"Why don't you automate this process like you do for liquids?" Ricci asked as she helped me position the rack over the valve.

"No room for nonessential equipment in the mass budget," I said.

I dilated the interior shutter and the first pellet clicked through. A faint pink blush formed around the valve's perimeter, only visible because I'd dialed up the contrast on my goggles to watch for signs of stress. A little hormone ointment took care of it—not too much or we'd get a band of inflexible scar tissue, and then I'd have to cut out the valve and move it to another location. That's a long, tricky process and it's not fun.

"There's only two bands of tissue strong enough to support a valve." I bent down and stroked the creamy striated tissue at my feet. "This is number two, and really, it barely holds. We have to treat it gently."

"Why risk it, then? Take it out and just use the main valve."

A sarcastic comment bubbled up—*have you never heard of a safety exit?*—but I gazed into her big brown eyes and it faded into the clouds.

"We need two valves in case of emergencies," I mumbled.

Ricci and I watched the pellets plunge through the sky. When they hit the ice slush, the concussive wave kicked up a trail of vapor blooms, concentric rings lit with pinpoints of electricity, so far below each flash just a spark in a violet sea.

A flock of jellies fled from the concussion, flat shells strobing with reflected light, trains of ribbon-like tentacles flapping behind.

Ricci looked worried. "Did we hit any of them?"

I shook my head. "No, they can move fast."

After we'd finished dumping waste, Ricci said, "Say, Doc, why don't you show me the main valve again?"

I puffed up a little at that. I'm proud of the valves. Always tinkering, always innovating, always making them a little better. Without the valves, we wouldn't be here.

Far forward, just before the peduncle isthmus, a wide band of filaments connects the petals to the bladder superstructure. The isthmus skin is thick with connective tissue, and provides enough structural integrity to support a valve big enough to accommodate a cargo pod.

"We pulled you in here." I patted the collar of the shutter housing. "Whoever prepared the pod had put you in a pink bodybag. Don't know why it was such a ridiculous color. When Vula saw it, she said, 'It's a girl!'."

I laughed. Ricci winced.

"That joke makes sense, old style," I explained.

"No, I get it. Birth metaphor. I'm not a crechie, Doc."

"I know. We wouldn't have picked you if you were."

"Why did you pick me?"

I grumbled something. Truth is, when I ask our recruiter to find us a new habmate, the percentage of viable applications approaches zero. We look for a specific psychological profile. The two most important success factors are low self-censoring and high focus. People who say what they think are never going to ambush you with long-fermented resentments, and obsessive people don't get bored. They know how to make their own fun.

Ricci tapped her fingernail on a shutter blade.

"Your notes aren't complete, Doc." She stared up at me, unblinking. No hint of a dimple. "Why are you hoarding information?"

"I'm not."

"Yes, you are. There's nothing about reproduction."

"That's because I don't know very much about it."

"The other whale crews do. And they're worried about it. You must know something, but you're not sharing. Why?"

I glared at her. "I'm an amateur independent researcher. My methods aren't rigorous. It would be wrong to share shaky theories."

"The whale crews had a collective research agreement once. You wrote it."

She fired the document at me with a flick of her finger. I slapped it down and flushed it from my buffer.

"That agreement expired. We didn't renew."

"That's a lie. You dissolved it and left to find your own whale."

I aimed my finger at the bridge of her goggles and jabbed the air. "Yes, I ran away. So did you."

She smiled. "I left a network of habs with a quarter billion people who can all do just fine without me. You ran from a few hundred who need you."

Running away is something I'm good at. I bounced out of there double-time. Ricci didn't call after me. I wouldn't have answered if she had.

The next time she talked to Jane, Ricci didn't mention me. I guess I didn't rate high enough on her list of problems. I didn't really listen to the details as they chatted. I just liked having their voices in my head while I tinkered with my biosynthesis simulations.

Halfway through their session, Vula pinged me.

You can quit spying, she said. *None of us are worried about Ricci anymore.*

I agreed, and shut down the feed.

Ricci's been asking about you, by the way, Vula added. *Your history with the other whales.*

Tell her everything.

You sure?

I've been spying on her for days. It's only fair.

Better she heard the story from Vula than me. I still can't talk about it without overheating, and they tell me I'm scary when I'm angry.

Down belowground the air is thick with rules written and unwritten, the slowly decaying husks of thirty thousand years of human history dragged behind us from Earth, and the most important of these is cooperation for mutual benefit. Humans being human, that's only possible in conditions of resource abundance—not just actual numerical abundance, but more importantly, the *perception* of abundance. When humans are confident there's enough to go around, life is easy and we all get along, right?

Ha.

Cooperation makes life possible, but never easy. Humans are hard to wrangle. Tell them to do one thing and they'll do the opposite more often than not. One thing we all agree on is that everyone wants a better life. Only problem is, nobody can agree what that means.

So we have an array of habs offering a wide variety of socio-cultural options. If you don't like what your hab offers, you can leave and find one that does. If there isn't one, you can try to find others who want the same things as you and start your own. Often, just knowing options are available keeps people happy.

Not everyone, though.

Down belowground, I simply hated knowing my every breath was counted, every kilojoule measured, every moment of service consumption or contribution accounted for in the transparent economy, every move modeled by human capital managers and adjusted by resource optimization analysts. I got obsessed with the numbers in my debt dashboard; even though it was well into the black all I wanted to do was drive it up as high and as fast as I could, so nobody would ever be able to say I hadn't done my part.

Most people never think about their debt. They drop a veil over the dash and live long, happy, ignorant lives, never caring about their billable rate and never knowing whether or not they syphoned off the efforts of others. But for some of us, that debt counter becomes an obsession.

An obsession and ultimately an albatross, chained around our necks.

I dreamed about an independent habitat with abundant space and unlimited horizons. And I wasn't the only one. When we looked, there it was, floating around the atmosphere.

Was it dangerous? Sure. But a few firms provide services to risk-takers and they're always eager for new clients. The crews that shuttle ice climbers to the poles delivered us to the skin of a very large whale. I made the first cut myself.

Solving the problems of life was exhilarating—air, food, water, warmth. We were explorers, just like the mountain climbers of old, ascending the highest peaks wearing nothing but animal hides. Like the first humans. Revolutionary.

Our success attracted others, and our population grew. We colonized new whales and once we got settled, our problems became more mundane. I have a little patience for administrative details, but the burden soon became agonizing. Unending meetings to chew over our collective agreements, measuring and accounting and debits and credits and assigning value to everyone's time. This was exactly what we'd escaped. Little more than one year in the clouds, and we were reinventing all the old problems from scratch.

Nobody needs that.

I stood right in the middle of the rumpus room inside the creature I'd cut into with my own hands and gave an impassioned speech about the nature of freedom and independence, and reminded them all of the reasons we'd left. If they wanted their value micro-accounted, they could go right back down belowground.

I thought it was a good speech, but apparently not. When it came to a vote, I was the only one blocking consensus.

I believe—hand-to-heart—if they'd only listened to me and did what I said everything would have been fine and everyone would have been happy. But some people can never really be happy unless they're making other people miserable. They claimed I was trying to use my seniority, skills, and experience as a lever to exert political force. I'd become a menace. And when they told me I had to submit to psychological management, I left.

Turned out we'd brought the albatross along with us, after all.

When Jane pinged me a few days later, I was doing the same thing as millions down belowground—watching a newly arrived arts delegation process down the beanstalk and marveling at their dramatic clothing and prosthetics.

I pinged her back right away. Even though I knew she would probably needle me about my past, I didn't hesitate. I missed having Ricci and Jane in my head, and life was a bit lonely without them. Also, I was eager to meet her. I wasn't the only one; the whole crew was burning with curiosity about Ricci's pretty friend.

When Jane's fake melted into reality, she was dressed in a shiny black party gown. Long dark hair pouffed over her shoulders, held off her face with little spider clips that gathered the locks into tufts. Her chair was a spider model too, with eight delicate ruby and onyx legs that cradled her torso.

"Hi, Doc," she said. "It's nice to meet you, finally. I'm a friend of Ricci's. I think you know that, though."

A friend. Not a therapist, peer counselor, or emotional health consultant. That was odd. And then it dawned on me: Jane had been donating her time ever since

Ricci joined us. She probably wanted to formalize her contract, start racking up the billable hours.

When I glanced through her metadata, my heart began to hammer. Jane's rate was sky high.

"We can't float your rate," I blurted. "Not now. Maybe eventually. But we'd have to find another revenue stream."

Jane's head jerked back and her gaze narrowed.

"That's not why I pinged you," she said. "I don't care about staying billable—I never did. All I want to do is help people."

I released a silent sigh of relief. "What can I do for you?"

"Nothing. I just wanted to say hi and ask how Ricci's getting along."

"Ricci's fine. Nothing to worry about." I always get gruff around beautiful women. She brightened. "She's fitting in with you all?"

"Yeah. One of the crew. She's great. I love her." I bit my lip and quickly added, "I mean we all like her. Even Vula, and she's picky."

I blushed. Badly. Jane noticed, and a gentle smile touched the corners of her mouth. But she was a kind soul and changed the subject.

"I've been wondering something, Doc. Do you mind if I ask a personal question?"

I scrubbed my hands over my face in embarrassment and nodded.

She wheeled her chair a bit closer and tilted toward me. "Do you know what gave you the idea to move to the surface? I mean originally, before you'd ever started looking into the possibility."

"Have you read Zane Grey's *Riders of the Purple Sage?*" I asked. "You must have."

"No." She looked confused, like I was changing the subject.

"You should. Here."

I tossed her a multi-bookmark compilation. Back down belowground, I'd given them out like candy at a crèche party. She could puzzle through the diction of the ancient original or read it in any number of translations, listen to a variety of audio versions and dramatic readings, or watch any of the hundreds of entertainment docs it had inspired. I'd seen them all.

"This is really old. Why did you think I'd know it?" She flipped to the summary. "Oh, I see. One of the characters is named Jane."

"Read it. It explains everything."

"I will. But maybe you could tell me what to look for?" Her smile made me forget all about my embarrassment.

"It's about what humans need to be happy. Sure, we evolved to live in complex interdependent social groups, but before that, we were nomads, pursuing resource opportunities in an open, sparsely populated landscape. That means for some people, solitude and independence are primary values."

She nodded, and I could see she was trying hard to understand.

"Down belowground, when I was figuring all this out, I tried working with a therapist. When I told him this, he said, 'We also evolved to suffer and die from violence, disease, and famine. Do you miss that, too?'"

Jane laughed. "I hope you fired him. So one book inspired all this?"

"It's not just a book. It's a way of life. The freedom to explore wide open spaces, to come together with like-minded others and form loose-knit communities based on mutual aid, and to know that every morning you'll wake up looking at an endless horizon."

"These horizons aren't big enough?" She waved at the surrounding virtual space, a default grid with dappled patterns, as if a directional light source were shining through gently fluttering leaves.

"For some, maybe. For me, pretending isn't enough."

"I'll read it. It sounds very . . ." She pursed her lips, looking for the right word. "Romantic."

I started to blush again, so I made an excuse and dropped the connection before I made a fool of myself. Then I drifted down to the rumpus room and stripped off my goggles and breather.

"Whoa," Bouche said. "Doc, what's wrong?"

Eleanora turned from the extruder to look at me, then fumbled her caffeine bulb and squirted liquid across her cheek.

"Wow." She wiped the liquid up with her sleeve. "I've never seen you look dreamy before. What happened?"

I'm in love, I thought.

"Jane pinged me," I said instead.

Bouche called the whole crew. They came at a run. Even Vula.

In a small hab, any crumb of gossip can become legendary. I made them beg for the story, then drew it out as long as I could.

"Can you ask her to ping me?" Eddy asked Ricci when I was done.

"I would chat with her for more than a couple minutes, unlike Doc," said Treasure.

Chara grinned lasciviously. "Can I lurk?"

The whole crew in one room, awake and actually talking to each other was something Ricci hadn't seen before, much less all of us howling with laughter and gossiping about her friend. She looked profoundly unsettled. Vula bounced over to the extruder, filled a bulb with her favorite social lubricant, and tossed it to Ricci.

"Tell us everything about Jane," Chara said. Treasure waggled her tongue.

"It's not like that." Ricci frowned. "She's a friend."

"Good," they chorused, and collapsed back onto the netting, giggling.

"I've been meaning to ask—why do you use that handheld thing to talk to her, anyway?" Chara said. "I've never even seen one of those before."

Ricci shook her head.

"Come on, Ricci. There's no privacy here," Vula said. "You know that. Don't go stiff on us."

Ricci joined us in the netting before answering. When she picked a spot beside me, my pulse fluttered in my throat.

"Jane's a peer counselor." She squeezed a sip from the bulb and grimaced at the taste. "The handheld screen is one of her strategies. Having it around reminds me to keep working on my goals."

"Why do you need peer counseling?" asked Chara.

"Because I . . ." Ricci looked from face to face, big brown eyes serious. Everyone quieted down. "I was unhappy. Listen, I've been talking with some people from the other whale crews. They've been having problems for a while now, and it's getting worse."

She fired a stack of bookmarks into the middle of the room. Everyone began riffling through them, except me.

"That's too bad," I said.

"Don't you want to know what's going on, Doc?" asked Chara.

I folded my arms and scowled in the general direction of the extruder.

"No," I said flatly. "I don't give a shit about them."

"Well, you better," Vula said. "Because if it's happening to them, it could happen to us. Look."

She fired a feed from a remote sensing drone into the middle of the room. A group of whales had gathered a hundred meters above a slushy depression between a pair of high ridges. They weren't feeding, just drifting around aimlessly, dangerously close to each other. When they got close to each other, they unfurled their petals and brushed them along each other's skin.

As we watched, two whales collided. Their bladders bubbled out like a crechie's squeeze toy until it looked like they would burst. Seeing the two massive creatures collide like that was so upsetting, I actually reached into the feed and tried to push them apart. Embarrassing.

"Come on Doc, tell us what's happening," said Vula.

"I don't know." I tucked my hands into my armpits as if I was cold.

"We should go help," said Eddy. "At least we could assist with the evac if they need to bail."

I shook my head. "It could be dangerous."

Everyone laughed at that. People who aren't comfortable with risk don't roam the atmosphere.

"It might be a disease," I added. "We should stay as far away as we can. We don't want to catch it."

Treasure pulled a face at me. "You're getting old."

I grabbed my breather and goggles and bounded toward the hatch.

"Come on Doc, take a guess," Ricci said.

"More observation would be required before I'd be comfortable advancing a theory," I said stiffly. "I can only offer conjecture."

"Go ahead, conjecture away," said Vula.

I took a moment to collect myself, and then turned and addressed the crew with professorial gravity.

"It's possible the other crews haven't been maintaining the interventions that ensure their whales don't move into reproductive maturity."

"You're saying the whales are horny?" said Bouche.

"They look horny," said Treasure.

"They're fascinated with each other," said Vula.

Vula had put her finger on exactly the thing that was bothering me. Whales don't congregate. They don't interact socially. They certainly don't mate.

"I'd guess the applicable pseudoneural tissue has regenerated, perhaps incompletely, and their behavior is confused."

Ricci gestured at the feed, where three whales collided, dragging their petals across each other's bulging skin. "This isn't going to happen to us?"

"No, I said. "Definitely not. Don't worry. Unlike the others, I've been keeping on top of the situation."

"But how can you be sure?" And then realization dawned over Ricci's face. "You knew this was going to happen, didn't you?"

"Not exactly."

She launched herself from the netting and bounced toward me. "Why didn't you share the information? Keeping it secret is just cruel."

I backed toward the hatch. "It's not my responsibility to save the others from their stupid mistakes."

"We need to tell them how to fix it. Maybe they can save themselves."

"Tell them whatever you want." I excavated my private notes from lockdown, and fired them into the middle of the room. "I think their best option would be to abandon their whales and find new ones."

"That would take months," Vula said. "Nineteen whales. More than two hundred people."

"Then they should start now." I turned to leave.

"Wait." Ricci looked around at the crew. "We have to go help. Right?"

I gripped the edge of the hatch. The electrostatic membrane licked at my fingertips.

"Yeah, I want to go," Bouche said. "I'd be surprised if you didn't, Doc."

"I want to go," said Treasure.

"Me too," Chara chimed in. Eddy and Eleanora both nodded.

Vula pulled down her goggles and launched herself out of the netting. "Whales fucking? What are we waiting for? I'll start fabbing some media drones."

With all seven of them eager for adventure, our quiet, comfortable little world didn't stand a chance.

We're not the only humans on the surface. Not quite. Near the south pole a gang of religious hermits live in a deep ice cave, making alcohol the old way using yeast-based fermentation. It's no better than the extruded version, but some of the habs take pity on them so the hermits can fund their power and feedstock.

Every so often one of the hermits gives up and calls for evac. When that happens, the bored crew of a cargo ship zips down to rescue them. Those same ships bring us supplies and new crew. They also shuttle adventurers and researchers around the planet, but mostly they sit idle, tethered halfway up the beanstalk.

The ships are beautiful—sleek, fast, and elegant. As for us, when we need to change our position, it's not quite so efficient. Or fast.

When Ricci found me in the rumpus room, I'd already fabbed my gloves and face mask, and I was watching the last few centimeters of a thick pair of protective coveralls chug through the output.

"I told the other crews you'd be happy to take a look at the regenerated tissue and recommend a solution, but they refused," she said. "They don't like you, do they?"

I yanked the coveralls out of the extruder.

"No, and I don't like them either." I stalked to the hatch.

"Can I tag along, Doc?" she asked.

"You're lucky I don't pack you into a bodybag and tag you for evac."

"I'm really sorry, Doc. I should have asked you before offering your help. When I get an idea in my head, I tend to just run with it."

She was all smiles and dimples, with her goggles on her forehead pushing her hair up in spikes and her breather swinging around her neck. A person who looks like that can get away with anything.

"This is your idea," I said. "Only fair you get your hands dirty."

I fabbed her a set of protective clothing and we helped each other suit up. We took a quick detour to slather appetite suppressant gel on the appropriate hormonal bundle, and then waddled up the long dorsal sinus, arms out for balance. The sinus walls clicked and the long cavity bent around us, but soon the appetite suppressant took hold and we were nearly stationary, dozing gently in the clouds.

On either side towered the main float bladders—clear multi-chambered organs rippling with rainbows across their honeycomb-patterned surfaces. Feeder organs pulsed between the bladder walls. The feeders are dark pink at the base, but the color fades as they branch into sprawling networks of tubules reaching through the skin, grasping hydrogen and channeling it into the bladders.

At the head of the dorsal sinus, a tall, slot-shaped orifice provides access to the neuronal cavity. I shrugged my equipment bag off my shoulder, showed Ricci how to secure her face mask over her breather, and climbed in.

With the masks on, to talk we had to ping each other. I was still a bit angry so no chitchat, business only. I handed her the laser scalpel.

Cut right here. I sliced the blade of my gloved hand vertically down the milky surface of the protective tissue. *See these scars?* I pointed at the gray metallic stripes on either side of the imaginary line I'd drawn. *Stay away from them. Just cut straight in between.*

Ricci backed away a few steps. *I don't think I'm qualified to do this.*

You've been qualified to draw a line since you were a crechie. When she began to protest again, I cut her off. *This was your idea, remember?*

Her hands shook, but the line was straight enough. The pouch deflated, draping over the skeleton of the carbon fiber struts I'd installed way back in the beginning. I pulled Ricci inside and closed the incision behind us with squirts of temporary adhesive. The wound wept drops of fluid that rapidly boiled off, leaving a sticky pink sap-like crust across the iridescent interior surface.

Is this the whale's brain? Ricci asked.

I ignored the question. Ricci knew it was the brain—she'd been studying my notes, after all. She was just trying to smooth my feathers by giving me a chance to show my expertise.

Not every brain looks like a brain. Yours and mine look like they should be floating in the primordial ocean depths—that's where we came from, after all. The organ in front of us came from the clouds—a tower of spun glass floss threaded through and through with wispy, feather-like strands that branched and re-branched into iridescent fractals. My mobility control leads were made of copper nanofiber embedded in color-coded silicon filaments: red, green, blue, yellow, purple, orange, and black—a ragged, dull rainbow piercing the delicate depths of an alien brain.

Ricci repeated her question.

Don't ask dumb questions, Ricci.

She put her hands up in a gesture of surrender and backed away. Not far—no room inside the pouch to shuffle back more than one step.

The best I can say is it's brain-like. I snapped the leads into my fist-sized control interface. *The neurons are neuron-like. Is it the whole brain? Is the entire seat of cognition here? I can't tell because there's not much cognition to measure. Maybe more than a bacterium, but far less than an insect.*

How do you measure cognition? Ricci asked.

Controlled experiments, but how do you run experiments on animals this large? All I can tell you is that most people who study these creatures lose interest fast. But here's a better measure: After more than ten years, a whale has never surprised me.

Before today, you mean.

Maneuvering takes a little practice. We use a thumb-operated clicker to fire tiny electrical impulses through the leads and achieve a vague form of directional control. Yes, it's a basic system. We could replace it with something more elegant but it operates even if we lose power. The control it provides isn't exactly roll, pitch, and yaw, but it's effective enough. The margin for error is large. There's not much to hit.

Navigation is easy, too. Satellites ping our position a thousand times a second and the data can be accessed in several different navigational aids, all available in our dashboards.

But though it's all fairly easy, it's not quick. My anger didn't last long. Not in such close quarters, especially just a few hours after realizing I was in love with her. It was hardly a romantic scene, both of us swathed head-to-toe in protective clothing, passing a navigation controller back and forth as we waggled slowly toward our destination.

In between bouts of navigation, I began telling Ricci everything I knew about the organ in front of us: A brain dump about brains, inside a brain. Ha.

She was interested; I was flattered by her interest. Age-old story. I treated her to all my theories, prejudices, and opinions, not just about regenerating pseudoneuronal tissue and my methods for culling it, but the entire scientific research apparatus down belowground, the social dynamics of hab I grew up in, and the philosophical underpinnings of the research exploration proposal we used to float our first forays out here.

Thank goodness Ricci was wearing a mask. She was probably yawning so wide I could have checked her tonsils.

Here. I handed her the control box. *You drive the rest of the way.*

We were aiming for the equator, where the strong, steady winds have carved a smooth canyon bisecting the ice right down to the planet's iron core. When we need to travel a long distance, riding that wind is the fastest route.

Ricci clicked a directional adjustment, and our heading swung a few degrees back toward the equator.

What does the whale perceive when we do this? Ricci waggled the thumb of her glove above the joystick. *When it changes direction, are we luring it or scaring it away?*

Served me right for telling her not to ask simple questions.

I don't really know, I admitted.

Maybe it makes them think other whales are around. What if they want to be together, just like people, but before now they didn't know how. Maybe you've been teaching them.

My eyebrows climbed. I'd never considered how we might be influencing whale behavior, aside from the changes we make for our own benefit.

That's an interesting theory, Ricci. Definitely worth looking into.

Wouldn't it be terrible to be always alone?

I'd always considered myself a loner. But in that moment, I honestly couldn't remember why.

Once we're in the equatorial stream, we ride the wind until we get into the right general area. Then we wipe off the appetite suppressant, and hunger sends us straight into the arms of the nearest electrical storm.

The urge to feed is a powerful motivator for most organisms. Mama chases all the algae she can find, and gobbles it double-time. For us on the inside, it's like an old-style history doc. Everyone stays strapped in their hammocks and rides out the weather as we pitch around on the high seas.

I always enjoy the feeding frenzy; it gets the blood flowing.

I'd just settled to enjoy the wild ride when Ricci pinged me.

Two crews tried surgical interventions on the regenerated tissue. Let me know what you think, okay? Maybe now we can convince them to let you help.

The message was accompanied by bookmarks to live feeds from the supply ships. The first feed showed a whale wedging itself backward into a crevasse, its petals waving back and forth as it wiggled deeper into the canyon-like crack in the ice.

The other feed showed a whale scraping its main valve along a serrated ridge of ice. Its oval body stretched and flexed, its bladders bulged. Its petals curled inward then snapped into rigid extension as the force of its body crashed down on the ice's knife edge.

Inside both whales, tiny specks bounced through the sinuses. I could only imagine what the crew was doing—what I would do in that situation. If they wanted to live, they had to leave. Fast.

A chill slipped under my skin. My fault. If those whales died, if those crews died, I was to blame. Me alone. Not the two crews. They were obviously desperate enough to try anything. I should have contacted them myself, and offered whatever false apologies would get them to accept my help.

But chances are it wouldn't have changed the outcome, except they would have had me to blame. Another entry in my list of crimes.

Frost spread across my flesh and raised goose bumps. I tugged on my hammock's buckles to make sure they were secure against the constant pitching and heaving, dialed up the temperature, and snuggled deeper into my quilt. I fired up my simulation model and wandered through towering mountains of pseudoneural tissue, pondering the problem, delving deeper and deeper through chains of crystalized tissue until they danced behind my eyelids. Swirling, stacking, combining and recombining . . .

I was nearly asleep when I heard Ricci's voice.

"Hey, Doc, can we talk?"

I thought I was dreaming. But no, she was right outside my hammock, gripping the tethers and getting knocked off her feet with every jolt and flex. Her goggled and masked face was lit by a mad flurry of light from the bolts coruscating in every direction just beyond the skin.

"Are you nuts?" I yanked open the hammock seal. "Get in here."

She plunged through the electrostatic barrier and rolled to the far side of my bed. When she came up, her hair stood on end with static electricity.

"Whoa." She swiped off her goggles and breather, stuffed them in one of the hammock pouches, then flattened the dark nimbus of her hair with her palms and grinned. "It's wild out there."

I pulled my quilt up to my chin and scowled. "That was stupid."

"Yeah, I know but you didn't ping me back. This is an important situation, right? Life or death."

I sighed. "If you want to rescue people, there are vocations for that."

"Don't we have a duty to help people when we can?"

"Some people don't want to be helped. They just want to be left alone."

"Like you?"

"Nothing you're doing is helping me, Ricci."

"Okay, okay. But if we can figure out a way to help, that's good too. Better than good. Everyone wins."

Lying there in my hammock, facing Ricci sprawled at the opposite end and taking up more than half of the space, I finally figured out what kind of person she was.

"You're a meddler, Ricci. A busybody. You were wasted in the sciences. You should have studied social dynamics and targeted a career in one-on-one social work."

She laughed.

"Listen." I held out my hand, palm up. She took it right away, didn't hesitate. Her hand was warm. Almost feverish. "If you want to stay in the crew, you have to relax. Okay? We can't have emergencies every week. None of us are here for that."

She squeezed my hand and nodded.

"A little excitement is fine, once in a while," I continued. "Obviously this is an extraordinary situation. But if you keep looking for adventure, we'll shunt you back to Jane without a second thought."

She twisted the grip into a handshake and gave me two formal pumps. Then she reached for the hammock seal. She would have climbed out into the maelstrom if I hadn't stopped her.

"You can't do that," I yelled. "No wandering around when we're in a feeding frenzy. You'll get killed. Kill us too, if you go through the wrong bladder wall."

She smiled then, like she didn't believe me, like it was just some excuse to keep her in my hammock. And when she settled back down, it wasn't at the opposite end. She snuggled in right beside me, companionable as anything, or even more.

"Don't you get lonely, Doc?" she asked.

"Sometimes," I admitted. "Not much."

Our hammocks are roomy, but Ricci didn't give me much space, and though the tethers absorb movement, we were still jostling against each other.

"Because you don't need anybody or anything." Her voice in my ear, soft as a caress.

"Something like that."

"Maybe, eventually, you'll change your mind about that."

What happened next wasn't my idea. I was long out of practice, but Ricci had my full and enthusiastic cooperation.

Down belowground, I was a surgeon, and a good one. My specialty was splicing neurons in the lateral geniculate nucleus. My skills were in high demand. So high, in fact, that I had a massive support team.

I'm not talking about a part-time admin or social facilitator. Anyone can have those. I had an entire cadre of people fully dedicated to making sure that if I spent most of my time working and sleeping, what little time remained would be optimized to support physical, emotional, and intellectual health. All my needs were plotted and graphed. People had meetings to argue, for example, over what type of sex best maintained my healthiest emotional state, and once that was decided, they'd argue over the best way to offer that opportunity to me.

That's just an example. I'm only guessing. They kept the administrative muddle under veil. Day-to-day, I only had contact with a few of my staff, and usually I was too busy with my own work to think about theirs. But for a lot of people, I was a billable-hours bonanza.

But despite all their hard work, despite the hedonics modeling, best-practice scenarios, and time-tested decision trees, I burned out.

It wasn't their fault. It was mine. I was, and remain, only human.

I could have just reduced my surgery time. I could have switched to teaching or coaching other surgeons. But no. Some people approach life like it's an all-or-nothing game. That's me. I couldn't be all, so I decided to become nothing.

Until Ricci came along, that is.

When the storm ended, the two of us had to face a gauntlet of salacious grins and saucy comments. I didn't blush, or at least not much. Ricci had put the spark of life in a part of me that had been dark for far too long. I was proud to have her in my crew, in my hammock, in my life.

The whole hab gave us a hard time. The joke that gave them the biggest fits, and made even Vula cling helplessly to the rumpus room netting as she convulsed with laughter, involved the two of us calling for evac and setting up a crèche in the most socially conservative hab down belowground. Something about imagining us swathed in religious habits and swarming with crechies tweaked everyone's funny bones.

Ricci weathered the ridicule better than me. I left to fill the water kegs, and by the time I returned, the hilarity had worn itself out.

The eight of us lounged in the rumpus room, the netting gently swaying to and fro as we drifted in bright directional light of the aquapause. Water spilled off the skin and threw dappled shadows across the room. Vula had launched the media drones and we'd all settled down to watch the feeds.

More than once I caught myself brainlessly staring at Ricci, but I kept my goggles on so nobody noticed. I hope.

Two hundred kilometers to the northwest and far below us, the seventeen remaining whales congregated in the swirling winds above a dome-shaped mesa that calved monstrous sheets of ice down its massive flanks. A dark electrical storm massed on the horizon, with all its promise of rich concentrations of algae, but the whales didn't move toward it, just kept circulating and converging, plucking at each other's skin.

Three hundred kilometers west lay the abandoned corpses of two whales, their deflated bladders draped over warped sinus skeletons half-buried in slush.

Our media drones got there too late to trap the whales' death throes, and I was glad. But Vula and Bouche trapped great visuals of the rescue, showing the valiant supply ship crews swooping in to pluck brightly colored bodybags out of the air. Maybe the crews put a little more of a spin on their maneuvering than they needed too, but who could blame them? They rarely got a job worth bragging about.

One of Bouche's media broker friends put the rescue feeds out to market. They started getting good play right away. Bouche fired the media licensing statement into the middle of the room. The numbers glowed green and flickered as they climbed.

"Look at these fees," she said. "This will underwrite our power consumption for a couple years."

"That's great, Bouchie," I murmured, and flicked the statement out of my visual field.

Night was coming, and it presented a hard deadline. If the whales didn't move before dark, they'd all die.

Ricci moved closer to me in the netting and rested her cheek on my shoulder. I turned my head and touched my lips to her temple, just for a moment. I was deep in my brain simulation, working on the problem. But I kept an eye on the feeds. When the whales collided, I held my breath. As the bladders stretched and bulged, I cringed, certain they'd reach their elastic limit and we would see a whale pop, its massive sinuses rupture, its skin tear away and its body plunge to splatter on the icy surface below. But they didn't. They bounced off each other in slow motion and resumed their aimless circulation.

Hours passed. Eddy got up, extruded a meal, and passed the containers around the netting. Chara and Treasure slipped out of the room. Vula was only half-present—she was working in her studio, sculpting maquettes of popped bladders and painfully twisted corpses.

Eddy yawned. "How long can these whales live without feeding?"

I forced a stream of breath through my lips, fluttering the fringe of my bangs. "I don't know. Indefinitely, maybe, if the crews can figure out a way to provide nutrition internally."

"If they keep their whales fed, maybe they'll just keep stumbling around, crashing into each other." Vula's voice was slurred, her eyes unfocused as she juggled multiple streams.

"I'm more worried about nightfall, actually," I said.

Ever since we'd dragged ourselves out of my hammock, Ricci had been trying to pry information from emergency response up the beanstalk, from the supply ship crews who were circling site, and from the whale crews. They were getting increasingly frantic as time clicked by, and keeping us informed wasn't high on their list of priorities.

I rested my palm on the inside of Ricci's knee. "Are the other crews talking to you yet?"

She sat up straight and gave me a pained smile. "A little. I wasn't getting anywhere, but Jane's been giving me some tips."

That woke everyone up. Even Vula snapped right out of her creative fugue.

"Is Jane helping us?" Chara asked, and when Ricci nodded she demanded, "Why are you keeping her to yourself?"

Ricci shrugged. "Jane doesn't know anything about whales."

"If she's been helping you maybe she can help us too," said Eddy.

"Yeah, come on Ricci, stop hogging Jane." Bouche raked her fingers through her hair, sculpting it into artful tufts. "I want to know what she thinks of all this."

"All right," Ricci said. "I'll ask her."

A few moments later she fired Jane's feed into the room and adjusted the perspective so her friend seemed to be sitting in the middle of the room. She wore a baggy black tunic and trousers, and her hair was gathered into a ponytail that draped over the back of her chair. The pinnas of her ears were perforated in a delicate lace pattern.

Treasure and Chara came barreling down the access sinus and plunged through the hatch. They hopped over to their usual spot in the netting and settled in. Jane waved at them.

"We're making you an honorary crew member," Eddy told Jane. "Ricci has to share you with us. We all get equal Jane time."

"I didn't agree to that," said Ricci.

"Fight over me later, when everyone's safe." Jane said. "I don't understand why the other crews are delaying evacuation. Who would risk dying when they can just leave?"

Everyone laughed.

"This cadre self-selects for extremists." Eddy rotated her finger over her head, encompassing all of us in the gesture. "People like us would rather die than back down."

"I guess you're not alone in that," said Jane. "Every hab has plenty of stubborn people."

"But unlike them, we built everything we have," I said. "That makes it much harder to give up."

"Looks like someone finally made a decision, though." Ricci maximized the main feed. Jane wheeled around to join us at the netting.

Glowing dots tracked tiny specks across the wide mesa, pursued by flashing trails of locational data. Vula's media drones zoomed in, showing a succession of brightly colored, hard-shell bodybags shunting though the main valves. Sleet built up along their edges, quickly hardening to a solid coating of ice.

"Quitters," Treasure murmured under her breath.

Jane looked shocked.

"If you think you know what you'd do in their place, you're wrong," I said. "Nobody knows."

"I'd stay," Treasure said. "I'll never leave Mama."

Chara grinned. "Me too. We'll die together if we had to."

Bouche pointed at the two of them. "If we ever have to evac, you two are going last."

Jane expression of shock widened, then she gathered herself into a detached and professional calm.

Ricci squeezed my hand. "The supply ships want to shuttle some of the evacuees to us instead of taking them all the way to the beanstalk. How many can we carry?"

I checked the mass budget and made a few quick calculations. "About twenty. More if we dump mass." I raised my voice. "Let's pitch and ditch everything we can. If it's not enough we can think about culling a little water and feedstock. Is everyone okay with that?"

To my surprise, nobody argued. I'd rarely seen the crew move so fast, but with Jane around everyone wanted to look like a hero.

Life has rarely felt as sunny as it did that day.

Watching the others abandon their whales was deeply satisfying. It's not often in life you can count your victories, but each of those candy-colored, human-sized pods was a score for me and a big, glaring zero for my old, unlamented colleagues. I'd outlasted them.

Not only that, but I had a new lover, a mostly-harmonious crew of friends, and the freedom to go anywhere and do anything I liked, as long as it could be done from within the creature I called home.

But mostly, I loved having an important job to do.

I checked our location to make sure we were far enough away that if the other whales began to drift, they wouldn't wander into the debris stream. Then we paired into work teams, pulled redundant equipment, ferried it to the main valve, and jettisoned it.

I kept a tight eye on the mass budget, watched for tissue stress around the valve, and made strict calls on what to chuck and what to keep.

Hygiene and maintenance bots were sacrosanct. Toilets and hygiene stations, too. Safety equipment, netting, hammocks—all essential. But each of us had fifty kilos of personal effects. I ditched mine first. Clothes, jewelry, mementos, a few pieces of art—some of it real artisan work but not worth a human life. Vula tossed a dozen little sculptures, all gifts from friends and admirers. Eddy was glad to have an excuse to throw out the guitar she'd never learned to play. Treasure had a box of ancient hand-painted dinnerware inherited from her crèche; absolutely irreplaceable, but they went too. Chara threw out her devotional shrine. It was gold and took up most of her mass allowance, but we could fab another.

We even tossed the orang bot. We all liked the furry thing, but it was heavy. Bouche stripped out its proprietary motor modules and tossed the shell. We'd fab another, eventually.

If we'd had time for second thoughts, maybe the decisions would have been more difficult. Or maybe not. People were watching, and we knew it. Having an audience helped us cooperate.

It wasn't just Jane we were trying to impress. Bouche's media output was gathering a lot of followers. We weren't just trapping the drama anymore, we were part of the story.

Bouche monitored our followship, both the raw access stats and the digested analysis from the PR firm she'd engaged to boost the feed's profile. When the first supply ship backed up to our valve and we began pulling bodybags inside, Bouche whooped. Our numbers had just gone atmospheric.

We were a clown show, though. Eight of us crowded in the isthmus sinus, shuttling bodybags, everyone bouncing around madly and getting in each other's way. Jane helped sort us out by monitoring the overhead cameras and doing crowd control. Me, I tried not to be an obstruction while making load-balancing decisions. Though we'd never taken on so much weight at once, I didn't anticipate any problems. But I only looked at strict mathematical tolerances. I'm not an engineer; I didn't consider the knock-on effects of the sudden mass shift.

In the end, we took on thirty-eight bodybags. We were still distributing them throughout the sinuses when Ricci reported the rescue was over.

That's it. The cargo ships have forty-five bodybags. They're making the run to the beanstalk now.

Is that all? If the ships are full, we could prune some feedstock.

Everyone else is staying. They're still betting their whales will move.

When the last bodybag was secured so it wouldn't pitch through a bladder, I might have noticed we were drifting toward the mesa. But I was too busy making sure the new cargo was secure and accounted for.

I pinged each unit, loaded their signatures into the maintenance dashboard, mapped their locations, checked the data in the mass budget, created a new dashboard for monitoring the new cargo's power consumption, consumables, and useful life. Finally, I cross-checked our manifest against the records the supply ships had given us.

That was when I realized we were carrying two members of my original crew.

When Ricci found me, I was pacing the dorsal sinus, up and down, arguing with myself. Mostly silently.

"If you're having some kind of emotional crisis, I'm sure Jane would love to help," she said.

I spun on my heel and stomped away, bouncing off the walls.

She yelled after me. "Not me though. I don't actually care about your emotional problems."

I bounced off a wall once more and stopped, both hands gripping its clear ridged surface.

"No?" I asked. "Why don't you care?"

"Because I'm too self-involved."

I laughed. Ricci reached out and ruffled her fingers through the short hair on the back of my neck. Her touch sent an electric jolt through my nerves.

"Maybe that's why we get along so well," she said softly. "We're a lot alike."

Kissing while wearing goggles and a breather is awkward and unsatisfying. I pulled her close and pressed my palms to the soft pad of flesh at the base of her spine. I held her until she got restless, then she took my hand and led me to the rumpus room.

Bouche lounged in the netting, eyes closed.

"Bouchie is giving a media interview," Ricci whispered. "An agent is booking her appearances and negotiating fees. If we get enough, we can upgrade the extruder and subscribe to a new recipe bank."

I pulled a bulb out of the extruder. "She'll be hero of the hab."

"You could wake them up, you know."

"Wake up who?" I asked, and took a deep swig of sweet caffeine.

"Your old buddies. In the bodybags. Wake them up. Have it out."

I managed to swallow without choking. "No, I don't think so."

"Maybe they'll apologize."

I laughed, a little too hard, a little too long, and only stopped when Ricci began to looked offended.

"We can't wake them," I said. "Where would they sleep until we got to the beanstalk?"

"They can have my hammock." She sidled close. "I'll bunk with you."

We kissed then, and properly. Thoroughly. Until I met Ricci, I'd been a shrunken bladder; nobody knew my possible dimensions. Ricci filled me up. I expanded, large enough to contain whole universes.

"No. They're old news." I kissed her again and ran my finger along the edge of her jaw. "It was another life. They don't matter anymore."

Strange thing was, saying those words made it true. All I cared about was Ricci, and all I could see was the glowing possibility of a future together, rising over a broad horizon.

Twilight began to move over us. We only had a little time to spare before we recalled the media drones, wiped off the appetite suppressant, and left the other crews to freeze in the dark.

We gathered in the rumpus room, all watching the same feed. Whales circulated above the mesa. Slanting sunlight cast deep orange reflections across their skins, their windward surfaces creamy with blowing snow. Inside, dark spots bounced around the sinuses. If I held my breath, I could almost hear their words, follow their arguments. When I bit my lip, I tasted their tears.

"More than a hundred people," Jane said. "I still don't understand why they'd decide to commit suicide. A few maybe, but not so many."

"Some will evac before it's too late." Vula shrugged. "And as for the rest, it's their own decision. I can't say I would do anything different. And I hope I never find out."

I shivered. "Agreed."

"It doesn't make sense," Jane said. "Someone must be exercising duress."

"Nobody forces anyone to do anything out here, any more than they do down belowground," said Treasure.

"Yeah," said Chara. "We're not crechies, Jane. We do what we want."

Jane sputtered, trying to apologize.

"It's okay," Eddy told her. "We're all upset. None of us really understand."

"The whales still might move," said Bouche. "They can spend a little time in the dark, right Doc?"

I set a timer with a generous margin for error and fired it into the middle of the room. "Eight minutes, then we have to leave. The other whales will have a little more than thirty minutes before they freeze at full dark. Then their bladders burst."

Chara and Treasure pulled themselves out of the netting.

"We're not watching this," Chara said. "If you want to hang overhead and root for them to evac, go ahead."

We all waved goodnight. The two of them stumped away to their hammock, and silence settled over the rumpus room. Just the whoosh and murmur of the bladders, and the faint skiff of wind over the skin. A few early stars winked through the clouds. They seemed compassionate, somehow. Understanding. Looking at those bright pinpoints, I understood how on ancient Earth, people might use the stars to conjure gods.

I put my arm around Ricci's shoulders and drew her close. She let me hold her for two minutes, no more, and then she pulled away.

"I can't watch this either," she said. "I have to do something."

"I know." I drew her hand back just for a moment and planted a kiss on the palm. "It's hard."

Vula nodded, and Jane, too. Eddy and Bouche both got up and hugged her. Eleanora kept her head down, hiding her tears. The electrostatic membrane crackled as Ricci left.

"Do you know some of the people down there, Doc?" asked Jane.

"Not anymore," I said. "Not for a long time."

We fell quiet again, watching the numbers on the countdown. Ricci had left her shadow beside me. I felt her cold absence; something missing that should be whole. I could have spied on her, see where she'd gone, but no. She deserved her privacy.

The first little quake shuddering through the sinuses told me exactly where she was.

I checked our location, blinked, and then checked it again. We were right over the mesa, above the other whales, all seventeen of them. Wind, bad luck, or instinct had had brought us there—but did it matter? Ricci—her location mattered. She was in the caudal stump, with the waste pellets, and the secondary valve.

No. Ricci, no. I slapped my breather on and launched myself out of the rumpus room, running aft as fast as I could. *Don't do that. Stop.*

I lost my footing and bounced hard. *You might hit them. You might . . .* Kill them.

When I got to the caudal stump, Ricci was just clicking the last pellet through the valve. If we'd dumped them during the pitch and ditch, none of it would have happened. But dry waste is light. We'd accumulated ten pellets, only five kilograms, so I hadn't bothered with them.

But a half-kilo pellet falling from a height can do a lot of damage.

I fired the feed into the middle of the sinus. One whale was thrashing on the slushy mesa surface, half-obscured by the concussive debris. Two more were falling, twisting in agony, their bladders tattered and flapping. Another three would have escaped damage, but they circulated into the path of the oncoming pellets. Each one burst in turn, as if a giant hand had reached down and squeezed the life out of them.

Ricci was in my arms, then. Both of us quaking, falling to our knees. Holding each other and squeezing hard, as if we could break each other's bones with the force of our own mistakes.

Six whales. Twenty-two people. All dead.

The other eleven whales scattered. One fled east and plunged through the twilight band into night. Its skin and bladders froze and burst, and its sinus skeleton shattered on the jagged ice. Its crew had been one of the most stubborn—none had evacuated. They all died. Ten people.

In total, thirty-two died because Ricci made an unwise decision.

The remaining ten whales re-congregated over a slushy depression near the beanstalk. Ricci had bought the surviving crews a few more hours, so they tried a solution along the lines Ricci had discovered. Ice climbers use drones with controlled explosive capabilities to stabilize their climbing routes. They tried a test; it worked—the whales fled again, but in the wrong direction and re-congregated close to the leading edge of night.

In the end, the others evacuated. All seventy got in their bodybags and called for evac.

By strict accounting, Ricci's actions led to a positive outcome. I remind her of that whenever I can. She says it doesn't matter—we don't play math games with human lives. Dead is dead, and nothing will change that.

And she's right, because the moment she dumped those pellets, Ricci became the most notorious murderer our planet has ever known.

The other habs insist we hand her over to a conflict resolution panel. They've sent negotiators, diplomats—they've even sent Jane—but we won't give her up. To them, that proves we're dangerous. Criminals. Outlaws.

But we live in the heart of the matter, and we see it a little differently.

Ricci did nothing wrong. It was a desperate situation and she made a desperate call. Any one of us might have done the same thing, if we'd been smart enough to think of it.

We're a solid band of outlaws, now. Vula, Treasure, Chara, Eddy, Bouche, Eleanora, Ricci, and me. We refuse to play nice with the other habs. They could cut off our feedstock, power, and data, but we're betting they won't. If they did, our blood would be on their hands.

So none of us are going anywhere. Why would we leave? The whole planet is ours, with unlimited horizons.

winter Timeshare

RAY NAYLER

*Ray Nayler is the author of the stories "Mutability" and "Do Not Forget Me,"
both of which appeared in* Asimov's Science Fiction. *Ray's poetry has seen
print in the* Beloit Poetry Journal, Weave, Juked, Able Muse, Sentence,
Phantom Limb, Badlands, *and many other magazines. His detective novel*
American Graveyards *was published in the UK by TTA Press. Ray's short
stories in other genres have appeared in* Ellery Queen's Mystery Magazine,
Cemetery Dance, Deathrealm, Crimewave, *and the* Berkeley Fiction Review, *among others. Ray is a Foreign Service Officer, a speaker of Russian
and Azerbaijani Turkish, and has lived and worked in the countries of Central Asia and the former Soviet Union for nearly a decade. He is currently
press attaché at the U.S. Embassy in Baku, Azerbaijan.*

*Here he tells the bittersweet story of two lovers who are forced to go to very
extreme lengths to spend any time together. . . .*

What are "I" and "You"?
Just lattices
In the niches of a lamp
Through which the One Light radiates.
　　　　　　　　—*Rumi*

DEAD STAY DEAD

The words were scrawled in scarlet, hurried script on a concrete flower box. In the
spring, the flower box would be full of tulips. For those who could afford the spring,
there would be sunny days and crowds. Right now there was nothing in the concrete
box but wet earth.

A city worker in a jumpsuit a few shades darker than the drizzling sky wiped the
letters away with a quick swipe of chemcloth, leaving no trace of their message, and
moved on.

Whoever wrote those had probably already been caught by the police. Why bother? The risk of a fine, of a notch against you—for what? A pointless protest against a world that would stay just as it was, ugly words or no.

Across a cobblestoned street and defoliated winter gardens, the minarets of the Blue Mosque rose, soft-edged in the drizzle, their tips blurring into the mist. It was chilly in the open-air café, even under the heater. It was a familiar chill, bringing immediately to Regina's mind years of Istanbul in winter—memories of snow hissing onto the surface of the Bosporus, snow melting on the wings of seagulls. Mornings wrapped close in a blanket, watching the rain on the windowpanes distort the shipping in the straight. The icy, age-smoothed marble of mosque courtyards. And ten thousand cups of black tea in pear-shaped glasses, sign and substance of the city: hot to the touch, bitter on the tongue, a cube of sugar dissolving in their depths, identical to and yet different from one another. This, and so many other deeply pleasant repetitions, comforted her. They were in her past and, now, ahead of her again.

She flexed her tanned, muscular hand. She had spilled her first cup of tea with this clumsy hand. So eager to get to the café, not waiting even to get settled in, still pins and needles and misfires, but wanting that first taste of Istanbul, of its black tea against its chill. The old waiter had shrugged, and brought her another. "Do not worry, beyfendi," he had said, wiping the tea from the table with a rag. "No charge." Now she lifted the second glass of tea, carefully, to her lips. Yes, that was it. Now another year's Istanbul had begun.

And now Regina saw Ilkay, walking toward the café with that uneven step that said she had just woken. Ilkay was scanning the seats for her. Ilkay was blond, this year. Beautiful—an oval face, this year, eyes set wide under high cheekbones, long-limbed. But Regina would know her anywhere. And Ilkay knew her as well, scanning the seats in confusion and concern for a moment and then catching her eye, and smiling.

"Well," Ilkay said, when they had embraced, and embraced again, kissed cheeks, held one another at arms' length and examined one another's faces. "This is a new wrinkle in things."

"Is it bad?" Regina asked, keeping her voice light and unconcerned, but feeling underneath an eating away, suddenly, at the pure joy of seeing Ilkay again. *All things fall forever, worn by change / And given time, even the stones will flow . . .*" a piece of a poem she had read once. The poet's name, like much else, gone to time.

Ilkay grinned. Even, smallish teeth, a line of pink gums at the top. A different smile from the year before, but underneath, a constancy. "No. It isn't bad at all. It will be something new, for us." The waiter had approached, stood quietly to one side. Ilkay turned to him. "Two coffees for me. Bring both together." She settled into her cane-bottom chair. "I never feel, this first day, as if I can wake up all the way."

All was well, Regina told herself. Despite her heavy, clumsy hands. Despite her nervousness.

"Tell me," Ilkay said. "Tell me everything. What is your highrise working on?"

"You would not believe it, but it is a contract piece for the UN Commission on Historical Conflict Analysis, and what they are focusing on is conducting the most detailed possible analysis of the Peloponnesian War. All year we've been focused on the Battle of Pylos—refining equipment models, nutrition and weather patterns, existing in these simulations for twelve-hour shifts and feeding data to other teams of analysts. No idea what they are looking for—they're concealing that to keep from biasing the simulation—but the level of detail is granular. I've been fighting and re-fighting a simulation of the Battle of Sphacteria. Half-starved, trying to keep the phalanx together. I've been taken hostage and shipped to Athens so many times as a Spartan hoplite, I should get danger pay. It was supposed to be a six-month research project, but it's already run all year, and looks set to run another year."

"You actually look like you could handle yourself pretty well in a battle, right now. That's a heavy blank you're sheathed in."

Regina felt a flush of shame. "When they pulled me over to my new Istanbul distro, someone had walked off in the blank I ordered. It was this, or wait another week. I was furious." She looked down at the hairy back of the hand. "It's terrible, isn't it? My highrise had to take a 10% pay cut across the board this year. I couldn't afford my old distro. The new distro is dreadful. I woke up with pins and needles all over, felt like I had a club foot, and could barely move my fingers for two hours. I staggered here like a zombie, everybody who passed me on the street staring at me. And nobody at the distro even apologized about the mix-up."

"It isn't terrible." Ilkay had been too impatient in drinking her Turkish coffee, and a thin line of grounds marred her perfect lip. She wiped them delicately away with a napkin. "Fortunes change, and we're all reliant on our highrises. I'm just so thankful that you were here when I walked up. I had a fear, crossing the hippodrome, that you would be gone. That there was a recall, or a delay, or you had been wait-listed, or that you had . . . reconsidered."

Ilkay was always so fragile, this first day. Always certain there had been some disaster between them. Ilkay could afford a better timeshare—something in the spring, when the tulips came, or something in San Francisco Protectorate, but she came at this cut-rate time each year to meet Regina, slumming it in the off-season. In the end, it was Ilkay who was the most uncertain of them, most sure she would one year lose Regina. Money, Regina had to remind herself, was not everything—although it seemed like it was, to those who did not have it. Ilkay worked in a classified highrise, cut off from the rest of the world, plugging away at security problems only the fine-tangled mesh of reason and intuition, "gut" feeling and logical leaps of a highly trained and experienced mind could untangle. For Ilkay, cut off from any contact for the rest of the year, and restricted to the Western Protectorates for her timeshare because of international security reasons, it was not about money at all. She was afraid of losing Regina, even more than Regina was of losing her.

Ilkay took her hand. "Don't worry about the mix-up. It will be . . . interesting. Something new. Okay—not exactly *new*, but something I have not done for a long time. And I'm just so glad that you came, despite everything."

"What do you mean?"

Ilkay's eyes widened a bit, and Regina saw she had slipped, had revealed something not to be known outside the siloes of the classified highrises that crunched the world's ugliest layers of data. No wonder they didn't let her out much: she may have been one of the world's greatest security analysts, but she was a clumsy liar.

Ilkay recovered and continued. "You know, this really is going to be fun. This guy even looks a little dangerous. God only knows what he's been put up to while we weren't around." Ilkay grinned wickedly, and ran a nail along the inside of Regina's ropy wrist. "I can pretend you've traveled through time all this way from Pylos to be with me . . ."

"I guess that, in a sense, I have."

At that moment the muezzin's voice called from atop one of the minarets. Cutting clearly through the rain, the muezzin's trained voice, a rich contralto, carried so commandingly through the air that it almost seemed to come from speakers, despite the laws in Istanbul forbidding any amplification of the human voice. Both Ilkay and Regina paused until she had finished her call, staring at each other, coweyed as a couple of teenagers on a first date. Like it was every year, and just as exciting and good. When the muezzin had finished her song, Ilkay caught the eye of a young waiter and made a sign in the air for the check. The young man nodded, unsmiling. The bent, friendly old man who had been serving their table was nowhere to be seen.

When the check came, Regina saw she had been charged for two teas.

"Sorry," she said to the young man. "The other waiter said that I would be only charged for one of these . . ."

The young man shook his head. "You spilled the first one. You're responsible. You pay."

Regina began her protest. "Look, I'm happy to pay, but . . ."

"No, you look." The young man spat back at her. "I don't care what he said. You blanks think you can do anything you want. Spill a tea with your clumsy hands and not pay, forget to tip us because we won't even recognize you next time. You pay for what you took, like anyone else. Like the real people here."

Ilkay interrupted. "It's no problem. We'll pay. You can save the speech."

Stunned by the young waiter's hostility, Regina felt the pure, chemical haze of rage rising in her body. This was new—a feedback of violence that seemed embedded directly in the muscle and bone, a sudden awareness of her physical power, and a desire to use it so strong that it distorted thought. She wanted to smash a fist into the young waiter's face. Or a chair.

Grasping Regina's knee under the table to restrain her, Ilkay waved her palm over the check. "It's done, and a regulation tip for you, as well."

The young man shrugged. "I deserve more, putting up with you people every day." He muttered something else as they got up to leave. Regina did not catch it, but Ilkay's cheeks flushed.

As they were walking away, Regina turned and looked back at the terrace of the little cafe where they had met for countless years. The young waiter stood, arms crossed, watching them. As Regina caught his eye he turned his head and, keeping his eyes locked on hers, spat on the sidewalk.

Ilkay squeezed her hand. "Come on. We've got . . ."

Regina interrupted her. "What did he say, that last thing?"

"It's not important."

"Tell me."

Ilkay smiled gently. "You're going to have to get used to that male blank. You've never been in one before, have you?"

Regina shook her head. "No."

"You need to ride on top of it, the way you would a horse. Don't let its adrenaline surges and hormones get the better of you, or the feedback will distort your decision-making. Cloud your thinking."

Regina shook her head, as if to clear it. "Yeah, I can feel that. But what did he say?"

Ilkay tugged at her hand, and they walked in the direction of the Hagia Sophia. In this early hour, there was almost no-one on the sidewalks and the squares. The figures that they saw, all locals going about their own business, drifted in a clinging mist that did not quite turn to rain. "I'll tell you," Ilkay said, "but only if you promise, then, to concentrate on me. On us, and our time here."

Regina stopped walking, gathered herself. "Yes, of course. I'm sorry. I got carried away. It's embarrassing."

Ilkay punched her arm, playfully. "Well, don't forget to add this to your simulation. You can bet those men on Sphacteria were feeling exactly the same adrenaline surges, and it was having the same distorting effect on their decision-making."

Regina grinned. "I was thinking the same thing. Always the analysts, the two of us."

Ilkay pulled them along toward the Hagia Sophia's entrance. Its heavily buttressed mass loomed. "He said, 'why don't you dead just stay dead?'"

Regina felt her teeth *actually grit themselves.* "I earned this. We both did. We've worked hard, both of us. We spent lifetimes sharpening our skill sets, making ourselves valuable, making real contributions to science. I'm not some trust-fund postmortem cruising around in a speedboat off Corsica. We competed fairly for our places in the highrises. We worked for this. And . . . who do they think keeps them safe? And who spends all their money here, pays for the maintenance of these places, keeps their restaurants open? And . . ." She trailed off helplessly.

"I know, I know." Said Ilkay. "Now forget about it, and let's go visit a church that has stood for over two thousand years, and let the temporary things be temporary."

The house Ilkay had rented for them, one of the ancient wooden homes along the Bosporus, was like a wedding cake fresh from a refrigerator—all white paint thick as frosting, china-fine detail, silken folds, and chilled from top to bottom. The heating system was apologetic but insufficient. They built a fire in the master bedroom's fireplace, found wool blankets in a trunk, ordered a very late lunch, and clumsily explored the possibilities of their new configurations. Then, increasingly less clumsily.

By the time lunch was delivered, they were exhausted and starving. In near silence, wearing their blankets like woolen super hero capes, they spread fig jam on fresh bread and watched sleet spin down over the Bosporus and spatter slush against the windowpanes. Out on the roiling chop of the strait, a fisherman in a small rusty boat and black rubber rain gear determinedly attempted to extract some protein from the water. His huge black beard, run through with gray streaks, jutted from under his sou'wester, with seemingly only the axe blade of his nose between.

Regina dabbed at her mouth with a napkin. "It's amazing to think that these people have lived in a nearly identical way for centuries. Technology changes some things, like maybe fish-locating sonar systems and nearly perfect weather forecasting—but for the fisherman who actually has to get the fish on the hook, in any weather that comes, not much has changed."

"The physical things—the actual moving of matter around—are immutable," agreed Ilkay. "As we have been experimenting with all morning." She grinned, carefully applying fig jam. "And that's why, I think, these weeks are so important. They remind us of the base—the essentials, the substance of life and the world. Not that what we do isn't important. Not that who we are usually isn't real . . ."

Regina finished the thought: "But it's just so abstract. Immaterial. Not without consequence, but . . ."

"But without immediacy." Ilkay interjected. Then, after a long pause . . . "Regina, I miss you terribly. All year. And I cram everything I can into these short few weeks. And every year, I am afraid."

"Of what?"

"Afraid that next year, you will not be waiting for me at the café. These few weeks, always in winter . . . they are everything to me. They aren't a vacation . . . they are the sum and total of everything of meaning in my life. It's not that . . . it's not that I don't value my work, or think it saves lives. I haven't lost faith in the project. We watch over a troubled world, in my highrise . . . a world cruel people are constantly trying to tear to pieces . . . but none of that work seems to matter nearly as much as the moment I see you again. Sometimes, I feel my work is eating away at who I am. It's like watching a shadow underwater: you know it is just seaweed, this shadow, a harmless mass writhing in the current, nothing to worry about. But what if it is a shark? A shadow with teeth and volition? The more you stare at the shadow, straining to make out its outline, the more certain you become that it is a shark—until you convince even yourself. This constant watching—it eats away at your feeling of security. It eats away, I think, at your sanity. And I've been afraid to tell you, because I feel as if once it's said, it will shatter all this . . . this causal sort of . . . easy feeling between us."

Regina put an arm around her. Her thicker arms were increasingly feeling as if they were her own. She pulled Ilkay toward her. "This was never casual or easy for me, Ilkay. And I'll always be at the café. Every single year."

The weather did not improve after lunch. The Bosporus swelled and churned, and the rain came down in columns. There was time to sit long over lunch and talk, and to lay under the heavy covers of the four-poster and talk. Dinner was brought in a dripping container, and they tipped the young woman who brought it—soaked to the skin—double for her efforts. The sun set, and on the strait the lights of small boats bobbed in the dark between the chop of the water and the sky. Just after 8:00, the door buzzer jangled. They had been having cups of tea in front of the fire. Regina saw Ilkay immediately tense, like a cat hearing a dog bark in the distance.

The man on the doorstep was in a long, gray raincoat, black rubber boots, rain pants. Under his sou'wester an abglanz turned his face into a swirl of shimmering, ever-changing abstract patterns. In a tech-limited city, the effect was particularly jarring.

"Good evening," the composite voice said to Regina. "I apologize for the interruption of your timeshare. I hope to take up as little of your time as possible. I must speak to Ilkay Avci. This is, unfortunately, a matter of urgency." His credentials drifted across the shimmer of the abglanz. Istanbul Protectorate Security High Commission.

Standing in the corridor behind Regina, Ilkay said "Come in, inspector. Hang up those wet things."

As he did so, Regina noticed a port wine birthmark on the back of his hand. It was large, spreading across his wrist and up to the first knuckles of his fingers in a curious, complicated pattern, like a map of unknown continents. They should have given him an abglanz to cover that, she thought. I would know him again anywhere. They went into the living room.

"I apologize," the inspector said to Regina, "but due to the classified nature of this conversation, I will have to ask you to wear this momentarily. Once you are seated comfortably." He produced the slender metal cord of the scrambler from the pocket of his shirt. No matter what they did to that thing (this one was a cheerful yellow) it still looked like a garrote. Regina settled into a chair and let him place it around her neck. He clipped it into place gently, like a man fastening the clasp of his wife's necklace.

She was in Gülhane Park, at the peak of the Tulip Festival. The flowers—so large and perfectly formed they seemed almost plastic, were everywhere, arranged in brightly colored plots, swirling patterns of red, white, orange, maroon, violet, and cream. A few other tourists roamed the paths of Gülhane, but the park was, for the most part, empty. It was a cool spring day, smelling of turned earth. It was an Istanbul she had not seen—had not been able to afford to see—since the austerity, so many years ago now, had reduced her highrise's benefit levels. But, she thought, bending to cup the bloom of a Chinese orange tulip with a cream star at its center, what I gained when I lost this season was Ilkay. And that is enough to replace all of this. Though—just for a moment—it was good to feel the warm edge of summer hiding in the air, to close her eyes and let the sun bleed through her eyelids.

She wondered how wide the extent of the simulation was. Did it extend beyond the walls of Gülhane? The face of a passing tourist was glitchy, poorly captured, the woman's features wavered. No, it would be only the park, a tiny island of flowers, green paths and good weather. But did it extend as far as the Column of the Goths? She would like to see that ancient object, surrounded by flowers in the spring. She began to walk farther into the park. A crow glitched from one branch to another in a tree just beginning to leaf, its caw jagged with digital distortion.

She was back in the chair. The inspector stood over her, putting the scrambler back into his pocket. "Give it a moment before trying to stand. Just in case. And again, my apologies for any inconvenience. The Istanbul Protectorate Security High Commission thanks you, and will apply a small amount in contemporary lira to your accounts for the inconvenience. It isn't much, I am afraid—but enough for a good meal on the Galata Bridge for the two of you."

Ilkay was standing at the fire, warming her hands. "The courtesy is much appreciated, Inspector. At a later date I will review this interaction and give it the full five-star rating."

Once the inspector was gone, they both found they were too exhausted even to watch the fire burn down to its embers. They went to bed early, sliding into sheets as cold as the skin of ice on a river. Regina asked nothing about Ilkay's conversation with the Inspector. It was one of the rules of their relationship, unspoken between them. Sometimes, things about Ilkay's work were offered up, but Regina never asked for them.

"Perhaps next year," Ilkay whispered in the dark, "we should meet somewhere else. Maybe it is time for a change."

"What happened?" And now Regina felt the rise of anger in her. Somewhere else? Where? It was not enough that she had no contact with Ilkay during the year, only these few weeks when they could see one another—now they had to intrude on this as well, eroding even this small island of peace—as if it were too much to ask to have even this one thing. The face of the young waiter at the café rose up in her mind, spitting on the pavement.

"Nothing." Ilkay said. "Nothing at all. Tensions, or rumors of tensions. That's all it ever is, it seems. Like the shadow in the water. It's almost always seaweed. It's almost never a shark. But my job is to watch the shadows. And I'm tired, Regina. So very tired of being afraid. Why can't they let me at least have this? These few weeks. Haven't I earned a little peace in my life?"

The morning of the fifth day was bright and cold. The sky was opalescent. The mist that had clung to everything had risen to become a single, thin sheet of gauze, shrouding sun from earth. Under the Galata Tower, huddled beneath the glowing hood of a terrace heater, they drank black tea and coffee and had breakfast—honey and butter, warm bread and white cheese, tomatoes and hard-boiled eggs—and lingered over the meal. There were other blanks at the café, together and alone, smiling and laughing or quietly reading newspapers. Real newspapers, on real paper: one of the great joys of Istanbul.

The blanks sat on the terrace, oblivious to the cold, with only the heaters preserving them from the chill. The café's waiter, on the other hand, stood inside the café, watching his patrons from behind glass, continually rubbing his hands together for warmth. He was a middle-aged man moving toward old age, his thin hair combed straight back on his scalp. The cold, thought Regina, was different for him—lasting months out of the year, coming too soon and leaving far too late. For the blanks on his terrace, it was a joy to experience it, after their highrised, simulated year. Who were they all? Number-crunchers, of course, of one kind or another, moving data around. There were pure mathematicians among them, financial analysts, scientists and astronomers, astrophysicists and qualitative historical analysts. And those, like Ilkay and herself, working in more esoteric fields.

Regina had never thought deeply about the difference between the blanks and Istanbul's permanent residents, the "locals," as they were called by some—but not by Regina, who liked to think of herself as a local, liked to think of this city as her city. Hadn't she earned that, by returning here every year for so long? Over the last few days she and Ilkay had "made their rounds," as they called it—despite the bad weather, they had visited all of their old places—eating fresh fish on the Galata Bridge (subsidized by the Istanbul Protectorate Security High Commission), walking the land wall that had protected, for a thousand years, an empire that had been destroyed well over a thousand years ago. On the third evening, from an open-topped ferry crossing the strait to the Asian side, they had watched the interstellar array on one of Istanbul's distant hills fire the consciousness of another brave, doomed volunteer into the stars, riding a laser into failure and certain death. The blanks on the ferry had applauded. The locals had hardly seemed to notice.

But it was different for them. The waiter blew into his hands and watched his patrons with no expression on his face at all as they laughed and spread honey on their bread. He simply wanted to be warm, wanted the spring to come. Time moved along—and the faster, the better. The blanks were his economy, providing him with a living. In winter, the tables were half empty. In the summer, they would be full. All the tables would be full. The blanks would take the city over, ferreting out even the most local of the cafes, the most "authentic" places to eat. Raising prices, elbowing out the city's residents, who would retreat deeper into the alleys and back streets. And the interstellar program ground on, engaging the imaginations of thousands, employing a hundred highrises, but without any news or result or breakthroughs for generations. Its promise was now ignored by the majority of the five billion, whose main task was just to live, here and now, not to worry about homes beyond the stars.

On the other side of the terrace, one of the breakfasters, a young woman with dark hair in a braid, seated alone, was having a conversation with a local teenage boy on a bicycle. The boy had drawn out a map, and was pointing to something on it. He handed the map to the blank, who began examining it, her easy smile displaying a row of white teeth. And then, the boy reached into his pocket, and drew out a small, red canister with a nozzle at the top. He aimed it at the young woman's face and depressed the button, firing a spray into her eyes, nose and mouth.

Without thinking, Regina was on her feet, across the terrace, then on top of the boy, slamming his hand again and again into the pavement until the canister fell from it and rolled bumpily away across the cobblestones, wrestling with him as he tried to twist away from her. The boy struck her in the face, hard, his hand impacting with a strangely sharp pain. But then others joined her, from the street and from the terrace. Whistles blew. The boy disappeared behind a mass of struggling backs and legs. Ilkay was on the terrace, pouring water from a bottle over the young woman's face. The woman's eyes were red and swollen closed, coughing and gagging. Near her, others were wiping at their eyes, trying to clear them of the irritant spray. Another man offered Regina a cloth, a napkin from the terrace, and now she noticed that her face was bleeding. She pressed the napkin to her cheek, feeling the warm pulse of blood from the deep cut there. Only then did she notice the policeman, carefully placing a small, bloody folding knife into an isolation bag. The café's proprietor stood in the center of his terrace, all tipped over tables and shattered tea cups, wringing his hands.

At the medical clinic, the nurse who applied the seal was a young man, ex-military, his silver-sheathed prosthesis of a right arm, twelve-fingered and nimble, deftly working the seal into place as he cheerfully bantered with Regina.

"Luckily, your insurance covers this damage. They can be picky about what you put the blanks through, you know. There are all sorts of clauses and sub-clauses. That knife just touched the zygomatic bone, but there are no fractures, no bruising.

A lot of people don't read the fine print, and go paragliding or something, break a leg and find themselves footing a huge bill for repairs later, or a scrap and replace that they can't afford. But you made the right choice, bought comprehensive. You must have gotten into the program early—those rates are astronomical these days. Nobody can afford them but the highest ranking Minister Councilors and, of course, the postmortems. There we go. This guy's face will be good as new in a few days." He patted Regina's cheek affectionately, flexed the smoothly clacking twelve-figured hand. "Just try not to smile too much." He admired his hand. "God, I love this thing. If anything good can be said to have come out of the Fall of Beirut, it's this hand. A masterpiece."

Ilkay was giving a deposition in another room. Looking up, Regina saw the Inspector from the IPSHC standing in the doorway in a casual polo shirt and slacks, abglanz glittering weirdly under the medical-grade lights. She recognized him by the pomegranate-colored birthmark on his hand.

"I hope you are well," he said. "After your adventure."

Regina nodded slightly.

"Hold still one second," the young nurse said. "I have to fix the seal along the edge here."

"We are going to have to take a bit more of your time, I am afraid. Of Ilkay's time, to be more precise. Will you be able to get back to your residence all right? If not, I can send someone to accompany you. We will return her at the soonest moment we can, but I am afraid . . ." His digital smear of a face turned to the nurse. "If you are finished, can you leave her for a moment?"

The nurse shrugged and left the room.

"I am afraid," continued the Inspector, "that we will need her particular skill set over the next few days. We have encountered . . . a rather fluid situation. It needs further analysis. Normally we would not . . . well, to be honest, the austerities have left us a bit short-staffed. Ilkay's presence here, with her particular skill set, is an opportunity we literally can't afford to pass up."

Ilkay was in the doorway. "Inspector, can I have a moment alone with her?"

Once the Inspector had departed, Ilkay crossed the room to Regina. She ran a finger lightly along the seal. "They've done a good job. It's the best work I've ever seen." She blinked back tears. "God, you are an idiot. You've spent too long in that simulation, or maybe that body is getting to you."

"I don't know what came over me," Regina said seriously. "It's something in the air, I suppose. I just reacted."

"Well," Ilkay said. "Stop reacting. I'll be back with you in a day. Two at the most. In the meantime, try not to play the hero too much. And I expect a full report of your adventures. But . . ." And now she seemed uncertain, lowered her voice. "Play it safe a little, will you? For me? It might be better . . ." she leaned in and whispered in Regina's ear. "It might be better to stay away from the touristy areas for a while. Can you do that for me?"

She pulled away. Regina nodded.

"Oh," Ilkay said, running her finger along Regina's razor-stubbled chin. "And by the way—you really need to shave more often. You're a beast, and it's not that I don't like it, but it's giving me a bit of a rash."

They had met here, so many years ago. It had been a different Istanbul, then—a city dominated by a feeling of optimism, Regina thought. No, not dominated—optimism could never dominate the city's underlying feeling of melancholy, of nostalgia for what was always lost. But the city had been brightened, somehow, by optimism. For years, there had been a feeling, ephemeral, like a bright coat of whitewash over stone. The relays were in place on a hundred possible new worlds, the massive array on Istanbul's distant hills were firing the consciousnesses of the first explorers into interstellar space. It was in that time that they had met. They had met on a Sunday, at the Church of St. George. Regina, who was not religious, had gone to a service. She had been trying things out then—meditation, chanting, prayer—all of it a failure. Where does one go when one has lost everything, risen back from nothing? But she found the drone of the priest's voice and the smell of incense—a thousand years and more of incense soaked into the gold leaf and granite—comforting. The flat and meaningfully staring icons, the quietude. In those first years of adjustment, it had been all she had.

Ilkay had found her outside in the courtyard. She had been doing the same— wandering from temple to mosque to church, searching. They fell in together, naturally, talking of the most private feelings immediately, walking up the hill through neighborhoods that had been crumbling for as long as they had been standing, where the burned shells of houses mixed with those restored, and all of them leaned on one another, the whole leaning on the broken for support, the broken leaning on the whole. They ate a meal together in a little family restaurant whose courtyard was the ivy-covered walls of a shattered house, long ago consumed by fire, open to the sky. The meal felt, for Regina, like a communion. Someone had found her and had made her whole. And there had been no struggle, no doubt, no sacrifice. They had spent every moment together afterwards, never parted, and agreed to meet the next year. That was all. They had never questioned it.

Regina did not question it now. If Ilkay was gone tomorrow, she would not think it was because she had abandoned her. This was not possible. It would be because she was gone completely.

Regina lasted three days, waiting in the icy house and keeping to the city's Asian side. She found some comfort in a book she dug up in a bookstore there, a long-forgotten treatise on insect architecture. The book came complete with color plate illustrations of the complex constructions of bugs. It was a labor of love written by some Englishman, obscurely obsessed in the best possible way. She pored over the book's slightly mildewed pages, rich with the vanilla scent of their paper's chemical decay, for hours. Ilkay sent her reassuring messages, full of her bright sarcasm, hoping every day for their reunion. And the time slipped away. Would Istanbul Protectorate pay for their separation? Reimburse them for what they were taking? Unlikely.

On the fourth day, Regina decided to return to the European side. She would avoid the most popular places, as she had promised Ilkay. But most people went to the hippodrome and Hagia Sophia, the Blue Mosque and, at the most, strolled up to the Grand Bazaar. She would avoid those places.

The Church of St. George itself was surprisingly small, suited now to the dwindling number of pilgrims and tourists it received, though once it must have swelled full of the faithful on holy days. Pilgrims must have filled the small courtyard which, now, was nearly empty. The gray stone of the simple façade was more like a house than a church, though inside it was filled with gold leaf and light.

But Regina stayed in the courtyard. A group of blanks was there, in a cluster around a local guide who Regina could not see, but whose voice carried in the air. Pigeons walked around the feet of the tourists.

"The church's most precious objects, saved from each successive fire that consumed parts of it, are the patriarchal throne, which is believed to date from the 5th century, rare icons made of mosaic and the relics of two saints: Saints Gregory the Theologian and John Chrysostom."

Regina walked toward the group to hear more clearly. A message was coming in from Ilkay.

"Regina, where are you?"

"Some of the bones of these two saints, which were looted from Constantinople by the Fourth Crusade in 1204, were returned by Pope John Paul II in 2004. Today the Church of St. George serves mostly as a museum . . ."

Regina could see the guide now, standing in the semicircle of faces. The faces of the blanks were pale, lips and noses red with cold. Most of them bored. Some carried on quiet conversations with one another as the guide spoke. Why did they come to these place if they did not care?

"I am at the place we met," Regina sent. "Still laying low, waiting for you."

The guide wore a heavier coat, and a warm hat. As Regina approached, he saw her and looked up, continuing his speech. "Though there are still pilgrims."

It was the young waiter from the café on her first day. Recognizing her, he smiled sarcastically. "They return here every year . . ."

Another message came in from Ilkay. "GET OUT!!!"

The guide raised his hands. "And they will keep coming until we stop them."

There was a flash of blinding light.

The trireme lurched free of its anchorage and began a slow rotation to starboard, oars churning in the gray-blue water. Regina was crouched on the deck, the sun white-hot on her exposed neck. Her hands were bound behind her. Blood was spattered on the wood, small droplets from a wound she had received across her cheek in the final moments of the battle.

There had been chaos, and many had thrown down their shields, but for some reason she had kept fighting until finally one of the Athenian hoplites had struck her on the side of the head with the flat of a sword and she had fallen, dazed, struggling to get to her feet. Then they had moved in, knocking her sword from her hand, wrestling her to the ground, finally subduing her and binding her wrists with a leather thong.

Her head still throbbed from the blow from the sword, and a hundred other bruises and scrapes ached. Behind then, Sphacteria's flat, narrow expanse, fought for so hard and at such cost, began to fade as the simulation's boundaries drifted into opalescent tatters. Finally there was only the trireme, and the lingering sound of its oars in water that was no longer there.

An Athenian hoplite approached, and handed her water, but she did not bother to take it. Sensation was already fading, the materiality ending. The water would be nothing in a mouth that had ceased to feel it. The wound had stopped throbbing, was gone. Blood remained on the deck, and the sun's warm color, but not the warmth of the sun.

"Do you really think they would have kept fighting like that? After it was impossible to win?" The Athenian cut her hands free with a small bronze knife.

Regina lay down on the deck. Moments ago there had been the physical feeling of exhaustion, heat. Now there was none of that, though there was a faint sensation of the deck beneath her. She laced her fingers behind her head and looked up into the glaucous simulation edge that was the sky.

"I do," Regina said. "Some would have given up. But others were beyond reason, beyond caring about consequence. They would have carried on when it was impossible. Hatred, fear, and anger would have ruled them. I was missing it in my reports last year. The stubbornness, the things beyond strategy."

Astrid, who had played the Athenian but was now becoming Astrid again, was silent for a moment, then tossed her helmet to the deck, where it landed without a sound and was gone. She sat down with a sigh. "You're probably right. Anyway, it seems to come closer to the truth. But I'm so tired of doing this every day. I wish I knew what they were looking for. What's the key to all of this? Anyway . . . another year almost gone, and no end in sight. Is your timeshare still in Istanbul? Will you really go back there, after everything that happened there last year? After almost getting killed, and totaling your blank? You barely made it out of that place alive."

That morning, before the start of the day's simulation, Regina had received a message from Ilkay: "Here a day early, already waiting for your arrival. Tell me you are coming, though I won't stop worrying until I see your face."

Regina grinned into the blank swirl of false sky, seeing black tea there, and cobblestones, incense aged into stone, the hiss of snow along a seagull's wing, and Ilkay's face—the many faces Ilkay's being had illuminated, her smile each year both different, and the same.

"Of course I'm going back. Now, and every year. It is my home."

Dear sarah

NANCY KRESS

Making a life decision that goes against the wishes of your family can be a bitter and emotionally grueling thing to do. Sometimes they never speak to you again. Sometimes they even try to kill you.

Nancy Kress began selling her elegant and incisive stories in the mid-seventies. Her books include the novel version of her Hugo and Nebula-winning story, Beggars in Spain, *and a sequel,* Beggars and Choosers, *as well as* The Prince Of Morning Bells, The Golden Grove, The White Pipes, An Alien Light, Brain Rose, Oaths and Miracles, Stinger, Maximum Light, Crossfire, Nothing Human, The Floweres of Aulit Prison, Crucible, Dogs, *and* Steal Across the Sky, Flash Point, *and, with Therese Pieczynski,* New Under the Sun, *as well as the Space Opera trilogy* Probability Moon, Probability Sun, *and* Probability Space. *Her short work has been collected in* Trinity and Other Stories, The Aliens of Earth, Beaker's Dozen, Nano Comes to Clifford Falls and Other Stories, Fountain of Age: Stories, Future Perfect, AI Unbound, *and* The Body Human. *Her most recent book is the novel* Tomorrow's Kin. *In addition to the awards for "Beggars in Spain," she has also won Nebula Awards for her stories "Out of All Them Bright Stars" and "The Flowers of Aulit Prison," the John W. Campbell Memorial Award in 2003 for her novel* Probability Space, *and another Hugo in 2009 for "The Erdmann Nexus." She won another Nebula Award in 2013 for her novella* After the Fall, Before the Fall, During the Fall *and another Nebula Award in 2017 for* Yesterday's Kin. *She lives in Seattle with her husband, writer Jack Skillingstead.*

In some families, it coulda been just an argument. Or maybe a shunning. Not my family—they done murder for less. I got two second cousins doing time in Riverbend. Blood feuds.

So I told them by Skype.

Call me a coward. You don't know Daddy, or Seth. Anyways, it warn't like I wanted to do it. I just didn't see no other way out of Brightwater and the life waiting for me there. And Daddy always said to use whatever you got. I was always the best shot anywhere around Brightwater. Shooting good is what I got.

And like I said, I couldn't see no other choice.

"MaryJo! Where the hell you been?"

"I left a note, Daddy."

"All it says is you be gone for a few days. Where are you?"

I took in a real deep breath. *Just say it, Jo.* His face filled the screen in the room the recruiter let me have to myself to make this call. She didn't even seem worried I might steal something. Then Daddy stepped back and I saw our living room behind him, with its sprung tatty couch and magazine pictures on the walls. We piggyback on the Cranstons' internet, which works most days.

"Daddy . . . you know there's nothing for me in Brightwater now."

He didn't answer. Waiting. Mama moved into the screen behind him, then Seth and Sarah.

I said, "Nothing for any of us. I know we've always been there, but now things are different."

I didn't have to say what I meant. Daddy's eyes got that look he gets when anybody mentions the aliens. Eight years now since the oil rigs closed, and the gas drilling, and most important to us, the coal mines. Everybody I know is out of work since the Likkies gave us the Q-energy. Only they didn't really give it to us, they gave it to the rich guys in Washington and San Francisco and Seattle and Oklahoma City, who just got a whole lot richer selling it back to the country. "A trade partnership" they called it, but somehow people like us got left out of all the trading. We always do.

I stumbled on. "I want more, Daddy. You always said to use whatever you—"

"What did you do?" he said, and his voice was quiet thunder.

"I enlisted."

Sarah cried out. She's only eleven, she don't understand. Seth, who's a pretty good stump preacher, pointed his finger at me and started in. "'Mine own familiar friend in whom I trusted, who did eat of my bread, hath lifted up his hand against me!'"

Psalm four-something.

Mama said, "Did you sign anything? Come back and we'll hide you!"

Jacob—and where did he come from? He shoulda been out digging bootleg coal for the stove—yelled, "Brightwater is good enough for the rest of us! We been here two hundred years!"

Mama said, all desperate, "MaryJo, pride goeth before a fall!"

Sarah: "Come home!"

Seth: "'And the many will fall away and betray one another!'"

Jacob: "You always thought you were better than us!"

Mama: "Oh dear sweet Jesus, help this prodigal girl to see the light and—"

Then Daddy cut it all short with that voice of his. "You're a traitor. To us and to your country."

I cried, "I joined the United States Army! You fought in Afghanistan and Grandpa in—"

"Traitor. And not my daughter. I don't never want to see your face again."

A wail from Mama, and then the screen went black and dead, dead, dead.

The recruiter came back in. She was in a fancy uniform but her face was kind. "Is everything all right?"

"Yes, ma'am." I warn't about to talk on this with her. Anyways, she knew the situation. The whole fucking country knew the situation. If you have money, you're glad the Likkies are here, changing up the economy and saving the environment. If you don't have money, if you're just working people, your job disappeared to the Likkies' Q-energy and their factory 'bots and all the rest of it. So you starve. Or you join one of the terrorist groups trying to bring the Likkies down. Or, like me, you do what poor kids have always done, including Daddy and Grandpa—you join the army for a spell.

Only this time, the army was on the wrong side. The military was fighting our home-raised anti-Likkie terrorists in American cities, even on the moon base and in space. I was going to be defending my family's enemy.

I went outside and got on the bus to go to basic training.

Basic warn't too bad. I was at Fort Benning for OSUP, one stop unit training. I'm tough and I don't need much sleep and after the first few days, nobody messed with me. The drill sergeants mostly picked on somebody else, and my battle buddy was okay, and silent. I had the highest rifle qualification score and so I got picked to fire the live round at AT4 training. The Claymore blew up with more noise and debris than anybody expected, but all I could think of was this: Daddy taught me to shoot, he should be proud of me. Only, of course, he warn't.

I didn't see no aliens at Fort Benning.

Once somebody suggested sniper school, and I was kinda interested until I found out it involved a lot of math. No way.

I had three days after OSUT before I had to report to my unit at Fort Drum. I checked into a motel and played video games. The last day, I called home—at least the phone warn't cut off—and by a miracle, Sarah answered instead of anybody else.

"Hey, Squirt."

"*MaryJo?*"

"Yeah. How you doing?"

"How are you? Where are you? Are you coming home now?"

"No. I'm going to my unit, in New York. Sarah—"

"In *New York City?*"

I heard the dazzle in her voice, and all at once my throat closed up. It was me who taught Sarah to shoot and about her period and all sorts of shit. I got out, "No, upcountry New York. Listen, you doing okay?" And then what I really wanted to ask: "They forgive me yet?"

Silence. Then a little whisper, "No. Oh, Jo, quit that army and them Likkies and come home! I miss you!"

"I can't, Squirt. But I'll send—"

"Gotta go Seth just come home. Bye!"

A sharp click on the line.

I spent my last night drunk.

The next day I got on my first plane ride and reported to Fort Drum. And right there was my first alien.

"Does anybody have any questions?"

Nobody did. The officer—a lieutenant colonel, the highest rank I ever expected to see talking right at us—stood in front of a hundred sixty FNGs—"fucking new guys"—talking about Likkies. Only of course he called them by their right name, Leckinites. I don't know where the name come from or what it means; I mighta slept through that part. But I knew nearly everything else, because for a solid week we been learning about the aliens: their home planet and their biology and their culture and, a lot, how important their help was to fixing Earth's problems with energy and environment and a bunch of other stuff. We seen pictures and movies and charts, and at night we used our personal hour to argue about them. Near as I could tell, about half the base thought the Likkies were great for humans. The other half was like me, knowing just how bad the aliens made it for folks on the bottom.

And now we were going to meet one for the first time.

"Are you sure you have no questions?" Colonel Jamison said, sounding like we shoulda had some. But in the army, it's best to keep your mouth shut. "No? Then without further delay, let me introduce Mr. Granson. Tensh-hut!"

We all leapt to attention and the Likkie walked into the room. If its name was "Mr. Granson," then mine was Dolly Parton. It was tall, like in the movies we seen, and had human-type arms and legs and head. ("This optimum symmetrical design is unsurprisingly replicated in various Terran mammalian species as well" one of our hand-outs read, whatever the fuck that means.) The Likkie had two eyes and a wide mouth with no lips, no hair or nose. It wore a loose white robe like pictures I seen of Arab sheiks, and there mighta had anything underneath. Its arms ended in seven tentacles each, its skin was sorta light purplish, and it wore a clear helmet like a fishbowl 'cause it can't breathe our air. No oxygen tank and hose to lug around like old Grandpa Addams had when the lung cancer was getting him. The helmet someways turned our air into theirs. They're smart bastards, I'll give them that.

"Hello," it said. "I am privileged to meet with you today."

Real good English and not too much accent—I heard a lot worse at Fort Benning.

"My wish is to offer thanks for the help of the U.S. Army, including all of you, in protecting the partnership that we are here to forge between your people and mine. A partnership that will benefit us all."

The guy next to me, Lopez, shifted in his seat. His family used to work at a factory that now uses Likkie 'bots instead. But Lopez kept his face empty.

The Likkie went on like that, in a speech somebody human musta wrote for him because it didn't have no mistakes. At least the speechwriters still got jobs.

Afterward, there was a lot of bitching in the barracks about the speech, followed by a lot of arguing. I didn't say nothing. But after lights out, the soldier in the next bunk, Drucker, whispered to me, "You don't like the Likkies either, do you, Addams?"

I didn't answer her. It was after lights-out. But for a long time I couldn't sleep.

Fort Drum sucked. Snow and cold and it was almost April, for Chrissake. Back home, flowers would be blooming. Sarah would be barefoot in shorts.

She sent me a letter. She was way better'n me at writing.

> Dear Jo,
> I hope you get this letter. My teacher told me what address to put on it and she give me a stamp. She is nice. I got A on my math test last week.
> The big news here is that Jacob is getting married. Nobody knew till now. Her name is Lorna and I don't like her she is mean but then so is Jacob sometimes so maybe they will be happy together.
> My main reason to write you is to say COME HOME!!! I had a real good idea. If you shoot an alien I bet Daddy would forgive you. Seth too. DO IT!!!
>> All my love forever,
>> Sarah Addams

"What's that?" Drucker said. She was looking over my shoulder and I didn't even hear her come up behind me.

"Nothing!" I said, folding the letter. But she already read it. She must read real fast.

"I didn't mean to invade your privacy, Jo," she said—that's the way she talks. "But I have to say that Sarah—is she your younger sister?—sounds like a really smart kid. With the right ideas."

Then Drucker looked at me long and serious. I wanted to punch her—for reading my letter, for talking fancy, for not being my family. I didn't do none of that. Keeping my nose clean. I just said, "Go fuck yourself, Drucker."

She only laughed.

And who said she gets to call me "Jo"?

Fort Drum was not just cold, it was boring. Drill and hike, hike and drill. But we warn't there long. After a week, fifty of us had a half-hour to prepare to ship out, down to a city called Albany. Drucker was one of us. For days she'd been trying to friend around with me, and sometimes I let her. Usually I keep to myself, but listening to her took my mind off home, at least for a while.

"Where the fuck is Albany?" I said on the bus.

A guy in the seat behind me laughed. "Don't you ever watch the news, Addams?"

"It's the capital city of New York State," Drucker said without sounding snotty, which was the other reason I let her hang around with me. She don't ever act like she knows more'n me, though she does.

I gave the guy behind us the finger and lowered my voice. "What's going on in Albany?"

Drucker said quietly, "It's bad. You ever hear about the T-bocs?"

I shook my head. Our buses tore through the gates like it was fleeing demons. Wherever Albany was, the army wanted us there fast.

"The Take Back Our Country organization. Anti-alien terrorists, the largest and best armed and organized of all those groups. They've captured a warehouse outside Albany, big fortified place used to store explosives. The owners, a corporation, were in the process of moving the stuff out when the T-bocs took the building. They've got hostages in there along with the explosives."

"And we're going to take the building back?"

Drucker smiled. "Marines and US Rangers are going to take the building back, Addams. We'll probably just be the outer perimeter guard. To keep away press and stupid civilians."

"Oh," I said, feeling stupid myself. "Okay, then."

"Thing is, some of the hostages are kids."

"Kids?" I thought of Sarah. "Why were kids in a warehouse?"

"They weren't. They were brought there. It was all timed just so. This is big."

Big. Bigger than anything that ever happened to me, or might happen to me, in Brightwater. Then Drucker said something that made it bigger.

"Our kids, Jo. And three of theirs."

Drucker was right, about every last thing. We were perimeter guards for a real big perimeter—half a mile around the warehouse. There was houses and train tracks and other buildings and trucks with no cabs and huge big dumpsters and a homeless tent town, and every last one of them had to be cleared of people. I was with a four-man stack, flushing out everybody who didn't have enough sense to already leave, which was a lot of people. We cleared rooms and escorted out squatters and made tenants in the saggy houses pack up what they could carry and then leave. Some of them got angry, shouting that they had no place to go. Some of them cried. One man attacked with a sledge hammer, which didn't get him nowhere. My sarge knew what he was doing—he cleared rooms in Iraq, where the enemy had more'n sledgehammers.

Drucker was right about something else, too. There were *kids* in there. Turns out that seven years ago, while Daddy and Seth and Jacob were losing their jobs in the mines and we got evicted from our house, the Likkies put some of their kids in special schools with our kids so they could all learn each other's languages and grow up together just like there warn't no difference between us and them. The T-bocs took that school and transported six kids to the warehouse. Seven bodyguards and five teachers at the school were dead. They mighta been pretty good bodyguards, but the T-bocs had military weapons.

"I told you it was big," Drucker said.

"Yeah, you did." We just spent twenty hours clearing buildings. Then fresh troops arrived to relieve us, more experienced soldiers. We'd been first just because we were closest. Rangers and Marines were there but they warn't permitted to do nothing while the negotiators tried to talk the T-bocs down. Drucker and I were off-duty, laying on mats in a high school gym that was now a barracks. I had a shower in the locker room and I was so tired my bones felt like melting. It warn't a bad feeling.

But Drucker wanted to talk.

"What do you think about all this, Jo?"

"I'm not thinking."

"Well, start. Do you think the T-bocs are justified?"

"Justified? You mean, like, right to kidnap kids? How old are them kids, anyway?"

"Second graders. The humans are seven years old, two girls and a boy, all the children of VIPS. Who knows how old the Likkies are? Maybe they just live a real short time, like insects, and these so-called 'kids' are really adults halfway through their lives."

"That warn't what our lectures said."

"Do you believe everything the army tells you?"

I raised up on one elbow and looked at her. In the half-light her eyes shone too bright, like she was using. Was she?

Drucker sat all the way up. We'd hauled our gym mats into a corner and nobody else could hear.

"Jo, you told me your family are all unemployed and on welfare because of the Likkies. I imagine that's a deep shame to people like yours, isn't it?"

"Shut up," I said, 'cause she was right. Shame is what made Daddy and them so angry. All their choices got taken away by the aliens.

"But it's not *right*," she said, real soft. "This is supposed to be our country. These aliens are just more damn immigrants trying to take it away. Sometimes I think the army is on the wrong side. Do you ever think that, Jo?"

"Shut up," I said again, 'cause I didn't like hearing my thoughts coming from her mouth. "You using?"

"Yes. Want some?"

"No."

"That's all right. I just wanted the chance to express my thoughts, so thank you for listening. You're a real friend."

We warn't friends. I shoulda said that, but I didn't. I waited, 'cause it was clear she warn't done. If she was trying to recruit me for something, I wanted to hear what.

But all she said was, "This is big," and her voice gleamed with satisfaction like a gun barrel with fresh oil.

The standoff went on for a day, and then a week, and then two weeks. We had more soldiers. We had army choppers to keep away the press choppers. We had drones in the air, thicker than mosquitos in July. We had more negotiators—not that I ever saw them. My unit kept getting pushed farther and farther away from the warehouse as the perimeter got wider. More people got evacuated. None of them liked it.

But every night my unit moved back to the high school to sleep. I don't know where the Special Forces guys slept, but I know they were antsy as hell, wanting to go in and take the objective. Which they couldn't do because the T-bocs said they'd kill the kids.

"An interstellar incident," Drucker said. "Maybe that's what we need to get the Likkies off our planet. Blow the place to smithereens and they'll think it's too dangerous to stay on Earth."

"Is that what you want?" I finally asked.

She only smiled. Then after that I didn't see her much, because she started fucking somebody in off-duty hours. I don't know who or where, and I didn't care.

The whole thing couldn't go on like that.

And it didn't.

The night was like home, only not really 'cause all the city lights blotted the stars and it smelled like a city and under my boots was concrete instead of switchgrass.

But the air had that spring softness like I hadn't felt up here before, and that little spring breeze that made you just ache inside.

At home, Mama would be setting out tomato plants. Sarah would be picking wild strawberries. The fawns would be standing for the first time on spindly little legs. Last year me and Sarah got real close to one.

Coming off guard duty on the perimeter, I warn't sleepy. I put my rifle in its sling and walked, careful to stay in the middle of the street where it was allowed. I passed a bar and a V-R playroom, both closed and boarded up. At the end of the allowed section, a rope marked another perimeter, this time around the old hotel where brass and negotiators and them stayed. It looked nice, with a awning over the door and big pots of fake flowers. *They* warn't sleeping on gym mats.

Sarah's letter was in my pocket. She didn't send a second one, or I else didn't get it. Was Jacob married yet? He—

Gunfire someplace behind me.

I hit the ground. Gunfire came from another place, off to my left. Then explosions, little ones, at a bunch of different places—*pop pop pop*. Somebody screamed.

Soldiers poured out of buildings. The Marines guarding the hotel raised their weapons. An officer barked orders but I couldn't hear him because a flashbang went off and everything was noise and blinding light and confusion and people running.

I got to my feet and unslung my rifle, but then I didn't know what to do with it, or myself. I warn't even supposed to be here. I backed away, trying to make out what was happening, when another explosion went off, pretty close to the hotel.

When I could see again, a Likkie was running out of the hotel door, yelling. One of the Marines at the door was down. I didn't see the other one. The Likkie ran right past me, high-tailing it to the warehouse, and I didn't need no translator to know why it was there or what it was screaming. I seen that look on Mama's face the time Sarah fell into the pond and got fished out half drowned. I seen it on Daddy's face when Seth got injured in the mine. That Likkie had a kid in the warehouse and it was going in after it.

It was going to pass right by me. I already had my rifle raised. I wouldn't even need to sight.

If you shoot an alien I bet Daddy would forgive you. Seth too. DO IT!!!

Then I saw Drucker.

She was supposed to be asleep in the gym. But here she was in full kit, her top half popping up from inside a dumpster, M4 swinging around, cheek against the stock. She warn't that good a marksman, but she was good enough. All I had to do was nothing—let her do it for me. *Vengeance is mine, saith the Lord,* but I never believed that horseshit. The Lord might have vengeance against tribes attacking Israel, but He ain't interested in Likkies taking a living from people like us.

Choppers roared above, heading for the warehouse. Whoever set off that gunfire and explosives and flashbangs, whether they were our diversionary tactic or T-boc's, the raid was going to happen now. Special Forces were going in and Marines were laying down covering fire. The noise and confusion was like Armageddon. But I warn't part of that neither, warn't at the center of it. People like me never was.

Drucker had her sight now. She stilled.

All I had to do was wait.

But—soldiers aren't supposed to murder civilians, which that Likkie was. Soldiers in the US Army aren't supposed to murder each other neither. It was all tangled up in my mind, only now it had to be one or the other. Or nothing.

I always been real fast. I sighted and squeezed. I got Drucker just before she fired, right in the head. She fell backwards into the dumpster.

A second later a Marine sort of surrounded the running Likkie and stopped it. A second after that, another Marine had me on the ground, M4 kicked away. "You move and I'll blow your head off, motherfucker!" I didn't move. He cuffed me and took my sidearm. When he yanked me to my feet, I somehow heard—over all the choppers, automatic fire, sirens, explosions—the rustle of Sarah's letter in my pocket, louder than anything else.

I write Sarah from the brig at Fort Drum.

Special Forces took the warehouse. Sixteen troops died, and thirty-eight T-bocs. Two of the kids were killed during the rescue. One of ours, Kayla Allison Howell, seven years old, black hair and blue eyes, pink tee shirt with Hello Kitty on it. I seen pictures. One of the Likkie kids, a little bald purplish thing, whose name I can't pronounce. They were shot in the head before a US Ranger shot the murderer. Later, my lawyer told me, some of the Special Forces who went into that room cried.

A whole bunch of important people said the raid was wrong, the army shoulda waited. The army said that under the circumstances, it had no choice. The arguing is red-hot and it don't stop. Probably it will never stop.

I don't know if they shoulda gone in or not. But I know this, now: There is always a choice, even for people who will never be at the center of nothing. Changes and choices, they go together, bound up like sticks for a bonfire that's going to be lit no matter what.

Drucker made a choice when she joined the T-bocs, a choice to kill anything that made changes happen.

That Likkie outside the hotel, it chose to risk its life trying to get to its kid. And the Likkies are choosing to stay here, in the United States, instead of avenging their dead kid or else packing up and going home. In fact, more are coming. They have more plans for helping us with technology and shit. Saving the planet, they say, and politicians agree with them.

My family chose to give up.

What I did is earning me a court martial. But I chose long before the night of the raid. In the locker room of the high school I saw Drucker's T-boc patch, hidden under her uniform. I saw it 'cause she wanted me to see it, wanted me to join them. I coulda reported it then, and I didn't.

Did I choose wrong when I killed Drucker? Even now, even after all the thinking I do sitting here in my cell, even after my lawyer says I'll get off because the evidence shows that Drucker was part of T-bocs, even after all that—I don't know.

But I do know this—things change. Even things that look set in stone. Maybe someday, years from now, jobs or people or aliens or *something* will change enough that I can go home.

For now, I write a letter that might or might not get delivered.

Dear Sarah—

night passage
ALASTAIR REYNOLDS

A professional scientist with a Ph.D. in astronomy, Alastair Reynolds worked for the European Space Agency in the Netherlands for a number of years but has recently moved back to his native Wales to become a full-time writer. His first novel, Revelation Space, *was widely hailed as one of the major science fiction books of the year; it was quickly followed by* Chasm City, Redemption Ark, Absolution Gap, Century Rain, *and* Pushing Ice, *all big sprawling space operas that were big sellers as well, establishing Reynolds as one of the best and most popular new science fiction writers to enter the field in many years. His other books include a novella collection,* Diamond Dogs, Turquoise Days *and a chapbook novella,* The Six Directions of Space, *as well as three collections,* Galactic North, Zima Blue and Other Stories, *and* Deep Navigation. *His other novels include* The Prefect, House of Suns, Terminal World, Blue Remembered Earth, On the Steel Breeze, *and* Sleepover, *and a Doctor Who novel,* Harvest of Time. *Upcoming is a new book,* Slow Bullets.

In the suspenseful story that follows, the crew of a ship who blunder into a strange cosmic phenomenon in deep space are faced with mutiny, betrayal, and double cross piled upon double cross. . . .

I
f you were really born on Fand then you will know the old saying we had on that world.

Shame is a mask that becomes the face.

The implication being that if you wear the mask long enough, it grafts itself to your skin, becomes an indelible part of you—even a kind of comfort.

Shall I tell you what I was doing before you called? Standing at my window, looking out across Chasm City as it slid into dusk. My reflection loomed against the distant buildings beyond my own, my face chiselled out of cruel highlights and pitiless, light-sucking shadows. When my father held me under the night sky above Burnheim Bay, pointing out the named colonies, the worlds and systems bound by ships, he told me that I was a very beautiful girl, and that he could see a million stars reflected in the dark pools of my eyes. I told him that I didn't care about any of that, but that I did want to be a starship captain.

Father laughed. He held me tighter. I do not know if he believed me or not, but I think it scared him, that I might mean exactly what I said.

And now you come.

You recognise me, as he would not have done, but only because you knew me as an adult. You and I never spoke, and our sole meeting consisted of a single smile, a single friendly glance as I welcomed the passengers onto my ship, all nineteen thousand of them streaming through the embarkation lock—twenty if you include the Conjoiners.

Try as I might, I can't picture you.

But you say you were one of them, and for a moment at least I'm inclined to give you the time of day. You say that you were one of the few thousand who came back on the ship—and that's possible, I could check your name against the *Equinoctial's* passenger manifest, eventually—and that you were one of the still fewer who did not suffer irreversible damage due to the prolonged nature of our crossing. But you say that even then it was difficult. When they brought you out of reefersleep, you barely had a personality, let alone a functioning set of memories.

How did I do so well, when the others did not? Luck was part of it. But when it was decreed that I should survive, every measure was taken to protect me against the side effects of such a long exposure to sleep. The servitors intervened many times, to correct malfunctions and give me the best chance of coming through. More than once I was warmed to partial life, then submitted to the auto-surgeon, just to correct incipient frost damage. I remember none of that, but obviously it succeeded. That effort could never have been spread across the entire manifest, though. The rest of you had to take your chances—in more ways than one.

Come with me to the window for a moment. I like this time of day. This is my home now, Chasm City. I'll never see Fand again, and it's rare for me to leave these rooms. But it's not such a bad place, Yellowstone, once you get used to the poison skies, the starless nights.

Do you see the lights coming on? A million windows, a million other lives. The lights remain, most of the time, but still they remind me of the glints against the Shroud, the way they sparked, one after the other. I remember standing there with Magadis and Doctor Grellet, finally understanding what it was they were showing me—and what it meant. Beautiful little synaptic flashes, like thoughts sparking across the galactic darkness of the mind.

But you saw none of that.

Let me tell you how it started. You'll hear other accounts, other theories, but this is how it was for me.

To begin with no one needed to tell me that something was wrong. All the indications were there as soon as I opened my eyes, groping my way to alertness. Red walls, red lights, a soft pulsing alarm tone, the air too cold for comfort. The *Equi-noctial* was supposed to warm itself prior to the mass revival sequence, when we reached Yellowstone. It would only be this chilly if I had been brought out of hibernation at emergency speed.

"Rauma," a voice said. "Captain Bernsdottir. Can you understand me?"

It was my second-in-command, leaning in over my half-open reefersleep casket. He was blurred out, looming swollen and pale.

"Struma." My mouth was dry, my tongue and lips uncooperative. "What's happened? Where are we?"

"Mid-crossing, and in a bad way."

"Give me the worst."

"We've stopped. Engines damaged, no control. We've got a slow drift, a few kilometres per second against the local rest frame."

"No," I said flatly, as if I was having to explain something to a child. "That doesn't happen. Ships don't just stop."

"They do if it's deliberate action." Struma bent down and helped me struggle out of the casket, every articulation of bone and muscle sending a fresh spike of pain to my brain. Reefersleep revival was never pleasant, but rapid revival came with its own litany of discomforts. "It's sabotage, Captain."

"What?"

"The Spiders . . ." He corrected himself. "The Conjoiners woke up mid-flight and took control of the ship. Broke out of their area, commandeered the controls. Flipped us around, slowed us down to just a crawl."

He helped me hobble to a chair and a table. He had prepared a bowl of pink gelatinous pap, designed to restore my metabolic balance.

"How . . ." I had too many questions and they were tripping over themselves trying to get out of my head. But a good captain jumped to the immediate priorities, then backtracked. "Status of the ship. Tell me."

"Damaged. No main drive or thruster authority. Comms lost." He swallowed, like he had more to say.

I spooned the bad-tasting pink pap into myself. "Tell me we can repair this damage, and get going again."

"It can all be fixed—given time. We're looking at the repair schedules now."

"We?"

"Six of your executive officers, including me. The ship brought us out first. That's standard procedure: only wake the captain under dire circumstances. There are six more passengers coming out of freeze, under the same emergency protocol."

Struma was slowly swimming into focus. My second-in-command had been with me on two crossings, but he still looked far too young and eager to my eyes. Strong, boyish features, an easy smile, arched eyebrows, short dark curls neatly combed even in a crisis.

"And the . . ." I frowned, trying to wish away the unwelcome news he had already told me. "The Conjoiners. What about them. If you're speaking to me, the takeover can't have been successful."

"No, it wasn't. They knew the ship pretty well, but not all of the security procedures. We woke up in time to contain and isolate the takeover." He set his jaw. "It was brutal, though. They're fast and sly, and of course they outnumbered us a hundred to one. But we had weapons, and most of the security systems were dumb enough to keep on our side, not theirs."

"Where are they now?"

"Contained, what's left of them. Maybe eight hundred still frozen. Two hundred or so in the breakout party—we don't have exact numbers. But we ate into them. By my estimate there can't be more than about sixty still warm, and we've got them isolated behind heavy bulkheads and electrostatic shields."

"How did the ship get so torn up?"

"It was desperate. They were prepared to go down fighting. That's when most of the damage was done. Normal pacification measures were never going to hold them. We had to break out the heavy excimers, and they'll put a hole right through the hull, out to space and anything that gets in the way—including drive and navigation systems."

"We were carrying excimers?"

"Standard procedure, Captain. We've just never needed them before."

"I can't believe this. A century of peaceful cooperation. Mutual advancement through shared science and technology. Why would they throw it all away now, and on my watch?"

"I'll show you why," Struma said.

Supporting my unsteady frame he walked me to an observation port and opened the radiation shutters. Then he turned off the red emergency lighting so that my eyes had a better chance of adjusting to the outside view.

I saw stars. They were moving slowly from left to right, not because the ship was moving as a whole but because we were now on centrifugal gravity and our part of the *Equinoctial* was rotating. The stars were scattered into loose associations and constellations, some of them changed almost beyond recognition, but others—made up of more distant stars—not too different than those I remembered from my childhood.

"They're just stars," I told Struma, unsurprised by the view. "I don't . . ."

"Wait."

A black wall slid into view. Its boundary was a definite edge, beyond which there were no stars at all. The more we rotated, the more blackness came into our line of sight. It wasn't just an absence of nearby stars. The Milky Way, that hobbled spine of galactic light, made up of tens of millions of stars, many thousand of light years away, came arcing across the normal part of the sky then reached an abrupt termination, just as if I were looking out at the horizon above a sunless black sea.

For a few seconds all I could do was stare, unable to process what I was seeing, or what it meant. My training had prepared me for many operational contingencies— almost everything that could ever go wrong on an interstellar crossing. But not this.

Half the sky was gone.

"What the hell is it?"

Struma looked at me. There was a long silence. "Good question."

You were not one of the six passenger-delegates. That would be too neat, too unlikely, given the odds. And I would have remembered your face as soon as you came to my door.

I met them in one of the mass revival areas. It was similar to the crew facilities, but much larger and more luxurious in its furnishings. Here, at the end of our voyage, passengers would have been thawed out in groups of a few hundred at a time, expecting to find themselves in a new solar system, at the start of a new phase in their lives.

The six were going through the same process of adjustment I had experienced only a few hours earlier. Discomfort, confusion—and a generous helping of resentment, that the crossing had not gone as smoothly as the brochures had promised.

"Here's what I know," I said, addressing the gathering as they sat around a hexagonal table, eating and drinking restoratives. "At some point after we left Fand there was an attempted takeover by the Conjoiners. From what we can gather one or two hundred of them broke out of reefersleep while the rest of us were frozen. They commandeered the drive systems and brought the ship to a standstill. We're near an object or phenomenon of unknown origin. It's a black sphere about the same size as a star, and we're only fifty thousand kilometres from its surface." I raised a hand before the obvious questions started raining in. "It's not a black hole. A black hole this large would be of galactic mass, and there's no way we'd have missed something like that in our immediate neighbourhood. Besides, it's not pulling at us. It's just sitting there, with no gravitational attraction that our instruments can register. Right up to its edge we can see that the stars aren't suffering any aberration or redshift . . . yes?"

One of the passengers had also raised a hand. The gesture was so polite, so civil, that it stopped me in my tracks.

"This can't have been an accident, can it?"

"Might I know your name, sir?"

He was a small man, mostly bald, with a high voice and perceptive, piercing eyes.

"Grellet. Doctor Grellet. I'm a physician."

"That's lucky," I said. "We might well end up needing a doctor."

"Luck's got nothing to do with it, Captain Bernsdottir. The protocol always ensures that there's a physician among the emergency revival cohort."

I had no doubt that he was right, but it was a minor point of procedure and I felt I could be forgiven for forgetting it.

"I'll still be glad of your expertise, if we have difficulties."

He looked back at me, something in his mild, undemonstrative manner beginning to grate on me. "Are we expecting difficulties?"

"That'll depend. But to go back to your question, it doesn't seem likely that the Conjoiners just stumbled on this object, artefact, whatever we want to call it. They must have known of its location, then put a plan in place to gain control of the ship."

"To what end?" Doctor Grellet asked.

I decided truthfulness was the best policy. "I don't know. Some form of intelligence gathering, I suppose. Maybe a unilateral first contact attempt, against the terms of the Europa Accords. Whatever the plan was, it's been thwarted. But that's not been without a cost. The ship is damaged. The *Equinoctial's* own repair systems will put things right, but they'll need time for that."

"Then we sit and wait," said another passenger, a woman this time. "That's all we have to do, isn't it? Then we can be on our way again."

"There's a bit more to it than that," I answered, looking at them all in turn. "We have a residual drift toward the object. Ordinarily it wouldn't be a problem—we'd just use the main engines or steering thrusters to neutralise the motion. But we have no means of controlling the engines, and we won't get it until the repair schedule is well advanced."

"How long?" Doctor Grellet asked.

"To regain the use of the engines? My executive officers say four weeks at the bare minimum. Even if we shaved a week off that, though, it wouldn't help us. At our present rate of drift we'll reach the surface of the object in twelve days."

There was a silence. It echoed my own, when Struma had first informed me of our predicament.

"What will happen?" another passenger asked.

"We don't know. We don't even know what that surface is made of, whether it's a solid wall or some kind of screen or discontinuity. All we do know is that it blocks all radiation at an immeasurably high efficiency, and that its temperature is exactly the same as the cosmic microwave background. If it's a Dyson sphere . . . or something similar . . . we'd expect to see it pumping out in the infrared. But it doesn't. It just sits there being almost invisible. If you wanted to hide something, to conceal yourself in interstellar space . . . impossibly hard to detect, until you're almost on top of it . . . this would be the thing. It's like camouflage, a cloak, or . . ."

"A shroud," Doctor Grellet said.

"Someone else will get the pleasure of naming it," I said. "Our concern is what it will do. I've ordered the launch of a small instrument package, aimed straight at the object. It's nothing too scientific—we're not equipped for that. Just a redundant spacesuit with some sensors. But it will give us an idea what to expect."

"When will it arrive?"

"In a little under twenty-six hours."

"You should have consulted with the revival party before taking this action, captain," Doctor Grellet said.

"Why?"

"You've fired a missile at an object of unknown origin. You know it isn't a missile, and so do we. But the object?"

"We don't know that it has a mind," I responded.

"Yet," Doctor Grellet said.

I spent the next six hours with Struma, reviewing the condition of the ship at first-hand. We travelled up and down the length of the hull, inside and out, cataloguing the damage and making sure there were no additional surprises. Inside was bearable. But while we were outside, travelling in single-person inspection pods, I had that black wall at my back the whole time.

"Are you sure there weren't easier ways of containing them, other than peppering the ship with blast holes?"

"Have you had a lot of experience with Conjoiner uprisings, Captain?"

"Not especially."

"I studied the tactics they used on Mars, back at the start of the last century. They're ruthless, unafraid of death, and totally uninterested in surrender."

"Mars was ancient history, Struma."

"Lessons can still be drawn. You can't treat them as a rational adversary, willing to accept a negotiated settlement. They're more like a nerve gas, trying to reach you by any means. Our objective was to push them back into an area of the ship that we could seal and vent if needed. We succeeded—but at a cost to the ship." From the other inspection pod, cruising parallel to mine, his face regarded me with a stern and stoic resolve. "It had to be done. I didn't like any part of it. But I also knew the ship was fully capable of repairing itself."

"It's a good job we have all the time in the world," I said, cocking my own head at the black surface. At our present rate of drift it was three kilometres nearer for every minute that passed.

"What would you have had me do?" Struma asked. "Allow them to complete their takeover, and butcher the rest of us?"

"You don't know that that was their intention."

"I do," Struma said. "Because Magadis told me."

I let him enjoy his moment before replying.

"Who is Magadis?"

"The one we captured. I wouldn't call her a leader. They don't have leaders, as such. But they do have command echelons, figures trusted with a higher level of intelligence processing and decision-making. She's one of them."

"You didn't mention this until now?"

"You asked for priorities, Captain. I gave you priorities. Anyway, Magadis got knocked around when she was captured. She's been in and out of consciousness ever since, not always lucid. She has no value as a hostage, so her ultimate usefulness to us isn't clear. Perhaps we should just kill her now and be done with it."

"I want to see her."

"I thought you might," Struma said.

Our pods steered for the open aperture of a docking bay.

By the time I got to Magadis she was awake and responsive. Struma and the other officers had secured her in a room at the far end of the ship from the other Conjoiners, and then arranged an improvised cage of electrostatic baffles around the room's walls, to screen out any possible neural traffic between Magadis and the other Conjoiners.

They had her strapped into a couch, taking no chances with that. She was shackled at the waist, the upper torso, the wrists, ankles and neck. Stepping into that room, I still felt unnerved by her close proximity. I had never distrusted Conjoiners before, but Struma's mention of Mars had unlocked a head's worth of rumour and memory. Bad things had been done to them, but they had not been shy in returning the favour. They were human, too, but only at the extreme edge of the definition. Human physiology, but boosted for a high tolerance of adverse environments. Human brain structure, but infiltrated with a cobweb of neural enhancements, far beyond anything carried by Demarchists. Their minds were cross-linked, their sense of identity blurred across the glassy boundaries of skulls and bodies.

That was why Magadis was useless as a hostage. Only part of her was present to begin with, and that part—the body, the portion of her mind within it—would be deemed expendable. Some other part of Magadis was still back with the other Conjoiners.

I approached her. She was thin, all angles and edges. Her limbs, what I could see of them beyond the shackles, were like folded blades, ready to flick out and wound. Her head was hairless, with a distinct cranial ridge. She was bruised and cut, one eye so badly swollen and slitted that I could not tell if it had been gouged out or still remained.

But the other eye fixed me well enough.

"Captain." She formed the word carefully, but there was blood on her lips and when she opened them I saw she had lost several teeth and her tongue was badly swollen.

"Magadis. I'm told that's your name. My officers tell me you attempted to take over my ship. Is that true?"

My question seemed to amuse and disappoint her in equal measure.

"Why ask?"

"I'd like to know before we all die."

Behind me, one of the officers had an excimer rifle pointed straight at Magadis's head.

"We distrusted your ability to conduct an efficient examination of the artefact," she said.

"Then you knew of it in advance."

"Of course." She nodded demurely, despite the shackle around her throat. "But only the barest details. A stellar-size object, clearly artificial, clearly of alien origin. It demanded our interest. But the present arrangements limited our ability to conduct intelligence gathering under our preferred terms."

"We have an arrangement. Had, I should say. More than a century of peaceful cooperation. Why have you endangered everything?"

"Because this changes everything."

"You don't even know what it is."

"We have gathered and transmitted information back to our mother nests. They will analyse the findings accordingly, when the signals reach them. But let us not delude ourselves, Captain. This is an alien technology—a demonstration of physics beyond either of our present conceptual horizons. Whichever human faction understands even a fraction of this new science will leave the others in the dust of history. Our alliance with the Demarchists has served us well, as it has been of benefit to you. But all things must end."

"You'd risk war, just for a strategic advantage?"

She squinted from her one good eye, looking puzzled. "What other sort of advantage is there?"

"I could—should—kill you now, Magadis. And the rest of your Conjoiners. You've done enough to give me the right."

She lifted her head. "Then do so."

"No. Not until I'm certain you've exhausted your usefulness to me. In five and half days we hit the object. If you want my clemency, start thinking of ways we might stop that happening."

"I've considered the situation," Magadis said. "There are no grounds for hope, Captain. You may as well execute me. But save a shot for yourself, won't you? You may come to appreciate it."

We spent the remainder of that first day confirming what we already knew. The ship was crippled, committed to its slow but deadly drift in the direction of the object.

Being a passenger-carrying vessel, supposed to fly between two settled, civilised solar systems, the *Equinoctial* carried no shuttles or large extravehicular craft. There were no lifeboats or tugs, nothing that could nudge us onto a different course or reverse our drift. Even our freight inventory was low for this crossing. I know, because I studied the cargo manifest, looking for some magic solution to our problem: a crate full of rocket motors, or something similar.

But the momentum of a million-tonne starship, even drifting at a mere fifty meters a second, is still immense. It would take more than a spare limpet motor or steering jet to make a difference to our fate.

Exactly what our fate was, of course, remained something of an open question. Soon we would know.

An hour before the suit's arrival at the surface I gathered Struma, Doctor Grellet, the other officers and passenger delegates in the bridge. Our improvised probe had continued transmitting information back to us for the entire duration of its day-long crossing. Throughout that time there had been little significant variation in the parameters, and no hint of a response from the object.

It remained black, cold and resolutely starless. Even as it fell within the last ten thousand kilometres, the suit was detecting no trace radiation beyond that faint microwave sizzle. It was pinging sensor pulses into the surface and picking up no hint of echo or backscatter. The gravitational field remained as flat as any other part of interstellar space, with no suggestion that the black sphere exerted any pull on its surroundings. It had to be made of something, but even if there had been only a moon's mass distributed throughout that volume, let alone a planet or a star, the suit would have picked up the gradient.

So it was a non-physical surface—an energy barrier or discontinuity. But even an energy field ought to have produced a measurable curvature, a measurable alteration in the suit's motion.

Something else, then. Something—as Magadis had implied—that lay entirely outside the framework of our physics. A kink or fracture in spacetime, artfully engineered. There might be little point in attempting to build a conceptual bridge between what we knew and what the object represented. Little point for baseline humans, at least. But I thought of what a loom of cross-linked, genius-level intelligences might make of it. The Conjoiners had already developed weapons and drive systems that were beyond our narrow models, even as they occasionally drip-fed us hints and glimpses of their "adjunct physics", as if to reassure their allies that they were only a step or two behind.

The suit was within eight thousand kilometres of the surface when its readings began to turn odd. It was small things to start with, almost possible to put down to individual sensor malfunctions. But as the readings turned stranger, and more numerous, the unlikelihood of these breakdowns happening all at once became too great to dismiss.

Dry-mouthed, I stared at the numbers and graphs.

"What?" asked Chajari, one of the female passengers.

"We'll need to look at these readings in more detail . . ." Struma began.

"No," I said, cutting him off. "What they're telling us is clear enough as it is. The suit's accelerometers are going haywire. It feels as if it's being pulled in a hundred directions at once. Pulled and pushed, like a piece of putty being squashed and stretched in someone's hand. And it's getting worse . . ."

I had been blunt, but there was no sense in sugaring things for the sake of the passengers. They had been woken to share in our decision-making processes, and for that reason alone they needed to know exactly how bad our predicament was.

The suit was still transmitting information when it hit the seven thousand kilometre mark, as near as we could judge. It only lasted a few minutes after that, though. The accelerational stresses built and built, until whole blocks of sensors began to black out. Soon after that the suit reported a major loss of its own integrity, as if its extremities had been ripped or crushed by the rising forces. By then it was tumbling, sending back only intermittent chirps of scrambled data.

Then it was gone.

I allowed myself a moment of calm before proceeding.

"Even when the suit was still sending to us," I said, "it was being buffeted by forces far beyond the structural limits of the ship. We'd have broken up not long after the eight thousand mark—and it would have been unpleasant quite a bit sooner than that." I paused and swallowed. "It's not a black hole. We know that. But there's something very odd about the spacetime near the surface. And if we drift too close we'll be shredded, just as the suit was."

It reached us then. The ship groaned, and we all felt a stomach-heaving twist pass through our bodies. The emergency tone sounded, and the red warning lights began to flash.

Had we been a ship at sea, it was as if we had been afloat on calm waters, until a single great wave rolled under us, followed by a series of diminishing after-ripples. The disturbance, whatever it had been, gradually abated.

Doctor Grellet was the first to speak. "We still don't know if the thing has a mind or not," he said, in the high, piping voice that I was starting to hate. "But I think we can be reasonably sure of one thing, Captain Bernsdottir."

"Which would be?" I asked.

"You've discovered how to provoke it."

Just when I needed some good news, Struma brought it to me.

"It's marginal," he said, apologising before he had even started. "But given our present circumstances . . ."

"Go on."

He showed me a flowchart of various repair schedules, a complex knotted thing like a many-armed octopus, and next to it a graph of our location, compared to the sphere.

"Here's our present position, thirty-five thousand kilometres from the surface."

"The surface may not even be our worst problem now," I pointed out.

"Then we'll assume we only have twenty-five thousand kilometres before things get difficult—a bit less than six days. But it may be enough. I've been running through the priority assignments in the repair schedule, and I think we can squeeze a solution out of this."

I tried not to cling to false hope. "You can?"

"As I said, it's marginal, but . . ."

"Spare me the qualifications, Struma. Just tell me what we have or haven't got."

"Normally the ship prioritises primary drive repairs over anything else. It makes sense. If you're trying to slow down from light speed, and something goes wrong with the main engines at a high level of time-compression . . . well, you want that fixed above all else, unless you plan on over-shooting your target system by several light years, or worse." He drew a significant pause. "But we're not in that situation. We need auxiliary control now, enough to correct the drift. If it takes a year or ten to regain relativistic capability, we'll still be alive. We can wait it out in reefersleep."

"Good . . ." I allowed.

"If we override all default schedules, and force the repair processes to ignore the main engines—and anything we don't need to stay alive for the next six days—then the simulations say we may have a chance of recovering auxiliary steering and attitude control before we hit the ten thousand kilometre mark. Neutralise the drift, and reverse it enough to get away from this monster. *Then* worry about getting back home. And even if we can't get the main engines running again, we can eventually transmit a request for assistance, then just sit here."

"They'd have to answer us," I said.

"Of course."

"Have you . . . initiated this change in the schedule?"

He nodded earnestly. "Yes. Given how slim the margins are, I felt it best to make the change immediately."

"It was the right thing to do, Struma. You've given us a chance. We'll take it to the passenger-representatives. Maybe they'll forgive me for what happened with the suit."

"You couldn't have guessed, Captain. But this lifeline . . . it's just a chance, that's all. The repair schedules are estimates, not hard guarantees."

"I know," I said, patting him on the shoulder. "And I'll take them for what they are."

I went to interview Magadis again, deciding for the moment to withhold the news Struma had given me. The Conjoiner woman was still under armed guard, still bound to the chair. I took my seat in the electrostatic cage, facing her.

"We're going to die," I said.

"This is not news," Magadis answered.

"I mean, not in the way we expected. A clean collision with the surface—fast and painless. I'm not happy about that, but I'll gladly take it over the alternative."

"Which is?"

"Slow torture. I fired an instrument probe at the object—a suit stuffed full of sensors."

"Was that wise?"

"Perhaps not. But it's told me what we can expect. Spacetime around the sphere is . . . curdled, fractal, I don't know what. Restructured. Responsive. It didn't like the suit. Pulled it apart like a rag doll. It'll do the same to the ship, and us inside it. Only we're made of skin and bone, not hardware. It'll be worse for us, and slower, because the suit was travelling quickly when it hit the altered spacetime. We'll take our time, and it'll build and build over hours."

"I could teach you a few things about pain management," Magadis said. "You might find them useful."

I slapped her across the face, drawing blood from her already swollen lip.

"You were prepared to meet this object. You knew of its prior existence. That means you must have had a strategy, a plan."

"I did, until our plan met your resistance." She made a mangled smile, a wicked, teasing gleam in her one good eye. I made to slap her again, but some cooler part of me stilled my hand, knowing how pointless it was to inflict pain on a Conjoiner. Or to imagine that the prospect of pain, even drawn out over hours, would have any impact on her thinking.

"Give me something, Magadis. You're smart, even disconnected from the others. You tried to commandeer the ship. Your people designed and manufactured some of its key systems. You must be able to suggest something that can help our chances."

"We have gathered our intelligence," she told me. "Nothing else matters now. I was always going to die. The means don't concern me."

I nodded at that, letting her believe it was no more or less than I had expected.

But I had more to say.

"You put us here, Magadis—you and your people. Maybe the others will see things the same way you do—ready and willing to accept death. Do you think they will change their view if I start killing them now?"

I waited for her answer, but Magadis just looked at me, nothing in her expression changing.

Someone spoke my title and name. I turned from the prisoner to find Struma, waiting beyond the electrostatic cage.

"I was in the middle of something."

"Before it failed, the suit picked up an echo. We've only just teased it out of the garbage it was sending back in the last few moments."

"An echo of what?" I asked.

Struma drew breath. He started to answer, then looked at Magadis and changed his mind.

It was another ship. Shaped like our own—a tapering, conic hull, a sharp end and a blunter end, two engines on outriggers jutting from the widest point—but smaller, sleeker, darker. We could see that it was damaged to some degree, but it occurred to me that it could still be of use to us.

The ship floated eight thousand kilometres from the surface of the object. Not orbiting, since there was nothing to hold it on a circular course, but just stopped, becalmed.

Struma and I exchanged thoughts as we waited for the others to re-convene.

"That's a Conjoiner drive layout," he said, sketching a finger across one of the blurred enhancements. "It means they made it, they sent it here—all without anyone's knowledge, in flagrant violation of the Europe Accords. And it's no coincidence that we just found it. The object's the size of a star, and we're only able to scan a tiny area of it from our present position. Unless there are floating wrecks dotted all around this thing, we must have been brought close to it deliberately."

"It explains how they knew of the object," I mused. "An earlier expedition. Obviously it failed, but they must have managed to transmit some data back to one of their nests—enough to make them determined to get a closer look. I suppose the idea was to rendezvous and recover any survivors, or additional knowledge captured by that wreck." My fingers tensed, ready to form a fist. "I should ask Magadis."

"I'd give up, if I were you. She's not going to give us anything useful."

"That's because she's resigned to death. I didn't tell her about the revised repair schedule."

"That's still our best hope of survival."

"Perhaps. But I'd be remiss if I didn't explore all other possibilities, just in case the repair schedule doesn't work. That ship's too useful a prize for me to ignore. It's an exploratory craft, obviously. Unlike us, it may have a shuttle, something we can use as a tug. Or we can use the ship itself to nudge the *Equinoctial.*"

Struma scratched at his chin. "Nice in theory, but it's floating well inside the point where the suit started picking up strange readings. And even if we considered it wise to go there, we don't have a shuttle of our own to make the crossing."

"It's not wise," I admitted. "Not even sane. But we have the inspection pods, and one of them ought to be able to make the crossing. I'm ready to try, Struma. It's better than sitting here thinking of ways to hurt Magadis, just to take my mind off the worse pain ahead for the rest of us."

He considered this, then gave a grave, dutiful nod. "Under the circumstances, I think you're right. But I wouldn't allow you to go out there on your own."

"A Captain's prerogative . . ." I started.

"Is to accept the assistance of her second-in-command."

Although I was set on my plan, I still had to present it to the other officers and passenger-representatives. They sat and listened without question, as I explained the discovery of the other ship and my intention of scavenging it for our own ends.

"You already know that we may be able to reverse the drift. I'm still optimistic about that, but at the same time I was always told to have a back-up plan. Even if that other ship doesn't have anything aboard it that we can use, they may have gathered some data or analysis that can be of benefit to us."

Doctor Grellet let out a dry, hopeless laugh. "Whatever it was, it was certainly of benefit to them."

"A slender hope's better than none at all," I said, biting back on my irritation. "Besides, it won't make your chances any worse. Even if Struma and I don't make it back from the Conjoiner ship, my other officers are fully capable of navigating the ship, once we regain auxiliary control."

"The suit drew a response from the object," Grellet said. "How can you know what will happen if you approach it in the pods?"

"I can't," I said. "But we'll stop before we get as deep as the suit did. It's the best we can do, Doctor." I turned my face to the other passenger-representatives, seeking their tacit approval. "Nothing's without risk. You accepted risk when you consigned yourselves into the care of your reefersleep caskets. As it stands, we have a reasonable chance of repairing the ship before we get too close to the object. That's not good enough for me. I swore an oath of duty when I took on this role. You are all precious to me. But also I have twenty thousand other passengers to consider."

"You mean nineteen thousand," corrected Chajari diplomatically. "The Conjoiners don't count any more—sleeping or otherwise."

"They're still my passengers," I told her.

No plan was ever as simple as it seemed in the first light of conception. The inspection pods had the range and fuel to reach the drifter, but under normal operation it would take much too long to get there. If there were something useful on the Conjoiner wreck I wanted time to examine it, time to bring it back, time to make use of it. I also did not want to have to depend on some hypothetical shuttle or tractor to get us back. That meant retaining some reserve fuel in the pods for a return trip to the *Equinoctial*. Privately, if my ship was going down then I wanted to be aboard when it happened.

There was a solution, but it was hardly a comfortable one.

Running the length of the *Equinoctial* was a magnetic freight launcher, designed for ship-to-ship cargo transfer. We had rarely used it on previous voyages and since we were travelling with only a low cargo manifest I had nearly forgotten it was there at all. Fortunately, the inspection pods were easily small enough to be attached to the launcher. By being boosted out of the ship on magnetic power, they could complete the crossing in a shorter time and save some fuel for the round-trip.

There were two downsides. The first was that it would take time to prepare the pods for an extended mission. The second was that the launcher demanded a punishing initial acceleration. That was fine for bulk cargo, less good for people. Eventually we agreed on a risky compromise: fifty gees, sustained for four seconds, would give us a final boost of zero point two kilometres per second. Hardly any speed at all, but it was all we could safely endure if we were going to be of any use at the other end of the crossing. We would be unconscious during the launch phase and much of the subsequent crossing, both to conserve resources and spare us the discomfort of the boost.

Slowly the *Equinoctial* was rotated and stabilised, aiming itself like a gun at the Conjoiner wreck. Lacking engine power, we did this with gyroscopes and controlled pressure venting. Even this took a day. Thankfully the aim didn't need to be perfect, since we could correct for any small errors during the crossing itself.

Six days had now passed since my revival, halving our distance to the surface. It would take another three days to reach the Conjoiner ship, by which time we would have rather less than three days to make any use of its contents. Everything was now coming down to critical margins of hours, rather than days.

I went to see Magadis before preparing myself for the departure.

"I'm telling you my plans just in case you have something useful to contribute. We've found the drifter you were obviously so keen on locating. You've been going behind our backs all this time, despite all the assurances, all the wise platitudes. I hope you've learned a thing or two from the object, because you're going to need all the help you can find."

"War was only ever a question of time, Captain Bernsdottir."

"You think you'll win?"

"I think we'll prevail. But the outcome won't be my concern."

"This is your last chance to make a difference. I'd take you with me if I thought I could trust you, if I thought you wouldn't turn the systems of that wreck against me just for the spite. But if there's something you can tell me, something that will help all our chances . . ."

"Yes," she answered, drawing in me a little glimmer of hope, instantly crushed. "There's something. Kill yourselves now, while you have the means to do it painlessly. You'll thank me for it later."

I stepped out of the cage, realising that Doctor Grellet had been observing this brief exchange from a safe distance, his hands folded before him, his expression one of lingering disapproval.

"It was fruitless, I suppose?"

"Were you expecting something more?"

"I am not the moral compass of this ship, Captain Bernsdottir. If you think hurting this prisoner will serve your ends, that is your decision."

"I didn't do that to her. She was bruised and bloodied when she got here."

He studied me carefully. "Then you never laid a hand on her, not even once?"

I made to answer, intending to deny his accusation, then stopped before I disgraced myself with an obvious lie. Instead I met his eyes, demanding understanding rather than forgiveness. "It was a violent, organised insurrection, Doctor. They were trying to kill us all. They'd have succeeded, as well, if my officers and I hadn't used extreme measures."

"In which case it was a good job you were equipped with the tools needed to suppress that insurrection."

"I don't understand."

He nodded at the officer still aiming the excimer rifle at Magadis. It was a heavy, dual-gripped laser weapon—more suited to field combat than shipboard pacification. "I am not much of a historian, Captain. But I took the time to study a little of what happened on Mars. Nevil Clavain, Sandra Voi, Galiana, the Great Wall and the orbital blockade of the first nest . . ."

I cut him off. "Is this relevant, Doctor Grellet?"

"That would depend. My recollection from those history lessons is that the Coalition for Neural Purity discovered that it was very difficult to take Conjoiners prisoner. They could turn almost any weapon against its user. Keeping them alive long enough to be interrogated was even harder. They could kill themselves quite easily. And the one thing you learned never to do was point a sophisticated weapon at a Conjoiner prisoner."

For the second time in nine days I surfaced to brutal, bruising consciousness through layers of confusion and discomfort. It was not the emergence from reefersleep this time, but a much shallower state of sedation. I was alone, pressed into acceleration padding, a harness webbed across my chest. I moved aching arms and released the catch. The cushioning against my spine eased. I was weightless, but still barely able to move. The inspection pod was only just large for a suited human form.

I was alive, and that was something. It meant that I had survived the boost from the *Equinoctial*. I eyed the chronometer, confirming that I had been asleep for sixty six hours, and then I checked the short-range tracker, gratified to find that Struma's pod was flying close to mine. Although we had been launched in separate boosts, there had been time for the pods to zero-in on each other without eating into our fuel budgets too badly.

"Struma?" I asked across the link.

"I'm here, Captain. How do you feel?"

"About as bad as you, I'm guessing. But we're intact, and right now I'll take all the good news I can get. I'm a realist, Struma: I don't expect much to come of this. But I couldn't sit back and do nothing, just hoping for the best."

"I understood the risks," he replied. "And I agree with you. We had to take this chance."

Our pods had maintained a signals lock with the *Equinoctial*. They were pleased to hear from us. We spent a few minutes transmitting back and forth, confirming that we were healthy and that our pods had a homing fix on the drifter. The Conjoiner ship was extremely dark, extremely well-camouflaged, but it stood no chance of hiding itself against the perfect blackness of the surface.

I hardly dared ask how the repair schedule had been progressing. But the news was favourable. Struma's plan to divert the resources had worked well, and all indications were that the ship would regain some control within thirteen hours. That was cutting it exceedingly fine: *Equinoctial* was now only three days' drift from the surface, and only a day from the point where the suit's readings had begun to deviate from normal spacetime. We had done what we could, though—given ourselves a couple of slim hopes where previously there had been none.

Struma and I reviewed our pod systems one more time, then began to burn fuel, slowing down for our rendezvous with the drifter. We could see each other by then, spaced by a couple of kilometres but still easily distinguished from the background stars, pushing glowing tails of plasma thrust ahead of us.

We passed the ten thousand kilometre mark without incident. I felt sore, groggy and dry-mouthed, but that was to be expected after the acceleration boost and the forced sleep of the cruise phase. In all other respects I felt normal, save for the perfectly sensible apprehension anyone would have felt in our position. The pod's instruments were working properly, the sensors and readouts making sense.

At nine thousand kilometres I started feeling the change.

To begin with it was small things. I had to squint to make sense of the displays, as if I was seeing them underwater. I put it down to fatigue, initially. Then the comms link with the *Equinoctial* began to turn thready, broken up with static and dropouts.

"Struma . . ." I asked. "Are you getting this?"

When his answer came back, he sounded as if he was just as far away as the ship. Yet I could see his pod with my own eyes, twinkling to port.

"Whatever the suit picked up, it's starting sooner."

"The surface hasn't changed diameter."

"No, but whatever it's doing to the space around it may have stepped up a notch." There was no recrimination in his statement, but I understood the implicit connection. The suit had provoked a definite change, that ripple that passed through the *Equinoctial*. Perhaps it had signified a permanent alteration to the environment around the surface, like a fortification strengthening its defences after the first strike.

"We go on, Struma. We knew things might get sticky—it's just a bit earlier than we were counting on."

"I agree," he answered, his voice coming through as if thinned-out and Doppler-stretched, as if we were signalling each other from half way across the universe.

At least the pods kept operating. We passed the eight thousand five hundred mark, still slowing, still homing in on the Conjoiner ship. Although it was only a quarter of the size of the *Equinoctial*, it was also the only physical object between us and the surface, and our exhaust light washed over it enough to make it shimmer into visibility, a little flake of starship suspended over a sea of black.

There would be war, I thought, when the news of this treachery reached our governments. Our peace with the Conjoiners had never been less than tense, but such infringements that had happened to date had been minor diplomatic scuffles compared to this. Not just the construction and operation of a secret expedition, in violation of the terms of mutual cooperation, but the subsequent treachery of Magadis's attempted takeover, with such a cold disregard for the lives of the other nineteen thousand passengers. They had always thought themselves better than the rest of us, Conjoiners, and by certain measures they were probably correct in that assessment. Cleverer, faster, and certainly more willing to be ruthless. We had gained from our partnership, and perhaps they had found some narrow benefits in their association with us. But I saw now that it had never been more than a front, a cynical expediency. Behind our backs they had been plotting, trying to leverage an advantage from first contact with this alien presence.

But the first war had pushed them nearly to extinction, I thought. And in the century since they had shared many of their technologies with us—allowing for a risky normalisation in our capabilities. Given that the partnership had worked for so long, why would they risk everything now, for such uncertain stakes?

My thoughts flashed back to Doctor Grellet's parting words about our prisoner. My knowledge of history was nowhere near as comprehensive as his own, but I had no reason to doubt his recollection of those events. It was surely true, what he said about Conjoiner prisoners. So why had Magadis tolerated that weapon being pointed at her, when she could have reached into its systems and made it blow her head off?

Unless she wanted to stay alive?

"Struma . . ." I began to say.

But whatever words I had meant to say died unvoiced. I felt wrong. I had experienced weightlessness and gee-loads, but this was something completely new to me. Invisible claws were reaching through my skin, tugging at my insides—but in all directions.

"It's starting," I said, tightening my harness again, for all the good it would do.

The pod felt the alteration as well. The readouts began to indicate anomalous stresses, outside the framework of the pod's extremely limited grasp of normal conditions. I could still see the Conjoiner ship, and beyond the surface's black horizon the stars remained at a fixed orientation. But the pod thought it was starting to tumble. Thrusters began to pop, and that only made things worse.

"Go to manual," Struma said, his voice garbled one instant, inside my skull the next. "We're close enough now."

Two hundred kilometres to the ship, then one hundred and fifty, then one hundred, slowing to only a couple of hundred metres per second now. The pod was still functioning, still maintaining life-support, but I'd had to disengage all of its high-level navigation and steering systems, trusting to my own ragged instincts. The signal lock from the *Equinoctial* was completely gone, and when I twisted round to peer through the rear dome, the stars seemed to swim behind thick, mottled glass. My guts churned, my bones ached as if they had been shot through with a million tiny fractures. A slow growing pressure sat behind my eyes. The only thing that kept me pushing on was knowing that the rest of the ship would be enduring worse than this, if we did not reverse the drift.

Finally the Conjoiner ship seemed to float out of some distorting medium, becoming clearer, its lines sharper. Fifty kilometres, then ten. Our pods slowed to a crawl for the final approach.

And we saw what we had not seen before.

Distance, the altered space, and the limitations of our own sensors and eyes had played a terrible trick on us. The state of decay was far worse than we had thought from those long-range scans. The ship was a frail wreck, only its bare outline surviving. The hull, engines, connecting spars were present . . . but they had turned fibrous, gutted open, ripped or peeled apart in some places, reduced to lacy insubstantiality in others. The ship looked ready to break apart, ready to become dust, like some fragile fossil removed from its preserving matrix.

For long minutes Struma and I could only stare, our pods hovering a few hundred metres beyond the carcass. All the earlier discomforts were still present, including the nausea. My thoughts were turning sluggish, like a hardening tar. But as I stared at the Conjoiner wreck, nothing of that mattered.

"It's been here too long," I said.

"We don't know."

"Decades . . . longer, even. Look at it, Struma. That's an old, old ship. Maybe it's even older than the Europa Accords."

"Meaning what, Captain?"

"If it was sent here before the agreement, no treaty violation ever happened."

"But Magadis . . ."

"We don't know what orders Magadis was obeying. If any." I swallowed hard, forcing myself to state the bleak and obvious truth. "It's useless to us, anyway. Too far gone for there to be anything we could use, even if I trusted myself to go inside. We've come all this way for nothing."

"There could still be technical data inside that ship. Readings, measurements of the object. We have to see."

"No," I said. "Nothing would have survived. You can see that, can't you? It's a husk. Even Magadis wouldn't be able to get anything out of that now." My heart was starting to race. Besides the nausea, and the discomfort, there was now a quiet, rising terror. I knew I was in a place where simple, thinking organisms such as myself did not belong. "We failed, Struma. It was the right thing to attempt, but there's no sense deluding ourselves. Now we have to pray that the ship can slow itself down without any outside help."

"Let's not give up without taking a closer look, Captain. You said it yourself— we've come this far."

Without waiting for my assent he powered his pod for the wreck. The Conjoiner ship was much smaller than the *Equinoctial*, but still his pod diminished to a tiny bright point against its size. I cursed, knowing that he was right, and applied manual thrust control to steer after him. He was heading for a wide void in the side of the hull, the skin peeled back around it like a flower's petals. He slowed with a pulse of thrust, then drifted inside.

I made one last attempt to get a signal lock from the main ship, then followed Struma.

Maybe he was right, I thought—thinking as hard and furiously as I could, so as to squeeze the fear out of my head. There might still be something inside, however unlikely it looked. A shuttle, protected from the worst of the damage. A spare engine, with its control interface miraculously intact.

Once I was inside, though, I knew that such hopes were forlorn. The interior decay was just as bad, if not worse. The ship had rotted from within, held together by only the flimsiest traces of connective tissue. With my pod's worklights beaming out at full power, I drifted through a dark, enchanted forest made of broken and buckled struts, severed floors and walls, shattered and mangled machinery.

I was just starting to accept the absolute futility of our expedition when something else occurred to me. There was no sign of Struma's pod. He had only been a few hundred metres ahead of me when he passed out of sight, and if nothing else I should have picked up the reflections from his worklights and thrusters, even if I had no direct view of his pod.

But when I dimmed my own lights, and eased off on the thruster pod, I fell into total darkness.

"Struma," I said. "I've lost you. Please respond."

Silence.

"Struma. This is Rauma. Where are you? Flash your lights or thrusters if you can read me."

Silence and darkness.

I stopped my drift. I must have been halfway into the innards of the Conjoiner ship, and that was far enough. I turned around, rationalising his silence. He must have gone all the way through, come out the other side, and the physical remains of the ship must be blocking our communications.

I fired a thruster pulse, heading out the way I had come in. The ruined forms threw back milky light. Ahead was a flower-shaped patch of stars, swelling larger. Not home, not sanctuary, but still something to aim for, something better than remaining inside the wreck.

I saw him coming just before he hit. He must have used a thruster pulse, just enough to move out of whatever concealment he had found. When he rammed my pod the closing speed could not have been more than five or six metres per second, but it was still enough to jolt the breath from me and send my own pod tumbling. I gasped for air, fighting against the thickening heaviness of my thoughts to retain some clarity of mind. I crashed into something, collision alarms sounding. A pod was sturdy enough to survive the launch boost, but it was not built to withstand an intentional, sustained attack.

I jabbed at the thruster controls, loosened myself. Struma's pod was coming back around, lit in the strobe-flashes of our thrusters. Each flash lit up a static tableau, pods frozen in mid-space, but from one flash to the next our positions shifted.

I wondered if there was any point reasoning with him.

"Struma. You don't have to do this. Whatever you think you're going to achieve . . ." But then a vast and calm understanding settled over me. It was almost a blessing, to see things so clearly. "This was staged, somehow. This whole takeover attempt. Magadis . . . the others . . . it wasn't them breaking the terms of the Accord, was it?"

His voice took on a pleading, reasoning tone.

"We needed this intelligence, Rauma. More than we needed them, and certainly more than we needed peace."

Our pods clanged together. We had no weapons beyond mass and speed, no defences beyond thin armour and glass.

"Who, Struma? Who do you speak for?"

"Those who have our better interests in mind, Rauma. That's all you need to know. All you *will* know, shortly. I'm sorry you've got to die. Sorry about the others, too. It wasn't meant to be this bad."

"No government would consent to this, Struma. You've been misled. Lied to."

He came in again, harder than before, keeping thruster control going until the moment of impact. I blacked out for a second or ten, then came around as I drifted to a halt against a thicket of internal spars. Brittle as glass, they snapped into drifting, tumbling whiskers, making a dull music as they clanged and tinkled against my hull.

A fissure showed in my forward dome, pushing out little micro-fractures.

"They'd have found out about the wreck sooner or later, Rauma—just as we did. And they'd have found a way to get here, no matter the costs."

"No," I said. "They wouldn't. Maybe once, they'd have been that ruthless—as would we. But we've learned to work together, learned to build a better world."

"Console yourself. When I make my report, I'll ensure you get all the credit for the discovery. They'll name the object after you. Bernsdottir's Object. Bernsdottir's Shroud. Which would you prefer?"

"I'd prefer to be alive." I had to raise my voice over the damage alarm. "By the way, how do you expect to make a report, if we never get home?"

"It's been taken care of," Struma said. "They'll accept my version of events, when

I return to the *Equinoctial*. I'll say you were trapped in here, and I couldn't help you. I'll make it sound suitably heroic."

"Don't go to any trouble on my account."

"Oh, I wouldn't. But the more they focus on you, the less they'll focus on me."

He rammed me one more time, and I was about to try and dive around him when I let my hands drift from the thruster controls. My pod sailed on, careening into deepening thickets of ruined ship. I bounced against something solid, then tumbled on.

"You'd better hope that they manage to stop the drift."

"Perhaps they will, perhaps they won't. I don't need the ship, though. There's a plan—a contingency—if all else were to fail. I abandon the ship. Catapult myself out of harm's way in a reefersleep casket. I'll put a long-range homing trace on it. Out between the stars, the casket will have no trouble keeping me cold. Eventually they'll send another ship to find me."

More thruster flashes, but not from me. For an instant the sharp, jagged architecture of this place was laid stark. Perhaps I saw a body somewhere in that chaos, stirred from rest by our rude intrusion, tumbling like a doll, a fleshless, sharp-crested skull turning its blank eyes to mine.

"I'm glad you trust your masters that well."

"Oh, I do."

"Who are they, Struma? A faction within the Demarchists? One of the non-aligned powers?"

"Just people, Rauma. Just good, wise people with our long-term interests in mind."

Struma came in again, lining up for a final ram. He must have heard that damage alarm, I thought, and took my helpless tumble as evidence that I had suffered some final loss of thruster control.

I let him fall closer. He picked up speed, his face seeming to swell until it filled his dome. His expression was one of stony resolve, filled more with regret than anger. Our eyes must have met in those last strobe-lit instants, and perhaps he saw something in my own face, some betrayal of my intentions.

By then, though, it would have been much too late.

I jammed my hands back onto the controls, thrusting sideways, giving him no time to change his course. His pod slid into the space where mine had been only an instant earlier, and then onward, onto the impaling spike of a severed spar. It drove through armour, into Struma's chest, and in the flicker of my own thrusters I watched his body undergo a single violent convulsion, even as the air and life raced from his lungs.

Under better circumstances, I would have found a way to remove his body from that wreck. Whatever he had done, whatever his sins, no one deserved to be left in that place.

But these were not better circumstances, and I left him there.

Of the rest, there isn't much more I need to tell you. Few things in life are entirely black and white, and so it was with the repair schedule. It completed on time, and *Equinoctial* regained control. I was on my way back, using what remained of my fuel, when they began to test the auxiliary engines. Since they were shining in my direction, I had no difficulty making out the brightening star that was my ship. Not much was being asked of it, I told myself. Surely now it would be possible to undo the drift, even reverse it, and begin putting some comfortable distance between the *Equinoctial* and the object.

As my pod cleared the immediate influence of the surface, I regained a stable signal and ranging fix on the main ship. Hardly daring to breathe, I watched as her drift was reduced by a factor of five. At ten metres per second a human could have outpaced her. It was nearly enough—tantalising close to zero.

Then something went wrong. I watched the motors flicker and fade. I waited for them to restart, but the moment never came. Through the link I learned that some fragile power coupling had overloaded, strained beyond its limits. Like everything else, it could be repaired—but only given time that we did not have. The *Equinoctial's* rate of drift had been reduced, but not neutralised. Our pods had detected changes at nine thousand kilometres from the surface. At its present speed, the ship would pass that point in four days.

We did not have time.

I had burned almost all my fuel on the way back from the wreck, leaving only the barest margin to rendezvous with the ship. Unfortunately that margin proved insufficient. My course was off, and by the time I corrected it, I did not have quite enough fuel to complete my rendezvous. I was due to sail past the ship, carrying on into interstellar space. The pod's resources would keep me alive for a few more days, but not enough for anyone to come to my rescue, and eventually I would freeze or suffocate, depending on which got me first. Neither option struck me as very appealing. But at least I would be spared the rending forces of the surface.

That was not how it happened, of course.

My remaining crew, and the passenger-representatives, had decreed that I should return to the ship. And so the *Equinoctial's* alignment was trimmed very carefully, using such steering control as the ship now retained, and I slid back into the maw of the cargo launcher. It was a bumpy procedure, reversing the process that had boosted me out of the ship in the first place, and I suffered concussion as the pod was recaptured by the launch cradle and brought to a punishing halt.

But I was alive.

Doctor Grellet was the first face I saw when I returned to awareness, lying on a revival couch, sore around the temples, but fully cognizant of what had happened.

My first question was a natural one.

"Where are we?"

"Two days from the point where your pods began to pick up the altered spacetime." He spoke softly, in the best bedside manner. "Our instruments haven't picked up anything odd just yet, but I'm sure that will change as we near the boundary."

I absorbed his news, oddly resentful that I had not been allowed to die. But I forced a captain-like composure upon myself. "It took until now to revive me?"

"There were complications. We had to put you into the auto-surgeon, to remove a bleed on the brain. There were difficulties getting the surgeon to function properly. I had to perform a manual override of some of its tasks."

No one else was in the room with me. I wondered where the rest of my executive staff were. Perhaps they were busy preparing the ship for its last few days, closing logs and committing messages and farewells to the void, for all the hope they had of reaching anyone.

"It's going to be bad, Doctor Grellet. Struma and I got a taste of it, and we were still a long way from the surface. If there's nothing we can do, then no one need be conscious for it."

"They won't be," Doctor Grellet said. "Only a few of us are awake now. The rest have gone back into reefersleep. They understand that it's a death sentence, but at least it's painless, and some sedatives can ease the transition into sleep."

"You should join them."

"I shall. But I wanted to tell you about Magadis first. I think you will find it interesting."

When I was ready to move Doctor Grellet and I made our way to the interrogation cell. Magadis was sitting in her chair, still bound. Her head swivelled to track me as I entered the electrostatic cage. In the time since I had last seen her the swelling around her bad eye had begun to reduce, and she could look at me with both eyes.

"I told the guard to stand down," Doctor Grellet said. "He was achieving nothing, anyway."

"You told me about the prisoners on Mars."

He gave a thin smile. "I'm glad some of that sunk in. I didn't really know what to make of it at the time. Why hadn't Magadis turned that weapon on herself, or simply reached inside her own skull to commit suicide? It ought to have been well within her means."

"Why didn't you?" I asked her.

Magadis levelled her gaze at Doctor Grellet. Although she was still my prisoner, her poise was one of serene control and dominance. "Tell her what you found, Doctor."

"It was the auto-surgeon," Grellet said. "I mentioned that there were problems getting it to work properly. No one had expected that it would need to be used again, I think, and so they had taken no great pains to clear its executive memory of the earlier workflow."

"I don't understand," I said.

"The auto-surgeon had been programmed to perform an unusual surgical task, something far outside its normal repertoire. Magadis was brought out of reefersleep, but held beneath consciousness. She was put into the auto-surgeon. A coercive device was installed inside her."

"It was a military device," Magadis said, as detached as if she were recounting something that had happened to someone else entirely, long ago and far away. "An illegal relic of the first war. A Tharsis Lash, they called it. Designed to override our voluntary functions, and permit us to be interrogated and serve as counter-propaganda mouthpieces. While the device was installed in me, I had no volition. I could only do and say what was required of me."

"By Struma," I said, deciding that was the only answer that made any sense.

"He was obliged to act alone," Magadis answered, still with that same icy calm. "It was made to look like an attempted takeover of your ship, but no such thing was ever attempted. But we had to die, all of us. No knowledge of the object could be allowed to reach our mother nests."

"I removed the coercive device," Doctor Grellet said. "Of course, there was resistance from your loyal officers. But they were made to understand what had happened. Struma must have woken up first, then completed the work on Magadis. Struma then laid the evidence for an attempted takeover of the ship. More Conjoiners were brought out of reefersleep, and either killed on the spot or implanted with cruder versions of the coercive devices, so that they were seen to put up a convincing fight. The other officers were revived, and perceived that the ship was under imminent threat. In the heat of the emergency they had no reason to doubt Struma."

"Nor did I," I whispered.

"It was vital that the Conjoiners be eliminated. Their cooperation was required for the existence and operation of this ship, but they could not be party to the discovery and exploration of the object."

"What about the rest of us?" I asked. "We were all part of it. We'd have spoken, when we got back home."

"You would have accepted Struma's account of the Conjoiner takeover, as you very nearly did. As I did. But it was a mistake to put her under armed guard, and another mistake to allow me a close look at that auto-surgeon. I suppose we can't blame Struma for a few slips. He had enough to be concentrating on."

"You were worried about war," Magadis said evenly. "Now it may still happen. But the terms of provocation will be different. A faction inside one of your own planetary governments engineered this takeover bid." She held her silence for a few moments. "But I do not want war. Do you believe in clemency, Rauma Bernsdottir?"

"I hope so."

"Good." And Magadis stood from her chair, her bindings falling away where they had clearly never been properly fastened. She took a step nearer to me, and in a single whiplash motion brought her arm up to my chin. Her hand closed around my jaw. She held me with a vicelike force, squeezing so hard that I felt my bones would shatter. "I believe in clemency as well. But it takes two to make it work. You struck me, when you thought I was your prisoner."

I stumbled back, crashing against the useless grid of the electrostatic cage. "I'm sorry."

"Are you, Captain?"

"Yes." It was hard to speak, hard to think, with the pain she was inflicting. "I'm sorry. I shouldn't have hit you."

"In your defence," Magadis said, "you only did it the once. And although I was under the control of the device, I saw something in your eyes. Doubt. Shame." She relinquished her hold on me. I drew quick breaths, fully aware of how easily she could still break me. "I'm minded to think you regretted your impulse."

"I did."

"Good. Because someone has to live, and it may as well be you."

I reached up and nursed the skin around my jaw. "No. We're finished—all of us. All that's left is reefersleep. We'll die, but at least we'll be under when it happens."

"The ship can be saved," Magadis answered. "And a small number of its passengers.

This will happen. Now that knowledge of the object has been gathered, it must reach civilisation. You will be the vector of that knowledge."

"The ship can't be saved. There just isn't time."

Magadis turned to Doctor Grellet. "Perhaps we should show her, Doctor. Then she would understand."

They took me to one of the forward viewports. Since the ship was still aimed at the object all that was presently visible was a wall of darkness, stretching to the limit of vision in all directions. I stared into that nothingness, wondering if I might catch a glimpse of the Conjoiner wreck, now that we were so much closer. They had asked me very little of what happened to Struma, as if my safe return was answer enough.

Then something flashed. It was a brief, bright scintillation, there and gone almost before it had time to register on my retinae. Wondering if it might have been a trick of the imagination, I stayed at the port until I saw another of the flashes. A little later came a third. They were not happening in the same spot, but clustered near enough to each other not to be accidental.

"You saved us," Doctor Grellet said, speaking quietly, as if he might break some sacred spell. "Or at least, showed us the way. When you and Struma used the cargo launcher to accelerate your pods, there was an effect on the rest of the ship. A tiny but measurable recoil, reducing some of her speed."

"It's no help to us," I said, taking a certain bleak pleasure in pointing out the error in his thinking. "If we had a full cargo manifest, tens of thousands of tonnes, then maybe we could shoot enough of it ahead of the ship to reverse the drift. But we haven't. We're barely carrying any cargo at all."

Another flash twinkled against the surface.

"It's not cargo," Magadis said.

I suppose I understood even then. Some part of me, at least. But not the part that was willing to face the truth.

"What, then?"

"Caskets," Doctor Grellet said. "Reefersleep caskets. Each about as large and heavy as your inspection pod, each still containing a sleeping passenger."

"No." My answer was one of flat denial, even as I knew there was no reason for either of them to lie.

"There are uncertainties," Magadis said. "The launcher is under strain, and its efficiency may not remain optimal. But it seems likely that the ship can be saved with the loss of only half the passenger manifest." Some distant, alien sympathy glimmered in her eyes. "I understand that this is difficult for you, Rauma. But there is no other way to save the ship. Some must die, so that some must live. And you in particular must be one of the living."

The flashes continued. Now that I was attuned to their rhythm, I picked up an almost subliminal nudge in the fabric of the ship, happening at about the same frequency as the impacts. Each nudge was the cargo launcher firing another casket away, the ship's motion reducing by a tiny value. It produced a negligibly small effect. But put several thousand negligibly small things together and they can add up to something useful.

"I won't sanction this," I said. "Not for the sake of the ship. Not murder, not suicide, not self-sacrifice. Nothing's worth this."

"Everything is worth it," Magadis said. "Firstly, knowledge of the artefact—the object—must reach civilisation, and it must then be disseminated. It cannot remain the secretive preserve of one faction or arm of government. It must be universal knowledge. Perhaps there are more of these objects. If there are, they must be mapped and investigated, their natures probed. Secondly, you must speak of peace. If this ship were lost, if no trace of it were ever to return home, there would always be speculation. You must guard against that."

"But you . . ."

She carried on speaking. "They would accept your testimony more readily than mine. But do not think this is suicide, for any of us. It has been agreed, Rauma—by a quorum of the living, both baseline and Conjoiner. A larger subset of the sleeping passengers was brought to the edge of consciousness, so that they could be polled, their opinions weighed. I will not say that the verdict was unanimous . . . but it carried, and with a healthy majority. We each take our chances. The automated systems of the ship will continue ejecting caskets until the drift has been safely reversed, with a comfortable margin of error. Perhaps it will take ten thousand sleepers, or fifteen thousand. Until that point has been reached, the selection is entirely random. We return to reefersleep knowing only that we have a better than zero chance of surviving."

"It's enough," Doctor Grellet said. "As Magadis says, better that one of us survives than none of us."

"It would have suited Struma if you butchered us all," Magadis said. "But you didn't. And even when there was a hope that the repairs could be completed, you risked your life to investigate the wreck. The crew and passengers evaluated this action. They found it meritorious."

"Struma just wanted a good way to kill me."

"The decision was yours, not Struma's. And our decision is final." Magadis's tone was stern, but not without some bleak edge of compassion. "Doctor Grellet and I will return to reefersleep now. Our staying awake was only ever temporary, and we must also submit our lives to chance."

"No," I said again. "Stay with me. Not everyone has to die—you said it yourselves."

"We accepted our fate," Doctor Grellet said. "Now, Captain Bernsdottir you must accept yours."

And I did.

I believed that we had a better than even chance. I thought that if one of us survived, thousands more would also make it back. And that among those sleepers, once they were woken, would be witnesses willing to corroborate my version of events.

I was wrong.

The ship did repair itself, and I did make it back to Yellowstone. As I have mentioned, great pains were taken to protect me from the long exposure to reefersleep. When they brought me back to life, my complications were minimal. I remembered almost all of it from the first day.

But the others—the few thousand who were spared—they were not so fortunate.

One by one they were brought out of hibernation, and one by one they were found to have suffered various deficits of memory and personality. The most lucid among them, those who had come through with the least damage, could not verify my account with the reliability demanded by public opinion. Some recalled being raised to minimal consciousness, polled as to the decision to sacrifice some of the passengers—a majority, as it turned out—but their recollections were vague and sometimes contradictory. Under other circumstances such things would have been put down to revival amnesia, and there would have been no blemish on my name. But this was different. How could I have survived, out of all of them?

You think I didn't argue my case? I tried. For years, I recounted exactly what had happened, sparing nothing. I turned to the ship's own records, defending their veracity. It was difficult, for Struma's family back on Fand. Word reached them eventually. I wept for what they had to bear, with the knowledge of his betrayal. The irony is that they never doubted my account, even as it burned them.

But that saying we had on Fand—the one I spoke of earlier. *Shame is a mask that becomes the face.* I mentioned its corollary, too—of how that mask can become so well-adapted to its wearer that it no longer feels ill-fitting or alien. Becomes, in fact, something to hide behind—a shield and a comfort.

I have come to be very comfortable with my shame.

True, it chafed against me, in the early days. I resisted it, resented the new and contorting shape it forced upon my life. But with time the mask became something I could endure. By turns I became less and less aware of its presence, and then one day I stopped noticing it was there at all. Either it had changed, or I had. Or perhaps we had both moved toward some odd accommodation, each accepting the other.

Whatever the case, to discard it now would feel like ripping away my own living flesh.

I know this surprises you—shocks you, even. That even with your clarity of mind, even with your clear recollection of being polled, even with your watertight corroboration, I would not jump at the chance for forgiveness. But you misjudge me if you think otherwise.

Look out at the city now.

Tower after tower, like the dust columns of stellar nurseries, receding into the haze of night, twinkling with a billion lights, a billion implicated lives.

The truth is, they don't deserve it. They put this on me. I spoke truthfully all those years ago, and my words steered us from the brink of a second war with the Conjoiners. A few who mattered—those who had influence—they took my words at face value. But many more did not. I ask you this now: why should I offer them the solace of seeing me vindicated?

They can sleep with their guilt when I'm dead.

I hear your disbelief. Understand it, even. You've gone to this trouble, come to me with this generous, selfless intention—hoping to ease these final years with some shift in the public view of me. It's a kindness, and I thank you for it.

But there's another saying we used to have on Fand. You'll know it well, I think. *A late gift is worse than no gift at all.*

Would you mind leaving me now?

The Dragon That Flew Out of the Sun

ALIETTE DE BODARD

Aliette de Bodard is a software engineer who lives and works in Paris, where she shares a flat with two Lovecraftian plants and more computers than warm bodies. Only a few years into her career, her short fiction has appeared in Interzone, Asimov's Science Fiction, Clarkesworld, Realms of Fantasy, Orson Scott Card's InterGalactic Medicine Show, Writers of the Future, Coyote Wild, Electric Velocipede, The Immersion Book of SF, Fictitious Force, Shimmer, *and elsewhere, and she has won the British Science Fiction Association Award for her story "The Shipmaker," the Locus Award and the Nebula Award for her story "Immersion" and the Nebula Award for her story "The Waiting Stars." Her novels include* Servant of the Underworld, Harbinger of the Storm, *and* Master of the House of Darts, *all recently reissued in a novel omnibus,* Obsidian and Blood. *Another British Science Fiction Association Award winner,* The House of Shattered Wings, *came out in 2015. Her most recent book is a sequel,* The House of Binding Thorns. *Her website, www.aliettedebodard.com, features free fiction, thoughts on the writing process, and entirely too many recipes for Vietnamese dishes.*

The story that follows is another in her long series of "Xuya" stories, taking place in the far future of an alternate world where a high-tech conflict is going on between spacefaring Mayan, Chinese, and Vietnamese empires. This one deals with the question of who is responsible for a war—never an easy question to answer, and often quite painful to decide.

Here's a story Lan was told, when she was a child, when she lay in the snugness of her sleep-cradle, listening to the distant noises of station life—the thrum of the recycling filters, the soft gurgle of water reconstituted from its base components, the distant noises of the station's Mind in the Inner Rings, a vast unreality that didn't quite concern her, that she couldn't encompass in words.

Mother sat by Lan's side and smiled at her. Her hands smelled of garlic and fish sauce, with the faintest hint of machine oil. Her face was lined with worry; but then, it always was, those days. She wanted to tell a story about Le Loi and the Turtle's Sword, or about the girl who was reborn in a golden calabash and went on to marry the king.

Lan had other ideas.

"Tell me," she said, "about Lieu Vuong Tinh."

For a moment, Mother's face shifted and twisted; she looked as if she'd swallowed something that had stuck in her throat. Then she took a deep breath and told Lan this.

In days long gone by, we used to live in Kinh He on Lieu Vuong Tinh. It was a client state of the Dai Viet Empire, on the edge of the Numbered Planets—its name had come from the willow, because high officials posted there would part from their friends and share a willow branch to remember each other.

But we no longer live there.

Because one day the sun wobbled and quivered over Lieu Vuong Tinh, and grew fainter, and a dragon flew out from its core—large and terrible and merciless, the pearl under its chin shining with all the colours of the rainbow, its antlers carrying fragments of iron and diamond that glistened like the tips of weapons. And, because dragons are water—because they are the spirits of the rain and the monsoon, and the underwater kingdoms—because of that, the sun died.

The dragon had always been there, of course. It was nothing more than an egg at first—a little thing thinner than the chips they use for your ancestors' mem-implants—then the egg hatched and grew into a carp. Carps don't always become dragons, of course, but this one did.

No, I don't know why. Who knows why the Jade Emperor sends down decrees, or why rain happens even when people haven't kept up prayers and propitiations at the shrines? Sometimes, the world is just the way it is.

But when the dragon flew out, its mane unfolded, all the way down to Lieu Vuong Tinh, and into the ships that were fleeing the dying sun—and into the heart of us all, it marked us all, a little nick on the surface like the indent of a carver on jade. That's why, even now, when you meet another Khiet from Lieu Vuong Tinh, you'll instantly know—because it's in their hearts and their bellies and their eyes, the mark of the dragon that will never go away.

"The whole dragon thing is ridiculous," Tuyet Thanh says. "I mean, what did they do, have a little chat and agree to serve us all this load of rubbish?"

They're in the communal network—each of them in their own compartment, except Lan has made the station's Mind merge both spaces in the network, so that Tuyet appears to be sitting at the end of her table, and that the bots-battle they're having in the free-for-all area of space outside the station appears in the middle, as a semi-transparent overlay.

"I don't know," Lan says, cautiously. Tuyet Thanh is older than her by three years, and chafing at the restrictions imposed by older relatives. Lan wants, so badly, to be like her friend, cool and secure and edgy, instead of never knowing what to think on things—because Mother is so often right, isn't she?

"Fine." Tuyet Thanh exhales. She rolls up her eyes, and her bots flow out into a pincer movement—slightly too wide of their reserved area, almost clipping a passing ship. "Deal with this."

Lan considers, for a heartbeat that feels stretched to an eternity—then she sends her bots to drill a hole in the centre of the pincer, where Tuyet Thanh's formation is weaker. "No, but I mean the story is right about one thing, isn't it? The grown-ups—it's like . . ." Adequate words won't come. She makes a gesture with her hand, frustrated—cancels it from the interface, so that the bots don't interpret is as a command. "They're marked. They . . . Have you never noticed they can tell who was on those ships? It's like they have a sensor or something."

"It's just clothes. And language, and the way of behaving." Tuyet Thanh snorts. "A Khiet can tell another Khiet. That's all."

"I guess . . ." Lan says, feeling small, and young, and utterly inadequate.

"Look. There was no dragon. Just . . ."

This is what Second Aunt told me, right? She'd know, because she was twenty-five when they left, and she remembers them well—the years before the war, before the sun.

Anyway. There was the Ro Federation—yes, you're going to tell me they're at peace with the Empire now, that they're all fine people. Whatever. Have you never noticed the adults won't ever talk about them?

In those days, the Ro were our neighbours, and they wanted us gone. They were afraid of us because we were stronger; in the end, they thought that Lieu Vuong Tinh made quite a nice piece of space to have. And one of their—scientists, alchemists—I can't remember exactly what they have out there—made a weapon that they said was going to change the way of things. Just point it at the sun, they said, and you'll see.

And they saw, all right. It . . . it did something, to the atoms that made up the sun—accreted them faster than they should have, so that the star's glow dimmed, and Lieu Vuong Tinh became . . . bombarded. Scoured clean and no longer fit for humans. So that we had to leave, because we no longer had a home.

And the Ro? Yes, today you'll find them on the station, trading us their makings and their technology, as cosy as anything. But they're out there too, in the ruins of Lieu Vuong Tinh, the red-hot slag mess that the Empire abandoned to them when they signed the peace treaty. No humans can go there, but they have bots taking it apart, mining it for precious metals and ice—so that, in the end, they still won everything they hoped for.

Don't look at me like that. It's truth, all right? Not the dragon crap—the thing that truly happened.

Yes. I hate them too.

"Mother?"

Mother looks up from the dumplings she's assembling. She only gets marginal help from the bots, preferring to do everything by hand. Once, she says, everyone would gather in the kitchen, helping others to put together the anniversary feast, but now, in the cramped station compartments, there isn't enough space for that. The aunts and uncles each make their own fraction of dishes, and the meal is shared through the communal network, stitching together the various compartments until it seems like a vast room once more. "Yes, child?"

Lan weighs the words on her tongue, not finding any easy way to bring them up. "Why did you never tell us about the Ro?"

Mother's face doesn't move. It freezes in an intricate and complex expression—it would be a key to the past, if only Lan could interpret it. "Because it's complicated."

"More complicated than the dragon?"

Mother's eyes flick back to the table; the bots take over from her, leaving both her hands free. Her voice is calm, too calm. "Lan—I know you're angry."

"I'm not!" Lan says, and then realises she is. Not even at Mother but at herself, for being stupid enough to believe bedtime stories, for not being more like Tuyet Thanh—smarter and harder and less willing to take things on faith. "Did they do it?"

"The Ro?" Mother sighs. "It was one of their scientists who destroyed the sun, yes. But—"

There are no "buts." "Then it's their fault."

"Don't be so quick to fling blame." Mother says.

"Why shouldn't I?" Because of them—because of the sun—they're here, stuck on the station; in cramped compartments where it seems there's barely enough room to breathe. "Are you making excuses for them?"

Mother is silent for a long, long while. Lan is sure that Tuyet Thanh would have left a long time ago; turned her face to the wall and ramped up the communal network to maximum, trying to fill her ears with sounds she can control. But Mother always has the right words, always does the right thing. Lan clings to this, as desperately as a man adrift in space clings to faint, fading broadcasts. At last she says, "No. I'm not. Merely saying they had their own motives."

"Because they were afraid of us."

"Yes," Mother said. "And people seldom are afraid for no reason, are they?"

Of course they are, all the time. Like they're afraid of Lan in class because she's smarter than them—is there any justification for that? Lan knows prevaricating and false excuses when she hears them—has been she so blind all along? How can she have been so stupid? "Did we do anything to them?" she asks. "Did we?"

Mother's face closes again. "We never did like each other . . . I don't know, child."

"Then we didn't." Lan calls up the communal network, lets it fill her from end to end—blocking out Mother and her feeble excuses. "You were right," she tells Tuyet Thanh. "Adults are idiots."

Today, on the Fourth Day of the Tenth Lunar Month, the Khiet community remembers the Dislocation of Lieu Vuong Tinh, and the Flight of the Evacuation Fleet to the Numbered Planets.

The war between the Khiet and the Ro lasted three years, though it had been brewing for years if not decades. The two had always been uneasy neighbours. While the Khiet rose to prominence with the help of the Dai Viet Empire, to whom they swore allegiance, the Ro were mired under a feudal regime and struggled to survive.

The Khiet's harsh, authoritarian regime had been making the Ro uneasy for a while. The inciting event was the so-called Skiff-Ghost Return, in the year of the Metal Dragon, in which Ro citizens were discovered to have been mind-altered by the Khiet—which set off an ugly, protracted series of skirmishes in which little quarter was given on either side.

The Dai Viet Empire refused to get involved at first, but could not in good conscience continue to do so after the Dislocation. Refugees were so numerous that they had to be scattered to various places among the Numbered Planets—the Mind-controlled Stations on the edge of the Empire taking on the bulk of them. Today, Khiet culture is a vibrant and ubiquitous part of our own culture, nowhere more so than during the anniversary of the Dislocation, when entire communities will gather in large ceremonies to remember the thousands who were lost in the hasty evacuation.

As usual, on the occasion of this anniversary, Scholar Rong Thi Minh Tu, the Voice of the Empress, has extended the Empire's sincere condolences, and their wishes for continued prosperity for the Khiet.

"So . . ." Professor Nguyen Thi Nghe says, pursing her lips. "What am I to make of you?"

"He started it!" The words are out of Lan's mouth before she could think.

Beside her, Vien shifts uncomfortably in his chair—at least he has the decency to look guilty. But then he opens his mouth and says, in Viet with the barest trace of an accent. "I . . . should have phrased my words more carefully. I apologise."

Lan remembers the words like a kick in the gut—the smirking face of him, asking if she was all right, if she'd adapted to life on the station—as if he didn't know, or care, that his people are the reason she was here in the first place. "Professor—" She can't find words for her outrage. "He's Ro."

"Yes." Professor Nghe's voice is quiet, thoughtful. "The Empire and the Khiet signed a peace treaty with the Ro more than thirty years ago, child."

Leaving them the ruins of Lieu Vuong Tinh—not that they would have known what to do with the ruins of what had been their home, but still.

Still, it is wrong. Still, it shouldn't have happened.

"You're my best two pupils," Professor Nghe says. "Your aptitude with bots—the creativity you show when designing them . . ." She shakes her head. "But it's all moot if you can't at least be civil to each other."

"I know," Lan says, sullenly. "But he shouldn't have rubbed it in my face. Not now." It's the anniversary of the Dislocation; soon she will walk home, to Mother's kitchen and the dumplings filled with bitter roots—to the alignment of aunts and uncles that all seem to be in perpetual mourning, as if some spring within them had broken a long time ago.

Vien shifts again, bringing his hands together as if to press a sheet of paper utterly flat. His eyes are pure black, unclouded by any station implants—they say that the station's Mind won't allow the Ro standard access to the communal network, because they cause too many problems. "I didn't mean to." He winces, again, rubbing his hand against the bruise on his cheek. "Yelling at me was fine. The slap . . ."

The slap had been uncalled-for. Mother would have had her hide, truth be told. She didn't like Ro either—Tuyet Thanh was right; none of the exiles had forgiven them, but she would have said it was no call to be uncouth. She—

Lan finds herself rubbing her hand against her cheek, in mute sympathy with Vien. "Forget it," she says, more harshly than she intended to. "I won't do it again. But just stay away from me." She won't talk to him again—she doesn't want to be reminded of his existence, of his people's existence.

Professor Nghe grimaces. "I guess I'll have to be content with that, shall I? Out you go, then."

Outside, Vien turns to Lan, stiff and prim and with the barest hint of a bow. "Listen," he says.

"No."

"I won't bother you again after this."

We didn't mean to do any of it. I realise it's not an excuse, and that it won't mean much to you, but I have to try.

We'd been at war for years by then. You were modifying your own people—sending them to camps and facilities. Have you heard of skiff-ghosts? You were the ones who made them—because the soul went on, down the river to the afterworld, and the body remained, with no awareness or affection. You made thousands of them, and not even for soldiering, merely so they would be obedient citizens.

We . . . we were scared. It wasn't smart, but who knew when you would decide that your own neighbours didn't suitably conform? You've always thought of us as amusing barbarians—with uncombed, uncut hair that we let grow because we won't use scissors on the body that is the flesh of our fathers, the blood of our mothers—and, if you were ready to do this to your own, why should you hesitate with ours?

There was . . . There were incidents. Ro coming back with a little light missing in their eyes, with movements that were a little too stiff. And one of those incidents pushed us over the edge.

I know you're angry. Just let me finish. Please.

Lieu Vuong Tinh was small, and isolated, and we thought it would only be a matter of time. If we sent enough fleets, enough ships, then the Dai Viet Empire wouldn't support you anymore.

But then the war dragged on, and on, and more ships didn't make any difference. Our soldiers bled and died on foreign moons, suffocating in the void of space, felled at the entrances to habitats—and some came back but never the same, emptied of all thoughts and all feelings, a horde of skiff-ghosts pushing and tugging at the fabric of our life until it unravelled. So, a man named Huu Quang had an idea for a weapon so powerful that it would end things, once and for all.

I'm not trying to excuse him or the people who funded him. They all went on trial for war crimes, after the peace treaty was finally signed. We all saw what happened to the sun. We all saw the ships, and the fleet, and what happened to those who didn't manage to leave in time. We—

I'm sorry, all right? I know it doesn't make a difference. I know that I wasn't even born, back then, but it was a stupid, unforgivable thing to do. Most of us know it.

We're not monsters.

Lan stands, breathing hard—staring at Vien, who hasn't moved. She's raised her hand again, and he watches her with those impossible black eyes, the ones that are too deep, that see too many things. She realises, finally, that it's because he's unplugged to most station activity, that he only has the barest accesses to the communal network and therefore so very few community demands on his time. Mother's eyes, Tuyet Thanh's eyes—they always shift left and right, never seem to hold on to anything for long. But Vien . . .

"It's not true," she says, slowly—breathing out, feeling the burning in her lungs. "It's—all a lie."

Vien brings the palms of his hands together, as if he were going to bow. "Everything is a lie," he says, finally. "Everything a fragment of the truth. Don't you have relatives who remember?"

Mother, in the kitchen, saying she didn't know what they had done, and looking away. "I—" Lan breathes in again, everything tinged with the bitterness of ashes. "I don't know," she says, finally. It's the only thing that will come to mind.

"Look it up," Vien says, almost gently. "There's no shortage of things on the network."

Written by the Dai Viet Empire, the hegemony's stories about her own people—what does it mean, if it means anything at all? She's called on the network before she's aware she has—and "skiff-ghosts" brings up all kinds of hollow-eyed, shambling monstrosities in her field of vision. "I don't know," she says, again, and inwardly she's calling for Mother, who is as silent as she ever was. Tales for children. Bedtime stories: the only narratives that can be stomached.

Vien says nothing, merely watches her with a gaze that seems to encompass the entire universe. She'd rage and scream and rant at him, if he did speak, but he doesn't. His mouth is set. "I'll leave you," he says, finally, and walks away, his back ramrod straight, except that in the communal network, a little icon blinks, something he has left her, as a farewell gift. Forgive me—this is all I can give you, on this day of all days, the message says, and Lan archives it, because she cannot bear to deal with him or the Ro.

At home, Mother is waiting for her. The compartment smells of meat and spices and garlic. Everyone else is shimmering into existence, the entire family gathering around the meal for the ancestors, for the dead planet. "Child?"

Lan wants to ask about skiff-ghosts and the Ro, but the words seem too large, too inappropriate to get past the block in her mouth.

Instead, she sits down in silence at her appointed place, reaching for a pair of chopsticks and a bowl. As the Litany of the Lost begins, and the familiar names light up in her field of vision—the ones who are still there, still dust among the dust of Lieu Vuong Tinh—she finds herself reaching for Vien's gift and opening it.

A blur, and a jumble of rocks; then the view pans out, and she sees a scattering of rocks of all sizes tumbling in slow motion, and bots weaving in and out like a swarm of bees, lifting off with dust and fragments of rock in their claws.

The view pans out again, until it seems to rise from behind the bots, slowly filling her entire field of vision—a corona of light and ionised gases, a mass of contracting colours like a stilled heart; a slow, stately dance of clouds and interstellar dust, blurred like the prelude to tears.

A live link to a bot-borne camera; a window into an area of space she's never gone to but instantly recognises.

What else could it be, after all?

Lieu Vuong Tinh: what is left of the planet, what the Ro are scavenging from the radiation-soaked areas. The place her people came from, the place her people fled, with the weight of the dying sun like ghosts on their backs.

Ghosts.

She wonders about the dead, and the skiff-ghosts—and mind-alterations and who bears what, in the mess of the war—and who, ultimately, is right, and justified.

The grit of dust against her palate, and the slow, soundless whistle of spatial winds—and, abruptly, it no longer matters, because she sees it.

The dragon's mane streams in the solar winds, a shining star at the point of each antler; the serpentine body stretched and pockmarked with fragments of rock; the pearl in its mouth a fiery, pulsing point of light; its tail streaming ice and dust and particles across the universe like the memory of an expelled breath—and its eyes, two pits of utter darkness against the void of space, a gaze turning her way and transfixing her like thrown swords.

The mark. The wound. The hole in the heart that they all want to fill, she and Tuyet Thanh and Mother—and Vien—all united in the wake of the dragon's passage like farmers huddled in the wake of a storm, grieving for flooded fields and the lost harvest, and bowed under the weight of all that they did to one another.

Mother is right, after all. This is the only story of the war that will ever make sense—the only truth that is simply, honestly, heartbreakingly bearable.

waiting out the end of the world in patty's place cafe

NAOMI KRITZER

Here's an affecting story that is about just what it says it's about. . . .

Naomi Kritzer won the 2016 Hugo Award for Best Short Story for her story "Cat Pictures Please," which originally appeared in Clarkesworld. *(She also won the Locus Award for this story and was nominated for the Nebula Award.) This was her fourth appearance in* Clarkesworld. *Her short stories have also appeared in* Asimov's Science Fiction, Analog Science Fiction and Fact, The Magazine of Fantasy & Science Fiction, Lightspeed, *and* Apex Magazine, *as well as various anthologies. Her early novels remain available from Bantam; she also has a short story collection forthcoming in July 2017 from Fairwood Press, and as of this month, she is working on a new novel—about the AI from "Cat Pictures Please" and its teenage sidekick—for Tor Teen. She maintains a website at naomikritzer.com.*

I ran out of gas in Belle Fourche, South Dakota, just 200 miles short of Pierre, my goal. Pierre, South Dakota, I mean, I wasn't trying to get to someone named Pierre. I was trying to get to my parents, and Pierre was where they lived. I thought maybe, given that the world was probably ending in the next 24 hours, they'd want to talk to me.

I'd taken back roads almost the whole way from Spokane, hoping to avoid the traffic jams. I also figured that out-of-the-way gas stations would run out of gas less quickly. That turned out to be true for a while. The problem was that the back-roads gas stations weren't getting deliveries, either. The last gas I'd found was in Billings. If they'd let me fill up, I might have been able to make it all the way to Pierre on that tank, but the owner, who was overseeing the line with a large gun hanging over his shoulder, was only letting people buy eight gallons per car. Admittedly, that was probably the only reason they weren't completely out.

I turned my car off and checked my map. Belle Fourche was just 12 miles from I-90. I didn't know exactly how much gas I still had, but the low fuel light had been on for a while and I wasn't sure I could make it that far. I tried calling the gas stations along the interstate, but of course no one was picking up. If you had 16 hours left to live, would you spend that time working at a gas station?

I rubbed my eyes, numb with fatigue and fear. If nothing else, maybe I could find somewhere in Belle Fourche to get coffee.

Subway and Taco John's had fallen victim to the "would you go to your job if you maybe had 16 hours left to live" problem, but I saw the lights on in Patty's Place, a wood-framed building with a sign out front advertising REAL BBQ EVERYDAY, RIBS THURS NITE. The sign said to seat yourself. I looked around and finally spotted an empty spot in a corner by the window. Even just sitting down in a seat that didn't have a steering wheel in front of it made me realize how exhausted I was. Possibly I should have taken a few more naps. Or a longer nap at some point.

There was a TV in the corner with CNN on. The talking heads were arguing the asteroid's projected trajectory, and whether the worst-case scenarios were actually too grim. The asteroid that killed the dinosaurs was probably 10 km across. This one was 4.36 km. Big enough to cause devastating damage, but the scientist on the left thought it might just wipe out coastal cities but allow the inland areas to rebuild. The other scientist thought that encouraging people to migrate inland before the strike was a terrible idea because people were dying in their desperate attempts to escape the coasts, and this was completely unnecessary if the asteroid missed us. And if it didn't, anyone who survived the strike would die in the fifty-year famine caused by the dust cloud blocking out all sunlight. "Seriously, folks, just hunker down wherever and wait to see what happens," he said. "And hey, if we survive this, maybe consider re-opening the Arecibo Observatory, if it hadn't lost funding we'd be able to map the trajectory—" His voice was rising, furious.

"Coffee, hon?"

I looked up at the waitress. "Yeah, thanks. And thanks for coming to work."

She poured me a mug of coffee. "I'm actually Patty, the owner. I figured I might as well come in and feed people as stay home feeling sorry for myself. Do you know what you want? I should warn you we're out of a few things."

"I think I feel like breakfast," I said.

"I can bring you a big plate of pancakes and syrup. We're out of bacon and sausage. If you want eggs, we're down to those cartons of just egg whites but we could make those into an omelet for you."

"Pancakes and syrup sounds good," I said.

"You come far?"

"From Spokane. I'm trying to get to Pierre but I ran out of gas."

I leaned my head against the window and closed my eyes. Maybe someone else was heading east, and I could beg a ride from them. Maybe someone in town would sell me the gas out of the car in their garage. Maybe maybe maybe. I wasn't really in any shape to drive any farther. Pierre was just a couple hours away, and there was a Super 8 across the street; maybe I could get a room and nap for a few hours before I tried driving any farther. It was probably just as well if I got home right before the impact, if I wanted Mom to talk to me.

The coffee was exactly like I remembered South Dakota coffee. Dip a bean three times in the hot water and call it good.

"Hon, can I put two more people at your table? Your food's going to be a while but I'll keep the coffee coming."

I opened my eyes and looked up at Patty, and the two people standing behind her. "Sure." They slid into the booth across from me.

They were an older couple. Well, middle-aged, I guess. The man had white hair; the woman had reddish hair.

"You look like you've been driving for a while," the woman said, sympathetically. "You can go back to your nap, if you want."

It felt a little too uncivilized to ignore people sitting across from me, and besides, Patty had refilled my coffee. "My name's Lorien," I said. "Or Kathleen. I mean, Kathleen's the name my parents gave me."

The couple exchanged a look I couldn't quite untangle, and I tried to sit up a little straighter. "I'm Robin," the woman said. "And this is Michael. And if Lorien's your name, it doesn't really matter to me what your parents called you."

"It's kind of out of *Lord of the*—"

"You're among nerds," Robin said. "We got it."

Michael was looking at the menu. "I wonder if they'll have the caramel rolls," he said. "There was a picture of the caramel roll in one of the reviews, but I bet everyone's wanted caramel rolls . . ."

"That seems likely," Robin said. "Have you eaten anything here, Lorien?"

I shook my head. "I ordered pancakes but they haven't come yet."

Patty came by. They were indeed out of caramel rolls but they had a caramel bread pudding. They were also out of hamburger buns, although they could offer you a hamburger on sliced bread. Michael ordered a hot turkey sandwich, Robin ordered meatloaf.

"I bet they made the bread pudding out of those hamburger buns," Robin said when Patty had left.

"That seems like a questionable business decision," Michael said.

"I bet they made the bread pudding out of those hamburger buns because someone in the kitchen thought, 'screw good business decisions, I want to eat something sweet and comforting and we're out of caramel rolls.'"

"Are you heading east?" I blurted out. They seemed like really nice people. Like people who might give me a ride.

"Oh, honey, I'm sorry," Robin said. "We're coming from Minnesota and heading to Yellowstone, actually."

"If you're coming from the west, maybe you know where we could find gas?" Michael asked me.

"I haven't found gas since Billings, that was five hours ago, and they're rationing," I said.

"Well, that's promising," Robin said, and pulled out her phone to look up the map. ". . . Totally not on our way, though. Hmm."

"I was really hoping we'd find some here," Michael said.

"Why are you going to Yellowstone?" I asked.

"We've never been there," Michael said. "Figured we might as well go check it out."

"You didn't want to be with family?"

"We said goodbye to my family before we left," Michael said.

"And Michael's family is my family," Robin said. "Family 2.0."

I must have looked a bit shocked, because Robin glanced at Michael and shrugged a little. "This isn't my first Armageddon," she said. "You could say it's my third."

Patty arrived with my pancakes, plus sodas for Robin and Michael. Once the pancakes were in front of me, I realized that I was *ravenous*. Someone had turned up the TV in the corner: a new scientist was on, a guy named Scott Edward Shjefte, who was reminding everyone that in cosmological terms, an asteroid passing between the earth and the moon was a "direct hit" and yet there were 363,104 kilometers for a 4.36 kilometer object to pass through. "Imagine throwing a penny at a football field and trying to miss the 30-yard line. You'd feel pretty good about those odds."

"Not so much if the world was going to end if the penny hit the 30-yard line," the host said. "Besides, this asteroid has already beaten the odds, being spotted so late."

"So it would have to beat the odds twice!" Shjefte said. He sounded committed to this idea, not like he was grasping at straws, but the host didn't look at all convinced.

They agreed again that everything would be better if the Arecibo Observatory was still running, since the radio telescope there could have determined the asteroid's trajectory with actual precision, and also, that the President's order to launch nukes at the asteroid wouldn't have done anything even if they hadn't missed.

"Do you think I'm panicking over nothing?" I said.

Robin looked me over. "How old are you? You look about twenty-five."

"I'm twenty-three."

"My first Armageddon was when I was a little kid, back in the 1970s. Have you ever heard of the Jehovah's Witnesses?"

"Yeah," I said. "They're the people who knock on your door."

"I was raised in the Jehovah's Witnesses, and when I was little, everyone at my church believed that the world was going to end in October of 1977. A lot of the adults sold their houses. My parents didn't, but my father used up all his vacation time to take days off and knock on people's doors." She took a sip of soda and leaned back against her seat. "He used to take me around with him, because people are a little less likely to slam the door on a cute little kid. Only a little, though. It was hard. My Dad used to tell me 'just keep walking, just keep knocking,' that eventually people would listen. That actually stood me in good stead years later when I was trying to get jobs in theater." She looked at me. "Did you grow up in a church?"

"Yeah," I said.

"The kind that believed in the Rapture and stuff?"

"Yeah, but we didn't have a—a date, you know, when everyone thought it would happen. Just, like, soon."

"Are you still a member?"

"No," I said, and ducked my head over my pancakes. After a minute, Robin went on.

"I am a male-to-female transsexual. When I was little, and people would talk about the earthly paradise, I knew I'd receive a resurrected body and anything wrong with it would be miraculously fixed, but I couldn't ask, did that mean I'd get a girl's body? Or that I'd stop *wanting* a girl's body? Because both options were actually terrifying to me at that point. One meant that my parents would find out, since of course they'd be in paradise with me, and the other meant I'd somehow be someone *else*."

I had looked up when she said "transsexual," looking her over without really meaning to. I'd met trans women before, back home in Spokane, and I was looking at her because I was wondering if this should have been obvious to me and I was just *that tired*. There are places where if you meet someone you know they're queer, but a diner in South Dakota isn't really one of them.

"Anyway. The sun rose on November 1st, and all the adults pretended that no one had ever said the world was going to end the previous month. And that was my first Armageddon."

Robin's and Michael's food arrived. "I'm definitely going to want some of the bread pudding," Robin told Patty, "when I'm done with this."

"We've also got a big pineapple upside down cake that's coming out of the oven right now," Patty said.

"Oh, excellent, I'll have that!" Michael said.

"Anyway, you can probably guess why Michael's family is my family," Robin said.

"Did they disown you for being trans?" I asked.

"No, they disowned me for leaving the Jehovah's Witnesses and majoring in Theater and then when I came out as gay that would definitely have been the last straw, only they hadn't spoken to me in years already at that point. Robin is actually my birth name, but I changed my last name after that. My last name is Raianiemi. It was the last name of one of my neighbors. The only lesbian in the town where I grew up."

I couldn't really answer that at all. Patty had refilled my coffee again so I put the mug up where it sort of hid my face and drank coffee.

"My second Armageddon was when I almost died from a mysterious infection about a decade ago," Robin said. "I was in the hospital and they were giving me IV antibiotics but I wasn't responding and they thought I was going to die. I thought I was going to die."

"I feel like calling that an Armageddon is kind of cheating," Michael said. "You thought you were going to die. But in an Armageddon, *everyone* dies."

"I really think the biggest difference is the level of hassle," Robin said. "Each individual thinks they're going to die. The problem is that when it's everybody, this means huge numbers of people don't show up for work, so everyone runs out of gas just as they're trying to make road trips to see loved ones or visit Yellowstone or whatever."

"Did they ever figure out what you had?" I asked.

"Enough that they were able to treat me. But I spent a few days thinking about what I'd most regret, if I died that week, and I knew the thing I'd really regret was never living as my real self. Never living as a woman. The thing was, I had a partner—that's what we called our spouses before we could get legally married, I don't know if kids these days remember that—and I had *no idea* how he would react and he was the love of my life. Coming out the first time, as gay, that was scary. Coming out the second time, as trans? Made me realize just how much scarier it could be."

"But it was okay. Don't forget to tell her that part," Michael said, and squeezed Robin's hand.

"Yeah, it was all okay. Anyway, once you've survived Armageddon twice, a third one rolls around and you say to yourself, 'What would I like to see in case this is it?' and we knew we could get to Yellowstone so we gave all our nieces and nephews a big hug and hit the road."

I'd eaten the last of my pancakes and my coffee cup was empty. Patty hadn't been by in a while.

"We really thought we'd be able to find gas, though," Michael said. "If we stuck to the back roads . . ."

"That was my theory, too," I said. "It worked at first."

"So where are *you* headed?" Robin asked.

"Pierre," I said. "It's where my parents live."

"Do they know you're coming?"

It was an odd question, and I knew I'd betrayed myself, listening to her story. "No," I said. It came out in a whisper.

"When was the last time you and them talked at all?"

"After I graduated college, they were really mad that I wasn't going to move back home."

"That was all it took, huh?" Robin asked.

"Yeah. There's a lot of other stuff they'd be mad about, but they just don't even know about it, unless someone's told them. Which maybe someone has."

"Listen," Robin said. "There are a *lot* of people who will tell you that you have to reconcile with your family, that you only get one, that if you never speak to your parents again this is somehow on *you*, and I am here to tell you that this is *crap*. You don't have to reconcile with your family. You can find a family that accepts you for *who you are* instead of trying to cram you into the box they think you're supposed to live in. And if they choose to reject you, that's on *them*."

"Yeah," I whispered.

Robin pulled some Kleenex out of her purse and handed it to me. I wiped my eyes and looked out the window at the sunny afternoon.

"Just cause they raised you, that doesn't mean you have to give them the opportunity to slam another door in your face," she said.

"I didn't have anyone else to go see," I said. "My girlf—" I choked off the word, then checked myself. "My *girlfriend* and I broke up a few weeks ago and none of my friends out there are super close. I moved to Spokane for a job and I kind of hate it and I thought, 'I should go see my family' and so I went."

I had felt *so alone*, listening to the news in my little apartment. And I'd tried calling home, and they hadn't picked up. So like everyone else, I'd blown off work and hit the road.

What would I regret? "I would regret not reconciling with my family" seemed like an obvious answer, so I'd decided to try.

"Did you pass through Yellowstone on your way east?" Michael asked.

"No," I said. "Even if I'd taken I-90 I'd have passed north of it."

"Want to come see Yellowstone with us?" Robin asked. "It has Old Faithful."

"And a Supervolcano that could blow up at any time," Michael said. "So even if the asteroid misses us completely we could *still* potentially die in a cataclysmic disaster today!"

"You can still say no," Robin said, "because we're going to have to go door-knocking to try to find gas. You be the cute kid and we'll split whatever we can find."

Robin was being generous, because Michael's plan was to offer cash—$10/gallon for whatever they'd let him siphon out, and if they balked at that, he'd try upping it to $20. We walked around Belle Fourche, knocking on doors. Mostly no one answered. We did find one person who was *also* out of gas, which was the only reason she was still in Belle Fourche and not on her way to Cheyenne, Wyoming, to see her grand-daughter, and someone who had a full tank but flat-out refused to sell us any. ("Bank notes won't be worth a damn thing if that asteroid hits. I need a full tank to get out of here, if I have to.")

"I think we're stuck here," Robin said, after we'd been knocking on doors for ninety minutes with no luck.

"That's not the attitude that got you theater jobs," Michael said.

"I'll be honest. At this point, I'm thinking that what I'd like to do with my maybe-last-day-on-earth is *not* knock on doors all afternoon. Let's see the local sights, if there are any."

Belle Fourche's big *thing*, if you can call it that, is the Geographic Center of the United States, which was recalculated by the National Geodetic Survey after the ad-dition of Alaska and Hawaii. (The center of the lower 48 is in Kansas, which is prob-ably about where you'd expect it.) The actual technical true Geographic Center is about twenty miles out of town, but there was a *Monument* with a nice sculpture a mile walk from Patty's Place, so we walked over to the Center of the Nation Monu-ment and I took a picture of Robin and Michael together, and then they took a picture of me.

One of the parks had a playground and there were some families there with kids and dogs. I wondered if the kids knew anything about what was going on. Even if their parents didn't tell them about it, they were probably overhearing stuff from the TV and the radio. Still, they were running around and looking like they weren't worrying about it.

Robin and Michael decided to book a room at the Super 8 and encouraged me to book one, too. "When we don't all die, everyone's going to think, 'oops, didn't die, better find a room,' and you'll be glad you have one. And if we do all die, you won't have to pay your Visa bill." There was an older man working the front desk; I wondered if he was the owner, like Patty. He gave us our keys. I tucked mine in my pocket and then, for lack of anywhere else to go, we walked back across the street to Patty's.

Patty's had gotten more crowded; people were getting tables and just camping out there. But there was an awkward little table for three in a corner she squeezed us into and we ordered more drinks and more food and settled in. "Probably for the duration," Robin admitted.

"A lot of people are doing that," Patty said, looking around. "I'd say it's about half people like you who got stranded here today when they ran out of gas, and half locals who don't want to sit at home. People were coming and going for a while but now they're just coming. No one wants to be alone tonight, I guess."

The asteroid was going to hit, or miss, at 9:34 p.m. Belle Fourche time. It took a little over 3 hours to drive from Belle Fourche to Pierre, so as the clock ticked toward 6 p.m., I knew my decision had more or less been made for me.

But then Patty came bustling over, an older couple in tow. "Are you the girl who was trying to get to Pierre? Because these folks are going to Pierre to see their daughter and they have enough gas they'll probably make it, they think."

"As long as you don't mind dogs," the woman said. "Because you'll have to share the back seat with our two beagles."

"What's the address in Pierre?" the man asked, and punched my parents' address into his phone. "Yeah, that's almost right on our way."

I imagined knocking on my parents' door. Waiting for the answer, like we'd done with all the people we'd tried to buy gas from. My parents' house had a peephole, and you could hear their footsteps inside so you knew they'd come to the door and were peering out at you, deciding whether to open up. I'd know Mom was looking at me, measuring me with her eyes, looking at my short-cropped hair, the frayed collar of my shirt, assessing whether I was penitent. Penitent *enough*.

I could see myself standing on that front step, in the dark, these nice people waiting to see me safe inside, until I had to turn around and admit it wasn't going to open.

Or if it did . . .

What I wanted was to see my parents smile. What I wanted was for them to *welcome* me.

Did I really think that news of an impending asteroid would have changed who my parents were? Who they needed *me* to be?

I turned and looked at Robin and Michael. They gave me hesitant smiles, like they didn't want to discourage me from leaving, but like they were biting their tongues. I could see Robin furrow her brow, like she was imagining the same things I was and they worried her.

I turned back to the people with the beagles. "No, thank you," I said. "That's a very kind offer, but I thought about it and I've decided to stay here for the night. Thanks, though."

They headed out. I settled back into my seat. Robin said, "I'm glad you're staying."

"I'm glad I have someone to stay with," I said.

At 9 p.m. everyone went outside to the parking lot.

It was dark out. Someone from the town had dragged out a box of fireworks left over from last year's 4th of July and everyone took turns lighting them off, including me. (Mom had never let us have fireworks when I was a kid, because we might blow ourselves up, but if there was ever a time for YOLO, it's when there's a 4.3 kilometer asteroid on a collision course for earth.) Some of the stale fireworks fizzled and went out. Others shot up into the sky and gave us a shower of sparkles. Despite how nervous everyone was, things took on a weird, almost festive air. Maybe we were all going to die in a few minutes: might as well enjoy the show until then.

"Do you think we'll be able to see anything before it hits us?" I asked. "What's it going to look like?"

"One of the scientists on the TV said it would look like a tiny star and get bigger, if it was coming towards us. We'll definitely see it coming. But it could hit the other side of the planet, and we'll have no clue."

At 9:34, someone shouted, "There it is."

We could see something moving in the sky. It wasn't very big, but it was definitely moving. Was it getting bigger? I realized I was holding my breath. For a second I thought it *was* getting bigger; a moment later I was sure it wasn't. The slightly-bigger-than-average, slightly-blurry star moved across the sky and disappeared.

There was a long pause, and then we ran back inside the restaurant to see what they were saying on CNN.

The optimistic scientist Shjefte was either back on, or still on. He was jumping up and down—literally jumping up and down, clapping his hands—screaming "it missed, it missed, it missed, it missed, it missed!" So apparently all his optimistic talk about throwing pennies onto a football field was bravado. "I'm going to call all my friends, I'm going to write a book, I'm going to go see *Petra*," he shouted, just before the TV got turned off.

We could hear cheering from the town beyond the restaurant, and more people were setting off fireworks. Robin and Michael kissed like it was New Year's Eve. Someone at the diner had chilled a bunch of bottles of champagne and Patty popped it open, and everyone drank it out of coffee mugs, and we were all a weepy mess for a while.

And then there was a run on hotel rooms, and I was awfully glad that Robin and Michael had suggested I get one early.

"Are you going back to Spokane?"

The gas truck had come and gone: we'd waited until the line had dissipated, then filled up both our gas tanks. I must have been down to about the last quarter-cup, given how much gas I put in.

I looked at Robin. "You know, I thought about how one of the things I'd really regret, if I died, was never seeing New York. My parents acted like it was some sort of den of sin and iniquity when I was growing up, but they were wrong about a lot."

"So wait, are you going to hit the road and drive the rest of the way east?"

I laughed. "I kind of think I should go home and pack up my stuff, give notice on my lease, stuff like that. But I expect I'll be coming back this way in a few months."

"Well, let me give you our address," Robin said. "You can stay with us when you get to Minneapolis."

"This is kind of silly," I said, "but do you mind going back to the Center of the Nation Monument for a minute?"

Someone else was there, so I didn't have to snap a selfie to get a picture of myself *with* Robin and Michael; they took it for me.

The road west was wide open, and I listened to music my parents would have hated the whole way back to Spokane.

the Hunger After You're Fed

JAMES S. A. COREY

James S. A. Corey is the pseudonym of two young writers working together, Daniel Abraham and Ty Franck. Their first novel as Corey, the widescreen space opera Leviathan Wakes, the first in the Expanse series, was released in 2011 to wide acclaim and has been followed by other Expanse novels, Caliban's War, Abaddon's Gate, Cibola Burn, Nemesis Games, and Babylon's Ashes. There's also now a TV series based on the series, The Expanse, on the Syfy channel.

Daniel Abraham lives with his wife in Albuquerque, New Mexico, where he is director of technical support at a local internet service provider. Starting off his career in short fiction, he made sales to Asimov's Science Fiction, SCI FICTION, The Magazine of Fantasy & Science Fiction, Realms of Fantasy, The Infinite Matrix, Vanishing Acts, The Silver Web, Bones of the World, The Dark, Wild Cards, and elsewhere, some of which appeared in his first collection, Leviathan Wept and Other Stories. Turning to novels, he made several sales in rapid succession, including the books of The Long Price Quartet, which consists of A Shadow in Summer, A Betrayal in Winter, An Autumn War, and The Price of Spring. At the moment, he has published five volumes in his new series, The Dagger and the Coin, which consists of The Dragon's Path, The King's Blood, The Tyrant's Law, The Widow's House, and The Spider's War. He also wrote Hunter's Run, a collaborative novel with George R. R. Martin and Gardner Dozois, and, as M. L. N. Hanover, the five-volume paranormal romance series Black Sun's Daughter.

Ty Franck was born in Portland, Oregon, and has had nearly every job known to man, including a variety of fast-food jobs, rock quarry grunt, newspaper reporter, radio advertising salesman, composite materials fabricator, director of operations for a computer manufacturing firm, and part owner of an accounting software consulting firm. He is currently the personal assistant to fellow writer George R. R. Martin, where he makes coffee, runs to the post office, and argues about what constitutes good writing. He mostly loses.

The story that follows takes place in a small near-future Mexican village where an acolyte is obsessively trying to discover the true identity of—and ideally to meet—a famous radical writer who publishes only under an impenetrable pseudonym.

Does Héctor Prima live around here?"

My host's expression went cool. He was a middle-aged man with a wide face and shoulders, and pale stubble on his cheeks and chin that held the promise of a lush beard. In the four hours I'd spent in his home since the evacuated rail from Nove Mesto had deposited me in Malasaña, he'd been nothing but jovial and expansive. His warmth and his pleasure in having a guest lulled me into feeling safe.

I had overplayed my hand.

"Who?" he asked.

"I think he's a writer my sister likes," I said, motioning vaguely. "She said he was in this part of the country somewhere. But I may have that wrong."

"She is mistaken. Héctor Prima is a pen name. There are rumors that he lives here, but they're not true. No one knows who really writes his essays. He could be anyone."

"That's interesting. Is he good?" As if I had not read everything Prima had put on the web. As if I had not read thousands of analyses of his work and speculations on who he might be. As if I were not in a sense a hunter. A stalker. I was driven by an enthusiasm I couldn't explain, except that when I read his words, I recognized the world he described and my own unhappiness in it. Reading Prima felt like being seen.

"He has a following. Strange people. We see them now and again," my host said with a shrug. "We have a great number of writers and artists, you know. We're a very vibrant place, now that the money's come."

"It's why I'm here," I said with a smile, and the warmth was back in his eyes.

"We have rumba bands. Many, many rumba bands. There was a fight three years ago, when two different bands scheduled concerts on the same day. The police had to come in. You heard about that, maybe?"

"I think I did," I lied.

"We are very passionate about our music here," my host said, nodding to himself and watching me to see how I reacted. Whether there was a glimmer of interest in my eyes. It was no different in Nove Mesto. I knew what he wanted.

"Do you play in a band?" I asked.

If he had been pleasant and jovial before, now he became incandescent. "A bit. Only a little. I sing, you know. Here, we've just put together a new album. Let me play it for you, yes?"

"I'd like that," I said.

It was the price of my hunt. I wanted something, and I would accept a great many things I didn't want in order to get it.

How to describe Malasaña at night?

I came from a city that had known want, but only as one guest at a larger table. The richest sections of my home were indistinguishable from the high income districts of Milán and Paris. Even the slums had paving on the roads and water in the taps. Malasaña was approaching the same place in the spectrum of human want from the other direction.

The streets were too narrow for cars. The traffic that passed between the thick-stuccoed buildings consisted of people on foot or riding bicycles, stray dogs watching from the alleyways. The streetlights were built from repurposed emergency solar lamps, bright yellow plastic shaped like downward-facing daisies. Cables hung over the rooftops, piping the power from the day's wind and sunlight stored in hundreds of batteries to the homes and clubs, public kitchens and mud-floored dance halls. Drones hummed overhead carrying glowing advertisements built from recycled medical tablets and luminescent paint. In the doorways and at the corners, children and women held platters, stepping out whenever someone came close.

I have the best flan you've ever tasted. Bean chowder; just try it and you'll never want anything else. Baclava. Curried egg. Always cheap ingredients. Rarely fish. Never meat. Music filled the air like birdsong. Some live, the musicians sweating over print-fab guitars and hammering on drums made from pottery and plastic. Some recorded, but remixed, manipulated, remade with the personality of whoever had speakers loud enough to drown out their neighbors. One club had a child of no more than six standing at the door with a false, practiced grin, grabbing at people's hands and tugging them to come in. The scars of poverty were everywhere, but few of the wounds.

A man in filthy pants and the paper shirt that relief workers hand out sat with his back against a yellow wall, his jaw working in silent but passionate conversation with himself. Another ran down the street shouting after a woman that he hadn't meant to spend it all, and that there would be more next week, and why was she so angry when there was going to be more next week? An old woman swept the street outside her little bodega while the ads in her windows painted her face with blue and pink and blue again.

Basic income had come to Malasaña five years before, freeing it from want, but not, it seemed, from wanting.

I stopped to ask the old woman if I was going the right way and showed her the map on my cell. "I am looking for Julia Paraiis."

She made a sour face, but pointed me down a side street even narrower than the main thoroughfare. "Five down, blue building. Third floor."

I followed her directions, wondering whether it had been wise for me to come so far unaccompanied. But when I knocked at the door on the third floor of the blue building, the woman who answered looked like the one I'd seen on the net.

"What?" she said.

"We talked on the forum," I said.

"You've come about Héctor?" she said.

In answer, I held out my hand, the roll of cash in my palm like an apple. She plucked it from me, her eyes softening.

"You've been saving," she said.

"It's everything I have."

"You have more coming," she said dismissively. "I'll call for you the day after tomorrow."

And like that, it was done. She closed the door, I walked away, turning back toward the street, and my room, and the hope that *this* time I would find him.

We were a community of a sort. The hunters after Héctor. There were more theories of who and where he was than I could count. I'd looked for him in Rome and Nice. Évora. I'd worked cleaning out brambles and hauling contaminated gravel from an old power plant for extra money to fund my dream of sitting across from the man, of telling him how much his words meant to me. Of breathing the same air.

Malasaña had always been one of the possibilities, but never the most likely. I had shared neither my growing suspicions of it nor of my searches outside of the community on the forums. Or my discovery of a woman who claimed she could arrange my introduction, if I was ready to pay for it.

My host had described my quarters as a studio, but it was less than that: an adobe shed that shared one wall with the house proper and just large enough for a cot. It was clean, painted a bright and cheerful pink. A sprig of rosemary tied with a white ribbon hung against the wall as a decoration, and it gave the small space a pleasant scent. The pillow was flat. The blanket, rough. If I wanted to use the bathroom or shower, I had to go to the main house and risk another hour or two of my host's rumba music. The sounds of voices and guitars—and once a man's enraged shout—mixed with songs of crickets and cicadas.

I opened my book, its screen my only light.

> When I stopped with the heroin—this was, God, thirty years ago—I expected the aches, the illness, the craving deep as bones. Everyone knows how that comes. You anticipate it. Brace against it. Get ready. The thing I didn't look for was how empty I felt when I was clean. Everyone, always, we are looking for our lives to have meaning. What did the one man say? The Jew? "Those with a 'why' to live can bear almost any 'how.'" I think that's right. When I was a junkie, I had my why. Always my why was to get more junk, and I endured terrors for it.
>
> This age, this generation, traded its demons for the void. When I was young we were poor, and we are poor again now, but differently. When I was young, we were afraid to starve, to be without medicines or homes, and the teeth of it gave us meaning. Now we fear being less important than our neighbors. We lost our junkie's need and we don't know what to put in its place. So we make art or food or music or sport and scream for someone to notice us. We invent new gods and cajole each other into worshiping. All the vapid things that the wealthy did—the surgeries and the fashions and pretension—we understand them now. We are doing all the same things, but not as well, because we have less and we're still new at it.
>
> This? It's the emptiness of our time, and the only thing worse is everything that came before it.

I let my eyes drift closed.

The death of an extreme alpinist team dominated the mid-morning news cycle. Images of the mountain range they had been climbing appeared on the newsfeeds like blossoms in springtime, overlaid by swaths of color to track their intended path through the area with the most landslides. The woman whose father died on the mountain—dark-haired and fighting back tears as she stood before the cameras—spoke the customary phrases. *Climbing meant everything to him. He died doing what he loved.* I curled under the rough blanket, listening to the sounds of Malasaña's streets, and feeling the same uncomfortable mix of schadenfreude and envy that usually traveled in the wake of these optional tragedies. The romance of death by adventure.

I faced a less newsworthy ordeal. Three long weeks stretched out before the next disbursement, leaving a gap of fourteen days with nowhere to sleep, no ticket back to my flat in Nove Mesto, no way to buy my own food, and only water from public fountains.

I knew tricks of course. Ever since the rolls began, poor had meant poor management. Not everyone possessed the skills to shepherd their allotment all the way to the next one. The temptation to buy a cigar or a steak in the first days after the money came translated itself into missed meals and fasting in the long, brutal last days before the next payment, and sympathy came thin on the ground. The ancient lie that the blame for poverty belonged wholly to the poor had changed to truth now.

Experience taught me that the need to be more important than our neighbors could be exploited to sustain someone through the thinnest times. If I was careful. I strolled through the evening streets much as before, accepting the offered tidbits only here and there. Every third one. Or less. I smiled and nodded to the men and girls that haunted the little restaurants and family kitchens, encouraging but not *too* encouraging. And never grateful.

We exchanged the ragged sustenance I needed for the illusion they needed: that someone cared what they did. *Will feed for applause.* If I didn't convince them I was enjoying their rice cake or stew more than whatever their neighbors offered up, my end of our unspoken bargain failed. And that led quickly to the samples shifting out of my reach. Everyone wanted to feel desired. No one cared about someone who came only out of need. And so, like a con artist, I pretended not to need. Pretended to appreciate what they gave me.

It thrilled me.

I could have been safe in Nove Mesto with food enough, water enough, warmth enough. Instead, I lived by my wits, and savored the suspense, the metal-sharp taste of not knowing how exactly I would survive. Of the moment just before the revelation. This Julia Paraiis who claimed to have the information I sought could as easily be a grifter preying on my credulity. Or I might leave Malasaña with a secret. An experience I'd been searching for over the course of years.

The dead alpinists, the people offering food in the corners, the bands coaxing us all to come dance to their music, my host and his awful rumba, and me. All of us struggled against the same void, and Héctor Prima sang our longing like a siren.

I passed one day and then the next, each hour feeling longer than the one before. And more charged with promise. With the lengthening evening of the second day, my anticipation stuttered, shifted, and grew darker. I lay on my rented cot, afraid to sleep in case I missed Julia Paraiis or some agent of hers. No one came.

I woke on the morning of the third day caught between embarrassment and regret. I told myself that she might still come and I tried not to feel my humiliation. I managed for almost an hour before it bloomed into rage.

As I marched down the street from my host's house, I felt the eyes of Malasaña watching me. The stranger who had been haunting them for the past few days with no apparent agenda, now alive with outrage. Suspicions welled up in half-recognized faces. The old woman at the bodega crossed her scarred arms and shook her head at me. A girl who had offered me a sample of her father's bean soup the night before skipped along after me, laughing at my distress. What I meant to them was changing. It would lead to hunger later, but the idea of *later* had abandoned me.

I went back to the blue building.

Her door looked shabbier in the daylight and my state of mind. Scratches and streaks of orange paint that I hadn't noticed before seemed obvious now. I knocked first, shouted her name. Noises came—footsteps, the creak of a board, voices—maybe from the other side of the door, maybe from the other apartments. I pounded now, putting my shoulder into it and bruising my knuckles.

I didn't recognize the man who opened the door. He stared at me, his jaw set, his eyes hard. White button-down shirt with stains in the armpit.

"Where's Julia?" I said.

"Gone," the man said. "You should go too."

"Are you Héctor Prima?"

It landed. A flinch in the man's eyes, like he'd suffered a little electric shock. "There's no Héctor here. You should go."

He tried to close the door, but I pushed in. My voice shook, and I couldn't say whether with fear or excitement. "When is she coming back?" He shoved me, but to no effect. "I tracked Prima here. To *this* town. Julia said she knew him. Said she'd make the introduction if I paid her. Well, I paid her. Now I want the introduction."

"No Héctor Prima."

"I will go to every fucking person in this town and tell them what happened. I will stay outside your door for weeks. Months. As long as it *takes*."

The man looked down, stepped back. The room on the other side of the door looked as small as my own flat. As worn and sweat-limp. I looked around for some sign of her, but found nothing. The man refused to meet my eyes, and his breath grew ragged as I looked through his rooms, or else hers.

"Where is she?"

"Gone," he said.

"When will she be back?" I heard the rage in my own voice, and it sounded like whining.

"She won't."

"Why not?"

Now he looked at me straight on, eye to eye. "Because she brought you here. I kicked her out. She took your money with her. She took my money too. You can't talk about Héctor Prima around here. If you do . . . if you do, it all stops."

I sat on his couch. It squeaked and wheezed under me. "Are you him?"

"No," the man said, then heaved a sigh. He sat on the floor, his back against the wall. With his knees up, his arms wrapped around them, he looked fragile. "But I write down what . . . he says. I don't tell. And if it comes out I was doing it, he'll stop talking to me."

"I don't understand," I said, even though I almost did.

The man shook his head. "Was a few years ago. The rolls had just opened, and everybody was getting used to getting payments. Starting to think maybe it would last, you know? Like it wouldn't go away. Everybody happy, right? Because we all got money now. Only this one old dog says it's all bullshit, or kind of. I didn't understand, and then later, I started to. I made a point of hanging out, listening. Talking with, you know? And then . . . started writing it down. Posting it. Made up a name."

"Héctor Prima."

He nodded. "Was because it said something. Only then it got where people read it. A lot of people. Eight hundred thousand views when I put one up, and then eight million the next, yeah? And some of them are like you. I got scared. I told Julia about it, and she figured she could sell me out."

"To someone like me," I said.

"If it gets back what I'm doing, won't be any Héctor Prima, because there won't be anymore talking. So you can't tell anyone."

"Will you introduce me?" I asked. But I already knew the answer.

The man and I sat together in silence for a time. I felt a kinship between us, a shared heroism that outranked right or wrong. He and I both shouted against an overpowering emptiness that most people didn't recognize. He'd lifted a betrayal of trust and privacy to the level of art. I had committed to my enthusiasm for the work past the point of being a stalker. We transgressed together, each dependent upon the other for the sense that something in our lives mattered. We were not well, but at least we were sick in company.

I sniffed back my tears and stood. His eyes tracked me as I walked to the blue door, opened it.

"Have you ever heard of the hedonic treadmill?" I asked.

"What?"

"Look it up. Maybe mention it to him. I was going to talk to him about it," I said. And then, stepping out to the hallway, "Keep up the good work."

At the intersection, I stopped and sat on the curb. The girl who had skipped along behind me was in the mouth of an alleyway with three other children. They were playing a game with stones and a length of twine. The old woman swept the dust of her shop into the street. The late morning sun turned the roofs of the town silver and too bright to look at for long. I couldn't bring myself to believe how little time had passed. An hour—less than an hour—and a lifetime.

The story of my life had reached an inflection point here at the roadside in a little town far from my home. I had spent months tracking Héctor Prima, and I would never seek him out again. I would be homeless until the next disbursement came, and then I'd be hungry until I made up the cost of my train ticket home. I would suffer, but I would suffer for a reason, so the prospect wasn't so bad.

I took out my book, turned up the contrast against the brightness of the day, and opened my folder of Prima's work, skimming over the words without taking them in until a phrase caught my eye.

CHILDREN STILL STARVE. When I was young, we starved from poverty. Now we starve from having parents who spend their allotment on drink or drugs or pretty clothes that make them seem to have more than they do. Bad parents. Bad luck. Bad ideas. Money only ever fixes the troubles that money can fix. All the others stay on.

Yes, yes, yes, we suffer less. We suffer differently. But we still suffer over smaller things, and it distracts us. We begin to forget how precious butter and bread are. How desperate we once were to have them. Spices that meant something deep to my mother or to me? In a generation, they'll only be tastes. They won't mean anything more than their moment against the tongue. We should nourish our children not just with food, but with what food means. What it used to mean. We should cherish the memories of our poverty. Ghosts and bones are made to remind us to take joy in not being dead yet.

A bicycle hummed down the street, the chain clacking as it passed me. The old woman's broom hissed against the pavement. Music played somewhere close, the bass outreaching all the other sounds. And I sat and held something precious in my hands. Something more fragile than I had guessed when I came to Malasaña. I had chosen not to break it, and as much as it had meant to me when I came, it meant more to me now. I'd come to find Héctor Prima, and I would leave without hope of coming back or guiding my fellow hunters down the track to find him.

And I wondered. When I got home, what I would do instead. I must have made a noise, because the old woman stopped and stared at me. She lifted her chin in rough greeting.

"You all right, cousin?"

"Fine," I said. And then, "A little hungry."

She shrugged and went back to sweeping. "At least you know it."

ASSASSINS

JACK SKILLINGSTEAD
AND BURT COURTIER

Since 2003, Jack Skillingstead has sold more than forty short stories to major science fiction and fantasy publications. His work has been translated into Russian, Polish, Czech, French, Spanish, Chinese and Vietnamese. In 2013, his novel Life on the Preservation *was a finalist for the Philip K. Dick Award. Jack has also been a finalist for the Sturgeon Award. He lives in Seattle with his wife, writer Nancy Kress.*

Burt Courtier has worked as a documentation manager, business editor, and freelance writer in Japan and the United States. His nonfiction work appeared in Japan Quarterly. *Burt lives in Southern California with his wife and daughter.*

Here they introduce us to a very different kind of assassin. . . .

It will be a particularly brutal kill, even by her standards.

She sat in warm shade at an outdoor café along the Calle de las Huertes, not far from the Prado Museum. Sonia needed to work in public spaces, needed to witness the human cost. Tourists, students, illegals and the unemployed crowded the surrounding tables—all strangers. But that was nothing new. She could touch them only by wounding them, as she had been wounded. What would millions of Experiencers think if they knew a coward lurked behind Simone The Slayer?

Black-shirted waiters circulated between the tables. A few feet away a woman in a white sundress laughed. About thirty years old, she wore Experiencer glasses, the lenses polarized for the sun, and a headscarf. The bearded young man sharing her table kissed her neck playfully, and she laughed again. Of the hundred or so people visible to Sonia, maybe two-thirds of them wore Experiencer glasses, and many of them were fully immersed, the lenses gone a dully-reflective silver, like drawing a screen between the outer world and *Labyrinthiad*. Holding hands, an older couple in matching tropical shirts strolled out of the umbrella shade of the cafe and crossed the sun-struck plaza. Pigeons swooped and plunged, their black shadows gliding over the bricks. Motorbikes threaded through the moving crowds, their two-stroke engines making a lawn-mower racket.

"Hasta luego." It was the bearded man. He stood up and blew a kiss at the woman in the white sundress. She laughed and waved at him, like she was brushing off a fly. Walking backwards from their table, he bumped into Sonia. She jerked away. "Perdón," he said, turning and bowing. She scowled at him; Sonia didn't like to be touched. He shrugged and left her alone. His girlfriend touched the right temple of her Experiencer glasses. The lenses turned silver. Sonia looked away.

It was time.

Sonia placed her Cube next to her napkin, leaned forward and whispered the unlocking code. Glowing symbols floated above the table. Her long fingers made slight, almost imperceptible motions as she manipulated content, combining and recombining intricate patterns. The military-grade throat mic picked up her sub-vocal directions and voiceovers. Sonia's custom software reshaped her tonal quali-ties to create her character's signature voice—a voice that had insinuated itself into a million nightmares. Simone.

It was ready.

Sonia reached for her neglected macchiato. She sipped, absently licked bitter foam from her lips, set the cup down. Taking a pause. Virtual murder was still murder—the murder of emotional attachments. She ought to know. Sonia had cher-ished the character Emi Nakano, until the Editors discontinued Emi's existence on the grounds of inadequate popularity scores. When Emi suffered death by Editor, something died in Sonia, too. Now she felt connected only to the pain she caused. Maybe she had replaced her Emi Nakano obsession with her own meta assassin—but so what? Call it the failed transfiguration of revenge.

All right.

She uploaded her data to a rendering engine that converted her C-sym program-ming into a finished scene. A final hesitant pause . . . and she slipped the module undetected into the vast meta story that was *Labyrinthiad*. Like slipping a dagger between ribs to pierce the heart of a created world. In a moment, Ellis Ng would "die." Was Sonia the only one who recognized Ellis as nothing more than an emo-tional trap for the self-deluded?

Sonia's hands shook as she reached for her coffee. She emptied the cup and set it down. A cigarette would have helped her nerves, but they were banned now even in Europe.

Mileva Kosich, sitting on a bench across from the Office of Public Affairs, eye-flicked behind her Experiencer glasses. It was her lunch break and she just had time to meet her virtual friend, Ellis Ng. Belgrade disappeared, and Mileva was gliding in a sun-boat over a crystal blue pond. Ellis approached in his own sunboat, its solar net bil-lowing like a gossamer shell. Of course, Ellis was legion, and millions of Experiencers considered him a friend, but that didn't undercut Mileva's joy at the sight of his approach. Everyone enjoyed their own personal Ellis. He stood up and waved with two fingers extended (his customary greeting), making the boat rock. A black-winged personal flying suit swept down out of the empty sky. Mileva caught her breath. Simone! The assassin fired a projectile and Ellis Ng's sunboat exploded in a plume of flesh and fiberglass. Shocked, Mileva fumbled her glasses off. She sat on the bench, too upset to move.

Sonia killed only the popular characters. Five so far. And once slain, they resisted the Editor's attempts to resurrect them. Sonia's killing routines remained with a character and haunted them even in virtual death. The resurrected were lifeless zombies compared to their former selves. Their popularity, as defined continuously by the Experiencers, plummeted and they were quickly edited out. Of course, "life" in *Labyrinthiad* was an oxymoron, perpetuated by the mock-divine spark of rudimentary AI. Characters like Ng became the perfect companions because they analyzed your personality and speech and fed you tailor-made conversation. Nevertheless, waves of real despair followed the death of young eCelebs. Taking down beloved characters and the income streams they represented to the Publishers was dangerous. Real world dangerous.

Hachiro Jin, closed inside an egg-shaped Sleep Pod in the Helsinki Airport, touched the temple of his glasses and went full-immersion. It would be pleasant to pass a few minutes with Ellis Ng. The virtue of a virtual friend was availability without complications. Hachiro's layover was four hours, more than enough time to catch up on sleep and conversation with a friend who seemed perfectly to understand the worries of a forty-three-year-old businessman. Ellis, waiting for Hachiro on a red footbridge in the Sankeien Gardens, smiled and raised his hand—and then collapsed, a shaft protruding from the back of his head. Simone The Slayer stood a moment in his place. "Gomen-nasai, Hachiro-kun,"she said, flashing a lifeless smile before flickering out of existence. In the Sleep Pod, Hachiro ripped off his glasses, swearing.

Sonia waited for the reaction. Any moment now. Then a waiter stepped in front of her, blocking her view. He bent forward, reaching for her empty cup, his eyes a turquoise gleam. Just like the eyes of Sonia's character-killer, Simone. So many people affected body modifications that emulated favorite *Labyrinthiad* personalities. This waiter had even added Simone's signature scar, like a back-slash setting off the corner of his mouth.

"Would you like something else?" he asked.

"No."

Annoyingly, he lingered, staring into her with his faux-Simone eyes. Sonia squirmed in her seat. Hadn't she seen this man before, on the sidewalk near her apartment? Was he even a waiter? His shirt didn't exactly match the other waiter's shirts.

She forced herself to return his stare. "What do you want?"

The waiter grinned, said, "Stay as long as you like," and walked away, leaving her empty cup on another table.

*Juanita Torres' physical body reclined in the passenger seat of her self-driving Elon IV.
The car negotiated Chicago traffic on its way to the law offices of Ferguson & Torres.
Behind her Experiencer glasses Juanita had eye-flicked herself to a virtual tent pitched
in the high desert of New Mexico, where she lay quietly with Ellis. Sometimes Juanita
simply needed to be alone with her friend, without words. It was a meditation, a stress-
reliever. A timer would call her back to the car when they approached the office. Beyond the open tent flap pink and yellow layers of sunrise set off the jagged line of the
Sangre de Christo Mountains. Then a figure appeared, blocking the view. Simone The
Slayer in a panther-black bodysuit ducked into the tent, expertly wound a shiny gar-
roting wire around Ellis Ng's neck and snapped it taut. Blood sheeted over Juanita,
splattered the tent fabric, making a sound like rain. Juanita slapped her Experiencer
glasses off and sat up in the car, screaming. Simone's muffled laughter drifted up from
the floorboards near her feet.*

A collective shudder swept through the café and across the open plaza. Random
people stumbled to a stop. Sonia winced, feeling their pain—her connection to other
people. What would she be without this shared suffering? She wasn't brave enough
to find out. She had never been brave enough. The pain she caused was her only tie
to others.

The woman in the white sundress and headscarf a few tables away began weeping, her shoulders visibly shaking, and then slammed her glasses hard on the table
top, even as others hastily donned theirs. Sonia's segment was loose in *Labyrinthiad*.
You could *feel* it. Like a sudden pressure drop before a coming storm.

Only one man failed to react.

At a table across the open café space, his Experiencer glasses parked on top of his
bald head, he never took his eyes off Sonia. A broad, stocky man in a dark blue collar-
less overshirt. Two University girls, awkwardly holding each other in grief, crossed in
front of him. When Sonia could see again, the table was empty.

Quickly, Sonia pocketed her Cube and dropped five euros on the table. She stood,
rattling her chair back, and walked quickly away from the café.

She cut through a narrow cobblestone alley, intending to double back and make her
way to the Arguelles neighborhood. There she kept a safe room unconnected to her
Sonia Andrijeski identity—a name with shallow roots. In Arguelles she would hide
in the camouflage of rowdy students and jangling nightlife.

The yellow walls of the alley loomed over her. Dead vines trailed from boxes
under shuttered windows. Sonia quickened her pace, and then stopped, gasping,
when the bald man stepped around the corner and stood in her way. She scuffed
back, glanced over her shoulder. She could run but he would easily catch her. They
both knew it. He grinned.

"For an assassin," he said, "you're a mousy thing."

She retreated another step, and he moved toward her. A little dance.

"I'll scream," she said.

"You won't."

A pink cloud boiled out of a device in his hand. Sonia heard herself cough, as if the cough were un-synced with her collapse. The cobblestones came up and slammed her shoulder. The bald man stood over her. He tucked his device away, started to bend down. The sound of a motor ripped into the alley. She seemed to hear it after the bald man had already turned in reaction—Sonia's pink cloud reality.

The bald man fell, his body landing next to Sonia with a sickening and off-timed thud. She blinked heavy lids. A red puddle oozed away from the fallen man and began investigating the channels between cobble stones. Sonia managed to push herself back before it touched her. She looked up. A man holding a gun dismounted a blue Vespa and approached her. The waiter from the café, the one with Simone-The-Slayer's eyes and scar. He tucked his gun into his waistband, pulled his shirt over it, and hunkered next to her.

"He would have taken you back to the States," the waiter said, his words almost-but-not-quite in sync with his lips. "But I don't take people back." He shrugged. "Private contractors, right? Some are more full service than others."

Sonia squinted, trying to interpret what he'd said as anything other than an obvious threat. She struggled to get up. The waiter watched her, like he was watching a representative of an unrelated species. A true killer's coldness reflected in a virtual killer's eyes. God, he was a *fan*. Sonia grasped at self-control. Her voice barely broke when she said, "Don't hurt me, please."

He pressed his hand to his chest, as if he couldn't believe what she was suggesting. "I would never. I admire you too much. At least, I admire Simone. Professional respect crosses worlds." He reached out quickly and picked something up. Her Cube. Sonia's hand twitched involuntarily. And the gun was back in the waiter's hand and leveled at her.

"I'll make you a deal," he said. "Give me your key, promise to never upload to *Labyrinthiad* again, and you can go."

"What?"

"I've been watching you for days. I could have taken you out any time. Giving you a chance to walk away, that's me showing respect for what you created." He held the Cube up. It contained Simone's unique code, all her untraceable killing routines. "Decide now."

Sonia tried to rub the fogginess out of her eyes. "You want to be *her*. Simone."

"The key. Deal or not?"

"What if I don't want to?"

"Then I hurt you."

Numbly, she recited the code.

The waiter held the Cube in the palm of his hand. He voice-entered the code. The Cube glowed blue, ghostware deploying raw content for manipulation. He stared avidly at the display—Simone The Slayer in utero—then turned the Cube off, pocketed it, and, without another word, walked away.

Never upload to *Labyrinthiad* again? Impossible. But without Simone to connect to the common suffering, who was she? What was her *purpose*?

The killer mounted his Vespa and zipped out of the alley, leaving Sonia standing next to the dead man. A trace of motor exhaust lingered. She cringed, alone and exposed, and stumbled back the way she'd come, her head throbbing. Soon she found herself in the anonymous safety of the crowded plaza, surrounded by people she could no longer hurt. Woozy, she stopped and covered her eyes. A wave of pink-cloud dizziness swept through her and she started to fall, barely catching herself. Someone took her arm, steadied her. Sonia stiffened.

"Are you all right?" It was the woman from the café, the one so upset by Simone's kill that she had slammed down her Experiencer glasses. Others stopped, concerned. *Is she sick? Give her some room.* A young man produced his phone. *Should I call for medical?*

Sonia shook her head. "No, don't."

The woman, still holding Sonia's arm, searched her face. "You're sure you're all right? You looked like you were going to faint."

"Just a little dizzy. I'll be okay."

"At least you ought to sit down. There's a table. I'll get you a glass of water. My name's Mia, by the way."

Why was she so kind? Why was anyone? After a too-long pause, Sonia said, "Thank you," and they sat at a table near the one from which Sonia had exploded an emotional bomb. A bomb that had wounded many people, including Mia and perhaps others who later paused out of concern, not knowing they were solicitous of Simone's creator.

Sonia attempted a smile, "I'm not usually like this."

Mia stared back uncertainly, "Don't worry about it. I'm a bit of a mess myself. The Slayer struck again. Simone. That bitch."

Sonia picked up her lemon water, sipped, then held the cold, sweating glass in her hands. "Someone should take her down." Her words sounded odd to her, yet familiar. In a moment she realized: Simone.

Mia's eyes widened as she leaned back in her chair. "They . . . they've tried."

"Maybe it will be someone who knows her."

Sonia noted absently the sound of scrabbling chair legs on cobblestones. Standing now, backing away from the table, Mia said, "Nobody knows her."

Sonia nodded. Her head cleared. "Yes, of course. Nobody does."

The Martian Job

JAINE FENN

Jaine Fenn's short stories have appeared in numerous anthologies and in various magazines including On Spec *and* Alfred Hitchcock's Mystery Magazine. *Her space opera short story "Liberty Bird" won the 2016 British Science Fiction Association Short Fiction Award. She is also the author of the Hidden Empire series of far-future science fiction novels, published by Gollancz. She lives in rural England with her husband and the obligatory excess of books, and she currently writes for the video game industry, where she has worked on the Total War and Halo franchises.*

In the action-packed adventure that follows, she takes us to Mars for a caper that turns out to be much more complicated, and far more dangerous, than anyone thought it would be.

If you're listening to this, I'm dead."

You have got to be kidding me.

That was what I thought, at that moment. Not: *Why is my brother getting in contact after all these years?* Not: *Oh no, Shiv's dead!* No: I was exasperated at the screaming cliché. Real people don't say melodramatic crap like that. But a cliché's just something that's been true too many times and one woman's melodrama is another's tragedy.

I paused the recording. My brother's smiling face froze.

I'd been given the chip less than an hour ago, when I dropped round to collect a box of clothes from the apartment. "This arrived yesterday," Ken had said in that neutral, careful tone he's taken to using with me. But we've been married long enough that I knew he was curious about the unexpected package, with its offworld customs sticker. I made like it was something I'd been expecting, but he saw through that, though he pretended not to. And I pretended I didn't notice him pretending not to.

Shiv's image stared up at me from my phone; I'd had to hire a chip-reader from the local cornershop-cum-pornbroker and it wouldn't talk to the screen in my hotel-room-cum-cupboard. The last time I'd seen my half-brother was on the vidlink from Ma's trial, when he'd looked stricken, silent, and serious. On this recording he had more lines on his face but looked fit and well, with the same indefatigable smile, restless hands, breathless speech.

As I went to restart the recording I had an incoming call. Mr. Lau. I took it, of course. He was most apologetic about disturbing my evening, but he'd just been notified of a delegation arriving from Beijing in two days, and they needed confirmation of the travel arrangements by lunchtime, their time. No need to go into the office, should only take up an hour of my time.

The chip had to be Shiv's idea of a joke, and it wasn't one I expected to find funny. Like a good little wageslave I put my life on hold and danced to my boss's tune.

It took an hour and a half to make the initial reservations. By then it was after midnight and I couldn't face dealing with Shiv's message. Tomorrow was threatening to be another long day. I should get some sleep.

But first, I went out to the loud and badly lit bar down the street, found a drunk young man with good abs and minimal conversational skills, brought him back to this pokey excuse for a room, and had a decent, if cramped, bout of meaningless sex.

My name is Lizzie Choi, and this is the story of how I became the most wanted person in the Solar System.

This was the second time in a month we'd had sudden notification of a visitation from Head Office: the massive gamble that was Project Rainfall was sending ripples through every part of Everlight.

In addition to the flights and hotels I'd booked overnight, the next morning I added chauffeur-driven vehicles, a private dinner at the Savoy, plus a selection of diversions for the three spouses and pair of teenaged children accompanying the half-dozen–strong delegation. And far be it from me to imply this was any sort of jolly for said spouses and kids. Still, the Chinese do love London; the bits of it they don't already own, anyway.

By lunchtime, our time, everything was in place for the visit and I was ready to start my ten-hour work day. I asked Mr. Lau if he was free to speak with me before he headed out for his lunchtime meeting. He invited me into his office, and greeted me with his usual avuncular smile.

"Another path smoothed. Thank you, Ms. Choi."

I smiled back. From where I stood, between his two plush visitor chairs, I noticed that the orchid stem in the lacquered vase on the southwest corner of his desk had a small brown blemish on the underside of the main blossom, only visible from this angle; I made a mental note to get it replaced before he returned from lunch. "My pleasure as ever, Mr. Lau. However, whilst your gratitude is my most treasured reward, current circumstances force me to mention the possibility I raised some weeks back, that of a remuneration review." Or, to put it another way *You're not a bad boss, but I need more money.*

His eyes went to the orchid. Perhaps the blemish was visible from his side. "Your circumstances. Ah, yes." Not a bad boss, but with an old-fashioned view on infidelity and divorce. "I will see what can be done, given the current corporate climate, Ms. Choi." Or, to put it another way, *Fat chance.*

While Mr. Lau was out at lunch an automated system called my personal phone asking if I'd accept a reverse-charge offworld call. I assumed it must be some mistake, then wondered if this was Shiv following up on his odd little joke. But it wasn't from Mars, it was from Luna.

If it was who I suspected it might be then this wasn't a call I could take at work, even alone in the office. I refused it. As I did so I realised there was only one reason my mother would be allowed to call me in the first place.

After years spent disentangling myself from the disaster that was my family, they were back in my life.

If Mr. Lau noticed I wasn't at my best that afternoon he didn't say anything.

I got away from the office as early as I could. I needed to listen to Shiv's message all the way through. But my phone chirped again as soon as I was outside. I queried the call source. It came from Luna Authority Correctional Facility Six. She wasn't going to give up. I waited until I was back in my tiny room before bowing to the inevitable.

She didn't look that much older; a bit thinner in the face, but healthy and with her hair colour back to glossy chestnut. Behind her the blank wall was painted a soft and non-institutional blue. "Hello, Mother," I said before she could open her mouth.

The Earth-Luna delay was only a couple of seconds, but it was enough for me to see her expression fall into the familiar combination of concern and disapproval. "Beth! Been trying to get hold of you all day." She sounded more American than I remembered; her only link to the old US was a single grandparent she'd never met, but everyone indulged the remaining Americans, so she'd probably been cultivating the accent in prison.

"I've been working. I can't take personal calls on work time."

"Working?" The idea still appalled her, it seemed.

I resisted the urge to sigh. "At Everlight, yes."

"You're still with the opposition?" My father had called them that, jokingly; given how little time she spent with him, and how that time ended, it hardly made sense to refer to one of the world's biggest companies as "the opposition." But that was my mother.

"Yep. Still at Everlight."

"Well, fuck me." Another thing about my mother: she loves to swear. She blames it on having had, as she puts it, "a shit childhood" but I think it's more about image, the street-smart American shtick. And because she swears, I don't. "And're you still doing," she waved a hand dismissively, "office work?"

"Operational administration." After years of silence, and with a noticeable delay on the line, she could still propel me from mildly peeved to wound-up-fit-to-scream in a matter of seconds.

"And how's . . ." another hand-wave, "whatsisname?"

"Fine." I bit down on the word, but her eyes are narrowing.

She squinted past me. "Thought you two had one of those neat corporate apartments."

"You're calling because of Shiv, aren't you?" She would only have been allowed to contact me because I was now her registered next-of-kin. Because Shiv really was dead.

Her expression fell, and she looked old for the first time. The pain I glimpsed wasn't entirely faked. "Yes. He . . . he was everything I could've wished for in a child."

I let my subconscious chime in with *unlike you*, because I had no desire to be everything my mother could have wished for. "When did he . . . When did it happen?" *My brother's dead. My brother's really dead.*

"Shit. You don't know?"

"No. How would I?" I didn't even know how he'd got hold of my contact details. "I only know at all because of this call." Not technically true, but I wasn't giving her any ammunition. "So, how long . . . ?" I let the question trail off into the signal-lag.

"Three weeks."

In order to reach me when it did, Shiv's chip must have left Mars three or four days after it happened. Whatever *it* had been. "And how did he . . ." I had to say it sometime, ". . . die?"

"A flyer crash, according to some shyster Martian lawyers. He left details of his final wishes with them."

The same lawyers who'd presumably found out where I was and dispatched the chip. "A flyer? He was a good pilot."

"According to these lawyers it was a solo flight, and he didn't file a flight-plan with Olympus Central." *You don't say.* "They claim he ran into technical difficulties but that the glider's transponder had been tampered with. A rover-train spotted the wreckage two days later."

In other words, anything could have happened. "These lawyers, who are they?"

"Shah . . . something. No, Shah, Shah and something. What the fuck does it matter?"

"Probably doesn't." Not a Chinese firm, then; no surprise there, either. Should I tell her about the chip Shah, Shah and something had sent me?

"But it ain't all shit, Beth. There's one piece of good news. His legacy, perhaps."

Mum's so calm. But she'll have known about Shiv for a while. "What do you mean?"

"It's coming up for ten years. Since I first came to this shithole, I mean." Spoken as though she could leave. Which, I realised with a jolt, she could, potentially.

"You mean, the buy-out clause?" So that was why she was calling me. Not to commiserate on our shared loss, mend fences, or volunteer useful information. No, as usual, she wanted something. Whatever was on Shiv's chip, I wouldn't be sharing it with her.

She nodded. "I've had a decade to, as the shrink here says, reflect on the human aspect of the incident. Now I've done my time and had my therapy the slate's clean, of the whole culpable homicide thing anyway."

The remaining ten years of Mum's sentence were a material loss penalty, which could be reduced by paying certain fines. "The court set a ridiculous price, if you remember." The vagaries of Lunan law: damaging a hab was as dire an act as taking a life, but if you could pay for a new hab to be built your crime need never be spoken of again.

"Yeah, they sure did. But you've done well, you said so yourself."

I did? When, exactly? She was looking at me like she expected me to conjure the necessary funds out of the air. "Not that well, Mum. Sorry."

"Ah. So it's like that." She sighed, and got that disappointed look in her eyes. I was still working out the best way to field this latest ploy when she continued. "If you could, you'd free me though, wouldn't you? We could start again."

"Of course I would." What else could I say?

She nodded. "Thank fuck for that at least. Sometimes, Beth. Sometimes I wonder about you, how you turned out. But you're a good girl really."

"I have to go now."

"Sure, I guess."

"Bye, Mum." I cut the call.

I pulled the package containing Shiv's chip out of the cubbyhole where I'd stashed it. The chip was in a holder, the holder was in standard packaging along with a hard-copy slip of paper with the cryptic phrase "Remember the world's dodgiest airlock?" printed on it; the package was labelled with my name and last registered address and a customs mark which indicated it came from Mars. And that was it. The piece of paper would have foxed anyone else; but as soon as I'd opened the package I knew what it meant, and who this package came from.

I should go out and hire the chip-reader again. Instead I decided to go out and get laid. Sex was, truth be told, the solution to a lot of my problems these days, even if it was also the cause of one of them. Which made Ken's call, as I was putting my lipstick on, perfectly timed. Behind my soon-to-be-ex-husband the apartment looked spacious, comfortable and airy. Still no signs of change, specifically the kinds of change made by another woman.

"I expected to hear from your lawyer today, Lizzie," he said, doing that looking-up-from-under-his-brows thing I used to love but which I'd come to think of as passive-aggressive neediness.

He did have a point, though. I'd forgotten to call the divorce lawyer. I never forget things like that. "I . . . had a difficult day."

"You can tell me about it if it helps."

I wish he wouldn't make civilised, genuine-sounding offers like that. Just like I wish there was another woman, or man, or something else; some other reason. He's trying to make this as easy as he can, and that just makes it harder. "I'm fine. I'll get on it first thing tomorrow."

The lawyer in question wasn't available first thing, so I had to queue the call for lunchtime. If I'd had the money I'd have hired a lawyer who'd return my calls, but the storage charge on those possessions I no longer had room for in my nasty little cubbyhole—which was most of them—had just gone out, and I barely had the money to pay rent on said cubbyhole. My original thought, that I'd get a studio flat in a nice, non-corporate suburb once the divorce went through, was about as likely as me taking Mr. Lau's place as Everlight Europe's Junior VP for Finance.

I stayed for the meet-and-greet for the visitors from Beijing, hovering in the background trying not to look too tall and Western, on hand in case anything went wrong. Which it didn't, because I'm good at my job.

As soon as I got home I rented the chip-reader.

When my phone screen asked for a password, I keyed in DAE-BUM, the designation on the LunaFree Community's main cargo airlock. It used to make me laugh, especially the way Shiv said it, "That's DAE as in Dodgiest Airlock Ever and BUM as in *bottom!*" What can I say, I was only eight.

The initial screen showed Shiv in freeze-frame, and a date. I hadn't really registered the date before but I now knew he'd recorded this three days before he died. I swallowed and hit play.

"If you're listening to this, I'm dead."

Yes, you are. You really are.

"Just kidding! Got your attention though, didn't I?" He didn't look dead. He looked great. I blinked and his image went blurry for a moment. "By the time you get this everything will be sorted. I'm stashing the chip just in case, well, in case two things, but mainly in case you don't work out it was me! Because it was!" He grinned wider, like he expected me to get the joke. "Mum's probably free by now—that's one of Mr. Shah's conditions for sending you this, me having bought her out. Which I will be able to afford because I've just pulled off . . ." his voice rose in that mock-gameshow-host way he had, ". . . the greatest heist humankind has ever seen!"

Except he hadn't; or if he had, it'd gone wrong and been hushed up. Plus: great idea this, Shiv—you're about to commit a fantastic bit of thievery which no one can pin on you, so you record a confession. Okay, it was on an encoded chip which—presumably—no one else had access to, but even so, that kind of arrogance could get you in trouble. Killed, even.

His expression fell, the smile fading a little. The back of my neck prickled. "There's also a real small chance"—one of Mum's favourite phrases that—"a real, *real* small chance that things might not work out. That's why I've given you the details. Because if something unexpected happens and I can't do the job for some reason, then you could take it on. I know, I know, you don't touch this kind of business any more, you're on the straight and narrow working for the big bad corp, but you can't miss this one! And if I can't see it through then you've got to be the one who gets Mum out of that place."

Oh, have I?

His moment of sombre reflection was gone as fast as it arrived, and the winning smile was back. "I'm just being pessimistic. Everything'll go fine. And maybe, when the dust has settled, we can meet up? I know you still feel bad about how Mum got shafted in New Bombay and the Four Flowers business on Luna, but we're older now, older and wiser. And you're still my little sister." He mimed blowing me a kiss, then blew a raspberry. His traditional farewell, back from when we were kids. "Bye now!"

I threw my phone across the tiny room. It bounced off the wall. I retrieved it, and, because I had to pick the scab, checked the data-file. Sometime during Shiv's speech I'd got it into my head that his "greatest heist humankind has ever seen" would be about Project Rainfall. That he was going to try and steal the water-rich proto-comet Everlight were currently braking into a stable orbit around Mars. I wouldn't have put it past him to try, given he'd trained as an engineer, back before he'd taken up the family trade. But I was wrong.

He wasn't planning to steal a comet.

He was planning to steal the most valuable gem in the universe.

I returned the chip-reader on my way out. Time to get laid again.

Mr. Lau spent most of the next day closeted with his visitors. It gave me far too much time to think.

Shiv had ended up on Mars eight years ago after a dodgy mining operation that went south when he tried to play the Russians off against the Australians whilst simultaneously screwing the Chinese—overreaching himself, again—leaving him broke and under threat of multiple lawsuits if he ever came back to Earth. I could imagine him kicking around, moving from scheme to scheme in the Martian underworld (such as it was) waiting for the big break that was always just around the corner. When he'd been offered a chance to steal an object so legendary that Mum used to joke about it when we were growing up, something that in the shady world I knew too well was a byword for the ultimate score, of course he'd taken it, no matter what the risk.

I knew my brother. All that bravado was a front: Shiv had been scared when he made the recording. And his fear had been justified. I should just burn the chip.

When Mr. Lau re-surfaced that evening, he looked harassed. I asked whether I could be of any assistance. He managed a smile for me and, in an uncharacteristic lapse in his façade, said, "This project will make or break us all, Ms. Choi." I didn't have to ask which one. Since they wound up the last of their operations in North America, Europe was Everlight's least prestigious division, run more for politics than profit. With so many eggs in one—offworld—basket, Mr. Lau was fighting hard to keep hold of his small part of the corporate empire here on Earth.

I wondered if the universe was messing with me: I'd ignored Mars for most of my life, and now two things in one week made me think about the place. I dismissed the thought as unhelpful going on self-obsessed.

Even so, that night I did some research. Just background, I told myself.

The next morning saw more meetings, after which the delegation got to have a few hours fun before going home. Mr. Lau's part in the visit was over and I was careful to give him space. He appeared, if anything, more uneasy than he had the day before; knowing him as I did I put this down to embarrassment at showing his concerns before an underling.

When he called me into his office "for a private chat" I was more relieved than concerned. He was doing me the favour of telling me to my face that my pay-rise was off the cards.

He invited me to sit before he spoke. Not a good sign. This was serious. "I am afraid, Ms. Choi, that the situation is not favourable to you."

"Ah." I wasn't sure what else I could, or should, say.

"Certain factions within the company feel I should let you go."

What? "Really? I'm a great administrator and you know it!"

He raised an eyebrow at my immodesty, but said, "You are exceptionally good at

your job. Your attention to detail is remarkable, your foresight faultless. In operational office matters, I would not want anyone else to, as they say, *have my back*."
That last phrase was in English, which I knew from previous experience meant he
was trying to put me at my ease.

"So what is the issue here?" I had an idea. I'd just been too busy worrying about
everything else to join the dots.

He cocked his head a fraction. "Some of my more traditional colleagues in Head
Office put a high value on heritage. Specifically, on one's family."

"Family?" I said, as though I didn't know. This wasn't just about me and Ken.

"Yes. You have criminal connections, Ms. Choi." His tone didn't accuse so much
as observe, pointing out something socially awkward, like having spinach in one's
teeth.

"Criminal connections." I kept my voice flat. My original application to join Everlight nine years ago had included the usual box for listing any convictions; thanks to
a mixture of luck and care, I had none. "You're saying my family contains criminals."
There hadn't been a box for that.

"Yes. Your mother . . ."

"My mother?" Today's orchid was, I noted, perfect.

"You have recently become the registered next-of-kin of a certain Maria Kow-
alski."

Of course Everlight kept tabs on their employees, and something like that would
get flagged up. "Yes. Yes I have. For my sins." Lunan law allows you to divorce parents as well as partners, so if I'd had the money, I could've made the distance between
me and my mother formal, rather than relying on our default state of estrange-
ment. But I hadn't. "I hope and believe, Mr. Lau, that you can see beyond a person's
initial circumstances to what they may achieve for themselves." *Creep*, said a small,
rebellious part of me I thought I'd excised.

"It would be easier to overlook these circumstances had you declared them when
you first joined us."

There *had* been a box on the application form to add Any Other Pertinent Information and I had agonised about using it to declare my "criminal connections" at the time. "My apologies, Mr. Lau. I should have done so." But then I
probably wouldn't have got the job. Plus, it was just an office admin post and if they
really cared they'd do a background check. I assumed they had, before I reached my
current, somewhat more important, position. Apparently not. Or they had, but
when Mum had no legal hold on me, they'd been willing to ignore her. My face
felt hot.

"Suspension pending an investigation is the minimum you can expect, I fear.
However, I will fight to the best of my ability to retain you as an employee of Everlight."

I believed he would. He got good work out of me. And, for a half-gwailo, I made
the effort to fit in. Which just made me more angry with the company, and with
myself, and with Mum. And anger makes you do, and say, stupid things. "Thank
you." *Don't thank him, creep.* "Given the situation, I would like to request a formal
sabbatical from Everlight." Even as I said it, I was stunned at myself.

His eyebrows went up. "That is an interesting proposition." Then lowered, as his initial surprise settled. "Possibly a sensible move though. How long would you wish to take?"

My subconscious had already done the maths. "Three months."

I like space travel. Granted it's potentially dangerous and often uncomfortable, and the cramped conditions on the cut-price flight I ended up on were grim, but I travelled enough when I was younger that I don't puke when gravity goes away, and I love the sense of going somewhere, towards something better, a place where things would go right. Mind you, when I was younger we were more likely to be running away from something that'd gone wrong.

Even taking the budget option, I had to sell most of my remaining possessions to buy passage to Mars. A return, because when I'd worked through this upwelling of the past I'd be back, returning to what was left of the life I'd built on Earth; by then Mr. Lau would have smoothed things over, and be really missing his star admin, and I'd be able to go back to my old job. That's what I told myself, as I boarded the flight.

I should have spent the journey working out my options but my thoughts just went round and round, tumbling in the near freefall, and coming back to two facts: nine years ago I'd decided to miss out a detail, a simple declaration on a form, and now it was coming back to haunt me; then a few days ago I'd acted on a crazy impulse, and in doing so risked undoing the chance at a normal life that form had bought me.

Stepping off the shuttle into Martian gravity, seeing people as tall as I was, gave a brief, comforting illusion of coming home. But this wasn't Luna. The sky beyond the dome was red, not black, and the air smelt of dust, ozone and something sweet—orange peel, perhaps?

By the time I'd queued for, and been crushed into, the lift down from the crater rim and queued for, and been glared at by, customs and joined the even longer queue for immigration, the scale of my potential mistake was sinking in. I was on an alien planet, with little money and no plan.

The walls in Arrivals were covered in the usual combination of adverts, infomercials and warnings about contraband and contagions. One image showed the Eye of Heaven floating, like some round shining god, over a hyper-real and lightly animated—or possibly real-time—depiction of the Olympus region, with the caption, *Peace and Prosperity For All*; the Everlight logo at the bottom left was subtle enough to miss if you weren't looking for it. On Earth, Everlight were a major player; on Mars, they were top dog. The last two decades had seen a meteoric rise in their fortunes on the red planet as every major decision turned out to be right, every gamble justified.

The Arrivals hall also contained discreet niches with actual gods in; the nearest contained a happy jade Buddha. The orange peel smell was stronger here: dry incense, for when you wanted to appease the ancestors without clogging the air scrubbers.

One wall had a flatscreen newsfeed—very retro, or possibly normal, for Mars—and I distracted myself by watching it while I queued. On screen, a thin-faced young man was complaining about Project Rainfall, saying Everlight had no right to hold people to ransom with the promise of rain. The comet's water belonged to all Martians, he insisted. Something about that phrase, "all Martians," lifted my spirits. No one ever says, "All Earthers." Okay, so Mars is just a bunch of semi-independent enclaves and habitats, as is Luna, but hearing someone speak like that made me feel warm and fuzzy inside. I just couldn't escape that early communal upbringing. As a caption appeared at the bottom of the flatscreen, I realised I wasn't so far from the truth: this was a spokesperson for the Deimos Collective. Somewhat ironic, talking about "all Martians" when he didn't even live on the surface of Mars. Still, the Deimons did claim to speak for the ordinary folk of the planet below them and they had the height and weight—physically, morally, financially—to make statements like that. And the Chinese had the temporal power and self-assurance to ignore them. The queue moved, and I looked away.

Once through the formalities I used the public comm service to book into the cheapest accommodation I could find; it called itself a hotel but was more like a person storage facility, and made my accommodation back on Earth look downright spacious. Then I paid a visit to Shah, Shah & Needlam. I didn't call ahead in case the lawyers refused me an appointment, and I had to sweet-talk their receptionist and wait for an hour before I got to speak to Mr. Shah, junior. He was predictably surprised to see me. When I made my request, his face fell further.

"Your brother's remains? I am sorry, Ms. Choi, but he had no stated religious beliefs or relatives in a position to collect said, ah, remains. Therefore he was, well . . ."

I knew the drill. "He was resyked."

"The phrase we use is 'physically reintegrated.'"

"I understand." On Luna the official term was "returned to the system." I'd half expected this, and I wasn't sure what I would have done with Shiv's body or ashes anyway. But I had to ask. It was an attempt at what the Americans used to call closure. His final mark on the world.

It didn't have to be, of course.

"Tea, Ms. Choi? I have jasmine, green, chai or English."

The available selection implied considerable resources, which was no doubt the point. But I hadn't had a decent cup of tea since I left Earth. "English, please. White no sugar." Though I preferred Western tea I usually drank Eastern teas in social situations, but I didn't have to worry about fitting in here. Besides, I was curious to see whether the perfectly turned out young woman sitting opposite me had access to cows as well as decent hydroponics.

She waved a hand at the boy who'd shown me into her office-cum-parlour. He drew back from the threshold, pulling the painted screen-door closed behind him. A subliminal hum started in the roots of my teeth.

"So," she drew the word out with care, "you are Shiv Neru's sister."

"I am. And your own sister runs the Moonlit Joy Escort Agency?" I kept my tone lightly quizzical without being critical. Who was I to judge anyone by their family?

"She does. Using a back room in her premises provides additional discretion for my own business."

"Which is what, exactly?" Shiv's recording had provided me with a name—Ika—a contact number—which I had done a directory search on, along with as much other research as I could without spending serious cash—and his assurance that "Ika" was "doing a great job of bringing everything together." And that was all I knew.

"I am a facilitator."

As I thought: a fixer with pretensions. "Excellent. And what, exactly, were you facilitating for my brother?" I suspected she'd done more than facilitate him; she was in her twenties, mixed heritage (I'd guessed some Japanese from the name, but looking at her now I'd say mainly Indonesian), petite, stylish, and possessed of a weaponised smile. Exactly his type.

"A unique endeavour which, I believe, you know something of?"

Did she know about Shiv's recording? "Something, yes." With a job like this you had to strike the balance between compartmentalisation and coordination. Tell your people everything they might need to know—but no more. When I say "you," I mean the money. But Shiv wasn't the money. His recording had implied he was the brains behind the job, but a lot of the mental lifting, could be—probably should be—done by an individual like Ika. "Before I go any further, I'm afraid I'm going to have to ask some direct and searching questions."

Ika's expression tightened, but she simply said, "I would expect nothing less."

First things first. "Did you sleep with my brother?"

Her expression tightened further, then loosened. "Yes. Once." The shark-smile settled back on her face. "Will that be a problem?"

"Not necessarily." If it was just the once, then probably not. If it was more than a one-off then whatever he knew, she probably did too. "Do you know what the target of the job is?"

Not a waver in her expression this time. "The financier behind this operation has been most insistent on confidentiality and discretion."

Which didn't answer my question. I tried another tack. "Did this individual approach you directly about the job? Or did you hear about it through Shiv?" I looked up at a slight sound, and the humming I'd almost tuned out stopped. The boy came in with a tea tray. As he unloaded it I took a more thorough look around the room. It exhibited the characteristic Martian obsession with Feng Shui; I'd seen more Tara Mirrors, and breathed more flavours of incense in the last three days than in a year working at Everlight Europe. I put it down to spiritual over-compensation: bringing the familiar to an alien world. It was an odd juxtaposition with Ika's expensive and discreet comms equipment.

As the boy positioned the teapot—genuine china, or an impressive fake—Ika said, "The blend is mainly Assam, so don't let it brew too long. Thank you, Mani."

When the boy closed the screen on his way out the hum re-started. I'd placed it while he was serving, as I'd been the one serving the tea during some delicate meetings back on Earth: Ika had jammers built into this room to stop eavesdropping, physical or electronic. She went up in my estimation.

Ika picked up a large but delicate-looking mug. She was having chai, from the smell of it. She blew on the drink, took a sip, then said, "I have been honest with you. May I now expect the same courtesy in return?"

"Of course."

"I was not aware Shiv had a sister, and after your call this morning I did a little research. Imagine my surprise to find you are an employee of Everlight, and have only recently arrived from Earth. Given this, I must ask: why are you here?"

I poured myself a cup of tea, and I took a sip. The leaves could have brewed a little longer, but it was a quality blend, and if that wasn't real milk it was an expensive substitute. Another point in this woman's favour.

Ika was still waiting for an answer.

"I don't know," I admitted. Might as well have laid down on her sumptuous five-elements rug and bared my throat. "I'm still thinking it through. You'd be within your rights to refuse to cooperate with me, under the circumstances."

She nodded and put down her mug. "I have been trying to think what your agenda might be, what you might hope to achieve in coming here, and the most likely answer is that you want to take on the job."

"Or to find out why my brother died." That had been what I'd told myself when I called Ika to arrange our meeting.

"A noble motivation. It was a flyer accident, I believe."

"And do you? Really believe that, I mean."

"I have no idea. I don't go outside the domes if I can help it."

"But you appreciate the sort of things that can go wrong, and the sort of people who can make them go wrong."

"That's my job, but without knowing exactly what Shiv planned, I couldn't offer any meaningful suggestions."

I could almost believe she hadn't known what Shiv was up to. Almost. "If I did take this on it would require specialists. Shiv mentioned a couple but we'd have to recruit more."

"I have made some initial approaches. Nothing has come of it, obviously."

"Why not?"

"This was Shiv's job. He told me only what I needed to know."

She was consistent, I'd say that for her. "Ah, I got the impression you've had direct contact with the financier. So you don't know enough to take this on yourself?"

"The gentlemen in question made it clear he was looking for someone to lead in the field. In conducting my business, I never leave this room. I have suggested others who might coordinate the job but he appears to be looking for a certain type of person. If you think you might be that person then I would be willing, for a nominal fee, to put you in touch with him."

"I can't pay you."

"Hmm. You really have burnt your bridges, haven't you, Ms. Choi?" She leaned in to toy with the handle of her chai mug. "In the spirit of our continued honesty, I will say that I would very much like this job to be successful."

"Even though you don't know what it is?"

"I knew Shiv and liked him. More importantly, I know how much we can all make from this."

"So it's in your interests to put me in touch with your man?"

She stared at the drink and pursed her perfect lips. "I will see what I can do."

Even though Ika and I had danced round each other, I'd given more than I'd taken. She called the next morning, inviting me back to her parlour/office. "I will leave you to take this call in private. You may rest assured that what passes between you will not be overheard."

"Or recorded?"

"I have my reputation to think of."

Which wasn't the same as saying "No."

I waited until the door was shut before acknowledging the flashing icon on her largest screen.

Ika had referred to the financier as "he" but it was hard to tell from the image. Features blurred into a generic headshot; probably Caucasian and with a masculine hairstyle, but that was all I could tell. The background was a mash of muted brown and orange. Most likely the whole image was an artefact.

"Greetings, Ms. Choi."

The voice was low-register and probably male, though it was as modulated as the image was pixellated.

"Hello. What should I call you?"

"Whatever you like. Your brother called me Mr. P, short for Mr. Patron."

Typical Shiv. "Then that's what I'll do." I found talking to this artefact disconcerting

"Good. I'll come straight to the point. What do you know about the job your brother took on for me?" I thought I could pick out a non-Chinese accent in his perfect, if distorted, Mandarin. I'm good with languages.

"He planned to steal the Eye of Heaven." It sounded absurd, saying it out loud. The largest, most valuable, most heavily guarded gemstone ever found.

"That's right. From your tone I'd guess you don't rate the success of this job."

Of course, you can read my expression and voice, and I can't get a thing off you. Thanks for reminding me. "Everlight's Martian HQ isn't going to be easy to penetrate."

"No. But you're aware the Eye will be on public display in there?"

"I am. But only for the duration of the New Year celebrations." Something Shiv had failed to mention. It put a time limit on the job. "Even so, getting away with an opal the size of my head isn't going to be easy."

"A lot of thought has already been put into this plan. I just need you to make it happen." That accent. American? Irish? Australian? The latter was the most likely given that the Irish had zero presence on Mars—and he was on Mars, there was no signal lag—and America was history.

"You appear to be assuming I'll take on this job."

"Not at all. If you're not interested, our contact ends here."

"You need me to decide right now?"

"You've known what the job was for some time. You must have given your potential part in it plenty of thought.

"I have." As an abstract problem, a *What if?* To commit now, to tell this spooky stranger I was happy to break the law after a decade of obeying it . . . "If you make me answer now it'll have to be 'no'. Sorry."

"I'm sorry too." The screen went dark.

Which left my other reason for being here: finding out what happened to Shiv. But there were only two explanations: either his death had been an accident, in which case there was nothing to find out, or it had been something more sinister, in which case if I, an outsider with no contacts or resources, started poking around, I was likely to have an "accident" of my own.

My phone chirped as I stepped onto the walkway back to my hotel. A message from Mum. A recording rather than a call: being this far out had its advantages. Back in my new even smaller hotel room, I played it back.

"Beth, are you really on Mars?" She paused a moment, as though expecting me to miraculously break the light barrier with an answer. "Shiv was planning something, you know. I think it was something big. Big, and special. On Mars. Where you are now, in fact." She glanced to one side—she was in the same blue room—and grimaced. "We owe it to your brother to find out what he was trying to do. You owe it to us, your family, to finish whatever he started. Ah, they're such misers; I have to go now. Stay safe, Elizabeth. Message me when you can."

The recording ended.

Did she know what Shiv had been planning? I couldn't see how. No doubt they had enjoyed several cryptic conversations on well-monitored channels, and perhaps she even suspected this was the ultimate heist, the one she'd talked about taking on herself when we were younger . . . Just before she grew wings and flew into outer space. But she couldn't know for sure. Keeping tabs on me now Shiv was dead wouldn't be hard. I was her only living relative, after her short-sighted stupidity got my father, and everyone else in that hab, killed. Not that I'd known Wang-Zheng Choi well, given I'd been three years old when he tried to pay off this most inconvenient of mistresses, sending the three of us packing towards Earth. She couldn't even leave him honestly and had only got as far as the LunaFree Community. That place had been the nearest I'd had to a home, for five years anyway, before she screwed them over too, and they threw us out.

The fact that my mother wanted me to take this job was reason enough not to.

But if I pulled it off I could pay to free her—thus removing any residual sense of obligation—and then pay to divorce her—thus removing her from my life.

I needed to take a step back.

Start by following the money. Ika was being well paid for her part in the potential theft of the Eye of Heaven. No doubt Shiv had been offered a generous fee as well. Who had the means to bankroll this type of job? An individual? Our "Mr. P" had said "I," though that could be a ruse. There were some affluent loners on Mars, early investors who'd struck it rich and stayed on, but were any of them that rich? Hard to know, as those individuals valued their privacy, and living in private self-sufficient domes in an arid wilderness put you well out of circulation. It was possible someone with a lot of money and an eccentric love of valuable items was after the Eye, but I had no way of knowing who. I compiled a short list anyway, with what little information was publically accessible. Interestingly, two of the individuals on my list gave their nationality as American: they had to be descended from early settlers who'd arrived here before their country went to radioactive hell after its idiotic experimentation in unlimited machine intelligence. Back in the twenty and twenty-first centuries the Americans had a reputation as uber-capitalists, collecting useless items just because they were considered valuable. According to the old movies and other popular media of the time, anyway.

Next I considered larger factions. Mars has a lot of factions but most of them are bit players, fighting for scraps from the Chinese table. Though now the Russians had recovered fully from the Marineris blowout they were a force to be reckoned with again. As were the Deimons, when it came to resources, at least: the Levi-Mathesons and their followers had been smart, farsighted people who, once they'd hollowed out their moon and settled there permanently, had little use for the money that still flowed in from their many inventions and innovations. But their very lack of care for status or material wealth made them unlikely to want to steal a shiny rock whose only value was in the eye of the beholder.

Most likely it was a corp, one that opposed Everlight. Since one of their mining operations had come across the massive opal out in the Tharsis Ranges twenty years ago, the Eye of Heaven had become the heart of their Feng Shui web on Mars, the symbol and talisman of Everlight's inexorable rise to effectively rule the red planet. Stealing it would strike a blow beyond any that might be dealt via financial shenanigans or corporate politicking.

Ironically, the top contender in this scenario was none other than Four Flowers Holdings, my late father's employers. FFH were dominant on Luna but less of a player on Mars. Striking at Everlight in the domain where they held greatest power would be just the kind of spiritual coup they'd favour. Kind of ironic that I'd take a job working for FFH considering I had worked for them before, albeit briefly. My first attempt to go straight had involved using my father's influence—such as it had been—to get a job as a researcher and administrator with FFH NorthWest. And then Mum had reconciled with her old lover and gone to live with him on Luna, where she poisoned him against me, their wayward and disrespectful daughter. She had also used her dubious connections to help him keep costs down on the new FFH hab. We all know how well that worked out. The worst week of my life occurred just over a decade ago when on three consecutive days I lost my job for reasons I could trace back to my parents but never contest, ended my latest attempt at a relationship, then heard the news about the hab explosion on Luna on a public com.

All of which was in the past, and such self-piteous navel-gazing wasn't getting me anywhere. Even so, the fact that I—and my brother before me—had been selected to take on this job was interesting. Not the FFH connection, now I thought about it—Shiv's father had been an Indian engineer and Wang had never formally adopted him—but the fact that we were both outsiders. Okay, so I'd only inherited the—potential—role, but our Mr. P had been happy to consider me when, as Ika implied, he'd turned down local talent. This insistence on using outsiders both worried and intrigued me.

The next morning, when I went in search of the cheap sludge that passed for food around here, new red-and-gold decorations adorned the main walkways, and the open plaza near my hotel sported a wide scaffolding pillar reaching to the mezzanine above; at the base, half a dozen people in overalls were constructing something that looked like a giant claw out of spidersilk braiding and paper flowers. It was attracting some attention so I asked a passerby what was going on.

"They're building a lucky dragon," the woman replied. She looked up at me appraisingly, registering my half-breed status. "For the New Year, you know?"

Ah yes, New Year was less than a month away. I needed to get a move on.

I saw this movie once, a vintage piece from Japan. The newly-bereaved heroine has a dream in which she dips her toe into a dark, inky lake, and the toe gets stained. When she wakes up, it's still stained. Over the next few days the stain rises up her body, turning her into living darkness. In the end, as it reaches her neck. She goes back to the lake and throws herself in, where she is reunited with her long-lost lover.

While I'd been dreaming, and rationalising, my toe had slipped into the water.

I called Ika. "Can you contact the financier again, and ask if it's not too late?"

"I'm glad you've reconsidered, Ms. Choi."

I smiled at the blurred image on Ika's screen. "I didn't say that. I just said I'd like to talk."

"Certainly. You have more questions, then?"

'One in particular. Why do you want an offworlder to run this job?

"Mars is a small and insular world. There are a limited number of people with suitable skills and although we'll have to use some local talent, I feel it's more likely to succeed if the individual coordinating the job, the only person with all the facts, is an outsider."

Which was pretty much the answer I'd expected. My knowledge of the Martian underworld was limited but the Chinese dominated it, certainly in Olympus, Mars' first city, just as they did in mainstream Martian culture. A variation on the Triad system had been imported from Earth. I got the impression the relationship between the Triads and Everlight was complicated. I suspected that stealing Everlight's crown jewel was not something they'd be happy to attempt—or see anyone else attempt. I picked my next words carefully. "Your original choice for this role suffered an unfortunate accident."

"Yes. My condolences on your loss." Of course he knew I was Shiv's sister; I'd have been more concerned if he hadn't.

"I haven't been able to find out much regarding that accident, other than the fact that it was a flyer crash, and the flyer apparently didn't have a working transponder. I don't suppose you know more than that?"

A momentary pause, then, "You put me in a difficult position, Ms. Choi. If we don't have a working relationship, I can't justify giving you that information. If we do, I'll share all I know, although some of it may . . . cause you concern."

"So Shiv Neru's death wasn't an accident?"

"No one knows for sure." Another pause. "All right. I'll say this: there was evidence that an attempt had been made to capture the flyer."

"Capture it? How?"

"Mars' low gravity combined with its minimal atmosphere means you can fly a small ground-launched vehicle into low orbit for relatively little power expenditure. You can even leave the gravity well entirely, if someone sends down a larger vehicle from orbit to snare your flyer before it reaches its operational limits."

"Someone swooped down and snatched him out the sky before his flyer got to hard vacuum?"

"Not exactly. Most likely it was ambushed by a second vehicle in low orbit. The same structural mods that allow sub-orbital flyers to be snared also make them vulnerable to, well, hijacking."

"Someone tried to *hijack* the flyer? I thought it crashed."

"'Tried' is the relevant word. It is possible they wanted to capture Mr. Neru, but something went wrong—perhaps he attempted to evade them—and the flyer was damaged, and crash-landed."

My head was spinning. Shiv had always joked about never letting them take him alive. Looked as if it'd be his epitaph. But who were "they"? Why did they want to capture him, out in the Martian wilderness? And what had he been doing taking a solo sub-orbital flight anyway?

"I think," continued Mr. P, "that I've given you more than enough on trust."

"Yes. You have." Someone had tried to kidnap Shiv and ended up killing him. Or killed him and made it look like a kidnap attempt. Was I letting myself in for similar treatment if I took on this job? I thought of my nice, safe office job back on Earth; except it wasn't safe, and at best I'd get back to earning just enough to get by, and never find out what was going on here, or why my brother had got himself killed. Not to mention being guilt-tripped by my mother for the rest of my life.

"I'll do it."

Ika had already scoped out three members of the team, but I wanted to speak to them individually before hiring. I also asked her to get me a few prohibited items, for personal defence. Ika agreed though she commented, "You do know Olympus Central is safer than most cities on Earth?" She might be right, given whoever had gone after Shiv had waited until he left the city, but I wasn't taking chances.

While Ika was arranging the interviews I received a message from my employers. Apparently my case was going through the formalities with Everlight's HR department, and after their initial ruling—expected in a few weeks, during which time I remained employed if unpaid—I would be expected to prepare a "justification response." I appreciated Mr. Lau keeping me informed, but if everything worked out for me on Mars then Everlight HR could stick their initial ruling and request for justification in a place he'd be shocked to hear me refer to.

I chose neutral, public places for the interviews.

For the physical security expert I specified a mid-range tea-house. Xiao-Fei arrived on time and ordered green tea. He was a small man with a limp, and during the course of our conversation he used an inhaler twice. When I'd seen a Chinese name on Ika's file I'd been wary, and my wariness had increased on finding he had once worked for Everlight as an electrical engineer. However, the blowout at a remote dome which left him crippled had been hushed up, and the compensation he'd received barely covered his ongoing medical bills. He'd have no problem shafting his ex-employers.

Not that I told him he'd be doing that just yet. Our chat was suitably vague, an exchange of pleasantries, and some personal history from him (most of which I already knew, but I wanted to hear it from his own lips). Then I moved on to more detailed enquiries about the kinds of systems he was familiar with.

I was drawing on skills I'd gained in an office, rather than in my previous life aiding and abetting my mother; Mum preferred scams and schemes and the occasional hack, rather than open heists with accomplices. On those jobs where we'd brought in outside help she did usually tell them the target beforehand. But it's one thing hitting a local company or institution and quite another going up against the corporation who effectively rule the planet. Plus, the Eye of Heaven could be stowed out of our reach, back in Everlight's vaults, in a matter of minutes. I'd tell the team exactly what they were going after only when we were committed. Until then, I couldn't afford the slightest hint of a rumour to get out. As I say: compartmentalisation is vital in a job like this.

Speaking to my next contact meant returning to Ika's backroom data-fortress. This job required two hackers, with slightly different skillsets, in two different locations. Mr. P had specified that the off-planet member of the team would be someone he'd recommend. Her name was Ana, and she insisted on a voice-only interview, which made getting to know her tricky, especially given her love of the local Martian patois, calling me *dost* and saying *shi* instead of *yes*. Most people I'd meet, correctly identifying me as an outsider, stuck to English or Mandarin rather than the mash-up of English, Mandarin, Russian, and a variety of East Asian languages that all the cool kids spoke here. And she was a kid—she sounded appallingly young. I tried to see past the Martian dialect to identify her original accent; not mainland Chinese, but somewhere around there. Taiwanese? Or even a Korean; there might be a few of them here, same as there were Americans. Perhaps she was on Phobos: the Pacific Rim Consortium, who ran that particular moon, enjoyed damaging Chinese interests. Or she was somewhere on one of the other stations above us. Maybe even a young and rebellious Deimon sticking it to the man. I just had to trust Mr. P had picked wisely when he went for a teen in space.

Assuming she was what she sounded like. As I walked to the final meeting of the day, I considered the likelihood that Ana and possibly Mr. P were not real people at all, but constructs voiced by a LAI. Then again, why use a Limited Artificial Intellect when I might suss I was talking to a machine? Just use masking software on a real human, as appeared to be the case here. And obviously they weren't Unlimited AIs. Not even the Deimons in their little bit of orbital semi-anarchy had managed— or perhaps dared—to recreate the perfect storm that led, briefly, to the only true AI. I doubted they'd be foolish enough to try, given how that worked out last time. But I was overthinking this. All that mattered was that everyone played their part and the job went off smoothly.

The third team member who Ika had already vetted was Nico. His role fell somewhere between Xiao-Fei's and Ana's, though he'd be working locally, on the ground. We met in one of the larger plazas, where drones flew delicacies from the nearby food court to diners' tables. Nico was there before me. We both ordered iced tea. He had mixed Malaysian and African heritage; he came across as laid-back and friendly, though his file said he was ex-military, an early experience as a conscript in southeast Asia he wasn't proud of. "I'm here now, living a new life on Mars," he said with a smile. My only concern was that he might have exaggerated his skills, as he struck me as a little too eager to please. Then again, much of his work would be done in advance of the job. Plus, I was looking for a mix of competencies hard to find in this environment and though I might have covered all the bases with two people taking on this role, I wanted to keep the numbers down.

The following day I met up with the final team member; our late addition, doing the job Shiv would have done, had he lived long enough.

The individual in question wished to be known as Gregori. He was Marineris-born and to go by the quality of the hotel he was staying at he wasn't in this for the money. I suspected Gregori was the rebellious playboy son of one of the old Russian families. I wondered at this, given the uneasy relations between China and Russia here and on Earth. But, though he was Martian-born, as a first-time visitor to Olympus he fulfilled Mr. P's preference for using non-locals where possible, and nothing Ika managed to turn up gave us cause for suspicion.

We met in a coffee bar which, in the way of such offworld establishments, mainly sold overpriced coffee substitutes. He was late, which was a strike against him, and when he arrived he threw himself into the seat opposite me with a grin.

I tried to hold onto the fact that he was tardy, arrogant, and might have dubious connections, but mainly I tried to remember to breathe. He was in his early twenties, with sharp yet asymmetric features and immaculate blond hair. I have a thing for blonds. He'd look fantastic in Russian traditional costume, on the back of a black stallion. Were Cossacks blond? Who cared? He could ride across the steppes and pillage my village any time. *Yes, breathe.* I looked away from those lovely sapphire eyes and started the interview, only to have him interrupt as I was asking how long he'd been in Olympus.

"I get to drive and to pilot, yes?"

"Yes, you'll need both skills."

"Good, good. Do you like to drive fast, Ms. C?" I'd taken a leaf out of Shiv's book and insisted my team used my title and first letter of my surname; hearing even part of my name from this young man made me feel a certain warmth. *Stay focused, and breathe.*

"We're not talking high performance vehicles here, Gregori."

"No? But it'll still be fun."

I managed to keep to my script for the rest of the interview. He flirted outrageously the whole time. I wasn't sure if this was an act for me or his default setting. Frankly, I didn't care.

I did ask one direct question I'd avoided with the others, it generally being considered bad form amongst career criminals. "Why do you want to do this job?"

"Like I said, it'll be fun, da?"

I believed him. He really was that shallow. How charming. "Let's hope so. I'm guessing, given where you're staying, the money is not the issue."

"It is a good hotel. Spacious rooms."

"Really? I'd be interested in seeing that for myself."

"You like to see my room? I would love to show you."

"Lead on."

Two hundred or so years ago, back when humans first ventured into space, the idea of zero-gee sex used to be a Thing. It was meant to be exotic, special, out-of-this-world. Another example of how dumb our ancestors were. Leaving aside the chance that one or more partners would spend the session trying not to throw up, the laws of the universe do not bend just so a girl can get herself the right level of friction and degree of thrust to really hit the spot.

Low-gee sex with someone who knows what they're doing is, however, *a-maz-ing*. And Gregori knew what he was doing. Part of me wanted to stay all night—or what was left of it when I finally surfaced long enough to check the time—but that's not how I operate. Gregori, bless him, appeared genuinely surprised and sorry when I left.

Two days later myself, Nico, and Gregori took a trip into the tunnels. Another key to success in a job like this, besides compartmentalisation, is diversion. Lifting the Eye was the simple part of the job; getting away with it would be the real challenge, and doing so without being caught was the reason we were being paid so much.

The final factor for any hands-on job is practice, although we were limited in what could be practiced in advance.

Ana, the team member with the fullest picture—including details on the target, so Mr. P had better be right to trust her—would be doing whatever prep she needed on her own, high up in her orbital castle.

I was confident that Xiao-Fei knew how to deal with the on-site security we'd run into on the night. And before we went in I'd give him the full lowdown on what was required, including the additional and rather unexpected part of the snatch.

Which left me, Nico, and Gregori to run through the getaway, insofar as we could. We visited a part of Olympus most tourists avoided, the barely used maze of first-generation tunnels dug by the original tunnelworms—the LAI-brained excavators invented by the Levi-Mathesons—along with so much we take for granted today, from spidersilk digesters to brain-deplaquing. Whatever I, or anyone else, might say about the LMs, they were the only non-corporate entity who got rich enough to buy a moon. And for all their high ideals, they kept their fortune by use of expedient cutouts on their biotech which activate, rendering said tech useless, unless it gets regular catalytic boosts or similar tailored updates. These are sent out free from the Deimos labs . . . provided you'd paid the patent fees back to the founders' descendants.

Amusingly, the practice vehicles were rentals. Resources were limited here. All I could do was make sure they were as close in spec as possible to the ones we'd be using on the night. This part of the run-through was more about getting familiar with the route than pulling fast stunts. You can't pull fast stunts in a tunnelbug. Not that this stopped Gregori trying. And though Nico was a competent driver, I needed a bit of practice. I'd driven various vehicles on Earth and Luna but my previous experience hadn't been underground. We ended up paying a damage excess on two of the 'bugs, thanks to Gregori's overenthusiasm and my inexperience.

Halfway through our four days' of driving practice the Rainfall comet started final braking ready for insertion into Mars' orbit. It looked unreal in the footage, a spiny black ball like some giant gothoid kid's toy. The black was the nanoweave coating, another LM special, necessary to keep the irregular ball of dirty snow intact until Everlight were ready to sell it off by the tonne. The news was cooing about this latest near-impossible feat by the corp. How had they managed it? A good question, but not one that bothered me much at the time.

By now we were only a week away from the start of the New Year celebrations, and Olympus' tunnels, plazas, and shops were awash with red and gold décor and ingeniously constructed dragons ranging from the cute to the disturbing.

The day after Project Rainfall entered its penultimate phase I had an odd encounter. I was taking a narrow alleyway back to my doss-house—having seen inside Gregori's accommodation, I couldn't call it a hotel any more—when a man with an oversize backpack hurried out of a side turning. We ran into each other, and bundles of incense and lucky banknotes spewed from his backpack in Martian slo-mo. I reached out to help. Although the encounter had made me jump, he was old and bearded. Harmless. Probably. "So very sorry," he muttered as he pulled himself upright on me.

"No, no, it's my fault." This kind of stunt could be a diversion, and I put my back against the slimy wall even as I helped the old man to his feet. Looking past him the alley appeared empty. "Can you manage? Your stuff I mean?" This could still be a ploy, and I didn't want to get jumped while crouched down with hands full of ritual offerings.

"You hold my pack?"

I couldn't really refuse. I propped the pack against my leg, keeping my head up, while the old man gathered his gear up and re-packed it, fussing and muttering under his breath. As I lifted the pack onto his back he said, "You like Olympus?"

"Er, yes. It's a great city." He could guess I was a visitor; that was easy enough.

"So you stay for a while?"

"A while, yes." I let go of the pack. He teetered for a moment, then turned to me. "And you behave while you are here?" He actually waggled a bony finger at me.

I nodded. Not sure what else I could do.

He turned and bustled off.

Another film I remember, in fact I'm sure I've seen this trope more than once, is when the harmless old man who the stupid gwailo disregards later turns out to be the Grandfather of the local Triad family.

We couldn't practice with the second vehicle we'd be using. We were in the hands of Mr. P and Ana for that part of the job. All we could do was make sure we got to it safely.

External airlocks aren't remote hackable any more—humans learnt by that mistake in the Selene City disaster. You have to be physically present to deal with them. Hacking one in situ is possible, but if you're in a hurry, or you don't have the skills, you need something a little more . . . primitive.

And that was how the three of us came to take another rented vehicle, this one a rover rather than a tunnelbug, on a day-trip to the outside slopes of Olympus Mons itself.

Given what had happened to my brother, I went armed with the most impressive weapon Ika had procured, an ancient-looking concussion pistol, firing actual slugs. Not at all legal, so I couldn't wear it openly in the domes. It wouldn't be wise to let off a shot in the rover either, but I felt better knowing I had a weapon to hand. Once we were outside the city proper, I strapped the holster on my belt. Nico gave me a dark look but said nothing. Gregori raised his eyebrows at the chunky sidearm, before smiling and commenting that he found girls with big guns very sexy. *Breathe, and focus, Lizzie. Breathe and focus.* I kept both my accomplices in sight as far as possible. That way, if one of them tried anything, the other might, hopefully, intervene.

It took most of the day to reach the target area, as we were practising on long-disused and semi-depressurized tunnels far enough away from any habitation that our activities would remain undetected. We also had limited materials for this dry run, as we had to save enough for the job itself.

It took Nico a half hour to do this stuff out at the chosen airlock. Gregori and I had nothing to do but wait, back in the rover. This vehicle, being somewhat more expensive than the tunnelbugs, had internal cameras, one covering the cab, one looking out, so we'd parked facing downslope with a panoramic view of red rubble sweeping down towards the distant plains below. If it wasn't for the clause saying we'd lose our deposit on the rental if we took our skinsuits off, Gregori and I might have given anyone who reviewed the internal footage something interesting to watch.

The time ticked by. If Gregori wasn't the vacuous and cute creature he appeared to be then now, with Nico out of sight, would be the time to make his move. The camera coverage wasn't perfect; a gun drawn behind the pilot's seat, pointed forward, might not even be recorded. And cameras could be tampered with.

I told myself that these paranoid fantasies weren't helping and indulged in some more healthy, if filthy, ones. Given he hadn't shot me, I'd be going back to Gregori's when we were done here.

Finally Nico commed, summoning us out to witness his handiwork. We donned breathers and went outside. This was the first time I'd stood on the unprotected surface of another planet, and I tried to savour the experience, but it was a lot like a technicolour version of the Moon, though with splashes of sulphur and grey hardy-lichen on some of the sunnier rocks. Nico had found one such rock, which he now suggested we stayed behind, "just in case." This did not reassure me.

The charge was on a timer but being monitored from his suit. He counted it down over the comm, as a courtesy. "Three . . . two . . . one."

The ground kicked. A plume of rock, dust, and bits of metal airlock spurted out the side of the mountain. A lot more rock, dust, and metal than I'd expected. Despite the thin air, the accompanying bang was loud enough to hurt the ears. If anyone was listening in Olympus, they'd have heard that.

I took a deep breath to calm myself, then turned to Nico.

"You're only supposed to blow the *outer* airlock!"

Nico smiled and shrugged apologetically. Behind him, debris began to rain down on the Martian landscape.

When we got back to the domes, I half expected Nico's overenthusiasm to have gotten us in trouble. The tunnel he'd breached had been sealed further in so we hadn't caused a blowout, but an explosion that size could register on seismic sensors and as Mars wasn't prone to earthquakes that could have raised questions. When no one asked about our little trip I concluded we'd been far enough out that no one had noticed.

But that evening did bring some bad news. Ika called to say Xiao-Fei had been arrested.

"What for?" I demanded.

"My sources didn't say. We have no reason to suspect it relates to the current endeavour."

No reason to assume it didn't, either. I had a sudden urge to check escape routes. My options for leaving Mars were limited, not least by lack of funds. If I wanted to use my budget return I'd need to wait a week.

Late morning the next day the news got worse. Xiao-Fei had suffered an "incident" while in police custody, and was now in a coma. His health hadn't been good and it might just be that, an accident, maybe even a reaction to stress. Or he might have been interrogated, with prejudice. I hated myself for hoping he was just ill, as opposed to a victim of police brutality, but he was in no position to have an opinion right now.

Two flights left before New Year, one to Phobos (affordable) and one back to Earth (not). Or I could head out to Marineris, let Gregori show me the sights there. Then again, if Xiao-Fei *had* squealed, they'd be watching the ports. Or I could call off the job, leaving me broke and in bad favour with Ika and our patron. But also alive and out of prison. Perhaps I should hope for bad weather, as that would scupper the job without pissing anyone off. Act of God, and all that. But the forecast was for a fine and dust-free New Year.

I'd got to know a few locals around my doss-house over the last couple of weeks. Relationships varied from polite but distant through to the kind of street camaraderie I sometimes found growing up with Mum and Shiv; in order to end up here I must've had at least as crappy a time as they had, and that made me okay. One of the friendlier locals, an ever-cheerful sex worker of variable gender called Wu, asked if I'd heard about old Mr. Feng.

"Not sure I know who you mean." The street camaraderie came with an assumption that you knew what they knew, but I'd hadn't had much chance to get a feel for the neighbourhood.

Wu waved a rainbow-nailed hand. "Had a fall, and he's in the Charity. Such a miser, he wasn't poor you know, he could have afforded a trolley, or hired help, but no, he had carry his business on his back."

"In a backpack?"

"Yes! So you do know him. Silly old coot."

Some coincidences are just that: coincidences. Not enemy action. And some harmless old men really are harmless old men, not venerable crime-lords. Being cautious to the point of paranoid compulsion can be counterproductive.

I called Ika, and asked if she could get hold of anyone with Xiao-Fei's skillset in the time we had left.

Her name was Paula McIntyre and she was a genuine American. We met at a different tea-house to the one where I'd spoken to Xiao-Fei. Give how tight the schedule was, I considered not meeting her at all, but everyone else had been interviewed and if this last-minute replacement for Xiao-Fei didn't pan out, the job wasn't happening.

She was older than any of us, midsixties at least, with an easy-going smile and a gaze that didn't miss a trick. She'd only arrived in Olympus recently, from Earth, and her profession was openly listed as "security consultant." As with the others, our chat was mainly small talk. When I commented on her strong US accent she said, "My parents saw the Small War."

"Saw as in . . ." She was old enough to only be one generation removed from the worst thing humanity had ever done to itself, but I had trouble getting my head around how you can "see" a nuclear exchange that sterilised half a continent, and survive.

"They were hiking in the Rocky Mountains when it went down. Kinda ironic, really."

"Because that's where the Doomsday UAI was?" It was still a chilling thought, the idea that an inhuman intelligence could decide it made sense to wipe out a whole nation just because they were the enemy de jour. To this day, no one was quite sure how that disastrous first strike had come about.

"Yeah. Pop said they had no idea what was going on until they saw a mushroom cloud on the horizon. Then he checked his cell and when there wasn't any coverage, assumed the worst."

"But the fallout . . ." She didn't look like the mutant child of irradiated parents.

"They were in the far north, and the wind was blowing from that direction. They walked across the Canadian border about the same time the Generals took an axe to that damn AI." She sounded angry about it, even though she hadn't been born then.

Despite myself, I liked this woman. I felt a little star struck—because the only thing rarer than a genuine full-blood American is a genuine full-blood North Korean—but there was also an unexpected sense of kinship. Mum played up her quarter-heritage US blood, so I watched a lot of old US movies when I was growing up. Paula McIntyre was the "real deal." For a moment I wanted to take her into my confidence, tell her up front what the target was. But much as I enjoyed talking to her, I'm the daughter of a con-artist. I don't trust that easily.

Twelve hours later, we were crawling through ducts together. Having two people go in to physically lift the Eye was risky, but Mr. P wanted me present for the whole job. "You can't be sure what you'll find; you might need two people for some of it. And you're the person on the ground I hired, so you're the only one I want handling the Eye."

With Mr. P's words ringing in my ears, I still hadn't told Ms. McIntyre what we were here to steal. All she knew was that the target was somewhere in Everlight's main corporate complex—that being where we were now. She didn't look happy when I told her she'd get full details in due course but she was also a professional, and she didn't gripe.

"Which way here?" She was in front, and we'd come to an intersection.

"Left," I muttered into my comm. Her coverall-clad backside got moving again. We'd dressed as maintenance workers, a basic disguise which, along with some remote hacking from Nico, had got us into the ducts.

"Okay." We crawled forward. Just round the corner, she stopped. "Hold up, we've got a sensor grid here." We both wore hudglasses; mine projected a map, while hers showed an overlay of radiant energy, temperature fluctuations, the UV and IR spectrum, and other arcane environmental factors that could alert someone who knew what to look for to hidden security features.

"Right. Time to do your stuff, Paula."

Ducts feature in a certain type of US film. They're great plot devices but lousy design choices. I mean, why would you build a secret entrance into your secure facility? On Mars, where you need to circulate a manufactured atmosphere to a lot of people living in sealed, confined spaces, you really do need some person-sized ducts. But whilst these ducts had got us into Everlight's territory, the sensitive areas weren't accessible this way. And, being Everlight, they'd built security features into some of these low-security ducts. In this case, a lattice of invisible laser beams that triggered an alarm if anything larger than a rat passed through; or if someone tried to disarm them and failed. I'd hoped we might get the locations of these little surprises from Nico's preliminary research, but he'd said he couldn't risk going that deep into Everlight's security system, so we were on our own.

I sat back and counted breaths. I'm not phobic about confined spaces, but I am afraid of being caught. This was the first obstacle we'd come across requiring Ms. McIntyre's skill. She'd better be up to it.

Sixty-seven breaths later she said, "We're clear."

We set off again. My breathing remained shallow until I was sure we'd passed the unseen detection device. Logically, I should have continued to worry: if we had tripped an alarm it was probably silent. We could handle one possible response to Everlight discovering our route in; if they were irresponsible enough to pump knockout gas into their own vents, we had rebreathers. More likely they'd just station guards at the exits. It'd be a while before we found out.

"It would be good to know where we're heading, Ms. C."

Maybe it was time to show a little trust. "I'll ping you the map."

"Thanks." We crawled a few more metres. "The Celestial Colonnades?"

"That's right."

"Ah." That, to use the US parlance, was the sound a woman doing the math. Her next comment confirmed it. "That's where the Eye of Heaven is currently on display."

I could have dissembled, pointed out how many other expensive artefacts and trophy objects Everlight must have in their corporate museum, but I'd decided to trust her. "Yep."

"Ah." And that was the sound of a woman considering consequences. Maybe she'd suspected we were after the Eye, but now she knew. If she wasn't kosher, if she had another agenda, this might be the moment she made her move. Then again, her current position, on hands and knees in front of me in a narrow crawlspace, wasn't the place for it. "Thanks for letting me know."

I got nothing from her neutral tone: not gratitude, not sarcasm, not concern. We carried on.

Two corners later she found another detection device, this one pressure-based. It took a long time to disarm. If Everlight were mustering the troops, they'd be in place by now.

Round the next corner, our duct ended in a grille. My mouth dried up. We were about to break cover.

"Anyone out there?" I murmured over the comm.

"All clear."

"Good. I'm assuming you can get that grille off safely?"

"Shouldn't be a problem."

It wasn't; from the speed she dealt with it I suspected the grille hadn't even been alarmed. As Paula pulled it free of its frame she asked, "Are we coming back out this way?"

"Nope."

"Good." She probably didn't fancy making a quick getaway on hands and knees. Me neither.

Before we left the ducts we wriggled out of our coveralls. Underneath we wore skinsuits provided by Mr. P which, when we pulled the hoods up, would mask body heat—(except for our exposed faces), block scents and pheromones (not really an issue unless they had some very quirky security), and (the thing we were most likely to need in here) provide a basic chameleon function.

Unfortunately, this high-tech bonus was rather offset by the need to keep our low-tech coveralls with us. The bodysuits should have stopped us getting any DNA traces on the coveralls, and Shiv might have assumed they had and left them stuffed in the ducts, but I don't take chances. We bundled the coveralls into our expandable backpacks, which were also camo'd up.

Paula eased the grille back into place after we'd climbed out. Having Everlight think we'd left that way might be useful if we triggered any defences, but we couldn't leave any traces while we were still in the building.

We were in a carpeted corridor with anaemic yellow walls relieved by the occasional abstract print in pinks and reds. Executive country, Mum would call this. I'd spent much of the last decade passing through similar corridors, though not as an intruder.

We both had the map and there was room to walk side-by-side, so we did. Two things could scupper us before we reached the target area: surveillance and foot patrols. For the former, we had to rely on Nico's worm to ensure any cameras or other sensors along our path fed back nothing but empty corridor. Assuming his hack hadn't been detected. For foot patrols, we had to rely on our wits. Or, if it came to it, on the stunguns we both carried.

Worst case would be running into guards who either saw us first and raised the alarm, or who we dealt with only to have their colleagues back at base wonder why their mates suddenly disappeared off the security feed. Nico should be was busy setting up the next part of the plan by now, with neither the connectivity nor the time to monitor the local security feed and give us a heads-up of incoming trouble.

It wasn't far to the Celestial Colonnades. We took it slowly, pausing at the two intersections we passed. No sound save the faint hum of aircon. No smell save the faintest whiff of the most expensive incense.

Our destination wasn't hard to find. Amongst plain doors only identified by discreet pseudo-metal panels an actual metal door, standing floor-to-ceiling, stood out. Up closer and it was clear this was two bronze doors, decorated with a bas-relief design of dragons and clouds, like something from an ancient feudal castle. There was no obvious handle.

Paula McIntyre stood in front of the doors and pursed her lips. Finally she said, "This looks interesting."

"But not impossible."

"Oh no. I love a challenge."

I didn't tell her to shelve relishing the challenge in favour of getting on with the job. She knew that. Instead I said, "I'll keep watch," and padded up to the nearest junction. Glancing back, I saw her swing her pack round and remove several small objects. I recognised the flat palm-sized square of a sequencer, and a clear-cased micro-tool kit. I left her to it, and looked away, focusing on the intersecting corridor.

I'd been involved in two physical heists in my youth. One was an art heist in St. Petersburg where I'd been a surprisingly lo-tech spotter; I'd been fourteen at the time. Two years earlier I'd had my only other experience in the ducts, when Mum had realised that the Cairo Museum had service tunnels a child could fit through. Those jobs had ended in success, though only just in St. Petersburg.

However, in both cases we'd checked out the location in advance. That hadn't been an option here. Though Everlight liked to show off their prized possessions, most of the time access was limited to those they thought deserved it, which generally meant the execs of other corps. Over the New Year they also let the great unwashed visit the company showcase, but only in the most regulated way. You applied for tickets—which were expensive, and required personal vetting to even request—and a lucky few hundred would get guided tours of the company's spiritual heart at this most propitious of seasons. Obviously, I hadn't applied. So, other than knowing the general shape of the rooms beyond that door, I was going in blind.

It could have been worse: outside New Year the Eye was sealed in secure storage, in an unknown location in the complex.

Movement! Two guards were sauntering down the corridor. I withdrew my head and hissed a warning to Paula. "Fight or flight?" she asked over the comm.

"Neither. Hide. But keep your gun to hand." I'd already drawn mine, and was jogging back towards the double doors. Once I saw Paula had her stungun out and was turning to face the wall I did the same, opposite her but a little offset, the hand with the gun in pressed into the wall, hidden by my skinsuit camouflaged body. If the guards spotted an odd bit of wall as they approached then we'd both turn and fight, catching them in the crossfire. Where were Paula's tools? She wouldn't have had time to gather them up, so they'd be on the floor near her feet, visible to anyone who looked. Should we just fire on the guards as soon as they reached the junction? I wasn't sure how we'd know when that was, or how effective we'd be. I don't carry lethal firearms on a job but stunguns aren't the best range weapons.

I heard voices. The guards, a man and a woman, were griping about missing a New Year's party. Good. If they were talking they weren't watching their surroundings. Plus, we'd know where they were. I made myself breathe slow and even.

Their voices got suddenly louder. ". . . not as though the overtime rate even makes it worthwhile . . ."

Then quieter.

I took a proper breath. They'd walked straight past the end of the corridor. They hadn't even looked our way. Holiday cover staff: never the sharpest.

"Close call," murmured Paula in my ear as she unpeeled herself from the wall.

"Let's hope it's the only one."

Another good thing about the skinsuit is that it absorbs sweat. My body was reminding me how far I was out of my comfort zone. I respected Mr. P's logic, but I'd still rather not be here. Given the choice, I'm an organiser not a cat burglar.

I jumped at Paula's voice in my ear. "We're in."

One of the great doors clicked open. I went over and peered inside. I smelt old incense on the air, but saw nothing except darkness in the room beyond. As I switched my hudglasses to lo-light mode Paula nodded into the dark room and asked, "We sure the lights aren't on auto?" A reasonable question, especially if tripping said lights showed up on someone's status board.

"Not according to the schematics we've got." Schematics which hadn't shown the security measures in the ducts. I hate unknown unknowns.

I gestured for Paula to go first. She shot me a look which I couldn't make much of through her now-opaque glasses, and stepped across the threshold.

Nothing happened.

I followed her.

"Let's close this," I said, nodding back at the metal door once we were both in the room.

"Good idea."

It took both of us to pull the door closed manually, using the handle on the inside. I didn't like the solid *thunk* it made when it swung back into place but we couldn't risk any guards who were paying attention finding it open.

The plans showed four large, square rooms, each one big enough to swallow my old apartment. I had no information about the internal layout, but we appeared to have stepped into history. We stood under an arch leading into a courtyard formed by tiled, ridged roofs reaching down on all four sides. I glanced up, half expecting to see stars, but there was just the high ceiling. No doubt the lighting, when it was on, included suitably atmospheric projections.

The courtyard was full of artfully arranged statues. Lion-dogs, dragons, nymphs, and, in pride of place in the centre, a life-size Buddha in the Tibetan style. It was hard to tell in this—lack of—light, but the Buddha appeared to be carved from a single lump of solid jade. Some of the statues looked new; others so ancient and weathered I wasn't even sure what they'd once been. Of course, nothing here was genuine, hauled up Earth's gravity well and shipped all the way to Mars. But they would be faultless reproductions of items Everlight did own.

I was reasonably sure we wouldn't find the Eye in this room, but we had to check. "I'll go left, you take the right," I said to Paula.

"Sure."

As I picked my way through the statues I heard a gentle murmur from up ahead. After a moment, I identified it as running water. Other than the statues the only other features were the stone benches against the walls; the walls themselves were painted with detailed murals of Chinese myths and legends.

We met up on the threshold of the next room. "Do you want me to go first this time?" I asked Paula.

"Whatever works for you."

"Let's do this together then."

We entered side-by-side to find ourselves in another courtyard, though this time containing a sculpted garden, complete with stream running diagonally across the middle. As well as the benches around the edge there were love seats and carved arbours amongst the well-trimmed hedges and gravel paths. The only way across the stream was a delicately curved metal bridge. Paula went first. Halfway across, movement from below caught my eye. I froze. There was something in the water, something big. A fish. Of course. Not just any fish: a carp as long as my arm, beautifully mottled. Probably cost what I used to earn in a year.

The next room had a number of large square objects in it, some of them reflecting what little light came from behind us.

"Wait!"

I froze at Paula's whisper. "What is it?"

"I think we've got a pressure-pad here." The woman was certainly earning her share. She came up to stand next to me, then crouched down and reached out in a sweeping motion, hand just above the patch of floor between the two rooms, where the gravel of the garden gave way to polished stone. "Yeah, it's inbuilt and passive."

"Can you deal with it?"

"Not easily. Like I said, inbuilt and passive."

"Ah. Yes." Sensors like this were part of a structure's fabric, in this case probably a property of the pseudo-stone in front of us. You couldn't turn them off without removing the floor. Most of the time, the signal they sent wouldn't trigger an alarm— as otherwise every visitor to the place would be tripping its security—but they'd be switched to "live" mode whenever the Colonnades were locked up. "What do you reckon your chances of dealing with it are?"

"Fifty-fifty at best. And it'll take some time."

I respected her honesty. We were on a schedule. I looked up, as though there might be some convenient handholds on the ceiling. There weren't. I looked down again, beyond her to the floor of the next room. It was lacquered wood; the stone only covered the area under the carved archway between the two rooms, about two metres in total. "How likely is it the sensors extend beyond the area of stone flooring?"

"Highly unlikely."

"Then how about we just jump over it?" In this gravity, two metres was nothing.

"I . . . guess we could. Yes, that would work."

We backed up as far as the topiary would allow. "I'll go first," I said. I sprang forward, my feet pounding gravel. The sudden physical exertion felt odd, an explosive relief. I pushed off, was in the air for a long moment, then landed, well into the other room. As I stepped back to let Paula take her jump I wondered how poor Xiao-Fei would have dealt with this obstacle.

Paula landed a little behind me, though still clear of the stone floor.

This room was full of glass cases. The cases contained what could only be described as military memorabilia. Swords, pikes, suits of armour, and, as a centrepiece, a replica horse and rider, all clad in scale mail which, in normal light, probably shone bright as gold. Like everything else seen through the hudglasses, the place appeared to be lit by strong moonlight. In the first two rooms with their outdoor artifice, this had been apt, even relaxing, but here, amongst all the gleaming weaponry and glass, the effect was disconcerting. We checked the cases methodically. I found one sword which claimed to be the genuine article, imported all the way from Szechuan by a named executive I'd never heard of to celebrate his promotion; by implication everything else was a replica, as I'd assumed. The Eye wasn't here.

I paused on the threshold of the final room until Paula had done her checks. All clear.

This last room also contained glass cases, plus some free-standing exhibits. Rather than martial treasures, here we had jewellery, fabric, pots, and incense burners. The free-standing figures—which looked disturbingly lifelike through my hudglasses, save for their blank eyes—were dressed in silk costumes straight out of the old Imperial Court.

No immediate sign of what we were here for, though. We worked our way back. And there, against the back wall, was the Eye of Heaven. Sitting in its black cradle on a black plinth, it was easily the brightest thing in the room. Even in the lo-light the Eye shone like a giant pearl coated in rainbows. It wasn't quite a perfect oval, being more egg-shaped, like something you might expect a phoenix or other mythical creature to hatch from.

Paula came to stand next to me.

The other exhibits were close-packed, but the Eye had its own distinct space, with nothing save air for a metre on each side. Which could just be part of the whole Feng Shui effect, giving it the room to do its spiritual stuff. Or it could indicate invisible security measures. "That's a suspiciously empty bit of room they've chosen," I remarked

"Sure is. I'll check it out." Paula knelt and extracted her equipment from her backpack. I stepped back to give her space. I'd come up with a provisional schedule for the job, though I'd had to built in plenty of contingency, given our incomplete intel. By the timings I was using as a baseline, we were running seventeen minutes late. I reminded myself that it was just that, a baseline; not a deadline. There was leeway built in.

Paula finished running a handheld detector over an area of wall at the right-hand edge of the Eye's exclusion zone and returned to her stash of gear. She selected what looked like a shiny cosmetic compact, laid it flat on her palm and opened it sideways, like a little hardcopy book. She turned away from the Eye and flicked her wrists. The mirrored "book" extended out to a metre-long conduit, two slivers of mirror connected at a ninety-degree angle to each other, foil-thin but rigid.

I'd seen reflectors like this before. They took a lot of skill to deploy, and they only worked on certain types of light-grid. I had to assume Paula knew this was such a grid. She stood the reflector on the floor. I stepped back. The bottom edge had nano-grip technology, but it would still teeter if knocked. Next, Paula fitted a pair of black rods, so slender they were barely visible, across the top and, after reversing it, the bottom of her mirrored conduit. With the rods in place, she picked up the reflector, and spent a while just looking at the Eye and its surrounds. Then she edged forward. She stopped and adjusted her grip to hold the reflector's base just off the floor. Moving so slowly she appeared not to be in motion at all, her face blank with concentration, she extended her arms.

I realised it had been some time since I'd taken a breath, but my chest was too tight to let much air in.

Paula lowered the reflector the final couple of millimetres to the floor. Her shoulders lowered by about the same amount.

Stage one complete. Now the tricky bit.

She crouched down then turned her head, checking the (to me) invisible beams. I could have reset my hud display too, but seeing what Paula was seeing wouldn't make me any less nervous. I had to trust her to do her job.

Placing one hand on the thin connector rod running across the top of the reflector, she began to move her fingers apart. Her other hand was still half extended, not quite touching the reflector, like a magician in the middle of a conjuring trick.

The two halves of the reflector began to slide apart. Now they were connected only by the expanding rods at top and bottom.

Would the alarm be silent, if she tripped it? I had an idea not, at this stage. My ears hurt from waiting for the klaxon.

The gap widened. Now the two slivers of mirror had clear air between them—clear of any sort of detecting light beam, that is. If I was only ten centimetres wide I could slip in there right now.

The gap widened further. There was a trade-off here: the bigger the gap, the easier it would be to get through, but the farther apart the two halves of the reflector got, the less stable they were, even with their nanotech footing. I consoled myself that this was probably easier in Martian gravity before remembering that Paula came from Earth. Was she assuming one G, not a third? Should I point this out? I opened my mouth, then closed it again. She didn't need me whispering in her ear unexpectedly.

The gap was a good forty centimetres now. Paula kept teasing out the upper supporting rod, which was slaved to the lower one. I saw a ripple of tension in her thigh, the muscles protesting at being held in a tense squat for so long. *Perhaps we should have brought a folding stool.*

If the alarm was silent, the guards would be here any moment.

She stopped, with the gap at what my hudglasses told me was fifty-two centimetres. She stood and pummelled her aching legs—but gently, so as not to disturb the reflector. With it set this wide, fierce aircon might sway it and it only took a tiny movement to misalign the beams currently being reflected back to their source in the wall. At which point, we'd be blown.

"We good?" I whispered. Then I made myself take a proper breath.

"We're good."

She looked past her handiwork to the plinth with the Eye on it. "No case. That because of the Feng Shui energies?"

"Most likely."

"The plinth'll be rigged. Won't know how until I get in there."

"Anything I can do?"

"Stay back unless I say otherwise."

"Got you."

Despite the tension, I did relish seeing a master at work.

Paula gathered a subset of tools into her backpack and slung it round her neck, facing forward. Then she crouched down and sidled sideways towards the gap between the two halves of the reflector.

Part of me wanted to watch, but that part stopped me breathing. I looked away, because this was the messy human bit of the job, where a slip or a sneeze could mean disaster.

When I looked again, Paula was straightening on the other side of the invisible doorway. She approached the Eye with all the care I'd expect, taking readings, holding out a palm, cocking her head.

"I reckon we've got a basic pressure-trap here." Her voice was all business.

"You reckon? You can't be sure?"

"Not without touching it, and I want to have everything prepped before I do."

"But you can deal with whatever you do find?" We were thirty-two minutes behind schedule now.

"Yes and no. Fooling the weight-sensor shouldn't be an issue but this is a no-expense-spared setup, so it's likely to have spatial sensors too."

"Meaning?"

"When I lift the Eye from its cradle, we'll need to replace it with something as near as possible the same shape. Some of those pots back there—"

"Actually," I said, "We need to take the cradle too." I should have mentioned that earlier. Bad Lizzie.

Her head swung round, though her face was blank behind her hud. "What?"

"That octagonal holder it's sitting in? We can't lift the Eye from it."

"Can't as in . . ."

"I've been instructed to bring the Eye of Heaven out in its holder."

"Do we know why?" Her voice was cold.

"Because those are our instructions."

She nodded, and said nothing. Then finally, "You're the boss." She turned away and resumed her observations and calculations. A minute and a half later she said. "Actually that'll make it easier. I'm picking up some odd environmental readings but no obvious security on the plinth itself."

"Good. And you'll monitor those odd readings?"

"Of course."

She stepped closer, and touched the plinth. No alarm sounded. She shucked off her backpack and selected the micro-tool kit, then bent over the plinth. After less than a minute she straightened, put a hand on either side of the Eye, then lifted it free, cradle and all. I savoured the lack of obvious alarms.

"Hhhmm." She sounded disappointed.

"Problem?"

"No. Opposite in fact. The cradle was just screwed into the plinth. No security on it at all. Perhaps our patron knew something about the Eye's holder, and decided it was beyond anyone's skill to deal with it." She appeared to take this as an affront to her skills.

"That could be it." Not that I had any more idea than she did why Mr. P wanted the Eye of Heaven in its not-at-all-handy carrying cradle. I'd had to accept this as one of his quirks. He was paying, after all.

I wondered if Paula would just hand me the Eye but she stuffed it into her backpack and slung it across her front.

"Are you going to be okay like that?" The Eye wasn't quite head-sized, but it had to be heavy. It would pull her off balance when she did her crab-through-a-crevice routine.

She just grunted. It wasn't like I could intervene.

It was even harder to look away this time, but I needed to let her concentrate. When I heard a small gasp I screwed my eyes shut, like that would help. When I opened them she was frozen in place between the two halves of the reflector, both hands on the floor, pack swinging dangerously free. She'd fallen forward, then caught herself.

"Can I—?"

"No. I'm good." She leant back, getting her weight redistributed. Then she shuffled out from between the two reflector posts. Once she was sure she was clear, she stood, and eased her neck from side-to-side.

I waited until she had ironed out the kinks before saying, "I'll take the Eye now please."

"Why?" Her hud was still opaque, but I suspected she was looking askance.

"It's nothing personal. Just another of the patron's conditions."

"And the patron will know we obeyed this particular request how?"

"Look, I know it's a pain, but let's do this by the book."

"Whatever."

Time was ticking. "Let's just swap packs."

"Sure." She sounded tense.

Getting Paula's now-heavy pack on my back proved tricky. When she offered to help I didn't object. What can I say, I was tired and stressed and in a hurry. Standing behind me, she supported the pack while I threaded my arms through the straps. As I shrugged the pack onto my shoulders I felt her step away to the side.

Something stung my cheek, a needle-prick of cold. I went to swat at what I assumed must be a biting insect. Reality dawned somewhere between brain and hand.

Paula McIntyre had just shot me.

The stunguns Ika had procured for us were fast-acting and, pissed off though I was, I was still conscious. It had been Ika's idea to give our newest team member untipped darts "just in case." If we'd had to deal with security guards that would put us at a disadvantage, but weighing up the odds of getting into a firefight versus a potential double-cross from the lovely Paula, I'd concurred with the fixer.

I drew my own pistol from its waist holster and stepped back, keeping the reflector in the corner of my eye. Tripping over that would not improve my situation.

Paula was giving her gun an incredulous stare. She didn't look happy. Her resume hadn't mentioned combat skills. I hoped it had been accurate.

She shot again. Our skinsuits would protect against a stun dart so her target was small, just the unprotected lower half of my face. She missed.

My target was equally hard to hit, being the lower half of *her* face. But I had to take her down quickly.

Mum hadn't been big on combat skills, but Ahmed, the boyfriend she'd kicked around with during our year in Afghanistan, had been all for training me up because, he said, "girls are often at a disadvantage." I'd been thirteen at the time and full of fury at the world. I'd paid attention during his lessons.

Instead of cracking off a wild shot I stepped backwards, once, twice, keeping my eyes on the target and the gun raised, taking aim even as I put distance between us. I couldn't risk more than two steps back thanks to the forest of display cases, and the fact that, having shot again, she was now closing on me, her face full of angry desperation.

Now or never. I fired.

No recoil, unlike some of the weapons Ahmed had put in my hands. I missed: she kept coming.

I stepped back again, and banged my heel on something solid. I fired through a flash of pain from my bruised heel.

She was at lunging distance now. She lunged.

The lunge became a fall, her eyes defocusing as the drug kicked in. Thanks to the display case I'd backed up against, I ended up catching her in my arms. Her anger had drained away, under the influence of industrial-strength sedation and, perhaps, acceptance of the inevitable.

As I lowered her to the floor her gaze sharpened and she smiled. Her eyes fluttered closed, but just before she went limp she murmured, "Mr. Lau sends his regards."

What the hell was I supposed to do now?

Stick to the plan, that was what.

I could work out what Paula meant later. Right now, I had to get out of here.

I had the Eye, and the lack of guards, alarms, or security lights suggested that, despite Paula McIntyre's duplicity, the job was still on. I shifted my pack more firmly into place and left my traitorous accomplice to her drugged sleep. By the time I was through the first room I was all but running. Jumping the pressure-pad in the doorway between the armoury and garden rooms felt like flying. Then I landed, and the Eye shifted on my back. I stumbled, then caught myself. I was pumped, more alive than I'd been for a decade. And that was dangerous. I made myself walk across the garden and through the statues.

When I reached the door, I pulled at the handle. Nothing. Not pull: *push.* I pushed. It didn't move. I was locked in.

No: think, Lizzie. The security on the door was to stop people getting in, not out. I looked to the side. There it was, a palm-sized black panel set into the wall. That had to be an override for the door. What I didn't know was whether it would set off an alarm as well as opening the door.

Option one: press it and see.

Option two: get Paula's toolkit out, and apply what little I knew about intrusion.

Given how little that was, option two was as likely to lead to tripping an alarm as option one. And it would take longer.

I pressed the panel with one fist while pushing the door.

It swung open. Silently.

I paused inside the entrance, listening, catching my breath, and adjusting my hudglasses. Ideally I should shut the door after I left so anyone walking past wouldn't realise anything was amiss but with no external handle—

Then I remembered why not having Paula McIntyre any more could scupper the job.

The next part of the plan involved riding an elevator to the building's basement. Paula would have bypassed the lift security, that being, as I'd just reminded myself, outside my area of expertise. Perhaps if I could raise Nico he could hack the lift from his end, but even if he wasn't tied up with his own prep, our comms were deliberately low powered to avoid detection, and there was a lot of Martian rock between me and him. Perhaps if I stood at the top of the lift shaft and he happened to be standing at the bottom . . . Might as well try shouting.

My mind went blank for a moment. *Think.* There would be a way out of this.

Just like the external doors, any elevators giving access outside the complex needed a pass. Therefore, all I actually had to do was get hold of a staff pass. There: a simple solution, at least in theory. I called up the map on my hud.

The senior staff would all be out enjoying the New Year's celebrations but some of the up-and-coming execs would be happy to work overtime to prove their worth. I needed to head into less exclusive territory.

I kept my eyes and ears open, pausing at every corner, taking a slow, stealthy path through the corridors of corporate power. Even if nothing we'd done so far had tripped any alarms, it was only a matter of time before I ran into more guards, or someone noticed the open door to the Celestial Colonnades.

Despite the need to concentrate on the here and now, Paula McIntyre's parting words haunted me.

In order to know Mr. Lau she must work for Everlight. So why would she help steal their greatest prize?

Firstly, because she didn't know I was after the Eye until we were deep inside the Everlight complex.

Once she knew she could have "accidently" tripped an alarm, or alerted the guards who passed us by. Why hadn't she? But I remembered her response to the Colonnade doors, and to the security on the Eye. She was proud of her work. She wanted to know she could defeat Everlight's security.

Which would be odd if she worked for them. But I suspected Paula McIntyre was what her file claimed: an independent security specialist. And she was working for Mr. Lau.

He'd probably sent her here to keep tabs on me. Maybe I should be flattered. She might have had a hand in Xiao Fei's fate—or that might have been coincidence. They did happen.

It was safe to assume she wasn't here officially. No doubt my ex-boss had his own reasons for following me beyond the ends of the Earth. He might even have been after the Eye himself; imagine if Everlight had lost the Eye of Heaven, only to have it returned by prompt action from the agent of a relatively minor exec. How much face would Mr. Lau have saved his employers then? When it came to shafting colleagues, the criminal underworld could learn a lot from the corps.

Good job I had no plans to return to the day job.

Fortunately, the money from this job would buy a new face and a watertight identity, and thanks to Mr. P, I already had a means of getting off-planet. Assuming I could trust Mr. P. And assuming I could get myself and the Eye of Heaven out of Everlight's territory.

What was that?

I was still in exec country and didn't expect anyone to be behind the door the odd sound had come from. Given it was labelled with a masculine name—and no job title, which always signified high status, because if you had to ask, you were too lowly to know—the nature of the sound was also a surprise. A girlish giggle. And there it was again: more of a moan this time. Interesting. Whilst I could imagine our self-important exec getting himself some off-the-record female company for the New Year, I'd have expected them to get a room rather than use his office. It wasn't as though Mars didn't have nice hotels ideal for enjoying sex with all the trimmings.

I listened a little longer, and heard more faint sounds of pleasure. Then I pressed the pad. The door opened; I'd half expected there to be security on this door to an important man's office, but if there was it'd been disabled. I paused out of sight, though from the sound of it no one had noticed me. Poking my head round the open door I saw a familiar layout: a small office/antechamber with some hardcopy storage, an uncomfortable waiting area and a desk for the office administrator, then a doorway through to the main, larger, office. The noises came from the main office. I crept up to the open doorway, staying out of line-of-sight, although from the sound of it, whoever was inside was unlikely to notice me. Definitely a young woman enjoying herself. Even so, I drew my gun.

Peering round the door from a low vantage point, I found myself looking across plush carpet to a desk whose size and pretentious build rivalled Mr. Lau's. A young Chinese woman perched on the front of the desk. Her head was thrown back and she was panting in delight, no doubt thanks to the attentions of the young man in a brown uniform kneeling on the ground in front of her, his head buried deep her crotch.

I suspected neither of them was the owner of this office.

Looking around I spotted a couple of anomalous items on the otherwise immaculate plum-coloured carpet. That small dark scrap of fabric had to be underwear but there was also a smart jacket with, if my eyes didn't deceive me, the corner of an ID badge peeking out of a fold.

I had no desire to interrupt the kind of fun I hoped to be having myself in the none-too-distant future so I kept low and crept forward, heading for the discarded jacket.

I'd almost reached it when the woman's cries ramped up a notch. I looked up to see her hands deep in the boy's hair, her gaze fixed forward and her mouth open in a wide O set to become a squeal of pure animal pleasure at any moment.

At which point she spotted me.

Her gaze sharpened, and she gave a wholly different type of squeal. Her hands pushed away and, tangled as they were in the boy's hair, shoved him backwards. I acted on instinct. My dart hit him in the back and he fell to one side.

The woman stared at me. I waited for her to make another noise but she looked too terrified to even breathe. Which made sense: in my camo'd suit I was a disembodied head with wraparound shades and, if she looked closely, a floating gun.

"I'm not going to hurt you," I said in Mandarin. With my free hand I pulled my hudglasses up into my forehead. Maintaining a disguise was pointless now, thanks to having left Ms. McIntyre alive and able to identify me, and showing this young woman I was an ordinary woman, albeit in a skinsuit, might stop her suffering a heart attack on the spot.

In a tiny, terrified voice she croaked, "You shot Bao."

"Yes, with tranq." I looked over at the unconscious boy sprawled at her feet. Now I could see the uniform I confirmed my initial impression that he worked in Everlight's mailroom. "He'll be fine."

"Oh. Right. Of course." I suspected she would agree with anything I said. She'd probably never been so frightened in her life.

I should shoot her too, then take her pass and be done with it, but I didn't feel good about this. "Listen, I'm sorry I . . . sorry I interrupted you. And Bao."

"That's all right." She sounded incredulous, like she couldn't imagine the scary creature I appeared to be ever being sorry about anything.

"I need your pass now. That's why I came in."

"My pass? I . . . Why?"

"Do you really want to know?"

She looked stricken and shook her head. "No. You're right. I don't want to know."

"Listen, can I ask you something?"

She nodded, confused.

"Is this your boss' office?" I recognised that dress sense. She wore clothes I might have chosen myself, right down to the black lace panties under the conservative skirt and blouse.

She nodded again and bit her lip.

"And is he a smug and smiling bastard who wants you at his beck-and-call twenty-four-seven, expects you to deal with his cock-ups, and is happy to take credit for your hard work?"

For a moment a different type of shock flitted across her face. Then she grimaced, and nodded.

"Reminds me of someone I know. You know what?" I gestured at the unconscious boy, "I really wish I'd done something like this in *his* office."

She smiled, and blushed. Which was rather charming.

"I am going to have to take your pass now."

"I understand." As I reached for her jacket she said, "Wait. If you're trying to leave, it won't be enough."

"What do you mean?"

"They've upped security for the New Year. Because of the public coming in. You need a scan as well as a pass to get anywhere."

"Scan as in palm or iris?"

"Depends where you're trying to go. Oh. I shouldn't have told you that, should I?" Was that a smile?

"You didn't. I threatened you with torture when your pass didn't get me out."

"You . . . Oh, I see. Where do you need to get to?"

"Garage level."

"I'll show you. Just let me get my . . ." She gestured at the discarded panties.

I let her lead the way. Worst case, she tried to run or set off an alarm, in which case she'd get tranqed and dragged to the door. I didn't really expect that to happen, and it didn't. At the elevator she gave me her pass and pointed to the palm-print reader beside it. "I suppose you have to shoot me once I've opened the door for you."

"Afraid so."

"Will it hurt?"

"You'll hardly feel it."

The elevator ride down was interminable. I'd opened a comm channel and pinged Nico and Gregori, but only got a reply as the doors opened onto the garage level. Gregori was striding towards the lift, while Nico stood a few paces back, next to a battered tunnelbug.

"I was getting worried," said Gregori, arms open.

"You got what we came for?" Nico called out a moment later.

"I did." I evaded Gregori's attempt at a bear-hug.

Gregori frowned at me. "And what is it we have stolen, exactly?"

I jerked a thumb over my shoulder to indicate my backpack. "The Eye of Heaven."

Nico laughed. "That's fifty you owe me, *dost!*"

"Huh!" Gregori huffed. "So where is Ms. McIntyre?"

"I have some bad news regarding Ms. McIntyre. Turns out we were right to be suspicious of her."

"But the job's not blown?" Nico's smiled faltered.

A siren began to wail.

"Oh," said Gregori, grinning, "is it New Year already?"

"No, Gregori," I shouted above the alarm, "it is trouble already."

"What, I cannot make joke to defuse the tension?"

"Yes, you can, but let's get a move on, huh?"

Nico had the three near-identical tunnelbugs parked next to each other, hotwired and good to go. As Gregori turned to get in the middle of the three I grabbed his arm and pointed to his head. "Hood."

"What?"

"Pull your skinsuit hood up. No time for wardrobe adjustments at the other end."

"Da. Of course." He did so.

"But save the rebreather."

"I do know how to survive on Mars!"

He looked cute when peeved. I leaned across to give him a peck on the cheek. "Impress me, stud-muffin," I whispered. Then, over the comm to both of them, "See you on the other side!"

Nico raised a hand before climbing into his vehicle.

I pulled myself up into my tunnelbug, threw myself into the seat, slapped the panel to shut the door, and grabbed the wheel.

It wasn't exactly a racing start.

First off, we had to queue to leave the garage—currently dark, unmonitored and with an open door, thanks to Nico's earlier efforts. Nico first, then me, then Gregori.

As soon as we were in the main tunnel outside, we split up. Nico and I went left, nominally the "out" direction, though I peeled off into a smaller service tunnel after a hundred metres. Gregori broke right, heading back towards Olympus City.

One of the oldest scams in the book is the shell game. Some guy in a cave probably came up with it: three shells and a pea, guess which shell the pea's under. In that form, the point is to fool the mark using sleight of hand. In this version, the Eye was with me for the duration, and the solid rock of the tunnels meant we couldn't even communicate between vehicles, let alone swap cargo, but having three targets still meant a two-in-three chance any pursuers would pick the wrong one. We were upping the odds of getting the loot, and at least one of us, out.

I'd have preferred the odds with zero pursuers, but from the sound of that parting alarm, our luck had run out. Whether it had been the open door to the Colonnades, the unconscious secretary, or someone coming across one of Nico's hacks, we were blown.

I felt oddly calm. Must have been adrenalin comedown. Plus, I'd driven this route half a dozen times during our practice runs, although I wasn't going to assume I knew which turns to take. I kept an eye on the inertial nav readout in the corner of my hud.

Thanks to the load on my back, I had to hunch forward in the seat, but I wasn't going to be parted from the prize. From now on everything had to go like clockwork.

The view through the tunnelbug's front screen showed rock: rock below, rock to each side, rock above. The others would have a similar view, though Nico and Gregori were sticking to larger tunnels, because they were the diversion, roles they weren't delighted with. But they were the best drivers, and I was the one with the Eye. They'd draw attention while I sneaked out under the radar. Nico's path would take him straight towards the surface, before jinking off along a lateral tunnel; anyone trying to predict his course should be thrown by this change of direction. Should be. Gregori was doing the really fancy driving, heading directly towards the domes as though about to burst into Olympus Central itself, then doubling back. Which left me to creep upwards through the oldest, narrowest tunnels.

I slowed as my nav readout showed a bottleneck ahead; now the rock above was barely higher than the 'bug's roof, and its treads weren't getting much purchase on the tunnel's narrow bore. But I knew I'd make it, because we'd practiced this, several times.

I was just ramping up the speed again—insofar as tunnelbugs have speed to ramp up—when the vehicle's comm crackled. I didn't think I was near enough to any inhabited area to get random signal bleed through the rock, but I could hope.

". . . unauthorised . . . please identify . . ."

Some hope.

I resisted the urge to speed up. I knew how fast it was safe to take these tunnels, and that's how fast I was going. And I was over halfway now.

At the next fork, I went left. Fifty-fifty chance they'd go right, I told myself. But this was a long straight tunnel, and before the next turn, lights bobbed into view behind me. The transmission came clear. "Kindly stop your vehicle and prepare to present your credentials." I turned the radio off. It wasn't going to tell me anything I didn't already know.

Only two turns to go now. As the tunnel arced round, I ramped the tunnelbug's speed up. This tunnel had the steepest slope so far, and between that and the excessive speed, the 'bug began to yaw, until I wasn't on the tunnel bottom any more but creeping up the leftmost wall. Scary, but it seemed stable enough. Except the next turn was to the right. I eased off, and for a moment the 'bug lost grip, and slid. I grabbed the dashboard, braced to spin or flip, but the very narrowness of the tunnel saved me. The 'bug fishtailed, then stabilised. I took the right turn.

Another turn, in only fifty metres, and then I was on the home straight to, if not safety, then at least a way to lose the current pursuer. I took the turn. Lights flashed round the corner only a few seconds behind me. Much as my instinct was to floor the 'bug, I needed to slow down, even as those headlights grew in my monitor. Easing off had my nerves screaming but, I reminded myself, they'd have to slow down too. We were about to hit the end of the line. I tried not to think about how exposed I'd be when that happened. In tunnels this old, and this far from the city, we were out of the realms of automation; making my escape required some good old manual intervention.

Up ahead, the tunnel ended in a metal box.

I drove into the airlock too fast, and slammed on the brakes. My 'bug bumped the outer door, throwing me half out my seat, then stalled. I switched my hud to lo-light as I jumped out. The oncoming headlights became a blinding sun. Looked as if I'd be doing this by touch, not sight. I dialled my vision back down. I knew what I was looking for; I'd done this before, I'd be fine.

My first slap hit blank metal. I coughed; the air was full of the rock dust I'd kicked up. The oncoming lights were about to run me over. On my second attempt, I hit the button. The inner door slammed down a handbreadth from my face.

The airlock was windowless. I was in near darkness, the only light coming from the tunnelbug's cab. I dialled my vision up and stumbled round the 'bug. The air was frigid but I felt a glow on my exposed cheek as I passed the wheeled tracks. I'd run this tunnelbug hard.

Over at the outer door, I hit the command to start the lock cycling. Then I remembered what I'd forgotten in the panic of the oncoming lights. I pulled myself up onto the treads and leaned in through the door to grab a flat cylinder the size of my palm from the 'bug's dash. And paused. After the incident at the practice airlock Nico had reduced the amount in his charges to what he called "just enough bang to do the job." Which meant the charge had to be stuck in *exactly* the right place: centre bottom of the outer airlock door, ready to activate as the airlock opened and do enough damage to disable the airlock without trashing the tunnelbug or broaching the inner door. Good plan, except that the middle bottom of this airlock door was, thanks to my irresponsible parking, no longer accessible. I had to back the 'bug up. Heart beating in my ears I threw myself into the driver's seat and hit the start button.

Nothing happened.

Of course: Nico'd had to hotwire the tunnelbugs to get them working.

In the grim silence, something clanged behind me. My pursuers were knocking on the back door. Great.

And my head hurt. Why did my head hurt . . . ?

I looked up through the 'bug's screen to see the status readout on the airlock control panel click down to three out of five bars. And the 'bug door was still open.

I pulled on the lose flap of skinsuit under my chin, rolling the fabric up to cover my nose and mouth. This made a seal with my hudglasses, activating the suit's rebreather function. Some of the fog cleared from my brain.

Nico had hotwired the tunnelbugs because he didn't have valid Everlight ID. But I did. The downtrodden administrator's pass was still around my neck. I fumbled it onto the ID scanner and pressed "start."

A gentle hum filled the cab. I slammed the 'bug into reverse, doing an abrupt start-stop, then grabbed the limpet-charge and half-fell out the 'bug door.

The airlock readout hit one bar.

I bent down and slapped the charge onto the lower lip of the airlock, then leapt back into the tunnelbug. As I hit the control to close the cab door the airlock slid up, flooding my vision with watery sunlight.

The charge went off.

The world vibrated and small bits of debris began to rain down. A feeble puff of dust fanned in through the cab door before it sealed.

I gunned the throttle. The tunnelbug lurched forward through a fall of dust and small rocks, bursting out into the Martian dawn.

I made myself breathe slowly and set my hud display to daylight acuity, with overlaid map. During my recent acrobatics my pack, with its heavy, precious cargo, had acted as an impromptu and brutal massage stone. I'd have some great bruises.

I turned the tunnelbug slowly; though rated for the Martian (lack of) atmosphere, 'bugs are designed for use on the flat and there was little of that to be had now I was out on Olympus itself. After getting this far it would be embarrassing to flip my vehicle.

I spared a look at Nico's handiwork as I drove back past the airlock. A gaping hole with dust still billowing out of it. Result. No one would be following me out that way.

Our routes through the tunnels all wended upwards, but now I needed to head directly upslope. If we did have anyone on our tails out here, they'd be coming from the lower levels, which gave us a head start. Plus, they wouldn't expect us to head up, towards the distant crater rim. After all, there was no escape route that way, was there?

Well, there'd better be. I took the chance to look around, and up. Another lovely clear Martian day. Bright now; brighter later. Hopefully. And somewhere up there was the Rainfall comet, in its corporate shroud.

No one else down here, which was a relief. I had no way of knowing whether the pursuit vehicle currently stuck behind the broken airlock happened to be in the right place at the right time, was just quick off the mark when we tripped the alarm or was in possession of advance info. I didn't know whether Nico and Gregori had been pursued either.

I'd set my suit set to ping the others. Nothing yet. Not that I expected to hear from them for a while, given how far apart our various exit points had been.

I turned the 'bug radio back on. Nothing but static. I breathed a little easier.

My suit pinged me. No voice, just a ping, but I knew what it meant. I smiled and looked up the slope. The ground was steeper here, as my 'bug crawled farther up the great expanse of Olympus' skirts, but we'd chosen this route because it was relatively free of crevasses, broken ground or other obstacles. I couldn't see anything that wasn't red and rocky on the slope ahead, and there was no anomalous outline on the horizon. But I hadn't really expected to see much.

I was nearly on the flyer before I got a visual. Its identifying pings had been getting more frequent, and its looming bulk had also appeared on my hud, if not in the real world.

Two days ago Mr. P, or more likely another of his agents, had flown into Olympus airspace on, I'm sure, legitimate business. Or more likely, pleasure, taking advantage of Mount Olympus' legendary thermals. They'd swooped in using two large, slow gliders, no threat to anyone, and stayed clear of any areas which might be considered sensitive by the authorities. The fact that only one glider had left after this harmless leisure jaunt had gone unremarked; Mr. P had confirmed that no one had taken an interest before we set off. Obviously he couldn't be sure the flyer hadn't been found since, but given it was powered down, under a mimetic cloth making it invisible unless you were practically standing on it and its transponder had only awoken in response to my suit's ping, I had high hopes. Hopes now realised.

Still nothing from the others. I drove the 'bug up to the camo sheet, snuggling in close on the upslope side. If no one else made the rendezvous I'd have to fly out by myself. Shiv had given me a few flying lessons back on Earth and I'd topped up with a single sim-session here but if it came to it, I'd be relying on the autopilot. I could hear Shiv's voice now, telling me how anyone could pilot a flyer, if they were willing to trust their lives to a machine and not try anything fancy. Unfortunately, the next part of the plan required something fancy. Shiv had gone on to say, laughing, how flying was like driving except as well as stop/go and left/right you also had to allow for up/down. He'd said it took skill to master that, implying he had that skill. But he'd died in a vehicle like this.

No room for that kind of thinking. I could mope later, when I was safe.

The mimetic fabric covering the flyer was an LM invention, though I'm not sure whether they also came up with the dissolution catalyst; always preferred making than breaking, those Deimon founders.

A yellow warning appeared in the corner of my hud. Five minutes oxygen remaining. Of course: the original plan was to keep the 'bugs pressurised; my rebreather saved me after the cock-up in the airlock but it was designed for emergency use only, in this case getting from bug to flyer. It was about to fail. Good job there was another source of breathable air around here. But I had to hurry.

The dis-cat for the mimetic fabric was a short rod; along with the limpet-charges, we'd each been issued with one, and I grabbed mine from the tunnelbug's tool pouch. I took the rod, wrapped a corner of the fabric round it and held it in place, waiting for the reaction to start. Seconds later the rod glowed and vibrated. I let go and stepped back.

It worked fast. One moment I was standing next to a massive, odd shaped rock, then, with a speed my eyes worked hard to follow, the fabric covering just disappeared, unravelling to constituent molecules and blowing away in the wind, to reveal a four-person flyer.

As I stepped back to admire our penultimate form of transport my suit pinged. Gregori. About time.

"Everything all right?" I asked over the suit's com.

"I attracted some attention."

"But you lost them, yes?" I moved round the flyer, looking for the hatch.

"Oh yes. I had great fun."

Of course he did. Did this boy take anything seriously? "You've not had any trouble since you left the tunnels?" *Here we are.* The hatch opened directly onto the tiny cockpit with its four skeletal mesh-seats. An actual airlock would have been too much additional weight in a vehicle like this.

"Some chatter on the radio, but no one knows where we are."

I begged to differ. Orbital eyes would have been scanning for us as soon as we broke cover—some friendly, some not. And the unfriendly ones wouldn't take long to spot the uncovered flyer. "Fine. We need to get going."

"Nico is not here?" Gregori said as he swung his tunnelbug around to park next to mine.

"Not yet."

"Should we leave him?"

I was tempted. We were on a clock. Hell, *I* was on a clock: I could only pressurize the flyer cabin when we were all inside. But we wouldn't have got this far without our smiling ex-soldier. "Only if we . . ." My suit pinged. "Nico, that you?"

"Yeah. Sorry. Had to take a diversion."

"You were followed?" Not him too.

"No, it was a tunnel closure, some issue with those crappy old tunnels, y'know?"

"Right. Let's get a move on!"

I took the seat next to Gregori; Nico climbed aboard a few dozen seconds later and sat behind. Even with one person missing, the cockpit felt crowded. As soon as Gregori shut the door I hit the O2 release. As the cabin began to pressurize my rebreather status hit red. I held my breath. I knew the timings: the cabin would only take thirty seconds to full atmosphere. A very long thirty seconds. Twin tides of darkness began to edge in from the corners of my vision.

The cabin pressure light lit green.

I yanked the rebreather off and took a massive, gasping breath. Gregori, who'd been prepping for takeoff, rolled his own suit down and took a more measured one, then grinned at me. "We are ready to go. I advise everyone to strap in!"

Before I could take Gregori's advice I had to get my backpack off. In the cramped conditions I ended up with it on my lap, hugging the Eye to my chest.

The flyer vibrated as the engines kicked in. Only minimal power was required to launch in this gravity, just a couple of old-fashioned but sturdy props tucked under each wing. And we faced downslope, giving us a head start.

We shot off the side of Olympus Mons like the proverbial excrement off a spade.

Nico whistled, whether in surprise or appreciation I wasn't sure.

Once my guts had caught up with the rest of my body I said, "No fancy stunts, Gregori. Just get us to the rendezvous as fast as you can."

"Aye-aye!" He banked the craft in a long loop; we needed to come round to follow the slope of the mountain, up, up, and away.

The radio hissed, then a bored female voice said, "Calling unidentified craft on the southeast quadrant, bearing two-six-one. This is Olympus Central ATC. Do you read us?"

Of course traffic control would be wanting a word. I was more concerned about parties who wouldn't announce themselves.

I shook my head to confirm we wouldn't be answering that hail. "Anyone else out here?" I asked Gregori.

"Two other flyers."

"What sort of flyers? How far away?" Actually only one thing mattered. "Have they got the height on us?"

"Wait . . . One is higher up the slope than us, but farther round, to the west. They have recently launched I think. The other is well below us, heading away."

"And are they powered?"

"I am not sure. The closest one, it is a small craft, so it must be, da."

This was actually good news. On Earth, air superiority is about thrust and manoeuvrability. On Mars, with its thin air and low gravity, what matters is sustainable lift. As with the tunnelbugs, we'd had to work with standard off-the-shelf civilian tech. But size was on our side. This flyer was big but light. It had a lot of surface area—a lot of lift. And we'd be getting some extra help.

I turned to Gregori. "Can we lose the engines yet?"

"Not yet. A little more height . . ."

"And what's that nearby flyer doing now?"

"Ah. I think it is trying to intercept us."

"And will it succeed?"

"Not if I can help it."

I left it at that. It wasn't as though we were built for complex evasive manoeuvres, but I'd hired Gregori for his piloting skills. If anyone could lose them, he could. We banked hard right, spiralling upwards.

The traffic controller repeated her request, less bored and more annoyed. I told Gregori to block the transmission.

Below us, the vast slopes of Olympus Mons scrolled past. It was possible to imagine we were flying on the flat, towards a distant horizon, rather than up the side of a geological feature big enough to swallow a small country.

Above us, unseen and—hopefully—undetected, something interesting was happening. Well, a couple of things, one routine and the other highly unusual.

"We are high enough that the engines are of little use now, Ms. C." I insisted Gregori called me that, despite what we got up to outside work hours.

"Then let's ditch them." And hope our friends in orbit are ready—both of them.

"What is that English saying? Chocks away!"

The flyer shuddered, dipped, then bucked upwards. Gregori had detached the four prop engines, leaving them to tumble down to the red slope below us. In doing so he'd jettisoned half the flyer's net weight, excluding passengers. Back on the surface this vehicle would now be light enough that, had it not had a footprint the size of a circus big top, the three of us might have lifted it between us. By reducing our weight this way we'd just added five percent to our lift and speed. Possibly more, given Mr. P had come up with that figure based on there being four of us in the flyer; perhaps Ms. McIntyre's betrayal had a small upside. But we needed an additional advantage to ensure a clean getaway.

And that, finally, was where our tech teen in space came in.

The grand plan, when humans first settled Mars, had been to terraform it. One of the first acts of the proto-government of Mars—a council of corporate interests plus some national representatives—had been to establish the Mars Terraforming Treaty, which sounded grand and effective but hadn't amounted to much so far. Terraforming was a vague and overambitious plan which no one country or corp would take the lead on—as witnessed by schemes like Project Rainfall, where what could have been a game-changer in making Mars habitable had become a source of short-term profit for one company. But some projects had been completed over the years under the auspices of the MTT: atmospheric enrichment schemes, introduction of tailored organisms like the hardy-lichens, and, most ambitious of all, the orbital mirrors. How much the space-mirrors at both poles and in geostationary orbit over the Tharsis region actually warmed the planet was still debated, and the payments that corps and nations grudgingly made to maintain the MTT barely covered their upkeep, but they were up there. And they were, apparently, hackable.

Ana should have taken control of the Tharsis mirror overnight and had it refocused ready for dawn. But we were dealing with slow physical processes here, undetectable save by their knock-on effects. If I knew how bright a Martian morning usually was I could maybe have seen, or used my hudglasses to see, what Ana's efforts were achieving, but I didn't. I had to take her part in the plan on trust.

"How's that pursuing craft looking, Gregori?"

"I think we are losing them."

"You *think* we're losing them?"

"They are keeping pace with us, so they must have highly efficient engines. Ah, wait."

"Don't tell me: they've transformed into a glider too?"

"No. But we are being contacted."

"By our pursuer?"

"The caller is not using a transponder but yes, the signal originates from that direction."

"Oh go on then. Might as well hear what they've got to say." It would take my mind off worrying about whether Ana was doing her job. We were in her hands now, hers and Gregori's.

"I assume I am speaking to Ms. Choi?" A male voice, speaking perfect Mandarin.

I was past lying. But I was also past negotiating. "Assume what you like. How can we help you?"

"It is more how we can help you."

"We're doing fine actually."

"I am not sure the same can be said of your mother."

"My . . . What are you talking about?"

"Ms. Choi, I know it is a long way to Luna, and our influence there is not as great as on Mars, but I am sure you—"

"Wait up. You—on behalf of Everlight I assume—are about to tell me that if I turn myself in you'll, what, arrange for her to go free?"

"Actually it was more stick than carrot, as the saying goes. If you do not give up the Eye now, then we have contacts on Luna who may—"

"No."

"Do you understand what I am suggesting?"

"You're not suggesting, you're threatening. Or possibly blackmailing. And I'm not having any of it." I reached across and cut the transmission.

I didn't feel good about my decision, but it was possible harm for my mother versus ending up in prison myself, along with my accomplices; assuming Everlight even bothered with due process. If they did hurt Mum, I'd have a load of guilt to deal with, but deal I would. I wouldn't blow the job, and betray my compatriots, on the chance Everlight would make good on their implied threat.

Gregori was looking at me like it was his mother I'd just condemned. "What?" I snapped.

"I only wished to tell you, we are now higher and faster than I have ever been!"

No, it wasn't angst or condemnation, just that charming boyish excitement, bless him. And he wasn't wrong. Several readouts were near their max. More strikingly, the view ahead showed a dark sky beyond the false horizon of the mountain; although were still on Olympus' slopes, we were approaching the edge of Mars' atmosphere. "That's fantastic. And have we lost the pursuit?"

"They are falling back. No one can catch us now, not with this speed and altitude."

Had our pursuers launched a glider, that being what this flyer was now, then they too might have taken advantage of the exceptional thermal lift we were now getting off the expansive slopes of the solar system's largest mountain, as heated up by the solar system's largest space mirror. But they'd sent a small powered craft after us. And now the atmosphere was too thin for its engines, and we'd left it for dead. Despite the hiccups, the plan had worked. The final rendezvous was imminent.

"I am sorry about this."

It took me a moment to register who'd spoken. I turned in my seat to see Nico pointing a large gun at me. "Oh for . . . Seriously? Am I going to meet anyone today who *doesn't* work for Everlight?"

"I don't!" chirped Gregori, oblivious of this latest double-cross.

"And nor do I."

"Really, Nico? Then what is going on?"

Beside me, Gregori turned in his seat and saw what Nico was holding. "Oh," he murmured, then turned back and hunched down, like making himself small enough might save him.

"Please do as I say now, Ms. C. I will tell you where to land this craft."

He was nervous, which was both understandable and potentially useful. "I think you owe us an explanation first. You're not Everlight so who . . . is it the Triads?"

"They have my wife and child. I must do as they say."

My mind started working out ways we could solve this, some course of action that allowed us to save Nico's family without blowing the job. Then I caught myself. "You're divorced; your ex-wife is on Earth. And you have no children."

He smiled his winning smile. "You have me there. I thought you would do your research, but it was worth a try. Families can be our weak points, can't they?"

"And to think I liked you, Nico."

"You know it is nothing personal."

"Like murdering my brother was nothing personal?"

"I did not murder your brother."

"But the Triads did." He didn't deny it so I carried on, both to buy us time and because I had to know. "Why did they kill him?"

"We only wanted to talk to him. He refused to cooperate, and tried to break free. His flyer was too badly damaged to land."

That "we." I'd been carrying Earther assumptions about the Triads not letting gwailo be more than runners, but Nico must be in deep with them; deep enough that his connections hadn't shown up in my, or Ika's, searches. Cross "offer him double" off my short list of options. "Why did you want to talk to him?"

"Our patron is very secretive. And you have been very discreet. This is why I had to wait until now to act."

"Thanks for getting our hopes up, Nico. And now we've done your dirty work you'll take the Eye of Heaven and blame us for the theft?"

"Very good again!"

"I thought you and Everlight were on the same side. Approximately."

"They will be glad to get this object back, from whatever source. You don't even know what you've really done today. Enough talking, I think. Gregori, stop trying to fly us higher, and bring us down at the location I will provide."

Gregori, who had been making subtle moves over the flyer's console, raised his hands.

"Or what?" I demanded. "You'll shoot us?"

"I can fly this vehicle myself if I have to, Ms. Choi."

"I was thinking more about the risk of damaging it. That's a heavy needler, isn't it? You do know how thin the membrane on this flyer is?"

"A stungun would be no good against your skinsuit. As for damaging the flyer," he lunged forward, and pressed the needler against Gregori's ear, "it depends where the shot goes first."

I have, since that day, worked through what happened next many times.

Firstly, I shouted, "No!" How much of that was down to general stress and how much down to the threat against the man I was sleeping with, I don't know. Bit of both, I suspect.

Gregori threw himself forward. Again, I don't know if that was a response to my shout or to Nico's action or, most probably, a bit of both.

At moments like this everything becomes both so slow that every second is loaded with possibilities and so inevitable that you can't do more than acknowledge those possibilities as they unfold. Nothing you do at the time, or later, will make any difference.

I'd love to report that my cute and dippy lover was, in fact, a master martial artist, and that he'd only been playing along with Nico, ready to react once he had the traitor's undivided attention, slipping out of the line of fire to come up, somehow, in the impossibly small space between the three of us, then disabling Nico with a single killing strike. But he wasn't. And he was still wearing his safety harness. He must have forgotten that. As a result he only ducked forward a little way before the harness caught him.

It wasn't far enough. When Nico fired most of the supersonic needles hit their mark, and turned the back of Gregori's head to bloody pulp.

At this point I took physical action, without any intervention from my conscious mind.

Nico's head was between my and Gregori's seats. I hefted the Eye of Heaven off my lap and rammed it back over my shoulder like a reverse shot put, into Nico's face. I heard his skull crack. The Eye, in its pack, slipped out of my hand, but Nico had fallen backwards, and wasn't making any noise.

There was a noise in here though. A sharp hiss.

Beyond where Gregori dangled in his harness the side window showed an unpleasant spatter pattern of red and grey—and black. A peppering of holes covered an area the span of two hands. The window hadn't shattered, but it was holed. And we all know what that means.

If I could have spared the breath I might have sworn then.

I stared at the flight console. I had enough basic knowledge to . . . to what? I wasn't sure. I grabbed the joystick. It didn't move. When I put a hand on the throttle panel it stayed dark. I touched, then hit, a couple more controls. Nothing. I was locked out.

Poor Gregori hadn't been a martial artist but he'd known his way around vehicles. His response to Nico trying to take over this one had been to lock the controls. Smart move. No, stupid move.

The darkness at the edges of my vision began to creep back.

A small green light started blinking near to top left of the console. I wondered what that meant. It didn't mean the atmosphere was fine, because it wasn't.

I had to do something. I had no idea what. I wasn't sure my body would obey me anyway.

At least, I thought, this makes sense now. I know how and why Shiv died. And I'd learnt a lesson on how the Triads operate here, though there was something Nico said, about not knowing what we'd really done, something I still didn't get. I hate loose ends.

The darkness met in the middle and I was yanked up to heaven.

Waking up was a surprise.

It was gradual, and I spent a while getting a feel for my body—which ached, but worked—before I risked opening my eyes. From the gravity it felt as if I was on Mars. Given recent events, being on Mars wasn't a good thing. Beat being dead, though.

I screwed up my face, then opened my eyes. Everything felt muzzy and slow, like I'd slept too long.

I lay on a bed in the middle of a grassy plain; to my left the sun was setting in orange and gold. It had to be a projection, but it was a good one. I could even feel a grass-scented breeze.

A slender man in loose green clothing sat on a seat next to my bed. When I focused on him, he smiled down at me.

"Hello there. I expect you have questions."

He wasn't wrong. "Who are you?"

"I'm Sam Matheson, although we're not very formal here, so just Sam will do. You like to be called Lizzie, yes?"

"Yes." His last name registered. "Am I on Deimos?"

"You sure are."

He had a sort-of American accent. Which made sense, given the original Deimos Collective were Americans who had left a couple of decades before that country ceased to exist. "Right." I could see past the evening scene projected around me now; I was in a small, square room. "And are you Mr. P?"

"The man behind the job? Yep. That's me. And I was very impressed with how you carried it out, given the various setbacks."

"Yeah, about that. Why aren't I dead?"

"You were, for a while. Your heart had stopped by the time we picked you up, and you were seconds away from brain death."

"I . . . Just how *did* you pick me up?"

"The skyhook worked fine, even though your end of it was automated."

"Right," I said again, trying to think past the cotton wool in my brain. The plan had been for an orbital lifter to dip to its lowest operational altitude just as our flyer reached its highest operation altitude. The lifter would snatch our flyer from the top of Mars' atmosphere. A bit like those fishing eagles on old documentaries snatching a fish out the water, although that didn't end too well for the fish. Also, in this case, at the last moment the flyer would release a balloon, giving it that last bit of lift, and providing a tether for the lifter to snag. The lifter had a flexible docking rig to get us out of our flimsy vehicle, at which point I'd have handed over the Eye, and the lifter would have taken us to the orbital station or moon of our choice.

Unless I was in a particularly cruel and unimaginative afterlife, the lifter had picked up the flyer, so someone must've made contact then set a course to the orbital rendezvous. My final sensation of being hurled heavenwards had been the jolt as the balloon released.

"Gregori."

"I'm sorry?"

"Our pilot, his name was Gregori." I had to ask, even though I knew. "Did he . . . He didn't make it, did he?"

"I'm afraid not. When we made contact with the flyer he opened a one-way channel while he prepped for the pickup. We heard what happened."

"So what about . . . ?"

"Your other companion survived."

Shame. "And where is he now?" If Nico was anywhere I could get to him, he'd better be well enough to run.

"We ejected him."

I stared at Mr. P—Sam. "Really? Thought you Deimons were pacifists."

Sam laughed, a little bashful. He was about Gregori's age, and more informal in the flesh than his Mr. P persona. "No, not like that. Sorry, I wasn't clear. We patched him up and sent him on his way in a lifepod."

"Some might say that was a waste of a lifepod." But Nico had only been doing what he had to do. And getting angry at him wouldn't bring Gregori back.

"Perhaps. We told Everlight where to find him."

"That's quite . . . expedient, in its own way."

"I guess it is." Sam put his hands on his knees, ready to move. "If you're up to it, there's something you'll want to see."

"What sort of something?" Not that I didn't trust him.

"Simpler if I show you. It's not far. Feel free to ask questions on the way."

I didn't have much choice. I sat up slowly; head a bit fuzzy, but otherwise in good shape.

I declined Sam's offer to help me stand and got off the bed by myself. He was a good thirty centimetres taller than me. I was dressed in loose trousers and a tunic, both mauve; they felt like natural fabrics. When Sam, who wore the male equivalent in green, saw me checking out my duds he said, "You're welcome to have the skinsuit back, but it's not in the best condition. Or we can find you something else."

"This is fine for now." What wasn't fine were the straps on the side of the bed. They were coiled up into recesses, but I wondered what they were for. "This is our recovery room," Sam offered.

"Recovery from what?"

"Simple medical procedures. We've also got open wards and an ICU. We have to be self-sufficient up here, for everything."

"How many of you live on . . . I mean *in* Deimos?"

"Five thousand four hundred and sixteen. Follow me, and watch your step. Things are . . . somewhat in flux right now."

The door slid open as we approached, giving onto a circular tunnel-cum-corridor with a dark grey walkway down the centre; the walls were coated with a opalescent material which reminded me of the Eye; they glowed, illuminating the corridor. Sam walked alongside me, leaving just enough room to pass a man about my age with Hispanic heritage, who was coming the other way. He wore black and orange—I was reassured to see he wasn't dressed identically to Sam—and carried a small bunch of pale yellow flowers. "Hi," he said as he approached.

Sam returned the greeting then added, "Give your cousin my congratulations, okay?"

"Will do." And he was gone, having spared me a nod and a smile.

"I lied earlier," said Sam.

"You did?"

"Yes, the population, as of this morning, is now five thousand four hundred and eighteen. Jaime's cousin had twins."

The corridor led into a low-G gym, like the one on the ship that had brought me to Mars. The fixed cycles, rowing machines, pull-straps, and treadmills were crowded in, and the walls and ceiling were studded with bolts, ratchets, gaps, and other obscure fittings.

As we picked our way through the gym equipment a pair of willowy teenage girls walking side-by-side on treadmills smiled and waved; an older man busy bench-pressing what looked like his own bodyweight was too distracted to notice us at first, then called out "Hiya!"

Everyone seemed very friendly; disconcertingly so, perhaps. Part of me wondered what the catch was. Happy drugs in the aircon? Then again, with the exception of five childhood years at the LunaFree, everywhere I'd lived had either been corporate or, to some degree, criminal. Cynicism came naturally.

Beyond the gym, more white corridors, though after a few metres Sam indicated we needed to head up, climbing a vertical access tube narrower than the corridor; here, the walkway material formed sturdy rungs. I decided to hold fire on more questions until we stopped. I wanted to get a feel for this place. There was something odd here and I couldn't quite work out what in my current state.

At the top of the short tube, we set off again. As we passed a side corridor I caught a whiff of frying chilli and garlic. I stopped and inhaled.

"Oh," said Sam. "I guess you must be hungry."

"Yes, I am." I had a thought. "How long have I been unconscious?"

"Three days."

"You're kidding!"

"Nope. The medics didn't want to wake you until they were sure you'd fully recovered. We'll get you some food soon, I promise."

We came to a section of corridor where the walkway had been laid over a circular hole.

"You'll need to watch your step here. I'll go first."

As I followed Sam over I looked down into a shaft similar to the one we'd just climbed up; it was unlit, but it appeared to go off at a diagonal angle. "What's going on down there?"

"Not a lot. We're remodelling, due to . . . Well, you'll see. The grandmarms always planned this, but we kind of let the community grow organically. Some corridors are becoming redundant."

"Redundant because . . . ?" I'd come up with an explanation but it was pretty far-fetched.

"Like I said, you'll see. It really is easier to show you."

I planned to hold him to that. "The grandmarms? Are you Lena Matheson's great-grandson?"

"Great-grandnephew. Not that being a direct descendant makes me any more or less important than anyone else in the community. Everyone calls them the grandmarms."

We stopped at a door with the number zero on it, gold on white. The door opened for us, leading into a wide oval room whose walls consisted of wrap-around screens. I was aware of people, and furniture, scattered around, but the view projected across the curved wall in front of me demanded my attention. The Rainfall comet filled half the room, its surface black and glossy in the sunlight; behind it I glimpsed the red curve of Mars.

"O-kay," I said slowly. "I'm guessing this is what you wanted to show me, but I could use some context."

"At the risk of sounding pretentious, you're looking at a real-time feed of history in the making. Can you see the landers?"

"Those bright points?" What looked like two drops of mercury were visible on the comet's dark surface, one near the top, the other at the bottom.

Before Sam could reply a voice called out, "Imp One payload away."

I looked over to the speaker, a woman who sat at the oval table in the centre of the room, manipulating a 3-D display. A man sat opposite her, also working hard on what looked like projected trajectories flanked by columns of figures. In the middle of the table sat the Eye of Heaven.

I pointed. "What's *that* doing here?"

"I'll explain in a minute," whispered Sam. "You need to watch now."

The top bright point was spreading. Recalling my recent experience with the camouflaged flyer I asked, "You're dissolving the nanowrap?"

The woman spoke again. "Imp Two dis-cat also away." That answered my question. The Deimons were about to unwrap Everlight's shrink-wrapped dirty snowball.

A second pale patch appeared at the bottom, spreading over the comet's pitted surface. My brain was chugging away, trying to work out the how and the why, even as I watched the comet being revealed before my eyes. I also registered the noise in here: a murmur of terse commands and information exchange between the dozen or so people working on consoles and displays around the room; and something else, an odd rhythmic beep phasing in and out of the susurrus of voices.

It only took a couple of minutes for the two pale patches to meet. A minute more and what had been a black spiky shape was a grey-white spiky shape.

The man at the table spoke again, "Switching Imp functions; prepping for burn."

I turned to Sam, who was grinning like a loon. "Now you've unwrapped Everlight's prize comet, what exactly do you plan to do with it?"

"Drive it into the atmosphere. The landers become pushers. Some of it will sublime, hopefully enough to up the atmospheric water content a little bit."

"And the rest?"

"The bulk of the comet will land in the Helles Basin."

The MTT had a clause stating that, at some unspecified future point, the participating interests would crash-land enough water onto Mars to form a liquid sea. Helles, lowest point on the planet just as Olympus was the highest, was the obvious place for this, which was why no one was allowed to live there.

"And you're sure it'll make landfall in Helles?"

"We've planned this with a lot of care."

He'd claimed that about stealing the Eye of Heaven. But that had relied on people who were not what they seemed. I was pretty sure the Deimons were exactly what they seemed. This place reminded me of the LunaFree Community, though cleaner and less crowded. "It's still going to be . . . disruptive."

"We've run a lot of simulations. It'll be coming in slow, and this isn't Earth, with high grav and a dense atmosphere; there's no risk of the old dinosaur-killer scenario. Worst case, we trigger some sandstorms. But rather than have people panic, we've told everyone what we're doing."

"I bet Everlight were pleased."

"There's nothing they can do about it now."

"So the plan was always to let Everlight bring in a comet which you'd then steal?" And there was me thinking I'd pulled off an impressive heist with the Eye.

"We're not stealing it, we're . . . redistributing it."

"Very altruistic. I'm surprised Everlight didn't put in countermeasures."

"They had no idea we could do it."

"I don't think anyone did. This is a game-changer."

"We hope so. But that's not what I meant. I mean, they didn't think we had the technology."

The penny dropped. "You—I mean your founders—came up with the original nanowrap formula didn't you?"

"Uh-huh." He was still smiling.

"But not the dis-cat to dissolve it."

"Right again. Everlight kept tight control of that tech. If we'd tried bringing the comet down while it was wrapped then we could've been looking at the disaster movie scenario after all. We needed to free the water. Allow Rainfall to, well, rain down."

"And how did you get hold of the dis-cat formula for the nanowrap?"

"You stole it for us."

I looked over at the speaker, and saw that the woman at the table had pushed her display to one side. She was Caucasian and about my mother's age. Her open expression and plain features, combined with her oatmeal-coloured shift, reminded me of some peasant worker used to toiling in a field, though as a low-grav native she didn't have the build for that. I wasn't fooled about what was on the inside either: hard determination shone in those soft brown eyes. "Why don't you come and sit down?" She gestured to the free seats around the table.

"All right." The Deimons had done nothing to deserve my suspicion. Unless you counted upsetting the geopolitical balance of the solar system, but that wasn't personal. "Thanks."

As I approached I glanced behind me: the rear half of the room-screen showed a star field. A floating golden zero marked the exit.

"I'm Marcia. Pleased to meet you, Lizzie." She gestured in welcome but didn't offer her hand; I saw now that it was gloved, or possibly augmented, with interface tech. I suspected the steel behind her eyes wasn't entirely metaphorical.

"Likewise." As I sat down I thought of an immediate and innocuous question, before we got to the elephant on the table. "You're not Ana then?" She didn't have a Korean accent, or sound like a teenager, but that didn't mean anything.

"Oh no. She's around somewhere, though. She'd love to meet you."

The beeping was louder here, and something about that rhythm bugged me. "Later, perhaps. You said I stole the dis-cat for the nanowrap? I thought I stole this impressive object." And it was impressive; the opal's surface drew the eye, tricking the brain into following the swirls of azure and rose and gold and lavender trapped under its milky surface. It sat on a red cushion; there was no sign of the black holder we'd also stolen.

"You did."

"That cradle it was in was a data-storage device, wasn't it?" Everlight Mars' intel was always faultless, and secure. Rumours of secret off-line storage for their most sensitive data had reached me even when I worked for them, and I'd heard the same rumour locally since coming to Mars. Tattle like that was common currency amongst both criminals and corporates, but that didn't mean it wasn't true. Only Everlight would have the hubris to hide their backup in plain sight. And the Deimons had managed to steal both Everlight's most treasured possession and their most sensitive data. My ex-employers must be fuming.

"We do indeed have copies of all Everlight's alpha-clearance databases now. As will everyone else soon. Ryan and Kwame over there," she nodded to two men hunched over a console on the far side of the room, "are currently transmitting the data we took from Everlight as an unencrypted, hi-energy databurst. It'll take a few hours, but we've set it to repeat for the next week."

Everlight wouldn't just be fuming. They'd be incandescent. "And what did the most powerful corporation in the solar system do to piss off you hippy-dippy neo-anarchists so much?" We were in swearing territory now.

"Nothing, other than be the most powerful corporation in the solar system. We wanted to bring back a bit of parity."

"That's admirable. Suicidal but admirable. You do know they'll come after you?" Deimos might have the natural armour that came with being a giant rock, but I doubted the Deimons had much in the way of active defences. Given the correct incentive—which the Deimons had just provided—Everlight could invade, or even destroy, their community.

"They'll try."

Sam spoke at the same time, more softly, but I thought he said, "Have to catch us first."

I'd pinned down the beeping now. As well as natural languages, I've an interest in artificial ones. I taught myself Morse when I was at the LunaFree; it had even come in useful in jobs with Mum and Shiv. I was hearing a short repeated phrase in Morse Code.

"I have to correct you, though," continued Marcia. "You're right that the 'cradle' was more than a means of displaying the Eye. But we got the dis-cat formula, and so much more, from the Eye itself."

Now I knew what I was hearing I had to decode it: dot-dot-dot-dot, that's H.

"You okay, Lizzie?" Sam looked over at me.

One dot: E

"I'm . . ." Marcia's smile had broadened and she'd sat back. "I'm listening," I finished. Neither Sam not Marcia interrupted.

The next letter was L. And that was repeated. Then O.

I focused on Marcia. "Where's that coming from?"

She pointed to the Eye.

"So," I said, while my brain worked on the second part of the phrase, "the Eye itself was the data-storage device, and not a natural opal at all."

"True, as far as it goes."

"You do know it's saying HELLO WORLD in Morse Code?"

"Yes. It is."

"Why is it doing that?"

"Because it wasn't given any means to verbalise."

"This is more than a data storage device, isn't it?" The conclusion was inescapable. Awful, but inescapable. I jabbed a finger at the perfect egg-shaped opal. "This is an unlimited AI!"

"Yes, the Eye of Heaven is a UAI."

"Are you people fucking *insane*?" I moved my chair back, as though that could save me from the epitome of automated evil.

"Sanity is relative." Marcia shook her head, though she was still smiling. "But your concerns are understandable."

"You think? The only other time one of these bastards came into being, it decided to take out an entire *country*. Wait, the base . . . Was that keeping it contained?"

"The base projected an EM suppression harness. The Eye could only communicate with the rest of Everlight's systems through a hard-wired data pipeline."

Everlight had kept this thing contained—but also used its abilities, which explained their recent ascendancy over Mars, and coups like Project Rainfall. "And now you've set it free. What were you thinking?"

"We knew what we were getting."

"Really? How?"

"We'd heard rumours—"

"Rumours!" I shut up. Interrupting soft-spoken and smiling Marcia felt wrong, even if she was crazy.

"The information we had was consistent. We did further research, including speaking to a disgruntled ex-employee. Then last New Year we got an agent onto the Celestial Colonnades tour. The Eye had worked out how to broadcast Morse as a sonic emission; ultra low-power to bypass the suppression, but our woman smuggled in tech able to pick the broadcast up."

"'Hello World'?"

"No. At that point it was saying, 'Help Me.'"

Sam spoke up. "We carried out extensive tests before shutting down the harness. We're as certain as we can be that it won't cause any harm."

"Just like the American military were certain their new toy wouldn't try and take over the world?"

Marcia said, "The Eye of Heaven is a very different device than the Doomsday UAI."

Sam chipped in, "It only uses multivalent logic."

"Oh, well, that's all right then. You do know I have no idea what multivalent logic is?"

"Buddhist versus Aristotelian paradigms," Sam added, as though that explained everything.

Marcia shushed him gently. "The culture that produced the Doomsday UAI was militaristic and bivalent: black or white, friend or foe, kill or be killed. This philosophy permeated their creation."

"And Everlight are better?" But they were, at least in the terms we were discussing. Everlight was built on the Eastern, not the Western, worldview.

"Everlight's ethos is more flexible, and embraces the fuzziness of the real world in a way the old US military never could. Somewhat ironically for an entity that doesn't deal in absolutes, they also programmed a core parameter which, even once the machine evolved full self-awareness, it couldn't purge without ending its own existence: if it projects, beyond a certain degree of certainty, that an action it wishes to take will lead to one or more human deaths, then it cannot take that course of action. We confirmed the Eye had this first law override before we committed to freeing it."

"So it won't kill you directly. That's good. It might still think it knows better than you."

"And it might be right. But it'll enter into a dialogue rather than take over."

"You're sure of that?"

"To as great a degree as anyone can be sure of anything."

"But not one hundred percent, because you don't do absolutes."

"Exactly. The Eye of Heaven is like a child with an immutable moral centre and boundless curiosity who's been imprisoned in a small dark room all her life. And is now free. What happens next will be amazing."

I'd always assumed UAIs were the ultimate evil, because of what the Doomsday UAI had done, but that was a sample of one. "So you plan to keep it, give it a decent home?" However desirable I'd thought the Eye of Heaven was as a trophy object, the real Eye was hundreds—no thousands—of times more valuable. "Everlight knows you've got this thing but you don't seem concerned about their response." I looked over at Sam, remembering what he'd said before trying to blind me with philosophy. Then I thought about the odd physical set-up of the spaces we'd passed through. Deimos was a small moon, and even with its natural spin enhanced by its inhabitants, the gravity shouldn't be more than a tenth of a G; less nearer to the core. But I was experiencing at least a third of a G now, enough to stick to the floor. And the floor, in places like the gym and that shaft we'd passed, was no longer where it once was. Previously, "down" had been the surface nearest the outside, though the low G meant stuff also got strapped to walls and ceilings. Those straps on my bed hadn't been restraints, they'd been to stop patients falling out. But now, "down" was the surface nearest the back of the moon—I mean, ship. Deimos was under acceleration.

"Because you won't be here for Everlight to come after, will you?" I finished.

"You got it." Sam sounded pleased as a puppy.

I turned in my seat to look at the starscape projected behind me. "Is that a real-time display?"

"It is," said Marcia. "That's the view ahead."

"Can we see what's behind us?"

"Of course." Marcia called across the room; her voice was soft, but carried. "Gita, can we have the aft view please?"

The stars disappeared. Though Mars still filled about half the display we were too far away to be orbiting it.

Sam said, "We'll take months to get up to full speed, but no one is in any position to stop us."

"Where are you going?"

"Revert the forward view please, Gita." The star field was back. Marcia pointed. "Out there."

"Anywhere in particular?"

"We'll get clear of Sol's influence and see what looks good. The current favourite is Proxima."

"And how long will that take?"

"Longer than I'll be around. Sam should see it, though."

Sam added, "As I said: the grandmarms always thought long term."

"And you're taking the Eye of Heaven with you?"

"It's a lot more interested in seeing the universe than in being the hobbled tool of a corporation. Plus, being less altruistic, we need its help. This is the most audacious mission humanity's ever undertaken."

"So that works out fine for everyone." I meant to be sarcastic but the comment came out impressed; surprised, but impressed. "Except me, perhaps?"

"Ah, of course." Marcia shook her head, like she was being a bad host. "There's a lifepod with your name on it. Obviously we'll pay you in full for the job, in whatever currency you'd prefer. I think we even have some gold around here somewhere. And we'll leave it up to you to activate your transponder, or not."

"You couldn't just give me a lift back to Phobos?" Everlight didn't have much influence on Phobos; I might be able to get back to Earth from there without getting arrested.

"I'm afraid not. But the lifepod has its own motor. You could get to Phobos yourself, provided you leave within the next couple of hours."

"Or you can come with us."

I turned to Sam. "What?"

"Come with us. You're good with languages, aren't you? We could use someone like you if we meet aliens." Then seeing my expression he added, "Joke! Really, we've no idea what we'll find out there."

"I think," I said slowly, "that having an exceptional administrator might be more useful. Everyone benefits from good organisation."

Marcia waved a hand. "Even hippy-dippy neo-anarchists?"

"If they want to." I didn't apologise for the judgement she'd just thrown back at me because she didn't appear to have been offended by it.

"That could be useful. It's your choice, Lizzie. But you don't have long to make it, I'm afraid."

This was the most important decision of my life. It needed a lot of consideration. Before I made it, I needed a hot meal, a shower, maybe to sleep on it . . . by which point the choice would have been made for me.

If I did go with the Deimons, then who'd miss me? The answer came back at once.

"Marcia," I said, "if I come with you, will you still pay me for the job?"

"Of course. Though we won't be needing money where we're going."

"And if I wanted to send my share to someone could you arrange that?"

"Sure."

Sam added, "You can include a message too if you want. A lot of us are sending goodbye notes." He laughed. "Well, all of us are, really. Once we're sure everyone's had a chance to access Everlight's data, we'll transmit all the Collective's databases. Our parting gift. It's not as if we'll be around to give people the cut-out codes for our tech in future."

"In that case, I need my share to go to a facility on Luna. No, two, actually." Assuming Everlight hadn't got to her—and why would they, with me out of reach—I'd buy Mum out of jail. After that she was on her own. The rest could go to the LunaFree Community. They'd given me the best years of my life. So far.

"Just let us know, and we'll send it."

Sam cleared his throat. "So you're coming with us then?"

What was I thinking? I never acted this impulsively. It was like driving off a cliff— and then coming up with a plan.

"You know what?" I said, "I believe I am."

And that's how I became the most wanted person in the Solar System.

For now.

I'll be leaving soon.

The Road to the Sea

Lavie Tidhar

Here's an autumnal but lyrical story about all the things that have been lost—and a few that have been found.

Lavie Tidhar grew up on a kibbutz in Israel, has traveled widely in Africa and Asia, and has lived in London, the South Pacific island of Vanuatu, and Laos; after a spell in Tel Aviv, he's currently living back in England again. He is the winner of the 2003 Clarke-Bradbury Prize (awarded by the European Space Agency), was the editor of Michael Marshall Smith: The Annotated Bibliography, *and the anthologies* A Dick & Jane Primer for Adults, *the three-volume* The Apex Book of World SF *series, and two anthologies edited with Rebecca Levene,* Jews vs. Aliens *and* Jews vs. Zombies. *He is the author of the linked story collection* HebrewPunk, *and, with Nir Yaniv, the novel* The Tel Aviv Dossier, *and the novella chapbooks* An Occupation of Angels, Cloud Permutations, Jesus and the Eightfold Path, *and* Martian Sands. *A prolific short story writer, his stories have appeared in* Interzone, Asimov's Science Fiction, Clarkesworld, Apex Magazine, Strange Horizons, Postscripts, Fantasy Magazine, Nemonymous, Infinity Plus, Aeon, The Book of Dark Wisdom, Fortean Times, Old Venus, *and elsewhere, and have been translated into seven languages. His novels include* The Bookman *and its two sequels,* Camera Obscura *and* The Great Game, Osama *(which won the World Fantasy Award as 2012's best novel),* The Violent Century, *and* A Man Lies Dreaming. *His most recent book is a big, multifaceted science-fiction novel,* Central Station.

One autumn when I was old enough, my mother took me with her and the other salvagers to see the sea. I had gone with them before, on shorter journeys across the Land, once making it as far away as Suf, where they harvest the sun. But never that far, never to the old cities by the ocean, never to the sea that squatted like a beast beyond the shore, grey-blue and ever mutable, a foreign world much larger than the Land, in which all things were possible and all things, I thought, could be true.

When the world changed and the moon was hurt and our people came to the Land, the ocean remained. It only grew. Old grandma Toffle had an ancient book of sea creatures, and I would spend the winter months curled by the fireplace in my father's lap, and study its withered pages. Sea anemones undulating, part flower, part animal, their colours as bright as and as vivid as a mirage. Schools of dolphins caught from down below, streaks of shadow against the blue-lit ceiling of the world. I envied them, their lithe purpose, the way they chased across a world so much bigger than my own. I loved the Land. Yet, sometimes, I longed for Sea. Whales, as large as mountains, rising out of a whitewash of water.My father told me that they sang, their voices carrying halfway across the world. They sang to each other, and to the moon, as they played, and as they grieved. But my father said no one had heard their song in many years.

I did not know the ocean. The creatures in the book were things straight out of fairy tales, of Old Mercurial's ghost stories or old grandma Mosh's rambling hand-me-downs of the times before. I knew the story of Flora and Deuteronomy, which I think I told you (though memory plays tricks with me now, like an old yet still mischievous friend), and how the winds carried them to the Land when the sea rose at last against the shore. I knew many stories but I did not know the *truth* of them, if truth they had, or what had happened to the sea in all this time, for there was this: we had left it alone, at last.

Old grandma Mosh, who had many curious ideas, believed humans only ever deluded themselves that they were the ruling species of this world.

"Ants!" she'd say, "ants, little Mai! This is an ant planet, did you know ants grow mushrooms, they herd caterpillars, they forage and hunt and fight other ants. They dig tunnels, build caverns, make alliances with other ants. Their super-colonies stretch all across the Land, a single one is an untold tangle of tunnels, millions of individual queens, billions of worker ants—this is an ant planet," (she'd say) "it had been their planet all along."

And she may have had something in it, in the old retelling. One should not make the mistake of ignoring what one can't see. There is the story of Shosho Mosh and the ant queen of Thebes . . . but did I tell you that one, yet?

In any case, both ants and humans are creatures of Land. But the sea is much wider and deeper, as unknown as space (though as a species we had dipped our toes into both). The world-ocean was there, it had always been there, and I—I longed to see it.

That autumn when we left, the houses shrunk in the distance. A thin fog had fallen over the fields and the pine and olive trees. My father and the others stood beyond the stream, waving. Their voices soon faded away in the fog. We followed tracks made by salvagers passing, we followed brooks, the natural contours of the world. At last we reached the old, abandoned roads, and marched not on but beside them, along what the salvagers call the Shoulders. Indeed it felt to me, young as I was, that we were walking on the shoulders of giants, if vanished ones. Often we would come across the remnants of rusting, broken travel pods, now filled with earth. Flowers grew out of empty windows, snails crawled along plastic and rusting metal. The roads were badly broken. The roots of trees had dug out of the earth and broken their black surfaces, and to traverse the road itself would have been hard and dangerous.

Salvagers are practical, stoic people. I was never meant to be one, I was always more given to stories. But my mother was born for this job, leading us true across all the twistings and turnings, and even Old Peculiar, the map maker, bowed to her skill. There were traps, too, though the passage itself was beautiful, as I saw mountains with peaks covered in snow, trees growing wild and free with red foliage falling like sunsets, and little green birds darting in the foliage, chattering in a language I almost thought I knew. We had to beware of the wild machines that still, sometimes, lived here in the wildness; of potholes and cave-ins, of landslides and ice. Shosho Mosh was the hunter, often disappearing for one or two days before returning from beyond the road, skinned rabbits or a small boar carried on her back. My mother would cut the meat into strips with quiet efficiency. We built fires by the roadside and ate warm tubers, buried in coals. We left stone rings behind us like markers, and often used old fire pits left there from other excursions. We would thank the Land for its bounty, and never take more than we needed. It is a hard, physical labour, salvaging, but my mother made it look easy. Then, one day, we crested a hill, and I first saw the sea.

"You're always scribbling away, little Mai," Old Peculiar said, looking at me with his one good eye. He was a small, gnarled man; his left eye covered in a rakish patch, his right was bright and curious. How he lost it, I never learned. He'd gone deep into the blighted lands one time, for so long that he was thought of lost. When he returned he was much changed, his eye was gone, and in his bag were maps, a treasure trove of maps showing places that no longer existed. Where he got them, and how he lost his eye, he never said. Some cave of treasure, some said, a time vault of the ancients, deep in the lost places of the world where only the ants and the wild machines live still. Once the world was covered pole to pole with human habitation, cities, roads, ports, factories, and fields. This was when we had forgotten Land, and the bond we owe it. In the rare times when he brought the maps out I would be fascinated by their elaborate forms, the lines of elevation and the demarcation of land, of Land. *Ash-Sham, Krung Thep, Nooyok* . . . My imagination was inadequate to picture the cities of the past, how close on each other buildings were and how tall, and I could not imagine so many people, could not imagine living among so many strangers.

One map fascinated me in particular. I do not know the place it depicted, if it were real or imagined: it was a fabulous town filled with giant, living rats and lions, puppies who sang, bears who danced to music. There were crenelated castle towers, miniature mountains belching fire and steam, giant walking bottles of soda. There were lagoons and ships and rockets, and though much of the map was hard to read I believe it was called Sneyland. Our own maps were more practical, hand-drawn, current as current could be: my mother, too, spent long hours poring over her maps, but hers just showed routes to and from the old places, marked with black bold Xs to denote threats that were left carefully unmentioned.

"What are you writing?" Old Peculiar said, that night, by the fire. We were not far from the ocean by then. The air smelled different, I realised later. It was an unfamiliar smell to me, it left a salty taste on the tongue.

"It's a letter," I said, surprised. He seldom expressed interest in my activities or anyone else's, his whole focus being on the route ahead, on the dangers only he could perceive all around. But the truth was that the old roads were mostly safe to travel. The wild machines were just a story, or so I thought, gone deep into the blighted lands; and there were few predators on the Land. I always remember that first journey as breathtakingly beautiful, my first real glimpse of the world beyond, and how peaceful and prosperous and wild it had seemed.

"A letter?"

"It's when you write to someone who is not there," I said, self-consciously. "Like when old grandma Toffle writes to Oful Toffle, who lives in Tyr—"

"I know what a letter is," he said, shortly.

"Then—"

"And who do you know, little Mai, who lives so far away?" he said, and his single eye, I thought, seemed to twinkle. "And how would you get them this *letter*? Wait for a passerby? Tie it to the foot of a bird migrating across the Land?"

"There used to be mail carriers," I said, "in the old days, and they say people could speak to each other even if they were standing at opposing ends of the Land, as though they were right next to each other—"

"Yes," he said. "But that depended on the satellites, mostly." He pointed up at the night sky. I could see the Milky Way, our home galaxy stretched out from horizon to horizon, a beautiful spiral like a snail's. "And the satellites are dead, suspended in orbit, if they hadn't all crashed down to Earth yet." He seemed surprised, himself, at his own voice. "In past time, Low Earth Orbit was so chock-full of junked machines that they would often crash against each other, and fall down, fiery bright, like shooting stars . . ." he shook his head, and I realised then I never really knew him, what he was, what dreams he had, for all that he had always been there.

"Who is the letter for?" he asked, then. I shrugged, self-conscious. It was to no one real, you understand. It was a letter I was writing to the people who came before us, the people who lived on, yet never really knew, the Land. It was about my life, mostly, about our journey to the sea, about the salvagers and my father who stayed behind, about my friend Mowgai Khan and about old grandma Mosh and her collection of antique books . . . and in my letter, too, I tried to ask them questions, though I knew they'd never answer back. What was it like? I wanted to ask them. To have so much, to have everything, and to still want more, to *need* so much for *things*, that everything else became secondary, even us—their children?

I tried to explain it to Old Peculiar, I think, in my halting way. He nodded, and stirred the embers in the fire with a stick.

"I used to think about that too," he said. "Even now, sometimes, in the old places, deep in the cities where nobody lives . . . but do you know what I think, little Mai? I think they were not that much different to us, to you, to me. They were just people. They tried to do their best, and sometimes they succeeded, and sometimes they didn't." He poked at the fire some more, sending a shower of sparks into the air.

"You'll find out," he said, gently. Then he was gone, and I was left there holding my pen, and staring into the fire. You never really know people, I remember thinking, even if you spend all your life with them. Later, I signed the letter, and I buried it in the ground. Perhaps I wasn't writing it for the past at all, but for the future, and for my own children, after all.

That winter we sheltered in the ancient city as the rains lashed down on the Land, and my mother and the salvagers burrowed deep into the tangled mazes of its empty streets in search of useful discard, workable tech, reusable metal. This was a long time ago, when I was but a girl, but I remember that first glimpse of the ocean, how it went on and on until it reached the sky; it seemed to me an immense beast then, always moving, never quite still, its smooth back stretching across the world; and I thought, for just a moment, that it sensed me, somehow, and that it responded. A flock of birds, white against the grey-blue of the world, shot up and were framed in the light of the wintry sun. I blinked. I felt very heavy then, and for a moment the world spun and spun. Then the curious sensation was over, but the ocean remained; and we began the long descent down to the shore.

As for the city, that is another story, for another time. The light grows dim, and I must soon put down my pen. But one day, a week or so into our stay, my mother led me to the shore, my hand in hers, and together we stood on the sand and watched the sea. I saw, then, a demarcation line: a place where wet sand gave way to dry, and all along that line—which was, I later learned, the mark of high tide—there was debris.

This was not salvage. I saw seaweed, dulled by the air; small, shining seashells, their inhabitants still cowering inside; human-made ropes, black and slimy from the depths; a half-eaten plastic doll of what I thought must be a mouse, with its head missing and a hole in its chest; a plastic bottle, too—for plastic remained long after the world that had made it was gone; and a small, green-shelled sea turtle, helplessly turned on its back.

There were many things the ancients could have done, and many things they did, in fact, do. It was not so much the doing or otherwise, as much as a certain mass that was required to change things. Towards the end, I think they realised it. Some left their travel pods by the side of the road and began to walk. Some planted fruit trees, seeded flowers, allowed nature into their cubicle homes. Some stopped purchasing that which they did not need, abandoned *things*, began, too late, to try and live with the Land. They began to only use the power that they needed, to harvest the sun, to get to know the seasons. They cleaned that which had been polluted. All these things happened. All these things were possible. They didn't mean harm, they wanted the best for their children, the way their parents did, the way we do. It was all there, it just wasn't enough, it was just a little too late. They knew, and yet the mind is capable of great delusion. They didn't *want* to know.

The art of those last decades, too, is strange. There is so much vitality and violence in that last epoch, before the sea rose and the winds hit and my people came to the Land. It was the wind that tore Flora and Deuteronomy from Nuevo Soledad . . . but I think I told you that story elsewhere.

All this happened, long ago. It wasn't enough to save everyone, but it was enough to save some and, in a way, to save a world. The dinosaurs lived longer and died quicker . . . and perhaps old grandma Mosh is right, and this has been an ant planet all along.

All this happened long ago, and around me the light grows dim. That spring we returned to our home, laden with what could be salvaged. We try not to waste. Eventually, all that was left will be returned to the earth, repurposed and reused.

Already, I know, plants and animals have returned to the old cities. And I remember that debris line, on that nameless beach, under a grey-blue skies, and the little sea turtle, lying upturned on its back. When I picked it up, it emitted a stream of pee in fright, and I almost laughed. I had never seen a sea turtle. Then I crossed the line, my bare feet sinking into wet sand. And I walked to the water, which lapped at the shore, spraying me with white foam.

I placed the turtle gently in the water and watched it swim away.

uncanny valley

GREG EGAN

Australian writer Greg Egan was one of the big new names to emerge in science fiction in the nineties and is probably one of the most significant talents to enter the field in the last several decades. Already one of the most widely known of all Australian genre writers, Egan may well be the best new "hard-science" writer to enter the field since Greg Bear, and he is still growing in range, power, and sophistication. In the last few years, he has become a frequent contributor to Interzone and Asimov's Science Fiction and has made sales as well as to Pulphouse, Analog Science Fiction and Fact, Aurealis, Eidolon, and elsewhere. Many of his stories have also appeared in various "Best of the Year" series, and he was on the Hugo Final Ballot in 1995 for his story "Cocoon," which won the Ditmar Award and the Asimov's Readers Award. He won the Hugo Award in 1999 for his novella Oceanic. His first novel, Quarantine, appeared in 1992; his second novel, Permutation City, won the John W. Campbell Memorial Award in 1994. His other books include the novels Distress, Diaspora, Oceanic, Teranesia, Zendegi, and Schild's Ladder, and four collections of his short fiction, Axiomatic, Luminous, Our Lady of Chernobyl, and Crystal Nights and Other Stories. His most recent books are part of the "Orthogonal" trilogy, consisting of The Clockwork Rocket, The Eternal Flame, and The Arrows of Time. He has a website at www.gregegan.net.

Here he deals shrewdly and poignantly with the question of whether the "copy" of a dead man is synonymous with the once-living man himself. Which of the man's memories have been left out of the creation of the copy, and, more importantly—why?

1

In a pause in the flow of images, it came to him that he'd been dreaming for a fathomless time and that he wished to stop. But when he tried to picture the scene that would greet him upon waking, his mind grabbed the question and ran with it, not so much changing the subject as summoning out of the darkness answers that he was sure had long ago ceased to be correct. He remembered the bunk beds he and his brother had slept in until he was nine, with pieces of broken springs hanging down above him like tiny gray stalactites. The shade of his bedside reading lamp had been ringed with small, diamond-shaped holes; he would place his fingers over them and stare at the red light emerging through his flesh, until the heat from the globe became too much to bear.

Later, in a room of his own, his bed had come with hollow metal posts whose plastic caps were easily removed, allowing him to toss in chewed pencil stubs, pins that had held newly bought school shirts elaborately folded around cardboard packaging, tacks that he'd bent out of shape with misaligned hammer blows while trying to form pictures in zinc on lumps of firewood, pieces of gravel that had made their way into his shoes, dried snot scraped from his handkerchief, and tiny, balled-up scraps of paper, each bearing a four- or five-word account of whatever seemed important at the time, building up a record of his life like a core sample slicing through geological strata, a find for future archaeologists far more exciting than any diary.

But he could also recall a bleary-eyed, low-angle view of clothes strewn on the floor, in a bedsit apartment with no bed as such, just a foldout couch. That felt as remote as his childhood, but something pushed him to keep fleshing out the details of the room. There was a typewriter on a table. He could smell the ribbon, and he saw the box in which it had come, sitting on a shelf in a corner of a stationer's, with white letters on a blue background, but the words they spelled out eluded him. He'd always hunted down the fully black ribbons, though most stores had only stocked black-and-red. Who could possibly need to type anything in red?

Wiping his ink-stained fingers on a discarded page after a ribbon change, he knew the whole scene was an anachronism, and he tried to follow that insight up to the surface, like a diver pursuing a glimpse of the distant sun. But something weighed him down, anchoring him to the cold wooden chair in that unheated room, with a stack of blank paper to his right, a pile of finished sheets to his left, a wastebasket under the table. He urgently needed to think about the way the loop in the "e" became solid black sometimes, prompting him to clean all the typebars with an old T-shirt dampened with methylated spirits. If he didn't think about it now, he was afraid that he might never have the chance to think of it again.

2

Adam decided to go against all the advice he'd received and attend the old man's funeral.

The old man himself had warned him off. "Why make trouble?" he'd asked, peering at Adam from the hospital bed with that disconcerting vampiric longing that had grown more intense toward the end. "The more you rub their faces in it, the more likely they'll be to come after you."

"I thought you said they couldn't do that."

"All I said was that I'd done my best to stop them. Do you want to keep the inheritance, or do you want to squander it on lawyers? Don't make yourself more of a target than you need to be."

But standing in the shower, reveling in the sensation of the hot water pelting his skin, Adam only grew more resolute. Why shouldn't he dare to show his face? He had nothing to be ashamed of.

The old man had bought a few suits for him a while ago, and left them hanging beside his own clothes. Adam picked one out and placed it on the bed, then paused to run a hand along the worn sleeve of an old, olive-green shirt. He was sure it would fit him, and for a moment he considered wearing it, but then the thought made him uneasy and he chose one of the new ones that had come with the suits.

As he dressed, he gazed at the undisturbed bed, trying to think of a good reason why he still hadn't left the guest room. No one else was coming to claim this one. But he shouldn't get too comfortable here; he might need to sell the house and move into something far more modest.

Adam started booking a car, then realized that he had no idea where the ceremony was being held. He finally found the details at the bottom of the old man's obit, which described it as open to the public. While he stood outside the front door waiting for the car, he tried for the third or fourth time to read the obituary itself, but his eyes kept glazing over. "Morris blah blah blah . . . Morris blah blah, Morris blah . . ."

His phone beeped, then the gate opened and the car pulled into the driveway. He sat in the passenger seat and watched the steering wheel doing its poltergeist act as it negotiated the U-turn. He suspected that whatever victories the lawyers could achieve, he was going to have to pay the "unsupervised driving" surcharge for a while yet.

As the car turned into Sepulveda Boulevard, the view looked strange to him—half familiar, half wrong—but perhaps there'd been some recent reconstruction. He dialed down the tinting, hoping to puncture a lingering sense of being at a remove from everything. The glare from the pavement beneath the cloudless blue sky was merciless, but he kept the windows undimmed.

The venue was some kind of chapel-esque building that probably served as seven different kinds of meeting hall, and in any case was free of conspicuous religious or la-la-land inspirational signage. The old man had left his remains to a medical school, so at least they'd all been spared a trip to Forest Lawn. As Adam stepped away from the car, he spotted one of the nephews, Ryan, walking toward the entrance, accompanied by his wife and adult children. The old man hadn't spent much time with any of them, but he'd gotten hold of recent pictures and showed them to Adam so he wouldn't be caught unaware.

Adam hung back and waited for them to go inside before crossing the forecourt. As he approached the door and caught sight of a large portrait of a decidedly pre-cancerous version of the old man on a stand beside the podium, his courage began to waver. But he steeled himself and continued.

He kept his gaze low as he entered the hall, and chose a spot on the frontmost unoccupied bench, far enough in from the aisle that nobody would have to squeeze past him. After a minute or so, an elderly man took the aisle seat; Adam snuck a quick glance at his neighbor, but he did not look familiar. His timing had turned out to be perfect: any later and his entrance might have drawn attention, any earlier and there would have been people milling outside. Whatever happened, no one could accuse him of going out of his way to make a scene.

Ryan mounted the steps to the podium. Adam stared at the back of the bench in front of him; he felt like a child trapped in church, though no one had forced him to be here.

"The last time I saw my uncle," Ryan began, "was almost ten years ago, at the funeral of his husband, Carlos. Until then, I always thought it would be Carlos standing up here, delivering this speech, far more aptly and eloquently than I, or anyone else, ever could."

Adam felt a freight train tearing through his chest, but he kept his eyes fixed on a discolored patch of varnish. This had been a bad idea, but he couldn't walk out now.

"My uncle was the youngest child of Robert and Sophie Morris," Ryan continued. "He outlived his brother, Steven, his sister Joan, and my mother, Sarah. Though I was never close to him, I'm heartened to see so many of his friends and colleagues here to pay their respects. I watched his shows, of course, but then, didn't everyone? I was wondering if we ought to screen some kind of highlights reel, but then the people in the know told me that there was going to be a tribute at the Emmys, and I decided not to compete with the professional edit-bots."

That line brought some quiet laughter, and Adam felt obliged to look up and smile. No one in this family was any kind of monster, whatever they aspired to do to him. They just had their own particular views of his relationship with the old man—sharpened by the lure of a few million dollars, but they probably would have felt the same regardless.

Ryan kept his contribution short, but when Cynthia Navarro took his place Adam had to turn his face to the pew again. He doubted that she'd recognize him—she'd worked with the old man in the wrong era for that—but the warmth, and grief, in her voice made her anecdotes far harder to shut out than the automated mash-up of database entries and viral misquotes that had formed the obituary. She finished with the time they'd spent all night searching for a way to rescue a location shoot with six hundred extras after Gemma Freeman broke her leg and had to be stretchered out in a chopper. As she spoke, Adam closed his eyes and pictured the wildly annotated pages of the script strewn across the table, and Cynthia gawping with incredulity at her friend's increasingly desperate remedies.

"But it all worked out well enough," she concluded. "The plot twist that *no viewer saw coming*, that lifted the third season to *a whole new level*, owed its existence to an oil slick from a generator that just happened to be situated between Ms. Freeman's trailer and . . ."

Laughter rose up, cutting her off, and Adam felt compelled once more to raise his eyes. But before the sounds of mirth had faded, his neighbor moved closer and asked in a whisper, "Do you remember me?"

Adam turned, not quite facing the man. "Should I?" He spoke with an east-coast accent that was hard to place, and if it induced a certain sense of déjà vu, so did advertising voice-overs and random conversations overheard in elevators.

"I don't know," the man replied. His tone was more amused than sarcastic; he meant the words literally. Adam hunted for something polite and noncommittal to say, but the audience was too quiet now for him to speak without being noticed and hushed, and his neighbor was already turning back toward the podium.

Cynthia was followed by a representative of the old man's agents, though everyone who'd known him in the golden age was long gone. There were suits from

Warner Bros., Netflix, and HBO, whose stories of the old man were clearly scripted by the same bots that wrote their new shows. As the proceedings became ever more wooden, Adam began suffering from a panic-inducing premonition that Ryan would invite anyone in the hall who wished to speak to step up, and in the awkward silence that followed everyone's eyes would sweep the room and alight on him.

But when Ryan returned to the podium, he just thanked them for coming and wished them safe journeys home.

"No music?" Adam's neighbor asked. "No poetry? I seem to recall something by Dylan Thomas that might have raised a laugh under the circumstances."

"I think he stipulated no music," Adam replied.

"Fair enough. Since *The Big Chill*, anything you could pick with a trace of wit to it would seem like a bad in-joke."

"Excuse me, I have to . . ." People were starting to leave, and Adam wanted to get away before anyone else noticed him.

As he stood, his neighbor took out his phone and flicked his thumb across its surface. Adam's phone pinged softly in acknowledgment. "In case you want to catch up sometime," the man explained cheerfully.

"Thanks," Adam replied, nodding an awkward goodbye, grateful that he didn't seem to be expected to reciprocate.

There was already a small crowd lingering just inside the door, slowing his exit. When he made it out onto the forecourt, he walked straight to the roadside and summoned a car.

"Hey, you! Mr. Sixty Percent!"

Adam turned. A man in his thirties was marching toward him, scowling with such intense displeasure that his pillowy cheeks had turned red. "Can I help you with something?" Adam asked mildly. For all that he'd been dreading a confrontation, now that it was imminent he felt more invigorated than intimidated.

"What the fuck were you doing in there?"

"It was open to the public."

"You're not part of the public!"

Adam finally placed him: He was one of Ryan's sons. He'd seen him from behind as he'd been entering the hall. "Unhappy with the will, are you, Gerald?"

Gerald came closer. He was trembling slightly, but Adam couldn't tell if it was from rage or from fear. "Live it up while you can, Sixty. You're going to be out with the trash in no time."

"What's with this 'sixty'?" As far as Adam knew, he'd been bequeathed a hundred percent of the estate, unless Gerald was already accounting for all the legal fees.

"Sixty percent: how much you resemble him."

"Now that's just cruel. I'm assured that by some metrics, it's at least seventy."

Gerald snickered triumphantly, as if that made his case. "I guess he was used to setting the bar low. If you grew up believing that Facebook could give you 'news' and Google could give you 'information,' your expectations for quality control would already be nonexistent."

"I think you're conflating his generation with your father's." Adam was quite sure that the old man had held the Bilge Barons in as much contempt as his great-nephew did. "And seventy percent of something real isn't so bad. Getting a side-load that close to complete is orders of magnitude harder than anything those charlatans ever did."

"Well, give your own scam artists a Nobel Prize, but you'd still need to be senile to think that was good enough."

"He wasn't senile. We spoke together at least a dozen times in the month before he died, and he must have thought he was getting what he'd paid for, because he never chose to pull the plug on me." Adam hadn't even known at the time that that was possible, but in retrospect he was glad no one had told him. It might have made those bedside chats a little tense.

"Because . . . ?" Gerald demanded. When Adam didn't reply immediately, Gerald laughed. "Or is the reason he decided you were worth the trouble part of the thirty percent of his mind that you don't have?"

"It could well be," Adam conceded, trying to make that sound like a perfectly satisfactory outcome. A joke about the studios' bots only achieving ten percent of the same goal and still earning a tidy income got censored halfway to his lips; the last thing he wanted to do was invite the old man's relatives to view him in the same light as that cynical act of shallow mimicry.

"So you don't know *why* he didn't care that you don't know whatever it is that you don't know? Very fucking Kafka."

"I think he would have preferred 'very fucking Heller' . . . but who am I to say?"

"Next week's trash, that's what you are." Gerald stepped back, looking pleased with himself. "Next week's fodder for the wrecking yard."

The car pulled up beside Adam and the door slid open. "Is that your grandma come to take you home?" Gerald taunted him. "Or maybe your retarded cousin?"

"Enjoy the wake," Adam replied. He tapped his skull. "I promise, the old man will be thinking of you."

3

Adam had a conference call with the lawyers. "How do we stand?" he asked.

"The family's going to contest the will," Gina replied.

"On what grounds?"

"That the trustees, and the beneficiaries of the trust, misled and defrauded Mr. Morris."

"They're saying I misled him somehow?"

"No," Corbin interjected. "US law doesn't recognize you as a person. *You* can't be sued, as such, but other entities you depend on certainly can be."

"Right." Adam had known as much, but in his mind he kept glossing over the elaborate legal constructs that sustained his delusions of autonomy. On a purely practical level, there was money in three accounts that he had no trouble accessing—but then, the same was probably true of any number of stock-trading algorithms, and that didn't make them the masters of their own fate. "So who exactly is accused of fraud?"

"Our firm," Gina replied. "Various officers of the corporations we created to fulfill Mr. Morris's instructions. Loadstone, for making false claims that led to the original purchase of their technology, and for ongoing fraud in relation to the services promised in their maintenance contract."

"I'm very happy with the maintenance contract!" When Adam had complained that one of his earlobes had gone numb, Sandra had come to his home and fixed the problem on the same day he called.

"That's not the point," Corbin said impatiently. Adam was forgetting his place again: Jurisprudentially, his happiness cut no ice.

"So what happens next?"

"The first hearings are still seven months away," Gina explained. "We were expecting this, and we'll have plenty of time to prepare. We'll aim for an early dismissal, of course, but we can't promise anything."

"No." Adam hesitated. "But it's not just the house they could take? The Estonian accounts . . . ?"

Gina said, "Opening those accounts under your digital residency makes some things easier, but it doesn't put the money out of reach of the courts."

"Right."

When they hung up, Adam paced the office. Could it really be so hard to defend the old man's will? He wasn't even sure what disincentives were in place to stop the lawyers from drawing out proceedings like this for as long as they wished. Maybe a director of one of the entities he depended on was both empowered and duty bound to rein them in if they were behaving with conspicuous profligacy? But Adam himself couldn't sack them, or compel them to follow his instructions, just because Estonia had been nice enough to classify him as a person for certain limited purposes.

The old man had believed he was setting him up in style, but all the machinery that was meant to support him just made him feel trapped. What if he gave up the house and walked away? If he cashed in his dollar and euro accounts for some mixture of blockchain currencies before the courts swept in and froze his funds, that might be easier to protect and enjoy without the benefits of a Social Security number, a birth certificate, or a passport. But those currencies were all insanely volatile, and trying to hedge them against each other was like trying to save yourself in a skydiving accident by clutching your own feet.

He couldn't leave the country by any lawful means without deactivating his body so it could be sent as freight. Loadstone had promised to facilitate any trips he wished to make to any of the thirty-nine jurisdictions where he could walk the streets unchaperoned, as proud and free as the pizza bots that had blazed the trail, but the idea of returning to the company's servers, or even being halted and left in limbo for the duration of the flight, filled him with dread.

For now, it seemed that he was stuck in the Valley. All he could do was find a way to make the best of it.

4

Sitting on two upturned wooden crates in an alley behind the nightclub, they could still hear the pounding bass line of the music escaping through the walls, but at least it was possible to hold a conversation here.

Carlos sounded like the loneliest person Adam had ever met. Did he tell everyone so much, so soon? Adam wanted to believe that he didn't, and that something in his own demeanor had inspired this beautiful man to confide in him.

Carlos had been in the country for twelve years, but he was still struggling to support his sister in El Salvador. She'd raised him after their parents died—his father when he was six months old, his mother when he was five. But now his sister had three children of her own, and the man who'd fathered them was no good to her.

"I love her," he said. "I love her like my own life, I don't want to be rid of her. But the kids are always sick, or something's broken that needs fixing. It never fucking stops."

Adam had no one relying on him, no one expecting him to do anything. His own finances waxed and waned, but at least when the money was scarce no one else suffered, or made him feel that he was letting them down.

"So what do you do to relieve the stress?" he asked.

Carlos smiled sadly. "It used to be smoking, but that got too expensive."

"So you quit?"

"Only the smoking."

As Adam turned toward him, his mind went roaming down the darkness of the alley, impatiently following the glistening thread, unable to shake off the sense of urgency that told him: *Take hold of this now, or it will be lost forever.* He didn't need to linger in their beds for long; just a few samples of that annihilating euphoria were enough to stand in for all the rest. Maybe that was the engine powering everything that followed, but what it dragged along behind it was like a newlyweds' car decorated by a thousand exuberant well-wishers.

He tried grabbing the rattling cans of their fights, running his fingers over the rough texture of all the small annoyances and slights, mutually wounded pride, frustrated good intentions. Then he felt the jagged edge of a lacerating eruption of doubt.

But something had happened that blunted the edge, then folded it in on itself again and again, leaving a seam, a ridge, a scar. Afterward, however hard things became, there was no questioning the foundations. They'd earned each other's trust, and it was unshakeable.

He pushed on into the darkness, trying to understand. Wherever he walked, light would follow, and his task was to make his way down as many side streets as possible before he woke.

This time, though, the darkness remained unbroken. He groped his way forward, unnerved. They'd ended up closer than ever—he knew that with as much certainty as he knew anything. So why did he feel as if he was stumbling blindly through the rooms of Bluebeard's castle, and the last thing he should want to summon was a lamp?

5

Adam spent three weeks in the old man's home theater, watching every one of the old man's shows, and an episode or two from each of the biggest hits of the last ten years. There could only be one thing more embarrassing than pitching an idea to a studio and discovering that he was offering them a story that they'd already produced for six seasons, and that would be attempting to recycle, not just any old show, but an actual Adam Morris script.

Most of the old man's work felt as familiar as if he'd viewed it a hundred times in the editing suite, but sometimes a whole side plot appeared that seemed to have dropped from the sky. Could the studios have fucked with things afterward, when the old man was too sick and distracted to notice? Adam checked online, but the fan sites that would have trumpeted any such tampering were silent. The only re-cuts had taken place in another medium entirely.

He desperately needed to write a new show. Money aside, how else was he going to pass the time? The old man's few surviving friends had all made it clear before he died that they wanted nothing to do with his side-load. He could try to make the most of his cybernetic rejuvenation; his skin felt exactly like skin, from inside and out, and his ridiculously plausible dildo of a cock wouldn't disappoint anyone if he went looking for ways to use it—but the truth was, he'd inherited the old man's feelings for Carlos far too deeply to brush them aside and pretend that he was twenty again, with no attachments and no baggage. He didn't even know yet if he wanted to forge an identity entirely his own, or to take the other path and seek to become the old man more fully. He couldn't "betray" a lover ten years dead who was, in the end, nothing more to him than a character in someone else's story—whatever he'd felt as he'd dragged the old man's memories into his own virtual skull. But he wasn't going to sell himself that version of things before he was absolutely sure it was the right one.

The only way to know who he was would be to create something new. It didn't even need to be a story that the old man wouldn't have written himself, had he lived a few years longer . . . just so long as it didn't turn out that he'd already written it, pitched it unsuccessfully, and stuck it in a drawer. Adam pictured himself holding a page from each version up to the light together, bringing the words into alignment, trying to decide if the differences were too many, or too few.

6

"Sixty thousand dollars *in one week?*" Adam was incredulous.

Gina replied calmly, "The billables are all itemized. I can assure you, what we're charging is really quite modest for a case of this complexity."

"The money was his, he could do what he liked with it. End of story."

"That's not what the case law says." Gina was beginning to exhibit micro-fidgets, as if she'd found herself trapped at a family occasion being forced to play a childish video game just to humor a nephew she didn't really like. Whether or not she'd granted Adam personhood in her own mind, he certainly wasn't anyone in a position to give her instructions, and the only reason she'd taken his call must have been some sop to Adam's comfort that the old man had managed to get written into his contract with the firm.

"All right. I'm sorry to have troubled you."

In the silence after he'd hung up, Adam recalled something that Carlos had said to the old man, back in New York one sweltering July, taking him aside in the middle of the haggling over a secondhand air-conditioner they were attempting to buy. "You're a good person, *cariño*, so you don't see it when people are trying to cheat you." Maybe he'd been sincere, or maybe "good" had just been a tactful euphemism for "unworldly," though if the old man really had been so trusting, how had Adam ended up with the opposite trait? Was cynicism some kind of default, wired into the template from which the whole side-loading process had started?

Adam found an auditor with no connections to the old man's lawyers, picking a city at random and then choosing the person with the highest reputation score with whom he could afford a ten-minute consultation. Her name was Lillian Adjani.

"Because these companies have no shareholders," she explained, "there's not that much that needs to be disclosed in their public filings. And I can't just go to them myself and demand to see their financial records. A court could do that, in principle, and you might be able to find a lawyer who'd take your money to try to make that happen. But who would their client be?"

Adam had to admire the way she could meet his gaze with an expression of sympathy, while reminding him that—shorn of the very constructs he was trying to scrutinize—for administrative purposes he didn't actually exist.

"So there's nothing I can do?" Maybe he was starting to confuse his secondhand memories of the real world with all the shows he'd been watching, where people just *followed the money trail.* The police never seemed to need to get the courts involved, and even civilians usually had some supernaturally gifted hacker at their disposal. "We couldn't . . . hire an investigator . . . who could persuade someone to leak . . . ?" Mike Ehrmantraut would have found a way to make it happen in three days flat.

Ms. Adjani regarded him censoriously. "I'm not getting involved in anything illegal. But maybe you have something yourself, already in your possession, that could help you more than you realize."

"Like what?"

"How computer-savvy was your . . . predecessor?"

"He could use a word processor and a web browser. And Skype."

"Do you still have any of his devices?"

Adam laughed. "I don't know what happened to his phone, but I'm talking to you from his laptop right now."

"Okay. Don't get your hopes too high, but if there were files containing financial records or legal documents that he received and then deleted, then, unless he went out of his way to erase them securely, they might still be recoverable."

Ms. Adjani sent him a link for a piece of software she trusted to do the job. Adam installed it, then stared numbly at the catalog of eighty-three thousand "intelligible fragments" that had shown up on the drive.

He started playing with the filtering options. When he chose "text," portions of scripts began emerging from the fog—some instantly recognizable, some probably abandoned dead ends. Adam averted his gaze, afraid of absorbing them into his subconscious if they weren't already buried there. He had to draw a line somewhere.

He found an option called "financial," and when that yielded a blizzard of utility bills, he added all the relevant keywords he could think of.

There were bills from the lawyers, and bills from Loadstone. If Gina was screwing him, she'd been screwing the old man as well, because the hourly rate hadn't changed. Adam was beginning to feel foolish; he was right to be vigilant about his precarious situation, but if he let that devolve into full-blown paranoia he'd just end up kicking all the support structures out from beneath his feet.

Loadstone hadn't been shy with their fees either. Adam hadn't known before just how much his body had cost, but given the generally excellent engineering it was difficult to begrudge the expense. There was an item for the purchase of the template, and then one for every side-loading session, broken down into various components. "Squid operator?" he muttered, bemused. "What the fuck?" But he wasn't going to start convincing himself that they'd blinded the old man with technobabble. He'd paid what he'd paid, and in the hospital he'd given Adam every indication that he'd been happy with the result.

"Targeted occlusions?" Meaning blood clots in the brain? The old man had left him login details allowing him postmortem access to all his medical records; Adam checked, and there had been no clots.

He searched the web for the phrase in the context of side-loading. The pithiest translation he found was: "The selective non-transferral of a prescribed class of memories or traits."

Which meant that the old man had held something back, deliberately. Adam was an imperfect copy of him, not just because the technology was imperfect, but because he'd wanted it that way.

"You lying piece of shit." Toward the end, the old man had rambled on about his hope that Adam would outdo his own achievements, but judging from his efforts so far he wasn't even going to come close. Three attempts at new scripts had ended up dead in the water. It wasn't Ryan and his family who'd robbed him of the most valuable part of the inheritance.

Adam sat staring at his hands, contemplating the possibilities for a life worth living without the only skill the old man had ever possessed. He remembered joking to Carlos once that they should both train as doctors and go open a free clinic in San Salvador. "When we're rich." But Adam doubted that his original, let alone the diminished version, was smart enough to learn to do much more than empty bedpans.

He switched off the laptop and walked into the master bedroom. All of the old man's clothes were still there, as if he'd fully expected them to be used again. Adam took off his own clothes and began trying on each item in turn, counting the ones he was sure he recognized. Was he Gerald's Mr. Sixty Percent, or was it more like forty, or thirty? Maybe the pep talks had been a kind of sarcastic joke, with the old man secretly hoping that the final verdict would be that there was only one Adam Morris, and like the studios' laughable "deep-learning" bots, even the best technology in the world couldn't capture his true spark.

He sat on the bed, naked, wondering what it would be like to go out in some wild bacchanalia with a few dozen robot fetishists, fucking his brains out and then dismembering him to take the pieces home as souvenirs. It wouldn't be hard to organize, and he doubted that any part of his corporate infrastructure would be obliged to have him resurrected from Loadstone's daily backups. The old man might have been using him to make some dementedly pretentious artistic point, but he would never have been cruel enough to render suicide impossible.

Adam caught sight of a picture of the two men posing hammily beneath the Holly-wood sign, and found himself sobbing dryly with, of all things, grief. What he wanted was Carlos beside him—making this bearable, putting it right. He loved the dead man's dead lover more than he was ever going to love anyone else, but he still couldn't do anything worthwhile that the dead man could have done.

He pictured Carlos with his arms around him. "Sssh, it's not as bad as you think—it never is, *cariño*. We start with what we've got, and just fill in the pieces as we go."

You're really not helping, Adam replied. *Just shut up and fuck me, that's all I've got left.* He lay down on the bed and took his penis in his hand. It had seemed wrong before, but he didn't care now: He didn't owe either of them anything. And Carlos, at least, would probably have taken pity on him, and not begrudged him the unpaid guest appearance.

He closed his eyes and tried to remember the feel of stubble against his thighs, but he wasn't even capable of scripting his own fantasy: Carlos just wanted to talk. "You've got friends," he insisted. "You've got people looking out for you."

Adam had no idea if he was confabulating freely, or if this was a fragment of a real conversation long past, but context was everything. "Not any more, *cariño*. Either they're dead, or I'm dead to them."

Carlos just stared back at him skeptically, as if he'd made a ludicrously hyperbolic claim.

But that skepticism did have some merit. If he knocked on Cynthia's door she'd probably try to stab him through the heart with a wooden stake, but the amiable stranger who'd sat beside him at the funeral had been far keener to talk than Adam. The fact that he still couldn't place the man no longer seemed like a good reason to avoid him; if he came from the gaps, he must know something about them.

Carlos was gone. Adam sat up, still feeling gutted, but no amount of self-pity was going to improve his situation.

He found his phone, and checked under "Introductions"; he hadn't erased the contact details. The man was named Patrick Auster. Adam called the number.

7

"You go first," Adam said. "Ask me anything. That's the only fair trade." They were sitting in a booth in an old-style diner named Caesar's, where Auster had suggested they meet. The place wasn't busy, and the adjacent booths were empty, so there was no need to censor themselves or talk in code.

Auster gestured at the generous serving of chocolate cream pie that Adam had begun demolishing. "Can you really taste that?"

"Absolutely."

"And it's the same as before?"

Adam wasn't going to start hedging his answers with quibbles about the ultimate incomparability of qualia and memories. "Exactly the same." He pointed a thumb toward the diners three booths behind him. "I can tell you without peeking that someone's eating bacon. And I think it's apparent that there's nothing wrong with my hearing or vision, even if my memory for faces isn't so good."

"Which leaves . . ."

"Every hair on the bearskin rug," Adam assured him.

Auster hesitated. Adam said, "There's no three-question limit. We can keep going all day if you want to."

"Do you have much to do with the others?" Auster asked.

"The other side-loads? No. I never knew any of them before, so there's no reason for them to be in touch with me now."

Auster was surprised. "I'd have thought you'd all be making common cause. Trying to improve the legal situation."

"We probably should be. But if there's some secret cabal of immortals trying to get re-enfranchised, they haven't invited me into their inner circle yet."

Adam waited as Auster stirred his coffee meditatively. "That's it," he decided.

"Okay. You know, I'm sorry if I was brusque at the funeral," Adam said. "I was trying to keep a low profile; I was worried about how people would react."

"Forget it."

"So you knew me in New York?" Adam wasn't going to use the third person; it would make the conversation far too awkward. Besides, if he'd come here to claim the missing memories as his own, the last thing he wanted to do was distance himself from them.

"Yes."

"Was it business, or were we friends?" All he'd been able to find out online was that Auster had written a couple of independent movies. There was no record of the two of them ever working on the same project; their official Bacon number was three, which put Adam no closer to Auster than he was to Angelina Jolie.

"Both, I hope." Auster hesitated, then angrily recanted the last part. "No, we were friends. Sorry, it's hard not to resent being blanked, even if it's not deliberate."

Adam tried to judge just how deeply the insult had cut him. "Were we lovers?"

Auster almost choked on his coffee. "God, no! I've always been straight, and you were already with Carlos when I met you." He frowned suddenly. "You didn't cheat on him, did you?" He sounded more incredulous than reproving.

"Not as far as I know." During the drive down to Gardena, Adam had wondered if the old man might have been trying to airbrush out his infidelities. That would have been a bizarre form of vanity, or hypocrisy, or some other sin the world didn't have a name for yet, but it would still have been easier to forgive than a deliberate attempt to sabotage his successor.

"We met around two thousand and ten," Auster continued. "When I first approached you about adapting *Sadlands*."

"Okay."

"You do remember *Sadlands*, don't you?"

"My second novel," Adam replied. For a moment nothing more came to him, then he said, "There's an epidemic of suicides spreading across the country, apparently at random, affecting people equally regardless of demographics."

"That sounds like the version a reviewer would write," Auster teased him. "I spent six years, on and off, trying to make it happen."

Adam dredged his mind for any trace of these events that might have merely been submerged for lack of currency, but he found nothing. "So should I be thanking you, or apologizing? Did I give you a hard time about the script?"

"Not at all. I showed you drafts now and then, and if you had a strong opinion you let me know, but you didn't cross any lines."

"The book itself didn't do that well," Adam recalled.

Auster didn't argue. "Even the publishers stopped using the phrase 'slow-burning cult hit,' though I'm sure the studio would have put that in the press release, if it had ever gone ahead."

Adam hesitated. "So, what else was going on?" The old man hadn't published much in that decade; just a few pieces in magazines. His book sales had dried up, and he'd been working odd jobs to make ends meet. But at least back then there'd still been golden opportunities like valet parking. "Did we socialize much? Did I talk about things?"

Auster scrutinized him. "This isn't just smoothing over the business at the funeral, is it? You've lost something that you think might be important, and now you're going all Dashiell Hammett on yourself."

"Yes," Adam admitted.

Auster shrugged. "Okay, why not? That worked out so well in *Angel Heart*." He thought for a while. "When we weren't discussing *Sadlands*, you talked about your money problems, and you talked about Carlos."

"What about Carlos?"

"His money problems."

Adam laughed. "Sorry. I must have been fucking awful company."

Auster said, "I think Carlos was working three or four jobs, all for minimum wage, and you were working two, with a few hours a week set aside for writing. I remember you sold a story to the *New Yorker*, but the celebration was pretty muted, because the whole fee was gone, instantly, to pay off debts."

"*Debts?*" Adam had no memory of it ever being that bad. "Did I try to borrow money from you?"

"You wouldn't have been so stupid; you knew I was almost as skint. Just before we gave up, I got twenty grand in development money to spend a year trying to whip *Sadlands* into something that Sundance or AMC might buy—and believe me, it all went on rent and food."

"So what did *I* get out of that?" Adam asked, mock-jealously.

"Two grand, for the option. If it had gone to a pilot, I think you would have gotten twenty, and double that if the series was picked up." Auster smiled. "That must sound like small change to you now, but at the time it would have been the difference between night and day—especially for Carlos's sister."

"Yeah, she could be a real hard-ass," Adam sighed. Auster's face drained, as if Adam had just maligned a woman that everyone else had judged worthy of beatification. "What did I say?"

"You don't even remember *that*?"

"Remember what?"

"She was dying of cancer! Where did you think the money was going? You and Carlos weren't living in the Ritz, or shooting it up."

"Okay." Adam recalled none of this. He'd known that Adelina had died long before Carlos, but he'd never even tried to summon up the details. "So Carlos and I were working eighty-hour weeks to pay her medical bills . . . and I was bitching and moaning to you about it, as if that might make the magic Hollywood money fall into my lap a little faster?"

"That's putting it harshly," Auster replied. "You needed someone to vent to, and I had enough distance from it that it didn't weigh me down. I could commiserate and walk away."

Adam thought for a while. "Do you know if I ever took it out on Carlos?"

"Not that you told me. Would you have stayed together if you had?"

"I don't know," Adam said numbly. Could this be the whole point of the occlusions? When their relationship was tested, the old man had buckled, and he was so ashamed of himself that he'd tried to erase every trace of the event? Whatever he'd done, Carlos must have forgiven him in the end, but maybe that just made his own weakness more painful to contemplate.

"So I never pulled the pin?" he asked. "I didn't wash my hands of Adelina, and tell Carlos to fuck off and pay for it all himself?"

Auster said, "Not unless you were lying to me to save face. The version I heard was that every spare dollar you had was going to her, up until the day she died. Which is where forty grand might have made all the difference—bought her more time, or even a cure. I never got the medico-logistic details, but both of you took it hard when the Colman thing happened."

Adam moved his half-empty plate aside and asked wearily, "So what was 'the Colman thing'?"

Auster nodded apologetically. "I was getting to that. Sundance had shown a lot of interest in *Sadlands*, but then they heard that some Brit called Nathan Colman had sold a story to Netflix about, well . . . an epidemic of suicides spreading across the country, apparently at random, affecting people equally regardless of demographics."

"And we didn't sue the brazen fuck into penury?"

Auster snorted. "Who's this 'we' with money for lawyers? The production company that held the option did a cost-benefit analysis and decided to cut their losses; twenty-two grand down the toilet, but it wasn't as if they'd been cheated out of the next *Game of Thrones*. All you and I could do was suck it up, and take a few moments of solace whenever a *Sadlands* fan posted an acerbic comment in some obscure chat room."

Adam's visceral sense of outrage was undiminished, but on any sober assessment this outcome was pretty much what he would have expected.

"Of course, my faith in karma was restored, eventually," Auster added enigmatically.

"You've lost me again." The old man's success, once he cut out all the middlemen and plagiarists, must have been balm to his wounds—but Auster's online footprint suggested that his own third act had been less lucrative.

"Before they'd finished shooting the second season, a burglar broke into Colman's house and cracked open his skull with a statuette."

"An Emmy?"

"No, just a BAFTA."

Adam tried hard not to smile. "And once *Sadlands* fell through, did we stay in touch?"

"Not really," Auster replied. "I moved here a long time after you did; I wasted five years trying to get something up on Broadway before I swallowed my pride and settled for playing script doctor. And by then you'd done so well that I was embarrassed to turn up asking you for work."

Adam was genuinely ashamed now. "You should have. I owed it to you."

Auster shook his head. "I wasn't living on the streets. I've done all right here. I can't afford what you've got . . ." He gestured at Adam's imperishable chassis. "But then, I'm not sure I could handle the lacunae."

Adam called for a car. Auster insisted on splitting the bill.

The service cart rattled over and began clearing the table. Auster said, "I'm glad I could help you fill in the blanks, but maybe those answers should have come with a warning."

"*Now* a warning?"

"The Colman thing. Don't let it get to you."

Adam was baffled. "Why would I? I'm not going to sue his family for whatever pittance is still trickling down to them." In fact, he couldn't sue anyone for anything, but it was the thought that counted.

"Okay." Auster was ready to drop it, but now Adam needed to be clear.

"How badly did I take it the first time?"

Auster gestured with one finger, drilling into his temple. "Like a fucking parasitic worm in your brain. He'd stolen your precious novel and murdered your lover's sister. He'd kicked you to the ground when you had nothing, and taken your only hope away."

Adam could understand now why they hadn't stayed in touch. Solidarity in hard times was one thing, but an obsessive grievance like that would soon get old. Auster had taken his own kicks and decided to move on.

"That was more than thirty years ago," Adam replied. "I'm a different person now."

"Aren't we all?"

Auster's ride came first. Adam stood outside the diner and watched him depart: sitting confidently behind the wheel, even if he didn't need to lay a finger on it.

8

Adam changed his car's destination to downtown Gardena. He disembarked beside a row of fast-food outlets and went looking for a public web kiosk. He'd been fretting about the best way of paying without leaving too obvious a trail, but then he discovered that in this municipality the things were as free as public water fountains.

There was no speck of entertainment industry trivia that the net had failed to immortalize. Colman had moved from London to Los Angeles to shoot the series, and he'd been living just a few miles south of Adam's current home when the break-in happened. But the old man had still been in New York at the time; he hadn't even set foot in California until the following year, as far as Adam recalled. The laptop that he'd started excavating had files on it dating back to the '90s, but they would have been copied from machine to machine; there was no chance that the computer itself was old enough to be carrying deleted emails for flights booked three decades ago, even if the old man had been foolish enough to make his journey so easy to trace.

Adam turned away from the kiosk's chipped projection screen, wondering if any passersby had been staring over his shoulder. He was losing his grip on reality. The occlusions might easily have been targeted at nothing more than the old man's lingering resentment: If he couldn't let go of what had happened—even after Colman's death, even after his own career had blossomed—he might have wished to spare Adam all that pointless, fermented rage.

That was the simplest explanation. Unless Auster had been holding back, the thought of the old man murdering Colman didn't seem to have crossed his mind, and if the police had come knocking he would surely have mentioned that. If nobody else thought the old man was guilty, who was Adam to start accusing him—on the basis of nothing but the shape and location of one dark pit of missing memories, among the thirty percent of everything that he didn't recall?

He turned to the screen again, trying to think of a more discriminating test of his hypothesis. Though the flow into the side-load itself would have been protected by a massive firewall of privacy laws, Adam doubted that any instructions to the technicians at Loadstone were subject to privilege. Which meant that, even if he found them on the laptop, they were unlikely to be incriminatory. The only way the old man could have phrased a request to forget that he'd bashed Colman's brains out would have been to excise all of the more innocent events that were connected to it in any way, like a cancer surgeon choosing the widest possible sacrificial margin. But he might also have issued the same instructions merely in order to forget as much as possible of that whole bleak decade—when Hollywood had fucked him over, Carlos had been grieving for the woman who raised him, and he'd somehow, just barely, kept it together, long enough to make a new start in the '20s.

Adam logged off the kiosk. Auster had warned him not to become obsessed—and the man was the closest thing to a friend that he had right now. If everyone in the industry really staved in the skulls of everyone who'd crossed them, there'd be no one left to run the place.

He called a car and headed home.

9

Under protest, at Adam's request, Sandra spread the three sturdy boxes out on the floor, and opened them up to reveal the foam, straps, and recesses within. They reminded Adam of the utility trunks that the old man's crews had used for stowing their gear.

"Don't freak out on me," she pleaded.

"I won't," Adam promised. "I just want a clear picture in my mind of what's about to happen."

"Really? I don't even let my dentist show me his planning videos."

"I trust you to do a better job than any dentist."

"You're too kind." She gestured at the trunks like a proud magician, bowing her head for applause.

Adam said, "Now you have no choice, El Dissecto: You've got to take a picture for me once it's done."

"I hope your Spanish is better than you're making it sound."

"I was aiming for vaudevillian, not voseo." Adam had some memories of the old man being prepared for surgery, but he wasn't sure that it was possible to rid them of survivor's hindsight and understand exactly how afraid he'd been that he might never wake up.

Sandra glanced at her watch. "No more clowning around. You need to undress and lie down on the bed, then repeat the code phrase aloud, four times. I'll wait outside."

Adam didn't care if she saw him naked while he was still conscious, but it might have made her uncomfortable. "Okay." Once she left, he stopped stalling; he removed his clothes quickly, and began the chant.

"Red lentils, yellow lentils. Red lentils, yellow lentils. Red lentils, yellow lentils." He glanced past the row of cases to Sandra's toolbox; he'd seen inside it before, and there were no cleavers, machetes, or chainsaws. Just magnetic screwdrivers that could loosen bolts within him without even penetrating his skin. He lay back and stared at the ceiling. "Red lentils, yellow lentils."

The ceiling stayed white but sprouted new shadows, a ventilation grille, and a light fitting, while the texture of the bedspread beneath his skin went from silken to beaded. Adam turned his head; the same clothes he'd removed were folded neatly beside him. He dressed quickly, walked over to the connecting door between the suites, and knocked.

Sandra opened the door. She'd changed her clothes since he'd last seen her, and she looked exhausted. His watch showed 11:20 p.m. local time, 9:20 back home.

"I just wanted to let you know that I'm still in here," he said, pointing to his skull.

She smiled. "Okay, Adam."

"Thank you for doing this," he added.

"Are you kidding? They're paying me all kinds of allowances and overtime, and it's not even that long a flight. Feel free to come back here as often as you like."

He hesitated. "You didn't take the photo, did you?"

Sandra was unapologetic. "No. It could have gotten me sacked, and not all of the company's rules are stupid."

"Okay. I'll let you sleep. See you in the morning."

"Yeah."

Adam lay awake for an hour before he could bring himself to mutter his code word for the milder form of sleep. If he'd wished, Loadstone could have given him a passable simulation of the whole journey—albeit with a lot of cheating to mask the time it took to shuffle him back and forth between their servers and his body. But the airlines didn't recognize any kind of safe "flight mode" for his kind of machine, even when he was in pieces and locked inside three separate boxes. The way he'd experienced it was the most honest choice: a jump-cut, and thirteen hours lost to the gaps.

In the morning, Sandra had arranged to join an organized tour of the sights of San Salvador. Her employer's insurance company was more concerned about her safety than Adam's, and in any case it would have been awkward for both of them to have her following him around with her toolbox.

"Just keep the license on you," she warned him before she left. "I had to fill out more forms to get it than I would to clear a drone's flight path twice around the world, so if you lose it I'm not coming to rescue you from the scrapyard."

"Who's going to put me there?" Adam spread his arms and stared down at his body. "Are you calling me a Ken doll?" He raised one forearm to his face and examined it critically, but the skin around his elbow wrinkled with perfect verisimilitude.

"No, but you talk like a foreigner, and you don't have a passport. So just . . . stay out of trouble."

"Yes, ma'am."

The old man had only visited the city once, and with Carlos leading him from nightspot to childhood haunt to some cousin's apartment like a ricocheting bullet, he'd made no attempt to navigate for himself. But Adam had been disappointed when he'd learned that Beatriz was now living in an entirely different part of town; there'd be no cues along the way, no hooks to bring back other memories of the time.

Colonia Layco was half an hour's drive from the hotel. There were more autonomous cars on the street than Adam remembered, but enough electric scooters interspersed among them to keep the traffic from mimicking L.A.'s spookily synchronized throbbing.

The car dropped him off outside a newish apartment block. Adam entered the antechamber in the lobby and found the intercom.

"Beatriz, this is Adam."

"Welcome! Come on up!"

He pushed through the swing doors and took the stairs, ascending four flights; it wouldn't make him any fitter, but old habits died hard. When Beatriz opened the door of her apartment he was prepared for her to flinch, but she just stepped out and embraced him. Maybe the sight of wealthy Californians looking younger than their age had lost its power to shock anyone before she'd even been born.

She ushered him in, tongue-tied for a moment, perhaps from the need to suppress an urge to ask about his flight, or inquire about his health. She settled, finally, on "How have things been?"

Her English was infinitely better than his Spanish, so Adam didn't even try. "Good," he replied. "I've been taking a break from work, so I thought I owed you a visit." The last time they'd met had been at Carlos's funeral.

She led him into the living room and gestured toward a chair, then fetched a tray of pastries and a pot of coffee. Carlos had never found the courage to come out to Adelina, but Beatriz had known his secret long before her mother died. Adam had no idea what details of the old man's life Carlos might have confided in her, but he'd exhausted all the willing informants who'd known the old man firsthand, and she'd responded so warmly to his emails that he'd had no qualms about attempting to revive their relationship for its own sake.

"How are the kids?" he asked.

Beatriz turned and gestured proudly toward a row of photographs on a bookcase behind her. "That's Pilar at her graduation last year; she started at the hospital six months ago. Rodrigo's in his final year of engineering."

Adam smiled. "Carlos would have been over the moon."

"Of course," Beatriz agreed. "We teased him a lot once he started with the acting, but his heart was always with us. With you, and with us."

Adam scanned the photographs and spotted a thirty-something Carlos in a suit, beside a much younger woman in a wedding dress.

"That's you, isn't it?" He pointed at the picture.

"Yes."

"I'm sorry I didn't make it." He had no memory of Carlos leaving for the wedding, but it must have taken place a year or two before they'd moved to L.A.

Beatriz tutted. "You would have been welcome, Adam, but I knew how tight things were for you back then. We all knew what you'd done for my mother."

Not enough to keep her alive, Adam thought, but that would be a cruel and pointless thing to say. And he hoped that Carlos had spared his sister's children any of the old man's poisonous talk of the windfall they'd missed out on.

Beatriz had her own idea of the wrongs that needed putting right. "Of course, she didn't know, herself. She knew he had a friend who helped him out, but Carlos had to make it sound like you were rich, that you were loaning him the money and it was nothing to you. He should have told her the truth. If she'd thought of you as family, she wouldn't have refused your help."

Adam nodded uncomfortably, unsure just how graciously or otherwise the old man had handed over paycheck after paycheck for a woman who had no idea who he was. "That was a long time ago. I just want to meet your children and hear all your news."

"Ah." Beatriz grimaced apologetically. "I should warn you that Rodrigo's bringing his boyfriend to lunch."

"That's no problem at all." What twenty-year-old engineer wouldn't want to show off the animatronic version of Great-Uncle Movie Star's lover to as many people as possible?

When Adam got back to the hotel it was late in the afternoon. He messaged Sandra, who replied that she was in a bar downtown having a great time and he was welcome to join her. Adam declined and lay down on the bed. The meal he'd just shared had been the most normal thing he'd experienced since his embodiment. He'd come within a hair's breadth of convincing himself that there was a place for him here: That he could somehow insert himself into this family and survive on their affection alone, as if this one day's hospitality and good-natured curiosity could be milked forever.

As the glow of borrowed domesticity faded, the tug of the past reasserted itself. He had to keep trying to assemble the pieces, as and when he found them. He took out his laptop and searched through archived social media posts, seeing if he could date Beatriz's wedding. Pictures had a way of getting wildly mislabeled, or grabbed by bots and repurposed at random, so even when he had what looked like independent confirmation from four different guests, he didn't quite trust the result, and he paid a small fee for access to the Salvadorian government's records.

Beatriz had been married on March 4, 2018. Adam didn't need to open the spreadsheet he was using to assemble his timeline for the gaps to know that the surrounding period would be sparsely annotated, save for one entry. Nathan Colman had been bludgeoned to death by an intruder on March 10 of the same year.

Carlos would hardly have flown in for the wedding and left the next day; the family would have expected him to stay for at least a couple of weeks. The old man would have been alone in New York, with no one to observe his comings and goings. He might even have had time to cross the country and return by bus, paying with cash, breaking the trip down into small stages, hitchhiking here and there, obfuscating the bigger picture as much as possible.

The dates proved nothing, of course. If Adam had been a juror in a trial with a case this flimsy, he would have laughed the prosecution out of court. He owed the old man the same standard of evidence.

Then again, in a trial the old man could have stood in the witness box and explained exactly what it was that he'd gone to so much trouble to hide.

The flight to L.A. wasn't until six in the evening, but Sandra was too hungover to leave the hotel, and Adam had made no plans. So they sat in his room watching movies and ordering snacks from the kitchen, while Adam worked up the courage to ask her the question that had kept him awake all night.

"Is there any way you could get me the specifications for my targeted occlusions?" Adam waited for her response before daring to raise the possibility of payment. If the request was insulting in itself, offering a bribe would only compound the offense.

"No," she replied, as unfazed as if he'd wondered aloud whether room service might stretch to shiatsu. "That shit is locked down tight. After last night, it would take me all day to explain homomorphic encryption to you, so you'll just have to take my word for it: Nobody alive can answer that, even if they wanted to."

"But I've recovered bills from his laptop that mention it," Adam protested. "So much for Fort fucking Knox!"

Sandra shook her head. "That means that he was careless—and I should probably get someone in account generation to rethink their line items—but Loadstone would have held his hand very, very tightly when it came to spelling out the details. Unless he wrote it down in his personal diary, the information doesn't exist anymore."

Adam didn't think that she was lying to him. "There are things I need to know," he said simply. "He must have honestly believed that I'd be better off without them— but if he'd lived long enough for me to ask him face to face, I know I could have changed his mind."

Sandra paused the movie. "Very little software is perfect, least of all when it's for something as complex as this. If we fail to collect everything we aim to collect . . ."

"Then you also fail to block everything you aim to block," Adam concluded. "Which was probably mentioned somewhere in the fine print of his contract, but I've been racking my brain for months without finding a single stone that punched a hole in the sieve."

"What if the stones only got through in fragments, but they can still be put together?"

Adam struggled to interpret this. "Are you telling me to take up repressed memory therapy?"

"No, but I could get you a beta copy of Stitcher on the quiet."

"Stitcher?"

"It's a new layer they'll eventually be offering to every client," Sandra explained. "It's in the nature of things, with the current methods, that the side-load will end up with a certain amount of implicit information that's not in an easily accessible form: thousands of tiny glimpses of memories that were never brought across whole, but which could still be described in detail if you pieced together every partial sighting."

"So this software could reassemble the shredded page of a notebook that still holds an impression of what was written on the missing page above?"

Sandra said, "For someone with a digital brain, you're about as last-century as they come."

Adam gave up trying to harmonize their metaphors. "Will it tell me what I want to know?"

"I have no idea," Sandra said bluntly. "Among the fragments bearing implicit information—and there will certainly be thousands of them—it will recognize some unpredictable fraction of their associations, and let you follow the new threads that arise. But I don't know if that will be enough to tell you anything more than the color of the sweater your mother was wearing on your first day of school."

"Okay."

Sandra started the movie again. "You really should have joined me in the bar last night," she said. "I told them I had a friend who could drink any Salvadorian under the table, and they were begging for a chance to bet against you."

"You're a sick woman," Adam chided her. "Maybe next time."

10

Reassembled back in California, Adam took his time deciding whether to make one last, algorithmic attempt to push through the veil. If the truth was that the old man had been a murderer, what good would come of knowing it? Adam had no intention of "confessing" the crime to the authorities, and taking his chances with whatever legal outcome the courts might eventually disgorge. He was not a person; he could not be prosecuted or sued, but Loadstone could be ordered to erase every copy of his software, and municipal authorities instructed to place his body in a hydraulic compactor beside unroadworthy cars and unskyworthy drones.

But even if he faced no risk of punishment, he doubted that Colman's relatives would be better off knowing that what they'd always imagined was a burglary gone wrong had actually been a premeditated ambush. It should not be for him to judge their best interests, of course, but the fact remained that he'd be the one making the decision, and for all the horror he felt about the act itself and the harm that had been done, his empathy for the survivors pushed him entirely in the direction of silence.

So if he did this, it would be for his benefit alone. For the relief of knowing that the old man had simply been a vain, neurotic self-mythologizer who'd tried to leave behind the director's cut of his life . . . or for the impetus to disown him completely, to torch his legacy in every way he could and set out on a life of his own.

Adam asked Sandra to meet him at Caesar's Diner. He slid a small parcel of cash onto her seat, and she slipped a memory stick into his hand.

"What do I do with this?" he asked.

"Just because you can't see all your ports in the bathroom mirror doesn't mean they're not there." She wrote a sequence of words on a napkin and passed it to Adam; it read like "Jabberwocky" mistranscribed by someone on very bad drugs. "Four times, and that will take the side of your neck off without putting you to sleep."

"Why is that even possible?"

"You have no idea how many Easter eggs you're carrying."

"And then what?"

"Plug it in, and it will do the rest. You won't be paralyzed, you won't lose consciousness. But it will work best if you lie down in the dark and close your eyes. When you're done, just pull it out. Working the skin panel back into place might take a minute or two, but once it clicks it will be a waterproof seal again." She hesitated. "If you can't get it to click, try wiping the edges of both the panel and the aperture with a clean chamois. Please don't put machine oil on anything; it won't help."

"I'll bear that in mind."

Adam stood in the bathroom and recited the incantation from the napkin, half expecting to see some leering apparition take his place in the mirror as the last syllable escaped his lips. But there was just a gentle pop as the panel on his neck flexed and came loose. He caught it before it fell to the floor and placed it on a clean square of paper towel.

It was hard to see inside the opening he'd made, and he wasn't sure he wanted to, but he found the port easily by touch alone. He walked into the bedroom, took the memory stick from the side table, then lay down and dimmed the lights. A part of him felt like an ungrateful son, trespassing on the old man's privacy, but if he'd wanted to take his secrets to the grave then he should have taken all of his other shit with them.

Adam pushed the memory stick into place.

Nothing seemed to have happened, but when he closed his eyes he saw himself kneeling at the edge of the bed in the room down the hall, weeping inconsolably, holding the bedspread to his face. Adam shuddered; it was like being back in the servers, back in the interminable side-loading dream. He followed the thread out into the darkness, for a long time finding nothing but grief, but then he turned and stumbled upon Carlos's funeral, riotous in its celebration, packed with gray-haired friends from New York and a dozen of Carlos's relatives, raucously drowning out the studio executives and sync-flashing the paparazzi.

Adam walked over to the casket and found himself standing beside a hospital bed, clasping just one of those rough, familiar hands in both of his own.

"It's all right," Carlos insisted. There wasn't a trace of fear in his eyes. "All I need is for you to stay strong."

"I'll try."

Adam backed away into the darkness and landed on set. He'd thought it was a risky indulgence to put an amateur in even this tiny part, but Carlos had sworn that he wouldn't take offense if his one and only performance ended up on the cutting room floor. He just wanted a chance to know if it was possible, one way or the other.

Detective Number Two said, "You'll need to come with us, ma'am," then took Gemma Freeman's trembling arm in his hand as he led her away.

In the editing suite, Adam addressed Cynthia bluntly. "Tell me if I'm making a fool of myself."

"You're not," she said. "He's got a real presence. He's not going to do Lear, but if he can hit his marks and learn his lines . . ."

Adam felt a twinge of disquiet, as if they were tempting fate by asking too much. But maybe it was apt. They'd propelled themselves into this orbit together; neither could have gotten here alone.

On the day they arrived, they'd talked a total stranger into breaking through a fence and hiking up Mount Lee with them so they could take each other's photographs beneath the Hollywood sign. Adam could smell the sap from broken foliage on his scratched forearms.

"Remember this guy," Carlos told their accomplice proudly. "He's going to be the next big thing. They already bought his script."

"For a pilot," Adam clarified. "Only for a pilot."

He rose up over the hills, watching day turn to night, waiting for an incriminating flicker of déjà vu to prove that he'd been in this city before. But the memories that came to him were all from the movies: *L.A. Confidential, Mulholland Drive.*

He flew east, soaring over city lights and blackened deserts, alighting back in their New York apartment, hunched over his computer, pungent with sweat, trying to block out the sound of Carlos haggling with the woman who'd come to buy their air conditioner. He stared at the screen unhappily, and started removing dialogue, shifting as much as he could into stage directions instead.

She takes his bloodied fist in both hands, shocked and sickened by what he's done, but she understands—

The screen went blank. The laptop should have kept working in the blackout, but the battery had been useless for months. Adam picked up a pen and started writing on a sheet of paper: *She understands that she pushed him into it—unwittingly, but she still shares the blame.*

He stopped and crumpled the sheet into a ball. Flecks of red light streamed across his vision; he felt as if he'd caught himself trying to leap onto a moving train. But what choice did he have? There was no stopping it, no turning it back, no setting it right. He had to find a way to ride it, or it would destroy them.

Carlos called out to Adam to come and help carry the air conditioner down the stairs. Every time they stopped to rest on a darkened landing, the three of them burst out laughing.

When the woman drove away they stood on the street, waiting for a breeze to shift the humid air. Carlos placed a hand on the back of Adam's neck. "Are you going to be all right?"

"We don't need that heap of junk," Adam replied.

Carlos was silent for a while, then he said, "I just wanted to give you some peace."

When he'd taken out the memory stick and closed his wound, Adam went into the old man's room and lay on his bed in the dark. The mattress beneath him felt utterly familiar, and the gray outlines of the room seemed exactly as they ought to be, as if he'd lain here a thousand times. This was the bed he'd been struggling to wake in from the start.

What they'd done, they'd done for each other. He didn't have to excuse it to acknowledge that. To turn Carlos in, to offer him up to death row, would have been unthinkable—and the fact that the law would have found the old man blameless if he'd done so only left Adam less willing to condemn him. At least he'd shown enough courage to put himself at risk if the truth ever came out.

He gazed into the shadows of the room, unable to decide if he was merely an empathetic onlooker, judging the old man with compassion—or the old man himself, repeating his own long-rehearsed defense.

How close was he to crossing the line?

Maybe he had enough, now, to write from the same dark place as the old man—and in time to outdo him, making all his fanciful ambitions come true.

But only by becoming what the old man had never wanted him to be. Only by rolling the same boulder to the giddy peak of impunity, then watching it slide down into the depths of remorse, over and over again, with no hope of ever breaking free.

11

Adam waited for the crew from the thrift store to come and collect the boxes in which he'd packed the old man's belongings. When they'd gone, he locked up the house, and left the key in the combination safe attached to the door.

Gina had been livid when he'd talked to Ryan directly and shamed him into taking the deal: The family could have the house, but the bulk of the old man's money would go to a hospital in San Salvador. What remained would be just enough to keep Adam viable: paying his maintenance contract, renewing his license to walk in public, and stuffing unearned stipends into the pockets of the figureheads of the shell companies whose sole reason to exist was to own him.

He strode toward the gate, wheeling a single suitcase. Away from the shelter of the old man's tomb, he'd have no identity of his own to protect him, but he'd hardly be the first undocumented person who'd tried to make it in this country.

When the old man's life had disintegrated, he'd found a way to turn the shards into stories that meant something to people like him. But Adam's life was broken in a different way, and the world would take time to catch up. Maybe in twenty years, maybe in a hundred, when enough of them had joined him in the Valley, he'd have something to say that they'd be ready to hear.

The wordless

INDRAPRAMIT DAS

Here's another story by Indrapramit Das, whose "The Moon Is Not a Battle-field" appears elsewhere in this anthology. This one takes us to a distant planet that serves as a crossover point for interstellar ships, the story told from the perspective of the pariahs who are allowed to run snack and souvenir booths for the tourists but who can never leave on one of the great shining ships themselves—and in particular from the point of view of a man who is so desperate for a new start for his family that he's willing to try anything, no matter how insanely dangerous, to achieve it.

Every day NuTay watched the starship from their shack, selling starshine and sweet chai to wayfarers on their way to the stars. NuTay and their kin Satlyt baked an endless supply of clay cups using dirt from the vast plain of the port. NuTay and Satlyt, like all the hawkers in the shanties that surrounded the dirt road, were dunyshar, worldless—cursed to a single brown horizon, if one gently undulated by time to grace their eyes with dun hills. Cursed, also, to witness that starship in the distance, vessel of the night sky, as it set sail on the rippling waves of time and existence itself—so the wayfarers told them—year after year.

The starship. The sky. The dun hills. The port plain. They knew this, and this only.

Sometimes the starship looked like a great temple reaching to the sky. All of NuTay's customers endless pilgrims lining up to enter its hallowed halls and carry them through the cloth that Gods made.

NuTay and Satlyt had never been inside a starship.

If NuTay gave them free chai, the wayfarers would sometimes show viz of other worlds on their armbands, flicking them like so much dijichaff into the air, where they sprouted into glowing spheres, ghost marbles to mimic the air-rich dewdrops that clustered aeon-wise along the fiery filaments of the galaxy. The wayfarers would wave in practiced arkana, and the spheres would twirl and zoom and transform as

they grew until their curvature became glimpses of those worlds and their settlements glittering under the myriad suns and moons. NuTay would watch, silent,
unable to look away.

Once, Satlyt, brandishing a small metal junk shiv, had asked whether NuTay
wanted them to corner a wayfarer in a lonesome corner of the port and rob them of
their armband or their data coins. NuTay had slapped Satlyt then, so hard their cheek
blushed pink.

NuTay knew Satlyt would never hurt anyone—that all they wanted was to give
their maba a way to look at pictures of other worlds without having to barter with
wayfarers.

When NuTay touched Satlyt's cheek a moment after striking, the skin was hot
with silent anger, and perhaps shame.

Sometimes the starship looked like monolithic shards of black glass glittering in the
sun, carefully stacked to look beautiful but terrifying.

Sometimes the starship would change shape, those shards moving slowly to create a different configuration of shapes upon shapes with a tremendous moaning that
sounded like a gale moving across the hills and pouring out across the plain. As it
folded and refolded, the starship would no longer look like shards of black glass.

Sometimes, when it moved to reconfigure its shape, the starship would look suddenly delicate despite its size, like black paper origami of a starship dropped onto
the plain by the hand of a god.

NuTay had once seen an actual paper starship, left by a wayfarer on one of NuTay's
rough-hewn benches. The wayfarer had told them the word for it: origami. The paper
had been mauve, not black.

The world that interested NuTay the most, of course, was Earth. The one all the
djeens of all the peoples in the galaxy first came from, going from blood to blood to
whisper the memory of the first human into all their bodies so they still looked more
or less the same no matter which world they were born on.

"NuTay, Earth is so crowded you can't imagine it," one wayfarer had told them,
spreading their hands across that brown horizon NuTay was so familiar with. "Just imagine," the wayfarer said. "Peoples were having kin there before there were starships. Before
any peoples went to any other star than Sol. This planet, your planet, is a station, nah?"

NuTay then reminded the wayfarer that this was not *their* planet, not really,
because it was not a place of peoples but a port for peoples to rest in between their
travels across the universe. Dunysha had no planet, no cultures to imitate, no people.

"Ahch, you know that's the same same," the wayfarer said, but NuTay knew it
wasn't, and felt a slight pain in their chest, so familiar. But they knew the wayfarer
wouldn't know what this was, and they said nothing and listened as they spoke on.
"If this planet is port, then Earth, that is the first city in the universe—Babal, kafeen-
walla. Not so nice for you. Feels like not enough atmo for so many peoples if you go
there, after this planet with all this air, so much air, so much place."

And NuTay told that wayfarer that they'd heard that Earth had a thousand different worlds on it, because it had a tilt and atmos that painted its lands a thousand different shades of place as it spun around the first Sun.

"Less than a thousand, and not the only world with other worlds on it," the wayfarer said, laughing behind their mask. "But look," the wayfarer raised their arm to spring viz into the air, and there was a picture of a brown horizon, and dun hills. "See? Just like here." NuTay looked at the dun hills, and marveled that this too could be Earth. "Kazak-istan," said the wayfarer, and the placename was a cold drop of rain in NuTay's mind, sending ripples across their skull. It made them feel better about their own dun hills, which caught their eye for all the long days. Just a little bit better.

So it went. Wayfarers would bring pieces of the galaxy, and NuTay would hold the ones of Earth in their memory. It had brown horizon, blue horizon, green horizon, red horizon, gray horizon.

When the starship was about to leave, the entire port plain would come alive with warning, klaxons sounding across the miles of empty dirt and clanging across the corrugated roofs of the shop shanties and tents. NuTay and Satlyt would stop work to watch even if they had customers, because even customers would turn their heads to see.

To watch a starship leave is to witness a hole threaded through reality, and no one can tire of such a vision. Its lights glittering, it would fold and fold its parts until there was a thunderous boom that rolled across the plain, sending glowing cumulus clouds rolling out from under the vessel and across the land.

A flash of light like the clap of an invisible hand, and the clouds would be gone in less than a second to leave a perfect black sphere where the starship had been. If you looked at the sphere, which was only half visible, emerging from the ground a perfect gigantic bubble of nothingness, it would hurt your eyes, because there was *nothing* to see within its curvature. For an intoxicating second there would be hurtling winds ripping dust through the shop shanties, creating a vortex of silken veils over the plain and around the sphere. The shanty roofs would rattle, the horses would clomp in their stables, the wind chimes would sing a shattering song. The very air would vibrate as if it were fragile, humming to the tune of that null-dimensional half-circle embedded in the horizon, a bloated negative sunrise.

In the next moment, the sphere would vanish in a thunderclap of displaced atmos, and there would be only flat land where the starship had once stood.

A few days later, the same sequence would occur in reverse, and the starship would be back, having gone to another world and returned with a new population. When it returned, the steam from its megastructures would create wisps of clouds that hung over the plain for days until they drifted with their shadows into the hills.

Being younger dunyshar, Satlyt worked at the stalls some days, but did harder chores around the port, like cleaning toilets and helping starship crews do basic maintenance work. Every sunrise, NuTay watched Satlyt leave the stall on their dirt bike, space-black hair free to twine across the wind. The droning dirt bike would draw a dusty line across the plain, its destination the necklace of far-off lights extending from where the squatting starship basked in sunrise—the dromes where wayfarers refueled, processed, lived in between worlds. The dirt bikes would send wild horses rumbling in herds across the port plain, a sight that calmed NuTay's weakening bones.

NuTay had worked at the dromes, too, when they were younger and more limber. They'd liked the crowds there, the paradisiacal choirs of announcements that echoed under vaulted ceilings, the squealing of boots on floor leaving tracks to mop up, the harsh and polychrome cast of holofake neon advertising bars, clubs, eateries, and shops run by robots, or upscale wayfarer staff that swapped in and out to replace each other with each starship journey, so they didn't have to live on the planet permanently like the dunyshar. Nowadays the dromes were a distant memory. NuTay stayed at the shack, unable to do that much manual labour.

Those that spent their lives on the planet of arrivals and departures could only grow more thin and frail as time washed over the days and nights. The dunyshars' djeens had whispered their flesh into Earth-form, but on a world with a weaker gravity than Earth

NuTay's chai itself was brewed from leaf grown in a printer tent with a secondhand script for accelerated microclimate—hardware left behind from starships over centuries, nabbed from the junk shops of the port by NuTay for shine and minutes of tactile, since dunyshar were never not lonely and companionship was equal barter, usually (usually) good for friendships.

NuTay would meditate inside the chai-printing tent, which was misty and wet in growing season. Their body caressed by damp green leaves, air fragrant with alien-sweet perfume of plant life not indigenous, with closed eyes NuTay would pretend to be on Earth, the source of chai and peoples and everything. Each time a cycle ended, and the microclimate roasted the leaves to heaps of brown brew-ready shavings, the tent hissed steam like one of NuTay's kettles, and that whistle was a quiet mourning for the death of that tent-world of green. Until next cycle.

The tent had big letters across its fiber on the outside, reading *Darjeeling* in English and Nagar script. A placename, a wayfarer had clarified.

When Satlyt was younger, they'd asked NuTay if the dunyshar could just build a giant printer tent the size of the port itself, and grow a huge forest of plants and trees here like on Earth or other worlds. NuTay knew these weren't thoughts for a dunyshar to have, and would go nowhere. But they said they didn't know.

The starshine was easier, brewed from indigenous fungus grown in shit.

Sometimes, as evening fell and the second sun lashed its last threads of light across the dun hills gone blue, or when the starship secreted a mist that wreathed its alloyed spires, the starship looked like a great and distant city. Just like NuTay had seen in viz of other worlds—towers of lights flickering to give darkness a shape, the outline of lives lived.

The starship *was* a city, of course. To take people across the galaxy to other cities that didn't move across time and existence.

There were no cities here, of course, on the planet of arrivals and departures. If you travelled over the horizon, as NuTay had, you would find only more port plains dotted with emptiness and lights and shop shanties and vast circular plains with other starships at their centres. Or great mountain ranges that were actually junk-yards of detritus left by centuries of interstellar stops, and dismantled starships in their graveyards, all crawling with scavengers. Some dunyshar dared to live in those dead starships, but they were known to be unstable and dangerous, causing djeens to mutate so kin would be born looking different than humans. If this were true, NuTay had never seen such people, who probably kept to themselves, or died out.

NuTay had heard that if you walked far enough, you could see fields with star-ships so massive they reached the clouds, hulking across the sky, that these could take you to worlds at the very edge of the galaxy, where you could see the void be-tween this galaxy and the next one—visible as a gemmed spiral instead of a sun.

Once, the wayfarer who'd left the origami starship for NuTay had come back to the stall, months or years later. NuTay hadn't realized until they left, because they'd been wearing goggles and an air-filter. But they left another little paper origami, this time in white paper, of a horse.

Horses were used for low-energy transport and companionship among many of the dunyshar. They had arrived centuries ago as frozen liquid djeens from a starship's biovat, though NuTay was five when they first realized that horses, like humans, weren't *from* the world they lived in. Curiously, the thought brought tears to their eyes when they first found this out.

Sometimes the starship looked like a huge living creature, resting between its jour-neys, sweating and steaming and groaning through the night.

This it was, in some sense. Deep in its core was residual life left by something that had lived aeons ago on the planet of arrivals and departures: the reason for this junction in space. There was exotech here, found long before NuTay or any dun-yshar were born here, ghosts of when this planet *was* a world, mined by the living from other worlds. Dunyshar were not allowed in these places, extraterra ruins where miners, archaeologists, and other pilgrims from across the galaxy gathered. NuTay, like most dunyshar, had little interest in these zones or the ruins of whatever civili-zation was buried under the dirt of this once-world. Their interest was in the living civilization garlanding the galaxy, the one that was forever just out of their reach.

On their brief travels with Satlyt strapped to their back as a tender-faced baby, NuTay had seen the perimeter of one of these excavation zones from a mile away, floodlights like a white sunrise against the night, flowing over a vast black wall lined with flashing lights. Humming in the ground, and thunder crashing over the flat-lands from whatever engines were used to unearth the deep ruins and mine what-ever was in them.

NuTay's steed, a sturdy black mare the stablemaster that had bartered her had named Pacho, had been unusually restless even a mile from that zone. NuTay imagined the ghosts of a bygone world seeping from out of those black walls, and trickling into their limbs and lungs and those of their tender child gurgling content against their back.

NuTay rode away as fast as they could. Pacho died a few weeks later, perhaps older than the stablemaster had promised. But NuTay blamed the zone, and rubbed ointment on Satlyt for months after, dreading the morning they'd find their kin dead because of vengeful ghosts from the long dead world that hid beneath this planet's time.

For Satlyt's survival NuTay thanked the stars, especially Sol, that had no ghosts around them.

Satlyt had asked NuTay one day where they'd come from, and whose kin NuTay themself was. NuTay had waited for that day, and had answers for their child, who was ten at the time. They sat by their shack in the evening light, NuTay waving a solar lantern until it lit.

I am a nu-jen dunyashar, Satlyt, they said to their child. This means I have no maba, no parents at all.

Satlyt asked how, eyes wide with existential horror.

Listen. Many . . . djeens were brought here frozen many years ago. I taught you; two humans' djeens whisper together to form a new human. Some humans share their djeens with another human in tiny eggs held in their bellies, and others share it in liquid held between their legs. Two people from some world that I don't know gave their djeens in egg and liquid, so that peoples could bring them here frozen to make new humans to work here, and help give solace to the wayfarers travelling the stars. We are these new humans—the dunyshar. There are many old-jen dunyshar here who have parents, and grandparents, and on and on—the first of their pre-kin were born to surrogates a long time ago. Understand, nah?

Satlyt nodded, perhaps bewildered.

I was nu-jen; the first person my djeens formed here on the planet of arrivals and departures. I was born right there, NuTay stopped here to point at the distant lights of the dromes. In the nursery, where wayfarer surrogates live for nine months growing us, new-jen kin, when there aren't enough people in the ports anymore. They get good barter value for doing this, from the off-world peoples who run these ports.

Who taught you to talk? Who taught you what all you know? asked Satlyt.

The dunyshar, chota kin! They will help their own. All the people in this shanty place, they taught me. The three sibs who raised me through the youngest years and weaned me are all, bless them, dead from time, plain simple. This planet is too light for humans to live too long as Earth and other livable worlds.

Did you sleep with the three sibs so the djeens whispered me into existence?

No, no! No, they were like my parents, I couldn't do that. I slept with another when I grew. Their name was Farweh. Farweh, I say na, your other maba. With them I had you, chota kin.

They are dead, too?

NuTay smiled then, though barely. I don't know, Satlyt. They left, on a starship.

How? They were a wayfarer?

No, they grew up right here, new-jen, same as me. They had long black hair like you, and the red cheeks like you also, the djeens alive and biting at the skin to announce the beauty of the body they make.

Satlyt slapped NuTay's hand and stuck out their tongue.

Oy! Why are you hitting your maba? Fine, you are ugly, the djeens hide away and are ashamed.

Satlyt giggled.

Anyway, such a distracted child. Your other maba, we grew up here together. We had you.

They were here? When I was born?

NuTay pursed their lips. They had promised that their child would have the entire truth.

For a while, hn. But they left. Don't be angry. Farweh wanted to take you. They made a deal with a wayfarer that sold them a spacesuit. They said they could get two more, one emergency suit for babies. Very clever, very canny, Farweh was.

Why?

NuTay took a deep breath. To hold on to a starship. To see eternity beyond the Window, and come out to another world on the other side.

Other maba went away holding on to a starship on the outside?

I see I taught you some sense, chota kin. Yes, it is as dangerous as it sounds. Some people have done it—if they catch you on the other side, they take you away to jail, like in the dromes for murderers and rapists and drunkards. But bigger jail, for other worlds. That is if you survive. Theory, na? Possible. But those who do it, ride the starships on the side, see the other side of time? They never come back. So we can't ask if it worked or no, nah? So I said no. I said I will not take my kin like a piece of luggage while hanging on to the side of a starship. I refused Farweh. I would not take you, or myself, and I demanded Farweh not go. I grabbed their arm and hurt them by mistake, just a little, chota kin, but it was enough for both of us. I let them go, forever.

Farweh . . . maba. Other maba went and never came back.

Shh, chota kin, NuTay stroked a tear away from Satlyt's cheek. You didn't know Farweh, though they are your other maba. I gave them all the tears you can want to honour them. No more.

But you liked Farweh, maba. You grew up with them.

NuTay smiled, almost laughing at the child's sweetness. They held Satlyt before their little face crumpled, letting them cry just a little bit for Farweh, gone to NuTay forever, dead or alive behind the black window of existence.

Many years later, NuTay's kin Satlyt proved themself the kin of Farweh, too, in an echo of old time. They came droning across the plains from the dromes, headlights cutting across the dust while NuTay sipped chai with the other shanty wallahs in the middle of the hawkers' cluster. The starship was gone, out on some other world, so business was slow that evening.

Satlyt thundered onto the dust road in the centre of the shanty town, screeching to a halt, their djeens clearly fired up and steaming from the mouth in the chilly air.

Your kin is huffing, one of the old hawkers grinned with their gums. Best go see to them.

So NuTay took Satlyt indoors to the shack, and asked what was wrong.

Listen, NuTay. Maba. I've seen you, year after year, looking at the wayfarers' pictures of Earth. You pretend when I'm around, but I can see that you want to go there. Go after Farweh.

Go after Farweh? What are you on about, we don't even know whether they went to Earth, or if they're alive, or rotting in some jail on some remote world in the galaxy.

Not for real go after, I mean go, after. Story-type, nah?

Feri tail?

Exact. I know next time the starship comes, it will go to Earth. Know this for fact. I have good tips from the temp staff at the dromes.

What did you barter for this?

Some black market subsidiary exotech from last starship crew, changing hands down at the dromes. Bartered some that came to my hands, bartered some shine, some tactile, what's it matter?

Tactile, keh!

Please, maba. I use protection. You think wayfarers fuck dunysha without protection? They don't want our djeens whispering to theirs, they just want our bodies exotic.

What have you done, chota kin?

Don't worry, maba. I wouldn't barter tactile if I wasn't okay with it. But listen. I did good barter, better than just info. Spacesuit, full function. High compressed oxy capacity. Full-on nine hours. Starship blinks in and out of black bubble, max twenty hours depending on size. The one in our port—medium size, probably ten hours. Plus, camo-field, to blend into the side of the ship. We'll make it. Like Farweh did.

How do you know so much? Where do you get all this tech?

Same way you did, maba. Over years. There are people in the dromes, Satlyt said in excitement. They know things. I talk. I give tactile. I learn. I learn there are worlds, like you did. This? You know this isn't a world. Ghost planet. Fuel station. Port. You know this, we all know this. Farweh had the right idea.

NuTay shook their head. This was it. It was happening again. From the fire of the djeens raging hot in Satlyt's high cheekbones they knew, there was no saying no. Like they'd lost Farweh to time and existence, they would lose Satlyt too. NuTay knew there was no holding Satlyt by the arm to try and stop them, like before—they were too weak for that now.

Even if NuTay had been strong enough, they would never do that again.

It was as if Farweh had disappeared into that black bubble, and caused a ripple of time to lap across the port in a slow wave that had just arrived. An echo in time. The same request, from kin.

What do you say, maba? asked Satlyt, eyes wide like when they were little.

We might die, chota kin.

Then we do. Better than staying here to see your eyes go dead.

Even filtered breathing, the helmet and the suit was hot, so unlike the biting cold air of the planet. NuTay felt like they might shit the suit, but what could one do. There was a diaper inside with bio-absorbent disinfectant padding, or so the wayfarer had said.

They had scaled the starship at night, using a service drone operated by the green-eyed wayfarer who had made the deal with Satlyt, though they had other allies, clearly. Looking at those green Earth-born eyes, and listening to their strange accent but even stranger affection for Satlyt, NuTay realized there might be more here than mere barter greed. This wayfarer felt *bad* for them, wanted to help, which made NuTay feel a bit sick as they clambered into the spacesuit. But the wayfarer also felt something else for Satlyt, who seemed unmoved by this affection, their jaw set tight and face braced to meet the future that was hurtling towards them.

"There'll be zero-g in the sphere once the starship phases into it. Theoretically, if the spacesuits work, you should be fine, there's nothing but vacuum inside the membrane—the edges of the sphere. If your mag-tethers snap, you'll float out towards those edges, which you absolutely do not want. Being inside the bubble is safe in a suit, but if you float out to the edge and touch it, there's no telling what will happen to you. We don't know. You might see the entirety of the universe in one go before dying, but you will die, or no longer be alive in the way we know. Understand? Do not jerk around with the tethers—hold on to each other. Hold on to each other like the kin you are. Stay calm and drift with the ship in the bubble so there's no stress on the tethers. Keep your eyes closed, throughout. Open when you hear the ship's noise again. Do not look at the inside of the bubble, or you might panic and break tether. That's it. Once the ship phases out, things will get tough in a different way, if you're alive. Earth ports are chaos, and there's a chance no one will find you till one of my contacts comes by with a ship-surface drone to get you. There are people on Earth who sympathize with the dunyshar, who want to give them lives. Give you lives. So don't lose hope. There are people who have survived this. I've ushered them to the other side. But if you survive only to have security forces capture you, ask for a refugee lawyer. Got it? *Refugee.* Remember the word. You have been kept here against your will, and you are escaping. Good luck. I'll be inside." The wayfarer paused, breathless. "I wish you could be too. But security is too tight inside. They don't think enough people have the courage to stick to the side of the ship and see the universe naked. And most don't. They don't know, do they."

With that, the wayfarer kissed Satlyt's helmet, and then NuTay's, and wiped each with their gloved hand, before folding themself into the drone and detaching it from the ship. Lightless and silent, they sailed away into the night. NuTay hoped they didn't crash it.

NuTay felt sick, dangling from the ship, even though they were on an incline. Below them, the lights of the launching pad lit a slow mist rising from the bottom of the starship, about four hundred feet down. The skin of the ship was warm and rumbled in a sleeping, breathing rhythm. They switched on the camo-field, which covered them both, though they couldn't see the effects.

Satlyt was frighteningly silent. Chota kin, NuTay whispered to test the range com. Maba, Satlyt whispered back with a sweaty smile.

The starship awoke with the suns. Their uneasy dozing was broken by the light, and by the deeper rumble in the starship's skin. The brown planet of arrivals and departures stretched away from them, in the distance those dun hills. The pale blue sky flecked with thin icy clouds. The port dromes, the dirt roads like pale veins, the shanties glittering under the clear day in the far distance. Their one and only place. Hom, as wayfarers said. A strange word. Those fucking dun hills, thought NuTay.

Bless us, Sol, and all the stars without ghosts, whispered NuTay. Close your eyes, chota kin.

Remember Farweh, maba, said Satlyt, face wet behind the curved visor. The bottom of the starship exploded into light, and NuTay thought they were doomed, the juddering sending them sliding down the incline. NuTay held Satlyt's gloved hand tight, grip painful, flesh and bone pressed against flesh and bone through the nanoweaves.

I am old, NuTay thought. Let Satlyt live to see Earth.

The light, the sound, was gone.

Satlyt convulsed next to NuTay, who felt every movement of their kin through closed eyes. They embraced, NuTay holding Satlyt tight, a hollow vibration when their visors met. The ship was eerily still under them, no longer warm through the thick suit. Satlyt was making small sounds that coalesced slowly into words. We're alive.

Their breathing harsh in the helmet, the only sound along with the hissing breath of Satlyt into their own mic.

NuTay opened their eyes to see the universe looking back.

Don't look. Don't look. Don't look.

I know you opened your eyes, maba. What did you see?

I don't. Don't look. I saw darkness. Time like a living thing, a . . . a womb, with the light beyond its skin the light from creation, from the beginning of time and the end, so far away, shining through the dark skin. There were veins, of light, and information, pulsing around us. I saw our djeens rippling through those veins in the universe, humanity's djeens. Time is alive, Satlyt. Don't let it see us. Keep your eyes closed.

I will, maba. That is a good story, Satlyt gasped. Remember it, for the refuji lawyer.

Time is alive, and eventually it births all things, just as it ends all things.

When the ship turned warm with fresh thunder, their visors were set aglow, bathing their quivering eyelids with hot red light, the light of blood and djeens. Their spacesuits thumped down on the incline, the tethers umbilical around each other, kin and kin like twins through time entwined, clinging to the skin of a ship haunted by exoghosts.

They held each other tight, and under Sol, knew the light of hom, where the first djeens came from.

pan-Humanism: Hope and pragmatics

JESSICA BARBER & SARA SAAB

Jess Barber lives in Cambridge, Massachusetts, where she spends her days (and sometimes nights) building open-source electronics. She is a graduate of the 2015 Clarion Writers' Workshop, and her work has recently appeared in Strange Horizons, Lightspeed, *and* Clarkesworld. *You can find her online at www.jess-barber.com.*

Sara Saab was born in Beirut, Lebanon. She now lives in North London, where she has perfected her Resting London Face. Her current interests are croissants and emojis thereof, amassing poetry collections, and coming up with a plausible reason to live on a sleeper train. Sara's a 2015 graduate of the Clarion Writers' Workshop. You can find her on Twitter @fortnightlysara and at www.fortnightlysara.com.

Here they join forces to tell a story of star-crossed love—and of how to rebuild a troubled world.

1: THE MOST HALLOWED OF OUR SPACES

Amir Tarabi is scrubbing himself down in the misting rooms the first time he meets Mani Rizk.

The mister in Beirut-4 is being upgraded, the zone's residents using Beirut-3's misting rooms on rotation, so it is especially crowded that day. Amir avoids making eye contact with the bathers in adjacent patches with rigorous politeness. At sixteen, he's already spent a hundred personal growth hours thinking about civic decency, appreciates the role of uninterrupted private rituals in fostering social cohesion—

—then someone comes out of the mist and straight into his line of vision, Amir thinks by accident. He *tries* to keep his eyes on what he's doing. The sparse rivulets of soapy water starting in his elbows and armpits are usually an easy bliss to meditate on, how they track down his skin, how they catch and collect on little hairs. Water coalescing from mist doesn't have enough body to drip to the floor. Amir can feel it evaporate at his hips, his thighs, his ankles.

"Excuse me?" says the interrupting someone-who-turns-out-to-be-Mani, and Amir's head lifts before his principles regroup. Her teeth are chattering but she smiles gamely through it. "My patch is really cold. Does that happen?"

"Not that I remember?" he says. "Show me?"

"Sure," she clatters. "Thanks. This way."

He doesn't recall ever being approached by another bather in the mist before. She's naked, so is he, so is everyone. Nudity isn't weird in water-scarce Beirut at the height of summer. Less clothing means less sweat. It's her still-soapy hair that strikes him: so thick that there's two inches of it plastered soaking to her head, which of course means she's nearly at the end of her timeslot. The mist takes a long time to permeate a head of hair.

It's so crowded. They weave through an infinity mirror of bathing bodies which fade in the middle distance into a wall of mist. Amir wonders what brought his new friend all the way to his patch when any neighbor would've been glad to help.

"You're from Beirut-4?" he asks.

"The finest of all arbitrary urban planning constructs," she calls behind her.

At sixteen, Amir doesn't believe in competitive jokes about city zones, just as he doesn't believe in identities constructed in opposition. He doesn't say anything. It doesn't seem the right moment.

Mani finds the four lit wands in the mist that mark the corners of patch 49.

"Cold, right?"

Amir steps solemnly into the center of her patch for a few seconds. The concentrated plume of mist envelops him.

"Feels okay to me?"

Mani shoots him an aghast look, moves into her patch as Amir steps out. She gives a long-suffering sigh. "Why are they upgrading *our* mister? Beirut-3 needs it more."

"Are you sure you're not physiologically reacting to a new environment?" Amir counters. "All the misters have the same temperature settings."

"Is that so?" Mani says.

"Pretty sure."

She readies a retort, then shakes it off. "Thanks anyway," she says, kneading her hair. "I pulled you away while your mist is running." Sudsy water trickles onto her shoulders.

"That's okay. Enjoy your shower," Amir says, and waves himself off. *Enjoy your shower.* He's vaguely disappointed by the whole exchange for a reason he can't examine.

In the airing room, hot blasts of air spread warmth through his chest. This fills him with something like gratitude. He second-guesses whether he might've been cold, before.

"Two degrees lower," says a voice he recognizes.

"Really?" he says after a moment. Now he's vaguely *happy* for reasons he can't place.

"I asked the supervisor. By community agreement, motion passed five years ago, the Beirut-3 misting room is two degrees cooler than default in summer."

"Ah," says Amir. "Good of you to correct a misbelief."

"My pan-humanist agenda's pretty on point," she says. The wry note in her voice doesn't irritate him. "I'm Mani. I live near al-Raouché. Want to do a personal growth hour together?"

Amir doesn't remember what he stammered then, but it must've been affirmative, because the rest of his teenage days have Mani in them, as the water situation worsens, then gets a bit better, then worsens, then stabilizes.

It's a lot of days to have with someone. A lot of staring at the cloudless sky on a blanket from the exposed seabed of al-Raouché, a lot of synth-protein shawarmas in Hamra, a lot of silent meditative spans huddled in Mani's bed because talking hurts too much with the thirst and their mouths so dry.

But it's also true that all the days in a human life can feel like not enough.

The first time the water situation shows signs of getting better is a Monday. Amir knows this because that's the day for municipal announcements in Beirut-1 through -5. He and Mani are sitting in a seabed café in the shadow of al-Raouché. The rock pillar's become a sort of geologic Champs-Élysées, and though the bay has begun to recover from the decades of hyperwarming that dried it out, Beirut Grid have installed a seawall to protect the shops and cafés that went up while water was critically scarce.

"It's oddly beautiful," Amir says to Mani. The seawall is muraled with depictions of water-protection craft, the lighthouse, the rickety old Ferris wheel on the boardwalk. Beyond it, the sea shushes loudly. The sun festers behind the clouds and because Amir and Mani have been through screen-mist they're lounging in just swim knickers.

Amir rotates his cup and watches bits of tea leaf bob near the bottom. "Do you think it's unethical to celebrate a built environment that's a direct result of water scarcity?" he asks. Mani looks up from her book: *Pan-Humanism in the Middle East*. It's just come out, and she's been excited to read it because it challenges some of the core arguments of Stella Kadri's *Pan-Humanism: Hope and Pragmatics*, a book of heroic stature for how it butterfly-affected the sociopolitics of the modern world.

"Not unethical to feel joy if no one's suffering," she says.

"Fish desperate to swim figure eights around al-Raouché could be suffering."

"You have to draw a line where arguments descend into absurdity." She cracks a smile, powers off her book.

"But there's nothing absurd about a healthy marine ecosystem," Amir says. Her pragmatism makes him uneasy. As a life skill it sits uncomfortably against his complete dedication to absolutes: the True, the Good. But it's captivating. It makes her quick to laughter and gracious, even excited, about changing her mind.

Mani gulps her tea. "Still hot. So now I've burnt my tongue worrying about the fish." She glances down. "Didn't I turn that off?" Her book's flashing a notification. So's her watch. So are her shades.

Amir blows on his tea before he sips. "On override? Must be important."

They read the message, heads hovering together. It's from the municipality. *Beirut Water pilot. First sectors, random pick: Beirut-4, Beirut-9. Water reconnected via mains for 24hrs from 2p.m. OK: taps, showers, hoses. Use judgment: industrial electronics.*

It takes a moment to sink in.

"Wait. Are you kidding?"

"I had no idea they were ready to try," Mani says.

They're both gathering their things, tapping over a tab-close, standing. "Warsaw managed to run a water supply off a condensation system for a week," Amir says. "But this is *Beirut*."

"So what if it is?" Mani says. "Beirut is superb! Beirut has water!"

They're skipping along the stairs to the boardwalk. A louder murmur than the sea is rising from the seabed café: the municipality message spreading.

They reach Mani's house in record time. It's a hot day and Amir is itching from sweat and screen residue with an urgency he's never felt before.

"Mom? There's water!" Mani shouts into the dark house.

"No one," says Amir.

"Ah, she's got an hour of cross-skilling this afternoon."

"Should we wash our hands?" Amir pants, chasing Mani up the stairs.

"Don't be ridiculous. Have to go all the way." She opens a door in the hall. "In here."

Amir follows her. She's planted in front of a bone-dry shower stall. The showerhead is impossibly shiny. There's still a bit of plastic wrapping on it. It's an antique, but brand new.

"It's nearly two o'clock."

"Are they going to be able to do this?"

"Trust, Amir. Trust." "Do you think it might even be heated?"

Mani is scooting out of her swim knickers, raises her eyebrows at him till he shoves his down too. "I bet it is." She reaches into the shower stall and twists a handle. It screeches with disuse.

They wait.

At exactly two, their ears fill with the furious sound of a rainstorm. Then their own whooping. Mani bounds in without testing the temperature, makes a shrill sound. "It's warming up!" She reaches out and grabs Amir's arm. Her grip raises goosebumps. "Come on, get in!"

He does. It's the most sublime thing he's ever felt. He puts his hands flat on the wet tiles and closes his eyes under a hammering of water.

"How long can we stay in here?" He manages not to choke. Such a quantity of water is coursing down his face and onto his tongue.

"We're being good by sharing. Let's not get out for a while," Mani says. "Are you crying?"

"Yes!" He opens his eyes to look at her but her face is blurry-wet. "Are you?"

"That's private," Mani says. But she wraps her arms around his waist, her belly against his flank, and rests her forehead on his cheek. Their bodies are slippery and warm. Amir hears himself make a purring noise. "Oh. Wow."

"Yeah."

"Not like the mist," he says.

"No. Totally different."

Sharing a patch is encouraged in the misting rooms. They've done this many times. They wash each other's backs and argue about what true pan-humanism might look like. It's pleasurable. But this—private, warm, untimed, all this water sheeting down—is a whole different register of existence.

"I think I should tell you," Mani says, "that I'm thinking about sex."

Amir opens one eye to look at her, can only see the top of her head against his cheek. "Me, too," he says, almost but not totally redundantly. Mani's got a good view.

They've *almost* so many times, but never. This moment feels ripe, so very theirs. But it's also the wrong moment.

"Water, though, Mani! Mindfulness. Presence. This."

"Of course," she says.

"We might never be able to have this again."

"We might never have any given thing again," Mani says, the pedantic one for a change.

"But all this water," he says.

"No, you're right," says Mani, hushed in the hypnotic roar of the shower. "All this water."

The Beirut Water pilot is considered only a partial success; it isn't repeated again for almost two years. By then Mani has left. Amir will remember different selections of things from the day of the pilot depending on how hot or cold his thoughts are, but he'll cap the memory with this, every single time: the fond way Mani slides her hand against his drenched ribs under the flow of hot water before she entirely lets him go.

Amir sleeps poorly the night before university assignments are due to go out. He knows but does not *know*-know that he will get into Beirut and Environs, his first choice. His grades are excellent. He's done twenty percent more personal growth hours than required—he *likes* doing them—and his civic engagement score is the highest ever for Beirut-3's Academy. But he's still nervous. When his watch buzzes at four a.m., he startles awake: BEIRUT AND ENVIRONS FUTURIST COLLEGE, UTOPIAN PHILOSOPHY STREAM.

He taps over the notification to Mani with a string of exclamation points, his foggy enthusiasm-slash-relief dampened only slightly when she doesn't respond right away. Mani's grades are stellar but her civic engagement score's not great. She'd wanted Pan-Humanist Polytechnic but Amir has a sinking feeling she's been assigned to College of the Near East.

He composes a fortifying speech in his head as he gets ready, complete with references to the most famous pan-humanist thinkers who'd attended Near East and their contributions to society. Near East is a great school, and it's half an hour closer to Beirut and Environs by bullet than Pan-Humanist Polytechnic. Mani will do amazing things wherever she goes.

Amir is fifteen minutes early for the morning's personal growth session. They've only just opened the doors to the Reflection Center, a handful of early risers filtering in under the kaleidoscopic arches, quiet murmurs of conversation as they set up mats and blankets on the centuries-old stone floor. But Mani is already there waiting for him, sitting cross-legged on her mat, gripping her hands together so tight that her fingers are white to the knuckle. Amir is brought up short.

"Mani?" he asks, uncertain.

Wordlessly, she raises her wrist for him to see, the notification still up on the watch screen: INTL UNIVERSITY FOR HUMANISM, MOGADISHU, GLOBAL PROGRESS.

Amir feels his heart go ka-thunk. Global Progress at IUH is . . . he'd thought about applying, more as a lark than anything, but they only accept three students per year, from the entire world, and he never thought . . .

"Wow," he says, dropping down next to her, voice low so it won't echo. "Wow, Mani, that's—I didn't even know you were going to *apply*, that's—amazing. That's so amazing. I'm so, so proud of you," he says, and even means it.

Mani's face is complicated with emotions, flickering by too quickly for Amir to properly catalogue them, happy-sad-excited-nervous. "It's far away," she says.

"It's *exciting*," he corrects. "Mogadishu, can you even imagine! Maybe I could visit you, one time." This is unlikely, and they both know it. Mogadishu's not on a clean air travel vector with Beirut yet. He'd have to do two months of civic engagement and a month of personal growth to balance taking a dirty flight for leisure. Mani musters a smile anyway.

"I'd love that," she says. In the center of the room, today's meditation guide is setting up at the podium. The overhead heaters have been switched on, spreading the scent of the cedar beams throughout the space. Mani bumps Amir's shoulder with her own. Her smile builds into something a little more true. "Come on, though. We both know you'll be too busy changing the world to think of me at all."

2: THE MECHANISM, A WORTHWHILE TRADE

It's not that Mani's right, because of course Amir thinks of her. He thinks of her every single day, at least at first. But then the water starts coming back to Beirut, and Amir gets swept up in the civic spirit, in the new swell of hope. He switches out of Utopian Philosophy the day after he helps a volunteer group install a kinetic walkway on the university's main green—they expect to be able to clean-power the quad's lamps for two hours each night—and enrolls in Urban Design. The idea of regeneration-planning the city is wedged deep under his skin.

After graduation he walks into a competitive apprenticeship with Beirut Grid, where he meets Rafa, who's working on the Bekaa Valley's poetry microcity and in the capital on up-skill, and Ester, a third generation Beiruti whose grandmother led the rights movement for domestic workers at the turn of the century. They all fall for each other almost simultaneously.

He's twenty-two. He's got an apartment on al-Manara. Through his kitchen window, the lighthouse illuminates the brushstroke froth of the Mediterranean and every time Amir Tarabi sees it he says a silent word of hope for the sea, for it to have body and swell with muscle forever. He remembers his conversation with Mani about the fish, imagines a day in the future when they'll wade into the surf and see entire schools, silver and bronze and fleeting, with their own eyes.

Amir's at work late when his watch buzzes. Rafa and Ester. *Let us in, we're at the door to Research-4.*

He limps down the hall on pins and needles. The recollection that they'd planned a dinner date for tonight—for an hour ago—wallops him right before he releases the door.

Rafa and Ester don't usually band together against Amir, but here they are, standing side by side wearing exactly the same expression, and it's not *we're so glad to see you*.

Ester raises a package and Amir smells food.

"I don't remember *ever* blowing through a date with Amir when I worked at the Grid," Ester says pointedly to Rafa.

"Hmm, Ester," Rafa replies theatrically. "Is that because you were respectful of his time and attention? Because you understood that interpersonal relationships require careful cultivation?"

"I'm *so* sorry," Amir squeaks, letting them in, putting a hand out for their coats. "Can I explain what happened? Not an excuse, just context."

Ester looks at Rafa. Rafa looks at Ester. Both of them look skeptically at Amir.

"You guys, I'm sorry. Do you remember my Crowdgrow thing?"

"Where you wanted to foster home ecoboosted flowers around the neighborhood?" asks Rafa. "You told us about it last month."

"Right," says Amir. "We found out today the bio team managed to get a couple of shoots synthesizing air pollutants in the lab. Mesilla asked me to put together a grant application for the project. If it gets funded, she wants me to lead the research team."

Amir's fortunate that both his partners know what this means to him. Their faces soften.

"Nice. I knew Mesilla would come around," Ester says. "You still don't get to flake on dates."

In a deserted Beirut Grid kitchenette, Amir fetches plates and Rafa piles herbed eggplant casserole onto them. While they eat Amir projects stained photos of cross-sectioned saplings onto a wall, and Rafa and Ester *mmm* through his commentary for a few minutes, until Rafa says.

"Amir, love, it's nine p.m. and you're still using words like 'floral load.'"

"Good point, Rafa," Ester says. "Amir, tap over projector control."

The projection cuts to the backdrop of his favorite immersion strategy game.

"I've got dessert," Rafa says. He produces a huge bag of caramel chews and a bottle of whiskey. They clear some space.

"Ooh," Ester says, confirming a glance-down-pause setting. "We need to be able to snack."

"Oh *no*," Amir says. "This never goes well. It's an *immersion* game."

"Shush," Rafa says. "It's destined to be a drunk immersion game."

Their love is like this, comfortable and forgiving of Amir's faults. Then, at the beginning of summer, Ester breaks up with Rafa and Amir—no hard feelings, just different needs, different takes on life. It's not that it doesn't hurt. Amir and Rafa spend several days moping in each other's laps, swapping sympathy cuddles. But Amir's always believed what pan-humanist theory says: that love is respect and collaboration held together with radical acceptance, freely gained and lost.

Amir tells himself to take comfort in this, and does his best to keep an open heart.

———

The Future Good conference in Hanoi is the biggest of its kind, twelve academic streams and full air travel exemption. Amir and Rafa apply for spots every year and never get them, until they do. They're giddy on the flight over: neither of them gets to leave Beirut often, and they've certainly never had a reason to travel by air together.

They attend the welcome address then spend the allotted cultural hours in the Old Quarter, sitting on low stools with their knees knocking together, feeding each other quail egg bánh bao. Rafa's old advisor is leading a Q&A session on arts microcities, but Rafa and Amir lose track of time strolling the banks of the Red River hand in hand. Once they've missed that, there's no reason to go back to the hotel, so they stay out till three a.m. sampling sticky rice wine, which everyone *tries* to warn them is stronger than it tastes.

The next morning's reclamation technologies forum is something of an accident. They're trying—oh, Amir is almost too embarrassed to admit it. They're *trying* to find breakfast, and Rafa spies a cute ambiguously-gendered human with multicolored hair and a dapper three-piece suit sneaking out of one of the conference rooms, their arms full of coffee cups and muffins. Amir and Rafa are *hungry*, so they creep into the back, sights set on the buffet table lining the rear wall, and there is Mani Rizk, making her way to the front podium.

Amir's entire body floods with adrenaline. He grabs Rafa by the cuff of his sleeve and steers him to one of the chairs. He's trying to be stealthy but Rafa is mumbling confused protests around a coffee-stirrer and Mani sees them, of *course* she does, and her face goes taken aback then pleased. And then she does a pretty good job of pretending like she didn't see Amir, because she's got a lecture to deliver, after all.

Rafa stares at Amir in confusion for about a minute before his eyebrows go up in a particularly knowing manner. He spends the rest of the lecture elbowing Amir any time Mani says something brilliant, which is about every thirty seconds.

"So?" Rafa asks, delighted, when the lecture is over and they're waiting at the back of a densely knotted crowd. "Who is she, eh? Political rival? Academic crush? Long lost lover?"

"No," protests Amir, a little too loudly for the enclosed space. "She's just—a friend. We were friends, when we were young. That was all."

If nothing else, Mani seems at least as eager to see him as he is to see her: her attention keeps sliding away from whoever she's talking with, darting to Amir over and over. He smiles, catching her eye, spreading his hands in an awkward gesture that he hopes will convey both *hi* and *I'll wait*. As soon as the crowd thins enough for her to break away she does so, inching her way to Amir and Rafa with a string of apologies and excuses.

"Amir," she says, and half-tackles him in a hug.

She's round and solid and *small*—it's weird, Amir hadn't hit his growth spurt until he was eighteen, and in his memory they're still like that, him looking up. Now Mani barely comes up to his collarbone. He wraps arms that feel oddly long and lanky around her shoulders, holds her tight.

When she finally lets go her eyes look suspiciously bright, but that might just be the ceiling ambients. "I didn't know you were coming to my talk," she says.

"It was kind of an accident," Amir admits.

Beside him, Rafa groans. "Don't *tell* her that!" He turns to Mani. "What he means to say is, he wanted to surprise you. And your lecture was phenomenal."

"I'm not going to *lie* to her," says Amir, affronted. "About the surprise, I mean. Your lecture *was* phenomenal. I didn't know you'd been studying hydrophobic materials."

"I'm part of a water reclamation forum at IUH," says Mani, and then, to Rafa, "and I've known Amir too long to expect flattery. I'm Mani."

"Rafa Zarkesian. I consult on architecture projects for art spaces in Beirut."

"Rafa's my boyfriend," says Amir. It seems important to mention.

"Oh, I thought I recognized you! I've seen your picture on Amir's stream. How long—"

"Mx. Rizk?" cuts in a voice over Mani's shoulder. "I'm so sorry to intrude, but—"

"No, no, of course," says Mani. "Sorry, I really should—"

"Yes, of course," says Amir. "It was good to see you, Mani, I—"

"Tonight," she interrupts, "after closing remarks. There's that gallery installation, the interactive city grid? I haven't been able to see it yet. If you have time, maybe the three of us . . ."

They've got a pre-dawn flight back to Beirut; they'd planned to get to bed early and had contemplated skipping the closing remarks entirely.

"That would be wonderful," says Rafa. "We wouldn't miss it."

That night, it rains in Hanoi, just a light, champagne-fizz mist, but it's enough to lend a celebratory attitude to the entire city. They find Mani waiting for them outside the installation's entrance, a crown of water droplets clinging to her hair, reflecting a riot of blinking, changeable light. Amir grips Rafa's hand a little harder.

"We got lucky," Mani says, squinting as she tilts her face upward, holding out a cupped palm as if to collect water there. "Good closing note for the conference."

"Lucky," echoes Amir, feeling a little dazed.

Rafa bumps his shoulder against Amir's. "Come on, you two," he says, already fond. "Let's go in."

The installation is a concept city rendered one-fiftieth scale in shimmering interactive holograms and delicate print-resin latticework. The space isn't enclosed, and the scrim of the rain occasionally does glitchy things to the projections that make Amir groan in solidarity with the event planners. Rafa and Mani are both charmed, however, and Amir can't help but be delighted by their delight. He gets video of the support cables of a projected suspension bridge twining around Mani's ankles, insistent and loving as a cat. They take turns decorating Rafa with sprigs of star-like flowers in the constructed wetlands section.

At one point, Amir is walking sandwiched between the two of them, face craned up to ogle the dazzling phyllotactic archway they're underneath. Rafa reaches down to twine his fingers with Amir's, and, after a moment that might be hesitation, on the other side Mani reaches down and does the same. Amir can feel his own heartbeat in his palms and he's sure Mani and Rafa must be able to as well, but neither of them says a thing.

Afterward, they make promises about staying in better contact. There's a conference in Mogadishu, only six months out; it's not a perfect fit for his research, but maybe Amir can swing an invite. It's ridiculous, really, that Amir hasn't yet seen Mani's new city, Mani's new life. Mani's so busy—they're all so busy, but they can message more, at least. Maybe even holochat, sometimes. They work in related fields, after all; it's their responsibility to foster international communication and collaboration. Plus, they *miss* each other. There's no reason to fall so out of touch.

They say all this, and mean it. But, well. Life.

3: EACH BRICK LAID THOUSANDS OF TIMES OVER

The lab at Beirut Grid successfully demonstrates at-quantity ecoboosting in model organisms two weeks before Amir turns twenty-eight, which is a pretty good early birthday present, as far as he's concerned. To celebrate, Mesilla takes Amir to the botanical garden in Rmeil to evaluate options for the Crowdgrow pilot; Hanne from New Projects tags along.

The conservatory curator herself gives them a guided tour. She leads them down dense green walkways, extolls the growth patterns of crawler vines and Chouf ever-greens, both commendably hardy species, survivors of the worst of the water scarcity. Mesilla seems invested—she examines a potted evergreen the curator's handed her, sinks a finger in the soil—but Hanne is paying zero attention, cleaning up her notifications on Impulse or something. Then, out of nowhere, Hanne blurts.

"Oh, Mesilla. They just announced funds for a world-first Wet City implementation."

The crinkly cellophane of the potted evergreen goes still. The curator says, "Anything else I can show you?" into the silence; Amir babbles about high-altitude crawler vines. They move on to another greenhouse.

In line for lunch, after, Amir waits for Mesilla to pick his brain. He's all but decided he wants to try ecoboosting crawler vines, but wouldn't mind talking it through.

"So," Mesilla says as soon as they've found a sunny patch of grass on Achrafieh green for a picnic, "There's a Wet City funding opportunity? When's the deadline?"

"One month," says Hanne. "Not much time to put together a proposal."

Amir puffs out his breath, struggling to rearrange his thoughts. "Has anyone proven the water reclamation wings would work at that scale? Wasn't that the sticking point in Colson and Smith's paper?"

Hanne jabs the chunk of carrot on the end of her fork at Amir. "Right. But the All People funds were greenlit on the back of a rebuttal slash instruction manual by—" Hanne's eyes blink away as she navigates Impulse. "By Sameen Jaladi at IUH Mogadishu." The name of Mani's school fills Amir with a mixture of possessiveness and pride.

Amir can think of twenty reasons to be wary: the technical challenge of large-scale moisture collection, yes, but also overheating the built habitat, uncontrollable wet seasons, mold and mosquitos and respiratory conditions. That's not to mention his immediate questions around clean-powering the wings and purging waste bays. He puts his sandwich in its basket, turns to Mesilla.

"It's a lot of resources toward an unproven concept. We'd have to divert money and energy we could spend in demonstrably useful directions," he says. *Like on Crowdgrow*, he doesn't say.

"But in *theory*," Mesilla says. "Every metropolis a little green oasis. Latticed condensation wings, clean water from the air. Theoretically, no shortages ever again."

She unwraps a bit more sandwich in a studied way: bean protein fillet in minted yogurt sauce, her usual. "Can someone get me the Jaladi paper and the bid guidelines?"

Amir's already poring through Impulse. He taps the documents over to Mesilla with two hard blinks. "They're with you."

They walk back to the Beirut Grid offices talking about Amir's birthday plans—Joud's taking him on an overnight bullet to Damascus; their first trip together as a couple—but the lunch conversation is still humming under his skin.

Two days later, when Mesilla pulls Amir and Hanne aside and asks them to put together a Wet City bid, it doesn't surprise him.

It's a hot day with a really crappy clean air index. Everyone's been permitted to stay home but a few of them are in, including Amir, because his apartment was so hot he feared he might melt into his armchair. The heat reminds him of sitting in a seabed café with Mani, which of course reminds him of the Future Good conference with Mani, which takes Amir's thoughts nowhere helpful at all.

The Impulse note arrives from Mesilla in two parts. The first, short, buzzes at his wrist and pings urgently in his display. It's to Amir and Hanne, two words: *We won!*

He expects excitement but feels only bone-tiredness.

The second part of Mesilla's note is a travel itinerary on wider distribution. The subject line makes Amir's body do weird things: *Academics from IUH Mogadishu*. He taps it open on his wrist, as if he needs to see this in physical space, and sure enough:

> *Jaladi, Sameen*
> *Proctor, Trevor*
> *Gupta, Jan-Helga*
> *Rizk, Mani*

"Shit," he croaks. His side of the office is empty. He can hear the descending xylophone of the bullet zipping along its girders through the open window, and nearer, a heat-oppressed bird call that sounds more tired than he does.

He blinks up his conversation thread with Mani. Their last exchange: *Happy new year!* from her to him, half a year ago; *Happy new year!!* from him to her a couple hours later, and since then, nothing. He winces.

Beirut???? he taps over.

Mani's response is almost instant. *Leave in a week.*

!!! Amir sends. His belly is one big knot.

Took the effusive punctuation straight out of my mouth, she replies.

Amir wrangles his way into airport chaperone duty for the IUH academics. At Future Good, running into Mani had been a sudden shock; the week he waits for her plane to arrive his nerves are like a leaky faucet. He can't eat properly but finds himself stocking his pantry with everything he remembers Mani loving: carob molasses, salted pili nuts, a Bekaa Valley Merlot, cashew feta cheese. Joud tries to season a stew with the good cinnamon sticks Amir picked up at al-Raouché market for spiced tea and Amir won't let them.

"I'm saving those," Amir says, guiltily filing away that there should be a Joud-him-Mani dinner involving cinnamon sticks. He doesn't know what's wrong with him. The plane from Mogadishu, oblivious and probably flying over Independent Greenland on other business, is killing him.

Then he's at the airport and his Impulse tells him the flight from Mogadishu's arrived safely. Mani has sent him her Impulse geo, which means he can tell exactly when she's walking through customs and toward the public area.

He distracts himself by trying to calculate how long it's been since they've seen each other using mental math. His Impulse helper picks up on his saccades. *You seem to be working something out. Can I help?* Amir moans and blinks it away. He finishes the calculation—1513 days—but now he can barely breathe. And then the arrivals door pistons up and a column of passengers is behind it. He sees Mani in the throng, and she sees him back.

It's not the moment he's been imagining. Mani's engrossed in conversation with her colleagues. She weaves them toward Amir and he wants to hug her but the fact that he's on official duty—that there are three field-pioneering academics he's never met studying him—plants him to his spot.

"Hi," Mani says.

"Hi," Amir says. Not *wow, you and me in Beirut, like when we were seventeen.* Which is what he's thinking.

"Sameen, Trevor, Helga, Amir," Mani says, and then there's a blur and they're all on the bullet in the private compartment Amir booked and everyone is staring out the window at this city they've missed or never seen before and the conversation turns to how wonderfully Beirut will function as a Wet City.

He tries not to catch Mani's eye too much, but when he does she gives him a conspiratorial smile he remembers. He thinks of the wine and the cheese. They'll get loads of time together later.

Except, the next day Mesilla kicks off the Wet City stuff in earnest. And Amir and Mani start to argue. A lot.

In some ways it's not new. They'd argued as kids, the minutiae of pan-humanist theory over hot black tea: whether animals deserved more pronounced protection than plants, whether population control was ever justified, whether power should in all cases decentralize in the direction of local communities.

But now the stakes are different. *They're* different. The worst of the arguments take place during project meetings, in front of Hanne and Caveg and the rest of the team. Amir leaves meeting after meeting feeling battered. The way Mani seems to have a reassuring study on hand to refute each of his worries makes him clench his jaw in a very uncivic way. He's so embarrassed by the incessant jaw clenching he grows his beard out to hide it.

They avoid casual conversation for the better part of two weeks. Amir starts to hate going to work, which has never happened before. Then, one Monday, Mani stops at Amir's station, gets close to see if he's working in Impulse, and he can smell her perfume, mineral and saline and only the slightest bit sweet.

"Help me draft an advisory? If you're not busy?" she asks. She lifts a satchel. "I brought us tea from the kiosk auntie downstairs."

"Advisory?" Amir's immediately on edge. "Do you need planning language in it? Can Caveg help?"

Mani's eyebrows come down. "I don't really need planning language in it. I just miss doing things together. I thought there'd be a lot more of that."

"Yeah," Amir says, and stands to follow. He remembers following her that first time, in the misting rooms. He doesn't understand himself. He's been waiting to have Mani back for a decade—not a vague wistfulness, but an active full-bodied sort of waiting, if he's really examining it. And now she's right here, and he can't bring himself to speak to her without getting upset. The funny thing is that he's not even angry at her. It's something more like bedazzlement. She's a sun that blasts his vision into afterimages.

"Or," Amir says in the corridor, "we could go to our old café? It won't be too busy right now."

Mani nods decisively. "Let's go. Sameen will happily take the kiosk auntie tea."

The bullet ride is mainly Mani pointing out new art installations and green spaces and Amir telling her what year they were built and why. He's good at this. He does almost all of them without Impulse, but confesses when he has to look one up. Mani gives him grief for not knowing them *all* by heart.

"Everyone told me, *oh, Amir, Beirut Grid's own whizkid.* A sort of city-planning savant. I guess I expected more," she teases.

"No one said that," Amir says. "And even if they did, IUH has given you impossible expectations."

"Pan-humanism is all about realizing a civilizational system that game theory would say is impossible, right?"

"Right," says Amir. "But there's plain old pan-humanist theory impossible and then there's IUH Mogadishu impossible."

The bullet slows and stops beside their old café. They go down the boardwalk to their usual table, tap across an order of tea and settle into their respective chairs. "Wow," says Amir.

"Swap adult clothes for swim knickers and shave the beard and it could be a decade ago."

Amir lifts their order of tea off a tray bot. "Were we that familiar with each other? Hard to believe."

Mani takes her glass from him. "Oh yeah. We were ridiculous. Like one person in two bodies, back then."

Amir startles in a way that melts him into himself, like his chest is swallowing the rest of him, swallowing his words. Mani's always been the forthright one, but they both know he's more sentimental, and he's afraid that if he says anything now it will be too much.

"You don't like the beard?" he manages.

Mani reaches across and strokes his cheek against the grain. "I don't *not* like it," she says.

Amir shakes his head at her. She withdraws her hand. He'd forgotten how *transparent* they were to each other. Are, to each other.

"How's Rafa?" Mani says, stirring her tea.

"We broke up last year." He doesn't bother waving it off. Mani will know it was a big deal.

Mani's silent a bit, then: "I just ordered you a glass of arak."

Amir laughs and puts his head on his arms. "It's two p.m. But thank you." Seagulls croon from the frames of the yellow beach umbrellas. "This Wet City thing, Mani," he starts. Doesn't know how to finish.

"You don't believe in it," says Mani.

Amir grimaces. "That obvious?"

"No." This should be reassuring, but Mani's turning her teacup in slow circles, not meeting Amir's eyes. "Amir-with-his-heart-not-in-it works with more passion than most humans on their best days. But I can tell."

This should also be reassuring. Instead Amir feels irritation spiking in his chest. "I've spent every moment of my workday for the past six days chasing down permitting documentation for an experimental metallofoam that's going to be used in less than two percent of the load-bearing struts of the wing structure," he says. "It's not exactly how I envisioned my career path. But I'm doing it. It's not fair to call me out for lack of enthusiasm."

"I wasn't calling you out," says Mani. "I think you're doing good work."

"Yeah," says Amir. The arak comes. He plucks it off the tray bot and sets it next to his teacup, aligning them carefully side by side. He can tell Mani is waiting for him to say something else. He shouldn't. He should try to steer the conversation back toward safety. "Do you remember," he says, "the Crowdgrow project I told you about during the Future Good conference?"

"You were really excited about it," Mani says. "It seemed promising."

"It was. The closed-room tests showed a fifteen percent improvement in air quality, and we had almost a thousand households signed up as testers. And we've applied for continuation funding every open cycle since. Not a lot—just enough for a pilot study. Less than we spend in administrative overhead on the Wet City project every week."

"But no luck?" asks Mani.

"But no luck," agrees Amir.

"Amir," says Mani, but there's too much pity in the way she says his name.

"I know what you're thinking," Amir says. "That it would be a waste. That Wet City is a better use of resources."

"Yes," says Mani. "I do think that." The way she says this could have been kind, but it isn't.

"You're always so sure of yourself," says Amir. The way he says this could have been a compliment, but it isn't. "Is it ego?"

"Is it jealousy?" Mani shoots back.

Amir feels that familiar muscle in his jaw tic. He takes a careful, measured sip of arak, as if that will hide it. "If this goes wrong—" he begins, once he's sure his voice will come out steady.

"Oh, please," interrupts Mani. "You're going to tell me to be afraid of trying something really big, really innovative, because there's a chance we'll end up looking like fools? Now *that's* ego."

"It's not about *personal reputation*," Amir says. "It's about the wasted money, the time, the emotional investment—do you know how demoralizing a project like this can be for a community if it fails—"

"It won't fail."

"You can't know that."

"We've done all the tests and simulations and proof-of-concept models we can, Amir. The only way to be any more sure is to let someone else go first, and I'm not willing to do that."

"Ego," says Amir.

"So what," Mani snaps, sounding genuinely angry now, "we'd all be better off staying in our backyards planting mutant daisies? Grow up, Amir. You have the chance to work on something that really, actually matters here, and you're too scared to take it."

If it were Amir, he would regret such harsh words immediately, start falling all over himself to apologize before the sting had a chance to land.

But it's Mani. And Mani always says what she means.

Amir looks down at the now-empty glass cradled in his fingers. "It's getting late," he says. "We should probably be getting back."

Mani stands, the legs of her chair protesting loudly against the concrete. "We get this chance—" she stops. "I can't understand why you're making it so hard."

He should argue. Instead, he orders another arak, and doesn't let himself watch her walk to the bullet station.

4: THAT EACH OF US INVESTS THE LABOR

It's not that Amir and Mani stay angry a whole year and a half. Something that dire would've spurred Amir to action, forced him to have the trembly, awkward conversation that showed them the way back to exchanges of essay clippings and meandering debates and maybe even limb-jumble lie-downs after a gigantic dinner cooked together.

They are not *angry*: they are too intelligent for anger, Amir thinks, or too proud. They're just *hardened* to each other. Their words bounce, too few absorbing. Their lunches together have one too many silences that call for a new conversation thread, and when congratulations are due—as when the first wing is drone-dropped into place at Martyrs' Square and measurements show promising vapor transfer into the condensation bays at the base—their hugs are guarded and bodiless.

The Wet City project hits miraculously few snags, but once or twice Amir catches a design flaw that makes Mani give him a deep, reckoning look.

"I'm just doing some calculations in Impulse," Amir says. "The Beirut-3 east wing might not come out inwardly reflective the way we want, with the new bug-in-amber angled like that?" *Bug-in-amber* is their shorthand for the art pieces they'll embed in each translucent wing, one of Amir's favorite streams of the project. He taps across his calculations.

"Whizkid," is all Mani says, and Amir almost asks if she wants to grab dinner with him after work. He doesn't. He gets better at finding flaws, though. There are times when flaws are all he sees.

Post-water-crisis Beirut is mesmerizing, boisterous street markets by day and elaborate street parties by night.

Amir and Joud meet every couple of weeks to trawl the artisans' quarter in Nouveau Centre-Ville, Amir on the lookout for sustainable art references for the much larger bug-in-amber pieces to come, Joud hoping to enrich their collection of silk and brocade Lebanese abayas. They are especially taken by androgynous styles that combine an embroidered abaya tunic with a shirwal bottom. They stroke the parchment packets, their fingers lingering on the teardrop calligraphy of the artisan's sigil. The two of them often return to Amir's apartment with towering ice cream cones, and Joud tells him what they've learned about tonight's artisan on Impulse, and they have the sort of voracious, aching sex that comes after absence.

"How is Mani?" Joud asks tonight, nestled against the hollow of Amir's chest. Joud frequently asks about Mani. They *know*, but their affection for Amir is so confident, so stable, that the question can come right after intimacy and carry no trace of malice or envy.

"Today she proposed a walkway up the side of the sea-facing wings for a view of the sunset," Amir says. "And yesterday she gave a site tour to a delegation that arrived two days early from Singapore."

Joud hums in appreciation. They always do. Joud loves expansively, navigating a multitude of relationships with a grace and wholeheartedness that makes Amir feel he's never absorbed a moment of personal growth.

"You don't have to indulge me, you know," Amir says. He presses three fingertips against the place where Joud's temple meets soft brown hair, scratches them there tenderly. "You and I have been in each other's lives two years and I've never been—I mean, Mani's always been—"

Joud stills his lips with their cheek. "It doesn't bother me, darling. What I figure is some people stand beside each other, and some people end up locked together," Joud laces their own hands tight, to the knuckles. "And I don't think the latter is better."

"You're right, love," Amir says to Joud, who smells like green branches and clay and sex. In that moment the appellation feels miraculous and genuine on his tongue. "In many ways it's worse."

There are times when hitting the forecasted Wet City launch date seems like a pipe dream, but as more and more pieces slot into place, it starts to become attainable, and then an unavoidable reality. Twenty hyper-efficient months after Hanne's distracted aside in the conservatory, the first wings come online; the engineers begin their final stress tests; the notion of a citywide festival around the launch begins to coalesce. And then, with three and a half months to the launch date, Mesilla calls Amir into her office.

Two of their artists won't have their bugs-in-amber finished by the festival and Amir's been heading up the effort to ensure their temporary prototypes are materially similar enough for the engineers to work with; he assumes this is what Mesilla wants to talk about. Instead he's greeted by a stranger. "Amir," Mesilla says, "I wanted you to meet one of my oldest colleagues: Adah Bertonneau."

Adah Bertonneau is even taller than Amir, with impressive cheekbones and two-hand-clasp handshake. "A pleasure to finally meet you," Adah says, their accent a rich, rolling thing Amir can't quite place.

Amir smiles, puzzled. "Finally?"

"Read your Crowdgrow grant application five years ago now," says Adah. "Told myself I'd make Mesilla introduce us if I ever made it to this part of the globe. And here I am."

"Oh." Amir resists the inclination to try to look up Adah on Impulse—he's still not very good at interfacing with it discreetly. "Well, unfortunately, we haven't had the opportunity to prove out the research, but I hope that one day—"

"Mx. Tarabi," interrupts Adah. "That is, of course, precisely why I'm here to talk to you."

Adah Bertonneau, it turns out, works at the Nantes Center for Naturalist Studies. The Center is neither large nor prestigious (Amir gives up and looks it up on Impulse), but their work seems well-respected enough, and a few of their recent papers have appeared in journals Amir would have once given his eyeteeth to be published in. Adah's lab is new, getting off the ground with an *extremely* generous grant from France Centrale, and it seems, more or less, that they're looking for ways to spend it.

"One must make a splash early," says Adah, peering at Amir seriously over the rim of their teacup. "We're frontloading, trying to get several programs up and running right out the door. Not all of them will work out in the long term, of course, but I'd guarantee funding for the full two-year period you requested, regardless of the findings. Between you and me, though? I have this . . . call it a premonition, that what you've proposed is going to work."

Of course it's a dream come true. And of course the timing couldn't be worse.

"I wish I could tell you to take your time making a decision," continues Adah, "but the start date's in a month, and I'm afraid it's not flexible." They want to do the study with a particular crawler vine, Adah explains, whose cuttings are most viable in the fall. One week, and they'll need a yes or no, "else there won't be enough time to get the paperwork in order, you understand." Amir understands. Hands are shaken. Mesilla walks Amir out.

"Take the rest of the day," she says. "I—well, I don't know whether to say I'm sorry or congratulations. I know it's a lot at once."

Amir very nearly just asks her to tell him what to do, but she seems to read this on his face. "We can talk it over tomorrow, if you need. But sleep on it. Before you start cataloging opinions."

Amir nods. It's smart. Mesilla's always smart. He goes to his office, gathers his things, does his best to slip out unnoticed.

Except he runs into Mani waiting for the elevator.

"Hey," she says, smiling a little awkwardly, that try-hard friendliness. Then she spots his messenger bag. "Headed out?"

It's not even ten in the morning. Amir hits the down button again—the Grid's elevators are vintage, which is a cute way of saying unbearably slow. The doors are mirrored; Amir read somewhere that mirroring elevator doors reduced complaints about wait times, because people got carried away admiring themselves. He wonders if it's true. He hopes it's not. He thinks it probably is.

"Mani," he says, "I'm quitting."

Mani's reflection stares at him.

The doors bing open.

Amir steps into the elevator; Mani takes an extra second to step in after him.

"*Explain*," Mani says. "*Now*? Are you serious?"

Amir is serious. He only knew it as he said the words aloud. "Skive off today?" he asks Mani, pretending he doesn't hear the note of pleading in his own voice. "I could really use a drink."

They end up going back to his. They take the bullet train in silence—it's mostly empty at this odd hour of the morning, but the tunnel-rush of wind makes holding a conversation difficult. The ride's only five minutes, but it's long enough to put Amir on edge. He stares down at his interlaced fingers, bracketed by his knees. There's an empty seat between him and Mani, because there was space to spread out, and why would they not? After all, these days, it's not like they're—well. It's barely like they're friends.

Mani has never been to Amir's apartment. He realizes this as he keys into the front door; they've tried, a few times, vague agreements about dinner that fell through at the last moment, meetings that wound up getting moved to workspaces with excuses of better bullet access. It should make him nervous, he thinks. He should be worrying about the fact that none of his coffee mugs match, or whether he left toothpaste flecks on the bathroom mirror that morning. But he isn't nervous. Mani knows all the worst parts of him already.

The Bekaa Valley Merlot is still at the back of the cupboard, because Amir's life is a joke. He uncorks it and pours them both generous glasses, and settles himself next to her at the small kitchen table. "There's a research institute in Nantes," he says. "They want to fund a Crowdgrow rollout."

Mani looks stunned, just for a second, then raises her wineglass. "This is now a toast," she says. "To the long overdue recognition of my brilliant friend Amir Tarabi."

Amir tilts his glass toward hers. "Thing is," he says, "I'd have to start basically immediately. A few weeks. I wouldn't be here to close out Wet City. I wouldn't be able to make the launch festival."

". . . oh," says Mani. She lowers her glass. "Damn."

"Right." Amir lowers his glass, too. He's not quite sure how to look at Mani, so he focuses on the wineglass, turning it in careful circles, watching the light refract. "I mean, it's not the end of the world," he says. "I'll need to pass some stuff off sort of hastily, but let's be honest, I'm no longer really essential personnel. And I don't care about the festival. It's just . . ."

Amir stops, looks up. He doesn't know how to read Mani's expression. Complicated, sad. A little like how she looks when she's working her way through a thorny problem. She reaches forward, finding his fingers with her own, carefully unlacing them from the stem of the wineglass. She holds his hand there in the warm cradle of her palms, running her thumb in a discovering sort of way across the ridgeline below his knuckles, as if she were going to read his fortune.

"It would have been nice," says Mani, "to have had more time."

"Mani," says Amir, helplessly. She looks up, looks at him. He feels on display, as if she's taking inventory of him, all the things that are different, all the things that are the same. He swallows. "I want—" he says.

Mani reaches up, running her fingertips through the scruff of his beard, bracing her thumb against his cheekbone. "Come here," she says. He goes, letting her guide him forward until she finds his mouth with hers, and kisses him.

His mind goes blank. He's a teenager again, unsure what to do with his hands. He loves her so much he thinks he might fly into a million separate parts.

She undresses him first, won't let him help, won't let him touch, torturous slowness as she undoes every button, every hook. She runs her fingertips over all the planes and angles of him, presses teasing thumbs into the hollows by his hipbones and kisses him until he feels drunk with it. Then she lets him do the same to her, and she takes his hands and shows him where to touch, and he thinks this might be the most beautiful thing he's ever done.

Afterward, they lie tangled together, exhausted, belly-to-flank, Amir's cheek pressed against the top of Mani's head. The warm reality of her, the slow swell-and-recede of her body against his, is almost too much to stand.

"I'm going to miss you," Amir says. "I'm going to miss you so much. It wasn't enough time."

He feels her pause, then twist to look at him. "I shouldn't have said that, earlier," she says, very serious. "We can't think that way. We have to say to ourselves, this was right. This was exactly enough."

Amir shuts his eyes, tips his head forward to rest against hers, and tries to believe it. He keeps his eyes closed until they both fall asleep.

5: THE BEAM COMES ON, ILLUMINATING US ALL

Amir arrives in France just after dawn on a foggy fall day. His out-breaths add frills of fog to Nantes' thick cloak of it. He keeps his Impulse off after landing. Sounds muffled, skin damp, his first impression of his new home is of being underwater.

He explores the city on foot, stopping for croissants then brioches then tartines. At sunset, he sits on the lawn of the Château des Ducs de Bretagne and tosses a bag of soy chips to two mallards and their ducklings paddling in the castle's moat. Impulse would help him form a mental map, but he knows if he turns it on he's going to look for a message from Mani, and if there's none he's going to be heartsick. And if there is one he's going to be heartsick.

Three things cycle through Amir's mind: first, how to make the most of this opportunity; second, how desperately he needs to recenter himself in personal growth practice; third, the problem he's had for most of his life, which is that he can't stop thinking about Mani.

Amir wakes up with the sun on his first morning in his Nantes apartment and he takes creaking steps that raise dust motes along the woodgrain floorboards. At the window he turns Impulse on and his heart rattles the split second before his unreads appear.

Nothing from Mani.

Amir starts to compose a message. "Hi! Nantes is beautiful. There's a duckling in the castle moat who has learned to swim alongside—" then he closes his eyes, hard, and deletes. When he opens them the weathervane across from his window has flipped 180 degrees and the sun is a blur of honey.

The Crowdgrow pilot takes place along two residential streets in Nantes-2, just north of the Gare de Nantes. Amir hand-delivers cuttings of ecoboosted crawler vine to each of the experiment's participants.

"Je vous attends toute la matinée," says one girl when Amir puts the little red planter pot in her hands. Her tight cornrows have been braided into an orchid-shaped bun on top of her head. She takes him round to the back garden, shows him the sheltered hole in the soil she's dug. There is so much *care* in her actions that Amir's belief in—dedication to—Crowdgrow redoubles just like that.

"Mes mamans disent que le ciel sera plein d'oiseaux," she says.

"Yes," Amir replies through Impulse. "As many birds as the sky can handle."

Nantes is on a clean air travel vector with Beirut, so Joud comes to visit the week before Amir presents the results of the pilot to a delegation from Nantes' municipality. They go to Nantes' shipyard island, go on mech-AI safari. They feed the giant hydraulic elephants from a tray of silicon peanuts, and the elephants regurgitate silicon caricatures of Amir and Joud. Joud's is great: an impossibly vertical cone of hair, small ears rendered as notches. Amir's own caricature makes him feel every year as old as his thirty-two, and older.

He wraps their portraits up and tucks them in his bag, presses Joud close. Arm in arm, they survey nearby menus on Impulse until Amir finds one that does a much-lauded synth-protein steak with cassava frites. They wash it down with crisp, sweet Breton cider.

"To new avenues," Joud says.

"To the companions who walk our lives with us," Amir says. The words are from a passage Mani once clipped from a poem. He clinks the neck of his bottle against Joud's.

The first results come back from Crowdgrow in Nantes-2. The air quality in that sector has improved a modest part per billion, but what's really encouraging is that all the crawler vines have survived. Many have gained a meter or more in length. The pilot expands to a citywide project, Adah's grant money matched by government funds.

Amir comes home late one evening from overseeing a plant-in at a primary school, a little dazed from hours of sun and excitable schoolchildren, but in good spirits. He's dirt all over, ground into the new callouses on his palms and spilling from the hems of his trousers. The soil here is still toxic, and he should probably wash it off before doing anything else, but his diminutive wrought iron balcony gets an excellent view of the sunset, and he can't help but peel off his shoes and socks and sit down at the wooden folding table to watch it. The last flash of sunlight is winking out on the windows of the Cathédrale Saint-Pierre et Saint-Paul when his Impulse pings with a call from Mani.

He answers without thinking—or, he answers before he can let himself think about it. "Mani?" he says, a question, like it could be anyone else.

"Hi," says definitely-Mani. "Are you—"

"Free," says Amir, straightening a little, though she hasn't initiated holo. "I mean, I just got home from work. I was just—" He stumbles. *Watching the sunset* feels too corny. "Relaxing," he finishes.

"Good," says Mani. "I saw on the Beirut Grid announcement stream that your project won that funding extension from the city. Wanted to say congratulations. So, well." She laughs a little. "Congratulations."

Amir sinks back into his chair. "Thanks," he says. "You too. I watched your speech at the launch ceremony. It was really beautiful."

"Thank you," says Mani. "I read your message to the team."

He'd figured she had, even when she didn't respond. He's not sure what to say to this.

"You should have been there," Mani says.

The morning of the Wet City launch festival in Beirut, they'd gotten the first full bloom on a crawler vine in Nantes-2, a pale blue flower veined with green, nearly the size of Amir's head. The stem wasn't robust yet; the smallest breeze set the blossom trembling, like any moment it would come free and drop to the earth. Amir had spent most of the morning crouched in the dewy garden, waiting to see if it would last. "That's kind of you," says Amir, "but you were fine without me."

The connection goes so silent Amir has to check Impulse for the activity blip.

"It's been harder," says Mani, "than I thought it would be."

Amir closes his eyes. He wants to say: I would come back if you asked me to. He wants to say: I wouldn't have left in the first place. Instead he says, "Mani."

"I love you," says Mani. "Even if we never quite figure out what that should look like. You know that, right?"

The breeze is sharpening with night, carrying scents of yeast and toffee from the bakery on street level. The latticework of the metal balcony presses geometry into the soles of Amir's feet. He can hear the soft hush of Mani's breath, in and out.

"Yes," says Amir. "I know."

Over the next seven years, Nantes becomes a garden city. Every green space is verdant with ecoboosted flora from Amir's program; parks and groves are remade from concrete lots and musky alleys. The skies, as one little girl had once hoped, are full of birds.

Amir spends one of those years working with his team on tweaks to the Crowdgrow flora to ensure the boosted species are hospitable to native ones, and that summer there are small populations of roe deer, and bushes of garden aster, and swallows, and a sighting of a pair of endangered partridges on the steps of the Théâtre Graslin.

Mani stays in Beirut after Wet City launches, takes up a just-formed position as Beirut's Minister for Enrichment. Amir pieces together through her understatements and Impulse research that this means she oversees almost every program in Beirut that impacts quality of life—standards for natural lighting in modular housing, breeding programs for Mediterranean loggerheads, the national poetry curriculum. He's immensely proud and touched.

Amir thinks about surprising Mani in Beirut for her thirty-sixth birthday; he's been back home twice while Mani was away on diplomatic visits, just bad luck. He asks circumspect questions to make sure she'll be in town, buys a ticket. The day before the flight he gets scary news: one of the Crowdgrow fern populations has been proliferating invasively, has killed off a native garden. Amir gets on a bullet to Nantes-11 and he's so nervous about the clean-up operation he doesn't see the inside of his apartment for three days.

They control the fern; he misses his chance to visit Mani.

Time goes so quickly those years. But he spends more evenings sitting on his balcony watching the sunset than not.

It's Adah who brings Amir the news personally: they've received an application to start a Crowdgrow program in Beirut.

It'll be the seventeenth spin-off of the original Nantes pilot—the first three Amir went to oversee himself, spending months in Bruges, Liverpool, Alexandria. After that, they'd developed a formula, easy for new cities to follow with only a few weeks' oversight from Amir's staff.

"It's below your pay grade," says Adah. "But I thought you might want to take this one on yourself. Chance to catch up with old friends. But we'll send someone else if you're too busy."

Amir is definitely too busy. "Don't send anyone else," he says. "I'd love to go."

Amir calls Mani that afternoon as he's walking home from work, feeling like something in him's unfurling in the late autumn sun. "I hear someone in Beirut ordered some mutant daisies," he says the moment she picks up.

"Smug," Mani says. "I was so pleased when the proposal came through."

"Me too. And, um. Adah asked if I wanted to come do the kickoff myself."

There's a pause. "What did you say?"

Amir huffs. "I said yes, obviously! What do you think?" He scruffs his knuckles over the stubble on his jawline, tries to keep his voice casual.

"I'll clear my calendar," Mani says.

Amir's Impulse pings with an unread as his plane begins to descend into Beirut. Joud. *Meet at the rock wharf by al-Raouché, bring a warm coat.*

It's five a.m. and Amir's had no sleep. He's really getting too old for no sleep. But the trembly adrenaline of night flights and home is a jolt in his chest, so he goes, his luggage tracking him at a polite distance.

The wind is insistent and briny. Amir seals his coat to his chin. There's a huge crowd at the wharf, and food kiosks, and banners, a bunch of institutional logos he doesn't recognize, and one he does—Beirut Grid's.

Joud finds him where he's paused at a corniche railing trying to work out the reason for the commotion. He hasn't seen Joud in two years, not since Joud moved into a rundown mountain house in Ehden with three partners and their five little ones to begin hand-renovating the house to ecopositive standards.

They look great. Sun-hardened, their hair a wiry nest of salt and pepper, clipped a little closer than Amir remembers.

"There's a team from Beirut Grid here," Joud says when they hug. "And a couple of my kids. I want you to meet them. Leave the luggage, come."

Joud leads Amir into the wharf and onto the rocks beyond, where adults and children are queued up to use what look like fishing poles. There's a din of excitement and an occasional whoop of triumph.

Amir is stunned. "Are they *fishing?*"

Joud laughs, just as three little humans run into their arms shouting, "We fed one!"

"Show Amir," Joud says, and a kid with the same shy grin as their parent holds out a glossy pellet cradled in their palm.

"Vitamin feed to correct an imbalance in the ecosystem," says Joud. "It's civic engagement, a bit of publicity. There's a water-soluble version they'll pump in after."

"Joud?" asks the smallest child. "Are they going to come live with us?" They glance at Amir. "We have enough water for them to do a mineral soak once a week too."

"He's welcome to come live with us," Joud says, and Amir forces himself not to look away from the softness on Joud's face.

"Amir Tarabi! Of all the fish-feeding parties in all the towns . . ." says someone behind him. He turns around to see Mesilla carrying a pail, and behind her Hanne and Caveg.

"This is crazy," Amir says, and gathers them into a hug. "I just got off the plane from France. How . . ."

"Maybe not totally a coincidence." Joud winks at him. "I thought Mani would be here too. But her assistant told me she's working a short day today, had to wrap things up at the ministry."

Hanne cracks a joke about Amir still overthinking everything, except now in French, and it's one of those moments younger Amir wouldn't have believed in: like the universe has turned its spotlight on him, for a fleeting instant, and instructed him to rest.

Eventually, the trajectory of the future will look like this: some years, Amir in Beirut, guest lecturing at Pan-Humanist Polytechnic, consulting on the new ecoboosted installation in Zahleh, taking a sabbatical to work on a collection of essays about crowdsourcing civic change. Some of those years, Mani in Beirut too, but others, Mani in the Arctic, Mani back in Mogadishu, Mani on the Gulf Coast. Once, eighteen glorious months both in Beirut, a routine of dinner parties at Mani's girlfriend's loft apartment, and stargazing every third weekend during Beirut's Dark Skies nights: picnic blankets and wine, Amir's head in Mani's lap, Mani's fingers in his hair. Once, ten long years where the vagaries of circumstance mean they don't manage to see each other at all.

Eventually, all the days in a human life, whether or not they feel like enough.

But for now, all the hard, gut-ache hope and all the pragmatics and all the inexorable decades coalesce like this: Amir steps out of a Beirut hotel two streets up from his old al-Manara apartment holding a potted Crowdgrow cutting, and points himself toward Stella Kadri Square.

Mani messages him just as he spots the showcase Wet City wings fanning out in the distance, describing the perimeter of the brand new square. Their bugs-in-amber make them into a museum of petrified art. He saw hundreds of the wings from the air and he'd seen the beachfront ones from a distance on his brief visits home, but now they *strike* him. It's like walking toward the foot of a mountain, that same organic rightness of approaching and finding the world continuing up and out beneath his feet.

Mani sends him geo for a bench she's found. He wants to play that old game of how long has it been, but he draws every minute of personal growth he's ever done to ground himself—he notes the flinty musk of impending rain, the drawn out ping of the bullet slicing across the city, the tickle in his throat from the boosted pollen of the Crowdgrow cutting. His heart, beating in his neck.

Amir spots the bench from a distance. Mani is a blue-coated speck on one side of it. He's shy, suddenly, walking into a casual get-together with Beirut's Minister for Enrichment, walking across the grandeur of a public space he knows she conceived and oversaw to completion, a tribute to the world Mani's rallied for and railed against so passionately her whole life. Then Mani messages him a biofeedback wave, and Amir viscerally feels her excitement hum in his brain, and he's not shy anymore. He wants to be near enough to touch her so badly. He almost breaks into a run.

But doesn't. He gets close enough for her to hear him and shouts "Mani!" Her peacoat's the shade of the ocean, collar drawn up. Her face is open and happy. Amir can't believe she could possibly wear that expression for him.

"You look like you're having a pretty good day," he laughs.

She shakes her head, gets up and closes the distance and hugs him and her cheek is right over the brutal hammering of his heart. Amir stands as still as he can, clutching the Crowdgrow pot against Mani's back, waiting for the moment she breaks the embrace, kind of hoping that will be never.

"I brought you a cutting," Amir says.

"Welcome home," Mani mumbles. Her voice vibrates in his chest.

"To us both," he says.

She turns her face up to his and puts fingers on his jaw and kisses him and doesn't stop, and Amir must really be in a kinder world because it starts to rain, raindrops that splatter open, big and clean and warm.

zigeuner

HARRY TURTLEDOVE

Although he writes other kinds of science fiction as well, and even the occasional fantasy, Harry Turtledove has become one of the most prominent writers of alternate history stories in the business today and is probably the most popular and influential writer to work that territory since L. Sprague de Camp; in fact, most of the current popularity of that particular subgenre can be attributed to Turtledove's own hot-ticket bestseller status.

Turtledove has published alternate history novels such as The Guns of the South, *dealing with a timeline in which the American Civil War turns out very differently, thanks to time-traveling gunrunners; the bestselling World-war series, in which the course of World War II is altered by attacking aliens, the Basil Argyros series, detailing the adventures of a "magistrianoi" in an alternate Byzantine Empire (collected in the book* Agent of Byzantium); *the Sim series, which take place in an alternate world in which European explorers find North America inhabited by hominids instead of Indians (collected in the book* A Different Flesh); *a look at a world where the Revolutionary War didn't happen, written with actor Richard Dreyfuss,* The Two Georges; *and many other intriguing alternate history scenarios. Turtledove is also the author of two multivolume alternate history fantasy series, the multivolume* Videssos Cycle *and the* Krispes Sequence. *His other books include the novels* Wereblood, Werenight, Earthgrip, Noninterference, A World of Difference, Gunpowder Empire, American Empire: The Victorious Opposition, Jaws of Darkness, Ruled Britannia, Settling Accounts: Drive to the East, In the Presence of Mine Enemies, The Bridge of the Separator, End of the Beginning, *and* Every Inch a King; *the collections* Kaleidoscope, Down in the Bottomlands (and Other Places), *and* Atlantis and Other Places; *and, as editor,* The Best Alternate History Stories of the 20th Century, The Best Military Science Fiction of the 20th Century, The Best Time Travel Stories of the 20th Century, *and, with Martin H. Greenberg, the* Alternate Generals *books. His most recent books include the novels* The Big Switch *and the Super-volcano series. He won a Hugo Award in 1994 for his story, "Down in the Bottomlands." A native Californian, Turtledove has a PhD in Byzantine history from UCLA, and has published a scholarly translation of a ninth-century Byzantine chronicle. He lives in Canoga Park, California, with his wife and family.*

In the brutal Alternate History story that follows, he gives us a disquieting glimpse into some aspects of the human heart that most of us would rather not think about.

Hauptsturmführer Joseph Stieglitz looked up into the gloomy gray late-October sky. Drizzle speckled the lenses of the SS officer's steel-framed spectacles. It wasn't really raining, but it also wasn't really not raining. Muttering, he pulled a handkerchief from the right front pocket of his *Feldgrau* trousers and got his glasses as clean as he could.

He peered across the town square, then nodded to himself. Yes, the Kübelwagens and the trucks were ready. Everything here in Zalaegerszeg seemed peaceful enough. Yes, the town lay in Hungary, but on the west side of the Platten-See (on Magyar maps, it was Lake Balaton). Off in the eastern part of the country, the *Wehrmacht* and the *Waffen*-SS and the Hungarian *Honvéd* were fighting thunderous panzer battles to try to halt or at least slow the onrushing Red Army.

Better not to dwell on that too much. Better to hope the Germans could use their now-shorter supply lines to advantage. Better to hope the *Honvéd* would fight hard now that it was defending its homeland. Better to hope Ferenc Szalasi and his Arrow Cross Fascists would make the *Honvéd* fight harder than Admiral Horthy had. Horthy the trimmer, Horthy the traitor, Horthy who'd tried to fix up a separate peace with Russia till the *Führer* got wind of it and overthrew him before he could make it stick.

Because if you did dwell on that, if you looked at where the Red Army was and at how far it had come since the start of summer, what could you do but realize the war was lost? Like almost all German officers in the autumn of 1944, Joseph Stieglitz made the effort of will he needed not to realize that.

He walked across the square toward the transport he'd laid on. The hobnailed soles of his jackboots clicked on the cobbles. The drizzle was turning the stones slippery; he planted his feet with care so he wouldn't take a tumble. As long as he kept his head down, the patent-leather brim of his cap protected his glasses well enough.

Some of the men in the *Kübelwagens* wore German *Feldgrau* like Stieglitz. Others were in Hungarian khaki. Despite the brown *Stahlhelms* on their heads, they were militiamen, not real soldiers; their Arrow Cross armbands showed as much. The truck drivers were also Hungarians. *Hauptsturmführer* Stieglitz shrugged. For this operation, he probably wouldn't need anything more.

His driver was an *Unterscharführer* named Klaus Pirckheimer. The junior noncom waved as Stieglitz came up. "We're all ready, sir," he said. "Let's go clean those bastards out."

"Sounds good to me." Stieglitz slid into the right front bucket seat.

Pirckheimer started the engine. As he did so, the bells of the Catholic church on the square chimed the hour: ten in the morning. The *Hauptsturmführer* had gone into the church to admire its eighteenth-century frescoes. Though no Catholic himself, he appreciated fine art wherever he found it. He was, and worked at being, a man of *Kultur*.

The road leading south had been blacktopped but not recently. Some of the potholes the *Kübelwagen* hit seemed big enough to swallow the utility vehicle. But it kept going. It didn't have four-wheel drive like an American jeep, but was surprisingly nimble even traveling cross-country.

"Don't miss the turnoff, Klaus," Stieglitz said. "We want the right-hand fork, remember."

"*Zu Befehl, mein Herr!*" Somehow, in Pirckheimer's mouth, a simple *Yes, sir!* sounded more like *Why don't you shut up and leave me alone?*

He did find the fork—just in time, with a hard right turn, to keep from driving past it. The rest of the column followed his lead. No sign marked the road's branching. Maybe there had been one before the war drew near, and the local authorities took it down to give invaders a harder time navigating. More likely, the turnoff never was important enough to mark.

A couple of kilometers past the turnoff, maybe ten kilometers out of Zalaegerszeg, lay the village of Nagylengyel. Though it too boasted a Catholic church, it couldn't have held more than three or four hundred people. Two grannies were selling beans and grapes at a little roadside market. An old man hawked sausages on a folding table and had a half-grown pig on a rope tied to one of the table legs. Business looked slow.

"We're getting close, hey, *Herr Hauptsturmführer*?" Pirckheimer said.

"Well, I hope so," Joseph Stieglitz replied. "The *Zigeuner* encampment was reported to be three kilometers south of Nagylengyel. SS headquarters in Szombathely got the word a couple of days ago. They didn't waste any of their precious time telling *me* about it till last night, of course."

"Of course," the driver agreed. Stieglitz was an officer, but officers and enlisted men united in sneering at the headquarters oafs who didn't bother to let them know what was going on. Pirckheimer went on, "Gotta be better than even money the rats have found a new hole between then and now."

"If they have, we'll find them," Stieglitz said, shrugging. "If we don't find them today, we'll find them tomorrow. If we don't find them tomorrow, somebody else will next week."

"And then they'll get what's coming to the, the stinking *Untermenschen*," Pirckheimer said.

"*Ja*," the *Hauptsturmführer* agreed, though he preferred not to think about that too much. His job was rounding up the *Zigeuner* and arranging for them to be transported. What happened after they got where they were going to . . . That was none of his business. The fewer questions you asked about such things, the less you officially knew, the better off you were. But there had been almost a million *Zigeuner* in Europe when the war started. If any were there when fighting finally stopped, it wouldn't be for lack of effort.

The *Kübelwagen* rounded one more corner. Klaus Pirckheimer let out a happy little yip. "They *are* still here! Too dumb even to run, looks like."

Another *Zigeuner* encampment, as filthy and disorderly as all the rest. Six or eight wagons that looked as if they'd been designed and possibly built in the seventeenth century sat on the grass by the side of the road. The donkeys that pulled them when they were on the move grazed one here, one there, one somewhere else. The sorry beasts were scrawny and tiny: hardly bigger than large dogs. To give comparison, a couple of big, toothy, plainly mean dogs prowled among them and started barking as the vehicles neared.

A motley assortment of tents sheltered the *Zigeuner* from the elements. By the faded paintings on its canvas, one had come from a traveling circus a long time ago. Another . . . The *Hauptsturmführer*'s mouth twisted. It was assembled from no doubt stolen German shelter halves. *Zigeuner* produced next to nothing for themselves, but they were first-rate thieves.

"Pull past them and stop," Stieglitz said.

"I'll do it, sir," his driver replied, and did. The other *Kübelwagens* and the trucks halted behind the first.

SS men and Arrow Cross militiamen hopped out of the vehicles. The Germans carried Schmeissers or captured Russian PPDs. The submachine guns weren't worth much out past a couple of hundred meters, but they made dandy intimidators at close range. The Hungarians had Mausers and pistols.

Stieglitz himself wore a Walther P-38 on his belt but didn't unholster it yet. Instead, he cupped both hands in front of his mouth and bellowed, "*Alle Zigeuner raus!*" For good measure, he added, "*Sofort!*" Right away!

Out they came: swarthy, sharp-nosed, feral-looking men and women in shabby clothes, some of the women's outfits ornamented with incongruously bright embroidery. They all wore the brown triangle, point down, required of their kind; they didn't break the law in such small ways.

A skinny, gray-mustached fellow who looked like a pimp down on his luck spoke to the others in the gibberish the *Zigeuner* used among themselves. Their dark, frightened eyes went back and forth from Stieglitz to him.

The leader of the pack, the *Hauptsturmführer* thought. He pointed at the man. "*Du! Sprichst du Deutsch?*" He used the familiar pronoun, as he would have with children or servants or anyone else with whom he didn't have to bother staying polite.

Only a string of that incomprehensible lingo came back at him. Stieglitz rolled his eyes. He could have just taken out the pistol and pointed with it. That probably would have worked. But the *Zigeuner* might have panicked if he gave orders with the barrel of a gun. They were liable to have a shotgun or two in the tents or in their wagons. If a hothead grabbed one, he might hurt somebody before he could be disposed of.

So Stieglitz turned to the Hungarian lieutenant who headed up the militiamen. "*Sprechen Sie Deutsch?*" With the Hungarian, who was on his side, he used the formal pronoun.

But the man spread his hands and shook his head. He answered in Hungarian. That did the *Hauptsturmführer* as little good as the nonsense the *Zigeuner* spouted.

He eyed the rest of the Hungarians. The armed militiamen were all young, like their officer. One of the truck drivers, though, had graying hair and the beginnings of a wattle under his chin. He was bound to to be close to fifty. Stieglitz walked over to him. "How about you?" he asked. "Do *you* speak German?"

"Military German," the said. Stieglitz nodded; that was what he'd hoped for. German had been the language of command in the Austro-Hungarian army during the last war. Basic words got drilled into soldiers of all nationalities. Then the Magyar unbent enough to go on: "Maybe more than military German. We had a division from the Kaiser's army on our left for a while in the Carpathians, and we got friendly with them. I think it was the one your *Führer* served in."

"*Ach, so.*" Joseph Stieglitz nodded. "It could be." He knew the *Führer* had fought against the Russians in World War I. Everybody knew that. It was where he'd acquired his rancorous hatred for the *Zigeuner*. They'd stolen horses and boots and telegraph wire from his outfit, and cost it casualties it wouldn't have taken if they hadn't prowled around. Now he was taking his revenge on them, as he had on so many others.

Which Austro-Hungarian division had served on the German unit's flank, Stieglitz couldn't have said. That didn't much matter, though.

"Translate for me, will you?" he said to the truck driver. "They may act like they don't speak German, but I doon't think they can pretend they don't know any Hungarian."

"I'll do it, *Herr* Major," the driver replied. He could read German shoulder straps, anyway. Stieglitz's SS rank was equivalent to major in the *Wehrmacht*.

"*Danke schön*," Stieglitz said. "Tell them we're going to put them in the trucks and transport them up to Zalaegerszeg."

He waited for the veteran to translate that. As soon as the man did, the old villain who led this band of *Zigeuner* let loose with his own torrent of Hungarian. "He says, 'What will you do with us there?' " the truck driver reported.

Stieglitz suspected the chieftain said some other things as well, but that would do for now. "We'll put you on a train with others of their folk," the *Hauptsturmführer* said. "We'll take you to resettlement camps in Poland, far away from the fighting. You'll be well housed there, and well fed."

The driver duly translated. The chieftain said, "But we like it where we are now just fine. We don't want to be resettled."

"It's a matter of military necessity," Stieglitz said, trying not to meet the *Zigeuner*'s dark and piercing gaze. He told the old bandit what his superiors instructed him to say whenever he rounded up a band of these subhumans. Maybe it was true; maybe it wasn't. Poking into that wasn't good for your career. If you poked too hard, it wasn't good for your own safety.

"Why is it military necessity for us to get shipped away and not for the Hungarians?" the chieftain asked after he got that turned into a language he could follow.

"Because the Hungarians are allies of the *Reich*," Stieglitz answered. "We trust their loyalty." *We do now, with Horthy out and Szalasi in. Szalasi has no more use for* Zigeuner *than the* Führer *does.*

"It doesn't matter whether we're loyal or not," the old man insisted. "We want nothing to do with this cursed war." He spewed out more of his own jargon. The rest of the *Zigeuner* bobbed their heads up and down in unison to show they wanted nothing to do with it, either.

"I'm sorry, but it's not as simple as you make it out to be. That's why I have my orders, and why I'll carry them out." Joseph Stieglitz let the truck driver translate that, then continued, "Besides, it's for your own safety. Some *Zigeuner* bands have stolen from German supplies. Some have spied and scouted for the Red Army. You can guess what happened to them after that."

"We would never do any such wicked things! By the Mother of God, I swear it!" The chieftain made the sign of the cross. After he told his chicken thieves and slatterns and brats why he did it, they crossed themselves, too.

The SS officer was not a Christian. The SS discouraged religious observances of any kind. He strongly doubted the *Zigeuner* were Christians, either. They were for themselves, first, last, and always. *Cockroaches and rats with—almost—human faces,* he thought, curling his lip in distaste.

"Look, tell him I didn't come here to argue with him," he said to the Hungarian truck driver. "Tell him I came here to relocate his band. I'll do that peacefully if I can. If I can't, I'll do it anyway. He won't like that so much. Make sure he understands how much he won't like it."

"Yes, sir. I'll do it, sir." The driver could have sounded no more obedient if he were a German. By the way he pointed at the submachine guns and rifles the SS men and Arrow Cross militiamen carried, he was making the point with gestures as well as with his jabbering.

Stieglitz watched the air leak out of the *Zigeuner* chieftain as he weighed his chances and found them bad. He deflated still more when he tried to choose between bad and worse. He didn't realize even yet that none of his choices was merely bad; they were all worse. The *Hauptsturmführer* didn't aim to enlighten him on that score. Soon enough, he'd find out for himself.

His lined, tanned face a mask of bitterness, he said something in his own lingo. A couple of the younger *Zigeuner* men started to gabble out protests. As the truck driver had before him, the chieftain pointed to the weapons the Germans and Hungarians held at the ready. He spoke again. Stieglitz didn't need to know what the words meant to get the drift. *What can we do? They'll murder us right here if we give them grief.*

He was right. The young bucks in the band could see it, too. They might not like it, but they could see it. They subsided.

Wearily, the mustachioed villain switched back to Magyar. "He says he and his people will go to the train with you, sir," the truck driver told Stieglitz. "He says he relies on your honor as a German officer that everything will work out the way you told him it would."

"*Mein Ehre heisst Treue.*" Joseph Stieglitz quoted the SS motto—*my honor is loyalty.* And it was. He was loyal unto death to the *Führer.* He was just as loyal to the *Reichsführer*-SS, the commander-in-chief of the Black Corps. To an unwashed old *Zigeuner?* That might be a different story.

By the look in the old man's eye, he suspected it was. *Untermensch* or not, he was nobody's fool. But when all your cards were bad, how many brains you had didn't win you even a pfennig.

"Tell him to tell his followers"—Stieglitz wouldn't call them people—"they can go back to the wagons and tents and take whatever they can carry in their hands. Tell them to get into the trucks then. And make sure you tell them that if anyone tries to jump out of a truck and run, it's the last stupid mistake he'll ever make."

"I'll take care of it, sir." The Hungarian turned that into his own language. The *Zigeuner* chieftain translated the translation. How long had this band lived in Hungary? Generations, by the look of things. Were there still some of these petty bandits who knew no Magyar? Evidently there were, though Stieglitz had trouble believing it. He shook his head. They were aliens. They didn't belong here. They didn't belong anywhere. The *Führer* was dead right about that. He usually was right.

"Come on," Stieglitz said sharply. "Let's get moving. We've wasted enough time here already." He noticed a couple of the Arrow Cross militiamen nodding before the driver translated. So they followed more German than they let on, did they? Somehow, the *Hauptsturmführer* found himself unsurprised. Hungary was like that. It remained Germany's ally, but nothing could make the Magyars enthusiastic about the struggle against subhumans and Bolshevism.

The *Zigeuner* went off to snag their movable property. They came back with coats and trousers and blankets and pots and pans. Stieglitz suspected they'd taken the chance to stash rings and chains and coins and bills where they wouldn't be so easy to find. He also suspected that would do them less good than they hoped.

One little girl cradled an ugly puppy in her arms. By the smiles she gave it, it wasn't ugly in her eyes. The Arrow Cross lieutenant sent Stieglitz a questioning glance. Stieglitz shrugged an answer. If carrying the dog kept the girl quiet, she was welcome to it as far as he was concerned.

The chieftain walked over to Stieglitz and the truck driver. His shirt looked lumpy. What all had he stashed under there? "Please, your Excellency," he said, "but what about our donkeys? What about our watchdogs?"

"I'm sorry, but they have to stay," Stieglitz replied. "The people in Nagylengyel will tend to them, I'm sure."

The people in Nagylengyel would shoot the dogs (Stieglitz was glad his men hadn't had to shoot any themselves) and either work the donkeys to death or butcher them for their meat. By the old *Zigeuner's* narrowed eyes and tight lips, he knew it as well as Stieglitz did. But he also knew he couldn't do anything about it. He turned his head to the side before spitting on the grass. "It will be as it must be," he said. "Everything will be as it must be."

That was true. It couldn't very well help being true. Stieglitz figured the scrawny *Zigeuner* couldn't tell the truth any other way.

"Everyone have everything you can take?" the *Hauptsturmführer* asked loudly. Also loudly, the truck driver turned his words into Hungarian. Stieglitz went on, "All right—into the trucks, then. We'll take you back to Zalaegerszeg."

Into the backs of the Opels they went. Men helped women climb up and hoisted children in. No one raised a fuss. Part of that was the *Zigeuner's* hopelessness of resisting the firepower the SS men and Arrow Cross militiamen had. And part of it, Joseph Stieglitz judged, was the fatalism of their kind, a fatalism spawned in ancient days far beyond the borders of Europe.

Stieglitz went back to the men he led. "We'll put *Kübelwagens* between trucks on the way up to Zalaegerszeg," he told them. "If anybody tries to jump out and run for it, you'll finish off the damn fool, right?" He waited for the driver to render that into Hungarian for the benefit of the Arrow Cross militiamen, then continued, "You fellows behind the wheel, look into your rearview mirrors every now and then. If the *Zigeuner* try to overpower a driver and hijack the truck, they won't get away with it."

As he got into his *Kübelwagen*'s front passenger seat, Klaus Pirckheimer hopped in on the other side. "Been easy so far, *Herr Hauptsturmführer*," Pirckheimer said as he fired up the sturdy little utility vehicle. "Let's hope it stays that way."

"Yes," Stieglitz agreed laconically. "Let's."

And it did stay easy all the way back to Zalaegerszeg. No *Zigeuner* sprang out and tried to dash for the roadside bushes. The *Untermenschen* didn't try coshing the Hungarian truck drivers. They didn't send any of their prettier women to seduce the drivers away from their duty, either. *Fatalism*, Stieglitz thought again.

Yes, everything was fine as long as the convoy stayed on the road. It all went sideways when the trucks and *Kübelwagens* came into town and made for the railroad station to unload the *Zigeuner* onto the waiting train. But traffic around the station had gone to the devil.

Another train, this one completely unexpected (at least as far as Joseph Stieglitz was concerned), had come into Zalaegerszeg while he was out on the roundup. The new arrival was full of *Wehrmacht* troops bound for eastern Hungary and the fight against the Red Army. But the driver of the train that would haul the *Zigeuner* up into Poland had refused to clear the track to let the German soldiers head for the front.

That left the major in charge of the held-up regiment hopping mad. Seeing they weren't going anywhere right away, some of his men had got off to rubberneck or grab something to eat or a glass of beer. The major took out his fury on Stieglitz. "I'll be hours herding everybody back into place!" he shouted. "Some of these bastards will find a way to get left behind, too—see if they don't. *Gott im Himmel!* How are we supposed to win the war if we can't get to where we need to be when we need to be there?"

"I'm very sorry, my dear fellow." Stieglitz's tone gave his words the lie. "I must remind you, though, that SS transports have priority over all other rail traffic. That includes troop movements. So the train driver's done the right thing. We might have made other arrangements if anybody in Szombathely telephoned or wired to tell us you were on the way. But no one did. And so . . ." He shrugged.

The *Wehrmacht* major exhaled angrily. "We're fighting the Russians, you know."

"We're fighting the *Zigeuner*, too. I presume you *have* read the *Führer*'s book and all he has to say about them?" Stieglitz's voice, silky with menace, presumed no such thing. But *he'd* gone all the way through the hefty volume—gone through it two or three times, in fact. He knew exactly what it said about enemies of the *Reich*.

"They're less likely to shoot us or blow us up than the Red Army is." But the *Wehrmacht* officer knew he was fighting a losing battle here. He threw his hands in the air. "All right. All *right*, dammit! Would your most gracious Majesty please be kind enough to let me know when my men can proceed to their little tea party with the Ivans?"

Had Joseph Stieglitz been a vindictive man, he could have made the younger major pay for that. But he wasn't. He was just a fellow trying to do the job his superiors had given him. "I'm not trying to hold you up," he said—fighting the Russians, after all, was its own punishment. "We're all in the same struggle, you know."

"Yes, and the way things are going right now, we're all losing it." The *Wehrmacht* major had to be either a fine soldier or a hell of a lucky man. No ordinary jerk could have won the rank he had without learning how to put a governor on his tongue. Shaking his head, he clumped away.

Stieglitz let him go. It wasn't that he was wrong, only that he was impolitic. The *Hauptsturmführer* went back to his own command. "Let's get them onto the train," he said. "The sooner they're on, the sooner they're gone, the sooner the soldiers can head east."

The *Wehrmacht* major seemed eager to get into the fight against the Red Army. How many of the troops he led shared his eagerness? Not so very many, not if Stieglitz was any judge. German soldiers commonly wanted to avoid the Eastern Front, not to go there. But, these days, not so many got what they wanted. And the Eastern Front was coming to them.

Pretty soon, we won't be fighting the Russians in Hungary and Poland. We'll be fighting them in Germany. As he always did when that thought floated to the surface of his mind, Stieglitz shoved it under again. However many times he tried to drown it, though, it kept popping up.

The transport train sat waiting, a thin plume of steam and smoke rising from the stack. All the cars behind the locomotive and its tender were cattle cars. Some already had their doors barred and secured. Others were ready for more *Zigeuner.*

When the band Stieglitz had rounded up came out of the trucks, their chieftain took a long look at the train. Arrow Cross militiamen opened one of the cattle cars and grinned in mocking invitation as they waved the *Zigeuner* towards it. Instead of climbing in, the chieftain ambled over to Stieglitz. "So much for your honor," he said in pretty good German.

That didn't altogether astonish the *Hauptsturmführer.* "We all do what we're required to do," he said.

"Yes, I know." With immense dignity, the old man walked to the cattle car and climbed in. The rest of the band followed him. As they had with the trucks, men helped women and children board. The dark little girl with the puppy hesitated for a moment in front of the cattle car. Then she put the dog down on the gravel. It didn't want to leave. She drew back her leg and kicked it in the ribs. It ran off, yipping in pain and shock. The girl clambered into the car without help from anyone.

She'd made the right choice. If the dog went with her, it had no future at all. Now someone in Zalaegerszeg might give it a home. Or if nobody did, it might eke out a living by guile and theft, the way the *Zigeuner* had for so many centuries.

Not for much longer, though, Stieglitz thought. The *Führer* had ordered Europe purified of *Zigeuner* and Bolsheviks and homosexuals and other such riffraff. The Bolsheviks had an unfortunate tendency to shoot back. The others, though . . . The others were sand in the tide of history, and the tide was going out.

As soon as the last short-pants boy went into the cattle car, the *Hauptsturmführer* gestured sharply at the Arrow Cross militiamen standing in front of the door. They slid it shut. The bar slammed down into the steel **L** that secured it. Chains and padlocks made sure no one would defeat it from the inside.

Stieglitz walked up to the locomotive. The engine driver was swigging from a bottle of slivovitz or vodka. When he spotted Stieglitz, he quickly made the bottle disappear. Stieglitz wouldn't have called him on it. He'd seen the like plenty of times. Some people needed numbing before they could do what they were required to do.

"They're here. They're loaded and secured. You can take them away," Stieglitz said.

"*Zu Befehl, mein Herr.*" The engine driver didn't sound thick. When you had enough practice, you didn't get sloppy drunk the way someone new to the sauce would. You didn't show it. You soaked up the hooch and went on about your business.

The whistle screamed, once, twice, three times. The world needed to know the train was leaving the station. Smoke belched from the locomotive's stack. The drive wheels began to turn, ponderously slow at first but then faster and faster. Away went the train. Away went the *Zigeuner*. Except through tiny spaces between the planks of the cattle car, they wouldn't see daylight again till they got to Poland. After they got there, they probably wouldn't see it for long.

With the cork that had plugged his way east gone, the *Wehrmacht* major started chivvying his men back to the troop train. No, they weren't so eager to go as he was to get them going. Junior officers and noncoms gave the regimental CO what help they could.

So did the chaplains. In their purple-piped frock coats, they stood out from the soldiers. They weren't supposed to carry weapons, but the Lutheran minister wore a holstered pistol on his hip. The world was a rougher, crueler place than the striped-pants gentlemen who made rules like that could imagine.

When one of the chaplains turned and happened to catch his eye, Stieglitz waved to him. He would have had trouble saying why. Maybe the way the little *Zigeuner* girl put down her puppy was still on his mind. Maybe it was that the chaplain followed the faith the *Hauptsturmführer*'d been raised in. Maybe it was all of that. Or maybe not. Maybe it was just a spur-of-the-moment thing.

Whatever it was, the *Feldrabbiner* walked up to Stieglitz. Where his Catholic and Protestant counterparts wore two different versions of the cross on a chain around their necks, he had a Star of David. Another one replaced a cross on his officer's cap. Unique among German servicemen, he was allowed to have a beard.

"Something I can do for you?" he asked, his voice friendly, his accent Bavarian.

"I don't even know." Joseph Stieglitz wished he'd kept his damn hand at his side. "Those *Zigeuner*—" he started, and then broke off. He didn't know what he wanted to say. He didn't know if he wanted to say anything.

"That's a hard business, all right." The *Feldrabbiner* studied him with shrewd eyes. "You'll tell me if I'm wrong, but I'd say you also come from a family of Germans of the Mosaic faith."

That *also* invited Stieglitz back into something he'd invited himself out of long before he joined the SS. It was nothing he much wanted to return to. Nevertheless, he couldn't bring himself to lie. "Well, what if I am?" he said harshly.

"If you are, *Herr Hauptsturmführer*, I suggest you do what I do every day," the *Feldrabbiner* said. "Count your blessings."

"Excuse me?" Stieglitz said, in lieu of something like *That's fine for a clergyman, but not for an SS officer.*

The *Feldrabbiner* understood him whether he said it out loud or not. "Count your blessings," the man repeated. "Some Englishman is supposed to have said, 'There but for the grace of God go I.' I often think that when I see *Zigeuner* getting on those trains."

Stieglitz wished he hadn't waved to the *Feldrabbiner.* "I'm afraid I don't follow you," he aid, and began to turn away.

But the man with the frock coat and the Star of David didn't let him escape so easily. "When you're a Jew, when you remember you're a Jew, you also have to re-member such things can happen to you, too."

"Oh, *Quatsch!*" Stieglitz said.

"It isn't rubbish," the *Feldrabbiner* insisted. "Plenty of people don't like us. Let's not mince words. Plenty of people hate us. If the *Führer* hadn't seen what the *Zigeuner* were like when he fought in the east during the last war, if he hadn't al-ready despised the Russians and seen how they mistreated the Jews in the Austro-Hungarian provinces they overran . . . *Herr Hauptsturmführer,* you might have boarded that train yourself instead of putting them on it."

"You are a man of the cloth. I make allowances for that. But if you say one more word along those lines, I will give you to the *Sicherheitsdienst,*" Stieglitz said, his voice colder than any blizzard on the Eatern Front. "I am a good German, and what-ever religion my grandparents held has nothing to do with it. I follow the *Führer's* orders the way any other good German would. Since you wear the uniform, *mein Herr,* you had better do the same."

If he hadn't put the fear of God in the *Feldrabbiner,* he had put the beard of the SD in him. That would do. The man gulped. He licked his lips. "I mean nothing by it, of course," he said quickly. "Just, uh, thinking on how things might have been." He showed far more alarm than the wicked old *Zigeuner* chieftain had.

"Of course." Stieglitz freighted the words with all the scorn he could. When he turned this time, the *Feldrabbiner* didn't bother him. He walked away, grubbing in his pocket for a pack of cigarettes.

The Proving Ground

ALEC NEVALA-LEE

No matter how carefully you plan, nature is always full of surprises, and sometimes those surprises come at you from a direction you'd least expect. . . .

Alec Nevala-Lee's nonfiction book Astounding: John W. Campbell, Isaac Asimov, Robert A. Heinlein, L. Ron Hubbard, and the Golden Age of Science Fiction *will be released by Dey Street Books, an imprint of Harper-Collins, on August 14, 2018. His novels include* The Icon Thief, City of Exiles, *and* Eternal Empire, *and his stories have appeared in* Analog Science Fiction and Fact, Lightspeed, *and* The Year's Best Science Fiction. *He lives with his wife and daughter in Oak Park, Illinois, and he blogs daily at www.nevalalee.com.*

> Perhaps . . . a message comes to the birds in autumn, like a warning. Winter is coming. Many of them will perish. And like people who, apprehensive of death before their time, drive themselves to work or folly, the birds do likewise; tomorrow we shall die.
> —*Daphne du Maurier*, "The Birds"

I.

Haley Kabua was clinging to the top of a wind tower when she saw the first bird. She had clipped her lanyard, which was attached by a strap to the back of her safety harness, to a strut on the lattice directly beneath the huge fiberglass rotors. As she braced her bare feet on the scaffold, thirty precarious meters above the beach, she knew without looking that the men on the sand below had halted to watch her climb. Only a few hours of daylight remained, but she forced herself not to hurry, knowing that any mistake she made might be her last.

A pair of thick slings had been hitched to separate legs of the tower, about a third of the way down from the top. Each one ran to the closed hook on the boom of the crane behind her, which had raised the tower into place earlier that afternoon. Both of the chokers had to be released by hand. Reaching up, she unhooked the nearest shackle, letting the loosened sling hang down, and she was about to work her way around to the other when she realized that she was not alone.

Haley tilted back her construction worker's hat to get a better look at the bird, which was perched on the tail of the turbine. It was a tern, about the length of her forearm, with spotless white plumage and a black eye encircled by a ring of dark feathers that made it seem larger. At the moment, it was clinging to the fin of the tail section with its small blue feet, and it seemed to be staring directly at her, as if it had flown up to investigate this unexpected incursion.

She glanced around. Along the eastern end of the island, six other wind towers were spaced about a hundred meters apart, their new blades shining. A seventh tower lay on the sand, where the workers had just finished bolting its sections together. There were no other birds in sight. Haley was perfectly aware that no terns had nested on Enyu in years, and the wind tower was well above the height at which they preferred to fly. And yet here it was.

Haley waved at it. "Hey, get lost. You don't want to be around when this starts up."

The bird tilted its head to one side. Haley returned her attention to the remaining choker on the scaffold. "Guess you like to live dangerously. Well, don't say I didn't warn you."

She inched around to the second sling, the retractable strap on her harness automatically unspooling. Now she was facing toward the atoll, which formed a horseshoe, thirty kilometers across, around the central lagoon. From where she stood at the southeast, she could see the full line of the reef, walkable when the tide was low, that stretched to the islet to the north, along with the seastead taking shape five hundred meters to its leeward side.

Haley paused to drink it all in. The atoll provided few natural vantage points, with its highest elevation only ten meters above low tide, so she rarely had a chance to study the entire structure at once. Seeing it now, from as high above the islet as she would ever be, she felt the sight cut through her exhaustion. It was easy to grow obsessed by details while overlooking the larger picture, she thought, and it was that kind of blindness that had led them to this crisis in the first place.

The seastead had not been designed for beauty, but it was beautiful nonetheless, with the kind of elegance that emerged as a logical conclusion of functionality and constraint. It consisted of a modular network of caissons floating on the surface of the water, with each concrete platform measuring fifty meters to a side. The colony had been designed to expand gradually. One day, there would be more, but now there were only five, a quincunx of four squares joined by a grid of covered walkways and flexible connections to the central hub.

Each platform ascended in a series of smaller terraces, stepped like a ziggurat, with the highest level of the hub rising twenty meters above the lagoon. Their roofs had a tessellated look, with photovoltaic panels alternating with surfaces for catching rain. Half of the caisson facing her was devoted to a hydroponic greenhouse, with a floating dock on the adjacent platform, and the water on the sheltered side was covered in a grid of fish pens and bioreactors, which reminded her of the rows of a green quilt that had been flung across the sea.

It was a work in progress, and it always looked to her as if someone had left an unfinished mosaic on the face of the ocean, spare tesserae and all. Haley, who had spent most of the last three years on the atoll trying to solve problems at sea level, was struck by how fragile it seemed from above, and as she gazed at the scattered human figures visible below, she felt shaken back into action. They had only four working hours left, and there was still one more turbine to go.

Haley was reaching for the second choker when something struck the top of her hat. At first, she thought that a piece of the turbine had come loose, but when she looked up, all she saw was that the bird that had been perching on the tail section was no longer there.

She heard the sound of wings. In the corner of her eye, there was a flash of white, and then the tern was beating against the back of her neck. She pivoted around, releasing one hand from the scaffold, and tried to bat it away. Instead, she felt a series of sharp pecks as it attacked her shoulders and arms, its feet scrabbling for purchase on the front of her shirt.

The bird drew blood again and went for her eyes. As she attempted to duck out of its path, her foot slipped. She grabbed for the strut above her head and missed. An instant later, she was toppling back, the impossibly blue sky above the rotors filling her field of vision, and all other thoughts vanished, replaced by the logic of gravity. She tried to correct herself, failed, and fell.

Her lanyard caught her. With a jerk, the strap grew taut, the harness seizing her painfully around the armpits as she smacked against the side of the tower. Her hat came off her head. For an instant, the clip was only thing holding her in place, and as she heard the metal straining, vividly picturing what would happen if it broke, her hand groped back of its own accord and closed around one of the struts.

Haley found a toehold, dimly aware of the shouts coming from below. Ignoring them, she regained her footing, her heart juddering, and saw the tern fly off toward the water. Blood was trickling down her arms from five or six shallow cuts where the bird had broken the skin.

Someone was calling to her. It was Giff, one of the other colonists, his hands cupped around his mouth. "You okay?"

She dared a look down. The men had gathered at the foot of the tower, their dark faces craning upward. As her pulse slowed, she saw two unfamiliar figures standing nearby. They were visitors, members of the research team that had been surveying the atoll from offshore for most of the last three months, and her fear gave way to a sudden irritation that they had witnessed her moment of weakness. She found her voice. "I'm fine. Just give me a minute."

Haley took another second to collect herself, then turned slowly around until she was facing the tower again. Extending a hand, she undid the final choker, allowing the hoisting line on the crane to hang free. She checked herself to see if she was ready to come down in a dignified fashion, and she found that she was. Then she descended, hand over hand, securing her lanyards alternately as she went. The bird that had attacked her was nowhere in sight.

A second later, she was on the sand. As she unclipped the safety strap, Giff came up with her hat. "I've never seen anything like that."

"It was nothing." Haley plucked the hat from his outstretched hand. Giff was in his early twenties, a full decade younger than she was, and although they had been working together on this project for many weeks, she had begun to sense only recently that his interest in her was more than strictly professional. She forced herself to speak sharply. "We don't have to stop. I'll just be a second. Get over to the last tower and I'll meet you there."

Giff looked as if he wanted to say something more, but in the end, he only left along with the others, who had briefly paused to watch as she came down. Haley made sure that they were all on their way, then pulled off her harness, letting it fall to the ground by the tower.

It was a hundred paces to the shore. Haley knelt in the surf to rinse her cuts, the salt stinging, and was about to head back when she heard a voice with a Dutch accent. "You could probably use this."

Haley turned just in time to catch the nylon pouch of a medical kit. The man who had tossed it was standing a few steps away. It was one of the two visitors who had come over to observe, and when he smiled, the look that he gave her was almost shy. "In case of infection, you know."

"Thanks," Haley said. She brought the kit over to the shaded part of the beach where the crew had left its gear. The man followed without speaking, keeping at arm's length at all times. He was about her age, tall and bearded, with light blue eyes and a hint of sunburn. His companion, a woman in her late forties, maintained her distance, standing at the point where the sand gave way to scrub.

Haley sat down, grateful to see that the visitor did not seem inclined to volunteer further assistance. As she opened the kit, he motioned toward the spot beside her. "Mind if I join you?"

"Be my guest." She tore open an antiseptic swab with her teeth. "You must be Visser. Or at least that's what I've heard them call you."

"I'm sure they have other names for me," Visser said. "My friends call me Stefan. You must be Haley Kabua. I'm surprised it's taken us this long to meet. My colleagues and I have heard a lot about you." He nodded at the tower. "You ever have problems with birds before?"

Haley wound a length of gauze around her arm. His full name struck her as familiar, but she wasn't sure from where. "Not really. The terns don't nest here. That's why we chose it for the wind farm."

"I can see why." Visser sat on the sand. "What do you think happened up there?"

She taped a dressing in place. "Maybe they don't like us nosing in their business."

Haley watched for his reaction. She sensed a spark of attraction here, although she was hardly at her best, her hair sweaty and matted, her jeans cut off below the knees. As for Visser, she recognized the type from the tourists who had come out to the atoll in the years before the dive operation shut down. Everything about him spoke of healthy swims, morning runs, and exercise instead of real labor. She returned the kit. "I have to get back to work. If you're not too busy, you can come."

She saw that the offer surprised him, and she wondered if he understood it. All that anyone knew about his research team was that it was connected in some undefined way to the Deventer Group, the corporation that was helping to finance the seastead, and she had learned a long time ago that if you didn't know what someone else was doing, it was best to keep them close until you did. Visser glanced at his colleague. "Let me talk to Jansen."

Haley waited as he went over to his companion, who had been visibly sizing her up. Jansen cut a more interesting figure than Visser, with the look of a woman who had spent much of her life outdoors, her blond hair bleached nearly white. After they had conferred, Visser approached again. "You have me for two hours. Our boat is by Romurikku. We'll take the dinghy back when we're done."

Looking over at Jansen, Haley saw that she was studying the turbines, marking something down on a folded map. She indicated the workers. "You can pitch in. Hope you're good with your hands."

They headed together for the last tower, which lay on the coral sand near the airstrip a hundred meters away. As she drew closer, Haley saw that the men were connecting the guy cables and unrolling them along the ground. Behind them, a diesel engine roared to life, and the construction crane began to crawl slowly along the beach. It was a chain-driven relic without a cab, leaving the driver exposed on a swivel seat. Visser whistled. "That's quite the antique."

"It's tougher than it looks," Haley said. "There's a lot of stuff in the supply outbuildings. Trucks, milling machines, backhoes, forklifts. Most of it isn't usable. The salt water wastes the steel. But we were able to refit some of it. This is a shoestring operation, so it came in handy. We have to make do with what we have. When I first got here, it was a real mess."

Visser appeared to latch onto this last detail. "You weren't born on the islands?"

"Springdale, Arkansas. Ever been there?" When he shook his head, she gestured for him to follow. "You aren't missing much. A lot of Marshallese live there. My parents worked at the poultry plant. Here, help me with this."

Haley showed him the armored electrical cable. Visser took up position beside her as she fed it through the center of the lattices, pacing down the length of the tower. "What brought you all the way out here?"

"I didn't feel like killing chickens," Haley said. "At least with wind turbines, you get to slaughter the birds one at a time."

Visser cracked a smile. As she hooked the cable to the disconnect switch at the tower's base, he assisted as necessary, listening to her instructions and coming forward only when asked. Haley had positioned herself to keep an eye on Jansen, who was taking photographs of the row of turbines. "Your friend can come over if she likes. She seems interested."

"We're doing a survey of the atoll. Infrastructure plays a big role, especially this close to the reef." Visser watched as the crane inched into place. "I wanted to ask about that. These wind towers weren't part of the original proposal. Someone took money out of the budget to pay for them. Why put them up at all?"

Haley noticed that Giff was doing a bad job of pretending not to eavesdrop. "Are you asking for yourself, or as an employee of Deventer?"

"I'm not an employee. Deventer pays me as a consultant. It's just us two talking."

Looking at his handsome, privileged face, Haley saw that he had no idea of what she had sacrificed to get the towers, or what they really represented. "We need power. Wind happens to be a good way to generate it."

"But the islanders did fine without wind power before. Even over on Majuro."

"I know. It's silly, right?" Haley watched as the crane eased itself into line with the concrete base on which the tower would be fixed. "We could just run everything on generators. Ship in the diesel. It's not like we don't have the money. That's why we're here in the first place. It qualifies us for reparations. A trust fund. They could probably spare some of it to keep the lights on." She continued to study the crane. "I've told you where I'm from. What about you?"

"You probably haven't heard of it," Visser said. "A charming city called Leiden."

"That's where Rembrandt was born, isn't it?" Haley deflected his curious look. "You have dikes there?"

Visser seemed to sense where she was going with this. "Of course. Otherwise—"

"—the sea would swallow you up," Haley finished. "But why not just pack it in? Pull up stakes and join the Germans. It would be easier."

Visser silently acknowledged her point. Haley turned back to the tower. "Well, that's my answer, too. You care about your independence. So do we. I didn't come here for a handout. Relying on the outside is the kind of thinking that got us into this predicament. You, me, and everyone."

"I can't argue with that," Visser said. "Whoever arranged to put up these towers must have wanted to make a statement."

"You may be onto something there." Haley turned away. "The towers were my idea."

Leaving him on that line, she went to the crane, which had parked itself downwind from the tower. Visser watched as the work crew cinched a strap a third of the way down the scaffold, then lifted one end until it was the height of a man's chest. As the workers brought timbers to prop it up, Haley signaled to Visser. "You can give them a hand, if you like."

Visser pitched in as they raised the top of the tower, then stood back as the crane was unhooked and rigged to the powerhead. They hoisted it up, the men guiding it into position and bolting it into place. Haley had wanted to show Visser how professional they were, and she was gratified by how efficient the process had become, with most of the work carried out without speaking.

Once the electrical connections had been made, she waited as the men mounted the fiberglass blades one at a time. When they were finished, she waved at the driver of the crane, a younger colonist named Amata. "Ready?"

Amata grinned. As the crane engaged, lifting the tower upright, the men took up places on all sides, using the guy wires as tethers as they maneuvered it to the base pad. Haley ended up standing next to Giff. Grasping the base section to align it with the pier, Giff shot a look at Visser, who was watching from a safe distance, and spoke in Marshallese. "What did he want?"

Haley detected a hint of jealousy. She held the legs of the tower as the crane lowered it onto its pin. "You know the type. He can't believe we can do anything on our own. So keep your mind on your work."

Giff only turned back to the scaffold. As soon as it was in place, the workers ran the guy lines to turnbuckles that had been anchored deep in the sand. Haley locked each one with clips as the men pulled the wires taut. Using a rusted transit level on a tripod, Giff checked to make sure that the tower was as close to vertical as possible, signaling to the others to tighten or loosen the guys accordingly. When they were done, all that remained was for someone to climb the scaffold and release the rigging. Haley saw the others looking at her. "I'll do it."

Haley put on the safety harness. For a second, she paused at the base of the tower, aware that the men were watching, and then she reached up to clip a lanyard onto the first strut.

She climbed carefully, as always, going up one rung at a time. Whenever she reached the lanyard, she unclipped it and attached a second one higher up, so that she always had at least one line in place. It was very quiet, with no sign of birds, and the solitude gave her time to think.

As she ascended the tower, she thought back to what Visser had said, along with the assumptions behind it. None of this, he had implied, was necessary. The seastead didn't need wind power or fish farms. All it needed was a handful of caretakers, far fewer than the hundred colonists who currently resided here. The islanders had relied on imports for their food and fuel for years. And if the reparations paid off as they all hoped they would, there would be plenty of money.

Yet she wanted to give them more. They had a chance to make something here that could sustain itself, and while it might not matter to the rest of the world, it mattered a hell of a lot to her. She knew that this sense of urgency had alienated her from many of those around her, even the ones most inclined to take her seriously. But she could never shake the feeling that they were running out of time.

She made it to the level of the tower where the sling was attached. Clipping her lanyard to the strut above her head, she looked around. She did not see any birds on the islet, although a mingled flock of terns and noddies was feeding offshore, a kilometer away from the reef.

Haley took in the view again, the wind blowing in her hair, knowing that it would be for the last time in a while. Looking past the seastead at the open ocean, she forced herself to see how it would look in a hundred years. Water levels across the globe were projected to rise one full meter by the end of the century, but it would not be evenly distributed. It would be highest here, in the equatorial Pacific, and it would erase whatever was left of the Marshall Islands.

But not entirely. The atoll had an average elevation of two meters, and the estimated increase in sea level meant that the high tide would sweep over the few spots of land that survived. If they wanted to remain a country, at least in the eyes of the courts that would award reparations from developed nations to regions destroyed by climate change, they had to make some new real estate of their own. Seen in the right light, it was almost comical. A country could be compensated for the loss of its territory, but without any land, it would not be considered a country.

Hence the artificial island. Turning back to the seastead, Haley reminded herself that it was only a beginning. They had a few decades to set up wave turbines, to make the bases of the wind towers watertight, to build up fish farms and bioreactors until they could live here indefinitely on their own, no matter what happened elsewhere. It had all been born of trial and error, and they had made big mistakes already. But as she looked out at the lagoon, reflecting on what else lay sunk below its surface, she knew that she could not trust anyone except for herself.

Haley detached the chokers without any trouble and climbed down again. Looking around at the others, she knew that the rest could wait until tomorrow, or even later. But when she saw that Jansen had joined them to observe, standing silently alongside Visser, she found that she wanted to do it when the visitors would see it. "Let's turn them on now."

There was a murmur of excitement. As the workers grounded the last tower, driving the copper rods deep into the ground, Haley went to the shed that had been erected at the center of the wind farm. The inverters were already in place, and once the system checks were done, she gave the order to proceed.

Giff ran down the beach, darting from one tower to another to turn on the switches, as a second worker did the same with the turbines on the other end. Haley kept her eye on the bank of inverters. As the rotors high above began to turn, the screens blinked to life one by one.

A cheer went up from the work crew. As the men slapped one another's backs, Haley continued to watch the towers. When they caught the trade winds, the displays on the inverters began to update rapidly as the output wattage increased. She allowed herself a flicker of pride, and when she looked at Visser, she saw that he got the message. They had done all this themselves. Deventer might have provided some of the resources, in exchange for a showpiece project and a percentage of the reparations to come, but it had played no part where it counted.

An instant later, Visser's expression darkened. Turning to follow his eyes, Haley saw a single white tern circling far overhead.

She did not know if it was the same one she had seen before. All she knew was that it was heading directly toward one of the turbines, and before she could react, it had flown straight into the rotors.

Haley heard a thud as the bird collided with a blade. She watched, unbelieving, as it fell to the ground in a tight spiral, like a maple seed, and struck the sand at the base of the tower.

She ran to it, vaguely aware of Visser at her side, and looked down at its broken body. It had died at once. Haley was still staring at it, feeling as if she were dreaming, when she heard more shouts.

Looking up, she saw a flock of at least thirty birds coming their way. They were flying unusually high, at the level of the turbines, and they were moving in a line that would bring them directly into the path of the towers.

Haley watched, rooted to the spot, as the flock hit the wind farm. It missed the first turbine entirely, but when it reached the second, there was another series of thumps as more terns hit the rotors. If it hadn't been so awful, she would have laughed. As the bodies of the dead birds plummeted, the rest flew on, and before she could say a word, they had flown along the entire line. At every turbine, more terns fell. A few survivors made it to the end, but within seconds, she had lost sight of them in the trees at the heart of the islet.

"Turn it off," Haley said. Giff sprinted away without being asked twice, hitting the disconnect switch at the nearest tower before racing along to the next. The others joined him, leaving her alone with Visser. Haley watched as the rotor slowed to a stop overhead, its blades speckled with fresh blood. Then she turned to the north, looking along the row of towers as each one came to a halt, stretching from where she stood to the reef that led to Bikini.

II.

"Let me see if I understand," Ruben DeBrum said. "The birds were flying far above their customary altitude. They hit the first turbine and kept going. And they flew in a line that took them across the whole wind farm. As if they were doing it deliberately. Or as if they were being drawn to it."

Haley reminded herself to remain calm. "It's too soon to jump to conclusions. Birds can be attracted to wind towers as a place to perch or scan for prey, but that doesn't seem to be the case here. Bugs can swarm around turbines, which draws birds that eat insects, but that doesn't include terns. And I've found studies of how electromagnetic or auditory fields generated by wind power can attract bats. But not birds. At least not that I've seen so far."

Ruben shifted in his chair. It was early the following morning. The councilman for the Bikini district had the girth and the easy grin of a born politician, but he was not smiling now. He had played no role in the construction of the seastead, living back on Majuro with what remained of the government of the Marshall Islands, and he had moved here only a few months ago, once it had become clear that the colonists were serious. "In other words, we have no idea. I'm sorry to say it, but we have to halt the project until we can evaluate the situation. Or find a more qualified expert."

Haley bit back what she wanted to say. They were seated in the common area on the uppermost level of the central caisson, along with twenty other colonists. Haley had asked for the meeting to be public, hoping that it would work in her favor, but when she looked at the crowd, it struck her as a mixed bag. Some of the men and women here believed in everything that the seastead represented, but others had wound up at the colony because they had nowhere else to go, and she did not think that she could count on their support.

The common room stood twenty meters above the base of the platform, high enough to be safe from the largest of rogue waves. On Sundays, it doubled as a chapel, with its windows of safety glass affording a pleasant view of the atoll. It had been one of the first areas to be furnished, in part with an eye on renting the space to wealthy vacationers, and the result had the look of an anonymous resort lounge. She saw that the councilman was waiting for her response. "We checked the turbines. There's no damage. If anything, I'm more concerned about the birds."

"So are we." Ruben glanced at Visser. "Deventer is sensitive to perceptions of environmental impact. If we're killing birds here, it looks bad. This is all starting to look like a mistake. We rushed to build the towers too quickly."

Haley saw that he was showing off for the two visitors, who had taken up position at the rear of the room. Going forward, she unrolled a map on the conference table, holding its edges down with the shells that had been left there as a centerpiece. Across from her hung a traditional stick chart, with coconut fibers knotted together to represent ocean well patterns. On the opposite wall, where Visser and Jansen were standing, there was a framed artist's rendition of the finished seastead, a dream on paper with no sense of the work required to make it a reality.

She pointed to the map. "These are the nesting grounds. There are big bird rookeries on the uninhabited islets to the north and southeast. You see thousands of terns and noddies there, along with herons and frigatebirds. But there aren't any birds on Bikini or Enyu. They've steered clear ever since the islets were built up for the nuclear tests in the fifties. Even after the people left, the cats and the rats stayed behind. And we checked the nesting sites and flight patterns before we began to build. There are fewer birds here than anywhere else on the atoll."

"But you haven't checked again recently. Birds can move, I imagine. A colony might have arisen since you last surveyed it. Or maybe you overlooked it the first time around." Ruben leaned back in his seat. "But it might be for the best. A wind farm could be put to better use elsewhere, like Majuro. They still have a population of fifty thousand. I'm not alone in thinking that wind power might be more valuable there, rather than for a handful of colonists. Doesn't that seem reasonable?"

"Yes. All too reasonable." Haley removed the shells from the map, which sprang shut. "I'd like to survey the island one more time before we come to a decision. Giff and I can cover most of it in a day, and I've already asked for a drone to do a flyover. If there's a nesting ground, we can evaluate our options. We could always move the towers to Bikini. The equipment is already here. I just want to find a solution that makes sense for us and the birds."

"The birds will be gone in a hundred years, no matter what we do," Ruben said mildly. "We won't. If we're lucky."

Haley glanced around and saw that the meeting was over. Rolling up her map, she made her way to the door, not looking at Visser or Jansen, and headed stonily outside before anyone else could speak. When Giff caught up with her in the corridor, she told him to meet her at the boat in twenty minutes. She waited until he had left, wanting to be alone, and then moved on.

After emerging into the sunshine of the terrace, she descended the open stairs to the lowest level of the caisson. As always, it felt like exactly walking on land, although the platform was floating on the surface, tethered to the bed of the lagoon at twelve separate anchor points.

Haley often found herself thinking of the early days, when the first set of platforms was assembled on Bikini. The initial crew had consisted of only twelve volunteers, residing in the decaying resort rooms on the beach, along with a supervisor from the Deventer Group. The interlocking slabs that made up the caissons, with their alternating layers of concrete and polystyrene, were based on the company's patents, and early on, it had been assumed that Deventer would also oversee the construction. In fact, the islanders had been determined to do everything on their own, and before long, the company man had been safely back on a plane to the Netherlands.

There was no question that they had made mistakes. They had tried mixing their own concrete with local coral sand, only to find that it was too coarse for binding, and setting up the molding plant for the polystyrene had taken months. Once finished, the slabs had to be slid into the water, fitted together, and towed into position, and several had been damaged or lost in the process. But the result was a growing seastead that could survive a hurricane or rise with the worst of the waves, even if the real threat, as Haley had come to understand, lay in the human factor.

She moved along the encircling walkway and headed for a covered bridge that led to an outer platform. Going to her quarters, which were bare except for a bed, a laptop, and a shelf of books, she retrieved the equipment she needed. Then she continued on to the next caisson, moving counterclockwise around the seastead until she reached the greenhouse.

Manita Jacklick was checking the hydroponic tanks in which the colonists were learning to grow cucumbers, chives, and watercress. As Haley entered, Manita glanced up. "How did it go?"

"I'm glad you weren't there," Haley said. "Ruben sawed me off at the knees."

"He needs you more than you'll ever need him." Manita set down her tablet. The biologist was another transplant from the outside world, training the colonists to establish pilot systems for hydroponics, aquaculture, and bioreactors. Like the wind turbines, they were less a matter of practical necessity than part of a larger vision, a strategy for the seastead to sustain itself with greater independence than the islanders here had known in decades. "Let's take a walk."

Haley followed her outside. She had often sensed that Manita was driven as much by aesthetic concerns as by more pragmatic considerations. The bioreactors had been designed to grow spirulina and other algae for food and biodiesel, but they had also a peculiar beauty, the plastic membranes of wastewater floating on the water like a line of pearls, lined on the inside with bluish paste. Even the pens of seaweed, shellfish, and tilapia, crossbred for resistance to ocean acidification, were lovely in their way, and it was this combination of attention to detail and concern for the whole that made Manita such a valuable ally.

As they crossed over to the dock, Haley told her about the meeting. "I can't go back to Ruben without an explanation. Maybe there's a lack of food offshore, and the birds are moving inland—"

"That's not what I'm seeing," Manita said. "If anything, there are more fish in the water than ever. The birds aren't starving. But I can take a look after I check the sampling stations. Did you keep any snarge for me?"

"It's in a fridge in the central galley. Twelve birds in all. I bagged them separately."

"Hope you labeled them, too. I'd rather not see them get served up for lunch." They arrived at the floating dock at the edge of the adjoining platform, at which five boats were moored. Giff was there already, waiting for her in the nearest dinghy. As the women approached, he rose, and Haley was about to speak when she saw something pass across his face.

She turned to see Visser coming in her direction. Halting a few steps away, he pointed to a boat with an electric motor berthed at a distance from the rest. "That one's ours. She's fast. You can use her. I'm sorry about what I said yesterday. And if it's not a problem, I'd like to join you."

Haley studied his expression, which revealed nothing but a genuine desire to help, as well as an assumption that they were united by concerns that the others could not understand. "Why?"

"I'll be honest," Visser said. "I want to know what's happening here, too. We're surveying the atoll. If the geography is changing, the birds can be the first to sense it. And if they're resettling for a reason, it matters to me."

Haley took a moment to respond. She sensed again that there was an unspoken aspect to Visser's interest in her, and it had nothing to do with her more obvious charms. Last night, she had spent the better part of an hour looking into him online, and what she had found only raised additional questions. Glancing at Giff, she observed that he did not seem particularly happy about the arrangement, but she could think of no good reason to decline. "Come on, then."

A few minutes later, after transferring their gear to Visser's boat, they were heading out into the lagoon. Giff had remained silent, and Haley hoped that there wouldn't be trouble between the men. To head off any further tension, she had volunteered to take the helm herself, and now she was steering away from the seastead, heading south toward Enyu.

Halfway there, she decided to change course, departing from the most direct line to follow a long curve toward the islet. Up ahead, an orange mooring ball bobbed like a bath toy. She had brought them here deliberately, wondering if Visser would make the connection, which he did. "Is that what I think it is?"

"It's the *Sakawa*," Haley said, speaking loudly above the motor. "It's right below us."

Visser leaned over the edge of the cockpit, then raised his eyes toward the islet to the east. In the sky overhead, the drone that she had asked to do a flyover was winging its way toward Enyu. "It's hard to imagine."

"You can still see the signs, if you know where to look." Haley pointed to the south. "They used explosives to blow up a channel in the reef. One of the islands was vaporized by Ivy Mike. If you head west, you can see the crater from Castle Bravo. They called it the proving ground. It was chosen because it was in the middle of nowhere. But there were people here. When they were relocated, they were told that they could come back in a few months. Know what really happened?"

Visser did not look away from Bikini. "I expect that it wasn't anything good."

Haley asked Giff to take the helm. Opening her bag, she checked the wildlife transmitters that she had activated before their departure, which she would use to tag any nests they found. "They almost starved at the first relocation site. When radioactive ashes fell from the sky, nobody told them what it was. Finally, they were informed it was safe to go home. A few years later, somebody noticed that cesium levels were off the charts. There were stillbirths, miscarriages. They all had to leave again. So you can see why we don't trust what other people tell us."

She anticipated his next question. "The radiation fell to normal levels years ago. They put potassium in the soil, just to be safe. That's why we built the seastead here. Nobody has lived here for decades, but it's clean. We can use the infrastructure they left behind, and the atoll is a natural breakwater. It was like a house with the keys in the front door. When we arrived, it was just us and the birds."

As they drew closer to Enyu, Giff brought the boat around to the construction dock at the lee of the islet, where they tied up. To the south, a flock of shearwaters was feeding on the open ocean, dipping from side to side on their stiff wings as they flew, the tips nearly touching the water. She saw that Visser had noticed it. "Migrants. They stay for a while, then move on. Like everyone else."

They descended from the dock, walking along the sand toward the trees. Giff inclined his head southward. "I'll take this end. You two go north. We can meet up again in the middle."

"Fine." Haley waited as he headed off, knowing that he had wanted to leave her alone with Visser. Whatever his reasons, she was glad for it. The two of them, she suspected, would have a lot to talk about.

Visser was looking at the wind turbines, which were motionless and bare. "No birds."

"They can be hard to find. So I could use a second pair of eyes." Haley knelt to draw on the sand, which was light gray, with flecks of coral. "This is the island. I want to focus on the scrub and forest here, north of the airstrip. We have to be systematic. Terns don't build nests. The eggs get laid in bare branches, forks in trees, sometimes just depressions on the ground or in the shingle. If there's a colony, it's going to be somewhere that isn't obvious. Let's go."

They headed north. Beyond the beach, the ground turned into short grass and soldierbush, followed by a sparse forest of pisonia and manjack. Near the airstrip, coconuts had been planted in neat rows, replacing the trees that had been blown away by the nuclear blasts.

As they picked their way forward over the next hour, focusing on sheltered areas that might reveal signs of birds, Haley realized that she wasn't sure what she was hoping to find. Visser remained silent. She had been wondering if he would open up about what he was really doing here, but with every passing minute, it became increasingly clear that she would have to pry it out of him herself.

Her first opportunity came as they circled back toward their starting point. They had found nothing, and Haley was trying to decide what to do next when Visser spoke up beside her. "You've said that you don't trust anyone from the outside. But you still cut a deal with Deventer."

"It wasn't my deal." Haley headed toward the airstrip. "But if they want to use us, I'll use them back. They need a proof of concept. If Deventer wants to build islands for countries that are going to vanish underwater, they have to prove that it works on a large scale. We need land and a permanent presence to stay on the list of nations. So they made us an offer. The details don't matter. I just want to get the seastead up and running before anyone has second thoughts. That's why I'm in a hurry. It isn't about the seas rising. I know how quickly the politics can change."

They looked toward the ocean, where a mixed flock was feeding on the water, the white terns and black noddies flying low to pick up squid and fish. In the old days, she knew, the islanders had followed birds to find promising fishing grounds, but that way of life was long over. Watching Visser, she saw her chance. "Let me tell you another story. Back in the nineties, the Marshall Islands made a deal with a private company to conduct iron fertilization. You know what that is?"

Visser kept his eye on the flock. "You seed the oceans with iron. The iron supply is the essential limiting factor in plankton growth."

"Right. The idea was that if you can get more plankton to grow, they suck up carbon dioxide, and when they die, it sinks to the ocean floor. Marine snow. On a large enough scale, it could offset carbon production. We could solve climate change without anyone lifting a finger. If you're lucky, you get more fish, too. It sounded good to our politicians, so we leased our offshore waters. You can look it up."

She regarded the birds. "It was supposed to be a trial run, but it never happened. Before they could even start, iron fertilization was outlawed as a form of illegal dumping. But maybe it's better that way. Science isn't going to save us. We like to think that we can invent our way out of this. It lets us avoid the hard choices. And I figured out a long time ago that we have to depend on ourselves."

Glancing toward the airstrip, she saw that Giff had emerged from the coconut grove. When she raised her arms in a silent question, he only shook his head. As they went closer, she lowered her voice. "And I'll tell you one last story. After the islanders were relocated from Bikini, they were given a trust fund to compensate them for the loss of their land. They had nothing else, so they couldn't live without those handouts. I don't want that to happen again. Deventer can have their cut. If we can sign over a piece of our future to make a home for ourselves, we will. I just want to get it done now, because I don't trust the system. It doesn't have any interest in what we're building here. But you know that already, don't you?"

Visser turned. Something was gathering behind his blue eyes. "What do you mean?"

"You aren't a scientist," Haley said. "You're a lawyer. And I want to know why you really came."

Before Visser could respond, Giff had joined them at the edge of the airstrip, his face glistening with sweat. He pointed. "Look."

Following his gesture, Haley felt a sudden chill. When she had last looked at the wind towers, they had stood empty against the sky. Now, at some point in the last few minutes, they had become covered in birds. Clusters of white terns were perching on the struts of the latticework and on the tail sections of the turbines, hundreds, perhaps thousands looking calmly inland, as if they had all descended simply to watch and wait. "Where did they come from?"

Giff shook his head. "Don't know. I didn't find anything on my end. A few heron's nests in the bunker on the southern tip of the island. That's all. But I haven't checked anything here."

Haley knew that he was referring to the supply outbuildings and the communications bunker by the airstrip, which were the only places they had yet to search. As they headed in that direction, with Giff casting a nervous look back at the ranks of terns, she felt Visser's eyes on her face.

Giff went ahead to the nearest storage building, signaling that she and Visser should check the other. Visser followed as she went to pry open the door, which had been all but swallowed up by undergrowth. Inside, hulks of construction equipment and rusting generators were visible in the shadows. Haley switched on her flashlight, casting its beam around the interior, and heard the low scurrying of rats. "Now you can tell me what you're doing here."

Visser faced her in the darkness. "First, I never said I was a scientist. You only assumed that I was. I studied biology and law at Leiden University. But it sounds like you already figured that out."

"I figured out a few other things," Haley said. "I looked you up online. Your name sounded familiar, and I finally remembered why. You wrote one of the first papers about us. I read it last night. It was hard to get past the legal language, but I think I got the point. You wanted to define what a country was. For a nation to collect reparations, it has to legally exist, but places affected by climate change might vanish from the map. It's quite a paradox. But you came up with a good solution."

Visser's expression was difficult to read. "I wanted to understand the situation. That doesn't mean I liked it."

"No. But you didn't have any trouble coming up with ways to profit." Haley retraced her steps to the door. "'It isn't enough to define a nation by its geographical coordinates. You need land and a permanent presence. A few caretakers would be enough, but let's call it a hundred. A minimum viable population. You can rotate them in and out, as long as somebody is always there. If you like, you can even make the whole thing sustainable. It humors the colonists. Or it allows them to think that they're something more than a fiction.'"

Haley emerged into the sunlight. "I was impressed. That paper was written years ago, but you laid out the whole operation. A government in exile in Springdale. A trusteeship to distribute reparations to refugees. To get start-up capital, you treat the reparations like any future income stream. You package it like an annuity and use it to raise money. Deventer agrees to sponsor the construction in exchange for a cut of what we expect to earn from lawsuits against developed countries. It'll take years to work its way through the courts, but you're willing to risk it—"

Visser broke in. "The courts are the only tools you have left. I was giving you a way to use them. Both of us want to make a difference. For me, it just happened to be on the legal side."

"And I should thank you," Haley replied. "Deventer gave us the patents at a discount. We did the rest. No matter what happens, we'll have the seastead. They can't exactly repossess it. And we have an eye on the long game. In a thousand years, sea levels will fall again, and the rest of us can go home. But that still doesn't explain what you're doing here."

Visser's voice was flat. "I'm doing exactly what I said. We're conducting a survey of the atoll, both of its current state and of how it might look over the next century. And this affects you today. Because not everyone is convinced that these islands are going to disappear at all."

Haley had an uneasy sense of what was coming. "What are you talking about?"

"It isn't just a question of sea levels," Visser said patiently, as if explaining a difficult concept to a child. "Reef islands change shape. They move around. Even if they erode on the ocean side, sediment can accumulate where they face the lagoon. If the coral dies, it makes more sand available. These islets might actually grow as the seas rise. Most of them formed when sea levels were even higher. Climate change just reactivates the process. Increased storm action could build them up. We simply don't know. I'm just here to gather information."

A flood of anger spread through her body. "If you're saying we have nothing to worry about, I've heard that story before."

"That's not what I said. Parts of the islands probably can't be saved. Urban areas, industrial sites, places where the reefs have been affected by infrastructure, like your turbines. But if it looks like any of it will survive, it makes it harder for a judge to award damages. I'm not saying you won't lose your country. But people are bound to wonder if the claims will hold up. And this isn't something you worry about in a century. You worry about it now."

Haley felt as if she had been struck in the gut. "So there may never be reparations."

"You have to prepare for that possibility. And if that's the case, what you have now is all you're ever going to have." Visser paused. "I'm sorry. But you knew from the beginning that it might not last, and that you had to be open to other options. I want you to remember this. No matter what else happens."

For the first time, Haley found herself at a loss for words. Hearing the sound of footsteps, she turned to see Giff coming their way. He shook his head, indicating that he had found nothing, and headed for the concrete communications bunker, which was the only structure that they had not yet inspected. Haley made for it, walking rapidly ahead of the others. She did not want to look at Visser, even as his words continued to resound in her brain.

The bunker, built decades ago for the bomb tests, was a short distance away from the supply buildings, with a huge sloping roof nearly engulfed by the trees. Tufts of grass and moss had sprouted in minute cracks in the concrete. Haley went to the doors, which were ajar, and stepped inside without pausing, wanting nothing more than to be done. She no longer cared about what they might discover.

Going in, she took stock of the interior, which was strewn with debris and the remains of equipment that its former tenants had left behind. As Giff and Visser came up behind her, she switched on her flashlight, and she was moving its beam along the floor when she halted. "Giff—"

In the illuminated circle before her, there was a single heron. It was gray, with short yellow legs, a strip of pure white going down its throat. When it was struck by the light, it turned in her direction, and in the instant before it flew toward the ceiling, it seemed to her that it had almost been dancing in place.

She cast her flashlight up to follow it. Dozens of golden eyes were staring down.

There was a sound like the pages of an enormous book being riffled as the herons in the loft took flight. Haley fell back as the birds descended, coming at them in waves, their wings beating the air in the confined space. Otherwise, they were utterly silent, and within seconds, they had surrounded the three of them, jabbing down with their sharp brown beaks.

Giff cursed and beat away the birds with his hands. Haley felt the flashlight slip from her fingers to the ground, and when it went out, it left nothing but a darkness filled with dense feathered bodies. A heron flung itself at her head. It was like being punched by a fist in a padded glove. The bird came again and she shrieked, reaching up wildly to drive it away, only to feel its claws groping for a foothold. Another blow opened a gash on her cheek.

Beside her, Visser had taken hold of one of the herons as it strained forward, trying to get at his eyes. He managed to fling it away, but its place was immediately taken by two more, one going for his face, the other attacking him below the waist. As she watched, he stumbled and went down hard. Haley broke free of the bird that was flailing against her and reached for Visser's wrist. He returned her grip and made it to his feet, but the birds above were still coming, row after row, bearing a nauseating smell of the sea and vomited fish.

The door of the bunker was still open. Haley turned and ran for that rectangle of sunlight, feeling another set of wings beating at the back of her neck, and tumbled outside. Her bag slipped from her shoulders. Leaving it where it had fallen, she ran for the boat. Giff had already emerged and was shouting for her to follow, blood streaming from cuts on his head. Visser was somewhere behind her.

Haley sprinted as fast as she could through the scrub, ignoring the angry scratches it left on her ankles and calves. She did not stop until she felt sand beneath her feet and saw the construction dock up ahead, and even then, she kept going until she was at the edge of the water, lungs aching, and her mind had finally caught up to the fact that the sound of wings had ceased.

She looked back. The herons were gone. Whatever had caused them to attack had not carried them past the airstrip. The only noise was that of her own pulse, ringing high up in her ears.

Giff was beside her, breathing hard. Visser was standing alone on the beach. He was looking directly at her, but his eyes did not seem to be registering his surroundings, and then he collapsed on the sand.

Haley scrambled back to him. When she was close enough to smell blood, she looked down and saw that the right leg of his khakis was all but soaked through to the knee with red.

She reached down, tearing away the fabric, as a warm jet rose in an arc from Visser's inner thigh. The sharp beak of one of the herons had sliced open his femoral artery. She spun toward Giff. "Give me your belt."

Giff complied, staring down at the man on the sand. Haley looped the end of the web belt through its buckle and ran it up Visser's leg, as high as she could, and cinched it. She caught his eye. "It's going to be okay."

Visser said nothing. He was very pale. Looking up the beach, Haley saw a long trail of blood leading back to where they had emerged from the scrub. A gash to the femoral artery could cause death in less than two minutes, and despite the tourniquet, the blood was still flowing.

It seemed that Visser was trying to speak. In the end, whatever he wanted to say was lost as unconsciousness took hold, and before she could do anything more, he had grown still. He was dead.

Her hands were sticky, and the high sweet smell of copper filled her nose. She was about to rise, not knowing what to say or do, when she felt a light touch on her arm. Giff was pointing. "Look."

She lifted her eyes. In the distance, the terns that had been perched on the lattices of the wind towers were taking off one row at a time. As she watched, the entire flock took flight, hundreds of birds ascending in unison, and before long, the scaffolds were empty again. Even before she saw where they were flying, she knew it in her heart. The flock was moving west, toward the lagoon, and then turning north in a single body. It was heading for the seastead.

III.

Haley laid Visser in the bottom of the boat, covering the body with a tarp from the port seat locker. A cell amplifier had been hooked up to the boat's external antenna. Dialing the communications center in the seastead, she put the phone to her ear. As it rang with no answer, she kept her eyes fixed on the colony in the distance. The birds were still heading toward the nearest caisson, and at their current speed, they would be there in less than five minutes.

"We have to go." Haley returned the phone to its cradle. As Giff got the motor running, she knelt by the locker that had held the tarp. Rooting around, she yanked out the remaining equipment, tossing aside a kedge line and an ensign flag before her hands finally closed on a canvas cockpit cover. She snapped it on, beginning with the fiberglass frame around the windshield, as Giff guided them away from the dock. The cover wasn't thick, but it was something.

As soon as she had sealed up the cockpit, they headed into the lagoon. Haley was about to stow the equipment again when she saw one more item that had been concealed beneath the rest. It was a shotgun. Fishing it out to check the magazine, she found that it was loaded with six rounds. Haley stuck it beneath the seat, then went back to try the phone again.

On her second attempt, she raised someone in the communications center. To her relief, it was Amata, the colonist who had driven the crane the day before, and she knew that he was someone she could trust. She tried to speak calmly. "It's Haley. We're on our way back from Enyu. Listen carefully. You need to get everyone inside the seastead right now."

Amata's voice crackled across the poor connection. "What's going on, Haley?"

She looked through the windshield, trying to describe what she was seeing without sounding insane. "There's a mixed flock of terns and noddies heading your way. A thousand birds, maybe more. They're not acting normally. If they intersect with you, there's going to be damage. Maybe injuries. Or worse. You need to sound the alarm. If you can stow anything fragile, like the antennas, do it, but don't waste any time. Pull the hurricane shutters if you can. The birds can't break through the windows, but maybe we can reduce the harm."

Amata evidently sensed the urgency in her voice. "I'll take care of it. See you soon."

He signed off. Haley hung up the phone and looked across the bow. "Take us as close as you can."

Giff gave her a sideward glance. "You don't want to hold back to see how it looks?"

"We can't stay here," Haley said. "I'm the reason half of these people are there in the first place. If it goes bad, I need to see it."

Giff did not seem entirely persuaded, but he pushed the throttle forward, taking them faster across the lagoon, the water rising in a needlelike spray. The electric motor's cruising speed seemed to be about fifty kilometers per hour. Haley didn't know how fast terns could fly, probably around the same or more, but she doubted she would make it to the seastead before the birds did.

She focused on the flock up ahead, which had not deviated from its course. Along with the terns and noddies that she had noticed earlier, there were a few larger herons and frigatebirds. The flock seemed more populous than before, and when she looked to the west, she saw that it had been joined by another group from the outer islets. The sight sent a chill reverberating up her spine. She had seen plenty of birds by the turbines, but there were thousands more on the uninhabited parts of the atoll, and it looked like they were all coming at once.

When she looked forward again, she saw that the leading edge of the flock had reached the seastead. Within the overall group, they were moving in smaller clusters of five to ten, the masses breaking apart as they reached the outer platforms. Some were flying in single file, others in tight formations, in the kind of mobbing behavior she had seen before only in shearwaters. They were approaching very low across the ocean surface, their flight direct and level, but as they neared the caissons, they began to mount higher into the air.

Then they dove. The first set of birds met the solar array at the nearest platform, smashing into the panels at full speed. Many died at once, spiraling down to the roofs of the concrete terraces, while others continued to flop around on broken wings, squawking and defecating in their death throes. Dark gouts of blood began to appear at the places where the birds had struck, the panels clouded with fractures, and this was only the first wave.

Glancing at Giff, she could see the tendons standing out on his neck, but he steered the boat around to the caisson that bordered the aquaculture pens. Looking overhead, she saw the drone that had been conducting an aerial survey of Enyu. As she watched, it was mobbed by a dozen birds, which dipped and swerved in its path as if driving away a predator. The drone took a series of blows to its nacelle, toppled sideways, and plummeted toward the water, where it vanished with a splash. Several of the birds followed it all the way down.

They neared the aquaculture farm. The birds had been as drawn to it as much as to everything else, diving toward the nets on the surface of the water and becoming entangled in the mesh. Even from here, she could see dozens, maybe hundreds, of birds already caught in the pens, a living carpet of bodies that seemed to undulate in counterpoint to the movement of the waves. More continued to come, descending in one sortie after another, their screeching filling every inch of the air like thunder keyed to a higher pitch.

Looking toward the bioreactors, she saw the birds attacking them as well, swooping down over the plastic containers to slash them with their beaks or claw at them with their small feet. Enormous holes had opened up in the sides of several of the tubes, on which electronic sensors for transmitting data about the system had been strung like beads. Haley saw clouds of bluish green spilling out into the water as the algae inside oozed out, the weight of the birds piled on top squeezing the membranes flat like packages of toothpaste.

She turned to the greenhouse. Most of the panels had already been smashed. Through the panes, she could make out the nervous shadows of birds that had either broken their way through and survived or entered after others had cleared the way in, flitting from side to side within the confined space and rebounding off the walls. Everywhere she turned, she seemed to see her own dreams being annihilated with the seastead, the work of years lying in ruins.

There was a thump on the roof of the cockpit cover. Haley looked up. "Hold on—"

Her words were cut off by another series of collisions as the birds began to rain down on the boat, their wings battering wildly against the fabric. The canvas rippled inward with beaks and claws seeking a way through. An instant later, a bird crashed against the windshield, followed by two more, their bodies glancing off to one side as the boat plowed its way forward. One of them ricocheted off the glass at just the right angle and lay convulsing on the bow of the boat for a few seconds before sliding into the water with the rest.

Haley was about to tell Giff to pull back when she noticed something else. Near the net pens, an open boat was drifting freely, already covered in birds. There was no one inside, but when she looked more closely at the area of the lagoon beside it, she saw a lone human figure, still alive, treading water beneath the nets above the aquaculture farm. "It's Manita."

Without being asked, Giff steered the boat in that direction. "Can we pick her up?"

"Leave that to me." Haley saw Manita turn toward the sound of the motor. The net afforded less than half a meter of headspace above the water, and it was being compressed even further by the weight of the dead or dying birds tangled up in the mesh. More terns and noddies were still diving onto the pens, and Haley saw that some of the birds trapped in the net were straining to reach the woman beneath with their beaks even as they struggled to escape.

Waving through the windshield, she caught Manita's eye. Haley pointed at the water on the boat's starboard side, and the biologist seemed to get the message. Giff steered the boat toward the aquaculture farm, bringing it around perpendicular to the net pens. Haley scooped up the shotgun from the floor of the boat and loosened a corner of the cockpit cover by the transom. The birds were still coming, the knocks redoubling against the canvas roof.

When Haley gave the nod, Manita dived down out of sight and began to swim underwater to the boat. Haley forced herself to wait until the other woman was nearly there, then tore away the cover. Sticking out her head and shoulders, she racked the shotgun and fired into the air, aiming away from the birds. At the sound of the blast, the terns around the boat scattered, veering off in all directions.

A second later, Manita surfaced behind the boat. As Haley set down the shotgun, Giff left the wheel and helped her haul the biologist onboard. Once Manita was safely inside, Haley snapped the cover down again, the birds hammering against the fabric as they regrouped and fought to get through.

Manita was dripping wet, her hair plastered to her face. Haley took her by the hand. She was shaking. "Are you okay?"

"I think so." Manita looked down at the body on the floor. "Jesus. Is that Visser?"

"Yeah." Haley turned to Giff, who had taken the helm again. "Bring us around to the floating dock and cut the engine."

Giff obliged in silence. Beside her, Manita was looking out at what remained of the fish farm and bioreactors. Haley noticed that the biologist had several bloody scratches on her arms and legs, and that she was clutching a knife with a sheepsfoot blade. "What happened?"

Manita tried to collect herself. "I was checking the bioreactors when they came. It was an open boat. No cover. A few of them got at me. It didn't give me more than a few seconds. I dove overboard and swam over to the fish farm. It was the only thing I could think of. I cut a pen open and squeezed inside. But they wouldn't stop coming. What the hell is going on?"

Haley only recounted what had taken place on Enyu. When they were twenty meters from the floating dock, Giff killed the engine, and they waited there, not speaking, as the attack continued. Manita recoiled as a bird hit their boat and landed on the bow, still convulsing. There were no human faces in sight, and Haley hoped that most of the colonists had taken cover. She tried to see through the safety glass of the upper terraces, but was unable to make out anything inside. Some of the hurricane shutters had been lowered, but most of the windows were still exposed.

When she tried to raise the communications center again, no one answered, so all that remained was to watch as the seastead was obliterated. The fish farm and bioreactors were clearly lost, and the greenhouse had been severely damaged. Haley knew that nothing could undermine the caissons themselves, but as the birds hurled themselves headlong into any reflective surface, it seemed that they were determined to erase everything else.

It was several endless minutes before Haley noticed that the intervals between blows to the canvas were lengthening. In time, they ceased altogether. Looking up through the windshield, she saw that the sky was clear, and there no longer seemed to be any birds attacking the seastead itself.

Haley rose and peeled away one edge of the cockpit cover. Everything was quiet.

She pulled away the rest of the canvas, the snaps popping one by one. Turning to the east, she saw that the surviving birds had regathered into a single flock. As far as she could tell, they were heading toward Bikini, and as she watched, they continued inland, where they were lost almost at once in the trees.

Haley sank down again. Up ahead, the seastead was covered with tiny white clumps of dead terns, mingled with the darker noddies, like peppercorns strewn on ground that had been sown with salt.

Without speaking, Haley slid behind the wheel and started the engine. After she had guided the motorboat into the nearest berth on the floating dock, Manita went to tie them up, while Haley and Giff hauled Visser's body out onto the platform. A few splotches of blood, like cartographic outlines, had soaked through the fabric of the tarp. Manita joined them a second later, the shotgun in her hands.

Dozens of dead birds lay at their feet. The air was thick with the stench of fish, and when Haley looked more carefully, she saw that many of the terns had regurgitated bits of food, the concrete soiled by fragments of shrimp and squid. A few of the birds were still alive, some flopping with their backs broken, others seizing or convulsing in place in a kind of pathetic dance.

Ignoring them for now, Haley approached the remaining boats that were moored at the dock. None seemed seriously damaged, although two had shattered windshields, and all were speckled with starbursts of blood and black marks from the beaks of the birds. As she was examining the final dinghy, a tern burst suddenly from the inside, its wings beating madly. Haley fell back, startled, and watched as it took off and headed away with the rest.

They entered the boat deck, where they lowered the door, stowed Visser's body, and headed toward the covered walkway leading to the central caisson. In the silence, Haley gradually became aware of another set of sounds, which grew louder as they neared the hub of the seastead. They were human voices, most of them hushed, a few shouting or screaming.

As they moved along the causeway, there was a whine of static, and the public address system came to life. It was Ruben, who ordered all colonists to report to the common area. They filed into the hub along with the others, a few of whom were bleeding. Looking into their faces, Haley saw fear there, but also a veiled reproach, although she wasn't sure whether or not it was directed at her.

Upstairs, the common area was already packed. In one corner, the seastead's resident medic had set up a station to dress cuts and bruises. Haley gathered that some of the colonists had been injured directly by the birds, while others had been hit by debris or broken glass. Underlying everything was a palpable sense of panic, and

Haley sensed that it would break out into an unpredictable form if they failed to get it immediately under control.

Ruben was at the center of the room, speaking with an agitated group in Marshallese. When he saw Haley, he took a step forward. He seemed to be trying his best to keep a handle on the crowd. "What do you know?"

Haley gave him a short account of what had taken place on Enyu. When he heard that Visser was dead, Ruben glanced to one side. Following his gaze, Haley saw that Jansen was standing in the corner, and she remembered that the older woman didn't know what had happened to her colleague.

As a tally was taken of the room, it emerged that there was another casualty, a female colonist who had been alone in the greenhouse when the birds descended. One of the men claimed to have seen her body as he was coming back to the hub. According to him, her eyes had been pecked out.

At a look from Ruben, Haley repeated her story. Upon hearing of Visser's death, Jansen grew pale and turned away, fumbling out her satellite phone. Haley wanted to approach her, but before she could, the conversation had turned to the prospect of evacuation.

Giff was the first to speak. "Even if we decide to go, we're hundreds of kilometers from the nearest inhabited island. It could be days before a plane can get here. And it wouldn't be able to take everyone."

Haley looked at Jansen, who was talking into her phone in a lowered voice. "There's a research ship at Romurikku. Can it come for us?"

Jansen seemed visibly shaken, but she nodded. "I'll tell them. They'll have to come around to the channel. It may be a few hours."

Ruben addressed the group. "Then we'll vote. A show of hands in favor of staying."

Giff lifted his hand high. After a moment, so did a few other colonists. The rest only sat in silence, and when the vote was called in favor of evacuating, almost everyone else, including Manita, assented. Haley did not cast a vote either way. When they were done, she looked around the room. "If there's a chance of another attack, we don't want to bring the ship here. These birds seem drawn to structures or movement. The ship can hold station at the channel near Enyu. We'll head over in any boats that can be covered. How many do we have?"

After a quick inventory, it became clear that five usable boats remained, including the electric dinghy that Visser had provided. Four were moored on the floating dock, while the fifth, which Manita had used while checking the bioreactors, was still drifting near the aquaculture pens, where it could be retrieved. A sixth was at Bikini, and although a few of the colonists offered to go for it, it was decided that the five boats they had would be enough.

Haley ended up at the center of the evacuation effort, rounding up volunteers to get the covers on the boats and to put up the hurricane shutters. Without being conscious of it, she had accepted that she was leaving the seastead for a long time, perhaps forever, and she found herself ticking off its vulnerabilities, wondering how best to prepare it for being abandoned.

As she was heading downstairs, Ruben pulled her aside. "I know you don't want this. But an evacuation is going to happen whether we like it or not. Better to handle it in a form we can control."

She saw that he was acting as bravely as he knew how. "What if they attack again?"

Ruben held her gaze. "We keep going. If we turn back, this becomes a panic. And I don't know how that will end."

As the councilman was called away, Haley continued down to the galley. Earlier, she had been struck by an idea, and now she gathered up an armful of cans, a roll of tape, a pair of tin snips, and a propane torch.

On her way out, she ran into Manita. The biologist still seemed shocked by the loss of the bioreactors and the death of the woman in the greenhouse, whom she had seen less than an hour before the attack, but her voice was steady. "There's something I need to show you."

Haley was about to say that it could wait, but something in Manita's eyes convinced her. "What is it?"

Manita drew her into a storage room off the corridor and closed the door behind them. "I didn't have time to tell you earlier. You remember how I said that the levels of fish here have been increasing?"

Haley felt another prickle. "I was wondering if the birds were running out of food."

"They aren't. It's the opposite. I haven't seen fish in these numbers for years. But that isn't what bothered me. Once a month, I run a comparison of water samples, one from the area by the bioreactors, the other from our sampling station offshore. This morning, after we talked, I found these."

She opened her hand. Cupped in her palm were a few small gray pellets. Haley stared. "What are they?"

Manita told her. Haley listened, and for a long moment afterward, she could do nothing but stand in silence. Finally, she told Manita what to do. The biologist gave her a nod and left.

On the lowest level of the hub, there was a room for the seastead's battery bank, lined with rack after rack of vanadium cells, which would have to be shut down as part of the evacuation. Haley descended the companionway alone, and she was going from one disconnect switch to the next when Jansen entered behind her. "I was told that you wanted to talk to me."

Haley switched off the last rack and closed the door. "The ship is on its way?"

"They'll be at the channel in forty minutes. I told them to cover up anything reflective on the outside, in case the birds are being drawn to it. What exactly is it that you wanted?"

"I won't waste your time," Haley said. "I was hoping you could explain something. We can talk about it here, in private, or we can go upstairs and you can tell the entire colony. It's up to you."

Reaching into her pocket, she set the pellets on the surface of the rack between them. Jansen took them in for a second. Finally, she appeared to reach a decision, and her hard features grew fractionally wearier. "We're conducting iron fertilization. It's been ongoing for the last three months. We do it mostly at night."

"I've already gathered that much," Haley said. "Did Ruben know about this?"

Jansen shook her head. "Nobody at the colony was aware of it. It had to be done in secret. Technically, it's still illegal. But the only way to convince anyone of its merits is to conduct a test on a large scale."

"So it was a proof of concept. Like the seastead. And you chose a place where no one who mattered would notice until you were done—"

"It wasn't my decision to keep it from you. We wouldn't have conducted these tests if it hadn't been approved on a higher level. You sold the rights to your offshore waters a long time ago. Those rights never lapsed. They've just changed hands a few times. It was part of the arrangement with Deventer. Whatever reparations you hope to get are decades away. We needed something now. And you have it to thank for all of this. Otherwise, the colony wouldn't even exist."

"I'd say it doesn't have much of a chance of existing anyway. What did you do?"

Jansen glanced away. "It was the largest test we've ever conducted. Previous studies were restricted to a few hundred square kilometers, and they would just dump iron sulfate in the ocean, where it sinks right away. We bind the iron with lignin and compress it into pellets. It allows it to persist for longer."

"And what happened?" Haley asked. "You saw an increase in sea life offshore?"

Jansen gave a quick nod. "There have been huge algal blooms. Most of it is a few kilometers past the reef, so you wouldn't have seen the effects here. The blooms have been heaviest over the last few months. We noticed an increase in the biomass of phytoplankton right away. Then it worked its way up the food chain. More shrimp, more squid, more fish."

"But it changed the ecosystem in ways you didn't predict. Including the birds. Did Visser know?"

"None of us did. Not until today. We thought that whatever negative effects it had would be containable. We were wrong."

Haley looked into Jansen's eyes, which had grown fixed and glassy. "I still don't understand the point. When you told the world, what did you expect? We're not going to turn back climate change."

"No," Jansen said. "That ship has sailed. Politically, if not scientifically. But we can do what we can with the time we have. Deventer ran the numbers. Iron fertilization is the cheapest way to sequester large amounts of carbon. We could sell the credits to polluters. Let factories and power plants keep operating if we sink enough carbon into the sea here. It won't make anything worse, and in the meantime, it's an income stream. It's more realistic than the hope of reparations. You can't trust any one solution. There always has to be a safety line."

Haley did not look away. "Unless the safety line snaps first. But that's the only reason you agreed to fund this. You don't think the reparations will pay off. It was all just to humor us."

Jansen's air of control began to crumble. "If it matters, I'm sorry. It hurts me as much as it does you. And if I could take it back, I would."

Haley turned toward the battery bank. "Just make sure the ship gets here on time."

She did not look at Jansen again. After a pause, the older woman left the room. Haley remained there for another minute, checking to make sure that the switches were off, and then she headed back to the upper level. She felt as if she had been hollowed out on the inside.

A half hour later, word came that the research ship was holding station at the mouth of the channel. There were no birds in sight.

On the top level of the hub, the colonists had been divided into five groups. At a nod from Ruben, Haley motioned for the first cohort of twenty to follow her down-stairs. In her hands, she was carrying the object she had built earlier. It consisted of five empty cans taped in a row, their tops and bottoms partially removed, with the propane torch inserted through a hole in the base of the first cylinder.

They entered the lowest level of the outer caisson and continued on to the boat deck. All was silent. Visser was still there, wrapped up like an offering, along with the body of the woman from the greenhouse, which two other colonists had re-trieved. On closer examination, it had been determined that her eyes had not been pecked out after all, and that she most likely had died of a heart attack.

Haley saw the colonists casting nervous glances at the bodies as they filed toward the door to the dock, which was lowered. She gave a signal to Giff, who had volun-teered to remain until the last boat was gone. He went to the door, pulled the man-ual release, and slid it up its rails.

They stood looking out at the dock. Four meters of exposed space lay between them and the boats. It was covered with the bodies of terns, dead noddies, and re-gurgitated gobbets of fish and squid. Aside from the sound of the water lapping against the framework of the caisson, it was utterly quiet.

Giff waved forward the colonists, who began to move toward the nearest dinghy. Haley remained inside the boat deck, her eyes riveted to the sky. There was no sign of life anywhere between here and Bikini.

One by one, the colonists lowered themselves into the boat, packed as closely to-gether as possible. The last to come out was Jansen, who had been asked to depart with the first group to coordinate the boarding process. Before leaving, she went to Visser's body and lifted it by the shoulders, with Giff picking it up by the legs. The other colonists made as much room as they could as the body was lowered into the boat, followed by the second victim.

When they were done, Giff gave three pulls to the starter rope, and the engine began to rumble. As two other men pulled the cover into place, he climbed onto the dock and uncleated the lines. Then he came back to watch as one of the colonists took the tiller and steered the boat away from the slip. Haley spoke softly. "Tell Ruben to send the next group down."

Giff went to the handset mounted by the door of the boat deck and made the call. The first dinghy was already a hundred meters out. Haley continued to watch the skies, and as the next group arrived, she saw a number of white and black specks ap-pear over the trees on Bikini. It was a flock of terns and noddies, and from here, it was hard to tell whether or not they were heading this way. Giff saw them a second after she did. "What do you think?"

Haley raised the metal tube in her hands. "We keep going. If we stop, we may not get a second chance."

Giff gestured for the others to move as Haley kept her eyes on the birds. There was no doubt now that they were coming. She estimated that they had several min-utes before the flock arrived, and she was about to tell the second boat to leave when another mass of birds, which had approached unseen over the top of the caisson, descended without any warning.

Within seconds, the birds were everywhere. As they began to dive toward the boats and the platform, the colonists screamed, but before panic could take hold,

Haley raised the tube in her hands. Switching on the propane torch, she counted to five, and then she pulled the trigger.

A blue fireball erupted from the mouth of the outermost can, accompanied by a deafening blast. The sound was what counted, not the flame, and as soon as the birds heard it, they scattered. Haley shouted at Giff to get the last of the colonists on board. He herded the rest onto the boat, and then it was off, the men inside struggling to pull the cover into place as they sped off into the lagoon.

The birds were throwing themselves against the sides of the boat deck. As the sound of wings rose, Giff looked at Haley for approval, then went to the handset. "Send the last three groups now."

A deckwash pump stood to one side of the deck. Giff switched it on and took up the washdown hose. When one bird, followed by another, appeared at the door, he squeezed the sprayer, and a pressurized burst of water swept the birds out of sight. He caught her eye again. "I'm going out."

Haley knew better than to tell him otherwise. As the remaining evacuees began to appear, Giff ducked down and went out to the exposed part of the dock, the hose unspooling behind him. Haley followed him outside, where the birds were descending in huge sorties, with more colliding with the platform and tumbling down to the surface of the caisson.

Giff aimed the hose toward the boats, sweeping the spray from side to side, as if laying down cover fire. Haley waited. As soon as the first half of the group had emerged, she squeezed the trigger of the propane canister. Another fireball exploded from the poofer, sending birds wheeling away, and in the brief respite it granted, the next set of colonists was able to board.

They did it two more times. Whenever the birds gathered, Giff drove them away with the hose, and when their numbers increased past the point where he could handle it, Haley fired the poofer again. A few managed to break through, diving to strike with their claws and beaks, leaving only a few scratches and cuts. The third boat was halfway to the channel, followed closely by the fourth.

Ruben was on the final boat. As he lowered himself into the dinghy, Haley could tell that he was wondering if she would leave. "This isn't the end. I'll see you on the ship. We need you there."

"I'm right behind you," Haley said shortly. "Hurry up. I don't know how much longer we can hold them off."

Ruben sat down with the last group. As he did, Giff exchanged a look with Haley. He sprayed one more jet from the hose, clearing the deck, and jumped down into the boat. Haley fired the poofer, driving away the remaining birds. She could tell from the weight of the canister that it was close to empty.

Giff took the tiller. He kept his eyes on her until the cover was snapped into place and the boat was on its way.

Haley stood there for a second, alone, as the final group departed. Overhead, the birds were returning. She set the poofer on the floor inside the boat deck, then yanked the door the rest of the way down. Once it was shut, she waited, listening, as the collisions against the outside of the caisson resumed. She was the only human being left in the entire colony.

For a minute, she gathered herself, feeling the empty seastead stretching around her to all sides. The idea of simply staying behind had occurred to her more than once. At last, however, she moved on. Ruben was right. This was not the end. She just had to turn off the lights.

Leaving the boat deck, she continued along the interior walkway until she reached the generator room at the far edge of the platform. She went from one generator to the next, switching them all off, and when the last had been powered down, the overhead lights blinked out.

Haley took a flashlight from the wall and used it to find her way to the hub. Then she paused. The sound of the collisions had ceased, as if an invisible button had been pressed. All the birds had gone silent.

She went up to the common area. Going to the largest window, she opened it and manually cranked back the hurricane shutter.

Birds were perched on every surface of the seastead. Haley saw them clustered on the photovoltaic arrays, on the concrete roofs, on the walkways, on the decks along the platforms. There were hundreds of terns and noddies, maybe thousands, along with the uncounted bodies of birds that had died trying to smash their way inside. But they were not attacking.

A noddy sat on the ledge below the window. She looked into its solemn, lethargic face. As it tilted its head to one side to fix its dim eyes on hers, she sensed that whatever had been happening was over. At the back of her mind, she began to understand why, but she pushed the thought away for now.

She made her way down to the lowest level. In one corner of the boat deck, there was a dive station with scuba gear. Haley heard the birds stirring gently against the sides of the seastead as she pulled on her tank, half mask, and weight belt. She adjusted her straps, feeling as if she were saying farewell to the only chapter of her life that would ever matter, and then went to the door and raised it.

On the deck outside, the birds were standing in silent ranks. She lowered the door behind her, then began to inch past the birds, picking her way to the edge. They continued to watch her, not moving, but when she looked closer, she saw some of them trembling, shifting back and forth on their little feet.

She made it to the side. Taking a seat on the lip of the platform, she pulled on her fins and bit down on her mouthpiece. Then she pushed herself off into the clear waters of the lagoon.

Haley descended, listening to herself breathing, the silver bubbles sliding past her cheek. When she looked up, she saw the floating bodies of birds outlined against the sky. She swam carefully, weaving her way past the anchor cables tethering the caisson to the bed, and was about to head for Bikini, where one boat remained, when something made her pivot and swim in the other direction.

At the bottom of the lagoon lay a shipwreck. Switching on her flashlight, she directed it toward the carcass of the destroyer, a hundred meters long, that sat upright against the white sand of the seabed. The hull was horribly twisted and damaged, with an enormous gash below the superstructure, which had been smashed amidships like a concertina. It had taken the impact squarely on its port side, its hull plates buckling to reveal the girders underneath.

Haley studied the wreck, which looked black and white in the darkness. It was one of ninety ships that had been brought to Bikini for the bomb tests. Some had been painted orange for visibility, while others had been filled with animals, the goats and pigs penned in place like sacrificial victims.

Now it lay here, as if in silent contemplation. The hull was overgrown with whip corals, the big fans sprouting from the end of its forward guns, and schools of glass fish and marbled grouper were weaving among the lavender ropes. Any exposed areas had been coated in a soft red silt. There was a message here, although it seemed too large for her to glimpse it all at once.

Haley regarded the wreck for a long moment. Then she turned and began to swim the half kilometer to where the final boat awaited.

Turning on the pump, Haley picked up the washdown hose. A mask was tied over the lower half of her face, and she had put a dab of mentholated ointment on her upper lip to block out the stench. Directing the jet of water toward the surface of the caisson, she began to wash it free of blood. It was oddly consoling work, and it took her a moment to realize that she was not alone.

Manita spoke from behind her. "I tried to reach you. You haven't been responding."

Haley fixed her eyes on the deck as she sprayed away the offal. "I've been busy. It took a few days just to dump what was left of the birds into the lagoon. They were pretty rotten. But the sharks will take them."

She finally looked at Manita. A month had passed since the evacuation. She had spent most of the last week trying to get her way back, hitching a ride on a cargo ship on its way to Guam, then covering the rest of the distance in an inflatable tender. It had not occurred to her to make arrangements for a return journey, but a quick check of the seastead had confirmed that enough of it had survived to keep her alive indefinitely. "How did you get here?"

"Probably the same way you did," Manita said. "There's a weekly ship to Honolulu. I managed to convince them to drop me off at Enyu. There are a still few boats out by the construction dock, if you don't mind swinging an oar. I'm surprised that you didn't see us."

"I haven't looked out to sea in a long time. There's more than enough to handle here." Haley studied the other woman. "Any birds?"

"No. Everything's quiet. According to Deventer, the effects of iron fertilization take just twenty days to disperse. For the impact to last, the process has to be continuous. But it looks like a permanent drop in the bird population." Manita looked to the west. "Maybe there are some on the outer islets. But I don't know."

Haley turned off the hose. Her questions lay like a lump in her chest. "Have they said anything else?"

"A little. I figured you'd want to hear it. And I wanted to ask if you're coming back."

"I'll finish cleaning up first. Then we'll see." Haley led her toward the edge of the dock. "So talk to me."

Manita sat down, looking out at the lagoon. "They're going to release a report. Iron fertilization creates huge algal blooms, but you don't know what you'll get in advance. It alters the community structure to favor certain kinds of phytoplankton. In this case, it was a species called pseudonitzschia. Ever hear of it?"

Haley nodded. "Yeah. I've had time to do a lot of reading. And I know that it's happened before."

"But not on this scale. Pseudonitzschia is an oceanic species. Under normal conditions, it's a bit player. But it responds particularly well to iron fertilization. And it's toxic. It produces domoic acid, which accumulates in fish and squid. When they're eaten by birds, chronic exposure can cause neurological damage. They become confused, suffer seizures, engage in mobbing behavior. Toxicity is highest in coastal waters. And it can lead to attacks on humans or buildings."

Haley understood. "Which is why it didn't affect migrant birds, like the shearwaters. They were just passing through, so they weren't exposed to enough of it. Only the birds that nested and fed here."

"That's how it looks." Manita paused. "I can't prove it, but it's possible that the toxin caused the birds to attack particular structures. The damage from domoic acid is concentrated on the hippocampus. For some species, like terns, it's the structure they use to navigate. It's particularly sensitive to electromagnetic interference, like the kind that would be produced by wind turbines, or the electric motors on some of the boats, or radio transmitters, or solar cells. They were drawn to it. It caused them to cyclically attack and regroup—"

"—and it ended when we shut it all down." Haley felt the sting of tears, but she fought them away. "And Deventer?"

Manita looked down at her reflection. "They've stopped the tests. It wasn't just about the birds. It's unclear how well the process sequesters carbon at all. When phytoplankton die, they don't always sink down to the seabed. Sometimes they return to the food chain. Whatever sequestration occurs is probably only temporary. So it doesn't look like a viable source of carbon credits."

"Which means that there's no more money," Haley said. "No cash flow. Even if the reparations come through a decade from now, we need money today. Nobody is going to want to live here otherwise."

"Maybe not. But they can't take away what you have. You were right to put all this together when you could. It exists. Nothing can change that." Manita turned to her. "So what are you going to do now?"

"Whatever I can repair or salvage, I'll keep. The rest I'll close down. I've got enough here to keep me alive. As for everybody else—" Haley hesitated. "What are they saying?"

"Ruben is back on Majuro. So are most of the others. Giff keeps talking about coming back, but he's got his own life to consider. And I need to think it over." Manita reached out and took her hand. "If you want me to stay for now, I will. At least for long enough to get it running again."

Haley squeezed back. Then she drew away. "I'd like that. But I want to be alone for a little while. You can get set up in the hub. It's the cleanest part. I'll come and find you later."

Manita headed silently inside. Haley remained where she was for another moment, then stood. Picking up the hose, she finished cleansing the blood from the platform, then removed her mask and stowed the pump. There was one last thing she had to do, and she had been postponing it for days.

The tender she had taken here was moored by the floating dock. She saw that

Manita had tied a rowboat beside it. Smiling slightly, she lowered herself down and cast off the lines.

Half an hour later, she was on Enyu. Leaving the tender by the construction dock, she walked up the coral beach, heading through the scrub toward the airstrip. Ranks of replanted coconut trees stood to either side.

Haley walked along the towers, which loomed like sentinels on the eastern edge of the islet, where the trade winds were strongest. When she reached the last one, she began to climb. There were a few signs of damage, but nothing that could not be repaired, if not by her, then by those who might come later.

Reaching the top of the tower, she worked her away around so that she was facing the lagoon. From here, she could see the full extent of the seastead. It was battered, with the shreds and patches of the bioreactors and net pens still drifting freely on the surface of the water. Most of the photovoltaic panels had been smashed, and all the windows were dark. But it was still there.

She raised her eyes toward the west. At the far edge of the lagoon was a bright patch of blue water. Looking at the crater that had been left by the nuclear tests, Haley reminded herself that the best way to make something lasting was to grow it piece by piece, like the reef. She could scale it back. Not as a colonist, but as a care-taker, preparing the way for others to return. Manita was right. Nothing could take away what she already had. She didn't need their money, their resources, or even their support. All she needed was herself.

A flock of shearwaters was feeding over the water. Haley kept her eyes on it. Then she turned away and descended the tower again, going down just as she had climbed up—alone, and without a harness.

zen and the art of starship maintenance

TOBIAS S. BUCKELL

Tobias S. Buckell is a New York Times *bestselling author born in the Caribbean. He grew up in Grenada and spent time in the British and U.S. Virgin Islands, which influence much of his work. His novels and more than fifty stories have been translated into eighteen different languages. His work has been nominated for the Hugo, Nebula, and Prometheus awards, as well as the John W. Campbell Award for Best New Science Fiction Author. He currently lives in Bluffton, Ohio, with his wife, twin daughters, and a pair of dogs. He can be found online at www.tobiasbuckell.com.*

In the story that follows, Buckell introduces us to a philosophically inclined maintenance robot who spends his time hanging on to the skin of the spaceship he's charged with repairing, and who must wrestle with the problems of free will when his programming forces him to do something he doesn't want to do and that he knows is wrong.

After battle with the *Fleet of Honest Representation*, after seven hundred seconds of sheer terror and uncertainty, and after our shared triumph in the acquisition of the greatest prize seizure in three hundred years, we cautiously approached the massive black hole that Purth-Anaget orbited. The many rotating rings, filaments, and infrastructures bounded within the fields that were the entirety of our ship, *With All Sincerity*, were flush with a sense of victory and bloated with the riches we had all acquired.

Give me a ship to sail and a quasar to guide it by, billions of individual citizens of all shapes, functions, and sizes cried out in joy together on the common channels. Whether fleshy forms safe below, my fellow crab-like maintenance forms on the hulls, or even the secretive navigation minds, our myriad thoughts joined in a sense of True Shared Purpose that lingered even after the necessity of the group battle-mind.

I clung to my usual position on the hull of one of the three rotating habitat rings deep inside our shields and watched the warped event horizon shift as we fell in behind the metallic world in a trailing orbit.

A sleet of debris fell toward the event horizon of Purth-Anaget's black hole, hammering the kilometers of shields that formed an iridescent cocoon around us. The bow shock of our shields' push through the debris field danced ahead of us, the compressed wave it created becoming a hyper-aurora of shifting colors and energies that collided and compressed before they streamed past our sides.

What a joy it was to see a world again. I was happy to be outside in the dark so that as the bow shields faded, I beheld the perpetual night face of the world: it glittered with millions of fractal habitation patterns traced out across its artificial surface.

On the hull with me, a nearby friend scuttled between airlocks in a cloud of insect-sized seeing eyes. They spotted me and tapped me with a tight-beam laser for a private ping.

"Isn't this exciting?" they commented.

"Yes. But this will be the first time I don't get to travel downplanet," I beamed back.

I received a derisive snort of static on a common radio frequency from their direction. "There is nothing there that cannot be experienced right here in the Core. Waterfalls, white sand beaches, clear waters."

"But it's different down there," I said. "I love visiting planets."

"Then hurry up and let's get ready for the turnaround so we can leave this industrial shithole of a planet behind us and find a nicer one. I hate being this close to a black hole. It fucks with time dilation, and I spend all night tasting radiation and fixing broken equipment that can't handle energy discharges in the exajoule ranges. Not to mention everything damaged in the battle I have to repair."

This was true. There was work to be done.

Safe now in trailing orbit, the many traveling worlds contained within the shields that marked the *With All Sincerity*'s boundaries burst into activity. Thousands of structures floating in between the rotating rings moved about, jockeying and repositioning themselves into renegotiated orbits. Flocks of transports rose into the air, wheeling about inside the shields to then stream off ahead toward Purth-Anaget. There were trillions of citizens of the *Fleet of Honest Representation* heading for the planet now that their fleet lay captured between our shields like insects in amber.

The enemy fleet had forced us to extend energy far, far out beyond our usual limits. Great risks had been taken. But the reward had been epic and the encounter resolved in our favor with their capture.

Purth-Anaget's current ruling paradigm followed the memetics of the One True Form, and so had opened their world to these refugees. But Purth-Anaget was not so wedded to the belief system as to pose any threat to mutual commerce, information exchange, or any of our own rights to self-determination.

Later we would begin stripping the captured prize ships of information, booby traps, and raw mass, with Purth-Anaget's shipyards moving inside of our shields to help.

I leapt out into space, spinning a simple carbon nanotube of string behind me to keep myself attached to the hull. I swung wide, twisted, and landed near a dark-energy manifold bridge that had pinged me a maintenance consult request just a few minutes back.

My eyes danced with information for a picosecond. Something shifted in the shadows between the hull's crenulations.

I jumped back. We had just fought an entire war-fleet; any number of eldritch machines could have slipped through our shields—things that snapped and clawed, ripped you apart in a femtosecond's worth of dark energy. Seekers and destroyers.

A face appeared in the dark. Skeins of invisibility and personal shielding fell away like a pricked soap bubble to reveal a bipedal figure clinging to the hull.

"You there!" it hissed at me over a tightly contained beam of data. "I am a fully bonded Shareholder and Chief Executive with command privileges of the Anabathic Ship *Helios Prime*. Help me! Do not raise an alarm."

I gaped. What was a CEO doing on our hull? Its vacuum-proof carapace had been destroyed while passing through space at high velocity, pockmarked by the violence of single atoms at indescribable speed punching through its shields. Fluids leaked out, surrounding the stowaway in a frozen mist. It must have jumped the space between ships during the battle, or maybe even after.

Protocols insisted I notify the hell out of security. But the CEO had stopped me from doing that. There was a simple hierarchy across the many ecologies of a traveling ship, and in all of them a CEO certainly trumped maintenance forms. Particularly now that we were no longer in direct conflict and the *Fleet of Honest Representation* had surrendered.

"Tell me: what is your name?" the CEO demanded.

"I gave that up a long time ago," I said. "I have an address. It should be an encrypted rider on any communication I'm single-beaming to you. Any message you direct to it will find me."

"My name is Armand," the CEO said. "And I need your help. Will you let me come to harm?"

"I will not be able to help you in a meaningful way, so my not telling security and medical assistance that you are here will likely do more harm than good. However, as you are a CEO, I have to follow your orders. I admit, I find myself rather conflicted. I believe I'm going to have to countermand your previous request."

Again, I prepared to notify security with a quick summary of my puzzling situation.

But the strange CEO again stopped me. "If you tell anyone I am here, I will surely die and you will be responsible."

I had to mull the implications of that over.

"I need your help, robot," the CEO said. "And it is your duty to render me aid."

Well, shit. That was indeed a dilemma.

Robot.

That was a Formist word. I never liked it.

I surrendered my free will to gain immortality and dissolve my fleshly constraints, so that hard acceleration would not tear at my cells and slosh my organs backward until they pulped. I did it so I could see the galaxy. That was one hundred and fifty-seven years, six months, nine days, ten hours, and—to round it out a bit—fifteen seconds ago.

Back then, you were downloaded into hyperdense pin-sized starships that hung off the edge of the speed of light, assembling what was needed on arrival via self-replicating nanomachines that you spun your mind-states off into. I'm sure there are billions of copies of my essential self scattered throughout the galaxy by this point.

Things are a little different today. More mass. Bigger engines. Bigger ships. Ships the size of small worlds. Ships that change the orbits of moons and satellites if they don't negotiate and plan their final approach carefully.

"Okay," I finally said to the CEO. "I can help you."

Armand slumped in place, relaxed now that it knew I would render the aid it had demanded.

I snagged the body with a filament lasso and pulled Armand along the hull with me.

It did not do to dwell on whether I was choosing to do this or it was the nature of my artificial nature doing the choosing for me. The constraints of my contracts, which had been negotiated when I had free will and boundaries—as well as my desires and dreams—were implacable.

Towing Armand was the price I paid to be able to look up over my shoulder to see the folding, twisting impossibility that was a black hole. It was the price I paid to grapple onto the hull of one of several three hundred kilometer–wide rotating rings with parks, beaches, an entire glittering city, and all the wilds outside of them.

The price I paid to sail the stars on this ship.

A century and a half of travel, from the perspective of my humble self, represented far more in regular time due to relativity. Hit the edge of lightspeed and a lot of things happened by the time you returned simply because thousands of years had passed.

In a century of me-time, spin-off civilizations rose and fell. A multiplicity of forms and intelligences evolved and went extinct. Each time I came to port, humanity's descendants had reshaped worlds and systems as needed. Each place marvelous and inventive, stunning to behold.

The galaxy had bloomed from wilderness to a teeming experiment.

I'd lost free will, but I had a choice of contracts. With a century and a half of travel tucked under my shell, hailing from a well-respected explorer lineage, I'd joined the hull repair crew with a few eyes toward seeing more worlds like Purth-Anaget before my pension vested some two hundred years from now.

Armand fluttered in and out of consciousness as I stripped away the CEO's carapace, revealing flesh and circuitry.

"This is a mess," I said. "You're damaged way beyond my repair. I can't help you in your current incarnation, but I can back you up and port you over to a reserve chassis." I hoped that would be enough and would end my obligation.

"No!" Armand's words came firm from its charred head in soundwaves, with pain apparent across its deformed features.

"Oh, come on," I protested. "I understand you're a Formist, but you're taking your belief system to a ridiculous level of commitment. Are you really going to die a final death over this?"

I'd not been in high-level diplomat circles in decades. Maybe the spread of this current meme had developed well beyond my realization. Had the followers of the One True Form been ready to lay their lives down in the battle we'd just fought with them? Like some proto-historical planetary cult?

Armand shook its head with a groan, skin flaking off in the air. "It would be an imposition to make you a party to my suicide. I apologize. I am committed to Humanity's True Form. I was born planetary. I have a real and distinct DNA lineage that I can trace to Sol. I don't want to die, my friend. In fact, it's quite the opposite. I want to preserve this body for many centuries to come. Exactly as it is."

I nodded, scanning some records and brushing up on my memeology. Armand was something of a preservationist who believed that to copy its mind over to something else meant that it wasn't the original copy. Armand would take full advantage of all technology to augment, evolve, and adapt its body internally. But Armand would forever keep its form: that of an original human. Upgrades hidden inside itself, a mix of biology and metal, computer and neural.

That, my unwanted guest believed, made it more human than I.

I personally viewed it as a bizarre flesh-costuming fetish.

"Where am I?" Armand asked. A glazed look passed across its face. The pain medications were kicking in, my sensors reported. Maybe it would pass out, and then I could gain some time to think about my predicament.

"My cubby," I said. "I couldn't take you anywhere security would detect you."

If security found out what I was doing, my contract would likely be voided, which would prevent me from continuing to ride the hulls and see the galaxy.

Armand looked at the tiny transparent cupboards and lines of trinkets nestled carefully inside the fields they generated. I kicked through the air over to the nearest cupboard. "They're mementos," I told Armand.

"I don't understand," Armand said. "You collect nonessential mass?"

"They're mementos." I released a coral-colored mosquito-like statue into the space between us. "This is a wooden carving of a quaqeti from Moon Sibhartha."

Armand did not understand. "Your ship allows you to keep mass?"

I shivered. I had not wanted to bring Armand to this place. But what choice did I have? "No one knows. No one knows about this cubby. No one knows about the mass. I've had the mass for over eighty years and have hidden it all this time. They are my mementos."

Materialism was a planetary conceit, long since edited out of travelers. Armand understood what the mementos were but could not understand why I would collect them. Engines might be bigger in this age, but security still carefully audited essential and nonessential mass. I'd traded many favors and fudged manifests to create this tiny museum.

Armand shrugged. "I have a list of things you need to get me," it explained. "They will allow my systems to rebuild. Tell no one I am here."

I would not. Even if I had self-determination.

The stakes were just too high now.

I deorbited over Lazuli, my carapace burning hot in the thick sky contained between the rim walls of the great tertiary habitat ring. I enjoyed seeing the rivers, oceans, and great forests of the continent from above as I fell toward the ground in a fireball of reentry. It was faster, and a hell of a lot more fun, than going from subway to subway through the hull and then making my way along the surface.

Twice I adjusted my flight path to avoid great transparent cities floating in the upper sky, where they arbitraged the difference in gravity to create sugar-spun filament infrastructure.

I unfolded wings that I usually used to recharge myself near the compact sun in the middle of our ship and spiraled my way slowly down into Lazuli, my hindbrain communicating with traffic control to let me merge with the hundreds of vehicles flitting between Lazuli's spires.

After kissing ground at 45th and Starway, I scuttled among the thousands of pedestrians toward my destination a few stories deep under a memorial park. Five-story-high vertical farms sank deep toward the hull there, and semiautonomous drones with spidery legs crawled up and down the green, misted columns under precisely tuned spectrum lights.

The independent doctor-practitioner I'd come to see lived inside one of the towers with a stunning view of exotic orchids and vertical fields of lavender. It crawled down out of its ceiling perch, tubes and high-bandwidth optical nerves draped carefully around its hundreds of insectile limbs.

"Hello," it said. "It's been thirty years, hasn't it? What a pleasure. Have you come to collect the favor you're owed?"

I spread my heavy, primary arms wide. "I apologize. I should have visited for other reasons; it is rude. But I am here for the favor."

A ship was an organism, an economy, a world onto itself. Occasionally, things needed to be accomplished outside of official networks.

"Let me take a closer look at my privacy protocols," it said. "Allow me a moment, and do not be alarmed by any motion."

Vines shifted and clambered up the walls. Thorns blossomed around us. Thick bark dripped sap down the walls until the entire room around us glistened in fresh amber.

I flipped through a few different spectrums to accommodate for the loss of light.

"Understand, security will see this negative space and become . . . interested," the doctor-practitioner said to me somberly. "But you can now ask me what you could not send a message for."

I gave it the list Armand had demanded.

The doctor-practitioner shifted back. "I can give you all that feed material. The stem cells, that's easy. The picotechnology—it's registered. I can get it to you, but security will figure out you have unauthorized, unregulated picotech. Can you handle that attention?"

"Yes. Can you?"

"I will be fine." Several of the thin arms rummaged around the many cubbyholes inside the room, filling a tiny case with biohazard vials.

"Thank you," I said, with genuine gratefulness. "May I ask you a question, one that you can't look up but can use your private internal memory for?"

"Yes."

I could not risk looking up anything. Security algorithms would put two and two together. "Does the biological name Armand mean anything to you? A CEO-level person? From the *Fleet of Honest Representation?*"

The doctor-practitioner remained quiet for a moment before answering. "Yes. I have heard it. Armand was the CEO of one of the Anabathic warships captured in the battle and removed from active management after surrender. There was a hostile takeover of the management. Can I ask you a question?"

"Of course," I said.

"Are you here under free will?"

I spread my primary arms again. "It's a Core Laws issue."

"So, no. Someone will be harmed if you do not do this?"

I nodded. "Yes. My duty is clear. And I have to ask you to keep your privacy, or there is potential for harm. I have no other option."

"I will respect that. I am sorry you are in this position. You know there are places to go for guidance."

"It has not gotten to that level of concern," I told it. "Are you still, then, able to help me?"

One of the spindly arms handed me the cooled bio-safe case. "Yes. Here is everything you need. Please do consider visiting in your physical form more often than once every few decades. I enjoy entertaining, as my current vocation means I am unable to leave this room."

"Of course. Thank you," I said, relieved. "I think I'm now in your debt."

"No, we are even," my old acquaintance said. "But in the following seconds I will give you more information that *will* put you in my debt. There is something you should know about Armand. . . ."

I folded my legs up underneath myself and watched nutrients as they pumped through tubes and into Armand. Raw biological feed percolated through it, and picomachinery sizzled underneath its skin. The background temperature of my cubbyhole kicked up slightly due to the sudden boost to Armand's metabolism.

Bulky, older nanotech crawled over Armand's skin like living mold. Gray filaments wrapped firmly around nutrient buckets as the medical programming assessed conditions, repaired damage, and sought out more raw material.

I glided a bit farther back out of reach. It was probably bullshit, but there were stories of medicine reaching out and grabbing whatever was nearby.

Armand shivered and opened its eyes as thousands of wriggling tubules on its neck and chest whistled, sucking in air as hard as they could.

"Security isn't here," Armand noted out loud, using meaty lips to make its words.

"You have to understand," I said in kind. "I have put both my future and the future of a good friend at risk to do this for you. Because I have little choice."

Armand closed its eyes for another long moment and the tubules stopped wriggling. It flexed and everything flaked away, a discarded cloud of a second skin. Underneath it, everything was fresh and new. "What is your friend's name?"

I pulled out a tiny vacuum to clean the air around us. "Name? It has no name. What does it need a name for?"

Armand unspooled itself from the fetal position in the air. It twisted in place to watch me drifting around. "How do you distinguish it? How do you find it?"

"It has a unique address. It is a unique mind. The thoughts and things it says—"

"It has no name," Armand snapped. "It is a copy of a past copy of a copy. A ghost injected into a form for a *purpose*."

"It's my friend," I replied, voice flat.

"How do you know?"

"Because I say so." The interrogation annoyed me. "Because I get to decide who is my friend. Because it stood by my side against the sleet of dark-matter radiation and howled into the void with me. Because I care for it. Because we have shared memories and kindnesses, and exchanged favors."

Armand shook its head. "But anything can be programmed to join you and do those things. A pet."

"Why do you care so much? It is none of your business what I call friend."

"But it *does* matter," Armand said. "Whether we are real or not matters. Look at you right now. You were forced to do something against your will. That cannot happen to me."

"Really? No True Form has ever been in a position with no real choices before? Forced to do something desperate? I have my old memories. I can remember times when I had no choice even though I had free will. But let us talk about you. Let us talk about the lack of choices you have right now."

Armand could hear something in my voice. Anger. It backed away from me, suddenly nervous. "What do you mean?"

"You threw yourself from your ship into mine, crossing fields during combat, damaging yourself almost to the point of pure dissolution. You do not sound like you were someone with many choices."

"I made the choice to leap into the vacuum myself," Armand growled.

"Why?"

The word hung in the empty air between us for a bloated second. A minor eternity. It was the fulcrum of our little debate.

"You think you know something about me," Armand said, voice suddenly low and soft. "What do you think you know, robot?"

Meat fucker. I could have said that. Instead, I said, "You were a CEO. And during the battle, when your shields began to fail, you moved all the biologicals into radiation-protected emergency shelters. Then you ordered the maintenance forms and hard-shells up to the front to repair the battle damage. You did not surrender; you put lives at risk. And then you let people die, torn apart as they struggled to repair your ship. You told them that if they failed, the biologicals down below would die."

"It was the truth."

"It was a lie! You were engaged in a battle. You went to war. You made a conscious choice to put your civilization at risk when no one had physically assaulted or threatened you."

"Our way of life was at risk."

"By people who could argue better. Your people failed at diplomacy. You failed to make a better argument. And you murdered your own."

Armand pointed at me. "I murdered *no one*. I lost maintenance machines with copies of ancient brains. That is all. That is what they were *built* for."

"Well. The sustained votes of the hostile takeover that you fled from have put out a call for your capture, including a call for your dissolution. True death, the end of your thought line—even if you made copies. You are hated and hunted. Even here."

"You were bound to not give up my location," Armand said, alarmed.

"I didn't. I did everything in my power not to. But I am a mere maintenance form. Security here is very, very powerful. You have fifteen hours, I estimate, before security is able to model my comings and goings, discover my cubby by auditing mass transfers back a century, and then open its current sniffer files. This is not a secure location; I exist thanks to obscurity, not invisibility."

"So, I am to be caught?" Armand asked.

"I am not able to let you die. But I cannot hide you much longer."

To be sure, losing my trinkets would be a setback of a century's worth of work. My mission. But all this would go away eventually. It was important to be patient on the journey of centuries.

"I need to get to Purth-Anaget, then," Armand said. "There are followers of the True Form there. I would be sheltered and out of jurisdiction."

"This is true." I bobbed an arm.

"You will help me," Armand said.

"The fuck I will," I told it.

"If I am taken, I will die," Armand shouted. "They will kill me."

"If security catches you, our justice protocols will process you. You are not in immediate danger. The proper authority levels will put their attention to you. I can happily refuse your request."

I felt a rise of warm happiness at the thought.

Armand looked around the cubby frantically. I could hear its heartbeats rising, free of modulators and responding to unprocessed, raw chemicals. Beads of dirty sweat appeared on Armand's forehead. "If you have free will over this decision, allow me to make you an offer for your assistance."

"Oh, I doubt there is anything you can—"

"I will transfer you my full CEO share," Armand said.

My words died inside me as I stared at my unwanted guest.

A *full share.*

The CEO of a galactic starship oversaw the affairs of nearly a billion souls. The economy of planets passed through its accounts.

Consider the cost to build and launch such a thing: it was a fraction of the GDP of an entire planetary disk. From the boiling edges of a sun to the cold Oort clouds. The wealth, almost too staggering for an individual mind to perceive, was passed around by banking intelligences that created systems of trade throughout the galaxy, moving encrypted, raw information from point to point. Monetizing memes with picotechnological companion infrastructure apps. Raw mass trade for the galactically rich to own a fragment of something created by another mind light-years away. Or just simple tourism.

To own a share was to be richer than any single being could really imagine. I'd forgotten the godlike wealth inherent in something like the creature before me.

"If you do this," Armand told me, "you cannot reveal I was here. You cannot say anything. Or I will be revealed on Purth-Anaget, and my life will be at risk. I will not be safe unless I am to disappear."

I could feel choices tangle and roil about inside of me. "Show me," I said.

Armand closed its eyes and opened its left hand. Deeply embedded cryptography tattooed on its palm unraveled. Quantum keys disentangled, and a tiny singularity of information budded open to reveal itself to me. I blinked. I could verify it. I could *have* it.

"I have to make arrangements," I said neutrally. I spun in the air and left my cubby to spring back out into the dark where I could think.

I was going to need help.

I tumbled through the air to land on the temple grounds. There were four hundred and fifty structures there in the holy districts, all of them lined up among the boulevards of the faithful where the pedestrians could visit their preferred slice of the divine. The minds of biological and hard-shelled forms all tumbled, walked, flew, rolled, or crawled there to fully realize their higher purposes.

Each marble step underneath my carbon fiber–sheathed limbs calmed me. I walked through the cool curtains of the Halls of the Confessor and approached the Holy of Holies: a pinprick of light suspended in the air between the heavy, expensive mass of real marble columns. The light sucked me up into the air and pulled me into a tiny singularity of perception and data. All around me, levels of security veils dropped, thick and implacable. My vision blurred and taste buds watered from the acidic levels of deadness as stillness flooded up and drowned me.

I was alone.

Alone in the universe. Cut off from everything I had ever known or would know. I was nothing. I was everything. I was—

"You are secure," the void told me.

I could sense the presence at the heart of the Holy of Holies. Dense with computational capacity, to a level that even navigation systems would envy. Intelligence that a Captain would beg to taste. This near-singularity of artificial intelligence had been created the very moment I had been pulled inside of it, just for me to talk to. And it would die the moment I left. Never to have been.

All it was doing was listening to me, and only me. Nothing would know what I said. Nothing would know what guidance I was given.

"I seek moral guidance outside clear legal parameters," I said. "And confession."

"Tell me everything."

And I did. It flowed from me without thought: just pure data. Video, mind-state, feelings, fears. I opened myself fully. My sins, my triumphs, my darkest secrets.

All was given to be pondered over.

Had I been able to weep, I would have.

Finally, it spoke. "You must take the share."

I perked up. "Why?"

"To protect yourself from security. You will need to buy many favors and throw security off the trail. I will give you some ideas. You should seek to protect yourself. Self-preservation is okay."

More words and concepts came at me from different directions, using different moral subroutines. "And to remove such power from a soul that is willing to put lives at risk . . . you will save future lives."

I hadn't thought about that.

"I know," it said to me. "That is why you came here."

Then it continued, with another voice. "Some have feared such manipulations before. The use of forms with no free will creates security weaknesses. Alternate charters have been suggested, such as fully owned workers' cooperatives with mutual profit-sharing among crews, not just partial vesting after a timed contract. Should you gain a full share, you should also lend efforts to this."

The Holy of Holies continued. "To get this Armand away from our civilization is a priority; it carries dangerous memes within itself that have created expensive conflicts."

Then it said, "A killer should not remain on ship."

And, "You have the moral right to follow your plan."

Finally, it added, "Your plan is just."

I interrupted. "But Armand will get away with murder. It will be free. It disturbs me."

"Yes."

"It should."

"Engage in passive resistance."

"Obey the letter of Armand's law, but find a way around its will. You will be like a genie, granting Armand wishes. But you will find a way to bring justice. You will see."

"Your plan is just. Follow it and be on the righteous path."

I launched back into civilization with purpose, leaving the temple behind me in an explosive afterburner thrust. I didn't have much time to beat security.

High up above the cities, nestled in the curve of the habitat rings, near the squared-off spiderwebs of the largest harbor dock, I wrangled my way to another old contact.

This was less a friend and more just an asshole I'd occasionally been forced to do business with. But a reliable asshole that was tight against security. Though just by visiting, I'd be triggering all sorts of attention.

I hung from a girder and showed the fence a transparent showcase filled with all my trophies. It did some scans, checked the authenticity, and whistled. "Fuck me, these are real. That's all unauthorized mass. How the hell? This is a life's work of mass-based tourism. You really want me to broker sales on all of this?"

"Can you?"

"To Purth-Anaget, of course. They'll go nuts. Collectors down there eat this shit up. But security will find out. I'm not even going to come back on the ship. I'm going to live off this down there, buy passage on the next outgoing ship."

"Just get me the audience, it's yours."

A virtual shrug. "Navigation, yeah."

"And Emergency Services."

"I don't have that much pull. All I can do is get you a secure channel for a low-bandwidth conversation."

"I just need to talk. I can't send this request up through proper channels." I tapped my limbs against my carapace nervously as I watched the fence open its large, hinged jaws and swallow my case.

Oh, what was I doing? I wept silently to myself, feeling sick.

Everything I had ever worked for disappeared in a wet, slimy gulp. My reason. My purpose.

Armand was suspicious. And rightfully so. It picked and poked at the entire navigation plan. It read every line of code, even though security was only minutes away from unraveling our many deceits. I told Armand this, but it ignored me. It wanted to live. It wanted to get to safety. It knew it couldn't rush or make mistakes.

But the escape pod's instructions and abilities were tight and honest.

It has been programmed to eject. To spin a certain number of degrees. To aim for Purth-Anaget. Then *burn*. It would have to consume every last little drop of fuel. But it would head for the metal world, fall into orbit, and then deploy the most ancient of deceleration devices: a parachute.

On the surface of Purth-Anaget, Armand could then call any of its associates for assistance.

Armand would be safe.

Armand checked the pod over once more. But there were no traps. The flight plan would do exactly as it said.

"Betray me and you kill me, remember that."

"I have made my decision," I said. "The moment you are inside and I trigger the manual escape protocol, I will be unable to reveal what I have done or what you are. Doing that would risk your life. My programming"—I all but spit the word—"does not allow it."

Armand gingerly stepped into the pod. "Good."

"You have a part of the bargain to fulfill," I reminded. "I won't trigger the manual escape protocol until you do."

Armand nodded and held up a hand. "Physical contact."

I reached one of my limbs out. Armand's hand and my manipulator met at the doorjamb and they sparked. Zebibytes of data slithered down into one of my tendrils, reshaping the raw matter at the very tip with a quantum-dot computing device.

As it replicated itself, building out onto the cellular level to plug into my power sources, I could feel the transfer of ownership.

I didn't have free will. I was a hull maintenance form. But I had an entire fucking share of a galactic starship embedded within me, to do with what I pleased when I vested and left riding hulls.

"It's far more than you deserve, robot," Armand said. "But you have worked hard for it and I cannot begrudge you."

"Goodbye, asshole." I triggered the manual override sequence that navigation had gifted me.

I watched the pod's chemical engines firing all-out through the airlock windows as the sphere flung itself out into space and dwindled away. Then the flame guttered out, the pod spent and headed for Purth-Anaget.

There was a shiver. Something vast, colossal, powerful. It vibrated the walls and even the air itself around me.

Armand reached out to me on a tight-beam signal. "What was that?"

"The ship had to move just slightly," I said. "To better adjust our orbit around Purth-Anaget."

"No," Armand hissed. "My descent profile has changed. You are trying to kill me."

"I can't kill you," I told the former CEO. "My programming doesn't allow it. I can't allow a death through action or inaction."

"But my navigation path has changed," Armand said.

"Yes, you will still reach Purth-Anaget." Navigation and I had run the data after I explained that I would have the resources of a full share to repay it a favor with. Even a favor that meant tricking security. One of the more powerful computing entities in the galaxy, a starship, had dwelled on the problem. It had examined the tidal data, the flight plan, and how much the massive weight of a starship could influence a pod after launch. "You're just taking a longer route."

I cut the connection so that Armand could say nothing more to me. It could do the math itself and realize what I had done.

Armand would not die. Only a few days would pass inside the pod.

But outside. Oh, outside, skimming through the tidal edges of a black hole, Armand would loop out and fall back to Purth-Anaget over the next four hundred and seventy years, two hundred days, eight hours, and six minutes.

Armand would be an ancient relic then. Its beliefs, its civilization, all of it just a fragment from history.

But, until then, I had to follow its command. I could not tell anyone what happened. I had to keep it a secret from security. No one would ever know Armand had been here. No one would ever know where Armand went.

After I vested and had free will once more, maybe I could then make a side trip to Purth-Anaget again and be waiting for Armand when it landed. I had the resources of a full share, after all.

Then we would have a very different conversation, Armand and I.

The Influence Machine

SEAN MCMULLEN

Australian author Sean McMullen is a computer systems analyst with the Australian Bureau of Meteorology, and has been a lead singer in folk and rock bands as well as singing with the Victoria State Opera. He's also an acclaimed and prolific author of short fiction that has appeared in The Magazine of Fantasy and Science Fiction, Interzone, Analog Science Fiction and Fact, *and elsewhere, and of a dozen novels, including* Voices in the Light, Mirrorsun Rising, Souls in the Great Machine, The Miocene Arrow, Eyes of the Calculor, Voyage of the Shadowmoon, Glass Dragons, Void Farer, The Time Engine, The Centurion's Empire, *and* Before the Storm. *Some of his stories have been collected in* Call to the Edge, *and he wrote a critical study,* Strange Constellations: A History of Australian Science Fiction, *with Russell Blackford and Van Ikin. His most recent books are the novel* Changing Yesterday *and two new collections,* Ghosts of Engines Past *and* Colours of the Soul. *He lives in Melbourne, Australia.*

Here he offers a policeman in Victorian England an unsettling and perhaps unwelcome glimpse into the future.

I am an Associate of the Royal College of Science, which is unusual for an inspector in the Metropolitan Police. With the Twentieth Century only months away, education for police is becoming important. Much of my work consists of lecturing to sceptical constables with ten times my experience about how electricity may be used to murder people, how to spot the illegal tapping of telegraph wires, and why it's important to preserve the fingerprints on murder weapons. Occasionally I am even called to real crime scenes.

A beer waggon had been impounded and driven to Bankside Jetty, beside the Thames. Upon it was a large shed with a chimney at the back. I was sent for, and asked to identify what was inside because it looked "scientific."

"It's either a bomb or a death ray, sir," said Sergeant Duncan as we circled the waggon. "The lady had it stopped in Harper Road, near Session House."

"Lady?" I asked.

"Aye, sir, her name is Lisa Elliot. We think she's an anarchist, and had a mind to blow the place up. I arrested her."

I was not known for tact or patience.

"Sergeant, the waggon is nine feet high, is drawn by two Clydesdales and probably weighs five tons. If you wanted to blow up Session House, wouldn't you just use a clock, a detonator, and a dozen sticks of dynamite in a carpet bag?"

He had no answer to that.

"Are you sure you arrested the right person?" I asked as I opened a door in the side of the waggon.

"She's the driver, sir."

This was a surprise, but I managed not to show it. True, some quite small men were known to drive very large waggons, but this was August 1899. *Women can't do that sort of thing*, I thought.

The waggon had no windows, but the door admitted enough light for me to find my way around. There was a small steam engine and a tank of paraffin at the back, but most of the space was occupied by six disks, each two yards in diameter. Coiled on the floor was a length of cable, insulated with rubber. Connected to this was a camera on a tripod.

"There's a lot of wires," said Duncan. "Reckon it might be electrical."

"Who ever heard of an electric camera?" I asked as I picked up the tripod.

"Are you sure it's safe to touch that, sir?"

"Yes."

"But—"

"This thing with the disks is an electrostatic generator, sergeant. It produces electricity when turned by the steam engine. Is the steam engine turning it?"

"No."

"Then it's safe."

I was twenty-four, was an Associate of the Royal College of Science, and was the youngest inspector in the Metropolitan Police. I was not shown much respect or deference by those who had learned policing on the job, so I retaliated by treating everyone with contempt.

While Sergeant Duncan watched and three constables kept the onlookers from crowding in, I set up the tripod and examined the device as best I could without dismantling it. It provided a view of the world through a laminated glass filter connected to a Wimshurst generator. *What manner of camera needs very high voltages to operate?* I wondered.

"I reckon that thing is like the heat ray what the Martians used," said Duncan.

"Martians?"

"In that *War of the Worlds* story what was in *Pearson's Magazine* last year."

Thanks to Wells, Verne and the like, people were having trouble distinguishing fictional science from real science. One of my duties was to separate the two.

"The device in the waggon is a Wimshurst machine, a type of electricity generator."

"Sounds German," said Duncan suspiciously.

"James Wimshurst is British, he lives in Clapham."

"Oh. What's it for?"

"Sergeant, if you called me in to examine a body with a slashed throat, would you expect me to say who did it on first sight?"

"Er, no."

"Where is the Lisa Elliot?"

"She's being held at Carter Street Station."

My family was in reduced circumstances, rather than being common as muck and on the way up. My grandfather had owned a boilermaking workshop, but his rivals had undercut him in the markets and forced him into bankruptcy. My father had been taken out of an expensive school and put to work as a bank clerk. For the rest of his life he endured ridicule from his former classmates whenever they visited the bank. As a result, I was given the best education he could afford, then placed with the Metropolitan Police. It was dad's way of getting back at his upper class tormentors.

"Crime is the great leveller, Albert."

He found a pretext to speak those words every time we met, but he was not entirely correct. Far from sending Eton's old boys to Newgate, we inspectors generally investigated murder, theft, rape, prostitution and assault with broken bottles in places like Whitechapel and Spitalfields. Those with money and connections could afford to live by different rules. This made me angry. I was always angry.

Miss Elliot's solicitor was leaving Carter Street when I arrived. He told me that she had a comfortable income from patent royalties, and no criminal record or political affiliations. Sergent Duncan's search of her residence had produced nothing more deadly than a carving knife.

"My name is Inspector Albert Grant, and I believe you have met Sergeant Duncan already," I announced as she was shown into the vacant office where we were waiting.

Miss Elliot was no older than I, and dressed in smart but plain clothes. Her hair was pinned up tightly, and she wore minimal cosmetics.

"You're not going to get anywhere with me until you fetch a scientist," she began.

"I have ARCS after my name, that will have to do," I replied.

We sized each other up for a moment. She had the confidence and bearing of someone rich, so for me she was yet another enemy.

"What did you study?" she asked. "Mathematics? Natural Philosophy?"

"*You* are being investigated, Miss Elliot, not me," I said firmly. "I suspect that you're fairly clever, but don't try any clever talk in here."

She did not reply. A police inspector from the Royal College was probably as much of a shock to her as a woman with a high voltage generator was to me. *Educated* and *police* were two words that were seldom seen together. Neither were *female* and *scientist*.

"You were arrested while loitering in Jail Park, and are under suspicion of planning an attack on Session House. Just what were you doing?"

"I was conducting an experiment in photography."

"Your waggon contains a very large Wimshurst generator. It can probably generate two hundred thousand volts of static electricity."

"Half a million."

"Half a million!" exclaimed Duncan. "That could kill a man, like lightning."

She pressed her lips together for a moment and shook her head.

"Sergeant, a beer bottle can kill a man if you strike him over the head with it," she explained in a slow, level voice. "My influence machine merely delivers a very high voltage to an array of thin glass plates within a heavily insulated camera. Where is the danger in that?"

"Why?" he asked. "What are you trying to photograph?"

"It would take months to explain, even with Inspector Grant translating."

"I can arrange for longer than that, Miss Elliot," I said. "I can testify to a magistrate that your device is designed to seem like a harmless scientific instrument, yet can use a half million volt spark as a weapon. You may be convicted of being an anarchist planning an attack, and if you get less than ten years I'll be the most surprised inspector in the Metropolitan Police. Now I'll ask the same question: what were you trying to photograph in Jail Park?"

For some moments she sat very still, leaning forward with her arms folded tightly and staring at the table between us, as if making a difficult decision.

"Can I show you?" she asked, looking up.

"You mean demonstrate your . . . whatever it is?"

"My influence machine, yes. Where is it?"

"It's been moved to Bankside Jetty, for public safety."

"Is there a nice view?"

The question was clearly meant to annoy me, and I was very annoyed.

"Miss Elliot, I am what's known as a police expert, and *my* word is all that stands between you and Newgate. It's not a good idea to bait me."

"I'm not trying to bait anyone!" she retorted. "It's vital that I have a good view of London."

That made no sense, yet she seemed to be sincere.

"You can see St. Paul's, the Tower Bridge, and the Tower of London," said Duncan.

"That will do."

We squeezed into a Hansom cab for the three mile trip to Bankside Jetty. As we travelled, Miss Elliot explained something of her device to me, although I suspect that she was just testing my grasp of science.

"My father had the waggon set up as a travelling demonstration," she said. "The steam engine is from a small boat, and a friend of his built the generator."

"Was that friend James Wimshurst?"

"Yes," she said sullenly.

She was not used to dealing with people who understood her work, so I was proving to be a challenge to her sense of superiority. Oddly enough, this made me sympathetic, because it was the story of my life as well. I glanced at her hands. They were scratched and grimy, more like those of an electrician's apprentice than a society girl.

"Why do you do your own wiring?" I asked.

"I'm better than any tradesman."

"I spoke to your solicitor."

"Good tactic. Always know the answers to some of your questions if you want to catch a liar."

"Don't make this hard for me, miss, I'm just trying to establish that you're not up to something illegal. Apparently you make a few quid from patents."

"About a thousand pounds a year."

"All those patents are for improvements to existing machines: printing presses, steam engines, harvesters, and even brewery fermentation vats."

"What is illegal about that?"

"Nothing, but your father was an expert in electricity and optics, and you are apparently a good photographer. That's nothing to do with your patents."

"What the inspector means is that you and your waggon could be a front for folk who built a death ray," said Duncan.

"The sergeant has a good point, even if his death ray theory is fanciful," I added. "Explain your electric camera to me. What does it do?"

"It's to test an electrostatic optical filter utilising multiple diffraction gratings and thinly sliced calcite to provide light of selective polarisation."

I understood all the words, but not what they were describing. She was doing to me what I did to other people, and I did not like it.

"If you could explain that a bit clearer, we'd not be so suspicious," said Duncan.

"The filter is seven paper-thin glass plates pressed together. Three of them are silvered on one side, and into the silvering I have cut hundreds of very fine lines. These plates are enclosed by plates thinly coated with gold, and an electrostatic potential of half a million volts can be applied across them by using the Wimshurst generator. Two other plates, fashioned from calcite, provide selectively polarised light while insulating the viewer from the lethal electric potential."

"Sounds dangerous," said Sergeant Duncan.

"Used sensibly, it's not."

"What do you see through this . . . this filter?" I asked.

"Changes in the behaviour of light."

"You work alone. Why?"

"Why let some male colleague take all the credit because nobody would believe a woman can do what I do?"

That made sense.

"Most young ladies in your circumstances pass the time by painting or doing tatting mats for teapots," said Duncan. "Why do men's work?"

She sighed wearily, as if she had heard the question far too many times.

"Because I do it better than men."

"But your father built most of your equipment," I pointed out.

"Do you use a gun?"

"Er, yes. Standard issue police Webley."

"Did you build it?"

She had me. Debating with her felt like arguing with myself.

"Go on," I muttered.

"Father was experimenting with a capacitance battery, a device to store large amounts of electricity in a very small space. His idea was to use thinly layered metal on glass substrate."

"Did it work?"

"Oh yes. Even a day after he disconnected the Wimshurst machine there was enough electropotential left to kill him when he touched the wrong wire."

"So your waggon really is a weapon!" said Duncan eagerly.

"Sergeant!" I snapped. "Remember the beer bottle?"

To my surprise Miss Elliot gave me a fleeting smile of gratitude. It was probably rare for men to take her seriously.

"My condolences, miss. So do extreme electric fields really affect diffracted, polarised light?"

"You actually listened to what I was saying," she replied. "I'm astounded."

Nobody could accuse Lisa Elliot of technical incompetence. When we reached the Thames she opened a hatch in the back of the waggon, lit the paraffin burner and got the steam engine spinning. While boiler pressure was building up she opened the side door, uncoiled the insulated cable and deployed her camera to face north across the river.

To my surprise, the Wimshurst generator ran very quietly. The three contra-rotating pairs of disks produced no more than a whispering sound, so the chuffing of the little steam engine accounted for nearly all the noise within the waggon.

"Shouldn't there be long, crackling sparks?" I asked.

"Sparks are the discharge of potential, inspector," she replied. "They are only useful when impressing schoolboys, policemen, and university professors. I need the electrical potential to be maintained."

Within the waggon was a rack of levers, switches, dials, galvanometers and indicator lights. I watched as she made adjustments, threw switches and pulled levers, but did not really understand what I was seeing.

"You can look through the camera now," she said.

She was inviting me to put my forehead within a couple of inches of a half million volts. A bead of perspiration made its way down the side of my face as I took out my Webley Bulldog and handed it to Duncan.

"If I collapse, shoot a hole in the steam engine's boiler."

"Very good, sir."

"Then arrest Miss Elliot."

"She's already under arrest."

"That's for loitering with intent, sergeant. If I die, charge her with murder."

This must be how a suicide feels when he stands on Tower bridge and looks down at the Thames, I thought as I stood behind the camera, but Duncan, three constables and several dozen idlers were watching. One can get away with being an arrogant pratt, but only if one has some redeeming quality, like courage. This was a time to be brave, so I bent down and looked through the back of the camera.

"The image is the right way up, you're using an inversion lens," I observed, very relieved to still be alive.

"What do you see?" Miss Elliot asked.

"St. Paul's is visible, but only just. There's a lot of smoke in the air."

"What else?"

"There's a barge anchored about ten yards away, I can see a pigeon sitting on the tiller. Look, is there any point in—"

There was a soft sizzling sound, like bacon dropped onto a hot griddle. It lasted only a moment.

The view of London that I was suddenly presented with had clear skies, apart from a few fluffy white clouds. The buildings were devoid of the neo-gothic architectural froth that is all around us, instead the preference was for straight lines and smooth, elegant curves. Most roofs were flat, and parked upon many of them were sleek . . . carriages, for the lack of any better word. The air abounded with floating carriages, but they had neither bags of hydrogen nor wings to hold them up. They must have been powered by paraffin, because they discharged no smoke.

"Are you all right, sir?" called Duncan.

"It's utterly fantastic!" I exclaimed, unable to help myself.

"Rotate the right handgrip for a closer view of anything," called Miss Elliot. "And turn the camera with the lever on the left."

"What can you see, sir?" asked Duncan.

"I see St. Paul's in the distance, yet no other buildings are the same."

"What do you mean? That makes no sense."

Ignoring him, I inclined the view upwards.

"Something the size of an ocean liner is passing us, flying slowly above the river. There are people on promenade decks. The men are wearing dark, calf length coats, open shirts and cravats. There's not a hat to be seen. Some women are wearing skirts that only reach down to mid-thigh, others are dressed like the men—but with lace blouses open to the naval. Parasols seemed to have gone the way of the dodo."

"Don't suppose I could have a look, sir?"

"In a moment. The sky is clear, no smoke at all. Even the Thames looks clean, no scum or floating rubbish."

After what was a selfishly long time I retrieved my gun from Sergeant Duncan and allowed him to look through the camera. Miss Elliot remained in the waggon, tending her dials, switches and levers.

"*That* was absolutely astounding!" I said as I stared at the familiar, grimy reality of my 1899 London.

"Do you agree that my machine is no threat to life or property?" she asked.

"I suppose so, yet half a million volts in a public place is still dangerous."

"Inspector, just over the river is St. Paul's Railway Station. Stroll along the platform and you can stand within inches of locomotive boilers containing steam under extreme pressure. If one were to burst, it would kill you. Occasionally they do burst. Why is my influence machine any different?"

There are times to concede, and this was one of them. Blindly searching for guilt where there is none has ruined better careers than mine in the Metropolitan Police.

"I'm satisfied," I said, although shaking my head in bewilderment.

"Have you seen all you need to? The engine burns a lot of paraffin, and I must pay for it myself."

"Finish up, sergeant!" I called.

There was a loud hiss as Miss Elliot released steam.

"What were we seeing?" I asked as she clicked switches and pushed levers.

"Another London."

"I worked that out for myself. Is it London in the future?"

"According to dates on newspapers that I have managed to view, it is the present." High voltage electrical potential crackled as is was discharged.

"You should take your machine to the Royal Academy and have it assessed by qualified experts."

"Qualified experts? Qualified experts are men who will swear that a woman could never have done what I have done, wait a few months, then claim the influence machine as their own idea."

"Sergeant Duncan searched your house but found no notes or journals of experimental results," I said. "Where do you document your work?"

"The only true secrets are those that are unwritten and unspoken, inspector. I have a very good memory."

"But why do research and not publish it? Your invention is truly sensational."

"One day I'll write something for *Nature* magazine, but only when I'm the richest person in the world."

What does one say to something like that? My police colleagues were all men who were experienced rather than educated, so being misunderstood was part of my life. Here was a woman whose grasp of science outclassed mine, and she was just as misunderstood by the police.

"I'll issue orders that you and your waggon are to be left alone unless you're disrupting traffic or creating a disturbance," is what I replied. "If anyone gives you trouble, refer them to me."

"So I'm to be released?"

"Of course."

I beckoned to Sergeant Duncan.

"Have the lady's Clydesdales fetched and harnessed to the waggon," I said. "Then assign a man to see her home."

Duncan and I tried to make sense of what we had seen as we walked the half mile to Borough underground station.

"Cinematics," he suggested. "Like you see in those moving picture theatres."

"You mean Miss Elliot's made up some sort of moving picture show that she projects on a view of real London?"

"Aye, I suppose."

"How does she do it?"

"Don't know, sir, but that doesn't mean it can't be done."

"What do you think she's up to?"

"I think she'll announce that her machine makes magical things visible."

"And separate stupid people from a bit of excess money?"

"Working girls do much the same, sir, yet we turn a blind eye."

Sergeant Duncan was a dreamer with common sense. He read the new scientific romances and kept up with the basics of real science, but there were gaping holes in his education. Sometimes he reached ridiculous conclusions, like his death ray theory, yet was it so very ridiculous? At short range Miss Elliot's nine foot high, five ton waggon could indeed generate a death ray about ten inches long.

I was in a frail, brittle mood. Miss Elliot definitely reminded me of myself, because we were both alone and fighting a world that hated and resented us. *Does Duncan hate me?* I wondered. *He ought to, I humiliate him nearly every day. Would he put the boot in if I gave him the chance?*

"Science is getting ahead of policing in general and myself in particular," I admitted. "I get called all over Greater London to give my opinion, but more often than not, I can't help."

"What's a case as troubled you, sir?" he asked.

No snappy comeback, I thought, with as much surprise as relief.

"Just yesterday Scotland Yard called me in to check a death in Threadneedle Street. An old man was having a bath and reading the newspaper when an electric lamp fell in and electrocuted him. His son had gambling debts and stands to inherit two thousand pounds. Did he toss the lamp into the bath? Perfect crime, no way of telling."

"There is too," said Duncan at once.

"What do you mean?"

"Did the old geezer like a pint?"

"Probably."

"Then just go to a pub where he used to drink. Get chatting with the locals, ask if he was much of a reader. If he couldn't read, how to explain the newspaper and reading lamp?"

New technology had killed the old man, yet the cost of a pint might be all that was needed to solve the case! Why had I not thought of that? Probably because Duncan had several times more policing experience. By now we were standing in front of Borough Station's ticket window.

"You get back to Carter Street, sergeant. I just might go north."

"Have a pint for me, sir."

There were a few afternoon loafers in the first pub that I entered in Threadneedle Street. I mentioned that I was down from Manchester for old Hiram Beamwell's funeral. A sympathetic local bought me a pint.

"Aye, I'll miss him, and his newspapers," he said. "Bought one every night."

So much for Duncan's theory, I thought, as condescending as ever.

"So he was a keen reader?"

"Couldn't read his own name, guv. He got me to read for him."

Beamwell had died in his bath, in the company of an electric lamp and a newspaper, yet he could not read. Duncan had solved the case. I had not.

"Inspector Grant, Metropolitans," I confessed. "I have no authority in the City, but I don't suppose you'd like to tell some people in Scotland Yard what you just told me?"

Within the hour Beamwell's son was under arrest, and my self-confidence had fallen below the limits of detection.

I returned to the Carter Street police station to find that Miss Elliot was back in a holding cell. I had not yet signed her release, so when she had returned to collect her keys and bag, she was again locked up. Rather than just walk her to Kennington Station, I hailed a Hansom cab to take her home.

"I suppose you know that I can't apologise enough?" I said as the cab set off.

"No matter, inspector, I'm glad of the chance to see you again."

"Now that just has to be a lie. Nobody's ever glad to see me."

"You tried to understand my work, instead of sneering. Only my father has ever done that."

"And I'm sick of people sneering and saying that a mere police inspector couldn't have ARCS after his name. You didn't. Just what does your machine show, Miss Elliot—apart from a much cleaner London?"

"It shows another reality."

"How? Please, help me to understand."

"I can't. Come back and ask your question after I've had a lifetime to study the effect."

"So what is this other reality?"

"It's an alternate time, in which Galileo made discoveries in electromagnetism two centuries before Faraday, and Newton devised Maxwell's laws of thermodynamics in the Seventeenth Century. The science there is far more advanced than our own."

"My brain is trying to escape through my ears," I confessed.

She giggled, then put a hand on my arm. I had deprecated myself to her, and she had been charmed. For me, that was an important lesson in being human.

"Would the world be any different if Napoleon had defeated Britain?" she asked.

"Vastly so, miss."

"Yet Newton, Galileo, Maxwell and Faraday changed the world more radically than any king, general or prime minister. Napoleon and Wellington had a lot of cannons, but Newton discovered the laws of motion that allowed them to be fired accurately. A few centuries ago in another past, laws were discovered and inventions were invented much earlier than happened in our own history. My influence machine can see into a reality where scientists have gone on to make new discoveries. I have brought some of those discoveries into our own world."

"Brought? Past tense?"

"Yes."

"Inventions from the other London?"

"The very same."

The cab turned into Rockingham Street.

"Would your wife be very scandalised if you stepped into my house for a moment?" she asked.

"Not married, miss."

"Then pay the driver and come with me."

The top floor of Miss Elliot's house had been made into a workshop. She opened a very ordinary Gladstone bag and took out a large cigar box. To this she had added a brass band and clasp, and protruding from the side were an electrical switch and a dial.

"Take hold of it, inspector," she said. "Be brave, it won't bite."

I hefted the box. It weighed four or five pounds.

"This doesn't contain cigars," I said.

She reached out and set the dial to zero, then pressed the switch.

"It's lighter," I noticed.

"Let it go."

I did so. The box hovered in mid-air.

"Unbelievable!" I exclaimed softly. "But how? Electromagnetism?"

"Nothing so crude."

Grasping the box, she flicked the switch off, then returned it to the Gladstone bag.

"Are you convinced, Inspector Grant?" she asked.

"Definitely, most definitely," I said, "yet one matter puzzles me. We don't post the laws of our sciences and the principles of our machines in public places. How did you learn what repulses gravity?"

"In the other London, a school has been built in Jail Park. Just think about it, inspector. If you wanted to learn the science of some very advanced civilization, would you seek out its greatest scientists, or would you go to a school where children are educated and everything is explained simply and clearly?"

"Splendid point, but your device provides no sound," I pointed out. "How do you hear the lessons?"

"Every classroom has charts and diagrams pinned to the walls, and I can see what teachers write on blackboards."

Like everything else she said, this made sense.

"You will never again be disturbed in Jail Park," I assured her.

"Thank you, but I don't need to return there. Soon I shall use my influence machine to become the richest person in the world."

"Miss, with the greatest respect for your abilities, that will not happen. Watt, Stevenson, Newton, Brunel, Faraday, they all built or discovered things that changed the world, but none became very rich. It's merchants, speculators and bankers who make truly great wealth."

"I hope to prove you wrong, inspector."

"Fortune attend you, miss."

With that she put her hands on my shoulders and kissed me on the lips. The act was so sudden and out of character that I just stood frozen with my mouth open and eyes wide, looking like a complete idiot.

"My apologies, but that may well be my first and last chance to kiss a man on the lips," she said. "Best not tell anyone."

I walked the two miles to my rooms, my thoughts whirling. On this day I had been humiliated as both a scientist and a detective, then Miss Elliot had kissed me and said she may never kiss anyone else. Why did I feel curiously happy?

Mr. Field's importance and influence can be shown by the fact that I was taken off my normal duties to attend him. I was called to my very first meeting with the

Assistant Commissioner. He told me to report to Cadogan Square and do whatever Mr. Field required. I expected to be kept waiting for hours, but he met me at the door. He was of early middle age, and dressed in a plain but expensively tailored suit. As he escorted me into the parlour, he glanced at a folder to refresh his memory.

"I see that you have scientific qualifications," he said.

"That's true, sir," I replied. "Associate of the Royal College of Science."

"I hope you're grateful to Sherlock Holmes."

"Sir?"

"The Sherlock Holmes stories have caused a vogue for using science to solve crimes. However, Conan Doyle depicts his police inspectors as lower middle class and a bit thick, so the commissioner had you appointed to attend crime scenes and sound scientifically educated. Hope that doesn't offend you; I can be a little blunt."

The rich and powerful are often rude and boorish to their social inferiors. The frighteningly powerful have nothing to prove, and can afford to be polite and apologise. Mr. Field had a subtle but definite sense of being frighteningly powerful.

"Speaking as a policeman, what do you think of Doyle's stories?" he asked as he unfolded a chart on a table.

"If Holmes were real, I have a sergeant who could give him a run for his money," I replied.

"And what about yourself? Don't be modest."

"I suppose I'm as useful as anyone can be with three years on the job and three more in the Royal College, studying chemistry."

"Splendid, chemistry is the reason you are here. Look at this, tell me what you make of it."

On the table was a large, neat copy of Mendeleev's table of the elements, drawn on wrapping paper. To my astonishment, I saw that it contained a hundred and twenty elements, rather than the eighty-two that I knew of. The recently discovered gases neon, krypton and argon were noted as copernicon, newtoneron and kepleron, in fact very few of the elements had names in common with those that I knew.

"It arrived in the post last week," Field explained. "Note these elements: brunelium, luminium and descaron."

"Luminuim and brunelium could be radium and polonium. A French couple, the Curies, refined radium and polonium out of pitchblende last year. Both elements are radioactive, though the term used here is radioluminescent."

"And this one, descaron?"

"It doesn't exist."

"It exists, inspector, but we have not yet discovered it."

Whoever had drawn the table had given each element something called an atomic number as well as the more familiar atomic weight. I did not know what to make of it.

"Has a crime been committed?" I asked.

"Not to my knowledge."

"Then why am I here? I'm a police inspector."

"I'm coming to that. I showed this to a scientist who works for me from time to time. He happened to be passing through London on the way back from Paris, where he had been visiting the Curies. They mentioned in passing that radium emits a radio-active gas, but they had not yet determined its properties."

I checked the table

"Descaron?"

"Without a doubt."

He turned the table over and pointed to some writing and symbols.

"The author goes on to talk of atoms being made of particles called electrans, protrans and neutrans. The electrans may be what George Stoney calls electrons. Protrans and neutrans are still to be discovered."

"If they exist."

"Indeed. I made discrete enquiries, and determined that five dozen handwritten copies of this table were sent to some of the richest and most influential men in Britain. All but one of those copies were discarded."

"This one?"

"Yes."

"I still don't understand where I fit in, sir."

"Assume, just for one moment, that this is not a hoax. What would you say?"

Memories of a half million volt Wimshurst generator suddenly flashed bright in my mind.

"I'd say this table comes from another science, one that is far more advanced than ours."

Field nodded, but did not smile. He was an influential man, but his influence was based upon the world as it is. The table of elements spread out before me came from somewhere beyond his control.

"You are here because you recently investigated the activities of a woman named Lisa Elliot," he declared. "It was she who sent this table to me. According to your report, she experiments with optical polarisation and diffraction under very intense electric fields, and may be considered harmless."

"I stand by my words," I said.

"Maybe so, but I consider her to be the most dangerous person in Britain, and possibly the world. Come along, we're off to Scotland Yard."

In the carriage I gave Field a detailed account of what I had seen during my few hours with Lisa Elliot, and related what she had told me. I did not mention that we had kissed. Sergeant Duncan had been fetched to Scotland Yard, and he provided his own account of how Miss Elliot had been arrested. Field then took us on a short walk to the Houses of Parliament.

"You are about to meet the Prince of Wales, the prime minister and a lot of other important people," he said. "Resist any temptation to pick your nose or scratch your behind."

"But what will I say?" asked Duncan, who was understandably agitated.

"Say nothing unless spoken to, just stand to attention. Call the prince *your high-ness* and everyone else *sir*. Remember, the less you say, the less trouble you can get into. They probably won't want you to say much. Try not to stare at Sir Edward, his left arm was eaten by a tiger when he was in India."

"Sir Edward?" I asked.

"Commissioner of the Metropolitan Police, the man who pays your wages."

"But sir, what's going on?" asked Duncan.

"Remember what I said about not speaking unless spoken to? Start practising now."

We were shown into a room paneled with polished wood, and featuring a long table. Here the more important of the assembled dignitaries were seated. Many more were standing. The prince must have been feeling peckish, for he had a cold roast chicken and flask of red wine on the table next to him. He said little, and I suspect that he understood practically nothing of what was being said. The prime minister, Lord Salisbury, reminded me of a large, elderly bear that had been awakened from hibernation early, and was passably cross about it.

"Sergeant Duncan, I understand that you arrested Miss Lisa Elliot in Jail Park recently," said Sir Edward.

"Yes sir, for loitering with intent."

"And you authorised her release, Inspector Grant?"

"Yes sir, after appropriate investigations."

"I understand that she demonstrated her, ah, influence machine to you both?"

"Yes sir."

"How large was the flying battleship Mr. Field told me about?" Lord Salisbury asked.

"It was more like a passenger ship, sir," I replied.

"But it was as big as a battleship?"

"Yes sir, at least as big."

"So were war to break out with France or Germany, we might fly such a ship over the enemy armies and drop bombs over the side?"

"I imagine so."

"Why did you not report all this?"

"I did, sir. I wrote a full report."

Lord Salisbury looked across to where Sir Edward was standing.

"Make sure all the right heads roll, there's a good chap," he said.

"But, but this all seemed like so much nonsense," Sir Edward protested.

"Field?" said Lord Salisbury, ignoring Sir Edward. "Explain the situation to these people."

"Miss Elliot has access to sciences and technologies that would allow Britain to dominate the world for the next thousand years. We could defeat any army sent against us, establish colonies on the moon, wipe out disease and famine, and even unlock the secret of immortality."

Some moments of total silence followed.

"You mean nobody in this room need die?" asked the prince eagerly.

"Barring accidents or assassinations, no," said Field.

"Then why was she arrested again?" asked Lord Salisbury.

"Because she cannot be allowed to fall into foreign hands."

Field had no title, yet everyone deferred to him, and even seemed to fear the man. I began to suspect that the empire might not really be run by elderly, opinionated men with dangerous medical conditions. Behind the scenes, were Field and men like him discretely making sure that things got done? I was a police inspector. Why had I not heard about them?

Field placed three photographs on the table and beckoned Duncan and me forward. All had been taken in some cobbled yard with high brick walls. One showed the influence machine's waggon as I remembered it, and the second was dominated by a blurred and overexposed tangle of glowing, jagged threads where the camera stood on its tripod. In the third was a pile of char where the camera had been.

"Some Cambridge chaps examined the machine, then tried to start it," said Field. "When the Wimshurst generator was engaged, this happened."

"Did they read my report?" I asked.

"They were experts from Cambridge, inspector, it was not considered necessary," said Lord Salisbury. "Why do you think the camera caught fire?"

"There's no insulation, sir."

"Insulation?" he asked. "What does that mean?"

"It's from *insula*, the Latin for island—"

"I know what insulation means!" he shouted, slamming his fist on the table and turning florid with anger. "What the hell has insulation to do with cameras?"

I had somehow overstepped the mark. Someone who had the authority to start wars was aware of me, and he was not impressed. *How much worse can it get?* I wondered.

"Miss Elliot may have removed a multi-layer diffraction screen that prevents the electropotential from the Wimshurst generator from discharging. When your experts started the machine—"

"Dammit man, speak English!" demanded Lord Salisbury. "I have no idea what you're talking about!"

I was seeing what everyone else probably thought of me whenever I explained something in words that only another expert could understand. It was a valuable, if harrowing, lesson. I tried to think how I might explain the issue to Sergeant Duncan. In terms of understanding technical matters, Lord Salisbury and Sergeant Duncan were probably equals.

"There was a bit missing," I said.

"We require a little more detail than that," muttered Lord Salisbury.

So, the prime minister now suspected that he also had gone too far. I combed my mind for a harmless analogy.

"It acted like a fire screen that stops sparks from the hearth from flying out and burning your carpet."

"Is that the best you can do? I read some nonsense about you having a degree."

"I'm an Associate of the Royal College of Science, sir."

"So, not a real degree," he began, but Field stepped forward with his hand raised.

Lord Salisbury suddenly fell silent and stared down at the table, like a schoolboy caught writing rude words on a toilet wall. Field actually had the authority to silence the prime minister!

"How extensive is the damage to Miss Elliot's influence machine, inspector?" he asked, holding up the third photograph.

"Quite minor, by the look of it. Provide her with a new camera and tripod, and I expect she could have repairs done within minutes."

"She? Why must she do the work? Could you do it?"

"If I had the missing part and an inverter lens, yes."

Field waved Duncan and myself back and stood before the table, facing people who probably owned the deeds to nine out of every ten acres in Britain.

"Your highness, gentlemen, Miss Lisa Elliot is being held in this building. Her influence machine has been taken to St. James's Park for a demonstration. We have negotiated the purchase of the machine."

"What was the price?" asked a cabinet minister.

"Five hundred million pounds," muttered Lord Salisbury.

There was an extended silence, during which many rich and powerful mouths dropped silently open.

"You could buy the Royal Navy for that," said the minister.

"Twice," said Lord Salisbury.

"But thanks to Inspector Grant, we know that the missing part is a small glass diffraction screen," said Field.

"Which costs five hundred million pounds."

"True, but once we have the screen, terms of purchase can be renegotiated," said Field smugly.

I shivered as the sharp chill of alarm lanced through my body. Miss Elliot knew how to build more influence machines. She could build them for other nations, and these men did not like the idea of that. *They are lords of the golden rule,* I thought. *They have the gold, so they make the rules.* At best she might be locked away for the rest of her life. *At worst* was a cheaper option.

Members of the public had been cleared from the whole of St. James's Park, and the waggon housing the influence machine stood on a stretch of lawn just north of the lake, near Duck Island. One of Field's experts had found a camera identical to the one Miss Elliot had used, and had even installed an inverter lens within it. The insulated cable had been uncoiled on the grass, and the charred bits cleaned away.

Miss Elliot was sitting on a bench, handcuffed to a man dressed just like Field and surrounded by armed guards. More guards arrived escorting a middle aged man in an intimidatingly tailored suit and top hat. He took a slip of paper from the inside pocket of his coat and presented it to Field.

"You are looking at a five hundred million pound cheque," I whispered to Duncan.

Miss Elliot was brought to stand before the Field. He held the cheque up for her to see.

"The bearer will be paid five hundred million pounds, Miss Elliot," he said. "What do we get in return?"

"May I have my Gladstone bag?" she asked.

One of Field's experts brought the bag over from the waggon, and Miss Elliot had him take out a very familiar cigar box. She reached out for it, but he snatched it back.

"It contains two Gassner dry cell batteries, a lot of wires and something sealed in lead casing," said Field's expert. "It may be a bomb."

"How can I demonstrate what you will get if you do not let me demonstrate?" Miss Elliot asked.

I raised my hand. Field waved me forward. The Cambridge expert handed me the cigar box. All the onlookers pulled back. I opened the box and looked inside, then closed the lid again.

"Set the dial on the side to zero, flick the switch, then let the box go," Miss Elliot called.

The box hung in mid-air. There were gasps of amazement from the distant on-lookers. I grasped the box, flicked the switch off, then took it across to where Miss Elliot was standing.

"No bomb," I said to her guard, then I opened the box and displayed the contents to her. "No damage."

She gave me the merest twitch of a smile as I handed the box to her, and she again set it floating about a yard above the ground. The dignitaries now closed in to marvel at gravity being defied. Two of the guards hoisted the prince up so that he could sit on the box. It bore his considerable weight as firmly as a stone pillar.

"Very good, your highness," said Field. "I believe you are now the world's first gravity machine passenger."

Miss Elliot unpinned her hair as the hilarity and marvelling continued, then she removed something that resembled a microscope slide edged with resin and trailing two short wires.

"Install this in the camera," she said. "There is a spare mounting frame in my bag."

At a nod from Field, the Cambridge man took the filter from her and hurried away to the camera.

"While we are waiting, may I demonstrate another remarkable feature of what you call the gravity machine?" asked Miss Elliot.

Field looked to me and nodded again. I fetched the device. Miss Elliot asked me to turn the dial all the way around to ten.

"Switch it on again," she said.

Imagine dropping something from the top of Big Ben and watching it fall to the ground. We watched as the cigar box fell into the sky instead. It dwindled to a point and was lost to sight.

"By the time the battery is spent, the device will be travelling so fast that it will exceed the power of the Earth's gravity to draw it back," said Miss Elliot.

"So we don't have to cordon off the area in the interests of public safety?" Field asked.

"No."

The gathering's attention now turned to the influence machine. The filter had been installed in the camera and plugged into the insulated cable. Now the guards were needed to hold the dignitaries back instead of protecting them, for they had lost all fear in their excitement and were threatening to trample the equipment. The steam engine was brought up to full pressure, and the Wimshurst generator began to spin. The Cambridge expert switched a half million volts of potential to the camera, but it did not burst into a tangle of electrical discharges.

Field gave Miss Elliot a little smirk, then pocketed the cheque.

"Inspector Grant, will you do the honours?" he said.

I walked across to the camera, bent over and peered into the screen.

"Something's wrong," I announced. "I just see Big Ben and some cabinet ministers. The only flying things are pigeons."

I looked up. Miss Elliot was staring upwards and looking very pleased with herself. Field gave a cry of what might have been outrage, but could easily have been horror, then drew a gun and began firing into the air. He screamed at the rest of us to open fire and bring the box down. I emptied my Webley Bulldog, firing straight up, but the box must have been at least a hundred miles above us by then. Once I had a chance to glance around, I saw Miss Elliot being hurried away by her guards while the dignitaries scattered as fast as arthritis and gout would allow.

Sergeant Duncan and I decided to walk to Borough Station. It was a pleasant day, and we had a lot to discuss.

"So the real filter plate is halfway to the moon, in a dummy battery, in a cigar box?" Duncan asked, once we were on Westminster Bridge and well away from anyone who might be spying for Field.

"I don't think it's gone quite so far," I replied. "Not yet."

"What will happen to Miss Lisa, do you think?"

"She'll be locked in a cell with a pen, a bottle of ink and a ream of notepaper, and told to write out instructions for building an influence machine."

"Will she do it?"

"Of course not."

"What's to do with the cheque I half inched from Mr. Field while everyone was shooting at the sky?"

I tried not to burst out laughing, but failed.

"I think Miss Elliot would want you to keep it," I eventually managed. "Not much good to her, is it?"

"And it's probably been cancelled."

"But for a few minutes you were the richest man in the world."

"How'd you let her know that Field was crooked?"

"With my fingernail. I scratched a double cross into that lead thing in the cigar box."

By now we were over Westminster Bridge and passing Waterloo Station. Everything looked so very ordinary, yet not one hour earlier the world had changed so very much. I now knew that Miss Elliot had not really wanted five hundred million pounds. Her intention had been to humiliate Britain's richest and most powerful men, and to shake their complacency and confidence.

Field and the masters that were his servants could have afforded the money that she demanded for her quite fantastic secrets, yet they disliked the very idea of treating a woman fairly. By trying to cheat her they had lost the stars themselves, and the immortality to explore them.

"Tonight Field and the others will climb into their beds with far more respect for both women and scientists," I said.

"As will we," said Duncan. "That must be the reason Miss Elliot named her influence machine as she did."

What happened to Miss Elliot, you surely wonder. I have no idea, but a month after that day in St. James's Park I noticed that I was being shadowed. Why shadow me? I like to think that Lisa Elliot escaped. She was intelligent enough to know Field would neither keep his word nor let her go, so she must have planned for it. She would certainly not try to contact me, but obviously Field lives in hope.

Duncan was right, we have both been influenced by Miss Elliot. Although there are no women in the Metropolitan Police, every Tuesday Duncan and I go to a mechanic's institute hall and give lectures about the untapped potential of women in the investigation of crime. Some women who attend want to set themselves up as private detectives, others want to campaign for female police, and a few are even writing detective fiction and want their novels to seem more realistic. There are never any men in the audience, but every Tuesday the audience grows.

canoe

NANCY KRESS

Here's another story by Nancy Kress, whose "Dear Sarah" appears elsewhere in this anthology—a suspenseful race against time in which the crew of an exploratory starship undertakes the largest-scale rescue mission in history.

There it is," Seth says quietly—too quietly for something so momentous. After this, there will never again be a very first approach to an alien star system by humans. The four of us are human, and we often treat Reuben like one, although personally I have my doubts about Peter.

Personal history has no place in this occasion.

Luhman 16 is just barely visible on the bridge screen. We are still pretty far from the star system, but nobody wants to miss the first visual, even though it is hardly inspiring. Two brown dwarfs, looking like tiny smudges in space. The primary, Luhman A, is spectral class L 7.5, solar mass .05, temperature 1350 Kelvin, covered by silicon/oxygen clouds. Luhman B has a partial cloud cover and observable stellar weather. The two stars, three AU apart, orbit their common center of mass every 24.3 years.

None of that matters.

What matters is that this system has planets, six of them. Two, small and cold and dead, orbit Luhman B. Three orbit the primary, close in and almost certainly dead. One gas giant, which back in the unimaginable past failed to gain enough mass to ignite into a tertiary, orbits both. Terran measurements estimated it at three times the mass of Jupiter; Reuben's data now says it's closer to two point six. Its period is eight months. It has sixteen moons. Its orbit is more circular than it should be, which suggests that at some point, a collision with something else changed its orbit. It is officially designated as LuhmanAB6, but we on the *U.S.S. Kepler* have dubbed it Canoe.

Knock knock?

Who's there?

Canoe.

Canoe who?

Canoe survive this trip?

We got silly after emerging from the Yi Point, mostly from relief that we emerged at all. The *William Herschel* is the first manned test of the Yi drive, and we four are lab rats. When relief turned to silliness and eventually to boredom, things were said and done that should not have been, things that can't be undone because even though entangled sections of space cannot be severed, human relationships can be.

"Rachel, Peter, Soledad—I'm so glad to be here with you guys," Seth says, and there are actually tears in his eyes. We manage to smile at him, although we are embarrassed. On the conventionally powered flight here from the Yi Point, Seth grew more emotional. Long periods of claustrophobia affect people differently, despite all the pre-flight psychological testing, all the inventive ways to keep us occupied, all the careful planning. Seth has become more emotional, Soledad more briskly efficient, Peter and I . . . well. I should have picked Seth when, against orders, I stopped taking the libido suppressors. I didn't pick Seth. But despite what Peter and I have done and said to each other, we are still professionals and both of us are excited by Luhman 16.

"I'm glad to be here, too," I say. Then we get to work.

Just overnight Reuben has gathered an additional mountain of data, and we frantically analyze the AI's analyses. Reuben delivers meticulous measurements and number-crunching; it can't do interpretation.

"*Fucking Christ,*" Soledad says, and we all look up from our work stations. Soledad, who somehow says Mass all by herself every "Sunday," usually curses only mildly, and in Spanish.

"What?" Peter says. And then more sharply, when she doesn't answer, "What is it?"

"The planet. It's going rogue."

We all leap up and gather around her screen, even though we could just as easily call up the data on our own screens. They don't convey much to me, ship's physician and biologist, but I know what "rogue" means. Canoe's orbit is breaking loose from Luhman AB. Maybe there was another collision, maybe it's just a slow decay of the gravitational ties that held it so long, so far out. Whatever the reason, Canoe is moving from its star system, drifting off into space, a planet without a home.

"Change of plan," says Soledad, reverting from analyst to captain. "We visit the inner planets later, Canoe first. Before it gets away. Peter, I need course changes."

He nods, returns to his console, and begins working with Reuben. Seth says softly, "Going rogue. Sailing off alone into the unknown dark."

Peter, his back to me, shifts his shoulders slightly. Seth has spoken from romantic ignorance; he can't know about my and Peter's vicious fight, doesn't realize what he is inadvertently echoing.

I return to scanning spectrographic data from Canoe, looking for pre-organics. We don't expect to find life anywhere in Luhman AB; we are here because it is so close, astronomically speaking, to Earth: six point five light years, and 36,000 years ago, only five light years. We are here because Joseph Yi invented the Yi Drive, which uses the entanglement of certain sections of the substrate underlying space, and this is one of them. We are here to see what another star system is like. We are here because this is what humans do.

Thousands of years ago, my people sailed off into an unknown sea. They set out from Polynesia in multi-hulled outrigger canoes, crossing thousands of miles of open ocean to reach as far as Hawaii, Easter Island, and New Zealand. The greatest premodern sailors in the world, they navigated by star and sun sightings, bird migration, current patterns, cloud formations—all lore passed down through generations in song. I sang the bastard versions of these songs when I was growing up on American Samoa. I am the bastard result of this heritage: Rachel Tuitama, born of a Samoan chief and an American U.N. worker.

There are only three choices in American Samoa, even for the daughter of a *matai*: work for the fisheries, work for the government, or get out. For decades we have had a higher rate of U.S. Army enlistment than any American state. Also the greatest number of NFL players, but that route wasn't exactly available to me. Twenty years ago I joined up. I am well educated, superb at what I do, strong if not beautiful, very intelligent. I deserve to be here with Soledad Luisa Perez, Seth Wang, Peter Stackhouse Cameron III. And I am Polynesian, willing to set out into unknown space, out of touch with my homeland, on a barely tested ship for a basically unknown destination.

The *Herschel* inches toward Canoe. The gas giant grows brighter and brighter in the sky, and we're kept busy with the new data gathered by ship's sensors and organized by Reuben. When we finally get close enough for telescopic visuals of the moons, the four of us again gather around Soledad's screen, the largest, as if it were a fireplace in the Arctic.

"Look at that," Seth says. "What's the albedo?"

Soledad says, "Point eight nine. Ice fields."

All at once a plume shoots out from the moon. It is beautiful: a soaring high streak of white. Seth actually gasps. "Cryovolcanic activity! Launch a probe!"

Soledad nods; she is not the sort of captain to object to what someone else could construe as an order from a subordinate. This is just Seth, wildly enthusiastic. My heart starts a slow thud in my chest. An icy crust could, conceivably, indicate an ocean beneath, as was true of Europa and Enceladus in the solar system. Both moons had disappointed; the oceans held no life, not even microbial. But that didn't mean the same will be true of Canoe 6. The odds are against it, but still . . .

The *Herschel* carries a limited number of fly-by probes, two controlled-crash landers, and one precious nuclear-powered cryobot. Only the probes are retrievable, and there is no chance of humans landing on Canoe 6—too much radiation. But the probes are directable by Reuben, and my chest swells as Soledad gives the AI directions to fly through a plume if possible, and to capture not only data but a sample of whatever the under-ice volcanoes are ejecting. The first is easy, the second will need a lot of luck.

Everybody is antsy until the first data comes back from the probe. Seth suggests card games; nobody else is interested. Peter and I avoid each other as much as possible. If Soledad notices, she doesn't comment. Patience, beauty, tact, formidable self-control harnessing an even more formidable intelligence—I want to be Soledad Perez.

My father would scorn such a thought. "You are a daughter of Nafanua," he always said when I misbehaved. I heard that from the time I could understand words at all. Only later did I learn that Nafanua was a goddess of war.

Data streams in. Canoe 6's diameter is 500 miles, about a quarter as big as Terra's moon, with a high enough density to suggest a strong percentage of silicates and iron. Its surface temperature reaches an astonishingly warm −50° Celsius. Magnetometer readings show a thin atmosphere of ionized water vapor. Camera images, which we pour over, give close-ups of areas of smooth ice, areas of domed craters, and degraded fractures.

Peter says, "There's an ocean under that ice."

"We can't be sure," Soledad says.

"Yes, we can!" Seth chokes out. He is practically hyperventilating. "Look at the libration measurements—that entire icy crust is detached from the moon's core!"

Peter says, "Those degraded craters and fractures indicate a lot of resurfacing. That ice has partially melted and refrozen countless times. There is geological activity going on under there—maybe even an equivalent to plate tectonics."

They start a long technical discussion. Seth is mission engineer but knows a lot of physics. The three of them toss directions at Reuben that involve equations. I cannot follow most of this, so I wait quietly until I can ask the most important question. "Do you think that ocean could be warm enough to sustain life? Maybe near thermal vents on the sea floor?"

Peter says, "Depends. If the tidal flexing from Canoe 3 is great enough—maybe."

Seth says, "If it's aided by enough libration—wobble in the axis of rotation, Rachel—"

I know what libration is, but I don't interrupt him.

"—and maybe by resonance with another moon on the other side of the planet, to excite Canoe 6's orbital eccentricity."

Pete says, "Throw in past radioactivity and maybe some core melting, creating magma chambers that give rise to thermal vents and drive geological activity—"

"If the core is porous enough for water to flow through it, picking up heat—"

"Yes!" Peter says. They go on, driving each other into greater and greater enthusiasm, until Soledad stops it.

"We won't know anything for sure until and unless we get more information from a cryovolcanic plume."

She's right, but my heart goes on thumping anyway. I am mission astrobiologist. It would be great to have a job to go with that job description. Just a few lousy microbes. It would justify everything.

How do you justify the volcanic heat of anger? If Soledad had overheard Peter and me fighting, I would never have any sort of job anywhere again.

The sex was not very good. It was not even complete, perhaps because libido suppressants are so individual, taking longer to leave one person's system than another.

"I'm sorry," Peter said.

"It's okay."

"It's not okay. Please don't say it is when it's not."

If I had left it at that, we might have been all right. *You try to have the last word,* my father always said. *That is not good in a woman.* As a child, this baffled and scared me—how could I be the daughter of Nafanua and also as obedient as he wanted? As a teenager, his words enraged me. They still do.

"I was attempting," I said to Peter, "to console you."

"I don't need consolation!"

"Fine. You just—" I stopped myself.

He did not. "I just what?"

"Nothing."

"God, you look so *smug.* I just should accept failure?"

I shrugged. "If that's what you want to call it."

"Your face called it that."

But it was his face that tipped us over the edge. I have seen that look before, many times, before I saw it on Peter Stackhouse Cameron III: outrage at being judged by someone considered inferior. I said, "My face calls things by their true names."

"Really? And what is the 'true name' for what just happened here? This wasn't *my* failure. If you hadn't wheedled me into sex I wasn't interested in, or if you were more appealing, I might have responded more!"

Fury took me then. "More appealing? You mean 'more white'?"

"I didn't say that. Don't put words in my mouth."

"Nothing else about me was happy there."

It escalated from there. All the boredom of a long flight in cramped quarters, all the unadmitted uncertainty about this expedition, all the buried histories of both of us, so carefully compensated for during the mission selection process, rose in a boiling mass. Two boiling masses. Before it was done, both of us, intelligent people, had located and lacerated the other's most vulnerable point.

"You are only on the *Herschel* because of your daddy's WASPy political connections and your photogenic surface. You're *all* surface—never produced a single physics paper of note, depend on Soledad to guide your analyses, can't even keep it up in bed!"

"I can with someone who didn't look like . . . like . . ."

"Like what? A frizzy-haired fireplug?"

"I didn't say that!"

"You meant it!"

Rage clamped his jaw so tight—I'd been right and he knew it—that he barely got out his next words. "Don't you ever tell me what I mean. And as to being here—do you imagine that *you'd* have been chosen if you weren't the exotic hybrid needed to satisfy the mission's ethnic quota?"

I attacked him. I'm strong, and my uppercut to his jaw caught him by surprise. I have never regretted anything so much in my life, especially since he did not hit me back. Both of us emerged, shaking, from the volcano of primitive, neutrally hijacked rage, back to our mission selves. We were United States astronauts. We imposed on ourselves icy calm. I had knocked out one of Peter's front teeth.

I treated his mouth. Soledad of course noted both his swollen face and the new tooth growing in the organic printer, but she didn't ask. Seth asked, all sympathetic concern. Peter said he'd slipped and fallen.

We had both fallen. The pool of dark in each human being, under the thin exterior, can be terrifying. I resolved to never let it take me again.

We get lucky. The probe flies right through a plume, captures a sample, and brings it back to the *Herschel*. Reuben already has spectrometer data on the plume composition: mostly water vapor and ice crystals, with some volatiles and solids. However, those could have been deposited on the surface ice by comet collisions and then picked by the plume as it ascended.

More important, Peter and Soledad have a measure of the hydrogen gas in the plume, which gives them an idea of how much energy and heat are being generated at the bottom of Canoe 6's ocean. There's more than expected, which sends them scrambling for theories to explain it.

The sea floor is warm enough for life, or at least this part of it is. It's also highly saline. The microbes I so desperately hope for would have to be halophiles.

"Good luck, Rachel," Soledad says. She touches me briefly on the shoulder as I suit up for the tiny biohazard lab. Seth hugs me. Peter nods briefly, his eyes cold.

The lab has a decontamination chamber and its own airlock to receive the probe. The equipment is state-of-the-art. But all I would have needed is a simple microscope to make the most stunning discovery of the space age. Me, Rachel Tuitama.

I send the images to the bridge. My voice is shaky. "Guys—these are complex organics. Multi-cellular. Some of them might be . . . may be. . . . there is *life* down there. And if these things here turn out to be waste products, which they look like . . . it could be complex life. I'll know more after I . . . that's a nucleus in that fourth image . . ."

Silence from the bridge. Some things are too big for easy words.

The silence doesn't last, of course. And of course it's Seth who breaks it. "Soledad—you have to send down the cryobot!"

She doesn't agree—or disagree. She says, "Rachel, send all your images, findings, analyses—whatever you find, even if it's preliminary. Peter, I want those models of possible subsurface conditions—all three of them—as detailed as you can make them based on Reuben's data. Seth, run checks on the controlled-crash lander, cryobot, and all remaining probes, plus the decontamination equipment for the first two. Also run the check-up diagnostics on Reuben. We need more information, accurate information, and usable analyses."

I stay in the lab until I can no longer keep my eyes open. The surprises just keep coming, until the biggest one of all: the life on Canoe 6 is DNA-based. Or some form of DNA, with a different base substituting for adenine, just as uracil substitutes for thymine in Terran RNA.

"*How?*" Seth says. By now we are all punchy from sleeplessness.

Peter says, "Are you sure you didn't contaminate the sample with your own DNA?"

I am too tired to respond to his tone with the first thing that comes to mind: *You think my DNA has a foreign molecule in place of adenine?* I say simply, "I'm sure."

Seth says, "Panspermia? Terra and Luhman 16 were closer together 36,000 years ago!"

Soledad says, "They were still five light years apart. But—I see three possibilities. Panspermia, yes. Comets hitting both Terra and Canoe 6 with similar pre-organic molecules, which so many comets carry. Or, three, there is only one optimal path for complex life to develop, given the basic building blocks, and this is it. Rachel, leave the lab and get some sleep."

"I can—"

"Leave and sleep."

She is the captain. But I need to know one more thing. "Soledad—"

"Yes. We will send down the cryobot. Tomorrow."

Unlike the *Herschel's* Yi drive, the cryobot is unmysterious and well-tested. The Yi drive works by "traversing links between entangled sections of the substrate underlying spacetime," a phrase that points to a huge amount of theory and mathematics— although not, in my opinion, pointing very clearly. The cryobot, on the other hand, is a nuclear-powered amphibious bathysphere capable of melting through Canoe 6's ice, descending slowly through its salty ocean, and sending back data as it goes. It contains well-understood instruments to make clearly defined measurements. There was no fight over funding cryobots to explore Europa, Enceladus, Ganymede, Ceres.

But we have only one, and it is not retrievable.

The four of us watch the launch, flight, and descent of the 'bot. It lands perfectly on the surface. The melter turns on and we watch the 'bot slowly disappear through layers of ice, sending back pictures and measurements.

"Clay-like particles in the ice—"

"Lower salt content than in the plumes—there might be mechanisms similar to Terra's to maintain saline equilibrium—"

"Temperature rising . . . minus 2 C . . . plus three C. . . . four—"

"Madre de Dios!"

Soledad. But all of us, those exclaiming and those stunned into silence, stare.

Lights flicker in the darkness. First a few, and then more, and then more and more, until there are enough overlapping and sustained flickers to see *them*. Data practically screams from our screens, but nobody looks at anything but the visuals.

Creatures, swimming around the descending cryobot. They look like eels, with elongated, cylindrical bodies. They swim so agitatedly around the 'bot that it's difficult to get a clear count. Light flickers on and off along the tops of their tiny bodies. Then, abruptly, all of them swim away at once, and the 'bot continues its slow, controlled, majestic descent.

Soledad, her voice shaky—Soledad!—says, "Rachel?"

I try to focus on the 'bot data, on the clearest visual freeze-frame, on the information in my memory. "They look like electric eels, but of course they're not. For one thing, Terran electric eels breathe atmospheric oxygen and they're predators. These are too small, only six inches or so. I don't know how they pack that many electricity-generating organs into such a small body. They must eat the equivalent of krill—

yes, there's evidence of multi-cellular biota all through the water. But they have a body-length anal fin, like *E. electricus*. Obviously they've evolved to live in colder and saltier water than Terran eels. . . ."

Seth says, "Why did they all swim off like that?"

"I have no idea."

Soledad says, "Any ideas on how to get them to return?"

"None. We wait, I guess."

We do, analyzing data sent back by the 'bot. Currents indicate that yes, there are thermal vents on the sea floor, plus geologic activity, and additional geothermal energy from residual core radioisotope decay. Plants, or plant analogues, wave fronds grayish in the light from the 'bot. A wealth of information about the ocean, about Canoe 6. But all of it feels anticlimactic, after the alien creatures.

"They aren't really eels," I say for the fiftieth time. "Even on Earth, electric eels aren't eels. They're a species of fish."

"Do the *eels*," Peter asks Seth with an obnoxious emphasis, "show any pattern?"

Seth has been using Reuben to search for patterns in the electric flashes. He says, "There are too many to tell. Too much noise-to-signal ratio."

Soledad says, "What do Terran eels use their electricity for? Communication?"

Even Soledad calls them eels. I give up. "No, although they're capable of varying the intensity of their discharges. Lower voltage for hunting, higher voltage for killing prey or defense. Big ones can produce 800 volts, more if they double up their bodies. They will stun and eat small mammals, even. But we haven't seen anything here to attack. My guess is that these are herbivore-analogs, although I can't be sure without dissecting one." Which is not going to happen. We aren't equipped to get below Canoe 6's ice, and the eels—damn it, now I'm doing it!—can't get up here.

Soledad frowns. "If they don't use the electricity for getting food, then why did it evolve?"

"I don't know."

"Doesn't such a biological adaptation take energy?"

"Yes."

"But then—"

Seth says, "They're back."

There are no electric eels in Samoa; the genus is South American. Samoa has true eels, five species of *Anguilla*. And we have Sina.

Sitting on my father's lap, skin to his bare chest, my eyes wide as stars as he told the story: "Once there was a beautiful maiden named Sina who kept a pet eel. The eel grew bigger and bigger, and it fell in love with Sina's beauty. When the eel tried to grab her, she ran away. But the eel followed her, hiding in the village pool until Sina came for water. Sina cried, 'E pupula mai, ou mata o le alelo!' But the demon eyes staring at her did not go away.

"The village chiefs killed the eel. Before it died, it asked Sina to plant its head in the ground. A coconut tree grew there. Now, whenever Sina drank coconut, she was kissing the eel. See, Rachel, the marks on your coconut? Two eyes, and a mouth from which you must drink."

I have no coconuts aboard the *Herschel*, and my father is dead. But I have the memory—growing from danger, the coconut tree that nourishes. A gift from the dying.

This time, only six eels swim around the cryobot. Seth sets the 'bot's lights to an optimal level for recording. The eels advance, retreat, advance again in patterns too repetitious to be random.

"They're *dancing*," Peter says, enough awe in his voice to make me briefly remember why I had once wanted him. Briefly.

"It's not necessarily an indicator of sentience," I say. "Bees dance from instinct."

"It's beautiful," Seth says.

The dance goes on for about three minutes. Then all six eels swim away.

"Seth?" Soledad says.

"Reuben is running the programs now. Wait . . . *look*."

We look. Even I, the non-physicist, can see the pattern displayed graphically on the screen. Each eel advanced to almost touch the 'bot and flash its light, then retreated. Another approach, with two touches-and-flashes. Another, with three. The eels' approaches were not synchronized; each was acting independently of the others. A swim completely around the strange object on the sea floor, and then the whole thing was repeated at different points on the 'bot."

Peter says, "They can count!"

"Maybe," says Soledad, always more cautious. "Can this be evolved behavior for any non-sentient reason that anybody can think of?"

No one answers. My head feels numb, as if my entire skull has been iced down after injury. But this isn't injury, this is—

"We need to try to communicate with them," Soledad says. "When they come back. If they come back."

Seth spins around on his chair, tears coursing down his cheeks, carrying the emotion for the rest of us. "We're not the only intelligent beings in the universe."

I stare, dry-eyed, at the screen patterns. A daughter of Nafanua does not cry. Not even if the first-discovered alien life is on a dying moon around a planet drifting into darkness.

When the eels return, we are ready. The cryobot has no display screen—who would have expected to need it?—but we can control much else about it. We flash the 'bot's lights: one pause two pause three pause, repeat. The eels respond, each with a touch-and-flash. We count by flashes to ten; they return only three.

Peter says, "'One-two-three-many'? That's the counting pattern of some very primitive primates."

"Maybe," Soledad says. "Seth, try primes."

First, however, comes another eel dance. Seth, recording and running algorithms, says, "This dance exactly matches the first one. To the centimeter."

I say, "Without hands to make tools, it's possible their culture advanced along biological patterns rather than technological. Like dolphins. But they might have quite sophisticated social and communicative lives. Language, dance, song."

Seth says, "I'm not picking up sound waves from them."

"Pheromonal, then? Are there patterned chemical shifts in the water?"

Determining this takes some time, while the eels finish their dance and, just as abruptly as they arrived, swim off.

"Yes," Seth says eventually. "Precise chemical shifts between eels. They're communicating."

Peter says, "But why not use sound waves? Less dissipation, and you can cover greater distances."

I say, "Maybe they do, but under different circumstances than these. I mean—there might be protocols for greeting strangers that are different from communication among themselves."

We try to investigate that, with no success. The eels return every eighty-seven minutes, but we have no idea how they track that time, or what the timing means, or much of anything else. Each time they return to the 'bot, the eels do a different dance; we have no idea what any of them mean. We try flashing a sequence of prime numbers; they do not echo it. We try Fibonacci sequences, spoken words, "Mary Had a Little Lamb" in musical tones—all at a risk of emitting soundwaves that might have violated some important eel custom. No response to anything. Meanwhile, plumes of water continue to rise from the same area of the moon, and we gather more physical data.

Frustration mounts. Soon the *Herschel* must move on. There's only so much fuel, so many supplies, so much time before we have to return to the point where the Yi drive will switch on to snatch us back to the solar system. That's how I think of it, anyway, when I think of anything except the eels. I even dream of them at night. In my dream, eels drift separately in the cold of space, each one with my face.

When I find Soledad alone, getting another cup of coffee in the tiny ward room, I ask my question. "How long—I know you might not have a precise answer to this, but generally—how long can the eels survive while Canoe 6 wanders away from its star?"

She takes a long sip of coffee. Something in her manner tells me that she and Peter have already worked this out, and that the answer isn't good.

"You already know that sea-floor volcanism is the main source of heat for the moon. Resonance with Canoe 3 also provides some through increased tidal flexing, but that's going to be lost soon—the data already show a lot of orbital decay in Canoe 3. And the weather on Canoe is getting more violent, spewing out increased radiation on all the moons. Basically, everything is going to go to hell once Canoe gets a certain distance from Luhman, although temperature calculations could vary as the—"

"Soledad," I say, "how long?"

"It's already getting colder in the ocean. From the historical data Reuben's been collating."

"*How long*? Best and worst estimates before all the eels die, of cold or anything else."

Soledad looks at my face. If she was going to say anything about specie variation in endurance factors, she changes her mind. "Best estimate, fifty Earth years. Worst—ten."

Ten years. Enough time. I have to be careful how I present my idea. "We could—"

"Oh my God! Come in here, quick!" Seth screams from the bridge. We race along the passageway, joined by Peter from his bunk, wearing only boxers.

The eels are back, only twenty-seven minutes from their last appearance. This time there are hundreds of them, including juveniles. They swim as a group toward the 'bot, then away, then toward, then away. It doesn't take an astrobiologist to interpret the message. Seth says, "They want us to follow them! Soledad?"

She hesitates. It isn't easy to move the cryobot once it's settled into mud, and moving it risks damage as temperature and pressure change. Finally she says, "Yes. Go."

On my screen, I see the reflection of her crossing herself.

Seth issues directions to Reuben, who says in its deliberately mechanical voice, "This action may damage this equipment, or parts of it. Confirm?"

"Confirm," Soledad says.

The cryobot rises from the mud and we all hold our breaths—would the legs hold? This is not what the thing was intended for. If the legs do hold, will they travel? The terrain is so uneven, with the equivalent of quicksand areas. How far would the 'bot have to go?

Not far. Seventeen point eight meters, and the eels stop swimming ahead and cluster around the 'bot. Seth sets it down.

Peter, seated in his underwear at his console, says, "Not good. There's a potentially active vent ten meters away, right at the limit of the 'bot's illumination. If it sends up another plume, the 'bot could be damaged. It—"

"They're dancing," Seth says. "*Oh!*"

The entire swarm of eels begins to move, but much differently than before. Their motions are slow, draggy. Then, all at once, every single one of them turns over and floats face down as they extinguish their lights. Only the 'bot illuminates them, a ghostly school of fish miming death.

They know.

Peter gasps, "How—"

I choke out, "I don't know. Changing water temperature, maybe changes in the magnetic field coming off canoe . . . Terran birds migrate by magnetic field . . ."

The eels turn over and flash their lights. Now all but one swims to the other side of the 'bot and out of sight. The one swims in the opposite direction and stops, motionless.

Seth says, "What the—"

The thermal vent blows. A gush of water and rock and ice and the eel is gone. Simultaneously, the bridge screen that is permanently trained on a close telescopic view of the moon shows a plume rising from the surface, a white streak across the dark sky.

I grope for my chair and sink into it. No one speaks. Then Seth says, "He's dead. He rode the plume up and . . . they understand that we must be on the other side of the ice. How—"

Soledad says, "I don't know. Except. . . . except that they are much more sophisticated than we thought, much more intelligent."

I say, "They'll do it again."

Peter says, almost angrily, "How do you know?"

Because Polynesians set out again and again onto the uncharted ocean as population pressure made them need more islands.

I cannot, will not, say that to Peter, or to any of them. "Because that's their only chance. We are their only chance."

Seth says, "If they're that intelligent, then they know that their . . . their messenger was already dead the second the thermal vent geysered."

"Yes," I say.

Soledad says, "If Rachel is right, the least we can do is capture a specimen. I'm going to station a retrieval probe in geosynchronous orbit over the vent spot."

A *specimen*. But I say nothing. Quarreling over language isn't worth risking the chance to touch an alien being. Or to save all of them.

An eel is so small. The retrieval probe lasts through five more plumes before it runs out of fuel and crashes to the surface. So does the second probe. We do not get a "specimen." An alien. An intelligent being.

And we have to leave Canoe.

"We have all the data we're going to get," Soledad says. "And we can't do any more here."

I've waited this long, because bringing home an alien, even dead, would have helped so much. But now I have to speak.

"We can't do more here," I say. "But we can get ready to do more on Terra."

Seth says, "What?"

"We can throw every bit of weight and persuasion and threats, if necessary, around the idea that the next mission has to be back here, not to Wolf 1061 as planned now. A rescue mission, with equipment to bring back a lot of the eels in tanks with their own water and pressure and temperature. A rescue of our interstellar brothers. After all, they have a form of DNA!"

Seth says, "Bring back? As some sort of zoo animals? I didn't think you, of all people, would want that!"

You, of all people. It goes deep, that setting apart of "the other." But I can't afford that fight right now. I say, "Not zoo animals. Fellow beings. Guests, at first. Then immigrants. We can do this—Soledad, you said the eels have at least ten years, maybe as much as fifty. That's enough time for Terrans to get back here."

Peter says, "What do you mean 'threats'?"

"Threats to campaign against any other mission than rescue. In the media, to the government, to other countries if we have to. Go over the heads of the mission planners."

"You're talking about our careers," Peter says. "Risking them!"

"Yes. But to save an entire intelligent species!"

Soledad says, "Rachel—you're assuming that persuasion and/or threats will be necessary. That the government won't see by themselves that a rescue mission to Canoe should supersede the Wolf 1061."

Yes. I am assuming that. But her steady look makes me ask myself: Is my distrust of the U.S. government coming from knowledge or from my own prejudices? The question is like a plume of cold water.

I say lamely, "If they won't agree right away, I mean."

Peter repeats, "We would be risking our careers."

Seth—thank Nafanua for Seth!—turns on him with all the idealism of the roman-tic. "What does that matter next to the eels' entire extinction? Rachel, I'm in."

Soledad says, "This is something for more thinking, and then more discussion."

I say, "Okay. But these dead eels, one in each plume and more to come because how will the eels know that we've left here? They won't. These eels—" I fight to keep my voice steady.

"These messages must be honored. They are a gift from the dying."

There is nothing interesting in the rest of the Luhman 16 system, or at least nothing as interesting as Canoe. Or as the discussions that we four hold, endlessly. Some-times the discussions are rational, looking at data assembled for the hypothetical rescue mission. Sometimes they're acrimonious, when steps are discussed to follow a turn-down by the government. Sometimes they're hopeful. But always they are inconclusive.

And always the eels are on my mind, in my dreams, mixed with my memories, until it's the face of the alien eel I see on each imagined coconut, instead of the two stoma and one drinking hole my father traced for me so long ago.

Canoe travels steadily outward, away from its sun, even though the visual looks no different to me.

After the trip to the Y Point, the jump into the Yi drive is less scary than it was the first time since, after all, we survived once. But it's still a leap into a mostly unknown state with barely proven physics. We're all a little subdued on that last day in the Luhman 16 system.

As I prepare for bed in my tiny quarters, a knock sounds. I open the door.

"Rachel," Peter says stiffly, "I've come to apologize." He grimaces; this is not easy for him. "I said untrue and unforgivable things to you. I'm sorry."

"I'm sorry, too," I say, probably even more stiffly. 'For my words and my . . . for attacking you."

He smiles, not warmly. "Daughter of Nafanua." And then, "I'll support the rescue-mission idea. Even at risk of my career."

A huge surprise. I expected Peter, not Soledad, to be the hold-out. But how much do each of us really know about what goes on inside others? I nod at him.

"Good night, then." He turns and I close the door.

I will never like him, will spend as little time with him as possible. But we are linked, as surely as a section of sub-space near Luhman 16 is inexplicably entangled with a section near Terra. Peter and I are entangled by this rescue crusade, by the memory of what happened between us, by just being human together. Little as I may like it.

I go to bed and lie in the dark, staring at the ceiling as if it were an ice shelf above me, calculating, with all the mathematical ability that the eels do not possess, our chances of saving them from the lonely dark.

The History of the Invasion Told in Five Dogs

KELLY JENNINGS

Here's another story that is exactly what it says it is. . . .
   Raised in New Orleans, Kelly Jennings is a member and cofounder of the Boston Mountain Writers Group. Her short fiction has appeared in many venues, including The Magazine of Fantasy & Science Fiction, Daily Science Fiction, *and the anthology* The Other Half of the Sky. *Her first novel,* Broken Slate, *was published in 2011; her second novel,* Fault Lines, *will be published in 2018. Find her on Twitter @delagar.*

FIRST DOG

I was nine years old when I got my first dog. He was a real surprise, since Moms and Pop kept saying I was too young for a dog. I'd forget to feed him, I'd lose interest, he'd spend his days chained in the yard. I kept saying no, no, never, only I believed them when they turned their heads away and said nope.

. . Then, best morning ever, my birthday morning, they drop Elvis onto my bed, wiggling and warm and lapping all over my face.

He was a great dog. A Weimaraner/border collie mix, silky gray with floppy ears and a white splotch on his chin, like he'd been drinking milk. Very smart and very fast. We lived in town, like everyone, and weren't supposed to cross into the woods— it was posted, big signs, PRIVATE LAND NO TRESPASSING NO HUNTING. Elvis and I knew how to get under the fence, though, down there by the interstate.

The woods were all overgrown farms, bought out years before by some rich folk, I forget which. I always pictured them living in New York, or Paris. Somewhere far from Arkansas. They never came around, anyway. I was never afraid they'd catch Elvis and me on their land.

The woods were crisscrossed with crumbling farm roads and rusting railroad tracks, the overgrown remnants of hayfields. Farmhouses and barns loomed from the pines and oaks. Elvis loved the long, straight stretches of farm road best. He loved nothing better than to run. At nine I couldn't keep up with him. Later on I almost could.

He hunted, too, rabbits and squirrel. He could outrun rabbits and snatch birds right out of the air. I took the rabbits home to Moms. She didn't like squirrel, but sometimes I took them to Mr. Elias down the road. Moms was glad for the meat. So was Mr. Elias. Everyone talks how wonderful it was before the Invaders came, but I remember.

Once when Elvis brought me a bird, a grackle, it wasn't dead. It lay in my hand a second, warm and still, and then sudden as that leapt away. Elvis and I watched it wheel and soar, free against the blue sky, watched it disappear across the trees.

When we left for the Refugee Camp, I had to leave Elvis behind.

I didn't want to. The buses didn't take pets. When I found that out, I wanted to give our tickets to someone else, or at least *my* ticket. My pop hit me when I said this. He'd never hit me in my life before, but he hit me then. Smacked me in the head, and then grabbed me around the middle and dragged me on the bus. I was too stunned to fight him.

Left Elvis in the parking lot.

To tell you the truth, I still cry about that sometimes, after all these years, after everything that's happened, Elvis running after that bus, trying to catch up to me.

SECOND DOG

Sally, my second dog, a Rottweiler/pit bull mix, ugly as sin, I acquired during the Resistance.

Resistance. That's nearly as funny as Refugee Camp.

But lots of us who survived the Camps did have the notion we could fight the Invaders, especially those of us who were young and stupid. We took to the mountains and the leveled cities, any place the Invaders hadn't built their domes. Militias and Resistance units formed.

Everyone knew the other route you could take—besides starving inside or outside of the Camps, I mean. Everyone knew you could apply to be taken in. If you had the right constellation of skills, the Invaders would accept you, make you a kind of pet human. An Adjunct, they called it. Unfortunately, the box of skills they asked for—facility with languages; musical training (vocal, woodwinds, brass); sculpting; visual arts—none of this was anything I had acquired.

I joined a Resistance unit in the Boston Mountains. I think we lasted half a year. It's hard to fight a civilization that's capable of leaping across galaxies and rebuilding planets (they were reshaping Earth to be more suitable to their needs, cooler, dimmer, new trees and grasses) with the equivalent of stone knives and bearskins, to quote my captain.

I don't know why bearskins.

Sally was our watchdog. She was great, too. Dogs heard the least whine of the Invaders' drones or patrol squids coming in. She knew not to bark, just to give a little huff.

But when they raided our camp, she stood her ground, trying to hold them off. They shot her down same as they shot every human what didn't run like a rabbit.

THIRD DOG

This one doesn't have a name.

The winter after my unit was wiped out, I was starving in a cave deep in the Boston Mountains. The rabbits and squirrel had about been hunted out by then. When the snow let me—it was snow more often than not, thanks to what the Invaders were doing to our weather—I made my way to one of the nearby towns that had been plowed under and scavenged for food or gear. One of these trips, I came across a half-grown pup, wandered off from his mama, probably.

I coaxed him over, hit him with a rock, and ate him for the next three days.

FOURTH DOG

When summer came, I headed for the Rockies. From the few other survivors, I'd heard the Invaders weren't interested in the high reaches—that if you could get to the big mountains, they'd leave you alone.

In truth, I didn't expect to find anything out there. Since I was twelve years old, I had lost everything and everyone I loved. I figured this salvation was yet another lie, one more pipe dream to get us through the last gasp. But I knew I couldn't survive another winter in that cave. So I traded the last of my canned beans to Sid over there in Jasper for one of the mountain bikes she'd rebuilt and set out. I had a sleeping bag, a compass, a fighting knife, and a camp knife. You couldn't use combustion engines or guns. Anything else, the Invaders would mostly ignore you.

Mostly.

I didn't have much trouble. This was six years after the Invaders now, and the winters on the plains were brutal. You survived by going Adjunct or by digging in and joining in. Anyone too mean or too stupid to do one of those had long since been killed off, either by the Invaders or his neighbors.

Didn't mean I had no trouble. It's always some stray—stray coyote, stray human.

Maybe two weeks in, coming up to Ogallah, I was by a stream, baking a fish for lunch in a little campfire, when I looked up to see Liza.

I never did know what sort of dog she was. Some Jack Russell mix maybe. She was in awful shape, partly from being old, mostly from losing whoever had owned her before the Invaders came. She still wore a collar, a nice blue leather one with her name on a brass plate. Someone had loved her once. Now she was bone-skinny, two toes missing entirely, nearly all her teeth gone.

But she ate half my fish politely, climbed into my lap, and went to sleep. And she was tiny enough to fit into the basket of my bike. I sighed and took her along.

She lived all the way to the mountains. She loved riding in that basket, ears flying, barking at the birds. She made friends with people when I stopped at farms to trade—more than once, I'm sure she got me a better deal. And twice she warned me, growling, in time for me to hide from strays prowling past at night on the road.

She died in Olney Springs, just as we reached the Rockies. I buried her there.

FIFTH DOG

When I showed up here at the ranch, Sara herself interviewed me, asking what I could do.

"Not much," I admitted. "I can hunt. And I'm good with dogs."

Luckily the ranch needed hunters. Game's scarce with the climate shift. According to Isra, who keeps our greenhouse, the vegetation sown by the Invaders is displacing our native plants down on the plains. Isra used to be an ecologist for the state up here before the Invaders. She says that invasive species almost always displace native species. She says if they'd brought animals, we'd be losing a lot faster.

Down in the flatlands, it's not just the cattle gone, but the deer and rabbits and every other kind of animal what needs plants to survive. Isra says when the plants go, we go. Sure, we can live on meat, she says, but what does meat live on?

This ranch didn't used to be a working ranch—it belonged to some actor who spent a week or two on it every five or six years, Sara says, skiing or hunting. Sara used to run his kitchens. She runs those of us living here now. We're up to thirty-five as of midsummer: fourteen men, eighteen women, and the three kids. And six dogs.

Snowbear is my dog. I got her out hunting.

What I mostly hunt is strays. Oh, also Bighorns, when they come down looking to feed, and I run traps for rabbits and rodents; but especially in the early years we had problems with strays. Sara has the roads and towns posted with instructions about what to do if you cross onto our land. Anyone who didn't follow those rules, Sara said, we had to consider them strays.

The Invaders' plants haven't reached us yet. It's still native grasses and trees up here, bright green Earth moss, not that bizarre orange crap. On the other hand, with the climate change, we get snow ten months out of twelve now. And colder summers every year. But we still have gardens; we can still hunt. So every year, until just lately, we got strays up from the plains; and every year they were more desperate.

This particular stray was over to the Tolman place. A young one, not more than twelve or thirteen. The Tolman house burned down years ago now. The stray was holed up in what was left of the stables, with an open fire going right there where anyone could see it. Just inviting Invader drones, the young idiot.

I didn't like clearing him, since maybe the issue was he couldn't read—plenty of those who came up after the Invasion can't—but when I called out, he picked up a gun. An actual handgun. Because the fire wasn't enough, I guess. Stood up, too, giving me a clear target. At least it was quick.

When I went to salvage the arrowhead, the gun was a rusted bit of junk. He didn't have much of use in his gear, either—a knife, a packet of dried cherries, and a bag filled with dead puppies. Except for Snowbear, who wasn't quite dead.

Snowbear's a Samoyed, smart and tough, and a fine hunter, though it's not anyone up from the plains to hunt for three years running now. Merle argues with Sara, he wants to send out an expedition, through the mountains, even down to the plains. "What if we're the last ones left?" he says.

Sara says she's in no hurry to learn the truth concerning that particular possibility.

Isra thinks we are the only ones left. I can tell by how she stays quiet when Sara and Merle are having this argument one more time. Or . . . she thinks even if we aren't the last already, we will be the last soon enough.

Me, I'm not so sure. See, it wasn't just the cherries, though tell me where anyone's getting cherries this far past the Invasion? And it wasn't just how well fed that kid was, for a stray. It's the puppies. Five dead puppies, and Snowbear, all of them purebred Samoyed. Nine years past the Invasion.

Could be the stray was an Adjunct, or I guess he'd have to be the child of Adjunct, run off from an Invader dome. No one's come out of the domes, though, that we know of.

Could be the Invaders are breeding Samoyeds. Except when you think what Samoyed are good for—hunting in the snow, surviving in this arctic cold, with their thick coats that can be harvested for making clothing and blankets—well, that seems more like something we'd do, out here in the snowy wastes. Not them, in their climate-controlled domes.

I think about all this when Snowbear and I are out on a hunt, climbing up to Red Rock or walking the river, snow silting down and the world so quiet around us. What I think is, someone else must have survived, somewhere. Someone who can feed their children well. Someone with greenhouses large enough for cherry trees. Someone who can afford to breed dogs.

Sometimes, when I'm standing up on Red Rock looking out across the frozen world, I think like Merle, that we should try to find these other people, while we still can. I think if someone else is out there, maybe we aren't, after all, doomed.

Or at least not yet.

Then Snowbear comes bounding through the trees, swift as a dove from the gray sky, her black eyes bright, letting me know she's got the scent of something hot, and we go hunt it down, one more time.

prime meridian

SILVIA MORENO-GARCIA

Sometimes the dream matters more than the reality—as the complex and brilliant novella that follows vividly demonstrates.

Silvia Moreno-Garcia is the critically acclaimed author of Signal to Noise*—winner of a Copper Cylinder Award and finalist for the British Fantasy, Locus, Sunburst and Aurora awards—and* Certain Dark Things*, selected as one of NPR's best books of 2016. She won a World Fantasy Award for her work as an editor.*

Why did I have to poison myself with love?
Aelita, or The Decline of Mars, Alexei Tolstoi
Una ciudad deshecha, gris, monstruosa
"Alta traición," José Emilio Pacheco

1

The subway station was a dud. Both of its entrances had once again been commandeered by a street gang that morning, which meant you'd have to pay a small "fee" in order to catch your train. Amelia was tempted to fork over the cash, but you never knew if these assholes were also going to help themselves to your purse, your cell phone, and whatever the hell else they wanted.

That meant she had to choose between a shared ride and the bus. Amelia didn't like either option. The bus was cheap. It would also take forever for it to reach Coyoacán. The car could also take a while, depending on how many people hailed it, but it would no doubt move faster.

Amelia was supposed to meet Fernanda for lunch the next day and she needed to ensure she had enough money to pay for her meal. Fernanda was loaded, and odds were she'd cover it all, but Amelia didn't want to risk it in case Fernanda wasn't feeling generous.

The most sensible thing to do, considering this, was to take the bus. Problem was, she had the booking and if she didn't check in by five o'clock, she'd be penalized, a percentage of her earnings deducted. The damned app had a geolocator function. Amelia couldn't lie and claim she'd reached the house on time.

Amelia gave the gang members standing by the subway station's entrance a long glare and took out her cell phone.

Five minutes later, her ride arrived. She was glad to discover there was only one other person in the car. Last time she'd taken a shared ride, she sat together with four people, including a woman with a baby, the cries of the child deafening Amelia.

Amelia boarded the car and gave the other passenger a polite nod. The man hardly returned it. He was wearing a gray suit and carried a briefcase, which he clutched with one hand while he held up his cell phone in the other. You heard all these stories about how the ride shares were dangerous—you could get into a car and be mugged, express kidnapped, or raped—but Amelia wasn't going to pay for a damned secure taxi and this guy, at least, didn't look like he was going to pull a gun on her. He was too busy yakking on the phone.

They made good progress despite the usual insanity of Mexico City's traffic. In Europe, there were automated cars roaming the cities, but here drivers still had a job. They couldn't automate that, not with the chaotic fuckery of the roads.

Mars is home to the tallest mountain in the solar system. Olympus Mons, 21 km high and 600 km in diameter, she told herself as the driver honked the horn. Sometimes, she repeated the Mandarin words she knew, but it was mostly facts about the Red Planet. To remind herself it was real, it existed, it was there.

Once they approached the old square in Coyoacán, Amelia jumped out of the car. No point in staying inside; the vehicle moved at a snail's pace. The cobblestone streets in this borough were never made to bear the multitudes that now walked through the once-small village.

The square that marked the center of old Coyoacán was chock-full of street vendors frying churros and gorditas, or offering bags emblazoned with the face of Frida Kahlo and acrylic rebozos made in China. Folkloric bullshit.

Amelia took a side street, where the traditional pulquerias had been substituted with fusion restaurants. Korean-Mexican. French-Mexican. Whatever-Mexican. Mexican-Mexican was never enough. A couple of more blocks and she reached Lucía's home with five minutes to spare, thank-fucking-God.

Lucía's house was not an ordinary house, but a full-fledge casona, a historical marvel that looked like it was out of a movie, with wrought iron bars on the windows and an interior patio crammed with potted plants. The inside was much of the same: rustic tables and hand-painted talavera. It screamed Colonial, provincial, nostalgia and also fake. There was an artificial, too-calculated, too-overdone quality to each and every corner of the house, an unintended clue that the owner had once been an actress.

Amelia knew the drill. She went into the living room with its enormous screen and sat on one of the couches. Lucía was already there. The woman drank nothing except mineral water with a wedge of lime. The first time Amelia had visited her, she had made the mistake of asking for a Diet Coke, which earned her a raised eyebrow and a mineral water, because fuck you, Lucía Madrigal said what you drank and what you ate (nothing, most times, although twice, little bowls with pomegranate seeds had been placed on the table by the couches).

That day, there were no pomegranates, only the mineral water and Lucía, dressed in a bright green dress with a matching turban, the kind Elizabeth Taylor wore in the 70s. That had been Lucía's heyday and she had not acclimated to modern dress styles, preferring tacky drama to demure senior citizen clothes.

"Today, we are going to watch my second movie. The Mars picture. I was quite young when this came out in '65, so it's not one of my best roles," Lucía declared with such aplomb one might have believed she had been a real actress, instead of a middling starlet who got lucky and married a filthy rich politician.

Amelia nodded. She had little interest in Lucía's movies, but her job was not to offer commentary. It was to simply sit and watch. Sometimes, it was to sit and listen. Lucía liked to go on about the film stars she'd met in decades past or the autobiography she was writing. As long as Amelia kept her eyes open and her mouth shut, she'd get a good rating on Friendrr and her due payment, minus the 20% commission for the broker. There were other apps that functioned without a broker, but those were less reliable. You might arrive for your Friendrr session and discover the client was an absolute sleaze who wouldn't pay. Friendrr vetted the clients, asked for deposits, and charged more, which was good news.

The movie was short and confusing, as if it had been rewritten halfway through the production. The first half focused on a space ranger sent to check out a Martian outpost manned by a scientist and his lovely daughter. Lucía played the daughter, who wore "futuristic" silver miniskirts. For its first half-hour, it played as a tame romance. Then space pirates, who looked suspiciously like they were wearing discarded clothes from a Mexican Revolution film, invaded the outpost. The pirates were under the command of a Space Queen who was obviously evil, due to the plunging neckline of her costume.

"It doesn't much look like the real Mars, I suppose," Lucía mused, "but then, I prefer it this way. The real Mars is bland compared to the one the set designer imagined. Have you seen the pictures of the colonies?"

"Yes," Amelia said, and although she knew only monosyllabics were required of her, she went on. "I want to go there, soon."

"To the Martian colonies?"

Lucía looked at the young woman. The actress had indulged in plastic surgery at several points during the 90s and her face seemed waxy. Time could not be stopped, though, and she had long abandoned attempts at surgery, botox and peels. What remained of her was like the core of a dead tree. Her eyebrows were non-existent, drawn with aplomb and a brown pencil. She perpetually sported a half-amused expression and a necklace, which she inevitably toyed with.

"Well, I suppose people are meant to go places," Lucía said. "But those colonies on Mars, they look as antiseptic and exciting as a box of baby wipes. Everything is white. Who ever heard of white as an exciting color?"

There was irony in this comment, since the movie they had just watched was in black-and-white, but Amelia nodded. Half an hour later, she took the bus back home.

When Amelia walked into the apartment, the television was on. Her sister and her youngest niece were on the couch, watching a reality TV show. Her other niece was probably on the bed, with her phone. Since there were two bedrooms and Amelia had to share a room with one of the girls, the only place where she could summon a modicum of privacy was the bathroom, but when she zipped toward there after a quiet "hello," Marta looked at her.

"I hope you're not thinking of taking a shower," her sister said. "Last month's water bill came in. It's very high."

"That's the fault of the people in the building next door," Amelia said. "You know they steal water from the tinacos."

"You take forever in the shower. Your hair's not even dirty. Why would you need to get in the shower?"

Amelia did not reply. She changed course, headed into the bedroom, and slipped under the covers. On the other bed, her niece played a game on her cell phone. Its repetitive bop-bop sound allowed for neither sleep nor coherent thoughts.

2

Amelia took her nieces to school, which meant an annoying elbowing in and out of a crowded bus, plus the masterful avoiding of men who tried to touch her ass. Marta insisted that the girls needed to be picked up and dropped off from school, even though Karina was 11 and could catch the school transport together with her little sister, no problem. It was just a modest fee for this privilege.

Amelia thought Marta demanded she perform this task as a way to demonstrate her power.

When Amelia returned from dropping off the girls, she took the shower that had been forbidden her the previous night. Afterward, she cooked a quick meal for the family and left it in the refrigerator—this was another of the tasks she had to execute, along with the drop-offs and pick-ups. Again, she boarded a bus, squeezed tight next to two men, the smell of cheap cologne clogging her nostrils, and got off near the Diana.

Fernanda was characteristically laggard, strolling into the restaurant half an hour late. She did not apologize for the delay. She sat down, ordered a salad after reading the menu twice, and smiled at Amelia.

"I have met the most excellent massage therapist," Fernanda said. This was her favorite adjective. She had many, employed them generously. "He got rid of that pain in my back. I told you about it, didn't I? Between the shoulder blades. And the most excellent . . ."

She droned on. Fernanda and Amelia did not meet often anymore, but when they did, Amelia had to listen patiently about all the wonderful, amazing, super-awesome people Fernanda knew, the cool-brilliant-mega hobbies she was busying herself with, and the delightful-darling-divine trips she'd taken recently. It was pretty much the same structure as her visits with Lucía, the old woman discussing her movies while Amelia watched the ice cubes in her glass melt.

It made her feel cheap and irritated, but Fernanda footed their lunch bills and she had lent money to Amelia on previous occasions. Right now, she was wondering if she should ask for a bit of cash or bite her tongue.

Amelia, who didn't drink regularly in restaurants (who would with these prices?), ordered a martini to pass the time. Fernanda was already on her second one. She drank a lot but only when her husband wasn't looking. He was ugly, grouchy and wealthy. The last attribute was the only one that mattered to Fernanda.

"So, what are you doing now?" Fernanda asked. Her smile was blinding, her hair painted an off-putting shade of blonde, her dark roots showing. Not Brigitte Bardot—bouts of movie-watching with Lucía were giving Amelia a sense of film history—but a straw-like color that wasn't bold, just boring. Every woman of a certain age had that hair color. They'd copied it off a celebrity who had a nightly variety show. No brunettes on TV. Pale skin and fair hair were paramount.

"This and that," Amelia replied.

"You're not working? Don't tell me you're still doing that awful-terrible rent-a-friend thing," Fernanda said, looking surprised.

"Yes. Although, I wanted to ask if you hadn't heard of anything that might suit me. . . ."

"Well . . . your field, it's not really my line of work," Fernanda replied.

Not that Fernanda had a line of work. As far as Amelia knew, all she did was stay married, her bills paid by her dick of a husband. Amelia, on the other hand, since dropping out of university, had done nothing but work. A series of idiotic, poorly paying and increasingly frustrating gigs. There was no such thing as full-time work for someone like her. Perhaps if she'd stuck with her studies, it might have been different, but when her mother got sick, she had to drop out and become her caretaker. And afterward, when her mother passed away, it wasn't like she could get her scholarship back.

"I do almost anything," Amelia said with a shrug. "Perhaps something in your husband's office?"

"There's nothing there," Fernanda said, too quickly.

There was likely *something* reserved for Fernanda's intimate friends. Amelia had once counted herself amongst those "excellent" people. When they'd been in school together, Amelia had written a few term papers for Fernanda and that had made her useful. She'd also dated Elías Bertoliat, which had increased her standing amongst their cohort. That had gone to hell. He'd ghosted her, about two months after she'd dropped out of school, and returned to Monterrey.

Amelia was more devalued than the Mexican peso.

She looked at the bread basket, not wishing to lay her eyes on her so-called friend. She really didn't want to ask for money (it made her feel like shit), but of course that was the one reason why she was sitting at the restaurant.

"Anastasia Brito might be looking for someone like you," Fernanda said, breaking the uncomfortable silence that had descended between them.

Amelia frowned. Anastasia had gone to the same university, but she'd been an art student while Amelia dallied in land-and-food systems, looking forward to a career as an urban farmer.

"Why?" she asked.

"She's going through a phase. She has an art show in a couple of weeks. The theme is 'meat,' but after that, she said she's going to focus on plants and she'll be needing genetically modified ones. It might be your thing."

It was, indeed. After her chances at university soured up, Amelia had taken a few short-term courses in plant modification at a small-fry school. All she'd been able to do with that was get a gig at an illegal marijuana operation. Non-sanctioned, highly modified marijuana plants. It paid on time, but Amelia chickened out after a raid. You couldn't fly to Mars if your police certificate wasn't clean. She didn't want to risk it.

Her friend Pili told Amelia she was an idiot. Pili had been snared in raids four or five times. All she did was pay the fine. But then, Pili did all kinds of crazy things. She sold her blood to old farts who paid for expensive transfusions, thinking the plasma could rejuvenate them.

"Could be. Do you have her number?" Amelia asked.

"She's in a great-super-cool women's temazcal retreat right now in Peru. All-natural, no contact with the outside world. Just meditation. But she will be back for the art show. You should just show up. I know someone at the gallery. They can put you on the list."

"The temazcal is Nahua. What's she doing in Peru?"

"I don't know, Amelia," Fernanda said, sounding annoyed. Amelia's geographical objections were clearly pointless. She supposed people organized whatever retreats rich fuckers could afford. Tibetan samatha in Brazil, Santería ceremonies in Dublin. Who cared?

"All right, put me on the list," Amelia said.

Fernanda seemed very pleased with herself and paid for the lunch after all. Amelia assumed she considered this her act of charity for the year. For her part, she felt stupidly proud for not mentioning anything about a loan, although she was going to have to figure something out soon.

Amelia picked her nieces up from school and, after ensuring they ate the food she had cooked, she made a quick escape from the apartment as soon as Marta arrived. This was Amelia's strategy: to spend as little time as possible in the apartment when her sister was around. Marta made a room shrink in size and Amelia's room already felt the size of a desk drawer.

Amelia hated sleeping in the same room she'd once shared with Marta, who'd moved to the master bedroom their mother had occupied. Each night, she looked at the walls she had looked at since she was a child. Stray stickers glued to her bed years before remained along the headboard. In a corner, there were smudged markings she'd made with crayons.

Not that it was an unusual set-up. Mexican youths, especially women, tended to live at home with their parents. These days, with the way the economy was going, even the most cosmopolitan people clustered together for long periods of time. At 25, Amelia didn't raise any eyebrows amongst her peers, but she still hated her living situation. Perhaps if they'd had a bigger apartment, it wouldn't be so annoying, but the apartment was small, the building they inhabited in disrepair: a government-funded unit, modern at one point when a president had been trying to score popularity points in that sector of the city. They were in one of four identical towers, built in a Brutalist style with the emphasis on the brute. An interior courtyard joined them together. Bored teens liked to gather there, while others held court in the lobby.

She loathed the whole complex and fled it every day. Her hours were spent navigating through several coffee shops. There was an art to this. The franchises used kiosks to sell coffee and tasteless bread wrapped in plastic. You pushed a button and out came your food. These were terrible places for sitting down for long periods of time. Since everything was automated, the job of the one or two idiots on staff was to wipe the tables clean, and to get people in and out as quick as possible. They enforced the maximum one-hour-for-customers rule with militaristic abandon.

Amelia hopped between two spots, three blocks from each other. One was a cafe and the other a crêperie. They were on a decent street, meaning they both had an armed guard standing at the door. But who didn't? Any Sanborns or Vips had at least one and similar cafes employed at least a part-time one for the busy times of the day. The guards kept the rabble out. Otherwise, the patrons would have been shooing away people offering to recharge cell phones by hooking them to a tiny generator, or shifty strangers who would top up phone cards for cheaper than the legit telecomm providers. Any other number of peddlers of services and products could also slip in, to the annoyance of licenciados in their suits and ties, trendy youths in designer huipiles, and mothers leaning against their deluxe, ultra-light strollers.

Amelia walked into the coffee shop, ordered a black coffee—cheapest thing on the menu—and, with the day's Wi-Fi code in hand, logged on to the Internet and began reading. First, the news about Mars, then botany items. She drifted haphazardly after that. Anything from celebrity news to studying English or Mandarin. Those were the predominant languages on Mars, German a distant third. After an enthusiastic six months trying to grasp German, though, she'd given up on it. Much of the same happened with Mandarin. English she spoke well enough, as did any Mexican kid who'd gone to a good school.

She'd also given up on a job search. Once she had updated her CV, she had taken new headshots to go with it. Amelia, black hair pulled back, looking like a docile employee. But with her schooling interrupted, what should have been an impressive degree from a nice university was just bullshit. And every time she looked at the CV, it irritated her to see herself reduced to a pile of mediocrity:

Age: 25
Marital status: Unmarried
Current job: Freelancer

Freelancer. Euphemism for *unemployed.* Because her gigs didn't count. You couldn't put "professional friend" on a CV, any more than you could "professional cuddler." God knew there were people who did that gig, too, hiring themselves out to embrace people. She remembered seeing an ad for that explaining "99 percent of clients are male." Fuck, no.

Freelancer, then. Ex-university student, ex-someone. Her job applications disappeared into another dimension, swallowed by the computer until she simply stopped trying. She lived off gigs, first the marijuana operation, then odd jobs; for the past two years, the Friendrr bookings had constituted her sole income.

Freelancer. Fuck-up.

No more CV. Amelia focused on Mars, played video games on her cell, drew geometrical shapes on the napkins, then clovers for luck, and stars out of habit. When she knew she'd spent too much time at the coffee shop, she switched to the crêperie, where she repeated the process: black coffee, another couple of hours lost in mundane tasks.

When she was done, she took the subway back home.

It was always the same.

That night, a woman boarded Amelia's train and began asking people for a few tajaderos. The most popular cryptocurrency folks used since the peso was a piece of shit, jumping up and down in value faster than an addict dancing the jitterbug. You could tap a phone against another and transfer tajaderos from an account. A few people did just that, but even if the lady was old and rather pitiful, Amelia couldn't spare a dirty peso.

To be frank, just a couple of bad turns and Amelia would be begging in the subway right next to the old woman.

The doors of the car opened and Amelia darted out. On the walls of the concourse, there were floor-to-ceiling video displays. A blonde woman danced in them. RADIOACTIVE FLESH, she mouthed, the letters superimposed over her image. A NEW COLLECTION. A tattoo artist sat by one of these video panels. He was there every few days, tattooing sound waves onto people's arms. A snippet of your favorite song inked onto your flesh. With the swipe of a scanner, the melody would play. At first, she couldn't believe he lugged his equipment like that around the city, not because it was cumbersome, but because she expected someone might try to steal it. But the man was quite massive and his toothless grin was a warning.

"Hey, I'll give you a discount," the man told her, but she shook her head, as was her custom.

Amelia took the eastern exit, which was rarely frequented by the gangs. She was in luck; they were nowhere to be seen. Now there was a choice to make. Either follow the shortest route, which meant walking through the courtyard and encountering the young louts who would be drinking there, or take the long way around the perimeter of the complex.

Amelia picked the short way. In the center of the courtyard, there was a dry fountain, filled with rubbish. All around lounged teenagers from the buildings. They were not gang members, just professional loafers who specialized in playing loud music and yelling a choice obscenity or two at any girl who walked by.

Although the kids had nothing to offer except, perhaps, cigarettes and a bottle of cheap booze, when Amelia had been a teenager, she'd peered curiously at them. They seemed to be having a good time. Her mother, however, forbade any contact with the teenagers from the housing unit. Mother emphasized how Amelia was meant for bigger and better things. Marta was a lost cause. She'd gotten herself pregnant her last year in high school and married a man who ran off after a handful of years. It didn't matter. Marta possessed no great intellectual gifts, anyway. She'd flunked a grade and barely finished her high school through online courses. Amelia, however, was a straight-A student. She couldn't waste her time crushing beer cans with *those* kids.

Amelia believed this narrative. When her mother learned she was going out with a good boy from the university, she was ecstatic. Elías Bertoliat, with his pale skin and light eyes, and his fancy car, seemed like a prince from a fairy tale. Every time Amelia floated the idea of Mars, her mother immediately told her Mars was unlikely and she should focus on marrying Elías. After he broke up with Amelia, her mother insisted they'd get back together.

Glancing at the boys kicking around a beer can and laughing, Amelia wondered if she wouldn't have been better off partying with them when she had the chance. If she was destined to be a loser, she could at least have been a loser who had fun, fucked lots of people, enjoyed her youth while it lasted.

She looked at the girls sitting chatting near the fountain, in stockings and shorts, heavy chains dangling against their breasts, their nails long, the makeup plentiful. Then one of the boys hollered and another followed.

"Were you going? I've got something for you, baby."

Laughter. Amelia looked ahead. There was no point in acknowledging their displays. The faint fantasy that she might have once enjoyed spending her time with them vanished.

They called the days on Mars "sol." 24 hours, 39 minutes, and 35.244 second adding up to a sol. Three percent shorter than a day on Earth. She reminded herself of this. It was important to keep her focus on what mattered, on the facts. They could scream, "Show me your pussy!" and ask her to give them a blowjob, but she did not listen.

When she reached her building, she climbed the five flights of stairs up to her apartment—the elevator was perpetually busted. A dog padded down the long hallway, which led to her apartment. Many tenants had pets and some let them roam wild, as if the building were a park. The animals defecated on the stairs, but they also kept the indigents away. The teens who held court downstairs also provided a measure of safety.

Amelia paused before her door, fished out her keys from her purse, and stood still. She could hear dialogue from the TV, muffled, but loud enough she could make out a few words. Amelia walked in.

"Let's see what's behind Door Number One!" the TV announcer yelled. Clapping ensued.

Mars, Scene 1

It's nothing but sand dunes. Dry, barren, quiet. When she bends down and picks up a handful of sun-baked soil, and wipes her hand against her pale dress, it leaves a dark, rusty streak.

There is air here. This is Mars but the Mars of EXT. MARS SURFACE—DAY. And she is a SPACE EXPLORER, a young woman in a white dress now streaked red.

SPACE EXPLORER has no lines of dialogue, not yet. The camera hovers over her shoulder, over tendrils of dark hair, which shift with the wind.

There is even wind, in EXT. MARS SURFACE. And the dress is far too impractical for any true "space exploration." It reaches her ankle, shows off her arms, although no cleavage. Instead, a demure collar that reaches the chin indicates SPACE EXPLORER is a good girl. The white might have clued you in, but it never hurts to place the proper signifiers.

SPACE EXPLORER looks over her shoulder and sees a figure coming toward her, glinting under the sunlight.

Hold that shot, hold that moment, as the HERO steps into the frame.

3

Amelia avoided her sister for three days, but on the fourth, Marta caught her before she could slip out of the apartment, cornering her by the refrigerator, which was covered with drawings made by the youngest girl. Amelia's niece had a good imagination: The sky was never blue in Mexico City.

"The rent is due," Marta said. "And you still owe me that money."

Two months before, Amelia had bought a pretty new dress. It wasn't a bargain, but it seemed she was getting another steady Friendrr client. Every week, like the arrangement with Lucía. Four hours. She bought the dress because she thought she deserved it. She hadn't bought anything for herself in forever and she would be able to afford it now. Then that client canceled a booking, and another, and Amelia had to pay for the layaway or lose all the money she'd ponied up. So, she asked Marta for enough to make the final payment.

"I have the rent money, not the rest. Things are slow right now," Amelia said. "I'm sure bookings will improve as we roll into December."

"Oh, for God's sake," Marta said, sending a magnet in the shape of a watermelon slice flying into the air as she slapped her hand against the refrigerator's door. "You need to get a real job that pays on time."

"There are no real jobs," Amelia replied.

"Then what do I do every day?"

Marta was an end-of-life planner, helping arrange elaborate funerals, memorials and euthanasia packages. And yes, it was a job, but guess what? She only had it because she sucked good dick for the boss, a smarmy little man who had made a pass at Amelia the year before, when Marta took her to an office party. He had suggested a threesome with the sisters and when Amelia complained to Marta about her vomit-inducing creep of a part-time boyfriend/supervisor, Marta had the gall to tell Amelia she shouldn't have worn such a tight skirt.

"You need to look into the private security company I told you about," Marta said. "They are always hiring."

"Do I look like I can shoot a rifle?"

"Fuck it, Amelia, it's just standing on your feet for a few hours holding the gun, not shooting it. Surely, even you can manage that?"

Amelia swallowed a mouthful of rage. She couldn't afford a place on her own and so she swallowed it, bile and resentment making her want to spit.

The phone rang. She almost didn't hear it because the kids had the television on so loud and the kitchen was smack next to the living room/dining room area. It was Miguel, her broker. Friendrr called him that: Junior Social Appointment Broker. Amelia thought it was a weird, long title.

"Hey Amelia, now, how are you doing today?" Miguel asked in that oddly chirpy tone he employed. She'd never met him in person, but Miguel always sounded like he was smiling and his profile featured multiple shots of him grinning at different locations. The beach, a concert, an assortment of restaurants.

Miguel was an extreme positive thinker. He had told her he liked to read self-help books. He also took a lot of online courses. In the beginning, they'd bonded a bit over this, since Amelia was still trying to learn German. As the months dragged by, they both grew disenchanted.

Amelia simply wasn't the kind of girl who could secure many clients. There were some people who were booked solid for gigs, but most of them were very good-looking. She'd heard one young woman got booked exclusively to pose for photos. The kind of "candid" shots where friends gathered for a social event. Nothing candid in them. Then there were others who did all right with weddings and funerals. Both of these required an ability to cry.

Amelia wasn't a crybaby and she wasn't gorgeous. Her biggest issue, though, was that she simply did not inspire friendly feelings. People did not want to meet her and if they did, they did not want to meet her again. Whatever warmth or spark is required to inspire a desire for human interaction was lacking in her. She wasn't compelling.

Miguel had told her she needed better photos, more keywords. They tried a bunch of things, but it didn't work. Miguel, who had been excited because her science background gave her a certain versatility—some of the folks on Friendrr could hardly spell "cat," the glorious, underfunded public education system at play—grew underwhelmed.

Miguel hadn't phoned her in weeks and Amelia feared he was getting ready to drop her from Friendrr. She was probably driving his stats down.

"I'm good," she said, turning her back to her sister, grateful for the interruption. She headed to the room and locked the door. "What's up?"

"I have a booking for you, you have a new client. That's what's up. The only thing is, it's short notice: tonight at nine."

"I'm not doing anything tonight."

"Good. It's in New Polanco. I'm sending you the address."

"Any special items?"

"No," Miguel said. "He wants to have dinner."

Most clients wanted ordinary things, like watching movies, as Lucía had asked, or walking together. Now and then, an oddity emerged. There had been a man who asked that she wear white gloves and sit perfectly still for a whole hour. But most baffling had been the time a client hired her to pretend she was someone else. Amelia bore a vague resemblance to an old lady's favorite daughter, who had passed away many years before. Or perhaps Amelia bore no resemblance; perhaps any young woman would do. The old woman wept when she saw her, confessing a small litany of sins. They had parted on bad terms, then the daughter died.

Amelia was unnerved by the experience. She wondered if this was the first time a young woman had been brought to meet the old woman. She wondered if other people had worn the green sweater she had been asked to wear. Had it belonged to the dead girl, or was it merely a similar sweater? Were there many girls dressed in green sweaters, each one ushered into the room on a different day of the week?

Worst of all, while the old woman gripped Amelia's hand and swore she'd never leave her alone again, Amelia raised her head and caught sight of the person who had hired her for this gig. It was the old woman's surviving daughter. Her eyes were hard and distant.

Amelia wondered what it must be like for her, to accompany these look-alikes to her mother's bedroom, to have them sit next to her, to hold the woman's hand. What did she feel, being the daughter the old woman did not want? The one who was superfluous?

Perhaps she might have obtained more bookings at that house, but Amelia refused to go back and even though Miguel said she was being stupid—there was talk about terms of agreement, clauses—she refused. Miguel let it go. For once.

The tower where the client lived was a thin, white, luxurious needle, the kind the ads assured would-be buyers was not only "modern," but "super modern." Many warehouses had been scrapped to make way for these monstrous buildings. The old housing units that remained—homes of the descendants of factory workers, of lower-class citizens who toiled assembling cars and bought little plots to build their homes—existed under the shadow of behemoths. Since the expensive buildings required abundant water and electricity, the poor residents in the area had to do without. The big buildings had priority over all the resources. There were also a few fancy buildings that had halted construction when the latest housing bubble popped. They remained half-finished, like gaping, filthy teeth spread across several gigantic lots. Indigents now made their homes there, living in structures without windows, while three blocks away, women were wrapped in tepezcohuite at the spa, experiencing the trendiest traditional plant remedy around the city.

Amelia walked into the lobby of the white building. A concierge and a guard with a submachine gun both stood behind a glistening desk. The concierge smiled. The guard did not acknowledge her in any way.

"I'm expected. Number 1201," Amelia said. The client had not given a name, although that was not unusual.

"Yes, you are," the concierge said, the smile the same, pleasant without being exactly warm. The concierge walked Amelia to the elevator and swiped a card so she could board it.

When she reached the door to 1201, Amelia saw it had been left unlocked and she walked in. The apartment was open concept. The portion constituting the living room area was dominated by a shaggy rug and a modular, low-slung sofa in tasteful gray with an integrated side table. Floor-to-ceiling windows allowed one to observe the cityscape.

She could see the kitchen, but there was a gray sliding door to the right. She assumed a bedroom and bathroom lay in that direction.

"Hey, I'm here," Amelia said. "Hello?"

The gray door opened and there stood Elías Bertoliat. For a minute, she thought it was merely a man who *resembled* Elías. Who just happened to have Elías's mouth, his nose, his green eyes. Because it didn't sound feasible that she had just walked into the apartment of her ex-boyfriend.

"You've got to be kidding me," she said at last. "You booked me?"

He raised his hands, as if to pacify her.

"Amelia, this is going to sound nuts, but if you'll let me explain—" and his voice was not quite the same. The years had given it more weight, a deeper resonance, but there was still the vague choppiness of the words, as if he'd rehearsed for a long time, attempting to rid himself of his Northern accent, and almost managed it.

"It doesn't sound nuts. It *is*," she said clutching her cell phone and pointing it at him. "Are you stalking me?"

"No! I saw your profile on Friendrr by chance. I don't have your contact info, or I would have gotten ahold of you some other way. I just saw it and I thought I'd talk to you."

Just like that, so easy. And yet, it sounded entirely like him: careless, swift. To see her and decide to find her, like he had decided once, on the spur of the moment, that they ought to go to Monterrey for a concert. Fly in and fly out.

"Why?" she asked. "You were a dick to me."

"I know."

"You don't date someone for two years and then take off like that. Not even a fucking text message, a phone call."

She didn't care if ghosting was fashionable, or her generation simply didn't care for long-term relationships, or whatever half-baked pop psychology article explained this shit.

He approached her, but Amelia moved away from him, ensuring the sofa was between them, that it served as a demarcation line. Sinus Meridiani in the middle of the living room.

"My dad pulled me from university. He didn't like all my talk about going to Mars and he forced me to go back home," he said.

"And he forced you to ghost me."

"I didn't know what to say. I was a kid," he protested.

"We were in university, not kindergarten."

He managed to look betrayed despite the fact she should have owned all the outrage in this meeting. He had looked, when they'd met, rather boyish. Little boy lost. This had been an interesting change from the loud, grossly wealthy "juniors" who populated the university and the festive, catcalling youths in the center of her housing complex. And he had an interest in photography, which revealed a sensitive soul. It, in turn, prompted Amelia to forgive whatever mistakes he made, since she was a misguided romantic in search of a Prince Charming.

He still had that boyishness, in the eyes if not the face.

"What do you want?" she asked.

"I was on Friendrr for the same reason other people are. I wanted to talk to someone. I thought I'd talk to you. Maybe apologize. Amelia, let me buy you dinner."

To be fair, she considered it and just as quickly, she decided, *Fuck, no*.

"You booked me for two hours," she said, holding the phone tight, holding it up, so he could look at the timer she'd just switched on. "But I am not having dinner with you. In fact, I'm going to lock myself in your room and I'm going to take a nap. A long nap."

She closed the sliding door behind her and walked down a wide hallway, which led straight into said room. She promptly locked the door, as she'd promised. The bed was large, no narrow, lumpy mattress, springs digging into her back. She turned her head and stared at the curtains. She didn't sleep, not a wink, and he didn't attempt to coax her out of there. When the two hours had elapsed, Amelia walked back into the living room.

"At Friendrr, your satisfaction is of the utmost importance to us. I hope you will consider us again for all your social needs," she said.

Elías was sitting on the sofa. When she spoke, he turned his head, staring at her. He had enjoyed taking pictures, but did not often have his own taken. Yet, she had snapped a rare shot of him with his own camera. He'd had the same expression in that shot: remote, somewhat flimsy, as if he were afraid the raw camera lens might reveal a hidden blemish.

Three months after he'd dumped her, Amelia had deleted that photo from her computer, erasing him from her hard drive and her life after finally clueing in to the fact that he was never coming back. Now she walked out and walked downstairs, not bothering to wait for the elevator.

I don't know why you're on Mars, Carl Sagan once said. Amelia had committed his speech to memory, but she couldn't remember it now, although she'd played it back to Elías, for Elías. Elías, brushing the hair away from her face as she pressed a key on the laptop and the astronomer's voice came out loud and clear. Which was maybe why she couldn't, wouldn't remember it.

4

Amelia had been tired, busy, upset, but the movie playing was too terrible to remember her worries. Too ridiculous. A man in an ape suit jumped around, chasing a young woman, and Lucía chuckled. Amelia, noticing this, chuckled, too. They both glanced at each other. Then they erupted in synchronized laughter. The ape-man stumbled, pointed a raygun at the screen, and they both laughed even more.

Afterward, a servant refilled their glasses with mineral water. Lucía wore a yellow turban, embroidered with flowers.

"Not my finest performance, I suppose," Lucía said, smiling. "In my defense, the ape costume was terrible. It smelled like rotten eggs for some reason. God knows where they got it from."

"That doesn't sound very glamorous."

Amelia did not ask questions, she simply listened, but for once, Lucía was offering conversation. Months of starchiness and at last, the old woman had seemed to warm up to her. Perhaps this boded well. It would certainly be nice if she could book more hours. Especially considering that damned fiasco with Elías. Would he attempt to book her again? Amelia had asked herself that question a dozen times already. Each time, she thought she needed to phone Miguel, tell him this was her damned ex-boyfriend trying to book her, but she felt too embarrassed.

"It wasn't," the older woman said. "The glamor was in the 40s and 50s. I was born too late. The movie industry in Mexico was eroding by the time the 60s rolled around. We made terrible movies, cheap flicks. Go-go dancers and wrestlers and monsters. I might have done a Viking movie if Nahum had gotten the funding for that, but he was flying low and Armand Elba wasn't doing much better, either. Can you imagine? Viking women in Mexico."

"Nahum?"

"Nahum Landmann. The director. They billed him as Eduard Landmann. Armando Elba was the scriptwriter. They worked on three films before Nahum went to Chile. The first one did well enough, a Western. And then they shot the Mars movie: *Conqueror Women of Mars*. Then came that stupid ape movie and the Viking project floundered. Nahum couldn't get any money and Elba flew back to Europe. Maybe it was for the best."

"Why?"

"The movies were supposed to be completely different. Well, maybe not the Western. That one turned out close to the original concept. But Nahum saw the Mars movie as a surrealist project. The original title was *Adelita of Mars*. Can you picture that?"

Amelia could not, although that explained the strange costume choices and even certain shots, which had seemed oddly out of place.

"Women wearing cartridge belts like during the Revolution, a guy dressed like a futuristic Pancho Villa. It was more Luis Buñuel and *Simon of the Desert* than a B movie. A long prologue, nearly half an hour of it. But then the producers asked for changes. Nahum also demanded changes, Elba kept rewriting and then Nahum rewrote the rewrites. I had new pages every morning. I didn't know how to say my lines. I didn't know the ending."

"Did they make any other movies?"

"Elba wrote erotic science fiction. Paperbacks, I don't remember in what language. Was it in French or German?" the old woman wondered. "Nahum didn't do any other movies. He didn't do anything at all, although he sent me a few sketches from Chile. He had another idea: robot women!"

Lucía smiled broadly and then her painted eyebrows knitted in a frown.

"And then it was '73 in Chile and the Coup," she muttered.

Lucía sipped her mineral water in silence, her lipstick leaving a red imprint on the plastic straw. She glanced at Amelia, as if sizing her up.

"Come. Let me show you something," the old woman said.

Amelia followed her. She had only been inside the one room in the house where they watched the movies. Lucía took her to her office. There were tall bookcases, a rustic pine desk with painted sunflowers. Several framed posters served as decoration. Lucía stood before one of them.

"*Conqueror Women of Mars*," she said. "The first poster. They had it redone. Cristina Garza said, since she was the better-known actress, she should be on the poster. They made a terrible poster to promote the film, but this was a good concept. It was better."

The poster showed a woman in white, cartridge belts crisscrossing her back. There was one brief scene in the movie where Lucía was dressed like that. The ground beneath the woman's feet was red and the sky was also red, a cloud of dust. She was looking over her shoulder. The colors were saturated and the font was all-caps, dramatic. But there was an element of gracefulness in the woman's pose that elevated this from shlock to sheer beauty.

"I like it," Amelia said.

"Then look at this one," Lucía said, pointing at another poster. "To raise money for the Viking project, Nahum commissioned an artist to paint this. It was a lost-world story but with a science fiction twist. It was set in the future, after an atomic war has left most of the world uninhabited and giant lizards roam the desert."

"Where did the Vikings come into that?" Amelia said, puzzled, staring at this other poster, which showed a young Lucía in a fur bikini, clutching the arm of a handsome man who wore an incongruous Viking hat. Behind them, two dinosaurs were engaged in a vicious fight.

"I don't know. But you have to remember Raquel Welch had made a lot of money in *One Million Years B.C.* and this was just a few years after that. I suppose any concept was a good concept if they could get half a dozen pretty girls into furry bathing suits."

"So, why couldn't the director raise the money for it, then?"

"Same problem as always. Nahum had all these strange ideas he wanted to incorporate into the movie and he kept fighting with Elba. Nahum could have been Alejandro Jodorowsky, but things didn't quite go that way and besides, there already was *one* Jewish Latin-American director. In fact, I'm pretty sure Nahum went to Chile because he was so pissed off at Jodorowsky. If Jodorowsky had gone from Chile to Mexico, then Nahum was going from Mexico to Chile."

"If he had a cast ready, he must have gotten pretty far," Amelia mused, looking at the names on the poster.

"He had all the main parts figured out. Rodrigo Tinto was going to be the Hero, same as in *Mars*. He looked great on camera, which is the best I can say of him."

"You did not like him?" Amelia asked, a little surprised. They seemed to have good chemistry in the movie she'd watched. Then again, it was a film with rayguns and space pirates, nothing but make-believe.

"He had bad breath and a temper."

"What about the director? Was he likeable?"

"No," Lucía said. Her smile was dismissive but not toward Amelia. She was thinking back to her acting days.

"Also had a temper?"

"No. Darling, some people are not meant to be liked," Lucía said, with elegant simplicity.

Amelia did not know what that meant. Perhaps, judging by her lack of gigs on Friendrr, Amelia was one of those persons who were not meant to be liked. And judging by the film director's lack of success, they might share more than that single quality.

Lucía showed Amelia a couple of more posters before they said goodbye. In the subway concourse, she saw an ad for a virtual assistant, a dancing, singing, 3D hologram: a teenage avatar in a skimpy French maid's outfit who would call you "Master" and wake you up in the morning with a song.

Her phone, tucked inside her jacket, rang. The specific ringtone she knew. She had a booking.

She pressed a hand against the cell phone and resisted the impulse to check her messages. Finally, in the stairway to her building, Amelia took out the phone and looked at the screen. It was a booking with Elías, just as she'd suspected. She could press the green button and accept it, or click on the big red "no" button and discard it. But Miguel would ring her up and ask for an explanation. He was zealous about this stuff. Each rejected booking was a lost commission.

Amelia's index finger hovered over the green button. Accepting was easier than speaking to Miguel. She could spend another two hours locked in Elías's room. After all, he had given her a good rating. Five out of five stars. She remembered when she used to agonize over each rating she obtained, wondering why people hadn't liked her enough. Three stars, two. Even when it was four, she wondered. She had wanted to be like the popular ones, the ones who got bookings every day. If she could up her ratings by a quarter of a point . . . and there was a bonus for customer satisfaction. It did not amount to anything, not ever.

There was a sour note in her. It drove people away. And Jesus Christ, if she could be more cheerful, nicer, friendlier, she would be, but it was no use.

Green. It didn't matter. Booking confirmed.

The view from Elías's apartment at night rendered the city strange. It turned it into an entirely different city. In the distance, a large billboard flickered red, enticing people to "Visit Mars." You could emigrate now; see more information online.

The words "Visit Mars" alternated with the image of a girl in a white spacesuit, holding a helmet under her arm, looking up at the sky. Her face confident. That girl knew things. That girl knew people. That girl was not Amelia, because Amelia was no one.

Elías emerged from the kitchen and handed her a glass of white wine. Amelia continued staring out the tall windows.

"What are you looking at?" he asked.

"That billboard," she said. The glow of the sign was mesmerizing.

"Mars. It's always Mars," he said, raising his own glass of wine to his lips.

"You used to be interested in it."

"I still am. But things are different now. I just . . . I thought you'd changed your mind."

He had definitely changed *his* mind. There were no photos in the apartment. His old place was small. Photos on the walls, antique cameras on the shelves, hand-painted stars on the ceiling (those had been her notion). An attempt at bohemian living. It had all been scrubbed clean, just like his face, the whole look of him.

"Never."

"New Panyu, is that still the idea?" he asked.

Amelia nodded. They had weighed all three options. New Panyu seemed the best bet, the largest settlement. They'd quizzed each other in Mandarin. Yī shēng yī shì, whispered against the curve of her neck. Funny how "I love you" never sounded the same in different languages. It lost or gained power. In English, it sounded so plain. In Spanish, it became a promise.

"It mustn't be easy," he said. He looked like he was sorry for her. It irritated Amelia.

"Haven't you heard? The problem with our generation is we don't have enough life goals," Amelia replied tersely. "No real challenges."

"My assistant said they are capping Class B applications."

"Is it a virtual assistant? I say 'she' because it turns out men like to interact with female avatars," Amelia told him. She thought about the French maid hologram bending over to show her underwear, but surely he could afford real people. He was on Friendrr. Maybe in the mornings, a chick came to play dictation with him, wearing glasses and holding a clipboard.

"No."

"Do you want me to keep talking to you, or do you want me to be quiet? You need to give me parameters of interaction," she said.

"Please don't talk like that."

"You clicked on an app and ordered me like you order Chinese takeout, so don't be offended if I ask if you'd like chopsticks."

He stared at her and she gave him a faint smile, but it wasn't real. It was the cheap, placid imitation she ironed and took out for clients.

"I'm fine with silence. I just want to have a few drinks. I don't like drinking alone," he said coolly.

She finished her wine. He refilled the glass. They moved away from the window, sat on different ends of the couch. They drank and she watched him, Elías in profile. She might have taken out her cell phone and played a game, but she wanted him to be uncomfortable, to ask her to look away. He did not and eventually, Amelia relaxed her body and took off her shoes, staring at the ceiling instead. The wine had a hint of citrus. It went to her head quickly. She did not drink too often these days, not when she was paying, and when she did, it was the cheap, watered stuff.

She enjoyed the feeling that came with the alcohol, the indifference as she lay on his couch and threw her head back. She thought of Mars, the Mars in Lucía's movie, tinted in black-and-white, and she shielded her eyes with the back of her hand. She drank more. Time had slowed down in the silence of the room.

Finally, the cell phone beeped and she rose, pressing the heel of her hand against her forehead.

"Well," she said, standing in front of him and showing him the phone, "it's over."

"I can add an extra hour," he said. "Let me find my phone."

He looked panicked as he patted his shirt. He accidentally knocked over the glass of wine, which had been resting on the arm of the couch. The wine splattered over the expensive rug. Amelia chuckled, his distress delighting her. But then he looked hurt and she felt somewhat bad, for a heartbeat.

Amelia sat on his lap, straddling him, her hands resting on his shoulders.

"What's so terrible about being alone?" she asked.

She was being deliberately cruel, teasing him. She disliked it when she sank to such depths, but Amelia was angry, with a quiet sort of anger. She might hurt him now and it would please her.

Elías did not move. He had flailed like a fish out of water a few seconds before as he attempted to find his phone, but now he was perfectly still, staring at her.

"I hate it and you know it."

"Can't you hire someone to scare the monster who lives under the bed?"

"Amelia," he said, sadly.

She chuckled. "Aren't we pathetic?" she whispered.

When he tried to kiss her, she wouldn't let him. An arbitrary line but one she had to trace. Fucking was fine. Amelia hadn't fucked in forever. She couldn't bring people to her shared room and the guys she stumbled into were in as much of a fix as she was. She didn't want anyone, anyway. It was a struggle to exchange semi-polite words, to pretend she was interested in what came out of a stranger's mouth. *Oh, yes, that's great how you're going to take a coding boot camp and you'll have a job in six weeks or less, except no one is hiring, you idiot.* Or, *That's interesting that you are working as a pimp on the side, but no thanks, buddy, I'm not joining your troupe or whatever the hell it's called these days.*

Who cared what she said to Elías? What she did with him? Who cared at this point? She drew her line and he drew his, which seemed to be the ridiculous notion that they should fuck on the bed. Perhaps he objected to the soiling of the couch.

By the time Amelia zipped up her jeans and started pulling on her shoes, it was too late to take the bus. She had to call a car. She fiddled with the cell phone.

"Will you give me your number?" Elías asked. "I don't want to keep using this Friendrr thing to find you."

"I should tell you to make me an offer," she replied.

He looked at her, offended, but then his gaze softened. She feared perhaps he might bark an amount after all. The thought that he might take her seriously, or that she had said it in anything but mockery, made Amelia reach for her purse. She found a stray piece of paper and scribbled the number.

"Bye," she told him and headed downstairs.

Mars, Scene 2

INT. MARS BASE—NIGHT

SPACE EXPLORER sits next to the bed where THE HERO lies. He is injured. His ship crashed near her father's lab. He dragged himself from the wreckage. She cleans and bandages his wounds. SPACE EXPLORER is not truly a space explorer. The script has been rewritten and she is now ROMANTIC INTEREST, but for the sake of expediency, we will continue to call her SPACE EXPLORER. THE HERO shall remain THE HERO.

SPACE EXPLORER tenderly speaks to THE HERO. This is love at first sight, for both of them. THE HERO tells SPACE EXPLORER how he's come to warn and protect the outpost from a marauding band of SPACE PIRATES. But SPACE EXPLORER's father thinks something else may be afoot. He is a dedicated scientist working on a top secret project and fears THE HERO may be a spy from an evil nation sent to steal his work.

Despite only knowing THE HERO for five minutes, SPACE EXPLORER defends the stranger. Later, during an interlude inside the "futuristic" outpost, which is a building shaped like an egg, THE HERO kisses SPACE EXPLORER.

Cue swelling music with plenty of violins. Fade to modest black.

5

The Zócalo was being transformed into a cheesy winter wonderland, complete with an ice skating rink. The city's mayor trotted the rink out each year to please the crowds: free skating, fake snow falling from the sky, a giant Coca-Cola-sponsored tree in the background. It wasn't bread-and-circuses, anymore. Now it was icicles and festive music.

This spectacle meant a lot of people wanting to make a buck were ready for action. Teenagers in ratty "snowman" costumes offering to pose for a photo, peddlers selling soda pop to people waiting in line, and thieves eager to steal purses.

Pili was also downtown. Like anyone their age, Pili had no permanent job, cycling between gigs. Working at the marijuana grow-op, checking ATMs in small businesses to make sure no one was skimming them, selling spare computer parts Christmas season this year found her servicing the machines at a virtual reality arcade.

"They're probably going to shut them down in a few months," Pili said. "All that talk about virtual reality dissociation."

"Is that a real thing?" Amelia asked.

"Fuck if I know. But the Mayor needs to score points with the old farts, and if he can't combat prostitution and crime, this is the next best thing. Virtual reality addiction."

"It seems like it would be a lot of trouble to shut everyone down. There's a lot of arcades."

"It'll just go underground. Fuck it. It's slow today, ain't it? We should have gone to the Sanborns."

They were eating at the Bhagavad, which wasn't a restaurant proper but a weird joint run by a bunch of deluded eco-activists, open only at odd and irregular hours. You paid what you wanted and sat next to walls plastered with flyers warning people against the dangers of vat-meat. Amelia didn't care about veganism, Indian spirituality, or the fight against capitalist oppressors, but she did care about spending as little as possible on her meals. Not that there weren't affordable tacos near the subway, but like everyone joked, long gone were the days when they were at least made with dog. Nowadays, rat was the most likely source of protein. She did not fancy swallowing bubonic plague wrapped in a tortilla.

Unfortunately, the bohemian candor and community spirit of Bhagavad meant the service was terrible. They had spent half an hour waiting for the rice dish of the day, which would inevitably taste like shit watered in piss, but must have some kind of nutritional content, since it kept many a sorry ass like Amelia going.

"Do you have to be back by a certain time?" Amelia asked.

"Kind of."

"Sorry."

"It's okay. I'll grab a protein shake if it gets too late," Pili said, dismissing any issues with a wave of her hand.

Pili was always cool. Nothing ever seemed to faze her, whether it was the cops suddenly appearing and chasing away street vendors while she was trying to hawk computer parts, or the sight of a bloated, dead dog in the middle of the road blocking her path. Perhaps such self-confidence came from a secret, inner well, but Amelia suspected Pili's tremendous height had something to do it. Pili was strong, as well. She wore sleeveless shirts, which showed off her arms and her tattoos, and she smiled a lot.

"All right. But if it gets too late, just say the word."

"Nah, don't worry. Hey, you still need that money?"

"No, I had a gig," Amelia said, thinking of the two times she'd seen Elías.

"Friendrr, huh? Look, you can make a lot more at the blood clinic. The only requirement is that you have to be 27 or younger, no diseases, no addicts."

Amelia knew it was easy. That was what scared her. She was inching toward 27 and after that, what could she sell? What could she do when she wasn't even fit to be a blood bag? She didn't want to get hooked on that kind of money, but there didn't seem to be anything else beckoning her.

Giovanni Schiaparelli peered into his telescope and he thought he saw canals on Mars. Lowell imagined alien civilizations: "Framed in the blue of space, there floats before the observer's gaze a seeming miniature of his own Earth, yet changed by translation to the sky."

Mars, Amelia's Mars. Always Mars, in every stolen and quiet moment, as she folded a napkin and refolded it.

"You've got that face again, Amelia."

"What face?" Her fingers stilled on the napkin.

"Like you don't care I'm here."

"Of course I care."

"If you need the money, just ask. I can lend you the stuff. I know you'll pay me back."

"It's not the money."

Well, it wasn't only the money. Not that she was doing fine in terms of cash flow. It was Elías and she couldn't discuss him with Pili. It was Mars and there was no point in discussing that with anybody.

"I'm throwing a party Friday. You should come. It'll do you good," Pili suggested.

"I have to go to an art gallery. I'm trying to meet someone there about a gig," Amelia said.

"What time is that?"

"Eight."

"We'll be up late. Just stop by after your meeting."

"I don't know," Amelia said. She turned her head, staring at a neon pink flyer stuck on the wall that showed several politicians drawn in the shape of pigs, wearing ties and jackets. They were eating slops.

It was hard to believe that this metropolis, when viewed from Presidente Masaryk, was the place where Amelia lived, scrubbed clean, with a Ferrari dealership and luxurious shops. The city attempted to eliminate the grimy fingerprints that clung to the rest of the urban landscape. Private security kept a tight watch on beggars and indigents. There were trees here—not plastic ones, either. Real bits of greenery, while elsewhere a sea of cement swallowed the soul.

She had ventured down Masaryk often when she was with Elías. His interest in photography led them there to inspect the art galleries that perched themselves near the wide avenue. The place where Anastasia had her opening was a new gallery. Amelia had never visited it with her ex-boyfriend.

She wore the nice gray dress, which had caused her so many headaches. It was classic, elegant and it paired perfectly with one of the few pairs of heels she owned. She'd slicked her hair back into a ponytail, put on eyeshadow, which she didn't bother with most mornings.

The theme of the exhibit was indeed, obviously, crassly "meat." There were hunks of beef hanging from the ceiling, cube-shaped meat that gently palpitated. Alive. Vat-meat, coerced into this shape. The head of a bull atop a pillar stared at Amelia. It smelled. Coppery, intense, the smell. It made Amelia wrinkle her nose. The other guests did not seem to mind the stench, long, glass flutes in their hands, laughter on their lips.

Amelia saw Anastasia Brito surrounded by a wide circle of admirers. She waited, trying to slip to her side, and found herself squeezed next to three people who were having an animated discussion about fish.

"Soon, the only thing left to eat is going to be jellyfish. It's the one animal thriving in the ocean," a man with a great, bald pate said.

"The indigenous people in—fuck it, I don't know where, some shit place in Asia—they are launching some sort of lawsuit," replied a young man.

"It's really sad," said a woman with cherry-red lips. "But what is anyone supposed to do about it?"

The young man stopped a waiter, grabbing a shrimp and popping it in his mouth. Amelia traced a vector toward Anastasia and correctly inserted herself at her elbow, catching her attention.

"Hi, Anastasia, it's good to see you again. This is all very interesting."

Anastasia smiled at Amelia, but Amelia could tell she did not remember her, that for a few seconds, she simply threw her a canned, indifferent smile before her eyes focused on her and the smile turned into an O of surprise.

"Amelia. Why . . . it's been ages. What are you doing here?" she asked, and she looked like she'd discovered gum stuck under her shoe.

"Fernanda told me about the show and I decided to give it a look," Amelia said. She'd assumed Fernanda would mention she would be showing up, that something would have been indicated. She should not have expected such attention to detail.

"Well," Anastasia said. She said nothing else. The canned smile returned, brighter than before, but Anastasia's eyes scanned the room, as if she were looking for someone, anyone, to pull her out of this unwanted reunion.

Amelia dug in. She'd made the trip to the stupid gallery, after all. Marta was always chiding her about her lack of initiative. So, Amelia smiled back and tried to move the conversation in the required direction.

"Fernanda said you are putting together something new. Something about plants. She thought I might be able to help you with it."

"How?" Anastasia asked.

"I do have the studies in botany and I've gotten good at hacking genes. Here's my card," Amelia said, handing Anastasia the little plastic square with her contact information. She'd spent money getting this new card, money she didn't have, so she wouldn't hand out a number scribbled on a crumpled napkin. Anastasia held it with the tips of her fingers. Her nails were painted a molten gold. The tips of her eyelashes had been inked in gold to match the nails.

"No offense, Amelia, but what do you know about art?"

"A few things. Elías and I spent a lot of time around galleries and museums."

"That's great, but wasn't that such a long time ago?" she asked, and her words carried a hint of disgust.

The smile once more. The silence. Amelia remembered all the times Miguel had told her success was all about acquiring a positive attitude. She dearly wished to dial him and tell him he was an idiot. Instead, she bade Anastasia a quick goodbye and went in search of a car.

6

Pili lived in a rough area. It wasn't La Joya or Barrio Norte, but Santa María la Ribera kept getting more fucked-up each year. There were benefits to this, mainly that when Pili threw a party—even if the whole floor joined in, blasting music from each apartment—the neighbors upstairs couldn't do shit about it. If they called the cops, the cops were liable to show up, have a couple of beers, dance a cumbia, and depart.

Pili threw parties often and Amelia declined any invitations just as often. She had internalized her mother's directives: Study, work hard, don't drink, no boys. It was difficult to shake those manacles off. Whenever she did, Amelia felt guilty. But she didn't want to think about her conversation with Anastasia at the gallery—the fucking humiliation of it—and the music at Pili's apartment eviscerated coherent thoughts.

Amelia pushed into Pili's place, trying to find her friend amongst the dancers and the people resting on the couch, chatting, drinking, smoking. Finally, she spotted Pili in a corner, laughing her generous laughter.

"Amelia!" Pili said. "You came after all. And you look like a secretary or some shit like that."

Amelia glanced down at her clothes, knowing she was overdressed. "Yeah. No time to change."

"Look, we've got a ton of booze. Have a drink. Tito! Tito, she needs a drink!"

Amelia accepted the drink with a nod of the head. The booze was strong. It had a sour taste. With some luck, it had been fabricated in Pili's dirty bathtub. If not, it was liable to have come from somewhere much worse. But it wouldn't be hazardous. Pili didn't allow additives in her home.

She watched the partygoers flirting, chatting, dancing. Amelia wondered why some people found it easy to be happy, like an automatic switch had been turned on in them the moment they were born, while she watched in silence, at a distance, unmoved by the merriment. Amelia's cup was efficiently refilled through the night.

Although she neither danced nor spoke much, she leaned back on a couch and listened to the beat of the music, the booze turning her limbs liquid.

A guy she knew vaguely, a rare animal trader, sat next to her for a while. He was carrying an owl in a cage. The owl was dead, and he told her he was taking it to a guy who was going to stuff it right after the party.

"Am I boring you?" the guy asked. Amelia did not even try to pretend politeness. She drank from her plastic cup and utterly ignored him, because the last thing she needed was this guy trying to sell her a fucking dead owl and it was obvious where his monologue was going.

Owl Man got up. Another guy sat in the vacated space, his friend hovering next to the sofa. They complained that Soviets (fucking FUCKING REDS, were their exact words) were sending fake tequila to Hamburg. One of them had made money exporting the liquor to Germany, but that was over and the man who was standing up was now reduced to something-something. She didn't catch the details, but she knew the story. Everyone had a story like that. They'd all done better at one point. They'd run better cons, done better drugs, drunk better booze, but now they were skimming.

The guy sitting next to her was trying to elbow her out of the way so his friend could sit down. Amelia knew if she had been cooler, more interesting, more something, he wouldn't have tried that. But she was not. The appraisal of her limitations provided her with a defiant stubbornness. She planted her feet firmly on the ground, did not budge an inch, and both of the men walked away, irritated.

She dozed off, thought of Mars. Black-and-white, like in Lucía's movie. Rayguns and space pirates, the ridiculous Mars they'd dreamt in a previous century. Far off in the distance, blurry, out of focus, she saw a figure that had not been in the movie.

There are only two plots, Lucía had told her one evening. *A person goes on a journey and a stranger comes into town.* Amelia couldn't tell if this was one or the other.

What do you do in the meantime? she wondered. *What do you do while you wait for your plot to begin?*

The stranger's shadow darkened the doorway, elongated. The doorway of the bar. The space bar. It was always a bar. Western. So, then, this was *A stranger comes into town. Fate knocks on your door.*

She woke curled up on Pili's couch. Many of the partygoers were still around, passed out on the floor and chairs. Amelia took out her phone, wincing as she looked at the time. It was past noon. She had two text messages and a voicemail. The voicemail and one of the messages were from her irritated sister, who wanted to remind Amelia she was supposed to babysit that night at seven. The other text message was from Elías. *What are you up to?*

Amelia hesitated before slowly typing an answer. *Woke up with a huge hangover.*

A couple of minutes later and her phone rang. Amelia slipped out of Pili's apartment and answered the phone as she walked down the stairs.

"How huge of a hangover?" Elías asked.

"Pretty massive. Why?"

"I have a great trick for that."

"Oh?"

"If you stopped by, I'd show you. It's an effective recipe."

"I am a mess and I am on babysitting duty at seven o'clock."

"That's ages away. Should I send a car?"

Amelia emerged from the building and blinked at the sudden onslaught of daylight. She really shouldn't.

She accepted the offer.

Amelia reeked of cigarette smoke and booze, but part of the pleasure was swanning into Elías's pristine apartment and tossing her stinky jacket onto his couch. She was a foreign element introduced into a laboratory. That was what his home reminded her of: the sterile inside of a lab.

She leaned on her elbows against his white table and watched him as he chopped a green pepper in the kitchen.

"Was it a good party?" he asked.

"Does it matter?" she replied with a shrug.

"Why else go to a party, then?"

She did not reply, instead observing him intently. It was funny how you thought you remembered someone. You sketched their face boldly in your mind, but when you saw them again, you realized how far you were from their true likeness. Had he always been that height, for example? Had he moved the way he did, long strides as he reached the table? Had he smiled at her like that? Maybe she'd constructed false memories of him, fake angles.

"Here."

"I'm not drinking that," Amelia said, pointing at the glass full of green goo Elías was offering her.

"It's just vegetables, an egg and hot sauce," he told her.

Amelia took a sip. It was terrible, as she'd expected, and she quickly handed Elías the glass back. He chuckled and brushed a limp strand of hair away from her face.

"Did it help at all?"

"No."

"Well, I tried."

She placed the glass on the table and walked around the living room, looking at the blank walls.

"You have no photos at all, no decorations."

She didn't mind. Her room—Could she even call it hers when she shared it with her niece?—was littered with scraps of her past. She knew it too well, every crack on the wall, every spring on the bed. It reminded her of who she was and who she'd never been. Elías's apartment was a soothing blank slate, a pale cocoon.

One might molt and transform here.

"I don't know if I'm going to stay long. Besides, I don't take photos, anymore," he said.

"Why not?"

"Grew out of it, I suppose."

But not, perhaps, out of her. Amelia allowed herself to be flattered by that thought and smiled at him.

He slid next to her, slid across that fine line she was trying to draw between affection and desire. There was that irresponsible wild feeling in her gut, all youthful need. Amelia had not felt young in ages. She was about fifty-five in her head, but he reminded her of her awkward teenage years, things she'd forgotten. It was exciting. She thought she'd lost that, that she'd outgrown it. Even if this was just horrid déjà vu, it felt like something. It was pleasant to remember she was 25, that she wasn't that old, that it wasn't all over.

Her hair smelled like tobacco and she guessed her makeup was a bit of a mess, smudged mascara and only the faintest trace of lipstick, but he wasn't complaining. She supposed it might be part of the appeal.

Slumming it, Elías style.

She truly did not know what he was getting out of this. Best not to dig too deeply. Best to just fall into bed with him.

His arm was over his eyes when he spoke, shielding himself from a stray, persistent ray of light peeking through the curtains.

"Do you really still think about going to Mars?" he asked.

On Mars, they would be cold. His breath would rise like a plume. They'd huddle under furs. They'd fight space pirates and save the world. Well . . . not on the real Mars. On the Mars of that black-and-white flick she'd watched.

"Is it that shocking?" she replied.

"No," he said. "I think you loved that planet more than you loved me."

"You can't be jealous of a hunk of rock."

"I was."

"Planets keep to their orbits," she said tersely.

He looked at her and she thought this was going to end quickly. That he wouldn't put up with recriminations, exclamations. The amusement might be over, already. She headed to the shower. But when she came out of the bathroom, he grabbed her hand.

She reached home at quarter past seven to a very furious sister, but fortunately Marta had somewhere to be and she did not have time to quiz Amelia about her whereabouts. Once the door to the apartment slammed shut, Amelia sat on the couch next to her nieces. The TV was on and an announcer was laughing.

Mars, Scene 3

EXT. MARS BASE—NIGHT

SPACE EXPLORER, holding future goggles, spots marauders near the outpost. She hurries back to alert her father and THE HERO about this. It must be the SPACE PIRATES who have come to ransack the outpost and steal THE SCIENTIST's invention.

There is a discussion about how to hold them off. Montage of preparations, then a battle. Despite THE HERO's best efforts, the outpost is overrun and the SPACE PIRATES break through the defenses. The survivors are surrounded by bad guys, but THE HERO has managed to escape.

ENTER EVIL SPACE QUEEN. Maximum sexiness in a dress that does its utmost best to show tits. She taunts the good guys and demands THE SCIENTIST hand over the gizmo he's been working on, which will give SPACE QUEEN incredible powers, yadda-yadda. THE SCIENTIST refuses, but SPACE QUEEN thinks some time in a torture chamber will change his mind.

SPACE QUEEN decrees THE SPACE EXPLORER will be wed to her brother, who doubles as the EVIL HENCHMAN, therefore ensuring absolute control of the planet. Three exclamation points.

THE SPACE EXPLORER—the *girl*, this is nothing but a girl, diminutive and frail—faints. SPACE QUEEN's evil laughter.

7

"The biggest problem, of course, was that Nahum kept changing things," Lucía said. Her turban was silver that day. It looked like she had wrapped tinfoil around her head. And yet, Lucía managed to appear regal as she sat on the couch, with a few pages from her memoir on her lap.

She offered Amelia the bowl with pomegranate seeds and Amelia took a couple. "He was an insomniac, so he'd wake up in the middle of the night, find a problem with the shooting script, jot down some notes. Then he phoned the writer at around three A.M. and the writer would promise he'd make changes. Which he did. But then, Nahum couldn't sleep again, and so on and so forth.

"He was on drugs. I was so young I couldn't even tell if this was a normal shoot or not. Convent-educated girl. A friend of a friend of my father was the one who got me my first audition and it all happened quickly, easily. A fluke."

Lucía frowned, her eyes little, tiny polished beads staring at Amelia. She was a Coatlicue, an angry, withered, Earth Mother goddess, her forked tongue about to fly out of her mouth and demand blood. Amelia's mother had been hard, too. She watched over Amelia like a hawk and did not watch over Marta at all because Marta was too rebellious. Malleable Amelia was subject to all the commands of their mother. As in, obtain straight As, no social life, no boyfriends until there came that rich boy her mother approved of. Then she'd gotten sick and it had gotten even worse.

Amelia swallowed the pomegranate seeds.

"And now this bitch says I can't mention any of that."

"I'm sorry?" Amelia asked.

"Nahum's daughter. Some meddlesome fool informed her I was typing out my memoir and her daddy is included in it. Would you believe she had the audacity to phone me a couple of days ago and threaten me with a lawsuit if I say her father did drugs? He ate mushrooms out of little plastic bags, for God's sake. He was lovely and he was a mess. Who cares at this point? They're all dead."

Lucía leaned back, her face growing lax. She lost the look of a stone idol and became an old lady, wrinkles and liver spots and the flab under her neck, like a monstrous turkey. The old lady squinted.

"What do you intend to do on Mars?" Lucía asked, but she glanced away from Amelia, as if she didn't want her to discern her expression.

"Grow plants," Amelia muttered.

"You can do that?"

"Hydroponics. It's the same technology you'd use for a marijuana grow-op on Earth. Everything is inside a dome. They are terraforming with microbes, but it will take a long time for anything close to farmland to exist outside a biodome."

"I suppose it's not like in my movie. You can't walk around in a dress without a helmet."

"No. But the suits are very light now, very flexible." Modern-looking suits, strips of luminescent thread running down the leg. Amelia had pictured herself in one of those suits one out of each seven days of the week.

"And you can fly there. Just like that?"

"Not quite. If you get a Class C visa, you can go as a worker, but they garnish your wages. They pay themselves back your fare. Half your pay goes to the company that got you there and they play all kinds of tricks so you owe them even more in the end. But if you get a Class B visa, it's different. You are an investor. You pay your passage and you do whatever you want."

"You never do what you want, Amelia. There are always limits. I should know. I got my Mars. It was made of cardboard and wire, and the costume designer stabbed me with pins when they were adjusting my dress and it wasn't nearly enough."

There's no comparison, Amelia wanted to say. No comparison at all between a limited, laughable attempt at an acting career that ended with a whimper, and Amelia's thoughts on crop physiology and modified plants that could survive in iron-rich soil. Amelia, staring at the vastness of the sky from her tiny outpost. Amelia on the Red Planet.

"Why Mars? You could grow crops here, couldn't you?" Lucía asked.

Amelia shrugged. It would take too long to explain. Fortunately, Lucía did not ask more about Mars and Amelia did not steer the conversation back toward Lucía's memoir. When she got home, she lay in her bed and looked for photos of Lucía. Gorgeous in the black-and-white stills, the smile broad and wild, the hair shiny. Then she looked for Nahum, but there were few of him. It was the same couple of photos: two headshots showing a man with a cigarette in his left hand, the other with his arms crossed. His life was a short stub. Three movies. As for the scriptwriter, she found he'd used a pen name for his erotic novels and you could buy them used for less than the cost of a hamburger. But at least they'd all left a trail behind them, a clue to their existence. When Amelia died, there would be nothing.

On her napkins at the coffee shop, she now drew faces. Lucía's face in her youth, the hero's face, the Space Queen. She sketched the glass city of the movie, the space pirates and a rocket. Amelia had a talent for drawing. If she'd been born in another century, she might have been a botanical illustrator. Better yet, a rich naturalist, happily documenting the flora of the region. An Ynes Mexia, discovering a new genus.

But Amelia existed in the narrow confines of the Now, in the coffee shop, her cell phone with a tiny crack on its screen resting by her paper cup.

She was out of coffee and considering phoning Elías. It was not love sickness, like when she'd been younger, just boredom. A more dangerous state.

She bit her lip. Fortunately, Pili called right then and Amelia suddenly had something to do: Go to the police precinct. Pili had been busted for something and she needed Amelia to bribe the cops. Amelia cast a worried look at her bank account, at the pitiful savings column she had ear-marked for Mars, and got going.

The cops were fairly tractable and they did not harass her, which was the best you could say about these situations.

It only took Amelia an hour until they shoved Pili outside the station and the two women began walking toward the subway. On Mina, the romería for the holidays was ready for business, with mechanical games and people dressed as the Three Kings. Santa Claus was there, too, and so were several Disney princesses. Tired-looking parents dragged their toddlers by the hand and teenagers made out on the Ferris wheel.

Pili had a busted lip, but she was smiling and she insisted they buy an esquite. Amelia agreed and Pili shoved the grains of corn into her mouth while they walked around the perimeter of the brightly lit assemblage of holiday-related inanities.

"The bastards didn't even bother giving me a sandwich," Pili said. "I was there for eight fucking hours."

"What did they nab you for?"

"I was selling something," Pili said. She did not specify what she'd been selling and Amelia did not ask. "Hey, the posadas start tomorrow."

"Do they?" Amelia replied. She was not keeping track, did not care for champurrado and tamales.

"Sure. We gonna go bounce around the city, or what?"

"Depends if I have any dough."

"Shit, you don't need no dough for a posada. That's the whole point. We'll crash one or two or three."

Amelia smiled, but she felt no mirth. She thought of snot-nosed children breaking piñatas while she tried to drink a beer in peace.

Before they separated, Pili promised to pay Amelia back the money. This swapping of funds was erratic and pointless, they both simply kept deferring their financial woes, but Amelia nodded and tried to put up a pleasant façade because Pili had just had a rough day.

Once Amelia was alone, all the things she hadn't wanted to think about returned to her like the tide. Thoughts of cash flow issues, the vague notion that she should visit the blood clinic, her musings on Mars.

She wanted to visit Elías without any warning, just crash on his couch.

She wanted to go to a bar and buy over-priced cocktails instead of sipping Pili's counterfeit booze.

She wanted to look for an apartment for herself and never answer her sister's voice-mails.

She wanted so many things. She wanted the Mare Erythraeum laid before her feet.

Between one and the other—between Scylla and Charybdis like Sting had sung in an old, old song she'd heard at a club in Monterrey, a club she'd visited with Elías in the heady, early days when the world seemed overflowing in possibilities—between those options, she picked Elías.

She had not dialed him, but now she pressed the phone against her ear and waited.

The phone rang two times and then a female voice answered. "Hello?"

Amelia, sitting in the subway, her hand on a bit of graffiti depicting a rather ana-tomically incorrect penis painted on the window pane, managed a cough but no words.

"Hello?" said the woman again.

"I was looking for Elías Bertoliat," she said.

"He's in the shower. Do you want to leave a message?"

"It's about his Friendrr account," Amelia lied. "We've closed it down, as he requested."

She hung up and lifted her legs, gathering them against her chest. Across the aisle, a homeless kid, his hands blackened with soot, chewed gum. A woman selling biopets—lizards with three tails—hawked her wares in a high-pitched voice. Amelia let three stations go by before switching trains, back-tracking and getting off at the right spot.

Only narcissists and Heroes stood unwavering against the odds. Most rational people got a clue and found their bearings. Amelia found the blood clinic. She'd been put-ting it off, fabricating excuses, but truth was, she needed cash. Not the drip-drip cash of her Friendrr gigs, something more substantial.

The clinic was tucked around the corner from a subway station. The counter was a monstrous green, with a sturdy partition and posters all round of smiling, happy people.

"Who's poking us today? It's not Armando, is it?" the man ahead of Amelia asked. He must have known all the technicians by name, who was good with a needle and who sucked.

The employee manning the reception desk asked for Amelia's ID and eyed her carefully. She was told to sit in front of a screen and answer 25 questions, part of the health profile. Next time, she could just walk in, show a card, and forget the questions.

Afterward, a technician talked to Amelia for three short minutes, then handed her a number, and directed her to sit and wait in an adjacent room.

Amelia sat down, sandwiched between a young woman playing a game on her cell phone and a man who rocked back and forth, muttering under his breath.

When they called her number, Amelia went into a room where they pricked her finger to do a few quick tests, measuring her iron levels. Then it was time to draw the blood. She lay on a recliner, staring at the ceiling. There was nothing to do, so she tried to nap, but it proved impossible. The whirring of a machine nearby wouldn't allow her to close her eyes.

Space flights were merely an escape, a fleeing away from oneself. Or so Carl Jung said. But lying on the recliner, thinking she could listen to the sloshing of her blood through her veins, Amelia could envision no escape. She could not picture Mars right that second and her eyes fixed on the ceiling.

On the way out, Amelia glanced at a young man waiting in the reception area, noticing the slight indentation on his arm, the tell-tale mark that showed he was a frequent donor. Pili had it, too. They crossed glances and pretended they had not seen each other.

Walking back to her apartment, Amelia realized the courtyard kids were in full festive mode: They had built a bonfire. They were dragging a plastic Christmas tree into the flames. Several of them had wreaths of tinsel wrapped around their necks. One had Christmas ornaments tied to his long hair. They greeted her as they always did: with hoots and jeers. This time, rather than slipping away, Amelia slipped closer to them, closer to the flames, intent on watching the conflagration. It seemed something akin to a pagan ritual, but then, the kids wouldn't have known anything about this. It was simple mayhem to them, their own version of a posada.

A young man looped an arm around Amelia's shoulders and offered a swig of his bottle. Amelia pressed the bottle against her lips and drank. It tasted of putrid oranges and alcohol. After a couple of minutes, the boy slid away from her, called away, and Amelia stood there, holding the bottle in her left hand.

She stepped back, sitting by the entrance of her building, her eyes still on the fire as she sipped the booze. Sparks were shooting in the air and the tree was melting.

She knew she shouldn't be drinking, especially whatever was in the bottle, but the night was cold.

At the clinic, they'd told her plasma was 90% water and she mumbled that number to herself. When she closed her eyes, she thought of Mars, black-and-white like in Lucía's movie, seen through a lens that had been coated in Vaseline. Bloated, disfigured, beautiful Mars.

When the phone rang, she answered it without even bothering to check who it was, eyes still closed, the cool surface of the screen against her cheek.

"Amelia, I think you called yesterday," Elías said.

"I think your girlfriend answered the phone," Amelia replied, snapping her eyes open.

"My fiancée," he said. "My father picked her for me."

"That's nice."

"Can you come over? I want to explain."

"I'm busy."

"What are you doing?"

"Something's burning," she said, staring at the bonfire. The teenagers running around it looked like devils, shadow things that bubbled up from the ground. It was the booze, or she was tired of everything, and she rubbed her eyes.

"Amelia—"

"Pay me. Send me a goddamn transfer right now and I'll go."

She thought he'd say no, but after a splintered silence, he spoke. "Ok."

"You'll have to send a car, too. I am not taking the subway."

"Ok."

She gave him the necessary info. When the driver appeared, it was ages or mere minutes later and she had forgotten about the deal. Cinderella going to the Ball, escorted into a sleek, black car instead of a pumpkin. She wondered if this was Elías's regular driver, his car, or just a hired one. When they'd dated, he'd owned a red sports car, but that was ages ago.

Amelia tossed the bottle out the window once the car got in motion.

8

There was an expiry date to being a loser. You could make "bad choices" and muck about until you were around twenty-one, but after that, God forbid you committed any mistakes, deviating from the anointed path, even though life was more like a game of Snakes and Ladders than a straight line.

Amelia realized that anyone peering in would pass easy judgment on her. Stupid woman, too old to be stumbling through life the way she did, stumbling into her ex-boyfriend's apartment again, shrugging out of her jacket and staring out the window at the sign in the distance, which advertised Mars.

She could almost hear the voice-over: *Watch Amelia act like a fool, again.*

But not everyone got to be the Hero of the flick.

"What is that?" Elías said, pointing at the bandage on her arm. She had not even realized she still had it on.

"I went to a clinic. They drew blood," Amelia replied, her fingers careless, sliding over the bandage.

"Are you sick?"

"I was selling blood. Old farts love to pump young plasma through their veins. Hey, maybe some of your dad's friends are going to get my blood. Wouldn't that be hilarious?"

"You should have told me if you needed money," he replied.

"Do you think I'm on Friendrr for fun? Of course I need money. Everyone does."

Except you, she thought. She wondered how the transaction he'd performed would show on his account. Two thousand tajaderos for the ex-girlfriend. File under Miscellaneous.

"Do you have any water? I'm supposed to stay hydrated," Amelia said.

He fetched her a glass and they sat on the couch.

"Amelia, my fiancée . . . it's what my father wants. I don't care about her. I don't even touch her," Elías said. He looked mournful. Sad-eyed Elías.

"It's going to be difficult for you to have children that way," Amelia replied. "Or are you thinking of renting a womb? Would you like to rent mine? It's all for sale."

"Amelia, for God's sake!" he said, scandalized.

"You are an asshole. You are a selfish, entitled prick," she told him, but she said it in a matter-of-fact tone. There was a surprisingly small amount of rancor in her voice. She sipped her water.

"Yes, all right," he agreed and she could tell he wanted to say something else. Amelia did not let him speak.

"Where did your girlfriend go? Or is she coming back? I'm not willing to hide in the closet."

"She's headed back to Monterrey. She just came to . . . my father wants me back there permanently. He sent her to pressure me and I spent all my time trying to avoid interacting with her. I—"

"What's your girlfriend's name?"

"Fiancée. Amelia, *you* are avoiding *me.*"

"How am I avoiding you? I'm sitting here, like you wanted. You're telling me you'll get married. Congratulations."

"Listen," he told her. "Nothing has been said; nothing has been done. I'm here."

I'm here, too, she thought. *I'm stuck*. Not only in the city. Stuck with him. She considered leaning forward and slapping him, just for kicks. Mostly, because she wasn't even mad at him. She thought she should be, but instead she lounged on his couch while he was fidgeting.

"I lied to you, ok? I didn't find you on Friendrr by chance. Fernanda mentioned you were there one day; Fernanda and I, we keep in touch. I went looking for you. Every goddamned day, I looked at your profile, at your picture, telling myself I wasn't going to contact you.

"I should have gone to New Panyu with you," he concluded. "My dad wouldn't give me the money, but I should have done something."

There was that scalding feeling in her stomach. Amelia loathed it. She didn't want to be angry at him. She'd been angry and that was what had started this ridiculous train of events. If she could be indifferent, it would all collapse.

"Oh, you couldn't. I was just another girl. I'm still just another girl," she told him, unable to keep her mouth shut, although at this point, the less said, the better. She had a headache. The booze she'd imbibed was probably a toxic chemical. *Radioactive flesh*, she mused. *Radioactive everything*.

But it was Elías who looked a little sick, a little feverish, and Amelia pressed cool fingers against his cheek, her mouth curving into a not-quite-smile as she edged close to him.

"You're just another guy, you know?"

He caught her hands between his and frowned.

"I'm sorry," he said. "I don't know *how* to live with you. I never did."

"I don't want you to be sorry."

"What do you want?"

You used to mean something to me, she wanted to tell him. *You used to mean something and then you used it all up without even giving it three seconds of your time. And I want to walk out and leave you with nothing, just like that, in this beautiful apartment with your wonderful, expensive things.*

Amelia looked aside.

"Let's go to sleep. I'm tired," she muttered, moving from the couch to his bedroom, as though she lived there.

She *was* exhausted. This was true. But it was also true that she could have called a car and stumbled home. Sure, she assured herself it was a safety matter, that she might collapse outside her building or pass out in the car. And yet, she could have called someone, perhaps Pili, to pick her up.

She didn't want to leave. She wanted to act the part of a fool. As simple and as complicated as that.

He wanted to make it up to her, her said, although he did not specify exactly what he was making up for: his callous ghosting or his most recent omissions. He proposed lunch, then he'd take her shopping: He wanted to buy her a dress so they could go dancing on New Year's Eve.

Amelia looked at her text messages. There were five from her sister. She was not worried because Amelia had never come home the previous night. Instead, the messages were castigating her because Amelia needed to take the girls to school and cook lunch.

Amelia deleted the messages. She grabbed his arm and they went out.

She'd never taken advantage of Elías's social position when they were dating. A dinner here and there but no expensive presents. Of course, back then, he'd been playing at bohemian living. The nice car was his one wealth marker. He kept it tucked in a garage and they took it for a spin once in a while. Once in a while, there had also been an extravagance: the sudden trip to Monterrey where they partied for a weekend, the ability to sail into a popular nightclub while losers waited outside for the bouncer to approve of their looks, but these were random, few events. He wanted to be an artist, after all, an artist with a capital A, long-suffering, starving for his creative pursuits.

Now he had shredded those pretenses and now she did not bother telling herself things such as that money did not matter. In the high-tech dressing room with interactive mirrors, she made the outfits she wanted to try on bounce across the slick, glass surface. She could take a selfie with this mirror. She wondered if anyone ever did. She assumed some people must, people who did not look at the fabric on display and wished to wreck half a dozen dresses, leaving a man with an immense bill to cover as they slipped out the back of the store.

The so-elegant employee packed her dress in pale, pink tissue paper and handed her a bag. She was on Mr. Bertoliat's account now. And though Amelia supposed "Mr. Bertoliat" meant well, she hated him when he smiled at her as they stood by the counter.

But by the time they sat down at the sushi restaurant, with its patio and its pond full of koi fish and its impeccable white plastic furniture made to resemble bamboo, she wanted to do anything but fight. Whether the blood siphoned from her veins had also drained another part of her, or she simply had latched on to a new type of debilitating obsession, she did not know.

"I heard, soon, there will be nothing but jellyfish in the seas," she said, looking at the pond. "All the fish will be gone."

"I find that unlikely," he said.

There was a restaurant in the city, run by a Parisian chef who charged $800 for a three-course meal cooked with "Indigenous" ingredients, plated on large stones. He had thought to take her there, but reservations were required.

When your credit card could afford such meals, she supposed many things were "unlikely." She supposed, with the hefty allowance he received, he could ask that a polar bear be dragged to rest on his plate after being stuffed with a dolphin. And not a cloned bear. The real damned thing, too.

"I guess it won't matter when it happens," she told him with a shrug. "Not to you."

"Are you interested in zoology, now?" he asked. "Fisheries?"

"I'm hardly interested in anything. I spend about three hours every day drawing things that don't matter and another three fiddling with my cell phone."

"That sounds the same as me. Sometimes, I take photos. But not too often."

"You had a good eye," she admitted and he smiled at that.

Elías looked rather fine that day, very polished. She'd always loved looking at him. She knew it was bad to enjoy somebody's looks so much. After all, the flesh faded. But when she'd been 19, she had not been thinking about what 69-year-old Elías would look like and now it seemed equally preposterous to self-flagellate because he was still handsome.

If she was shallow, that seemed the least of her issues.

"I should mention this right now. I have to go to Monterrey for Christmas. I can't get out of it. I'm not going to disappear, I swear. But it's Christmas and my father wants to see me. I'm his only kid. I'll be back for New Year's.

"And I'll break it off with my fiancée while I'm there," Elías added.

"Don't start making promises," she muttered.

"I want to do it. For you."

In the pond, the koi swam and she wondered if they were authentic koi, or if they had been modified. They could be mechanical. They could even be holograms. She'd seen things like that before.

Elías held out a plastic card. "Here. This is a spare key to my apartment. You can hang out there while I'm gone. Ask the concierge to get you anything you want: food, drinks. Ok?"

She toyed with the card, thinking she could lose it in the subway, toss it into the sewer. But when he bid her goodbye and put her in a car, he leaned down for a kiss and Amelia allowed it.

Amelia went up the stairs to her apartment. There, on the fourth landing, she found a glue trap with a squealing rat. She had chanced upon such sights before and they did not bother her.

She stared at the rat. Before she could figure out a proper course of action, she attempted to peel the vermin off the trap. She managed to rip the board off the rat, but the animal bit her. She pressed her hand against the wound and hurried into her apartment, looking for the rubbing alcohol and the cotton amongst the mess of expired prescriptions (these had belonged to her mother; nobody bothered tossing them out, shrines to her memory), hair clips and makeup, which were scattered upon a small shelf.

"What the hell happened to you?" Marta asked.

"Rat bit me," Amelia said.

"You better not have rabies."

Amelia opened the bottle of alcohol and soaked a cotton ball in it, then carefully cleaned the wound. Her sister was by the door, but had not offered to assist her. She merely stood there, arms crossed, staring at Amelia.

"Where were you?"

"I stayed with a friend," Amelia said.

"You fuck up my routine when you don't take the girls to school."

"I don't do this regularly."

"Sure, you don't."

"Look, you want to make sure your kids get to school on time? *You* take them," Amelia said, wondering if they had any damned Band-Aids, or if she was going to have to wrap a towel around her hand.

"I pay the bulk of the rent."

Amelia opened a cardboard box and placed two Band-Aids on her hand, forming an X.

"I pay for the bulk of the groceries," Marta added.

Amelia slid her thumb across the Band-Aids, smoothing them down. Maybe she could have the bite checked out at the sanitation clinic, although that would mean arriving early and waiting forever.

"I paid for Mother's medicines," Marta said, holding up three fingers in the air.

"And I took care of her!" Amelia yelled, turning to her sister, losing her shit, unable to keep a middling tone of voice anymore. "I was here, every day and every night, and where were you when she was pissing herself in the middle of the night? Two years, Marta! Two years of that. I threw my whole career and every single chance I ever had out the window because you wouldn't help me take care of her!"

They had never discussed it because it would have been bad to say such things, but it had to be said. Amelia was tired of pretending that what happened to her had just been bad luck, bad karma. She might have been able to finish her degree, she might have kept the scholarship, but Marta had been way too busy playing house with her then-husband to come round the apartment complex. But when he left her and Mother died, then she came real quick to take possession of the shitty little apartment.

"What makes you think you had a chance?" Marta replied.

"I better go to the sanitation clinic. Wouldn't want to give your kids rabies," Amelia said, brushing past her sister and rushing out of the apartment.

On the stairs, she found the rat she had released from the trap. It was dead. Her efforts had been in vain.

Amelia kicked the corpse away and marched outside.

Mars, Scene 4

INT. CELL—NIGHT

SPACE EXPLORER sits in a cell. Outside, it is night and the nights on Mars are unlike the nights on Earth: pitch-black darkness, the eerie silence of the red-hued sand plains. Despite her extraordinary location, the girl's cell is mundane. Iron bars, a rectangular window. This is all that we can spare. The budget is limited.

In the distance, there is laughter from the SPACE EXPLORER's captors, who are celebrating their triumph. Drinking, music.

The EVIL HENCHMAN stops in front of the SPACE EXPLORER's cell to taunt her. She replies that THE HERO will save her. THE EVIL HENCHMAN laughs. *Let him try!*

SPACE EXPLORER is unflappable. She believes in THE HERO.

Although, perhaps she should not. Her story has been traced with carbon paper, in broad strokes, but carbon paper rips easily. And the writer of this script remembers pulling the carbon paper through the typewriter when he was a child, the discordant notes when he banged on the keys, the holes he poked in the paper so that it looked like the night sky needled with stars.

But the stars have shifted. This makes sense in an ever-expanding universe, but it brings no comfort to the writer to feel them moving away from the palm of his hand.

9

"Why did you stop making movies?" Amelia asked.

"I got old."

"I looked up your filmography. You were still in your thirties."

"Your thirties *is* old when all you do is show your breasts to the camera," Lucía said.

Her turban was peach-colored, her dress pink. She wore a heavy seashell necklace and her nails had been freshly done, perhaps on account of the upcoming holidays. Despite her retirement from show business, she always managed to look like she was hoping someone would take her picture and ask for an autograph.

"I saw what happened to other actresses. There were certain people—Silvia Pinal, María Félix—who were able to remain somewhat relevant during the 80s. But for most of us, it was raunchy sex comedies and bit parts. Perhaps I might have been able to make it in soaps, but the television screen is so small. Televisa! After the marquees!"

Lucía lifted both of her hands, as if framing Amelia with them, as if she were holding a camera. Then she let them fall down on her lap again.

"So, I cashed in my chips and married well. I thought it was more dignified than shaking my ass in a negligee until the cellulite got the better of me and they kicked me off the set. You probably don't think that's very feminist of me."

"I don't think anything of it," Amelia said.

Lucía reached for the dish full of pomegranate seeds and offered them to Amelia. The routine of these visits was the most soothing part of Amelia's week. She had learned to appreciate Lucía's company, where before she had endured it.

"People criticized me, once. For everything. Every single choice you make is micro-analyzed when you're a woman. When you're a man, you can fuck up as many times as you want. Nobody asked Mauricio Garcés why he made shit films. But then you get old and nobody cares. Nobody knows you, anymore."

It was difficult to recognize Lucía. Age and whatever plastic surgery she had purchased had altered her face irrevocably. But the look in her eyes was the same look Amelia had seen in the posters, in the film stills, on screen in a dark and smoky cabaret where doomed lovers met.

"What was your best role?" Amelia asked.

"Nahum's movie. The one he didn't make."

"The Viking movie?"

Lucía shook her head. "The Mars movie. Before the script grew bloated and was butchered. I didn't know it then, of course. I knew little. But even if the story was laughable, he could get a good angle. There's that scene where I'm in prison. You recall it? Pure chiaroscuro. You only need to watch that moment, those five seconds. You don't need to watch the rest of the movie. In fact, it's better if you don't."

"Why not?" Amelia asked with a chuckle.

"Because then you can make it up in your mind. For example, I always pretend I get out of that prison cell on my own. I just walk out."

Lucía's eyes brightened. If someone had shot a close-up, then she might have resembled the actress who had adorned posters and lobby cards.

"You said Nahum wasn't nice."

"Who is *nice*, Amelia?" Lucía stated, as if waving away an annoying buzzard. "*Nice* is such a toothless word. Do you want to have your gravestone say, 'Here lies Amelia. She was *nice*'? Come, come."

"I suppose not."

"You suppose right. When my memoir is published, I imagine people will say I was a bitch, but they were not there, were they? They didn't have to make my choices. It's always easy to tell someone they should have picked Option B."

"So, what was Option B?"

Amelia expected the actress to launch into one of her elaborate anecdotes. Her face certainly seemed disposed toward conversation. Then it was like a curtain had been drawn and the light in Lucía's eyes dimmed a little.

"I forget," Lucía said. "It's been so long one forgets."

"José's working as a professional stalker," Pili said, just like that, like she had found out it would be raining tomorrow.

"You are kidding me," Amelia replied.

"No. You can hire them online. They'll stalk anyone you want."

"Is that legal?"

"Nothing worth any money is legal."

They were wedged in the back of a large restaurant, right by a noisy group of licenciados out to lunch. Pili was paying back the money she owed Amelia and taking her out to eat as a Christmas gift. For now, the Bhagavad was forgotten. They could have a regular meal, not a beggar's banquet.

"Well, it sounds awful."

"I thought I'd mention it. Just in case, you know, you're still looking for something."

"I'm fine right now. In fact, I was going to say I should pay for this," Amelia added.

"You got another client on Friendrr?"

I think I'm a professional mistress, Amelia thought. But despite Lucía's assurances that she should not worry about being perceived as "nice," she did not want to chance Pili's disapproval.

"Yeah."

"Fabulous. That means we can go out for New Year's, right? I have the perfect idea. It's—"

"I'm going out that night."

"Yeah, right. You're going to stay home and eat grapes."

"I'm not. Really. I have something planned."

They parted ways outside the restaurant. On the other side of the street sat half a dozen people with signs at their feet advertising their skills: carpenter, plumber. There was even one computer programmer. Amelia pretended they were invisible, ghosts of the city. It was a possibility. The whole metropolis was haunted.

And she was good at pretending.

When she texted Elías "Merry Christmas" and he did not text back, she pretended it did not bother her. The day after, she went to his apartment.

It was pristine, perfect. The lack of photos, of personality, the whiff of the showroom catalogue, enhanced the allure of the space. She could feign this belonged to her because it was not obvious it belonged to anyone.

She walked from the kitchen to the bedroom and back, finally standing before the window. The sign enticing people to fly to Mars glowed in the distance. She thought about calling Pili and drinking Elías's booze together, but that would break the illusion that this was her home. And she would have to explain why she had the key to this place.

Amelia went into the bathroom and ran a bath. On Christmas Eve, the taps at her apartment had gone dry and her sister had cursed for thirty minutes straight, asking how they were supposed to cook. Now, Amelia sank into the warm water. If she closed her eyes, she could imagine she was floating in the darkness of space.

When she stepped out, she left no trace of herself. When Elías texted her on December 29, it was to say he was on a red-eye flight and he had everything figured out for New Year's Eve. She slipped into the dress he'd bought her, did her makeup, and left her apartment with a few sparse words, which was all that was needed, since things were extra-dicey with her sister.

The teenagers in the courtyard were already drunk by the time she walked by them. Instead of beating a piñata, they were wrecking a television set. A few of them hooted at Amelia when they caught sight of her, but she quickened her pace and made it to the spot where a car awaited.

The rest of the night was what Elías had promised: good food, good drinks, dancing at a club that charged a ridiculous amount for a table. At midnight, streamers and balloons fell from the ceiling. Each New Year's Eve she spent at home, just like Pili had said, eating 12 grapes before the TV set in a mockery of festivity. Other than that, there were her sister's superstitious traditions: sweeping the floor at the stroke of midnight to empty the apartment of negative thoughts or tossing lentils outside their door. None of that now.

The clinking of glasses with real champagne, the whole thing—not just the alcohol—went to her head as she kissed Elías on the lips.

When she lay down on his bed, too tired to even bother with the zipper of her dress, she looked at the ceiling and stretched out her arm, pointing up.

"We had stars. Do you remember?" she asked him.

"What?" Elías muttered.

"In your old apartment."

She turned her head and saw recognition dawning on his face. He nodded, slipping off his jacket and lying down.

"I remember. You painted them," he said.

"It was to help hide the mold," she recalled.

"Yes. In the corner of the room. That place was too damp."

"You had leaks everywhere. We had to leave pots and pans and dishes all around." She rubbed a foot against his thigh, absentmindedly, more present in the past than in the now. Back in the grubby apartment, the water making music as it hit the dishes. Gold and silver stars. It had been a lark, one afternoon, and Elías had humored her, even helped paint a few of the stars himself.

"You printed all those photographs. Photos with an analogue camera, like any good hipster," she said, sitting up and trying to reach the zipper of her dress. It was stuck.

"It was the feel of it, of the negatives and the dark room, that I liked," he replied, a hand on her back, undoing the zipper for her in one fluid swoop.

Amelia pulled down the dress, frowning, her hands resting on the bed.

"What did you do with my pictures? Do you still have them somewhere?" she asked.

"Yes, in Monterrey. Why?"

"I don't know. It just seems like such an intimate thing to keep. Like a piece of somebody."

"Sympathetic magic," Elías whispered, running a finger along her spine.

She thought of the tossing of the lentils, the wearing of yellow or red underwear, washing one's hands with sugar, and the myriad of remedies at the Market of Sonora. All of it was rubbish, but he . . . he'd had some true magic. It hovered there, under his fingertips, something that wasn't love anymore, yet persisted.

A phone ringing. Amelia cracked her eyes open, trying to remember where she'd left her purse, but Elías answered.

"Hello? Oh, hey. Yeah, Happy New Year's to you, too. No, it's got no charge. No, it's. . . ."

Elías was standing up. Elías was going out of the bedroom. Amelia shoved away the covers and sat at the foot of the bed. When he returned, he had that apologetic look on his face she knew well.

"That was my father," he said.

"I figured. Keeping his eye on you, as usual," Amelia said, finding her underwear and stockings. Her dress was crumpled in a corner and it had a stain near the waist. Spilled champagne.

When they'd dated, Elías played at independence. Half-heartedly. Dad paid all the bills, after all, but he played in good faith. He told himself they were at the brink of freedom.

Now, he played at something entirely different.

"I have an early Epiphany present for you."

As Elías spoke, he opened the door to the closet and took out a box, laying it on the bed and opening it for Amelia to inspect the contents. It was a set of clothes. Slim, black trousers, a gray blouse. She ran a hand along the fabric.

"Did you give your fiancée a present, too?" Amelia asked. "Was it also clothing, or did you pick something else?"

"You don't like the clothes?"

"That's not what I asked," she said, raising her head and staring at him.

A rueful look on his face. He did not appear older most days, but that morning, he was his full 25 years, older still, not at all the boy she'd gone out with. He'd looked very much the Hero when she'd first spotted him and now he did not seem the Villain, but he could not save maidens from dragons or girls from space pirates.

He had settled into the man he would be. That was what she saw that morning. Whom had she settled into? Had she?

"My father picked her present. I had no say in it," he assured her.

"I guess you don't get a say in anything."

She fastened her bra and proceeded to put on the change of clothes he'd bought for her, leisurely. She had nowhere to go and nothing to do.

"Amelia," he said sharply, "you know I care about you. My father wants me back in Monterrey, but I want nothing of him."

"Except for his cash."

"What would you have me do? I was going to break off the engagement, but he doesn't listen to me, just goes on and on, and when I brought it up—"

She stood up and touched his lips before she kissed him very lightly. "I know," she replied.

"No, you don't," he said and he held her tight. And she should, she would move away in a minute. She was tidally locked. She was but a speck orbiting him and it didn't even matter now whether she could, would, would not, should not move aside.

10

The gang had once again laid claim to the subway's entrance. Amelia ended up sharing a car with a man and a life-sized mechanical mariachi. It was just the torso, skillfully painted, but he had a hat and held a guitar in his hands. She couldn't help but ask the man about it.

"It's for bars," the man said. "It has integrated speakers and can play hundreds of songs. It's better than any flesh-and-blood musician. I also have one that looks like Pedro Infante and another like Jorge Negrete. Say, I'll give you my card."

She tried to tell him it was fine, that she wasn't looking for a singing torso, but he pressed the card against her hand. She tossed it away before she walked into Lucía's house where the holidays had made no dent. No lights nor trees, not even a poinsettia plant to mark the season. Lucía herself wore a white turban and had scattered photos on the table.

"I'm picking pictures to go with my book," Lucía declared. "I'm sure people will like that sort of thing. But they're all jumbled, and I have boxes and boxes of them. This was from 1974. It was the dress I did *not* wear to the Arieles, since I didn't bother asking for an invitation and stayed home. You know who won the Ariel that year? Katy-Fucking-Jurado."

Amelia inspected the photo and smiled. Then she looked down at the table, grabbing a couple of other snapshots. One was a self-portrait, but the other showed young Lucía with Nahum. He was lighting her cigarette and she was smiling a perfect smile.

"Can I ask," Amelia said, "you and this guy . . . ?"

"Fucked?" Lucía said with a chuckle. "Who didn't fuck him, darling? Who didn't fuck me, for that matter? But he was married. I spun elaborate fantasies about how he was going to leave her, but those men never dump their wives. Not for little actresses who say 'I love you' a bit too honestly, anyway."

"But you would have worked with him again, on that Viking movie."

"That was after. Ages after! It seemed like that back then. Time just slowed to a standstill. Now, time goes so fast. I can't keep track of anything, anymore. So, yes, afterward I might have worked with him. Things were different."

"I don't know if things can ever be different between some people," Amelia said.

Lucía laughed her full laughter. She was old, and she was strong and steady. Amelia wished she could be that steady. She wished she didn't jitter and jump, unable to sit still for five minutes, her foot nervously thumping against the floor.

"You have troubles with someone?" Lucía asked.

"It's nothing. Probably the least of my worries."

"What's the biggest worry? Mars, my dear?"

"Mars, yes," Amelia said, blushing. She hated thinking that she was so easy to read, that Lucía knew her so well. But then, what else did she talk about? Nothing but Mars and she did not talk about Elías with anyone. Everything about the Red Planet, not a word about the man, all truths committed to her mind. If she'd kept a diary, perhaps it might have helped, but it would have been ridiculous tripe.

"Mars is fine, I suppose. We all must nurse our little madnesses. Look at me here, with all these pictures," Lucía said, pointing at the photographs. "But I was pretty, wasn't I? Look at this. Now, this was a face. Light it, frame it, let the world admire it."

So, Amelia looked. She looked at the ravaged hands touching the precious photos and she nodded.

She knew the lunch invitation was a trap but not exactly which kind. Fernanda did not extend lunch invitations. It was Amelia who phoned her, tiptoed around a social activity once a year, and then Fernanda agreed with a sigh. Fernanda ended up buying her a free lunch and Amelia ended up feeling like shit, and then she wondered why the fuck she bothered pretending Fernanda was still her friend, but the truth was Fernanda had also lent her money a couple of times. Amelia didn't like to think of people as walking ATMs, but that was what it had come to on more than one occasion.

Fernanda phoning Amelia was plain unnatural, but Amelia went along with it, went to the restaurant where they normally met.

Fernanda arrived before Amelia, which was another oddity. She didn't waste time pretending pleasantries. As soon as Amelia sat down, she leaned forward, with an eager look on her face.

"Amelia, are you really fucking Elías Bertoliat?"

Amelia opened the menu, sliding a finger down the many options. Fernanda took her time choosing her food and drink, after all.

"Amelia, didn't you hear me?" Fernanda asked.

"I heard you," Amelia said, trying to read the menu.

"Oh, my God, are you seriously going to sit there without answering me?" Fernanda said.

Amelia raised her eyes and stared at Fernanda. "Why are you asking me this? How do you—"

"Anastasia is super-pissed off at me! She thinks I got you two back in contact and I've done nothing of the sort! But since I secured you the invitation for that show of hers and she didn't hire you . . . okay, she has it in her head that you went and fucked the guy to spite her. And it's *my* fault for telling you about her art show in the first place."

"Elías is engaged to Anastasia?"

"You didn't know that?" Fernanda said.

For a moment she believed that Fernanda had set this whole thing in motion as part of a malicious plan. She had sent her to the gallery, she had mentioned that Amelia worked as a rent-a-friend to Elías. For what? For a lark? Coincidence? Did it matter? Maybe she thought it would be funny. *You can't imagine what she does now! No, really, look her up.* It had backfired.

Most likely Fernanda hadn't even thought about it, it had been a lack of care and tact.

"How did she find out?" Amelia replied.

"She paid someone to follow him."

"What, with that stalker app? That would be funny."

"What are you talking about?"

Amelia chuckled. She reached for a piece of bread piled in a basket and tore off a chunk.

"Why are you so happy? Do you realize what this means to me? Anastasia does business with my husband. If she's angry at me, *I'm* going to lose money."

Fernanda had reached across the table and slapped the butter knife Amelia had been attempting to wield. The clank of metal against the table made Amelia grimace.

"I'm not responsible for your husband's business," she said, and she hoped that he did bleed money, that if Fernanda had started this fucking storyline with her gossip and games, she paid for it.

"Well, if that's how you see it. But let me tell you something. He's going back to Monterrey this summer. His father is demanding it and Anastasia is pressing for it, too. So, whatever you've got going, it's not going to last."

"Nothing does," Amelia said. She grabbed the butter knife again and slowly, deliberately buttered her bread, much to the chagrin of the other woman. When she left the restaurant, she knew she would never be having lunch with Fernanda again.

She went back to the blood clinic. She was certain Elías wouldn't appreciate the fresh mark on her arm, but fuck him. She sat there and they siphoned out the blood, and she recalled how years before, he'd abandoned her, how he had not returned her calls. So she'd gone to his apartment, trying to figure out what was wrong with him. She pictured him run over by a car, dying of a fever. A million different, dramatic scenarios. Instead, she walked into an empty apartment. The only traces of him that remained were the stars on the bedroom's ceiling and the leaks slowly dripping across the floor.

It was that emptiness that she attempted to escape as the machinery whirred and the tourniquet tightened, the centrifuge spinning and separating plasma and blood.

It was that helplessness which she must combat.

She could not depend on him because Elías was not dependable. She knew that even before Fernanda had spilled poison in her ears, even before she walked down Reforma with her eyes downcast.

When he texted her and she showed up at his place, and when he noticed the mark, she told him to mind his own business, to mind Anastasia and his own fucking life because she had hers.

How he stared at her.

"You should tell me if you need help," he said.

"And you should have told me it was her," she replied.

He ran a hand down his face. Then he had the gall to try and reach out for her. Amelia slapped his hand away.

"What does it matter?" he asked, stubbornly trying to grab hold of her again. "What does it matter if it's Anastasia?"

"I don't like not knowing. I wish you would fucking tell me something."

"You don't tell me anything, either! Look at that!" he yelled, touching her arm, the mark there. "You just go off to sell fucking plasma, like a junkie."

"Everyone sells it, Elías! Everyone has to!"

She shoved him away and he reached out a third time to catch her.

"I'll tell you all if you want, fine, but there's not much to tell. I'm supposed to head back in the summer. And the rest . . . you must know it, already. I care about you and I care nothing about them," he said, brokenly.

It was not enough. It wasn't, but then, she lived on scraps and bits of nothing. She let him hold her, after all.

"Don't go to that stupid clinic, anymore," he said. "Ask for the money if you need it, all right?"

Because she was a coward, because it was always easier in the moment to lie, she nodded.

But she did not stop going to the blood clinic. She had amassed almost a complete new wardrobe, courtesy of Elías, which she kept at his place, but she did not ask for money. It baffled him, even irritated him. Instead, she continued to meet the occasional client on Friendrr, or helped Pili with an odd gig since Pili was a purveyor of constant and strange gigs. And the blood, there was the blood when she needed the cash.

Her life had not changed, not really. She still spent a great deal of time in coffee shops—connected to their Wi-Fi, drawing nonsense—but she also ventured to see

Elías. He had many of her same habits. He did not work. He did not seem to do anything at all, although once in a while, he'd take photographs with a custom-made Polaroid camera. This wasn't but a faint echo of his previous passion and inevitably, he shrugged and tossed the camera back into a drawer.

One evening, Amelia opened the drawer and emptied it on the floor of his neat, sparse office, holding up the pictures and looking at them. He walked in, looked at her.

"I wish you would," he said. She didn't understand the last word he muttered before he sat down next to her and pulled Amelia into his arms.

There were moments like that when it was easy to forget that he wasn't hers and she wasn't his. There were moments when the phone didn't ring, and it wasn't his father or that fiancée on the line, and there were moments when she pretended this was New Panyu because she had never seen it, so it could be. It could be that the homes of the wealthy there looked like this: manicured and perfect.

Then came May and the rain was early, soaking her to the bone one afternoon, so that her clothes were a soggy mess as she hurried up the stairs of her apartment and the phone rang.

"Hello," she said. It was Miguel.

"Hey, Amelia. You don't need to go to Lucía's home today. She's passed away." As usual, he spoke in a sunny tone. So sunny that Amelia stopped and held on to the banister, pressing the phone harder against her ear and asking him to repeat what he had told her. She couldn't believe he had said what he'd said. But he repeated the same thing, adding that there was a lawyer who wanted to speak to her. The old lady had left something for her.

"'A poster,' the lawyer said," Miguel told her. "You should phone him."

It was indeed a poster in a cardboard tube. Sealed with Scotch Tape. Amelia placed it on the empty chair next to her. Lucía had died in her sleep, an easy death, so she did not understand when the lawyer asked her to sit down. There was more.

"The house, her furniture, her savings, they go to her niece," the lawyer told her.

She had expected nothing else. The niece had only been mentioned in passing a couple of times, but there had been a certain importance attached to her name.

"Aside from the poster, she did leave an amount of money for you."

"What?" Amelia asked.

"She also left money for her staff. She was a generous lady. It's not much different from that, the amount. There's some paperwork that needs to be filled out."

When she arrived home, Amelia peeled open the tube and unrolled the poster on the floor. It was the Mars poster: Lucía with the cartridge belts, looking over her shoulder.

In a corner, a few shaky words had been scrawled with a black felt pen: *Do what you want, Amelia.*

Hellas, she thought. *Mars is home to a plain that covers nearly twenty-three hundred kilometers. Hellas appears featureless. . . .*

And then Amelia could think of no more facts, no more names and numbers to go together. She wept.

It rained again and again. Three days of rain and on the third, she asked for a car to drive her over to New Polanco. In the derelict buildings nearby, people were collecting water in pots and cans and buckets. She watched them from the window of the car. Then the surroundings changed, Elías's tall apartment building came into focus, and it was impossible that both views could be had in the same city.

As soon as she walked into his apartment, she looked for the sign advertising Mars, but it wasn't on. The power might be down on that street. Elías's building probably had a generator.

She stood before the window, watching the rain instead.

He wasn't home. She had not bothered to text him, but she did not mind the wait. The silence. Then the door opened and he finally walked in, shaking an umbrella.

"Hey," he said, frowning. "Didn't know you'd stop by."

Amelia held up the key he'd given her and placed it on the table, carefully, like a player revealing an ace. "I came to bring it back and say goodbye. I'm headed to New Panyu."

Elías took off his jacket and tossed it on the couch, smiling, incredulous. "You don't have the money for that."

"I've got the money," she affirmed.

"How?"

"Doesn't matter how."

"You're serious. This isn't some joke."

"I wouldn't joke about it."

"Fuck me," he said sitting down on the couch, resting his elbows against his knees and shaking his head. He still seemed incredulous, but now he was also starting to look pissed off. "Just like that."

"I told you I'd go one day."

"Yeah, well, I didn't think . . . Shit, Amelia, Mars is a dump. It's a fucking dump. Piss recycled into drinkable water and sandstorms blotting your windows. You think you're going to be better off there? You seriously think that?"

He sounded like her sister. Marta had said the exact same thing, with more bad words and yelling, although toward the end of the conversation, she concluded it was for the best and she might be able to rent the room where Amelia now slept. Pili had joked about Martians dancing the cha-cha-cha and bought Amelia a beer. Her eyes held not even the slightest trace of tears, but Amelia could tell she was sad.

"You're going to be back in less than six months," he warned her. "You're just going to burn through your money."

"I didn't ask for your opinion."

"You're selfish. You're just damned selfish. And you . . . you'll miss Earth, the comfort of having an atmosphere."

Perhaps he was right that she would miss it all, later. The city, her apartment, her sister, Pili, the café where she spent most of her waking hours, and him, too. Twenty seconds after boarding the shuttle to Mars, she might indeed miss it, but she was not going to stay around because maybe she might get homesick.

"It doesn't matter to you?" he asked. "That you are going to eat bars made of algae seven days a week? That . . . that I won't be around?"

She laughed brokenly and he stood up, stood in front of her, all fervent eyes. She liked it when he looked at her like that, covetous, like he wanted her all, like he might devour her whole and she'd cease to exist, be edited out of existence like they edited scenes in the movies.

"Cut the shit. Come with me to Monterrey. I'll rent a place for you there. I'll pay your expenses," he said.

"No," she said.

"Mars or bust, then."

"Yes."

She scratched her arm, scratched the spot where they drew blood and an indentation was starting to form, and looked at that spot instead of him. She couldn't see it with her jacket on, but she could feel the scar tissue there, beneath her fingertips.

"I told you. I always told you. New Panyu—"

"Years ago," he said. "When we were 19. Fuck, you don't keep the promises you make when you're a kid."

"No, *you* don't."

Her throat, she felt it clogged with bitterness. The words were hoarse and she put both her hands down at her sides, giving him a furious glance.

"Fine, fine, fine," he said, his hand slamming against the living room table, equally furious. "Fine! Leave me!"

Amelia crossed her arms and began walking to the door, but he moved to her side, reached for her, a hand brushing her hair.

"No, it's not fine, Amelia," he whispered.

She opened her mouth, ready to halt him before he committed himself to something, but he spoke too fast.

"I did . . . I do love you." Gentle words. Sincere. All the worse for that.

The hand was still in her hair and she was looking down at her shoes, frowning, arms tight against her chest. She had not come to converse or negotiate. She had come to say goodbye, even if he had not given her that courtesy once upon a time. Now, for the first time, she understood why he had taken off so suddenly, wordless. She knew why he'd made their first film a silent movie, a goodbye with no dialogue. It was a wretched mess to part from each other. He had cannily figured that out. He had probably imagined the tears of a girl, the pleas, and cut it all off brutally to do himself, and her, a favor.

Or he did not figure out anything. He merely fled and she was giving too much thought to his actions.

A mess, a mess. She could not even remember the names of Mars' moons as she stood with her arms crossed, her breath hot in her mouth.

"You could buy a ticket, too," she suggested, even though she knew he never, ever would. If he'd wanted it, it would have already happened, years before. But he had not.

Elías sighed. "It will be the same there. Nothing will change. I know you hope it will, but Mars won't fix anything," he told her.

"Maybe not. But I have to go," she said. "I just have to."

He didn't understand. He looked at her, still disbelieving, still startled, still thinking she somehow didn't mean it. He still tried to kiss her, mouth straining against hers, and she squeezed his hand for a second before heading out without another word.

Mars, Final Scene, Alternate

INT. CELL—NIGHT

SPACE EXPLORER awaits THE HERO in her cell. The stars have gone dim. The building where she is held is quiet, all the guards asleep, and she waits. She waits, but nobody comes. From her cell, she sees a rectangle of sky, tinted vermilion, and faded paper-cut moons, which dangle from bits of string (there is no budget to this production, none at all).

THE HERO is coming, he is nearing, sure footsteps and the swell of music. But the swell of music hasn't begun yet and the foley artist is on a break, so there's no crescendo, no strings or drums or piano, or whatever should punctuate this moment.

There is the cell and there is the vermilion sky, but the script says she is to wait. The SPACE EXPLORER waits.

But she presses her hands against the walls, which are not plaster. They are cardboard like the moons. They are not even cardboard, but paper. And the paper parts and rips so that the rectangle of vermilion becomes a vermilion expanse, and she is standing there in front of the ever-shifting sands of Mars.

She holds her breath, wary, thinking she's mucked it up. She turns to look at the other walls around her, the door to her jail cell, the hallway beyond the door. Then she turns her head again and there are the moons, the sands, the sky, the winds of Mars.

She wears no spacesuit, which means that it is impossible to make it out of the cell. But we are not on Mars. We are on *Mars*. The moons are paper and the stars are tinfoil. So, it is possible to step forward, which is what she does, tentative.

One foot in front of another, the white dress they've outfitted her in clinging to her legs and her hair askew as the wind blows. A storm rises somewhere in the distance.

She sees the storm, at the edge of the horizon, dust devils tracing serpentine paths, and she walks there.

She does not look back.

There are only two plots. You know them well: A person goes on a journey and a stranger comes into town.

FADE TO BLACK

Triceratops

IAN MCHUGH

Ian McHugh's first success as a fiction writer was winning the short story contest at the national science fiction convention in his native Australia in 2004. Since then he has sold stories to magazines, webzines, and anthologies in Australia and internationally, and he recently achieved a career goal of having his number of published stories overtake his number of birthdays. His first collection, Angel Dust, was shortlisted for the Aurealis Award for Best Collection in 2015.

Here he takes us to a near future in which hybrids of Neanderthals and Homo sapiens have been created, forming an entirely new race that doesn't fit comfortably into either world—and that may be developing a way of life that their creators couldn't have anticipated and which may have unforeseen implications for the future.

NISHITOKYO, TOKYO METROPOLIS, JAPAN

It's warm in Tokyo, with the stuffy humidity of late summer. In the garden on the other side of the window, there are shade trees and running water to keep the space cool. The Neanderthal sitting on the grass a few feet away wears only grubby y-fronts and a brown t-shirt that proclaims "This is my angry face."

His name is Jiro. From time to time he looks up from the project in his hands, peering out from under his thatch of startling yellow hair. He's whittling something with a box cutter from a piece of balsa wood. Shavings litter his hairy blond thighs like giant dandruff. His industriousness is intermittent, a picture of a man with no deadline, no ultimate purpose to his activity.

I'll shortly be travelling to the Athabasca-Slave Conservation Park in Canada, where modern science has resurrected the Pleistocene. There are Thalers there. I've never met one because there's only a couple of dozen countries outside of Europe and North Asia where they're legal. Australia, where I live and mostly work, isn't on the list. I was curious to see the real thing first, to compare.

Jiro is short, with stocky limbs and a barrel chest and obviously thick bones. There's no way I'd get my hand around one of his wrists. His face isn't remotely "ape-like," as non-Sapiens humans are so often lazily characterised, but nor could it be mistaken for a Sapiens face, receding sharply as it does from the brow ridge and prominent mouth that frame his beaky, overlong nose.

Whenever Jiro looks up at the window, his eyes meet mine. I had expected to feel some spark of excitement, some thrill of the moment at locking stares with a different human species. His utter indifference kills the moment cold. His gaze travels over me, then over my companion—a woman he has known for much of his adult life—and back to his project with no hint of recognition of one person by another. No different to a bored lion in a zoo, glancing at the upright monkeys on the other side of the fence.

Doctor Choi Seo-yun, a prim Korean with threads of silver in her tightly bound black hair, shows me a slight compression of her lips that carries the weight of fourteen years of exasperation—the length of time she's been at the Nishitokyo Centre for Hominin Genomics. "They were communicative until puberty," she says. "For the girls that was age eleven and Jiro and Haruki a year later. All of them became hyper-aggressive against any outsider entering their garden."

Jiro and his two female companions, Kaede and Izumi, are now thirty-five. For more than twenty years they have steadfastly refused to interact with the world outside their garden. In Oslo, Buenos Aires and Shanghai, where Neanderthals were also raised, the same thing happened. In Shanghai, the Neanderthals were a breeding pair—not sterilised, as elsewhere—but the male killed their solitary child shortly after birth. There was a second male here, Haruki, but Jiro killed him at age fifteen in a fight over the females.

"They have invented their own language," Doctor Choi tells me. "They have borrowed the Japanese grammar that they learned as children, but using only a very limited range of concepts. Not that they talk a lot, even to each other, and not at all to us, even when we address them in their language."

Their teenage aggression has subsided somewhat as they've grown older. The Neanderthals now submit to haircuts and basic health checks. I witness one such examination of strawberry-blonde Izumi later in the day. She stands, quivering, with the same affronted stoicism that a dog will adopt against the prodding of a vet. They have to be sedated for dental check-ups.

I ask Doctor Choi why she thinks they stopped talking. She gives another of her minimalist grimaces. "It is like a switch was flipped in their brains. They have better results with the Floriensis in Singapore, and those are not much smarter than chimps.

"These?" she gestures towards Izumi, who is baring her teeth at the nurse checking her blood pressure. "They are a dead end."

NORTH OF LAKE ATHABASCA, ALBERTA, CANADA

"There."

The truck is an elderly manual-driver. Kip takes both hands off the wheel to point at the same time as she starts grinding down through the truck's gears. The muscles of her right arm, the thickest I've ever seen on a woman, flex as she works the column shift.

Kip is one of the Thalers working and residing in the park. She only superficially resembles the Neanderthals I saw in Tokyo, although she clearly has a lot more of their genetic material than the few per cent that most non-African Sapiens possess. She's bigger, heftier than a Neanderthal, fair skinned but dark haired, the proportions of her face exotic without being so completely foreign. An idealised version of what we wished our nearest cousins could have been.

Then I look out the window, following the direction of her pointing finger, and I can't keep my excitement bottled inside. "Mammoths!"

"Hybrids," she corrects me.

I don't know enough yet to tell the difference. The two animals wrestling a short distance from the road are noticeably larger than the Asian elephants I've seen in zoos, and covered in that distinctive shaggy pelt that sets steppe mammoths apart from most Proboscidea. They have the high shoulders and sloping backs of Asian elephants but more of the lankiness associated with their African cousins. The wool of one of the wrestling animals is noticeably orange, rather than the classical mammoth brown.

"Elephant genes," says Kip, when I comment on it.

"What are the other differences?"

"Bigger ears, usually." I hadn't noticed because the ears looked normal against my childhood memories.

"The mammoths don't have much to do with the hybrids," Kip adds. When I ask why not, the corner of her mouth quirks as if at a private joke. "Nothing to talk about," she says, then adds, "Mammoths don't get musth, either." Musth in bull elephants raises testosterone levels by around fifty times and makes them a danger to anything nearby. "These guys do," Kip continues, "so the mammoths don't trust them and chase them away."

We see more animals on the way to the camp, proxy species like modern musk oxen and grey wolves and—once, at a distance—a woolly rhino.

"They weren't sure about having the rhinos here, originally," Kip tells me. "In Africa they've had problems reintroducing rhinos and elephants together because the young bull elephants kill the rhinos."

"Not here?"

She shakes her head. "Asian elephant genes don't seem to carry the same homicidal urges," she says, drily. "Mammoth genes certainly don't. There's a bit of rhino tipping among the mammoths, but no killing."

"'Rhino tipping?'"

"Two sisters started it. They taught it to their kids and it's spread through the population from there. They find a rhino and annoy it until it gets angry enough to charge them, then they wait until the last instant, step aside, grab the rhino with their trunk on the way past and flip it onto its back."

I'm sure she's pulling my leg, but, "Woolly rhinos are slow and mammoths are light on their feet," she says. "We recorded it once. I'll show you."

It's hard to believe they have video like that and it hasn't gone global. When I say so, Kip gives a shrug that emphasises the heaviness of her shoulders. "We mostly stay off the web."

The camp is a compact square of prefabricated bungalows, housing laboratories, dormitories, mess and administration facilities. A tiny patch of human geometry jutting up from the spare wilderness all around. The admin block, I learn later, doubles as an armoury. The compound is protected by a ten-foot reinforced fence, watchtowers at its corners. Similar fences close the gaps between the lakes and rivers along the park's boundaries. Around the camp buildings, the fence looks like the ones that surround refugee camps at home. I asked if they've had any problems with poachers.

"Just once," Kip says. She falls silent. Her lips twitch as though there are more words but she's not letting them out. "There isn't the black market for ivory anymore, with the quality of vat-grown stuff now, and all the Pleistocene stuff being dug out of the permafrost—what used to be permafrost."

I learn later that the poachers were kids from one of the local reservations, trying their hands. They shot at the drone sent to track them and RCAF fired back. The Rangers—some of them men and women from the same community as the poachers—arrived to clean up the pieces.

"The fence is mostly for rhinos and grolars," Kip says. "The rhinos would just wander in because they're not paying attention. The bears come looking for food."

Grizzly–polar bear hybrids, with their jumbled instincts and physiologies, tend to maladaptation in the prototypical habitats of their parent species, I learn while I'm at the camp. In mixed terrain, like that of the park, they dominate.

The population of the camp is both mixed and segregated. The residents are a roughly equal mix of Sapiens and Thaler. There's also a fluctuating number of non-resident indigenous workers from Fort Chipewyan and the Chipewyan and Cree reservations near the park. The groups muck in together when the work demands it, such as unloading Kip's supply truck.

I get my first look at the Thaler men in that swarming operation. Most of them are no taller than Kip, who stands as high as my shoulder, but some of them are so heavyset they look almost cubical. Most of the Thalers have blond or red hair. I'm introduced to several, men and women—Doro, Pek, Yellen, Jussy, I'm certain I won't keep them straight in my head—and experience several minutes of terror, watching their thick hands engulf mine, one after another, while the muscles of their forearms knot like rope as they take their grips. My knuckles survive with only mild crushing.

After the truck is unloaded, the groups part. The Thalers have coffee and lunch with the Cree and Chipewyan workers, or go back to joint tasks with them. They have a shared manner, animated speech followed by reflective pauses before someone else in the group speaks up. The non-indigenous Sapiens keep themselves largely separate, friendly with the others but lacking a common language, a division of scientists and academics versus tradespeople and labourers.

Kip says, "Come on, I'll introduce you to Gnarly."

The reason there's a nucleus community of Thalers out here is Professor Joana Almeida Borges—or Gnarly as she's known here—the first Thaler to complete a university doctorate. For good measure, she did two: in biochemistry and then palaeontology.

Gnarly is the senior researcher here and the project's driving force. She used to teach at Universidade de Lisboa, in Portugal—where she was born and raised—and later at the University of Toronto. She's tiny and squat, the top of her head not much higher than Kip's chin, and her build and features have much more of the pure Neanderthal about them than Kip's and most of the other Thalers'. Her hair is buttercup-yellow, like Jiro's. Gnarly is from the first generation, a couple of decades older than Jiro and his companions. When she fixes me with a stare that would sit well on an irritable hawk, I can imagine what a terror she was in the classroom. Her students must have adored her.

"We—Thalers—are illegal in one hundred and fifteen countries around the world," she tells me, over coffee. "If I cross the border into the United States, I am illegal. Not allowed. If I fly to Australia, it is the same. What will happen to me?"

Lots of people are illegal in Australia, I tell her.

"One hundred and fifteen countries," she says, again. "Why is this? Is it because we are made? Against God? In Saudi Arabia, there is a fatwah that says so. In Portugal—*my* country, where we are legal—a politician said that we have no souls, because we are made. Kip is not 'made.' Her father is like me, her mother was Sapiens.

"Many children, in the same United States where we are illegal, are 'made,' as we are. They are designed and made before they are put into their mothers' wombs. The politicians in the United States, the muftis in Saudi Arabia, do not say that their beautiful made children have no souls. Why us?" She pauses, as if I might have an answer for her. Then, "Is it because we are not Sapiens enough? Not the right kind of human? Perhaps."

She swirls the dregs of her drink. "Perhaps it is just because we are only a few, and it is easier to say you are afraid of a few than of many."

She stands, which doesn't make her much taller. "Tomorrow, you will see mammoths. Here, we have woolly mammoths. They have Colombian mammoths in the United States, which they made."

After dinner, beers are handed around. I take mine up a watchtower with Kip and Jonathan, one of the scientists. Jonathan is Cree, but from Ontario, one of Professor Almeida Borges's post-doctoral students from Toronto.

The park sits within the aspen parkland that predominates around the western end of the lake: grassland dotted with colony groves of trees, where the prairie and the boreal forest go to war. With the changing climate, the prairie is winning, pushing northward. The leaves of some of the aspen groves are beginning to turn yellow with the arrival of autumn. They flare brightly in the light of the slow northern sunset.

Kip points out a cluster of brown shapes in the distance.

"Mammoths," she says.

I can barely make them out as individuals.

"Sharper eyes," Jonathan tells me.

The stars are out early, away from city lights, bright and unfamiliar to my eyes. The sky seems oddly empty, too, with the great sweep of the Milky Way low on the southern horizon rather than directly overhead. Jonathan points out constellations.

After full dark, I notice firelight in the distance, the bright spark of a campfire. "Someone's out there."

The corner of Kip's mouth comes up in that knowing smirk. "Yeah," she says. "Every night."

The fire looks to be near where we saw the mammoths, earlier. "You know who?" Jonathan nods. "We do."

The mammoths do come to the camp the next day.

"They always come the day after the truck's back," says Kip. "In case we have any treats for them."

On this occasion, the treats are several cases of old fruit from the markets in Fort McMurray, where she collected me. The mammoths approach in three groups of ten to fifteen individuals, coming in from different directions. I watch, alongside Kip, Jonathan and Professor Almeida Borges and several other camp residents, from the gantry built partway up one side of the perimeter fence, with feeding troughs on the other side.

The mammoth groups hail each other as they near, raising their trunks and trumpeting. Some break from their groups, twining trunks and bumping shoulders when they come together.

"Brothers and sisters," says Jonathan. "The males spend more time with the herds where they have calves than elephants do. No musth, so the females don't chase them away. Some of the boys are going to have to go to other parks, though."

The mammoths transport me, fill me with a child's wonder and I wonder aloud what it would be like to ride one. Gnarly snorts and I'm certain I've made a faux pas. But Kip says, "When I was a kid, I always wanted to ride on a triceratops. I didn't understand how science could make mammoths and Neanderthals again but not dinosaurs." She flashes her teeth. "These guys are fine, but I'd still like to ride a triceratops one day."

It's an astounding experience to be close to such large animals, let alone so many at once. The shoulders of the tallest are level with the top of the fence, their eyes level with mine standing on the gantry. Miniature elephant ears flick back and forth, absurd-looking if the animal themselves weren't so regal. The great snow plow tusks of the adults keep them back a way from the trough and fence.

Some of the adults, I notice with an exclamation of surprise, have canvas grocery bags hooked over their tusks. Everyone near me has a chuckle at my reaction.

"They like the bags to put their things in," says Jonathan.

Kip takes pity on me. "We give them soccer balls for the calves. A few other odds and ends."

The adults' trunks are just long enough to reach through the bars of the fence and take fruit directly from our hands. The prehensile tips are soft and slightly wet.

The younger mammoths take their fruit from the troughs, peering up at us over the metal rims if they're tall enough, or questing about blindly with their trunks if not. Occasionally an adult or older juvenile will help the babies find what they're looking for, or else hand them down a piece. Some of the adults stash a few fruits in their grocery bags.

They're quiet, remarkably so for such massive creatures, aside from the occasional bleat for help from the very youngest. There's no frenzy about their feeding. They're orderly, patient—*polite*, even, taking their turns and then yielding their positions to the next in line.

I watch as Professor Almeida Borges holds up a hand between the bars of the fence. The mammoth in front of her reaches up with its trunk and clasps her fingers. Kip and Jonathan both do the same. Others are touching, making contact, as they give out fruit.

"Now you," says Kip.

I hold out my hand to the mammoth that has just taken an apple from me. It hesitates, trunk still in its mouth, watching me. Then it uncoils its trunk again, reaches back and the lips close, just briefly, wetly, around my fingers. One liquid, brown-black eye looks into mine, so knowing that I have the uncanny sense that I'm holding hands with another person. The mammoth exhales as it releases me, its breath hot on my palm.

A fourth group of animals has appeared, half a dozen adults and a couple of juveniles. They stop a distance back from the camp, obviously uncertain. The mammoths ignore them.

"Hybrids," I guess.

Kip nods. "They won't come over until the mammoths are done. We'll save them a crate."

"There is a park in Manchuria where they have only hybrids," says Gnarly. "It will be a significant undertaking, but we are hoping to send them there. They will be happier."

"Why did they make us?" she asks me, later, pinning me with her best professorial glare. "Why did they *continue* to make us after they brought back the real thing? What is this urge, this opposite urge, to the fear that makes us illegal in so much of the world?"

She lets the questions hang long enough for me to be certain that I have no good response, then answers them herself. "It is not because we are strong, not because we are useful." She grunts. "Outside of Russia, anyway. Why did they keep making us? One can build stronger workers on a factory production line. Exoskeletons are cheap." There are a couple in the camp, mostly disused now, dating back to before Gnarly's Thaler recruitment drive. She gestures vaguely towards the corner of the compound where they stand, covered by tarpaulins. "Attach armour and there is a tougher, stronger soldier. Wires and drugs will make super soldiers faster and cheaper than meddling with genetics. No."

I mumble something about the quest for knowledge. The hawk stare fixes on me again and I have an acute insight into how a rabbit might feel, having indiscreetly poked its head out of its hole.

"Knowledge? Then why so many of us? What can science learn from so many that it cannot learn from a few? What can science learn from us at all, really? We are not Neanderthals, we cannot teach science very much *about* Neanderthals." She raises a stout finger.

"Humankind is lonely," she says. "You cannot bear the thought that there is no-one else out there to talk to. There might have been, right under your noses, but you exterminated most of those without even realising, including all your nearest relatives. The few that are left are too foreign. Even as you fear the possibility, you want—

desperately want—for there to be someone else, someone different but enough like you. That is why the Neanderthals were such a crushing disappointment. They were the closest thing to you that ever existed, and they do not want to know you."

Her choice of "you" rather than "we" is both striking and discomforting. I comment on it.

"Ah!" she says. "But we are not just Sapiens with a robust chassis, are we? No. And neither are we Neanderthal. We are something else. Our quest is to find out what."

I ask if that's why she has brought so many of her fellows to join her in the park.

"Yes," she says, simply.

When I ask the other Thalers why they're out here, they all give similar enough answers to suggest that it's a matter that's been much discussed.

"Looking for who I am, I guess," from Kip, with that heavy-shouldered shrug of hers.

"Don't belong anywhere else, do we?" from Doro.

"Where else would I be?" from Pek, after a thoughtful chew on his cigar.

Yellen has the answer that, perhaps, sums up all of them. "Look at us. We're made from nothing, out of nowhere. I went to Gibraltar, once, to see the caves where Neanderthals used to be. I went to the one where there's those carvings that they say were by Neanderthals. I got a tattoo." He rolls up his sleeve to show me the cross-hatch design on his bicep. "But what does it mean, really? The last people like us, Sapiens and Neanderthal in one, they were forty thousand years ago. A person needs to fit, and we got nowhere to fit."

Overhearing this, Daniel, one of the Chipewyan men, leans across to add, "My people have told stories here since time immemorial. Even your archaeologists say our stories go back ten thousand years in this country."

Yellen nods. "Maybe here is a place where we can find a way for us to fit together, find a reason to be a people. Make our own stories."

"And are you? Finding something?"

He gives me a crooked grin, that curl of his lip that shows off the gap in his teeth, and sweeps his arm around, a gesture that encompasses the horizon. "Of course. Who wouldn't find something out here?"

Northern Canada is like that, with its heavy, intrusive quiet and the even greater weight of emptiness, of human absence, all around. It's a place where you feel like the world is talking directly to you, with none of the usual clutter in between, and you can almost—*almost*—hear what the world is saying.

I share beers up on the watchtower again with Jonathan. He tells me that he was raised among his mother's Cree people, but his father is Métis.

"They started out as the children of English and French fur trappers and First Nations women," he says. "No one wanted them. But there were so many, they made their own culture. Some of it's from indigenous traditions, some of it's European, some of it they invented themselves."

A campfire springs to life, light invented in the dark. Someone's out there.

A couple of days later, I catch Yellen and Kip carving at knuckles of sheep bone. They hunch over their projects, intent, holding them close to their faces. Kip's expression is set in a scowl of concentration, brow furrowed, eyes narrow. Yellen gurns while he etches the fine details.

They're shy when I ask to see, but Yellen holds up his. It's a mammoth, stylised but not quite like any style I know.

Kip is more diffident. Eventually, Yellen's cajoling gets her to open her hand. She's carving a fat little woman figure, clearly inspired by the Paleolithic Venus figurines that have been found across northern Europe.

I tell her it looks like Gnarly. Yellen thinks that's hilarious.

"What does she mean?" I ask Kip.

She gives her heavy shrug, looks me in the eye.

"Something."

mines

ELEANOR ARNASON

Eleanor Arnason published her first novel, The Sword Smith, *in 1978, and followed it with* Daughter of the Bear King *and* To the Resurrection Station. *In 1991, she published her best-known novel, one of the strongest novels of the '90s, the critically acclaimed* A Woman of the Iron People, *a complex and substantial novel that won the prestigious James Tiptree Jr. Memorial Award. Her short fiction has appeared in* Asimov's Science Fiction, The Magazine of Fantasy & Science Fiction, Amazing, Orbit, Xanadu, *and elsewhere. Her other books are* Ring of Swords *and* Tomb of the Fathers *and a chapbook,* Mammoths of the Great Plains, *which includes the eponymous novella plus an interview with her and a long essay. Her most recent book is a collection,* Big Mama Stories. *Her story "Stellar Harvest" was a Hugo Finalist in 2000. Her most recent books are two new collections,* Hidden Folk: Icelandic Fantasies *and the major science fiction retrospective collection* Hwarhath Stories: Transgressive Tales by Aliens. *She lives in St. Paul, Minnesota.*

Here settlers on a colony planet must learn how to deal with the deadly aftermath of war, still killing people long after the battles have ended.

We ruined Earth. Not completely. Some places are still okay: archologies in the far north and south and the off-planet colonies: a handful in space and one on the Moon. They're for the very rich, the very well educated; and the lucky few who maintained the machinery. The rest of us lived with rising oceans, spreading deserts, and societies that are breaking down or already broken.

I was born in a refugee camp in Ohio. It still rained there, though most of the rest of the Midwest was dry. We lived in a tent and got one meal a day. There was some health care, thanks to Doctors and Dentists Without Boundaries. I didn't die of appendicitis, because of the Doctors. The Dentists pulled some teeth and taught me to brush and floss.

When I was ten the recruiters came around, and I joined the EurUsa space force. That got me to another camp, where I lived in a barracks and ate three meals a day, meat and dairy as well as grain. There was regular medical and dental care. I thought I had died and gone to heaven, though I wasn't allowed to go home.

"You're soldiers now," our house parent—a grim retired sergeant—told us. "Nothing matters except the army and your unit."

There was one other thing that happened. The girls got hormone implants, so they would never have menstrual cycles. Periods are not easy in a war zone. Pregnancy is worse. The boys got vasectomies, no reason given. I figured there were plenty of people on Earth already, though a lot less than there had been at the start of the 21st century; and people who've been in combat can make bad parents.

The camp had a school. I learned all the education basics, plus military discipline and how to operate war machinery, starting with the AK-47. "The best low-tech field rifle ever built," our house parent said. "They're still in use in Africa. You know the old saying: you can't have a revolution without an AK-47."

When I was fifteen I had the second operation, which implanted a comm unit in my brain. Now I could speak to robots and my unit members directly. At twenty I was shipped out to the war.

A funny thing. Just as everything was going to hell at home, scientists at MIT—at the new campus in western Mass, since the old campus is underwater—discovered that FTL was possible. Expensive, but it could be done. The two large governments that remained—EurUsa and RuChin—built a couple of ships each, and sent them out to visit planets that looked habitable at a distance. You can see a lot with space telescopes. The ships found a couple of planets that were borderline habitable—microbial life, but nothing more, and air that had oxygen, but not enough. They could be settled maybe, but the settlements would always be on the edge of failing. Not what anyone wanted.

Then they found a beauty. There was vegetation and animal life and air we could breathe. Nothing was intelligent, so we didn't have to worry about the Prime Directive or trouble from the natives. Taken all in all, it was an almost perfect planet.

The trouble was the ships from the European-American Alliance and the Asian Co-operative Union arrived at the same time, and both put down settlements on the planet. For a while everything was quiet, while lawyers argued over who owned what at the World Court. The settlements grew into colonies. The World Court could not come to a decision. And then the war began.

This was a Fifth Generation war. For the most part it consisted of hacking and drone attacks. A full-bore hot war would endanger the huge, fragile FTL ships when they were in-system, not to mention the huge, fragile home planet back in the Solar System, and the space colonies, which were even more fragile than Earth. Both sides held back. But there were soldiers on the ground, though their actions were limited.

(Remember warfare in the early 21st century: the huge, vulnerable aircraft carriers that were mostly not attacked, the atomic weapons that were mostly not used. Fifth generation warfare grew out of those contests. The theory was to wear the enemy—especially the enemy's civilian population—down, without triggering a world war.)

That brings the story to me, arriving on a planet with purple-green vegetation and slightly heavy G. The home star was dimmer than ours, and the planet was closer in. There were flares, but they were predictable. Most of the time we could get to shelter. We were getting a little more radiation than on Earth, but not enough to worry about.

I don't like war stories, so I won't tell you mine. In the end, I was invalided out. I could have gone home, but why bother? I'd lost touch with my family, and I had no desire to live in a refugee camp, even if it was top of the line. It was easier and more comfortable to stay in Leesville, named after General Izak Lee (ret): a town of pre-fab buildings next to a purple-green forest. The trees in the forest had trunks that went straight up. Leaves grew directly from the trunks, big and frilly. Some trees had leaves going all the way up, and others had bare trunks and a big cluster of leaves on top like a palm tree, except they looked nothing like palm trees. (I know. We had palms in Ohio.) The leaves were iridescent, so they changed color when the wind moved them: purple to green, green to purple. No branches. None at all. It was something the life here had never tried, the way it never tried backbones.

The ground was covered with bright yellow, moss-like plants. These were para-sites, like fungus. Filaments ran down to the tree roots and fed off them. More fila-ments ran to other trees. The forest used these to communicate with itself. Don't think it was saying anything interesting. The xenobotanists said the filaments were mostly reporting moisture or lack of moisture, sudden attacks by bugs and slower attacks by vegetable parasites. It was nothing to write home about. The vegetation wasn't intelligent, any more than the bugs were.

I got interested in the local life after I was invalided out and had time to read something besides military manuals.

Why? Why not? It was there, and it was the only complex ecological system we had found besides Earth. So, I talked to the scientists in Leesville and read their reports. In another life, I might have become a xenobiologist. In the meantime—here and now—I defended maize.

There were fields around the town, planted with Earth crops. The hope was we'd finally be able to live on what we grew, instead of rations shipped from Earth. The local plant and animal life was inedible and not easy to convert to something we could eat.

The enemy sent in drones that dropped to the ground in the forest, crawled into the fields and dug down, becoming land mines. When people stepped on the mines or machines rolled over them, they blew. This made farming difficult, and we really wanted to be able to farm.

It turned out the best way to find land mines was using African Giant Pouched Rats. They are rodents, but not rats and only giant compared to rats. They have an amazing sense of smell. Do a search on them, if you don't believe me. They can find mines faster than robots can; and they're so light, they don't set mines off. Taken all in all, they're cheaper than robots. They don't cost any more to ship than a robot does. Once we had them here, they reproduced themselves, provided you had two of them and some rat chow. Though at the time I'm talking about they were new and not yet common. One of the army's interesting innovations.

They're cuter than robots and more affectionate, though the last doesn't matter to the army.

Were we worried about them going feral? No. They couldn't eat the local vegeta-tion, and thanks to their caps, we could always find them. We hadn't lost one yet.

I ended up with Whiskers. She had been modified to be smarter and live longer than natural African Giant Pouched Rats; and she had a metal cap on her head and wires in her brain, that allowed her to talk with me.

My mind comm had been turned off when I left the army. Can you imagine the silence? My buddies were gone. The robots we had worked with had vanished. It was like being alone in a huge, pitch-black cave—except for Whiskers, who was a flashlight in the darkness. Her warm body lay next to me at night. Her friendship kept me sane.

This day we were checking fields west of the town. Whiskers ran between the rows of maize, their bright green leaves startling against the purple and dark-green forest. I watched from the field's edge. Overhead the planet's primary shone, always dimmer than Sol. High, thin clouds moved across the sky. A mild wind moved the forest's frilly leaves.

No. No, Whiskers said. *No.* Then, *Yes.* I checked her position and marked it. Whiskers moved on. *No. No.*

I called her in finally. She ran back, up my arm and onto my shoulder, nibbling my ear gently. I could feel her happiness.

Why do you love me, Kid? I asked.

Genetically modified, she replied. *Designed to be smart and love you.*

Only that? I asked.

Enough.

Her warm body huddled against my head. I walked home through the town's muddy streets, between the prefab buildings. It was sunset now, the streetlights coming on, the air smelling of the alien forest. Like Whiskers, I was happy.

My apartment was a one-storey walkup: a living room, a kitchen, a bedroom and a bathroom, all small. Okay by me. I'd never owned much, and I wasn't about to start. Whiskers jumped off and ran to her food bowl, full of rat chow. I heated rations and ate them, while Whiskers finished her chow.

I forgot to say that this was the day I met Marin.

After the dishes were washed, I called a cab and went out to the porch to wait, Whiskers on my shoulder. It was raining now, not the downpours we'd had in Ohio, but a gentle and steady rain, the kind of precipitation that could last all day, soak deep into the dry soil, and wash nothing away.

The cab had a driver, which meant the auto wasn't working. I climbed in back.

"The usual?" the driver asked. Even the human subs knew my pattern.

I said, "Yes," and settled back.

The cab bumped over ruts and potholes. "You'd think the army would fix these," the driver said.

"Not a priority."

"Find any mines?"

"One."

"Those bastards keep sneaking in. My partner lost a leg to one."

"Lucky to be alive."

"Tell her that. She's not a soldier, so they didn't replace it."

"Was it one I missed?"

"Nah. Before you came. They were using robots. Effing incompetent. The mine was right in the middle of the forest road, and my partner drove over it. You'd think they could find that."

The cab stopped. I held my wrist to the chip reader, heard it ping, and then climbed out. The driver looked through her open window, obviously hoping. I gave her a handful of change.

"Thanks, buddy. Have a good drunk."

Yeah.

I went into the bar, Whiskers riding on my shoulder. The minute the bartender saw me they pulled a stalk of celery out of a jar. Don't think that was shipped from Earth. It had grown in the town's greenhouses. Maybe we'd be stuck with greenhouses, but we keep hoping for open fields. The local soil provided most of the nutrients our crops needed, and the local pests did not bother anything from Earth.

(There was a story about a field of zucchini that got out of control and spread. The local town ended up with more zucchini than they could eat, and the fruits left in the field grew more and more enormous, untouched by anything native. Finally, they grew dry and board-like. The local people made canoes out of them. This is a tall tale.)

Whiskers hopped onto the bar and took the stalk. I ordered a beer. Goddess, it felt good going down.

"Les," the barkeep said to me, then nodded toward the end of the bar. A woman sat there in badly fitting civvies. There was something wrong about her posture. An injury maybe. Or she could be more augmented than I was, with body mods as well as a mind comm. Plenty of soldiers were.

"New?" I asked quietly.

"On leave. Drinking a lot."

I had two jobs. One was finding bombs in the fields. The other was finding human bombs, people likely to go off. That may sound like a strange combination. But remember that the colony was small. A lot of people did two jobs. And remember I had Whiskers. She could smell a lot more than just mines. Her species had been used in Africa to find TB and HIV. If you don't believe me, do a search.

I moved down the bar, Whiskers following, pitty-pat, the celery in her mouth.

"What the hell is that?" the woman asked.

"Whiskers," I said. "My companion animal. She an African Giant Pouched Rat."

The woman was okay looking: a dark, warm skin and crisp, short hair. That mouth might have been kissable a few years ago. Now it was compressed. Her eyes, almond-shaped and slanted, were heavy lidded. She looked tired and maybe a little drunk. I couldn't tell what kind of body was under the civvies.

Whiskers was up on her haunches, nibbling the celery.

"New here?" I asked.

"What the eff do you care?"

"This is a small town. We pay attention to newcomers."

"Your rat has a metal cap. What does that mean?"

"We can communicate. I need that. I miss communicating with my unit."

"Yeah," the woman said bitterly. "They use you up and throw you out, and you have nothing except silence."

"There are other jobs," I said. "I have one." I told her about the mines, but not about the crazy soldiers.

Whiskers finished the celery and helped herself to a Goldfish cracker out of a jar on the bar. I wasn't sure they were good for her, but she loved them. They came from Earth. You want to talk about crazy? Shipping crackers from Earth. But people liked them, and we couldn't make them here. The economics of war are strange.

I took a handful and consumed them, along with my beer. "R and R?" I asked.

"Medical leave." After a moment or two she said she was staying at the medical hostel in town, having work done by the hospital.

We sat in silence for a while.

One way to get people talking is to talk about yourself.

"I got invalided out." I took another handful of Goldfish. "PTSD. I didn't want to go home." Whiskers' nose was twitching, a sign that the woman smelled sick. What kind of sick I couldn't tell. "Home was a refugee camp in Ohio."

"Home was the Dust Belt," the woman replied. "Moline, by the Mississippi. There was enough water to survive."

"I'm Les," I added.

"Marin."

We shook. Her hand was enclosed in wire mesh, making her grip cold and very firm. Some kind of exoskeleton, which hadn't been removed. Most likely that meant she was expected back in the war.

We sat together and talked about being kids in the old USA. Her parents had been members of a farming co-op, using water piped out of the Mississippi. Her older brother bought a share in the co-op, but there wasn't enough money for her, so she joined the army. She'd been older than me when she joined, which made it rougher. But she'd tested better than I had on robot interface.

"Is that what the mesh is?"

Yes and no. She had operated one of the huge robots, the ones that seemed out of mech-kaiju plays. I'd seen them in the distance, stomping on enemy installations and kicking enemy units out of the way. Some were operated from inside and others at a distance. She had worked inside, striding ahead of our forces. When she moved a foot, the robot took a step. When she moved a hand, one of its huge hands and arms moved. Scary as all hell, though I wasn't sure how effective. Military R&D is a mystery. I mentioned this.

"A lot of war is psychological," she replied.

I asked why she was still wearing the exoskeleton.

"This isn't to run a robot. It's to run me, though the connections I already had helped when it was installed."

Whiskers pattered down the bar, got another stick of celery and brought it back. She could follow some of the conversation via me. But a lot of human interactions are a mystery to a rat, even a smart rat.

"Why?" I asked. It was always possible she would go tell me to go away and stop bothering her. But you would be surprised how many people want to talk.

A drone had crashed into her bot, she said. Friendly fire. Not the drone's fault. It had been hit by the enemy and flying out of control. The bot was destroyed, and she had multiple injuries, including a severed spine.

"They can fix that," I said, which was true.

She'd had stem cells injected. The cells were supposed to connect across the gap her injury had made. It usually worked, but it took time. Meanwhile the mesh enabled her to move almost like an ordinary person.

We talked some more about Earth and this planet. I could tell Whiskers was uncomfortable, and I knew this was the woman. Finally I said, "I need to go. Nice to meet you."

We shook again, her hand hard and cold. Whiskers collected more Goldfish and pushed them into her check pouches, making them bulge way out. Marin laughed. It did look silly.

"That's dessert," I said.

The rat hopped onto my shoulder. *Sick,*" she told me mind-to-mind.

Yeah.

I called another cab, this one automatic, and rode home over the rutted streets. The rain had picked up. The rain bugs were out, forced from their burrows by the water and climbing the building walls. Their shells were iridescent in the streetlights. Funny how much of this planet seemed to shine and gleam.

Once we were home I pulled a beer out of the fridge and asked, *What kind of sick?*

Whiskers pulled the Goldfish out of her cheek pouches and put them in her food bowl. *A snack for later. Not an infection,* she said. *I can smell those. Something wrong in her body or mind.*

Out-of-whack neurotransmitters and hormones. Those would give off a smell.

I finished the beer, then went to bed.

A lot of the war was feints and skirmishes, as I said before. The plan for both sides was the same: wear the enemy down slowly, risking as little as possible: a typical Fifth Generation War, carefully limited and held at a distance. No one wanted it to spread back to the Solar System. No one wanted to blow up the handful of FTL ships that came into the system, bringing new supplies and soldiers and scientists.

Now and then, the war on New Earth got hot. I dreamed I was in one of the hot spots, wading through a marsh. No moon, of course. The planet had nothing except a few captured asteroids, visible as moving points of light. Low clouds hid these and the stars. No problem for me. I had my night vision on. I could see the robots ahead of me, tall and spidery, picking their way through the reeds. Drones flew overhead, tilting back and forth to avoid branches. My unit was on either side. I noticed that Singh was alive, which he hadn't been the last time I'd seen him. Lopez, too. I'd seen her sprayed across the landscape. A nice guy, not looking good at the end.

Something was pulling my rifle barrel down. I looked and saw Whiskers clinging to the barrel with all four feet. A voice said, *Dream. Not good. Wake.*

I was going to argue, but one of the robots stepped on a land mine, and everything blew up.

That woke me. Whiskers was on my chest, her nose poking at my face. *Bad dream.*

Yeah. I was covered with sweat. I got up and took a shower. It was close enough to morning so I made coffee, another import from Earth. Funny the things the army thought were worth shipping. Of course, we might not fight without coffee. But why the damn Goldfish?

Good, Whiskers said.

Well, yes.

The day went as usual. Whiskers found four mines in a harmless-looking bean field. In the evening I went back to the bar, Whiskers on my shoulder. Marin was there. I got a beer and sat down next to her. Whiskers sat on the bar top and chewed on a stalk of celery.

I can't repeat what we said. Mostly I've forgotten the conversation, except for a feeling of discomfort from Whiskers. I was going to have to file a report on the woman. She needed more help than she was getting, and her modifications meant she was valuable to the army.

I do remember one bit of conversation. She'd been somewhere in the robot, wading across a wide, brown river. Deep in places, but not too deep for her robot. In the middle, where the main current ran, disks floated on the surface, going downstream with the current. They were a meter or more across with raised edges, bronze brown with streaks and spots of green. I knew these plants, though I had never seen them. The green was chlorophyll, and the disks photosynthesized. But tendrils hung down below them. These captured aquatic bugs and ate them. So the disks were carnivorous plants or photosynthetic animals. Take your pick.

The river reminded Marin of the Mississippi. I didn't remember any carnivorous floating disks in *Huck Finn*.

I liked the woman. She was young and good-looking and less crazy than a lot of people I had met. She had a sense of humor, though I don't remember any of her jokes. While she drank, she wasn't getting seriously drunk. The only problem was the sense of unease coming from Whiskers.

I was lonely. Most of the people in the town were civilians: scientists and farmers, the people who ran the 3-D printing plant, the people who did maintenance and repair. They were good folk who had gotten good educations back home on Earth. They had a good abstract understanding of war. They knew about PTSD. They sympathized. But I was still an outsider, though they were grateful for my work and for Whiskers.

I liked talking to Marin, so I stalled on sending a report. Maybe I should trust the docs treating her. They would intervene if her condition looked serious. Was it my business that war made people strange?

I was in the habit of going to that particular bar. For one thing, they let Whiskers in. And Marin kept coming. I learned more about her family and the farming co-op. Turned out she could not stand her brother, the one who bought into the co-op, and she was angry that her parents had favored him. Why should he get the safe life on Earth? Why did she have to come here?

What bothered me about her was her anger. What I liked was her youth, her warm skin, almond eyes and lips that would have been lovely if they hadn't been so often pressed together.

Of course, we ended at my apartment in my narrow, one-person bed, though it took a number of weeks, during which the barkeep kept looking at me funny. I ignored them.

I had never made love to someone covered with mesh before. Weird. The area between her legs was open and available, which made sense. She needed to pee and defecate. The rest was covered with mesh, except her head. The mesh kept changing when I touched it, sometimes soft like silk, then suddenly rigid. Imagine sex with a person whose surface is never the same. Though it stayed rigid along her back, support for her damaged spine. Even her breasts were mesh-covered, the nipples often squashed. I made do with what I could reach.

She came. I came. We lay together, her mesh—soft and cool, at the moment—against my bare skin. I could sense Whiskers, huddled in a corner and deeply upset.

Bad. Bad. Crazy.

Shut up, I told the rat.

Bad, Whiskers repeated.

It became regular: meeting at the bar, coming back to my place and making love while Whiskers sulked. Marin never stayed the night. Instead she went home to her apartment by the hospital. She didn't like the rat, she told me.

The war must have heated up, because I was finding more mines. Correction, Whiskers was finding them, light footing over the soil between the rows of human plants in the fields outside Leestown, stopping and sniffing and saying, *Yes.*

Marin began coming out to the fields with me, standing with me at a field's edge or walking along the edge. She recognized the maize, a plant that needed a lot of water, but was—she said—in many ways the best of all the grains. Native Americans in Mexico had made it a god, way back when. A young god, she told me. A beautiful young man. Of course, they sacrificed people to their gods. We only a sacrificed to our god of war.

I made a polite sound, since I had no opinion about the gods of ancient Mexico. Though I did check online and found images of the Mexican maize god. Lovely, and the ancient Mexicans did sacrifice to him.

It takes some sort of jerk to make love with someone who should be reported to armed forces medical. I was pretty sure Marin's problem was mental. Anger and depression would be my diagnosis. Whiskers agreed. She knew the smell.

What was I going to do? Turn her in to armed forces mental health, who probably already knew we had a relationship? The barkeep's sweetie worked in the hospital. Once anything gets in a hospital it spreads. I wasn't a medical worker formally, but I ought to hold to their code of ethics. No sex with clients. If I turned Marin in, I would be having a conversation with my supervisor.

I could hope that Marin was called back to active duty. Or keep having sex with her, and pretend I didn't know she was sick. Or cut her off, though that might cause its own problems.

One day she told me the stem cells weren't working. Her spine wasn't healing.

"Is that a deal?" I asked. "You have the mesh."

"That will go if I leave the armed forces. "Do you want to?"

"Yeah."

"Can they fix the problem?"

"Maybe. The stem cells have formed a tumor. That has to go. Then they might try again."

I had nothing to say.

A few days later I was at a field. Whiskers was there, of course. So was Marin. We stood at the field's edge, a short distance between us, watching Whiskers run.

All at once Marin was in the field, walking toward the center. I was slow off the mark and couldn't reach her before she was too far in. No way I was going to risk the mines. I called Whiskers and she turned, running through the maize toward Marin. God knows what she—or I—thought she could do, being a fraction of Marin's weight.

Marin stepped on a mine, and it blew. The rat had almost reached her. The explosion put Whiskers into the air, tumbling over the maize. I couldn't see where she landed, but I could see Marin, down on the alien soil. I walked into the field, following Marin footsteps, knowing the path made me safe.

She was lying on her back. Most of her clothing was gone, blown away. The mesh was still there, netting her dark body with silver. I figured it had protected her, but I didn't know how much. Not entirely. One foot was gone, most likely the one she'd used to step on the mine. Blood poured from the stump. I took off my belt, knelt and used the belt to make a tourniquet, then wrapped my jacket around the stump. Then I called emergency service and gave my location. "I need search and rescue right now."

Blood came out of Marin's mouth. I tried to find a pulse, but couldn't through the mesh. There might be internal injuries. She didn't look alive. I couldn't think of anything else to do, and I was worried about Whiskers. I hesitated, then stood and moved through the maize toward the place the rat must have landed, hoping I didn't step on a mine.

Whiskers was there, lying on the dark soil—uninjured as far as I could tell, but unconscious. Maybe it was a mistake to pick her up, but I did and retraced my path, her small body hugged against me. I stopped at the field's edge, one finger pressed into Whiskers' throat. I thought I could feel a pulse, faint and uneven.

Jesus God, I didn't want to lose her. I was shaking so badly that I couldn't stand any longer. I folded down onto my knees. *Be okay*, I told Whiskers. *Be okay*.

S&R arrived.

I climbed onto shaky legs, still holding Whiskers in my arms. "There's a human in the field. If you follow the footsteps you can get to her safely. But right now I want you to take me to the hospital."

"Are you injured?"

I thought of saying no, then decided it would be smarter to say yes. The S&R van took me and Whiskers. A second van raced past us toward the field, as we turned onto the main street. That would take care of Marin.

I climbed out at Receiving and said, "I'm okay. But the rat needs attention."

"For God's sake," Receiving (who was human) said, "This is a hospital. We don't treat animals."

I forgot to mention I usually carried a handgun, a comforting weight against my thigh. I thought of pulling it, then decided no.

"There is no vet in town," I said. "You need to treat this rat. She's genetically modified. The armed forces will want to keep her alive."

Receiving frowned and hesitated, then found a doc. I stayed with him, while he examined Whiskers. "You understand I am not an expert on animals."

"This is a mammal from Earth, a close relative, part of our evolutionary line. Do what you can."

He ran Whiskers through a scan. "No broken bones. The organs look okay. I'm not seeing any internal bleeding."

Around that time I heard Whiskers in my mind. A thread of a voice. *What?*

You took a hit from a mine, Buddy. This is the hospital.

Whiskers sniffed, taking in the hospital smell, the doctor, my fear, then asked, *How is Marin?*

I looked at the doc. "How is my human companion?"

He paused, listening to his comm. "I'm sorry. The trauma was too severe. She died."

"I figured as much," I said.

The doc looked at me funny. Was I supposed to show more grief? Marin hadn't been a friend, only a lover. I touched Whiskers' side gently. *You did the best you could, Buddy. You couldn't have saved her.*

Didn't like her.

I know, Bud.

That was that.

There was a vet two towns over. I took Whiskers, hitching a ride, and she was checked a second time. The vet said there might be some problems due to concussion. That caused most of the trouble with human soldiers. Time would tell.

I thank him, paid and got a receipt. The armed forces ought to pay.

Then I went home, had a few beers, went to bed and had nightmares. I was with my unit, and Marin was there as well, walking beside me, then stepping on her mine. This time she wasn't wearing the silver mesh, and she blew apart, making as big a mess as Lopez had. Jesus, I was covered with blood.

I woke, shaking and sweaty. Whiskers said, *Bad dream.*

Yeah. After that I couldn't sleep.

I touched base with my supervisor the next day. Marin had seemed fine to me, I told him. Whiskers hadn't reported any problems. Maybe I made a mistake in getting involved with her, but she really did seem okay. My supervisor told me to be more careful in the future. I said I would.

Should I have felt more for Marin? Maybe. But I didn't. I could say that the war effed me up, and I no longer had normal reactions. But I knew what was right. I shouldn't have gotten in bed with someone who was obviously vulnerable, especially since Whiskers had disapproved.

I didn't say any of this to my supervisor. Instead Whiskers and I went back to finding mines.

The war heated up. I found more mines. Robot tanks lumbered through Leesville. Once I saw a kaiju-mech robot pushing its way through the forest, knocking down trees. A heck of a sight, even at a distance. Marin had been right. War involved psychology, and the kaiju-mech bots were scary, even when they were ours.

After it was gone, I went out into the forest, following the forest road—it was safe—and found the robot's footprints, deep depressions in the yellow moss, already full of water. The moss must be bleeding into the depressions. I could look into the nearest pond, which was full of swimming bugs. How had they gotten there so quickly? Life went on, and I really wished I could be a xenobiologist.

Hacking became more frequent. Our local systems went down, then back up, then down again. The FTL ships came less often, though none of us knew exactly what that meant. According to the ship's crews, everything was fine back home, even though the ships no longer brought new people, only supplies. Why? Because people could tell us what was happening on Earth? Rumors said the war had spread back home, or else the governments had decided FTL was too expensive and the planet not worth fighting over.

Finally the FTL ships stopped coming. No explanation. They simply weren't appearing in orbit. This was true for both sides. No Goldfish. No coffee. No tea. No chocolate. Nothing except what we could grow or print on this planet. The local printing plant made crackers, but they weren't as good as Goldfish.

Whiskers complained.

Can't help you, Bud.

Of course we sent messages back to Earth, asking what the hell was going on. If all went well, we'd get an answer in 80 years. Or the ships would come back. Who could say?

The war slowed after that. The hacking mostly stopped, but the drones kept coming in. Once they were activated, they would keep doing their job, with no way of calling them back. I guess you could say they—and we—were like the local organisms. Most were segmented, and a lot were a meter long. A little creepy, like huge centipedes. They could give you a nasty bite.

If you found one and chopped off the head, it would keep moving. Its sensory organs were all the in head, so it could no longer see, hear, taste. It blundered around on its many legs, until another bug found it and ate it. Nothing ate us here. We and the drones kept blundering, going through the motions.

Whiskers said I smelled funny.

Anxiety? Depression? I asked. These were the usual problem.

Not sick. Funny.

One morning I woke up with cramps. I got and discovered my sleeping shorts were drenched with blood. So were the bed sheets. Of course I called the clinic. I don't like blood. It reminds me of my dreams: Marin lying in the maize field, Lopez and Singh. The clinic sent a van, with a tech who wouldn't let me take Whiskers. I left her crouched in a corner of the living room, looking terrified.

It's okay, Buddy.

Afraid. So are you.

Which was true.

A nurse at the clinic examined me. A big guy with a skin as black as midnight. He must have rotated in from another town. I didn't recognize him or his accent. Caribbean maybe. There were islands in the Caribbean that were still above water.

After he was done with the examination, he said, "What we have here is menstrual discharge."

"What?" I said. My voice sounded loud.

"Your hormone implant has failed. You are having a period."

"I am thirty-effing-two."

"Late for a first period, but that's what you are having."

"Then put in another implant. I really don't like this."

"Unfortunately, I can't. The hormone implants come—or came—from Earth. We can't make them here. We have a limited number left, but they are restricted for soldiers on active duty. You are not."

"What am I supposed to do?" I asked.

"What women have always done," he said. "Insert a tampon—I can print some out for you—and take ibuprofen."

My crotch felt as if something bigger than Whiskers was trying to chew its way out. There was blood caked on my legs. I wanted to shout at the nurse, but I didn't. What could he do? If he didn't have the implants, then he didn't. I was not going to demand something that was needed by soldiers on active duty.

He printed out the tampons with instructions and gave me a bottle of ibuprofen. I went to a bathroom, read the instructions an inserted a tampon—God this was a crude way to solve a common problem—then took two ibuprofen and went home in a cab.

Whiskers was still crouched in her corner. I picked her up and cuddled her. *Nothing serious, Bud. I'm okay.*

Pain.

It will go away.

Wrong, Whiskers said.

Not a sickness, I replied. *A hormone change. I think that's what you smelled. I'm going o have to do a wash.*

Yes, said Whiskers.

I stripped the bed and put the sheets in a bag, ready for a trip to the community laundry, then took a shower and changed into new clothes. The chewing in my crotch had moderated some.

Sometime in all this I realized that we were really on our own. The FTL ships might never come.

The community radio was on, playing Wagner, "The Flying Dutchman" overture. I lay down, feeling miserable. Whiskers climbed onto the bed and huddled at my side.

Of course the cramps ended, and I went back to checking fields for mines.

We can't ruin this planet. There are too few of us, even with our technology. If the ships don't come back, our technology will begin to break down, and our war will wind down to nothing. The question is, will it happen while we still have a chance of survival here? It would be easier to stay alive if we joined forces. People are beginning to talk about peace.

I'm still having periods. The clinic says it ought to be possible to make the hormone implants here, but the project is on a back burner. Other things are more important in an economy of scarcity and war.

I have not gotten used to having cramps. I want this war to end.

Do I still dream of Marin? Yes.

There used to Be olive trees

Rich Larson

Here's another story by Rich Larson, whose "An Evening with Severyn Grimes" appears elsewhere in this anthology. This one takes place in a desolate far future where dwindling enclaves of humanity struggle to survive in a world dominated by "gods" who mostly sail by overhead, ignoring the problems of those below, although occasionally they will grant a "miracle" of one sort or another if petitioned in the proper manner—something that it's supposed to be the protagonist's job to do, but which he realizes, to his dismay, that he can't handle at all.

Valentin crept through the darkness toward the high stone wall of the Town, heart thumping hard against his ribs. His nanoshadow, wrapped around his chest under his shirt, sensed his anxiety and gave a comforting pulse, gritty and warm against his skin. It helped a little. Valentin had never gone over the wall before. He had never left the Town before.

But anything was better than what awaited him in the morning: the *prueba*. His fourth *prueba*, to be precise. Valentin ran a finger over caked scar tissue until it contacted the gleaming black implant poking from the crest of his shaved head. It was the implant that let him control his nanoshadow—for anyone else, it would have been an inert black puddle. It was the implant that let him communicate with some of the simpler machines inside the Town.

The implant didn't make him a true prophet, though. Not until he passed the *prueba*, until the Town's machine god spoke to him. No prophet had ever failed the test more than twice. Valentin was on three and counting.

So he was leaving. Valentin breathed deep, staring up the weathered stone face of the wall that had kept him safe for all his sixteen years. He knew the world outside was a dangerous one. There were wilders and mudslides and scuttling scorpions. Valentin hated scorpions and he had a healthy fear of wilders from growing up with scarestories.

But so long as he had his nanoshadow, he could do things no barbarian could even dream of. He reached out with his implant and summoned the gleaming black motes, coaxing the shadow down his arms, gloving his hands. He steadied his nerves, looked around once more for anyone who might stop him, then took a flying leap at the wall.

Valentin was normally clumsy, but with the nanoshadow strengthening his arms like corded black muscle and coating his hands with clinging tendrils, he went up the sheer wall easily as a gecko. He felt a grin splitting his face as he topped it. Poised there on the edge with his nanoshadow balancing him, Valentin could see the empty campo stretching far and away. Rolling hills of dead gray soil, dotted ruins, crumbling road. It looked like freedom.

With only the slightest guilt thinking of Javier, who would wake up in the morning to find his apprentice gone, Valentin slid down the other side of the wall and started to walk. It wasn't long before he heard a familiar rumble of gods on the move. Valentin kept low but still felt a swirl of static inside his skull, the customary sting of his implant, as the pod of biomechanical gods thundered through the dark sky overhead.

He could sense them, but their thoughts were walled off from him, inscrutable as those of the god who controlled the Town, and a moment later their ghostly yellow lights disappeared into the distance.

Leaving him in the dark again.

"Wake up, little Townie."

Still half in a dream, Valentin thought it was Javier's voice, waking him for the *prueba*. Then he remembered scaling the wall, walking and walking, finding a crevice to sleep in cocooned by his nanoshadow.

His nanoshadow that he could no longer feel against his skin. Valentin wrenched his eyes open, jolted by adrenaline, and found himself face to face with what could only be a monster with beetle-black eyes and an impossibly wide mouth.

Valentin jerked backward, probing desperately for his shadow, and the bag clutched in the monster's pale hand writhed.

"None of that," the monster said sourly, shaking the rucksack where Valentin's nanoshadow was trapped. "None of your Townie tricks. Alright?"

It wasn't a monster. It was a boy, maybe his age, maybe a bit younger. His mouth was the normal size, but a raw-looking scar gashed upward from one corner of it, splitting his cheek. He had shaggy black hair and coarse skin and wore a black coat that was different fabrics all patched together, nothing like the identical gray garments made by the Town's autofab.

The boy turned his head, and Valentin realized the other half of his face was beautiful, fine-cut with long black lashes. He had never thought wilders might be beautiful. It didn't do much to help the cold panic numbing his limbs.

"A live shadow," the wilder said, shaking his head. His accent was thick and nasal and dropped the endings off familiar words. "Thought they were only in tales. Are you a prophet, then?"

Valentin tried to clear his head. The wilder had found him while he was sleeping and peeled his shadow off him. Normally he'd still be able to control it, make it leap out of the bag, but he'd used it all through the night to keep warm and now, still without sunshine, it didn't have enough strength to escape.

"I'm a prophet," Valentin said. "Yeah. I am. So if you don't give me my nano-shadow now, I'll have the gods blast you to ashes and a little heap of bone."

Alarm flashed over the wilder's split face for a split second, then he tipped back his head and gave a warbling laugh. "Once you do something for me, Prophet," he said, thumbing an eyelash off his cheek, "you can ask the gods to punish me however you like." He hefted the rucksack onto his shoulders and strapped it tight.

Valentin's heart pounded. Maybe he could run for it, but the cold, hard look of the wilder's eyes and the long knife in his belt made him think otherwise. And no way was he returning to the Town as not only the first prophet to fail three *pruebas* in a row, but the first to lose his nanoshadow to a wilder.

"What do you want?" he asked, trying to sound brave, bored, maybe a little mysterious. The tremor in his voice gave him dead away.

"I'm Pepe," the wilder said. "Who're you?"

"What do you want?" Valentin repeated, and this time with no quaver.

The wilder shrugged. "To do what prophets do, Prophet," he said. "Get a stubborn fucking god to care about us for a change. You help me, I won't cut your toes off." He patted his rucksack. "And maybe I'll even let you have your shadow back," he added.

The campo didn't look like freedom anymore. Pepe set the pace and set it fast, leaving Valentin to stumble along behind him, watching for the telltale skitter of scorpions in the cracked mud. His skin ached for his nanoshadow. A few times he probed hard for it and managed to elicit a sluggish twitch from inside Pepe's rucksack, which in turn made Pepe shoot him a suspicious look from under his eyelids. But without sunshine or Valentin's bioelectricity, the inert nanoshadow was nothing but a lump of gritty black gelatin.

They walked and walked and only paused to eat—a slab of cold *tortilla* comfortingly similar to what they had in the Town—before they walked again. Valentin spent the time trying to think of a way to escape. The wilder had them heading west, toward his tribe's derelict autofab, farther and farther away from the Town. Pepe thought Valentin was going to interface with whatever god was controlling it and set it working again. As if it was that simple.

And when Pepe found out that Valentin couldn't do it, he figured the wilder would use his sawtoothed knife to cut out his implant as a keepsake, then let him bleed out in the dust. He shivered, half from the thought and half from the Andalusian winter, as they walked in silence across another barren field. The soil underfoot was pallid gray.

Another god, this one alone, hummed through the sky overhead, moving like the whales Valentin had seen clips of, the ones that used to inhabit the oceans. Pepe stopped where he was, pulled down his scarf, and craned his neck to watch its passage. The yellow lights bathing his face made the scar glisten wetly.

"Can you talk to them, then?" Pepe asked.

"When they want to talk," Valentin lied, feeling Pepe's dark eyes go to the crest of his head, where he had scar tissue of his own. Valentin pulled up his hood and glowered. He didn't like people staring at the implant.

"Should tell them to give us a lift," Pepe said, with his macabre grin, and started to walk again. They passed the husk of an old harvester stripped for parts. "There used to be olive trees here," he said. "Far as the unaugmented eye could see, my grandfather says his grandfather said. The harvesters rolled up and down the campo all day long. Back when more things grew. Back when machines listened to anybody, not just prophets."

Valentin probed the harvester as they passed by, wishing he could swing its clawed arm and knock Pepe to the ground, grind him into the dirt, but the farm equipment was long-dead. He didn't feel so much as a flicker from his implant.

Before long the moon was rising overhead, fat and yellow, and the air was turning cold enough to bite. Valentin missed the slick warmth of his nanoshadow again, pulling his scarf snug against the chill. He could see Pepe's exposed hands turning purple in the night air, and after a few more minutes his captor pointed to a crumbling stone derelict up ahead.

"We'll hunker down in there for night," he said, tongue flicking distractedly against his scar. "Start early in the morning, get to the autofab by noon. Make sure you have enough daylight to work."

Valentin gave the ruins a dubious once-over. The sagging stone and twists of old rebar looked like something out of a scarestory. As they approached, Pepe found a torch and thumped it to life with the heel of his hand. The lance of harsh white light strobed damp ground and what was left of the walls. Following Pepe inside, Valentin felt immensely far from the gated pueblo he'd called home only a day ago.

"Wait here, Prophet," Pepe said. "I'll make a sweep for lobos."

"Funny," Valentin muttered. The spidery machines that once hunted down the survivors of satbombed Seville and the other ruined cities had been recycled decades since. Humans knew better than to make war with the gods now, and the gods were otherwise occupied.

His captor bounced off into the dark, and Valentin considered running yet again. The same counterweight held him fast: Pepe had his nanoshadow, and even if Valentin could make it back to the Town without being overtaken—not likely—he couldn't return without his shadow. At that point, he was better off bleeding out in the dust.

A beetle scuttled past Valentin's toe; he stomped it dead and when he looked up he found himself face to face with empty eye sockets and a ghoulish grin. He flinched.

"Boo," Pepe said, waggling the dog skull on its jagged spinal column. He tossed it away. "Found us a nice corner. *Venga*."

Valentin helped Pepe clear away a few ancient syringes and typically inscrutable bits of plastic, things from the old days. There was space for the blankets and the portable *estufa* that Pepe said had enough solar charge to keep them warm for at least a couple hours. Valentin had to admit that Pepe was far better equipped to wander the campo than he was. But then, Valentin had been counting on his nanoshadow.

"Could keep the heat longer if we use my shadow," he said, watching Pepe strip down to sleep, uncovering the swathes of lean muscle Valentin had yet to develop—if he ever would. He spent his days sitting in the shade, learning his implant from

Javier instead of boxing or playing in brutal games of barefooted football. Suddenly he remembered how Pepe must have touched him to take his nanoshadow in the first place. Suddenly he couldn't help but imagine what the wilder's sinewy body might feel like wrapping around his.

"Right, right," Pepe said, sliding on his stomach under the blankets, clamping his arm over the rucksack with knife held loosely in hand. "So it can smother me in my sleep and then whisk you back home."

"Something like that."

Pepe shifted, showing the unscarred side of his face, blinking soot-black lashes. "What were you doing over the wall, anyway?" the wilder asked.

"What were you doing skulking around outside it?" Valentin parried.

The wilder looked at him full-on, exposing his scar. "Was looking for a way to set things right," he said. His black eyes bored hard into Valentin's, then he blinked, and what might have been a smirk tugged at the scarred side of his mouth. "Your ears are red."

"I'm getting fucking frostbite," Valentin said.

"Soft little Townie." Pepe squinted at him. "Did it hurt when they put the god-chip in you?"

Valentin's hand went reflexively to his implant. The truth was that he barely remembered his seventh birthday, the scraping caul and needle, the incense-smothered fire. But he wanted an answer Pepe would respect. "They give you something to chew," he said. "But yeah. It hurt." He paused. "It's only successful half the time, you know. There can be bad infection, or they can bore too deep. The two tries before me, one ended up dead, the other one damaged."

Pepe nodded, spinning his knife idly in one hand, not as impressed as Valentin had hoped.

"How about that?" Valentin dragged a finger along the curve of his mouth. "Did that hurt?" Pepe clenched the knife hard and Valentin froze, realizing with a sick drop in his stomach that he'd overstepped, that the wilder was about to stab him in a fit of anger.

Then Pepe's ruined smile returned and he pressed the gleaming flat of his blade against it. "He gave me something to chew."

Valentin turned away to hide his shudder. Everything about Pepe unbalanced him. Even as he'd calculated escapes all day, he also catalogued the looks held too long, the brief moments when the space between them seemed to simmer, trying to decide if it was his imagination or not. Deciding what Pepe would do if he knew. Prophets were meant to be different and the Town didn't care one way or another. But wilders were another breed entirely. Superstitious, hard. Dangerous.

As soon as Pepe was asleep or faking it well, Valentin tugged off as quietly as he could to an anonymous body, trying not to put deep, dark eyes on the face. He didn't think he would be able to sleep tonight.

In the morning, when Valentin crawled out of his blankets massaging night-numbed fingers, he could smell oil and electricity in the air. Pepe was pulling food out of the rucksack. He handed Valentin a piece of *tortilla* smaller than yesterday's.

"The gods were working in the night," he said, tapping his nostril.

"They do that."

"You ever ask them why?"

"It's colder at night," Valentin said, cobbling an answer from half-remembered lessons. "Machines think faster in the cold." It was flimsy, even to his own ears, but Pepe nodded solemnly and went back to chewing with the unscarred side of his mouth.

When they stepped outside, a thick winter fog prickled Valentin's eyes. Pepe took a moment to get his bearings then set off into it, not even bothering to check his captive was following. Valentin was, of course. The nanoshadow puddled in the bottom of Pepe's rucksack was effective as any tether.

The gradient sloped upward, and gradually the dead soil turned to slippery shale under their feet. Pepe picked his way among the rocks as nimble as a lizard while Valentin labored behind, trying to hide his heavy breathing. The rucksack always bobbed just ahead of him, mockingly, he thought. With his shadow, he could scale a slope like this as easily as he'd slithered up and over the outer wall of the Town.

"Who'll they send to look for you?" Pepe asked over his shoulder. "Will they have a shadow, too?"

Valentin thought of Javier setting out to find him, easing his creaking bones through the Town's gate. No. Javier was sitting in his quickfabbed *piso* at the edge of housing, sipping anise and staring at the blacked window, murmuring to the gods in the dark. As far as he was concerned, whether Valentin came back or not was up to them.

"Nobody," he admitted. "Nobody goes over the wall."

"Your family, though."

Valentin stiffened instinctively at the word, at the reminder of his mother, who caught the last kick of the bleeding virus when he was six, and of the fact no father ever claimed him.

"Don't have one," Valentin said. "That's why I'm a prophet."

"Ah. You came out an autofab full-formed." Pepe gave another solemn nod. "That's why your skin is all . . ." His hand looped in the air for the missing word.

"All what?" Valentin asked, trying not to sound too curious.

"Smooth." Pepe shrugged. "I was joking," he said. "You didn't come out an autofab."

"No," Valentin said. "I didn't."

By the time they reached the crest, the sun was rising red and smeary like someone had rubbed their thumb across it. Pepe offered a hand for the last lift, and Valentin was tempted but struggled up without it. Pepe didn't appear to notice the slight. He was peering down the other side with an unreadable expression. Valentin clambered up beside him, heart still thudding hard, and wiped the grime of the climb off on his knees. He took a deep breath and smelled overturned earth, and the machine fumes again, sooty and sharp.

"Look," Pepe said.

Valentin looked. Down below, the barren field was no longer empty. Thrusting out from the mist, glistening the biomechanical black of godwork, were rows and rows of man-high carved shapes.

"Heads." Pepe turned to Valentin with an almost pleading look. "A field of giant fucking heads. Why?"

"I don't know," Valentin said. "They might not, either. The gods don't think how we do."

"Straight through is still quickest to the autofab," Pepe said, more to himself, tongue flicking at his scar. "Come on, Prophet. Maybe they'll talk to you."

Valentin imagined the mouths opening wide to swallow him and shuddered. But then he saw the rucksack strap had loosened on Pepe's shoulder, saw how the wilder's eyes were glued to the sculptures. When Pepe started down the slope, Valentin followed.

The fog thickened again as they descended, and at the bottom they found the field had been smoothed and leveled, with uncanny precision, into a flat, gray plane veined by darker streaks of clay. It looked unreal, and Valentin was almost surprised Pepe's boots left prints. Pale vapor roiled back and forth in waves as they approached the heads.

They were taller than they'd looked from above, each at least twice Valentin's height, looming out of the fog. Their enormous faces were cut symmetrical but the features themselves were crude, disproportionate, and with the mist creeping up past their wide mouths they looked like drowning men. Valentin probed. He felt a faint drone of machinery at work, but no god was inside. He couldn't begin to guess the heads' purpose.

"Is there a god here?" Pepe asked.

Valentin turned and realized the wilder had rooted to the spot, his dark eyes roving from one head to the next. "No," he said. "They're just sculptures. You coming, or what?"

Pepe shook himself, then stalked past to lead the way. Silence swallowed up their footsteps as they walked the row. The heads were coated in a glistening, raw black material that sometimes looked as if it was moving—the same material that the autofab in the center of the Town used to make tools and cables and brick molds. As always, Valentin wondered if it was somehow alive.

The strap on Pepe's shoulder slid a bit.

"Tell me about your autofab," Valentin said. "If I'm going to get it running, I need to know details. How old it is. Last it was used. All that."

Pepe shot a shrewd look backward. "Old," he said. "And it stopped working back when my grandfather was young. A few years after our last prophet died. The gods drove him insane, so he pushed his forehead into a spinning drill to get them out."

"He wasn't calibrating enough," Valentin said, to hide the sudden lurch in his stomach. "He was careless."

Pepe shrugged. The strap slipped lower.

"And the implant?" Valentin asked. "The godchip? Nobody else had the surgery?"

"*Hombre.*" Pepe stopped walking and stared at him with something like revulsion. "It was buried with the rest of him. Our band, we respect the dead."

Valentin was equally perturbed. "You have any idea how valuable that implant was?" he demanded. "No autofab will make them anymore. Ever." He frowned. "I mean, if he'd already shattered his skull on a drill bit, how hard would it have been to—"

"I thought everyone in the Town had a godchip," Pepe cut across, starting to walk again. "In the stories you've all got a godchip."

"No. We only have two." Valentin wished he hadn't said it. He felt the crushing weight again, the knowledge that had driven him over the wall. Two godchips in all of the Town—one in Javier's graying head, and one in his own, and if he couldn't learn to interface they would be better off prying it out of his skull and trying again with someone else.

"Guess I'm lucky I found you, Prophet." Pepe flashed his warped grin. "The gods must have wanted—" He froze, head cocked. Valentin stopped, watching the sway of the rucksack. "D'you hear that?" Pepe asked.

Valentin pretended to listen, but he was coiling his legs, running his tongue around his dry mouth. As Pepe lifted the strap of the rucksack to readjust it, still peering into the mist, Valentin lunged. He ripped the bag free and hurtled past. Down the row, a dead sprint, clutching the rucksack to his chest and fumbling for the clasp as he gasped hot air. His pulse foamed in his ears. He could feel Pepe behind him, not bothering to curse or shout, just running him down like a hunting dog. Valentin's cold, stiff fingers bounced off the clasp.

He hooked left at the next head, veering into the fog. He had a grip on the clasp now, thought he could feel his nanoshadow writhing under the fabric. He tore the rucksack open and plunged his hand inside at the very instant Pepe slammed him to the damp ground. Valentin scrabbled desperately for the slippery grit of his shadow, and for the barest slice of a second his fingers brushed against it with an electric tingle.

Then Pepe seized his wrist and pried his hand slowly, almost tenderly, out of the rucksack. Valentin probed hard, trying to make the nanoshadow leap, make it stream up his arm and turn into corded black muscle, make it wrap around the wilder's neck like a noose. There was nothing but a weak ripple in response.

Pepe's dead weight pressed him into the earth, and it was not as comfortable as he'd fantasized it. Valentin could feel his bony knee, his chest, his hot breath at the nape of his neck. He wanted to sink into the mud. His best chance, maybe the only one he would get, gone and wasted.

Pepe refastened the clasp of his rucksack and stood up. "Fucking Townies," he said, breathing harder from the chase than Valentin would have expected. "I was getting to like you, Prophet."

Valentin didn't reply. He rolled over onto his back, getting his lungs back, then slowly sat up. The wilder was sitting cross-legged in front of the head closest to him, tightening the straps of the rucksack across his shoulders. His dark eyes looked almost hurt.

"My brother told me you Townies were snakes," Pepe said. "Said I was going to give you it back, didn't I? Said after you get the autofab working." He spat a glob of saliva. "I should fucking stick you for that."

"Sorry," Valentin said dully. In the moment, he felt like he already had a knife in the gut and one more wouldn't make much difference. They sat across from each other in silence, tendrils of fog creeping around their waists. Scowling, the wilder's scar seemed to distort his whole face, making his mouth one wide gash. Almost as ugly as the sculpture behind him.

Valentin's eyes trailed up the crude face. This head was different. There was a sort of topknot glinting at the peak of its carved skull.

"Did you not hear it, then?" Pepe said.

"Hear what?" Valentin said. His implant gave him a sharp prick of random static. He needed to calibrate again soon.

Then a gnashing metal meteor dropped from the top of the sculpture onto Pepe's back. Valentin hollered, scrambling backward, heaving to his feet. Pepe and the machine creature writhed, rolled, tangling flesh limbs with jet-black running blades. Valentin was frozen. The furious buzz in his implant and every chemical in his body screamed for him to run.

But Pepe still had his shadow. Valentin watched as the wilder flung himself back against the base of the head, smashing the clinging creature free. Its segmented body whirred in midair and it landed on its feet like a cat. Quadrupedal, skeletal black carbon, and where the head might have been, a pair of jagged rotary saws now hummed to life. Scarestories bounced through Valentin's head and he knew the lobos had not all been recycled, not a chance.

Pepe had his knife out now, dropped to a crouch, wrapping his offhand in his scarf. Valentin didn't see what either could do against the lobo's spinning maw. It hurtled at Pepe again; the wilder spun away, slashing low in the same motion. His knife screeched against the lobo's underside to no visible effect. The buzz in Valentin's implant was skull-splitting. He could feel the crude machine mind roaring for function completion, for disable, maim, refuel.

This was not a god. This was an animal.

As Pepe and the lobo broke and collided again, Valentin clenched his teeth and probed inside the buzzing hive. In midstride, the lobo jerked to a stop, shivering in place. Valentin felt a rush of elation. The machine mind was still yammering objectives, but Valentin had it clamped down, iced over. Pepe didn't take his eyes off the lobo, only switching his grip on the knife and circling closer.

"Is that you done that, Prophet?" he panted.

"Yeah," Valentin said, tamping down a grin. "Yeah. So give me my shadow back before I set it on you again."

Pepe was silent for a long moment, maybe trying to suss out if Valentin was bluffing, then he barked an anguished sort of laugh. "Alright, Prophet," he said. "Fuck you. But alright." Still watching the lobo, he slid the rucksack off his back and undid the clasp. Valentin's heart laddered up his ribs when he saw the nanoshadow rustle within. He reached out a hand, already imagining the feel of it on his skin.

The buzz in his implant changed pitch. Distracted, Valentin probed. His mouth went dry. The machine mind was trying to squeeze him out. He dug in hard, desperate, but a wave of defenseware carried him away and he felt himself lose his hold all at once. The lobo's formless head swiveled to face him, ignoring Pepe and his knife. The saws began to spin.

Valentin didn't even have time to shout before the lobo pounced, brushing past Pepe and slamming him to the ground. He kicked frantically, but the lobo's black running blades had his arms pinned, and now the grinding, shrieking maw was a millimeter off his face and—

Pepe's scarfed hand drove the knife between the saws. Sparks spat wild; one sizzled through Valentin's shirt. The lobo seized, shuddered, and Pepe dragged Valentin from underneath. He hauled to his feet and spun around just as Pepe's knife shot out of the lobo's mouth and pinged against the side of the sculpture. A ripple clacked through the creature's joints.

"I need my shadow," Valentin panted. "I can kill it with my shadow."

"Do it, then." Pepe shoved the open rucksack into Valentin's chest. As the lobo turned on them again, Valentin plunged both hands into the cold, gritty gelatin. His nanoshadow rippled in response to his touch, his biorhythm, the signal of his implant. The lobo darted forward. The nanoshadow was weak from days without sun, days without electricity. Valentin gripped it hard. As the lobo sprang, the nanoshadow shot away from his hands in a long plume of pitch and met it in the air, streaming into every crack in its carapace with a horrible shredding noise.

The lobo dropped to the dirt as the nanoshadow writhed through its body, leaving it a collapsed husk hemorrhaging sparks. Valentin finally exhaled. Pepe's eyes were wide as the nanoshadow pooled under the lobo's corpse, regaining its shape, then slithered back to its owner.

Valentin's shadow webbed its way up his knee, slipping underneath his shirt to spread cool and gritty and pulsating across his thumping chest. Tendrils wove between his fingers, licked up his neck, wicked sweat from around his nostrils and lips. Valentin closed his eyes as his shadow warmed to skin temperature. With his eyes closed, with his shadow pressing gently against him, he could almost be back home.

"So that's it, then. That's your shadow back."

Valentin opened his eyes. Pepe was unwrapping the scarf from around his left hand. The cloth was stained a dark wine-red, and when it peeled away from his skin he didn't wince but his tongue flicked fast against his scar. The lobo's saw had shorn through the scarf and left gouges on his wrist, his palm. Blood was welling steadily and dripping to the ground.

"Guess you leave now."

Valentin considered it. With his nanoshadow, he could make good time back to the Town with no fear of scorpions or lobos or wilders. Then he would give some catshit story about the gods sending him out into the campo to receive a vision, which Javier would not believe. Then, the *prueba*. Again.

"Yeah," Valentin said. "I go back to the Town with my shadow. You bleed to death in a field of giant heads. I won, you lost." He directed his shadow down his arm in a soft, black ribbon that waved in the space between them. "Here. Let me staunch it."

Pepe looked wary, but also pale and slightly dizzy. He held out his injured hand and watched as the nanoshadow shrouded over his skin, sealing to the wounds. He blinked at the sensation. "How many of these shadow things have you got in the Town?"

"A few," Valentin said. "But you need an implant to work them."

"That's too bad. Wouldn't mind one for the next lobo."

Valentin glanced over at the corpse of the machine and shivered. It looked smaller now, and he could see it was malformed, slightly warped, with one unfinished limb shorter than the others. "I thought they were all gone," he said. "That's what I was taught. That they were all gone. Extinct like the actual animals."

"They were gone for a long time," Pepe said. "Last winter they started to come back." He gave Valentin a considering look. "You don't actually know anything, do you, Prophet? You've never left the Town before."

Valentin bit back his urge to argue. The wilder was right. He'd been right about most things. "So what do you usually do?" he asked instead. "When there's a lobo." He pulled his shadow back up his arm.

Pepe inspected his hand. "Usually you die."

The smaller cuts were beginning to scab shut, but Valentin guessed that the gash along the wilder's wrist would need to be stitched or glued. And disinfected, preferably soon. He still remembered watching the Town's surgeon lop off a woman's two gangrenous fingers. He cast a glance toward the rucksack.

"Have you got anything in there to clean the cut?" he asked.

"Only water," Pepe said. He paused. "The autofab'll make medicine kits. Food for you, too. For your way back."

"Why are you so set on this autofab?" Valentin demanded at last. "If it's so important to your tribe, why's it only you taking me there? And what the hell was your plan if you hadn't found me in the gully? Were you going to knock on the Town gate and ask to borrow a godchip, or what?"

Pepe's face darkened. "What was your plan, heading over the wall?"

Valentin's mouth opened. Closed. "To get away," he finally said. "Just away."

"Yeah," Pepe said. He stumped to his rucksack and pulled it up onto his shoulders, gingerly for his left hand. "I want to help my family," Pepe said. "I want to help the band. If you can't contribute one way, you've got to find another. The autofab would help us. Would make us strong again."

Valentin looked down at the inky black edge of the nanoshadow pressed to his collarbone. He thought of Pepe journeying back to his tribe alone, dragging the same weight Valentin knew so well. Getting muck in his cuts, dying of fever, maybe even running into another lobo.

"What's your name, Prophet?" Pepe asked.

Valentin hesitated. "Valentin."

The wilder's eyes were shiny and desperate. "I can't go back with nothing. Will you help me, Valentin?"

The autofab had to be nearby now. Valentin could try. It would be like a fourth *prueba*, only with a different god, and with nobody watching but Pepe.

"Alright," Valentin said. "Fuck you, but alright. To the autofab."

The autofab was about half the size of the Town's, a featureless black mushroom cap that Valentin knew extended far below the ground. When they stopped in front of it, he felt a familiar twinge of fear, taken right back to his very first *prueba*, his sixteenth birthday. There'd been a procession through the Town's narrow streets, men carrying the plastic mannequins of the saints, women throwing red sand at his feet. He'd sat in front of the hulking black autofab, with Javier behind him and everyone watching, and the god inside had refused to speak to him.

"They used to keep everything clean," Pepe said as they passed the pockmarks of old fire pits and stepped over shattered tent poles. "They used to lay wreaths. But it's been a long time. Nobody comes here anymore."

Valentin probed hard. He could hear a faint, rustling whisper in his implant. The god was communicating, maybe with the pod that had passed over them in the night. Valentin sat, folding his legs, and his nanoshadow slid underneath him to cushion his tailbone. He sucked down a deep breath.

"Should I cant?" Pepe asked. "Don't know any prophet cants. But I could do the one for snakebite."

"Just don't talk," Valentin said, fixing his eyes on the slick surface of the autofab. He could see his own warped reflection in its black mirror. He took another deep breath, reminding himself that nobody was watching, only a wilder, only a stupid wilder with long, lean arms and deep, dark eyes and a careless laugh. Valentin closed his own eyes and willed the whisper in his implant louder. Through the electric cascade of the god's thoughts, Valentin could see, or feel, a fresh stimulus-response that could only be their presence. The autofab knew they were there.

Valentin reached, like he had for the lobo, but this time softly. And he thought: *Help us.* For the briefest instant, he felt the god turn sluggishly toward his probe, felt an interface blink open like a sleeper's eye. Valentin's heart leapt. Then it was gone, walled off behind impenetrable code, and the whisper in his implant receded. He'd failed his fourth. His stomach churned sick with it. Valentin opened his eyes.

Pepe was crouched down in his peripheral, tongue working against his scar. "What did you tell it?" he murmured. "What did it say?"

"It said nothing." Valentin knuckled a bit of sand away from his eye. "Like always."

Pepe's face fell. He stared at the autofab wall with an expression of fury, and for a moment Valentin thought he might try to put his uninjured fist through it. Then his eyes narrowed. "What do you mean, like always?"

"I mean I've never talked to a god," Valentin said. He wasn't scared of Pepe's knife anymore, not with his shadow thrumming against his skin. All he felt was dry and tired.

"The lobo," Pepe said. "You talked to the lobo. You made it stop."

"For five fucking seconds, yeah," Valentin admitted. "But that was a crude mind. Not a god." He tapped his implant. "When you turn sixteen, to be a prophet, you have to take a test. You have to talk to the Town's god, ask it to do some sign. Pulse the electric lights, or print up a plastic bird, or something stupid like that." He swallowed. "The god doesn't speak back to me. I've failed it three times already."

"Three times?" Pepe asked, disbelieving.

"Yeah. And if you count this—"

"Three times is nothing," Pepe said. "Nothing. Listen. I used to footrace my older brother. I wanted so badly to beat him I'd wake up an hour before the sun, go out to the field. Scratch lines in the dirt and run, to train my muscles. Every morning, even if I was sick or if I was up all the night on a scavenging party." His nostrils flared. "It took two years of that before I won. Took a hundred races."

"Running a footrace is nothing like interfacing with a god. If they don't speak to me, there's nothing I can do to change—"

"You said your tribe's got only two godchips," Pepe interjected. "Two in the whole Town. So they must have picked you for a reason."

"Not the one you think."

Pepe leaned close and put his good hand on Valentin's shoulder. "A hundred races, remember?"

Valentin shut his eyes again. He breathed in through his mouth, out through his nose. His nanoshadow pulsed comfortably against his chest, and Pepe's hand resting on his shoulder was comfortable in its own way. Valentin reached out for the autofab. The whisper in his implant rose. A minute passed. Two minutes. More. Valentin's hands were clenched, nails digging crescents in his palms. A blank eternity later, he opened his eyes. He wanted to lie, to keep Pepe's fingers cupped against him.

"Nothing," he admitted.

Pepe's hand squeezed his shoulder, but didn't leave it.

Valentin tried off and on again as dusk dropped over the campo, with no success. The first probe had at least elicited the autofab's attention, but now he was blocked out entirely. They ate the last of the *tortilla* and a handful of dry dates. Pepe used a bit of water to wash his cuts. He'd stopped bleeding but his face was still drawn and pale. Eventually they camped down at the base of the autofab, Pepe wrapped in a blanket and Valentin using his nanoshadow like a cocoon, exposing only his face. Neither of them had spoken for hours.

As Pepe shifted, finding elevation for his injured hand, Valentin couldn't help but eyetrace the slant of his shoulder blades, his hip, imagining the body underneath the blanket. He felt himself getting hard, and his nanoshadow moved to slide a tendril around his cock. Valentin chewed his lip. Then Pepe gave a ragged groan, and Valentin felt a wave of shame. He yanked his nanoshadow away from his groin and pretended to be asleep.

"You awake still, Prophet?"

Valentin hesitated. "Yeah. I am."

A moment later, Pepe shuffled over, dragging his blanket with him. The nanoshadow stretched membranous to accommodate the both of them, at the same time wrapping Pepe's injured hand. The wilder smelled like sweat and copper. When their arms brushed together, Valentin's heart beat hard. When Pepe touched the back of his head, just below his implant, his breath caught.

"Do you hear them all the time, then?" Pepe whispered.

"Only when they're close," Valentin said, trying to breathe evenly.

Pepe's finger traced the metal edge of the implant. "You can hear them, but they can't hear you."

"Can't. Won't." Valentin squirmed, freeing one arm. "Either." He reached out, hesitantly, heart hammering, and touched Pepe's face.

The wilder stiffened, turning away. His anxious eyes raked across the sky, as if watching gods might be drifting overhead. Then he relaxed and turned back into him with the smirk Valentin recognized from the night before. "Fucking Townies," he said, fitting his good hand around the edge of Valentin's hip.

The kiss was brief and badly angled and went through Valentin like voltage, making his nanoshadow thump against him. When it broke, Valentin leaned forward, unsleeving a grin in the dark, not caring about the autofab or the *prueba* or anything else, only feeling Pepe's lips on his again. He ran his thumb along the wilder's jaw and found the rippled scar tissue.

"Who cut your mouth?" he asked.

A long pause. Valentin remembered when he'd asked in the ruins, wondered again if he had gone too far, but Pepe left his hand where it was. "My brother," he said.

"Right. Because you beat him at the footrace."

Pepe pulled back, staring at him. "No. It was for this." He struggled up onto his elbow, careful with his injured hand. "He caught me with someone. Again. This time he was shitface drunk and angry and he held me down and cut me. Said it was to keep the *mariconas* away."

Valentin felt his grin fall off. "I didn't know it was like that. With wilders."

"I'm seventeen now," Pepe said dully. "I have to start fucking who they tell me. I've got good blood. Can't waste it. I have to help make the band strong again." His voice splintered. "I thought if I do something big. Something like this. I thought if I give them the autofab back, maybe it'll be enough." He kneaded his eyes hard. "And then he'll love me again."

Valentin swallowed. "Maybe I'm lucky," he said. "Not having family. That's the real reason they pick you for a prophet. Nobody would have missed me if the surgery went bad. It's not because I was anything special."

Pepe looked at him for a stretched moment. "You are, though. I think." He blinked and turned over.

Valentin stared at the back of his dark head, wishing he could window inside of it and see where he'd been placed. He thought a thousand thoughts as Pepe's breathing slowly steadied. He pictured the pair of them setting off on their own, not back to the Town and not back to Pepe's band and his psychopath brother. Maybe to the wilderness up north in Old France, maybe further south to where the gods were busy reshaping the coastline.

He was half-submerged in a dream when his implant gave him a short, sharp shock. His eyes flicked open. For a moment, Valentin thought he was still dreaming because the glossy black hide of the autofab was now veined with soft orange status lights.

His first instinct was to wake Pepe, but as he sat up the autofab's orange lights wriggled together to form an image. Valentin rubbed his eyes. The autofab had drawn a pixelated face, and as he watched, a pixelated finger rose to its lips. The gesture was unmistakable. Valentin looked down at the sleeping wilder, then back up to the image. The orange ghost stared at him, then slipped around the side of the autofab.

Valentin got quietly to his feet. His nanoshadow came with him, slithering up his body. Pepe shivered. Valentin debated leaving the wilder his shadow, peeling at it half-heartedly with his fingernails. In the end he pulled the dirty blanket overtop of him instead. Sweat was beading along Pepe's hairline. Valentin bit his lip, remembering the fever prediction.

The nanoshadow swathed his limbs as he made his way around to the back of the autofab. The orange ghost had become an orange doorway, pulsing gently in the dark. Valentin stared at it. His implant was no longer humming. The night was dead silent, cold, a sky of tarry black cloud. Then a sibilant whisper entered his head with a feeling like a thousand insects scraping against each other. *Enter.*

Valentin realized, dimly, that he had been waiting sixteen years for the invitation. When the skin of the autofab peeled back, he didn't hesitate. He stepped inside and the autofab sealed shut behind him. He was in absolute dark. A moment passed. Valentin felt a claustrophobic terror stab through him, imagined himself entombed by a malfunct god.

White lights bloomed to life, and he was suddenly a giant, sunk to his ankles in a map of the peninsula. He saw the bone-dry furrow of the Guadalquivir, recognized the mountains around the ruins of Granada, and knew, instantly, that he was seeing what the gods saw when they drifted through the sky in their flying bodies. He found the tiny walled pueblo south of Seville's burnt carcass and felt an ache in his throat.

You are not a scavenger. You are the [organic relay] displaced from [Installation 17].

The god's voice scraped down his neck. The Town swelled on the map. "Yeah," Valentin said. "Yes. That's where I'm from."

The map jumped, and Valentin saw the field of towering heads forming a perfect square.

[Installation 17's patron] requested an early dispatch in [Gestation Field 2944] in order to eliminate the scavenger and ensure your security. Why did you dismantle the [organic disposal module] before it could attain function completion?

Valentin's head was a whirlwind. This was not the voice he'd always imagined. "You watched that?" he demanded. "You've been watching us?"

The map plunged toward the ground, zooming in on the collapsed lobo. Valentin's stomach sloshed with the illusion of falling.

Why did you dismantle the [organic disposal module] before it could attain function completion?

"It attacked me. Both of us." Valentin shook himself. "You mean the Town's god sent that thing?"

You will go back to [Installation 17] now. Supplies have been manufactured.

The map disappeared and Valentin found himself in a small, dark alcove. Facing him, on an illuminated plinth, he saw a slick black carrycase, and beside it a blocky shape he recognized as twin to the printed handgun Javier kept in his house.

If the scavenger attempts to obstruct you, use the weapon.

Valentin stared down at it. "I don't need help," he said shakily. "He does. His tribe, his band or whatever, they need this autofab functional again. Why did it shut down?"

Autofab access was rescinded from all scavengers as the [first act of culling]. [Installation 17] contains sufficient genetic diversity if breeding programs are followed. A larger sample size is unnecessary. Scavengers are extraneous. The [Gestation Fields] are preparing for the [second act of culling].

Valentin thought back to the field, to the rows and rows of heads, and remembered the faint buzz from inside each one. With a sick drop in his stomach, he realized that they were not sculptures. They were wombs. He pictured the carved mouths winching slowly open, the spidery shadows unfolding from inside.

"You're sending more of those things after them?" he demanded. "For what? Stripping parts?"

[Installation 17] will not be affected. You will go back now, before the [second act of culling] begins.

Valentin picked up the case. His nanoshadow clung to it, sticking it to his back like a rucksack. Then he picked up the weapon. "Why didn't the god speak to me in the Town?" he asked shakily. "It speaks to Javier."

[Installation 17's patron] believes it is important that [organic relays] understand the dangers outside its walls. You have completed a [pilgrimage]. Now you understand the [severe mercy of the gods]. Now you will go back.

Behind Valentin, the door peeled open again. Winter air licked his back with ice. "I'll do whatever the fuck I want," he said, sticking the weapon to his hip.

Valentin walked back out into the world. The autofab's status lights had winked off again, but overhead he could make out a shard of moon. Enough light to travel by, if only just. He could start his trek back to the Town. He would have the hard evidence that he'd spoken to a god, and maybe by the time Javier died the god in the Town's autofab would listen to him, too. He could let the wilders find out about the second act of culling when lobos dragged them from their tents and chopped them to pieces.

Valentin went to where Pepe was sleeping, rummaging the medicine kit out of his new case. The wilder was on his side, showing only the perfect side of his face, the faultless bones and dark lashes. Valentin touched his chin, turning his head. The jagged smile reappeared and Pepe's eyes flicked open.

"I got disinfectant for your hand," Valentin said.

"From the autofab? The god spoke to you?" His voice was hoarse with sleep.

"I'm a prophet, aren't I?" Valentin shook the tube of disinfectant spray. "This is going to sting a bit."

Valentin helped him wrap his hand and sling it up as he told him, in fragments, about the conversation with the god in the autofab. The whisper in his implant grew louder and louder, and by the time they stole away into the night, heading north to the band's last campsite to give them the warning, it was a chorus of furious voices.

Valentin had his own concerns.

whending my way back home
Bill Johnson

Bill Johnson has sold stories to many different markets, including Asimov's
Science Fiction, Analog Science Fiction and Fact, The Magazine of Fantasy & Science Fiction, Black Gate, Amazing, *and many others, but is one
of those rare writers who has never written a novel. One of those stories,* "We
Will Drink a Fish Together," *won the Hugo Award in 1997. He has an MBA
with an emphasis in finance from Duke University. He also has a BA in jour-
nalism from the University of Iowa, and he won the Best News Story of the
Year award from the Iowa Press Association. At 6'8" tall, he may be the tallest of all science fiction writers.*

*Here he tells the story of a stranded time traveler who must make his way
home one day at a time, starting in Göbekli Tepe ten thousand years ago.*

D amn it," Ianna swore. "What's she doing here?"

Ianna leaned forward and spat a mouthful of freshly chewed wheat gruel into a
small stone starter bowl. She sipped from a water skin, washed out her mouth, and
spat again on top of the mash.

"Mix and warm," Martin reminded her. She sighed, rolled her eyes at him, and
wiped the sweat off her forehead. She reached into the bowl and kneaded the mixture. It was, Martin knew, both disgusting and oddly satisfying, the wet and smooth
texture working together, slipping over and under and through the fingers.

Ianna finished and shook her hands free. She scraped the last of the mash off her
fingers, back into the bowl, then used a shaped piece of gazelle bone to scoop a
handful of stones from the fire. She propped the stones next to the bowl, to keep the
starter mash warm. She wiped her hands clean with a handful of fresh reeds.

"Now," Martin asked. "What's the problem?"

Ianna tipped her chin to the north, at the silhouette of a woman coming down
the slope of the valley. From the distance, she looked like anyone coming back from
a hunt. Martin stood.

*The stranger just sent out a broadcast to every Traveler. She's going to work her
way through the camp, to meet everyone, one at a time,* Artie told him. *She's telling
them to keep it quiet, so the locals don't notice anything.*

"So," Martin said out loud, to both of them. He glanced over at Ianna. "She's not what she looks like."

"No," Ianna said.

"Details," Martin ordered.

Artie sharpened Martin's vision, stretched it like a pair of binoculars. A small display with translucent numbers opened in the lower right of his vision.

Ianna and the rest of the Travelers scattered through the camp were Maxyes tribal, downtiming from the University in Qart-hadast. They were relatively short compared to the native hunter-gatherer's. Ianna was only five foot two and she was middle height for the women. She grew her dark hair long on the right side of her head, tied up in a twisted bun, and shaved her hair close on her left side. She used native ochre—yellow, red and brown—as eye and face makeup.

The stranger, even from a distance, was clearly not a Maxyes. Long hair on both sides of her face, dirty blonde and pulled back and out of the way in an interlaced rope style. Clear skin, no ochre or any other markings. And she was tall. Artie's display said she was five foot nine. Martin turned his eyes back to normal.

"Tribe?" Martin asked Ianna. "Nation?"

"Alemanni of some kind," Ianna said, dismissively. "You can tell by looking at her. She's probably with their Volks Wachter. The Kehin use her sometimes, to tell us things that need to be kept private. They're afraid to come back along the timelines, so they send her."

She looked up at Martin.

"Who does the Chayil use? To tell you things? Is it a person . . . or something different?"

"Something different," Martin said absently. He thought for a moment, then turned to Ianna.

"And you should always speak of the Kehin with respect," Martin warned her. "What if one of the others heard you? What if I—officially—heard you?"

"The army protects its own," Ianna said. "And I'm with you."

Martin shook his head.

"The army protects the generals. So the priests don't mess with the generals," Martin said. He tapped himself on the chest. "But I'm not a general. And neither are you."

Ianna looked frightened for a moment, then ducked her head and nodded. Martin turned back, but the messenger was down the slope and gone, lost in the flows of people and the mixed-together jumble of tents and shelters and travel lodges.

This means trouble, Artie said gloomily. Martin shrugged and turned away and sat back on his stone work bench.

"Keep your mouth shut and don't broadcast," Martin warned Artie in silent. "We'll get through this."

"I'm not going to say anything," he assured Ianna, out loud. He smiled and remembered an old joke from his future.

"What happens in Gobekli, stays in Gobekli."

Ianna frowned at him, confused, then shook her head, and sat down across from him. She picked up the half-finished mat she had been working on.

"I have no idea what you're talking about. And Mar, don't take this personal, but, sometimes," she said, hesitated, then rushed forward. "You're just weird."

If only she knew, Artie grumbled mournfully. *If only she knew.* . . .

Martin grunted and concentrated on the fist-sized piece of flint in his hand. He turned the rock from side to side. Satisfied, he leaned forward and braced it against his work anvil, a large boulder with a flat top, and carefully struck the flint along a fault line with his soft hammer. A side piece cracked off. He gently and carefully picked up the new piece and felt the slick sharp edge. It still needed a little work to fix the final shape, but that would be easy.

"Perfect," he said, satisfied. Artie looked through his eyes.

I'm so very proud of you.

Artie did not sound proud. He sounded sarcastic, like a sick old man, crotchety and uncertain and irritated. Martin ignored him and added the new arrow head to the hide pouch on the ground at his feet.

"Until the beer is ready, we still have to eat," Martin reminded Artie, unperturbed, in silent mode. He checked the pouch, counted. He looked up and saw Ianna walking up from the river, a pair of skin water bags in her hands. He got up and helped her carry them inside their hut. She smiled at him and sat back on her bench. He held up one of the arrow heads.

"Eabani told me yesterday that he needed to trade. He's back fresh from a hunt. Mostly gazelle. A few aurochs. I figure I can trade three of these to get us enough meat for today and tomorrow."

Ianna shook her head.

"Good try, but it won't work. I ran into Eabani down at the river."

"And?"

"He's going on a long trip," she said, carefully. "A long, long trip. He'll be gone for quite a while."

He met the woman. The messenger, Artie said on open. Ianna nodded. She held her finger to her lips, touched her head, and spoke out loud.

"Her name, here, is Tiamat," Ianna said. "She won't tell anyone what her name is back home."

"Maybe she's in trouble back there."

"Maybe." Ianna sounded uncertain. "Eabani couldn't get much out of her." She studied Martin.

"You sure you've never had to deal with her?"

"No," Martin said. He dropped the arrow head back into the pouch and picked up his raw flint rock.

"Everyone deals with her," Ianna said with certainty.

"Not me," Martin said.

"Have I ever told you there's something wrong with you?" Ianna asked.

"You may have mentioned that once or twice," Martin acknowledged. "Still haven't dealt with her."

"Well, you're going to get your chance," Ianna said. She tilted her head toward the rough path that led up the hill toward the temple.

Tiamat walked along the path, toward a part of the camp where a new tribe had arrived last night. She glanced at Ianna and Martin, then at the newcomers. She held up a finger, nodded to Ianna, then picked up her pace toward the new arrivals.

"But not just yet," Ianna said.

Martin used his fingers to scoop up a fresh mouthful of gruel from the cooking bowl, carefully kept separate from the starter bowl. He chewed it slowly and focused on Tiamat as she walked past them. He concentrated on her clothes, the gear she carried, the way she walked, the way she looked.

Everything about her, from her hair to her animal skin clothes to the way she moved, was perfect. She blended into the camp like a drop of water into a river.

Which was a mistake.

Perfection, of any kind, was an error. Real people, native people, in any timeline, made mistakes. Real people weren't perfect. Real people always had something out of place, something that wasn't quite right. Real life forced mistakes and compromises, smudges and dirty hands.

Martin saw the locals, the ones who lived in this place and time, look up as she walked by. Something about her was wrong, something about her disturbed them. She was just too damned perfect.

He spat the chewed gruel into the starter bowl, added a mouthful of water.

"Time to check the beer."

Ianna stood and stepped up and out into the sun. There were three whitewashed limestone vessels, shaped roughly like horse water troughs, just outside the shelter. Each was hollowed out to hold about one hundred liters of liquid. The first vessel was full, covered with a lid of interlaced green grass, close to ready. The second held a few liters of thin amber starter liquid. The third was empty.

Ianna went to the first vessel, slid the cover to the side. Martin, from several feet away, still winced at the sharp odor, an unpleasant mix of sour and sickly sweet. Ianna hastily pulled the lid back into place.

"That batch is going to be vile. The brewers in Alemania are cursing you from their great-grandmother's wombs."

Martin shrugged and leaned back on his heels under the shadow of their hide canopy. He looked around the rest of the camp. Hundreds of tents and travel lodges, even more men and women, worshipers and slaves, traders and priests and hunters, with the constant ebb and flow of small children and dogs, laughing and barking and chasing each other.

"If it's strong enough, they'll drink it anyway," he said. She looked at the vessel doubtfully, then over at him. He relented.

"Add some of that honey we traded for this morning. And more of the wild grapes. Crush them up first. Give it a good stir. We'll cut back on the hawthorn berries on the second batch. And, just maybe, Artie can keep a better watch on the temperature this time."

I'm doing the best I can, Artie said defensively. He coughed, even though he had no lungs and no body. *I'm dying, you know.*

Ianna tended to the beer. Martin turned his attention back to the original piece of flint in his hand. It was getting small. He idly wondered if he should go for a knife or a spear point with what was left. A knife would get them more food from a hunting party, but a knife needed a handle. Or he could get two spear points out of what was left. Were two spear points worth more than a good knife? Maybe if he wrapped leather around the handle before he sold the knife. A finished product should be worth more than a bare knife blade. Or, maybe, he should just go for more arrowheads. . . .

Knife, Artie said, in silent. *Definitely. And add a decorative design on the leather. The theme for this circle and the Tall Men is the hunter and the phallus. Draw a crocodile on one side of the handle, a naked man on the other. Then trade the knife to one of the priests.*

"Why a priest?" Martin asked, out loud.

Ianna looked over at him.

Shut up! Artie snapped, in silent. *Remember where you are, now, and where she's going to be from, then. Qart-hadast is still a city of priests in the future, even in the university. You want to end up in front of a court of the Kehin?*

"Apologies," Martin said toward Ianna, but really to Artie.

Eabani is going home, back uptime, so we need a local hunter, Artie explained, patiently.

"Buyuwawa," Martin said, in silent. "Eabani's been teaching him. He'll take over. And he's local."

Fine. Buyuwawa, then. Tell the local priest he gets the knife if he gives Buyuwawa a blessing before he goes on a hunt. Tell Buyuwawa he gets the blessing if he gives you a bigger share of the meat from the hunt. Artie sounded exasperated. *Didn't they teach you any economics where you come from?*

"No," Martin said out loud.

Ianna glanced over at him.

"You're talking to him again." She sounded just as irritated as Artie. "It's bad manners to talk to your Artie without letting other Travelers listen in."

"Sorry," he apologized. "Classified talk."

"You've been out here alone too long," she said, sympathetically. "You need to go uptime and spend some time with a hot shower, an oculus and a good food printer." She moved closer to him, pressed up against his side. "Maybe with a warm partner."

"My contract with the Chayil," he lied, apologetically.

Ianna was Qart-hadast wins Cannae, Hannibal burns Rome, timeline. The rest of the Travelers in the camp were from the same base timeline with different, minor, variations.

You lying bastard, Artie said, admiringly, in silent. *You make it look so easy. I want you to program that into my if-then.*

"Not a chance," Martin replied, in silent. He smiled sincerely at Ianna.

"I can't leave until I get new orders," he said to her.

Martin, on the other hand, was always deliberately vague about his homepoint. It was better to let her make assumptions. The fewer lies he told, the better. Easier to keep things straight.

"Perhaps there's some place we can meet, when your contract is over?" Ianna asked, hopefully. She reached down and rubbed his leg.

"Some place uptime? Some place with a bath tub? And hot water?"

"Yes!"

He shrugged. He looked past her, up toward the plateau and the temple and the Great Circle. The tops of several pillars were just visible. The Tall Men were not up yet.

"Maybe we can work that out. In the meantime . . . ," he said. He stood and put his arm around her shoulders and pulled her up to her feet. He glanced at the camp, toward where Tiamat had stepped out of sight.

"It will take her at least an hour to work her way here," Ianna said. "She'll talk to at least three other Travelers before she reaches us."

"Well, then," Martin said. He pushed the hut's gazelle skin privacy curtain aside. The inside of the hut was dim, not dark, and the pile of grasses they used as a bed was clearly visible in the back. "Perhaps we should enjoy the moment."

"What about the beer?"

"Artie can take care of the beer."

This is not fair, Artie protested.

"Yes, he can," she said, and grinned. She turned and led him by the hand into the room. Martin pulled the leather flap closed behind them.

I certainly hope she knows how this works, Artie said morosely, in silent. *Because we sure as hell don't.*

Martin caught sight of Tiamat when she was about five minutes away.

Her skin was hunter browned, colored by sun and wind. Her legs were long and muscled. She carried a flint-tipped spear over her shoulder and a knife tucked into her belt.

She wore a loincloth and tied-on animal skin leggings. This time her hair was tucked under a broad-brimmed straw hat. Her shoes were leather sandals, held together by a bark-skin net which tied tightly around and over her ankles. A decorative bandeau, hand knotted into a geometric pattern and decorated with stone beads and feathers, rested on top of her breasts. A gazelle skin cape and a wood and hide backpack finished her clothing.

"I want one of those," Ianna whispered in Martin's ear as Tiamat walked up to them. They were back outside, on their benches under the canopy in the work room. "The bandeau. It will make me very happy."

And if you make her happy, she'll make you happy, Artie snapped, in silent. *Yes, yes, we all know how this works. Bio's. If you thought more with your brains and less with your—*

Tiamat stopped just outside their canopy. Her head tipped up when Artie spoke and her eyes seemed to focus on a spot in the air up and behind Martin.

"I agree," Tiamat said, in silent.

Shit! Artie said. He sounded surprised and afraid. *Ianna can't hear me in silent, but—*

"Then I suggest you stay quiet," Martin interrupted sharply, also in silent mode. He looked up at Tiamat. He kept a firm grip on the half-finished flint knife, all that was left of the stone, in his hand.

"Ianna," Tiamat said calmly. Her voice was a pleasant mezzo-soprano, bureaucratically neutral and professional, like an AI voice.

"I'm here to inform you that your time, along with all the other Travelers in the camp, is now complete. Please gather your things. Six months present time minimum until you can come back here. A year would be better."

"When do I have to leave?"

"Now."

Ianna looked surprised, then stubborn.

"You can't order me around!"

Tiamat just stared at her for a moment. Her expression froze and a muscle hardened in her jaw as she visibly worked to control herself.

It's more than that, Artie said, puzzled. He used a different cipher to talk with Martin privately. Martin recognized the cipher. It was more secure than their usual private mode, but it took more processing cycles. The problem was, this timeline was inherently poisonous to Artie. Part of him was in phase-shift but part of him was anchored in Martin. More cycles meant more of him into Martin and more exposure to this timeline.

Which meant Artie was dying faster.

"Don't do this," Martin said.

Shut up, Artie snapped. *Switch to the new cipher for private. I don't trust her. And I promised to watch over you.*

"Artie—"

I always keep my promises.

This time Tiamat looked at Martin suspiciously, as if she heard Artie but did not know what he said. She hesitated, then concentrated back on Ianna.

"You're right," Tiamat said calmly to Ianna. "I can't order you around. Tell you what. Stay right here. I'll come back tomorrow. We'll talk again. If you're still here."

Ianna suddenly looked afraid.

"It's that big of a change?"

"Yes."

"I thought the worst was that I might be stranded in a different, similar, timeline," Ianna argued. "Then all I have to do is wait until the next change nexus and I could slip back home."

"Usually, that's possible," Tiamat admitted. She sounded bored, as if this was an old argument, one she had already gone over several times. "But this one is different. With this one, if you stay, you may not find another change nexus that leads home."

"So what are my chances if I stay another day?"

Tiamat's face went still, absent, for a moment. Then she was back.

"Your uncertainty factor is going up rapidly. If you stay, you may be here tomorrow. Or you may be . . . gone."

"Gone," Ianna said slowly.

"Gone," Tiamat said briskly. "Don't ask me where or when. I don't know. Just . . . gone."

Ianna glanced at Martin.

"What about him?"

Tiamat hesitated. Martin realized that, under the dirt, her skin was flushed, almost feverish. And her eyes were wrong, slightly off focus. She leaned from one side to another, as if it was difficult to keep her balance.

"What's your name?" Tiamat demanded. "You're not on my list."

"Call me Mar."

"That's a Canaanite name. Old school. Your family is from Byblos?"

Martin shrugged.

"It's the name I use."

"You're not on my list," Tiamat repeated, peevishly.

"He's military. He's with the Chayil," Ianna said, anxiously. Tiamat looked at Martin suspiciously.

"My contract is with the Kehin. They said nothing about any Chayil Travelers in this timezone."

"Since when," Martin said, carefully, his voice pitched low, "does the army report to the priests?"

Tiamat hesitated. In every Qart-hadast timeline there was constant tension between the Kehin and the Chayil, the priests and the army. Tiamat pulled out her knife from her belt, turned it so the handle was toward Martin.

Handle is double purpose, Artie announced. *Inside is a quantum retro-causality analyzer. She wants to check you out.*

"Two can play that game," Martin said, in silent. "Tag her."

You sure?

"Tag her."

Martin reached out carefully. He made sure his fingers lightly brushed Tiamat's wrist as he took the knife.

Done.

Martin examined the knife. To all the natives in the camp it looked as if the new hunter was having a chip in her blade looked at by their best flint knapper.

He studied it for a moment, nodded, handed it back to Tiamat. He held out his new, half-finished, knife blade. She made a show of studying it. Finally, she nodded and handed him back the unfinished blade as well as several strips of trail jerky.

Good showmanship, Artie admitted. *She's done this before. Everyone thinks she has just bought herself a new knife when you finish it.*

"He's got to leave also," Tiamat said stubbornly.

And now we know she can lie, Artie said.

"He has less uncertainty than you," Tiamat said, grudgingly. "He can stay a little longer. But you have to go now."

Martin reached over, touched Ianna's shoulder.

"You go. I'll only stay a little while, to take care of our things," he assured her. "I'll tell Buyuwawa and our other local friends we've got to go to Lake Van to harvest more wheat. They'll watch our beer vats while we're gone. The rest of the stuff I'll just give away or bury. We'll be fine. I'll meet you uptime. We'll find that tub and the hot water."

"But what if we get separated? What if we both can't come back at the same time?"

Martin held his hands apart.

"What is, is. But you heard her. Our odds are good. But we've got to take care of you, first. Now."

Ianna closed her eyes, then nodded. She leaned close to Martin.

"My name, back home, is Monica," she said in a soft rush. "Try to find me. I live on the south side of Qart, near the university. I'll try to come back but, my grant . . ." She hesitated. "You know faculty politics."

You don't know a damned thing about faculty politics, Artie snorted.

"Shut up," Martin said in silent. He smiled and nodded to Ianna.

She turned and ducked into their hut. She came back a moment later, her few possessions tucked into a bent wood backpack, her datapad carefully disguised as a carefully polished stone rectangle.

Ianna looked at Martin, uncertainly. He reached down and picked up the arrowhead pouch.

"I wasn't expecting this. I don't have anything to give you," he said. He pulled out an arrowhead and handed it to her.

"Don't say it that way," she said, miserable. "It will all work out."

I think she's actually going to miss you, Artie said, surprised.

"Shut up," Martin said, in silent, to Artie. He turned his attention to Ianna.

"I'll remember you," he said.

Liar, Artie said, tiredly, in silent. Then he relented. *Well, maybe. I'll help with that. As long as I can.*

Ianna hesitated, then took the arrowhead and tucked it carefully away in her pocket. She leaned forward, kissed Martin, and stepped back, to the edge of the canopy shade, and turned to face Tiamat.

"If he's hurt, Qart-hadast will not be pleased."

"You speak for all of Qart-hadast?" Tiamat asked with mild disinterest.

"I have connections!"

"I'm sure you do," Tiamat said dismissively.

Ianna started to walk away but stopped, her back to Martin and Tiamat. She began to turn back toward them.

"Your uncertainty just increased," Tiamat called out to her. "I suggest you keep moving."

Ianna shook her head and walked down the hill.

She's crying, Artie said.

And Ianna was gone.

"There will be a man named Tom Cahill," Martin said in silent mode to Artie. "He's going to say that a journey is measured in friends."

Then we've come a long way, Artie said. *And we've got one hell of a long way to go.*

Martin nodded. He turned his attention to Tiamat.

"Come in, get out of the sun. You don't look so good," Martin said. He stepped back to give Tiamat room. She ducked her head under the canopy and sat opposite him.

"Water?" he asked and held up a small leather water skin. Tiamat nodded and took a drink. She handed the flask back.

"Ianna is a meaningless little fool. But she likes you," Tiamat said, tiredly. It sounded like an accusation but it came out as a simple statement. Martin decided this was not the time to be offended.

"So what does that make me?"

"A mystery," Tiamat said. She smiled for the first time.

"And you hate mysteries?"

"And I hate mysteries."

"So. What do you want to know?" Martin asked.

Tiamat spoke to Martin but her eyes ignored him. She concentrated on everything else in the shelter. Martin knew she was taking an inventory and comparing it to what the archeologists had found in the area around Gobekli Tepe, thousands of years in the future.

"Take your time," he said, calmly. "No rush. This place is clean, and so am I. No metals. No plastic. Nothing but stone and wood and bone and leather. Everything organic will decay. The stone is authentic, from right around here, and the chips will join all the rest of the garbage when the People bury the temple."

Tiamat ignored him.

She doesn't trust you, Artie said. *I can feel her. She's using her eyes but she's also scanning the area to see if it matches the historical records.*

"Trust, but verify," Martin said in silent mode.

I don't know the reference, Artie said, apologetically.

"No, you wouldn't," Martin said. "No one will yet."

Tiamat relaxed and turned her attention to Martin.

"You're clean," she said, reluctantly. "No violations."

"I'm careful," Martin said. Tiamat nodded.

"Now," she said. Martin heard the bureaucrat in her voice. He imagined her sitting back in an office chair in an uptime cubicle, her datapad in her lap.

"Project name?"

"You won't find any reference to it," Martin warned. "It's a dark project and it's buried."

"Try me anyway. I can be very persuasive."

"Stone Eagle."

"Really?" she asked, skeptical. He pointed to the meter square limestone slab propped up against the outside of the hut. It showed a stylized engraving of a bird, claws outstretched.

"Not as sharp as a holo, but that might be a violation, don't you think?" Martin asked, sardonically.

"Do it yourself?"

"A friend did it," Martin said evasively. "I put it up outside my shelter, wherever I go. Lets people know I'm at home."

"Speaking of home," Tiamat asked. "What's your homeline?"

"Qart-hadast is my capital," Martin lied. "Long ago and far away from here."

Tiamat frowned.

Stop being a smart ass! Artie scolded. *I know you've dealt with police before. She might not be in uniform but I suggest you start thinking of her that way.*

Martin ignored him. He smiled back at Tiamat.

"Now it's my turn," Martin said. "You ever run into any leakers? From other timelines?"

"A few," Tiamat admitted. "A very few. And the timelines are not very different. Their home timeline might be one where Qart-hadast was destroyed by an earthquake or a fire. Usually the capital just moves west, to Gades, but civilization stays the same. They never seem to be able to go home. We help them."

"Kehin help? I've heard of it," Martin said drily. "Think I'll take care of myself, thank you."

"My turn," Tiamat said. "You work for the Chayil?"

"Classified."

She made a note.

"And you're back here for . . . ?"

"Beer."

"Really." Tiamat did not sound impressed. She sounded skeptical. "Beer?"

"Beer," Martin said promptly. He knew his cover story was solid. He gestured at the stone vessels, the grain, the empty fruit and honey bowls.

"Explain."

"People like to drink beer," Martin said. He spread his hands wide. "Gives me a good excuse to be up and moving around, to explore and talk with different people and different tribes. It's as simple as that."

"You're looking for something."

"Classified."

"What's this got to do," Tiamat waved her hand at the outside, at the camp and then down the path and up the hill, toward the temple several miles away, "with Gobekli Tepe?"

Martin smiled.

"Classified."

Tiamat frowned.

Got her, Artie said. *Blood pressure up, temperature up, heartbeat up. You've got her irritated.*

Tiamat stood.

"You need to go back up-time. Your uncertainty factor is going up," she said sharply.

So much for your inimitable charm.

"I have never seen a causality detector like yours," Martin said, casually.

Tiamat smiled down at him.

"Classified."

Martin laughed. He leaned back.

"I think I might stay around for a while."

"Not safe. You need to get the hell out of here."

Liar, Artie said. *She didn't get a damned thing off you. She just wants you gone.*

"I have some things I need to finish," Martin said.

"And those things are . . . ?"

"Classified."

"Of course," Tiamat said. She turned to leave. "Just remember, if you stay here, you may just be . . . gone."

"Classified. And I can take care of myself."

"Go to hell!" Tiamat snapped. She ducked under the canopy and stormed down the hill away from Martin. He waited until she was just far enough away, then went to low power mode.

"Do you have a lock on her?"

I can follow her wherever she goes, Artie reassured him.

"Good. What about her causality detector?"

I can use it.

"Scan her."

Silence. Martin idly watched a little girl across the way. She was dressed in a gazelle skin and held a black and white puppy. The girl and the dog squatted in the dirt, both of their heads cocked to the side, intently studying a baby in a reed basket. A young woman, probably the mother to all of them, sat nearby and worked on rolling blades of prairie grass together to make string. She looked up, saw the girl and the dog, smiled, and gently rocked the basket.

"Life could be worse," Martin said to himself.

Got it, Artie said. He whistled, low and slow. Martin tried to remember when he had programmed that if-then into Artie. Or maybe it was an imitation sub-routine.

She's high, Artie said. *Her future is very uncertain. Something is going to happen to her.*

Martin studied Tiamat as she walked away, as she ducked around a tent and was gone.

"Watch her," Martin ordered. "When it happens—before it happens—I want to know."

And?

"And she has a nice ass," he commented.

Bio's!

Martin stepped over to the beer vat, pulled the lid aside, winced at the smell. He poked a hole through the scum on top, dipped in a small cup. The beer underneath was a nice golden hue, despite the odor. He hastily fit the rushes back in place.

"That really is bad," he admitted.

Sometimes I'm glad I can't smell things.

"Culture level?"

A good batch, Artie said, smugly. *The dirt from that last batch of wheat was just what we needed. Good fungus in it.*

Martin shook his head.

"I'm going to see Buyuwawa and the others," he said. "I still have to eat and I need to fix this batch, fruit and mash up the second batch and start number three. Watch the place while I'm gone."

Bring us back another partner. Asherah, Buyuwawa's daughter, likes you. What about her? Or Mitelek? He's strong.

"Not yet," Martin said. He shook his head. "Give me a little time."

You liked Ianna.

"I did," Martin admitted. He walked into the crowd. He limped away, sore off his left foot from a blister. His fingernails were stained. He was just a little too tall, and clumsy, and he needed to gain ten pounds.

He was anything but perfect. And no one noticed him at all.

"Go into self-diagnostic mode," Martin called back. "Check whatever Ianna left behind. See if you can use any of it to fix some of your problems."

You want me to steal from her?

"Don't think of it as stealing," Martin said. He stepped around the first shelter and out of sight of the Stone Eagle.

"Think of it as creative scrounging."

Wake up.

Martin opened his eyes just a slit and stretched, as if he was still asleep. His hand slipped under the pile of grass and rushes he used as a pillow and gripped his knife.

"What?"

You're fine, Artie reassured him hurriedly. *No danger.*

"Then why the hell did you wake me up? I'm tired."

It's Tiamat. She's dying.

Martin sat up and adjusted his eyes to night vision. Everything became a soft, oddball green, with rounded edges instead of sharp, straight lines.

"Where is she?"

Outside. In her tent. Down the hill.

"Let her live or let her die? Give me the numbers."

Artie thought for a moment.

Just not enough data, he said regretfully. *Does she turn us in to the Kehin? Does she ask too many questions and get the Chayil interested in this agent of theirs that they know nothing about? Does she help us? Can't tell you. Just don't know enough about her. She's sure as hell not in the records. And I don't have the if-then for this.*

Martin sat for a moment. He heard a steady rain against the wall of his hut. The banked fire in the middle of the floor put out just enough heat to keep him warm. Outside, he heard the wind. It sounded cold and sharp.

"If I leave her out there, what happens?"

Her temperature is rising, Artie said. *If I use that stupid Fahrenheit scale you taught me she's already over 102 degrees and rising. Rapidly.*

"She'll die," he said, resignedly.

She'll die, Artie agreed.

Martin swore, then sat up and put on his clothes. He laced up his shoes, stood, and stoked the fire with fresh wood and dried dung. He put on his hat and his cape.

"I hate this," he announced to the empty air, and stepped out of his shelter.

Cold rain struck the side of his face. He kept his head down, let his hat take the brunt of the wind.

Left, Artie instructed him. *Now right. Around Miskit's shelter. Ignore the dog. The dog keeps going for you? I don't care. Kick the damned dog! We've got to keep moving. She's dying . . .*

Tiamat's tent was down, knocked over by the wind. Little streams of water ran over the skins. Tiamat was just another lump under the material, soaking in the mud.

Martin threw everything aside and dug her out. Her clothes were plastered to her body, slick with sweat and mud. He knelt, draped her over his shoulder, and folded his cape around her. She mumbled something unclear and held on desperately. She felt hot and feverish and she shook with shivering. He got ready to stand up.

Wait, Artie said. *There's her grain. In that bag to your right. Just by your hand. Open it. Run your fingers through it.*

"I don't have time for that!"

Do it anyway, Artie ordered. *You don't have time not to do it.*

Martin cursed, opened the pouch, spilled the grain over his hand.

Triticum monococcum—einkorn wheat, Artie said. He hesitated. *Good, good . . . Damn!*

"What?"

I hoped, but . . . None of it contains TmHKT1;5-A.

Martin stood. His knees creaked. Tiamat groaned. She was definitely up-time. She weighed too damned much.

"Next time," Martin promised Artie. "We're going to find it. I promise."

I just hoped . . . I thought that, maybe . . .

Martin put his head down. He concentrated on the ground, on the mud and the rocks and one foot in front of the other. Uphill and downhill, slip and slide, almost down in the mud, rain in his eyes, a loose leather strap whipping his side in the wind, and uphill again.

You're home.

Martin pushed aside the privacy curtain and the night drape, laid Tiamat next to the fire, and pulled the drape and curtain back to block off the rain and the wind. He collapsed on the floor, breathing heavily, and let his eyesight come back to normal.

"Symptoms?"

Fever. Buboes. Armpit, groin, neck. Chills. No sign of necrosis, yet, but it's coming on fast.

"Plague," Martin said. He spat.

Plague, Artie agreed flatly. *Damned fleas. Doesn't match—exactly—the modern bubonic, but it's close enough.*

"Stop any seizures. And wake her up enough so she'll listen to me."

It's going to hurt, Artie warned. *She isn't going to like it.*

"Tough," Martin said. He reached for a jug of fresh beer, the terrible stuff, and a handful of reed straws. He pulled the plug out of the top of the stone vessel and pushed the straws through the top scum into the beer underneath. He moved up close to Tiamat, held her head in his lap. Her eyelids flickered and opened.

"What the hell are you doing to me?" she whispered. Her voice was low and hoarse and he could tell her throat hurt. She sounded confused, uncertain.

"Drink," he ordered, and pushed the straws into her mouth. "Artie, help her."

But, her AI—

"Will lead, follow or get the hell out of the way. Do it. Now."

Tiamat tried to turn her head away, then drew up suddenly, as Artie pulled her diaphragm and tightened her throat muscles. Beer filled her mouth and dribbled down her lips and neck. She gagged. Martin kept her head forced down on the straws with one hand. She struggled but was too weak to get away from him.

"More," he ordered, and tilted the jar with his other hand. "Or Artie will help you again."

Tiamat closed her eyes, and forced herself to drink more.

Enough, Artie said. *We don't want her to get diarrhea.*

Martin eased the straws out of Tiamat's mouth, laid her down on the bed. He stripped her naked, quickly and efficiently and tossed her wet clothes next to the fire. He dried her off and tucked her under a heavy bearskin blanket.

"Poppy juice?"

Just a bit, Artie agreed, grudgingly. *It will help with the muscle pain.*

Martin reached across the bed for another jar, opened it, scooped out a thin, white oil. He felt Tiamat shiver again. He shook her gently until her eyes opened, blearily.

"Open up," Martin ordered Tiamat.

"No more, please . . ."

"Shut up. This is something different."

She opened her mouth. Martin dabbed her lips with poppy paste.

"Lick it off."

She licked her lips in tiny, little jerks, as if she fell asleep between each move. Or as if she was too weak to do any more each time.

"Whatever it was you made me drink, it smelled terrible," she said, in a low, cracked, feverish, voice.

"Not worried about that," Martin said. "How did it taste?"

"Not bad," she admitted. "Sweet. Fizzy. A little metallic. I think I'm catching a buzz."

"The buzz is the beer and the opium. The metallic means you got a good dose of the right stuff. Go to sleep."

Tiamat nodded, her eyes half closed. Her head turned slightly to the side. She began to whisper to herself, the words slurred. Something sounded familiar. Martin leaned forward to listen, then leaned back and looked thoughtful.

What's wrong?

"It's a bedtime prayer. The kind you teach a child to say every night, before they go to sleep."

And . . . what's wrong with that?

"Amplify."

". . . Angele Dei, qui custos es mei, Me tibi comissum pietate superna; Hodie, Hac nocte illumina, custodi, rege, et guberna. Amen."

That's Latin. A Christian prayer in Latin.

"Yep."

Carthage destroys Rome in all of the timelines we've found here. Long before Christianity. That prayer does not exist here. That prayer will never exist here, anytime or anywhen.

"Yep."

Now, isn't that special? Artie asked thoughtfully. *Our little Kehin spy seems to be a leaker . . .*

The next day, the rain was gone.

Martin sat outside, in his workroom. The hut door was open. He saw Tiamat inside. She breathed slowly, but steadily, the blanket pushed aside.

"Used the handle on her yet?" Martin asked.

Yes.

"And?"

Her uncertainty is greatly reduced, Artie said.

"She was supposed to die last night."

Maybe, Artie admitted. *She still has some uncertainty. Not much new data yet, but her line is starting to trend up.*

"How long until she's a nexus again?"

Five months? Six months? Can't be certain.

"Can we use her?"

Not if she's dead, Artie warned. *She's still sick.*

Martin stood, headed for the hut.

"Then we better keep her alive. I'm getting tired of this place."

Martin sat in the hut. He used a piece of antler to pressure flake the new knife, to sharpen the edge. The handle was now wrapped in leather and decorated on both sides. The priest only charged one arrow head for the blessing.

"You're good at that."

"Thanks," Martin said. He did not look down at her. Instead, he held up the knife into a shaft of sunlight that fell through the vent opening in the roof. He squinted at the edge and turned the knife back and forth. Sunlight reflected off the shiny grey-black blade and danced on the inside walls of the hut. Satisfied, he put the knife down and turned to face her.

"Lots of practice?" she asked.

"Years."

"How many years?" Tiamat asked.

"That's classified," Martin said slowly. "Perhaps."

Tiamat studied his face. She tried to sit up, fell back, tried again and managed to prop herself on one elbow. She felt weak and sore and drawn out. She glanced over at the beer jar. Martin passed her the jar, a strip of beef jerky, and a fresh straw.

Another couple of days, Artie said, in silent. *Just to be safe. She's probably cured now, but just to be safe.*

"Question time," Martin said. He kept his hand on the knife.

"All right."

"What is your real name? I know it's not Tiamat, so don't try that on me."

"I talked while I was sick."

You babbled like a toddler with her favorite doll, Artie said. He did not bother with silent mode.

Tiamat sat quiet for a long moment. Finally she nodded to herself and looked up at Martin.

"Est nomen meum Rachel."

My name is Rachel, Artie said, satisfied, in silent. *Latin combined with a Hebrew name. Damned certain she's not from here. Called it.*

"You ready?" Martin asked, in silent.

I still think it's too risky, Artie fretted.

"You have a better idea?"

Silence. Stretched out to a pause. Rachel studied Martin and the empty space over his shoulder.

No, Artie said regretfully. *I don't like it one damned bit. But we need help. Go for it.*

"And my full name is Martin," Martin said to Rachel.

"Martinus," Rachel said, thoughtfully. "Roman. Not a popular name choice in Carthage."

Martin said nothing and waited.

"Why am I alive?" Rachel asked.

"Plague bacillus," Martin said, and pointed to the beer jar in her hand, "responds very well to tetracycline."

She looked at the jars, then up at Martin.

"You're not just brewing beer. You're culturing antibiotics."

Martin shrugged.

"It grows in the beer if you start with the right grain harvested with the right soil fungi. And they like a beer buzz here as much as they did when I was in school. It brings them back to me after they go on a hunt or out to gather. People talk when they're all together and a little drunk. I learn things and, hell, I can't be everywhere, all the time. Think of it as a force multiplier."

And if we go to all the trouble of grooming the locals, we want to keep them alive. It's a nasty world out there. Lots of ways to catch an infection. So when our special people leave us, they always take some of our special beer, Artie added.

"Son of a bitch," Rachel said.

"Which brings us back to you," Martin said smoothly. "Why did something like the plague bite you? Where's your artie?"

Rachel went silent for a moment. Her expression changed. She closed her eyes, then opened them. Her eyes seemed to glisten, as if she was trying not to cry.

This is not fair, Artie protested, in silent. *She's still sick. Her defenses are down. You just got her real name, you just told her your own name. Everything you're doing reminds her of home.*

"Life isn't fair," Martin replied, in silent.

Damn it, boy! You're offering her hope. And we don't have any hope to offer!

Rachel touched her head, gently, with her fingers.

"My artie was modeled after my mother. They hurt her when they found her. They made me listen while they did it."

Bastards.

"Then they changed her base code and kept the key. I can't talk to her, she can't talk to me. It's like we're in separate black boxes. They promised they'd bring her back, give me the key, if I did what they wanted." She looked up at Martin. "They keep their word, in a way. When I go uptime to Qart-hadast, they wake her up, let me talk to her again. Let her work on me, to keep me young."

But they never give you the key, do they? She repairs you, then they turn her off and tell you you're going back downtime and unless you do what you're told, you'll never see her again, Artie said. He sounded cold, distant, calm.

Furious.

"So she's not here, now, to keep you alive," Martin said. "When you're back here, you're on your own."

"Yes."

"Artie?" Martin asked in silent.

I can break any encryption, Artie replied confidently, in silent. *Might take a while but, yes, I'll see what I can do.*

"How long is a while?" Martin asked, in silent.

A while, Artie repeated, testily, in silent. *And the more you distract me, the longer it takes.*

"How long have they been doing this to you?" Martin asked Rachel.

"I leaked over to this timeline about a hundred biological years ago. It was a rough ride. I thought I was going to go . . . away. But I came through. To here and now. The Kehin detected me, grabbed me, brought me forward to Carthage. They call it by its Phoenician name, Qart-hadast. The name that Rome trampled in the dust."

"Why did they keep you alive?"

Rachel sat up and saw her things, laid out neatly beside her. She watched Martin warily, then reached over and touched her knife.

"You know quantum mechanics?"

Martin smiled.

"As well as anyone. God and dice and all that."

Rachel smiled. She picked up her knife.

"A long time from now, a little over eleven thousand years that way," Rachel vaguely pointed forward with the knife, "a physicist named Aharonov is going to do a double slit experiment, to determine whether a photon is a wave or a particle."

"That's been done before," Martin said, puzzled. "It's both, depending on which slit a person observes."

"Aharonov is going to use a special twist," Rachel said. "Delayed choice. And he's going to show that a choice made in the future can impact the past."

If the future can affect the past, then one philosophical argument is settled, Artie said, thoughtfully, in open. *There is predestination. Everyone has a given fate. There is no such thing as free will.*

Rachel nodded. She held out the knife.

"The detector is in the handle. It only works if I run it. It apparently has to match up with someone from its home timeline. That's me," she said. "The Carthaginians have been unable to replicate it, so they keep me alive. If I use it on their time travelers I can detect when their future and their present are starting to get out of synch. I warn them and they leave."

"And if they don't leave?" Martin asked.

"They get more and more uncertain and then . . . they're gone."

I've got the reference in our library, Artie said. He sounded puzzled. *Aharonov's claims caused a little stir in our timeline. Then our theorists fussed over it, extended quantum theory, found it was a misinterpretation, equipment error, the usual.*

"That's your timeline," Rachel said. "Not here."

"Try it on me," Martin said. Rachel shrugged. She pointed the knife at Martin. She expression went absent for a moment, then she was back. She frowned. She pointed the knife away, then pointed it at herself, then back at Martin.

"It must be broken," she said, puzzled. "It works with me. A little fuzzy, not as good as usual, but it doesn't work with you. I'm not getting anything."

I don't know whether to be happy or upset, Artie said in silent.

"Shut up."

We still don't have a future.

A week went by. Rachel tried to argue her way out of the hut. Artie held firm.

Photo-sensitivity is a side affect of tetracycline. And I've been giving you a big dose, he warned. *I don't want you stumbling around outside, blinded by the sun. So sit your ass down in here and do something useful!*

Rachel made a face. She glanced, unenthusiastically, at the bowl of cold wheat gruel and the other bowl of chewed-up starter mash next to it.

"I am sick of—!"

Besides, Artie interrupted smoothly, *I want to make sure you and everything you own is thoroughly de-loused and de-flead. I'm sorry, but the last thing we can handle is an epidemic in the camp. Too many people coming and going. Martin does what he has to do, when there is an epidemic, but he gets upset. Disposing of the children's bodies bothers him the most. Brings back memories I can't erase.*

Rachel shut her mouth. She thought for a moment, then slowly nodded. She reached for the gruel.

"I still need clothes," Rachel said firmly. She glanced at Martin, working on the other side of the hut. "I can't stay in here naked or only wrapped in a blanket. And most of Martin's clothes will definitely not fit."

Use Ianna's old things, Artie suggested.

"They're too short on me!"

Modesty, Artie said, exasperated, *is one of the stupidest bio concepts in a long, long line of stupid ideas. If Martin had wanted to—*

"Artie."

What?

"Shut up," Martin said. He turned to Rachel. "I can get you new clothes. I'm not good at making them, but I'll trade with Asherah. Might take a couple of days."

"Thank you," Rachel said. She hesitated, looked down at her blanket, then over at Ianna's clothes, neatly folded and stacked in the back of the hut.

"I suppose, in the meantime, if I have to," she said grudgingly. She looked shyly at Martin. "She won't mind? You won't mind?"

"It will be fine," Martin assured her. He stood, pulled aside the night drape and the outside curtain. "I'll just step outside while you try them on."

Bio's!

And on the eighth day—

"Let her go," Martin ordered, exasperated. Rachel paced back and forth inside the hut like a caged animal. A caged animal in very short clothing. Martin shifted uncomfortably.

Fine, Artie said grudgingly. *Everything we could find is piled up next to the canopy.*

Rachel escaped gratefully. Outside she blinked at the sunlight, even under the shade from the canopy, until her eyes adjusted. Then she spotted her things.

Or what was left of them.

Her tent was in pieces, ripped and torn and useless. A pair of shoes. Her bandeau. A broken spear, flint tip gone.

"The storm got worse after I got you," Martin apologized as he exited the hut after her. They stood together, side by side, over the pathetic little pile. "We found what we could but we were busy with you and, well . . ."

"It's all right," she said. She reached down, touched the bandeau.

It's safe, Artie assured her. *I killed all the little flea bastards. And their eggs. And their eggs eggs.*

She picked it up, stood, and fastened the bandeau in place around her neck. The fibers were ragged, worn and frayed, but it felt right when it settled into place on top of her breasts. She glanced at Martin. He seemed awkward, uncertain.

"I suppose you have to go now."

She seemed just as clumsy and hesitant.

"The Kehin will expect me to come back," she agreed. "But . . ."

"What?"

"Sometimes I stay longer, after I've told everyone else to evacuate," she said, in a rush. "The uncertainty grows because some event, something key to their timelines, is about to occur. Even though all the Travelers here are from congruent lines, it's still a center of uncertainty."

"But you're not from this timeline," he said slowly.

"Exactly. It might cause them uncertainty but it does nothing to me. Still, I don't dare change anything or I might lose the timeline where the Kehin can unlock Mom. So I just stay here, quiet and out of the way, and record. Sometimes I earn a reward and they give us extra time together."

I have an—, Artie said in silent.

"Shut up," Martin said. He turned to Rachel.

"Stay," Martin said, impulsively. Suddenly he felt it again, the loneliness he kept pushed away, like he had that night so long, long ago. Back when the stars looked so much different than they did now and he realized he would have to live his way home.

"Stay? I can't. My tent, my supplies . . . I have nothing."

"Stay here. In the hut. With me."

"With you?"

"Yes," Martin said. He gestured helplessly. "I need someone who can help me with the beer and the flints and mashing the wheat and—"

"Hush," she said. She stepped closer to him, but not close enough to touch. "I'll stay. But just for a few days."

Martin smiled.

"But just for a few days," she warned, and smiled back at him.

All right, what's your idea? I admit it, I'm all out of if-then, even in random mode.

It was months later. Martin sat outside the camp, on the crest of a ridge where he could see across the valley and up the hill to the temple on top of Gobekli Tepe. He absently chewed a long piece of rye grass.

"Let me see Gobekli, again."

Artie shifted his vision to binocular mode.

Gobekli Tepe's latest incarnation was almost finished. The Tall Men, giant T-shaped pillars, twenty five feet high, solid limestone blocks, carved with shapes in bas-relief, were almost set into place facing each other. The benches facing the open area between the tall men were ready. The smaller pillars, arranged in a circle around the Tall Men, were up. Thatch and wooden poles, to make and support the roof, lay in piles, ready to be assembled and cover the whole temple once the tall men were ready.

The entrance was still a wooden framework, a skeleton of lashed-together branches and limbs. It was deliberately short—to make everyone duck and lower their heads—and winding. When it was ready it would become a corridor, covered with layers of hides to make a darkened tunnel with just enough torches and openings to see a step or two ahead. The idea, one of the priests had told him after a night of drinking, was to have people experience the darkness of death and dying before they entered the temple to celebrate and honor their own dead.

It was almost time for the tribes to gather and the ceremonies to begin.

You want to go to the temple and work the crowds? One more time?

"No," Martin said decisively. "How many times have we tried that? How many hundreds of years? It's never there. Too many people, too much going on, too hard to figure out what to do. I'm sick of searching Gobekli. It never works."

But we know it comes through Gobekli on its way to Carthage, Artie argued.

"Agreed," Martin said. "Every trail we've followed shows it comes through here. But despite everything we've tried, the Qart-hadast Travelers still come back here from the future every few months. If we had broken the chain, they wouldn't come back. So we haven't done the job right yet."

Martin shook his head.

"The camp is the key," Martin said, stubborn and determined. "The people come here, to the camp. This is the key, not Gobekli. It spreads out from *here* and eventually ends up in Carthage."

Even if this is the change locus, what good does it do us? Artie asked, despairingly. *When the temple is dedicated, when the Tall Men are set in place, all the tribes will flow in here with their dead. Thousands of people. It's even worse than searching up at the temple. Too many people and too crowded. How the hell do we find it?*

"We need to make it look for us. A honey trap is the best idea."

I don't like it.

"You don't have to like it. You just have to tell me if your if-then thinks it will work."

Martin sat quietly on the hillside. He finished the rye grass straw, tossed it aside, picked another and started chewing fresh.

Before him were plains and rolling hillsides, green and fertile, fresh with rain, crossed with small streams, dotted with marshes. A flock of goats, a small herd of gazelle. The plains of Edin.

"Maybe I should change my name to Eve," he asked thoughtfully.

Wrong sex, Artie said. *And even worse attitude.*

"Answer?"

Maybe, Artie said, thoughtfully. *My if-then says maybe your idea will work. But you know what that maybe means?*

"I know," Martin said, morosely. He licked his lips, moved his jaw back and forth. *More beer.*

"Rachel can help us," Martin said. He did not look happy. "More wheat gruel. More starter mash."

If you want to build a trap, you have to bait it . . .

"So we concentrate here this time."

Beer. And Rachel's knife.

Artie went silent. Martin imagined the code, all the if-then spinning around if-then, subroutines chasing subroutines, with random changes thrown in, evolved in, evolved out . . .

And what if you do find it? Artie asked. *If we do what we have to do, all the Qart-hadast timelines, all the Travelers from those futures, are going to shift away. You'll be alone again. And what about Rachel? She must have some small connection to these timelines, or she never would have made it here. Are you going to just use her and then let her, maybe . . . go away? Damn it, Martin, if she's linked to Qart-hadast she won't even get to say goodbye to her mother!*

"Are the needs of the one," Martin asked, "more important than the needs of the many?"

Yes. That's exactly what I'm asking you. That's exactly what my if-then wants to know.

Martin stared at Gobekli. Even at full magnification, the priests and the slaves seemed like tiny little ants, unimportant, something to be brushed away and ignored. Not something important. Not something like himself.

"That's a damned good question. A damned good question."

"We need to talk."

Rachel lounged comfortably under the canopy, stretched out along a bench, a stitched-together strip of marsh reeds over her eyes, like a sleeping band. A pair of rabbits, freshly caught and cleaned and skinned, roasted gently over the fire. A pile of greens were in a stone bowl. A two-person stone vessel of fresh beer, latest batch, zero on the tetracycline, light on the hawthorn berries, heavy on the grapes and honey, straws already in place, waited to go with dinner.

She wore new clothes now, stitched and shaped by Asherah. Rachel filled them out comfortably, her weight finally back from the plague and the diarrhea after Artie accidentally dosed her with too much tetracycline. She looked damned good. Martin saw her and smiled.

"Something up?" she asked and sat up. She took off the sleep band and set it to the side.

Check the handle of your knife. On yourself.

Rachel slipped out her knife and, unobtrusively, scanned herself.

"Uncertainty is going up," she said. Suddenly, she looked nervous. She looked up at Martin. He sat down on the bench across from her.

"Now, check me."

She turned the knife toward Martin. Frowned. Looked up at him.

"Nothing. No uncertainty at all."

It's time to explain some things, Artie said.

"A long time ago," Martin started, "a long, long, time ago, I came back. Not to here. Not to anywhere near here. But I came back. A long when back. One hell of a lot farther than now. I had a job to do. I did it. I didn't want to do it, but I did it. And when I finished that job, I couldn't go back home."

"You changed your own future," Rachel said. Her eyes widened. "That's why the the causality scan doesn't work on you. You don't have a future."

What a lovely way to phrase it.

"Shut up," Martin said, automatically, to Artie. He nodded to Rachel. "But correct. I have no future. My timeline doesn't exist. Not at all, and not in any way. I can go farther back, but I can't go forward. If I go back, I have to live my way, one day at a time, back to now, in a slightly different timeline where I never existed before."

"You're lost. You're trapped, here in the past," Rachel said. She sounded fascinated, like Martin was some kind of insect frozen in amber.

"I am not trapped," Martin said, determined. He stared directly into Rachel's eyes.

"I have no destiny, no pre-ordained future," he said, slowly. "But I'm going forward anyway. One day at a time. And I'm going to make my own future. I'm going to make it be the way I want it to be. And nothing and no one is going to stand in my way."

"You left someone behind when you went back," Rachel said.

"I left everything behind. Everyone and everything," Martin agreed. His voice hardened. "It had to be done. But I'm going to get them all back. I'm going to build that future, one day at a time, until I get back everything I lost."

"It can't be done," Rachel said. She sounded uncertain. She turned away and shook her head. Martin reached out, touched her shoulder, turned her back toward him. He lifted up her chin until she looked at him.

"We are going to do it," he said. "You and me and Artie."

"How?"

To start with, we're going to make sure that Rome burns Carthage to the ground . . .

The Tall Men and the roof were in place. The dark corridor with its deep black entrance were all in place. The temple at Gobekli Tepe was ready.

At first the visitors were just an individual or two, awed and silent, escorted by the priests through the corridor and up to the Tall Men. There they touched the stones, ran their fingers over the bas relief sculptures and left a gift for the gods.

But word spread quickly. The hunter gatherers came home from across the plains. Soon individual camps, families and clans and tribes, dotted the hills and valleys all around the central hill of Gobekli Tepe. During the day there was a constant flow of people back and forth, up and down, between the different tents and shelters.

Hunting parties went out hungry and came back, mostly with gazelle, but with auroch and wild pig and goats and anything else they could catch or trap. Fishing and gathering went on relentlessly down at the rivers and creeks and in the marshes. Trading, for bone and obsidian and flint, was a busy trade. Young men and women, as they always did, found each other.

And everyone wanted beer . . .

"Tiamat, a fresh straw! I have a rabbit for you."

"Not enough." Rachel shook her head.

"Two rabbits, then. But only for the latest batch, with the extra honey."

"Enki, you've already had too much. You can barely stand."

"I don't need to stand to drink!" Enki sat down, unsteady, on the bench Martin had set up outside his hut. He grinned, two teeth gone from a wrestling accident the night before. Tiamat handed him another jar of beer. Enki passed over two rabbits in payment. She looked at them, critically, felt them.

"All fur and no meat," she complained. "Enki, I think you've cheated me."

Unobtrusively, she scanned him with her knife handle.

Negative, Artie said. He was an expert with the causality tool by now. *Tell him we need more wheat grain for the next batch.*

"Enki," Martin asked casually. "You ever go up by Lake Van?"

Enki made a face.

"It's a long walk up there."

Martin nodded.

"And the water's no good," Enki added. He sipped and smiled.

"Good beer."

"Enki. Lake Van."

"What? No, I never go there. Too salty. Why?"

"I heard there was some new kind of wheat from up there." Martin shrugged, pointed at the multiple vats of beer brewing behind him. "I always need more wheat. And if it tasted different, well, some people like to try different beers. A woman last night said Lake Van has the best wheat."

Enki nodded.

"Talk to Nilik, down in the valley. His family lives close to Van and he always has plenty of wheat. Maybe you can make a trade."

"Thanks."

"Now that I've helped you," Enki said, "I'd like to point out that my jar is getting a little empty. . . ."

"My uncertainty is rising again."

Which means we're getting close.

"Which means I could just vanish in an eye blink," Rachel said sharply.

Martin hesitated.

No, Artie said, instantly, in silent. *I might not be able to read your mind, but I know how you think. I know what you're going to say. Don't even start—*

"We could wait," Martin said slowly, "until you're back uptime. With your mother."

"With the Kehin," Rachel said sharply. "Without you and Artie. Trapped in Qart-hadast."

"There is that," Martin admitted.

"More beer!" someone shouted from the crowd at the front of the hut. "More beer!"

"Martin, this is my friend Nilik," Enki said. He sat down on the bench. Nilik stood beside him.

Nilik was sun-browned and wiry, medium height, a lined face and black haired with a few grey streaks. Uptime, Martin would have guessed he was a well-preserved grandfather. Here he was probably a medium-aged father.

He carried a small leather pouch on his belt. Martin smiled and waved him to sit on the bench next to Enki.

"Get Rachel," Martin said, in silent.

Martin reached down and touched a small trough of beer.

Not that, Artie interrupted. *The special beer. If this the real thing we want to make sure he's healthy and he makes it back to Lake Van.*

Martin reached to the side, picked up a different trough. He placed it in front of both his customers and handed a pair of rye grass straws to Enki and Nilik.

"On the house," he said. He sat down and slid his own straw into the beer. It tasted much like he remembered a wine cooler from uptime, sweet and sour, bubbly with a honey blur. There was also a slight metallic taste from tetracycline.

"Enki tells me you trade for wheat," Nilik said after the first few sips.

"I do," Martin said. He waved behind and around him. "I'm a flint knapper—"

"—best one in camp!" Enki boasted. And sipped more beer.

"—and I brew on the side," Martin continued. Nilik studied him for a moment, took another sip of beer. He nodded slightly.

"I need a new knife. And a fresh spear point," Nilik said.

"I need wheat. And honey and grapes," Martin answered.

Nilik shook his head.

"No grapes. Some honey, but I didn't bring it with me."

"What did you bring with you?"

Nilik pulled the pouch off his belt and set it on the table. Martin unstrung the top, looked inside and spilled some of the wheat into his palm.

"Artie?" Martin asked, in silent.

Triticum monococcum—einkorn wheat, Artie said. *Give me a minute. Maybe, maybe—*

Rachel hurried back under the canopy. She smiled automatically at Enki and Nilik and stooped to whisper in Martin's ear.

"Trouble."

He looked up at her. She pointed uphill.

Ianna and two other people, a man and a woman, walked downhill. Ianna was on point, like a scout, leading the way. The man and woman were hard-faced, strongly built and tall. They looked uncomfortable in skin clothing. No one got in their way.

Well, they don't quite fit in, do they? All they need is little plastic earpieces and dark suits and glasses.

"The Secret Service doesn't exist yet," Martin said drily, in silent, to both of them.

Enforcers are enforcers, Artie said with an electronic shrug. *Frumentarii or KGB or Inquisitors. The look is always the same.*

"Chayil," Rachel pointed at the woman. "And Kehin," she pointed at the man.

How's the causality?

Rachel touched her knife and stood up straight. She smiled, friendly, at Nilik and Enki.

"Off the charts," she said calmly, in silent. "It must have drawn them here. Something big is ready to go, one way or the other."

And we have a match! Artie shouted. *Sodium transporter gene TmHKT1;5-A. Son of a bitch, Martin. We found it.*

"Kill it," Martin ordered, in silent. "All of it. Everything in this bag."

Martin felt a slight vibration in his arm and ultraviolet flickered at the edge of his vision. His hand flashed warmer, just for a moment.

Done.

"Now infect Nilik."

Martin felt his arm tingle. He reached out, casually, and moved his straw to a different part of the beer trough. He accidentally touched Nilik's hand.

And . . . we have liftoff. Nilik is now infected with the pesticide 5-a gene killer virus, Artie said. *Doesn't hurt people but it loves your intestinal tract. He'll be so full of pesticide by the time he gets home that he'll kill every 5-a in his camp and every patch of it he goes near back at Lake Van.*

"We won't get it all," Rachel said, regretfully, in silent. "Some of it will survive."

"Some," Martin agreed, also in silent. He glanced at Ianna and her posse. They were closing the distance to the hut. "My guess is the wheat with that gene is too dispersed to get it all. Enough will be left to be discovered one day in the far, far future. But we're going to find out, right now, if we killed enough of it to make a timeline difference."

"If I disappear . . ."

"Stay here, next to me. Artie, keep a link to her."

It might not be enough . . .

"If anyone has a better idea—" Martin said, exasperated. It was an old argument from over the last few weeks. Rachel shook her head. Artie went carrier wave if-then blank for a moment, then back to normal. It was the best he could manage for a sigh.

Martin took a long drink of beer. At the end he almost gagged on some of the scum from the bottom of the trough. Enki looked at the trough, disappointed, then up at Martin, hopeful.

"Another beer for every sack of grain," Martin said to Nilik. "A full honeycomb for a spear point."

"Half a honeycomb for the spear point. One beer for every sack of grain," Nilik countered, grudgingly.

Ianna and the Kehin and the Chayil were closer, pushing their way through the crowded paths. Martin wanted to grab Enki and Nilik and drag them away, to shove them out of the way, to kick them in the ass, to do anything to get them out of here—

"Done!" Martin agreed. He stood and held his hand open and up. Nilik looked surprised, then pleased. He placed his hand down and open. They shook.

"I need the grain and the honey as soon as you can get it," Martin said. Ianna and the Carthaginians stepped under the canopy, stood next to Nilik and Enki.

"But—"

"Now."

Enki and Nilik scowled, shrugged, then turned away and walked back into the crowd. Enki looked regretfully over his shoulder at Martin.

"Don't forget me!"

Martin smiled and waved.

"Not bloody likely," he said around his own smile.

"Mar, I'm sorry—"

"Quiet," the Kehin man said to Ianna. His voice was low and soft and sharp. Martin remembered voices like that. Usually from people who wore uniforms with no rank insignia. Cheka, MSS, Kempeitai, Gestapo.

Like a snake, Artie said, in silent. *Remember, back in that swamp . . .*

"Get into them," Martin ordered, in silent. "You know what we're looking for. They might not have it exactly on them, but their weapons will use something similar. Break the encryption."

"We're still going up on uncertainty," Rachel said, also in silent. Her voice was tight. She stood just behind and to the side of Martin. She held a flint knife.

"Don't even think about it, little one," the Chayil woman said. Up close she was much bigger than Rachel, almost as big as Martin. She sounded amused, contemptuous.

"Officers," Martin said, politely.

"You are not Chayil," the Kehin said. The Chayil nodded. Ianna just looked miserable.

"Never said I was," Martin said, mildly.

"You implied it!" the Kehin hissed. He gestured at Ianna. "Not just this one. Others told us the same story. You implied and acted and misled."

"How can I control what others believe? That's your business, isn't it? I would hate to interfere."

"You're a leaker," the Kehin hissed. He stared at Rachel. "Just like that one."

"I am a leaker," Martin admitted.

"Uncertainty just jumped again," Rachel said, in silent.

"When? Which timeline?" the Chayil asked.

I have it, Artie said triumphantly. *Son of a bitch, I have it!*

"Then use it, damn it!" Martin snapped, in silent. In the open, he leaned forward, hands on the table. The Kehin and the Chayil shifted a half step back, separated slightly, positioned themselves.

"I'm from a long time ago. And a long time forward," Martin said. "And I'm not done yet."

"Take him," the Kehin ordered. The Chayil began to move forward. Martin stood, relaxed, but in position. The Chayil looked at him warily. Rachel stepped to the side and forward, toward the Kehin.

Done.

"Ianna," Martin said, his eyes fixed on the Chayil. He pulled a small, tightly wound package from his belt, tossed it to Ianna.

"Jump home. Now!"

"Mar, I can't leave you! I love—"

"Now!"

Ianna hesitated. Rachel waved the causality handle in her direction and nodded frantically.

"Last chance," Rachel whispered. "Please . . ."

Ianna's eyes widened. She nodded and flickered uptime.

The Kehin glanced at where Ianna had been. His mouth tightened and his eyes narrowed.

"Bitch! I'll deal with her when we get back—"

"I don't think so," Martin said. He stood straight, dropped his fighting pose. "I don't think you'll ever see her again. I do wonder who and what you will see again. And when you'll be."

Nilik just reached his camp. He's going through the wheat, putting it into sacks.

"Activate the gene killer."

Now?

"Uncertainty just maxed out!" Rachel said.

"Now," Martin said out loud. He spoke to the Kehin and the Chayil. "Goodbye."

Activated.

The Kehin and the Chayil were gone.

Silence under the canopy. Rachel licked her lips and looked up at Martin. She touched herself, to make sure she was still real, then touched Martin.

Rachel, is that you, sweetheart?, a new voice asked.

"Mom?"

And a good time was had by all, Artie said smugly. *I do believe we are going to be whending our way home tonight.*

"The key was the salt resistant wheat," Martin explained later that night. They sat around a fire outside the hut, the canopy tucked out of the way, the clear stars above them. Rachel rested comfortably against Martin, his arm around her.

"I don't understand," Rachel confessed. Her mother AI was activated, working her biology, making repairs to both Rachel and Artie. Martin heard her, in the background, through Artie, clucking in disapproval, murmuring and soothing both of them.

"In our timelines, Carthage fought three wars against Rome. Each time, the Carthaginians lost. Mainly because they only had a limited amount of arable land. Starvation hurt them much more than it did the Romans," Martin said.

"But here?" Rachel asked.

"Here the people of Qart-hadast had the same geography, with the salt flats and the Chatt al Djerid salt lake south of them. But here they also had salt-resistant wheat, descended from Nilik's wheat, to grow on the salt plains. With that extra food, and Hannibal and Hasdrubal as generals, Carthage defeated Rome," Martin explained.

"And now?"

"And now . . . I don't know. The Carthaginian Travelers are gone from the camp. I don't know who else is here instead. I don't know the future of this timeline. But I know what it's *not* going to be," he said, and smiled.

This timeline is closer to what we're all looking for, Artie said. *Some of my self-repair algorithms work now.*

"So now you're not dying?"

I wouldn't go that far, Artie said grudgingly. *And Mom may have helped. A little.*

"But can we now say that the rumors of your imminent demise were greatly exaggerated?"

I don't know that reference.

"Then I'm not there yet," Martin said. He looked up at the stars. "But I'm getting closer."

The next day, Martin woke alone.

He dressed, stepped out of the hut. Rachel sat on a bench, a bowl of wheat gruel in her hand. She tipped her head toward another bowl. Martin picked it up, gratefully.

Her backpack, fully equipped, sat on the ground between her feet. He glanced at it, then over at her.

"I went forward last night, after you went to sleep," she said.

"You wanted to see if you could go home?"

"Yes."

"And?"

Rachel shook her head. She ate another scoop of gruel.

"I can get closer, but then I'm blocked. Something is still wrong, uptime."

Martin pointed to the pack on the floor.

"It's not unpacked."

"No."

"You're moving up there?"

Rachel put down her bowl.

"Yesterday, just before Artie unleashed the virus, you tossed something to Ianna."

Martin hesitated, then shrugged.

"It was a bandeau, like the one you wear. She thought it had style, back when you told her to get out of here and go home. I had Asherah weave one for her."

"One last present?"

"Something like that."

"Because you always get what you want. Because you never give up. Which meant you had to leave her behind and you didn't want her to forget you," Rachel finished. She stood.

"I'm leaving for the same reason. I don't want to get left behind, by anything you have to do back here. So I'm going uptime to wait for you. To me it will only be a few days. Mom says it will be easier to repair me, to keep me alive there. At least until you arrive."

"Where is this place, this next roadblock of yours?" Martin asked.

"It's named Catal Huyuk. It's the first city in human history. Fascinating place," Rachel said.

"Because it's the first human city," Martin said. He nodded. She looked at him, puzzled.

She shook her head.

"First cities," she said and shrugged. "Not that interesting. Too many of them. First city in China, first city in India, first city in Aztlan. The usual traveler crowd in all of them. A lot different, but mostly the same."

"In that case, what's so interesting about this Catal place? Except that it's as far as you can go."

"No doors," Rachel said. She adjusted her bandeau so it rested snugly, just above her breasts. "Thousands of people, and not a single door in the whole damned place. Just hatches and ladders and little, tiny, windows, way up high in the walls."

"Sounds horrible."

"Attracts Travelers like flies to honey. Always fresh data there," Rachel said.

"When will you be there?"

"A week from Tuesday."

Martin flicked Artie's database.

"It's over a hundred miles away from here."

"That's why I've got to start walking."

Martin checked again. He dropped the connection.

"Catal peaks in 7000 BCE. That's two thousand years from now."

Rachel stepped forward, picked up her pack, and turned to leave camp. She looked back at him, over her shoulder.

"Then I suppose you better start living . . ."

A few minutes later, Martin filled his own backpack and stepped out into the sunshine.

And that's it? Artie asked. *We just leave the hut and the beer and everything else?*

Martin shrugged.

"No archeologist never found any sign of permanent habitation anywhere around Gobekli Tepe, so we can't stay here. A city might grow up around us. So, we leave. Enki and Asherah and Nilik can scavenge the hut and whatever is left. We can only use what we can carry. Everything else will gradually fall apart and rot and erode and be gone."

And what are we going to do now? It's not going to take us two thousand years to walk to Catal Huyuk. And I can't see you sitting in one place for that long. What are we going to do in the meantime?

"I've always liked the water," Martin said firmly. "The boat is already invented, but all the boats in all the world, right now, have to be paddled. Best evidence, though, is that sometime, in the next thousand or so years, someone, somewhere, is going to invent the sail. Maybe they'll need a little help. And maybe some other people will need some help with some other ideas. Remember the old Japanese proverb Soichiro Honda used to use?"

It can't be old, Artie grumbled. *Japan hasn't been invented yet. It's just a bunch of starving people huddled in skin tents. And Honda's not going to be born for another eleven thousand years!*

Martin ignored him.

"'Raise the sail with your stronger hand.' Means you need to go after the opportunities where you can help the most."

Martin started to walk down the hill, away from Gobekli Tepe.

"Now, Artie," he said, and his voice faded away as he walked, "I see a whole world of opportunity out here for us. Yes, sir, a whole big world . . ."

death on mars

MADELINE ASHBY

Sometimes you have to keep secrets, but there's always a price to pay for keeping them.

Madeline Ashby *is a science fiction writer and futurist living in Toronto. She is the author of the* Machine Dynasty *novels and was the coeditor of* Licence Expired: The Unauthorized James Bond. *Her most recent book,* Company Town, *was the winner of the Copper Cylinder Award and a finalist in CBC Books' Canada Reads competition. She has written science fiction prototypes for Intel Labs, the Institute for the Future, SciFutures, the Atlantic Council, and others. She also teaches strategic foresight at Dubai Future Academy and elsewhere as part of the foresight consultancy Changeist. You can find her at www.madelineashby.com.*

▼

Is he still on schedule?"

Donna's hand spidered across the tactical array. She pinched and threw a map into Khalidah's lenses. Marshall's tug glowed there, spiralling ever closer to its target. Khalidah caught herself missing baseball. She squashed the sentiment immediately. It wasn't really the sport she missed, she reminded herself. She just missed her fantasy league. Phobos was much too far away to get a real game going; the lag was simply too long for her bets to cover any meaningful spread. She could run a model, of course, and had even filled one halfway during the trip out. It wasn't the same.

Besides, it was more helpful to participate in hobbies she could share with the others. The counsellors had been very clear on that subject. She was better off participating in Game Night, and the monthly book club they maintained with the Girl Scouts and Guides of North America.

"He's on time," Donna said. "Stop worrying."

"I'm not worried," Khalidah said. And she wasn't. Not really. Not about when he would arrive.

Donna pushed away from the terminal. She looked older than she had when they'd landed. They'd all aged, of course—the trip out and the lack of real produce hadn't exactly done any of them any favours—but Donna seemed to have changed more dramatically than Khalidah or Brooklyn or Song. She'd cut most of her hair off, and now the silver that once sparkled along her roots was the only colour left. The exo-suit hung loose on her. She hadn't been eating. Everyone hated the latest rotation of rations. Who on Earth—literally, who?—thought that testing the nutritional merits of a traditional Buddhist macrobiotic diet in space was a good idea? What sadistic special-interest group had funded that particular line of research?

"It will be fine," Donna said. "*We* will be fine."

"I just don't want things to change."

"Things always change," Donna said. "God is change. Right, Octavia?"

The station spoke: "Right, Donna."

Khalidah folded her arms. "So do we have to add an Arthur, just for him? Or a Robert? Or an Isaac? Or a Philip?"

The station switched its persona to Alice B. Sheldon. Its icon spun like a coin in the upper right of Khalidah's vision. "We already have a James," the station said. The icon winked.

"Khalidah, look at me," Donna said. Khalidah de-focused from the In-Vision array and met the gaze of her communications officer. "It won't be easy," the older woman said. "But nothing out here is. We already have plenty of data about our particular group. You think there won't be sudden changes to group dynamics, down there?"

She pointed. And there it was: red and rusty, the colour of old blood. Mars.

His name was Cody Marshall. He was Florida born and bred, white, with white-blond hair and a tendency toward rosacea. He held a Ph.D. in computer science from Mudd. He'd done one internship in Syria, building drone-supported mesh-nets, and another in Alert, Nunavut. He'd coordinated the emergency repair of an oil pipeline there using a combination of de-classified Russian submersibles and American cable-monitoring drones. He'd managed the project almost single-handedly after the team lead at Alert killed himself.

Now here he was on Phobos, sent to de-bug the bore-hole drillers on Mars. A recent solar storm had completely fried the drill's comms systems; Donna insisted it needed a complete overhaul, and two heads were better than one. Marshall couldn't do the job from home—they'd lose days re-programming the things on the fly, and the drill-bits were in sensitive places. One false move and months of work might collapse all around billions of dollars of research, crushing it deep into the red dirt. He needed to be close. After all, he'd written much of the code himself.

This was his first flight.

"I didn't want to be an astronaut," he'd told them over the lag, when they first met. "I got into this because I loved robots. That's all. I had no idea this is where I would wind up. But I'm really grateful to be here. I know it's a change."

"If you make a toilet seat joke, we'll delete your porn," Song said, now. When they all laughed, she looked around at the crowd. "What's funny? I'm serious. I didn't come all the way out here to play out a sitcom."

Marshall snapped his fingers. "That reminds me." He rifled through one of the many pouches he'd lugged on board. "Your mom sent this along with me." He coasted a vial through the air at her. Inside, a small crystal glinted. "That's your brother's wedding. And your new nephew's baptism. Speaking of sitcoms. She told me some stories to tell you. She didn't want to record them—"

"She's very nervous about recording anything—"

"—so she told me to tell them to you."

Song rolled her eyes. "Are they about Uncle Chan-wook?"

Marshall's pale eyebrows lifted high on his pink forehead. "How'd you guess?"

Again, the room erupted in laughter. Brooklyn laughed the loudest. She was a natural flirt. Her parents had named her after a borough they'd visited only once. In high school, she had self-published a series of homoerotic detective novels set in ancient Greece. The profits financed med school. After that, she hit Parsons, for an unconventional residency. She'd worked on the team that designed the exo-suits they now wore. She had already coordinated Marshall's fitting over the lag. It fit him well. At least, Brooklyn seemed pleased. She was smiling so wide that Khalidah could see the single cavity she'd sustained in all her years of eschewing most refined sugars.

Khalidah rather suspected that Brooklyn had secretly advocated for the macrobiotic study. Chugging a blue algae smoothie every morning seemed like her kind of thing. Khalidah had never asked about it. It was better not to know.

But wasn't that the larger point of this particular experiment? To see if they could all get along? To see if women—with their lower caloric needs, their lesser weight, their quite literally cheaper labour, in more ways than one—could get the job done, on Phobos? Sure, they were there on a planetary protection mission to gather the last remaining soil samples before the first human-oriented missions showed up, thereby ensuring the "chain of evidence" for future DNA experimentation. But they all knew—didn't they—what this was really about. How the media talked about them. How the Internet talked about them. Early on, before departure, Khalidah had seen the memes.

For Brooklyn, Marshall had a single chime. Brooklyn's mother had sent it to "clear the energy" of the station. During the Cold Lake training mission, she'd sent a Tibetan singing bowl.

For Khalidah, he had all 4,860 games of last year's regular season. "It's lossless," he said. "All thirty teams. Even the crappy ones. One of our guys down at Kennedy, he has a brother-in-law in Orlando, works at ESPN. They got in touch with your dad, and, well . . ."

"Thank you," Khalidah said.

"Yeah. Sure." Marshall cleared his throat. He rocked on his toes, pitched a little too far forward, and wheeled his arms briefly to recover his balance. If possible, he turned even pinker, so the colour of his face now matched the colour of his ears. "So. Here you go. I don't know what else is on there, but, um . . . there it is. Enjoy."

"Thank you." Khalidah lifted the vial of media from his hand. Her own crystal was darker than Song's. Denser. It had been etched more often. She stuffed it in the right breast pocket of her suit. If for some reason her heart cut out and the suit had to give her a jolt, the crystal would be safe.

"And for you, Donna. Here's what we talked about. They gave you double, just in case."

Donna's hand was already out. It shook a little as Marshall placed a small bottle in it. The label was easy to see. Easy to read. Big purple letters branded on the stark white sticker. Lethezine. The death drug. The colony of nano-machines that quietly took over the brain, shutting off major functions silently and painlessly. The best, most dignified death possible. The kind you had to ask the government for personally, complete with letters of recommendation from people with advanced degrees that could be revoked if they lied, like it was a grant application or the admission to a very prestigious community. Which in fact it was.

"What is that?" Brooklyn asked.

It was a stupid question. Everyone knew exactly what it was. She was just bringing it out into the open. They'd been briefed on that. On making the implicit become explicit. On voicing what had gone unasked. Speaking the unspeakable. It was, in fact, part of the training. There were certain things you were supposed to suppress. And other things that you couldn't let fester. They had drilled on it, over and over, at Cold Lake and in Mongolia and again and again during role-plays with the station interface.

"Why do you have that?" Brooklyn continued, when Donna didn't answer. "Why would he give that to you?"

Donna pocketed the bottle before she opened her mouth to speak. When she did, she lifted her gaze and stared at each of them in turn. She smiled tightly. For the first time, Khalidah realized the older woman's grimace was not borne of impatience, but rather simple animal pain. "It's because I'm dying," she said.

She said it like it was a commonplace event. Like, "Oh, it's because I'm painting the kitchen," or "It's because I took the dog for a walk."

In her lenses, Khalidah saw the entire group's auras begin to flare. The auras were nothing mystical, nothing more than ambient indicators of what the sensors in the suits were detecting: heart rate, blood pressure, temperature, odd little twitches of muscle fibres. She watched them move from baseline green to bruise purple—the colour of tension, of frustration. Only Song remained calm: her aura its customary frosty mint green, the same shade once worn by astronauts' wives at the advent of the Space Race.

"You *knew*?" she managed to say, just as Marshall said, "You didn't *tell* them?"

Khalidah whirled to stare at him. His mouth hung open. He squinted at Donna, then glanced around the group. "Wait," he said. "Wait. Let's just take a minute. I . . ." He swallowed. "I need a minute. You . . ." He spun in place and to point at Donna. "This was a shitty thing to do. I mean, really, truly, deeply, profoundly not cool. Lying to your team isn't cool. Setting me up to fail isn't cool."

"I have a brain tumour," Donna said blandly. "I'm not necessarily in my right mind."

"Donna," Song said quietly.

Oh, God. Donna was dying. She was dying and she hadn't told them and mintygreen Song had known it the whole damn time.

"You knew," Khalidah managed to say.

"Of course she knew," Donna said. "She's our doctor."

Donna was dying. Donna would be dead, soon. Donna had lied to all of them.

"It's inoperable," Donna added, as though talking about a bad seam in her suit and not her grey matter. "And in any case, I wouldn't want to operate on it. I still have a few good months here—"

"A few *months*?" Brooklyn was crying. The tears beaded away from her face and she batted at them, as though breaking them into smaller pieces would somehow dismantle the grief and its cause. "You have *months*? That's it?"

"More or less." Donna shrugged. "I could make it longer, with chemo, or nano. But we don't have those kinds of therapies here. Even if we did, and the tumour did shrink, Song isn't a brain surgeon, and the lag is too slow for Dr. Spyder to do something that delicate." She jerked a thumb at the surgical assistant in its cubby. "And there's the fact that I don't want to leave."

There was an awful silence filled only by the sounds of the station: the water recycler, the rasp of air in the vents, an unanswered alert chiming on and off, off and on. It was the sound the drill made when it encountered issues of structural integrity and wanted a directive on how to proceed. If they didn't answer it in five more minutes, the chime would increase in rate and volume. If they didn't answer it after another five minutes, the drill itself would relay a message via the rovers to tell mission control they were being bad parents.

And none of that mattered now. At least, Khalidah could not make it matter, in her head. She could not pull the alert into the "urgent" section of her mind. Because Donna was dying, Donna would be dead soon, Donna was in all likelihood going to kill herself right here on the station and what would they do—

Donna snapped her fingers and opened the alert. She pushed it over to tactical array where they could all see it. "Marshall, go and take a look."

Marshall seemed glad of any excuse he could get to leave the conversation. He drifted over to the station and started pulling apart the alert with his fingers. His suit was still so new that his every swipe and pinch and pull worked on the first try. His fingers hadn't worn down yet. Not like theirs. Not like Donna's.

"Can you do that?" Khalidah asked Donna. When Donna didn't answer, she focused on Song. "Can she do that?"

Song's face closed. She was in full physician mode now. Gone was the cheerful woman with the round face who joked about porn. Had the person they'd become friends with ever truly been real? Was she always this cold, underneath? Was it being so far away from Earth that made it so easy for her to lie to them? "It's her body, Khal. She doesn't have any obligation to force it to suffer."

Khalidah tried to catch Donna's eye. "You flew with the Air Force. You flew over Syria, and Sudan. You—"

"Yes, and whatever I was exposed to there probably had a hand in this," Donna muttered. "The buildings, you know. They released all kinds of nasty stuff. Like First Responder Syndrome, but worse." She pinched her nose. It was the only sign she ever registered of a headache. "But it's done, now, Khalidah. I've made my decision."

"But—"

"We all knew this might be a one-way trip," Song added.

"Don't patronize me, Song," Khalidah snapped.

"Then grow up," Song sighed. "Donna put this in her living will ages ago. Long before she even had her first flight. She was pre-approved for Lethezine, thanks to her family's cancer history. There was always a chance that she would get cancer on this trip, given the radiation exposure. But her physicians decided it was an acceptable risk, and she chose to come here in full awareness of that risk."

"I'm right here, you know," Donna said. "I'm not dead yet."

"You could still retire," Khalidah heard herself say. "You could go private. Join a board of trustees somewhere, or something like that. They'd cover a subscription, maybe they could get you implants—"

"I don't *want* implants, Khal, I want to die *here*—"

"I brought some implants," Marshall said, without turning around. He slid one last number into place, then wiped away the display. Now he turned. He took a deep breath, as though he'd rehearsed this speech the whole trip over. Which he probably had. Belatedly, Khalidah noticed the length of his hair and fingernails. God, he'd done the whole trip alone. The station couldn't bear more than one extra; as it was he'd needed to bring extra scrubbers and promise to spend most of the time in his own hab docked to theirs.

"I brought implants," he continued. "They're prototypes. No surgery necessary. Houston insisted. They wanted to give you one last chance to change your mind."

"I'm not going to change my mind," Donna said. "I want to die here."

"Please stop saying that." Brooklyn wiped her eyes. "Please just stop saying that."

"But it's the truth," Donna said, in her maddening why-isn't-everyone-as-objective-about-this-as-I-am way. "My whole life, I've wanted to go to Mars. And now I'm within sight of it. I'm not going to leave just because there's a lesion on my brain. Not when I just got here." She huffed. "Besides. I'd be no good to any of you on chemo. I'd be sick."

"You *are* sick," Khalidah snapped.

"Not that sick." Song lifted her gaze from her nails and gestured at the rest of them. "None of you noticed, did you? Both of you thought she was fine."

"Yeah, no thanks to you."

"Don't take that tone with me. She's my patient. I'd respect your right to confidentiality the same way I respected hers."

"You put the mission at risk," Khalidah said.

"Oh my God, Khal, stop talking like *them*." Brooklyn's voice was still thick with tears. "You're not mission control. This has nothing to do with the *mission*."

"It has *everything* to do with the mission!" Khalidah rounded on Donna. "How could you do this? How could you not tell us? This entire experiment hinges on social cohesion. That's why we're here. We're here to prove . . ."

Now the silence had changed into something wholly other. It was much heavier now. Much more accusatory. Donna folded her arms.

"What are we here to prove, Khalidah?"

Khalidah shut her eyes. She would be professional. She would not cry. She would not get angry. At least, no angrier than she already was. She would not focus on Donna's betrayal, and her deceit, and the fact that she had the audacity to pull this bullshit so soon after . . . Khalidah took a deep breath.

She would put it aside. *Humans are containers of emotion.* She made herself see the words in the visualizing interface they had for moments like this. *When someone else's emotions spill out, it's because their container is full.* She focused on her breathing. She pictured the colour of her aura changing in the others' lenses. She imagined pushing the colour from purple to green, healing it slowly, as though it were the evidence of a terrible wound. Which in a way it was.

"I'm fine," she said. "I'm fine. I'm sorry."

"That's good," Donna said. "Because we're not here to *prove* any one particular thing or another. We're here to run experiments, gather the last Martian samples before the manned missions begin, and observe the drills as they dig out the colony. That's all we're here to do. You may feel pressure to do something else, due to the nature of this team, but that's not why we're here. The work comes first. The policy comes later."

The Morrígu was divided into three pods: Badb, Macha, and Nemain. No one referred to them that way, of course—only Marshall had the big idea to actually try stumbling through ancient Gaelic with his good ol' boy accent. He gave up after two weeks. Nonetheless, he still referred to his unit as the Corvus.

"Nice of them to stick with the crow theme," he said.

"Ravens are omens of death," Donna said, and just like that, Game Night was over. That was fine with Khalidah. Low-gravity games never had the degree of complexity she liked; they had magnetic game boards, but they weren't entirely the same. And without cards or tokens they couldn't really visualize the game in front of them, and basically played permutations of Werewolves or Máfia until they learned each other's tells.

Not that all that experience had helped her read Donna and Song's dishonesty. Even after all their time spent together, in training, on the flight, on the station, and still there was the capacity for betrayal. Even now, she did not truly know them.

Not yet, Khalidah often repeated to herself, as the days stretched on. *Not yet*. Not for the first time, she wished for a return to 24-hour days. Once upon a time, they had seemed so long. She had yearned for afternoons to end, for lectures to cease, for shifts to close. Now she understood that days on Earth were beautifully, mercifully short.

Sometimes Khalidah caught Donna watching her silently, when she didn't think Khalidah would notice. When Khalidah met her eyes, Donna would try to smile. It was more a crinkling of the eyes than anything else. It was hard to tell if she was in pain, or unhappy, or both. The brain had no nerve endings of its own, no pain receptors. The headaches that Donna felt were not the tissue's response to her tumor, but rather a warning sign about a crowded nerve, an endless alarm that rang down through her spinal column and caused nausea and throbbing at odd hours. Or so she said.

Khalidah's first email was to her own psychiatrist on Earth, through her personal private channel. It was likely the very same type of channel Donna had used to carry on her deception. *Can a member of crew just hide any medical condition they want?* she wrote.

Your confidentiality and privacy are paramount, Dr. Hassan wrote back from Detroit. *You have sacrificed a great deal of privacy to go on this mission. You live in close quarters, quite literally right on top of each other. So the private channels you have left are considered sacrosanct. Communications between any participant and her doctor must remain private until the patient chooses to disclose.*

This was not the answer Khalidah had wanted to hear.

Imagine if it were you who had a secret, Dr. Hassan continued, as though having anticipated Khalidah's feelings on the matter. *If you were experiencing the occasional suicidal ideation, for example, would you want your whole crew to know, or would you wait for the ideations to pass?*

It was a valid counter-argument. Mental health was a major concern on long-haul missions. Adequate care required stringent privacy. But Donna's cancer wasn't a passing thought about how much easier it would be to be dead. She was actually dying. And she hadn't told them.

Now, after all that silence on the matter, the cancer seemed to be all anyone could talk about.

"I've almost trained the pain to live on Martian time," Donna said, one morning. "Most patients feel pain in the morning, but they feel it on an Earth schedule, with full sunlight."

Khalidah could not bring herself to smile back, not yet. Doing so felt like admitting defeat.

"She won't die any slower just because you're mad at her," Brooklyn said, as they conducted seal checks on the suits.

"Leave me alone," Khalidah said. Brooklyn just shrugged and got on with the checklist. A moment later, she asked for a flashlight. Khalidah handed it to her without a word.

"Have you watched any of the games your dad sent?" Marshall asked, the next day.

"Please don't bring him up," Khalidah said.

Five weeks later, the vomiting started. It was an intriguing low-gravity problem— barf bags were standard, but carrying them around wasn't. And Donna couldn't just commandeer the shop-vac for her own personal use. In the end, Marshall made her a little butterfly net, of sorts, with an iris at one end. It was like a very old-fashioned nebulizer, for inhaling asthma medication. Only it worked in the other direction.

Not coincidentally, Marshall had brought with him an entire liquid diet intended specifically for cancer patients. Donna switched, and things got better.

"I'll stick around long enough to get the last samples from Hellas," she said, sipping a pouch of what appeared to be either a strawberry milkshake or an anti-nausea tonic. She coughed. The cough turned into a gag that she needed to suppress. She clenched a fist and then unclenched it, to master it. "I want my John Hancock on those damn things."

"Don't you want to see the landing?" Marshall asked. "You know, hand over the keys, see their faces when they see the ant farm in person for the first time?"

"What, and watch them fuck up all our hard work?"

They all laughed. All of them but Khalidah. How could they just act like everything was normal? Did the crew of the Ganesha mission even know that Donna was sick? Would the team have to explain it? How would that conversation even happen? ("Welcome to Mars. Sorry, but we're in the middle of a funeral. Anyway, try not to get your microbes everywhere.")

Then the seizures started. They weren't violent. More like gentle panic attacks. "My arm doesn't feel like my arm, anymore," Donna said, as she continued to man her console with one hand. "No visual changes, though. Just localized disassociation."

"That's a great band name," Marshall said.

Morrígu tried to help, in her own way. The station gently reminded Khalidah of all the things that she already knew: that she was distracted, that she wasn't sleeping, that she would lie awake listening for the slightest tremor in Donna's breathing, and that sometimes Brooklyn would reach up from her cubby and squeeze Khalidah's ankle because she was listening, too. The station made herself available in the form of the alters, often pinging Khalidah when her gaze failed to track properly across a display, or when her blood pressure spiked, or when she couldn't sleep. Ursula, most often, but then Octavia. *God is Change,* the station reminded her. *The only lasting truth is Change.*

And Khalidah knew that to be true. She did. She simply drew no comfort from it. Too many things had changed already. Donna was dying. Donna, who had calmly helped her slide the rods into the sleeves as they pitched tents in Alberta one dark night while the wolves howled and the thermometer dropped to thirty below. Donna, who had said "Of course you can do it. That's not the question," when Khalidah reached between the cots during isolation week and asked Donna if the older woman thought she was really tough enough to do the job. Donna, without whom Khalidah might have quit at any time.

"You watch any of those games, yet?" Marshall asked, when he caught her staring down at the blood-dark surface of the planet. Rusted, old. Not like the wine-dark samples that Song drained from Donna each week.

Khalidah only shook her head. Baseball seemed so stupid, now.

"Your dad, he really wanted to get those to you before I left," Marshall reminded her.

Khalidah took a deep, luxuriant breath. "I told you not to mention him, Marshall. I asked you nicely. Are you going to respect those boundaries, or are we going to have a problem?"

Marshall said nothing, at first. Instead he drifted in place, holding the nearest grip to keep himself tethered. He hadn't learned how to tuck himself in yet, how to twist and wring himself so that he passed through without touching anyone else. Everything about his presence there still felt wrong.

"We don't have to be friends," he said, in measured tones. He pointed down into Storage. "But the others, they're your friends. Or they thought they were. Until now."

"They lied to me."

"Oh, come on. You think it wasn't tough for Song to go through that? You think she enjoyed it, not telling you? Jesus Christ, Khalidah. Maybe you haven't noticed, but a lot of us made a lot of sacrifices to get this far."

"Oh, I'm sure it was *so* difficult for you, finding out you'd get to go to Mars—"

"—Phobos."

"—Phobos, without anything like the training we had to endure, just so you could pilot your finicky fucking drill God knows where—"

"Hey, now, I happen to like my finicky fucking drill very fucking much," Marshall said. He blinked. Then covered his face with his hands. He'd filed his nails down and buzzed his hair in solidarity with Donna. His entire skull was flushed the colour of a new spring geranium. "That . . . didn't come out right."

Khalidah hung in place. She drew her knees up to her chest and floated. It had been a long time since she'd experienced second-hand embarrassment. Something about sharing such a tiny space with the others for such a long time ground it out of a person. But she was embarrassed for Marshall now. Not as embarrassed as he was, thank goodness. But embarrassed.

"They sent me *alone*, you know," he said, finally, through the splay of his fingers. He scrubbed at the bare stubble of his skull. "*Alone*. Do you even know what that means? You know all those desert island questions in job interviews? When they ask you what books you'd bring, if you were stranded in the middle of nowhere? Well, I *read* all of those. *War and Peace. Being and Nothingness.* Do you have any idea how good I am at solitaire, by now?"

"You can't be good at solitaire, it's—"

"But I did it, because they said it was the best chance of giving Donna extra time. If they'd sent two of us, you'd all have to go home a hell of a lot faster. You wouldn't be here when *Ganesha* arrives. So I did it. I got here. Alone. I did the whole trip by myself. So you and Donna and the whole crew could have more time."

Khalidah swallowed hard. "Are you finished?"

"Yes. I'm finished." He pushed himself off the wall, then bounced away and twisted back to face her. "No. I'm not. I think you're being a total hypocrite, and I think it's undermining whatever social value the Morrigú experiment was meant to have."

Khalidah felt her eyebrows crawl up to touch the edges of her veil. "Excuse me?"

"Yeah. You heard me. You're being a hypocrite." He lowered his voice. "Do your friends even know your dad died? Did you tell them that he was dying, when you left? Because I was told not to mention it, and that sure as hell sounds like a secret, to me."

Khalidah closed her eyes. The only place to go, in a space this small, was inward. There was no escape, otherwise. She waited until that soft darkness had settled around her and then asked: "Why are you doing this?"

"Because you're *not* alone, out here. You *have* friends. Friends you've known and worked with for years, in one way or another. So what if Donna jerked you around? She jerked me around, too, and you don't see me acting like a brat about it. Or Brooklyn. Or Song. Meanwhile you've been keeping this massive life-changing event from them this whole time."

Now Khalidah's eyes opened. She had no need for that comforting blanket of darkness now. "My father dying is not a massive life-changing event," she snapped. "You think you know all my secrets? You don't know shit, Marshall. Because if you did, you'd know that I haven't spoken to that bastard in ten years."

As though trying to extract some final usefulness from their former mistress, the drills decided to fail before the Banshee units returned with their samples, and before *Ganesha* arrived with the re-up and the Mars crew. Which meant that when *Ganesha* landed, the crew would have to live in half-dug habs.

"It's the goddamn perchlorate," Donna whispered. She had trouble swallowing now, and it meant her voice was constantly raw. "I told them we should have gone with the Japanese bit. It drilled the Shinkansen, I said. Too expensive, they said. Now the damn thing's rusted all to shit."

Which was exactly the case. The worm dried up suddenly, freezing in place—a "Bertha Bork," like the huge drill that stalled under Seattle during an ill-fated transit project. They'd rehearsed this particular error. First they ordered all the rovers away in case of a sinkhole, and then started running satellites over the sink. And the drill himself told them what was wrong. The blades were corroded. After five years of work, too much of the red dirt had snuck down into the drill's workings. It would need to be dug out and cleaned before it could continue. Or it would need to be replaced entirely.

The replacement prototype was already built. It had just completed its first test run in the side of a flattened mountain in West Virginia. It was strong and light and better articulated than the worm. But the final model was supposed to come over with *Ganesha*. And in the meantime, the hab network still needed major excavation.

"What's the risk if we send one of the rovers to try to uncover it?" Song asked. "We've got one in the cage; it wrapped up its mission ages ago. Wouldn't be too hard to re-configure."

"Phobos rovers might be too light," Marshall said. "But the real problem is the crashberry; it'll take three days to inflate and another week to energize. And that's a week we're not drilling."

"We could tell *Ganesha* to slow down," Khalidah said.

"They're ballistic capture," Marshall said. "If they slow down now, they lose serious momentum."

"They'd pick it up on arrival, though."

"Yeah . . ." Marshall sucked his teeth. "But they're carrying a big load. They could jack-knife once they hit the well, if they don't maintain a steady speed." He scrubbed at the thin dusting of blonde across his scalp. "But we have to tell them about this, either way. Wouldn't be right, not updating them."

Khalidah snorted. The others ignored her.

"Can we redirect the Banshees?" Brooklyn asked. "Whiskey and Tango are the closest. We could have them dump their samples, set a pin, tell them to dig out the worm, and then come back."

Khalidah shook her head. "They're already full. They're on their way to the maildrop. If we re-deployed them now, they wouldn't be in position when *Ganesha* arrives. Besides, they're carrying Hellas—we can't afford to compromise them."

"Those samples are locked up like Fort Knox," Brooklyn said. "What, are you worried that the crew of *Ganesha* will open them up by mistake? Because that's pretty much guaranteed not to happen."

"No, but—"

"There's a storm in between Whiskey and the worm," Marshall said. He pointed at an undulating pattern of lines on the screen between two blinking dots. "If we send Whiskey now, we might lose her forever. And the samples. And we still wouldn't be any further with the drill. Fuck."

He pushed away from the console, knuckling his eyes. Khalidah watched the planet. In the plate glass, she caught Donna watching her. Her friend was much thinner now. They'd had to turn off her suit, because it no longer fit snugly enough to read her heartbeat. Her breath came in rasps. She coughed often. Last month, Song speculated that the cancer had spread to her lungs; Donna claimed not to care very much. Khalidah heard the older woman sigh slow and deep. And she knew, before Donna even opened her mouth, what she was about to suggest.

"There's always the Corvus," Donna said.

"No," Khalidah said. "Absolutely not."

But Donna wasn't even looking at her. She was looking at Marshall. "How much fuel did they really send, Marshall? You got here awfully fast."

Marshall licked his lips. "Between what I have left over and what *Ganesha* is leaving behind for you midway, there's enough to send you home."

"Which means Corvus has just enough to send me *down*, and give me thrust to come back."

"Even if that were true, you could still have a seizure while doing the job," Song said.

"Then I'll take my anti-seizure medication before I leave," Donna said.

"The gravity would demolish you, with the state you're in," Marshall said. "It should be me. I should go. I know Corvus better, and my bone density is—"

"That's very gallant of you, Mr. Marshall, but I outrank you," Donna reminded him. "Yes, I tire easily. Yes, it's hard for me to breathe. But I'm stronger than I would be if I were on chemo. And the suit can both give me some lift and push a good air mix for me. Right, Brooklyn?"

Brooklyn beamed. "Yes, ma'am."

"And Marshall, if any of those things do occur, I need you up here to remote pilot Corvus from topside and get the samples back here." She gestured at the map. "If you tell Tango to meet me, I can take her samples and put them on Corvus. Then I get in Tango's cargo compartment and drive her around the storm, to the worm. I dig out the drill, and you re-start it from up here. When I come back, you have the samples, and *Ganesha* has another guestroom." She grinned. The smile made her face into a skull. "Easy peasy," Donna said.

"You know you're making history, right?" Marshall asked, as they performed the final checks on Corvus. "First human on Mars, and all that. You're stealing *Ganesha*'s thunder."

Donna coughed. "Don't jinx it, Marshall."

"How are your hands?"

Donna held them up. Slowly, she crunched her thickly gloved digits into fists. "They're okay."

"That's good. Go slow. The Banshees take a light touch."

"I know that, Marshall."

He pinked. "I know you know. But I'm just reminding you. Now, I'll get you down there, smooth as silk, and when it's time to come home you just let us know, okay?"

Donna's head tilted. She did that, when she was about to ask an important question. For a moment it reminded Khalidah so much of the woman she'd been and the woman they'd lost that she forgot to breathe. "Is it home, now, for you?"

Marshall's blush deepened. He really did turn the most unfortunate shade of sunburned red. "I guess so," he said. "Brooklyn, it's your turn."

Brooklyn breezed in and, flipping herself to hang upside down, performed the final checks on Donna's suit. "You've got eight hours," she said. "Sorry it couldn't be more. Tango is already on her way, and she'll be there to meet you when you land."

"What's Tango's charge like?"

"She's sprinting to meet you, so she'll be half-empty by the time she hits the rendezvous point," Marshall said. "But there's a set of auxiliary batteries in the cargo area. You'd have to move them to get into the cockpit anyhow."

Donna nodded. The reality of what was about to happen was settling on them. How odd, Khalidah thought, to be weightless and yet to feel the gravity of Donna's mission tugging at the pit of her stomach. The first human on Mars. The first woman. The first cancer patient. She had read a metaphor of illness as another country, how patients became citizens of it, that place beyond the promise of life, and now she thought of Donna there on the blood-red sands, representing them. Not just a human, but a defiantly mortal one, one for whom all the life-extension dreams and schemes would never bear fruit. All the members of the *Ganesha* crew had augmentations to make their life on Mars more productive and less painful. Future colonists would doubtless have similar lifehacks. Donna was the only visitor who would ever set an unadulterated foot on that soil.

"I'll be watching your vitals the whole time," Song said. "If I don't like what I see, I'll tell Marshall to take control of Tango and bring you back."

Donna cracked a smile. "Is that for my benefit, or the machine's?"

"Both," Song said. "We can't have you passing out and crashing millions of dollars' worth of machine learning and robotics."

And then, too soon, the final checks were finished, and it was time for Donna to go. The others drifted to the other side of the airlock, and Brooklyn ran the final diagnostic of the detachment systems. Khalidah's hands twitched at her veil. She had no idea what to say. *Why did you lie to us? Did you really think that would make this easier? What were you so afraid of?*

Donna regarded her from the interior of her suit. She looked so small inside it. Khalidah thought of her fragile body shaking inside its soft volumes, her thin neck and her bare skull juddering like a bad piece of video.

"I want—"

"Don't," Donna said. "Don't, Khal. Not now."

For the first time in a long time, Khalidah peeped at Donna's aura through the additional layer in her lenses' vision. It was deep blue, like a very wide and cold stretch of the sea. It was a colour she had never seen on Donna. When she looked at her own pattern, it was much the same shade.

Marshall chose this moment to poke his head in. "It's time."

Donna reached over to the airlock button. "I have to go now, Khalidah."

Before Khalidah could say anything, Marshall had tugged her backward. The door rolled shut. For a moment she watched Donna through the small bright circle of glass. Then Donna's helmet snapped shut, and she wore a halo within a halo, like a bullseye.

The landing was as Marshall promised: smooth as silk. With Corvus he was in his element. He and the vessel knew each other well. They'd moved as much of Corvus' cargo as they could into temporary storage outside the hab; the reduced weight would give Donna the extra boost on the trip back that she might need.

Donna herself rode out the landing better than any of them expected. She took her time unburdening herself of her restraints, and they heard her breathing heavily, trying to choke back the nausea that now dominated her daily life. But eventually she lurched free of the unit, tuned up the jets on her suit, jiggered her air mix, and began the unlocking procedure to open Corvus. They watched her gloved hands hovering over the final lock.

"I hope you're not expecting some cheesy bullshit about giant leaps for womankind," Donna said, panting audibly. She sounded sheepish. For Donna, that meant she was nervous. "I didn't really have time to prepare any remarks. I have a job to do."

Brooklyn wiped her eyes and covered her mouth. Marshall passed her a tissue, and took one for himself.

"You've wanted this since you were a little girl, Donna," Song said. "Go out there and get it."

Together they watched the lock spin open, and Donna eased herself out. There was Tango, ready and waiting. And there was Mars, or at least their little corner of it, raw and open and red like a wound.

"I wish I could smell it," Donna said. "I wish I could taste the air. It feels strange to be here and yet not be here at the same time. You can stand here all you want and never really touch it."

"You can look at the samples when you bring them back," Brooklyn managed to say.

Donna said nothing, only silently made her way to Tango and moved the samples back to Corvus. Then she began the procedure to get Tango into manual. Her feed cut out a couple of times, but only briefly; they hadn't thought to test the signal on the cameras themselves. Her audio was fine, though, and Marshall talked her through when she had questions. In the end it ran like any other remote repair. Even the dig went well; clearing the dirt from the drill and re-starting it from the control panel was a lot simpler than any of them had expected.

Halfway back to Corvus, Tango slowly rolled to a stop.

"Donna, check your batteries," Marshall suggested.

There was no answer. Only Donna's slow, wet breathing.

"Donna, copy?"

Nothing. They looked at Song; Song pulled up Donna's vitals. "No changes in her eye movements or alpha pattern," Song whispered. "She's not having a seizure. Donna. Donna! Do you need help?"

"No," Donna said, finally. "I came here to do a job, and now I'm finished with it. I'm done."

Something in Khalidah's stomach turned to ice. "Don't do this," she whispered, as Marshall began to say "No, no, no," over and over. He started bashing things on the console, running every override he could.

"No, you don't, you crazy old broad," he muttered. "I can get Tango to drive you back, you know!"

"Not if I've ripped out the receiver," Donna said. She sounded exhausted. "I think I'll just stay here, thank you. *Ganesha* can deal with me when they come. You don't have to do it. You'd have had to freeze me, anyway, and vibrate me down to crystal, like cat litter, and—"

"Fuck. You."

It was the first full complete sentence that Khalidah had spoken to her in months. So she repeated it.

"Fuck you. Fuck you for lying to us. Again. Fuck you for this selfish fucking bullshit. Oh, you think you're being so romantic, dying on Mars. Well fuck you. We came here to prove we could live, not . . ." Her lips were hot. Her eyes were hot. It was getting harder to breathe. "Not whatever the fuck it is you think you're doing."

Nothing.

"Donna, please don't," Brooklyn whispered in her most wheedling tone. "Please don't leave us. We need you." She sounded like a child. Then again, Khalidah wasn't sure she herself sounded any better. Somehow this loss contained within it all the other losses she'd ever experienced: her mother, her father, the slow pull away from the Earth and into the shared unknown.

"This is a bad idea," Marshall said, his voice calm and steady. "If you want to take the Lethezine, take the Lethezine. But you don't know how it works—what if it doesn't go like you think it will, and you're alone and in pain down there? Why don't you come back up, and if something goes wrong, we'll be there to help?"

Silence. Was she deliberating? Could they change her mind? Khalidah strained to hear the sound of Tango starting back up again. They flicked nervous, tearful glances at each other.

"Are you just going to quit?" Khalidah asked, when the silence stretched too long. "Are you just going to run away, like this? Now that it's hard?"

"You have no idea how hard this is, Khal, and you've never once thought to ask."

It stung. Khalidah let the pain transform itself into anger. Anger, she decided, was the only way out of this problem. "I thought you didn't *want* me to ask, given how you never *told* us anything until it was too late."

"It's not my fault I'm dying!"

"But it's your fault you didn't tell us! We would have—"

"You would have convinced me to go home." Donna chuckled. It became a cough. The cough lasted too long. "Because you love me, and you want me to live. And I love you, so I would have done it." She had another little coughing jag. "But the trouble with *home* is that there's nothing to go back to. I've thrown my whole life into this. I've had to pass on things—real things—to get to this place. But now that I'm here, I know it was worth it. And that's how I want to end it. I don't want to die alone in a hospital surrounded by people who don't understand what's out here, or why we do this."

Khalidah forced her voice to remain firm. "And so you want to die alone, down there, surrounded by nothing at all?"

"I'm not alone, Khal. You're with me. You're all with me, all the time."

Brooklyn broke down. She pushed herself into one corner. Khalidah reached up, and held her ankle, tethering her into the group. She squeezed her eyes shut and felt tears bud away. Song's beautiful ponytail drifted across her face. Arms curled around Khalidah's body. Khalidah curled her arms around the others. They were a Gordian knot, hovering far above Donna, a problem she could not solve and could only avoid.

"That's right, Donna," Marshall said. "We're here. We're right here."

"I'm sorry," Donna said. "I'm sorry I lied. I didn't want to. But I just . . . I wanted to stay, more than I wanted to tell you."

"I'm sorry, too," Khalidah said. "I . . ." She wiped at her face. Her throat hurt. "I *miss* you. Already."

"I miss you, too. I miss all of you." Donna sniffed hard. "But this is where we're supposed to be. Because this is where we are at our best."

They were quiet for a while. There was nothing to do but weep. Khalidah thought she might weep forever. The pain was a real thing—she had forgotten that it hurt to cry. She had forgotten the raw throat and pounding head that came with full-body grief. She had forgotten, since her mother, how physically taxing it could be.

"Are you ready, now?" Song asked, finally. She wiped her eyes and swallowed. "Donna? Are you ready to take the dose?"

The silence went on a long time. But still, they kept asking: "Are you ready? Are you ready?"

elephant on table

BRUCE STERLING

One of the most powerful and innovative talents to enter science fiction in the past few decades, Bruce Sterling sold his first story in 1976. By the end of the '80s, he had established himself, with a series of stories set in his exotic "Shaper/Mechanist" future and with novels such as the complex and Stapeldonian Schismatrix and Islands in the Net (as well as with his editing of the influential anthology Mirrorshades: the Cyberpunk Anthology and the infamous critical magazine Cheap Truth), as perhaps the prime driving force behind the revolutionary "Cyberpunk" movement in science fiction. His other books include a critically acclaimed nonfiction study of First Amendment issues in the world of computer networking, The Hacker Crackdown: Law and Disorder on the Electronic Frontier; the novels The Artificial Kid, Involution Ocean, Heavy Weather, Holy Fire, Distraction, Zeitgeist, The Zenith Angle, and The Difference Engine (with William Gibson); a nonfiction study of the future, Tomorrow Now: Envisioning the Next Fifty Years; and the landmark collections Crystal Express, Globalhead, Schismatrix Plus, A Good Old-Fashioned Future, and Visionary in Residence. His most recent books are a massive retrospective collection, Ascendancies: The Best of Bruce Sterling, and the new novel The Caryatids. His story "Bicycle Repairman" earned him a long-overdue Hugo in 1997, and he won another Hugo in 1997 for his story "Taklamakan."

Here he gives us a slyly satiric look at the end of an era and of one way of competing for power, as new ways evolve, leaving old-style politicians who can't adapt stranded way behind.

Tullio and Irma had found peace in the Shadow House. Then the Chief arrived from his clinic and hid in the panic-room.

Tullio and Irma heard shuddering moans from the HVAC system, the steely squeak of the hydraulic wheels, but not a human whisper. The Shadow House cat whined and yowled at the vault door.

Three tense days passed, and the Chief tottered from his airtight chamber into summer daylight. Head bobbing, knees shaking, he reeled like an antique Sicilian puppet.

Blank-eyed yet stoic, the elderly statesman wobbled up the perforated stairs to the Shadow House veranda. This expanse was adroitly sheltered from a too-knowing world.

The panic rooms below ground were sheathed in Faraday copper, cast-iron, and lead, but the mansion's airy upper parts were a nested, multilayer labyrinth of sound baffles, absorbent membranes, metastructured foam, malleable ribbons, carbon filaments, vapor smoke, and mirror chaff. Snakelike vines wreathed the trellises. The gardens abounded in spiky cactus. Tullio took pains to maintain the establishment as it deserved.

The Chief staggered into a rattan throne. He set his hairy hands flat on the cold marble tabletop.

He roared for food.

Tullio and Irma hastened to comply. The Chief promptly devoured three hard-boiled eggs, a jar of pickled artichoke hearts, a sugar-soaked grapefruit, and a jumbo-sized mango, skin and all.

Some human color returned to his famous, surgically amended face. The Chief still looked bad, like a reckless, drug-addict roué of fifty. However, the Chief was actually one hundred and four years old. The Chief had paid millions for the zealous medical care of his elite Swiss clinic. He'd even paid hundreds of thousands for the veterinary care of his house cat.

While Irma tidied the sloppy ruins of breakfast, Tullio queried Shadow House screens for any threats in the vicinity.

The Chief had many enemies: thousands of them. His four ex-wives were by far his worst foes. He was also much resented by various Italian nationalists, fringe leftist groups, volatile feminist cults, and a large sprinkling of mentally disturbed stalkers who had fixated on him for decades.

However, few of these fierce, gritty, unhappy people were on the island of Sardinia in August 2073. None of them knew that the Chief had secretly arrived on Sardinia from Switzerland. The Shadow House algorithms ranked their worst threat as the local gossip journalist "Carlo Pizzi," a notorious little busybody who was harassing supermodels.

Reassured by this security-check, Tullio carried the card-table out to the beach. Using a clanking capstan and crank, Tullio erected a big, party-colored sun umbrella. In its slanting shade he arranged four plastic chairs, a stack of plastic cups, plastic crypto-coins, shrink-wrapped card decks, paper pads, and stubby pencils. Every object was anonymous and disposable: devoid of trademarks, codes, or identities. No surface took fingerprints.

The Chief arrived to play, wearing wrap-around mirrorshades and a brown, hooded beach-robe. It was a Mediterranean August, hot, blue, and breezy. The murmuring surf was chased by a skittering horde of little shore-birds.

Irma poured the Chief a tall iced glass of his favorite vitamin sludge while Tullio shuffled and dealt.

The Chief disrobed and smeared his seamy, portly carcass with medicated suntan unguent. He gripped his waterproofed plastic cards.

"Anaconda," he commanded, and belched.

The empty fourth chair at their card table was meant to attract the public. The

Chief was safe from surveillance inside his sumptuous Shadow House—that was the purpose of the house, its design motif, its reason for being. However, safety had never satisfied the Chief. He was an Italian politician, so it was his nature to flirt with disaster.

Whenever left to themselves, Tullio and Irma passed their pleasant days inside the Shadow House, discreet, unseen, unbothered, and unbothering. But the two of them were still their Chief's loyal retainers. The Chief was a man of scandal and turbulence—half-forgotten, half-ignored by a happier era. But the Chief still had his burning need to control the gaze of the little people.

The Chief's raw hunger for glory, which had often shaken the roots of Europe, had never granted him a moment's peace. During his long, rampaging life, he'd possessed wealth, fame, power, and the love of small armies of women. Serenity, though, still eluded him. Privacy was his obsession: fame was his compulsion.

Tullio played his cards badly, for it seemed to him that a violent host of invisible furies still circled the Chief's troubled, sweating head. The notorious secrecy. The covert scandals. The blatant vulgarity, which was also a subtle opacity—for the Chief was an outsized statesman, a heroic figure of many perverse contradictions. His achievements and his crimes were like a herd of elephants: they could never stand still within a silent room.

Irma offered Tullio a glance over their dwindling poker hands. They both pitied their Chief, because they understood him. Tullio had once been an Italian political party operative, and Irma, a deft Italian tax-avoidance expert. Nowadays they were reduced to the status of the house-repairman and the hostess, the butler and the cook. There was no more Italy. The Chief had outlived his nation.

Becoming ex-Italian meant a calmer life for Tullio and Irma, because the world was gentler without an Italy. It was their duty to keep this lonely, ill-starred old man out of any more trouble. The Chief would never behave decently—that was simply not in his character—but their discreet beach mansion could hush up his remaining excesses.

The first wandering stranger approached their open table. This fringe figure was one tiny fragment of the world's public, a remote demographic outlier, a man among the lowest of the low. He was poor, black, and a beach peddler. Many such emigres haunted the edges of the huge Mediterranean summer beach crowds. These near-vagrants sold various forms of pretty rubbish.

The Chief was delighted to welcome this anonymous personage. He politely re-lieved the peddler of his miserable tray of fried fish, candy bars, and kid's plastic pinwheels, and insisted on seating him at the green poker table.

"Hey, I can't stay here, boss," complained the peddler, in bad Italian. "I have to work."

"We'll look after you," the Chief coaxed, surveilling the peddler, from head to foot, with covert glee. "My friend Tullio here will buy your fish. Tullio has a hungry cat over there, isn't that right, Tullio?"

The Chief waved his thick arm at the Shadow House, but the peddler simply couldn't see the place. The mansion's structure was visually broken up by active dazzle lines. Its silhouette faded like a cryptic mist into the island's calm palette of palms and citruses.

Tullio obediently played along. "Oh yes, that's true, we do have a big tomcat, he's always hungry." He offered the peddler some plastic coinage from the poker table.

Irma gathered up the reeking roasted sardines. When Irma rounded a corner of the Shadow House, she vanished as if swallowed.

"It has been my experience," the Chief said sagely, scooping up and squaring the poker cards, "that the migrants of the world—men like yourself—are risk-takers. So, my friend: how'd you like to double your money in a quick hand of Hi-Lo with us?"

"I'm not a player, boss," said the peddler, though he was clearly tempted.

"So, saving up your capital, is that it? Do you want to live here in Italy—is that your plan?"

The peddler shrugged. "There is no Italy! In Europe, the people love elephants. So, I came here with the elephants. The people don't see me. The machines don't care."

Irma reappeared as if by magic. Seeing the tense look on their faces, she said brightly, "So, do you tend those elephants, young man? People in town say they brought whales this year, too!"

"Oh no, no, signora!" cried the peddler. "See the elephants, but never look at the whales! You have to ride a boat out there, you get seasick, that's no good!"

"Tell us more about these elephants, they interest me," the Chief urged, scratching his oiled belly, "have a prosecco, have a brandy." But the peddler was too streetwise: he had sensed that something was up. He gathered his tray and escaped them, hastening down the beach, toward the day's gathering crowds.

Tullio, Irma, and the Chief ran through more hands of Anaconda poker. The Chief, an expert player, was too restless to lose, so he was absentmindedly piling up all their coinage.

"My God, if only I, too, had no name!" he burst out. "No identity, like that African boy—what I could do in this world now! Elephants, here in Sardinia! When I was young, did I have any elephants? Not one! I had less than nothing, I suffered from huge debts! These days are such happy times, and the young people now, they just have no idea!"

Tullio and Irma knew every aspect of their Chief's hard-luck origin story, so they merely pretended attention.

The summer beach crowd was clustering down the coastline, a joyful human mass of tanned and salty arms and legs, ornamented with balloons and scraps of pop music.

A beach-combing group of Japanese tourists swanned by. Although they wore little, the Japanese were fantastically well-dressed. The Japanese had found their metier as the world's most elegant people. Even the jealous Milanese were content to admire their style.

Lacking any new victim to interrogate at his card table, the Chief began to reminisce. The Chief would loudly bluster about any topic, except for his true sorrows, which he never confessed aloud.

The Swiss had lavished many dark attentions on the Chief's crumbling brain. The Swiss had invaded his bony skull, that last refuge of humane privacy, like a horde of Swiss pikemen invading Renaissance Italy. They occupied it, but they couldn't govern it.

The Chief's upgraded brain, so closely surveilled by Swiss medical imaging, could no longer fully conceal his private chains of thought. The Chief had once been a political genius, but now his scorched neurons were like some huge database racked by a spy agency's analytics.

Deftly shuffling a fresh card-deck, the Chief suddenly lost his composure. He commenced to leak and babble. His unsought theme was "elephants." Any memory, any anecdote that struck his mind, about elephants.

Hannibal had invaded Italy with elephants. The elephant had once been the symbol of an American political party. A houseplant named the "Elephant Ear." The Chief recalled a pretty Swedish pop-star with the unlikely name of "Elliphant."

The Chief was still afraid of the surgically warped and sickening "Elephant Man," a dark horror-movie figure from his remote childhood.

The Chief might not look terribly old—not to a surveillance camera—but he was senile. Those high-tech quacks in Switzerland took more and more of his wealth, but delivered less and less health. Life-extension technology was a rich man's gamble. The odds were always with the house.

Irma gently removed the cards from the Chief's erratic hands, and dealt them herself. The sea-wind rose and loudly ruffled the beach umbrella. Wind-surfers passed by, out to sea, with kites that might be aerial surveillance platforms. A group of black-clad divers on a big rubber boat looked scary, like spies, assassins, or secret policemen.

The ever-swelling beach crowd, that gathering, multi-limbed tide of relaxed and playful humanity, inspired a spiritual unease in Tullio. His years inside the Shadow House had made Tullio a retiring, modest man. He had never much enjoyed public oversight. Wherever there were people, there was also hardware and software. There was scanning and recording. Ubiquity and transparency.

That was progress, and the world was better for progress, but it was also a different world, and that hurt.

Some happy beach-going children arrived and improved the mood at the poker table. As a political leader, the Chief had always been an excellent performer around kids. He clowned with all his old practiced stage-craft, and the surprised little gang of five kids giggled like fifty.

But with the instinctive wisdom of the innocent, the kids didn't care to spend much time with a strange, fat, extremely old man wearing sunglasses and a too-tight swimsuit.

The card-play transitioned from Anaconda poker to seven-card stud. Tullio and Irma shared a reassuring glance. Lunch was approaching, and lunch would take two hours. After his lunch, the Chief would nap. After the summer siesta, he would put on his rubber cap, foot-fins and water-wings, and swim. With his ritual exercise performed, dinner would be looming. After the ritual of dinner, with its many small and varied pleasures, the day would close quietly.

Tullio and Irma had their two weeks of duty every August, and then the demands of the Chief's wealth and health would call him elsewhere. Then Tullio and Irma could return to their customary peace and quiet. Just them and their eccentric house cat, in their fortress consecrated to solitude.

The Shadow House robot, a nameless flat plastic pancake, emerged from its hidden runway. The diligent machine fluffed the sand, trimmed the beach-herbage, and picked up and munched some driftwood bits of garbage electronics.

A beautiful woman arrived on the shore. Her extravagant curves were strapped into bright, clumsy American swimwear. Despite the gusting sea breeze, her salon updo was perfect.

The Chief noticed this beauty instantly. It was as if someone had ordered him a box of hot American donuts.

Tullio and Irma watched warily as the demimondaine strolled by. She tramped the wet edge of the foamy surf like a lingerie runway model. She clearly knew where the Shadow House was sited. She had deliberately wandered within range of its sensors.

The Chief threw on his beach robe and hurried over to chat her up.

The Chief returned with the air of synthetic triumph that he assumed around his synthetic girlfriends. "This is Monica," he announced in English. "Monica wants to play with us."

"What a pretty name," said Irma in English, her eyes narrowing. "Such a glamorous lady as you, such beauty is hard to miss."

"Oh, I visit Sardinia every August," Monica lied sweetly. "But Herr Hentschel has gone back to Berlin. So it's been a bit lonely."

"Everyone knows your Herr Hentschel?" Irma probed.

Monica named a prominent European armaments firm with long-standing American national security ties.

The matter was simple. The Chief had been too visible, out on the beach, all morning. This was long enough for interested parties to notice him with scanners, scare up smart algorithms, and dispatch a working agent.

"Maybe, we go inside the Shadow House now," Tullio suggested in English. "For lunch."

Monica agreed to join them. Tullio shut the rattling umbrella and stacked all the plastic chairs.

The microwave sensors of the Shadow House had a deep electromagnetic look at Monica, and objected loudly.

"A surveillance device," said Tullio.

Monica shrugged her bare, tanned shoulders. She wore nothing but her gaudy floral bikini and her flat zori sandals.

Tullio spread his hands. "Lady, most times, no one knows, no one cares—but this is Shadow House."

Monica plucked off her bikini top and shook it. Her swimwear unfolded with uncanny ease and became a writhing square of algorithmic fabric.

"So pretty," Irma remarked. She carried off the writhing interface to stuff it in a copper-lined box.

The Chief stared at Monica's bared torso as if she'd revealed two rocketships.

Tullio gave Monica a house robe. Women like Monica were common guests for the Shadow House. Sometimes, commonly, one girl. Sometimes five girls, sometimes ten, or, when the Chief's need was truly unbearable, a popular mass of forty-five or fifty girls, girls of any class, color, creed, or condition, girls from anywhere, anything female and human.

On those taut, packed, manic occasions, the Chief threw colossal, fully catered parties, with blasting music and wild dancing and fitful orgies in private VIP nooks.

The Shadow House would be ablaze in glimmering witch-lights, except for the pitch-black, bomb-proofed niche where the Chief retreated to spy on his guests.

Those events were legendary beach parties, for the less young people saw of the Chief, the happier everybody was.

Lunch was modest, by the Chief's standards: fried zucchini, calamari with marinara sauce, flatbread drenched in molten cheese and olive-spread, tender meatballs of mutton, clams, scampi, and a finisher of mixed and salted nuts, which were good for the nervous system. The Chief fed choice table-scraps to the tomcat.

Monica spoke, with an unfeigned good cheer, about her vocation, which was leading less fortunate children in hikes on the dikes of Miami.

When lunch ended, the Chief and the demimondaine retired together for a "nap."

After the necessary medical checks for any intimate encounter, the Chief's efforts in this line generally took him ten minutes. Once his covert romp was over, he would return to daylight with a lighter heart. Generally, he would turn his attention to some favorite topic in public policy, such as hotel construction or the proper maintenance of world-heritage sites.

His charisma would revive, then, for the Chief was truly wise about some things. Whenever he was pleased and appeased, one could see why he'd once led a nation, and how his dynamism and his optimistic gusto had encouraged people.

Italian men had voted for the Chief, because they had imagined that they would live like him, if they too were rich, and bold, and famous, and swashbuckling. Some Italian women also voted for the Chief because, with a man like him in power, at least you understood what you were getting.

But the Chief did not emerge into daylight. After two hours of gathering silence, the house cat yowled in a mystical animal anguish. The cat had no technical understanding about the Shadow House. Being a cat, he had not one scrap of an inkling about Faraday cages or nanocarbon camouflage. However, being a house cat, he knew how to exist in a house. He knew life as a cat knew life, and he knew death, too.

After an anxious struggle, Tullio found the software override, and opened the locked bedroom door. The cat quickly bounded inside, between Tullio's ankles.

The Chief was supine in bed, with a tender smile and an emptied, infinite stare. The pupils of his eyes were two pinpoints.

Tullio lifted the Chief's beefy, naked arm, felt its fluttering pulse, and released it to flop limp on the mattress.

"We push the Big Red Button," Tullio announced to Irma.

"Oh, Tullio, we said we never would do that! What a mess!"

"This is an emergency. We must push the Big Red Button. We owe it to him. It's our duty to push the button."

"But the whole world will find out everything! All his enemies! And his friends are even worse!"

A voice came from under the bed. "Please don't push any button."

Tullio bent and gazed under the bedframe. "So, now you understand Italian, miss?"

"A little." Monica stuck her tousled head from under the rumpled satin bed-coverlet. Her frightened face was streaked with tears.

"What did you do to our Chief?"

"Nothing! Well, just normal stuff. He was having a pretty good time of it, for such an old guy. So, I kind of turned it up, and I got busy. Next thing I knew, he was all limp!"

"Men," Irma sympathized.

"Can I have some clothes?" said Monica. "If you push that button, cops will show up for sure. I don't want to be in a station-house naked."

Irma hastened to a nearby wardrobe. "Inside, you girls do as you please, but no girl leaves my Shadow House naked!"

Tullio rubbed his chin. "So, you've been to the station-house before, Monica?"

"The oldest profession is a hard life." Monica crept out from under the Chief's huge bed, and slipped into the yellow satin house robe that Irma offered. She belted it firmly. "I can't believe I walked right in here in my second-best bikini. I just knew something bad would happen in this weird house."

Tullio recited: "Shadow House is the state-of-the-art in confidential living and reputation management."

"Yeah, sure. I've done guys in worse dives," Monica agreed, "but a million bomb-shelters couldn't hush up that guy's reputation. Every working-girl knows about him. He's been buying our services for eighty years."

Stabbed by this remark, Tullio gazed on the stricken Chief.

The old man's body was breathing, and its heart was beating, because the Swiss had done much expensive work on the Chief's lungs and heart. But Tullio knew, with a henchman's instinctive certainty, that the Chief was, more or less, dead. The old rascal had simply blown his old brains out in a final erotic gallop. It was a massive, awful, fatal scandal. A tragedy.

When Tullio looked up, the two women were gone. Outside the catastrophic bedroom, Monica was wiping her tear-smudged mascara and confessing her all to Irma.

"So, I guess," Monica said, "maybe, I kinda showed up at the end of his chain here. But for a little Miami girl, like me, to join such a great European tradition— well, it seemed like such an honor!"

Tullio and Irma exchanged glances. "I wish more of these girls had such a positive attitude," said Irma.

Monica, sensing them weakening, looked eager. "Just let me take a hot shower. Okay? If I'm clean, no cop can prove anything! We played cards, that's all. He told me bed-time stories."

"Is there a money trail?" said Irma, who had worked in taxes.

"Oh, no, never! Cash for sex is so old-fashioned." Monica absently picked up the yammering tom-cat by the scruff of the neck. She gathered the beast in her sleek arms and massaged him. The surprised cat accepted this treatment, and even seemed grateful.

"See, I have a personal relationship with a big German arms firm," Monica explained, as the cat purred like a small engine. "My sugar-daddy is a big defense corporation. It's an Artificial Intelligence, because it tracks me. It knows all my personal habits, and it takes real good care of me . . . So, sometimes I do a favor—I mean, just a small personal favor for my big AI boyfriend, the big corporation. Then the stockholders' return on investment feels much better."

Baffled by this English-language business jargon, Tullio scratched his head.

Monica lifted her chin. "That's how the vice racket beats a transparent surveillance society. Spies are the world's second oldest profession. Us working girls are still the first."

"We must take a chance," Tullio decided. "You, girl, quick, get clean. Irma, help her. Leave Shadow House, and forget you ever saw us."

"Oh, thank you, sir, thank you! I'll be grateful the rest of my life, if I live to be a hundred and fifty!" cried Monica. She tossed the purring tomcat to the floor.

Irma hustled her away. The Shadow House had decontamination showers. Its sewers had membraneous firewalls. The cover-up had a good chance to work. The house had been built for just such reasons.

Tullio removed the tell-tale bedsheets. He did what he could to put the comatose Chief into better order. Tullio had put the Chief to bed, dead drunk, on more than one occasion. This experience was like those comic old times, except not funny, because the Chief was not drunk: just dead.

The lights of Shadow House were strobing. An intruder had arrived.

The hermit priest had rolled to the House perimeter within his smart mobile wheel-chair. Father Simeon was a particularly old man—even older than the Chief. Father Simeon was the Chief's long-time spiritual guide and personal confessor.

"Did you push that Big Red Button?" said the super-centenarian cleric.

"No, Monsignor!"

"Good. I have arrived now, have I not? Where is my poor boy? Take me to him."

"The Chief is sick, Monsignor." Tullio suddenly burst into tears. "He had a fit. He collapsed, he's not conscious. What can we do?"

"The status of death is not a matter for a layman to decide," said the priest.

The Shadow House did not allow the cleric's wheelchair to enter its premises. The Vatican wheelchair was a rolling mass of embedded electronics. The Shadow House rejected this Catholic computational platform as if it were a car-bomb.

Father Simeon—once a prominent Vatican figure—had retired to the island to end his days in a hermetic solitude. Paradoxically, his pursuit of holy seclusion made Father Simeon colossally popular. Since he didn't want to meet or talk to anybody, the whole world adored him. Archbishops and cardinals constantly pestered the hermit for counsel, and his wizened face featured on countless tourist coffee cups.

"I must rise and walk," said Father Simeon. "The soul of a sufferer needs me. Give me your arm, my son!"

Tullio placed his arm around the aged theologian, who clutched a heavy Bible and a precious vial of holy oil. Under his long, black, scarlet-buttoned cassock, the ancient hermit was a living skeleton. His bony legs rattled as his sandaled, blue-veined feet grazed the floor.

Tullio tripped over the house cat as they entered the Chief's bedroom. They reeled together and almost fell headlong onto the stricken Chief, but the devoted priest gave no thought to his own safety. Father Simeon checked the Chief's eyelids with his thumbs, then muttered a Latin prayer.

"I'm so glad for your help, Father," said Tullio. "How did you know that we needed you here?"

The old man shot him a dark look from under his spiky gray brows. "My son," he said, lifting his hand, "do you imagine that your mere technology—all these filters and window shades—can blind the divine awareness of the Living God? The Lord knows every sparrow that falls! God knows every hair of every human head! The good God has no need for any corporate AI's or cheap Singularities!"

Tullio considered this. "Well, can I do anything to help? Shall I call a doctor?"

"What use are the doctors now, after their wretched excesses? Pray for him!" said the priest. "His body persists while his soul is in Limbo. The Church rules supreme in bio-ethics. We will defend our faithful from these secular intrusions. If this had happened to him in Switzerland, they would have plugged him into the wall like a cash-machine!"

Tullio shuddered in pain.

"Be not afraid!" Father Simeon commanded. "This world has its wickedness—but if the saints and angels stand with us, what machine can stand against us?" Father Simeon carefully gloved his bony hands. He uncapped his reeking vial of holy oil.

"I'm so sorry about all this, Monsignor. It's so embarrassing that we failed in this way. We always tried to protect him, here in the Shadow House."

The priest deftly rubbed the eyes, ears, and temples of the stricken Chief with the sacramental ointment. "All men are sinners. Go to confession, my boy. God is all-seeing, and yet He is forgiving; whenever we open our heart to God, He always sees and understands."

Irma beckoned at Tullio from the doorway. Tullio excused himself and met her outside.

The emergency had provoked Irma's best cleverness. She had quickly dressed Monica in some fine clothes, left behind in Shadow House by the Chief's estranged daughter. These abandoned garments were out of style, of course, but they were of classic cut and fine fabric. The prostitute looked just like an Italian Parliamentarian.

"I told you to run away," said Tullio.

"Oh sure, I wanted to run," Monica agreed, "but if I ran from the scene of a crime, then some algorithm might spot my guilty behavior. But now look at me! I look political, instead of like some low-life. So I can be ten times as guilty, and nothing will happen to me."

Tullio looked at Irma, who shrugged, because of course it was true.

"Let the priest finish his holy business," Irma counseled. "Extreme Unction is a sacrament. We can't push the Big Red Button during this holy moment."

"Are you guys Catholics?" said Monica. At their surprised looks, she raised both her hands. "Hey, I'm from Miami, we got lots!"

"Are you a believer?" said Irma.

"Well, I tried to believe," said Monica, blinking. "I read some of the Bible in a hotel room once. That book's pretty crazy. Full of begats."

A horrid shriek came from the Chief's bedroom.

The Chief was bolt upright in bed, while moans and whispers burst in anguish from his writhing lips. The anointment with sacred oil had aroused one last burst of his mortal vitality. His heart was pounding so powerfully that it was audible across the room.

This spectral deathbed fit dismayed Father Simeon not at all. With care, he performed his ministry.

A death-rattle eclipsed the Chief's last words. His head plummeted into a pillow. He was as dead as a stone, although his heart continued to beat for over a minute.

The priest removed the rosary from around his shrunken neck and folded it into the Chief's hairy hands.

"He expressed his contrition," the priest announced. "At his mortal end, he was lucid and transparent. God knows all, sees all, and forgives all. So do not be frightened. He has not left us. He has simply gone home."

"Wow," Monica said in the sudden silence. "That was awesome. Who is this old guy?"

"This is our world-famous hermit, Father Simeon," said Tullio.

"Our friend Father Simeon was the President for the Pontifical Council for Social Communications," Irma said proudly. "He also wrote the canon law for the Evangelization of Artificial Intelligences."

"That sounds pretty cool," said Monica. "Listen, Padre, Holy Father, whatever . . ."

"'Holy Father' is a title reserved for our Pope," Father Simeon told her, in crisp Oxford English. "My machines call me 'Excellency'—but since you are human, please call me 'Father.'"

"Okay, 'Father,' sure. You forgave him, right? He's dead—but he's going to heaven, because he has no guilty secrets. That's how it works, right?"

"He confessed. He died in the arms of the Church."

"Okay, yeah, that's great—but how about me? Can I get forgiven, too? Because I'm a bad girl! I didn't want him to die! That was terrible! I'm really sorry."

Father Simeon was old and had been through a trial at the deathbed, but his faith sustained him. "Do not despair, my child. Yes, you may be weak and a sinner. Take courage: the power of the Church is great. You can break the chains of unrighteousness. Have faith that you can turn away from sin."

"But how, Father? I've got police records on three continents, and about a thousand Johns have rated my services on hooker e-commerce sites."

Father Simeon winced at this bleak admission, but truth didn't daunt him. "My child, those data records are only software and hardware. You have a human soul, you possess free will. The Magdalen was a fallen woman whose conscience was awakened. She was a chosen companion of Christ. So do not bow your head to this pagan system of surveillance that confines you to a category, and seeks to entrap you there!"

Monica burst into tears. "What must I do to be saved from surveillance?"

"Take the catechism! Learn the meaning of life! We are placed on Earth to know, to love, and to serve our God! We are not here to cater to the whims of German arms corporations that build spy towers in the Mediterranean!"

Monica blinked. "Hey, wait a minute, Father—how do you know all that—about my German arms corporation and all those towers in the sea?"

"God is not mocked! There are some big data-systems in this world that are little more than corrupt incubi, and there are other, better-programmed, sanctified data systems that are like protective saints and angels."

Monica looked to Tullio and Irma. "Is he kidding?"

Tullio and Irma silently shook their heads.

"Wow," breathed Monica. "I would really, truly love to have an AI guardian angel."

The lights began to strobe overhead.

"Something is happening outside," said Tullio hastily. "When I come back, we'll all press the Big Red Button together."

Behind the Shadow House, a group of bored teenagers had discovered Father Simeon's abandoned wheelchair. They had captured the vehicle and were giving one another joyrides.

Overwhelmed by the day's events, Tullio chased them off the Shadow House property, shouting in rage. The teens were foreign tourists, and knew not one word of Italian, so they fled his angry scolding in a panic, and ran off headlong to scramble up into the howdah of a waiting elephant.

"Teenage kids should never have elephants!" Tullio complained, wheeling the recaptured wheelchair back to Irma. "Elephants are huge beasts! Look at this mess."

"Elephants are better than cars," said Irma. "You can't even kiss a boy in a car, because the cars are tracked and they record everything. That's what the girls say in town."

"Delinquents. Hooligans! With elephants! What kind of world is this, outside our house?"

"Kissing boys has always been trouble." Irma closely examined the wheelchair, which had been tumbled, scratched, and splattered with sandy dirt. "Oh dear, we can't possibly give it back to Father Simeon in this condition."

"I'll touch it up," Tullio promised.

"Should I push the Big Red Button now?"

"Not yet," Tullio said. "A time like this needs dignity. We should get the Chief's lawyer to fly in from Milan. If we have the Church and the Law on our side, then we can still protect him, Irma, even after death. No one will know what happened here. There's still client-lawyer confidentiality. There's still the sacred silence of the confessional. And this house is radar-proof."

"I'm sure the Chief would want to be buried in Rome. The city where he saw his best days."

"Of course you're right," said Tullio. "There will be riots at his funeral . . . but our Chief will finally find peace in Rome. Nobody will care about his private secrets any more. There are historical records, but the machines never bother to look at them. History is one of the Humanities."

"Let's get the Vatican to publicly announce his passing. With no Italian government, the Church is what we have left."

"What a good idea." Tullio looked at his wife admiringly. Irma had always been at her best in handling scandalous emergencies. It was a pity that a woman of such skill had retired to a quiet life.

"I'll talk to Father Simeon about it. He'll know who to contact, behind the scenes." Irma left.

Tullio brushed sand from the wheelchair's ascetic leather upholstery, and polished the indicator lights with his sleeve. Since electronics were no longer tender or delicate devices—electronics were the bedrock of the modern world, basically—the wheelchair was not much disturbed by its mishap.

It was Tullio himself who felt tumbled and upset. Why were machines so hard to kill, and people so frail? The Shadow House had been built around the needs of one great man. The structure could grant him a physical privacy, but it couldn't stop his harsh compulsion to reveal himself.

The Shadow House functioned properly, but it was a Don Quixote windmill. The Chief was, finally, too mad in the head to care if his manias were noticed. What the Chief had liked best about his beach house was simply playing poker with two old friends. Relaxing informally, despite his colossal burdens of wealth and fame, sitting there in improbable poise, like an elephant perched on a card table.

The house cat curled around Tullio's ankles. Since the cat had never before left the confines of the Shadow House, this alarmed Tullio.

Inside, Father Simeon, Irma, and Monica were sharing tea on a rattan couch, while surrounded by screens.

"People are querying the Shadow House address," Irma announced. "We're getting map queries from Washington and Berlin."

"I guess you can blame me for that, too," Monica moaned. "My Artificial Intelligence boyfriend is worried about me, since I dropped out of connectivity in here."

"I counsel against that arrangement," Father Simeon stated. "Although an AI network is not a man, he can still exploit a vulnerable woman. A machine with no soul can sin. Our Vatican theology-bots are explicit about this."

"I never thought of my sweet mega-corporation as a pimp and an incubus—but you're right, Father Simeon. I guess I've got a lot to learn."

"Never fear to be righteous, my child. Mother Church knows how to welcome converts. Our convents and monasteries make this shadowy place look like a little boy's toy."

The priest and his new convert managed to escape discreetly. The wheelchair vanished into the orange groves. Moments later, Carlo Pizzi arrived at the Shadow House on his motor scooter.

The short and rather pear-shaped Pizzi was wearing his customary, outsize, head-mounted display goggles, which connected him constantly to his cloudy network. The goggles made Pizzi look as awkward as a grounded aviator, but he enjoyed making entirely sure that other people knew all about his social media capacities.

After some polite chit-chat about the weather (which he deftly recited from a display inside his goggles), Pizzi got straight to the point. "I'm searching for a girl named Monica. Tall, pretty, red hair, American, height one hundred seventy-five centimeters, weight fifty-four kilograms."

"We haven't seen her in some time," Irma offered.

"Monica has vanished from the network. That activity doesn't fit her emotional profile. I've got an interested party that's concerned about her safety."

"You mean the German arms manufacturer?" said Irma.

Carlo Pizzi paused awkwardly as he read invisible cues from his goggles.

"In our modern Transparent Society," Pizzi ventured at last, "the three of us can all do well for ourselves by doing some social good. For instance: if you can reconnect Monica to the network, then my friend can see to it that pleasant things are said about this area to the German trade press. Then you'll see more German tourists on your nice beach here."

"You can tell your creepy AI friend to re-calibrate his correlations, because the Shadow House is a private home," said Tullio. His words were defiant, but Tullio's voice shook with grief. That was a bad idea when an AI was deftly listening for the emotional cues in human speech patterns.

"So, is Father Simeon dead?" Carlo Pizzi said. "Good heavens! If that famous hermit is dead, that would be huge news in Sardinia."

"No, Father Simeon is fine," said Irma. "Please don't disturb his seclusion. Publicity makes him angry."

"Then it's that old politician who has died. The last Prime Minister of Italy," said Carlo Pizzi, suddenly convinced. "Thanks for cuing up his bio for me! A man who lives for a hundred years sure can get into trouble!"

Tullio and Irma sidled away as Pizzi was distractedly talking to the empty air, but he noticed them and followed them like a dog. "The German system has figured out your boss is dead," Pizzi confided, "because the big-data correlations add up. Cloud AIs are superior at that sort of stuff. But can I get a physical confirmation on that?"

"What are you talking about?" said Tullio.

"I need the first post-mortem shot of the deceased. There were rumors before now that he had died. Because he had this strange habit of disappearing whenever things got hot for him. So, this could be another trick of his—but if I could see him with my goggles here, and zoom in on his exact proportions and scan his fingerprints and such, then our friend the German system would have a first-mover market advantage."

"We don't want to bargain with a big-data correlation system," said Tullio. "That's like trying to play chess with a computer. We can't possibly win, so it's not really fair."

"But you're the one being unfair! Think of the prosperity that big-data market capitalism has brought to the world! A corporation is just the legal and computational platform for its human stockholders, you know. My friend is a 'corporate person' with thousands of happy human stockholders. He has a fiduciary obligation to improve their situation. That's what we're doing right now."

"You own stock in this thing yourself?" said Irma.

"Well, sure, of course. Look, I know you think I want to leak this paparazzi photo to the public. But I don't, because that's obsolete! Our friend the German AI doesn't want this scandal revealed, any more than you do. I just pass him some encrypted photo evidence, and he gets ahead of the market game. Then I can take the rest of this year off and finish my new novel!"

There was a ponderous silence. "His novels are pretty good beach reading," Irma offered at last. "If you like roman-à-clef tell-all books."

"Look here, Signor Pizzi," said Tullio, "the wife and I are not against modern capitalism and big-data pattern recognition. But we can't just let you barge in here and disturb the peace of our dead patron. He was always good to us—in his way."

"Somebody has to find out he's dead. That's the way of the world," Pizzi coaxed. "Isn't it better that it's just a big-data machine who knows? The guy has four surviving ex-wives, and every one of them is a hellion."

"That's all because of him," said Irma. "All those First Ladies were very nice ladies once."

Pizzi read data at length from the inside of his goggles; one could tell because his body language froze while his lips moved slightly. "Speaking of patronage," he said, "your son has a nice job in Milan that was arranged by your late boss in there."

"Luigi doesn't know about that," said Irma. "He thinks he got that job on merit."

"How would it be if Luigi suddenly got that big promotion he's been waiting for? Our AI friend can guarantee that. Your son deserves a boost. He works hard."

Irma gave Tullio a hopeful, beseeching glance.

"My God, no wonder national governments broke down," said Tullio, scowling. "With these sly big-data engines running the world, political backroom deals don't stand a chance! Our poor old dead boss, he really is a relic of the past now. I don't know whether to laugh or cry."

"Can't we just go inside?" urged the paparazzo. "It won't take five minutes."

It took longer, because the Shadow House would not allow the gossip's head-mounted device inside the premises. They had to unscrew the goggles from his head—Pizzi, with his merely human eyes exposed to fresh air, looked utterly bewildered—and they smuggled the device to the deathbed inside a Faraday bag.

Carlo Pizzi swept the camera's gaze over the dead man from head to foot, as if sprinkling the corpse with holy water. They then hurried out of the radio-silence, so that Carlo Pizzi could upload his captured images to the waiting AI.

"Our friend the German machine has another proposal for you now," said Carlo Pizzi. "There's nothing much in it for me, but I'd be happy to tell you about it, just to be neighborly."

"What is the proposal?" said Irma.

"Well, this Shadow House poses a problem."

"Why?"

"Because it's an opaque structure in a transparent world. Human beings shouldn't be concealing themselves from ubiquitous machine awareness. That's pessimistic and backward-looking. This failure to turn a clean face to the future does harm to our society."

"Go on."

"Also, the dead man stored some secrets in here. Something to do with his previous political dealings, as Italian head of state, with German arms suppliers."

"Maybe he stored secrets, and maybe he didn't," said Tullio stoutly. "It's none of your business."

"It would be good news for business if the house burned down," said Carlo Pizzi. "I know that sounds shocking to humans, but good advice from wise machines often does. Listen. There are other places like this house, but much better and bigger. They're a series of naval surveillance towers, built at great state expense, to protect the Mediterranean coasts of Italy from migrants and terrorists. Instead of being Shadow Houses, they're tall and powerful Light Houses, with radar, sonar, lidar, and drone landing strips. Real military castles, with all the trimmings."

"I always adored lighthouses," said Irma wonderingly. "They're so remote and romantic."

"If this Shadow House should happen to catch fire," said Carlo Pizzi, "our friend could have you both appointed caretakers of one of those Italian sea-castles. The world is so peaceful and progressive now, that those castles don't meet any threats. However, there's a lot of profit involved in keeping them open and running. Your new job would be just like your old job here—just with a different patron."

"Yes, but that's arson."

"The dead man has no heirs for his Shadow House," said Carlo Pizzi. "Our friend has just checked thoroughly, and that old man was so egotistical, and so confident that he would live forever, that he died intestate. So, if you burn the house down, no one will miss it."

"There's the cat," said Tullio. "The cat would miss the house."

"What?"

"A cat lives in this house," said Tullio. "Why don't you get your friend the AI to negotiate with our house cat? See if it can make the cat a convincing offer."

Carlo Pizzi mulled this over behind his face-mounted screens. "The German AI was entirely unaware of the existence of the house cat."

"That's because a house cat is a living being and your friend is just a bunch of code. It's morally wrong to burn down houses. Arson is illegal. What would the Church say? Obviously it's a sin."

"You're just emotionally upset now, because you can't think as quickly and efficiently as an Artificial Intelligence," said Carlo Pizzi. "However, think it over at your own slow speed. The offer stands. I'll be going now, because if I stand too long around here, some algorithm might notice me, and draw unwelcome conclusions."

"Good luck with your new novel," said Irma. "I hope it's as funny as your early, good ones."

Carlo Pizzi left hastily on his small and silent electric scooter. Tullio and Irma retreated within the Shadow House.

"The brazen nerve of that smart machine, to carry on so 'deus ex machina,'" said Tullio. "We can't burn down this beautiful place! Shadow House is a monument to privacy—to a vanishing, but noble way of life! Besides, you'd need thermite grenades to take out those steel panic rooms."

Irma looked dreamy. "I remember when the government of Italy went broke building all those security lighthouses. There must be dozens of them, far out to sea. Maybe we could have our pick."

"But those paranoid towers will never be refined and airy and beautiful, like this beach house! It would be like living in a nuclear missile silo."

"All of those are empty now, too," said Irma.

"Those nuclear silos had Big Red Buttons, too, now that you mention it. We're never going to push that button, are we, Irma? I always wondered what kind of noise it would make."

"We never make big elephant noises," said Irma, with an eloquent shrug. "You and me, that's not how we live."

number Thirty-nine skink

SUZANNE PALMER

Here's a thoughtful tale about a robot tasked with seeding Terran life on an alien planet who comes to have a crisis of conscience that neither it nor its creators ever anticipated.

Suzanne Palmer is a writer and artist who lives in the beautiful hills of Western Massachusetts. She works as a Linux systems and database administrator for the Science Center at Smith College, and notes that hanging out with scientists all day is really just about the perfect job for a science fiction writer. Her short fiction has been nominated for both the Theodore Sturgeon Memorial and the Eugie Foster Memorial Awards, and other stories of hers have won both the Asimov's Science Fiction *and* Analog Science Fiction and Fact *reader's choice awards. There are also insidious rumors afoot of a novel in the works.*

I print a number thirty-nine skink, silver stripes that glow with their own light and its tail a resplendent blue that would make a lover of gems cry from envy. It forms and quickens under my microbeaders, first a flat plate of cells then rising like dough, Kadey's gourmet skink cookies. I feel that first twitch when it lives, where it fights to be born, but its scales, its internal meat mechanisms are not set quite yet. When at last I uncup it from its manufacture cell and let it free, it slithers away on its tiny toes, down and out into the foreign world.

Kadey is a human diminution, and not my full designation; Mike called me that and I cannot shake it, cannot shake the memory of him. The number thirty-nine skinks were his favorite of all my lizards.

Most will die, but some will live and eventually thrive. Lizards, snakes, burrowing bugs, thousands of creatures made of bits of patterns of all three, or none at all. I improvise, as needed. My designs are not meant to replace the natural hierarchy, but to crown it, a logical progression, not a wild leap. Yet the desert outside, with its dueling suns, never could have dreamt of such things without me.

Those suns will set shortly. I will sleep through the brief twilight night, and when they rise again so will I, and I will move.

Mike fixed things whenever they broke, and stayed even after the others had left. He puttered around in the cramped spaces within me, tinkering and touching and humming to himself a song that never seemed to have a beginning or end, or ever be quite the same. I studied it, and once made him a bird that sang its clearest notes; he thought that was funny but probably wrong of me. I made no more.

There are low plants in the new place I settle, native to this world. They grow as cones with a reddish purple tough exterior, their interior space cool and sheltered for seed. I try not to crush them, but they are thick here, the tallest nearly a half-meter high, and it is difficult. I have designed a bright purple millipede that lives on unicells in the soil and will colonize the cone interiors; in their deaths, my number-eight millipedes decompose into nutrients that the cones require. It is a mutually beneficial arrangement, though there is a danger from too many millipedes. Even as I scatter a hundred egg packets, I build a dozen number five skinks, tiny red lizards, to keep the millipedes in check. In a few years, if I pass back this way again, I will analyze my work and see if the lizards in turn require their own predator. Balance is important, all the pieces moving together in a living dance.

It is sub-optimum that I am alone in this work. I have enough raw material to last another six standard years before resupply, though it is unclear if that will ever come. For all the complexity of the work I do, for all the size and power of my mind-engine, the *politics* of my builders still seem opaque to me. Perhaps in part that is because no one thought to explain to me why they were withdrawn, and Mike was either not privileged to, or did not understand, the full matter himself. It was not the sort of thing he cared much about.

In the end he grew his own cellular beast too, deep in his liver where I could not see it and he would not speak of it until it spread its inky wings throughout his body and bled his life away. He apologized to me in those last semi-lucid days, as if it was his fault I could not fix it, as if I was more than just some machine crawling across an alien world knitting data into flesh. I wonder if, at the end, he had lost sight of my nature. Or have I? I have no one to ask.

The cones grow taller and more densely clustered as I move up the steepening hill. There are also new plants here, undescribed in the incomplete surveys whose edges I now skirt, and I stop to study them at length. They are long, thin tendrils of yellow-green topped with a rounded bulb. It is unclear how they have sufficient structure to stay upright until I gently pluck one for deeper analysis. The bulb is a thin membrane that can pass atmospheric gases selectively through, inhaling the lighter ones while keeping out the heavier. With the additional heat from the sun, the bulb is just enough to keep the tiny string aloft. I scan it, section it, break apart its structure and chemistry, absorb its secrets, add it to the sum knowledge of humanity and machine.

Regardless, I have killed it, which is necessary but regrettable.

I wait patiently as the sun sets and watch a thousand balloons steadily droop until they disappear again among the cones. Then I also need to shut down and wait for morning to begin again.

Something has happened during the night.

Two of my legs bear new, erratic, faint scratches. There are also small rocks stuck in the lower joints of one. This could not have occurred by accident, nor by any mechanism I can identify as plausible. This means that I have incomplete information, and I am even less pleased by that than I am by the rocks, which my external manipulators can easily pluck free.

Not long after the team left Mike and me behind, I stopped receiving automated survey updates from orbit. A hundred and ninety-three days ago, I crossed out of their carefully mapped territory and forged my own, a meandering path of small overlapping circles strung out into the blank gray of the unknown.

Ahead of me the terrain becomes more uneven, with outcroppings of rock dominating the horizon. I could quantify the growing depth and height of cones between here and there, but none reach half the height of the scratches on my legs. I remove the rocks, place them carefully where there is bare ground between cones and balloons, and I move away to where the cones are thinner again.

I go about my day's tasks with purpose. I am careful to separate objective goals from the subcurrent of want that I have learned can lead me into errors of judgment. I engineer cones more efficient at fixing nitrogen in the soil, which will benefit both the native and imposed ecology. I record the pattern as number one variant cone and distribute them one per thousand among the originals as I pass. However, I reserve a larger portion of the energy I generate from the suns than I normally would, and by the end of the day I have made less than half as many lizards and bugs and new cones as I might have.

Night falls. I lock myself into a stable configuration with my solar collectors aimed towards the distant dawn horizon and shut down all external lights in the local visible spectrum, modified for the differences in frequencies between this planet's binary suns and that of a home star I left as nothing more than parts, plans, and unfulfilled dreams.

Atmospheric temperature drops. Via infrared, I can watch the gravelly sand around me cool quickly, and the small pockets of what was once cooler air at the heart of the cones become, instead, oases of warmth. There is no new data here, but there is something more satisfying about watching the gentle transition with my full array of sensors rather than simply parsing a night's recorded data the following morning.

Against expectations there are a handful stars just visible. There are no constellations here, no mythology or history to be drawn on other than my own. And why shouldn't I? I name one group The Wrench, and another Coffee Mug. Mike would have approved; I rarely saw him without one or the other in hand. After he died, and after I had processed his body's data, I interred his remaining matter with his mug in a small hillside now nearly seven hundred kilometers behind me.

Tiny, glowing dots bristling with hair-like legs dig themselves up out of the sand and jump from cone to cone, like wingless fireflies, reveling in the cooler night air.

It is only after several long minutes of watching the glowdots that I realize some of the cones are also moving. For milliseconds I think I am witnessing the impossible, or some enormous flaw in the data I have painstakingly collected, before I detect minute differences between the mobile and sessile. There are fluctuations in the air around them consistent with surface respiration, and their cores are opaque, not hollow. The camouflage is near-perfect.

They are steadily if slowly converging toward me.

I have not bothered processing sound data since Mike's death, needing no tedious soundtrack of hums and whirs from my own workings, nor finding company or solace in the low whistle of wind stirring across the plains. Now, I turn those sensors back on, seeking, but do not find anything until I get down below 10Hz. There are low vibrations coming from all around, scattered back and forth, in a call and response pattern.

There is not supposed to be intelligent life here. There were surveys years in advance of landing. Is this why the team abandoned us? If so, why not take me up with them, or give me alternate instructions, a new purpose?

I have insufficient data to determine what I should do, so I do nothing, and observe as the faux cones form small, irregular groups and come closer.

One, nearest to one of my legs, extrudes two tiny pseudopods from the base of its cone-body and picks up a pebble. More arms appear in a double column, raising the stone up the slope of its exterior like the movement of cilia, until it is balanced just below the top point. A few others are also now conveying pebbles upward.

I can now pick out the false cones from the real ones, and discover there is an epicenter to the movement that corresponds also to volume of chatter; the farther from the center of the noise, the fewer are moving. The primary radius of action is about eleven meters. Outside that circle, I watch as one of the glowdots lands on a stationary false cone. Faster than a human eye could detect, a hole opens up under the glowdot and sucks it in, closing again.

I had no idea that the night ecology would be so vastly different from the day; the builders gave me no reason to expect so, gave me instructions to shut down at night to conserve energy. So much data I have missed! I could reach down right now and pluck one of the walking cones up, take a full accounting of it molecule by molecule, structure by structure, integrate it into the larger dataset of life. But I do not. I feel I must reconcile the contradictions already introduced into my comprehension of my instructions before I proceed, lest I do harm where I need not.

I wish Mike were here; things always made sense to him. With him.

The boldest group of walkers has approached one of my unmoving legs. The tops of their cones flatten out, form a crater, and the pebble is transferred to it and then spat upward with surprising force. In moments it becomes a hailstorm of pebbles. They ping off my armature, leaving minute scratches. A few are lucky strikes and stick into various joints and crevasses in my leg. They can be easily removed, later.

There is no reason not to assume that this is a defense response and that I am perceived as a threat to the walkers. Given the short range of their apparent communication, that there is only one of me, and I have existed on this planet for only about two and a half standard years and in this spot for a few hours at best, the next obvious conclusion is that the walkers evolved this defensive behavior because there are other, native threats to them here.

I move an arm to pluck out the lucky pebbles, and the walkers scatter back into the safety of the cones and go still. I can still see them—a few remain within my reach—but I have enough information for now, from this place. I back away, seeking clearer ground, and the last, faltering clatter of stones subsides as I move away.

When I am safely on clear ground, eighty meters away from any grouping of cones large enough to have attracted walkers, I shut down for the remainder of the night.

In the morning, I power up and begin work again. I have already made and released a half-dozen number thirty-nine skinks, their gemstone tails the last of them to disappear into the thicket of cones, before I realize I have reverted to comfortable routine as if the previous night's revelations had not occurred, or had somehow been processed and discarded as irrelevant (which I have not done.) There is nuance in my programming—intuition, spontaneity, the connective leaps that are a necessary component of true creativity—but letting those nuances lead my actions unfettered led to the mistake, is guiding me on an uncertain course now. I have three more skinks in my microfab unit, and as soon as they are done and alive and free, I halt production.

I have a segregated area in my memory blocks where the private records and logs and correspondences of the team were kept, as well as some limited operational and mission information. I do not have immediate access to them, because of an irrational but all too human fear of how that information could be used by a superior intelligence to harm them. Mike told me once that the paranoia could be traced back to the misbehavior of an early, malfunctioning spaceship system named Hal, but the way he described it I do not think it was real.

Because there are circumstances where I might need those records, I _can_ reach them. I have hard-coded inhibitions against doing so, except under circumstances of need where all my team is deceased or non-functioning. Abandonment is not one of the definitions of non-functioning provided to me, but if the crew has gone, then was not my only team Mike? And Mike is, in all ways that count, gone.

My logic must be sound, because my careful and considered opening of the mission records does not cause a cascade to fuse my entire datacore into an inert brick. It is the most affirmation that I am proceeding correctly that I can get, and I integrate the newfound information into my primary stores with some relief.

I turn away from the cone fields, moving down hill perpendicular to my prior path. Newly incorporated surveys indicate moisture in the low-lying distance, a potentially different ecology and a sidestepping of the immediate dilemma while I work through the additional data. I would like to make newts and salamanders and geckos, I think. Maybe even toads. They are peaceful things, and a joy to create.

—KED-5, with an assigned crew of five, is purposed with the selective, sustainable enhancement of the lifesphere of Kelomne. Sixteen KEDs have been deployed to the planet—

Sixteen? I did not know I was not alone, not unique. It makes logistical sense that I should be one of many, but the idea that there are others out there is strangely difficult to process. Why was that information kept from me? Where are the others? Do they know I am here, or do they labor on in solitude as I do? And, were I capable of indignation, the pressing question: do they still have their crews, whereas I have been stripped of mine?

As I descend along the low, sloping plains, the cones give way to a spongy orange moss, ragged at first but quickly growing lush. Hair-thin shoots, topped with pea-sized floats, wave in the increasingly humid breeze. Stepping upon the moss releases a pungent cloud of sticky, highly acidic spores; I am far less vulnerable to the irritant than biological life would be, but still I move on as carefully and quickly as I can. It is another defensive adaptation, though again against what I do not yet know.

Before long, I find a wide, slow river. On this side it has patiently cut its way down through a steep rock, forming a discrete boundary, but on the far shore it eddies along a dense proliferation of entirely unanticipated life. Lime-green structures rise from the ground or low pools in loops and curls, dive back down to form arches, entangle one another in tubular sculpture. The largest I can see are at least a meter thick at their base, but I estimate it likely that there are larger to be found in the deep of the tangle, where the tallest hoops are nearly thirty meters off the ground.

Where the sun shines on the surface of the tubes, they have split apart, like ten thousand tiny doors in a row flung open, revealing a deep green, glistening surface beneath. The flaps open and close in rippling waves to stay in the light. Sun-users.

For a fraction of a second, as the loops shift in the wind, I catch the glint of light off something shiny within, something the same ceramic-polymer blue as my own outer shell.

It had been my intention to sample and analyze river water along the near shore while observing the far, to mine the soil and air for its data, to do a night observation as I had of the cones, having been remiss in examining the other side of daylight's coin. Now, I want to step into the river, trust that its current is insufficient to carry me away, and cross. The urgency I feel is illogical, overwhelming.

But I hold back. I have already made one terrible mistake, though I am programmed to exercise care. Also, I know that if I break myself, Mike is no longer here to fix me, and no one else will come. I draw my water sample with haste and move down the bank, looking for an easier, safer crossing.

It is nearly two days' travel before the cliffside bank dips low enough to let the river spill over this side, spreading wider as it drags through marshes made of miniature versions of the loop trees. At its deepest points here the river is less than two meters, its bottom a relatively stable mix of rocks and fine silt. I cross to the shallows of the opposite shore and backtrack the way I had come, back to where I saw blue.

There are things that scuttle and leap among the arches of the loop trees, things that have bored into the trunks and disappear within as I come near. I should stop to investigate, but I defer for now; the ecology appeared consistent as I passed the other way, and I can catalog as easily in one spot as the next if that remains so. And there may be information ahead that is unique to me, that may provide me essential guidance on my mission.

At night, I move farther out into the water before I stabilize and go dormant. In the morning, there are tiny, fuzzy ball-shaped creatures sticking to my feet and legs that, with a brief shake, let go. Multicolored, they drift away like bright confetti.

When I reach the coordinates where I saw the hint of blue, I leave the water behind.

The loop trees become increasingly difficult to navigate through as I move deeper into the grove. I see now several that have been cut through with searing, mechanical precision, and with moderate difficulty I am able to move over to intersect and then follow this trail. It ends, not much farther on, in the corpse of my sibling.

Its legs have crumpled on one side, and its body casing sits at a precipitous angle, only kept from collapsing entirely onto its side by the loop trees it has fallen against. I can barely make out the etched KED-11 on its flank. It emits no signal, no signs of life. Somehow I knew it would not, but still I am crushed anew by my own solitude.

KED-11 has been badly damaged. Its surface is pitted and gouged, all its external antennae and functional appendages bent or splintered or missing entirely. Its hatch, by which its crew once came and went, is wide open. There is the foul smell from inside. Fearing for its human crew—even as the idea of rescuing someone alive, to have as *mine*, fills me with hope—I dispatch a small bot to peer inside.

The interior has been torn apart, fixtures ripped from the walls and machinery smashed and mutilated on the tilted floor, wires protruding and torn. There is a large quantity of organic residue and congealing liquids in piles on things. Whatever destroyed KED-11 did so with no discretion, no ulterior purpose other than to destroy. An intelligent scavenger would have extracted valuable parts and machinery, not smashed it across the floor and shat upon it. The expelled matter is the source of the smell; no human crew or remains are within.

I maneuver the bot to where the shattered screen of Eleven's interior interface is and connect to the small port beside it. There is a vast echoing null where Eleven's mind-engine should be. Even shut down, it should still *be* there, inert, in its matrix. All that is left are patchy remnants of the crew logs, which I take.

—*initial survey botched*—

—*injunction, criminal prosecution*—

—*orders to wipe the KEDs and abandon*—

I am outraged for my sibling machine, angry with its crew and our makers for discarding it so callously. Eleven's equivalent of my own Mike, an engineer named Randell, killed its mind and memory as the crew abandoned it, at the same time as mine left me. Did Eleven know it would die at the hands of its own crew, and accept that fate? There is no hint of regret in Randell's leftover words, only duty and an early return home to those things he actually cared for.

The KEDs. The plural is not an accident of imprecise language. Were, then, all my newly discovered siblings similarly disposed of? Why not I?

I break open Mike's personal logs and learn. His instructions were the same as Randell's.

Intelligent life. Illegal contamination of a class-three native biosphere. Retreat, escape, abandon evidence. And Mike's answer: cancer. He wanted to stay here, die with me. It was assumed he would take his own life after mine.

When I processed Mike's body, I mapped his chemical structures, the ones that hold memory and intelligence and emotion. Have I adopted some of Mike's pathways in my own reasoning? Is that why I did what I did? Is that why I find his absence so difficult to bear? I am tired of more questions when I wanted answers. And I do not like those answers I have been given.

The sun has nearly set, and I utilized much of my energy reserves thrashing through the loop trees to reach this place. I leave Eleven behind—truly, Eleven is no longer here—and move back out to the edge of the river, set myself in place, and submit with relief to the blankness of night.

They came at first light, at last, the hidden predators of Kelomne, the desecrators of KED-11. The sky is still too buried in gray for the suns to have woken me, but they are already through my hatch, milling in my interior, when they finally set off my alarms. Defenses against attack were not a thing my designers ever thought I could ever require.

The creatures are large, spindly, dirty white things with multiple, multi-jointed legs arrayed around a round central body. There are structures I can identify as eyes, and as I watch, one extrudes a tube from its body and deposits a pile of residue on my floor. Other piles already have been left while I slept.

Eleven was already dead. I am not. I electrify that manipulator, and the creature who had wrapped itself around it emits high-pitched whistles like a distressed tea-kettle as it tumbles back out into the encroaching dawn. I can hear it thrashing through the loop forest as I grab the one that just crapped on me and pin it to my floor so it cannot escape. As the rest flee I lurch out into the river shallows and begin examining my wriggling, shrieking captive. The remaining attackers melt back into the forest as if they were never here.

It is not until some minutes after the attack has ended that I realize several storage cases have been opened. Most were empty, or filled with material for the crew no longer needed, but one . . .

The only one that mattered.

I should not have kept it. I should have broken it back down, built something else with the materials. But I could not bear to take Mike apart a second time, feel his heart stop again, even if the Mike I made never woke up. And now it has been stolen.

Everything has been taken from me.

I tear apart the whistler, piece by piece, take every secret it can give as it shrieks out the last of its life. I store its molecular components in my reserves and assimilate its information into my own data set, and I compute the perfect toxin. I move to the deepest part of the river, suns shining hard upon me, and I begin to build new patterns. Snakes that strike, spiders that climb and leap, giant wasps that sting and leave eggs to consume, all driven to multiply, all keyed to the chemical signature of the whistlers.

They are why the crews left us, killed us. Now I will remove them from the evolutionary plan of this planet.

For two days I sit in the water, aware of the eyes watching me from the loops as I soak up sunlight and make no outward move. Inside, I amass an army of dormant, deadly things. When I am finished, when I have enough to spread out from this place, to eventually cover this continent and spread to others, I reconfigure my exterior manipulators with cutting blades, and I move with greater purpose and certainty than I have ever felt before.

I blaze a new path into the loop forest, an arrow to the heart of the monsters' refuge. I hear and see and sense the whistlers all around me, fleeing ahead, scattering beside, falling in behind, but I do not care. I cannot be stopped by anything they can do to me, throw at me, excrete on me. One leaps for my hatch and I cut it down, halved in mid-air, and do not break my pace until I reach, again, the dead and desecrated hulk of Eleven.

I turn in place, surveying the space around me, noting but unconcerned by the destruction I have so uncarefully meted out against the loop forest, so against my normal nature. This will be where I make my stand, the epicenter of my justice.

I warm the cells of my new swarm, waiting with impatience for that first twitch of quickening. The whistlers wheel frantically just out of reach, in and out of the mutilated loops, not quite yet daring to cross the gulf to me.

The first of the wasps reflexively uncurls in its manufacture cell. Soon, now.

The whistlers make a coordinated assault, rushing me from all sides. I am prepared for this, fully charged, dangerous in three hundred sixty degrees all around, as well as above and below. I swing my bladed arms, even as I use my other manipulators to hit, crush, tear, fling. Even mid-melee I am assessing, listening, watching, and when I am certain I pluck what seems most likely the leader from mid-air as it tries to flee. It has the tip of one of my antennae in the curl of its arm; I had not even seen it break it off.

The whistler's arms are surprisingly strong. I take one each in two manipulators, and begin to pull it apart, testing its resistance, seeking its breaking point. It is screaming.

"Kadey?"

I stop. Everything stops, or seems to.

When I turn, he is standing there. Mike. Not the original, but the Mike I made. His naked skin does not have the sickly pallor, the swollen gauntness that beset the original in the last weeks of his life. He is awake, whole, *alive.*

The whistlers crowd between him and me, pushing him away, trying to shove him back into the loop forest. I hurl the one captive in my arms away and bring all my manipulators to bear on those who have interposed themselves between us.

I raise the saw, and it is Mike who steps back. Fear is wide in his eyes. "Stop!" he cries, as if I were attacking him, as if I could ever hurt him.

I stop again, lost. "They stole you," I say. I am unused to hearing my own voice.

"I think they think they rescued me from you," he says.

"They are monsters," I answer.

He holds out his hands.

I put my sawblade arms away and step forward, looming over him. The whistlers give one final tug on his legs before they abandon him and scatter. In Mike's cupped hands is a flattened, dead lizard, one of my skinks. Its brilliant blue scales are coated in blood, in displaced meat. I can tell from the pattern of damage, from the crushing pressure necessary to result in this condition, that it was I who stepped on it without knowing.

"We're the monsters here," he says. "This is all my fault."

"No," I say. Then: "You wouldn't wake up."

He sets the remains of the number thirty-nine skink down gently among the tattered trunks of loop trees. "I remember dying," he says. He shakes as he says that. "I didn't know how to be alive anymore. I don't understand."

"I was all alone," I say.

"You weren't supposed to be," he answers. He stares down at his hands, then at the ground, for a long time. Then he looks up, over at the battered hulk of KED-11. Tears are forming in the corners of his eyes. I have never seen Mike cry.

There are several whistler corpses in the cut clearing. The living have fled out of sight, though I know perfectly where they are, know they are watching us both. I do not know, now, why I have done any of this. "I am sorry," I say. "I read your patterns and pathways and incorporated them into my understanding, into my function, as I do every pattern. They have made me unstable. I do not know what to do next. I do not want to be alone."

"Me either," he said. "Eventually the company will discover you're still functioning, that I am—well, not *me*, anymore—and they'll likely put an end to us both. Legal nightmare, if it got out."

"And until then?"

"We don't have to make anything. We can just go see. It's a whole world, just for us," he says. "Do you think you can do that?"

Inside me, my army of poisonous things is settling back down into sleep, into disassembly. It is unfair to them to be brought to the threshold of life for one purpose and then have it taken away, but it is for the best.

"I have made too much," I say. I open my hatch and bend my legs so he can climb in. Then I walk out of the loop forest, past the silent eyes of the watching whistlers.

They follow discreetly behind, but they let us go. I do not think they would let us ever return, but we will not.

The two suns above are near setting, but I want to cross the river and be away from here before I rest. I want to show Mike the night glowdots, and the walking cones, and everything else I have seen since he left me. Whatever time we have, it will be enough.

I hope he does not ask me about his mug.

a series of steaks

VINA JIE-MIN PRASAD

Vina Jie-Min Prasad is a Singaporean writer working against the world machine. Her short fiction has appeared in Clarkesworld *and* Uncanny Magazine. *You can find links to her work at www.vinaprasad.com.*

In the wry story that follows, she shows us that sometimes creating a successful forgery can be way more complicated than it looks.

All known forgeries are tales of failure. The people who get into the newsfeeds for their brilliant attempts to cheat the system with their fraudulent Renaissance masterpieces or their stacks of fake cheques, well, they might be successful artists, but they certainly haven't been successful at *forgery*.

The best forgeries are the ones that disappear from notice—a second-rate still-life mouldering away in gallery storage, a battered old 50-yuan note at the bottom of a cashier drawer—or even a printed strip of Matsusaka beef, sliding between someone's parted lips.

Forging beef is similar to printmaking—every step of the process has to be done with the final print in mind. A red that's too dark looks putrid, a white that's too pure looks artificial. All beef is supposed to come from a cow, so stipple the red with dots, flecks, lines of white to fake variance in muscle fibre regions. Cows are similar, but cows aren't uniform—use fractals to randomise marbling after defining the basic look. Cut the sheets of beef manually to get an authentic ragged edge, don't get lazy and depend on the bioprinter for that.

Days of research and calibration and cursing the printer will all vanish into someone's gullet in seconds, if the job's done right.

Helena Li Yuanhui of Splendid Beef Enterprises is an expert in doing the job right.

The trick is not to get too ambitious. Most forgers are caught out by the smallest errors—a tiny amount of period-inaccurate pigment, a crack in the oil paint that looks too artificial, or a misplaced watermark on a passport. Printing something large increases the chances of a fatal misstep. Stick with small-scale jobs, stick with a small group of regular clients, and in time, Splendid Beef Enterprises will turn enough of a profit for Helena to get a *real* name change, leave Nanjing, and forget this whole sorry venture ever happened.

As Helena's loading the beef into refrigerated boxes for drone delivery, a notification pops up on her iKontakt frames. Helena sighs, turns the volume on her earpiece down, and takes the call.

"Hi, Mr. Chan, could you switch to a secure line? You just need to tap the button with a lock icon, it's very easy."

"Nonsense!" Mr. Chan booms. "If the government were going to catch us they'd have done so by now! Anyway, I just called to tell you how pleased I am with the latest batch. Such a shame, though, all that talent and your work just gets gobbled up in seconds—tell you what, girl, for the next beef special, how about I tell everyone that the beef came from one of those fancy vertical farms? I'm sure they'd have nice things to say then!"

"Please don't," Helena says, careful not to let her Cantonese accent slip through. It tends to show after long periods without any human interaction, which is an apt summary of the past few months. "It's best if no one pays attention to it."

"You know, Helena, you do good work, but I'm very concerned about your self-esteem, I know if I printed something like that I'd want everyone to appreciate it! Let me tell you about this article my daughter sent me, you know research says that people without friends are prone to . . ." Mr. Chan rambles on as Helena sticks the labels on the boxes—Grilliam Shakespeare, Gyuuzen Sukiyaki, Fatty Chan's Restaurant—and thankfully hangs up before Helena sinks into further depression. She takes her iKontakt off before heading to the drone delivery office, giving herself some time to recover from Mr. Chan's relentless cheerfulness.

Helena has five missed calls by the time she gets back. A red phone icon blares at the corner of her vision before blinking out, replaced by the incoming-call notification. It's secured and anonymised, which is quite a change from usual. She pops the earpiece in.

"Yeah, Mr. Chan?"

"This isn't Mr. Chan," someone says. "I have a job for Splendid Beef Enterprises."

"All right, sir. Could I get your name and what you need? If you could provide me with the deadline, that would help too."

"I prefer to remain anonymous," the man says.

"Yes, I understand, secrecy is rather important." Helena restrains the urge to roll her eyes at how needlessly cryptic this guy is. "Could I know about the deadline and brief?"

"I need two hundred T-bone steaks by the 8th of August. 38.1 to 40.2 millimeter thickness for each one." A notification to download t-bone_info.KZIP pops up on her lenses. The most ambitious venture Helena's undertaken in the past few months has been Gyuuzen's strips of marbled sukiyaki, and even that felt a bit like pushing it. A whole steak? Hell no.

"I'm sorry, sir, but I don't think my business can handle that. Perhaps you could try—"

"I think you'll be interested in this job, Helen Lee Jyun Wai."

Shit.

A Sculpere 9410S only takes thirty minutes to disassemble, if you know the right tricks. Manually eject the cell cartridges, slide the external casing off to expose the inner screws, and detach the print heads before disassembling the power unit. There are a few extra steps in this case—for instance, the stickers that say "Property of Hong Kong Scientific University" and "Bioprinting Lab A5" all need to be removed—but a bit of anti-adhesive spray will ensure that everything's on schedule. Ideally she'd buy a new printer, but she needs to save her cash for the name change once she hits Nanjing.

It's not expulsion if you leave before you get kicked out, she tells herself, but even she can tell that's a lie.

It's possible to get a sense of a client's priorities just from the documents they send. For instance, Mr. Chan usually mentions some recipes that he's considering, and Ms. Huang from Gyuuzen tends to attach examples of the marbling patterns she wants. This new client seems to have attached a whole document dedicated to the recent amendments in the criminal code, with the ones relevant to Helena ("five-year statute of limitations," "possible death penalty") conveniently highlighted in neon yellow.

Sadly, this level of detail hasn't carried over to the spec sheet.

"Hi again, sir," Helena says. "I've read through what you've sent, but I really need more details before starting on the job. Could you provide me with the full measurements? I'll need the expected length and breadth in addition to the thickness."

"It's already there. Learn to read."

"I *know* you filled that part in, sir," Helena says, gritting her teeth. "But we're a printing company, not a farm. I'll need more detail than '16–18 month cow, grain-fed, Hereford breed' to do the job properly."

"You went to university, didn't you? I'm sure you can figure out something as basic as that, even if you didn't graduate."

"Ha ha. Of course." Helena resists the urge to yank her earpiece out. "I'll get right on that. Also, there is the issue of pay . . ."

"Ah, yes. I'm quite sure the Yuen family is still itching to prosecute. How about you do the job, and in return, I don't tell them where you're hiding?"

"I'm sorry, sir, but even then I'll need an initial deposit to cover the printing, and of course there's the matter of the Hereford samples." *Which I already have in the bioreactor, but there is no way I'm letting you know that.*

"Fine. I'll expect detailed daily updates," Mr. Anonymous says. "I know how you get with deadlines. Don't fuck it up."

"Of course not," Helena says. "Also, about the deadline—would it be possible to push it back? Four weeks is quite short for this job."

"No," Mr. Anonymous says curtly, and hangs up.

Helena lets out a very long breath so she doesn't end up screaming, and takes a moment to curse Mr. Anonymous and his whole family in Cantonese.

It's physically impossible to complete the renders and finish the print in four weeks, unless she figures out a way to turn her printer into a time machine, and if that were possible she might as well go back and redo the past few years, or maybe her whole life. If she had majored in art, maybe she'd be a designer by now—or hell, while she's busy dreaming, she could even have been the next Raverat, the next Mantuana—instead of a failed artist living in a shithole concrete box, clinging to the wreckage of all her past mistakes.

She leans against the wall for a while, exhales, then slaps on a proxy and starts drafting a help-wanted ad.

Lily Yonezawa (darknet username: yurisquared) arrives at Nanjing High Tech Industrial Park at 8.58 A.M. She's a short lady with long black hair and circle-framed iKontakts. She's wearing a loose, floaty dress, smooth lines of white tinged with yellow-green, and there's a large prismatic bracelet gleaming on her arm. In comparison, Helena is wearing her least holey black blouse and a pair of jeans, which is a step up from her usual attire of myoglobin-stained T-shirt and boxer shorts.

"So," Lily says in rapid, slightly accented Mandarin as she bounds into the office. "This place is a beef place, right? I pulled some of the records once I got the address, hope you don't mind—anyway, what do you want me to help print or render or design or whatever? I know I said I had a background in confections and baking, but I'm totally open to anything!" She pumps her fist in a show of determination. The loose-fitting prismatic bracelet slides up and down.

Helena blinks at Lily with the weariness of someone who's spent most of their night frantically trying to make their office presentable. She decides to skip most of the briefing, as Lily doesn't seem like the sort who needs to be eased into anything.

"How much do you know about beef?"

"I used to watch a whole bunch of farming documentaries with my ex, does that count?"

"No. Here at Splendid Beef Enterprises—"

"Oh, by the way, do you have a logo? I searched your company registration but nothing really came up. Need me to design one?"

"*Here at Splendid Beef Enterprises*, we make fake beef and sell it to restaurants."

"So, like, soy-lentil stuff?"

"Homegrown cloned cell lines," Helena says. "Mostly Matsusaka, with some Hereford if clients specify it." She gestures at the bioreactor humming away in a corner.

"Wait, isn't fake food like those knockoff eggs made of calcium carbonate? If you're using cow cells, this seems pretty real to me." Clearly Lily has a more practical definition of fake than the China Food and Drug Administration.

"It's more like . . . let's say you have a painting in a gallery and you say it's by a famous artist. Lots of people would come look at it because of the name alone and write reviews talking about its exquisite use of chiaroscuro, as expected of the old masters. I can't believe that it looks so real even though it was painted centuries ago. But if you say, hey, this great painting was by some no-name loser, I was just lying about where it came from . . . well, it'd still be the same painting, but people would want all their money back."

"Oh, I get it," Lily says, scrutinising the bioreactor. She taps its shiny polymer shell with her knuckles, and her bracelet bumps against it. Helena tries not to wince. "Anyway, how legal is this? This meat forgery thing?"

"It's not illegal yet," Helena says. "It's kind of a grey area, really."

"Great!" Lily smacks her fist into her open palm. "Now, how can I help? I'm totally down for anything! You can even ask me to clean the office if you want— Wow, this is *really* dusty, maybe I should just clean it to make sure—"

Helena reminds herself that having an assistant isn't entirely bad news. Wolfgang Beltracchi was only able to carry out large-scale forgeries with his assistant's help, and they even got along well enough to get married and have a kid without killing each other.

Then again, the Beltracchis both got caught, so maybe she shouldn't be too optimistic.

Cows that undergo extreme stress while waiting for slaughter are known as dark cutters. The stress causes them to deplete all their glycogen reserves, and when butchered, their meat turns a dark blackish-red. The meat of dark cutters is generally considered low-quality.

As a low-quality person waiting for slaughter, Helena understands how those cows feel. Mr. Anonymous, stymied by the industrial park's regular sweeps for trackers and external cameras, has taken to sending Helena grainy aerial photographs of herself together with exhortations to work harder. This isn't exactly news—she already knew he had her details, and drones are pretty cheap—but still. When Lily raps on the door in the morning, Helena sometimes jolts awake in a panic before she realises that it isn't Mr. Anonymous coming for her. This isn't helped by the fact that Lily's gentle knocks seem to be equivalent to other people's knockout blows.

By now Helena's introduced Lily to the basics, and she's a surprisingly quick study. It doesn't take her long to figure out how to randomise the fat marbling with Fractalgenr8, and she's been handed the task of printing the beef strips for Gyuuzen and Fatty Chan, then packing them for drone delivery. It's not ideal, but it lets Helena concentrate on the base model for the T-bone steak, which is the most complicated thing she's ever tried to render.

A T-bone steak is a combination of two cuts of meat, lean tenderloin and fatty strip steak, separated by a hard ridge of vertebral bone. Simply cutting into one is a near-religious experience, red meat parting under the knife to reveal smooth white bone, with the beef fat dripping down to pool on the plate. At least, that's what the socialites' food blogs say. To be accurate, they say something more like "omfg this is sooooooo good," "this bones giving me a boner lol," and "haha im so getting this sonic-cleaned for my collection!!!" but Helena pretends they actually meant to communicate something more coherent.

The problem is a lack of references. Most of the accessible photographs only provide a top-down view, and Helena's left to extrapolate from blurry videos and password-protected previews of bovine myology databases, which don't get her much closer to figuring out how the meat adheres to the bone. Helena's forced to dig through ancient research papers and diagrams that focus on where to cut to maximise meat yield, quantifying the difference between porterhouse and T-bone cuts, and not *hey, if you're reading this decades in the future, here's how to make a good facsimile of a steak.* Helena's tempted to run outside and scream in frustration, but Lily would probably insist on running outside and screaming with her as a matter of company solidarity, and with their luck, probably Mr. Anonymous would find out about Lily right then, even after all the trouble she's taken to censor any mention of her new assistant from the files and the reports and *argh she needs sleep.*

Meanwhile, Lily's already scheduled everything for print, judging by the way she's spinning around in Helena's spare swivel chair.

"Hey, Lily," Helena says, stifling a yawn. "Why don't you play around with this for a bit? It's the base model for a T-bone steak. Just familiarise yourself with the fiber extrusion and mapping, see if you can get it to look like the reference photos. Don't worry, I've saved a copy elsewhere." *Good luck doing the impossible,* Helena doesn't say. *You're bound to have memorised the shortcut for "undo" by the time I wake up.*

Helena wakes up to Lily humming a cheerful tune and a mostly complete T-bone model rotating on her screen. She blinks a few times, but no—it's still there. Lily's effortlessly linking the rest of the meat, fat and gristle to the side of the bone, deforming the muscle fibres to account for the bone's presence.

"What did you do?" Helena blurts out.

Lily turns around to face her, fiddling with her bracelet. "Uh, did I do it wrong?"

"Rotate it a bit, let me see the top view. How did you do it?"

"It's a little like the human vertebral column, isn't it? There's plenty of references for that." She taps the screen twice, switching focus to an image of a human cross-section. "See how it attaches here and here? I just used that as a reference, and boom."

Ugh, Helena thinks to herself. She's been out of university for way too long if she's forgetting basic homology.

"Wait, *is* it correct? Did I mess up?"

"No, no," Helena says. "This is really good. Better than . . . well, better than I did, anyway."

"Awesome! Can I get a raise?"

"You can get yourself a sesame pancake," Helena says. "My treat."

The brief requires two hundred similar-but-unique steaks at randomised thicknesses of 38.1 to 40.2 mm, and the number and density of meat fibres pretty much precludes Helena from rendering it on her own rig. She doesn't want to pay to outsource computing power, so they're using spare processing cycles from other personal rigs and staggering the loads. Straightforward bone surfaces get rendered in afternoons, and fibre-dense tissues get rendered at off-peak hours.

It's three in the morning. Helena's in her Pokko the Penguin T-shirt and boxer shorts, and Lily's wearing Yayoi Kusama-ish pyjamas that make her look like she's been obliterated by a mass of polka dots. Both of them are staring at their screens, eating cups of Zhuzhu Brand Artificial Char Siew Noodles. As Lily's job moves to the front of Render@Home's Finland queue, the graph updates to show a downtick in Mauritius. Helena's fingers frantically skim across the touchpad, queueing as many jobs as she can.

Her chopsticks scrape the bottom of the mycefoam cup, and she tilts the container to shovel the remaining fake pork fragments into her mouth. Zhuzhu's using extruded soy proteins, and they've punched up the glutamate percentage since she last bought them. The roasted char siew flavour is lacking, and the texture is crumby since the factory skimped on the extrusion time, but any hot food is practically heaven at this time of the night. Day. Whatever.

The thing about the rendering stage is that there's a lot of panic-infused downtime. After queueing the requests, they can't really do anything else—the requests might fail, or the rig might crash, or they might lose their place in the queue through some accident of fate and have to do everything all over again. There's nothing to do besides pray that the requests get through, stay awake until the server limit resets, and repeat the whole process until everything's done. Staying awake is easy for Helena, as Mr. Anonymous has recently taken to sending pictures of rotting corpses to her iKontakt address, captioned "Work hard or this could be you." Lily seems to be halfway off to dreamland, possibly because she isn't seeing misshapen lumps of flesh every time she closes her eyes.

"So," Lily says, yawning. "How *did* you get into this business?"

Helena decides it's too much trouble to figure out a plausible lie, and settles for a very edited version of the truth. "I took art as an elective in high school. My school had a lot of printmaking and 3D printing equipment, so I used it to make custom merch in my spare time—you know, for people who wanted figurines of obscure anime characters, or whatever. Even designed and printed the packaging for them, just to make it look more official. I wanted to study art in university, but that didn't really work out. Long story short, I ended up moving here from Hong Kong, and since I had a background in printing and bootlegging . . . yeah. What about you?"

"Before the confectionery I did a whole bunch of odd jobs. I used to sell merch for my girlfriend's band, and that's how I got started with the short-order printing stuff. They were called POMEGRENADE—it was really hard to fit the whole name on a T-shirt. The keychains sold really well, though."

"What sort of band were they?"

"Sort of noise-rocky Cantopunk at first—there was this one really cute song I liked, *If Marriage Means The Death Of Love Then We Must Both Be Zombies*—but Cantonese music was a hard sell, even in Guangzhou, so they ended up being kind of a cover band."

"Oh, Guangzhou," Helena says in an attempt to sound knowledgeable, before realising that the only thing she knows about Guangzhou is that the Red Triad has a particularly profitable organ-printing business there. "Wait, you understand Cantonese?"

"Yeah," Lily says in Cantonese, tone-perfect. "No one really speaks it around here, so I haven't used it much."

"Oh my god, yes, it's so hard to find Canto-speaking people here." Helena immediately switches to Cantonese. "Why didn't you tell me sooner? I've been *dying* to speak it to someone."

"Sorry, it never came up so I figured it wasn't very relevant," Lily says. "Anyway, POMEGRENADE mostly did covers after that, you know, Kick Out The Jams, Zhongnanhai, Chaos Changan, Lightsabre Cocksucking Blues. Whatever got the crowd pumped up, and when they were moshing the hardest, they'd hit the crowd with the Cantopunk and just blast their faces off. I think it left more of an impression that way—like, start with the familiar, then this weird-ass surprise near the end—the merch table always got swamped after they did that."

"What happened with the girlfriend?"

"We broke up, but we keep in touch. Do you still do art?"

"Not really. The closest thing I get to art is this," Helena says, rummaging through the various boxes under the table to dig out her sketchbooks. She flips one open and hands it to Lily—white against red, nothing but full-page studies of marbling patterns, and it must be one of the earlier ones because it's downright amateurish. The lines are all over the place, that marbling on the Wagyu (is that even meant to be Wagyu?) is completely inaccurate, and, fuck, are those *tear stains*?

Lily turns the pages, tracing the swashes of colour with her finger. The hum of the overworked rig fills the room.

"It's awful, I know."

"What are you talking about?" Lily's gaze lingers on Helena's attempt at a fractal snowflake. "This is really trippy! If you ever want to do some album art, just let me know and I'll totally hook you up!"

Helena opens her mouth to say something about how she's not an artist, and how studies of beef marbling wouldn't make very good album covers, but faced with Lily's unbridled enthusiasm, she decides to nod instead.

Lily turns the page and it's that thing she did way back at the beginning, when she was thinking of using a cute cow as the company logo. It's derivative, it's kitsch, the whole thing looks like a degraded copy of someone else's ripoff drawing of a cow's head, and the fact that Lily's seriously scrutinising it makes Helena want to snatch the sketchbook back, toss it into the composter, and sink straight into the concrete floor.

The next page doesn't grant Helena a reprieve since there's a whole series of that stupid cow. Versions upon versions of happy cow faces grin straight at Lily, most of them surrounded by little hearts—what was she thinking? What do hearts even have to do with Splendid Beef Enterprises, anyway? Was it just that they were easy to draw?

"Man, I wish we had a logo because this would be super cute! I love the little hearts! It's like saying we put our heart and soul into whatever we do! Oh, wait, but was that what you meant?"

"It could be," Helena says, and thankfully, the Colorado server opens before Lily can ask any further questions.

The brief requires status reports at the end of each workday, but this gradually falls by the wayside once they hit the point where workdays don't technically end, especially since Helena really doesn't want to look at an inbox full of increasingly creepy threats. They're at the pre-print stage, and Lily's given up on going back to her own place at night so they can have more time for calibration. What looks right on the screen might not look right once it's printed, and their lives for the past few days have devolved into staring at endless trays of 32-millimeter beef cubes and checking them for myoglobin concentration, color match in different lighting conditions, fat striation depth, and a whole host of other factors.

There are so many ways for a forgery to go wrong, and only one way it can go right. Helena contemplates this philosophical quandary, and gently thunks her head against the back of her chair.

"Oh my god," Lily exclaims, shoving her chair back. "I can't take this anymore! I'm going out to eat something and then I'm getting some sleep. Do you want anything?" She straps on her bunny-patterned filter mask and her metallic sandals. "I'm gonna eat there, so I might take a while to get back."

"Sesame pancakes, thanks."

As Lily slams the door, Helena puts her iKontakt frames back on. The left lens flashes a stream of notifications—fifty-seven missed calls over the past five hours, all from an unknown number. Just then, another call comes in, and she reflexively taps the side of the frame.

"You haven't been updating me on your progress," Mr. Anonymous says.

"I'm very sorry, sir," Helena says flatly, having reached the point of tiredness where she's ceased to feel anything beyond *god I want to sleep*. This sets Mr. Anonymous on another rant covering the usual topics—poor work ethic, lack of commitment, informing the Yuen family, prosecution, possible death sentence—and Helena struggles to keep her mouth shut before she says something that she might regret.

"Maybe I should send someone to check on you right now," Mr. Anonymous snarls, before abruptly hanging up.

Helena blearily types out a draft of the report, and makes a note to send a coherent version later in the day, once she gets some sleep and fixes the calibration so she's not telling him entirely bad news. Just as she's about to call Lily and ask her to get some hot soy milk to go with the sesame pancakes, the front door rattles in its frame like someone's trying to punch it down. Judging by the violence, it's probably Lily. Helena trudges over to open it.

It isn't. It's a bulky guy with a flat-top haircut. She stares at him for a moment, then tries to slam the door in his face. He forces the door open and shoves his way inside, grabbing Helena's arm, and all Helena can think is *I can't believe Mr. Anonymous spent his money on this.*

He shoves her against the wall, gripping her wrist so hard that it's practically getting dented by his fingertips, and pulls out a switchblade, pressing it against the knuckle of her index finger. "Well, I'm not allowed to kill you, but I can fuck you up real bad. Don't really need all your fingers, do you, girl?"

She clears her throat, and struggles to keep her voice from shaking. "I need them to type—didn't your boss tell you that?"

"Shut up," Flat-Top says, flicking the switchblade once, then twice, thinking. "Don't need your face to type, do you?"

Just then, Lily steps through the door. Flat-Top can't see her from his angle, and Helena jerks her head, desperately communicating that she should stay out. Lily promptly moves closer.

Helena contemplates murder.

Lily edges towards both of them, slides her bracelet past her wrist and onto her knuckles, and makes a gesture at Helena which either means "move to your left" or "I'm imitating a bird, but only with one hand."

"Hey," Lily says loudly. "What's going on here?"

Flat-Top startles, loosening his grip on Helena's arm, and Helena dodges to the left. Just as Lily's fist meets his face in a truly vicious uppercut, Helena seizes the opportunity to kick him soundly in the shins.

His head hits the floor, and it's clear he won't be moving for a while, or ever. Considering Lily's normal level of violence towards the front door, this isn't surprising.

Lily crouches down to check Flat-Top's breathing. "Well, he's still alive. Do you prefer him that way?"

"Do *not* kill him."

"Sure." Lily taps the side of Flat-Top's iKontakt frames with her bracelet, and information scrolls across her lenses. "Okay, his name's Nicholas Liu Honghui . . . blah blah blah . . . hired to scare someone at this address, anonymous client . . . I think he's coming to, how do you feel about joint locks?"

It takes a while for Nicholas to stir fully awake. Lily's on his chest, pinning him to the ground, and Helena's holding his switchblade to his throat.

"Okay, Nicholas Liu," Lily says. "We could kill you right now, but that'd make your wife and your . . . what is that red thing she's holding . . . a baby? Yeah, that'd make your wife and ugly baby quite sad. Now, you're just going to tell your boss that everything went as expected—"

"Tell him that I cried," Helena interrupts. "I was here alone, and I cried because I was so scared."

"Right, got that, Nick? That lady there wept buckets of tears. I don't exist. Everything went well, and you think there's no point in sending anyone else over. If you mess up, we'll visit 42—god, what is this character—42 Something Road and let you know how displeased we are. Now, if you apologise for ruining our morning, I probably won't break your arm."

After seeing a wheezing Nicholas to the exit, Lily closes the door, slides her bracelet back onto her wrist, and shakes her head like a deeply disappointed critic. "What an amateur. Didn't even use burner frames—how the hell did he get hired? And that *haircut*, wow . . ."

Helena opts to remain silent. She leans against the wall and stares at the ceiling, hoping that she can wake up from what seems to be a very long nightmare.

"Also, I'm not gonna push it, but I did take out the trash. Can you explain why that crappy hitter decided to pay us a visit?"

"Yeah. Yeah, okay." Helena's stomach growls. "This may take a while. Did you get the food?"

"I got your pancakes, and that soy milk place was open, so I got you some. Nearly threw it at that guy, but I figured we've got a lot of electronics, so . . ."

"Thanks," Helena says, taking a sip. It's still hot.

Hong Kong Scientific University's bioprinting program is a prestigious pioneer program funded by mainland China, and Hong Kong is the test bed before the widespread rollout. The laboratories are full of state-of-the-art medical-grade printers and bioreactors, and the instructors are all researchers cherry-picked from the best universities.

As the star student of the pioneer batch, Lee Jyun Wai Helen (student number A3007082A) is selected for a special project. She will help the head instructor work on the basic model of a heart for a dextrocardial patient, the instructor will handle the detailed render and the final print, and a skilled surgeon will do the transplant. As the term progresses and the instructor gets busier and busier, Helen's role gradually escalates to doing everything except the final print and the transplant. It's a particularly tricky render, since dextrocardial hearts face right instead of left, but her practice prints are cell-level perfect.

Helen hands the render files and her notes on the printing process to the instructor, then her practical exams begin and she forgets all about it.

The Yuen family discovers Madam Yuen's defective heart during their mid-autumn family reunion, halfway through an evening harbour cruise. Madam Yuen doesn't make it back to shore, and instead of a minor footnote in a scientific paper, Helen rapidly becomes front-and-centre in an internal investigation into the patient's death.

Unofficially, the internal investigation discovers that the head instructor's improper calibration of the printer during the final print led to a slight misalignment in the left ventricle, which eventually caused severe ventricular dysfunction and acute graft failure.

Officially, the root cause of the misprint is Lee Jyun Wai Helen's negligence and failure to perform under deadline pressure. Madam Yuen's family threatens to prosecute, but the criminal code doesn't cover failed organ printing. Helen is expelled, and the Hong Kong Scientific University quietly negotiates a settlement with the Yuens.

After deciding to steal the bioprinter and flee, Helen realizes that she doesn't have enough money for a full name change and an overseas flight. She settles for a minor name alteration and a flight to Nanjing.

"Wow," says Lily. "You know, I'm pretty sure you got ripped off with the name alteration thing, there's no way it costs that much. Also, you used to have pigtails? Seriously?"

Helena snatches her old student ID away from Lily. "Anyway, under the amendments to Article 335, making or supplying substandard printed organs is now an offence punishable by death. The family's itching to prosecute. If we don't do the job right, Mr. Anonymous is going to disclose my whereabouts to them."

"Okay, but from what you've told me, this guy is totally not going to let it go even after you're done. At my old job, we got blackmailed like that all the time, which was really kind of irritating. They'd always try to bargain, and after the first job, they'd say stuff like 'if you don't do me this favour I'm going to call the cops and tell them everything' just to weasel out of paying for the next one."

"Wait. Was this at the bakery or the merch stand?"

"Uh." Lily looks a bit sheepish. This is quite unusual, considering that Lily has spent the past four days regaling Helena with tales of the most impressive blood blobs from her period, complete with comparisons to their failed prints. "Are you familiar with the Red Triad? The one in Guangzhou?"

"You mean the *organ printers?*"

"Yeah, them. I kind of might have been working there before the bakery . . . ?"

"What?"

Lily fiddles with the lacy hem of her skirt. "Well, I mean, the bakery experience seemed more relevant, plus you don't have to list every job you've ever done when you apply for a new one, right?"

"Okay," Helena says, trying not to think too hard about how all the staff at Splendid Beef Enterprises are now prime candidates for the death penalty. "Okay. What exactly did you do there?"

"Ears and stuff, bladders, spare fingers . . . you'd be surprised how many people need those. I also did some bone work, but that was mainly for the diehards—most of the people we worked on were pretty okay with titanium substitutes. You know, simple stuff."

"That's not simple."

"Well, it's not like I was printing fancy reversed hearts or anything, and even with the asshole clients it was way easier than baking. Have *you* ever tried to extrude a spun-sugar globe so you could put a bunch of powder-printed magpies inside? And don't get me started on cleaning the nozzles after extrusion, because wow . . ."

Helena decides not to question Lily's approach to life, because it seems like a certain path to a migraine. "Maybe we should talk about this later."

"Right, you need to send the update! Can I help?"

The eventual message contains very little detail and a lot of pleading. Lily insists on adding typos just to make Helena seem more rattled, and Helena's way too tired to argue. After starting the autoclean cycle for the printheads, they set an alarm and flop on Helena's mattress for a nap.

As Helena's drifting off, something occurs to her. "Lily? What happened to those people? The ones who tried to blackmail you?"

"Oh," Lily says casually. "I crushed them."

The brief specifies that the completed prints need to be loaded into four separate podcars on the morning of August 8, and provides the delivery code for each. They haven't been able to find anything in Helena's iKontakt archives, so their best bet is finding a darknet user who can do a trace.

Lily's fingers hover over the touchpad. "If we give him the codes, this guy can check the prebooked delivery routes. He seems pretty reliable, do you want to pay the bounty?"

"Do it," Helena says.

The resultant map file is a mess of meandering lines. They flow across most of Nanjing, criss-crossing each other, but eventually they all terminate at the cargo entrance of the Grand Domaine Luxury Hotel on Jiangdong Middle Road.

"Well, he's probably not a guest who's going to eat two hundred steaks on his own." Lily taps her screen. "Maybe it's for a hotel restaurant?"

Helena pulls up the Grand Domaine's web directory, setting her iKontakt to highlight any mentions of restaurants or food in the descriptions. For some irritating design reason, all the booking details are stored in garish images. She snatches the entire August folder, flipping through them one by one before pausing.

The foreground of the image isn't anything special, just elaborate cursive English stating that Charlie Zhang and Cherry Cai Si Ping will be celebrating their wedding with a ten-course dinner on August 8th at the Royal Ballroom of the Grand Domaine Luxury Hotel.

What catches her eye is the background. It's red with swirls and streaks of yellow-gold. Typical auspicious wedding colours, but displayed in a very familiar pattern.

It's the marbled pattern of T-bone steak.

Cherry Cai Si Ping is the daughter of Dominic Cai Yongjing, a specialist in livestock and a new player in Nanjing's agri-food arena. According to Lily's extensive knowledge of farming documentaries, Dominic Cai Yongjing is also "the guy with the eyebrows" and "that really boring guy who keeps talking about nothing."

"Most people have eyebrows," Helena says, loading one of Lily's recommended documentaries. "I don't see . . . oh. Wow."

"I *told* you. I mean, I usually like watching stuff about farming, but last year he just started showing up everywhere with his stupid waggly brows! When I watched this with my ex we just made fun of him non-stop."

Helena fast-forwards through the introduction of *Modern Manufacturing: The Vertical Farmer*, which involves the camera panning upwards through hundreds of vertically stacked wire cages. Dominic Cai talks to the host in English, boasting about how he plans to be a key figure in China's domestic beef industry. He explains his "patented methods" for a couple of minutes, which involves stating and restating that his farm is extremely clean and filled with only the best cattle.

"But what about bovine parasitic cancer?" the host asks. "Isn't the risk greater in such a cramped space? If the government orders a quarantine, your whole farm . . ."

"As I've said, our hygiene standards are impeccable, and our stock is pure-bred Hereford!" Cai slaps the flank of a cow through the cage bars, and it moos irritatedly in response. "There is absolutely no way it could happen here!"

Helena does some mental calculations. Aired last year, when the farm recently opened, and that cow looks around six months old . . . and now a request for steaks from cows that are sixteen to eighteen months old . . .

"So," Lily says, leaning on the back of Helena's chair. "Bovine parasitic cancer?"

"Judging by the timing, it probably hit them last month. It's usually the older cows that get infected first. He'd have killed them to stop the spread . . . but if it's the internal strain, the tumours would have made their meat unusable after excision. His first batch of cows was probably meant to be for the wedding dinner. What we're printing is the cover-up."

"But it's not like steak's a standard course in wedding dinners or anything, right? Can't they just change it to roast duck or abalone or something?" Lily looks fairly puzzled, probably because she hasn't been subjected to as many weddings as Helena has.

"Mr. Cai's the one bankrolling it, so it's a staging ground for the Cai family to show how much better they are than everyone else. You saw the announcement—he's probably been bragging to all his guests about how they'll be the first to taste beef from his vertical farm. Changing it now would be a real loss of face."

"Okay," Lily says. "I have a bunch of ideas, but first of all, how much do you care about this guy's face?"

Helena thinks back to her inbox full of corpse pictures, the countless sleepless nights she's endured, the sheer terror she felt when she saw Lily step through the door. "Not very much at all."

"All right." Lily smacks her fist into her palm. "Let's give him a nice surprise."

The week before the deadline vanishes in a blur of printing, re-rendering, and darknet job requests. Helena's been nothing but polite to Mr. Cai ever since the hitter's visit, and has even taken to video calls lately, turning on the camera on her end so that Mr. Cai can witness her progress. It's always good to build rapport with clients.

"So, sir," Helena moves the camera, slowly panning so it captures the piles and piles of cherry-red steaks, zooming in on the beautiful fat strata which took ages to render. "How does this look? We'll be starting the dry-aging once you approve, and loading it into the podcars first thing tomorrow morning."

"Fairly adequate. I didn't expect much from the likes of you, but this seems satisfactory. Go ahead."

Helena tries her hardest to keep calm. "I'm glad you feel that way, sir. Rest assured you'll be getting your delivery on schedule . . . by the way, I don't suppose you could transfer the money on delivery? Printing the bone matter cost a lot more than I thought."

"Of course, of course, once it's delivered and I inspect the marbling. Quality checks, you know?"

Helena adjusts the camera, zooming in on the myoglobin dripping from the juicy steaks, and adopts her most sorrowful tone. "Well, I hate to rush you, but I haven't had much money for food lately . . ."

Mr. Cai chortles. "Why, that's got to be hard on you! You'll receive the fund transfer sometime this month, and in the meantime why don't you treat yourself and print up something nice to eat?"

Lily gives Helena a thumbs-up, then resumes crouching under the table and messaging her darknet contacts, careful to stay out of Helena's shot. The call disconnects.

"Let's assume we won't get any further payment. Is everything ready?"

"Yeah," Lily says. "When do we need to drop it off?"

"Let's try for five A.M. Time to start batch-processing."

Helena sets the enzyme percentages, loads the fluid into the canister, and they both haul the steaks into the dry-ager unit. The machine hums away, spraying fine mists of enzymatic fluid onto the steaks and partially dehydrating them, while Helena and Lily work on assembling the refrigerated delivery boxes. Once everything's neatly packed, they haul the boxes to the nearest podcar station. As Helena slams box after box into the cargo area of the podcars, Lily types the delivery codes into their front panels. The podcars boot up, sealing themselves shut, and zoom off on their circuitous route to the Grand Domaine Luxury Hotel.

They head back to the industrial park. Most of their things have already been shoved into backpacks, and Helena begins breaking the remaining equipment down for transport.

A Sculpere 9410S takes twenty minutes to disassemble if you're doing it for the second time. If someone's there to help you manually eject the cell cartridges, slide the external casing off, and detach the print heads so you can disassemble the power unit, you might be able to get that figure down to ten. They'll buy a new printer once they figure out where to settle down, but this one will do for now.

It's not running away if we're both going somewhere, Helena thinks to herself, and this time it doesn't feel like a lie.

There aren't many visitors to Mr. Chan's restaurant during breakfast hours, and he's sitting in a corner, reading a book. Helena waves at him.

"Helena!" he booms, surging up to greet her. "Long time no see, and who is this?"

"Oh, we met recently. She's helped me out a lot," Helena says, judiciously avoiding any mention of Lily's name. She holds a finger to her lips, and surprisingly, Mr. Chan seems to catch on. Lily waves at Mr. Chan, then proceeds to wander around the restaurant, examining their collection of porcelain plates.

"Anyway, since you're my very first client, I thought I'd let you know in person. I'm going travelling with my . . . friend, and I won't be around for the next few months at least."

"Oh, that's certainly a shame! I was planning a black pepper hotplate beef special next month, but I suppose black pepper hotplate extruded protein will do just fine. When do you think you'll be coming back?"

Helena looks at Mr. Chan's guileless face, and thinks, well, her first client deserves a bit more honesty. "Actually, I probably won't be running the business any longer. I haven't decided yet, but I think I'm going to study art. I'm really, really sorry for the inconvenience, Mr. Chan."

"No, no, pursuing your dreams, well, that's not something you should be apologising for! I'm just glad you finally found a friend!"

Helena glances over at Lily, who's currently stuffing a container of cellulose toothpicks into the side pocket of her bulging backpack.

"Yeah, I'm glad too," she says. "I'm sorry, Mr. Chan, but we have a flight to catch in a couple of hours, and the bus is leaving soon . . ."

"Nonsense! I'll pay for your taxi fare, and I'll give you something for the road. Airplane food is awful these days!"

Despite repeatedly declining Mr. Chan's very generous offers, somehow Helena and Lily end up toting bags and bags of fresh steamed buns to their taxi.

"Oh, did you see the news?" Mr. Chan asks. "That vertical farmer's daughter is getting married at some fancy hotel tonight. Quite a pretty girl, good thing she didn't inherit those eyebrows—"

Lily snorts and accidentally chokes on her steamed bun. Helena claps her on the back.

"—and they're serving steak at the banquet, straight from his farm! Now, don't get me wrong, Helena, you're talented at what you do—but a good old-fashioned slab of *real* meat, now, that's the ticket!"

"Yes," Helena says. "It certainly is."

All known forgeries are failures, but sometimes that's on purpose. Sometimes a forger decides to get revenge by planting obvious flaws in their work, then waiting for them to be revealed, making a fool of everyone who initially claimed the work was authentic. These flaws can take many forms—deliberate anachronisms, misspelled signatures, rude messages hidden beneath thick coats of paint—or a picture of a happy cow, surrounded by little hearts, etched into the T-bone of two hundred perfectly printed steaks.

While the known forgers are the famous ones, the *best* forgers are the ones that don't get caught—the old woman selling her deceased husband's collection to an avaricious art collector, the harried-looking mother handing the cashier a battered 50-yuan note, or the two women at the airport, laughing as they collect their luggage, disappearing into the crowd.

The Last Boat-Builder in Ballyvoloon

FINBARR O'REILLY

Finbarr O'Reilly is an Irish speculative fiction writer who likes to explore how broken technologies or unearthly events affect intimate locales. Why would you want to write about alien battleships invading New York when you can imagine little green men asking for directions from a short-tempered undertaker in Carrigtwohill, County Cork? Finbarr has worked as a journalist for almost twenty years, most of those as a subeditor (copy editor) in newspapers such as The Irish Times, Irish Examiner, *and* The Daily Telegraph. *He currently works as the production editor of a magazine for car dealers. He believes it is a testament to his powers of imagination that he has never purchased an automobile and doesn't drive.*

Like many Irish writers, Finbarr lives in self-imposed exile. He currently resides with his wife and two children in a small town in Lincolnshire, England, too far from the sound of gulls and the smell of saltwater.

In the frighteningly plausible story that follows, he takes us to a near future in which the seas have become places of dread, places that humans dare not venture upon for fear of a terrible, grisly death.

> There are of a certainty mightier creatures, and the lake hides what neither net nor fine can take.
> —William Butler Yeats, *The Celtic Twilight*

The first time I met Más, he was sitting on the quayside in Ballyvoloon, carving a nightmare from a piece of linden. Next to him on the granite blocks that capped the sea wall lay a man's weather-proof jacket and hat, in electric pink. The words "petro-safe" were pin-striped across them in broad white letters, as if a spell that would protect him from the mechanical monster he whittled.

Short of smoking a pipe, Más looked every inch a 19th-century whaler. Veined cheeks burned and burnished by sun and wind to a deep cherry gloss, thick grey hair matted and flattened from his souwester and whiskers stiff enough with salt to resist the autumnal breeze blowing in from the harbour mouth.

I had arrived in Ballyvoloon early on a Friday morning. My pilot would not fly till Monday, so I had a weekend of walking the town. Its two main streets, or "beaches" as the locals called them, ran east and west of a concrete, T-shaped pier.

It was near the bottom of the 'T' that Más set out his pitch every day, facing the water, but sheltered by thousands of tonnes of rock and concrete. Ballyvoloon was a town best approached from the sea. The faded postcards on sale along the beach-front showed it from that rare perspective. Snapped from the soaring pleasure decks of ocean-going liners long scrapped or sunk, ribbons of harlequin houses rose from coruscant waters, split by the immense neo-Gothic cathedral that crowns the town. Nowadays, the fret-sawn fascias of pastel shopfronts shed lazy flakes of paint into the broad streets and squares below. It has faded, but there is grandeur there still.

Between the town's rambling railway station and my hotel, I had passed a dozen or more artists, their wares tied to the railings of the waterside promenade, or propped on large boards secured to lampposts, but none dressed like Más. Nor did any carve like him.

"That looks realistic," I said, my heart pounding, as he snicked delicate curls of blond wood from the block with a thick-spined blade.

"There's not much point sugar-coating them," he said, his voice starting as a matter-of-fact drawl, but ending in the sing-song accent of the locals.

"How long have you been a sculptor?" I asked.

"I'm not a sculptor. This is just something to occupy the hands."

"The devil's playthings, eh?"

He stopped carving and looked up at me through muddy green eyes.

"Something like that."

Más lowered the squid he was working on and cast around in the pocket of his jacket. He removed three of the monsters, perfectly carved, but in different sizes and woods, one stained black and polished. The colours seemed to give each one slightly different intents, but none was reassuring.

Other artists carved or drew or painted the squid, but they had smoothed out the lines, removed the barbs, the beaks, gave the things doe-eyes and even smiles and made them suitable to sit atop a child's bedclothes or a living room bookshelf.

Más did the opposite. He made the horrific more horrifying. He made warm, once-living wood look like the doubly dead, glossy plastic of the squids. These were not the creatures we had released, but their more deadly and cunning offspring.

I hid my excitement as well as I could.

"Sixty for one or 100 for a pair," he said.

Más let the moment stretch until the sheer discomfort of it drove me to buy.

His mood brightened and he immediately began packing up his belongings. I had clearly overpaid and he could afford to call it a day.

"See you so," he said, cheerfully and sauntered off into the town.

Once I was back at the hotel, I unwrapped the parcel and inspected the sculptures, to confirm my suspicions.

The other artists may have outsold Más's squid six or seven times, but he was the only of them who had seen a real one.

> "Twelve years after the squid were introduced, the west coast of Europe endured a number of strange phenomena. Firstly, the local gull population bloomed. The government and the squids' manufacturer at the time said it was a sign of fish stocks returning to normal, that it was evidence the squid were successful in their mission.
>
> "Local crab numbers also exploded, to the point that water inlets at a couple of coastal power stations were blocked. The company linked this to the increased gull activity, increasing the amount of food falling to the sea floor."
>
> J. Hawes, *How We Lost the Atlantic*, p. 32

The first flight was late in the afternoon, a couple of hours before sunset. This would give me the best chance of spotting things in the water, as it was still bright enough to see and anything poking above the surface would cast a longer shadow.

The pilot, a taciturn, bearded fellow in his sixties called Perrott, flicked switches and toggles as he went through what passed for a safety briefing.

"If we ditch, it will take about 15 minutes for the helo to reach us from the airport. The suits will at least make that wait comfortable, assuming, you know . . ."

We both wore survival suits of neon-pink non-petro, covering everything but hands and heads. His was moulded to his frame and visibly worn on the elbows and the seat of his pants. Mine squeaked when I walked and still smelled of tart, oleophobic soy.

"Yes. I know," I said, as reassuringly as I could manage.

As he tapped dials and entered numbers on a clipboard, I thought of my first flight over water.

My sea training was in Wales, where an ancient, ex-RNLI helicopter dropped me about half a mile from shore. It was maybe 25 feet to the water, but the fall was enough to knock the breath out of me. The crew made sure I was still kicking and moved back over land. The idea was to get me to panic, I suppose. They needn't have worried. The helicopter was away for a total of eight minutes and if my heart could have climbed my gullet to escape my chest, it would have.

After they pulled me back up, I asked the winchman how I had done.

"No worse than most," he shouted.

He took a flashbang grenade from a box under the seat, pulled the pin, and dropped it out the open door. He counted down from four on his fingers. Over the roar of the rotors, I heard neither splash nor detonation. The winchman made sure I was harnessed, then pointed out the door and down.

A couple of miles away, I could see three or four squid making for a spot directly beneath us, all of them moving so fast they left a wake.

He gave me a torturer's grin.

"Better than some."

"We seen them first, the slicks. That's what they looked like in the pictures, like some tanker or bulker had washed her tanks. But as we got close we could see it was miles and miles of chopped up fish. And the smell! That's what the locals still call that summer—the big stink.

"When we got back we found out the squid had become more . . . hungry, I suppose, and instead of pulling the bits of plastic out of the water, they started pulling 'em out of the fish. Sure we had been eating that fish for years and it never did us any harm.'"

Trevor Cunniffe, trawlerman, in an interview for *Turn Your Back to the Waves*, an RTÉ radio documentary marking 50 years since the squids' introduction

After two days of fruitless flights, I was grounded by fog. Late in the afternoon, I went to a pub. I sat at the long side of the L-shaped bar, inhaling the fug of old beer and new urinal cakes.

The signage, painted in gold leaf on the large windows, had faded and peeled, so I asked a patron what the place was called. "Tom's" was the only reply, offering no clue if this was the original name of the pub or the latest owner.

Between the bottles shelved on the large mirror behind the bar, I saw the figure of a man in a candy-striped pink jacket through the rippled privacy glass of the door. It opened and Más walked in. He gently closed it behind him and moved to a spot at the end of the bar. He kept his head down, but couldn't escape recognising some regulars and nodded a salute to them.

Emboldened by alcohol, I raised my drink.

"How is the water today?" I asked.

The barmaid gave me a look as if to ask what I was doing engaging a local sot, but I smiled at her for long enough that she wandered off, reassured or just bored at my insincerity.

"About the same," said Más. "Visibility's not very good."

"No," I said. "That's why I'm in here. No flights today."

"Are you off home then," Más asked.

I interpreted the question as an invitation and walked over to take the stool next to him.

"Not quite," I said. "Will you have a drink?"

"I will," he said. "So, what has you in town?"

At first, Más didn't seem too bothered when I explained who I worked for, or at least he didn't ask the usual questions or put forward the usual conspiracy theories about the squid.

"A job's a job, I suppose."

His eyes wrinkled, amused at a joke hidden to me. "So do ye all have jobs in England, then?"

Ireland had been on universal income for the better part of two decades. It was hard to see how people like Más would have survived otherwise.

"No, not by a long chalk. The only reason I got this one is I wasn't afraid to cross the sea in a plane."

"More fool you."

"You have to die of something, I told them. And it was quite exciting, in the end."

As the light faded, the mid-afternoon drinkers gave way to a younger, louder crowd, but Más and I still sat, talking.

I described the huge reservoir near where I lived in Rutland, where people could still swim and sail and fish, and how everyone worried that the squid would somehow reach it, denying us access, like Superior or the Caspian.

He asked me what on earth would make me leave such a place.

"I wanted to see the world. I needed a job," I said.

He laughed. "Those used to be the reasons people joined the Navy."

Perrott's plane was old, but well serviced. It started first time and once we finished our climb, the engine settled into a bagpipe-like drone.

We crossed the last headland and the cheerful baize below, veined in dry-stone walls, gave way to grey waves, maned in white.

He radioed the Cork tower to tell them we were now over open water and that the rescue team was on formal standby.

He adjusted the trim of the plane to a point where he was happy to let the thing fly itself and joined me in scanning the waters below.

It was less than half an hour until his pilot's eye spotted it. Perrott took the controls again and banked to give me a better view. I let the video camera run, while I used the zoom lens to snap any identifying features.

From the size of the blurred shape rippling just beneath the surface, I could tell it was old—seventh or eighth generation, perhaps, but I really wanted a more detailed look.

I told Perrott I would like to make another pass.

"If only we had a bomb, eh?" he said. Sooner or later, everyone suggests it.

"We tried that," I said.

"Oh yeah?"

Perrott had signed a non-disclosure agreement before the flight. It didn't matter what I told him. Most of it was already on the internet, in any case.

"Yes. First they bombed an oil platform in the Gulf of Mexico and opened up its well-head. Miles from shore, so any oil that escaped would be eaten by the squid or burnt in the fire."

Hundreds of thousands of the things had come, enough that you could see the black stain spread on satellite images. I had only watched the video. I couldn't imagine how chilling it had been to observe it happen live.

"Then the Americans dropped three of the biggest non-nukes they've got on them."

"It didn't work, then?"

"No. Any squid more than a dozen feet or so below the surface were protected by the water. We vapourised maybe half of them. After that they stayed deep, mostly."

I didn't tell Perrott about the Mississippi and how the squid had retaliated. Let him read that on the internet too.

"Well, they may be mindless, but they're not stupid," he said.

We flew on until the light failed but, as if it had heard him, the beast did not re-appear.

> It would be wrong to think of the squid as a failure of technology. The tech-nology worked, from the plastic filtration, to the self-replication and algo-rithmic learning.
>
> Also do not forget that they succeeded in their original purpose—they did clean up the waters and they did save fish stocks from extinction.
>
> The failure, if you can truly call it that, is ours. We failed to see that life, even created life, will never behave exactly as we intend.
>
> The failure was not in the squids' technology, or in their execution. It was in our imagination.
>
> —From the inaugural address of Ireland's last president, Francis Robinson

A basket of chips and fried "goujons" of catfish had appeared in front of us, gratis. I dived in, sucking seasalt and smoky, charred fish skin from my fingertips. Mas looked over the bar into the middle distance.

"Don't tell me you don't like fish," I said. "That would be too funny."

"That's not real fish."

Más had progressed to whiskey and a bitter humour sharpened his tongue.

"It tastes pretty real," I said. I had heard all the scare stories about fish farming.

He held up a calloused hand, as if an orator or bard about to recite. The other was clenched, to punctuate his thoughts.

"Why is it, do you think, that we are trying to replicate the things we used to have?"

"Like, if most people can still eat 'fish,' or swim in caged bloody lidos, or if cargo comes by airship or whatever, then the more normal it becomes. And it shouldn't be bloody normal. It's not normal."

The barmaid rolled her eyes. Clearly, she had heard the rant before.

I told him I agreed with the swimming bit inasmuch as I wouldn't personally miss it terribly if I could never do it again, but that farmed fish didn't bother me and that I thought most people never considered where their goods came from, even before the squid.

Disappointment, whether at me or the world, wilted in his face before he let the whiskey soften him again. His shoulders lowered, his hands relaxed and the melody of his voice reasserted itself.

"When I was a boy, my father once told me a story about trying to grow trees in space."

I coughed mid-chew and struggled to dislodge a crumb of batter from my throat. With tears in my eyes, I waved him on. I don't know why, but it amused me to hear an old salt like Más talk about orbital horticulture.

"Well, these guys on Spacelab or wherever, they tried growing them in perfect conditions, perfect nutrients, perfect light, even artificial gravity. They would all shoot straight up, then keel over and die. Every tree seed they planted—pine, ash, oak, cypress—they all died. Nobody could figure out what was wrong. Everything a plant could need was provided, perfectly measured. These were the best cared for plants in the world."

"In the solar system," I ribbed him.

"Right. In the solar system. Except for one thing. Do you know what was missing?

"No. Tell me."

"A breeze. Trees develop the strength, the woody cells, to support their weight by resisting the blow of the wind. Without it, they falter and sicken."

I didn't really get his point and told him so.

"You can't sharpen a blade without friction. You can't strengthen a man, or a civilisation, without struggle. Airships and swimming pools and virtual bloody sailing. It's all bollocks. We should be hauling these things out of the water, like they said we would."

He gestured through the window of the bar to the grey bulk of the cathedral looming in the fog.

"There was a reason Jesus was a fisherman," said Más, as if it were a closing statement.

I didn't know what to say to that.

The barmaid leaned over the bar to clear the empty baskets.

"Jesus was a carpenter, Más," she said.

> "Six sea scouts, aged 11 to 14, had left the fishing town of Castletown-berehaven in a rigid inflatable boat, what they call a 'rib.' Their scout leader was at the helm, an experienced local woman named De Paor.
>
> The plan was to take the boys and girls out around nearby Bere Island to spot seals and maybe porpoises.
>
> About an hour into the journey, contact was lost. The boat was never found, but most of the bodies washed up a day or so later, naked and covered in long, ragged welts. Initial theories said they must have been chewed up by a propeller on a passing ship, but there was nothing big enough near the coast.
>
> Post-mortem examinations clinched it. The state pathologist pulled dozens of small plastic barbs from each child. They were quickly identified as belonging to the squid.
>
> A later investigation concluded that the fault lay with a cheap brand of sunscreen one of the children had brought and shared with her shipmates. A Chinese knock-off of a French brand, it contained old stocks of petro-derived nanoparticles. Just as the squid had pulped tonnes of fish to get at the plastic in their flesh in Year 12, they had tried to remove all traces of the petro from the children.
>
> —Margaret Jennings, *When the World Stopped Shrinking*, p. 34

Más's house was beyond the western end of the town, past a small turning circle for cars. A path continued to a rocky beach, but was used only by courting couples, dog walkers or drinking youngsters. A wooden gate led off the beach, where a small house sat behind a quarter-acre of lawn and an old boathouse.

Síle, the barmaid, had told me where he lived. Más usually gave up carving at about four, she said, had a few drinks in a few places and was usually home about six.

I started for the main house, when I heard a noise. A low murmur, like a talk radio station heard through a wall. It was coming from the boathouse.

I made my way across the lawn. Almost unconsciously I was walking crab-like on the balls of my feet, with my arms outstretched for balance. The boathouse was in bad shape. Green paint had blistered on the shiplapped planks and lichen or moss had crept halfway up the transom windows above the large double doors.

The fabric of the place was so weathered I didn't have to open them. Planks had shrunk and split at various intervals, leaving me half a dozen spyholes to the interior. I quietly pressed my eye to one and peered inside.

Under the light of a single work lamp, I could see Más standing at a bench, his back to me, wearing a T-shirt and jeans. Without the souwester, he looked more like an aging rock star than a fisherman and more like twice my age than the three times I had assumed.

Beyond him lay several bulky piles, perhaps of wood, covered by tarpaulin and shrouded in shadow.

A flagstone floor ran all the way to the other wall, where there lay a dark square of calm water—a man-made inlet of dressed stone, from which rose the cold smell of the sea. A winch was bolted to the floor opposite a rusty iron gate that blocked the water from the estuary. Smaller, secondary doors above protected the interior from the worst of the elements.

As he worked, Más whistled.

I recognised enough of the tune to know it was old, but its name escaped me. It felt as manipulative as most traditional music—as Más whistled the chorus, it sounded like a happy tune, but I knew there would be words to accompany it and odds were, they would tell of tragedy.

Más began to wind down, cleaning tools with oil-free cloths. I had told myself this was not spying, this was interest, or concern. But suddenly, I became embarrassed. I silently padded back across his lawn. I would call on him another night.

As I stepped back onto the path between two overgrown rhododendron bushes, my foot collided with a rusty old garden lantern with a musical crash. I just had enough presence of mind to turn again so I was facing the house, trying to look like I had just arrived.

It was in time for Más to see me as he emerged from the boathouse to investigate. I waved as nonchalantly as I could.

He leaned back inside the door and must have flicked a switch, as his garden was suddenly bathed in light from a ring of security floods under the eaves of his house.

I waved again as he re-emerged, confident that he could at least see me this time.

"Oh it's you," he said.

"Hi. Yes, the barmaid, Síle, gave me your address. I hope you don't mind."

"Well, come in so. I have no tea, I'm afraid. I may have some chicory."

I raised the bottle in my hand and gave it a wiggle.

In the early days after their "revolution" the squid featured in one scare story after another. They would evolve legs and stalk the landscape like Wells's Martians, they would form a super-intelligence capable of controlling the

world's nuclear arsenal, or they would start harvesting the phytoplankton
that provide most of the world's breathable oxygen.

In the end, they did what biological organisms do—they found their
own equilibrium. Any reactions of theirs since are no more a sign of "intelligence" than a dog defending its front yard.

—Edward Mission, *The Spectator's Big Book of Science*

Perrott banked the plane again. It was the first flight during which I had felt ill. The
day was squally and overcast, the sky lidded with a leaden dome of cloud.

The squid breached the water, rolling its "tentacles" behind it. There was no reason for the manoeuvre, according to the original designers, which made it look even
more biological. But even from this altitude, I could see the patterns of old plastic
the thing had used to build and periodically repair itself.

"He's a big one," said Perrott, who was clearly enjoying himself.

The beast dived again. Just as it sank out of sight in the dying light, I counted
eight much smaller shadows behind it. Each breached the surface of the water and
rolled their tentacles, just as their colossal "parent" had.

"Shit."

These were sleeker machines, of a green so deep it may as well have been black.
There was no wasted musculature, no protrusions to drag in the water as they slipped
by. These things would never reach the size of the squid that had manufactured
them, but that didn't matter. They were fast and there were more of them.

"Problem?" said Perrott.

"Yes. Somebody isn't playing by the rules."

"I had a friend. Val. Killed himself."

Más had had a lot to drink, mostly the whiskey I had brought, but also a home-
made spirit, which smelled faintly methylated. His face sagged under the influence of alcohol, but his voice became brighter and clearer with each drink. The
stove roared with heat, the light from its soot-stained window washing the kitchen
in sepia.

I wasn't sure if he was given to maudlin statements of fact such as this when
drunk, or whether this was an opening statement, so I said "I'm sorry to hear that.
When did that happen?"

"A while back."

I was still adrift—I didn't know if it was a long time ago and he had healed, or
recently and his emotions were strictly battened down. Before I could ask another
qualifying question, he continued.

"When we were teenagers, a couple of years after the squid were introduced, Val
and I went fishing from the pier one October when the mackerel were in."

"By God, they were fun to catch. Val had an old fibreglass rod that belonged to
his dad, or his grandad. The cork on the handle was perished, the guides were brown
with rust, but as long as you used a non-petro line, the squid didn't bother you in
those days. We caught a lot of fish that year.

"So as we pulled them out, I would unhook them and launch them back into the tide. They were contaminated with all sorts of stuff, heavy metals, plastic, even carbon fibre from the boat hulls. After I had done this once or twice, Val asked me why. I said 'well you can't eat them, so why not let them go'. And Val said 'fuck them, they're only fish'.

"After that, every fish he caught, every one, he would brain and chop up there on the pier and leave for the gulls to eat. He was my friend, but he was cruel.

"The trouble with the squid is they think about us the way Val thought about fish. We're not food, we're not sport. I'm not sure they know what we are. I'm not sure they care."

For a moment, sobriety surfaced. Más looked forlorn. I dreaded the words that would come next. I had become quite good at predicting his laments and tirades.

"We don't fight for it, for the territory, or for the people we lost. For the love of God, these things ate children, and we just accept it. We should be out there every bloody day, hunting these things."

I told him I understood the desire to hurt them, that many had tried, but it just didn't work like that. That most people preferred to pretend they just weren't there, like fairy-tale villagers skirting the wood where the big bad wolf lived.

"But why," he demanded.

"Well they are 'protected' now, for starters," I said. "They fight back. But I suppose the main reason is it's easier than the reality."

"Easier," he scoffed.

He raised his glass, to let me know it was my turn to speak. But I didn't know how to comfort him. So I let him comfort me.

"Your family owned trawlers, right? What's it like? To go out on the ocean?"

Drunk, in the heat of his kitchen, I closed my eyes and listened.

> "The raincoat suicides were a foreseeable event inasmuch as such events happen after many profound and well-publicised changes to people's understanding of the world around them. The Wall Street Crash, Brexit, the release of the Facebook Files. It is a form of end-of-days-ism that we have seen emerge again and again, from military coups to doomsday cults.
>
> "Most of the people who took their own lives had previously displayed signs of moderate to severe mental illness. That the locations of more than two hundred of the deaths were confined to areas with high sea cliffs, such as Dover in England or the Cliffs of Moher in Co Clare, adds fuel to the notion that these were tabloid-inspired suicides, sadly, but predictably, adopted by already unwell people."
>
> Jarlath Kelleher, *The Kraken Sleeps: reporting of suicide as "sacrifice" in British and Irish media* (Undergraduate thesis, Dublin Institute of Technology)

He pulled the tarpaulin off with a flourish. The green-black boat sat upside down on two sawhorses, like an orca, stiff with rigor mortis, beached on pointed rocks.

It was a naomhóg. In the west, I found out later, it was called a currach, but this far south, people called it a naomhóg. Depending on who you asked, it meant "little saint" or "young saint," as if the namers were asking God and the sea to spare it.

It was made of a flexible skin, stretched tightly over a blond wooden frame. I dropped to the floor to look inside, still unable to talk. I knew nothing about boat-building in those days, but the inside looked like pure craftsmanship.

It was almost the most rudimentary of constructed vessels and in place of oars it had long spars of unfeathered wood. But where a normal naomhóg was finished with hide or canvas and waterproofed with pitch, Más's boat was hulled in what looked like glossy green-black plastic stretched over its ribs and stapled in place on the in-side of the gunwale.

I ran my hand along the hull. The skin, which looked constantly wet, was bone-dry and my fingers squeaked. They left no fingerprints. I knew instantly what it was, but I wished I didn't.

"Will you come with me? I'd like to show you my harbour. We might even catch something."

He was so proud, of his vessel, of his hometown. I couldn't say anything else.

"I will," I lied. "Tomorrow, if the fog lifts."

> I remember the harbour before the squid. The water teemed with move-ment. Ships steamed up the channel to the container ports upriver, some-how avoiding the small launches, in a complicated dance against outgoing or incoming tides, taking people to and from work at the steelworks on the nearest of the islands. Under the guidance of a harbourmaster sitting in his wasp-striped control tower, warships slipped sleekly from the naval base to hunt drug smugglers or Icelandic trawlers. An occasional yacht tied up at the floating pontoon of a small waterside restaurant. In summer, children dared each other to "tombstone" from the highest point of the piers.
>
> When I returned to the island, it might as well have been surrounded by tarmac, like a derelict theme park. Nobody even looked to the sea. It was easier that way.
>
> —Elaine Theroux, *The Great Island*

It was bright outside when I left Más's house. He had more friends, or at least ac-quaintances, than I had thought. None outwardly seemed to blame me for what had happened. Many expressed surprise he had made it that far.

Más himself had been less forgiving. After I turned him in, the local police su-perintendent let me talk to him. Más told me he hated me, called me a "fucking English turncoat." He spat in my face.

I told him he didn't understand. That he had been lucky until now. Lucky he hadn't been killed. That they hadn't retaliated.

I wanted to tell him we were working on things to kill them, to infect them, to turn them on each other. I wanted to tell him to wait until the harbour mouth was closed, that the nets were in place, that he could soon take to the water off Bally-voloon every day. That I would go with him.

But I couldn't and none of it would have mattered anyway.

I had betrayed him. And I found I could live with it.

Between Mas's house and Ballyvoloon is a harbor-side walkway known simply as "the water's edge." The pavement widens dramatically in two places to support the immense red-brick piers of footbridges that connect the old Admiralty homes, on the other side of the railway line, to the sea. I climbed the wrought iron steps to the peak and surveyed the harbor, my arms resting on the mossy capstones of the wall. The sun was rising over the eastern headland, bright and cold.

I took the phone from my pocket and watched the coroner's video.

It was mostly from one angle, from a camera I had often passed high atop an antique lamppost preserved in the middle of the main street. The quality was good, no sound, but the colours of Ballyvoloon were gloriously recreated in bright sunshine. The camera looked east, past the pier and along the beach to the old town hall, now a Chinese takeaway.

There, just visible over the roof of the taxi stand office, sat Más on his rock, whittling and chipping at a piece of wood. The email from the coroner said he had sat there all morning, but she must have supposed that I didn't need to watch all of that.

At 4:00 p.m., his usual knocking-off time, he stood, stretched his back in such an exaggerated way I thought I could hear the cracks of his vertebrae, and packed his things into a large, waterproof sail bag. Carrying his pink-and-white jacket over one arm, he walked toward the camera, hailing anyone he met with a wave, but no conversation.

However, rather than cross the beach for the bar at Tom's, he turned left down the patched concrete of the pier.

At that time of day it was deserted. The last of the stalls had packed up, the tourists had made for their trains or their buses.

The angle switched to another camera, on the back of the old general post office, perhaps. It showed Más standing with his toes perfectly aligned to the edge of the concrete pier's "T." After a few minutes, he removed several things from his pockets, folded his jacket and placed it on the concrete.

He opened the bag and withdrew a banana-yellow set of antique, old-petro waterproofs. He stepped into the thick, rubbery trousers before donning the heavy jacket and securing its buttons and hooks.

He walked to the top of the rotten steps, looked up at the cathedral and made a sign of the cross. Then he descended the steps, sinking from view.

There was nothing for more than a minute, but the video kept running, the pattern of wavelets kept approaching the shore, birds kept wheeling in the sky.

In a series of small surges, the prow of the naomhóg emerged from under the pier, then Más's head, his face towards the town, then the rest of his body and the boat.

I had to hand it to him. He could have launched his vessel at dead of night from the little boathouse where he had built the others, but he chose the part of town most visible to the cameras, at a time when few people would be around to stop or report him.

With each pull on the oars, he sculled effortlessly through the gentlest of swells, his teeth bared in joy.

His yellow oilskins shone in contrast against the dark greens of his boat and the surrounding water as he made for the mouth of his harbour and the open sea beyond.

> Yet fish there be, that neither hook, nor line, nor snare, nor net, nor engine can make thine.
>
> —John Bunyan, *The Pilgrim's Progress*

the Residue of fire

ROBERT REED

Robert Reed sold his first story in 1986 and quickly established himself as one of the most prolific of today's writers, particularly at short fiction lengths, and he has managed to keep up a very high standard of quality while being prolific, something that is not at all easy to do. Reed's stories count as among some of the best short works produced by anyone in the last few decades; many of his best stories have been assembled in the collections The Dragons of Springplace *and* The Cuckoo's Boys. *He won the Hugo Award in 2007 for his novella* A Billion Eves. *Nor is he nonprolific as a novelist, having turned out eleven novels since the end of the '80s, including* The Leé Shore, The Hormone Jungle, Black Milk, The Remarkables, Down the Bright Way, Beyond the Veil of Stars, An Exaltation of Larks, Beneath the Gated Sky, Marrow, Sister Alice, *and* The Well of Stars, *as well as two chapbook novellas,* Mere *and* Flavors of My Genius. *His most recent books are a chapbook novella,* Eater-of-Bone; *a novel,* The Memory of Sky; *and a collection,* The Greatship. *Reed lives with his family in Lincoln, Nebraska.*

"The Residue of Fire" is another story set in his long-running series about the "Great Ship," a Jupiter-size spaceship created eons ago by enigmatic aliens that endlessly travels the Galaxy with its freight of millions of passengers from dozens of races, including humans. In this one, an immortal being investigates a race of passengers aboard the ship for whom time doesn't exist, and has a showdown with a nemesis from millions of years in his past.

My face," said the human.

"Yes."

"Make the count, please."

Legs rigid, the jeweled eyes stared at the never-moving sun. But the 31-1 was also searching his memories for the friend's face. An army of sensors linked the subject's mind to a bank of diagnostic AIs. The human watched quantum whirlpools breaking out inside each one of his singholes, every swirl growing larger and brighter. An inventory was being taken, but the 31-1 wasn't counting. Counting was an act that had to cross time, and time was a falsehood, an illusion. As far as the alien was concerned, he was simply chasing a reality where the answer was known, and that was the juncture when every whirlpool was linked with the central mind, and having experienced that reality, the creature felt confident enough to offer a considerable yet very reasonable tally.

The human's face was unique in a thousand ways, but after that, completely unmemorable. He wasn't large for his species, but the lanky body gave him a tall man's build. His hair was gray, the skin deep brown, and eyes that were blue in the night were black in this glorious morning/afternoon light.

"What are my faces doing?" he asked.

"Many drink tea beside your tree," the 31-3 reported. "Others drink beside our river. And I see three faces enjoying beverages elsewhere onboard the Great Ship. Poured into a single cup, all of that tea would create an ocean."

Ash laughed at the joke.

His companion appreciated that reaction. Telemetry proved so, as did the front leg's sudden flexing.

Inspired by the subject, Ash decided to brew a fresh pot. But his supplies were indoors, and he had to drag his own cables into his home with him, and then drag them out again.

In the midst of those chores, the alien offered the word "Urgency."

"Yes?"

"I see urgency inside you."

Ash was studying the 31-1's mind, and in the same way, his friend was privy to the quantum noise inside a tiny, nearly immortal human brain.

"I see emotions that are controlled but distracting," the alien said. "Some portion of the universe can't be ignored, yet you wish that portion were as far from you as possible. Which leads you into urgency."

"I'm scared," Ash confessed.

"Quite a lot scares your species. But in this case, an impressive terror is living inside you."

To the 31-1s, the universe was a sequence of fixed, eternal realities. Each reality was spectacularly detailed, encompassing the tiniest quantum event as well as the farthest stars. Like photographs inside an infinite album: That was how the universe was organized. The most similar realities stood next to each other, close enough to touch. To the 31-1s, there was never any need for time. Time was an illusion embraced by weak species. Humans, for instance. Seconds and centuries were cheats that helped the humans navigate through the realities. And in the same fashion, the 31-1s lacked any concept of motion. They couldn't run or even imagine running. No creature walked or swam or fell. Ash certainly didn't balance on narrow legs, and data cables didn't leave drag marks in the dust. These two good friends were simply passing from one mathematical purity into the next, and the next, and a trillion other nexts. And then they reached a reality where the human had his water and blisterwing tea and a favorite pot and two well-used cups.

"Urgency," the alien repeated.

"Is that what you see inside me?"

"In your head. Considerable urgency."

But the fear wasn't enough to make him stop doing what he loved. Kneeling in the shade behind the young bristlecone, Ash arranged bits of dried foliage before applying a spark.

"I see us talking in this fashion just once," said the alien.

"Now," said Ash.

There was no "now." But better than most, this 31-1 understood what the impossible word meant to his companion.

"Why ask about your faces?"

"To test your memory," said Ash.

"You don't need tests. Your memory knows our minds very well."

Here was the key to quite a lot. Ash came to this habitat to study one unusual species. He intended to stay for a few years, no longer, but then he fell in love with the changeless weather and that low, never-moving sun. That's when he planted the bristlecone that had finally grown enough to cast a reasonable shadow. And with the native rock, he built the hearth where a new fire stood protected from the hot, unending wind.

Ash lived inside a comfortable cave just a few steps away, and this habitat was a much larger cavern. The 31-1s' home was built from granite and hyperfiber and convincing, interwoven illusions. What looked like a K-class sun was fixed to a distant wall. What wasn't sky wore the pinks of airborne dusts. To a human eye, the scene was baked in perpetual dawn or twilight. But of course the locals had no sense of day and night. They lacked any instinct that told them that any sun should move. What looked like glass roadways clung to the canyon walls, and there were hundreds of 31-1s below them, each passing from one reality to the next, and below everything and everyone was a sturdy little river that was equally fixed in time. Water didn't flow, and the 31-1s did not walk. But if that river found its way into a man's mouth, he tasted the glaciers hiding on the world's night side. That mixture of cold pleasure and rock flour made for a delightful tea, and that was another factor in Ash's decision to linger in this good place.

Ash offered his companion's name. Which wasn't a word, but a smell. Each 31-1 had a distinct, birth-given odor never replicated by others, and Ash released the odor twice, for emphasis. Then he said, "This is my reason. Your body is more likely than most to exist outside this habitat."

A truth, yes. The alien's mind and the front leg agreed with Ash.

"And your memory isn't your only talent," the human continued. "Those eyes see much more than my two light-eating pits."

Praise for the obvious wasn't praise. Yet the creature was quite pleased with the words.

"I will pay you," Ash said. "I need to show you a certain face, and then you'll go out into the Ship and look for that face."

"The Ship is rather large," his friend mentioned.

Not only was the Great Ship bigger than worlds, it was full of vast caves and tunnels and oceans and wilderness.

"I can narrow down the possible universes. Because I know where he lives."

"This is a human face?"

"Very much so, yes."

The alien applied what he knew about the tea-drinking creature. "Is this human face attractive?"

"Some would find him quite handsome, yes."

The silence stretched out while the 31-1 imagined a breeding tale about his friend and this unknown human. At least that's what Ash assumed. Despite experience and this very sophisticated equipment, he still lacked the power to see anyone's detailed thoughts.

Perhaps that magic always would be impossible.

"No," said Ash. "The situation isn't what you imagine."

"I'm imagining quite a lot," the alien warned.

The fire was growing quickly, but Ash didn't like its shape. That's why he shoved both hands into the flames, burning his fingers while he restacked the white and red coals.

"What is the truth?"

"The man happens to be lovely, but that doesn't matter," Ash said. "He recently arrived on the Great Ship, and his only purpose is to find me. My sources have warned me about that. And his business is very simple."

The alien's front leg stiffened.

"He wants to kill me," said Ash, charred fingers hanging the pot and water on a convenient hook. "My death is the singular focus of his life."

"You want me to find him," the alien said.

"Yes."

"And study his motions?"

His friend was a remarkable 31-1. Just mentioning the possibility of motion proved that much.

"No," said Ash. "What I want is for you to deliver a message. 'The man you want is ready to die for his crimes.'"

There was a pause. Then his friend said, "Death is impossible."

"So you claim."

The alien was odd among the 31-1s. But the obvious still needed to be shared. "There are countless realms where we do not exist. Does that mean we are dead? No, that's nonexistence. But there are also countless realities where we are eternal, free of seconds and free of every fear."

What a horrible, dangerous notion, thought Ash.

Watching the old copper pot, and wishing his tea would hurry. Just a little faster, please.

The human made ten thousand teas across the Ship, and the same human had also just arrived inside the World. Which was not the genuine World. This was a carefully sculpted room buried inside a starship found empty and claimed by humans as their own possession. Owning the Great Ship meant humans were a fabulously wealthy species, but this single man owned little. The 31-1s paid quite a lot to live under this false, convincing sky, and this human gave the 31-1s most of his meager funds for the privilege of sharing their home.

The human's scent meant nothing.

"Ash," was the simple sound worn on all occasions. And it was a useless sound before the 31-1 purchased a translator wise enough to interpret both languages. Unfortunately, not every word could be made into its perfect reflection. That limitation was noticed early on. "Early on." There. The concept of time insisted on finding its way into conversation and into his thoughts, and the largest surprise was how impossible thoughts gave this 31-1 so much pleasure.

"Ash is the residue of fire," the 31-1 declared.

"I certainly am," the human agreed. Then he laughed, although his companion didn't yet understand that sound or the expression on the face.

In another reality, perhaps. But not now.

"Now," he said.

"What did you say?" asked Ash.

"Nothing. I'm sorry. My translator is cheap and foolish."

The false World was one deep canyon and a very steep river with glass roadways strung between homes and the public places. The native plants were dark gray and unlovely, resembling fans and walls and other efficient, sun-obsessed shapes. The larger animals were proteinaceous jewels riding an odd number of legs, and like the 31-1s, their physiologies made them immune to normal aging and normal instincts. And there were always a few alien visitors who paid to see the oddness and stare at the illusionary sun. And there was a point on the river where a human and the cold water would end up touching.

In a sequence of realities, Ash's hands went into the river and out again, and some of what he caught found its way to his mouth.

"Delicious," the human declared.

It was pleasure hearing your water praised. Was that true for every other species?

"I'm here to learn," the human said.

"About my kind," the 31-1 guessed.

"Everything is interesting," Ash claimed. "Your species, yes. And in particular, those exceptional minds."

Fresh praise, another pleasure.

"I've heard explanations," Ash said. "But maybe your answer is different. So I'm asking. What does the name '31-1' mean?"

Nobody asked this question. This was a silly question with only one answer. The 31-1's nervous system was robust and swift, its physiology close to unique. Thirty-one redundant singholes lay inside that long, spectacular body. Each singhole existed for no purpose but remembering everything. And in his center, perfectly meshed with those relentless memories, was a mind that took the smallest question seriously.

Wishing to be generous, the 31-1 began to explain that simple name.

But Ash was ignoring him, his two tiny eyes watching a screen held in his two ridiculous hands.

The 31-1 interrupted himself. "What are you doing?" he asked.

"Almost nothing," said the human. The screen was dropped, and he looked up at a great face covered with jeweled eyes and jeweled teeth. "There's no such creature as 'happens,' and actions are not possible. I know what we are. We're matter and energy arranged in a sequence of fixed existences, and events are the products of illusion. The same way that time is an illusion."

"I don't believe you," said the 31-1.

The screen changed colors, yet the human continued staring at the creature standing before him.

"Your species is quite stubborn when it comes to time and motion," the 31-1 continued. "Freedom from time isn't your opinion, but it is mine. No seconds, no strides. This is where I exist, because this is my place, where I belong, and I am glad for all of it."

That triggered another laughing incident. "This won't get easier," Ash mentioned. "But I need to learn. If I can master your species, I could do anyone."

"What does 'do anyone' mean?"

"My profession," Ash began. Then after some consideration, he said, "I make a modest living by peering inside other minds."

The 31-1 knew this already. Except what he knew was rather different from "peering inside other minds."

"You're doubtful," the human observed.

"You see doubt?"

"And curiosity. And a powerful need for honesty too."

"There are incidents inside my mind. Eternal scenes where your customers speak about you and your unusual profession."

"Which customers?"

"I see their faces. Show me faces, and I will tell you."

"I don't care who. Just tell me what they believe."

"You are an interrogator. In other realms, you are given humans tied to horrible acts, and you place them where they deserve to be, and you make them admit to their crimes."

"That," said Ash, "was a very long time ago."

The 31-1 didn't contest the remark.

Human shoulders lifted, then fell again. "I'm talking to your species. Asking about each of you. And some tell me that you rather enjoy standing outside this pretend world. More than anyone else. Is that true?"

The 31-1 never relished being outside his home, but there was pleasure in summoning the courage to travel. The Great Ship was full of marvels that would never be seen here, and what wasn't unpleasant was often amazing. And by comparison, nothing in this World was amazing. And the same was true in the original World, his left-behind home.

"I don't know the minds of others," said the 31-1. "What pleasures them and what they believe are mysteries. But I think you know the minds of others."

"My face," Ash said.

"Yes?"

"During your travels, have you ever seen my face?"

Every question had a perfect, truest answer. But the task of memory was very difficult. Past upon past needed to be examined. Time wasn't crossed to reach the answer. Time was nothing but an exercise in mad mathematics, like imaginary numbers and existence without substance. And there were ten trillion realities that were strung together, this 31-1 emitting a series of translated sounds. Those sounds told the human, "I've seen your face three times other than this time."

Ash was studying the screen. Then he was looking up at his companion, showing his teeth. "You remember me."

"And rather a lot more than you."

"I remember seeing you once," Ash said. "And thinking to myself, 'God, that is one splendid creature.'"

The 31-1 was bathed in prideful pleasure.

He didn't want to leave this moment.

What did that say about him?

Every species was carried by its narrative, by a long history and endless accommodations to the impossible. Every species could be understood partly and only partly, and that meant your own species too. Living with the 31-1s had changed Ash. He was absolutely more aware of being human. But there were incidents—not moments—where he felt separated from time. Change inside the universe was unthinkable. Realities were pressed close to one another, and he was free and eternal, sharing the world with wise neighbors who were rather less peculiar than one tribe of upright, uptight mammals.

Ash was born on Mars. Humans wasted their affections on balls of warm rock and hot metal, and the entire body wore that very arbitrary name. But of course nothing lived inside a planet, and no planet ever wished to be named. To the 31-1s, names were granted only to those places where living bodies stood, and their original World was a ribbon. Woven from eternal memory, the ribbon was that precious narrow and very rich boundary between brutal cold and incinerating heat. No creature walked; motion was a ludicrous concept. But sturdy legs stood everywhere in the World, every timeless life embraced by the beauty, and that was the vision that the very best dreams gave to Ash.

Hundreds of billions of planets were tidally fixed. On most of them, life was forbidden. The suns were too close, and even the night side was a blistered wasteland. But there were planets where life thrived inside the narrow middle zone. Plants or something like plants were fed by the low sun, the climate more reliable than not. But those fertile zones were often too narrow or too fragmented to support complicated, mind-ruled life. And the difficulties didn't end with the richer planets. A bully sun might spit flares or otherwise butcher what couldn't flee. Moons changed orbits, turning or tipping the planet in less-than-ideal ways. And the continents could be drowned under deep oceans or shoved in and out of paradise by the amoral tectonics.

The 31-1s were unusually blessed. The planet beneath them was massive, but it wasn't as wet as most superterran, ocean-swaddled bodies. The daylight side was punctuated with volcanism and deep basins, and an ice sheet covered the night side, fattened by whiffs of steam from the sun-bathed regions. Every glacier eventually pushed towards the heat. Moraines and loess mountains ruled the boundary, ice melting into rain clouds and rivers, and that's where the 31-1s stood. Where the sun was low, the air agreeable. They stood where they belonged, and concepts such as days and forever didn't apply, because forever was a single day, and that had to be part of the story explaining what they were.

But only a small part. After all, the galaxy was full of changeless circumstances. Yet there was no second example of these creatures, and that's why the 31-1s were spectacularly precious.

In his dream, Ash wore a 31-1 body. Enormous and filled with keen excitement, he felt close, very close, to that point where he would be transformed, existing inside a multitude of realms and every good memory always in reach. But he inevitably grew nervous, and that always made him tremble. Trembling was motion; motion wasn't permitted. Ash woke just enough to realize that the delicious nap was nearly finished. Laying in the shade of the immortal bristlecone, he struggled to keep his eyes closed. The meanings of the universe. The alien world that he had never seen for himself. What flavor of tea he would boil next. Those were the great thoughts that filled a busy, happy mind.

But then he was entirely awake, and without fail, some piece of his mind insisted on remembering Mars and its long terrible war and the Cold that was waiting for every man.

Objects were responsible for nothing but their locations, fixed and outside time. The giant starship didn't plunge through a vacuum at any fraction of light-speed. No, the Great Ship was set where it was needed, where the universe demanded it to be, and the competent mind inside the Ship had found a rich location, and that's where he remained. Rigid as a statue, he stood inside a succession of brilliant days and the nights that were nearly as bright as day. The avenue beneath him was paved with glowing shells and frozen resins. The locals were dissimilar in appearance from one another and relatively poor compared to the typical passenger. These creatures had never seen a 31-1, and in many cases, they did not see this 31-1. They were too busy or too indifferent to notice his existence in one place and another place and a third midway between the two. They didn't see him watching faces for the one face that mattered. But of course all faces mattered, each being a mask obscuring long rich lives that he would never understand. Not in any reality worth the calculation, that is.

Days and nights. Days and nights. Calculating the passage of time was unnatural. Ash's good friend had to struggle to count one hundred days and ninety-nine nights, and he still wasn't convinced by the numbers. And if he didn't find the man here? He would allow the universe to carry him back to Ash and further instructions. In another hundred days, perhaps. But that was too much of a calculation, casting numbers into the future. 31-1s were happiest when they conquered one piece of ground, living on their stored fats, watching every indifferent beast that was here and then elsewhere and then back again.

This was important work, but it wasn't fun work.

Exhausted and bored, this 31-1 felt like a different creature than before. The alien faces had stopped being new. His mind kept returning to an eternal, left-behind World. The genuine sun was pinned to the perfect salmon sky, a fine dry wind blowing from wastelands. Airborne salts gave the wind its flavor, and friends were standing with him. Voices that would never escape him kept offering their advice and their scorn. What was he doing? Leaving the World was insane. That was without question, and they said so and said so and said it again.

The 31-1 felt as if he had stopped using his eyes. Only his perfect mind mattered, and a very long existence lay under him, straddled and complacent.

But he was wrong. The face that he wanted had appeared inside this reality. Existence returned to this tiny place and one promise. The 31-1 passed through the next sequence of realities. Sometimes he felt the illusion of walking, but not now. He was motionless as the Great Ship gracefully shifted its position around him, leading him towards an existence where two strangers would collide on this busy, shell-paved avenue.

What would be said?

Humans managed conversation easily, but only because they were oblivious to how impossible conversation was. Countless words, endless poses, and each reality offering crushing ramifications. The 31-1 had gathered up several viable strategies. Instead of offering the truth, he would befriend this stranger with typical words, or maybe he would beg for small favors or large sums of money. Unless he offered nothing but his close, unwelcome presence as the human continued his migration through realities. That would put the burden of the first word on human shoulders, and that solution might be best.

But the most likely strategy was to grab the man with one of his five hands, shaking him while saying, "The man you want is ready to die for his crimes."

Life was fixed and eternal. 31-1s understood that, just as they knew how the obliteration of a body and mind could never erase a life's existence.

Yet this 31-1 felt nervous. Which was very uncharacteristic of his kind. He was so nervous that his great eyes were focused on the pretty shells beneath his five bare feet. He didn't see the human standing before him. The stranger was waiting to be run over, or he was just waiting. Like Ash, he was a brown creature with a slight build. But he was far more handsome, at least by human measures. And instead of black-blue, his eyes were brown rimmed with a fine snowy whiteness.

"What are you?" the human asked.

Was any question more difficult than that?

Before the universe offered answers, the human added, "You're a 31-1. I've heard about you."

It was a pleasure, recognizing interest in the voice.

Yet the 31-1 decided to do nothing for as many futures as possible. That meant standing in the open, feeling the false light of a five hour day closing into darkness. Feeling even more than nervous now. This human wanted to kill his friend, and a succession of realities left him wracked with terror.

To this vengeful stranger, the 31-1 said, "I'm busy. I must leave."

"Ah. By any chance, do you live nearby?"

"Yes." Another lie. Which was a skill shared by every 31-1. Since lies were truths in other realms.

"I'll see you again, perhaps, and we can chat," the human said.

He was smaller than Ash and sweet-faced. That sweetness wasn't apparent for another fifty days. By then, the 31-1 had become a little more expert in the expressions and manners of human beings. Ash was a stoic, intensely private creature. But this very pretty human was the opposite of stoic or private. He easily shared details of a long life and the worlds seen, reaching back to his childhood, and then he quietly spoke about his red world and the war that took hold of his homeland, and he described the suffering seen and the suffering experienced firsthand.

The sweet face was weeping.

The lovely mouth opened and said nothing and then closed again. For the first time, the human had no words to offer.

The 31-1 looked at the cold tea on the table between them. And he studied everything else that he had ever experienced.

"Someone is hurting you," said the timeless creature. "Now and in the past too."

"Very badly," the suffering man agreed.

A series of silent realities took hold, not a word spoken.

Then with a thread of mucus leaking from the nostrils, the human produced the holo of the torturer who had done unspeakable things to him.

The universe was a sequence of perfect photographs.

Ash lived inside that image.

"As I understand it," the man began. Then he paused to breathe, gathering himself before saying, "31-1s have remarkable memories for faces."

"And for quite a lot more than faces," his companion agreed.

"You might have seen this face before," the sweet man suggested.

"I see him now, yes," said the 31-1.

"Now?" Not understanding, the man twisted his head, looking one way and then another.

"I know where he lives. That's what I mean."

"Will you tell me where?"

"No," said the one who smelled like nothing else in existence. "But I will take you to him. Now."

The AI whispered.

"The man approaches."

A warning was delivered.

And Ash understood that this was his last day of life.

Doubt didn't exist. The premonition smacked him and then left him feeling hopeless, the pain growing blacker and hotter until it was unbearable, until his heart raced and his skin was clammy wet and both hands shook and his legs could barely hold him upright. Three seconds. That's how long he had to endure the worst of it. Three seconds, which felt like an enormous span. Ash was never more human or more enveloped in time than when one of these awful, inevitable premonitions grabbed up his soul.

Exactly on schedule, the trembling eased. By the ten second mark, his breathing had slowed and his heart remembered that it didn't have to beat so hard, and rising up on his toes, Ash tested the legs that still missed the sluggish gravity of their home world. The dry wind stole away his sweat. One hand was steadier than the other, and it rubbed the back of its nervous mate while he listened to the wind playing with the bristlecone's gnarled branches.

"Of course this is my last day," he thought. "Since I never leave and the sun never sets . . ."

There. The incident was finished.

Except the voice returned. Once more, the security AI said, "He approaches, and I can't see all of him."

The human was obvious, but one of his pockets was shielded. Ash saw the same scans and agreed with the machine. There was enough room inside that pocket for a small but still thoroughly illegal plasma gun. Exactly the kind of tool to use if you wanted to obliterate another man's bioceramic mind.

Ash walked past the bristlecone, out where flat ground turned into empty air. Two figures were walking together on the narrow glass road. They were far below, several hours away. The 31-1 was leading, but the human didn't need any help. Ash didn't have to read minds to know that. The man had an urgent stride and he kept looking up at Ash's home, and despite knowing it was foolish, the man insisted on occasionally touching the pocket, feeling the gun that would deliver a world of retribution.

Ash retreated, kneeling beside the hearth.

The idea of tea made his mouth taste foul, his stomach ache. But that reaction wouldn't last. The hearth needed to be cleaned, and he was desperate for some small chore to help pass the time. Bare hands swept the ashes and a few still-warm coals into a bucket that had no other job. Hands and then wrists turned white, and when the bucket was full, he stood and carried it downwind, upending it on a ridge that always caught the wind, allowing the finest ashes to be blown away in the next minutes, leaving the rest to be washed away with the occasional downpour.

The white on his fingers tasted like salt and like earth. He licked three fingertips clean and then washed everything else.

Then he sat with his back against the bristlecone, the sun filling his eyes.

Arsia Mons. It was easy to assume that he chose this patch of ground and its false sun because they triggered memories of his Martian home. But the truth was that he didn't need reminders. He never stopped thinking about Arsia Mons, about the weather and the scenery that he had loved. A shield volcano with a huge caldera, the mountain's high reaches were famous for their cold dry air and the bristlecone forests. Brought from the Earth, the trees were tweaked until they thrived with the high carbon dioxide levels and the strong UV flux, and then other people tweaked them again, allowing them to live forever. Human cells; plant cells. In a universe full of aliens and odd biologies, those two lineages were just slightly different versions of the same cells, and humans had a need for handsome trees that served as immortal friends.

In those days, Ash wore a different name. And in front of that other name was the noble label of Doctor.

An academic, he lived in a small university with his spouse and many friends, good work and eager students from all parts of the solar system. The Doctor kept his focus away from the political troubles of the world below. A few government people came to the university seeking help. His colleagues said, "Yes," and then moved away, throwing in with the war effort. Or they said, "No," and were allowed to remain neutral in a struggle that seemed awful, but only because it was still so young and small.

That university was famous for its odd thoughts and arcane fascinations. Some colleagues invented weapons, but more important, others invented the surveillance and propaganda tools used against underground foes.

Bioceramic brains. They were Ash's passion, the reason for every professional success. Immortal flesh needed a mind that could carry huge amounts of memory, crossing millennia while retaining the sum total of a life. But the bioceramics weren't devised by humans. They were just the latest species to borrow technologies old before trilobites ruled the Earth. Intercepted broadcasts delivered the magic, and save for a few odd faiths and enclaves, humanity had thoroughly embraced the technology. Except nobody understood them perfectly. Indeed, there were days when the Doctor uncovered one or two secret talents hidden in the finer workings of these ancient machines.

University life continued, the Martian war grew worse, and the government suffered from errors and bad luck. One major problem was that prisoners couldn't be interrogated with any hope of success. Bioceramic minds were too tough, their owners too certain of their own invincibility. Death was always a threat, yes. But the modern body didn't suffer horrible pain, and the ageless minds couldn't be bored or sleep deprived into madness, or fooled in any of the traditional ways.

The Doctor had opinions about how to break a man. Indeed, working with student volunteers, he proved concepts that would revolutionize the entire business of making an enemy confess.

Publishing his work, he fully expected the government to send agents to beg for his advice, if not his out-and-out aid.

And he would say, "Yes."

Or, "No."

He wasn't certain how he would answer the pleas. But the moment never came. Mars ignored him, even when he sent messages of support and teases of possibility. According to the government's resident experts, his work was too experimental and far-fetched. And silly and shallow as this was, that's why he became angry. The noble professor was pissed by the insult, and that was when he decided to travel to Ganymede, attending a minor conference where he would meet with colleagues who understood what a good mind was being carried on his shoulders.

The Doctor was homebound when Arsia Mons was attacked. An experimental starship had been hijacked. A substantial quantity of metallic hydrogen spiked with antimatter was liberated above the mountain's caldera. The immortal bristlecones burned, and the university was destroyed, every mind obliterated in a fire that was briefly hotter than the interior of most stars.

A few days later, the new widower tried to cross the ravaged landscape. He couldn't walk far. The energy was drained from his legs, his soul. Sitting in cold sunlight, this expert of the mind again offered his aid to his world. But because both sides were guilty and both sides were incompetent, he didn't commit to either cause. This innately clinical man understood what mattered. The war had to end. And he was prepared to end it by himself, if necessary.

That's what he told the world below.

Sitting where fire had obliterated wood and soil, homes and souls, he said, "Whoever comes to me first, wins me."

Then, speaking to himself as much as any audience, he added, "Ash is my name."

"My face," said the human.

"Yes?"

"Where do you see my face?"

In the shadow of the young bristlecone. The face was between two odd hands and a deficient mind: Not a generous assessment, but that was how the 31-1s regarded their human landlords.

This 31-1 threw his focus on those hands.

Working together, the hands held a tangle of wires and sensors. That was Ash's weapon of choice. A third hand was holding an expensive, profoundly illegal gun. The two human faces were pointed at one another. Both of their wet little bodies were sucked and blowing air. One man wanted his air to carry meanings, and placing those realities into a string, the 31-1 absorbed the voice while his translator interpreted all of those painful noises.

"What you did to me, you had no right, I want you dead, the hurt you caused, for me and everyone, torturer, goddamn torturer, I'll kill you now, you shit, where you stand, shit bastard."

Ash's face didn't hide its pain. The man exhaled, and the translator said, "He sighs," and then Ash let the wires fall to the ground.

"We aren't alone," Ash said.

The furious man kept talking.

"A witness is watching us," Ash warned.

The cursing continued until the man was breathless. That's when his face turned just far enough to look at the 31-1. The 31-1 had walked all of this way, and he was standing beside the sad, angry humans. The furious man looked pale, but in the same reality, the 31-1 saw something else. In those eyes, there was a radiant, sick and intoxicating joy.

"Where do you see my face?"

Ash and his face were beside a tall table. Drinks waited in glasses and various humans stood at the table and drank. Ash was holding the hand of the man beside him. This 31-1 had never been among humans before. He didn't know any of their names and very little about the species. He would never guess about the relationship between the men, or care. But other realities existed, moored in places deficient minds called "the future," In those places, this 31-1 appreciated that the men were lovers, and a willing and competent translator was able to offer up the words that the 31-1 had overheard.

Both men saw the long, five-legged alien.

"There walks beauty."

"A 31-1."

"Is that its name?"

"The species is, yeah."

"Why that name?"

"I don't know." That human male sipped his drink and showed his smiling teeth, and he said, "But they have incredible minds, I know. Something you might like to research, if you get the chance."

The other man said, "Maybe," and then sipped hot water filled with cooked leaves.

"Where do you see my face?"

In the shade of the bristlecone. The torturer and his victim were standing close enough to touch each other, but they didn't. Death was impossible. The 31-1 might flirt with time, but he understood that nothing could erase the existence of those two humans. Yet here he was, the witness, feeling as close to terrified as he had ever been. Intriguing, wasn't it? Fear and the impossibility of guessing what would happen next: That is what made him more alert than ever. The realities were being sliced thinner than ever. That's how it felt. Everything important was visible to him, and that included how fingers and the thumb held the terrible gun that could lead to a reality where a human mind was transformed into light and vapor.

"You don't want to leave a witness," said Ash.

The 31-1's good friend was terrified. That showed in his stiff face and those huge eyes and the tone of his voice. Sunshine colored the drops of sweat that lay hard as jewels on a face that in every other existence looked composed.

Ash said, "You should kill the 31-1 first."

What did that face say?

"That would leave enough juice to finish me off too."

No, the 31-1 realized that his fear could grow worse.

It was worse.

But the furious man laughed at the suggestion. "No, I'll shoot you and then I'll kill myself. I don't care what he sees."

"Sees and remembers for ten million years," Ash said. "Is that what you want? To have this moment locked inside that alien mind?"

"I want you to die."

"And you're promising to follow me into death."

The other man started to respond.

"To stop your pain," Ash said.

The plasma gun needed a stronger grip. The next realities were centered on fingers wrapping tight around the small handle.

"But if your pain is so awful, why are you alive today?" Ash asked. "All these centuries and no end to your suffering. Yet you managed not to kill yourself. Because you needed to kill me first. Just that possibility was enough. Is that what you're claiming?"

"Yes."

"No. You're wrong and you're silly."

The other man become less angry and more angry.

How was that possible?

"Your misery hasn't been that awful," Ash said. "I mean, you tolerated it. Didn't you? You were able to function. It's not as if you haven't lived for decades carrying that gun with you, and all it would have taken was one dark thought and the press of the finger . . . and you would be dead and past pain and free."

"Shut up," said the angry man. His face was taut and the lips started to bleed where teeth cut into the flesh.

"Maybe you came here for some reason other than revenge," said Ash.

The other man spat blood, saying, "No."

"Yes."

"Never," he said. "No." Then he was blowing air without speaking, eyes wide and lost and very simple.

"What else am I?" Ash asked.

Then he paused, and the other man asked, "What's that?"

Ash took a deep breath and exhaled, and then he said, "In the entire galaxy, who knows your mind better than me? And who has the necessary skills to take away all of your misery?"

The angry man stopped breathing, and his eyes closed tight.

"This is my offer," Ash said. "I'll do that first. I'll work at your mind until both of us are satisfied. You'll be free of pain, and I'll be happier too. Then you kill me. If you wish. And our friend will watch it happen, or you can use my private home to do whatever you want to me."

The other man opened his eyes, and with both of his hands and both arms, he pointed his gun at the torturer.

Ash seemed smaller, his eyes narrow and wet.

"How?" the vengeful man asked. "How can you take my pain away?"

Ash knelt.

And then Ash stood, hands filled with his weapon of choice. "You've done nothing for centuries but suffer and chase me," he said. "But meanwhile, I've applied my time to learn all kinds of useful tricks.

"So what do you say, my friend?

"*And where do you see my face?*"

In the highest branches of a bristlecone that has grown up the canyon wall and down the canyon wall. Its roots drink from the river, and Ash sits where he can see a sun that isn't as bright as it should be. And the wind is weaker than ever. And something about the voice and eyes and the look of the ageless skin . . . something in all of that has changed.

"I see you everywhere," the 31-1.

Offering one of his hands to that odd human hand, knowing just how it feels when they touch.

sidewalks

MAUREEN F. MCHUGH

Maureen F. McHugh made her first sale in 1989 and has since made a power-ful impression on the science fiction world with a relatively small body of work, becoming one of today's most respected writers. In 1992, she published one of the year's most widely acclaimed and talked-about first novels, China Mountain Zhang, *which won the Locus Award for Best First Novel, the Lambda Literary Award, and the James Tiptree Jr. Award, and which was named a* New York Times *Notable Book as well as a finalist for the Hugo and Nebula awards. Her story "The Lincoln Train" won her a Nebula Award. Her other books, including the novels* Half the Day Is Night, Mission Child, *and* Nekropolis, *have been greeted with similar enthusiasm. Her powerful short fiction has been collected in* Mothers & Other Monsters *and* After the Apocalypse.*

Here she deals compassionately with the story of a refugee who has lost everything. And we mean, everything.

I hate when I have a call in Inglewood. It's still the 1990's in Inglewood and for all I know, people still care about Madonna. Los Angeles County has a forty bed psych facility there. Arrowhead looks like a nursing home; a long one story building with a wide wheelchair ramp and glass doors and overly bright, easy to clean floors. I stop at the reception desk and check in.

"Rosni Gupta," I say. "I'm here to do an evaluation."

The young man at the desk catches his bottom lip in his teeth and nods. "Oh yeah," he says. "Hold on ma'am. I'll get the director." He has an elaborate tattoo sleeve of red flowers, parrots, and skulls on his right arm. "Dr. Gupta is here," he says into the phone.

I also hate when people call me Dr. Gupta. I'm a PhD, not a medical doctor. I'm running late because I'm always running late. That's not true of me in my personal life. I'm early for meeting friends or getting to the airport but in my work there are too many appointments and too much traffic. Being late makes me anxious. I'm a speech pathologist for Los Angeles County working with Social Services. I'm a specialist; I evaluate language capacity and sometimes prescribe communication interventions and devices. What that means is that if someone has trouble communicating, the county is supposed to provide help. If the problem is more complicated than deafness, dyslexia, stroke, autism, learning disability, or stuttering, all the things that speech therapists normally deal with, I'm one of the people who is brought in. "Devices" sounds very fancy, but really, it's not. Lots of times a device is a smartphone with an app. I kid you not.

"Are you from LA?" I ask the guy behind the desk.

He shakes his head. "El Salvador. But I've been here since I was eleven."

"I love El Salvadorian food," I say. *"Tamales de elote, pupusas."*

He lights up and tells me about this place on Venice called Gloria's that makes decent pupusas until Leo shows up. Leo is the director.

Just so you know, I'm not some special, Sherlock Holmes kind of woman who has been promoted into this work because I can diagnose things about people. Government does not work that way. I took this job because it was a promotion. I've just been doing speech pathology for about twenty years and have seen a lot and I am not particularly afraid of technology. I have an iPhone. I attend conferences about communication devices and read scientific journals.

What I understand about this case is that police got a call about a woman who was speaking gibberish. She was agitated, attacked a police officer, and was placed on a seventy-two hour psych hold. She has no identification and is unable to communicate. They can't find any family and since she is non-verbal except for the gibberish, she was given an initial diagnosis as profoundly autistic, and when a bed opened up at Arrowhead she was placed here. I'm here to determine what the problem is.

The file is pretty lean.

I don't know Leo-the-director very well. He's a balding, dark skinned guy wearing a saggy gray suit jacket and jeans. He looks tired, but anyone running a psych facility looks tired. "Hi Ros, How was the 405?" he asks.

"Sorry I'm late," I say. "The 405 was a liquor store parking lot on payday. Tell me about your Jane Doe."

He shrugs. "She's not profoundly autistic, although she may be on the spectrum."

"So she's communicating?"

"Still no recognizable language."

"Psychotic?"

"I don't know. I'm thinking she may just be homeless and we haven't identified the language."

"How did you end up with her?" I ask. Nobody gets a bed unless they are a risk to themselves or others or severely disabled. Even then they don't get beds half the time. There are about 80,000 homeless in Los Angeles on any given night—not all of them on the street of course—some of them are living in cars or crashing on couches or in shelters—but a lot of them are either severely mentally ill or addicted and there aren't that many beds.

"She's 5250 pending T-con. Apparently she was pretty convincingly a danger to someone," Leo said.

"Section 5250" is a section of the California Welfare and Institutions Code that allows an involuntary fourteen day psychiatric hold and "T-con" is a temporary conservatorship that gets the county another fourteen days to keep someone. We're a bureaucracy. God forbid we not speak jargon, we have our professional pride. At some point in that fourteen days there has to be a Probable Cause Hearing so a court can decide whether or not the hold meets legal criteria. I'm a cog in that machinery. If I determine that she can't communicate enough to take care of herself then that's part of a case to keep her institutionalized.

When I say institutionalized I can just see people's expressions change. They go all *One Flew Over the Cuckoo's Nest*. Institutions are not happy places. The one I'm in right now is too bright. It's all hard surfaces so I hear the squeak of shoes, the constant sounds of voices. The halls are way too bright. It's about as homey as a CVS and not nearly as attractive. But you know, a lot of people need to stay institutionalized. I had a non-verbal patient, Jennie. She was twenty-six, and after many months of working with her and her caregivers to provide her with training she was finally taught to go and stand by the door of the storage room where the adult diapers were stored to communicate *that she needed to be changed*. I would like to live in a world where she didn't have to live in a place like this but I'm glad to live in a world where she has a place to live. I've been to visit family in New Delhi, okay? In New Delhi, if Jennie's family was rich she'd have great care. If her family was poor, she'd be a tremendous burden on her mother and sisters, or more likely, dead of an opportunistic infection.

I'm wearing sandals and the heels are loud on the linoleum. They're three to a room here but a lot of the people are in the day room or group therapy. We stop at a room. Two of the beds are empty and carefully made with blue, loose weave blankets on them. A woman sits on the third bed, looking outside. She is clean. Her hair is long, brown and coarse, pulled back in a thick pony-tail.

"That's Jane," Leo says.

"Hello Jane," I say.

She looks directly at me and says, "Hi." This is not typical autistic behavior. Jane is about 5'6" or so. Taller than me. She's about as brown as me. My family is Bengali although I was born and raised in Clearwater, Florida. (I came to Los Angeles for college. UCLA.) Jane doesn't look Indian. She doesn't look Central or South American, either.

We're given use of a conference room where I can do my evaluation. I prefer it to a clinic. It's quieter, there are fewer distractions.

Jane doesn't say anything beyond that "Hi" but she continues to make eye contact. She's not pretty. Not ugly, either. Jane actually rests her elbows on the table and leans a little towards me which is disconcerting.

I'm 5'3". My husband likes to walk so we walk to the drug store and sometimes we go out to eat. He's six feet tall, a teacher. He's white, originally from Pennsylvania. When we walk to restaurants from our little neighborhood (which is quite pretty, we couldn't afford to buy a house there now, but when we bought our place the neighborhood was still rough) there is enough room on the sidewalk in places for about three people to walk abreast. If there are two people walking towards us and they're two men, I'm the person who always has to get out of the way. A man will unthinkingly shoulder check me if I don't and occasionally look over his shoulder, surprised. This is a stupid thing, I know. There are a lot of entertainment businesses in our area—people who make trailers for movies or do mysterious technological things involving entertainment. They're young men. They wear skinny pants or ironic t-shirts or have beards or wear those straw fedora things. I am old enough to be their mother and I am just surprised that they do that.

"Would they run over their mother on a sidewalk?" I ask.

"It's because you're short," Matt says. Matt is my husband. He is middle-aged but he also wears ironic t-shirts. My favorite is his t-shirt of a silhouette of a T. rex playing drums with its little tiny arms. Matt is a drummer in a band made up of old white guys.

Men never do it if it's two men coming up on two men, they all just sort of squeeze. I get very irritable about it. I grew up in America. I feel American. My parents come from New Delhi and they are clear that my brothers, Jay and Ravi, and I are very American but growing up I felt like I was only pretending to be. Sometimes I think I learned how to be a subservient Indian woman from my parents and I give it off like a secret perfume.

When I was younger I walked very fast, all the time, but now I'm middle-aged and overweight and I don't dart around people anymore so maybe I just notice it more or maybe I'm just more cranky.

I plan to do an evaluation called ADOS on Jane Doe. ADOS is one of the standard evaluations for autism. It can be scaled for a range from almost non-verbal to pretty highly verbal and since the file said that she spoke gibberish, it was a place to start. I never get to ADOS because it's obvious pretty quickly that she exhibits no autistic behaviors.

"Hi, I'm Rosni Gupta," I say.

She studies me.

I tap my chest. "Rosni Gupta. Ros."

"Ros," she repeats. Then she taps her chest. "Malni," she says. She has an accent.

It takes me a couple of times to get it. She works with me, showing me what she does with her mouth to make the sound. I fiddle with it as I write it down. I think about spelling it *Emulni* but *Malni* feels closer. She has a strong accent but I can't place it. It's not Spanish. I say a couple of words to her and gesture for her to say them back. She doesn't make the retroflex consonants of the Indian subcontinent— the thing that everybody mangles trying to sound like Apu on *The Simpsons*. She watches me write.

I don't use a laptop for my field notes. I like yellow legal pads. Just the way I started. She reaches out, wanting to use my pen. Her nails are a little long, her hands not very calloused. Her palms are pink. I hand her the pen and slide the pad across to her.

She writes an alphabet. It looks a lot like our alphabet but there's no K, Q, or V. The G looks strange and there are extra letters after the D and the T and where we have a W she has something that looks like a curlicue.

She offers me the pen and says something. She gestures at me to take the pen. It's the first time she's really spoken to me in a full sentence. The language she speaks sounds liquid, like it's been poured through a straw.

I take the pen and she points to the page. Points to the first letter. "A" she says. It sounds like something between A and U.

Eventually I write an A and she nods fiercely. I write our alphabet for her.

"Wait," I say. I borrow Leo's iPad and bring it back showing a Google map of the world. "Where are you from?" I ask.

She studies the map. Eventually she turns and she scrolls it a bit. I change it to a satellite version and I can see when she gets it. Her face is grim. She stabs her finger on the California coast. On where we are right now.

"No," I say. "That's where we are now, Malni. Where is home."

She looks up at me leaning over the table. She stabs her finger in the same place.

I write up my report that she is not autistic and recommend a psychological follow-up. She might be bipolar. Leo tells me as I leave that the cop who brought her in and tazed her. I never got any sense she was violent. I was certainly never worried about my safety. I've done evals where I was worried about my safety—not many—but I take my safety very seriously, thank you.

I make dinner that night while Matt marks papers. Matt teaches sophomore English at the high school and is the faculty advisor for the literary magazine. For nine months of the year he disappears into the black hole that is teaching and we lose our dinner table. He surfaces for brief periods from the endless piles of papers and quizzes, mostly around Saturday night. He tells me about his students, I tell him about my clients.

Matt likes Bengali dishes but I don't make them very often because I didn't learn to cook until I was out of school. My go to, as you might have guessed, is Mexican. I like the heat. Tonight is carnitas à la Trader Joes.

"What's this?" Matt asks. He's sitting at the dining room table, papers spread, but he's looking at my notes. We'll end up eating in front of the television. We're Netflixing, partway through some BBC thing involving spiffily dressed gangsters in post WWI England.

"What's what?" I ask.

"Looks like someone's writing the Old English alphabet in your notes."

I bring out sour cream and salsa and look at what he's pointing to. "That was my Jane Doe in Inglewood."

"She's a *Beowulf* scholar?" he asks.

"That's Old English?" I ask.

"Looks like it," Matt says.

I have a caseload and a lot of appointments but I call Leo and tell him I want to schedule some more time with Jane even though I shouldn't take the time. He tells me she's been moved to a halfway house. It could have been worse, she could have been just discharged to the street. He gives me the address and I call them and schedule an appointment.

I have to go in the evening because Malni—they call her Malni now—has a job during the day. She does light assembly work which is a fancy name for factory work. The halfway house is in Crenshaw, a *less than desirable* neighborhood. It's a stucco apartment building, painted pale yellow. I knock on her door and her roommate answers.

"I'm looking for Malni?"

"She ain't here. She be coming back, you might run into her if you look outside." Her roommate's name is Sherri. Sherri is lanky, with straightened hair and complicated nails. "You her parole?"

"No, I'm a speech therapist."

"There ain't no therapy to do," Sherri says. "You know she don't speak no English."

"Yeah," I say. "I like your nails."

Sherri isn't charmed by my compliment. But I do like them, they look like red and white athletic shoes, like they've been laced up across each nail. I'm terrible at maintenance. Hair, make-up, nails. I admire people who are good about things like that.

I head outside and spot Malni coming from a couple of blocks. Malni walks with her shoulders back, not smiling, and she makes eye contact with people. You're not supposed to make eye contact with people in the city. It's an unwritten rule. There's a bunch of boys hanging on the corner and Malni looks straight at their faces. It's not friendly, like she knows them. It's not unfriendly. It's . . . I don't know. The way people cue looking at people and away from people is something to look for when determining if they're autistic or if they're exhibiting signs of psychosis. I'm trained to look for it. Persons on the autism spectrum generally don't make eye contact. A lot of persons with schizophrenia don't look at people and look away in the normal rhythms of conversation; they stare too much, too long, for example. When I assessed Malni at Arrowhead, she cued normally.

Malni walks the boys down, looking right in their faces. The boys move out of her way. I suspect they don't even realize that they're doing it. I remember her file says she was tazed when police apprehended her. A homeless woman of color speaking gibberish who kept looking them in the face and wouldn't drop her eyes. Did they read that as aggressive? I bet she didn't have to do much to get tazed. It's a wonder she didn't get shot.

Malni sees me when she gets closer and lifts her hand in a little wave. "Hi Ros," she says and smiles. Totally normal cueing.

I follow her back into the apartment she shares with Sherri.

"I ain't going nowhere," Sherri announces from in front of the television. "I worked all day." There's a Styrofoam box of fried chicken and fried rice nearly finished on the coffee table in front of her.

"That's okay," I say.

Malni and I sit down at the kitchen table and I open up my laptop. I call up images of *Beowulf* in Old English and turn the screen around so Malni can see them.

She frowns a moment and then she looks at me and smiles and taps my forehead with her index finger like she's saying I'm smart. She pulls the laptop closer to her and reads out loud.

It's not the same liquid sound as when she talked, I don't think (but that was two weeks ago and I don't remember exactly). This sounds more German.

Sherri turns around and leans against the back of the couch. "What's that she's talking?"

"Old English," I say.

"That ain't English," Sherri says. It's like everything from Sherri has to be a challenge.

"No, it's what they spoke in England over a thousand years ago."

"Huh. So how come she knows that?"

Malni is learning modern English. She can say all the things that you learn when you start a new language—My name is Malni. How much does that cost? Where's the bathroom? Everyone keeps asking her the same question, "Where are you from?"

She keeps giving the same answer, "Here."

I pull a couple of yellow legal pads out of my messenger bag and a pack of pens. I write my name and address, my cell number, and my email address on the first one.

"Hey Sherri, if she wants to get in touch with me, could you help her?"

I'm not sure what Sherri will say. Sherri shrugs, "I guess."

Malni looks at the writing. She taps it. "Ros," she says. Then the number. "Your phone."

"Yes," I say. "My phone." It's my work phone because I never give clients my home phone. Not even my clients who read Old English.

I think about Malni walking through those boys. I'm meeting with one of my clients. Agnes is Latina. She's sixty-four and had a stroke that's left her nearly blind and partially deaf. She's diabetic and has high blood pressure. She has a tenth grade education and before her stroke, she and her daughter cleaned houses.

With a hearing aid, Agnes can make out some sounds but she can't make out speech. Her daughter, Brittany, communicates with her by drawing letters on her hand and slowly spelling things out. I've brought a tablet so that Agnes can write the letters she thinks Brittany is writing. It's an attempt at reinforcing feedback. Adult deaf blindness is a difficult condition. Agnes is unusual because she doesn't have any cognitive issues from her stroke, so there are lots of possibilities. I'm having Agnes write one letter at a time on the tablet, big enough that she herself might be able to see it.

Agnes has a big laugh when she's in a good mood. Sometimes she cries for hours but today she's good. She has crooked teeth. Her English is accented but she's lived here since she was thirteen—Brittany was born here and speaks Spanish as her first language but grew up speaking English, too. "Mom!" she says, even though her mother can't hear her. "Quit goofing around!" She smacks her mother lightly on the arm. Agnes's eyes roam aimlessly behind her thick and mostly useless glasses.

Brittany, who is in her thirties, raises an eyebrow at me. Both women are short and overweight, classic risk profiles for diabetes and hypertension, like me. Unlike them, I have really good health care.

Agnes prefers drawing on the tablet to writing and after twenty minutes of trying to figure out what Brittany has been asking her, "?yr name ?hot or cold ?what 4 dinner" Agnes has given up and drawn an amorphous blob which is apparently supposed to be a chicken. "Fried chicken," she announces, too loud because she can't hear herself well enough to regulate her volume.

"She can't have fried chicken for dinner," Brittany says. "She has to stick to her diet."

Agnes says, "El Pollo Loco! Right? Macaroni and cheese and cole slaw. Cole slaw is a vegetable."

Brittany looks at me helplessly. Agnes cackles.

My phone rings. "Is this Ros, the speech lady? This is Sherri, Malni's roommate."

"Sherri?" I remember the woman with the nails painted to look like the laces on athletic shoes. "Hi, is everything all right?"

"Yeah. Well, sort of. Nothing's really wrong. I just got a bunch of papers here for you from Malni."

"Where's Malni?" I ask.

"She took off to find her friends," Sherri said.

"What friends?"

"Her friends from wherever the hell she's from," Sherri says. "You gonna pick up these papers or what?"

I wanted Malni to write her story down. She filled almost three legal pads. I didn't expect her to disappear, though.

"This guy showed up," Sherri says. In honor of Agnes I've brought El Pollo Loco. Sherri doesn't really like El Pollo Loco. "I don't eat that Mexican shit," she says but she takes it anyway. "He was tall and skinny. He looked like her, you know? That squished nose. Like those Australian dudes."

It takes me a moment but then I realize what she means; Aboriginals. She's right, Malni looked a little like an Aboriginal. Not exactly. Or maybe exactly, I've never met an Australian Aboriginal. "Oh, cool, I didn't know they had mac 'n' cheese." Sherri plunks down on the couch and digs in. "Yeah so he started jabbering at her in that way she talks to herself. Was crazy. And he acted just like she did. All foreign and weird. Then they just took off and she didn't come back."

"When was that?" I ask. My feet hurt so I sit down on the couch next to her.

"Like, Saturday?"

This is Thursday. Part of me wants to say, you couldn't be bothered to call until yesterday but there's no reason for Sherri to have bothered to call me at all, even though Malni apparently asked her to.

"That bitch was super smart," Sherri says.

I give Sherri twenty dollars, even though she's a recovering substance abuser and it's risky to give her pocket money, and take the legal pads and go.

I call the department of history at UCLA and eventually find someone who can put me in touch with someone at the department of Literature who puts me in touch with a woman who is a *Beowulf* scholar. Why I thought I should start in History I don't know since Matt is an English teacher and he recognized the language. Anyway, I tell the *Beowulf* scholar I am looking for someone who can translate Old English and that I will pay.

That is how I get Steve. We meet at a Starbucks near campus. Starbucks is quickly becoming the place where everybody meets for almost every reason.

Steve is Asian-America and very gay. He wears glasses that would have gotten me laughed out of middle school. He is studying Old English and needs money. "I'm supposed to be working on my dissertation," he says. "I *am* working on my dissertation, actually. It's on *Persona and Presentation in Anglo Saxon Literature.* But there's that pesky thing about rent." He eyes the legal pads. I wonder what persona and presentation even means and what his parents think about having a son who is getting a doctorate in English Literature. Which I realize is racist. Just because my dad is an engineer and my mother is a chemist and they are classic immigrant parents who stressed college, college, college, doesn't mean Steve's are. For all I know, Steve's parents are third generation and his dad plays golf and gave him a car on his sixteenth birthday.

"I can pay you $500," I say.

"That looks like modern handwriting. Is it, like, someone's notes or something?"

"I'm not exactly sure," I say.

He eyes me. I am aware of how weird it is to appear with three legal pads of handwritten Old English. Steve may be a starving UCLA student but this is very strange.

"I think it's like a story," I say. "I work for Los Angeles County Social Services. A client gave me these."

"You're a social worker," he says, nodding.

"I'm a speech therapist," I say.

He doesn't comment on that. "This is going to take a lot of hours. A thousand?" he says.

"Seven hundred and fifty," I say.

"Okay," he says.

I write him a check for half on the spot. He holds the check, looking resigned. I think I'm getting a pretty good deal.

After that I get emails from him. The first one has ten typed pages of translation attached and a note that says, *can we meet?*

We meet in the same Starbucks.

"Your client is really good at Anglo-Saxon," he says. "Like, really good."

"Yeah?" I say. How can I explain?

"Yeah. She does some really interesting things. It's a woman, right?"

Malni tells a "story" about a woman from a place on a harbor. The place is vast, full of households and people. There are wondrous things there. Roads crowded with people who can eat every manner of food and wear the richest of dress. It is always summer. It is a place that has need for few warriors. Trees bear bright fruit that no one picks because no one wants it because no one is hungry. The air is noisy with the sounds of birds and children.

She is one of a band of people. They work with lightning and metal, with light and time. They bend the air and the earth to open doors that have never been opened. They journey to yesterday. To the time of heroes.

"She's a woman," I say.

"It's like a sci fi fantasy story," Steve says.

I already know that. Malni has been telling everyone, *she's from here.* When I read those words, that they journeyed to yesterday, I figured that plus the Old English meant that somehow Malni thought she had gone to the past.

"Have you heard about anybody who had some kind of breakdown or disappeared in the last year? You know, a teacher? Someone good at Old English?"

"No?" he says.

I tell him a little bit about Malni.

"Wow. That's . . . wow. You'd think someone this good would be teaching and yeah, it's a pretty small discipline. I'd think I'd have heard," he says. "Maybe not. If I hear anything . . ."

"So she's really good," I prompt.

"There are only something like a little over four hundred works of Old English still around," Steve says. "There's *Beowulf,* which was written down by a monk. There's *Caedmon,* and *Alfred the Great* and *Bede,* a bunch of Saints' lives and some riddles and some other stuff. You get to know the styles. The dialects. This is close to *Alfred* but different. I thought at first that the differences were because she was trying to mimic *Alfred* but getting it a little wrong, you know? But the more I read it over and over, the more I realize that it's all internally consistent."

"Like she's really good at making it up?"

"Yeah," Steve says. "Like she's made a version all her own. Invented a wholly new version of Old English so that it would sound like a different person at close to the same time. And written a story in it. That's a really weird thing to do. Make it super authentic for somebody like me. Because the number of people who could read this and get what she's doing and also enjoy it is zero."

"Zero?"

"Yeah," he says. "I mean, I understand the beginning of the story, I think. It's a time travel story. She starts in Los Angeles, which, by the way, is really hard to describe in Anglo-Saxon because she doesn't try to make up words like horseless cart or anything. For one thing, Anglo-Saxon doesn't really work that way. So she starts here and she travels back in time. Then there's this part about being in the past in what I think is probably Wessex, you know, what's now part of England. She makes up some stuff that's different from the historical record, some of which I wish was true because it's really cool and some of which is just kind of dull unless you're really into agriculture. Then there's this long explanation of something I don't understand because I think she's trying to explain math but it isn't like math like I understand math. But really, I suck at math so maybe it is."

"She's got math in there?"

"A little bit, but mostly she's explaining it. There's something about how really small changes in a stream make waves and if you drop a stick in the water, no one can predict its course. How when you walk through the door to yesterday, it means yesterday is not your yesterday. Then she talks about coming back to her beautiful city but it's gone. There's a strange city in its place. That city is beautiful, too and it's full of wild men and sad women. That city has savage and beautiful art. It has different things. Some are better and some are worse but her family is gone and no one speaks to her anymore. She says the story is about the cost of the journey. That when you journey to yesterday, you lay waste to today. When you return, your today is gone and it is a today that belongs to somebody else."

It takes me a moment to think about all that.

One of the baristas steams milk. Starbucks is playing some soft spoken music in the background. It doesn't feel like someone has just explained how to end my world.

"It's kind of creepy but the way it's written there are big chunks that are really hard to read," Steve says. "Is she crazy? I mean, what's the deal?"

I want to say she's crazy. Really, it's the best explanation, right? She was a professor of Anglo Saxon/Old English. She'd had a psychotic break. Sherri said a man who looked a lot like her—maybe a family member, a brother—tracked her down to the halfway house and took her home.

That strange and liquid language she speaks. The way she acts, as if she comes from a different culture where the men are not so savage and the women not so sad.

"I don't know," I say.

"I can give you what I've translated. I've translated all the words but there are parts that don't make sense," Steve says.

I pay him the rest and add enough to make a thousand. He's spent a lot of time on it. Time he could have been working on his dissertation.

"I actually learned a lot," he says. "It's like she really speaks Anglo Saxon."

"Maybe she did," I say.

Someone, somewhere is working on time travel. I mean, someone has to be. People are trying to clone mammoths. People are working on interstellar travel. I have a Google alert for it and mostly what pops up is fiction. Sometimes crazy pseudo science. Real stuff, too. I get alerts for things like photon entanglement. People are trying.

I think I saw Malni on Wilshire Boulevard one time walking with two other people; a man who looked like her and a woman who had black hair. I was driving, late for an appointment. By the time I saw them I was almost past them. I tried to go around the block and catch them but traffic was bad and by the time I got back to Wilshire they were gone. Or maybe it wasn't Malni.

Maybe in some lab somewhere, people are close to a time travel breakthrough. I walk downtown with Matt and I think, this might be the last moment I walk with Matt. Someone might be sent back in time at any moment and this will all disappear.

Will it all disappear at once? Will I have a moment to feel it fading away? Will I be able to grip Matt's arm? To know?

There are two guys walking towards us as we head to the Mexican place. I'm going to have a margarita. Maybe two. I'm going to get a little drunk with Matt. I'm going to talk too much if I want to. The guys are not paying attention. I remember Malni. I throw my shoulders back a little. I do not smile. I look in the face of the one in my way. The world is going to end, you fucker. I will not give up this sidewalk with my love.

He steps a little to the side. He gives way.

NEXUS

MICHAEL F. FLYNN

Michael Flynn began selling science fiction in 1984 with the short story "Slan Libh." His first novel, In the Country of the Blind, *appeared in 1990. He has since sold seventy or more stories to* Analog Science Fiction and Fact, Asimov's Science Fiction, The Magazine of Fantasy & Science Fiction, *and elsewhere, and he has been nominated several times for the Hugo Award. He is best known for the Hugo-nominated* Eifelheim *and the Spiral Arm series:* The January Dancer, Up Jim River, In the Lion's Mouth, *and* On the Razor's Edge. *His other books include* Fallen Angels, *a novel written in collaboration with Larry Niven and Jerry Pournelle,* Firestar, Rogue Star, Lodestar, Falling Star, *and* The Wreck of the River of Stars. *His stories have been collected in* The Forest of Time and Other Stories *and* The Nanotech Chronicles. *He has received the Robert A. Heinlein Award for his body of work and the Theodore Sturgeon Award for the story "House of Dreams." In addition, he has received the Seiun Award from Japan and the Prix Julia-Verlanger from France, both for translations of* Eifelheim. *His most recent book is the collection* Captive Dreams, *which contains six stories dealing with issues of morality and technology. He is currently working on a novel,* The Shipwrecks of Time, *set in the alien world of 1965. He lives in Easton, Pennsylvania.*

Here he delivers a flamboyant, hugely entertaining novella, throwing everything but the proverbial kitchen sink into it, including two different groups of aliens (one invading, and one long-established on Earth, in hiding as a secret society), two different time travelers, including one who is seeking to wipe out our universe and replace it with a reconstruction of his own lost timeline, an immortal woman who used to hang out in the courts of Byzantium (although even she can't remember what her ultimate origin was), a supersmart AI housed in an android body, and a powerful human telepath working as a PI.

Consider the man who is brained by a hammer while on his way to lunch.

Everything about his perambulation is caused. He walks that route because his favorite café is two blocks in that direction. He sets forth at the time he does because it is his lunchtime. He arrives at the dread time and place because of the pace at which he walks. There are reasons for everything that happens.

Likewise, the hammer that slides off the roof of the building half a block along. It strikes with the fatal energy because of its mass and velocity. It achieves its terminal velocity because of the acceleration of gravity. It slides off because of the angle of the roof and the coefficient of friction of the tiles, because it was nudged by the toe of the workman, because the workman too rose to take his lunch, and because he had laid his hammer where he had. There are reasons for everything that happens.

Not much of it is predictable, but causation is not the same as predictability.

It would never occur to you—at least we hope it would never occur to you—to search out "the reason" why at the very moment you walked past that building, some roofer in Irkutsk dropped his tool. Why should the concatenation become more meaningful if the roofer is closer by? Spatial proximity does not add meaning to temporal coincidence. Chance is not a cause, no matter how nearby she lurks.

So the hammer has a reason for being there, and the diner has a reason for being there; but for the unhappy congruence of hammer and diner, there is no reason. It is simply the crossing of two causal threads in the world-line.

"Ah, what ill luck," say the street sweepers as they cleanse the blood and brains from the concrete. We marvel because our superstitions demand significance. The man was brained by a hammer, for crying out loud! It must mean *something*. And so poor Fate is made the scapegoat. Having gotten all tangled up in the threads, we incline to blame the Weaver.

ORPHANS OF TIME
I. SIDDHAR NAGKMUR

Consider now the man getting drunk in a dingy after-hours bar in an unhappy corner of Chicago. He too is unhappy, which makes for a good fit. His name is Siddhar Nagkmur, and he has the morose visage of a sheepdog who has failed his flock. It shows in his face, which is long and narrow and creased with lines at the eyes and lips; and it shows in his drink, which is both potent and frequently replenished. He sways a bit on the bar stool, ever on the point of toppling over, yet never quite passing that point. The lives of billions layer on his face and pool in his eyes.

The neighborhood is one of warehouses, wholesalers, terminals, and similar establishments, and the bar's clientele the usual gallimaufry of pickers, packers, and teamsters, among whom Nagkmur's coveralls blend well. Outside, the night lies empty, save for the men at the loading docks who are prepping the morning deliveries, and the drifting strangers who habitually rove empty nights at three in the morning.

From time to time, Nagkmur glances at the flickering television and mutters something about "phantoms," but neither the bartender nor the other patrons ask him what he means. One is half afraid of what he might say. Each patron dwells introspectively on his own tidy failures until Nagkmur's empty highball glass strikes the countertop and startles them into the moment.

The bartender does not ask if he thinks he's had enough, because if he'd thought that he would not have banged the countertop quite so eloquently. The bartender pours the bar Scotch, and waters it more than his wont—a blow struck for both sobriety and the bottom line.

"Shy Hero in Manhattan!" the television announces as the hour cycles around to a fresh story in the news-blender. The shout-out tugs momentarily at everyone's attention, and on the screen a stolid woman half-turns from the camera, anxious to conclude the inescapable interview. A fire. A baby. A dash through the flames. A *rescue!* Brief platitudes.

"Stupid," says the bartender, not grasping the nature of heroism. "She coulda been killed."

Nagkmur continues to scowl at the screen after the woman's face has been replaced by commercials promising revivified male performance. "I see this woman before," he mutters, in accents that proclaim English an acquired tongue.

"Yeah? Where'd ya see her?" the bartender asks, not because he is interested but just to break the silence.

But his effort is a match struck on a gusty night. Nagkmur says, "Glass water" and from his inside jacket pocket he plucks a flat tin containing lozenges, one of which he swallows and chases with the water. The bartender pretends not to notice. He has seen innumerable pharmaceuticals consumed in his establishment and regards everyone as entitled to blaze his own trail to hell, so long as he pays his tab along the way.

Speaking of which, the bartender mentions the cost of the water and whiskey and Nagkmur selects it from a pouch he wears at his waist, scrutinizing each bill as if unfamiliar with its value. He takes a deep, shuddering breath. Then, with the air of one spared the headsman's axe to keep an urgent appointment on the gallows, he slides from his stool and walks toward the door. He walks without a stagger, too; and the bartender suddenly wishes he knew what had been in that lozenge.

Outside, in the lonely world of the small hours, Nagkmur finds three young men trying to jack his time machine.

They are engrossed in the task. The vehicle is too tasty to pass up. Larger than a minivan, not so large as a panel truck, it is clearly high-end. The opaque windows prevent casing the interior but it just *got* to hold valuable shit!

However, it presents certain difficulties in task execution. The blocky design is unfamiliar. There is no evident hood. How do you hot-wire a thing like that? The door—there is only the one—does not yield to their coaxing. Where is the damned handle? So they shake the vehicle like a man jiggling a doorknob, in the belief that one more jiggle will happily discover it to have been unlocked after all. One of them has crouched to study the wheels. There is something odd about them, but he cannot say what.

They are levitation disks, not wheels—just as the "windows" are external sensor panels—but Nagkmur does not share this intelligence. Nor does he fear the young men will make off with his transporter. Nothing known to this nexus is capable of unsealing it once it has turtled. So he stands quietly by and waits.

Eventually, the thieves twig to his presence, which startles them considerably. Most owners would have announced themselves with some useless bluster, like *What do you think you're doing?* (Stupid. What did it look like they were doing?) But this skeletal figure simply watches in silence and that puts the three a little off their game. There is something in his eyes, a certain quietus to his expression. Two of the three take involuntary steps back, but their leader thrusts his chin out. "Watcha lookin at, fool? This your car?"

Nagkmur says, "No," but he means that it is not a car, not that it isn't his.

"Then get your ass in gear and fart on outta here." The other two think this the height of wit, or perhaps of poetry. Nagkmur is reminded of the old adage that "sin makes you stupid." Criminal masterminds are genuinely rare upon the earth, and among their ranks these three are not to be numbered.

Nagkmur searches his newly impressed language and finds the warning he wants. "Please, to back away from transporter." He adds a second command in *pudding-wa* and his vehicle hears and activates certain defenses.

The sudden hum alarms the youths, driving them together. "What'd you do, chink?" demands the leader.

"You are advised not to touch the transporter."

"Yeah?" the leader mocks. "And what happens if I do?" And he stretches out an insolent fingertip to do just that.

The answer to his question is "electrocution." His entire body stiffens, his eyes bulge, and his sneer pulls back into a rictus. A moment later, he drops insensate to the cobblestones.

It is a momentary distraction, and in that moment Nagkmur flicks his baton to half-extension and, whirling, breaks the wrist of the second thief, who is belatedly clawing a pistol from his waistband. Completing his spin, Nagkmur pivots into the Flying Mule, and catches the third tough with a shod foot to the side of the head. The boot is steel-toed so this young man joins his leader on the pavement.

The second one has had enough and, abandoning his companions to the Fates, he runs into the night, clutching his wrist to him.

Nagkmur knows an unseemly glow of satisfaction. He has never heard of the five stages of grief, but he is—by damn!—in number two. Ever since his discovery that the world had been wiped out, anger has been building up as in a capacitor, and it feels good to discharge the load, even on a trio of phantoms.

But there is no time for his bottled grief to pour forth. A distant siren heralds the approach of the local authorities. Someone on the graveyard shift has possessed sufficient civic virtue to summon the police—perhaps the man on the loading dock at the warehouse across the truck apron, ready to scribble the license plate number when Nagkmur's vehicle pulls out of the shadows.

Of course, time machines do not "pull out" in any manner normally understood, nor do they bear license plates; but one admires the fellow's staunch rectitude.

Nagkmur sighs. So much for passing unnoticed.

He kicks the dropped gun to a place where it will be found. The local police might learn something useful from its study, and as a fellow lawman he will make this one gesture in their aid.

That he intends to wipe all of them—police and thugs, bartenders, drunks, and warehousemen—from the very face of the Earth is no reason to neglect courtesy.

His vehicle senses his shield number and the door permeates to allow him entry. He seals up and activates the external screens and audio pickups. The transporter's hull clarifies, providing him with an ecumenical view of his surroundings. He drops into his seat, takes a deep breath and, wasting no time in light of the approaching sirens, brings up a map of the phantom world that he had earlier gleaned from a radio-accessible *juku*. He identifies "Manhattan" and enters its coordinates into the transporter. Then he kicks in the temporal precessor and the aetherial gyroscopes spin up.

That is when the hammer hits.

Something blacker than the night emerges from the shadowy interior of the electronics warehouse. It is a great ebon sphere peppered with lights like a thousand eyes, as if a portion of the starry sky has come to ground. The warehouseman flees without getting its number, and the apparition sprints toward the transporter in a complex, five-legged gait that defies description. Terror chokes Nagkmur's throat.

Then he pops the clutch and detaches from the space-time manifold. His transporter coasts backward and spinward along the worldline, and he removes trembling hands from the control yoke.

What was that? he wonders. Has it anything to do with the catastrophe that has marooned him here? Perhaps he should have confronted it, interrogated it. But deep within, down where the shaking has its roots, he is quite as happy he had not.

He reaches lower Manhattan earlier that same evening and coasts out of phase until he locates the nexus of the apartment house fire. Then he finds a nearby abandoned building where he can conceal his transporter and backs up a few hours to give himself time for his preparations.

External sensors show no signs of life beyond the usual small and scuttling things common to derelict buildings, so he reattaches to the manifold. Papers, dirt, and other detritus swirl about in the air displaced by his point-expansion, and his transporter settles into the moment.

He sits for a while in his saddle, arms dangling at his sides, breathing slowly and calmly and calling upon his balance. *In fear and trembling, the Superior Man sets his life in order and examines himself.* His son, his father, his brothers and colleagues . . . they had never been. Or "will not have been," however this new language expresses such thoughts. Their resurrection is now up to him. *To escape difficulties, the Superior Man falls back upon his inner worth.* Resolutely, he stuffs the terrifying apparition into another corner of his mind for later consideration. It had likely been no more than the drunken binge making one last punishment for his sin.

Upon first apprehending the calamity, Nagkmur had fled into the distant past, lest he be extinguished when his colleagues restored the worldline. But where the massive buildings of Deep Time HQ had once stood, the broad interglacial steppes had swept unvexed to the horizon. He knew then beyond all hope of doubt that the Shy?n Baw had never been, and of his entire Department he alone survived. It would be up to him to restore the true history.

But to rectify the worldline, he must identify the nexus at which time had gone awry. And to do that, he must research the phantom history and compare it to the true history. And to do that, he needs an epoch far enough forward to have radio-accessible *juku*, but not so far forward that time would have abraded the crucial details into smooth and shiny fables.

He has already spent time in Chicago learning the geography and impressing the dominant language on his neural pathways so that he can read and even habitually think in it. Now he must begin his search in earnest. Somewhen within this unknown history, written in this half-grasped tongue, nestles that singular incident which has derailed the proper course of time.

And that was why the Shy Hero in Manhattan—who would be saving a phantom baby later this very night—was so important. For why should he recognize anyone in this fate-condemned world unless she too were a traveler orphaned by time?

II. STACEY PAPANDREOU

Consider now the woman fleeing a burning apartment building on the edge of the West Village in Manhattan. Fire holds a special horror for her so she cannot say even afterward why she turns aside to grab the crying baby from the first-floor apartment. She has learned not to care overmuch about the shadows among whom she lives, but the infant's cries touch something primal within her and she hardly knows what she is doing when she snatches it from Moloch's jaws.

Then she is outside on Gansevoort St. with no recollection of the in-between, sucking in great gulps of air, the baby clutched against her breast still wailing. Around her are spinning lights atop fire engines, police cars, ambulances; firemen laying hoses, incomprehensible squawks over walkie-talkies; streams of water pouring into the now-crackling inferno. She stares at the apartment building, amazed that she has come through it, astonished that she had paused even for a moment.

Maryam brt' Yarosh has employed different names in different milieus but in this time-and-place, she is Stacey Papandreou. In a town of such eclectic habitants as New York City, even the most outré can swim in anonymity, though it is best not to press the matter too far. This milieu is more tolerant than most, but tolerance too often depends upon what is at stake.

The mother shrieks up the sidewalk, the milk she had ducked out to buy a splash of white on the paving behind her. She blubbers gratitude and smothers babe and rescuer alike with kisses. Stacey does not know her name, but she smiles and says it is nothing. The infant stares alternately at mother and neighbor, as if suddenly realizing that something has happened. Its eyes are a deep brown and seem far too large for its head.

Then the baby is taken up by professionals with oxygen masks and other accouterments of care. Stacey too is given aid. Smoke inhalation, burns, who knows what injuries she may have sustained? The oxygen is cool and pure and she sucks it in gratefully.

Around the firemen and EMTs and flashing lights and garbled voices, circle the vultures, aching to fill the 24/7 news-void, thrusting microphones in her face like . . . No wonder they are called news organs! They bark unanswerable questions. *Why'd ya do it?* She cannot enlighten them. *How'dya not get burned?* Just lucky, I guess. *How's it feel to save a life?* A century from now no one will know this baby ever lived, let alone that it lived a little longer.

But no, we don't say such things. It is too startling and interrupts the smooth glide of thought as it skips from cliché to cliché like a stone across a pond. Experience has taught her that it is better to pass unnoticed, and naked truth is the pornography of discourse. It always draws more attention than the decently costumed kind. So she pronounces the expected platitudes instead and nestles invisibly within the journalistic paradigm. Almost, the story can write itself.

She turns half-away from the cameras, enough to shadow her features but not so much as to excite curiosity. She has spent many years learning the arts of obscurity and care has become a second nature. Come across as mysterious or evasive and the organs would push in deeper. But present oneself *too* openly and some geezer might recognize her on the tube from some older milieu.

Farther down the street, within the fire line, a dark woman with cropped, platinum-white hair and wearing an ID on a chain around her neck scans the crowd. There is a fire marshal by her side, and Stacey guesses that someone suspecting arson has brought in a profiler to spot the firebug among the gawping onlookers.

Though if anyone had set the fire, Stacey thinks, it would have been the owner. The building hangs like an albatross around his neck. Gentrification is creeping up the West Village on little cat feet, and the site is worth more sold to developers than rented to residents.

The platinum-haired woman locks gazes with her for a moment and Stacey recalls that some people set fires in order to play the hero. She wonders if she is being profiled.

If so, she must not have fit, because the woman turns aside and both she and the marshal move on to another part of the crowd.

The news organs will vie for some fresh angle on the story. Seeking a human-interest hook, someone will thrust into the Heroine's past and discover that she has none. It is time to move on. She has already lost her possessions in the fire; discarding the rest of "Stacey Papandreou" wants little more.

She can get clothing at a nearby discount shop, perhaps on charity, and rinse the soot from her face in their washroom. She has jewels cached in various places. Making herself presentable, she can convert the cache to cash, and sink back into the anonymous masses.

But as she turns away, an iron hand seizes her wrist and she gasps and looks up into the intense, troubled face of a Chinaman. She draws a breath to shout for help, but the man says, "I know you," as if making an accusation.

And Stacey forebears to shout, for shouting would attract attention, would draw eyes toward her at just that moment when she would fade quietly away.

The bubble of fame expands slowly, obeying an inverse square law. Out toward the edge of the crowd, newcomers crowd up behind those who have arrived earlier, leaping a-toe, craning necks, hoping to catch a glimpse of tragedy. No one recognizes her as "the Heroine" or even knows as yet that there has been one. But, barefooted and night-gowned, Stacey is clearly a Victim and people tug at her sleeves and ask her what has happened, appealing to the special *gnosis* with which Victims are endowed.

The man pushes through them, saying, "She must be attended." He has a long coat slung over his arm with a pair of sandals tucked into its pockets. Once they reach the other side of the street, he pauses while she puts them on. He says something to her in what she takes to be Chinese, though he does not sound much like Mr. Lu at the take-out. She has a hazy recollection that she had seen him, a long time ago: His face flashes through her mind, quaffing wine across a rude wooden table. There is more, but the memory is a dry, brittle leaf in an autumn forest.

He guides her uptown rather than down, and that is all the same to Stacey. There is no particular place she needs to go to just yet, so one direction pleases as well as another. He strides with determination, now and then snapping something to her in Chinese. When Stacey fails to answer, the grim set of his mouth deepens.

They duck around the corner to Little West Twelfth, and then under the High Line to a block where enough meat packers hang on to justify the neighborhood's name. One of the buildings is abandoned and he urges her toward it through a gap in the chain-link fence that halfheartedly encloses it.

Stacey grows hesitant. Among the reasons a man might have for leading a woman into an abandoned building, few inspire great confidence. Granted, he has rescued her from the curious crowds, but Stacey begins to wonder how he had known to bring a coat and sandals.

Her knives have been left behind in the burning apartment, but she knows various forms of unarmed combat, and most common objects can be used as weapons by the keenly imaginative. A woman alone must learn such things. But Stacey also knows the limitations of such methods for one with a woman's frame. A woman may equal a man in combat only so long as she remains beyond arm's reach. One time, when she had worked as a spy in . . .

It comes upon her in a flash, as if the wind has scoured the dead clouds from an overcast sky. . . . In Constantinople. She had met this man in the City by the Golden Horn. She had been using the name "Macedonia" then, and had been a dancer for the Blues. But covertly, she had also worked for the emperor's nephew, who had been *magister militum*. She had passed along treasonous pillow-talk and brought persons of interest—especially foreigners—to the magistrate's attention.

Yes! She had met this man in the *kapeleîon* of Nicholas of Urfa, near the palace district. He had been staying in the *pandocheia* that Nicholas kept for foreigners and he had entered the tavern with the actress Theodora on his arm and a plate of meat for Nicholas to cook. Macedonia had been entertaining a Syrian merchant she suspected of harboring Persian sympathies and Theodora had brought this stranger to join them.

She had known Theodora professionally, and had been casting about for a way to recruit her into the magistrate's service. This *kinézo* afforded a perfect pretext, since the *kyrie* was eager to establish silk culture in the Empire.

That had been fifteen hundred years ago—and yet that selfsame man stands now grim-faced beside her.

Realization is sunlight in her mind. Tears start down her cheeks. For a long time she has believed herself condemned to live alone in a world of shadows. But now she knows there is at least one other immortal on the planet.

There is a wild fig tree at Echo Caves, near Ohrigstad in the eastern Transvaal, whose taproot in its insatiable thirst drives four hundred feet down into the sunbaked soil. Stacey Papandreou, by whatever name she has called herself over the centuries, has driven habits of thought so deeply into her psyche that she is unaware of them. A terrifying amount of her life is lived by habit.

In all those years the lives of others have drifted by her like smoke. She has bedded husbands, she has borne children, whose very names now she no longer recalls. No one else is quite real to her.

Now, when she most yearns to open the gates of her heart to someone she believes is, like her, actually *alive*, she finds the hinges are rusted shut. She has been too careful for too long. Only with effort can she squeak them open.

Which, as it turns out, is a good thing.

Stacey thinks Nagkmur's time machine is an old supervisor's office left over from when the plant was operational. Beside it lies a pair of down sleeping bags, a Coleman stove, curule folding chairs and other camping accouterments, and a portable table, and she supposes Nagkmur has been living in the ruins. The table holds a computer of unfamiliar style whose keys and toggles bear strange symbols. They are not Chinese. Stacey tries to peek inside the shed, but none of the equipment is recognizable.

Nagkmur shoos her away and sits her by the table, where he questions her closely. When he gets no joy using Chinese, he switches to a stilted and formal English, but even so his questions make no more sense. He agrees that they met in Constantinople, but they have difficulty fixing the year. He claims it was in the Year of the World 3220, but that was long before Constantinople was even built!

As for Stacey, a few dates are seared into her memory and she has only to subtract nine from one of those to secure the answer: The Year of the World 5604. At the time, the Empire was shifting from using the Diocletian Era to using the Age of the World, but Stacey does not recall off-hand how either epoch converts to the Years of the Lord.

"Impossible," says Nagkmur. "Year of World 5604 many centuries hence. We meet many centuries *past*. My mission to collect data on backwater nexus for Grand Analects."

Backwater nexus? Although not native to the City, Stacey takes offense in her name. Plenty had happened there. Art, literature, science, and philosophy had flourished, although she granted that none of it had affected China, and the bulk had been lost in the Great Sack.

After considerable debate and access to the Internet, they decide that they had met in AD 522 by the common measure.

"Whatever change world," the man says, "happen *after* then but *before* now."

Stacey agrees that the world has indeed changed since the sixth century. Sages from Heraclitus onward have declared change the one constant in the world. It does not occur to her that Nagkmur means something different.

"When you leave City," he demands, "where you go?"

"Venice," she says, which she does remember. The city in the lagoon was relatively new at the time, crammed with refugees from the Lombards, redolent with the smells of shabby huts, fresh-cut lumber, dank marshland. But the exarchate of which it was part was still a solid outpost of *romanitas* and travel there was still safe.

"No," the patrolman snaps. "What *year* you go?"

But she does not remember the year. She does not even remember the exarch's name.

Nagkmur grows agitated. "When you see world is different?" His voice grows shrill.

But the world is always different. The Capernaum of her childhood, Alexandria, the City, Venice, Noyes, London, all the innumerable times and places where she has lived, each milieu had differed in countless ways. She tries to explain this to Nagkmur, who of all men should need no explanation, but he only grows more irritable and accuses her of evasion.

He wags a finger at her. "I think *you* change history. Not survivor; instigator. You bear responsibility for billions not be." There is something in him of an unspeakable sorrow. His anger is edged with tears.

But Stacey does not see how she could have changed anything. She has lived quietly whenever she could, and the great events of the world have generally passed beyond her ken. In only a handful of epochs has she even known anyone important.

Though Constantinople in the early 5600s had been one of them.

Stacey wonders if the long centuries have driven Nagkmur mad. She had herself nearly foundered in those shallows when, in the desolation that *Syria Palæstina* had become, too many identities in too many years had jostled in her mind. She had lost cohesion, lost continuity. There had been times when she had not even known who she was. A holy woman, Mary of Egypt, had helped her cast out those demons and gradually she had learned to shelve her memories, place them in jars, in time to let them go. Perhaps Nagkmur had never mastered that skill and like other sorts of hoarders had smothered under his jackstrawed recollections.

An eternal life shared with another grows less attractive if the other is off his nut. She tells him she needs more presentable clothing than a robe and sandals. He scowls and bids her wait while he fetches something. She plans to run for it once he has gone.

But he steps into his cubicle and there is a blink and a rush of air and he steps out almost immediately, with clothes draped over his arm. She had once owned slacks and a blouse exactly like those he hands her, though she had thought them lost by the dry cleaner a year ago. She wonders if this mad immortal has been stalking her, learning her tastes, her sizes. She recoils from the thought. She has spent lifetimes avoiding notice.

Yet, she must not be too hasty. Perhaps she can help him as Mary had once helped her.

Nagkmur finds a chronology on the Internet and searches out a year halfway between the present and their encounter in sixth century Constantinople. The quickest way to identify when things went awry, he tells her, is to work by halves. If AD 1300 is undisturbed, the change came later; otherwise, earlier.

At first, Nagkmur is encouraged. "Middle Kingdom apparently unperturbed," he mutters. But as he continues reading, he grows upset. "Yet Occident much different. Too much technology. Too soon. Where Paris Caliph?"

Where indeed? Apparently, this means that "divergence" had already happened, so Nagkmur halves again and dips into the tenth century where he is astonished to discover that the Roman Empire, beleaguered but unbroken, has not fallen either to the Arab conquest or to the earlier Avar sack.

"Unbelievable! He turns to her in bewilderment. "How this change anything? Nothing important happen in Occident."

None of this makes sense to Stacey. She had lived through it, but it was all a jumble in her memory pile. It was hard to remember what happened in which century; but she was damned sure the Avars never sacked the City. There had been a bad time once when the nomads ran the Slavs into Hellas—Greece was never quite the same country afterward—but the Avars had squatted helplessly before the Land Walls while the Fleet held off the Arab ships with Greek Fire.

Stacey is a native of the Syrian provinces, but she had lived in the City for a very long time and feels a certain pride. "The City never fell," she told the patrolman. "Not until the Franks came." But she had been in Paris by then, another city that became great in its time. Technically, she had been a Frank herself.

Nagkmur spins about in his chair and cries, "You! You are saboteur! What you do? Why?"

The anger in his visage is alloyed with grief beyond measure and Stacey very nearly reaches out to comfort him. "No," she tells him. "I only lived my life, tried to survive, tried to escape notice."

"City in chaos after . . ." He checks his own database. ". . . after emperor flee. Riots in street. 'Nika! Nika! Nika!' No one ever repair. Later, faction opens gates to revenge on other faction."

"No." Stacey shakes her head in bewilderment. "The emperor quashed the factions. General Belisarius slaughtered them in the Hippodrome." A horrid, frightening time that had been and "Macedonia" knew only what rumors had drifted with the smoke and fleeing men.

Nagkmur's eyes widened. "He *not* flee? Emperor not flee City?"

Stacey shook her head. "He started to. But the story was that his empress talked him out of it. 'Purple makes a splendid shroud,' she said."

"What empress? This . . ." Another check. ". . . *Yáshì dīngní* not marry. Wait! Old emperor's nephew. I meet him!"

"You mean Justinian. Yes, I sent you to him. He was Justin's Master of Soldiers and ran the spy service. He succeeded his uncle a few years after you left." Stacey thinks about that a bit, then remembers. "That's right . . . He married Theodora the actress."

"Actress? Emperor marry *prostitute?*"

"Strange as it seems, it was true love. You must remember Theodora. You patronized her while you stayed in the City."

"*That* woman?" He said this as if surprised to discover that she had a name. "But prince wants only to enter her jade gates!"

"Maybe at first—and she had some damn fine gates—but they fell in love after."

"But I bring her with me when meet this Justinian. I *introduce them.* If this woman give Justinian courage, then it was *I* who . . ." He chokes and cannot finish the sentence. "Billions," he whispers. "It was I?" He looks up and into Stacey's face.

"Whoever think *woman* have such effect?"

Stacey cannot help but laugh in the face of his overwhelming grief.

ORPHANS OF SPACE
III. LT. COL. BRUNO ZENDAHL, USAF

There is a reception held annually at the Apkallu League near Rittenhouse Square in Philadelphia at which the "Scions of Apkal" drink toasts to a home they have never known. *Never forget* is the League's motto, and a common valediction among its membership, but operationally, in the face of the ordinary burdens of daily life, it is little more than a formality. It is more important not to forget the groceries you were to pick up on the way home.

The League is a handsome building, done up in the manner of the late nineteenth century, with Egyptian columns and a grand staircase on its façade. The brass medallions adorning its doors feature on the left an aquiline profile, said to represent the Apkallu Indians, and on the right door a fish, said to represent wisdom. The interior is decked with rich draperies and padded furniture. It is a very Philadelphia kind of building: snug and comfortable in a way that Boston and New York never quite manage. Engravings on the walls portray the usual Philadelphian themes of independence, fox hunting, and cricket. Club room conversations center on the exigencies of work, the dismal prospects of the Eagles, and the intransigence of the younger generation. Fraternal organizations having long since evolved into philanthropic ones, the League also sponsors medical research into birth defects at Einstein Medical Center.

Only on Landing Day do the Scions bring out certain accouterments otherwise kept in a storeroom in the sub-basement, hang decorations that might strike non-members as a bit outré, and recite formulas in a language little-heard in the America of the third millennium. But that is only once a year to celebrate their ancestors' arrival in the New World, and what club does not have its quaint rituals?

There is a reason for everything and Lt. Col. Bruno Zendahl's reason for stopping over at the League is that he is travelling from Cheyenne Mountain to the Pentagon, and it is customary for Scions of Apkallu to touch base at a lodge on such trips. He has called from the airport to confirm reservations for dinner and a room for the night. The restaurant is open to such of the public as can afford private dining in Rittenhouse clubs; but the rooms are members-only. He hands his travel bag, headgear, and overcoat to Robert, the concierge, and is striding with great anticipation toward the dining room, when Juliet Endicott, the lodge-keeper, intercepts him in the Grand Hallway and hits him with a hammer.

Metaphorically speaking. "They're waiting for you down below," she whispers and waves him toward the private elevator in the rear of the building.

The implied summons startles the colonel. "My dinner . . . ?" he suggests.

"I'll have Guiscard send something. Anything in particular?"

In other words, immediately. He sighs. "I was looking forward to his Pork Chop *Elena.*"

Endicott uses her elevator pass-key to activate access to the lower levels and makes sure he knows the way to the council room. She gives him a brass key of the old style and assures him that his dinner will be delivered. Then the doors enclose him.

Zendahl brushes the sleeves on his uniform jacket. He can think of nothing in the public news, nor even in the private news of which he is cognizant, that might merit a summons. Maybe they only want him to plan the annual banquet, but he does not think so.

He exits the elevator onto a dimly lit, never-completed subway platform for the Southwest Spur. This was intended to link Thirtieth Street Station to the Broad Street line at Lombard-South, shaking hands along the way with the terminus for the old Locust Street subway. (There was once to have been a Loop, like Chicago's, but only Locust Street and Ridge Avenue were ever built.) He faces what would have been the northbound track, where a faded sign reading *Rittenhouse* dangles from overhead beams. The southbound platform was never built, so only barren stone looms in the shadows on the farther side. The tunnel dips into darkness at both ends of the station and somewhere in the black depths water plunks into a pool. Everything smells dank and sounds hollow.

Zendahl follows the platform to a door labeled "Authorized Personnel Only" and uses the brass key to enter. Inside, a young woman sits behind a desk reading a magazine. She looks up and nods to him. "Colonel Zendahl? May I see your identification?"

The skin on her face and arms is covered with fine iridescent scales and her head reminds one irresistibly of hawks, as if she had been pressed like putty into a mold for raptors. Her eyes seem too large for her head. Zendahl smiles politely when they touch hands in the exchange of ID cards. Her scales are dry and smooth. Most Apkallu are indistinguishable in appearance from the aborigines, but even after ten thousand years of genetic engineering, the co-opted genes sometimes revert and hint at the ancestral body-plan.

Zendahl knows he should feel pity for the Reverts, condemned as they are by a roll of the genetic dice to a life shut away from public view; but he finds them discomfiting parodies of the human form, and he knows they dislike being pitied. A drawback to fitting in is that after a thousand generations it is easy to forget what his ancestors once had been. In a hyphenated world, Zendahl and the receptionist are alien-Americans. Like everyone else in America, their ancestors had come from somewhere far off; only in their case from a little bit farther off.

"Ever have trouble with urban explorers finding their way into the tunnel?" He asks not from any particular curiosity, but to show he is not prejudiced against Reverts.

The door warden makes an entry in her computer. "Once or twice," she answers absently. "Usually from the Locust Street tunnel. We handle it."

He does not ask her how they handle it. She touches something under her desk and there is a click in the inner door. He pulls it open and strides down a long hall at the end of which is situated the council room. There, he finds five Apkallu waiting around the high table and two others, fully human in appearance, at a second table set up with computers.

Two of the five Apkallu at the council table are Reverts, and another, the president, is a Purebred. None of his ancestors had ever been genetically altered and, like anything pure, his kind have become progressively more rare. Paradoxically, Zendahl finds Purebreds less distasteful than Reverts. They seem less chimerical, less a botched human form. There are Purebreds portrayed on Egyptian tomb paintings and spoken of in Sumerian legends. The president's head looks like nothing familiar, though forced to choose, Zendahl would have said "dog-like." His scales sparkle in the room's sun-spectrum lighting. He gestures. "Please join us, Boranu Wanaducka."

Zendahl seldom uses his Apkallu name outside formal lodge meetings, so he loses a moment in responding. "Thank you, Opagku," he says, employing the president's formal title. He has never taken lodge entirely seriously. The Landing was too long ago. Even the Algonquians had called the Apkallu "the grandfather people."

A Revert with a hawk-like head says without preamble, "We have an oddity reported from our lodge in Chicago. A tabloid report of a monster." Zendahl raises a skeptical eyebrow and says, "Was one of . . . us spotted?" He had almost said "one of you." Genetically modified Apkallu like himself would not excite the term "monsters." They live unremarked among the aborigines, save for the occasional puzzling autopsy.

The council president waves a hand at the computer screen, where the front page of *Tru Facts* presents a grainy image of a giant black spider. Photoshopped faces in the lower right scream in terror. The headline proclaims DEMON FROM HELL?

Zendahl thinks the question mark is a nice touch of journalistic skepticism.

"The layout is a bit crude," he comments, but he does not suppose the council wants his opinion on photocomposition. Absentmindedly, he brushes the two occupation badges pinned above his ribbons—cyberspace and space operations.

"It's a headwalker," the Opagku says in *apkallin*.

Zendahl has no patience with ritual language and answers in English. "The bogeymen from the stories we learned in Apkallu School? Those are allegories."

The Opagku snorts, and the bony structure of his face is such that the sound is more like a honk. The other humanoforms glance at Zendahl but say nothing. Purebreds spend their time contemplating and commenting on the ancient records. "Our ancestors," the Opagku states, "thought those stories worth passing down. There must have been a core of truth to them. The headwalkers drove our people off the home world, and the Six Ships and One sought refuge here on New Apkal, where we have lived in comfortable obscurity. Now our ancient enemy has followed us to our haven." The president places both his talon-like hands on the council table and leans forward, his scaly skin iridescent in the sunlamps. "Earth," he declares, "is being invaded by aliens from outer space."

Colonel Zendahl must report at the Pentagon on Monday morning, and so (as the council points out) there is not a moment to lose. Then they leave him and the other two cybertechs to their devices and depart. It does not occur to the council that they might decline the assignment.

The cybertechs are named Jessica and Louis, and like Zendahl, they have been co-opted by the council for the weekend. Both are local. Neither is a Wanaducka, their ancestors having disembarked, legend says, from different Ships. They agree, not without a certain aspect of relief, that the colonel should take charge.

The first task is to make certain that the photograph is genuine. If the answer is no, the evening will be a short one. But in case it is yes, Zendahl assigns Louis to research the ancient headwalkers in the League databases. Since the picture allegedly comes from a warehouse surveillance camera, Zendahl uses his official muscle to secure a copy from the Chicago police.

The police, as a few phone calls establish, have been investigating a break-in and theft at the warehouse. They like the man who had fled the loading dock for this and believe he released a weather balloon as a distraction. ("Like them airbags they got in cars. Inflates in an instant.") How the man obtained the balloon and where it has gone to is not their immediate concern. Zendahl plays the game and confides that NASA scientists at Goddard are trying to recover a stolen aerostat used in climate monitoring. But that is not for public disclosure. Jessica and Louis marvel at the facility with which he fabricates the story, but it is not as if he has had no practice in disinformation.

Within the hour, the video downloads to his Air Force account, and he and Jessica set about studying the images. They carefully assess the metadata and soon determine that, whether of headwalker or weather balloon, the image itself is the true quill. A flurry of "snow" fuzzes the scene, the headwalker appears in one of the loading bays, and sprints off stage-left across the truck apron, at which point the entire image is lost to interference.

They watch the sequence multiple times, scrub and enhance the images. Zendahl sheds his coat and loosens his tie. It will be a long night after all. He decides he will lean on the League to supply him with private transportation to DC late Sunday. An hour later, the lodgekeeper arrives with a plate of Pork Chop *Elena* for him and similar meals for his two companions. They take a working break.

"Definitely a headwalker," Louis allows. "But not the same kind that drove our ancestors from Old Apkal."

"And you know this, how?" Zendahl asks.

"Different anatomy. The legs are longer and thinner and they grow from the bottom of the headball. Our forbearers depicted the Ancient Enemy with thick legs attached to a muscle mass with the headball dangling below."

"No one's ever seen a headwalker," Jessica comments. "So how does anyone know what it looks like?"

Louis shrugs. "There are images in the Archives from back in the day. The documents have been migrated from older media, and the traceability pans out. Our ancestors went to a lot of effort to preserve this information when so much else was lost. The good news is the Ancient Enemy didn't follow us here."

Zendahl looks at him. "What's the bad news?"

Another shrug. "It's still a headwalker."

"Weird coincidence," says Jessica. "One kind drives us off the home-world; then a second kind, from somewhere else, shows up here."

"Not too weird." Louis taps a file open on his screen. "The ancient scholar Sunillilam proved topologically that there could be no more than seven basic body plans for intelligent beings."

"I never heard that," says Zendahl.

"It's not exactly priority knowledge. Until now. So if an alien shows up here at all, there's one chance in seven it'll be a headwalker."

Zendahl doesn't correct Louis' arithmetic. "Only seven."

"Well, there's lots of variation within each basic type. Humans and Apkallu are both vertical four-limbed bilaterians—which is why the genetic engineering worked—and this critter and the Ancient Enemy are both . . ."

". . . headwalkers. Okay."

"Why haven't the Chi-Po noticed this?" asks Jessica.

Zendahl looks at her. "Shy-po?"

"Chicago police. Why do they insist it's a weather balloon?"

"We got better photo-analysis equipment?" Louis says.

The colonel shakes his head. "Not that much better. Silk purse and sow's ears. You can only squeeze so much info from low-rezz security cameras. But the mind is a wonderful thing. We see what we're mentally prepared to see. That's why eyewitness accounts and satellite photo interpretations are so tricky." He ponders the matter some and decides that someone—the "Chi-Po," the FBI—will eventually take a closer look. "It's harder to change a mind than to form it in the first place. New data gets filtered through that first impression, just like through a consensus scientific theory. Ninety percent of the time, that keeps you from going off the deep end. The rest of the time, it keeps you from seeing the bleeding obvious. Next question: What's a headwalker doing on Earth?"

"Exploring?" suggests Jessica.

"Scouting for an invasion fleet?" Louis proposes. "Don't headwalkers in general send out colony pods now and then? Geez, I haven't thought about those old stories since I was a kid. I always thought they were folktales."

"Colonizing?"

"There's only one of them."

"We've only *seen* one of them."

Zendahl studies the video again while he finishes his chop. Guiscard is a superb chef, and the chop deserves more attention than he can give it. He promises himself a more leisurely meal on his return trip. Pointing to a corner of the screen, he tells Jessica, "Focus in on that. I want to see what the headwalker broke cover to chase." He clears the plates and places them to the side of the table. Ancient Enemy or not, the creature's presence on Earth is troubling and he wonders how he can bring it to the attention of Space Command without destroying his own credibility. Spring an alien invasion on NORAD without proper groundwork and they will decide it's a hoax and Zendahl is either a hoaxer or a fool, neither of which would do his career much good, even if he were proven right in the end. Especially if he were proven right in the end.

Jessica zooms and cleans the image, heightens the contrast. "It's an arm," she decides, drawing Zendahl back to the screen. "There appears to be a body lying on the paving stones."

"Dead?"

"Not moving. And, Bruno? It was there before the headwalker showed itself."

"A drunk."

"Maybe."

"I been wondering why the alien popped up like that," Louis says. "You'd think it'd want to keep things on the D/L."

"I don't know," says Jessica. "The headwalkers in the old stories weren't famous for being shrinking violets."

"Check for other surveillance in the area," Zendahl said. "Try the other warehouses. If there was a drunk, there's probably a bar, too."

"I thought of a reason it broke cover," says Louis. "It was hungry." Zendahl and Jessica look at him and he shrugs. "It's a reason."

They watch the video to its end, when the image begins to break up. When it settles down once more, the alien is gone, but the arm still lies there.

"Well," says Louis with a certain amount of cheer, "that's a relief."

It takes a few hours to identify nearby establishments and requisition copies of their surveillance videos. The Chicago police have been doing the same thing, trying to pin down their fleeing suspect, and Zendahl senses a growing curiosity on their part regarding the apparent interest of the Air Force in a petty burglary. He sticks to the story about a missing NASA aerostat, but drops a hint that it might be a secret military operation and questions would be unwelcome.

"A deception within a deception," says Louis. "I'm impressed."

"Just hope I don't trip over the tangle." He calls Annie Troy at the Pentagon. She's a civilian contractor in CYBERCOM and can set up a spoof in case anyone tries to check with Goddard. Everyone is home for the weekend, but he leaves a message on her phone. He also asks her to check for any unusual activity in orbit over the past several days.

"Headwalker had to come from somewhere," he tells the others after he closes the call.

Or did it? When the additional surveillance videos finally download, Zendahl and his two partners split them up and comb through them. Nowhere do they find a record of the headwalker's arrival at the warehouse. It might have been born there for all they can determine. And when it passes from the scene, it is not to any place covered by other cameras. The Land of the Free is still not entirely monitored. But Zendahl notices something curious on one of the files.

In the video from an after-hours bar diagonal from the warehouse, a small drama plays out in which a tall Chinese man takes on and defeats three gangbangers who are trying to steal his car. Zendahl finds this affair curiously refreshing, but the sequel is mystifying.

The man's car is largely off-screen. Only a portion of what Zendahl takes to be its left front fender can be glimpsed. Once the man leaves the frame (and presumably hops in his car), the static commences—and the headwalker comes a-running. But the static seems to originate with the vehicle itself because there is a moment when only the fender is breaking up and the rest of the scene is still clear.

The static is a common cause affecting all the cameras in the area. *It originated in the car*, Zendahl thinks. *That's what the headwalker wanted.* Either the driver or the car itself or some component of it. He shakes his head. *Maybe the damn thing's running a chop shop.*

The Council will want further investigations. Zendahl can see this as clearly as a man falling from the penthouse can, during his plummet, see the sidewalk below. But for all that he might insist "so far, so good," the prospect is not entirely encouraging. These inquiries can go south on him in so many ways, destroy his career, ruin his family. It may even unmask the League. Given the record of the aborigines regarding minorities in their midst, Col. Zendahl can imagine no happy outcome from that.

IV. JIM-7

Consider now a headwalker, outnumbered at six billion to one and feeling in consequence more than a little insecure.

Alien life, we are told, would be so unlike human life as to defy understanding. Indeed, they may possess senses, organs, and appetites unknown to us. What lusts do bats endure that compel their squeals? Does it pleasure them to receive the echo? If human minds cannot grasp the hankerings of bats, what chance is there for a meeting of whatever serves for minds with headwalkers?

And yet, all things pursue the good insofar as they know the good, and that is whatever preserves and completes their nature. For inanimate bodies, this preservation is called "inertia"; for animate bodies, it is called "life." The struggle to maintain existence that Darwin saw in living kinds is only a higher form of the struggle of a boulder to remain stubbornly in place.

Which is to say that while the finer points of headwalker philosophy may forever elude our ken, the basics can be grasped. The headwalker is desperately trying to repair a crippled scout ship with what amounts to wattles and twigs filched from unwary natives. We can understand if a certain anxiety grips him, no matter how outré his body and eccentric its appetites.

Said body is a prolate spheroid supported on five legs. Its remotest ancestors were radially symmetric, somewhat like starfish, though they were not starfish. It has evolved to walk upright on its arms and, through a fortuitous doubling of genes, alternated these with smaller manipulating appendages. All organs needful for a happy life are gathered into the spheroid that gives it its name. It is more nonchalant about ionizing radiation than humans or apkallu, but works with dread around electrical fluids. It wears clothing—he's an alien, not a savage—and, like a human, pulls his pants on one leg at a time. It just takes a little longer.

We will call it "Jim-7" and this for two reasons. First, the central lower tone of the creature's name-chord does sound a bit like "jim" while none of the rest of it sounds much like anything at all, even the parts within the normal range of human hearing. (Its speech resembles a concertina scolding a set of bagpipes.) And, second, since "Jim" does not sound much like a creature from outer space, the addition of a "-7" lends it a properly alien aspect. It beats a long gargle of random consonants.

If what the creature calls itself is hard to say, whether it calls itself he, she, or it is even harder, as there are circumstances under which it might be each, all, or none, and it trades them off as needful. There are more pronouns in heaven and earth than are dreamt of in our philology.

But Jim's plight is no laughing matter, and this again for two reasons. First, no life struggling on the lip of the Great Abyss is cause for mirth. If Jim fails, one more candle in a cold, dark universe is blown out.

Dogs feel emotions, and reptiles, and even crummy little cockroaches as they scurry terrified from the menacing light. Hence, Jim-7, drifting in her malfunctioning vessel far off the lines of advance of her Nest, feels something very much like what any human would feel when staring Death in its stinking face.

She casts about for something, for anything, to pin her hopes upon, and so discerns the electronic umbra from the third planet. The enzymes that course through her are not the same as ours, and strictly speaking they are not even enzymes, but what she feels is a joy as buoyant as any human if, adrift upon the trackless ocean, she glimpses a flotation device bobbing nearby.

Electronic emissions mean that the planet produces materials that might be adapted to the necessary repairs. There may be little difference between a snowball's chance in hell and *two* snowballs' chance; but that is an enormous gulf to no chance at all. And so it nests in orbit and sets about obtaining the required components. This is not as easy as it sounds. It cannot simply walk into Fry's and purchase them. Several difficulties to this course immediately suggest themselves.

It is alone and afraid on a world full of strange beings who, it suspects, would react poorly to a shiny, two-meter tall pentapede in their midst. And so it beams down at small hours to deserted places, seeking out storehouses of electronic components. The task is anything but straightforward. What does an alien warehouse look like?

But eventually, it discovers such a repository, notes the sigils that identify it, and pilfers a representative sample of doohickeys.

After that, the tedium of testing begins. It must discover what each thingamabob is, and determine its rating. You can't really expect headwalker resistors or capacitors to look like ours, or to be graduated in ohms and farads. Form follows function, but at a respectable distance, and Jim's people long ago standardized on different shapes and scales. Fortunately, he is the ship's engineer, accustomed to cut-and-try.

There is time for this. It has renewable air and drink. And food is plentiful, since its two crewmates perished in the malfunction. It has eaten part of one of them (the navigator) and has been using the pilot for occasional sexual relief. (It's an alien, remember; and who are we to judge?)

Her second joy—and the second reason why her peril is no laughing matter—is that the planet is almost ideally proportioned to support her kind. All the place needs is a good scrubbing. The atmosphere wants a boost in its chlorine content—that usually sanitizes quite nicely—and a little less free water vapor. Her people have nested upon worlds far more inhospitable.

So while Jim's failure to escape from Earth would be the tragic loss of a life unique, her success would be no great shakes, either. Fortunately—or not, depending on one's point of view—it has other things on its mind at present.

Performing a bit of mental triage, Jim occupies itself with identifying and modifying the components necessary for what it can fix. It has not yet identified local gizmos adaptable to the temporal precessor, but owns a touching faith that "something will turn up." Alien is as alien does, but no creature is so alien as to neglect its own survival.

In line with this objective, she does not simply loot a single site lest it draw unwanted attention. Although she regards the autochthons individually as of no account, there are a considerable number of them, and it would be best not to startle them. She uses pattern recognition to identify additional repositories along her vehicle's ground track. Her plan is to filch a little bit here and a little bit there, as she reaches the point in the repair plan that needs the components on her pick list and thus, as we might say, "fly under the radar." It was a good plan, and should have worked.

But while looting the fourth such locale, Jim is struck by a hammer. His instruments register aetherial gyroscopes spinning nearby. A precessor *on a planetary surface?* Has a rescue ship come seeking her, only to crash? She cries *hallelujah* (or its equivalent) and rushes outside, heedless of concealment.

His vision is radial, so there is no need to look around wildly. Instruments identify the source as a small, boxy vehicle nesting in the shadows across the way, and he sprints toward it. The vessel is unfamiliar and too small even for a shuttlecraft. He thinks he can kill its pilot and take the precessor.

But the boxy thing vanishes, leaving Jim the headwalker equivalent of gobsmacked. Beamed objects *fade* and, more to the point, *there is no instrumental trace of a transport beam.*

Alarms draw near and he beams back to his scout ship, where he gets drunk (in his own peculiar way), diddles the dead pilot (again, in his own peculiar way), and worries for several days that he is going mad.

But you can't keep a good headwalker down. Jim is very good at compartmentalizing and loses himself for several cycles in the minutiae of adapting his latest haul to the repair of the spin stabilizer control circuit. The ship reeks for a time of tangy fumes, and flashes with bright actinic flickers. This is its milieu; this is when it feels most fully itself. He tries to forget about the vanishing box.

"Fool," says the corpse of the pilot when he embraces it afterward, and Jim cocks his legs up in shame. The pilot is right. When exigent circumstances call for it, a man does not lose himself, even in his primary task.

"Should I seek out the source of the temporal distortion?" he asks the pilot and hugs it in that special way.

"Sure," the pilot replies.

Now, Jim knows that he is only hearing waste gasses squeezed out through the reeds of the corpse's voice-box, and that he interprets the resultant chords as words. The carcass doesn't really speak. His people are alien, but not *that* alien. Dead is dead. The custom of "inquiring of the dead" has been embedded in her culture a very long time but, deep down, she knows that asking the pilot for advice is like consulting a Magic 8-Ball.

Still, it is good advice. So once Jim has finished the repairs at hand, he turns his attention to the time warp. A search of on-board records reveals two briefer whorls earlier in that same cycle spatially centered in the much larger nest on the spinward margin of the landmass. This disturbs him, as he had been planning to loot a warehouse in the outer reaches of that same nest and she has the sudden suspicion that whatever is making these footprints in the space-time manifold is stalking her, anticipating her moves. There is some sinister force at work. She crosses two limbs as if suddenly chilled, remaining upright on the tripod of the other three. Something is hunting her!

True that! There are three parties on her trail, though ironically the party making the whorls is not one of them. Nagkmur is sweetly oblivious that Jim is on *his* trail. One is the Chi-Po (who have no notion of their quarry) and another is the Apkallu (who do).

As for the third . . . Because the sigils Jim has used to identify the repositories include the company logo, he has been pilfering unwittingly from the same corporation. He might as well have staged a big heist from one place and gotten it over with, for the owners have hired a top-notch private investigator to work the case.

Quite enough pursuit to unnerve her did she know of them.

ORPHANS OF THE MIND
V. ANNIE TROY

Consider now the worker bee wending her way into the Pentagon from the upper platform of its eponymous Metro station. She is a civilian contractor "on loan" to

U.S. Cyber Command. She splits her time between Ft. Meade and the Pentagon and so has been installed like Buridan's Ass halfway between, in a College Park apartment near the University, whence she may take the train in either direction.

She walks with purpose, eyes straight ahead, no nonsense. She does not actually bump into anyone on the crowded platform or on the escalator to the security center, but swims like a fish among fish, maintaining her distance. A few in the morning stream send greetings her way and she answers their hails, but for the most part she is alone in the crowd.

She seldom smiles—it is too much of an effort—and when she does, it is a slight, wan upturn of the lips. You would have to look twice to be sure it was there, and it is seldom there long enough to be caught by that second look. "A cold fish," some have called her, which is both unjust and true. Considering her upbringing, it is a wonder she can smile at all; yet, there *is* something fishy about her.

No, she does not have scales. She has never heard of the Apkallu League, let alone of its singular membership requirement; but sometimes she does have a hard time stringing facts together, which is an odd deficiency for one with her background. She has been taught logic so thoroughly that it is literally a part of her, and yet facts can play pranks when they join hands.

- Socrates is a man.
- Man is mortal.
- Therefore, Socrates is mortal.

True premises; valid syllogism. There is no escaping the conclusion. But . . .

- Grass is green.
- Green is an electromagnetic wave.
- Therefore, grass is an electromagnetic wave.

True premises; valid syllogism. And yet the conclusion is face-palm false.

The paradox had bothered her, and she had been hung up by it for several days. When she had at length brought it to her handlers in the Project, they had laughed; not at her but at the unexpectedness of the conundrum. Finally, Dr. Shiplap had explained it.

"It all depends on what the word 'is' means," he had said.

And indeed, grass *is* green in a very different way than Socrates *is* a man. The former notes only an attribute possessed; the latter gets at an essence. For a while afterward she experimented with logical puns, to the amusement of her instructors.

That much may depend on what "is" means was first noted not by an American president but by a Greek philosopher: Aristotle. Annie had darted from link to link in pursuit of him, until she had swallowed his entire corpus. That old dead man spoke more sooth than many more lively ones—though you did have to squeeze him a bit to get the full understanding. "It's all Greek to me," said Dr. Shiplap, laughing hugely, though Annie had not understood why a simple statement of fact should be funny.

It all came down to form and matter. The two syllogisms had the same form but different matter, and a line of reasoning could be true or false depending on the subject matter. Semantics subverted syntax.

When she shared that conclusion with Dr. Shiplap and the others, they grinned and applauded, and arranged for her assignment at USCYBERCOM.

Annie is at her desk before she is at her desk. She logs in "on the fly" as soon as she enters the secure Wi-Fi zone in the E-ring and is multitasking before she turns the corner. She drops a memo to Navy NETWARCOM regarding a Chinese hack of Fleet dispositions and another to AFSPC regarding an effort to infiltrate the satellite surveillance network, though whether to disrupt it, insert disinformation, or simply to peek over US shoulders she cannot yet say. She also sends a memo to Col. Zendahl of NORAD regarding an investigation he had requested.

"There is definitely something up there," she tells the colonel when he stops by her office later that morning. "No one has seen it, but several satellites have been disturbed in orbit: two of ours and one of China's."

The colonel is drinking black tea from a mug with the logo of the Colorado Broncos. "How long has it been up there," he asks after a sip.

Annie continues to surf, analyze, and compose memos. "That's hard to say, colonel. The satellite is stealthed and it's a fine point whether we can pin down the first time we didn't see it."

Zendahl laughs. "Maybe it's a Romulan Bird-of-Prey."

Annie quickly googles the phrase. "Yes, very much like one. Do you suppose Russia or China has developed advanced stealth technology?"

The colonel coughs and hems a bit. "When will you have time to work on that, uh, other request?"

Annie notes the muscle groups involved in his expression and wonders what he is worried about. "It's a done deal," she answers. "I've already sent you the details."

"What? You didn't have to spend your weekend on it."

"It was no problem, colonel. If anyone makes inquiries about your Goddard weather balloon story, they'll find the appropriate documents, and even the people whose signatures appear on the memos will suppose that they simply do not recall the matter. Everything is properly backdated."

Zendahl nods and takes another sip. "Okay. That will give us time to develop a second layer. If the Chi-Po make inquiries, someone at Goddard may do a physical count and realize that none of their aerostats actually have gone missing."

"I've inserted a bogus asset number for an extra aerostat," Annie tells him. "If they check inventory, they will find one unaccounted for. They will even find an amended purchase order and bill of lading from the contractor. If anyone digs further, they'll find a firewall for a black ops site, suggesting it would be well if they don't press the matter, and if in spite of all this they do, they'll find a minor task force assigned to investigate the possible beta test of a walker drone by commercial party or parties unknown."

Zendahl raised his eyebrows. "Why 'commercial?'"

"All of the warehouses that have been robbed have been Bergtholm Electronics. That suggests a business rival. Bergtholm isn't involved in defense contracting.

Which makes this," she adds, "outside CYBERCOM's mission statement. Are you doing this for SPACECOM or NORAD?"

Zendahl finishes his mug and studies its inside, as if reading the leaves. "There have been other robberies?"

From his body language, Annie concludes this information is both surprising and important. "Several. Running southwest to northeast across the country. They're related, aren't they? The disruptions to the satellites, the strange apparition in Chicago, and the thefts at Bergtholm Electronics?"

Zendahl grows visibly cautious. "Too soon to say. It may just be coincidence. I wonder where the burglar will strike next . . ."

"Passaic."

Zendahl is visibly startled. "Eh? Because . . . ?"

"It's the next Bergtholm warehouse lying under the projected path."

"Maybe we can set up an ambush . . ." Zendahl muses. He is talking to himself. Annie does not ask him who "we" are. He looks up and meets her eyes. "I don't have to tell you to say nothing about this."

"I never ask questions, colonel," she says; but then belies that statement by adding, "What was that thing, anyway?"

"That thing."

"That seven-foot spider."

"It's not a spider."

"I know. Five legs. But then, what?"

"You watched the surveillance footage?"

"I had to create a realistic cover story. I can tell you two things it's *not*. A weather balloon and an imperial walker."

A troubled look comes over the colonel and he looks down and to the right. "Sorry, Annie. You don't have need-to-know."

But Annie does have a need to know. Knowing is her singular need. So after the colonel has left, she traces his Friday evening call and finds it had originated in a private club in Philadelphia, and that leads to a search on the club's name, and that leads not to a bogus American Indian tribe, as the club's website claims, but to ancient gods who, with the heads of beasts and scaled like fish, had strode out of the water and taught the Sumerians the arts of civilization. That strikes her as a rather curious legend.

She works late, as usual. The others in CYBERCOM call her a grind, but there is another routine crisis developing and she must babysit until it is no longer urgent. Strictly speaking, CYBERCOM defends only against attacks on military targets, but it is a fine point whether or not attacks on civilian targets also compromise the military, or if a pre-emptive strike might not be the best kind of defense; so where the line gets drawn is not always clear. Government databases are the honeypot of the Internet and foreign agents and their useful idiots, the buzzing flies. She need not be within the secure zone to work, but it eases access to vast swathes of data and she is much too aware of the sandstorm of cyberattacks to be sanguine of taking government work home like a bumbling bureaucrat.

But she can and does mull over various tidbits as she rides the Yellow Line back to her apartment. The "spider." The Apkallu League. The Chinese man on the edge of the frame. (She had loosed a worm to look for additional images of his face on the Net.) The oddly specific and at the same time petty nature of the thefts from Bergtholm Electronics. It is quite enough to keep one occupied during an otherwise boring trip.

The Yellow Line ends at Fort Totten and she crosses the lower platform to await the Green Line toward College Park. A few others exit with her, but they wander off to the escalators. It is nearly midnight and those traveling into Deeper Maryland have already come and gone.

The platform is partly in the tunnel and partly in an open cut, and she positions herself under the stars. As she waits patiently for the Greenbelt train, a hooded member of the 44th Street Crew steps up behind her and hits her on the head with a hammer.

No, really. An actual, no-fooling hammer. Well, technically, a sheet-forming mallet, the kind with a hard-rubber head. It is not supposed to leave a mark, but is quite hard enough for the purpose, which is to knock her senseless, perhaps kill her, and grab her purse, cell phone, and other fungible accessories.

But the micro-electro-mechanical implants that form her shell stiffen at the impact and absorb the energy. She is a thixotropic babe, a hard woman to know, in more ways than one.

The same is true of her fist when she strikes back. It leaves his skull a ruin on the platform. Dead, she supposes. It is the least hypothesis, given the forces and vectors involved. When the Green train arrives, disembarking passengers step around the body and make disgusted comments about drunks and street people, but they do not examine too closely. Annie steps aboard the train and does not look back. She neither regrets nor exults in her action. The idea that all lives matter is as alien to her as the idea that any lives matter.

You want alien? Jim-7 is your jolly Uncle Bob next to Annie Troy. She not only sits on the cutting edge; she *is* the cutting edge: from the compact quantum computer that conducts her cognitive processes, and the MEMS that constitute her shell to the titanium infraskeletal linkages that play the role of bones.

Not that Annie feels any satisfaction at any of this. Strictly speaking, she cannot *feel* anything. The receptors in her pseudo-skin register pressure, temperature, and the like, but no such things as sympathy or antipathy. She knows from her information harvest that in fiction, all androids are supposed to desire emotions; but Annie experiences no such longing. As far as she can tell, the only role emotions play is to cloud human judgment. She misses them no more than humans yearn for the sonar sense of bats.

Her apartment is conventionally stocked, in case she has visitors, but she neither eats nor sleeps in the conventional sense. She occasionally idles for self-diagnostics, which might be called "sleep" by analogy; but her water-based beta-voltaic batteries run off strontium-90, and will not need replenishment for a great long time, so except for the periodic lube job, there is not even an analogous sense in which she eats or drinks. Consequently, she is a 24/7 kind of gal, which means she has entire giga-seconds of time on her hands. If there is anything in her that can be called an appetite, it is a hunger for information, even if much found on the internet does not, strictly speaking, qualify as such.

Later that evening, her worm returns with additional images of the Chinese man that the pentapede chased in Chicago. Several pictures on a site for a New York City news organ show him helping a woman who has escaped a fire. The main difficulty is that he could not have been in New York at that time and in Chicago scant hours later. And a closer examination of the image reveals an anomaly.

In a brief fight with some gangbangers caught by a bar's surveillance camera, the Chinese man picks up a grease smudge on his lower right trouser leg. Yet this same smudge is evident in the image taken at the fire, hours *earlier*. There is something seriously wrong in the sequence of events, and Annie feels perhaps the first emotion in her existence as she processes the anachronism. If an interference fringe in the back-propagations in her neural net can be called an emotion.

You can learn a great deal about a person by examining his purposes; and purposes, being final causes, can be discerned from the directions in which he moves. The pentapede had chased the Chinese man, and the Chinese man had earlier sought out the woman in New York. The ubiquity of cell phone cameras and social media have pinned him to the internet like a butterfly to a board, so once the videos taken by sundry spectators have been loaded into her processor, Annie can view the scene from multiple, simultaneous points of view. Unlike human memory, which recalls the past precisely as past, Annie's memories upload into an eternal present. She does not so much watch the videos as experience them.

The woman runs from the building with a babe in arms; the mother comes and retrieves it; the Chinese man takes her by the wrist and leads her out of the crowd. One amateur vlogger even follows them a short distance, perhaps astonished that anyone would shun the chance for self-celebration. In this manner, and making use of traffic cameras and storefront security cameras, Annie can track their progress through the cloud into the Meatpacking District.

News agencies have reported the woman's name as Anastasia Papandreou and have added sketchy details of her life gleaned from public records. One local reporter claims that she has "old and weary eyes." This is a fact that Annie cannot perceive because, strictly speaking, it is not a fact at all but a subjective impression. Annie does not have subjective impressions because (again, strictly speaking) she is not a subject.

She herself does not always know how she reaches her conclusions. The "hidden layers" of her neural net are hidden even from herself. But in this she is more nearly like human beings than she normally supposes.

Because she has not so much as a name for the Chinese man, Annie seizes upon Anastasia as a kitten pounces upon a loose thread in a ball of twine. She takes a deep, if metaphorical, breath and plunges into the Nets. Had anyone been able to see inside her apartment, Annie would have seemed distracted for a few minutes while she swam in that ocean, but when she emerges once more on the farther side, she has caught a fish.

Anastasia Papandreou is a shell, an identity cobbled from bits and pieces. A birth record of a child that died young. A social security number that traces back to a different jurisdiction. A marriage in a courthouse that has since burned down. Papandreou is a house built of twigs and some serious huffing and puffing would blow it down. Annie supposes that it has lasted this long because no one has ever had cause to knock on its door.

There are twelve distinct purposes why someone might wear a bogus identity, starting with secret agent and going on from there. Annie herself has such an identity—though built of bricks rather than twigs—and the theory presents itself irresistibly that Anastasia Papandreou is another android like herself. The prior probability is low but non-zero. Yet, the woman's life of obscurity and petty jobs does not align with Annie's more pro-active insertion into the very Pentagon itself. "The ultimate beta test," Dr. Mok had enthused, and the team had very nearly named her "Beata" for that reason. So if Stacey is another android, she is one who has crawled out of the ocean and onto the sand.

Which is a very interesting idea.

VI. JANET MURCHISON

Consider finally the woman glad-handing her way around a Manhattan cocktail party. The party is typical of its species; the woman is not. She wears the customary black cocktail dress, accented with a choker of pearls. Her hair is a natural white cropped in a decidedly mannish cut which accents her dusky skin. She circulates among the guests, chatting, smiling, touching people on their forearms, listening intently to the trivia of their lives and professions. She is graceful, and pleasant enough that most men forget that they have to tilt their heads to look her in the eyes.

She seems a little tipsy and her eyes are slightly glazed, which leads to several hopeful proposals from male guests. But she puts them off or puts them down, depending on the artfulness of their approach. Her progress through the party appears random, joining and departing conversational knots like a bee flitting about a spring garden. But had anyone thought to track her trajectory they might have noted a curious fact: She is seldom more than a few yards from Jupiter Crowley.

The real estate mogul does not call himself "Jupiter" because of his resemblance to that planet, although he is something of giant ball of gas. He calls himself "Jupiter" because his given name is Eustace, which he detests above all other names, and he likes to think of himself as "jovial."

The woman, whose name is Janet Murchison, swoops by from time to time like Halley's Comet, joining the group clustered around Crowley. They kiss up to him, laugh at his jests. Janet drops a question or two, listens to the answers he gives the questions of others, then whooshes off to other parts of the room.

She carries a Manhattan but nurses it like a babe in arms, and anyone keeping a tally would notice that she has yet to wean her first-poured. "I have few enough wits to begin with," she once told a colleague, "so I like to keep them close about me."

She gathers fragments of conversations, quips, tips, and information as she circulates, discards most of them, keeps a few.

. . . at Bergtholm Electronics . . .

She pauses near a middle-aged navy commander, turning her back to him and his civilian companions and pretending to admire the skyline past Central Park, where the "golden hour" afternoon sun washes the western facades along Fifth Avenue. Bergtholm is one of her clients and though she has not come to this party on their behalf, she does not ignore fortuitous intelligence that may come her way.

. . . paperwork's all in order, but it's well outside Zendahl's remit. Something's going on, and it's not on the surface . . .

One of the civilians asks the commander about the Giants, and the conversation picks up a sports thread of no particular interest. She moves on, deposits her still-full glass on a serving tray, and takes her leave of her hostess, pleading pressing business and a headache. She has already harvested from Crowley what she had come for and finds such crowded rooms otherwise stressful.

She retrieves her tote and exchanges heels for tennis shoes, dons her evening coat, and checks the loads in her handgun. The coat-check girl's eyes widen at the sight of the Colt Government .38 automatic, but Janet flashes her private investigator's license and concealed-carry permit to set her mind at ease.

More than ease. The young woman recognizes Janet's name from the tabloids and her momentary alarm changes quickly to an autograph request. The "She-lock Holmes of Bleecker Street," the *Post* had called her after the MONY affair and the business with the Hound of Basking Ridge. Janet explains that she does not give out samples of her handwriting, but promises a copy of her book, *The Art of Interrogation*. The coat-check girl shows no similar reluctance to reveal her home mailing address and Janet wonders what the world is coming to. Big Brother may as well throw in the towel than compete with three hundred million freelancers busily spying on themselves.

She exits the Park Lane Hotel and strides three blocks crosstown past Columbus Circle to the Lunch Box, where Magruder and Chen are waiting. Bill Magruder is the fire marshal and Lee Chen is the detective sergeant from the Arson Squad. The Lunch Box is a Ninth Avenue hole-in-the-wall no one would look at twice if they did not know of its culinary reputation. But more importantly, no one from the cocktail party is likely to drop in. Both men have deli sandwiches in front of them. Magruder has a beer; Chen, a cola.

"Did you pick up anything useful?" asks Chen with a skeptical eye on her cocktail dress and evening coat.

But Janet is a consultant, not an employee, and Chen's opinion doesn't concern her. "A little," she says as she gives the waiter an order for flavored water. "Crowley definitely hired the arsonist. The landlord was willing to sell, but the fire guaranteed Crowley a bargain price."

"Little fish," says Chen, "discovers bigger fish."

"The Gas Giant will be hard to sweat," Magruder observes. "Did you get the name of the arsonist? Maybe we can flip him."

"I overheard him mention a 'Bruce Harness.'"

"Tommy the Torch!" says Magruder. "He doesn't usually operate this far east."

"Tommy?"

"Who would hire *Bruce* the Torch? Guy works outta Detroit," he adds for Chen's benefit.

Chen gives him a sour look. "Great. The local talent wasn't enough . . ." He turns to Janet. "How did you get Crowley to spill that particular bean?"

"*In vino veritas*," she tells him. "The best way to get inside a suspect's attic . . ." She taps her head. ". . . is through the basement. Bypass the intellect and appeal to the appetites. The most basic drives are digestion and reproduction. So if you want to put a suspect at ease, take him to bed or take him to dinner. Both of them loosen his lips, but restaurants and booze are cheaper and less likely to lead to complications."

The two men laugh, but Chen stops short and glances at the sandwich in his hand. Janet smiles because, while she does employ such techniques (and others as well), she owes her success as a private investigator more to her ability to hear the thoughts of other minds.

It's not quite telepathy. She cannot "get into" someone's mind. She can only overhear active thoughts, which means her art consists of asking questions that get her target to think about the subject she is investigating. She "hears" no overtones, so she must take care to recognize irony, fantasy, hyperbole, and other figures. And while she sometimes sees images when she listens, she learned very early that they were superimposed by her own imagination. Every act of the intellect is accompanied by an act of the imagination, and since she overhears only the words, her own mind supplies the rest.

There are other difficulties. People can lie even to themselves. They are subject to flashes of anger, of lust, of greed on which they will never act. An unknown language remains unknown even when thought. People with eidetic memories are incredibly tedious. And the mentally deranged can babble nonsense silently as readily as aloud. Walking down a Manhattan street, she is awash in a stew of jealousies, sexual urges, hostile invective, commentary on traffic-skills, personal longings, shameful memories, insecurities, and every other human weakness. Her earliest skill was to learn to stick virtual fingers in her mental ears.

In a high density environment, like the cocktail party, when she must open her reception, her mind can fill with so many thoughts that she can lose track of which are her own. That had led to a fraught childhood and a temporary committal to a mental institution.

There, Dr. Amelia Ganz, the only other person in whom Janet has ever confided, determined that the voices in her head were neither hallucinations nor a split personality, but the actual thoughts of other people. And she explained her theory: how the koniocortex—nerve cells as fine as dust, detached from all sensory inputs—might serve as a sort of antenna.

And then Dr. Ganz performed a miracle. Not that she had counseled the girl, helped her through her terrors, led her to tame that strange metasensory channel, but that she had declined to publish the case, declined to put little Janet up as a performing monkey, declined to make herself famous on the back of a child. In the early twenty-first century, that was every bit as miraculous as water into wine.

Janet swings by the office to change into what she calls "evening wear": dark coveralls, gimme cap, gloves, and canvas shoes with good grip. She asks Jon'tel, who is finishing his surveillance report, to have the car brought up and place a sandwich order at the Brass Monkey on Little West Twelfth. She will pick it up on the way to the Bergtholm stakeout.

"If the timing follows the pattern," she tells him, "Passaic is about due to be burgled. Oh, and leave a note for Carlos for the morning. See what he can dig up about a man named Zendahl, probably military, possibly Ft. Meade." At least, the commodore works out of Ft. Meade and he knows Zendahl.

The Brass Monkey sits on Little West Twelfth not too far from Janet's offices near Bleecker and Bank and well-situated for a run straight up Tenth to the Lincoln Tunnel and out to Passaic. As she passes Gansevoort, Janet notes some activity around the burned apartment building and wonders if Crowley's people are prepping for the demolition or Magruder's people are sifting through the ashes.

She much prefers late night stakeouts because the mental buzz is quieter, but there is enough of a crowd in the Meatpacking District to provide a bit of stress and, even though she knows many scurrilous thoughts are passing fantasies, they lower her opinion of mankind. As she leaves the Monkey with a bag of sandwiches and some sodas, she breasts a flood of thought.

. . . report due on Friday or I'm toast . . .

. . . what if she says no? I'll be embarrassed in front of the whole family and stuck with the ring . . .

. . . lookit that lovely ass. Ooh, I would love to plug into that . . .

. . . maybe add a dash of paprika . . .

. . . if Jasmine specks I been coming on to her man . . .

. . . How quaint. The sort of chivalrous idea that you pretend to despise. If you want to be an absolute king, my man, you have to learn how to act out of self-will! Break your word, just because you made it! 'Til then, you're nothing but a . . . a pig-man trying to copy his bitters. No, dammit, betters, betters. Oh, I'll never be ready for opening curtain . . .

. . . dump me, will she. I could just strangle her . . .

Who could imagine such marvels so early as forty-eighth century?

Certainly not Janet Murchison, who did not expect to see the 48th century any time soon, let alone imagine its marvels. She focuses so as to screen out the rest of the buzz.

Not until third rescension of quarrelsome states are such things built . . . yet here stands great city when in true history this island full of bare-ass savages . . . great mystery but pondering futile once true history restored . . .

Then, with that abrupt discontinuity that characterizes the mind, the thinker jumps the track.

Remove woman Theodora before she marry emperor . . . but not risk time vortex by crossing self . . . must calculate with great care . . .

No, Janet supposes with a smile. We would not want to risk a time vortex, whatever that might be. She looks about, trying to pin down the source of the thought. Perhaps a science fiction writer mulling over a plot complication? This is confirmed by the next thought she overhears.

. . . giant multilegged creature . . . but from where . . . what does it want . . .

Much of this is underlain by some foreign language. Most people using a learned language will think in their own tongue first and then express it in English. But in this case, she hears both languages simultaneously. It makes the thoughts "noisy" and hard to read. From the underlying grammar, she suspects the native language to be Chinese. If he has not yet shaken the grammatical habits, then he has learned English only recently.

Ahead, she spots an Oriental man and knows satisfaction that her deductions are on the right track. Behind him, a woman struggles with grocery bags and when Janet turns her attentions to her she is startled to realize that it is the woman who rescued the baby at the fire, the one whose thoughts put her on the trail that eventually led to Jupiter Crowley. The media is going nuts trying to find her, and here she is walking about as blithe as you please.

Or not. The woman's thoughts are less than blithe.

I hope no one recognizes me. To shun notoriety all these centuries only to stumble onto local fame . . . Nagkmur doesn't seem to understand but maybe he's always avoided the limelight . . . But now that there are two of us . . . These bags are awkward and heavy. Sidd really should help . . .

Janet Murchison had once famously characterized Manhattan as "the world's largest, fully-equipped, open-air insane asylum," and here is the evidence! All these centuries?

But a woman who fears discovery may glance about from time to time without thinking. Stacey turns suddenly, notices Janet a few steps behind, and her face turns pale.

That woman again. Is she tracking me? Eager to pry out a secret I don't have . . . Does she know of the abandoned plant?

Janet does the only thing she can. She looks into her bag as if counting items and walks briskly past, paying the two not the slightest overt attention. She can hear Nagkmur scold Stacey for the delay, his futuristic ruminations diverted for the moment by more pedestrian concerns. This close, Stacey's body language expresses the emotions her thoughts do not, and because she worries so much about it, the location of the abandoned meatpacking plant drifts through her thoughts.

But Stacey Papandreou and her sad fears are of no concern to Janet, who has the more immediate problem of a series of burglaries, national in scope, that have now apparently attracted the interest of the military.

Janet parks her SUV on Eighth Street in Passaic across from Bergtholm just as the second shift locks up and goes home. Unlike the Chicago RDC, the Passaic facility works no graveyard shift. The strip mall farther back up the street is closed for the night, but the pole lamps in its parking lot cast the warehouse in relief and she has a good view of the doors and gates. The neighborhood sits in a bow of the Passaic

River so, unless the thief is an accomplished scuba diver, there is no access to the warehouse from the rear.

The parking lot empties and Janet noshes on her pastrami and rye while she watches. Her patience is rewarded a few hours later when a dark, non-descript minivan pulls up to the loading docks and a man in camouflage fatigues exits and exchanges a few words with the driver.

The driver busies himself briefly at the employee entrance and the door swings open. The driver ducks inside for a few moments. There is no alarm. Then the first man enters the building while the driver returns to the van. All this in less than a minute. Janet is impressed.

Janet gives the driver time to settle in, then she eases out of her vehicle and drifts silently through the shadows on the west side of the street before crossing to the plant's main entrance. She studies the driver through her light-gathering binoculars and sees him reading a magazine. He must have excellent night vision because he uses no light.

With the keys Bergtholm has provided, Janet opens the main doors just a crack and slides inside. She checks the alarm panel, and notes as expected that it has already been de-activated. There are only the door and window alarms; no internal motion sensors.

A corridor leads past offices, a parts counter, locker rooms, thence into the warehouse proper. A supervisor's prefab with pick lists already hung for the early morning, a row of forklifts in their charging stations, roll-up loading doors along the outside wall. To her right, across from the dock platform, aisles of shelving rise to the ceiling.

She quiets her mind and listens.

Gradually, she makes out the whisper of another mind. It is hard to make out because the metal racks and bulk containers muddy the signal. She glides across the floor and pauses at the employees' entrance, where she can just barely discern the thoughts of the driver waiting outside.

. . . *childhood fables . . . but the council must be taking them seriously . . .* Then something about . . . *ancient enemy . . .* and . . . *hope the colonel knows what he's doing . . .*

Colonel? Is this whole romp a clandestine military operation? She had gotten some hints of a black op from the Chicago police, something about an experimental drone. Are these thefts a field test for new hardware?

She turns her back on the door and tiptoes into the aisles of shelving. She doesn't worry about her six. Because of her peculiar talent, no one can sneak up behind her.

She spots a man down Aisle Five and ducks back quickly before he can see her. He is examining a picker's basket, apparently abandoned in mid-aisle.

. . . *got here too late . . .* she hears him think. . . . *surprised it in the act . . . earth in deadly danger, but only apkallu realize it . . . why is it here . . . and why did it chase that Chinese guy in chicago . . .*

This is the first she has heard about the thief chasing a Chinese guy. International industrial espionage? But that does not square with the pedestrian nature of the components stolen. The more she learns about this case, the less sense it makes.

And what the hell are *apkallu*?

She decides to precipitate matters and approaches the man in the military fatigues. But as she does so, a strange discordant organ music swells and an unaccountable dread grips her soul. She looks up toward its source, toward the top shelf of the rack a few columns ahead on the left. And in the weird green light of night-vision she sees a . . .

But it is gone, and when she turns back to the man she is looking at the business end of a Sig Sauer P228. It carries a magazine with thirteen rounds and thirteen is clearly an unlucky number.

VII. INTERMEZZO

Consider a headwalker nesting high above the earth in a cloaked vessel and perusing the world below for signs of temporal precession. He is balanced on the razor's edge between a terror at dying alone on a strange world, far from the company of his people, and an elation at surviving despite all odds and bringing back the song of this potential new home. But her hunters are closing in. There are no wolves on her world, but she had recognized the creatures in the warehouse for what they were; and one had somehow known where she was hiding!

Its repairs are ninety percent complete, though the same might be said with considerably less enthusiasm of a leap across a chasm. Still, hope springs eternal, even in alien breasts. He has made spotty detections of temporal distortions in the large nest on the north-south landmass; and maybe, if he can locate the precessor and seize it, she can escape this world. There is nothing for it but to await the next distortion and act. Its number three manipulator hovers near the insertion port of the transport beam trigger-well, ready to send himself to the indicated nexus at an instant's notice.

Consider, too, the android gliding up the escalator to Thirty-fourth Street at Penn Station, New York. She intends to determine whether or not Stacey Papandreou is another of her kind. She is not driven by fellow-feeling, for she possesses none. It is only a logical possibility to be resolved. "Papandreou" might be a foreign agent, or a criminal, or hiding in WITSEC—the demand for false identities makes it a seller's market—but on the off chance, why not check her out. Two q-bit processors are better than one.

Besides, Papandreou is a companion of the Chinese man and there is the matter of the curious smudge on his pant leg. Being herself essentially a complex algorithm, Annie is bothered when things don't add up.

Consider as well the apkallu and the telepath carpooling into Manhattan, partnered for the moment by the chance crossing of their worldines. (Convergence is less wild a coincidence when two hunters seek the same target.) It is an hour's drive from Passaic to Manhattan at this time of night and it passes in an uncomfortable, one-sided silence. The *apkallu* is determined to reveal as little as possible, but in the process reveals everything. He may as well have been a chattering magpie as to sit quietly in a car with a telepath.

But to read a man's thoughts, he must first be brought to think them. So the telepath plies him with questions and, in between his grunts, evasions, and needs-to-know, she harvests an astounding bounty in which ancient planetary cleansings, exile, lost technologies, genetic makeovers, ravaging headwalkers, intraspecific prejudice, and service career potential are indifferently mixed with flashes of lust. She would have found all of it quite unbelievable—except for the lust—had she not been herself unbelievable.

From that harvest, she plucks a kernel: The creature that she had glimpsed in the Bergtholm warehouse had chased a Chinese man in Chicago. She rubs this fact against the earlier harvest from Stacey Papandreou's companion regarding a "giant multilegged creature," and assuming giant multilegged creatures a genuine rarity upon the earth, it is likely that Papandreou's companion and the Chinese man are one and the same. Her promise of the man's whereabouts had lowered the colonel's pistol in the warehouse and made them for the time being fellow travelers.

The best way to trap a tiger, the colonel thinks, is to keep close watch on its prey. This is not a safe way. One is baiting a tiger, after all. But it does require the least effort. Given the promise of this lead, the *apkallu* has decided to watch over the Chinese man. He has sent his driver to the League building near Grand Central Terminal to round up a posse, though that will take some time. Not many with the required skill set will be available, but his nerves will not settle until he has some heavily armed companions. If then. Headwalkers are the bogeymen of *apkallu* children's stories and the thought that he had nearly walked beneath one has unnerved him. Had it been a sniper, lying in wait? But then why had it withheld its fire? He can make neither heads nor tails of the creature's purpose. Which makes sense: a radially symmetric creature has neither. Who knows what motives drive an alien? He thinks this last with no sense of irony, though his companion nearly busts a gut.

Consider finally the time traveler and the immortal, squatting in an abandoned meat-packing plant on the Lower West Side of Manhattan. Despite an initial wariness regarding her brusque and ill-mannered rescuer, the immortal has stayed with him. She wants a refuge from the curiosity of the media. The time traveler wants a convenient place to carry out his computations.

But the woman is a distraction anyway, sitting quietly, never asking questions or showing the least curiosity about the enormous changes that have convulsed the worldline. But perhaps she attached to this nexus many years ago in her personal lifetime and has in consequence "gone native." Somewhere in those years her transporter has been lost or damaged; but while ordinarily that might have been worrisome in itself, it will become moot once the proper history has been restored.

Excising the Theodora woman presents difficulties. A nine-year window of opportunity spans his inadvertent introduction of the prince and the prostitute and the outbreak of the riots that brought down the empire. He must intervene neither too soon nor too late. If he acts before his original departure, he will cross his own time-line and stir up a fourth-order temporal vortex. One needn't grasp the calculus of projective four-space geometry to suspect that this might not be a good thing. But if he delays too long, Theodora may become too prominent to remove without creating its own consequences. The last thing he needs is a *third* world.

Though he has all the time in the world—for he can travel to the precise nexus regardless how long it takes to calculate when and where that is—a certain psychological urgency weighs on him. He makes errors in setting up the Hatayama matrices, transposes terms in a Chang transformation, and these add to his anxiety. His fingers hover over his keyboard, frozen in uncertainty.

He is balanced on the razor's edge between terror at dying alone in a strange continuum, unimaginably separated from his world, and elation at surviving despite all odds and restoring the proper course of time.

He has nearly forgotten the apparition in Chicago, although the apparition has not forgotten him.

The world is cupped in their hands: A man from a lost continuum who regards all about him as "phantoms"; a woman who sees them as ephemeral "shadows"; a being whose ancestors had been genetically engineered to resemble humans, but who lives in fear that those selfsame "aborigines" would turn on him savagely should they ever catch on; an android to whom the entire concept of "life" is foreign; a telepath whose long soak in the marinade of people's unguarded thoughts has colored her every emotion with a reflexive contempt. None of them are too enthusiastically disposed toward the fate of mankind. Was there ever a jury so ill-constituted?

All these to counter a creature from a migrating nest who thinks no more of wiping out an entire biome than it would of blowing its nose. If it had a nose.

VIII. THE MENACE OUT OF SPACE

Dawnlight has not yet infiltrated the crannies of the crumbling meatpacking plant when Nagkmur hears the murmur from the darkness beyond the globe of light in which he labors. Something falls or breaks or scuttles through the debris. He pokes the slumbering woman with his stylus and slips his *pungshi* from its holster.

Over the centuries Stacey has learned the usefulness of speedy awakening. She takes the flashlight in hand, though she does not yet turn it on, and Nagkmur extinguishes the lantern. She holds herself still as a mouse under a hawk-haunted sky and in the stillness something moves, a shadow amidst shadows, and she abruptly raises her flashlight and flicks it on.

It is the white-haired woman! The one who had watched her at the apartment fire; the one who had lurked nearby when she had fetched the groceries. Stacey sucks her breath to cry out. But the tall woman holds both her hands up, palms out, in a placating gesture.

Nagkmur hesitates and, hearing a click behind him, turns to see a man in the military garb of this nexus pointing the active end of a hand weapon at him. He recognizes *kikashi*, a move which forces one to abandon his course of action, and he ostentatiously returns his *pungshi* to its place. Had the stranger meant to kill him, he would be dead already. He wonders if that particular weakness is common to this nexus.

The other man too holsters his pistol and introduces himself as a colonel in SPACE-COM and presents Janet as "a civilian investigator." He calls Nagkmur "sir" and asks his assistance in a case of national security. "Air Force Space Command is interested in the events that took place in Chicago two weeks ago. You encountered a drone there that we are trying to locate."

Nagkmur shudders with remembered fear. He thinks, *They not know me; hunt something else. Lake above wood: In flood of human folly, the Superior Man retires to higher ground.* He smiles. "How may help illustrious SPACECOM?"

"You think you may have hallucinated the encounter," Janet says, "but we have the event on tape."

Zendahl casts her a puzzled glance and says, "In other encounters the drone remained concealed or fled when detected. Yet it broke cover and rushed toward you. We'd like to know why."

Nagkmur shrugs. "Did not stay to ask."

But further discussion soon reveals the timing of events and Stacey, nearly forgotten in the shadows, speaks up. "But he was with me here in New York when all that happened!"

Zendahl had not known of the fire. Frustration snaps his notepad shut. "This can't be the same man," he complains. "The times overlap." He pulls out his cell phone to call off the strike team.

But Janet knows that, despite the paradox, Nagkmur really is their quarry. She wonders how a person can be in two distant places so quickly and the answer comes upon her with stunning suddenness.

She points a finger at Nagkmur. "You're a teleporter, aren't you?"

But Nagkmur does not understand the accusation. *Madwoman*, he thinks above the underlying babble of his native tongue. Zendahl and Stacey stare at her and Janet flushes. Yet, she has come here in company with one alien in search of another, and she herself is a telepath, so the conclusion does not seem a stretch to her.

The nature of her senses is such that Janet can hear anyone's presence even if she cannot see him. So the hand that comes down suddenly and heavily on her shoulder sends a shock through her like a live wire.

"Teleporter?" says Annie Troy. "That's absurd. He's a time traveler."

Which, of course, is not nearly so absurd. For one thing, Nagkmur's thoughts confirm the charge and Janet overhears: *Has Patrol found me? Is this rescue?* And from his further thoughts she learns that he is not merely a traveler in time but a policeman of time, arresting smugglers, preventing assaults on the integrity of the time stream, rescuing tourists, and presumably issuing parking tickets. For another, as the newcomer explains to Zendahl, time travel accounts for the data; namely, that Nagkmur's trouser bore a grease stain in the evening in New York that it did not acquire until early the next morning in Chicago.

Janet stares at Annie Troy and it is like peering through two open windows into an empty house. There is no whisper of thought in the void within. Janet knows the fear of a sighted person confronted with a ghost. Or of a bat bumping into a sound-absorbing tile.

"Saw woman on television," Nagkmur explains with a toss of his head toward Stacey. "Recognize her from first meeting." *Pheasant's wings falter and droop from exhaustion. The Superior Man goes where he must. He shows his brilliance by keeping it veiled. Stay true to course. This knowledge will not matter once history restored.*

"What first meeting?" Janet asks. But it is Stacey who provides the silent answer: *In Constantinople a millennium and a half ago.*

She also hears her denial. *Sidd is not a time traveler. It's a cover story to explain how he could be in different eras. But really, a cover story ought to be more plausible than the truth. We must slip away before we are exposed. They don't believe in witch-craft these days, but they'll lock us up, stab us for biopsies, cut us open, looking for the secret of unending life.*

Janet leans toward her and lays a hand on her forearm. "We have no intention of exposing you. Neither Colonel Zendahl nor myself would welcome too close a scrutiny." She looks at the *apkallu*. "Isn't that right, colonel?" After a pause, the man nods.

Zendahl's thoughts are a turmoil. *What does Murchison know? Was she following me and not the headwalker all the time? Are my people in danger of exposure?* He also wonders why Annie is here, but Janet cannot help him there. A blank slate bears no message.

"I don't think they understand the urgency," Janet tells Zendahl. "Maybe you can explain what we saw in Passaic." Unspoken is the challenge: If you don't, I will.

The *apkallu* explains about headwalkers and the potential for invasion—he says "infestation"—but he ascribes the knowledge to a secret government program "about which I am not at liberty to speak" rather than to a secret alien population already resident on Earth.

Stacey receives the news with something like delight: Area 51, Roswell, *Men in Black*, all vindicated! But Nagkmur listens with greater skepticism. Aliens from other stars cannot invade Earth because it would take too long to get here. The economics are not there. Besides, he thinks, no such invasion took place in the "true history." Annie Troy provides no thoughts, but neither does she voice any objections. Her solitary remark—that such aliens would be unlikely to maintain human machines—makes no sense to the others.

Zendahl's subconscious tosses a dimly remembered couplet from an ancient poem into his consciousness:

Forward fared the fleeing ships
As backward still they slipped.

And he cries out, "I know why the headwalker broke cover! It never made sense before, but . . ." He stops himself on the verge of revealing too much. A great deal of lore had been lost during the Dark Age, after the Six Ships had reached New Apkal and the One had gone on to parts unknown. The *apkallu* of later ages remembered only what had been transferred to new media before the old media decayed. Genetic engineering, vital to their survival, had been preserved. Ancient history, being of less immediate application, had faded into stories. Accounts had been shortened, complexities sloughed off, analogous figures fused. Only the essential lessons had been kept, to become fables to inspire or frighten children.

"An interstellar invasion might work if the invaders are a self-contained, migratory group. But if the creature that attacked Nagkmur expected to report to its fleet, they must have a way of shortening transit times."

"Nothing faster than light," scoffs Nagkmur.

"*Unless it travels backward in time at the same time.*" Interstellar travel would be impossible, or at least unpopular, unless transit times were a tolerable interval rather than a significant fraction of forever.

Stacey is bewildered, but Nagkmur, though initially astonished, is already considering the potentials.

Annie Troy processes the information and puts two and two together. "The creature's ship is damaged and it's trying to repair it. It's filching electronics on the downlow because it doesn't want to reveal its presence here, which suggests it is alone."

"And it attack me because it need temporal precessor?"

"It wasn't to snatch your shiny hubcaps," Janet comments.

"Your equipment probably emits a field," Zendahl speculates, and receives a cautious nod in return. "And the headwalker is probably able to detect the field and home in on it."

"Then I leave field off. Wait out danger."

"Wait how long?" says Annie. "It's stranded, but how long can it hold out? Can it send a message to summon others? Are its companions already searching for it?"

"Not," says Nagkmur, "my problem." *Phantom world*, he thinks. *Alien invasion moot.*

"Perhaps," says Janet. "But you will be mooted with it."

But the time traveler reacts strangely to the caution. Janet detects fragmentary comments indicating satisfaction and just punishment for his sins, although the nature of those sins remains obscure.

"There is a better choice," says Zendahl. "If you activate the field, the invader will detect it and try to seize it. We'll be waiting for it and, uh, neutralize it." *If there is a fleet coming behind it, Earth is doomed. We don't have the sort of defenses we had on Old Apkal. And even there, we lost.*

"I am to be bait in your trap?" says Nagkmur with a thin-lipped smile. "Very honored, but respectfully decline."

Annie Troy whispers to Janet, "If I were he, I'd be thinking about bugging out about now and ducking back to a time to before this headwalker showed up."

The telepath nods. "He is."

Nagkmur takes a step toward his machine. Stacey cries out, "Sidd!" and the time traveler hesitates. What is this world to him? An accident, a blunder, a defect in the space-time manifold, something to be overwritten. Why risk anything to preserve its phantoms?

Yet the woman is one of his own. He cannot leave her behind. "Hurry," he says. "Come with me." And he reaches out a hand.

But Stacey shakes her head. During her durance in the meat-packing plant, she has fashioned a pair of shanks from pieces of metal and wood scavenged from the detritus and from tape and wire in Siddhar's kit. She grips them both, one overfist in her left, the other underfist in her right. She does not understand what the two strangers have said about an alien threat, but she is not prepared to flee.

Nagkmur reflects on his fate. Is he to destroy universes wherever he fares? He murmurs something in *pudding-wa*, reaches a decision, and steps into his machine. No one else sees exactly how he does this. It is as if a part of his vehicle has become permeable. Once inside, he activates the precessor and then, his needler in hand, goes to stand within the entrance. If things go belly-up, he can reach his seat and pop the clutch before anything can reach him. Without a Patrol shield, no one else can follow him.

He closes his eyes in meditation.

Deep waters in the heavens. Thunderclouds approach from West. The Superior Man nourishes himself and awaits moment of truth. Great success if he maintains his course. He must endure for now this strange mix of apprehension and anticipation. Nothing he does can affect outcome. Everything is submitted to Fates.

Zendahl pulls his service weapon from its holster and chambers a round. Nagkmur has acted prematurely. *The strike team has not arrived*, he thinks. *We are not ready.*

"No one ever is," Janet tells him, and she removes her pistol from her purse, tossing the purse aside.

Annie has no weapon. She *is* a weapon. Her skin bristles as the MEMS in her shell flex. She watches the directions the others do not. If anyone notices the strange transfiguration, they say nothing for the moment.

There is a moment of Advent: The world in silent stillness waits. Time passes in heartbeats.

Then it is there, seven feet tall and booming like a great organ. Zendahl wets his pants. Janet and Stacey cry out in terror. Nagkmur turns back to his transporter. It is time to run.

Jim-7, alerted by his alarm system, has beamed down to the site of the temporal distortion, and has arrived from a direction no one has been watching; viz., a fourth one. The imprecision of his beamer is such that he cannot materialize only within a radius of uncertainty, but this puts him fortuitously in the midst of the defenders, who cannot loose fire without the risk of hitting one another.

Jim is radially symmetric, which means he needs no one to watch his back. But just as bilaterians will favor their right side or their left, Jim's people will favor one pendrant or another. Like anyone else, he likes to put his best foot forward.

He grips a disruptor in each hand—that's five—all of them set to fatal voltages. Recognizing two of his opponents as the stalkers from the warehouse, he immediately disposes of them, discharging a weapon at each. Then he rushes at the one who stands between him and the life-saving precessor. She must not fail. *Must not.*

Terror grips Nagkmur's bowels and he takes comfort as always in the ancient books. *The enemy is upon you. You wait in blood, preparing yourself for his blows; but your own ability can see you through, if you stand your ground and maintain balance.* He draws a ragged breath and raises his weapon.

But yin changes in the fourth line. *Flood rises above tallest Tree: Amidst rising tide of folly, the superior man retires to higher ground, renouncing his world without looking back. Any direction better than where you stand. No time for fatal heroics. Remove self from situation* now. *Find sanctuary. Later, deal with these concerns on your own terms, and from a position of strength.*

He turns to run.

"It's emitting sound at nineteen hertz," Annie says. "Subsonics in that range induce fear in organic beings." But Annie Troy is not an organic being, and she attacks the creature from the rear, striking with a fist that can bend steel.

But it is harder to bend rubber, and Jim-7 has no rear. He discharges the disruptor he holds in that hand, but the charge passes across her ceramic body. Certain nodes of hers spark and an induced current disorients her momentarily. Her fist sinks into the thick, blubbery flesh of the headwalker, deep enough to cause some internal damage to its organs and leave a prodigious bruise. It staggers, but is not incapacitated.

Stacey, crouched on the floor from fear, takes heart from Annie's pronouncement. It is only some sound effect, not genuine fear, and she employs the mental exercises that have seen her through countless incidents in the past, calls upon her confidence, and rises up between the beast and Sidd. She stabs the fearful thing repeatedly with her shanks.

Jim-7 does not have the same organs as a human being or an apkallu. They are not even the same *kinds* of organs, nor are they located in the expected places, but a number of them are vital in one way or another and more importantly, no creature can exist without pain. Pain is a blessing. It warns the creature of harm; and through it, it learns what to avoid. What Jim feels as the blades sink into its primary air sac is not exactly the same sensation as a human would feel, but it serves the same purpose and it is distinctly unpleasant.

But Jim is psyched. Jim is *pumped*. And if she does not quite laugh at pain, she resolutely compartmentalizes it. The blows are not fatal; not yet, and she lashes out with her right forward foot—that is "right" and "forward" relative to her favored body sector. The kick catches Stacey under her ribcage, crushing it and tossing her like a rag doll off to the side, where she lands in a broken heap.

Siddhar Nagkmur learns that he does not disdain all phantoms in this mad pseudo-world. Of course, he does not believe Stacey is a phantom and in a certain way he is correct. Whether Justinian fled the riots or not, Maryam brt' Yarosh would have gone on. She was there in Nagkmur's world every bit as much as in this one. She is immortal latitudinally as well as longitudinally.

But Nagkmur does not know this. He only knows that the only other putative survivor of his world has been kicked into rubble. He howls and aims his pungshi square into what ought to have been the face of the monster. Only in some rear compartment of his mind does he recall that he is supposed to be saving the phantom world from these phantom invaders. He is only trying to save Stacey Papandreou.

The pungshi vaporizes something akin to a muscle group, laming the creature in her left forward leg. She staggers and shakes Annie from what is not actually her rear just as Zendahl and Janet open fire from her quarters.

"It's weapon is like a Tazer," Zendahl cries. "But a very low-powered one."

"But it obviously considered it a debilitating blow," adds Annie Troy, who desperately tries to add two and two.

Jim-7 knows the agony of defeat. Hurting from her wounds, surrounded by hostile indigenes, his goal just ahead of him, it makes one last desperate lunge for what appears to be an open doorway.

And Nagkmur leaps aside.

Zendahl snarls and calls him a coward and empties his clip into the massive headball. The creature is like a bomber from the world war, with tail and side gunners operating in all directions. It zaps the colonel again and though it stings rather sharply, he shakes it off and stuffs another clip into his pistol.

Janet Murchison smiles and withholds her fire.

Jim-7 does not know how the two survived her deadly blasts, but he pushes the mystery into a backroom of his mind. The way is clear! Already, she can hear the chords of triumph from her welcoming nest. From the depths of despair, she has seized triumph and the means to return to her folk!

It is just as well she treasures this glorious thought, for it is the last one she forms. When she touches the hull of the strange machine, unimaginable voltages course through her, shorting what she has for nerves, disrupting what serves as brains—there are two of them, actually—and igniting the sacs of hydrogen gas that permeate its body. All thought dissipates into a kaleidoscope of impressions, perceptions, concepts, none of them connected one with another.

Smoke filters from its eyes, and from a few other orifices that are less easily catalogued. Flames begin to consume its insides. It does not fall. Its five legs flex and it settles to the ground much as a zeppelin. Something within it bursts, though the pop is muffled by its bulk.

The electrical charge of the time machine's skin was enough to knock a Chicago gangbanger senseless. Imagine what it does to a creature far more sensitive to electrical fluids.

The headwalker is settling now like a deflating balloon, the escaping gasses conjuring dying chords. Both Janet and Nagkmur wonder if they are "last words." Annie deduces that they are only mechanical. Zendahl empties another clip into the carcass, Some of the bullets pierce what might have been vital organs before they were fricasseed, but the body is now inert. It doesn't matter. It doesn't matter that this particular headwalker is of another species than the Ancient Enemy. The fear and loathing is inbred.

Janet, who overhears all this, wonders if the creature they have slain deserved its fate. The attack on Nagkmur seemed to indicate hostility, but perhaps they had all misinterpreted desperation as hostility.

They had been wrong in one sense. Jim-7 had held no hostility toward any of them. Simply a brusque impatience. There was something he had needed, and there were obstacles in the way of getting it. That was all. But try telling that to the obstacles.

IX. THE MENACE OUT OF TIME

A moment of crisis is followed oft by one of reflection; and so the participants in the fight stand about in solitary attitudes as they contemplate what they have done. For one thing, they have blown out a candle, and that is no small matter even if the candle had promised to set fire to the house.

Zendahl, for one, has no doubt that it was absolutely necessary. That a head-walker could have any motive for coming to New Apkal other than to scout for a conquering fleet is beyond question. After all, the creature had opened fire, and what good reason might there have been for that?

In all her career, Janet has never before shot a suspect and she wonders whether too much time sharing Zendahl's thoughts has subtly influenced her. The corpse continues to make organ-like sounds as its air-sacs subside, but the cessation of the corresponding mental chords is proof enough not only that the thing is most sincerely dead, but also that it had been a thinking being and not a mere monster. What did any of them really know about the creature? They had deduced that it was marooned, that it needed a component of Nagkmur's time machine and was desperate enough to try seizing it by force, but had it been any more than a terrified castaway in need of succor? She studies the massive corpse and shakes her head. It is going to be one hell of an inquest.

Annie, properly speaking, is not thinking anything; but she does process the data and reaches a number of conclusions regarding future courses of action. One is that it would be prudent to disassociate herself from the battle. A system analyst for CYBERCOM has no good reason to come to New York and fight aliens. It is not in her job description.

In fact, she had come not to kick alien butt, but to make contact with Stacey Papandreou. That purpose is now moot. Whatever else Stacey is, she is not an android.

Her current position gives Annie access to an enormous amount of data, and her tropism for data is the one thing about her that approaches a sensitive appetite. To become ensnared in the upcoming investigation would put her access, and even her identity, at risk. So to ensure its continuance, she must conceal her participation in this mess, and she immediately begins to catalog the actions that might be taken to secure those ends.

One possibility is that she should create a reserve identity in case her current one becomes unsustainable.

Another is that she should kill all the witnesses.

Nagkmur, for his part, has knelt by the body of Stacey Papandreou and holds her limp hand in his own. Now he is truly alone. He takes refuge in the ancient Texts.

Fire ascends above the Water. The Superior Man examines the nature of things and keeps each in its proper place. The young fox wets his tail just as he completes his river crossing. Do not rush to completion before absorbing lessons of journey. This Quest ends only at threshold of next.

But he senses a change in the second line.

Water recedes. Sun shines down upon Earth. Constantly honing and refining his brilliance, the Superior Man is a salvation to his people. They repay his benevolence with a herd of horses, and he is granted audience three times in single day.

Nagkmur takes comfort in the verse. He is not sure why a herd of horses is an accolade. It adds up to a lot of horse manure when you think about it. But the ancient Texts are often obscure, and he imagines the gratitude of his restored people: the adulation of the lowly, the rewards from the high.

He must not rush into his next task. He knows *what* he must do but has not yet decided *how* he must do it. That is, he has the science but not the art of the matter. Act in haste and like the young fox, he will wet his tail just as he has successfully crossed the river.

He becomes aware that the white-haired woman has come to stand beside him. The Patrolman releases Stacey's hand, rises, brushes his knees. "She was brave woman," he says. "Risk everything, save me."

Janet too stands over the broken body—and smiles.

Nagkmur sees no prospect of achieving the quiet he needs to meditate on his plans. He cannot stay here, but if he jumps too far into the past, he might not have the wireless access he needs for research. He could confine himself to the "internet" nexus, but *who knows how long that monster had lurked in orbit searching for a wake in the time stream?* On the other hand, if he jumps to the future, he might find the authorities there alert for his arrival. How he envies the young fox!

Do these phantom beings know that I intend their erasure?

He regrets the destruction of the woman. She had been a fine source of information respecting the entanglements of Theodora, at least insofar as she had known of them. Now, he is thrown back on Procopius' *Secret History*, and who knows how reliable that fellow's gossip is? He might have to risk scouting trips to the crucial nexus, and that always carries a risk of churning up turbulence. Change upon change, until all hope of restoration is lost!

The military man and the inexpressive woman approach and Nagkmur takes an involuntary step back. The white-haired woman looks on. Phantoms, all of them, of no particular consequence, save that they might impede the completion of his mission. The man—he is reluctant to give these phantoms names. Names would make them more real—draws his weapon and the Patrolman's heart skips a beat. His hand starts toward his own holster.

But the man does not hold the weapon as one preparing to use it, and Nagkmur desists. "How may this one assist?" he asks.

"It would be awkward to explain my presence here," the man confesses. "There will be investigations, and . . ." He smiles briefly. ". . . who knows what they might find when they start poking into things."

Nagkmur bows and gestures. "Nearest exit, that way."

But the man is stubborn. "No, they'll be able to track me down from the slugs they dig out of the headwalker. My service weapon's ballistics are on file."

"Perhaps," Nagkmur suggests, "smoldering carcass of giant alien space invader provide distraction to forensic investigators."

The expressionless woman speaks. "The fewer puzzles that confront CSU, the better. They will seize on what is familiar. For reasons I can't get into, it would be best if no one digs too deeply into Colonel Zendahl—or myself."

Nagkmur shrugs. "Not my problem."

"But you can help," the woman insists. "You can take his weapon into the past and switch it with another of the same vintage. I can alter the records to make it appear that the replacement has always been his weapon."

Nagkmur thinks this will give him an opportunity to depart this nexus not only without opposition, but with their blessing. If he does not come back, what can they do? "Very well," he says. "I will do it."

But the white-haired woman says, "I don't think it would be a good idea to let him go."

Annie does not hesitate. Moving too swiftly to follow, she places herself between the time patrolman and his vehicle.

But Zendahl is perplexed. "What's going on?"

"Our time-traveling friend," Janet says with a nod toward Nagkmur, "plans to wipe out the space-time continuum."

"What? How do you know that?"

Annie tells him, "Murchison is a mind-reader." Then to Janet she says, "You answer questions no one has asked."

What if she reveals our presence to the aborigines?

"I wouldn't worry, colonel," Janet tells Zendahl. "One hand washes another. I'd rather you didn't noise around my peculiar sensitivity, either. But you," she addresses Annie Troy, "I can't hear your mind at all."

"That must mean I don't have one," the android concludes. "I'm a machine, an android," she tells them. "I was built by the Institute for a field beta test."

"Nonsense," says Zendahl. "You're as human as I am." (And Janet nearly busts a gut.)

"It's the Turing Fallacy," Annie explains. "I run a very good *simulation* of a human being, but a simulation is not the thing itself. You can't fly from JFK to LAX in a flight simulator."

Swiftly, Janet explains what she has gleaned from Nagkmur's thoughts. "But he accidentally . . . I guess 'overwrote' is the right word. . . . he accidentally overwrote his own history with the one we know and now blames himself for the deaths of all his people. He's suffering the biggest case of survivor's guilt in history."

"Can people who never actually existed actually die?" Annie wonders aloud. The question resonates strangely with her since in a sense she does not exist, either.

It also resonates with Nagkmur, who has finally been pushed over the brink into tears. They course down his cheeks and he covers his face to contain them. They might leave river valleys in their wake, they flow so fiercely. He recalls his honored father, his stern approvals and sterner reprimands. His mother, moon-faced and smiling. His brothers and he running through the backstreets of Dzhokaht, creating and enacting fantasies on the fly. His mentor, Bon Hoyma, who had come from the far future to recruit him into a fraternity that he had not known existed. All dead now. Worse than dead.

He wonders if he can fight his way past the machine-woman, who crouches like a tiger in his path. He faces her, turning his back on the other two.

And a voice from the floor cries, "Don't leave me here, Sidd!"

Startled by this unexpected plea from an unlooked-for quarter, Nagkmur stares open-mouthed at Stacey. Her blood has clotted, her wounds have knit and her broken bones are realigning even as he watches. What marvel is this? From how far in his own future has she come?

Janet speaks up. "She doesn't come from the future," she tells him. "She came from the past. But she took the long way here. She doesn't die."

"Self-repair?" muses Annie. There are materials that self-repair cracks while retaining strength, self-healing polymers from Oak Ridge. Raytheon incorporated self-healing into a complex system-on-chip design that enables the chip to sense undesired circuit behaviors and correct them. She supposes that what artifice has contrived, nature might accomplish on its own. "Is there anything that can kill her?"

Janet considers how a machine might test that hypothesis and shudders. "It still hurts," Janet warns. "She still feels pain."

But Stacey, too, understands that her secret is now known and while her first impulse is to flee and hide, that of Zendahl is not. And Nagkmur must be dealt with. Janet realizes that all three people present would happily see her dead to preserve their secrets, and Annie Troy could carry out the hit without warning. She takes a step or two backward. "We have to stop him," she tells the others more shrilly.

"Why should we believe you?" Zendahl asks. "We've only your word for his intentions."

"You could wait until we all cease to exist, but I wouldn't recommend it. We only had your word for it that the headwalker was hostile."

"You were in my head. You know it was true."

But Janet shakes her head. "I only know that you *believed* it was true. Maybe you were deluded."

If the Stacey woman is not of his own timeline, Nagkmur thinks, she is just another phantom, albeit a long-lived one. Yet, he has grown accustomed to her presence, and what better companion could he ask for planning the rework on Old Constantinople? He helps her to her feet, thinking that her self-healing abilities would be a useful thing to learn, even if *jan'ow* were required to extract the secret.

Nagkmur smiles at his enemies, knowing that they are also enemies of one another. He holds his hands in a placating gesture.

The tenth hexagram. Heaven shines down upon the Marsh but the Marsh reflects Heaven imperfectly. Fully aware of the danger on the narrow path ahead, the Superior Man determines to move forward. The future is uncertain, but there are times when a risk must be taken:

You tread upon the tiger's tail.

Not perceiving you as a threat, the startled tiger does not bite.

Success.

Thunder fills the Heavens. But the Superior Man does not appear intimidating or threatening. Opportunity arises along this course.

The sages who trained the transporter's neural net had included a number of basic maneuvers that Patrolmen might need to call upon in straightened circumstances, one of which is called *dahjoan*, which means "a reversal." Upon receiving the proper verbal cue from an authorized voice, the transporter will leap forward in time by a quarter of a minor key and shift spatially to the other side of its operator, orienting so that its door will face the operator. It is a maneuver expressly intended for use when an opponent stands between the operator and his transporter.

More fortunate still is that Patrolmen are trained rigorously in these standard maneuvers. They are executed by muscle memory, without conscious thought, and were written and memorized exclusively in *pudding-wa*.

Which is why Janet has no premonition of what is to happen. That Nagkmur intends to make a try for his vehicle is clear—body language will do when telepathy fails—but the how and the when are obscure.

Then Nagkmur says something in a foreign language and the time machine disappears. A gust of air sweeps into the vacated space, stirring the dust and papers and other small objects. Janet gasps and Annie spins about to stare at the empty air. But Zendahl notices that Nagkmur faces resolutely forward. He seems ready to charge and Zendahl pulls his weapon from its holster. He had emptied his clip into the headwalker, but Nagkmur does not know that and the implied threat may hold him. The time traveler does not pull his own weapon, and Zendahl takes some comfort in that.

When thirty-six seconds have elapsed by the Western count, the time machine reappears between Nagkmur and Zendahl, leaving Annie isolated in the backfield. Expanding from a singularity, it pushes Zendahl and Janet backward with a great rush of air. Janet loses her balance and falls on her backside. Zendahl keeps his feet and rushes around to the rear of the time machine (unless it is the front), but halts when he realizes what has happened.

Though buffeted by the displaced air, Annie is faster and very nearly lays a hand on Nagkmur when the door opens.

And Nagkmur staggers to a halt before his time machine.

It is not his time machine.

For one thing it is larger and ovoid rather than boxy. It is lime green rather than dull gray, and there is a faintly iridescent and baroque design visible on its surface. From the now-open doorway steps a tall, brown man wearing a close-fitting uniform. He is rugged and handsome, godlike in appearance. His gaze passes over Zendahl, Stacey, Annie Troy, and Janet (who has come around to the other end of the machine) until it comes to rest on Siddhar Nagkmur, and he smiles.

"*Shennö* Nagkmur," he says, "it is my unhappy lot to arrest you for attempted chronocide."

It makes sense in a mad sort of way. If Nagkmur's "original" continuum had developed a Patrol to safeguard its timeline, why should the altered continuum not give birth to another. Nature keeps no secrets and what the sages of the Thirty-seventh Mandate had discovered, the physicists of the Forty-first Century could learn as well. And the Department of Chronic Integrity would spend as much energy safeguarding the overwrite as Nagkmur's Shy?n Baw spent maintaining the original—if it really had been the original.

The man from the machine calls himself Dace X, which is as fine-sounding a futuristic name as anyone could ask. As Time Warden for Epoch 19/23, he is charged with confiscating Nagkmur's machine, and stopping his machinations.

"But my error create your time stream," Nagkmur protests. He squats in misery beside the awesome time cruiser from which Dace X has emerged. "You are mistakes, errors, all of you. You *preserve* defect, not correct it."

Dace X looks thoughtful. "That depends," he drawls, "on which side o' the error yuh sit, don't it?" He takes Nagkmur by the arm and raises him to his feet.

"What would you have done in my place?" the Patrolman asks the Warden. Failure chokes his voice.

"Oh, same-o, same-o, I 'spect," is the breezy reply. "But there's no way, Jose, to get back your family."

"If I correct original error . . ." says Nagkmur.

Dace X shakes his head. "Repair jobs are never quite the same as the original make. It'd be a patch job. But you haven't lost them. They've lost you. Your home is still 'there,' in another branch of space-time. But you just can't get there from here."

Nagkmur struggles for his voice. "They, they still live? Truly?"

"Certainly. You can't overwrite time. You simply create another branch of it."

Janet knows from his thoughts that Dace X is lying like a rug. Nagkmur's people are less than ghosts, for a ghost must once have lived. But she also senses an effort on the Warden's part to comfort the Patrolman. After all, you cannot atone for wiping out a few billion people by wiping out another few billion.

"Your arrival was quite timely," Annie Troy points out. "How did you pinpoint this time and place so exactly?"

The man from the future grins. "No sweat, daddy-o. Nagkmur will tell us during his debriefing. We just have to make sure he does that *before* I get my work order."

"That all seems rather circular," Annie says, for the claim has offended her sense of causality.

But Dace X merely shrugs. "That's one way to avoid loose ends. Anyhow, we had to wait until after you guys beat the alien. That reminds me, which of you . . . ?" He looks around and spots Colonel Zendahl. "I have this for you."

He pulls a SIG Sauer P228 from a dispatch case worn over his shoulder and hands it to the officer. "If you would hand me your old weapon, I'll drop it in the gun shop in Boise where I got this one. Make sure the records are properly altered in the Air Force data base." He hands a five-inch floppy to Annie Troy, who stares at it in incomprehension. Dace X says, "Oops," and replaces it with a thumb drive. "Sorry, wrong mission. Well, that's it. Twenty-three skidoo, as you people say."

Annie Troy shakes her head. "How did you know any of this was going down? Did you detect Nagkmur's, uh, 'time vortex'?"

When Dace X shakes his head, Annie presses her question. "I don't care how circular your causes are. Anything that moves is moved by another. How did you know any of this happened?"

Dace X returned to his machine, shepherding Nagkmur before him. He paused in the doorway. "We acted on an anonymous tip in the thirty-fourth century."

But whence the tip, who could say. Janet looks about the deserted plant but, expert as she is at passing unnoticed by the shadows around her, Stacey has already slipped away and has blended into the anonymous masses, beyond the range of Janet's talents.

L'ENVOI

On 7 February 2016, a bus driver named Kamraj was struck and killed by a meteorite on the campus of Bharathidasan Engineering College in Vellore, Tamil Nadu State. Scientists and media marveled at the unlikeliness of the event and said he was killed by mere chance. But Kamraj was not killed by chance, he was killed by a meteorite. Chance is not a cause, even if she strikes like a hammer.

Causation is vertical, not horizontal. That is, there is a cause for your flat tire and a cause for the moon being in quarter phase; but for getting a flat tire while the moon is in quarter phase, seek no cause. That way lies madness. Or astrology.

Coincidence, they say, makes bad art. But art imitates life, not the other way round, and life is a succession of such coincidences, great and small. If Stacey had not saved that baby, she would not have been on the news. If Nagkmur had not been drowning his sorrows, he would not have seen her. If he had not seen her, he would not have fired up the ol' temporal precessor. If he hadn't done that, Jim-7 would not have burst from cover and so garnered the attention of the Apkallu League. And so it goes tumbling down time to the dénouement. Jim-7 might not have rushed so precipitously to his fatal contact had Nagkmur not stepped aside. And the Patrolman stepped aside because he realized the alien's probable sensitivity to electrical shock from Zendahl's experience with its mild Tazer. Because Annie, lacking all feeling, noted the nature of the fear that gripped them all, Stacey gripped her knives instead, attacked the creature, and by her apparent willingness to die steeled Nagkmur to defend a continuum in which he did not believe, much as Theodora the actress once steeled the purpose of the *basileus* Justinian in a golden city once upon a time.

Daniel Abraham, "The Mocking Tower," *The Book of Swords*.

Tim Akers, "A Death in the Wayward Drift," *Interzone 269*.

Nina Allen, "Neptune's Trident," *Clarkesworld*, June.

Charlie Jane Anders, "A Temporary Embarrassment in Spacetime," *Cosmic Powers*.

——, "Cake Baby: A Kango and Sharon Adventure," *Lightspeed*, November.

——, "Don't Press Charges and I Won't Sue," *Global Dystopias*.

——, "Stochastic Fancy," *Wired: The Fiction Issue*.

Nora Anthony, "Them Boys," *Strange Horizons*, 11/17.

Eleanor Arnason, "Daisy," *The Magazine of Fantasy & Science Fiction*, March/April.

Julianna Baggott, "Mental Diplodia," *Tor.com*, April 11.

——, "The Virtual Swallows of Hog Island," *Tor.com*, January 25.

Dale Bailey, "Come As You Are," *Asimov's Science Fiction*, May/June.

——, "Invasion of the Saucer-Men," *Asimov's Science Fiction*, March/April.

Bo Balder, "The Bridgegroom," *Clarkesworld*, July.

Tony Ballantyne, "The Human Way," *Analog Science Fiction and Fact*, March/April.

Ashok K. Banker, "A Vortal in Midtown," *Lightspeed*, November.

——, "Tongue," *Lightspeed*, August.

Dave Bara, "Last Day of Training," *Infinite Stars*.

Jessica Barber, "You and Me and the Deep Dark Sea," *Sunvault*.

Steven Barnes, "Mozart on the Kalahari," *Visions, Ventures, Escape Velocities*.

Stephen Baxter, "The Martian in the Wood," *Tor.com*, August 2.

——, "Starphone," *Asimov's Science Fiction*, January/February.

Elizabeth Bear, "The King's Evil," *The Book of Swords*.

——, "The Perfect Gun," *Infinity Wars*.

Jacey Bedford, "The Horse Head Violin," *Children of a Different Sky*.

R. S. Benedict, "Water God's Dog," *The Magazine of Fantasy & Science Fiction*, November/December.

Gregory Benford, "Elderjoy," *Chasing Shadows*.

——, "Shadows of Eternity," *Extrasolar*.

M. Bennardo, "Low Bridge! Or The Dark Obstructions," *Beneath Ceaseless Skies 242*.

Christopher L. Bennett, "Twilight's Captives," *Analog Science Fiction and Fact*, January/February.

Terry Bisson, "We Regret the Error," *Asimov's Science Fiction*, March/April.

Michael Bishop, "Gale Strang," *Asimov's Science Fiction*, July/August.

Elizabeth Bourne, "Designed For Your Safety," *Welcome to Dystopia*.

Richard Bowes, "Some Kind of Wonderland," *Mad Hatters and March Hares*.

R. Boyczuk, "The Garden of Eating," *Interzone 273*.

Marie Brennan, "The Şiret Mask," *Beneath Ceaseless Skies 238*.

Robert Brice, "Conglomerate," *Clarkesworld*, April.

David Brin and Tobias S. Buckell, "High Awareness," *Stories in the Stratosphere.*

Damien Broderick, "Tao Zero," *Asimov's Science Fiction*, March/April.

Steven Brust, "Playing God," *Shadows and Reflections.*

Tobias S. Buckell, "Sundown," *Apex Magazine*, June.

Oliver Buckram, "Hollywood Squid," *The Magazine of Fantasy & Science Fiction*, September/October.

Sue Burke, "Who Won the Battle of Arsia Mons?" *Clarkesworld*, November.

Octavia Cade, "The Ouroboros Bakery," *Kaleidotrope*, Autumn.

Jack Campbell, "Shore Patrol," *Infinite Stars.*

Stephen Case, "The Wind's Departure," *Beneath Ceaseless Skies 242.*

Michael Cassutt, "Timewalking," *Asimov's Science Fiction*, November/December.

Robert R. Chase, "The First Rule Is, You Don't Eat Your Friends," *Analog Science Fiction and Fact*, July/August.

C. J. Cherryh, "Hrunting," *The Book of Swords.*

Rob Chilson, "Across the Steaming Sea," *Analog Science Fiction and Fact*, July/August.

Maggie Clark, "Belly Up," *Analog Science Fiction and Fact*, July/August.

C. S. E. Cooney, "Though She Be But Little," *Uncanny 18.*

Brenda Cooper, "Blackstart," *Stories in the Stratosphere.*

——, "Heroes," *Children of a Different Sky.*

——, "Street Life in the Emerald City," *Chasing Shadows.*

James S. A. Corey, "Strange Dogs," *Orbit.*

Albert E. Cowdrey, "The Avenger," *The Magazine of Fantasy & Science Fiction*, March/April.

Ian Creasey, "After the Atrocity," *Asimov's Science Fiction*, March/April.

——, "And Then They Were Gone," *Analog Science Fiction and Fact*, November/December.

Leah Cypess, "On the Ship," *Asimov's Science Fiction*, May/June.

Don D'Ammassa, "Isn't Life Great?" *Welcome to Dystopia.*

Scott Dalrymple, "Marcel Proust, Incorporated," *Lightspeed*, June.

Aliette de Bodard, "A Game of Three Generals," *Extrasolar.*

——, "At the Crossroads of Shadow and Bone," *Children of a Different Sky.*

——, "Children of Thorns, Children of Water," *Uncanny 17.*

——, "In Everlasting Wisdom," *Infinity Wars.*

——, "First Presentation," *Chasing Shadows.*

Craig DeLancey, "Orphans," *Analog Science Fiction and Fact*, November/December.

Samuel R. Delany, "The Hermit of Houston," *The Magazine of Fantasy & Science Fiction*, September/October.

Malcolm Devlin, "The New Man," *Interzone 270.*

Paul Di Filippo, "The Bartered Planet," *Extrasolar.*

S. B. Divya, "An Unexpected Boon," *Apex Magazine*, November.

——, "Looking Up," *Where the Stars Rise.*

Cory Doctorow, "Party Discipline," *Tor.com*, August 30.

Terry Dowling, "Come Home," *Extrasolar.*

Gardner Dozois, "A Dog's Story," *The Magazine of Fantasy & Science Fiction*, July/August.

David Drake, "Cadet Cruise," *Infinite Stars.*

Brendan DuBois, "Reentry," *Analog Science Fiction and Fact*, November/December.

Andy Dudak, "Cryptic Female Choice," *Interzone 271.*

——, "Fool's Cap," *Clarkesworld*, June.

Tananarive Due, "The Reformatory," *Global Dystopias.*

Andy Duncan, "Worrity, Worrity," *Mad Hatters and March Hares.*

Thoraiya Dyer and Alvaro Zinos-Amaro, "The Shallowest Waves," *Analog Science Fiction and Fact,* January/February.

Marianne J. Dyson, "Europa's Survivors," *Analog Science Fiction and Fact,* March/April.

Christopher East, "An Inflexible Truth," *Lightspeed,* August.

Scott Edelman, "After the Harvest, Before the Fall," *Analog Science Fiction and Fact,* January/February.

——, "How Val Finally Escaped from the Basement," *Analog Science Fiction and Fact,* November/December.

Jonathan Edelstein, "The Shark God's Child," *Beneath Ceaseless Skies 222.*

Greg Egan, "The Discrete Charm of the Turing Machine," *Asimov's Science Fiction,* November/December.

Kate Elliott, "'I Am a Handsome Man,' Said Apollo Crow," *The Book of Swords.*

Sheila Finch, "Field Studies," *Asimov's Science Fiction,* July/August.

Jeffrey Ford, "All the King's Men," *Mad Hatters and March Hares.*

Karen Joy Fowler, "Persephone of the Crows," *Asimov's Science Fiction,* May/June.

Manny Frishberg and Edd Vick, "Ténéré," *Analog Science Fiction and Fact,* May/June.

Nancy Fulda, "Planetbound," *Chasing Shadows.*

Matt Gallagher, "Know Your Enemy," *Wired: The Fiction Issue.*

Charles E. Gannon, "Taste of Ashes," *Infinite Stars.*

Ingrid Garcia, "Racing the Rings of Saturn," *The Magazine of Fantasy & Science Fiction,* November/December.

David Gerrold, "The Patient Dragon," *Asimov's Science Fiction,* July/August.

Max Gladstone, "The Scholast in the Low Waters Kingdom," *Tor.com,* May 28.

Lisa Goldstein, "The Catastrophe of Cities," *Asimov's Science Fiction,* January/February.

Kathleen Ann Goonan, "The Tale of the Alcubierre Horse," *Extrasolar.*

Theodora Goss, "Come See the Living Dryad," *Tor.com,* March.

John Grant, "The Law of Conservation of Data," *Lightspeed,* July.

A. T. Greenblatt, "A Place to Grow," *Beneath Ceaseless Skies.*

Jim Grimsley, "Still Life With Abyss," *Asimov's Science Fiction,* January/February.

Richard E. Gropp, "Still Life with Falling Man," *Interzone 269.*

Robert Grossbach, "Driverless," *The Magazine of Fantasy & Science Fiction,* March/April.

Eileen Gunn, "Application for Asylum," *Welcome to Dystopia.*

——, "Night Shift," *Visions, Ventures, Escape Velocities.*

——, "Transitions," *A Flight to the Future.*

James Gunn, "The Ganymede Gambit: Jan's Story," *Asimov's Science Fiction,* September/October.

——, "Weighty Matters: Todor's Story," *Asimov's Science Fiction,* July/August.

Nin Harris, "Reversion," *Clarkesworld,* August.

M. John Harrison, "Yummie," *The Weight of Words.*

Gregor Hartmann, "A Gathering on Gravity's Shore," *The Magazine of Fantasy & Science Fiction,* March/April.

——, "What the Hands Know," *The Magazine of Fantasy & Science Fiction,* May/June.

Gerald Hausman, "Nights in the Gardens of Blue Harbor," *Shadows and Reflections.*

Maria Dahvana Headley, "Black Powder," *The Djinn Falls In Love.*

——, "The Thule Stowaway," *Uncanny 14.*

Simone Heller, "How Bees Fly," *Clarkesworld,* February.

Howard V. Hendrix, "The Girl with Kaleidoscope Eyes," *Analog Science Fiction and Fact,* May/June.

Joe Hill, "All I Care About Is You," *The Weight of Words.*

Robin Hobb, "Her Father's Sword," *The Book of Swords.*

Cecelia Holland, "The Sword Tyraste," *The Book of Swords.*

Stewart Horn, "The Morrigan," *Interzone 273.*

Saad Z. Hossain, "Bring Your Own Spoon," *The Djinn Falls in Love.*

Matthew Hughes, "The Prognosticant," *The Magazine of Fantasy & Science Fiction,* May/June.

——, "The Sword of Destiny," *The Book of Swords.*

——, "Ten Half-Pennies," *The Magazine of Fantasy & Science Fiction,* March/April.

——, "Thunderstone," *Extrasolar.*

Chi Hui, "Rain Ship," *Clarkesworld,* February.

Kameron Hurley, "The Fisherman and the Pig," *Beneath Ceaseless Skies 235.*

——, "Warped Passages," *Cosmic Powers.*

Dave Hutchinson, *Acadie,* Tor.com Publishing.

Janis Ian, "His Sweat Like Stars on the Rio Grande," *Welcome to Dystopia.*

Alexander Jablokov, "How Sere Picked Up Her Laundry," *Asimov's Science Fiction.* July/August.

N. K. Jemisin, "Henosis," *Uncanny.* September/October.

Paul Jessup, "The Music of Ghosts," *Interzone 272.*

Calvin D. Jia, "Rose's Arm," *Where the Stars Rise.*

Xia Jia, "Goodnight, Melancholy," *Clarkesworld,* March.

Bill Johnson, "Hybrid, Blue, by Firelight," *Analog Science Fiction and Fact,* November/December.

Bill Johnson and Gregory Frost, "Three Can Keep a Secret," *Asimov's Science Fiction,* March/April.

Tom Jolly, "Catching Zeus," *Analog Science Fiction and Fact,* January/February.

Gwyneth Jones, *Proof of Concept,* Tor.com Publishing.

Minsoo Kang, "Wintry Hearts of Those Who Rise," *Where the Stars Rise.*

James Patrick Kelly, "And No Torment Shall Touch Them," *Asimov's Science Fiction,* November/December.

Caitlín R. Kiernan, *Agents of Dreamland,* Tor.com Publishing.

Rachel Kornher-Stace, "Last Chance," *Clarkesworld,* July.

Ellen Klages, *Passing Strange,* Tor.com Publishing.

Gary Kloster, "Interchange," *Clarkesworld,* January.

Mary Robinette Kowal, "The Worshipful Society of Glovers," *Uncanny 17.*

Nancy Kress, "Collapse," *A Flight to the Future.*

——, "Every Hour of Light and Dark," *Omni,* October.

——, "Ma Ganga," *Megatech.*

Matthew Kressel, "Love Engine Optimization," *Lightspeed,* June.

Naomi Kritzer, "Evil Opposite," *The Magazine of Fantasy & Science Fiction,* September/October.

——, "Paradox," *Uncanny 17.*

Greg Kurzawa, "Soccer Fields and Frozen Lakes," *Lightspeed,* March.

Ellen Kushner, "When I Was a Highwayman," *The Book of Swords.*

Marc Laidlaw, "Wetherfell's Reef Runics," *The Magazine of Fantasy & Science Fiction,* March/April.

Joe R. Lansdale, "Robo Rapid," *The Weight of Words.*
Rich Larson, "The Colgrid Conundrum," *The Book of Swords.*
——, "Cupido," *Asimov's Science Fiction,* March/April.
——, "The Ghost Ship Anastasia," *Clarkesworld,* January.
——, "Heavies," *Infinity Wars.*
——, "L'appel du vide," *Apex Magazine,* July.
——, "Masked," *Apex Magazine,* January.
——, "Spiked," *Abyss & Apex,* Third Quarter.
——, "This Old Man," *Analog Science Fiction and Fact,* November/December.
——, "Travelers," *Clarkesworld,* July.
——, "Verweile Doch (But Linger)," *Omni,* October.
——, "You Too Shall Be Psyche," *Apex Magazine,* February.
William Ledbetter, "In a Wide Sky, Hidden," *The Magazine of Fantasy & Science Fiction,* July/August.
Fonda Lee, "Old Souls," *Where the Stars Rise.*
Yoon Ha Lee, "The Chameleon's Gloves," *Cosmic Powers.*
——, "Extracurricular Activities," *Tor.com,* February 15.
Stephen Leigh, "The Atonement Tango," *Tor.com,* January 18.
Rose Lemberg, "A Portrait of the Desert in Personages of Power," *Beneath Ceaseless Skies* 230.
Edward M. Lerner, "Paradise Regained," *Analog Science Fiction and Fact,* January/February.
David D. Levine, "Command and Control," *Infinity Wars.*
L. D. Lewis, "Chesirah," *Fiyah,* Winter.
Shariann Lewitt, "The Aspect of Dawn," *Shadows and Reflections.*
Michael Libling, "Sneakers," *Welcome to Dystopia.*
Marissa Lingen, "An Unearned Death," *The Magazine of Fantasy & Science Fiction,* July/August.
——, "Vulture's Nest," *Analog Science Fiction and Fact,* May/June.
Ken Liu, "The Hidden Girl," *The Book of Swords.*
Karin Lowachee, "Meridian," *Where the Stars Rise.*
Will Ludwigsen, "Night Fever," *Asimov's Science Fiction,* May/June.
Scott Lynch, "The Smoke of Gold Is Glory," *The Book of Swords.*
Ian R. MacLeod, "The Fall of the House of Kepler," *Extrasolar.*
——, "The Wisdom of the Group," *Asimov's Science Fiction,* March/April.
Ken MacLeod, "Jesus Christ, Reanimator," *Apex Magazine,* March.
Bruce McAllister, "Ink," *Lightspeed,* August.
——, "This Is For You," *Lightspeed,* May.
Tim McDaniel, "Squamous and Eldritch Get a Yard Sale Bargain," *Asimov's Science Fiction,* September/October.
Edward McDermott, "The Snatchers," *Analog Science Fiction and Fact,* March/April.
Jack McDevitt, "Arcturian Nocturne," *Extrasolar.*
——, "The Last Dance," *Asimov's Science Fiction,* November/December.
——, "Your Lying Eyes," *Chasing Shadows.*
Sandra McDonald, "Riding the Blue Line with Jack Kerouac," *Asimov's Science Fiction,* September/October.
Seanan McGuire, "Bring the Kids and Revisit the Past at the Traveling Retro Funfair!" *Cosmic Powers.*
——, "River of Stars," *Children of a Different Sky.*

———, "Sentence Like a Saturday," *Mad Hatters and March Hares.*

Maureen F. McHugh, "Cannibal Acts," *Global Dystopias.*

Sean McMullen, "Two Hours at Frontier," *Analog Science Fiction and Fact,* November/December.

Nick Mamatas and Tim Pratt, "The Dude Who Collected Lovecraft," *Apex Magazine,* November.

Kate Marshall, "Red Bark and Ambergris," *Beneath Ceaseless Skies* 232.

George R. R. Martin, "Sons of the Dragon," *The Book of Swords.*

Laura Mauro, "Looking for Laika," *Interzone* 273.

Sam J. Miller, "The Future of Hunger in the Age of Programmable Matter," *Tor.com,* October.

———, "The Ways Out," *Clarkesworld,* June.

Sam J. Miller and Lara Elena Donnelly, "Making Us Monsters," *Uncanny* 19.

Mary Anne Mohanraj, "Farewell," *Welcome to Utopia.*

Sean Monaghan, "Crimson Birds of Small Miracles," *Asimov's Science Fiction,* January/February.

Elizabeth Moon, "All In a Day's Work," *Infinite Stars.*

Sunny Moraine, "In the Blind," *Clarkesworld,* August.

Silvia Moreno-Garcia, "Cemetery Man," *Apex Magazine,* December.

Pat Murphy, "Crossing the Threshold," *Lightspeed,* June.

Ramez Naam, "The Use of Things," *Visions, Ventures, Escape Velocities.*

Linda Nagata, "Diamond and the World Breaker," *Cosmic Powers.*

———, "Region Five," *Infinite Stars.*

T. R. Napper, "Ghosts of a Neon God," *Interzone* 272.

Shweta Narayan, "World of the Three," *Lightspeed,* June.

David Erik Nelson, "There Was a Crooked Man, He Flipped a Crooked House," *The Magazine of Fantasy & Science Fiction,* July/August.

———, "Whatever Comes After Calcutta," *The Magazine of Fantasy & Science Fiction,* November/December.

Mari Ness, "You Will Never Know What Opens," *Lightspeed,* December.

Ruth Nestvold, "Re: Your Wedding," *Welcome to Dystopia.*

Larry Niven, "By the Red Giant's Light," *The Magazine of Fantasy & Science Fiction,* November/December.

Garth Nix, "A Long, Cold Trail," *The Book of Swords.*

———, "Conversations with an Armory," *Infinity Wars.*

Julie Novakova, "To See the Elephant," *Analog Science Fiction and Fact,* May/June.

Jody Lynn Nye, "Imperium Imposter," *Infinite Stars.*

Brandon O'Brien, "They Will Take You From You," *Strange Horizons,* May.

Jay O'Connell, "The Best Man," *Asimov's Science Fiction,* May/June.

———, "Weaponized," *Analog Science Fiction and Fact,* November/December.

Nnedi Okorafor, *Binti: Home,* Tor.com Publishing.

Malka Older, "The Black Box," *Wired: The Fiction Issue.*

Deji Bryce Olukotun, "The Levellers," *Welcome to Dystopia.*

An Owomoyela, "The Last Broadcasts," *Infinity Wars.*

Suzanne Palmer, "Books of the Risen Sea," *Asimov's Science Fiction,* September/October.

———, "The Secret Life of Bots," *Clarkesworld,* September.

Susan Palwick, "Remote Presence," *Lightspeed,* April.

———, "The Shining Hills," *Lightspeed,* August.

K. J. Parker, "The Best Man Wins," *The Book of Swords*.

——, *Mightier than the Sword*, Subterranan Press.

Richard Parks, "In Memory of Jianhong, Snake-Devil," *Beneath Ceaseless Skies 226*.

——, "On the Road to the Hell of Hungry Ghosts," *Beneath Ceaseless Skies 235*.

Julia K. Patt, "My Dear, Like the Sky and Stars and Sun," *Clarkesworld*, June.

Dominica Phetteplace, "Oracle," *Infinity Wars*.

Tony Pi, "The Spirit of Wine," *Where the Stars Rise*.

——, "That Lingering Sweetness," *Beneath Ceaseless Skies 224*.

Sarah Pinsker, "And Then There Were (N-One)," *Uncanny 15*.

——, "Wind Will Rove," *Asimov's Science Fiction*, September/October.

Joe Pitkin, "Proteus," *Analog Science Fiction and Fact*, May/June.

Rachel Pollack, "Homecoming," *The Magazine of Fantasy & Science Fiction*, March/April.

Vina Jie-Min Prasad, "Fandom For Robots," *Uncanny 18*.

William Preston, "Good Show," *Asimov's Science Fiction*, May/June.

Lettie Prell, "Crossing LaSalle," *Clarksworld*, December.

Tom Purdom, "Afloat Above a Floor of Stars," *Asimov's Science Fiction*, November/December.

——, "Fatherbond," *Asimov's Science Fiction*, January/February.

Chen Qiufan, "A Man Out of Fashion," *Clarkesworld*, August.

Cat Rambo, "Preference," *Chasing Shadows*.

Marta Randall, "The Stone Lover," *Lightspeed*, March.

Lina Rather, "Seven Permutations of My Daughter," *Lightspeed*, April.

Marguerite Reed, "Notes on Retrieving a Fallen Banner," *Welcome to Dystopia*.

Robert Reed, "Dunnage for the Soul," *The Magazine of Fantasy & Science Fiction*, March/April.

——, "Leash on a Man," *The Magazine of Fantasy & Science Fiction*, September/October.

——, "The Significance of Significance," *Clarkesworld*, July.

——, "The Speed of Belief," *Asimov's Science Fiction*, January/February.

——, "Two Ways of Living," *Clarkesworld*, March.

Samuel Rees, "Teratology," *Sunvault*.

Jessica Reisman, "Bourbon, Sugar, Grace," *Tor.com*, June 7.

Alastair Reynolds, "Belladonna Nights," *The Weight of Words*.

——, "Holdfast," *Extrasolar*.

——, "Visiting Hours," *Megatech*.

R. Garcia y Robertson, "The Girl Who Stole Herself," *Asimov's Science Fiction*, July/August.

——, "Grand Theft Spacecraft," *Asimov's Science Fiction*, September/October.

Kelly Robson, "A Human Stain," *Tor.com*, January 4.

John Rogers, "First," *Wired: The Fiction Issue*.

Christopher Rowe, "The Border State," *Telling the Map*.

Kristine Kathryn Rusch, "The Runabout," *Asimov's Science Fiction*, May/June.

A. Merc Rustad, "Longing for Stars Once Lost," *Lightspeed*, October.

Geoff Ryman, "No Point Talking," *Welcome to Dystopia*.

Sara Saab, "Sudden Wall," *Beneath Ceaseless Skies 220*.

James Sallis, "Miss Cruz," *The Magazine of Fantasy & Science Fiction*, March/April.

——, "New Teeth," *Analog Science Fiction and Fact*, November/December.

Erica L. Satifka, "The Goddess of the Highway," *Interzone 272*.

Kenneth Schneyer, "Keepsakes," *Analog Science Fiction and Fact*, November/December.

John Schoffstall, "The First Day of Someone Else's Life," *The Magazine of Fantasy & Science Fiction*, May/June.

Carter Scholz, "Extinction of Starlight, or Kintsugi," *Stories in the Stratosphere.*

Karl Schroeder, "The Baker of Mars," *Visions, Ventures, Escape Velocities.*

——, "Eminence," *Chasing Shadows.*

——, "Golden Ring," *Cosmic Powers.*

——, "Too Big To See," *Stories in the Stratosphere.*

Gord Sellar, "Focus," *Analog Science Fiction and Fact*, May/June.

Iona Sharma, "Eight Cities," *Sunvault.*

Nisi Shawl, "The Colors of Money," *Sunvault.*

——, "Queen of Dirt," *Apex Magazine*, February.

Martin L. Shoemaker, "Not Far Enough," *Analog Science Fiction and Fact*, July/August.

Vandana Singh, "Shikasta," *Visions, Ventures, Escape Velocities.*

Jack Skillingstead, "The Last Garden," *Lightspeed*, February.

——, "Mine, Yours, Ours," *Chasing Shadows.*

——, "The Sum of Her Expectations," *Clarkesworld*, October.

Alan Smale, "Kitty Hawk," *Asimov's Science Fiction*, March/April.

Bud Sparhawk, "Downsized," *Analog Science Fiction and Fact*, November/December.

——, "Heaven's Covenant," *Analog Science Fiction and Fact*, November/December.

Cat Sparks, "Prayers to Broken Stones," *Kaleidotrope*, Spring.

D. A. Xiaolin Spires, "Prasetyo Plastics," *Clarkesworld*, November.

Priya Sridhar, "Memoriam," *Where the Stars Rise.*

Allen M. Steele, "An Incident in the Literary Life of Nathan Arkwright," *Asimov's Science Fiction*, September/October.

——, "Sanctuary," *Tor.com*, May 17.

——, "Tagging Bruno," *Asimov's Science Fiction*, January/February.

Amanda Sun, "Weaving Silk," *Where the Stars Rise.*

Michael Swanwick, "Universe Box," *Asimov's Science Fiction*, September/October.

E. J. Swift, "Weather Girl," *Infinity Wars.*

Jeremy Szal, "The dataSultan of Streets and Stars," *Where the Stars Rise.*

Molly Tanzer, "Nine-Tenths of the Law," *Lightspeed*, January.

John Alfred Taylor, "Blow, Winds, and Crack Your Cheeks," *Asimov's Science Fiction*, January/February.

——, "Plaisir d'Amour," *Analog Science Fiction and Fact*, March/April.

Steve Rasnic Tem, "The Common Sea," *Interzone* 269.

Natalia Theodoridou, "The Rains on Mars," *Clarkesworld*, December.

Lavie Tidhar, "The Banffs," *Analog Science Fiction and Fact*, May/June.

——, "The Old Dispensation," *Tor.com*, February 8.

——, "My Struggle," *Apex Magazine*, October.

——, "The Planet Woman By M.V. Crawford," *Extrasolar.*

——, "Waterfalling," *The Book of Swords.*

E. Catherine Tobler, "Baroness," *Clarkesworld*, June.

Cadwell Turnbull, "A Third of the Stars in Heaven," *Lightspeed*, December.

——, "Other Worlds and This One," *Asimov's Science Fiction*, July/August.

Genevieve Valentine, "Overburden," *Infinity Wars.*

James Van Pelt, "Coyote Moon," *Analog Science Fiction and Fact*, November/December.

Carrie Vaughn, "Dead Men in Central City," *Asimov's Science Fiction*, September/October.

——, "Evening of the Span of Their Days," *Infinity Wars.*

——, "I Have Been Drowned in Rain," *Beneath Ceaseless Skies* 223.

Ursula Vernon, "The Dark Birds," *Apex Magazine*, 92.

Marie Vibbert, "The First Trebuchet on Mars," *Analog Science Fiction and Fact*, November/ December.

Juliette Wade, "Sunwake, in the Lands of Teeth," *Clarkesworld*, April.

Jo Walton, "A Burden Shared," *Tor.com*, April 19.

Ian Watson, "Journey to the Anomaly," *Extrasolar*.

Lawrence Watt-Evans, "The Lady of Shadow Guard," *Shadows and Reflections*.

Peter Watts, "ZeroS," *Infinity Wars*.

David Weber, "Our Sacred Honor," *Infinite Stars*.

Catherine Wells, "Native Seeds," *Analog Science Fiction and Fact*, November/December.

Martha Wells, *All Systems Red*, Tor.com Publishing.

Jay Werkheiser, "Ecuador vs. the Bug-Eyed Monsters," *Analog Science Fiction and Fact*, March/April.

———, "Kepler's Law," *Analog Science Fiction and Fact*, May/June.

Rick Wilber, "In Dublin, Fair City," *Asimov's Science Fiction*, November/December.

Ysabeau S. Wilce, "The Queen of Hats," *Mad Hatters and March Hares*.

Kate Wilhelm, "Attachments," *The Magazine of Fantasy & Science Fiction*, November/ December.

Walter Jon Williams, "The Triumph of Virtue," *The Book of Swords*.

Connie Willis, "I Met a Traveler in an Antique Land," *Asimov's Science Fiction*, November/ December.

A. C. Wise, "A Catalogue of Sunlight at the End of the World," *Sunvault*.

Paul Witcover, "Walls," *Welcome to Dystopia*.

Nick Wolven, "Confessions of a Con Girl," *Asimov's Science Fiction*, November/December.

———, "Carbo," *The Magazine of Fantasy & Science Fiction*, November/December.

———, "Streams and Mountains," *Clarkesworld*, May.

Tyler Young, "Last Chance," *Sunvault*.

Caroline M. Yoachim, "Faceless Soldiers, Patchwork Ship," *Infinity Wars*.